RED CENTRE

Moscow, 1986. The Chief Intelligence Directorate of the Soviet General Staff is preparing to launch the Death Bird, an ultra-secret assault satellite. A pre-emptive measure to ensure the West could never place in orbit any satellite deemed inimical to Soviet interests . . . And in the technological world of espionage, treachery, betrayal and sudden death, only British secret agent David Caine and the lovely Cuban-American widow Lynda Sanchez can prevent the master spy from achieving his ends . . .

FREDERICK NOLAN

RED CENTRE

Complete and Unabridged

LINFORD
Leicester

First published in Great Britain

First Linford Edition
published 2009

British Library CIP Data

Nolan, Frederick W., *1931* –
 Red centre. - - (Linford mystery library)
 1. Space weapons- -Fiction. 2. Soviet Union
 - -History- -*1985 – 1991*- -Fiction.
 3. Espionage, British- -Fiction. 4. Spy
 stories. 5. Large type books.
 I. Title II. Series
 823.9'14–dc22

 ISBN 978–1–84782–941–2

Published by
F. A. Thorpe (Publishing)
Anstey, Leicestershire

Set by Words & Graphics Ltd.
Anstey, Leicestershire
Printed and bound in Great Britain by
T. J. International Ltd., Padstow, Cornwall

This book is printed on acid-free paper

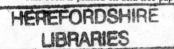

For my sons
Christian and André

Prologue

The Chief Intelligence Directorate of the Soviet General Staff — *Glavnoye Razvedyvatelnoye Upravleniye* — is smaller and less well-known than its sister organization. GRU does not advertise itself. Its head office is not a tourist attraction like the old insurance office building on Dzerzhinsky Square which houses the KGB, but hidden away in a suburban backwater by the central airport, the old Khodinka Field. It is no less deadly for that.

Patrolled night and day by armed guards and killer dogs, the area itself is bordered by restricted buildings, among which are the offices of three leading aviation firms, the Military Aviation Academy, and a rocket construction firm. On the fourth side of the rectangle formed by these buildings lies the Institute of Cosmic Biology.

The entrance to the central enclave, again guarded by dogs and electrified

1

sprung-steel S-wire, is down a narrow lane named for Richard Sorge, a famous Soviet spy. It leads through a blind wall ten metres high into the GRU complex. The main GRU operations executive building is a nine-storey extended rectangle, surrounded on all sides by a two-storey structure, the windows of which look down upon a central courtyard. The external walls have no windows at all, which may account for its being known, sardonically, as the Aquarium. No car — not even that of Marshal Sokolov, the Minister of Defence — is permitted to enter this restricted area. No one may take inside any metallic object, not a cigarette lighter, or a belt buckle, or still less a briefcase. Everyone entering or leaving, regardless of rank, is required to pass through a sophisticated electronic security check.

Most of the GRU's staff are based in the Aquarium, but its chief executive, Colonel-General P. I. Ivashutin, spends four or five hours of his eighteen-hour day in the rather less forbidding administration building on Znamensky Street,

just across the Yauza river from Moscow's famous Sokolniki Park. Between the hours of ten and midday, Ivashutin holds his daily briefings. These are invariably followed by a private conference with his First Deputy, Colonel-General A. G. Pavlov, which lasts until one. Sometimes, not invariably, they lunch afterwards in the ornately gilded dining room on the top floor, where the food is said to be the equal of anything in Europe.

It was 10.23 precisely, a brilliant June day. The morning sun shone brightly through the tall windows of the conference room. Around the beautifully polished conference table, on which, in 1914, the Tsar of Russia and his generals had signed the declaration of war against Germany and Austria, sat Ivashutin's eight deputies. With the exception of Pavlov, they were all in full uniform.

'You have all read the intelligence digests I circulated for your attention?' Ivashutin asked, lighting a cigar. They were a personal gift from his old friend Fidel Castro, specially flown in each week by Aeroflot. Someone had told Ivashutin

that Castro had given them up to encourage young Cubans not to smoke. Sometimes Fidel was a damned fool, the Russian thought.

Of course, the 'Grandfathers' said, undoubtedly. The digests confirmed that the United States was developing a new generation of space satellites, hardened against radiation and hostile laser beams, and capable of evading Soviet attack. These satellites, the report continued, would hover 22,000 miles in space, part of a worldwide network called Space-track, which would provide round-the-clock surveillance of all satellites in deep space. Five stations would track the satellites: one in New Mexico, another in Hawaii, a third in Korea. The fourth was under construction on the British-owned island of Diego Garcia in the Indian Ocean, and work on the fifth, in Portugal, would commence shortly.

'I am sure you all appreciate, then, the significance of the setbacks the Americans have received in this area recently,' Ivashutin said. 'Allow me to refresh your memory. On August 28, 1985, an

advanced Titan 34D rocket exploded at Vandenberg air force base in California, destroying what we believe to have been an 800-million-dollar satellite. On January 28, 1986, the space shuttle Challenger exploded soon after takeoff, killing everyone on board. On April 18, a second Titan 34D, carrying what the Americans call a 'Big Bird' satellite, blew up five seconds after takeoff at Vandenberg, wrecking two launch pads in the process. On May 3, a Delta rocket carrying a weather satellite broke up and was destroyed.'

The Grandfathers nodded, saying nothing. Ivashutin was going somewhere; when he was ready he would tell them. Inside nine months, Ivashutin went on, three of the four means the Americans had available to put heavy military payloads into orbit had failed. The fourth, the Atlas-Centaur, shared much of the Delta's engine design and was therefore suspect.

'Flights of all four have been suspended indefinitely. Even the most optimistic NASA planners do not foresee a resumption of the American space programme

until mid-1987, and possibly a great deal longer. Meanwhile, their surveillance capability is severely inhibited, presenting us with a unique opportunity to pre-empt their plans to dominate space with what they childishly insist upon calling 'Star Wars' hardware.'

He looked at each of them in turn. No one spoke, although he knew they had all guessed what was coming. Ivashutin permitted himself a frosty smile before continuing.

'In the light of these developments we have been invited — ' he paused on the word just long enough to make them smile at his irony, 'to submit this agency's recommendations, with especial reference to our own super-satellite, to the General Secretary and the Secretariat.'

The Grandfathers looked at each other. They had tried pre-empting the American Strategic Defense Initiative once before, with an ultra-secret assault satellite, nicknamed *Smert Ptytsa*, Death Bird, by the Space Agency scientists. Conceived as a means of ensuring the West could never place in orbit any satellite deemed

inimical to Soviet interests, the Death Bird had been identified for what it was by American satellite surveillance the moment it had appeared at the launch site two years ago. The result had been an eyeball-to-eyeball confrontation with the Western powers, who delivered an ultimatum: launch, and take the consequences. No one who remembered those tense meetings when the American missile-carrying F-16s were standing by to scramble, or the embarrassing climb-down by the General Secretary which ensued, wanted a repetition of that debacle.

'What about the Neighbours?' Pavlov asked, using the GRU nickname for the KGB. 'Do they also know of the Secretary's request?'

'Of course,' Ivashutin said, smoothly. 'And in their usual subtle way they have promised the Central Committee a scenario guaranteeing that it will be us, and not the Americans, who achieve domination of outer space.'

'And?' Pavlov prompted.

'Comrade Secretary Gorbachev replied,

7

as is his wont, 'Do you honestly believe what you are telling me?''

The Grandfathers around the table roared with loyal laughter. The Chief's impersonation of General Secretary Mikhail Gorbachev was wickedly accurate. Ivashutin held up a hand for attention. His deputies at once fell silent.

'I need not tell any of you that there is a wind of change blowing in the Kremlin,' he said. 'And I propose that we shall profit by it. We have in this matter an opportunity once and for all to demonstrate we are not only the equal but the superior of any espionage organization in the world!'

He laid his hand firmly on the table, giving his words more emphasis than if he had slammed it down hard.

'It was we, not the Neighbours, who ran Sorge in the Great Patriotic War,' Ivashutin said. 'We, not they, who obtained the atomic bomb from Nunn May. It was we who stole the American Sidewinder missile at Zell in 1967, we who obtained the plans of the French Mirage fighter. This new task is work we

can do better than the Neighbours. Better than anyone!'

He paused, looking at each of them individually, as if assessing them. They sensed the anger in him, the ambition. Times were changing, and Pyotr Ivanovich Ivashutin was not a young man. He needed a coup, a big success. They said of Mikhail Gorbachev that he had a nice smile but iron teeth. He had already flouted Kremlin protocol by reconstituting the Politburo, by replacing Gromyko, by putting Viktor Chebrikov, Yuri Andropov's hand-picked successor — and therefore, by definition his own, since he had been a protégé of the former KGB chief — at the head of the KGB. Providence had sent Ivashutin an opportunity to show the General Secretary that no stodgy, cliché-spouting party hack from Dnepropetrovsk could hope to compete on equal terms with a man who had given his whole life to the Great Game.

Ivashutin nodded abruptly, a mannerism they all knew well. It meant he had come to a decision.

'The Americans are in disarray. They have only one major surveillance satellite

in orbit. If it is neutralized long enough for us to put *Smert Ptytsa* into orbit, the Americans will be helpless. I want a scenario, gentlemen. An initiative so devious that the Neighbours will not even smell it. I want the very best brains put on this job, and the very best men to carry it out. Understand me — the best! Everything is to be subordinated to this task, everything! I want to go to the chiefs of the General Staff and tell them that we — we, no one else! — have found a way to make the undetected launch of our satellite possible. Is that understood?'

'But . . . Comrade General!' one of the deputies protested. 'The National Security Agency spends more than a hundred million dollars a year protecting its computer network. That's more than our entire budget for hardware. What you are asking is impossible. It can't be done.'

'It will,' Ivashutin said. 'It must.'

1

It took David Caine about twenty minutes to get from National Airport to Aurora Heights. He paid the cab off outside the Court House and walked south to Fourteenth. At an office building in the Twenty block, he inserted a plastic ID card into the slot in the wall beneath the plaque which read 'International Security Systems, Inc.' A buzzer sounded behind the solid oak door. He pushed it open and went inside.

The carpeted hallway was discreetly lit; several of Hugh Casson's distinctively economical watercolours hung on the hessian-covered walls. Caine went across to the reception desk and handed his personal ID to the athletic-looking Ryan O'Neal clone behind the desk. Beyond it, separated from the hallway by a smoked-glass wall, he could see the desks of the genuine security firm behind whose cover his own secret organization operated.

They didn't look very busy.

'Thank you, Mr Caine,' the young man behind the desk said. 'The Director is expecting you.'

Caine nodded and went across the hall to the elevator. There were no stairs in the front of the building. It was impossible to get from the reception area he had entered to the upper floors without using the elevators, in which concealed cameras with fibre-optic lenses kept all visitors under surveillance.

The soft chunner of electronic machinery and the muted chirr of telephone bells met him as he stepped out on the third floor into a small hallway decorated with the same green hessian. On either side, unmarked swing doors led into corridors with offices on either side. Kingly's office was at the far end of the corridor on the right. To get to it, you had to pass through an outer office occupied by Kingly's PA, Betty Torre. She was a lively, handsome woman in her mid-thirties who had been working for Kingly since he came to Washington from Berlin in 1983.

'Hello, David,' she said. 'That's a fine tan you've got.'

'The Sun Shines Bright on My Old Kentucky Home,' Caine replied. 'How are you?'

'Ginger peachy,' she said, and made a gesture with her head towards the door of Kingly's office. 'He's expecting you.'

'So I'm told,' Caine said. He knocked and went in.

'You got here fast,' Kingly said, looking up.

'Delta was ready when I was.' Kingly grimaced, and Caine instantly regretted his mild humour. He had forgotten Kingly's dislike of anything smacking of flippancy.

'Sorry I had to rush you,' Kingly said, with no trace of regret. 'No choice, really. Sit down, sit down.'

He was nearly fifty now, with a hairline that had not yet receded enough for him to be called balding, and an out-of-condition body not yet quite flabby enough to be called fat. He wore an immaculately-cut grey lightweight hounds-tooth suit from his Sackville Street tailor, a silk shirt, a

13

Traveller's tie, and shoes handlasted in St James's. Not for the first time, Caine wondered how Miles ran to it, even on Station Director's pay.

'What's the panic?' Caine asked. It must be something of more than usual importance for Control to have pulled him out of the field. All but the most sensitive assignments were handed out through the liaison desk, right here in Arlington.

'Priority signal from Station One,' Kingly told him, sliding a sheet of paper across the desk. 'A service job.'

'Is that all?'

A 'service job', in ISS jargon, was an in-depth check on an individual working within American intelligence. It was normally a very routine business, certainly nothing to fly to Washington for.

'This one would appear to be special,' Kingly said. 'So I thought I'd better brief you personally.'

'Who's the subject?' Caine said, turning the briefing sheet around to read it.

'A Company operative working undercover in Miami. Name of Genevevo.'

'Antony Genevevo, Clandestine Services,' Caine read. 'I thought they weren't allowed to operate domestically.'

'He's attached to Domestic Ops,' Kingly explained. The Domestic Operations Division was one of fifteen or so separate components of the CIA's Clandestine Services, or to give it its official title, the Directorate of Operations. Domestic Operations was, in essence, an area division, conducting its clandestine activities inside the United States. Caine's attention sharpened. If DOD was operating in his territory he wanted to know a lot more.

'Why don't London just ask the Company for sight of his dossier?' he asked.

'The inference is that Sam mustn't know of our interest.' Kingly never called the Americans the 'Cousins', as most people in the Service did. He said the terminology had been debased by too many thriller writers.

'It says we're to concentrate on any links Genevevo might have with the Comrades,' Caine noted. 'Do they think

he's turned Red?'

'It's possible. DGI' — the acronym stood for *Dirección General de Inteligencia*, the official title of the Cuban intelligence service — 'is very active there, and we all know the Cubans are just a branch office of Red Centre. Would you like some coffee or tea?'

'Coffee would be fine,' Caine said. Kingly pressed a button on his desk as Caine asked another question. 'Have we got any background on Genevevo?'

Before Kingly could answer the door opened, and Betty Torre came in.

'Coffee for David, tea for me,' Kingly said. 'And let's have some of those biscuits from Fortnums.'

'Germaine Greer, where are you when I need you?' Betty said to the ceiling. Kingly didn't smile. He waited till the door was closed, then swung his feet up on to the desk.

'Last summer, Six brought over a big one. A GRU colonel. Second Directorate, no less.'

'Quite a catch,' Caine observed, and it was true. GRU defectors were very much

rarer birds than KGB men. A colonel in the Second Directorate, which dealt with the Americas, Britain, Australia and New Zealand, was a real prize. DI6 — only lazy hacks who got their information from outdated spy books called the Secret Intelligence Service MI6 any longer — would really have their tails up.

'They brought him out through the Consulate in Berlin. Cheeky buggers, even flew him back on a commercial flight. They'd never have got away with that in my day.'

Kingly had been Station Director in Berlin for six years prior to this posting. He talked about it as if it had been the best time of his life, although as far as Caine had been able to ascertain Kingly's achievements there had been less than spectacular.

'They gave him a code name: Viktor,' Kingly went on. 'Put him in intensive care.'

More jargon: 'intensive care' meant non-stop, relentless debriefing which went on nine hours a day for week after week after week. Everything the defector said was checked, cross-checked, and

double-checked. They usually took them to a military establishment first: Saltdean Barracks outside Brighton was one of the more favoured places. Later, he would be taken to the safe house at the corner of South Audley Street and Adam's Row, and later still, to the secluded Winterbourne Hotel at Bonchurch on the Isle of Wight.

'They kept him to themselves as long as they could, of course,' Kingly went on. 'Wanted to be sure they'd emptied him out. But once the expulsions started, Sam knew we had a talker.'

The preceding September, Britain had ordered twenty-five Soviet officials out of the country — diplomats, embassy staff, trade officials and journalists. Calling this 'an unwarranted action of unfriendly character', the Russians riposted by kicking twenty-five British officials out of Moscow for 'engaging in activities incompatible with their status'. The formal expulsion of spies from any Western country was a sure sign to other intelligence agencies that a Soviet defector with a wide knowledge of field

activities was talking. It was clear now that it must have been 'Viktor', the GRU colonel.

'So now Sam is asking for equal time?'

'Right,' Kingly said. 'But Six won't be in any hurry to hand him over.'

'What's Viktor got to do with Genevevo?'

'Ah,' Kingly said, swinging his feet to the floor. 'Here's the tea.'

Betty Torre put the silver tray on the otherwise empty desk. 'Note: biscuits, not cookies,' she said to Caine. 'Flown in by diplomatic pouch.'

'Proper treasure, you are,' Caine said.

'Ain't it de troot,' Betty said, and went out. While Kingly poured his tea into a pretty Minton cup, Caine looked around his office. It was L-shaped, and unadorned, almost austere. Tinted windows kept out the glare of the Washington sunshine. The walls were covered with the same green hessian, the floors with the same darker green carpet as the outer offices. Kingly's desk stood in the lower horizontal of the 'L'. Behind it stood floor-to-ceiling bookshelves of Malabar teak, packed with government publications, military digests

and intelligence reports. The other part of the office contained a reproduction Regency table and chairs for Kingly's briefing meetings. There were no pictures, no personal touches. The only thing hanging on the walls was a large-scale Rand-McNally map of the United States.

'You were going to tell me what Viktor has to do with this Genevevo,' Caine said, watching Kingly munch the biscuits like a kid in a candy store.

'Ah, mm, yes,' Kingly said. 'One of Viktor's gifts to Six was a chap in DI5's F Section called Clive Jamison. Nasty little bugger. He'd made contact with the Comrades in London, and they flew him out to Vienna a couple of times to make sure he was kosher. He'd given them some Beta-level stuff: Five's assessment of the KGB order of battle in England, GRU infiltration of the IRA, that sort of thing. Viktor blew the whistle on him, and K Section took him to pieces. One of the people he named as an informant was Genevevo. The Joint Chiefs wanted to know more, but apparently preferred not to ask Sam direct. Which resulted in its

being handed to ISS.'

International Security Systems, Inc., Arlington, was part of a genuine world-wide network of security consultants, with head offices in Lincoln's Inn Fields in London. Its business, the supply of security equipment and expertise to government and private agencies, was a perfect 'cover' for the organization to which David Caine belonged.

Dating from the signing in 1947 of the still-secret UKUSA agreement, it had become a *sine qua non* of Western intelligence that America and Britain did not spy upon each other. Since the UKUSA agreement brought together under a single umbrella the SIGINT (Signals Intelligence), RADINT (Radar Intelligence), HUMINT (Human Intelligence) and ELINT (Electronic Intelligence)-gathering facilities of America, Britain, Canada, Australia and New Zealand, such surveillance was theoretically rendered unnecessary.

Then in 1982, a wretched paedophile named Geoffrey Prime confessed to his wife that he had been supplying the Soviets with secret documents from

GCHQ, the British cypher centre at Cheltenham where he had formerly worked. His wife, Rhona, informed the police and Prime was arrested.

It transpired that Prime, possibly alone, or possibly in concert with another man, killed in an unexplained glider accident near Cheltenham ten days later, had turned over to the Comrades not only thousands of pages of secret material relating to the most sensitive US-UK spy-satellite projects, but also details of the even more secret Sambo Project, a detection system used to locate Soviet submarines.

American reaction was Draconian. Claiming that British security was as 'leaky as an old scow', and that GCHQ was a 'negative asset', General Lincoln D. Faurer, head of the American National Security Agency, clamped down on the flow of information passing to Britain, and his formerly cordial relationship with Sir Brian Tovey at GCHQ deteriorated to one of the utmost formality. The same reticence became apparent in Five and Six's dealings with Sam. A solution was

sought, and found — the ISS organization.

Through a Hong Kong-based consortium managed by the Properties Division of the Department of the Environment, a controlling interest was acquired in the old-established London company. Funds approved by the Permanent Secretaries' Committee on the Intelligence Services were made available for the establishment, at each of the existing offices of ISS, of a separate, secret section whose task was to monitor American intelligence activities around the world.

The covert staff of ISS was recruited over a two-year period from every branch of the security services. In Caine's case it had been army intelligence. He had been given a six-week crash course at the DI6 school in Borough High Street and posted to the American branch as soon as he had completed it. ISS had come 'on stream' late in 1985, working alongside but not for DI6. Its director, Major-General Sir James Bamford, DSO, MC, listed in *Who's Who* as 'semiretired, on attachment to MoD', reported only to the

chairman of the Joint Intelligence Chiefs and the Prime Minister's COBRA committee.

'You say Jamison named Genevevo as a source?' Caine asked. 'A source for what?'

'Jamison did some liaison work on Operation Nightingale, which was set up to investigate heroin and cocaine smuggling between Florida, Nigeria and London,' Kingly explained. 'He went to Miami and the DEA people there put him on to Genevevo. This was before Genevevo went undercover, obviously. Apparently Jamison convinced him that he could crack the ring at the British end if Genevevo would feed him the names of the people running drugs across the Atlantic out of Miami.'

'And they gave them to him?' Caine said, incredulously.

'It was more like a swap. In return, Jamison gave the Americans some DI5 assessment papers on graft in the Bahamas that made their 'Blue Lightning' operation possible. Rather neat, really, a new twist on false-flag recruiting.'

'Genevevo thought he was helping

British intelligence to catch drug smug-
glers . . . '

' . . . while in fact Jamison was passing
the names of every federal undercover
agent he got direct to his Soviet case
officer, Arkady Semionov.'

'Who in turn, no doubt, passed them
straight to the Cubans.'

'Something like that,' Kingly said.

He pushed a six-inch-square envelope
across the desk. Caine slid out the
floppy disk, and read the coded formula
on the label: ISS/1/IT 300386/BABY
— STATUS VIPAR. This told him that
the interrogation transcript had been
prepared at ISS/1, London, on 30 March.
Jamison's codename was 'Baby', and the
security classification meant its contents
were highly restricted.

'I'd like to study this for a while,' he
told Kingly. 'Can I use the visitor desk?'

'Get Betty to fix it,' Kingly said.
'Anything else you need?'

'No, nothing,' Caine said. Kingly stood,
ending the interview.

'Must get on,' he said. 'I've got a lunch
date.'

'Anyone interesting?'

Kingly gave him a frosty smile and Caine shrugged. Kingly had always been extremely cagey about his contacts, just as he was almost paranoid about leaving sensitive materials in plain sight. That was why his desk was always empty. Either that, or he didn't trust even his closest associates, Caine thought. He picked up the file and went out, wishing now he'd taken another biscuit.

2

Caine spoke briefly to Betty Torre and then ambled along the corridor to the liaison office. The blue card in the slot outside the door told him the duty officer was Dick McClelland. He went in, and McClelland came across to meet him, smiling. He was like a jolly bear to look at, a big, grizzled man with a grin a yard wide. But the jolly bear appearance was utterly deceptive: McClelland was one of the most astute officers in the Service.

'How are you, Dick?' Caine asked. 'How's the book business?'

McClelland's wife Diane ran a book-shop which specialized in modern first editions. Caine had once bought a complete set of Ian Fleming's James Bond novels from them, all in fine mint-condition dust wrappers. Dick was always trying to buy them back.

'Prices keep going up and up since Joe Connolly wrote that book. I should think

those Flemings of yours — '

'Save your breath, Dick,' Caine smiled.

'Always worth asking,' McClelland grinned. 'What can I do for you?'

'Apart from a mint first of *The Godwulf Manuscript*, not a lot,' Caine said, 'Betty said I can use the visitor desk.'

'I assume she'll have already cleared it with Arthur?' Arthur Cotton was Head of Security. His responsibilities ranged from the use of the 'safe room' to the maintenance of the twin remote-controlled Mossberg 500 Bullpup shotguns behind the reception desk.

He walked with Caine to the safe room at the end of the corridor, unlocked the door and let him in. The room was simply furnished with a teak desk, a Naugahyde-covered swivel chair, and a desktop PC. There were no windows and no other exit.

'Anything else?' McClelland asked.

'See if you can raise Tom Crandon in Miami for me, will you?'

Caine closed the door and sat down. Switching on the IBM, he slid in the disk

and waited while the computer hummed and buzzed. The screen lit, the cursor blinking on a warning: *Awaiting Authorized Access.*

All secret information stored on disks was scrambled. This meant that it would appear on the screen as a meaningless mess unless it was used in conjunction with a Cryptag security key like the one that Betty had given him. It was a resin block, six millimetres thick, which contained a radio receiver, transmitter and microprocessor. He inserted it into the interrogator unit, keying in his personal password. Because the tag was interactive, the computer would now have a record of who had used it, and how much information had been requested.

The green-tinted screen filled with lines of information. Caine read the entire interrogation transcript through once, fast, then returned to the beginning and read it again, this time more slowly. He was into the fourth reading when the telephone on the desk beside him burred quietly.

'Miami,' McClelland said.

'Secure the line,' Caine told him. 'Hello, Tom.'

'Where are you?'

'Head office,' Caine said. 'Can you meet me tomorrow at your end? Fifteen hundred hours, Rendezvous Three?'

'No sweat,' Crandon said. 'You got something for me?'

'See you tomorrow,' Caine said, and hung up. Tom Crandon was the ISS 'specialist' in Miami. Within the firm, ranks were referred to in civilian terminology. Heads of Sections (there were seven in the United States) were called 'consultants'. Each consultant controlled five intelligence officers known as 'specialists', who in turn controlled a minimum of two, maximum of six field agents called 'technicians'. Caine's Section, 'F', covered the south-eastern United States, with headquarters in Louisville, Kentucky, and specialists in Miami, Memphis, Birmingham and Atlanta.

Caine lifted the phone to call Eastern Airlines. He booked a one-way coach seat to Miami on EA197, leaving National Airport at five thirty. Next, he called

Sheraton, and reserved a room at the River House near Miami International Airport. There was a Budget rental office a few blocks from the hotel. ISS expense accounts didn't run to renting cars at airport concessions.

He spent the rest of the afternoon reading and re-reading the interrogation transcript. By the time he was finished, he could have recited everything Clive Jamison had told the K-7 Interrogation Team — dredgers, as they were known in the trade. K Section, which operated from an anonymous-looking building at the Euston Road end of Gower Street, was the liaison branch of DI5 and DI6. K-7, counterintelligence, was headed by the man who had brought Caine into the service, Colonel Peter Harland.

Caine switched off the computer and took the disk back to Kingly's office. Betty Torre told him Miles was still out. She took the disk and put it into the security slot which fed it directly into the safe, for which only Kingly had the combination.

Turning down Dick McClelland's offer

of a lift, Caine checked out of the office and took a cab to the airport. It was three forty-five when he left; Kingly had still not returned from lunch. If the espionage business ever dried up, Caine thought, Miles could always get a job in publishing.

3

The mid-afternoon traffic was fairly light, and Caine made good time in the rented Omni. He paid the toll and rolled across the Rickenbacker Causeway towards Key Biscayne. Cormorants wheeled above the Marine Stadium. Sunshine glittered on the roofs of massed cars in the huge parking lots on the oceanside. The divided highway was lined with graceful coconut palms. Shortly after it became a two-way, Caine turned right on Harbor Drive and right again into the parking lot of the Yacht Club.

Despite its exclusive-sounding name, the bar and restaurant were open to the public. The bar looked out across the bay. It was decorated Trader Vic style, with lobster baskets and cork floats. Tom Crandon was already there, sitting by the window and gazing pensively at the sailboats on the bright blue water.

He was a tall, well-built, good-looking

man of thirty-three, with blond hair and blue eyes. He wore one of those shirts with no collar, a tan lightweight suit and loafers with matching tan woven tops. He turned as Caine came in, and a wide grin banished the thoughtful expression.

'David!' he said, coming across to shake Caine's hand. 'Let me get you a drink.'

'I'll take a Beck's,' Caine said to the bartender, a hulking young fellow with a Sundance Kid moustache and the beginnings of a beer gut. The bartender put the bottle and glass on the counter without a smile.

'Two fifty,' he said.

'That include service?' Caine asked.

The bartender didn't answer. He took Crandon's five, banged the change down, and went back to his cronies down the bar. Caine grinned.

'Oops,' Crandon said. 'You hurt his feelings.'

'I'm old enough to remember when people were polite down here,' Caine said, pouring the beer.

'You think this is bad?' Crandon said.

'Try the airport.'

'I already did,' Caine said. 'Even the British are rude out there. What are they trying to do, give New York a good name?'

'You snowbirds are all the same,' Crandon said. 'Bitch, bitch, bitch. Why don't you stay up north where you belong?'

A snowbird, in local jargon, was one of the pale-skinned, pudgy creatures that flew down to Florida at the first sign of cold weather up north. 'North' was a moveable feast: to a Miamian, Cape Canaveral was north.

'They used to have ads in the papers, 'When you need it bad, we got it good',' Caine said. 'You remember that?'

'I'm too young,' Crandon said. 'I don't even remember The Beatles. Come on, let's go sit at a table.'

The dining area was filled with round tables covered with checked tablecloths that were supposed to give the place the atmosphere of a bistro. It was empty, as they had expected it to be. Nobody came here to eat at this time of day. The

bleached-blond beach boys at the bar were talking spinnakers and trapezes, and showed not the slightest interest in them.

'OK,' Crandon said, sipping his beer. 'What's the panic?'

'A service job,' Caine told him.

'You flew here from Washington to tell me you want a service job?'

'It's a special.'

'It would have to be. Who's the subject?'

'CIA undercover operative, name of Tony Genevevo.'

'What's special about him?'

'He might be a Comrade.'

'What do we know about him?'

'He's Cuban-American. Born here in Miami. Divorced, with grown-up children. I've got a dossier for you.'

He didn't tell Crandon anything about Jamison, or what Jamison had told K-7 about Genevevo. Crandon needed to know only the identity of the surveillance target.

'OK, we can check him out. If he's Cuban, could be La Dirección has got an armlock on him.'

Tom was using the nickname local Cubans used for DGI, the Cuban intelligence organization. Although it kept pretty busy in the Miami area, 'La Dirección' was little more than a branch office of the KGB. Headed until 1985 by Ramiro Valdez, it was best known for its prize alumnus, Carlos the Jackal, who had been trained at a DGI camp in the Contramaestre mountains in Cuba prior to being sent to Patrice Lumumba University in Moscow.

'How's your workload?' Caine asked.

'The usual,' Crandon said. 'Four or five legit jobs. You know about them. The rest's routine, mostly to do with drugs. You in Co-Caine City, babe.'

'Anything special going down?'

'Word on the street is that there's a big one in the works. Which means big-big. It has to be, these days. Three years ago, a kilo of snow fetched between sixty and seventy-two thou. They're landing so much of the stuff now, the going price is down to between twenty and thirty, depending on the quality.'

'Any idea who, what, where?'

'Nothing definite, but it doesn't seem

to be any of the Colombian families.'

'Why would the Company be interested?'

'Everybody else is,' Crandon said. 'We got the Florida Cocaine Task Force, the Drug Enforcement Agency, FBI, armed forces, state police, Christ alone knows who else down here, all falling over each other. It figures the Company would be in there someplace. I can find out.'

'How soon?'

Crandon looked at him judiciously. 'A few days?'

'Be like Avis — try harder.'

'Oooh, I get goose bumps when you're mean,' Crandon grinned. 'OK, sooner. Earn my pension, right?'

'You won't live to draw a pension,' Caine told him. 'You'll screw yourself to death before you're forty.'

Tom grinned. He had no ties, no wife, no mortgage, not even a steady girlfriend. He drove a very expensive car, he snorkelled in St Maarten, he ski'd in Zermatt, spending his money as fast as he earned it, sometimes faster. The all-American male: Hugh Hefner would be proud of him, Caine thought. Tom's

lifestyle was a long way from being a low profile, but there were all sorts of covers, and Tom's seemed to work.

'That's the trouble with you old men,' he said. 'You see us younger guys living out your fantasies, and you're eaten up with jealousy.'

'I don't have fantasies,' Caine said. 'I'm saving myself for Susan Silverman.'

'Think she'd give you a tumble with me around?' Crandon scoffed, getting up out of his chair. 'Fat chance.'

They were both keen readers of Robert B. Parker's 'Spenser' novels. Caine was trying to put together a set of first editions. Last time someone had offered him an early Parker they'd wanted a couple of hundred dollars for it. If only Houghton Mifflin had known, he thought.

'You want another beer?' Tom asked.

'Not at these prices,' Caine said. 'Let's get out of here, Tom. I want to get started on this Genevevo thing right away. The works: friends, politics, money, sex life. Whatever.'

'Wouldn't all that be on his dossier at Langley?'

'We didn't pull it. Don't want to tip off Sam.'

They walked out into the spring sunshine. A light breeze came in off the bay. The steel and glass towers of Miami shone flat and hard across the water. It was the kind of day when shipping clerks dream of being millionaires.

'I might need to put on some extra people, David,' Crandon said. 'That OK?'

'Use your own judgement,' Caine told him. 'I want it fast, but I want it good.'

'I'll get right on it. You want to have dinner later?'

'Fine.'

'How does Joe's Stone Crab sound?'

'It goes 'eek, eek, eek'.'

'You got a sense of humour like the Incredible Hulk,' Crandon said. 'I'll pick you up, OK? Where you staying — the River House again?'

'I'm kinky for fat tourists.'

'You went to the right place.' Crandon walked across to his car, a silver-grey Porsche 944. All part of the golden-boy image, like the beach apartment, the four hundred dollar suits, the gold Oyster

Perpetual. Caine smiled as Crandon revved the engine and roared away. He got into the little Dodge and headed back across the Causeway to Miami. Two cars behind him, a couple of Cuban-Americans in a tan Thunderbird carefully matched their speed to his.

4

'Ya got trouble,' Crandon said. 'Right here in River City.'

It was Caine's third full day in Miami. Hamstrung by Kingly's injunction not to alert Sam, there was little he could do except kick his heels at the ISS office on Biscayne Boulevard while Tom Crandon set up surveillance on Tony Genevevo.

The office was a suite of three rooms in a fairly new building opposite the public library. It was furnished in a style which Crandon referred to as 'Filing Cabinet Modern', the walls decorated with photographic blow-ups of security equipment. Facing the entrance was a roster of some of the Florida companies for whom ISS acted as genuine security consultants. Crandon had a small personal office across the hall from the 'front'. It was functional and uncluttered a desk, a divan, a low table, a couple of easy chairs, the usual electronic gadgets.

'What kind of trouble?' Caine asked.

'We're not the only ones watching Genevevo,' Crandon said.

'What?'

'That's exactly the way I felt when I found out. I thought this was going to be a nice, simple service job, David. In, out, easy-peasy.'

'So did I,' Caine said.

The preliminary investigation into Genevevo's background had run into a brick wall. Crandon couldn't even get anything out of his police contacts downtown. Then he realized why: Genevevo was working for Pedro Avranilosa, a Cuban-born middleman who acted as ambassador for the South American cocaine dealers, putting them together with local buyers. Which meant one of only two things: either the Company had their man in deep, deep cover, or he had gone over to the other side and the Americans knew it.

In such circumstances, putting Genevevo under surveillance was a very delicate operation: if he was working undercover and they blew him, they could get

Genevevo killed. Avranilosa, *El Gordo*, was dealing in ten-figure sums. Wasting an informer was small-change stuff.

The surveillance itself could not have been more difficult to set up if Genevevo had deliberately set out to frustrate it. His house was on South Lake Drive, facing the lake. There was no way to keep a van on the street for more than an hour or two at a time. The same applied to 'sidewalkers': they stood out like spiders on a whitewashed wall on the wide, empty residential streets. Fortunately, Crandon's team had gotten lucky and obtained a short-term rental on a two-bed apartment on the next street, from whose back windows it was possible to obtain a clear view of Genevevo's house.

After all the bad luck, they got a break: on the third day of their surveillance, Crandon's watchers filmed a meet between Genevevo and his control, a Domestic Operations Division officer named Frank Forsyth. DOD involvement indicated that Langley suspected that *El Gordo*, the Fat Man, might be involved with what DOD liked to call 'foreign institutions'.

'So Genevevo's watching Avranilosa, who is probably working for the Cubans. OK,' Caine said. 'Then who's watching Genevevo? His own people?'

'They're not Feds, David. It's not local cops, either. I know most of the local boys. These guys are all Cubans. I don't know who the hell they are.'

'DGI? You think maybe the Fat Man's got his people checking Genevevo out?'

'It's possible.'

'Is Genevevo on to them?'

'He's doing a hell of an acting job if he is.'

'How did you spot them?'

'Pure accident,' Crandon said. 'Take a look.'

He pressed a button on the TV remote control. The big Mitsubishi rear-projection screen flickered to life, and the video-recorder began to turn. The videocamera had been positioned inside a parked vehicle. Genevevo, a good-looking, compactly-built Cuban-American, came out of his house and down the path to a blue '85 Dodge Daytona. The camera held on him as he got into the car. His dark hair was cut

very short and lay flat on his scalp like a yarmulka. He wore a seersucker jacket and dark blue slacks.

'Now watch,' Crandon said.

Genevevo's Daytona rolled away down South Lake Drive, and then, from behind what would have been the cameraman's right shoulder, a black Lincoln Continental slid into the picture and moved off after the Dodge.

'The limo was a rental,' Crandon said. 'It was hired by a man who gave his name as Luis Echeverria, with an address in Hialeah. And in answer to your next question, no, nobody of that name lives there.'

'Didn't he show ID when he hired?'

'Driving permit.'

'Forged, of course. How did he pay? Credit card?'

'Stolen. They're pros.'

'Cubans. Pros. It's got to be La Dirección.'

'Say it is. Why are they watching Genevevo?'

'Because Avranilosa called them in?'

'If he suspected Genevevo, he'd just

take him out. Why waste time having him watched?'

'There's a reason,' Caine said. 'We just haven't hit it yet. What else have your people come up with? Were you able to get peeps or sneakies into his place?'

In the jargon, 'sneakies' were listening devices, and 'peeps' were cameras with fibre-optic lenses no bigger than the head of a pin, which could be pushed through the cracks in walls or the joints in floorboards.

'Didn't even try. Genevevo's a pro, David,' Crandon reminded him. 'We put an induction tap on his line, just in case, but he's not going to use the phone for anything sensitive.'

'What are you using at the apartment?'

'I'm having to use shotgun mikes. They're not particularly effective, but at least they tell us when he's in the house.'

'So what have we actually got on Genevevo?' Caine asked.

'He's got himself in like Flynn with the Fat Man. He handles all Avranilosa's collections, and that is *dinero, hombre*. No special male friends we've been able

to spot. He lives high on the hog, higher than he could ever hope to live on a government salary.'

'What about women?'

'He plays the field. Only one he sees regularly is a woman called Lynda Sanchez, who runs a restaurant over on Key Biscayne.'

'And nothing to indicate he might be playing Comrades?'

'Nothing you could nail down.'

'What have we got on Avranilosa?'

'El Plenty,' Crandon said.

Pedro Avranilosa was the son of an American sugar importer and a Cuban woman. Born in Santiago in 1938, he had attended Havana High School and gone on to the university.

'His family knew the Castros well. Pedro was a real Fidelista,' Crandon went on. 'He was only twenty when they kicked Batista out. Then like a lot of others, he became disenchanted when Fidel started cosying up to the Russians. The US government airlifted him out in 1965. The Company vetted him, of course — I've seen his records. He came in

clean, but he's been playing dirty ever since. The local cops have rounded him up a few times on drug busts, but he's always walked away free.'

'And now DOD is interested. Why?'

'Could be a lot of things. Remember I told you there was word on the street that a really big deal is going down soon? That could be why Genevevo is in there. The Fat Man — Avranilosa — is a middleman, a fixer. Maybe he's connected to someone the Company is interested in. Maybe they think he's working for La Dirección.'

'Possible, I suppose,' Caine said, without enthusiasm. Cuban Intelligence frequently filtered their agents into mainland Florida. That might explain DOD's interest in Avranilosa, but it provided no clues at all to why someone in London thought Genevevo was working for the Comrades.

'Guilt by association?'

'He wasn't working for the Fat Man then.'

'What about this Lynda Sanchez you mentioned — have you talked to her?'

'Didn't want to tip Genevevo,' Crandon said.

Caine sighed. 'So we look at the surveillance films again,' he said.

'Ready when you are, C.B.,' Crandon replied. He switched on the video again, and for the next four hours they watched Genevevo at work. As Crandon had said, their man was living the lush life. He went to all the glitter palaces in Miami Beach and Coconut Grove, and the smiling welcome he got everywhere indicated he was a big tipper. He had a private box at the Hialeah track, a boat at the Miamarina, a light plane at Opa-Locka.

'Who wants to be a millionaire?' Caine said.

'I do,' Crandon replied.

They watched Genevevo going about his, or Avranilosa's, business. Hotels, used-car lots, pool halls, motels — like the trained operative he was, Genevevo made much use of bars, all-day porno cinemas, and massage parlours.

Crandon's watchers were very good: they only lost him a couple of times.

'Here's the meet with Forsyth,' Crandon said.

The film showed a man walking down a

street. He was about fifty-five, stocky, undistinguished-looking. He wore a dark suit, a white shirt and a neat tie. The only flamboyant touch was the bright ribbon hatband on his narrow-brimmed straw Stetson. Caine watched him duck into a massage parlour. The sign outside said: WHO SAYS YOU CAN'T HAVE IT BOTH WAYS?

A few minutes later, Genevevo's blue Daytona pulled up. Genevevo got out, looked around casually, and then went inside. The clock superimposed on the top right-hand corner of the frame moved another ten minutes. Then Forsyth came out. Meet concluded, drop made, Caine thought.

'What do we know about Forsyth?' he asked.

'Been down here since '82. The scuttlebutt is he was drinking heavily, and got demoted for insubordination. Around the same time his wife walked out on him. If he'd kept his nose clean he'd probably have his own station by now. But he's too much of a loner. You want me to switch this thing off?'

'It isn't telling us much,' Caine said.

'I know,' Crandon replied gloomily. 'The trouble was, David, you told us to watch Genevevo, not to see if anyone was watching him.'

'Have you got a cigarette?'

'I quit. I thought you did, too.'

'I did,' Caine said. 'Only sometimes I get the urge to — ' He sat up abruptly, staring at the screen. 'Stop the tape!'

'What?'

'Run the film back, Tom. Take it from the sweep of the street, before it picked up Forsyth.'

When making surveillance films, the watchers usually 'swept' the scene, so that the locale could be easily identified.

Caine waited impatiently as Crandon rewound the tape and switched the machine back to play.

'Slow it down when you come to the pan,' Caine said, leaning forward. 'Now . . . wait. There. Freeze it.'

The image on the screen was that of a short, wiry Cuban-American, walking towards the stakeout car. He had long sideburns and a gunfighter moustache.

52

He wore mirror sunglasses, a cheap straw hat with the brim turned down all round, and a pink shirt with a domino motif instead of a breast pocket.

'That shirt,' Caine said. 'That domino shirt. I've seen it before.'

'Jesus!' Crandon said. He knew what that meant. 'Shall I run it through from the beginning?'

'No, wait,' Caine said. 'Give me a minute.'

His head was spinning with the implications of what he had just seen. He pinched the bridge of his nose between his fingers and forced himself to concentrate. 'The art gallery,' he said. 'Go back to the art gallery.'

'Grove House,' Crandon said, snapping his fingers. 'I know the one you mean.'

He pressed the eject button, took out the cassette, slid in another, waited while it sighed metallically into the slot, then put it on fast forward. Figures flickered across the screen like the chases in Keystone Kops one-reelers.

'Here it is,' he said.

'Slow motion,' Caine told him. The

tape advanced jerkily in single frames, the resolution poor. The camera was panning across the junction of Main and Poinciana Avenue. A tan Thunderbird turned into a parking slot a few bays ahead of the vehicle from which the film was being shot. A man got out of the T-Bird and walked towards and past the cameraman's point of view.

'Shit!' Crandon said, disgustedly. 'It's him. Domino Shirt.'

'When was this film shot?'

Crandon looked at the logbook. 'Yesterday morning.'

'Who took it?'

'Butch Young. Len Wurzel was driving.'

'Where are they now?'

'At the apartment. Coral Way Village.'

'Are they armed?'

'What the hell would they be armed for?'

'I think we'd better pull them out, Tom,' Caine said. 'I don't like the way this is shaping up.'

'No sweat,' Crandon said, but he was sweating and so was Caine. He dialled the apartment and let the phone ring just

54

once, then hung up. That would tell his men to leave the place immediately and call in from a public phone as quickly as they could.

They waited.

Nobody called. After ten minutes, Caine stood up.

'We're blown, Tom,' he said.

He grabbed his jacket and the ASP Smith & Wesson M39 combat pistol in its shoulder holster, then ran out of the room and down the stairs, not bothering to wait for the elevator. Behind him he heard Crandon yelling into the phone.

5

The sleek, white Lincoln Continental Mark VII LSC slid on to Broad Causeway and across the narrow neck of Biscayne Bay. It headed through Bay Harbor Islands and on until it reached the ocean at Collins Avenue.

The man in the rear seat was a good-looking Cuban of thirty-two or-three, with dark hair and coffee-coloured skin. He wore a pale blue Gianni Versace cashmere jacket, dark blue slacks of imported mohair, a pale blue open-necked silk shirt with a monogram on the breast pocket, and neat Bruno Magli loafers. On his wrist was a heavy gold Cartier watch with a crocodile strap; round his neck was a fine solid gold chain.

At first glance, he might have been taken for one of the new breed of success-ful Cuban-American entrepreneurs who have grown rich with the Latinization of Miami; he had that same, sleek *made-it*

confidence. But Saturnino Baca was no run-of-the-mill businessman. That was why, nestling in a spring clip beside him in the door recess, was a 9mm Smith & Wesson automatic pistol. All perfectly legal, of course — Florida law permitted residents to carry handguns in their cars — but, in Baca's case, a necessary precaution, even on an errand as ostensibly safe as this. For Saturnino Baca, 'Mr B.' as he was known on Calle Ocho, was head of the most powerful Cuban family in Miami, and his businesses were those of extortion, prostitution and drugs.

The limo rolled on through picture-postcard scenery of languid coconut palms and lush tropical greenery. The sky was a brilliant blue, with hardly a cloud in sight. Past Balfour the driver made a left and came to a stop at the entrance to the Bay Harbor Estate, a palm-thatched wooden gatehouse with a striped pole like a frontier post. A red and white octagonal sign said: STOP HERE.

The security guard came out of the gatehouse. He wore a white shirt with dark blue epaulettes, white slacks and a

white pith helmet. On his left sleeve was a shield-shaped patch which bore the name of the security company he worked for. Around his bulging middle was a tan leather belt and a holster holding a .357 Magnum Mark III Lawman Colt. He bent down as the chauffeur rolled down the tinted window.

'Hi, Chico. Hello, Mr Baca,' he said, touching the brim of his helmet. 'Go right on through. You're expected.'

The man in the back of the car nodded, and they drove on. The whole estate was like a park, maintained without regard for cost. The sidewalks were litter-free, and there were no fallen coconuts or palm fronds in the road. Anti-speed ramps kept the big car to a ten mph crawl. Here and there, sun-stark white walls peeped through high hedges or banks of flowering plants. Once in a while they passed an ornate wrought-iron gate, or a driveway leading towards a large mansion half-hidden behind pal-metto and buttonwood trees.

'You see the piece that asshole at the gate had, Chico?' Baca said to his driver.

'I seen it, Mr B.,' Chico grinned. 'Old fart ever fire that thing, it gonna break his arm.'

The limo turned left into Hibiscus Close, following the road until it ended in a cul-de-sac, then stopped at a pillared gateway. The chauffeur got out, taking a telephone from a recess in the pillar. He listened, spoke, nodded, and put the phone back on the hook. The heavy gates swung open. A CCTV camera watched them as they drove in.

The house was huge, all white, with red roof tiles and green shutters on every window. The drive led to a turning circle with a covered walkway leading to the house. The garage doors were open: inside stood a Mercedes 300SL convertible and a Bentley Mulsanne. A smiling Chinese manservant came out of the house.

'Good day, Mr Baca,' he said. 'This way, please.'

Baca followed him up the walkway, through a foyer, and out to the huge patio at the rear of the house. Wide fieldstone steps sloped gently down from it to an

Olympic-sized swimming pool set among manicured lawns that stretched all the way down to the boat dock fronting the bay. Across the glittering water the skyscrapers of Miami stood stark against the empty sky.

The rear part of the house was a wall of glass, fifty feet wide and eighteen high, open now so that the inside and outside living areas were one. The floor of the enormous room inside was of imported marble. Twelve thousand square feet of house, with four and a half acres of land around it enclosing tennis courts, staff quarters, guest cabins. For a guy who had never taken a risk in his life, Baca thought, Avranilosa was doing all right. His host came out of the living room, a drink in his hand and a smile on his face.

'Nino!' Pedro Avranilosa said. 'Good to see you, *hombre*.'

He was a big man who had gone fat. He had black hair, dark brown eyes and the swarthy skin of a *mestizo*. He wore a LaCoste sport shirt, tan slacks, and Gucci loafers. On his wrist was a solid gold Rolex Explorer. A diamond twinkled on

his ring finger as he beckoned over the waiting houseboy.

'Lemme have a pisco sour,' Baca said. As the servant padded away, Avranilosa waved a hand towards a table and chairs in the shade. They were made of white-painted metal, with brilliantly coloured cushions on the chairs. A huge beach umbrella with the same pattern was angled over the table to keep the sun away.

'Listen, Nino, I want to thank you for coming out here,' Avranilosa said. 'I appreciate it.'

'You said it was urgent.'

'Damn right, it's urgent,' the Fat Man said. 'I got a big problem, Nino. I just found out Tony Genevevo is a cop. A goddamn Fed.'

'What?'

'It's true. That's why I called you.'

'I don't believe this,' Baca said in disgust. 'I don't believe what I'm hearing here. You're telling me the last, what? fifteen, eighteen months, right? the fuckin Feds have had a line in here?'

'Nino, listen to me,' Avranilosa pleaded. 'I know what you're thinking, but it's not

as bad as it looks.'

'You think so?' Baca snarled. 'We're talking a sixty-million-dollar deal, the Feds are listening to every word, but you don't think it's as bad as it looks. Is that what you're saying?'

Avranilosa silently cursed Havana for getting him into this. It was like walking on razor edges. But he danced to Havana's tune just as Havana danced to Moscow's music, and if Moscow wanted this Frederic Drosdow introduced to Baca as a Turkish cocaine dealer working out of Bogotá, Avranilosa didn't have much option but to do it. He had once asked Drosdow what the deal was all about. Drosdow just looked at him. 'You don't need to know that,' he said. 'Just do it.'

'Nino, listen,' Avranilosa said, placatingly. 'I talked to Drosdow. He says if we play this right, it can still go down.'

'Drosdow wants me to buy sixty mill of snow with some fuckin cop takin pictures?' Baca said, angrily. 'What are you, crazy?'

Avranilosa held up a finger as the

Chinese houseboy came out with Baca's drink. They waited until he had gone back into the house.

'When Drosdow told me Genevevo was a Fed, I told him he was out of his tree,' Avranilosa said. 'I brought him in off the street, taught him the business. He was good. You said so yourself, Nino.'

'I know, I know,' Baca said, grudgingly. 'And it was true. I never seen anyone could keep the peace between our people and the Colombians like Tony Genevevo. You say Drosdow fingered him? How the fuck does he know so much?'

'Drosdow said his source was impeccable,' Avranilosa said. 'I couldn't afford not to check it out. I put some of my people on him, and they spotted him making a meet with a CIA field man name of Forsyth. My first instinct was to waste him.'

'Un-hunh,' Baca said. 'The Feds react very bad when one of their people gets blown away.'

'I know. But I figured it was my responsibility. I brought him in. I was still thinking about it when my people picked

up a secondary surveillance.'

'On Genevevo?'

'I didn't believe it myself at first. But it's true: some rent-a-cop outfit called International Security Systems has a team watching Genevevo.'

'What the fuck is this, Pedro? What the fuck is goin on here?'

'I don't know. All I know is somebody's paying a security firm to watch Genevevo. The Feds got more undercover agencies in Florida than the rest of the country put together. It could be anyone: DEA, Task Force, Miami cops, state police . . . '

'It could be Disney fuckin Enterprises,' Baca said, impatiently. He stood up, getting ready to go. 'It doesn't make any difference. You tell Drosdow I'm out, *comprende*?'

'Nino, listen, don't fly off the handle,' Avranilosa said, placatingly. 'Let's try to find a way through this. I talked to Drosdow. He says — '

'Drosdow, Drosdow!' Baca said impatiently. 'That goddamned go-between! What the fuck does he know?'

'Give me a minute,' Avranilosa pleaded.

'A couple of minutes of your time. Is that too much to ask?'

Baca looked at the skyscrapers across the water, as if the view could help him decide. He shrugged, and sat down again.

'All right. What?'

'There's a way through this, Nino. A way we take out Genevevo, shake off these other people, and come out of it clean.'

'He's a Fed. You waste him, they'll take Miami to pieces. Didn't you read about that DEA agent that got killed in Guadalajara?'

'There's a way,' Avranilosa said. 'If you still want to go through with the cocaine deal.'

Avranilosa watched Baca carefully. He knew Baca needed the cocaine deal desperately: the Colombian families were making heavy inroads into what had formerly been exclusively Cuban territory. Baca nodded, indicating he should continue.

'Here's what we do,' he said.

Going slowly, making sure Baca understood every nuance, Avranilosa told Baca

what Frederic Drosdow had instructed him to tell the gang boss. It figured that Genevevo had already passed the word to the Feds that a deal was going down, he said. That was OK: Genevevo didn't know how big the thing was yet. He watched Baca closely as he went on, outlining the way the whole thing could be handled. Baca nodded, wary interest in his eyes. Maybe Drosdow had been right, Avranilosa thought. Maybe Baca would go for it, after all. He'd told Drosdow there wasn't a chance in hell he would, but it was beginning to look like Drosdow had been right and he had been wrong. The trick, Drosdow had told him when they'd discussed the proposition earlier that day, was to tell Baca everything he needed to know, but not everything.

'How will Baca react to the news about Genevevo?' Drosdow had asked.

'He'll want to walk away from the whole deal.'

'That can't be permitted,' Drosdow said, flatly.

'Now all we got to do is convince Baca,' Avranilosa said. Drosdow stared at

him with those empty blue eyes, and Avranilosa instantly regretted his jibe.

'Suppose we terminate Genevevo. Would that satisfy him?'

'Take Genevevo out and you'll have ten thousand cops up your ass before you can say FBI,' Avranilosa said, scornfully.

'Not my way,' Drosdow said.

'What have you got in mind?'

'Chaos,' Drosdow said.

He explained his plan. There was no doubt it would work, he said, if they could get Baca to go for it. As long as the Cubans didn't stage one of those Marielito chainsaw massacres they were so fond of, they could do their deal and walk away from it clean, with no DGI involvement and nothing to tie them to it.

'That's the way I want it,' Drosdow said, as if daring him to argue. 'You sell it to Baca.'

Avranilosa nodded his agreement; not that he had much choice. He wished he had the courage to tell Drosdow to take a flying fuck at a jumping marlin, but he did not dare. One word from this cold-eyed *sinverguenza* and Pedro Avranilosa

would spend the rest of his life cutting sugar cane back on the island.

He did not like Frederic Drosdow, nor did he trust him: if any of this went wrong, it was for Pedro Avranilosa that Saturnino Baca would come looking, not Frederic Drosdow who would by then be long gone. It was quite one thing for Nino to suspect but tolerate his, Avranilosa's, 'connection' to Cuban intelligence in Havana. It would be quite another if he thought he, Baca, was being manipulated by them.

'Well?' he said now, as he finished laying Drosdow's plan out for Baca. 'What do you think?'

'I like it,' Baca said. 'Chaos. That's good. I like it.'

'Do I tell Drosdow to go ahead?'

'Yeah,' Baca said. 'Tell him we can handle our end. Tell him to just make sure he handles his.'

'I'll pass the word,' Avranilosa said, hoping he was concealing his relief. 'How long do you think it will take to set up?'

'Coupla days,' Baca said. He shook his head, chuckling. 'Chaos. You got to hand

it to that fuckin Drosdow. He knows the way we operate.'

If you only knew, Avranilosa thought, remembering how sure Drosdow had been that Baca would take the bait. There was no way you could overestimate a Marielito's greed, Drosdow said. Avranilosa could still hear the contempt in his voice.

6

Crandon's Porsche was an easy car to follow. Caine knew that. He also knew it made him very hard to catch, if he didn't want to be caught. It was about three times faster off the mark than an American car, particularly one as soft-sprung and power-steered as the Buick Electra which was following him now.

Just past Flagler Memorial Park, SW55th Avenue Road cut diagonally away to the left. Caine made the left and rolled down to a junction where six streets met: 56th going north-south, 2nd going east-west, and the road he was on cutting diagonally across the intersection. He stopped at the junction and checked his mirror, smiling as he saw the Buick coast to a stop by the kerb a hundred yards back.

He put the Porsche into gear, floored the gas pedal and spun the wheel, using the handbrake to execute a 135-degree

turn on to 56th Avenue, pointing north. A block up, he turned left on to 1st Street and then left again on 57th going south. He was half a mile away before the driver of the Buick even worked out which way he might have gone. At the bottom of Red Road — the old name for 57th — he turned right into 40th, sped past Tropical Park Garden, and took 75th across the canal and on to the manmade island.

He drove as slowly as a pensioner towards the apartment block on SW72nd Court, half-expecting to encounter flashing police lights. It was early evening, and apart from a mother pushing a baby buggy loaded with groceries, the street was empty. The curtains in the first-floor apartment were still drawn. Young's VW Rabbit was still in its slot.

Caine got out of the car, leaving it open. Nothing for it but a blind walk-in, he decided. If there were Foreigners in the apartment, he would have to handle it. He glanced at his watch: seven ten. He unbuttoned his jacket for easier access to the shoulder holster, then went into the building. The apartment was on the right

at the head of the stairs. Using his own keys, he opened the door.

Silence.

Easing his ASP out of its holster, Caine moved into the corridor which bisected the apartment. The door of the living room was on his right. Taking a deep breath, he grasped the handle firmly, then went in all at once, fast and low and with the gun up ready.

There was no one there.

He stood upright, his breath coming raggedly now in the reaction. There were no signs of a struggle. The surveillance equipment was all where it was supposed to be. He checked the videotape boxes. They were all empty, as were the tape spools on the Akai. There was no film in any of the cameras.

Swiftly, silently, he checked the other rooms. All were empty, their tidiness mocking him. He went to the window and checked the street outside. It would not be long before whoever had been tailing him figured out his probable destination. They might have even put a beeper on the car: he'd had no time to check.

He ran downstairs and got into the Porsche, driving as fast as he dared off the island and down to Bird Road, the local name for 40th Street. He pulled into a Mobil station and ran for the phone booth.

'Any word?'

'All hell's broken loose, David,' Crandon replied. 'Where are you?'

'Near Tropical Park. Tell me.'

'Genevevo's been lifted.'

'What? When was this?'

'Couple hours back, near his home. Six heavies, all Cuban. They were driving — '

'Never mind that!' Caine said. 'Who's on them?'

'Pete Lavery,' Crandon told him. 'He just called in. Says they took Genevevo to a warehouse up near the airport. Acme Novelty, 1888 Northwest 29th Street.'

'Tom, the shit's hit it. The apartment has been sanitized. No sign of our people.'

'Jesus, David, you think — ?'

'I'll back up Lavery,' Caine said.

'I'll meet you there.'

'No, Tom!' Caine said. 'Stay put!' He

hung up before Crandon could argue. He ran for the Porsche and burned rubber getting back on the street. When Crandon thought about it, he would realize he had to stay where he was: with both of them on the street, no one at ISS would know what was going on. He drove fast and decisively, praying no rookie cop with a low arrest record would pick him up. Heavy traffic in Coral Gables slowed him down, and he cursed in frustration, willing himself back under control. The easiest way to total a motor was to drive with your teeth clamped together.

He turned north on Douglas and was able to make better time on the wide avenue. Off to his left the lights of the hospital gleamed brightly in the growing twilight. He turned left at the Tamiami bridge and saw the frontage of the Sheraton River House looming up ahead. On his right lay an industrial area, with single-storey units that housed building firms, cleaning companies and storage warehouses, all girded by the tracks of the Seaboard Coast Line railroad.

He parked the Porsche out of sight

behind a building and walked up to 29th Street, keeping in the shadows. The street was deserted and dark, except for one building on the opposite side. Acme Novelty, he read on the sign above the entrance.

A small sound caught his attention, and he saw Lavery in the dark entrance to a garage alongside an office building. The agent was wearing a Parrot Jungle T-shirt, oil-stained chino pants, battered Nike training shoes, and a plastic baseball cap from Disney World. Lavery, a thin-faced beanpole of a man, looked and sounded like anything but what he was, a *cum laude* graduate of the University of Miami who had chosen security work in preference to being the token black in a WASP practice.

'They're in there, boss,' he said, pointing at the lighted windows on the second floor of the Acme Novelty building.

'How many of them?'

'Six in the car. Other cars there already. What's happenin, man?'

'They took Genevevo in there?'

'Right. He was in no shape to argue.'

'You didn't see anyone else?'

'Like who?'

'Lennie Wurzel and Butch Young are missing.'

Caine scanned the building opposite, wishing there was something he could do. A shotgun mike would have been useful; at least they might have been able to hear what was going on inside. As it was, there was no way of getting closer to the Acme building without being spotted.

'Got any suggestions, Pete?'

'Bet your ass,' Lavery said, his teeth gleaming in the darkness. 'Let's get the fuck outa here.'

'You looked around already?'

'Some,' Lavery said. 'Nothin special about the place. It's L-shaped, long side facing the street. Parking in back, seven foot wire fence topped with barbed wire in back of that. Freight yard beyond it. See that furniture place next door? There's a alley runs between the two buildings, used as a freight entrance. Dead end. That's it.'

It was black dark now. Once in a while a big jet roared up into the sky from

Miami International, its navigation lights winking like moving stars. An hour went by. Nothing happened.

'I could kill for coffee,' Lavery said.

'Where's your car?'

'End of the street, near Lejeune.' He pronounced it Lee-June, Miami-style. They fell silent. The lights of the office across the street seemed artificially bright. The windows were curtained with white nylon net. Caine looked at his watch. Nearly ten.

'We got action!' Lavery hissed urgently.

A man came out of the Acme building. He could not see them. He went around the back, and they heard a car start up. Lights sliced through the darkness. Genevevo's Daytona swung into the dead-end alley. They heard the *graaack* of the emergency brake. The driver got out, leaving the headlights on, and went back into the building. A few minutes later the lights in the upstairs offices went out. The watchers heard voices, footsteps. The doors were opened, and they saw Young and Wurzel being frog-marched into the alley where the Daytona was parked.

When they got into the beam of the headlights the watchers could see blood on Young's face. Wurzel was slumped in the grip of the two men holding his arms.

Next, two men came out of the building carrying a body. One of them opened the driver's door of the Daytona and put the limp figure in the driving seat. It did not move.

'That's Genevevo!' Lavery hissed.

'I count nine of them, Pete,' Caine said. The ASP held seven rounds. He knew Lavery was not armed. There probably wasn't a telephone nearer than six blocks away.

'We got to do some — '

The sound of a single pistol shot silenced him. One of the Cubans had shot Genevevo through the forehead. Almost simultaneously, another shot was fired. Wurzel was slammed back against the wall of the building, then slid down it into a sitting sprawl, dead before he stopped moving. Young made a clumsy grab at the man with the gun. The man shot him, too hastily. The bullet tore through Young's throat, smacking him sideways off his

feet, kicking and flopping like a gutshot squirrel. The assassin skipped back to avoid being spattered with blood.

'Jesus Christ!' Lavery muttered.

'OK, let's go!' someone shouted. They ran out of the alley and into the parking lot. Car doors slammed; then two cars lurched out of the lot and turned on the deserted street. Their headlights swept over the prone bodies of Caine and Lavery, flat on their bellies in a patch of scrub.

'I got the lead car,' Caine said, memorizing its licence number, knowing Lavery would do the same with the second. Tail lights glowed briefly as the two cars braked on the corner of Lejeune. Then they were gone. Cicadas burred again in the warm darkness.

'Come on,' Caine said, urgently. 'We can't get ourselves tied into this, Pete.'

'What about Wurzel and Young? What about Genevevo?'

'They're dead,' Caine said harshly. 'There's nothing we can do for them.'

'And that's it? You just going to leave them there?'

'I'll call the police first chance I get,' Caine said. 'You get back to town and tell Tom Crandon exactly what happened. Tell him to get a make on those two cars. I'll contact him tomorrow. Got that?'

'Jesus fuckin Christ,' Lavery breathed. 'You cold-hearted bastard!'

Caine looked at Lavery for a moment, then shrugged. 'Let's go,' he said.

7

By the time Dade County's finest reached the scene of the killings — tipped off by an anonymous phone call — all three corpses had been stripped. The guns, of course, were gone. Wallets, credit cards, everything. The trunk of Genevevo's Daytona had been prised open, the spare wheel and the tools taken. The thieves had even taken the shoes off the dead men's feet. None of that surprised the prowl car boys. There were street vultures in Miami that made the ones in the Everglades look like lovebirds.

The Blues found Genevevo lying half in and half out of his car, and most of his brains on the rear window. Sprawled on the ground nearby was the body of another man. A third lay crumpled against the wall of the alley, between Acme Novelty and the Merritt Furniture Repository.

The two men were identified by their

fingerprints as Leonard Wurzel and Robert Young, employees of a Miami company called International Security Systems. Each of them had been shot once: Wurzel through the upper chest just above the heart, and Young through the throat. The ME's report said that Wurzel would have died almost instantly, whereas Young might have lived two or three minutes after he was shot. Preliminary ballistics findings indicated that two weapons had been used: both .38s.

The physical evidence posited the following scenario: Genevevo had met the two security men in the alley, possibly to consummate a drug sale — there were traces of cocaine on the carpets of the Daytona. A shootout had ensued, in which Genevevo killed Wurzel and fatally wounded Young without being hit. Then somehow Young, bleeding like a stuck pig, had put a bullet through Genevevo's head at close range.

Thomas Crandon, who ran the Miami branch of the security firm, said his people had been on a simple surveillance case in Coral Gables. The client was a

major credit company. He knew of no reason why his men should have met with Genevevo, who formed no part of their investigation. As for the shooting: it was against ISS policy for its personnel to carry firearms, although all were licensed to do so. He was shocked by what had happened, he said. It made no sense at all.

'No sense?' Frank Forsyth said, throwing the police dossier he'd 'borrowed' on the floor in disgust. 'Goddammit, it sucks!'

Damned if he didn't sometimes wish he was a thousand miles away from Miami, away from his chief of station Donald Bensen and, most of all, away from the drug scene. For all the newspaper headlines, drugs were at the not-very-important end of Company business: the CIA was spending more on covert operations in Afghanistan than the entire federal anti-drugs budget. So being at the not-very-important end of drug investigating did not carry a hell of a lot of clout at best, and if you were Frank Forsyth, even less.

He had been transferred to Miami in 1982, part of Shotgun Reagan's high-profile Operation Thunderbolt, 'the most massive war on drugs ever seen'. It had involved teaming army, naval and air force intelligence, Pentagon spy planes, the FBI, the DEA, and God alone knew who else. The thunderbolt had turned out to be a wet wick; far from wiping out the drug traffic, it seemed to have had the opposite effect. What had been a thirty billion dollar industry in 1981 was now estimated to be turning over four times that amount. Trying to stamp it out was like trying to put out Hell with a bucket of spit. The men who controlled the drug rackets could buy the goddamned world and still have change. Whoever they couldn't bribe or buy outright, they simply ran right over. Which, Forsyth was certain, was what had happened to Tony Genevevo.

For the past year and a half Genevevo had been working undercover, feeding information on Avranilosa's Cuban intelligence contacts and narcotics dealings through Forsyth to Domestic Operations

in Washington. Forsyth had put up the proposition that the Fat Man was high enough in DGI's Cuban hierarchy to be worth trying to 'double', and Tony had gone in undercover to send out enough information to make it possible. Somehow, God alone knew how, his cover had been blown, and now he was dead. And no matter what the police report said, Forsyth knew whose finger had been on the trigger.

Well, that was Pedro Avranilosa's mistake. When Forsyth had first come to Miami, embittered at what he still felt had been an unfair demotion, the only human being he found in the entire regional organization was Tony Genevevo, big, lanky Tony who'd buy him a drink, agree with him that Donald Bensen was full of what made the grass grow green, then take him off to some Cuban bordello and get him laid. He figured he owed Tony, and he planned to pay off.

He picked up the report Mickey Garrity down at police headquarters had copied for him, found his place again and read the rest. A check had been made on

Crandon's story, of course, and it held up. ISS had been employed by a New York credit company to report on a number of Miami corporations which were being remiss in loan payments. The list of the companies involved provided no clues. Until somebody could prove otherwise, they were clean.

There was a missing factor someplace, Forsyth thought. Like a signpost in a fog: it was there but he just couldn't see it. Any way you examined the killings, they came out looking like an execution. And if it had been an execution, it had to be Avranilosa's people who had carried it out. He could see where they might kill Genevevo if somehow they found out he was a cop. So Question Number One was, how did they find out? And Question Number Two was, why ice the security men?

Forsyth didn't do many things by the book, but this time he did. He handed the case over to the Sewer Squad, leaving that unsung Company department to tidy up the mess. They would liaise with the Miami police, take care of the funeral

arrangements, tie up the loose ends. Anyone on the team killed in the line of duty was always decently taken care of. Meanwhile, he had things to do.

Forsyth knew his reputation as a maverick was not entirely unjustified. He preferred working outside the system because he knew how the system worked, and how it worked was inefficiently. The system was in the hands of people like his Chief of Station, Donald Bensen, who would trade ten men like Genevevo for a jacket commendation, and sell his grandmother to a Chilean whoremaster for an overseas posting. So although Genevevo's murder had set off one of the biggest police operations in Miami history, Forsyth wasn't optimistic about the possible results. If anyone had asked him, he'd have told them not to waste their time. The police could question every deadbeat in the sovereign State of Florida and they'd get no nearer to Tony's executioners than they were right now. Forsyth planned to kill his own snakes.

He admitted — to himself, no one else, and especially not Bensen — that he'd

been worried about Genevevo. Tony had been 'out' a long time and, latterly, he hadn't been delivering the way he was supposed to. Forsyth had covered for him, wondering whether it was the right thing to do, but understanding better than most the pressures Genevevo was under.

There was a hell of a difference between how you lived on government pay and how you lived working for the Fat Man. Working for Avranilosa got you a fancy pad in Kendall, a white Mercedes convertible, a boat, a plane, and all the pussy you wanted to stroke. Working for Avranilosa got you reservations in fancy beachside restaurants where fawning maître d's greeted you by name and told you how happy they were to see you. It got harder and harder to remember you were a cop, dedicated to bringing all this down on the heads of the people you were sharing it with. The last time they'd talked, Forsyth remembered wondering: does he *want* to come out?

Can he?

Genevevo's assignment was simple: to

catch the Fat Man with his feet in the snow, then turn him around. Threaten to take away the house in Bal Harbor, the lithe young Cuban waiters he liked to entertain there; promise him twelve to twenty in the black wing at Tallahassee; and he'd crack. With the Fat Man in their pockets, they might be able to infiltrate DGI operations in Miami and south-east Florida, roll up Avranilosa's drug interests, and maybe as a bonus get an inside line on what the Comrades were up to in other parts of the country.

That was the proposition before Genevevo was killed. Go on, say it, Forsyth told himself: shot in the head, executed, assassinated. That was what didn't make sense. Espionage agencies went to extreme lengths to avoid assassination. Killing the other side's men threw a monkey wrench into the machinery: the game wasn't played that way. Counterespionage was a *react* discipline. You watched your quarry, waited till he made an overt move; then you responded to it. That way you found out whether his move had been made to provoke yours, or not. When you knew

that, you watched and waited to see what he would do next. According to what it was, you reacted again; and so on. Chess, played with live pawns.

And now dead ones, Forsyth thought.

Of course, he knew what Bensen, his Chief of Station, would say: that irrespective of Genevevo's death, their aims remained the same, to find a way of compromising Avranilosa and, if he really was working for DGI, to turn him. He would consider Forsyth's personal involvement unwise and unprofessional, so Forsyth had no intention of letting Bensen know how he felt.

Before he did anything else, however, Forsyth needed to know whether he, too, had been blown. Unlikely as it was, he took all the routine precautions. He closed down his apartment in Coral Gables and checked into the Holiday Inn at the Civic Center under the name of Cecil Smith. He verified with the Sewer Squad that the house on South Lake Drive and Genevevo's car had been properly vacuumed. They hadn't found anything, but then they hadn't expected

to. Their job was to make sure there was nothing there for anyone else to find.

After two days, during which the watchers in Coral Gables reported nil activity, he called them off. He had anyway decided to abandon that possibly compromised identity. In due course the apartment would be put up for sale by a Company realty front, and the neighbours would be told of an unexpected transfer abroad. The Joe Roberts who had lived there briefly would soon be forgotten.

Next, Forsyth checked with his Chief of Station, Donald Bensen. Given the choice, he would rather have eaten glass, but he knew if he wanted to get back in harness, he had to have Bensen's clearance. He called the office on Brickell Avenue.

'What have you got in mind?' Bensen asked.

'Among other things, I want to check out this security firm.'

'Haven't the police done that?'

'Not the way I'll do it,' Forsyth said.

'You think there's something there?'

'I don't know where else to look.'

'All right,' Bensen said. 'I'll get you operational clearance.' He sounded reluctant. Maybe he thinks he's doing me a favour, Forsyth thought.

ISS was as good a place to start as any. He recalled the old Company saying: if God had expected you to know all the answers, he wouldn't have invented Head Office. Smiling at the thought, he sat down to compile a shopping list. He used the same pay phone to dictate it to a coding clerk at Vanguard. Within an hour, it was being transmitted via the CIA's protected computer circuit to the office of the Divisional Director of Domestic Operations Division on Pennsylvania Avenue in Washington, DC.

8

Forsyth's signal was logged on the Domestic Operations computer at 11.04 and sent immediately to the office of the Divisional Director. A simultaneous print-out at CIA headquarters on its wooded 125-acre site at Langley, eight miles from the capital, was taken by internal courier to the office of the Area Divisional Controller. This procedure, in Langley as at the Pennsylvania Avenue building which housed Domestic Operations Division, in-volved the negotiation of numerous gates guarded by Internal Security officers in bulletproof glass kiosks. At these gates, each courier's ID badge was carefully checked for the appropriate security clearances.

On receipt, Forsyth's requests were graded for priority and authorization; since they appeared mainly routine, they were rerouted from the office of the Director to the Coordinator of Information, Stephen Greene. Greene was a suntanned man of fifty-nine

with neat, unsmiling features and iron-grey eyes which occasionally — but only occasionally — betrayed a faint hint of amusement. He did not drink anything stronger than tea. He smoked three cigarettes a day, no more, no less. He ran five miles every morning without fail.

Forsyth's signal was just one of many requiring his authorization that day. Immediately after he finished reading it, Greene picked up the direct phone link and spoke to his opposite number in Clandestine Services. CICS said he knew of no reason why the information should not be made available to Miami, whereupon Greene endorsed Forsyth's request for action and passed it to the Office of Communications in its IBM-designed underground bunker.

A copy was also sent to Intelligence Requirements Service, a division of the Directorate of Intelligence, asking for their input. By three that afternoon, the computers had correlated and printed out their information, ready for pre-transmission coding prior to being sent to Forsyth in Florida. The dossier was then

directed to the Pre-Transmission Coding (PTC) Section, where it arrived finally on the desk of Paul Bogdanovich, the senior of three coding clerks in office PTC/D/ 2857 on Level Four. Bogdanovich set to work immediately.

After first keying in the secret access codes which would protect the computer transmission, he began enciphering the dossier. It was a long and boring job, but all of Bogdanovich's work was boring, if you cared to look at it that way. He did not. There was always the element of the unexpected in PTC. And always the strange, inexplicable satisfaction of watching the powerful computers turn page after page of secret text into something that might easily have been Martian.

The material he was handling today was of more than usual interest. It was generally understood that the CIA was not permitted to operate within the United States, although in fact anyone with the slightest knowledge of intelligence operations knew this was nonsense. A whole area division, Domestic Operations, conducted clandestine activities in

the United States, not overseas. Exactly what those activities were was classified information; and, because he knew this, Bogdanovich's interest was immediately aroused. He was further intrigued by Forsyth's request for a full personnel breakdown on a British-owned security company operating in Miami. A familiar thrill of nervous anticipation coursed through his body as it always did at times like these.

He worked steadily until he had completed coding all the documents. When this was done, he picked up the phone on his desk and dialled the office of the Co-ordinator of Information, which gave him clearance to transmit to Miami. As soon as the transmission was effected and acknowledged, the computer memory was to be cleared and the unenciphered originals returned to their various points of origin.

While the computer hummed and buzzed, transmitting direct to Miami, Bogdanovich prepared security folders with Alpha Black tabs denoting the security rating of the material they would

contain. He then took the working papers he had used to encipher the dossier and pushed them into the shredder, watching impassively as they turned into paper spaghetti. Without haste or hesitation he took the unenciphered dossier and slid it into his briefcase. Into the security folders he had earlier prepared he now placed a set of completely unrelated documents. He placed the folders in his Out tray for courier pickup and pressed the button which would summon the messenger. A few minutes later the courier arrived, signed for the documents, and hurried away. Bogdanovich looked at the clock. His shift would be ending in an hour and twenty minutes.

He waited until Miami acknowledged that the transmission had been received and safely stored, then punched the keys on his pad to clear the computer's memory. He continued working steadily until the bell that marked the end of the second of the day's three shifts rang, a frown of concentration on his face. He went through his end-of-shift routine carefully, as if it were for the first time.

He put all his disks, papers and codebooks into the safe behind his desk, spinning the dials of the combination lock. He checked that the disk slots in the computer were empty, and the memory cleared. He then switched off the machine and locked it. Next he locked his desk. His two colleagues were doing the same thing.

'You wanna get a beer after work, Paul?' Marty Fielder asked him. Fielder was a tall, slat-thin man whose clothes always looked a size too big for him. He had worked in the same office as Bogdanovich for about six years. They usually played racketball on the Thursdays when they weren't on night swing. The third clerk, Harry Tracy, was a relative newcomer. He wasn't much of a talker. He looked up with interest when Fielder issued his invitation, as though hoping it included him.

'Can't tonight, Marty,' Bogdanovich said. He stretched his arms above his head, watching as Fielder and Tracy went through the same end-of-shift routine he had observed. He was tall, thin, and

weedy and his complexion was bad. He looked like what he was, a man with a sedentary job who spent most of his time indoors, and got nothing like enough exercise. 'I'm taking Eva to dinner.'

'You celebrating something?'

'Yeah,' Bogdanovich grinned. 'She gets paid today.'

They swapped gossip while they waited for the security officer to come and check them out, as he did every half hour or so. Anyone who left classified material unsecured got a VC in his jacket. So did the person in the office designated to check the others. That was why Bogdanovich always worked so methodically. The last thing he wanted in his personal file was a Violation Chit.

When the security officer had finished his perfunctory inspection and cleared them to leave, Bogdanovich and Fielder rode up to ground level in the elevator.

'Where you eating?' Fielder asked.

'Going to try a French place on 20th, Le Provençal. I'm told it's good.'

'I'm told it's expensive,' Fielder said. 'Maybe I oughta send Janie out to work,

we could join you.'

They passed out through the security gate, smiling at Charlie, the pot-bellied guard, who checked their passes. Bogdanovich said so-long to his colleague and walked across the parking lot to the numbered slot where his Toyota Tercel was parked. He drove to the gate of the compound where he again showed his ID to a security guard. The man hardly looked at it. He was there to stop people getting in, not to stop people getting out. Bogdanovich thanked him impassively and said good-night, even though his shirt was wet with sweat as he drove out.

On his way home to Pimmit Hills, he stopped for gas at an Amoco station on Route 650. While the attendant filled the tank and checked the oil, Bogdanovich made a call from the pay phone alongside the cashier's desk. He paid cash for the gas and drove on home. He did not put the car away when he got there. Eva came out to meet him. She got home before he did when he was on this shift.

'Hi,' he said, kissing her. 'Had a good day?'

'Not bad,' she said. 'Old Appleby was being a pain as usual. Otherwise fine.'

She was short, dark and, if not pretty, then so vivacious that people thought her attractive. She worked in a downtown ad agency. Bogdanovich put his arm round her waist and they went indoors. Eva had opened a bottle of Chablis. They poured two glasses and clinked them: their evening ritual.

'Ah,' he said. He took off his jacket and put it carefully on a hanger, which he then hung in the hall closet.

'I was looking at those garage doors, Paul,' Eva said. 'We're really going to have to do something about them.'

'We?' he grinned, leaning back on the sofa.

'You,' she said. 'You never do anything around the place.'

'Tomorrow,' he said. 'I'm taking you out tonight.'

'I bought pot roast.'

'Put it in the freezer. Tonight we dine de-luxe.'

'What's the occasion?'

'The anniversary of the invention of the

corkscrew,' he said. 'I just feel like eating out, OK?'

'OK,' she said, smiling. 'What time do you want to leave?'

'I've made a reservation for eight. I've got a couple of things to do. Work things. They won't take long. We'll leave around seven thirty, OK?'

'Do I dress up?'

'Put on that pink suit,' he said. 'I like that.'

'Where are we going?'

'That's for me to know,' he grinned. 'And you to find out.'

He finished his wine and then went into the little study on the far side of the hall. He drew the blind and switched on the tungsten lamp standing at one side of the desk. From his briefcase he took out the dossier he had earlier transmitted to Miami. Using a Minox ultra-compact 35GT camera, he carefully photographed every page twice. When he was finished, he put the dossier back into his briefcase. Tomorrow, when he went to work, he would discover his silly 'mistake' — an inadvertent substitution of one set of

papers for another — and send the correct dossier across to IR, explaining that it had been locked in his safe all night. It wouldn't even cause a raised eyebrow: such things happened all the time.

He took the roll of film out of the Minox and put the camera away. Next he took a pack of Lark cigarettes from his breast pocket, emptied it out, and put the roll of film into the pack. Then he put back as many cigarettes as would comfortably fit, putting the rest into a cigarette box on the desk.

He went into the bedroom. Eva was drying her hair. He took off his clothes, showered, shaved and got dressed. He decided to wear the dark blue lightweight mohair suit he'd bought at Wallachs on Fifth Avenue last time he was in New York. By the time he put on his jacket and tie, Eva was ready. She was wearing the pink Jaeger suit with a navy-blue polka dot blouse.

'Yum, yum,' he said, rolling his eyes.

'Oh, you!' Eva said.

The restaurant was a large, split-level

place with ceiling beams that radiated from a central point like the spokes of a great wheel. A collection of framed celebrity photographs and certificates from travel magazines flanked the doorway. The chill of the air-conditioning was like a blanket of cold. There were paintings on the walls of nymphs and shepherds.

They ate onion soup and steak *au poivre*. Bogdanovich ordered a bottle of Zinfandel. It was ten forty-five when he called for the check, and almost exactly eleven when they left the restaurant.

'That was lovely,' Eva said, contentedly. 'But I ate too much.'

'You always say that,' he said.

At that moment, a man came hurrying along, head down. He did not seem to see Bogdanovich, who held up his hands to fend the man off.

'Hey, watch it, Jack!' he snapped, angrily.

'Sorry, pal,' the man grunted. 'Din see ya.' He hurried away. Bogdanovich watched him go, feigning anger, then walked around the car and unlocked it.

'Are you all right?' Eva asked.

'Yes,' he said. 'Fine.'

'Want me to drive?'

'It's all right,' he said, and smiled to show her he was no longer angry. 'Get in.'

They drove past the Kennedy Center and across Roosevelt bridge. He pushed a cassette into the player, and the gentle voice of Karen Carpenter filled the car. Eva smiled: they would make love when they got home, she decided.

She had absolutely no idea of what had happened outside the restaurant on 20th Street. In the brief moment they had been in contact, Bogdanovich had passed the Lark pack containing the film to the man who had jostled him. By now, he imagined, it would already be in the hands of Stepan Lykov, his case officer at the Russian Embassy.

He smiled. Money in the bank, he thought, and put his hand on his wife's thigh. She put her hand on top of his and held it there. Karen Carpenter began to sing a rainbow.

9

During the three days following the killings David Caine spoke to Tom Crandon only once. His first priority, as he saw it, was to establish a new cover. That wasn't something you could do overnight, or alone. After he had called the police from the phone booth on Lejeune, Caine went directly to the River House. He had swapped cars with Lavery, who had taken the Porsche back to town, and reported to Crandon. Next morning, Lavery came back out to the River House in a cab to pick up his own car. At the same time, he dropped off the ISS PAPD — a people and places digest of the surveillance dossier on Genevevo — for Caine.

After five hours' fitful sleep, Caine picked up the dossier at reception, checked out of the hotel and got a ride in the hotel bus to the airport. From there he took a cab into town, telling the driver

he wanted to go to the Omni International. The man's expression of terminal boredom changed to cupidity.

'You want I should take the Expressway?' he said. 'Drops you right down on Biscayne.'

'Gosh,' Caine said. 'You know the way.'

It was a cheap shot, and he regretted making it the moment the words left his lips. Everybody hustles; it was the American way, and only a jerk complained, right? He heard the man mutter something uncomplimentary under his breath. Ah, well, he thought, there goes another potentially rewarding relationship. Ignoring the driver's surliness, he concentrated instead on the options he had left. There weren't too damned many.

First, it was logical to assume that Genevevo's case officer, Forsyth, would go after ISS like a coyote after a rabbit, the firm's Alpha-Alpha-Seven security clearance and friend-of-the-Company status notwithstanding. It would not take Forsyth long to establish that Wurzel and Young had been operating in Genevevo's backyard and, when he did, he was going to wonder why Tom Crandon had told the police the two

agents were working on an unrelated case. Which meant the next priority was taking Crandon out of the line of fire before that happened. And Crandon wasn't going to like that one damned bit. Well, tough!

The Omni complex was a ten-acre sprawl of boutiques, shops and movie theatres, restaurants, tennis courts, swimming pools and playgrounds, all topped off with a five-storey atrium in the new God-how-do-they-do-that? style of construction which is to architects what Oscars are to movie stars.

Caine checked into the hotel and, for a daily rate not much less than he had paid for the first car he ever owned, was given a room on the fourteenth floor. Everything in it was colour co-ordinated, modern and pseudo-luxurious. To Caine's eye, it had about as much personality as an egg carton. He picked up the telephone and called Memphis. The ISS specialist there was a lanky, slow-spoken Mississippian named Geoff Beale. Caine wasted no time in small talk.

'I'm at the Omni International in Miami. We've got problems here. Advise

Arlington I'm off the air until further notice.'

'You got it,' Beale said. 'Anything else?'

'I need a new set of clothes. Get over here as soon as you can.'

'There's a flight around four,' Beale said. 'I'll be on it. What name are you using?'

'Philip Howard.'

'Long stay, or short?'

'Depends.'

'Always admired decisive men,' Beale said. 'See you tonight.'

Next, Caine called Tom Crandon. He did not think he was taking too much of a chance, but even though he was fairly sure he hadn't been followed to the hotel and knew Crandon would sweep the office phones hourly in case the Company was bugging them, he avoided using his name.

'I've changed my address,' Caine said. 'And I'm getting a new set of clothes from Memphis.'

'Two smart moves. You're doing well.' In the jargon a new set of clothes was a legend, a completely new identity. 'What

do you want me to do?'

'Meet me at Rendezvous Two. Can you make noon plus one?' The phrase 'plus one' meant tomorrow and not, as any listener might assume, one p.m.

'You got the digest OK?'

'Sure.'

'Watch your ass.'

'I'll do my best.'

The rest of the day Caine stayed in his room, going over the surveillance reports on Tony Genevevo until the print blurred before his eyes. He stood for a long time by the window, looking down at the streets below where ordinary people were going about their everyday business, selling soap, buying clothes, drinking coffee, planning trips. He wondered whether any of them gave so much as a moment's thought to men like Tony Genevevo. Not hardly, as John Wayne used to say.

He had some lunch sent up, then returned to the dossier, studying it assiduously. There was nothing else he could do until Geoff Beale got in with the documents and accessories that would

provide him with a new identity. Genevevo's range of contacts had been wide: it would be hell's own job checking them all out. But there was one name that kept recurring, and he made a note of it: Lynda Sanchez, an address in Kendall, manageress of La Paloma restaurant on Key Biscayne. Genevevo had been a frequent visitor at both places. Caine put the woman high on his list of people to see.

Shortly after seven, reception called to say Geoff Beale had arrived. Caine told them to send him right up. As soon as the door closed behind him, Beale got straight down to business.

'Got you everything you asked for,' he said, lifting the small suitcase he had brought with him on to the bed. 'Clothes, car, new ID. That's the good news.'

'And the bad news?'

Beale tossed an envelope on to the writing table. Caine picked it up and opened it. Inside was a folded telex form addressed to the Memphis office. He read what it said: 'CAINE: KEEP ME INFORMED YOUR LOCATION AT ALL TIMES. REPORT

DIRECT TO ME BY LANDLINE ON UNLISTED NUMBERS MINIMUM TWICE DAILY NO EXCEPTIONS NO EXCUSES.'

It was signed, 'Kingly'.

'Boola boola,' Caine said. 'You eaten, Geoff?'

'On the plane.'

'Want a drink?'

'Why not?'

Beale collapsed into one of the armchairs like a shot heron, his long legs crossed. Caine got two miniature bottles of whisky out of the mini-bar and poured the golden liquid into glasses.

'Here's lookin at you, kid,' Beale said. 'You want to talk?'

Caine shrugged. 'There isn't all that much to say. I'm still trying things on to see if they fit. There's something about all this that gives me a bad feeling.'

'Go on.'

'The man Genevevo was working for, Pedro Avranilosa, is probably a Cuban agent of some kind. Let's suppose he found out somehow that Genevevo was a plant. He wouldn't be able to act independently, and I can't believe even

112

DGI would be dumb enough to sanction the assassination of a Federal agent. Even if they were dumb enough, why would they go after our people? It doesn't make any sense at all.'

'Maybe our people saw something DGI didn't want them to see.'

'That's possible. All their surveillance tapes and photographs were gone. Always supposing it was DGI who took them.'

'Who else would want them?'

'Someone who wanted us to think DGI. Whoever really did the shooting.'

'Someone like who?'

'I don't know. That whole business out there near the airport was set up to look as if Genevevo, Wurzel and Young had a shootout. Why go to so much trouble if all you want to do is take them out of the picture?'

'Maybe DGI wanted it to look like a gang shooting because, that way, there'd be no heat from the Feds about Genevevo's death.'

Caine shook his head in exasperation. 'There'd be heat from the Feds no matter which way it went down. There's an

element missing, Geoff, and I can't get a handle on it.'

'Maybe Crandon will come up with something.'

'Maybe,' Caine said.

Twelve hours later, he was still brooding about the slayings he had witnessed, trying to make sense of something that only made sense in a way he didn't choose to accept. Well, maybe Geoff Beale had been right, he thought. Maybe Tom Crandon would come up with something. He drew the drapes and looked out of the window. It was a bright sunny day. Surprise, surprise.

He went down to street level and picked up a copy of *Newsweek* at the newsstand. He dawdled for a while, watching people come and go. The people who had lifted Genevevo were Cuban, or Cuban-American. So were the men who had done the killings out near the airport. So were a lot of the people milling around the Omni complex. So what? A lot of them were fat; that didn't mean anything, either. It was impossible to be certain no one was watching him. In the end, Caine

said the hell with it, and went into the coffee shop for breakfast.

At eleven thirty, he went across to the elevators and rode up to the third floor. Nobody else got out with him. He walked down the stairs to the lobby and out into the street. Nobody took any notice of him. Nobody came after him. He flagged a cab and headed for the meet.

Long ago, he and Crandon had set up a series of prearranged meeting places they could refer to by number for maximum security. Rendezvous Two was the 16th Avenue entrance to the Orange Bowl Stadium. He had been waiting only a couple of minutes when Crandon eased up to the sidewalk in a beaten-up, anonymous-looking LTD. Caine got in, and Crandon gunned the car into the traffic, driving north on 18th.

'Nice car,' Caine said.

'Thought the Porsche might be a tad conspicuous,' Crandon grinned.

'Where is it?'

'Pete Lavery's driving it around,' Crandon grinned. 'Trying to attract attention.'

'You haven't got a tail?'

'Haven't seen anything. I took the usual precautions.'

'Keep your eyes skinned,' Caine said.

'Amen,' Crandon said. 'You see the paper?'

'I saw it,' Caine said, tossing his copy of the morning paper on to the rear seat. The headline glared at him: 'Police Still without Leads in Mystery Shootings'. 'You heard from the boys in blue, of course?'

'They were banging on my door ten minutes after they got a make from the Bureau.'

'What did you tell them?'

'Just what it says in the paper. Lennie and Butch were on a simple surveillance job. They had no reason to know or meet with Genevevo.'

'How long will it stick?'

'A little while, as long as it's only local police asking. We really are doing some work for Mercantile & Industrial of New York.' Crandon threaded the big car expertly through the traffic. 'Where we going, by the way?'

'Anywhere they got Rolling Rock.'

Caine knew his attempt at humour was strained, and knew Crandon understood. Neither wanted to broach the subject they had to discuss. Crandon drove in silence for a while, then pulled into a shopping plaza off Seventeenth.

'You serious about the beer?'

'Coffee would be better.'

'*Mens sana in corpore sano.*'

'I wish I could speak French,' Caine said.

They went into a deli and sat in a booth. A sour-faced waitress brought them menus they didn't need, then waited expectantly, hands on hips.

'Just coffee,' Crandon said.

'That all?' she asked.

Crandon looked at her. 'You wanna get me a caviar taco?' he asked.

'Anh,' she said, wearily. 'A wise-ass.' She went away to get the coffee pot.

'Don't you ever take anything seriously?' Caine said.

'I think,' Crandon replied. 'Therefore, I ham.'

'First Latin, now philosophy. I'm dazzled.'

'All right,' Crandon said. 'I heard Lavery's version. Now you tell me about it.'

Caine told him, pulling no punches, about the long vigil, the abrupt appearance of the men from the Acme building, and the brutal, unexpected murders.

'Bastards,' he said, softly. 'I want them, David.'

'I know,' Caine said. 'But first we have to find out who they were.'

'You know who they were!'

'Is that what I know, Tom? Or is it what I'm supposed to know?'

'What the hell does that mean?'

'It means don't jump to conclusions.'

'You saying it wasn't the Fat Man's people?'

'I'm saying don't jump. What about the cars?'

'I checked them. They were both stolen.'

'What about the warehouse? Acme Novelty?'

'It's owned by something called the Diversified Entertainment Corporation. Which is a subsidiary of another company

called Sunshine State Enterprises. Sunshine State is one of Saturnino Baca's fronts.'

'Who he?'

'Local hero,' Crandon said. 'King of the shitheap.'

In 1980, he told Caine, Fidel Castro had 'permitted' about 125,000 people to emigrate to the United States, a compassionate gesture which relieved him not only of the unskilled, the uneducated and the poor of his island, but also the scourings of his prisons, detention centres, hospitals and asylums. In among the huddled masses yearning to breathe free who embarked at the Cuban port of Mariel was the biggest assortment of junkies, rapists, extortionists, pimps and thieves ever to land on the shores of America.

In the makeshift camps set up for them beneath the highway ramps and overpasses of Miami, the Marielitos soon discovered that the only ticket out of the hell they were living in was one of the coveted green cards which entitled you to work in America. If you had a trade, no

119

problem. If you were a professional man, likewise no problem. If you were neither, maybe you could buy one from somebody who was. If you had no profession, no trade and no money, then maybe you got a knife or a gun, you killed someone who fulfilled all the legitimate requirements, and you took his place.

By the time anybody realized that Saturnino Baca was not a poor but honest union leader from the Havana electric company, he had a stranglehold on the South Beach area, he had his papers, and he had protection. Soon his reach extended to cover most of Miami south of Calle Ocho. His organization was so tight, it was almost impossible to infiltrate. The supply of Cuban-Americans willing to try it tended to diminish in direct proportion to the number of times TV newscasts showed police fishing another bound, battered, bloated body out of some swampy canal.

'You think Baca had anything to do with this?' Crandon asked.

'Suppose those Cubans weren't DGI. Suppose they were Baca's people,' Caine

said, thoughtfully. 'Suppose he was watching Genevevo — and us — all the time.'

'Not his style,' Crandon said, emphatically. 'Baca isn't the subtle type. His people go in for chainsaws.'

'That's not a reason, Tom, that's a prejudice.'

'Why would Baca want to kill our people? Or even Genevevo, come to that? It was Avranilosa he was after, not Baca.'

'But if he busted Avranilosa, wouldn't he be busting Baca at the same time? If Baca is the head drugs honcho in South Miami . . . '

'The word on the street is that Baca's hold is slipping badly,' Crandon said. 'The Colombians are slowly but surely taking over the trade, driving the Cubans out. Or killing them off. They're not too damned particular.'

'I still think Baca's a better bet than DGI. I can't believe Cuban intelligence ordered this done. They don't want to make those kind of waves. It doesn't make sense.'

'We'll crack it,' Crandon said. 'Don't worry.'

121

'No,' Caine said, flatly. 'Not 'we'. You're out of this, Tom.'

'The hell you say!'

'That's right, the hell I say.'

They glared at each other across the table. The waitress came back and put two mugs on the table. She sloshed coffee into them and went away. Her performance made them grin in spite of their own tension.

'All right,' Crandon said. 'All right. Tell me why.'

'It's not going to take Domestic Operations long to make a connection between ISS and Genevevo, Tom,' Caine said. 'When they do, I want you elsewhere. Like maybe Melbourne, Australia.'

'It won't make any difference whether I'm around or not. Those guys don't take 'I don't know' for an answer, David.'

'I just want to stall them as long as possible. That means putting you out of harm's way for a while.'

'David, I want to be in on this. I want — '

'Sorry, Tom,' Caine said, flatly. 'You're off the case, and that's final. Come on,

let's get out of here.'

Crandon paid the check and left seven pennies on the table as a tip. Caine smiled. Tom fought small wars with just as much enthusiasm as big ones. He felt a surge of affection for the rangy Miamian. There was no one he would have liked better at his side in the days ahead, but it was just not possible.

'I'm giving you twenty-four hours to git outa town, kid,' he said, doing his best John Wayne voice.

'Hey, Jimmy Stewart, right?' Crandon said. He got into the car and started the engine. Caine lifted a hand in salute, and Crandon touched his finger to his forehead in farewell. He looked over his shoulder to check the oncoming traffic.

Automatically following Crandon's glance, Caine halfsaw a blue Chrysler Fifth Avenue accelerating past the LTD, and hurled himself backwards as a staccato burst of bullets blazed from its open window. He heard screams, the whine of ricocheting slugs, glass smashing. He landed in a heap, sending a display of fruit outside a grocery scattering all over the sidewalk.

123

He scrambled to his feet. An elderly man sat with his back against the wall, his shirt stained with blood, a look of surprise on his face. Tom Crandon was slumped over the wheel of the LTD. The windshield was spattered with blood. There was no sign of the blue Chrysler. A burly, red-faced man came out of the store, gesticulating. Caine turned sharply away so that the man could not see his face, and walked briskly up the street.

'Hey!' someone shouted. 'Hey, you!'

Caine kept walking, not hurrying. The voices died as he put distance between himself and the scene of the shooting. There was a K-Mart at the next corner, its parking lot half full. He found a shopping cart, then walked with it between the rows of cars. In the third row, he spotted a Ford Tempo with the keys in the ignition. Swiftly checking that no one was nearby, he got into the car and started it up. Fifteen minutes later, he abandoned it near Highland Park, and walked back to the Omni International. By the time he got there, he had stopped shivering.

10

'*Otlitchno*,' Drosdow said in Russian, excellent.

Everything had gone well. With Avranilosa as his front, it had been easy to get Baca to take the bait he had offered. Baca was stupid and greedy, perhaps even stupider and greedier than the Fat Man. Drosdow liked working with such people. There were no nuances: you gave them money and they ate shit.

He smiled at the thought. It was not a sympathetic smile: Frederic Drosdow was not a sympathetic character. His brilliant blue eyes were hard and unforgiving, his mouth an uncompromising slash in a square, swarthy, pockmarked face. Saturnino Baca believed him to be Turkish: in fact, Drosdow had been born in the Zeravshan valley near Bukhara, in Uzbekistan, USSR. It was on Soviet orders that Avranilosa's Cuban masters had instructed the Fat Man to present Drosdow to Saturnino

Baca as a big-time supplier from Bogotá.

Drosdow had opened up the contact with ten kilos of hashish, the very finest Afghanistan, flown in direct from Moscow to Bogotá in the diplomatic bag and brought over by an airline pilot working for DGI. Once the connection was made, the bona-fides established, Baca asked for more. Drosdow got it for him, and then offered cocaine. Baca went after it like a shark after chum. Cocaine was the smart-money drug. Everyone wanted it, from ghetto kids sticking their money through the door slots of 'rock houses' to the super-rich of Miami Beach, who served it along with caviar at their flashy parties.

Drosdow's first shipment of cocaine had a street value of about three and a half mill. It came in by courier this time, two human mules each of whom had more than a hundred plastic sachets of cocaine in their stomachs. The next, much bigger shipment came in by air, landed on a field strip up around Loxahatchee. Then, finally, last night, the payoff shipment Drosdow had been

working up to: sixty million dollars' worth, brought in on a schooner and landed without incident at Lower Matecumbe Key.

He would be glad to get out of Miami. He had not much liked Bogotá, but Miami was even worse. How could people live in a place where alligators crawled out of the canals and ate their pets? The downtown streets were as sleazy as the ones in Havana, but without the Cuban city's character. As for the Cubans, they were irresponsible, unreliable, lazy and corrupt. Apart from their gilded, garish plaster saints, the only thing they believed in was money. They were good at only one thing: they hated, with a fine impartiality, anyone and anything not Cuban.

My kalutsky, he thought. It was an old Russian phrase that meant 'it's nothing to do with me'. The fate of men like Baca and Avranilosa was of no consequence. They deserved neither loyalty nor sympathy; they were mercenaries, to be used, like a Kleenex, then thrown away.

He turned north on Collins and drove

steadily, up through Haulover Beach Park golf course and the glitzy resort developments at Sunny Isles. At Interama he made a left, cruising the mile or so it took him to reach US-1. Billboards exhorted him to visit the Ancient Spanish Monastery of St Bernard and its gardens. A quarter of a mile north on One, he turned off into East Greynolds Park. A road ran down to the edge of Maule Lake, with a turning loop at the end. There were picnic tables and barbecue stands beneath the trees. The place was deserted. Drosdow checked his watch: four minutes to three.

At two minutes to three, a Cutlass coasted down the road and pulled up alongside his Mercedes. The man who got out was a short, barrel-chested man with cropped hair. He wore a rumpled light-weight suit and heavy leather brogues. He rapped on the window of the Mercedes and Drosdow opened it.

'Miami is pleasant at this time of year,' the stranger said, in Russian.

'I prefer Washington myself,' Drosdow replied, completing the recognition code. 'How are you, Comrade Lykov?'

'Good, fine, excellent,' the stranger beamed, getting into the Mercedes. His full name was Stepan Ivanovich Lykov, and he was a counsellor at the Russian Embassy in Washington. This rank, which placed him fifth in seniority to the Ambassador, was of course only a cover: Lykov was a GRU officer with special responsibility for 'illegals' — Soviet spies working in the United States as business-men, rather than members of the diplomatic establishment.

'What news have you for me?' Drosdow said.

'Good news, Comrade Major. Moscow advises us that *Smert Ptytsa* will be ready to fly on schedule. They are anxious to hear your report. Has everything gone to plan?'

'Everything,' Drosdow said.

Baca and his people had rented a vacation house on Lower Matecumbe Key, south of Miami, which had a dock big enough to accommodate the schooner bringing in the cocaine. The schooner was a local boat, with a sailing pattern familiar to the customs agents. For a fee of one

million dollars in cash, her skipper had agreed to pick up some goods — nobody said what, nobody needed to — from a cargo boat off Bimini. She slid in without incident an hour after dark, and by ten o'clock she was unloaded and on her way to Boca Raton, her home port. Long before she got there, Baca's chemists had done their alkaloid tests and pronounced themselves satisfied, and the cocaine had been transferred to three U-Haul trucks and driven north to Miami.

Neither Drosdow nor Baca was at Matecumbe; they waited together at the Indies Inn on Duck Key, and when Avranilosa called to say the shipment was cleared, the payoff was made: sixty million dollars, packed into cartons like so much waste paper. Which, in a way, it was, Drosdow thought.

'So the properties have been purchased?'

'I'll be finalizing that today,' Drosdow said. 'What about the girl?'

'She will be waiting for you at the Holiday Inn in Key Largo when you arrive. Her name is Katja Renis.'

'What are the paroles?'

'The first line of *Anna Karenina*.'

Drosdow nodded. 'And the clerk? Bogdanovich?'

'He has been programmed. He will leave Washington the day after tomorrow. As you instructed. What about Avranilosa?'

'Leave him to the CIA.'

'You're serious?'

'I've filled him full of disinformation. It will be no use if it doesn't get to them.'

'As you wish,' Lykov said. 'I'll talk to Havana. They'll withdraw their support. That should do it.'

'The poor fat bastard,' Drosdow said, unsympathetically. Avranilosa had been living like a prince for a long time. The man would have no grounds for complaint. In this business, nothing came with a guarantee.

He had been honest with Avranilosa about only one thing: the name of the game he was playing. It was *chaos*. He was sowing disinformation like a man planting corn and in his wake he would leave chaos.

'You're going straight back to Washington?' he asked Lykov.

'I'll go to the airport from here.'

'Then I'll be on my way. Good luck, comrade. Honour the work!'

'Honour the work!' Lykov echoed. He got out of the Mercedes and into the rented Cutlass. He raised a hand as he drove away. Drosdow did not return the compliment. His mind was already busy on what he must do next.

In due course, he had no doubt, Avranilosa would divulge what he had been programmed to reveal. As for Baca, fuck him. Sooner or later, the CIA would establish that he had executed their man Genevevo, and when they did, arrangements would be made for something unpleasant to happen to the Cuban: his limousine sideswiped by a truck on a freeway, an inexplicable gas leak at his home. While the security agencies went baying down the false trail he had laid for them to follow, Drosdow would be proceeding with the second phase of his plan, financed by the sale of the drugs in Miami. That was the sole reason for

everything which had happened so far: money.

Drosdow grinned.

They'll make an American of me yet, he thought.

11

'I want you to walk away from it, David,' Kingly said. His voice sounded tinny; was he recording what they were saying? 'You know the rules.'

'Go tell Tom Crandon the rules.'

'Don't get truculent with me,' Kingly snapped. 'If you were dead, I'd be saying the same thing to him. And you know it.'

He was right, of course. The organization's first priority was to protect its carefully constructed cover. Knowing he was right didn't make it any easier.

'I've got a new set of clothes. Nobody even knows I'm on the ground.'

'You can't be sure of that,' Kingly said. 'And even if you could, my answer would be the same.'

'What about Domestic Operations?' Caine said. 'What happens when they find out we were watching Genevevo?'

'I've anticipated that,' Kingly said, smugly. 'We're going to let it leak to Sam

that Tom Crandon was working freelance for our Customs and Excise people, acting on a tip that Genevevo might have been involved in running drugs to London. Of course, we'll assure them we had no idea he was working undercover — how could we?'

'It's pretty thin. You think they'll buy it?'

'The indications are they will,' Kingly said. 'Domestic Operations is already embarrassed — the last thing they want is to be visible on the mainland. So they're not going to make too many waves. If the matter is raised, our answer will be that Crandon was acting on his own initiative, and that was why we didn't know about the surveillance setup. Either way, our interest in Genevevo is terminated.'

'And what about whoever killed my people? Is our interest in them terminated, too?'

'I know how you feel, David, but — '

'One thing is certain, Miles,' Caine said. 'You do not know how I feel.'

He wasn't yet altogether sure how he did feel. The shock of the assassination

135

had ebbed, leaving a numb, undirected anger. Tom Crandon had been that rare thing in Caine's solitary life, a friend. Long-term relationships and the clandestine world tended to be mutually exclusive. You were taught not to believe even someone who said he was going to fetch the milk until he came back with the bottle in his hand. That was why so many agents were divorced. Or drunks. Or both.

'Even if you stayed down there, what could you hope to achieve?'

'I don't know. I've got the people and places digest. I want to follow up on a few things.' Caine heard the space-opera sounds of relays bleeping and pinging on the long-distance line as Kingly pondered.

'You're a stubborn bugger sometimes, David,' Kingly said. Caine didn't argue. 'All right. I'll give you another seventy-two hours. If you come up with anything, we'll review the situation. If not, you walk away. Fair enough?'

'Fair enough,' Caine said.

'I'll patch you through to McClelland,'

Kingly said. 'Give him your contact numbers and legend.'

And lots of luck, kid, Caine thought, as the connection closed. Well, that was Kingly's style. No use expecting a snake to tap-dance. After a few moments, Dick McClelland came on the line. Caine gave him the information he needed and hung up.

He tried to put himself into Forsyth's shoes. The Company's first priority was still Avranilosa: they would leave investigation of the murders to the FBI and the local police. If he stayed on the street and moved fast, he might be able to beat Forsyth to the punch. Forsyth had to go by the book: he would be hampered by the bureaucratic restraints he had to work with.

Caine's first task was to change his appearance. He darkened his hair with Clairol and put on heavy horn-rim glasses with plain lenses. He exchanged his grey Hart, Schaffner & Marx lightweight for a pale blue Dacron sports jacket, plaid slacks, a dark blue open-neck shirt, and Thom McAnn loafers. He packed his own

things into a Samsonite two-suiter and checked out of the hotel, paying cash.

The dark blue Chevrolet Impala was parked where Beale had said it would be. It looked clean inside and out. The tyres had plenty of tread on them, and the muffler was in good shape. He lifted the hood and checked the engine over. The wiring was tidy and the hoses looked all right. There were no oil leaks on the crankcase. He got in, started the engine: it ran without hunting. The odometer showed seventy something thousand miles.

He drove out of the parking lot and south through Shenandoah, where he picked up the South Dixie Highway, a continuous wilderness of billboards and neon signs, sprawling shopping plazas and clusters of stores, restaurants, laundromats, garages, clothing stores, repair shops, icecream parlours and greasy spoons.

It was hard to believe that this area had once been a tropical paradise where panthers lived among the mangroves, where ospreys and pelicans soared over manatees basking in the shallows of uninhabited keys. Now the ospreys nested

in TV aerials, the pelicans scavenged in the wake of tourist boats, and the manatees were all but gone.

Their world had been taken over by the realtors, the tourists and the retirees. Because of them, every vacant stretch of sand was a potential goldmine. Real-estate signs advertised 'residential communities' called Citrus this or Pine that, each with its own exclusive golf course — ten thousand dollars a year to join and another three to play. Over on the Gulf side, island houses were selling for seven million. Man was inexorably destroying all the beautiful things that had attracted him to this lovely land in the first place. Nobody seemed to care.

Caine grinned at himself in the driving mirror. He was beginning to sound like Travis McGee. Next thing he knew, his long-lost daughter was going to turn up and tell him what a schmuck he was.

He drove automatically, going through in his mind what he had read in the dossier about Lynda Sanchez. First-generation Cuban-American — her parents had come over in the same wave as Avranilosa — she

had worked as an auxiliary nurse at Jackson Memorial, where she met Jim Sanchez, an intern, whom she married in 1969. Sanchez had been killed near Danang in August 1972, just a few days before the last American ground troops left Vietnam. His widow found work in a restaurant in Key Biscayne, and became its manageress on the retirement of its owner in 1980. She had been running it, very successfully, ever since.

The Dadeland Mall loomed on his right, rows of parked cars behind it glittering in the sunshine. Lynda Sanchez lived on SW88th Street, about half a mile past the Mall. The building was a cream-coloured, U-shaped block with a Spanish tile roof. A sign over the door said El Palacio Apartments.

He went into the lobby. A middle-aged black man sat behind a desk facing the doors. He laid down his newspaper and got heavily to his feet, hitching up his belt.

'Whatever you sellin, we don' want none,' he said.

'I'd like to see Mrs Sanchez,' Caine

said, giving him the winning smile.

'Miz Sanchez ain't seein nobody.'

So much for the winning smile, Caine thought. 'Tell her it's in connection with Tony Genevevo.'

'*Sir*,' the man said, with long-suffering patience, 'I jus' got through tellin you, Miz Sanchez ain't seein . . .'

'Humour me,' Caine said. 'Tell her I'm here. Philip Howard, Alliance Interstate Mutual Insurance Corporation.' He handed the man one of the visiting cards Beale had given him as part of his new identity. The super took the card reluctantly, and went back to the desk, where he punched a button on his phone and waited.

'Oh, hi, Miz Sanchez. Got a guy here named Howard from the A-liance Interstate Mutual Insurance Corporation wantsa see you? Yeah, that's right, A-liance. Yessum, I *tole* him that. He say it's about Mr Genevevo? Ahuh. Oh? OK, if you say so.' He put down the phone and looked up. 'Miz Sanchez wants a word with you.'

Caine picked up the telephone. 'Hello, Mrs Sanchez. This is Philip Howard. I apologize for the intrusion. I'm making

inquiries into the death of Antony Genevevo?'

'What do you want to know?'

'I'd rather not discuss it on the telephone, Mrs Sanchez. This is a confidential matter.'

He heard her sigh. 'Very well,' she said. 'Let me speak to the super.'

Caine handed the phone back to the black man who listened and nodded. He put the phone on the cradle and looked up at Caine.

'She say you to go on up. Second floor, apartment two-twenty.'

Caine took the carpeted stairs two at a time, and walked down the mirrored corridor. Through the windows he could see the area enclosed by the wings of the building. Three women lay on loungers around the pool. The nearest of them was a slim brunette with a model's figure and a thousand-dollar tan. She was reading Kierkegaard. Whatever happened to dumb blondes? Caine wondered.

He knocked on the door of 220. It opened six inches. Caine held his card where Lynda Sanchez could see it. He

heard her release the chain and the door swung open.

'Mr Howard?' she said. 'Come in, please.'

She was not tall — few women of Cuban descent are — but she was unusually slender and carried herself well, giving an impression of height. She had on a linen and cotton blend white suit, with random horizontal stripes on the jacket and matching vertical ones on the skirt. She had dark, liquid eyes and a good figure. Her hair was black and long, and looked as if it was naturally waved. Her fingernails were well-kept, and she wore the minimum of makeup.

'You say you're investigating Tony Genevevo's death, Mr Howard?' she asked. 'Surely the police have done that already? I've told them all I know.'

'We prefer to conduct our own investigations. Particularly when there is such a great deal of money involved.'

'Tony had a big insurance policy? He never mentioned anything like that to me.'

'You were very close?'

He caught her reaction and made a deprecatory gesture. 'Forgive me, but we insurance investigators do sometimes have to ask personal questions. To find out, you know, what kind of man we were dealing with.'

'You want to know what kind of man Tony Genevevo was?' she said. 'I'll tell you. He was a bastard.'

12

'You surprise me, Mrs Sanchez,' Caine said. 'The local papers are making him out to be something of a hero.'

'He may well have been,' she said. 'He was still a bastard.'

'Why do you say that?' Caine asked.

She looked at the telephone and he knew what she was thinking. He took a card out of his pocket and gave it to her.

'That's the number of my Washington bureau if you want to call them,' he said. The number on the card was a hand-on phone somewhere in Annandale. If she rang it, she would be patched through to Dick McClelland, Caine's 'supervisor'. She looked at the card, and then at Caine. It seemed like a long moment.

'I'm sure that won't be necessary,' she said. 'Please, sit down. What about something to drink?'

'Coffee would be good.'

She went into the kitchen and Caine

looked around. To the right an archway led into a dining area with a walnut table and ladderback chairs. The furniture looked comfortable and lived-with; a brown, leather-covered three-seater sofa, two vast armchairs in dark brown Dralon, off-white shag pile carpeting, wall lights. Two bedrooms, Caine decided.

It was a very American-looking apartment. None of the usual Cuban touches, the Lazaro or Carita de Cobre shrine with flowers and food, or the photographs of family still 'on the island'. On one wall hung a large framed print of a Renoir painting; the garden of the rue Cortot. On the opposite wall was a bookcase, books piled into it in haphazard stacks. In one corner stood a Toshiba portable TV and a Panasonic hi-fi stack with a pile of records alongside it.

Lynda Sanchez came back with the coffee and caught the direction of his gaze. 'Show tunes,' she said. 'I collect everything. Like a squirrel.'

'You get to a lot of shows?'

'Tony and I used to fly up to New York. See everything, bam-bam-bam.'

146

'I thought you said — ?'

'That he was a bastard? Maybe I'm being too rough on him. I don't know. I've had a lot of time to think this past couple of days. About Tony. And myself. About our relationship.'

'And?'

'I've come to the unpleasant conclusion that he didn't give a damn about me, Mr Howard. He was just using me to get what he wanted.'

'That sounds pretty cold-blooded.'

'Yes,' she said, looking fiercely out of the window. 'It does, doesn't it?'

He let her fight with that until she felt she had it under control. He admired the way she did it without tears. If what she said was truly how she felt, her ego must be badly dented.

'I shouldn't have said what I did,' she said, turning to face Caine. 'Tony was a good man. Maybe I . . . expected more than he had to give.'

'How did you meet him?'

'I run a restaurant on Key Biscayne, La Paloma. He came in with some people I knew. They introduced us.'

'How long ago was that?'

'Two years, maybe a little longer.'

'Did you know what he did for a living?'

'Not then, not at first. He told me he worked for the government. Something to do with the State Department.'

'And later?'

'Later . . . he hinted. Never came right out with what he actually did. He said to forget he'd ever told me he worked for the government. If anyone ever asked.'

'That was when he went undercover.'

'I guess so. It's easy to understand in retrospect.'

'You went on . . . seeing each other?'

'He was . . . square. Going out with him was like going on a date with a college kid. All very formal. We held hands. He would bring me home and kiss me goodnight, then he'd leave.'

'It's none of my business, Mrs Sanchez . . .'

'No, I'm trying to see it clearly,' she said. 'I thought, maybe he's just shy. Now I wonder whether . . . whether he really didn't care for me at all. Just . . . used me.'

'How do you mean?'

'He said I could be very helpful to him in what he did. If I could keep my eyes and ears open.'

'In what way?'

'Before I answer any more questions, I want to ask you something, Mr Howard,' Lynda Sanchez said. 'Who are you? Who sent you here? Another of those faceless government agencies who tell you they prefer not to show identification?'

'I told you, I'm — '

'Mr Howard, you're no more an insurance investigator than I am. You ask all the wrong questions.'

Caine shrugged ruefully. When he did not speak, Lynda Sanchez's lips became a determined line.

'I guess I'd liked to see some real ID,' she told him. 'Or I call the police right now.'

'I'm a secret agent,' Caine said.

She laughed out loud in astonishment. 'You expect me to believe that?'

'It's true.'

'You sound . . . what is it, British?'

'The two men who were killed with Genevevo were working for me,' he

replied, evading the question. 'I'm trying to find out who killed them.'

'The papers said . . .'

'Forget what the papers said, Mrs Sanchez. They were all murdered, in cold blood.'

'Then why — ?'

'Why didn't all those quietly-spoken gentlemen in the lightweight suits who came to see you after Genevevo was killed, and told you not to talk to anyone about him, mention the fact that he had been murdered? It's called the need-to-know principle, Mrs Sanchez. Someone somewhere decided you didn't need to know.'

'They couldn't . . . would they do that?'

'They most certainly would.'

'And what about you?'

'I'm telling you the truth. You can believe it or not, as you please. If you tell me to get out of here, I'll go. I have no authority, no jurisdiction in this country. In fact, I would be deported at once if anyone knew what I just told you.'

'Then why did you tell me?' she asked, very quietly.

'Because I want you to trust me, and I don't know any other way to convince you that you can.'

'Trust you?' she said. 'Can I trust any of you?'

'It's up to you.'

She shook her head very slightly, as if to rid herself of her own disbelief. When she spoke, her voice was little more than a whisper. 'All right,' she said. 'What do you want to know?'

'What did Genevevo ask you to do?'

'He wanted information about my customers.'

'And you obliged?'

'I told him to go straight to hell.'

'That must have made his morning.'

'He said he admired me for saying that, but what he was asking me was important. He said there were Cubans, gangsters, giving the rest of us Cubans a bad name. He said it was his job to stop them, but he needed help. I tell you, I was glad to do it.'

'Why?'

'My parents came over here in '61, Mr Howard. They had no money, no place to

live. My father had been an electrical engineer in Cuba. Here, he couldn't get a job. He pushed a broom in a factory eight hours a day, then worked another six hours in a car wash. My mother cleaned house for rich American ladies, waited on tables. They didn't complain, they didn't ask for handouts. They worked and worked because they wanted us kids to have a better life than they had. And where we lived, we'd see them, those other Cubans, letting gangsters use their houses for drug deals, making more money in a day than my father made in a month. And we knew what people said: those Cubans, they're no good, any of them, they're all into drugs, they ought to be run out of the country, they ought to be sent back where they came from. And I thought of how hard my mother and father worked, and . . . I don't know how else to say it to you. I wanted to do a good thing for them. For America.'

'Genevevo must have known what he was asking you to do could be dangerous.'

'Not so dangerous,' she smiled. 'Cuban men are very, you know, macho. A

152

woman, bringing them food, they don't even see her.'

'How did it work — did Genevevo tell you who he wanted you to eavesdrop on?'

'He'd telephone, ask me who was in the restaurant. I'd tell him this man, that one. He'd say, see what you can get for me.'

'Like what?'

'Oh, who they saw, who they came in with, who they talked to.'

'Do you know why?'

'It was something to do with the man he was working for, a man called Pedro Avranilosa.'

'I'm afraid the name doesn't mean anything to me,' Caine told her.

'He claims to be a realtor. Tony said the real estate was just a front, that Avranilosa's real business was drugs.'

'How do you mean?'

'He's a middleman, a fixer. Tony said he brings together interested parties — the people selling drugs and the ones who want to buy them.'

'This Avranilosa — he came to your restaurant a lot?'

'Two, sometimes three times a week.'

'And you told Genevevo who he met, what he talked about.'

'That's right.' She hesitated. 'I . . . it wasn't the way I've made it sound. I was . . . I cared about Tony. What he was doing was brave. And dangerous. If by doing what he asked, I made it a little less dangerous, I was . . . I wanted to do it.'

'Have you any idea why he was killed, Mrs Sanchez?'

'No,' she said, shaking her head. 'It was . . . what the police told me, what it said in the papers, I couldn't believe it. I saw him the night before it happened. He was the same as always, you know, relaxed, buying drinks.'

'He didn't seem tense, or anything?'

'Not till I told him about Avranilosa meeting these men at the restaurant. I could always tell when he was excited. He'd talk staccato, words-all-strung-together-like-that, you know? I got the impression something important was breaking.'

'What exactly did you tell him?'

'Avranilosa had met two men. One of

them was from South America. Obviously, I didn't get all the details, but I heard enough to know they were talking about buying a property.'

'Did you get their names, Mrs Sanchez?'

'Yes. The swarthy one who said he was from Colombia was called Drosdow, and the other man's name was Percival.'

'First name, or surname?'

'I'm not sure.'

'What was so special about them?'

'I don't know. I gathered Drosdow had a lot of money, I mean really a lot, and was looking for a place to live.'

'In Florida?'

'I suppose so. But that wasn't what interested Tony. It was what I told him about Key Largo.'

'Key Largo?'

'I overheard Drosdow telling Avranilosa the sparrow was waiting in Key Largo. It was such nonsense it stuck in my mind. But when I told Tony, he got very excited.'

'Excited?'

'No, that's not the right word. Tony wasn't the excitable type. But . . . elated. He said I'd cracked it for him. He said

everything was coming together.'

'Are you sure that's what the man said, a sparrow?'

'No, wait a minute, not a sparrow. A swallow. He was going to Key Largo to see a swallow. I remember, Tony asked me the same thing.'

'What did Genevevo do then?'

'He couldn't wait to get out of there, like someone lit a fire under him.'

No wonder, Caine thought. Genevevo would have known the jargon and concluded, like Caine, that if Drosdow was going to meet a swallow — a female operative used to sexually entrap a targeted male — then the South American and Avranilosa were engaged in setting up what was known in espionage circles as a honey trap.

'This man Drosdow,' Caine said. 'Can you tell me anything about him? Where he stayed, what he looked like?'

'Not much,' she said. 'He was well-built, not tall. Good clothes, imported, I'd say. About fifty. Dark brown hair, very blue eyes, swarthy, pockmarked skin.'

'When you first mentioned him, you

said he *said* he was from South America. As if you weren't convinced.'

'Exactly,' she said.

'What kind of accent did he have?'

'I don't know. But he was no more South American than . . . than you are.'

'What about the other man, Percival?'

'Sixtyish. Tall, thin, stooped. Old-fashioned businessman look about him. I gathered he was some sort of realtor.'

'Local?'

'I don't know. But if I had to guess, I'd say no.'

'Tell me, was there anyone else Genevevo showed particular interest in? Anyone Avranilosa saw a lot of?'

She gave him a wry grin, and he interpreted it correctly. 'The button-down boys asked you the same thing, I take it?'

'Yes.'

'And what did you tell them?'

'I told them the one Avranilosa saw the most of was Saturnino Baca. Tony said he was the boss of all the rackets in South Miami.'

'Do you know what his special interest in Baca was?'

'Nothing you could use in a courtroom. But I gathered there was some kind of deal going on between Avranilosa and Baca. Maybe drugs, maybe something else. Baca is into a lot of things: numbers, loansharking, women.'

'Talking about women, did Avranilosa bring any to the restaurant?'

'Women?' She laughed. 'Avranilosa isn't interested in women.'

'How do you know?'

'I hear the waiters talking. That's what they say.'

'I think he and Baca murdered Tony Genevevo and my people, Mrs Sanchez. I don't know why. But I want to find out, and I need all the help I can get to do it. Will you help me?'

Lynda Sanchez stubbed out the cigarette she had lit and looked directly at Caine. 'There is a certain kind of Cuban that my people are not proud of, Mr Howard. The ones who make a lot of money, usually dirty money, and then forget who they are and where they came from. They exploit their own kind worse than the worst kind of American, they spit

on anyone who believes in hard work, a decent life. Avranilosa is one of those. Baca is another. If helping you will rid us of them and their kind, then yes, I will help you any way I can.'

He wondered whether what she was saying was genuine, or whether it was an act put on especially for his benefit. Her attachment to Genevevo seemed genuine enough, but there was no way of being sure about it. That was the trouble with this business: you ended up despising yourself because you were so far gone you could no longer trust anyone. Lynda Sanchez was a very attractive woman. It would not be difficult to get to like her. For a moment, he felt the ache of self-imposed loneliness.

'I'd better be going, Mrs Sanchez,' he said. 'There are a few more people I've got to see.'

'I wish you'd stop calling me Mrs Sanchez,' she said. 'You make me feel a hundred and four years old.'

'I'd hate to do that.'

'You said your name was Philip? Would you like to give me a ride as far as the

Mall, Philip? I've got some shopping to do. I can walk back.'

'I'd be glad to wait.'

'No, I want to dawdle,' she smiled. He waited while she took out the coffee cups and got her pocketbook and a shopping bag. They walked out through the lobby, and Caine blew the man at the desk a kiss. The super raised a rigid digit. They got into the car, and Caine moved the Impala into the slow-moving traffic, checking the mirror. As far as he could see, no one was tailing him. He drove around into the parking lot of the Dadeland Mall. Lynda Sanchez got out of the car and stood by the open door, smiling.

'Well,' she said. 'I seem to have done a lot of talking.'

'You've been very helpful, Lynda,' Caine said. 'It would be even more helpful if you didn't tell anyone I'd been to see you.'

She said nothing for a moment. Then she nodded.

'Thank you,' Caine smiled. 'Will it be OK if I call you?'

'I haven't heard that one for a long time,' she said, and for the first time he saw mischief dancing in the dark eyes.

'I'm old-fashioned.'

'Music by Kern, lyrics by Mercer,' she said. 'You are one of the good guys, aren't you, Philip? You are going to catch the men who killed Tony?'

'Yes,' he said. 'If I can.'

She smiled her brilliant smile again. In the context it was heartbreaking. She looked at him for what seemed like a long while, then shook her head slightly, as if to banish a dark thought.

'I can't think of one good reason for trusting you,' she said. 'But for some strange reason, I do.'

'Thank you.'

'I'm in the book,' she said. 'Call me.'

She walked away. He watched her go, knowing she was aware of his scrutiny. She had a good figure. Nothing noisy, but everything in the right places. Caine sighed. If he had been doing any other job than the one he was doing, he might have been tempted to take her up on that invitation. As it was . . . Next life, maybe.

13

Just one more, Forsyth thought.

He eyed the bottle of Johnny Walker Black Label judiciously: old Johnny had taken a beating tonight. One more smack over the head would just about finish him off.

He sloshed the whisky into his glass and stared moodily at the newspaper on the table in front of him. The headline mocked him: 'Gangland Links Seen in Downtown Slaying.'

'Goddammit!' Forsyth said, banging the empty glass down on the table. He had just returned from an interview with Bensen, who worked out of a front called the American Agency for International Development in a forty-storey, steel and glass block on Brickell Avenue. Forsyth had gone there expecting Bensen to tell him to give maximum precedence to finding out who had killed Tony Genevevo.

Fat chance.

'Crandon's death was inexpedient, Frank, but it's not our brief to go out on the streets looking for whoever killed him,' Bensen said, primly. 'Leave it alone.'

Inexpedient, for Christ's sake! First Genevevo and the two ISS men. Now somebody had burp-gunned Thomas Crandon in broad daylight on a city street and Bensen called it inexpedient!

The Miami police had come up with zilch: a dozen Ingram shells on the street, the testimony of an old man who'd taken a ricochet in the upper arm, and that of a few shocked bystanders who were seeing more every time they retold their story. The sum of it was that the shooting had been done by two, four or five men, who were either Cuban, Puerto Rican, black or white, and driving a late model blue, or black or purple Buick. Or maybe it was a Chrysler, or a Dodge. Or a goddamn flying saucer, Forsyth thought disgustedly, tossing the paper on the floor.

'You don't attach any special significance to the murder of Crandon, then?' he'd asked Bensen.

'Look, Frank, there are two, three hundred murders in Metro-Dade every year, half of them drug-related. We can't waste any more time on this. You've got to see the bigger picture.'

'The bigger picture.'

Bensen's head came up. Like all insecure men, he read criticism into irony, and was constantly on the alert for the imagined slight. He was a short man, thickset and balding, with rimless glasses that imparted a moonlike impassivity to his face. He was what Forsyth privately termed a break-dancer — impressive to look at, but when their act was finished, they hadn't produced a damned thing. There were a lot of them in the Company. Careful, reticent, petty men who never took risks and snapped up every break. College boys, success-oriented, upwardly-mobile, with the morals of the Great White.

'You've got a reputation as a maverick, Frank,' Bensen said. 'You've got to play with the team, or I'll take you off it. Make up your mind.'

'I'll stay,' Forsyth said, perhaps a shade

too quickly. He saw the little glint of triumph in Bensen's eyes and cursed himself. You never let a man like Bensen think you wanted something; that gave him the sadistic pleasure of making you sweat for it.

'You've read the option papers?'

'I'm not altogether in agreement with them. I'd still like to know why those ISS people were watching Tony.'

'Frank, Frank,' Bensen said, grindingly patient. 'You saw the memo from Langley. They were freelancing for the British Customs people.'

'That's not what Crandon said.'

'You didn't expect he'd be telling the truth, did you?'

No, of course not, Forsyth thought. Nobody told the truth. Everything, including the truth, was a lie. You could always draw two sets of vastly different conclusions from the same set of facts. Which was why he mistrusted Bensen's option papers and the analysts who prepared them. Analysts were to his line of work what lady detective-story writers were to homicide cops.

'Let me ask you something,' he said. 'How did the British Customs, or whoever the hell it is, latch on to Genevevo?'

'He gave one of their people some information.'

'Bullshit. I was his case officer, Donald. If he met any British agents, I'd have known.'

'You admitted yourself there was a possibility Tony was off the leash, Frank,' Bensen pointed out. 'If you'd lost him, he wouldn't have told you anything.'

'I hadn't lost him!' Forsyth snapped, feeling his own anger rise. Bensen knew all the cheap shots. 'But if Tony had gone over the line, there'd have been even less reason for him to talk to some British narc.'

'Well,' Bensen said. He always said that when he had no argument, but didn't want to be left with nothing to say. After a while, it just got tiresome. What am I fighting him for? Forsyth asked himself. Nobody cares but me.

'Just tell me one thing, Donald,' Forsyth said. 'On a scale of one to a hundred, how big is this?'

'I don't measure things that way,' Bensen said, prim as an old maid. 'And neither should you. Avranilosa is part of a bigger picture we're putting together. That's why I want you to give it all you've got.'

Give it all you've got? Did anyone still say things like that, for real? Yes, Forsyth thought. In his fifteen years with the Company, he'd met a lot of men like Bensen. They all seemed to think all they had to do was latch on to some inspiring phrase to quote you, and you'd go out and die for them.

Asshole, he thought, still angry over the interview. He knew what Bensen's 'bigger picture' was. Avranilosa, a junk peddler with less to recommend him to humanity than a bubonic rat, would provide a means by which Domestic Ops could infiltrate Cuban intelligence operations in the Miami area. Instead of frying the bastard's ass for his part in the death of Genevevo, they'd kiss it. They'd make him a government employee, and pay him more money in one lump than Forsyth could earn in five years. They'd give him

anything he wanted, including a pension.

He opened another bottle of Scotch and poured a good one. He wished he could get really drunk; he never did. It was as if he had some sort of built-in mechanism that prevented it from happening, although he often drank more than he should. Kidneys probably look like the sole of a running shoe, he thought.

Again he wished he was a thousand miles away from Miami, away from Bensen, away from acting for Domestic Ops in a scenario that nobody seemed to care shit about. The only thing that kept him from calling it a day and sending in his papers was the fact that Tony Genevevo's murderer was still at large. Somehow or other, he was going to find that turkey.

It was a cinch nobody else was going to: the death of one undercover operative was to Head Office what a pinprick might have been to a dinosaur. They had bigger things on their minds: SIGINT and RADINT and ELINT, destabilization in Nicaragua, troop movements in El Salvador, Afghanistan, Iran. Nuclear submarine bases at

Severomorsk, political assassination in Lebanon, multi-million-dollar covert operations in Kampuchea and Korea and Chile. Street killings were a local matter: let the head of station handle it.

So Forsyth was stuck with Bensen, who seemed to care even less about Genevevo than Head Office did. All Bensen wanted was to bring Avranilosa across, a nice little coup, one more commendation on his way to that overseas posting with virtually unlimited expenses and the chance to buy a duty-free Mercedes.

Screw him. Screw them all.

They could take their option papers and jam them where the sun never shone. Tony Genevevo had found out something that got him killed, and Crandon's security company was tied into it. Whatever it was, Forsyth promised himself, he was going to find out, then level the score. He didn't know how, yet. But he'd do it. Meantime, Bensen wanted Avranilosa turned. Forsyth grinned. He'd turn the fat bastard, all right.

Inside fucking out.

14

The Holiday Inn on Key Largo was at Mile Marker 100, on the western side of US-1, about a mile south of the entrance to the John Pennekamp State Park. Drosdow sighted the familiar sign with relief. The highway south from Miami was as ugly a road as he had ever travelled, and he had travelled some pretty ugly ones. To drive it was to be ceaselessly affronted by signs, hoardings and poster come-ons, mile upon mind-numbing mile of them. Eat at Beefsteak Charlie's, Burger King, MacDonalds, Wendy's, Hamburger Heaven, Leon's Bar-B-Que, Taco John's. Visit Tropical Dreams, Lion Country Safari, Planet Ocean, Parrot Jungle, Metrozoo, the Serpentarium, Monkey Jungle, Mossosukee Indian Village, Fairchild Tropical Garden, Six Flags Atlantis, Flipper's Key West, Orchid Jungle, Coral Castle. Stay at Holiday Inn, Best Western, Ramada Inn,

Flamingo Inn, Howard Johnson, Travelodge, Quality Inn, Marriott, Hilton, Hyatt. Rent from Quality, Budget, Avis, Hertz, Econocar, Olin, Alamo. Fly Delta, TWA, Eastern, Air Florida, American, United, Air Jamaica, Pan Am. Smoke Marlboro, Kent, More, Salem, Lark, Winston, Chesterfield. Drink Budweiser, Miller's, Michelob, Old Granddad, Jack Daniel's, Canadian Club, Smirnoff. Burritos, Tacos, Hot Dogs, Gator Burgers, Eats To Go. Ice Cold Drinks, Airboat Rides, Boat Rentals, Bike Rentals, Shells, Fishing Tackle, Guns, on and on, endless, unavoidable.

When he turned into the parking lot in front of the Holiday Inn, Drosdow was surprised to see a battered old boat on a huge trailer in front of the hotel. The boat looked spuriously old, like a fake antique. On its bow was the name *African Queen*. A sign on the towing truck announced that this was the original boat used in the movie of the same name.

Americans, he thought: they turn the sites of actual history into parking lots, but lovingly preserve artefacts from old movies. He got out of his car and walked

around the boat, remembering the scene where Humphrey Bogart got the leeches all over him and Katharine Hepburn rubbed salt on them to get them off. His memory told him that the boat had been sunk at the end of the film, ramming the German cruiser. Maybe they had two, he decided.

He went into the lobby. The registration desk was on his right. On the left a doorway led into the restaurant. The Bogart theme was continued: Casablanca Room, and so on. Probably nobody in America had ever heard of Key Largo till they used the name as a movie title, he thought. He asked for a room facing the pool, and the girl at the desk drew him a sketch to show him how to park his car in back. Nobody offered to help him with his luggage.

'Did Miss Jones check in yet?' he asked. 'Miss Mary Jones?'

The girl checked the register. 'She's in 115, Mr Smith,' she said. 'Three doors along from you.'

Drosdow nodded and went back out to his car. He drove around the back of the

hotel. The parking lot was enclosed by a chain-link wire fence. A sign offered rides in a glass-bottomed boat. Loud rock music blatted from a radio somewhere nearby. He parked the Mercedes close to the building, so that it would be in shadow in the morning, and carried his two-suiter to the room. It was like every Holiday Inn he had ever been in, phony but comfortable, ugly without being offensive, with carved wooden head-boards on the beds and huge lamps on the bedside tables that gave off just too little light to read by.

An armchair and a round glass-topped table stood between the air-conditioning unit beneath the window and the twin queen-sized beds. In the bathroom, a white paper strip across the toilet seat advised him that it had been sanitized for his protection. So, Americans still believed you could get clap off lavatory seats.

He opened his case and took out the bottle of Glenfiddich he'd bought at the liquor store in south Miami on the way down. He got the ice-bucket from the bathroom and padded around the

building to the machine, filled the bucket and went back to his room. Kids were screeching in and out of the pool. Water streamed across the pathway where the jungly plants were being hosed. Drosdow locked his door and poured himself a large drink. He put ice into the glass, although he knew that was no way to treat a good single malt. To hell with it. He needed a cold drink, and he had no intention of drinking the piss Americans drank under the delusion it was beer.

He looked at his watch. Five o'clock. He picked up the phone and dialled 115. A woman's voice answered, low-pitched, relaxed.

'Happy families are all alike,' he said.

'Every unhappy family is unhappy in its own way,' she replied, completing the opening sentence of *Anna Karenina* 'I've been expecting you. What room are you in?'

'One-oh-nine,' he said. 'Join me for a drink?'

'Give me a couple of minutes.'

While he waited, Drosdow reviewed in his mind what he knew about Katja

Renis. Born in Prague, she was the second of the three daughters of Hanna and Karl Malinkov. Her father was a lecturer at the University of Prague, where Katja had graduated in 1966. Fluent in Czech, Russian, French, German and English, she had no trouble in obtaining a job as an assistant news editor with FSZS, the Czech Federal News and Information Service. Very soon thereafter she became the mistress of Leszek Cubr, head of the Second Department of the StB — *Státni Tajná Bezpečnost*, the State Security Agency of the Interior Ministry. In 1973, after intensive training which included attendance at the assassination school, a former monastery on the banks of the Vltava in the Prague suburb of Vysehrad, she and her 'husband', Vaslav Renis, chosen by Cubr to accompany her, had made their way to the United States posing as anti-communist refugees. A year after their arrival they 'separated', and Katja moved to Washington. Before long, she obtained employment as an executive assistant at the School of Foreign Service at Georgetown University. This placed her ideally

for making contacts in the intelligence world — her boss was a former CIA White House briefing coordinator — as directed by her case officer, Arkady Shuvarov.

Shuvarov had protested bitterly when Katja was selected to work as Drosdow's swallow, claiming she was far too valuable to waste on one operation. His protests were overruled. The GRU *rezident* in Washington reminded him of Colonel-General Ivashutin's dictum that the neutralization of the American satellite was to be effected at all costs: nothing took precedence over Initiative Open Window.

Drosdow got up and opened the door when she knocked. He smiled and she came in. She was everything he had hoped for: tall, blonde, beautiful, with a good figure and that unmistakable Continental style that American women strive for but never achieve. She had blue eyes, a full mouth, elegant hands and ankles. Her skin was lightly tanned, with a scattering of freckles across the bridge of her nose. She wore a white linen suit, white shoes and a dark blue open-necked

silk blouse. Yes, he thought, perfect: a centrefold with a brain.

'Sit down,' he said. 'Do you want some whisky?'

'Thank you, no.'

'You have been informed about your assignment?'

'Only that it is a sanctification.'

'A very important one. Perhaps the most important one we have ever undertaken.'

'Then I am honoured to have been selected.'

'You come highly recommended. Not too highly, I hope. I do not tolerate failure.'

'I understand,' she said. 'Who is the subject?'

'His name is Butler Mitchell. He is a deputy chief of what is known inside the National Security Agency as the 'S' Organization. Its full name is the Office of Communications Security, COMSEC for short.'

COMSEC, he told her, provided the methods and equipment which protected the entire range of American intelligence

communications: command, control, voice, data, teletype and telemetry among them. It also prescribed the way these systems were used, from the scrambler phone in the presidential limousine to the banks of chattering crypto machines on the sixth floor of the State Department; and anywhere in between.

'Mitchell is directly responsible for the security of an NSA computer network known as Platform,' Drosdow said. 'It is the host environment for fifty-two separate computer systems all around the world, including the British GCHQ complex at Cheltenham. Our intention is to penetrate it.'

He took a folder out of his case and opened it, taking out an assortment of photographs, some of them Polaroids, others black and white ten-by-eights. Many of them had been taken with a very long telephoto lens. They showed a house, vacation photos, a man and a woman standing in front of two cars. The man in the pictures was dark-haired, in his middle forties, with the husky shoulders of a football player. Katja Renis went

through them in silence.

'This is his house?'

'And his wife. Study the pictures thoroughly. Then go through the dossier. A great deal of effort has gone into its compilation.'

'Later,' she said. 'Tell me something about the man. His personality.'

'He is forty-six,' Drosdow said. 'Born in Plymouth, Massachusetts, eldest of three brothers. An old family, originating in the South. They are what the British call snobs. They boast a great-grandmother who was a French aristocrat, one of those who fled the slave insurrection in Santo Domingo in 1794 and settled in Georgia. They put great value on such nonsense, and consider themselves a cut above the common herd. The parents virtually bankrupted themselves sending their children to the right schools. Mitchell, for instance, went to MIT and was recruited there. His wife's name is Catherine. He married her against his parents' wishes: they thought her a social inferior.'

'For a people who pride themselves on being a classless society, Americans are

very class-conscious.'

'That is because most of them are hypocrites. Now, the wife: Cathie, as she is known, works part-time in an office in Laurel, Maryland, near Fort Meade. She plays tennis at her country club most weekends, spends all her money on clothes she doesn't need, drinks too much. Typical American bourgeois mentality. The marriage is a sham, of course, as many of them are. There is no evidence that she sleeps around, but he has a reputation as a womanizer. He's not very imaginative on that front, but then, people who work with computers rarely are.'

'Likes, dislikes?'

'He likes people to think he's rich. He dresses well. As you see, he drives an expensive car, a Dodge 600 Turbo convertible. He takes a vacation trip two or three times a year, alone. Picks someone up, has a fling. He's a bad gambler, given to plunging. He lost a lot of money in Atlantic City last month; more than he could really afford.'

'He sounds like a very unhappy man.'

'That's precisely what makes him your meat,' Drosdow said. 'Not only is he dissatisfied with his personal life, he is unhappy at work. He has been twice passed over for promotion, and believes it is because of his wife. She's one of those women who drink too much at parties and get maudlin. As a security officer himself, Mitchell knows his superiors must view her lapses with some unease. The more he cheats on her, the unhappier she becomes. The unhappier she is, the more she makes a fool of herself. He hates her for that.'

'How long will we have?'

'The timing of every phase of this undertaking has been minutely planned. So far it is exactly on schedule. The financing has been effected, the properties purchased, the decoys set running. Now we need Mitchell in the bag, and sooner rather than later. Red Centre has scheduled the launch of our bird for October 3, four months from now. We must effect our brute force attack at the end of September.'

'I understand,' she said. 'Don't worry.'

'You sound very confident,' Drosdow said.

She smiled a feline smile, tossing her well-modelled head so that the long blonde hair swung away from her face. 'I am,' she said, silkily. 'I'm very, very good.'

Drosdow smiled, too. He kicked off his shoes and loosened his tie.

'All right,' he said. 'Show me.'

15

Somebody once described a CIA man as a cross between a Boy Scout and a mugger. There was enough truth in the description to make Forsyth grin as he made his preparations. He did not discuss his plans with Bensen or anyone else.

It was at times like this that being an old hand paid off: you knew how to cut any corner that needed cutting. Forsyth had been around since the days when filing cabinets were made of wood and you had to make a reservation if you wanted to call overseas. There might be more than one or two people in the Company who'd spit if you mentioned his name to them; but there were plenty of others who owed him.

One of them was Jack Dempsey in M & S. Management and Services was where you went if you needed manpower, money, transportation, untraceable weapons or cars, and Dempsey was the area

controller. On his desk was a sign that said: 'TELL ME YOU WANT IT YESTERDAY — I HAVEN'T HAD A GOOD LAUGH ALL WEEK.'

He asked Dempsey for a motor-driven Canon A1 with a 70-210mm zoom lens and a dozen rolls of XP1 black and white film. XP1 could be up- or down-rated in the camera, which made it the ideal any-light film.

'Don't log this, Jack,' he told Dempsey. 'I'm on a private shoot.'

'Frank, you know the rules,' Dempsey protested. He was a tall man with a long jaw, dark auburn hair that had thinned at the crown, and wide brown eyes which surveyed the world with benevolent amusement. Like Forsyth, Dempsey had been a Company man pretty much all his working life.

'Damned right, I know the rules,' Forsyth said. 'If you log this, I've got to give you a case number, and I don't have one, Jack. Trust me. I'll get it all back to you, don't worry.'

'Don't worry, he says,' Dempsey said. But he was grinning.

'Now, about wheels. Something anonymous, Jack.'

He decided on a panel truck, and Dempsey came up with a theatrically filthy GMC Safari with enough onboard equipment hidden inside to follow a fish up a river. Forsyth signed it out and hit the street. When he came back in, three days later, he had almost two hundred shots of the Fat Man going about his business.

He checked in the camera and took the elevator down to Archives. He fed his ID into a slot for computer scan, and after a few moments the unmarked door opened with a metallic clack. Beyond it was a desk at which he signed the log. He filled out a requisition form and took it across to the issue counter, where a clerk gave him a call unit with the number 38-F Dymo-taped to it. While he waited Forsyth got a cup of coffee from the dispenser.

After about ten minutes, the call unit gave its discreet signal and he went back to the issue counter and picked up the files he had requested. It took him most of the afternoon, but when he was done, he had a stack of perhaps twenty black

and white photographs set aside. He went back to the issue clerk and told him which photographs he wanted to sign out.

'OK, you've got to fill out an ATRD,' the clerk said. 'Five copies, press hard. Signature, authorization code and service number.'

'I know, I know,' Forsyth growled, impatiently. The man looked at him the way issue clerks always do. Forsyth filled in the Authorization To Remove Documents, then took the tie-flap envelope containing the prints up to the fifth floor, where he knocked on Jack Dempsey's door.

'Frank, not again,' Dempsey said, alarmed. 'What are you after now?'

'Relax,' Forsyth said. 'This is Ongoing Situation time. I just need some speciality work, Jack. These are from Archives. Sign the chit, will you?'

Dempsey signed the back copy of the release chit and put it into a cylindrical container with a red 'R' on top. He fed the container into a slot beside his desk. The machine gave a thud as compressed air sped the container to Archives,

verification that the photographs had reached their intended destination. The top copy would remain with Dempsey until the photographs were returned.

Dempsey opened the envelope and riffled through the photographs. 'Nasty-looking bunch of mothers,' he observed. 'Who are they, Frank?'

'Various kinds of Miami sewer life,' Forsyth said. He laid twelve rolls of XP1 on Dempsey's desk. 'I've got a couple of hundred shots of a man named Avranilosa on these,' he said. 'I want him married into as many of these pictures as possible.'

'You've indicated where?'

'On the back of each picture.'

'Some of these shots are blurred, Frank,' Dempsey remarked. 'It won't be easy.'

'Use maximum entropy,' Forsyth said.

'Know it all, don't you?'

'My momma didn't raise no fools,' Forsyth grinned. Maximum entropy was a mathematical principle invented by two Cambridge scientists named Skilling and Gull. Fed into a computer, the algorithm

could turn an out-of-focus blur into a sharp and recognizable picture. Dempsey's technicians could strip the picture of Avranilosa in, then defocus the result to restore the telephoto blur.

'What are you up to, Frank?' Dempsey asked, suspiciously. 'Who is this Avranilosa guy, anyway?'

'Don't ask,' Forsyth said. 'Can you get me these fast, Jack?'

'Couple of days. That OK?'

'It'll have to do. Lose it on another case, will you? Don't bill it to me.'

'Frank . . . '

'I know, I know. Just this once, Jack. OK?'

Dempsey shook his head, like a vexed uncle. 'One of these days, Frank . . . '

'You're a pal, Jack. Hey, what's green and smells?'

'I'll buy it.'

'Kermit's ass,' Forsyth said.

Three days later, on a bright sunny morning with a sky the colour of bleached denim, Forsyth drove out to Bal Harbor. He pulled the big Olds to a stop in front of the pole barrier at the gatehouse and

wound down the window as the guard came out. The man had on a white pith helmet and an all-white uniform with blue epaulettes. He had a beer belly and a gun that looked big enough to blow a hole in a battleship.

'The agency I work for prefers not to show ID,' Forsyth said to the man. 'If you insist, however, I will do so.'

The guard's eyes widened. He was an ex-policeman, and he knew the formula. 'CIA?' he said. 'What can I do for you?'

'What's your name?'

'Reilly, sir. John F. Reilly.'

'That your cruiser over there, John?'

'Yessir.'

'Let's you and me get in it, then, and you can give me a ride up to the Avranilosa house.'

'Uh . . . sir, I can't — '

'What, John?'

'I'm supposed to call the house first.'

'You know anything about Pedro Avranilosa, John? You know where his money comes from?'

'Look, whoever you are, it's not my responsibility, right? You take it up with

Armorgard Security. They send me here, I do my job. And my job is to call all residents before admitting visitors.'

'Today, you forget,' Forsyth said, getting out of the car. 'Come on, let's move it.'

They got into the cruiser, a white Ford Mustang with a dome light and a blue stripe along the body. Reilly drove slowly through the estate, easing the car over the ramps. The air smelled of flowers and wet grass. And money, Forsyth thought, as they rolled to a stop outside the gates of Avranilosa's house. He squinched down in the back as the CCTV cameras swung in their watching arc. Reilly picked up the phone, waited, and said what Forsyth had told him to say.

'John Reilly here. Got a special delivery package.'

There was a short wait, long enough for the camera to scan the car, and Reilly standing in the sunshine. Then the ornate gates swung back. Reilly drove up to the parking area and stopped by a covered walkway that led up to the house. He was sweating badly.

'Get lost,' Forsyth advised him. He got out of the car and walked up the ramp. Ahead of him, a young Chinese wearing a white coat and black trousers came out of the door.

'What you want?' he said. 'How you get in here?'

'Where's your boss?'

'You leave, now!' the Oriental said.

'Drop the Charlie Chan act, kid, and take me to your leader,' Forsyth said. The manservant moved in front of him, hands at his sides, face impassive. Forsyth took a step, and the houseman immediately fell into a karate fighting stance, a sibilant hiss coming from his lips. Forsyth grinned and flipped back his jacket.

'What I have here is a Model 92 SB-C Beretta,' he said, conversationally. 'It fires thirteen 9mm Parabellum slugs at a muzzle velocity of three hundred and ninety metres a second. Call it eight thousand five hundred miles an hour. What I want you to do is think about one of those bullets hitting your head.'

The manservant looked at the gun and then up into Forsyth's eyes. He shrugged

191

and put his hands down.

'I never was any good at that karate shit, anyway,' he said. 'He's out on the tennis court.'

'Who else is around?'

'Chauffeur's day off. Two maids in the house. Bodyguard is with the Boss. That's it.'

'Very good,' Forsyth said. 'Let's go surprise him.'

The manservant led him through a patio commanding a splendid view across Biscayne Bay. The lawns were like green carpeting. The water in the pool was pellucid. A Hatteras 36 Convertible swayed at its mooring. The wages of sin, Forsyth thought: luxury.

He kept the Beretta in his hand as he followed the servant to the raised tennis court. He heard the familiar *blop!* of racquet hitting ball, and then, as they turned the corner, he saw Avranilosa. The Fat Man was alone on the court, returning balls fired at him by one of those tennis-ball cannons. A young Cuban with a skeletal face sat slumped in a canvas chair off to one side, torpid in

the heat. Avranilosa swung angrily around when he saw them.

'What the — ?' he snapped. 'Lee, I told you never — '

'He's got a gun,' Lee said, laconically. The bodyguard snapped upright, his hand moving for the gun in its shoulder holster. Forsyth let him see the Beretta and he froze. Avranilosa looked left and right, edgy-eyed, like an animal seeking a hole.

'Stay put, Fat Man,' Forsyth said. 'Don't make me nervous, now.'

'How the hell did you get in here?'

'Free fall,' Forsyth said. He gestured at the bodyguard, come here. 'Take the gun out of the holster with your left hand, finger and thumb. That's it. Drop it on the ground, then step away from it.'

The pistol hit the lush grass almost soundlessly. The Cuban took two steps backwards, hands at his sides. His dark eyes glittered with anger.

'Face down on the ground,' Forsyth said. 'You, too, Confucius.' The body-guard and the servant stretched out prone, face down. Forsyth went across

and picked up the Cuban's gun. It was a .357 Combat Magnum Smith & Wesson with a two and a half inch barrel. Useful for hunting rhinoceros. He threw it into the swimming pool.

'I know you,' Avranilosa said. 'I know you from someplace.'

'The name is Forsyth. Is that any help?'

The Cuban's eyelids dropped, hooding his eyes. He put his tennis racquet down, and wrapped a white cotton towel around his neck.

'What happens now?' he said.

'You and I are going to talk, Fat Man.'

'I doubt we got anything to talk about.'

'We'll see. You boys stay right there, hear me?'

He gestured with the pistol towards the patio, where there was a white garden table shaded by a multi-coloured sun-shade.

'Let us cross over the river and rest in the shade of the trees,' he said.

'What?'

'Never mind, Fat Man. Lead the way.'

He sat in one of the chairs where he could keep an eye on the two men still

prone on the lawn. Avranilosa sat on his left.

'You know who I am?' Forsyth said.

'I know,' Avranilosa said. 'What you want with me?'

'I want to talk to you about Nino Baca, Pedro,' Forsyth asked. 'You do know him, don't you?'

'I know him.'

'Do business together?'

'I don't know what you're talking about.'

'Let me put it into words of one syllable for you,' Forsyth said. 'Co-caine.'

'I don't deal in drugs. My business is real estate. I'm a legitimate businessman, and you can't — '

Forsyth held up a hand. 'Cut the bullshit, Pedro. You're talking to a pro.'

Avranilosa started to say something, but stopped when Forsyth thrust the fat folder of photographs into his hands.

'Look what I brought you,' Forsyth said. The Cuban slid the ten-by-eights out of the envelope and shuffled through them, frowning. When he looked up, the anger in his eyes was burning bright.

'What is this?' he said.

'We call it 'compelled accommodation' these days,' Forsyth said, cheerfully. 'It used to be called a frame-up.'

'You out of your mind?' Avranilosa said, angrily. 'You think you can walk in here and pull a stunt like this?'

'Ask yourself a question,' Forsyth suggested. 'Ask yourself what I'm going to do with these pictures.'

'You can set fire to them and jam them up your ass for all I care!'

'I tell you, Pedro, I admire you,' Forsyth said. 'I admire any man that can make jokes while he's looking death in the face.'

Avranilosa frowned, 'Just what the fuck are you talking about, Forsyth?' The veneer of sophisticated wealth was slipping a little. Forsyth smiled benevolently. It was like bringing in a sailfish: you had to know when to reel in, when to give it slack.

'You haven't put it together yet, have you?' he said. 'I thought you were smart, Pedro.'

Avranilosa's eyes narrowed to slits. 'You

think you can get away with this?' he hissed. 'I make one call, you dead, man! Hear me? You fucking dead!' He slapped the table hard to emphasize his threat.

Forsyth made a little sound of annoyance and brought the butt of the Beretta down heavily on Avranilosa's hand. The Fat Man screeched with pain. Forsyth saw the bodyguard's hands curl tensely, but he didn't move. Smart cookie.

'I warned you, Pedro,' Forsyth said. 'This isn't a TV movie. You fuck with me, you're gonna get hurt.'

'Looka my hand!' Avranilosa wailed, his voice halfway between a sob and a shout. 'Look what you done to my hand!'

'I came here to get some information, pally,' Forsyth said, unsympathetically. 'And you are going to give it to me. If you want me to beat the shit out of you first, say the word.'

'I don't talk to you!' Avranilosa whined, nursing his hand beneath his arm and rocking from side to side. 'I don't tell you fucking nothing!'

'You still haven't got it through your thick skull, have you, you tub of lard?'

Forsyth said, putting all the contempt he could muster into his voice. 'You tell me what I want to know, you do like I say, or Nino Baca gets a complete set of these pictures. And you wind up in a canal in Hialeah with your dick in your mouth.'

'He wouldn't believe it!' the Cuban panted, his face slick with sweat. 'Those pictures are fakes, and you know it!'

'Sure I know it,' Forsyth said, equably. 'But your friend Baca doesn't. What you think he's gonna say when he sees this one, Pedro? That's you talking to Raoul Ramirez, deputy director of DGI. Or what about this one in the boat? You're shaking hands with Paco Ortiz, remember him? He went down for twenty years at Tallahassee a couple of months ago for smuggling coke. Didn't he try to muscle in on Baca's territory in south Miami? What you think Ninobaby would say if he saw this, Fat Man, or this one of you coming out of the Ministry of the Interior building in Havana?'

'I wasn't in any of those places!' Avranilosa whined. 'I've never seen Paco Ortiz in my life.'

'All you got to do now is get Baca to believe you,' Forsyth said. 'What you think he'll do when he finds out he's been doing La Dirección's dirty work for them?'

Avranilosa did not reply, although if he could have killed Forsyth without moving, Forsyth would have dropped dead on the spot. The silence lengthened. Forsyth was in no hurry. The hook was in and set. He could see the sweat beading on the Cuban's upper lip. A big jet roared somewhere up high. Bees hummed in the flower borders. A blackbird landed on the lawn, saw them and flew away.

'I can't talk to you,' Avranilosa mumbled. 'They would kill me for that.'

'This is really a nice place you've got here, Pedro,' Forsyth said.

'You don't realize what you're asking.'

'Pretty view,' Forsyth said, as if he hadn't heard the Cuban speak.

'You asking me to double, *hombre*,' Avranilosa said. 'I couldn't do it. I just wouldn't be able to cut it.'

'It's not as if you had a choice,' Forsyth said, turning to face him. 'Is it?'

Avranilosa sighed; his shoulders slumped.

'You hurt my hand real bad, you know that?'

'Tell me about Tony Genevevo,' Forsyth said. 'And the others.'

'Listen, I'm not talking to you till I get some guarantees. I don't even know for sure who the hell you are.'

'You know who I am, Fat Man. You know who I work for, just like I know who you work for. As for guarantees, I guarantee you I will shoot that bodyguard of yours right up the ass if he doesn't stop twitching.'

'Raoul!' Avranilosa said, sharply.

'That's better, Raoul,' Forsyth said, agreeably. 'Now, about Genevevo. Baca wasted him, right?'

'You know, why you asking?'

'What was in it for him?'

'You got any idea what it's like on the street right now, fucking Colombians taking over everything in sight? Nino had a big deal going down, he couldn't take any chances. Genevevo knew everything we were doing.'

'Too simple,' Forsyth said. 'Lay it out for me. Right from the beginning. How did you get on to Genevevo? Why were

the security people taken out? Whose idea was it to dress it up like that? What was the payoff? Let me tell you what I'm thinking, Fat Man. I'm thinking that all this stinks of smokescreen. Am I right? Was the whole thing pulled to cover something completely different, something put up by your friends in Havana?'

Avranilosa fell silent again, his only reply a shrug of the shoulders. Time to give the fish a few fathoms of line, Forsyth decided: there wasn't much more fight in him. He let the silence lengthen again, watching a sailboat on the bay, gulls soaring effortlessly above its wake.

'Tell you what I really want to know, Pedro,' Forsyth said, choosing his moment. 'Did Genevevo find out what DGI was up to? Was that why you conned Baca into killing him?'

The Fat Man stared past him out across the blue water. After what seemed like a very long time, he sighed.

'You ever heard of a man named Frederic Drosdow?' he said.

16

Eastern Airlines flight EA 173 from Baltimore touched down at Miami International dead on time, a few minutes after eleven a.m. As it was the only flight of the day from there, the plane was full, and there was a twenty-minute wait before Butler Mitchell got his luggage and headed for the cab rank. After a few minutes, the dispatcher signalled him to a Courtesy cab, and Mitchell told the driver to take him to the Fontainebleau Hilton at Miami Beach. Not for a moment did it occur to him that he was being watched.

At the hotel, he let the system wash over him. That was the great thing about luxury hotels: everywhere you went there were doormen, bellmen, reception staff and maids, smiling brightly, waiting to cater to your slightest whim. He always travelled with a wad of singles ready: everyone who lent a hand — and there

was always someone ready to lend a hand — got a dollar. It wasn't big tipping by Miami Beach standards, but he knew that if you tipped frequently, word soon got around, even in a place as big as the Fontainebleau.

As soon as he was unpacked, he phoned down to the Oceanfront Spa and told them he'd like a massage. He put on a white Ralph Lauren polo shirt, a pair of white Dacron slacks, white towelling socks and a pair of Adidas Oregon running shoes. Then he went down to the main gallery of the hotel, feeling the familiar excitement of anticipation.

He always came to the Fontainebleau: the place had class. Fourteen million dollars' worth, to be precise. That was what they'd spent refurbishing what had always been the most astonishing of all the 'flabbergast' hotels on the Beach. Soft lights, candelabra, real paintings on the walls. Class: the Fontainebleau had it in spades. Eighteen acres of tropical gardens, twelve hundred feet of private beach, a half-acre swimming pool, its own eighteen-hole golf course, three jacuzzis, a

bowling alley, six bars, a nightclub. In the Main Gallery restaurant, with its plants and antiques and statues, you could get the best prime rib in Florida. And in the Poodle Lounge, the best tail.

Mitchell went down to the restaurant in the tropically landscaped pool area. A calypso band beneath a thatched hut was playing a song about a little girl in Kingston Town. The maître d' showed him to a table beneath an umbrella.

'Welcome to Under the Trees, sir,' he said. 'Enjoy your meal.'

The sun was hot and strong, a wonderful change from the gusty winds and rain of Baltimore. The jungly smell of irrigated plants mingled with those of good food, suntan oil, perfume, perspiration, the sea. Mitchell felt good, relaxed. He had been glad to get away from Cathie, from her constant catalogue of dissatisfactions and her watery smile and the pathetic way she kept trying to get him to make love to her. He banished the picture of his wife from his mind: he had come to Miami for fun, not to think about Cathie.

The waitress came and took his order: two eggs over easy, Canadian bacon, hash browns, white toast, coffee. He leaned back in his chair, watching the lissome bodies of the young women around the pool with a fond, unfocused lust.

Six tables away, Drosdow watched the American and smiled. It looked as if this might be easier than he had thought.

* * *

That evening, relaxed after a whirlpool bath and a massage, Butler Mitchell patted some Aramis aftershave on his cheeks, looked at his watch, and then at his reflection in the bathroom mirror. Not bad, he thought. He had good shoulders, a deep chest, a flat belly. He was particularly careful about that. In his opinion, nothing turned a woman off faster than a fat gut.

He put on a cotton shirt with monogrammed French cuffs, fastening them with chunky gold cufflinks. He selected a dark blue silk Countess Mara tie with a narrow white diagonal stripe,

and then put on the Palm Beach suit he'd bought for this trip. He slipped on his tasselled Gucci loafers, picked up a pack of Winston 100s, his loose change, his wallet and his room key, and went out of the room.

He went straight down to the Poodle Lounge, which was on the same level as the starkly art-deco Steak House. The sounds of music, laughter and conversation washed towards him like surf as he went in. He walked over to the bar. The bartender, a tubby, balding man wearing a white jacket, wore a lapel nameplate.

'Hi, George,' Mitchell said, putting a twenty on the bar. 'Let me have a large whiskey sour. Make that very sour, okay?'

'You got it,' the bartender said, crashing a glass into the chipped ice. When the drink came, Mitchell left his change on the leatherette bar in front of him. Glass in hand, he swivelled around on his stool to look the place over. Most of the tables were occupied by formally dressed couples, or foursomes. Formally dressed for Miami, anyway. The trio were playing an uptempo version of 'My Funny

Valentine' for the dozen or so couples dancing in the centre of the room. Older couples sat together, not saying anything to each other. Younger women, obviously vacationers, sat together in pairs. A blonde woman with a suntan met Mitchell's gaze and held it. She wore a pale blue V-necked sleeveless dress. Her hair was cut short, Kim Novak style. Mitchell smiled at her and then looked away. There was no rush. He ordered another drink and invited George the bartender to join him. George drew a Cola from the mixer and took a five dollar bill from the pile on the bar.

'Pretty quiet, tonight,' Mitchell observed.

'Early yet,' George said, industriously polishing a glass. 'Another half an hour, the place'll be jammed. You just get in today?'

'Right.'

'Seen you before, though, ain't I?'

'I get down three, four times a year.'

'Thought I knew your face. You get so you remember the regulars.'

The man sitting next to Mitchell slid off his stool to leave and Mitchell glanced

at the newcomer taking his place. He was a swarthy, middle-aged man of medium height, with brilliant blue eyes and a pockmarked face. He wore a dark blue lightweight suit, a white shirt, and a neat tie. He ordered Glenfiddich on the rocks. Catching Mitchell's eye, he smiled sheepishly.

'Shouldn't do that to good whisky,' he said, apologetically.

'Diff'rent strokes for diff'rent folks,' Mitchell said.

'You on vacation?'

'Just taking a few days' break,' Mitchell said.

'Where you from?'

'Near Baltimore,' Mitchell said, half turning away. He didn't want to get tied up with some talkative travelling salesman or conventioneer.

'That's a coincidence,' the man said. He had a faint regional accent that Mitchell couldn't place. Hell, he thought, half of the population of America had some sort of accent you couldn't place.

'You live in Baltimore?'

'I've got a place in Easton.'

'Very nice,' Mitchell said. Easton was in the heart of what they called the Maryland Tidewater, full of tradition and old money. 'You on vacation, too?'

'Business and pleasure trip,' the man said. 'My daughter's down here with me. I'm in computer software. My own company. FD Associates.'

'Can't say I've heard of it.'

'We're small, but growing. Eight million turnover this year. It'll go to ten next year. The 'FD' stands for Fred Drosdow. That's me.'

'Butler Mitchell,' Mitchell said, reluctantly. The blonde girl with the great haircut gave him another long look. If he was going to make a move on her, it had better be soon, Mitchell decided.

'Let me get you another of those,' Drosdow said. 'George, give us the same again, here.'

'No, don't do that,' Mitchell said, hastily. 'Thanks all the same, Fred. I'm meeting someone. Don't want to be squiffed when they get here.'

It was at that moment that she walked in. She was about five feet eight, maybe a

hundred and twenty pounds. Blonde hair framed a heart-shaped face with violet-coloured eyes and a sprinkling of freckles across the bridge of a slightly retroussé nose. She wore a white Halston day dress and Ferragamo sandals. To Mitchell's astonishment she came directly towards him, smiling. Just as he thought she was about to speak to him, he realized she was looking at the man sitting next to him.

'I thought I'd find you here,' she said, shaking a finger at Drosdow mock-reprovingly. 'Can't take my eyes off you for a second, can I?'

'There you are, Kate,' Drosdow said. 'I was just talking to this gentleman here while I waited for you.'

'How do you do, Mr . . . ?'

'Mitchell,' he blurted, shaking the soft, slender, cool hand. 'May I offer you a drink, Miss Drosdow?'

'I think . . . not,' she said, looking around. 'I prefer somewhere a little . . . quieter.'

She happened to be looking right into Mitchell's eyes as she spoke and, for a moment, he thought there was a message

behind the words. She was still looking at him, the indigo eyes guileless. No, he told himself. He was imagining it. Still . . .

'Have you any plans for dinner?' he heard himself saying, astonished by his own temerity.

Drosdow looked at him, surprised. 'I thought you said you were meeting some friends?' he said. 'Anyway, we can't. Already got a date. Some other time, maybe.'

'You're staying here?'

'Penthouse,' Drosdow said. 'We'd better be going, Kate.'

'You will give us a raincheck, won't you . . . Mitch?' the girl said, touching the back of Mitchell's hand as Drosdow turned to leave. It seemed to him that there was something in the contact, a hint of a promise that made his heart bump suddenly. Their eyes met again. He had not been mistaken: there was frank invitation there now.

'Of course,' he mumbled, hoping his voice didn't sound as thick as it felt in his throat. He watched Kate Drosdow as she followed her father out of the room.

She made the other women in the place look dowdy. Class, Mitchell thought, you can always spot it. She had been wearing an emerald ring that must have been worth every cent of five thou. He finished his drink. The blonde woman was still sitting alone. She met his glance and smiled.

Much later, as she squirmed and moaned beneath his thrusting body, he tried to imagine that the blonde woman was Kate Drosdow. It was no use; he began to loathe her ten seconds after he climaxed. Her name was Martha Cobbett, a divorcée from Boston. As she got dressed, she asked him if he could loan her a hundred, you know, until her alimony came through. He gave her a fifty to get rid of her, then took a long, punishing shower to wash the bitch smell off him before he went to sleep.

Next morning he called the penthouse. Drosdow answered, and they arranged to meet for brunch in the Gallery Lounge. Mitchell made a reservation, then showered and shaved, putting on a pale lilac shirt and a white Calvin Klein suit. He

got to the restaurant ten minutes early and asked for the wine list. He knew only a little about champagne, so he played safe by ordering Dom Pérignon. He told the *sommelier* to bring it right away and open it. He was sipping his first glass, looking out over the tropical gardens and the rock grotto at the ocean when Drosdow and his daughter came in.

Kate Drosdow was wearing a lemon-yellow shift that bared creamy shoulders and elegant, lightly-tanned arms. The shift was gathered loosely at the waist by a thin gold chain. She wore no jewellery other than a tiny white-gold Rolex Cellini watch. She looked cool and very self-possessed.

'Champagne!' she said. 'How lovely!'

'Dom Pérignon, too,' Drosdow observed. He had on a dark blue Corbin blazer and pale grey slacks, a white shirt open at the neck to reveal a heavy gold chain. 'You must be doing well, Mr Mitchell. What line of business are you in?'

'I work for the government,' Mitchell said, giving the standard non-specific answer. 'Just another civil servant.'

'You must be a very well-paid one if you can afford Dom Pérignon in a place like this,' Drosdow said. 'What do they charge for that here?'

'I'm afraid I didn't look,' Mitchell said, hoping it sounded as casual as he wanted it to.

'Oh, Fred, stop being crass!' Kate said, fondly. 'Just ignore him, Mr Mitchell. It was a lovely thought.'

'Most people call me Mitch,' he said.

'What's your first name?'

'My mother called me after a character in a book,' Mitchell said. '*Gone With the Wind*. She said we had some vague family connection with the woman who wrote it.'

'I saw that movie,' Drosdow said. 'What was the man's name?'

'Clark Gable,' Mitchell said. 'He played the part of Rhett Butler.'

'I remember,' Kate said. 'He was quite a man.' She looked into Mitchell's eyes as she spoke and, yet again, he felt there was more coming at him than the words alone.

'Well, young fellow, are you ready to

214

eat?' Drosdow said.

'Thanks for the 'young fellow',' Mitchell smiled. 'It's very flattering, but a bit inaccurate, I'm afraid. I'm forty-six.'

'You don't look it,' Kate said. They went across to the buffet. Mitchell was pleased to see she wasn't one of those women who make a production out of what they can and cannot eat. It was one of the things about Cathie that gave him such a pain. Kate Drosdow selected herself a healthy meal.

'How old is your father?' he asked, as they walked back to their table.

'Let's see . . . I'm twenty-nine. So he's . . . fifty-five. Fifty-six this year. But don't tell him I told you.'

'So how come he called me 'young fellow'?'

She laughed. 'Anyone younger than him is a young fellow to my father.'

'Are you his only daughter?'

'That's right.'

'How come a beautiful woman like you isn't married?'

'Well, thank you, Mitch. As a matter of fact, I was married once. A long time ago. I prefer my freedom.'

'Me, too,' he said.

During the meal, he discovered that they had a lot in common. They agreed that Hawaii was ruined, Acapulco, too. They argued over which of the Caribbean islands was best, and whether the clams were better at Faidley's than Obrycki's. The talk turned to films, then books, then TV. They seemed fascinated by Mitchell's opinions. Drosdow ordered another bottle of champagne. People turned their heads when the cork popped. Mitchell feigned indifference. He felt witty, and worldly. The problems he had left behind him in Maryland seemed a million miles away.

' . . . if you ask me, Sondheim hasn't written anything to compare for sheer theatrical daring with *Pacific Overtures*,' he said, pouring the last of the champagne. 'There were magnificent things in *Sweeney Todd*, of course, notably that marvellous moment right at the end when Todd slams the door. But . . . '

'Mitch, I could sit here all day listening to you,' Drosdow said. 'But I've got to run. One of my people flew in from Rio especially to see me. He's got to fly back

216

tomorrow, so I've got no choice. You'll forgive me?'

'Don't give it a thought,' Mitchell said, waving a lordly hand. 'Let's do this again real soon.'

'Good idea,' Drosdow said. 'Kate, you coming?'

'I'm in good hands, Fred,' she said, smiling at Mitchell. 'You run along.'

When he was gone, she turned to Mitchell and smiled conspiratorially. 'I bet I know what you're thinking,' she said.

'What?' he said, startled, thinking *if you knew*.

'You're thinking, 'Oh, God, I'm stuck with this damned woman for the afternoon.' Well, you're not, so don't worry about it. I'm used to Fred dashing off and leaving me on my own.'

'I can't think of anyone I'd rather be stuck with, as you put it,' Mitchell said, with what he felt was clumsy gallantry.

'The man's a charmer!' she said, amazed. 'It must be the champagne.'

'You're very beautiful,' he said. The smile on her face did not change, but

217

again he thought he saw something in her eyes, and decided to believe it was encouragement. 'And I can think of nothing I'd like more than to be with you . . . as often as possible.'

He said it in a way that left her no room to doubt what he meant. He saw her expression change: impatience, annoyance, what? She looked away from him and then back again, and now the smile was gone.

'I think I'd better leave,' she said, coolly. She rose, and Mitchell stood, too, awkwardly uncertain. 'Thanks for brunch.'

'Please,' he begged. 'It came out wrong. I meant . . . '

'Goodbye, Mr Mitchell,' she said. He watched the soft, flowing movements of her thighs and body as she walked away, and he thought *shit!* Kate Drosdow wasn't some housewife from Oshkosh looking for a quickie to round out her Florida package tour. She was wealthy, sophisticated and intelligent, and he had gone at her like a drunken Marine in a Kobe whorehouse. *Jerk*, he told himself.

He called for the check. It was well over

a hundred dollars. Like all rich men, Drosdow hadn't given a thought to the second bottle of champage he'd ordered. Mitchell's dismay lasted only a few moments. Look at it as an investment, he told himself. So he'd been a jerk, that was no reason to go on being one. Anything in life worth having cost money. You had to go for it.

He went down to the florist in the shopping gallery and ordered two dozen long-stemmed roses for delivery to Kate Drosdow. He stared at the card for a long time trying to decide what to write. Finally, he wrote four words: 'Let me try again.' After much thought, he added another: 'Please.' Then he went back to his room and stayed there, smoking his way through a pack of cigarettes and staring sightlessly at the daytime soaps on TV. Shortly after five, the telephone rang. He pounced on it.

'Thank you for the flowers,' her soft voice said. 'They're lovely.'

'They ought to be ashamed to be in the same room as you,' he said. 'Kate? Are you still there?'

'I'm here.'

'I just . . . I apologize. But I'm not sorry for what I said. I meant every word of it. I want to — '

'Don't waste it on the telephone,' she said, and he thought she sounded as if she was smiling.

'Just say where,' he said, 'and when.'

'Fred's here, but he's got to go out again,' she said. 'Why don't you come up for a drink? Later we can go out to dinner.'

'Ten minutes,' he said, and hung up. *Later*, she'd said. He shaved carefully, cleaned his teeth, and changed his clothes from the skin out. When he was ready he looked in the mirror, a smile of triumph on his face. It would have vanished in an instant had he been able to overhear what was being said in the penthouse suite on the crescent-shaped top floor of the hotel.

'He's coming up,' Katja Renis said to Drosdow.

'You think he's hooked?'

She smiled contemptuously. 'He's hooked,' she said.

17

Once he accepted what had happened to him, Avranilosa became positively anxious to talk. That happened sometimes: you turned someone, and the information spilled out of him like a pan boiling over, as if the telling itself were an act both of confession and contrition. That was the good news.

The bad news was that, as usual, Forsyth's boss had gone for the glory. Avranilosa wasn't a very big fish, but Bensen acted as if they'd turned the chief of the KGB, firing off a series of memoranda to Washington to make it perfectly clear that if anyone deserved credit for rolling up the Cuban espionage operation, that someone was good old Donald Bensen.

Forsyth wasn't as worried about who got a gold star as he was about the fact that Bensen's memos would bring all sorts of I-Teams down from Head Office

to interrogate the Fat Man. Which meant he had to get what he wanted before they arrived. To his furious surprise, Bensen told him he was keeping Avranilosa under wraps until the dredgers arrived.

'They're sending specialists to debrief this man, Frank.'

'We don't need specialists. We don't need anybody!' he said, angrily. 'This honey trap thing is our baby, Donald. It's on our patch. It's my privilege, for Christ's sake, not Langley's!'

'You'll get your chance, Frank,' Bensen said. 'Lighten up.'

'What the hell kind of talk is that?' Forsyth said, savagely. 'If it means what I think it means, take it easy, I'm not in the mood. I want first turn with the Fat Man, Donald. Goddammit, I'm the one who brought him across.'

'I remember,' Bensen said, waspishly. 'And if I were to forget, I'm sure you'd remind me. But you'll have to wait, Frank. A lot of people — '

'Let *them* wait!'

'You want me to tell Langley they'll have to get in line because one of my field

agents wants priority?' Bensen said sweetly, twisting the knife of emphasis on Forsyth's rank. 'You'll just have to be patient a little longer.'

'Look, you've read my preliminary report,' Forsyth said. 'From what Avranilosa told me, it looks as if we've probably had Cuban — and for Cuban you can read Russian — military intelligence working right under our noses, and we didn't know a damned thing about it.'

'I'm aware of that,' Bensen said, tartly. He did not need reminding: some sharp words had been spoken when he talked to the head of DOD at Langley. 'All sorts of other people are interested now, Frank. Whether you like it or not.'

'Donald, let me have Avranilosa for a few hours, and I can wrap this thing up for you,' Forsyth said. 'Just a few hours.'

He watched Bensen carefully, saw the flicker of opportunism in the evasive eyes. He knew how the man's mind worked. To trash a Russian operation on home ground, on top of turning Avranilosa — it was too sweet for someone as greedy for

kudos as Bensen to resist. Come on, Donnie baby, he thought, go for it.

'Well,' Bensen said, pursing his lips and steepling his fingers. 'I don't know, Frank. How many men would it take?'

'Just a couple,' Forsyth said. 'I'll handle that. But I need the Fat Man, Donald.'

'Well . . . ' Bensen deliberated. 'Where do you plan to talk to him?'

'How about the Sonesta Beach Hotel on Key Biscayne? Tomorrow morning, ten thirty.'

Bensen drew in his breath sharply. 'Tricky, Frank,' he said. 'We'd be putting him in harm's way if he was on the street. I don't think that would be at all wise.'

'I want some psychological distance, Donald. I don't want to talk to him in the interrogation suite.'

'How long would you need? There's a team flying down from NSA. DEA are asking for him, too. And — '

'I'll have him back before you know he's been out.'

'I'm not sure — '

'Who is?' Forsyth said.

* * *

The Sonesta Beach Hotel looked like a pre-Columbian Mexican temple would have looked if the Mayans had known about pre-stressed concrete. It was about the last place on earth anyone would have chosen for an intelligence debriefing, which was why Forsyth selected it. The moment you walked into the place you became as anonymous as the plants. He took a luxury double on the fifth floor. The room had a king-sized bed with a coverlet that matched the drapes, a table, some chairs, a couch upholstered in white plastic. A balcony overlooked the beach. Some kids were sailing a catamaran on the ocean: its multi-coloured sails had the name of the hotel stencilled on them.

Two IS officers brought Avranilosa in. He looked tired, older. He was wearing a rumpled seersucker suit, a white cotton/poly shirt and scuffed loafers. He looked at Forsyth and then, without much interest, at the two men by the window.

'The tall one is Mike, the other one is Harry,' Forsyth said. Harry Lloyd was

forty-five, balding, short and overweight. His clothes looked as if they'd been bought at a K-Mart. Balfour was tall, thin and studious-looking. He wore a dark blue mohair suit, a white shirt and dark tie. He had the air of a small-town high-school teacher.

Avranilosa sat down and waited; he had become used to waiting. He was happy to have a change of scenery, to be in a room with real furniture, with a window with a view. Outwardly he appeared calm, but it was a pretence: inside him, fear seethed. He had been a fool. Suppose they weren't going to give him a pension and a new identity, as he'd thought? Suppose they were going to put him back on the street and use him as a double-agent? He would spend the rest of his life walking on eggshells.

'How've you been, Pedro?' Forsyth asked. 'They looking after you OK?'

'Oh, yeah, great,' Avranilosa said, heavily.

He was being kept in a safe house in Kendall. He never knew where he was, or whether it was day or night. Food came at

irregular intervals: he ate it automatically, as if it were a chore. He slept in an air-conditioned room which had no windows. Two doors: one that was always locked, except when the bland-faced orderly brought in his meals; the other leading into a second, equally anonymous room with a table and four chairs. There were no windows there, either; no clock, no calendar, nothing.

Forsyth began very slowly, asking innocuous questions that were easy to answer. He knew the secret was to make Avranilosa relax and lose his fear. They talked about what would happen after all the debriefings were over; Forsyth assured the Fat Man he'd see to it personally that they didn't put him back on the street. He understood him. He respected his views. They talked about the island, sport, anything. Avranilosa relaxed. His uneasiness began to abate.

'I guess I got to start talking to you guys, right?' he said.

'Sooner or later,' Forsyth said.

'Where you want me to begin?'

'Any place you like.'

Avranilosa began by describing how Havana had financed his real-estate operation so that he could provide cover residences in Miami for DGI agents. He laundered money which was used to fund the political campaigns of agents DGI wished to infiltrate into local government and law-enforcement agencies. He was supplied with narcotics connections in order to establish a relationship with Saturnino Baca, so that DGI could infiltrate the man's organization and monitor his activities.

'So DGI knew Baca was finding it harder to make good connections in Colombia,' Forsyth said.

'I told you. Them Indians, they won't deal with nobody but each other.'

'And when your friend Drosdow came along, it must have been like answered prayers — a reliable source for big shipments of top-quality cocaine.'

'Answered prayers is right.'

'Listen, Pedro,' Forsyth told him. 'What we're here for today is, I want you to tell Harry and Mike about your friend Frederic Drosdow.'

'Jesus, I already spent hours telling you about him,' the fat man said, wearily. 'Don't you ever quit, Forsyth?'

' "Winners never quit, Quitters never win",' Forsyth quoted sententiously. 'Old American saying.'

'Old American bullshit,' Avranilosa said, irritably. 'Why don't you guys just listen to the tapes I made for Forsyth here?'

'Drosdow, Pedro. Start at the beginning.'

'OK, OK. I got word from Havana, make contact with this guy Drosdow, staying at the Omni. Give him anything he asks for, *carta blanca*. I asked a few questions, but he wasn't giving anything away. They tell me his name, Drosdow, they say he's Turkish. Well, he's dark-skinned, he could be anything, but Turkish he isn't. So I figure he must be KGB: they usually are. Later I decided he might just be GRU. Whatever he was, he had a lot of juice, man. Havana couldn't do enough for him. So he tells me he's from Colombia, he's got a connection down there for cocaine. My job is to be

his guarantor, he wants to do business only with Nino Baca. I ask him why, he says I don't need to know.'

'Didn't you wonder what it was all about?'

'Of course I wondered. I couldn't figure it out. I thought, what's DGI doing, why are we helping Moscow to run snow? Then I thought, maybe he's doing it on the side, you know what I'm saying? Making a few bucks after hours, you know how they go for hard currency. Then I find out this guy was talking sixty million dollars' worth, man. And the best. I mean, the *very* best.'

'He told you he bought it in Colombia?'

'That's what he said.'

'Who was he dealing with?' Balfour asked, polishing his glasses like a fussy old maid. 'You got any names for us?'

Avranilosa shrugged. 'He never told me any more than he had to. Same as you people, right?'

'You're cute,' Lloyd said. 'How'd you like a smack in the mouth?'

'Let's try some on you,' Balfour

interrupted. 'How about O'Campo? No? What about Pablo Escobar? Alberto Prieto?'

'Prieto's all washed up, man,' Avranilosa sneered. 'Don't you guys know that?'

'Who, then?'

'Jesus, how many times have I got to repeat this? I don't know, man. You want me to guess, I'd say it was Fabio Ochoa. Drosdow once said something about seeing a *corrida* while he was down there. Ochoa's son Jorge thinks he's some kind of bullfighter. They fly *toreros* in from Mexico, Spain even, just so he can show off.'

'You think it's worth checking out Medellin, Frank?' Lloyd said.

'Suppose you go down to Medellin, what you think you gonna find out, man?' Avranilosa said patiently, as if explaining a complex mechanism to a child. 'This isn't some tourist you're dealing with here. You think he went down there and told them his real name, asked for a copy of *Pravda*, maybe? Shit, you can't be that dumb.'

'All right, let's move on. You made the intro, Drosdow checked out, Baca made the deal. They brought the coke in on a schooner,' Forsyth said. 'You were at Lower Matecumbe Key when it came in. What was the name of the boat?'

'I never even looked,' Avranilosa said, flatly. 'They told me, keep the hell away from the dock, I kept the hell away from the dock. I'm gonna get my throat cut just to look at a *boat*?'

'They moved the stuff in three trucks. Where did it go?'

'First, to Little Havana to be cut and packed. Then it was shipped north, like I said. They send it up in limos driven by women dressed as nuns. They make drops in New York, Washington, Atlantic City.'

'Names, names,' Lloyd said, impatiently. 'What about some names, Pedro?'

'I know nothing about that side of it,' Avranilosa said, shaking his head. 'I've never even been in Baca's warehouse.'

'You said Baca paid Drosdow off at the Indies Inn. Sixty million in cash?'

'If you want to be picky, it was actually sixty-one million,' Avranilosa said. 'But

yes, the payoff was in cash.'

'Trusting soul, your man Drosdow,' Harry remarked. 'What was to stop Baca feeding him to the sharks?'

'They were doing *business*, man!' the Cuban said, wearily. 'Why would Baca want to ice a good supplier?'

'Then Drosdow went to Key Largo.'

'That's what he said. To pick up the woman.'

'Ah,' Balfour said. 'Tell us about her.'

Avranilosa repeated it all: that he had never seen the girl, that her name was Katja, that she was to meet Drosdow at the Holiday Inn on Largo. That was it.

'He tell you how he planned to use her?'

'Not in so many words. But I knew this, I heard that, it wasn't too hard to figure out. The plan was to compromise some CIA guy, name of Bogdanovich or something. Drosdow had a contact in Washington who knew Bogdanovich, a guy named Crane. He gets Bogdanovich to come to Miami, where he introduces him to the girl. She takes him to Marco Island. You know how it goes.'

'What else do you know about this Crane?'

'Only what I told you. What Drosdow said.'

'We ran Bogdanovich through the computers till steam came out, Pedro,' Forsyth said. 'And we came up with zilch. Bogdanovich doesn't know anybody named Crane, or any imaginable variant of the name.'

'What do you want me to say?' Avranilosa said. 'I'm telling you what I heard. I'm not swearing that it's true. That bastard Drosdow lied to everyone else, why wouldn't he lie to me?'

'Something else, Pedro,' Lloyd said. 'Apart from the fact that Bogdanovich is clean enough to squeak, he's a nobody. If your friend Drosdow is GRU as you seem to think, why would he be going to so much trouble to recruit a lousy coding clerk?'

Avranilosa shrugged. 'You think he'd tell me?'

'Let's go over it again,' Balfour said, in his pedantic way. 'You're talking to Drosdow. He's telling you about the man

in Washington. What were his exact words?'

'He said he didn't want to spring the trap in Washington. Not enough psychological distance, he said. Fortunately, Bogdanovich is very friendly with this guy Crane who works for British intelligence in Washington. What Bogdanovich doesn't know is that Crane is a sleeper GRU turned in Germany, years ago.'

'You're sure he said Washington?' Forsyth insisted. 'He actually said that?'

Avranilosa frowned. 'No,' he said, slowly. 'Now you mention it, he just said the guy was a friend of Bogdanovich's. I assumed if he was, it would be in Washington.'

'Could the name you heard have been Caine?' Forsyth asked. 'C-a-i-n-e?'

'Just as easy,' the Cuban shrugged. 'I told you, I'm not sure, man.'

'Drosdow didn't by any chance mention Louisville, Kentucky?'

Avranilosa shook his head. 'No,' he said, decisively. 'I'd have remembered that.'

There was no doubt in Forsyth's mind

that Avranilosa was telling them the truth. Put a polygraph on him and you wouldn't get a flicker. Which wasn't the same as saying that what he was telling them was *true*. He was telling them what Drosdow had told him, or allowed him to know. And there lay the anomaly: if Drosdow had been feeding Avranilosa disinformation, that would suggest Drosdow knew what was going to happen to the Fat Man.

And there was no way he could have known that.

Was there?

'Who's Caine?' Harry Lloyd asked.

'Just a thought,' Forsyth muttered. The security firm which had been watching Genevevo had been working for the British Customs and Excise they said. The dossier he had requested from Langley had shown that their senior man in the south-eastern USA was called David Caine. The two names weren't all that dissimilar. It might be worth running a check on the offchance.

Forsyth decided to try the long shot. He went across to the phone and put in a

call to Jack Dempsey. Speaking quietly, so the others would not hear, he told Dempsey what he wanted, and asked him to get it on the mainframe as soon as he could. Then he turned back to Avranilosa.

'OK, Pedro,' Lloyd was saying. 'Exactly where on Marco Island is this house they're using?'

'I don't *know*, man!' Avranilosa shouted. 'How many times I got to say it, I don't *know!* Go put it through your fucking computer!'

'Tell you what,' Mike Balfour said, standing up to stretch his arms above his head and yawn cavernously. 'We're reasonable men. Let's go over it again. But this time we concentrate on Drosdow, right?'

'How many more times you gonna make me go through this?' Avranilosa complained. 'My throat's like a chemical toilet!'

'You want something?' Forsyth said. 'Coffee, tea?'

'How about a piña colada?'

'Sure,' Forsyth said. He dialled room service and told them to send up drinks.

Meanwhile, Harry Lloyd was telling Avranilosa he might as well get started.

'What you tryna do, man?' the Cuban complained. 'You tryna break my brain?'

'Don't tempt me,' Lloyd said.

'It's just as wearing for us, Pedro,' Balfour smiled, taking the sting away from his partner's retort. 'But you might just have forgotten something, some unimportant detail that will help us crack this. You never know.'

They went over it all again. The drinks came and were consumed. Another hour went by, and then another. They kept on at the Cuban, until they could think of nothing else to ask him, until they felt confident there was nothing more he could tell them.

'OK, Pedro, relax,' Forsyth said. 'Take it easy.'

'Listen, man, I need another drink,' Avranilosa said.

'Not worth bothering now, Pedro. Time for you to go back where you came from.'

'You guys are all fucking heart, you know that?' Avranilosa said, disgustedly. 'I break my ass for you here, what? Two,

three hours, what do I get? One lousy piña colada.'

'Tell you what,' Lloyd said, brightly. 'We'll lie awake tonight and feel bad about it.'

Forsyth went across to the telephone and called Internal Security. Then he hung up and dialled another number.

'Forsyth,' he said. 'We're through with the Fat Man. IS is on its way now. No, nothing new. Yes, Marco Island. We're flying out there in about an hour. Yes, Lloyd and Balfour. Ahuh. Ahuh. Did you talk to the local police, Donald? Who? Is that like Byron the poet? Lieutenant Tom Byron, Collier County Sheriff's Office. Got it. No, I can find it. OK, good.'

He hung up. Lloyd and Balfour were watching him expectantly.

'We're in business!' Forsyth said. 'The local police did the legwork for us. They've located the house on Marco Island. They're keeping an eye on the place till we get there.'

After about half an hour the IS escort arrived to take Avranilosa back to the safe house. Forsyth patted the Cuban on the

shoulder as he went out the door. 'Stay out of trouble, *amigo*,' he said.

'Thanks a lot,' Avranilosa said. 'What happens to me now, Forsyth?'

'A lot of people want to talk to you, Pedro. You're going to be kept busy for a long time.'

'I mean, when all this is over? What then?'

'You'll get a new name, money, a new place to live. You'll be OK.'

'You better be right, man. If Nino Baca or DGI ever get a line on me, I'm alligator food.'

'Any alligator tried to eat you would puke,' Forsyth said. 'Go on, get him out of here!'

The security men led Avranilosa out into the corridor, and down to the rear entrance in the freight elevator. All the way back to Miami, the Fat Man kept thinking about Forsyth. And Baca. And Drosdow. And how nice it would be if they all killed each other.

18

After two days of kicking his heels at the Willard waiting for the telephone call summoning him to Arlington, Caine's nerves were stretched thin. He knew Miles well enough to know he was being punished, not so much for his actual insubordination — if you wanted to call it that — as for flouting Kingly's direct order. He went through the usual check-in procedure and proceeded to Kingly's office. Betty Torre waved him in, avoiding his eyes.

The office looked just the same. So did Kingly. He was wearing another of his Tom Gilbey suits, with a pale blue silk shirt that looked like Turnbull & Asser. This time the tie was Stowe.

'Sit down,' he said. His manner was stiff with disapproval. He put the papers he had been working on into a drawer and leaned back in his chair.

'I've read your report,' he said. 'Interesting.'

'That's one way of describing it,' Caine replied.

'You believe this Sanchez woman?'

'No reason not to.'

'You followed up on what she told you?'

'It's all in the report.'

'You were supposed to check in twice a day. No excuses. You did not do so.'

'Miles, you knew where I was.'

'*Au contraire*, dear boy, I knew no such damned thing. And I am not best pleased with your conduct.'

'I made what seemed like a sensible decision. I'm sorry if it was wrong.'

'You didn't really think you were going to find this Drosdow in Key Largo, did you?'

'I thought it was worth checking out.'

'So you spent three days sitting by the pool of a Holiday Inn without feeling it necessary to tell anyone where you were.'

Caine did not speak. Kingly's attitude would have been quite different if he had located Drosdow; but he hadn't, and now it was time to pay the piper. Nothing he said would make any difference now, anyway.

Kingly folded his hands and unfolded

them again. 'There's no easy way of saying this. I imagine you know why I called you in, David. I'm taking you out of the field.'

'Damn it, Miles, I — '

'No arguments, please,' Kingly said, sharply. 'You're lucky I'm not sending you for a face job.'

Caine shrugged. It was *de rigueur* for consultants whose face had become the property of the opposition to be sent to Los Angeles for plastic surgery. At least he was being spared that.

'Who will you put on this?'

'We'll see,' Kingly said, evading the question. He took a batch of computer printout from the drawer of his desk and plonked it in front of Caine.

'I want you to look at something before you go,' he said. There was a strange, expectant look in his eyes.

'What's this?' Caine asked.

'Your friend Forsyth turned Avranilosa. He's singing like a nightingale.'

'I don't believe it.'

'It's all in the summary. Take it away and read it.'

Caine looked at the printout. It was an ISS summary of a DOD interrogation transcript, security code BLACKALP, dated three days earlier.

'How the hell did you get hold of this?' he asked. Kingly gave his non-committal ask-me-no-questions smile.

'Maybe I got it off the Comrades,' he said, playfully.

'Then you'd have to tell me how they got it.'

'All right, then, suppose I told you that the Joint Intelligence Chiefs got DI6 to request Langley's cooperation in an ongoing Customs and Excise investigation into cocaine smuggling out of Miami, and asked for anything they had on a man named Avranilosa. On a quid pro quo basis, of course.'

'Is that what happened?'

'It could be. Or it could be that I've got my own man inside Domestic Operations. Or that I put a squad of computer hackers on to it and they broke into the Domestic Ops mainframe?'

'That I'd find easier to believe.'

'Take your pick. My point is that you

don't need to know where I got it from,' he said, coldly. 'Just read it and tell me what your conclusions are.'

'Yes,' Caine said. 'Sir.'

He was still trying to figure out how Forsyth could have turned the Cuban so quickly. He must have gotten him between a rock and a very hard place, and Caine wondered what it had been. He realized Kingly was sitting back in his chair, steepled fingers touching his lips, as though he was expecting to be asked something. Caine could not imagine what it was.

'I'll use the visitor desk,' he said.

'Yes, do,' Kingly said, remotely.

An hour later, Caine put down the ITS, a frown of concentration creasing his brow. He went through it slowly in his mind, to fix it there once and for all. Frederic Drosdow, probably a GRU officer, had arranged to sell sixty-one million dollars' worth of cocaine to Saturnino Baca through Pedro Avranilosa, not realizing the latter was under surveillance by Genevevo. The Cubans got a tipoff that Genevevo was an undercover agent (from whom?

Caine wondered), and DGI surveillance not only confirmed it, but revealed the presence on the ground of ISS. Somehow Avranilosa had persuaded Baca that whatever Genevevo knew, ISS knew, too. The only way he could protect the drug deal was by killing Genevevo and at the same time neutralizing ISS.

With Genevevo and the ISS operatives out of the way, the drug sale was finalized, and now Drosdow was using the proceeds to finance a honey trap operation on Marco Island, near Naples, Florida. The 'target' was a senior coding clerk in CIA Communications, Paul Bogdanovich. Simple, except for the questions it raised. Like what possible reason could Russian military intelligence have for setting up so sophisticated an operation to suborn a low-level paperpusher? And what was Drosdow doing with the rest of the money?

Caine went back along the corridor to Kingly's office. Betty Torre waved him in.

'He's been waiting for you,' she said. Caine frowned; that wasn't Kingly's style at all.

'You've read the ITS, then?' Kingly said. 'What's your reaction?'

'Puzzlement,' Caine said. Kingly was watching him very closely. He wondered why. Was there something about this he hadn't been told?

'Because?'

'They're going to an awful lot of trouble for a low-echelon coding clerk.'

'They're not particular,' Kingly said.

'The Comrades never spend a dollar when a dime will do,' Caine retorted. 'Do you think Avranilosa could be lying?'

'Hardly likely,' Kingly said. 'They'll have dredged him pretty comprehensively.'

No doubt of that, Caine thought. The Russians had no monopoly on ruthlessness. The CIA would squeeze Avranilosa like a lemon, and then some more, and then some more. When they were through, they would know everything he knew about everyone he knew. Especially Saturnino Baca. The Company didn't like having its operatives killed by the opposition, especially on American soil. Sooner, rather than later, Baca would be involved in what the Punishment Squad

at Langley called, with typical gallows humour, a 'Pan Am', from the initials PAA, Pre-arranged Accident.

'There's an element missing somewhere,' he said to Kingly. 'Whatever Drosdow is up to, there's more to it than a honey trap in Florida.'

'We'll be keeping it under review,' Kingly said. 'Is that all?'

'What do you mean, all?'

'Was there anything else in the ITS you want to discuss?'

Caine frowned. 'No.'

'Very well,' Kingly said. 'Where are you going to take your gardening leave?'

'I'll leave it to you,' Caine said. 'Gardening leave' was civil service jargon for suspension time. 'London, perhaps?'

'See what we can do,' Kingly said.

'I'll need to pick up some things in Louisville,' Caine said. 'I can take the four o'clock plane.'

'Good,' Kingly said. 'Call McClelland when you're ready to travel. I'll be in touch as soon as you can be re-established.' He did not get up or offer to shake hands. Caine swallowed his frustration and went

248

out, squeezing Betty Torre's shoulder as he passed. She gave him one of those instant, on-off smiles. He decided to call in and see Dick McClelland, who had just returned from a courier trip to London. He beamed as Caine came through the door.

'Hello, old son, how are you?' he said, getting up to shake hands. 'I hear you had a bit of poor luck in Miami. Tea and sympathy?'

'Coffee would be better.'

McClelland waved him to a chair, and glanced over at his duty officer. Dave Hedges, a small, neat man, caught his chief's look, smiled, and went out, closing the door softly behind him.

'Damned good chap, that,' McClelland said.

'How was London?'

'Full of grockles,' he grumbled, using his pejorative word for tourists. 'Tubes are worse than bloody cattle trains, especially the ones from Heathrow. Harrods is full of people screaming 'Take my money, take my money, give me anything but take my money!''

'Any news?'

'Didn't Miles tell you? Curzon Street House is vibrating like a bloody Chinese gong, old lad. They lost Viktor.'

'What?'

'Disappeared without a trace, two months ago. Red faces all round. Nobody can figure it out.'

Caine recalled Kingly telling him about Viktor, the Colonel in the GRU's Second Directorate who had defected the preceding year. Viktor was the one who had named Jamison, the KGB mole at Curzon Street House, and precipitated the investigation of Genevevo.

'DI5's been sitting on it for two months?'

'I gather they thought he'd been lifted by his own people. They're leaning more now towards the idea that he's done a runner. Tony Duff is absolutely livid. They'd only had him six months. Nowhere near finished with him. Lots of other agencies waiting in line. I rather gather relations between DI5 and Langley have become somewhat strained.'

Caine recalled that the Americans had

been asking for their turn with Viktor. Was that why he had decided to disappear?

'What's the consensus?' he asked.

'There isn't one. If he ran, where did he run to, and why? If he was lifted, why hasn't there been a circus?'

When a defector was taken back by his own people he usually reappeared in Russia very soon thereafter, most often at a press conference stage-managed by the KGB. Before the world's press, he would protest at the outrageous methods of the British secret service, which had lured him to an hotel, drugged him, flown him to London, and forced him to write propaganda lies for the state-controlled newspapers. He would go on to reveal just enough real names and addresses in London to ensure that his story got front-page treatment all around the world.

For a couple of days the 'spy scandal' would give the Leader of the Opposition a club with which to belabour the Prime Minister, while the names of Blunt, Philby, Burgess and Maclean were once again exhumed from their dishonourable

graves. Then everything would go quiet. The defector would disappear from public view, and the Soviet news agency, Tass, would report a 'breakdown' caused by the treatment he had received in England. No one would ever hear of him again. His usefulness over, he would be disposed of as dispassionately as a paper cup. That was what Five had expected to happen in the case of Viktor, McClelland said, but it had not.

'What have we got on him, Dick?' Caine asked.

'Full dossier,' McClelland said. 'He's Most Wanted, old chap. Alpha Apple Red.'

'Is it on the box?'

'I can whistle it up for you if you like.'

'Do that for me, Dick.'

McClelland swivelled his chair round and switched on his PC. When the access code request appeared, he muttered something vivid under his breath, checked his log, and punched in the required sixteen digits. An index appeared on the screen. He rolled it over until he found what he was looking for.

'Access Viktor five eight seven four three one nine four,' he chanted as he tapped the keys, 'six nine nine six four oh oh five.'

He leaned back and waited while the computer whirred softly. Then lines of text began to zip across the screen. He got up out of his chair and gave Caine a stagey bow.

'Ta-daaaaaah!' he said.

Caine slipped into the chair and frowned at the monitor. The index to the dossier was formidably comprehensive. Biographies came in sections: ADK, all details known; APD, all personal details; AKA, all known associates; AAP, all available photographs; ATC, all telephone contacts made. Caine keyed in the letters ADK, and waited. The lines filled the screen. He stared at them in utter disbelief.

It was Guchkov.

. . . and every window in the front of the house blew in simultaneously, a shattering crash that was the echo of a harder, louder explosion outside. He ran out screaming his wife's name. The

253

Opel was lying upside down in the middle of the front garden, burst apart and burning furiously . . .

Andrei Ilyich Guchkov. He was fifty-three now. When Caine had crossed swords with him in Berlin, more than ten years earlier, he had only been a captain. He read the dossier, although he already knew much of what was in it. Born in Uzbekistan, fourth son in a family of eight, a graduate of the Lenin Military-Political Academy, Guchkov had found his way into GRU after distinguishing himself as an army officer during the Hungarian uprising of 1956. Since then he had seen service in Prague, Hanoi, Belfast, Berlin. In 1961, he had married Irina, daughter of his former army group artillery commander. There were no children. He spoke fluent English, French and German, which accounted for his being in the Second Directorate. There followed a complete listing of all the man's preferences: food, drink, sex; even the brand of cigarettes he smoked and the make of the clothes he had been wearing.

Andrei Guchkov, a defector?

Caine went methodically through the rest of the dossier, making notes on a small pad beside the monitor. Apart from Jamison, Guchkov's gifts to DI5 had included a bag of diplomats at embassies in Paris, Brussels, The Hague and London, all of whom had been given their walking papers. The rest were a curious mixture: seven servicemen at the Composite Signals Organization Station in Hong Kong who were selling secrets, and other agents in sensitive locations around the United Kingdom. A senior collection officer at the Morwenstow listening post near Bude, Cornwall; a supervisor of traffic at the Foreign and Commonwealth Office — DI6 — transmitting station near Aylesbury. Guchkov also named as a KGB plant an analyst working in the Palmer Street office of GCHQ in London, as well as a cipher officer in the three-storey computer annex at Century House, DI6's headquarters building on Westminster Bridge Road.

A motley bunch, Caine thought. Highly-placed defectors usually produced bigger rabbits out of their hats than these.

Guchkov might easily have been expected to name GRU operatives at all his earlier stations, not to mention the US, but he had notably failed to do so.

Next, Caine checked the debriefing schedule. It was much as he'd originally thought: Saltdean, the out-station at Vauxhall Bridge Road — he wondered whether they'd had the clock fixed yet: it had been stopped at 9.30 for as long as anyone could remember — the Old Felbridge Hotel at East Grinstead, then safe houses in Sheen Court, Richmond, and finally Redcliffe Square in Earl's Court. A whole series of intelligence officers had interviewed him, notably Colonel Peter Harland, head of K-7, and his deputy, Lieutenant-Colonel David Gill. Considering how long they'd had him, they had got a lot less out of Guchkov than Caine would have expected.

Caine keyed in another three-letter code, and watched as a sequence of photographs of Guchkov appeared on the screen. Many of them were surveillance shots, taken without the man's knowledge. One or two were studio pictures,

probably taken at Curzon by A2, the photographic section. He looked much the same: a little jowlier, a few more lines around the eyes, but that was all. It was still the same unforgettable face, the one Caine had seen in his nightmares for the last ten years, the face of the man who had killed his wife.

He kept his mounting excitement under control. The worst exercise your mind could get was jumping to conclusions. But if . . . if he was right . . . ?

Dick McClelland came back into the room.

'Well, genius?' the big man said.

'They did him proud, didn't they?' Caine said. 'Two passports, one British, one American. Both false names, of course. And forty thousand pounds sterling. He could be anywhere in the world.'

'And probably is,' McClelland grinned. 'More coffee?'

'A phone.'

McClelland tossed a Sanyo cordless across the desk, and Caine dialled Delta to make his reservation to Louisville. As

he passed the phone back, McClelland asked him if he wanted a lift to the airport.

'It'll give us a chance to talk,' he said.

He drove a red Subaru, a honcho wagon with big tyres and four-wheel drive on demand. Caine had once asked him why he needed such a vehicle; McClelland said he'd always wanted a car that would climb trees.

They came down through Fort Myer Heights. The Iwo Jima memorial slid past on the right, the gentle green wooded slopes of Arlington Cemetery behind it.

'I never drive past here without wondering how many of the men buried in there ever really knew what they were dying for,' he said. 'Like Tom Crandon, or Lennie Wurzel, or Butch Young. Christ, David, we work in a shitty business.'

'They knew, Dick,' Caine said. 'We all do.'

'I suppose so,' he said. He was silent for a while, the silence of someone who is working up to say something unpleasant.

'How do you get on with Kingly?' he asked, eventually.

'It's not a love affair,' Caine said.

'Does he trust you?'

'That's a strange question, Dick.'

'He wanted to know why you had asked for the file on Viktor. As a matter of interest, why did you want to see it?'

'I've got something going around in my brain, Dick. There's something about that whole Miami business . . . '

'Would it help to talk it through?' McClelland said. 'I can park the heap. You've got forty minutes till flight time.'

'It's too damned nebulous to put into words,' Caine said. 'Forget it. I'm probably just being an old woman.'

'You're sure there's nothing you want to tell me?'

Caine nodded, frowning at the way the question had been phrased. McClelland pulled to a stop behind a tan Buick Electra Park Avenue parked in front of the Delta bay, two army officers standing beside it. Caine got out, and McClelland came around the car as though to shake hands. As he did, Caine saw the two army officers start towards them. Alarm bells rang in his mind as McClelland grabbed

his arm and tried to hustle him towards the Buick.

'Get in the car,' McClelland gritted, 'you bloody traitor!'

Caine reacted without hesitation. Half turning, he drew his Nova stun-gun, jammed it against McClelland's sternum and pulled the trigger. McClelland's knees buckled and he lurched away, falling heavily. A woman screamed. The two army officers stopped dead in their tracks, confusion on their faces.

'Heart attack!' Caine shouted. 'I'll get a doctor!'

He ran into the terminal, heart pounding wildly. As soon as he was inside he slowed to a brisk walk. Nothing drew attention more quickly than a running man. He saw that there were crowds up around the car rental desks and the baggage claim area below Gates 1-8. Holding the stun-gun ready in his hand, he went out through the doors to the cab rank. He looked around warily. Nobody came towards him. Nobody shouted. He signalled a Barwood cab.

'Dulles,' he snapped. 'Fast!'

'Ya want I should go nort or sout?' the driver asked. He was a squat, bald-headed man. The licence shield on the dash gave his name as Zbigniew Bojak. 'I go nort we gonna hitta rushow traffic. Ya wan I should try Washenton Boulvar?'

'Just get this heap out of here!' Caine snapped, leaning well back in the seat. 'Move it, for Christ's sake!'

'Ah, shit,' Bojak said, resignedly, 'another nut.'

The cab lurched into motion. As they went by the Delta gateway, Caine saw the two officers standing beside the Buick, watching the entrance. One, a tall, cadaverous-looking individual with patches of grey hair, wore the insignia of a colonel. The second, a major, was shorter, with blond hair cut very close at the back and sides. There was no sign of McClelland.

Caine stowed the stun-gun, blessing the day he had bought it. No larger than an electric razor, it worked by shooting an electrical discharge which interrupted messages from the brain to the muscular system, causing severe disorientation in

the victim lasting between ten and fifteen seconds. It was otherwise quite harmless. Caine had picked it up in Austin, where it was manufactured. Some Texas police forces used it to pacify arrestees.

Zbigniew Bojak tooled up the George Washington Memorial Parkway, past the waterfowl sanctuary and the Marriott Twin Bridges Motel into a maze of feeder roads and overpasses. The great squat hulk of the Pentagon loomed on the right as he cursed his way through the clotted traffic on the Shirley Memorial Highway. He circled around the upper perimeter of the cemetery to Arlington Boulevard, and headed towards Falls Church. Caine hardly noticed. All he could hear, repeating itself in his mind like the non-stop tolling of a bell, was the name Dick McClelland had called him: *traitor*.

Why?

He was still asking himself the same question — and a lot of others — when they reached Dulles Airport. The cab driver's voice broke into his reverie.

'Take the lower drive,' Caine said. 'I'm meeting someone.'

He had never had any intention of flying anywhere. His dossier would already be on the wire from Langley, or Fort Meade, or wherever the military types had come from. His name would be on a high-priority list in a national surveillance trawl within hours. He paid off the cab and went to a pay phone. He took off his Omega chronometer, set the stopwatch to zero, and dialled ISS. It took them forty-two seconds to put him through to Kingly. He knew why, of course.

'Where are you?' Kingly said, without preamble.

'I'm timing this, Miles,' Caine told him. 'Don't bother putting a trace on me.'

'You're on a landline, of course.'

'Naturally. Would you like to tell me what the hell is going on?'

'You tell me, David.'

'McClelland called me a traitor.'

'That was . . . ill-considered,' Kingly said. His voice was placatory, even paternal. 'We just want to talk to you. Something that needs clarifying.'

Caine checked the watch: one minute.

He couldn't talk much longer. 'Why did McClelland have military waiting for me at National? Who were they, Miles?'

'I can't discuss this on an open line,' Kingly said. 'Tell me where you are and we'll come and get you.'

'Damned right you would.'

'Don't be foolish, David,' Kingly said, no trace any longer of friendliness in his voice. 'You can't run away from this. You've nowhere to hide. There's nowhere you can go that we can't find you.'

'He called me a traitor, Miles,' Caine persisted. 'Why?'

'I told you we can't discuss it on the telephone.'

'Has it got anything to do with the Drosdow case?'

'What makes you think that?'

Caine looked at the stopwatch: ninety seconds. He had another thirty seconds.

'Who said it, Miles? Who told you I was a traitor?'

'Are you telling me that you are?'

'Don't be so fucking dense!' Caine snapped.

'No point losing your temper,' Kingly

said. 'Think about it, David. Be sensible. Come in, and we can sort this whole thing out.'

'Which whole thing?' Caine shouted. 'For God's sake, Miles, tell me what I'm supposed to have done?'

'Of course I'll tell you. As soon as you come in. We can't do it any other way. You know that.'

Caine looked at his watch and hung up. He had nothing more to say to Kingly anyway. He strapped on the Omega and walked over to the car rental desks. With any luck at all, he would be able to put a few hundred miles between himself and Washington before they traced his reservation.

19

Drosdow hummed unmusically to an easy-listening programme on WBAL as he pointed the Mercedes 380SEL across the Severn river bridge en route to Easton. It was a bright blue day. Sailboats leaned away from the breeze off Annapolis. His meeting in Baltimore with Lykov had been highly satisfying: how many men had single-handedly effected a payment of over fifty million dollars in cash to GRU funds? The Soviet trading organization Amtorg would be able to buy a lot of hi-tech equipment with that kind of money.

'An Order of Lenin at least,' Lykov had beamed, 'when you get back to Moscow, my friend.'

I'm expecting more than that when all this is over, comrade, Drosdow said to himself as he recalled Lykov's words. He reviewed his plans in his mind as he drove. Red Centre was ready to move. And so was he.

Mitchell had been putty in Katja's experienced hands: he had never seen a man so sexually infatuated. The man hardly ever went home any more: he spent every moment he was not working — he had long since boasted to Kate about where he worked and what he did there — either with her at the house in Easton or on the town in Baltimore. They had gone away together for a weekend in New York, and now another in Atlantic City. It was time now to move Mitchell along to the next stage, which was why Drosdow was looking forward to getting back.

As for the rest of the plan, in spite of what the American security services no doubt by now believed, there was no honey trap on Marco Island. There *was* a house there, bought and paid for out of the cocaine deal, an eighty thousand dollar unit on Alamo Court with a nice view across Roberts Bay. He had set it all up, no expense spared: a powerboat moored at its berth, gassed up and ready to go, with fishing tackle and scuba gear on board. Bogdanovich could take his

choice of pleasures: he could swim, surfboard, scuba-dive, fish, play tennis or golf at the Marco Island Club on Nassau Road, sail, hunt shells, spot birds or, if the outdoor life was not to his taste, simply sit on the patio nursing a long, cold drink from the well-stocked refrigerator and watch the pelicans making wide circles over the emerald-blue water.

Bogdanovich should be there by now, he thought. Through his Washington case officer, Stepan Lykov, the American had been instructed to apply for leave, fly to Miami, stay overnight at the Marriott, then proceed in a rented car to Marco Island. On arrival, he was to go to a designated phone booth in the Island Plaza shopping centre, and from it call a number he had been given, telling whoever answered that Pimmit — his code name — was in place. After that, he was told, he could enjoy himself until he received further instructions.

Drosdow smiled. The whole thing was a nonsense, of course. The number Bogdanovich called would be linked to a tape recorder. The fact that 'Pimmit' was

'in place' would mean nothing to anyone, except possibly the CIA, and Bogdanovich's vacation would be short-lived. Lykov had confirmed that Avranilosa had dropped out of sight. An unexpected business trip, they were saying at his Miami office. Yes, and Drosdow knew what the business was. The Fat Man had 'made new friends', so by now the wheels were probably turning quite fast. Unless the Americans were even more stupid than he had imagined, Bogdanovich would already be under intensive surveillance.

It was common knowledge that every member of the intelligence community with access to secret materials was occasionally put under spot surveillance for a couple of days. Bogdanovich was no exception; but Lykov had run him so skilfully that Bogdanovich had never encountered any problems. Once surveillance became intensive, however, he would be finished. Drosdow had left a trail a blind deaf-mute could follow. What happened to Bogdanovich was of no importance whatsoever: the man was expendable, his involvement merely

another factor in Drosdow's chaos.

Outside Queenstown he turned south, following US-50 for another dozen miles past imposing mansions with magnificent landscaped gardens that stretched down to the shining bay. Just past the airport, he turned on to the Easton Parkway, then filtered left into Washington Street. When he got to the centre of town, he stopped at Trader's Pharmacy to make a brief call.

'Is everything ready?' he said, when Katja answered.

'He's here.'

'I'll be there in twenty minutes.'

He got back into the Mercedes and drove through Easton, Queen of the Maryland Tidewater, with its early colonial architecture and manicured streets. Sometimes it was hard to come to terms with just how wealthy some Americans were. They were like overgrown children, with wardrobes full of clothes they could never wear out, more shoes than they could use in a second lifetime. The men spent most of their adult lives making money, and with it they roamed the world, buying without pleasure or need.

South of town, he turned on to Route 333 to Oxford. It was pretty countryside, a neat pattern of spreading rivers and streams, large farms and fine homes. In some ways it reminded him of the Zeravshan valley in Uzbekistan, and he sighed. He hadn't been home for a long, long time. He turned off 333 on to a private road that led to an ornate gate between two massive stone pillars surmounted by griffins. He identified himself by means of the intercom unit set into one of the stone gateposts, and after a few moments the gates swung ponderously back. He drove on a paved driveway through a stretch of woods which opened up into pastures and parkland running down to the water's edge.

Before him lay Highfield, spacious and serene. The gracious old house stood on an inlet looking out over the Tred Avon river, almost a mile wide at this point. Built by the grandson of a Marylander from Calvert county who settled in Washington in 1798, Highfield was an imposing estate in an area where the word imposing was not a superlative.

Constructed of fieldstone and wood, the house was surrounded by spacious living porches at the ground level and several large screened porches above; their steeply-pitched roofs and wide, overhanging eaves made them a cool retreat on humid summer nights. The estate included a superintendent's cottage, stables, garages, two barns, greenhouses and other outbuildings. There were six servants: a cook, two maids, a manservant, a groom and a chauffeur: all, of course, supplied by GRU.

Four million dollars and worth every cent, he thought as he looked about him. The lawn and formal terraced gardens covered some five acres. There were two tennis courts and an Olympic-sized swimming pool. From now on, Drosdow thought as he got out of the car, all honey traps would be measured against this, the real one.

He heard music and the sound of voices beside the pool. He walked around the house and through the garden. Katja was swimming; Butler Mitchell sat on the apron of the pool, his legs dangling in

the water. He looked up as Drosdow's feet crunched on the gravel.

'Fred, hello!' he said, getting up to shake hands. 'Good to see you, good to see you.'

'You too, Mitch,' Drosdow said, watching Katja. She had on a one-piece Anne Cole swimsuit with diagonal violet and black stripes, cut high at the hip and low at the back. Her skin was beautifully tanned.

'Come on in!' she called. 'Wash the city away!'

'Later, maybe,' Drosdow smiled. He looked at Mitchell, who was watching Katja with adoring eyes. No question of it, the girl was as good as she had claimed to be. Mitchell caught Drosdow's look and gave him a sheepish grin.

'How was Atlantic City?' Drosdow asked.

'Windy,' Katja said, climbing out of the pool, and vigorously towelling herself dry.

'Where did you stay?'

'The Boardwalk Regency,' Mitchell said. 'They know me there.'

'You enjoyed yourselves?'

Mitchell hesitated. 'Go on, tell him,' Katja said.

'I lost,' Mitchell said, reluctantly. 'A bundle.'

Drosdow shook his head. 'You're a sucker for punishment, Mitch,' he said. 'How much?'

'Not enough to break the bank,' Mitchell said, forcing the laugh. 'More than I intended, though.'

'Well, you know what they say: you've got to lay it down to pick it up.'

'He was ahead fifteen thousand at one point,' Katja said.

'Some people like liquor. Some like fast cars. With me, it's the tables,' Mitchell said. 'I can't resist them.'

'Never mind, it's only money,' Katja said. 'We had a lovely time, and that's all that matters, isn't it, darling?'

'Absolutely,' Mitchell said, a shade too enthusiastically. Watching the man carefully, Drosdow saw the hint of a wince that had followed Katja's carefully-aimed shaft of disregard for the American's losses. Mitchell was overspending wildly to impress them. Correction: to impress Katja, who succeeded in remaining

utterly unimpressed.

'So how was Washington?' Mitchell said, changing the subject. 'Business good?'

'Just the opposite,' Drosdow said, gloomily. 'The software business is in hell's own shape at the moment.'

'Hell, I thought it was booming,' Mitchell said. 'I was reading about some guy named McGovern in Boston who — '

'That was some time ago, Mitch. And anyway, computer publishing isn't software. I'll bet even IDG is hurting at the moment.'

'If you two are going to talk business, I'll go on up to the house and change,' Katja said. 'Come on up for a drink in a little while.'

She kissed Mitchell on the top of his head and walked up to the house. She moved like a well-oiled machine, and Mitchell's eyes never left her until she was out of sight. Drosdow was reminded of a phrase he had heard Saturnino Baca use to describe one of his men who'd been on a three-day binge with a woman in Miami: *pussywhipped*. It fitted Mitchell perfectly.

'You listening to me, Mitch?'

'Sorry,' Mitchell grinned, blushing. 'What were you saying?'

'Software,' Drosdow said. 'Remember? There are a lot of people in Silicon Valley who thought they had a licence to print money, and have found out the hard way that they don't. I'm not planning to join them. I'm going to get me some of that government contract business.'

'Smart move,' Mitchell said. 'That's where the big bucks are.'

'Trouble is, Mitch, I don't know where to start.'

'There's a facility at the Pentagon that advises — '

'I don't care to stand in line, Mitch,' Drosdow interposed. 'You ought to know that's not my style. What I need is some introductions. Get to know the right people.'

'Easier said than done, Fred.'

'I was wondering . . . Kate told me you work at the National Security Agency. Couldn't you get me in?'

Mitchell shook his head. 'You'd have to go through channels, like everyone else.'

'You can't help me at all? Even though, in the long run, it's for Kate, too?'

'Fred, you know there's nothing I wouldn't do for Kate. Or for you. You've been more like an older brother to me than . . .'

'What were you going to say, father-in-law?'

'I'm sorry, Fred. Rules are rules, especially at NSA.'

'That is some place you work at, Mitch,' Drosdow said, noting how Mitchell had avoided the topic of marriage. He was still maintaining the pretence that he was a divorcé. It would make things that much easier when Drosdow began to turn the screws. 'The National Security Agency. It's enormous. I drove by it a few days ago. It's like a small town. How many people work out there, anyway?'

'Thirty-five, forty thousand, I believe.'

'Is that big nine-storey block the headquarters building?'

'At the moment. There are plans for a new one.'

'Which department deals with buying equipment?'

'It's called I&L — Installations and Logic.'

'That's not the division you work in.'

'We call them 'offices' at NSA, Fred. The one I work for is called the Office of Communications Security, COMSEC for short.'

'What about this other one, I&L? Who's the head guy there?'

Mitchell shook his head, uncomfortable yet determined. 'I'm not permitted to discuss other agency personnel, Fred. I'm sorry.'

'It's all right, it's all right,' Drosdow grinned. 'You and your goddamn secrets. Look, just tell me this: if I want to see someone over there to try to sell them something, what do I do?'

'You call Fort Meade and ask for OHP — that's the Office of the Head of Procurement, which is part of I&L. You request an appointment with a procurement officer. Then — '

'That could take weeks!' Drosdow said, feigning dismay.

'Sorry. That's the way it works, Fred.'

'Mitch, listen to me, I'm in a bind,'

Drosdow said. 'I can't wait weeks. I need turnover, and I need it now. Isn't there any way you could help me out? From what Kate told me, I figured you had some clout over there.'

'I do,' Mitchell said, nettled.

'Well, then, for Christ's sake, give me something, anything,' Drosdow said. This was a critical moment in their relationship. He was acting the supplicant while watching Mitchell very closely. 'You want to see me go to the wall?'

'Fred . . . ' Mitchell said, uncomfortably. 'It's not that easy.'

Drosdow felt a small glow of elation. The absence of refusal was the beginning of agreement, the first breakthrough. The next step was to test the man.

'Listen, isn't there some kind of organizational chart I could borrow?' he asked. 'Something that lists all the heads of department — sorry, offices.'

'There is, but it's restricted,' Mitchell said.

'What does that mean?'

'Documents have different security classifications. An organizational chart is

restricted, but not classified.'

'In other words, it's not secret.'

'I can see you're like most civilians, Fred. You don't understand how the system works. Everything is secret. But some things are more secret than others.'

Bravo, Drosdow thought drily. He's described the espionage business in one sentence. In spite of himself, he was tense. Getting Mitchell to this stage had taken a lot of careful manoeuvring. They had to establish the man's motivations, what he would accept, what balk at. A loan 'to tide him over' after a disastrous session at the Miami tables? No problem: it was implicit that Mitchell would pay it back 'as soon as he got himself straightened out'. A loan was not a gift, even if there was no term, no talk of interest, not even an IOU. In the world of espionage, this technique was known as expanding the area of conscience. It enabled Mitchell to accept and rationalize Drosdow's largesse without its becoming a constant burden.

'Well, never mind,' Drosdow said,

putting disappointment into his tone. 'It was just a thought.'

'I feel badly about this, Fred,' Mitchell said. 'I'd really like to help you out, but . . . ' He shrugged. 'You know how it is.'

'Listen, Mitch, forget it,' Drosdow said, as if to move away from the subject. 'I've embarrassed you. I never should have asked.'

He let the silence lengthen. Mitchell was staring at the water in the pool as if hypnotized by the dancing lights on its surface.

'How long would you need it for?' he said, so quietly that Drosdow almost missed the words. Christ, he thought, he's mine! Easy, now, easy.

'An hour, half an hour, even. But Mitch, I can't ask you . . . '

'Hell,' Mitchell said. 'I guess I could do that much for an old friend.'

And that was it. Drosdow felt the sweat trickling down inside his shirt. The threshold was crossed, the new relationship established. Drosdow let all the air out of his lungs and then took a long,

deep breath. He felt good.

'I won't forget this, Mitch,' he said, putting a hand on Mitchell's shoulder. 'It could be a life-saver.'

'Hell, I haven't done anything, yet,' Mitchell replied, forcing a grin. He was just realizing what he had agreed to. It was the natural, the inevitable reaction: Drosdow had seen it a hundred times. But if the manipulator had done his work well, there could be no going back. He stood up and clapped Mitchell on the back.

'Come on up to the house,' he said jovially, 'and I'll buy you a drink.'

'I could use one,' Mitchell said.

Kate was waiting for them in the drawing room, a bottle of Veuve Clicquot and three Waterford glasses beside her on a low table.

'I thought you men would probably have sore throats after all that business talk,' she smiled. 'So I opened a bottle of medicine.' She looked at Drosdow as she poured the champagne. His eyes told her what she wanted to know. A smile touched her lips.

'Bubbly?' Mitchell said. 'What are we celebrating?'

'Success,' Drosdow told him, smiling broadly.

'I'll drink to that,' Mitchell said. They all laughed.

20

A thousand miles and four stolen cars later, Caine pulled to a stop outside the La Paloma restaurant on East Drive in Key Biscayne. It was a long, low building with stone facings; the sign showed a dove with an olive branch in its beak. It was a prime location: directly opposite lay the Key Colony golf course. He stood outside for a moment, wondering whether to go through with this. Then he shrugged. He didn't have a hell of a lot of choice.

It was dark and cool inside. He paused on the threshold while his eyes adjusted. He was in a small foyer with stuccoed walls on which hung a bullfight poster and a Spanish guitar. Through an archway on the left he could see into the restaurant. It was empty at this time of afternoon. He went through the archway and saw that there was a well-stocked bar on the right. Lynda Sanchez was behind the bar. She looked up as he came in.

'Remember me?' he said.

She regarded him levelly, as if she was uncertain what to say next. She was wearing a sleeveless cream linen dress, buttoned down the front. She looked very cool and very beautiful.

'Yes,' she said. 'I remember you. What do you want?'

'I need your help, Lynda.'

'I think not,' she said, firmly. Her voice was cool, distant.

'The last time I saw you, you said — '

'Then was then,' she replied. 'Now is now. I had some . . . visitors after you left.'

'Ah,' he said. 'Not police, I assume.'

'Definitely not police. Nice business suits, like the ones who came to see me after Tony Genevevo was killed. Very quietly-spoken, very precise. They said they were from a government agency which prefers not to show identification.'

'When was this?'

'A week ago. Exactly.'

'Go on.'

'They wanted to know if I'd had anyone come around asking questions about Tony.'

'What did you tell them?'

'At first I said no.'

'But they already knew I had.'

'How did you know that?'

'I didn't know it. It just figured.'

'They described you. Perfectly. They asked me to tell them what you were wearing, what you said, anything I could remember.'

'And?'

'I told them. I said your name was Philip Howard and that you told me you were an insurance investigator.'

'They, of course, told you I was not.'

'They said you were an agent of a foreign power.'

'What did you say to that?'

'I told them you told me you were some kind of secret agent.'

'I bet that perked up their interest.'

'One of them got on the phone. He talked to somebody long distance and reported what I'd told them. They stayed a long while. They said they weren't supposed to say anything, but they thought I ought to know that everything you'd told me was a lie.'

'Not everything, Lynda,' Caine said.

'They said I should call them immediately if you contacted me again.'

'Are you going to?'

'I should. You did lie to me.'

'Only about my name. Everything else I told you is true.'

'What is your name, anyway?'

'Didn't your visitors tell you?'

'They didn't tell me anything. They said it was a matter of national security, and that I shouldn't discuss it with anyone, under any circumstances.'

'But you told them about Genevevo and Avranilosa. And Frederic Drosdow.'

'Yes.'

'Was one of them called Forsyth?'

'They never gave their names. Who is Forsyth?'

'He was Tony Genevevo's case officer.'

'What?'

'The man he reported to.'

'And you? You still haven't told me who you are.'

'My real name is Caine. David Caine.'

'Like the movie star Caine?'

'That's the only similarity.'

She shook her head. 'I don't know who to believe.'

'I understand that. I know it's difficult. But what I told you when I came to your house is true. I really am trying to find the man who had Tony Genevevo killed.'

'That's not what they said. They said you're wanted for questioning.'

'As of four days ago, I am. That's why I came here. You're the only one who can help me do what I set out to do.'

'Why should I believe you? Give me one good reason.'

'Because you want the man who had Tony Genevevo killed punished.'

'I do. But why do you?'

'I told you: the men who were killed at the same time as Genevevo were working for me. For my company. We had Genevevo under surveillance.'

'Your company.'

'We operate as a company.'

'Who is we?'

'I think you're better off not knowing that, Lynda.'

'Why did your . . . company have Tony under surveillance?'

'He was suspected of being involved in espionage.'

'Tony? I don't believe it!'

'You don't have to. It isn't true. But it was made to look as if he was by the man who had him killed. Do you remember Frederic Drosdow?'

'Of course.'

'He's the man.'

'Drosdow had Tony killed? Why?'

'It's a long story. Are you going to help me?'

'You mean you won't tell me if I don't.'

'That's right.'

'Why me?'

'That day at your apartment, when I first talked to you — I left there feeling sure I could trust you.'

'You, trust me? The question we ought to be discussing is, can I trust you?'

'What am I going to say, no?'

She was silent for a moment, her dark eyes thoughtful. 'You really had me convinced, you know that?'

'Lynda, what I told you is true.'

'If you're what you claim to be, why do you need my help?'

'I'm out in the cold, Lynda. You know what that means?'

'Only from spy books.'

'I've been fitted up. Framed, if you like. My own organization is after me as well as the CIA. The only way I can clear my name is to find Drosdow and to do that, I need you.'

'Why not just turn yourself in?'

'Because whoever fitted me up is working for the opposition himself. I wouldn't get to Washington. An accident, killed while trying to escape. There are all sorts of ways to shut me down.'

She shivered. 'I don't know that I want to get involved in your world, Caine. Or with you.'

'Yes,' he said, turning away. 'You're probably right. I won't bother you any more.'

'Wait a minute,' Lynda said. 'Just wait a damned minute. I didn't say I wouldn't help you. I said I shouldn't.'

'Then you will?'

'Supposing I say yes. What happens then?'

'You come with me to Marco Island.

Help me to find Drosdow.'

'Let me get this straight,' she said, leaning on the bar. 'You want me to drop everything, come with you to Marco Island for some unspecified time, looking for this Drosdow. You don't know where he is, and you don't know what you're going to do if you find him. And I've got to take it all on trust. Is that about right?'

Caine grinned ruefully. 'It's worse than that. I want you to pay for it.'

'Pay for it? What does that mean?'

'That's why I need you, Lynda. I've been able to get this far only because nobody knew where I was going or when I'd be there. But I can't get away with that on Marco Island. I need someone to front for me, someone to rent cars and book rooms and ask questions. Someone legitimate. You.'

'You don't want much,' she said. 'Just tell me one more thing. What have I done to deserve all this?'

'You said something when I first met you. It stuck in my mind. You said you wanted to do something good for America.'

'I remember.'

'That's why I'm asking you, Lynda.'

She was silent for a while. Then she nodded. 'I've got a feeling I'm going to regret this,' she said. She opened a drawer, took out a bunch of keys and put them on the bar in front of him.

'You know where I live,' she said. 'Go and get cleaned up, wait for me. I can't get away from here much before mid-night.'

'Midnight sounds fine,' Caine said.

'Caine?'

'Yes?'

She held her nose. 'Buy a clean shirt,' she said.

* * *

From the moment he had driven away from Dulles, Caine knew he could take absolutely no chances. The Company probably had him tabbed as their best possible lead to Drosdow. Finding him would be given maximum precedence. This would include blanket surveillance by the NSA, which immediately cut off

his access to credit, his possessions, his friends and acquaintances. His name and a number of other key words would go into the computers scanning hundreds of thousands of telephone calls per hour looking for him. Any credit card transaction, any reservation made via a computer system, any traffic violation, any bank withdrawal, any payment by cheque, any of the routine things millions of people do every day could be picked up in the surveillance trawl and lead them straight to him.

At Manassas he had scouted around till he found a car-parts dealer, where he bought a slide-hammer (the car thief's favourite tool) and a selection of switch assemblies. In a hardware store he picked up a small screwdriver and a log-splitting wedge and took a couple of yards of nylon packing-case tape from a pile of junk in the back of the store. Then he drove to the station parking lot where he abandoned the rental car and broke into a red Buick Somerset with Virginia plates. Stealing a car was almost ridiculously easy: car thieves never stopped seeing the

joke of car-makers putting a set of locks costing less than fifty dollars on a forty thousand dollar vehicle. He used the wedge to prise the door open enough to slide in the packing-case tape and lift the locks. Two smacks from the slide-hammer took out the ignition lock, and one turn of the screwdriver started the car. He looked around. There was no one in sight. Commuter stations were always a good place to steal from: the theft would not be discovered until six or even later that evening, by which time he would be long gone.

He had run out of gas in Emporia, just short of the North Carolina line. He left the Buick on the street, stole a Renault Encore he found parked in a blind alley — all he had to do was get in, whip out the starting switch and substitute one of the assemblies he'd bought in Manassas — and headed south again. At Fayetteville he paid thirty dollars cash for a motel room and slept six hours.

When he got up, he walked over to a shopping mall and hung around until he spotted a likely pigeon, a middle-aged

man in a yellow cotton polo shirt and grey gaberdine slacks, pushing a shopping cart while his wife shopped. A collision, profuse apologies, and Caine was on his way out of the market with the man's wallet in his pocket. He was in luck: as well as a MasterCharge, Diner's Club, and a Mobil gas card, it contained a hundred and four dollars in cash. With any luck they'd last him long enough.

He crossed the Georgia line and turned off on to State 21, parking the hot little Renault from Emporia at Savannah Municipal Airport. There, he selected a feisty-looking Honda Accord SEi, opened it up, and drove it away. That was the way the pros worked it: enter the short-term parking facility in a clapped-out wreck, dump it, and drive out in the new car of their choice, using the ticket they picked up on the way in.

He made a wide swing around Jacksonville, taking no chances on using its network of toll bridges: there were too many cops on toll bridges. Then it was due south on US-95 to St Augustine, where he made a night stop and ditched

the Honda in 'exchange' for a new-looking Toyota Cressida with Flagler County plates. It was his third day on the road. He needed a shave, clean clothes and, most of all, sleep. He was weary of the endless highway coming at him, the rush of trucks, the glare of headlamps, the blatting of horns, the sameness of the junk food he'd eaten at a dozen roadside diners.

He had spent most of his driving time on the journey south thinking through what had happened in Washington. The conclusion was unpleasant: because of his stupidity, Tom Crandon, Lennie Wurzel and Butch Young were dead; perhaps even Genevevo, too. Caine had committed the cardinal sin: he had vastly underestimated the enemy, rashly assuming they were unaware of his involvement. He was now faced with the inescapable realization that not only had the opposite been true right from the start, but that he, too, had been a target when Tom Crandon was killed. And when that did not work, they had painted him Red instead.

There could have been no other reason

for Dick McClelland's turning on him. His instincts told him that the only source for such an accusation was Avranilosa, but there had been nothing in the interrogation summary ... Then he remembered Kingly's unwonted tension, Betty Torre's uneasy smile, McClelland's questions. Whatever the Cuban had said had been expurgated before Kingly showed the summary to Caine. They had been waiting to see how Caine would react. When there was no reaction, Kingly had decided to give him to the Company, or to NSA, which explained the military types waiting at the airport. They would have driven him out to a helicopter on the tarmac and he would have spent the next six months under interrogation. While Frederic Drosdow got on with what he had come to America to do.

Why not call him by his real name, Andrei Guchkov?

The bastard had taken every trick so far. Whatever his true intent was, it was big enough for him to have sacrificed quite a few agents-in-place. Such actions would require sanction at the highest level

at Red Centre in Moscow. Could all this have been done merely to entrap a small-time CIA coding clerk? It seemed a long way less than likely, but if it wasn't that, what was it?

<p style="text-align:center">★ ★ ★</p>

'How much further is it?' Lynda asked, breaking into his reverie.

'Thirty miles, give or take a few.'

They had been driving along the Tamiami Trail for about an hour and a half. The dun-and-green sawgrass wetlands of the Everglades were behind them now; they would soon be out of Big Cypress National Preserve. They passed a roadside eatery with a fifteen-foot-high beer can advertising Budweiser. On the apron was a battered old Lincoln Continental; on top of it was a cut-out alligator with the word Gatorburgers painted on it.

'Half an hour,' she said. 'Do you want to talk, Caine?'

'What about? Drosdow?'

'Whatever.'

'That's not his real name,' he said. 'His real name is Andrei Ilyich Guchkov.'

'A Russian? He's a spy?'

'That's what all this is about, Lynda: espionage, not drugs. Tony Genevevo was killed because he found that out.'

He tried to explain it to her, not really expecting her to understand. He told her how Drosdow — Guchkov, he was sure of it now — had posed as a drug dealer, using Avranilosa as his guarantor. Whatever his plans were, they were important enough that he could not allow Genevevo or the ISS men to jeopardize them, so he used Avranilosa to convince Baca that the simplest solution was to get rid of all of them.

'Then when he realized Baca's hit men hadn't succeeded in killing me, he painted me Red.'

'You said that before,' Lynda said. 'What does it mean?'

'Sorry,' he said, smiling. 'Trade jargon. When you accuse someone of working for the other side, it's called painting them Red. Somehow Guchkov knew the CIA was going to put the screws on Avranilosa

299

— maybe he even engineered it — and fitted me into what he told the Fat Man. With the result that I am now on the CIA's books as a probable KGB agent, which will make me flavour of the month with the FBI.'

He didn't add that Kingly would certainly have put him on AI — Apprehension Imperative — status, permitting anyone from ISS to take him by any means short of actually killing him.

'What has all this got to do with what's happening in Marco Island?'

'Drosdow is trying to recruit a man named Paul Bogdanovich. To do that he's using a technique that's known in spookspeak as a honey trap, or sometimes a swallow's nest. It means using a woman to seduce the target man — '

'So that's why Tony was so excited that night when I told him about Drosdow going to Key Largo to look at a swallow!'

'That's right. He knew that if Drosdow and Avranilosa were talking in espionage jargon, that one or both of them were agents.'

'And you think Drosdow will be in Marco?'

'I hope so.'

'I hope so, too,' she said fiercely. She looked at him. 'There's more to it than that, though, isn't there?'

'What do you mean?'

'I want this man caught. I want him to pay for what he did. But it's more than that with you. There's another reason: something personal, isn't there?' Lynda said.

'Yes,' he said. 'There is.'

It didn't seem likely that Guchkov would have remembered his name, but it was possible. Caine had been a very lowly field agent in West Berlin then, part of a team that was bringing over a defecting East German HVA agent named Anatoli Shadrin. Caine and his partner, Jerry Hadfield, went to a *treff* in a house in East Berlin that looked out on the parish cemetery of the Sophienkirche. Through its grimy windows you could see the Wall looming ominously at the end of the street.

They had no inkling that Shadrin had been rumbled, or that the GRU *rezident* at HVA in East Berlin — Captain Andrei

301

Guchkov — had persuaded General Markus Wolff to make an example of them by fitting a bomb to Caine's car timed to go off after they had returned to West Berlin. The agent sent to do the 'wet job' botched it and, instead of exploding with the agents in it, the trembler didn't trip until two days later, when Caine's wife Jenny started up the Opel to run down to the commissary.

'Look,' Lynda said. Up ahead of them was the long, rising curve of the Collier Boulevard bridge. A sign beside the road said: MARCO ISLAND WELCOMES CARE-FUL DRIVERS. Down at the public boat ramp, a crew of suntanned kids were putting a sailboat into the water. Pelicans watched with wary detachment.

'Well, here we are, Caine,' Lynda said, turning to face him. 'What happens now?'

'I'm going to buy you some coffee,' he told her. 'Then I'm going to tell you what you need to know about Andrei Ilyich Guchkov. And then you're going to work.'

21

'You ever heard of Carl Sigman?' he said.

'Sure,' Lynda replied. 'He writes songs.'

'Somebody told me when he got the music for the theme song for that movie, *Love Story*, he tried about fifteen different lyrics, but the studio turned them all down, told him to try again. He was all out of ideas, and he turned to his wife, and he said, what am I going to do? And she said, try again. And he said, where do I begin?'

'And lo, A Song Was Born,' she said. 'Point, please?'

'I feel the same way. Where do I begin?'

'You said you figured Drosdow had bought a place somewhere on the island?'

'He wouldn't rent.'

'Then we hit the realty offices.'

'Saying what?'

'We'll tell them we're looking for our dear friend Fred Drosdow, who invited us down here for the week, only we lost his

address on the way.'

'Well,' Caine said. 'You seem to have the gift.'

They drove along the broad, palm-lined expanse of North Collier Boulevard until they spotted a Chamber of Commerce sign outside a building next to the starkly modernistic First Bank of Marco Island. A helpful lady named Fran Gilbert loaned them a phone book, and gave them a map of the island and a list of realtors. Five hot and tiresome hours later, they got lucky.

The Pearson & Leach Realty office was on San Marco, right next to the Deltona building. They told their story to a handsome, blonde woman in her mid-forties whose name was Jill Leach.

'We tried the Chamber of Commerce,' Lynda said. After so many performances, she knew her lines perfectly. 'And the Post Office. The only other thing we could think of was to make the rounds of the realty offices, describe Fred, and hope for the best.'

'Bright blue eyes, you say?' Mrs Leach said. 'Almost violet, right?'

'Pockmarked face, slight accent,' Caine confirmed. 'That sure sounds like Fred.'

'I remember the man,' Mrs Leach said, 'but . . . ' She shook her head, going through a card index. She frowned. 'Ah, here it is. I knew the name wasn't the same. It isn't Drosdow. It's Ziegelmann. Victor Ziegelmann. Number five, Alamo Court.'

The reason she remembered the transaction so well, she told them, was because not only had the man known exactly what he wanted, he had a bank draft waiting to cover the full cost of the house plus agency fees and title registration. The whole transaction had been finalized in two days.

'Well, gee, that couldn't be Fred,' Lynda said. 'I guess he must have a double. You've been very kind, Mrs Leach. Thank you very much for your help.' She turned to Caine. 'C'mon, hon, we'll just have to keep trying.'

Jill Leach came to the door with them. They thanked her again and got back into the car. He headed south on Heathwood Drive.

305

'You know what?' he said. 'You're terrific.'

'Shut up and drive,' she replied.

Everywhere they looked they saw boats: big, small, sail, power. The whole island was one vast marina. Seen from the air, it would look like one of those enlarged microscope photographs of a snowflake, each tiny frond branching into jetties, landings, and cutely named 'courts'. The Rotary Club map they'd picked up at the Chamber of Commerce indicated that any thoroughfare ending at water's edge was called a court.

He made a left on San Antonio Drive. Alamo Court was third on the right. The Texan theme was continued in the names of the others: San Jacinto, Goliad and Austin, on which new homes were being built. Each court was effectively a three hundred yard peninsula jutting into Roberts Bay. Each cul-de-sac had eight houses on it, surrounded by rectangles of artificial-looking fescue grass with carefully sited shrubs and trees. Caine turned the car around at the end of San Antonio and drove back the way he had come.

'Aren't you going to go and look at the place?' Lynda asked.

'Did you see that blue Safari parked on the corner?'

She twisted around in her seat. 'I see it now.'

'Mirror windows,' he said. 'Nobody in the cab.'

'So?'

'Surveillance truck,' he said. He drove straight along Winterberry to South Collier, then turned south. Condominiums stood like rows of roseate dominoes facing the pink-white beach, monuments to a collision between fantasy and greed, distinguishable one from the other only by their romantic names: Princess del Mar, Royal Seafarer, Summit House, Club Regency, Surf Club, The Palms. The coloured sails of boats and surfboards made kaleidoscopic patterns on the bright turquoise water.

The public boat ramp was at the far end of South Collier looking out to Henry Key. Caine rented a dinghy with an outboard Evinrude for an hour, started her up, and pushed off into

Smokehouse Creek, negotiating the turn into Roberts Bay, which was really a lagoon, never more than half a mile across.

'Where are we going, Caine?' Lynda asked.

'We need a better look at Alamo Court than we were going to get from the street,' he told her. 'Nobody takes any notice of two people pottering about in a boat.'

As they drew closer to their destination, on the northwestern edge of the Bay, they saw a twenty-four-foot twin-engined Seabird riding at anchor about twenty yards offshore. Caine eased back on the throttle and let the little dinghy idle northward. On the site where the new houses were going up, workmen in yellow hardhats moved about.

'Well?' she said.

'Van in the avenue, covering the front. Fast boat here in case he leaves this way. See the powered inflatable tied to the stern? Any move he makes, they can follow. They've probably got watchers on the building site as well. At night, they'll pose as security guards.'

'Who is 'they'?'

'CIA. FBI. Or both.'

He thought of the computers feeding their information into the inexhaustible maw of 'Bubbles', the $17.6 million Cray-2 computer at the NSA. Everything Bogdanovich had ever done, every transaction he had ever effected, every ticket he'd bought, every subscription he'd ever taken out, all the fine hairs of the strands of his life would be in there now for re-evaluation. There would be nothing about him, his family, his friends and acquaintances, the books he read, the trips he had taken, the mail he received, his bank, his phone, his tax, his social security records, that would not be scrutinized in the search for that one denominator, common or otherwise, that would tell the searchers they were on the right track.

The little boat rocked gently in the water as Caine thought it through. The moment he went anywhere near the house, tapes would start to turn, shutters begin to click. They'd have a make on him ten minutes after the pictures were

Faxed to Langley. So he had to make contact some other way: and once again, inescapably, Lynda was it. Nobody was looking for her.

'Why the long face?' Lynda said.

'Just thinking,' he said. 'We can go back now.'

'Do we have to?'

'We can take a ride, if you like.'

'I like,' she said. He revved the engine up and the little boat scooted over the water. The breeze was soft and refreshing. Lynda leaned back, her eyes closed, face lifted to the sun. Caine took the boat through the neck of the lagoon and out into the open water of Caxambas Pass. Ibis flew overhead in line astern. When the boat was in the lee of Henry Key, Caine cut off the engine. The only sound he could hear was the sound of water lapping against the hull. The setting sun bounced flashes of light off the windshields of cars moving along South Collier Boulevard.

'What was she like, Caine?'

'What was who like?'

'Your wife.'

310

'How did you know . . . ?'

'Someone once told me men over thirty are either married or singular.'

'I'm not . . . singular.'

'I never thought you were. What happened — divorce?'

'No. She died. She was just a kid. We'd only been married two years.'

'I'm sorry.'

'It's all right. It was a long time ago.'

'Was she beautiful?'

'Beautiful? No, not really. But she had an honesty that shone out of her, that made her attractive. She wasn't tall. Five three, five four. Very slim. She had green eyes, very fine brown hair that frizzed up when she washed it.'

'Where did you meet?'

'At a dance.'

'I can't imagine you going dancing.'

'That was the only time I ever went.'

'Then how — ?'

'I was sharing a flat with a guy. He arranged to meet a girl at a dance, but he didn't want to go alone. So he asked me to go with him, as a favour. Jenny had a friend . . . well, you can guess the rest.'

'Her friend was your friend's date.'

'Which kind of threw Jenny and I together. I liked her, she liked me. We made a date for the following Sunday. I didn't think she'd show up. Neither of us ever went out with anyone else after that.'

'Love at first sight?'

'Not quite,' he said. 'She didn't want to get married. She wanted to travel: work on a kibbutz, the Greek islands, Africa. But I talked her into it. I was being sent to Germany, and I asked her to come with me.'

'How . . . ?'

'How did she die? She was killed by a car bomb that was meant for me.' His voice was harsh. Lynda put a hand to her lips, her eyes wide with shock, and she fell silent. Waves slapped the side of the boat. After a while, Caine smiled at her. 'It's all right, Lynda,' he said, more gently. 'It was ten years ago. I've done all my grieving.'

'It was Guchkov, wasn't it? That's why you want him.'

'That's why.'

'Were you angry, David? I remember, I got so angry when my husband died in Nam. Like he'd got himself killed on purpose, to make life more difficult for me. It was so irrational. And yet I couldn't help it. I suppose I needed to be angry at someone, something. Otherwise it was all so pointless. Such a waste.'

'Yes,' he said softly. 'I was angry. For a long time. I'd forgotten how angry till I saw Guchkov's face in that dossier. Then it all came back.'

'And now?'

He shook his head. 'Not any more. Angry men make stupid mistakes. You can't afford to make mistakes with a man like Guchkov.'

The sun was down low over the Gulf now, tinting the sky with ribbons of pink and red. He started up the engine and headed for the boat ramp.

'Time to go back to the real world?' she said.

'I don't usually talk so much,' he said.

'You didn't mind? That I asked about her?'

He shook his head. 'I don't mind.

You're easy to talk to, Lynda.'

'Thanks for the boat ride.'

'Next time we'll do it properly.'

'I'll hold you to that.'

He turned in the boat, and made a call to the Post Office from the booth outside. They told him the mailman delivered to Alamo Court mid-morning.

It was safe to assume that the watchers would have someone at the Post Office opening any mail addressed to the house, just as it was safe to assume they were listening to the phones. While there was no way around the latter, there was a way to circumvent the readers.

'What now?' Lynda said, as he came out of the booth.

'We'd better check in someplace,' he said. 'How about the Marco Beach Marriott?'

'I only have a two thousand dollar credit line, Caine. Two rooms at the Marco Beach Marriott is going to knock a big hole in that if we're here for any length of time.'

'We'll just have to wing it, Lynda. Come on, let's get over there. We've got

an early start tomorrow, and you've got to look your best.'

'Why?'

'You're going to flirt with a postman,' Caine said.

22

'Hi,' Lynda said.

The mailman touched his cap, not stopping.

'I wonder if you could help me?' Lynda said.

'What's the problem, ma'am?' He was a tall, thin, fit-looking man with a short beard that made him look older than he probably was. Lynda guessed his age at about thirty.

'I got myself a little lost,' Lynda said. 'I wonder if you could help me out?'

'Glad to,' the man said. 'Where you trying to get to?'

'I'm trying to find the public library,' she said. 'I seem to have taken a wrong turning someplace.'

'Library's on Winterberry,' he told her. 'Where's your car?'

'Over there,' she said, gesturing vaguely.

'OK, here's what you do,' the man said. 'This here is San Antonio. Drive west till

you come to a Stop sign, make a right. The next intersection, you make a left. That's Winterberry. The library is two blocks along on your right. You can't miss it.'

'Well, thanks, uh . . . what's your name?'

'Owen.'

'First name or last?'

'First. Owen Davies.'

'This job must keep you pretty fit, Owen.'

'I do some running.'

'I thought it must be something like that. What kind of distances do you go?'

'Six, eight miles a day. Sometimes more.'

'You run on the beach?'

'Right,' he said. 'Listen, it was nice talking to you, ma'am. I got to get this mail delivered.'

'I'm sorry, I'm holding you up,' Lynda said. 'Thank you for your help, Owen.'

'Y'welcome,' he said.

He had gone about ten yards when she called his name. He turned, frowning.

'You dropped this,' Lynda said, handing him Caine's letter.

'How the hell . . . ?' he muttered, looking at it. He riffled the bundle he was carrying, shaking his head. He jammed the letter in with the others, thanked her and went on his way. Lynda went in the opposite direction, walking fifty yards to where Caine sat waiting in her car.

'Mission accomplished,' she said.

'Let's hope it works.'

They drove up to the Island Plaza shopping centre and had breakfast in a coffee shop. Lynda said only snowbirds were dumb enough to pay seven dollars for an egg in resort hotels. She ordered croissants with her coffee. Caine took blueberry muffins. She told him he should eat more. He said yes, Momma. The coffee was hot and strong. Pretty girls with long tanned legs giggled at the counter.

'Do you think he'll show?' Lynda asked.

'I'm working on the assumption he's expecting someone to contact him. Let's hope I'm right.'

'But . . . ?'

'Go ahead.'

'If he's under surveillance, they'll spot you the moment he makes contact with you.'

'Think you're pretty smart, don't you?'

'But not as smart as you, huh?'

'Just you wait and see.'

He paid for the breakfast and they walked over to the Winn-Dixie supermarket. He bought a pair of swim trunks, a bath towel, a pair of Ray-Ban sunglasses, sneakers and a straw hat. Lynda picked out a pair of short-shorts in blue denim and some cheap sandals, and T-shirts for both of them with the words 'Marco Island' set round a garish orange sunset and a palm tree. They changed clothes in the restrooms and went back to the car. On the way, Caine 'stressed' the straw hat, giving it a well-worn look.

It was only a short drive from Island Plaza to Tigertail Beach. They got there shortly after ten. It would be the best part of an hour before they could expect Bogdanovich. They sat and listened to the radio while they waited.

A bunch of shouting teenagers were playing volleyball on the beach and,

further over, two sun-bronzed hulks in cutoff jeans were tossing a frisbee at each other with a fine display of pectorals. Near the water's edge, kids were splashing about and screeching. A golden labrador dashed into the water and out again, barking. Girls nearby squealed as the dog shook himself dry. A long-haired, bearded proselytizer pushing a ten-foot wooden cross on a single wheel went from group to group, inviting them to open up their hearts and let in the sweet music of Jesus Christ.

'Shall we dance?' Caine said.

They walked down to the water's edge, feet crunching on the wide swathe of broken shells on the high-water mark. Shell hunters searched in the shallows, picking up and discarding, their faces intent and serious. Caine singled out a kid of about fifteen standing shin-deep in the water, a net bag of shells slung from his waist. He wore bathing trunks and one of those mass-produced baseball caps. On the white panel at the front were stencilled the words 'Chisum Trail Ride, 1980', and in smaller letters, 'Roswell, N.M.'

'Ten bucks for your shells,' he said. 'What do you say?'

The kid took off the baseball cap he was wearing. He squinted and rubbed his head.

'You crazy, or what?'

'What,' Caine said, and showed him the ten. The kid handed him the bag, took the money and walked off, looking back once. Caine stood in the shallows, the warm water swirling at his feet.

'You look like you've been here all morning,' Lynda said, joining him.

'That's the basic idea,' he said.

'You know anything about shells?'

'I used to.'

He tried to remember all the exotic names shellers gave to their treasures: pectins, jingles, boat shells, sun rays, Scotch bonnets, jewel boxes, lion's paws, cups and saucers, cat's eyes. He looked at his watch: five after eleven.

'OK, this is the plan,' Caine said. 'I've sent Bogdanovich a picture of you, and a note that says his life may depend on his meeting you here. I just hope to God it didn't spook him.'

'What do I do?'

'We've got to get him away from his watchers long enough for me to talk to him. If they see me, we're cooked. So it's up to you. Think you can do it?'

'How will I know it's him?'

'He'll ask you if you've found any yellow rough scallops. You say they're the hardest ones of all to find. But you've got some other stuff, if he's interested. He'll ask you what the hell all this is about.'

'And then?'

'You tell him you've got proof his life is in danger, and if he'll walk across to your car you'll show it to him. He'll probably be chary. He won't want to get in any car with a total stranger. Tell him he doesn't have to. Point out that the car is over there right out in the open, where nothing can happen without a hundred people seeing it.'

'And where will you be?'

'In the car, on the floor. So make sure he's close enough to hear me. Think you can do it?'

'Good job you brought me along, Caine.'

'The thought had occurred to me,' he grinned.

He pulled the straw hat down over his face and ambled up the beach, leaving her standing in the water, the bag of shells in her hand.

When he got to the car he looked back. A man was working his way slowly up the beach. Every so often he would stop and talk to one of the shellers. Caine checked the crowd for a watcher, but could see no one obvious. They'd be out there someplace, though. The man drew level, looked at Lynda with appreciative interest, then walked on by.

Caine stifled a curse. Wrong man. The man walked on about ten yards, stopped, turned back and spoke to Lynda.

'I don't suppose you've come across any yellow rough scallops, have you?' He was tall, but thin and weedy-looking. He wore a white cotton tennis shirt, black Pegasus shorts, and carried a pair of Adidas tennis shoes with white tube socks tucked into them.

'They're the hardest of all to find,' Lynda said. 'But I've got some other

stuff, if you're interested.'

'You the one sent the photograph?' Bogdanovich said. 'What is all this about?'

'Tell me how interesting the shells are,' Lynda said. 'Make like you never saw one in your life before.'

Bogdanovich did as he was bidden, picking up the shells one by one and examining them like a diamond cutter looking over an uncut stone. 'Who are you?' he said, his voice almost inaudible. 'What do you want?'

'You see the white Toyota parked over there?'

'What about it?'

'What I want to show you is in it.'

'What is this, lady?' Bogdanovich said. 'What are you after?'

'Look, you came this far. Trust me for another couple of minutes, OK? I couldn't bring what I want to show you down here. It's in my car. Just walk over there with me. You don't have to get in.'

Bogdanovich frowned, then gave a curt little nod of assent. They walked up the beach to where the car was parked. Lynda

noticed that one of the windows was wound right down. Bogdanovich stood by warily as she opened the door.

'Bogdanovich, can you hear me?' Caine said. The man outside jumped visibly.

'Wha . . . who is that?' he stuttered.

'Drosdow sent me.'

'Who's Drosdow? Who are you?'

'Where's the woman?' Caine said.

'You mean Eva?' Bogdanovich frowned.

'She's a plant, Bogdanovich. You know what a honey trap is?'

'Are you crazy, or what?'

'That's the second time today I've been asked that. Who owns the house? Who told you to come to Marco Island?'

'You'd better tell me who the hell you are, mister.'

'Somebody has set you up, Bogdanovich. Your own people have got you under intensive surveillance. Didn't you know?'

Bogdanovich looked as if he had been kicked in the belly. His pasty skin went grey and, for a moment, Lynda thought the man might pass out.

'Are you . . . who are you?' Bogdanovich managed.

'I told you, Drosdow sent me.'

'I don't know any Drosdow.'

He was looking around him edgily, as if he was convinced Caine was mad, and Caine was beginning to feel as if he might be. The more they talked, the less sense anything made. Something was vastly wrong.

'Listen to him, Mr Bogdanovich,' Lynda said. 'He's telling you the truth.'

'How do you know my name? What do you want?'

'Let's start over,' Caine said. 'The woman who brought you down here knows you work for the Company. She works for Russian Intelligence. Her job is to compromise you so Drosdow can recruit you as a spy.'

'You are crazy!' Bogdanovich said, angrily. 'Woman, Russian intelligence? I'm down here on vacation with my wife, for Christ's sake!'

'Listen, Bogdanovich,' Caine said, urgently. 'I know it must sound insane to you, but I swear what I'm saying is true. Hear me out, OK?'

'I'm listening,' Bogdanovich said.

'My name is David Caine. I work for a security firm called International Security Systems. You ever heard of it?'

'Nope.'

'I was assigned to a case in Florida. It concerned a Company operation headed up by a Domestic Ops agent, Frank Forsyth. Name ring any bells?'

'I don't know who the hell you are, mister. And I'm not discussing my business activities, with you or anyone.'

'All right, all right. Look, I know you work at the CIA. Let me assume you might know the name, and cut a long story short. Forsyth got on to a man named Frederic Drosdow who is probably a Russian intelligence officer. Drosdow sold drugs to raise finance for a honey trap. Let's also assume you know what that is. The swallow was a woman named Katja. The location was the house you are staying in. And the target was a senior Company coding clerk named Paul Bogdanovich. And that's why, right now, you are under intensive surveillance by the Office of Security. They think you've been lured down here for entrapment. The fact you

brought your wife may have thrown them a little, but that won't last long.'

'You're one of them, aren't you?' Bogdanovich said, a wary look in his eyes. 'This is the old double-whammy play, right?'

'Sure,' Caine said, scornfully. 'And Lynda is Mata Hari in disguise.'

'I've nothing to hide,' Bogdanovich said, defiantly. 'I haven't done anything wrong.'

'They haven't got round-the-clockers on you because they think you stole a few paperclips, sunshine,' Caine told him. 'You better talk to me.'

'Why should I even listen to you?'

'Who else have you got?'

Bogdanovich thought about that for a while. Caine saw him scan the beach furtively from beneath lowered eyebrows, looking for watchers. 'What did you say your name was?' he asked.

'David Caine. International Security Systems.'

'And what do you want?'

'I want to find Frederic Drosdow.'

'I told you, I never heard of him.'

'All right,' Caine said. 'We've talked

long enough. Take the shells, give Lynda some money. Meet me at Marco Bay marina tomorrow at nine thirty a.m. Bring your wife. Eva, you said?'

'I don't understand any of this,' Bogdanovich said. He looked suddenly haggard, worried. 'It doesn't make sense.'

'Tomorrow I'll charter a boat. We'll go for a cruise, talk, try to figure this out. OK?'

'The marina, maybe,' Bogdanovich said. 'If you think I'm going out on a boat with you or anybody else, forget it.'

'Nine thirty,' Caine said. 'Just be there.'

Bogdanovich walked back down the beach. Caine tried to spot the watchers and failed again. All he could see were brashly confident American kids, mindlessly enjoying the world's highest standard of living, waiting their turn with the Amex Gold cards and the Cadillac Sevilles.

'OK,' he said to Lynda. 'We move fast now before they can get a car up here. Walk down the beach till you come to Bayside Court. Walk up to Collier Boulevard. I'll pick you up on the corner.'

He watched her go, waiting to see if anyone would come over to check out the

329

car. No one came near. As he had suspected, the watchers had been caught flat-footed. One of them would stay with Bogdanovich. If there were two, the other would tail Lynda on foot. He grinned at himself in the driving mirror. 'Home, James,' he said.

He drove over to Collier and turned south. As he coasted to a stop at the corner of Bayside Court, he saw her coming. She ran the last ten yards and jumped into the car. They didn't speak until they pulled into the parking area at the Marriott.

'What do you think, Caine?' she said. 'Did he buy it?'

Caine shrugged. 'I think so. He looked pretty worried.'

'He looked sick,' Lynda said. 'As if he'd been betrayed.'

Caine shook his head in disbelief. Then he took her face in his hands and kissed her on the lips.

'Holmes,' he said, 'you amaze me!'

She stared at him in astonishment.

'What did I do?' she gasped.

'It'll come to you,' he replied.

23

When they were about an hour out, Hank Valdes broke out some Coors. The owner of the *Sea Wind* was a barrel-chested man with skin as brown as leather, a grizzled beard and a luxuriant thatch of black hair liberally streaked with grey. He wore a T-shirt that bore the legend '*Joggers do it with their earphones on*'.

The two women sat in deckchairs on the stern and watched the island dropping away. The sun was hot through the breeze of their passage. Valdes busied himself checking the leaders and swivels on the unused fishing equipment. The size of his fist made the beer can in it look small.

'Is there anything you'd like, Mrs Bogdanovich?' Lynda asked the woman sitting beside her. Eva Bogdanovich was petite and dark, attractive in a soap-powder commercial sort of way. Her face was set and tense.

'Nothing. Thank you.'

'Don't be afraid. There's nothing to be frightened of.'

'I don't understand what all this is about.'

'What did your husband tell you?'

'He said we had to go on this trip. That it was something to do with his work.'

'That's all?'

'We have a family agreement. We never discuss his work.'

'Did he tell you that you have been under surveillance the whole time you have been here on Marco Island?'

Eva Bogdanovich's eyes widened with alarm. She looked from right to left, as if seeking escape. 'He . . . he said you'd ask me questions. He said not to tell you anything.'

'But if you know nothing about his work, what could you tell me?'

'Who are you?'

'My name is Lynda Sanchez. I run a small restaurant on Key Biscayne called La Paloma.'

'Then why . . . ?'

'Why am I here? I've wondered that

myself once or twice. Let's just say we're trying to help your husband, Mrs Bogdanovich.'

'Help him?'

'He's in some sort of trouble. Espionage.'

'Oh, God!' Eva Bogdanovich said. Lynda looked at her more closely.

'Didn't you know?' she said.

'I told you, I don't know anything.'

'Talk to him, Mrs Bogdanovich. Try to make him realize we're the only ones who can help him.'

'I don't know what you're talking about.' Eva Bogdanovich stood up and went across to the rail, leaning out so she could see her husband sitting on the prow of the boat with Caine. They had been out there since soon after they sailed, more than an hour ago. 'How much longer are they going to stay up there, anyway?' she said, irritably.

'Didn't he tell you about the honey trap, Eva?' Lynda asked, gently. The other woman just shook her head, not replying.

'Do you know who owns the house you are staying in?' Lynda asked. Eva

Bogdanovich turned to face her, frowning.

'Of course I do,' she said. 'A friend of Paul's at work. A man called Marty Fielder.'

'He told you that?'

'Of course.'

'It's not true, Eva,' Lynda said. 'We talked to the realtor who sold it. The house was bought by a man who called himself Victor Ziegelmann. His real name is Frederic Drosdow.'

'I . . . we don't know anybody called Drosdow. Or Ziegelmann. Are they going to sit out there for the whole trip?'

'Caine is trying to convince your husband that he wants to help him.'

'You keep saying that. What has Paul done?'

'Here they are,' Lynda said. 'Ask him yourself.'

Bogdanovich's face was stiff and sullen. He clambered down into the well deck and sat down on one of the deck chairs. Caine sat opposite him. Eva looked at him and then at her husband.

'Paul,' she said. 'What's wrong? They

334

keep saying you're in some kind of trouble.'

'You don't understand,' he said.

'Let's all go sit up top,' Caine suggested. 'It's cooler up there, anyway.'

They went up to the flying deck. Valdes had rolled back the canopy so there was plenty of breeze. If by any chance Bogdanovich's watchers had put sneakies aboard, the sound of the wind and the waves was more than enough to ruin whatever they might pick up, Caine decided.

'How much has he told you, Eva?' Caine asked. Eva looked at her husband. He avoided her pleading eyes.

'She . . . ' Eva gestured towards Lynda. 'She says the house doesn't belong to Marty Fielder, Paul. Is that true?' He did not reply. 'She says it belongs to a man named Frederic Drosdow. Who is Frederic Drosdow?'

'He is a Russian military intelligence officer,' Caine told her.

'Russian?' she said. 'Here? In Florida?'

'The Russians have lots of agents working in Florida, Eva,' Caine said.

'Most of them are Cuban, but by no means all of them.'

'How would he know about us? We know no one like that.'

'That's what I keep hoping Paul will tell me.'

'Paul?' she said, saying his name the way she had before, with a note of pleading in it.

'No!' he said, sharply. 'He's trying to get me to incriminate myself. You think I'm stupid?'

'What do you mean, incriminate yourself?' Eva said, her face suddenly pale beneath the tan. 'How could you do that?'

'Tell her, Paul,' Caine said.

'There's nothing to tell.'

'You've been betrayed, Paul,' Caine said. 'They're throwing you to the wolves to protect someone — or something — much more valuable.'

'You're crazy!' Bogdanovich said, hoarsely, but the conviction had gone out of his voice. The grey pallor they had seen before had again taken away his colour.

'If he's crazy, why are we under surveillance?' Eva said.

'How do we know it's the Office of Security that's watching us?' he snapped. 'We've only got his word for it.'

'Who else could it be?' Caine said.

'Why are they watching us at all?' Eva asked, very quietly.

Bogdanovich shook his head. 'I'm saying nothing,' he said, doggedly. 'Nothing!'

'You were already working for them, weren't you, Paul?' Caine said, softly. 'That's how they knew you. What did they tell you — go to Marco Island, wait until you're contacted, something like that?'

'Tell her, Paul,' Lynda said, putting her hand on his. He looked out at the unchanging ocean. Tears glistened in his eyes.

'You're expendable. You knew it from the moment I told you about the honey trap yesterday. That's why you agreed to come out on the boat with us. You knew we were the only hope you had.'

'Why?' Bogdanovich whispered. 'Why me?'

'They probably have someone else who

can do what you were doing for them. You became a liability.'

'Are . . . will you help me, Caine?'

'If I can. You've got to help me first, Paul.'

'I'll be finished. You don't know.'

'Then don't lie down and let them do it to you. Fight back.'

'Who are you talking about?' Eva said, angrily. 'Who is 'them'?'

'The Russians, Eva,' Caine said.

'Oh, God!' she whispered. 'Oh, God, no.'

<p style="text-align:center">★ ★ ★</p>

By the time they got back to the marina that evening, Caine knew just about all there was to know about Paul Michael Bogdanovich. Born in St Paul, Minnesota, he was one of the four children of Harold Bogdanovich, a naturalized Czech refugee who had a General Motors dealership in Golden Valley. Usual middle-class family background of high school and college. Faced with the prospect of going to Vietnam, Paul had embraced the offer made to him

by a CIA recruiter who came out to UOM; his fluency in Czech made enrolment in the Company's junior officer training programme simple.

Caine knew the induction routine pretty well, but he let Bogdanovich talk about it at his own speed. It was all part of the debriefing technique, which varied only slightly from individual to individual. Caine's job was to make him relax, to allay his fears the way you do with a child: tell me the truth and nothing bad will happen to you. Once in a while he would throw in a deliberate error, to see if Bogdanovich would correct it.

Enrolment in the CIA in those days began with a series of interviews and tests which took place at Quarters Eye, near the Potomac in Washington. It was a non-stop exhausting programme that made no concessions to normal working hours or physical needs. You grabbed a sandwich from one of the blind stands — all Company snack concessions were run by blind people — between punishing sessions with the Wechsler, Guilford, Minnesota Multiphasics, Rohrschach, Strong,

Kudor and the rest of the tests. After more interviews, you signed an all-embracing secrecy agreement and were assigned to the Personnel Pool at 1016 Sixteenth Street. There you folded maps and competed in crossword puzzle contests until your final 'technical interview' — spookspeak for a polygraph test.

When you passed the lie-detector test, and only when, you got a provisional clearance to handle secret material. After a session on what was euphemistically called the Farm — the Company enclave on Camp Peary, near Williamsburg — Bogdanovich was assigned to East European Radio Transmissions as an analyst, reading radio traffic intercepts picked up by the NSA listening station at Menwith Hill, in Yorkshire, England.

'Menwith,' Caine said, raking through the cold ashes of old memory. 'Primary targets West and Eastern Europe, and Russia east of the Urals.'

'Let me ask you something, Caine,' Bogdanovich said. 'How do you know all this?'

'How did it happen, Paul?' Caine said,

ignoring the question. 'Did they come to you, or did you go to them?'

'Who are you, Caine? Who do you work for?'

'You know I can't tell you that.'

'How do I know I can trust you?'

'If I was hostile, I wouldn't be helping you, Paul,' Caine reminded him. 'You'd already be dead.'

'You could still do it,' Bogdanovich said. 'After you've got all the information you want.'

Caine shrugged. 'That's a risk you're going to have to take,' he said. Bogdanovich looked at his wife.

'You've got to trust someone, Paul,' she said.

'I did,' he said, bitterly. 'Look where it got me.'

Eva reached across and took his hand in hers. 'Tell him,' she said.

He took a deep, deep breath and then let it out slowly. 'All right,' he said. 'I'll tell you.'

'Go right back to when it first started,' Caine prompted.

'Everything seemed to go wrong all at

once,' Bogdanovich said. 'One minute everything was fine, the next . . . There was an appropriations cut, they said they were closing down my section. They told me I could take retirement on half pay or a downgrade in salary. I didn't have any choice. Then . . . it was . . . funny, really,' he said, staring out at a gannet swooping above the turning waters of the boat's wake. 'I was driving a Maverick back then. The transmission went. You remember, Eva?'

'I remember,' she said.

'I went to a car dealer in Pimmit Hills, just to look around. I couldn't afford what they had, we'd just bought the house. I didn't want to borrow. Then I got talking to this guy who was there. We went and sat in a coffee shop together, he told me maybe he could help me, he knew a guy who loaned money at very low rates to government employees. He gave me a number to call. I called the man and he arranged to meet me.'

'Where?'

'In the lobby of the Hay-Adams.'

'Didn't you suspect anything?'

'No. Yes. Yes, now I look back on it, I think I must have done. But I think I'd already decided, in my mind, if this was a pitch, I was going to listen to it. Especially after what happened at work. I thought, if that's how they repay me for twelve years, screw them. I guess I was ready to talk to someone, and that someone came along.'

'What happened then?'

'He asked me how much I needed, and I told him four thousand He said he could handle that, no problem. He counted out four thousand dollars in hundred dollar bills, right there in the hotel lobby. I couldn't believe it. I said, how do I pay this off, and he said, don't worry about that, I'll be in touch. Then he was gone. It sounds incredible, but that's what happened.'

'Let me guess what came next,' Caine said. 'Your friend had a friend he wanted you to meet.'

'Right,' Bogdanovich said. 'He called me at home, asked me if I could help him out, he had this friend who was being investigated by the FBI. He said the

343

friend would gladly pay a couple of K to see a copy of his dossier.'

'You got it?'

'You wouldn't believe how easy it was. I mean, most of what the guy wanted he could have gotten himself under the Freedom of Information Act.'

'Then what happened?'

'He asked me for some other things. Very low classification stuff. I couldn't believe the kind of money they were prepared to pay for what I was giving them. They could have read most of it in the *Washington Post*.'

'What was the name of the man you were dealing with?'

'He called himself Alexei. His real name is Stepan Lykov. He's a third attaché at the Kremlin in Washington.'

The vast new Soviet Embassy high on its hill, dominating the entire Washington skyline, was known as the Kremlin to civilians and military alike.

'How long did the honeymoon last?'

'Is that what they call it? A year, maybe two. Then Alexei told me that from now on, his requirements would be more

specific. He would give me assignments to fulfil, and I would fulfil them. Like he was a goddam general talking to a PFC.'

'You did what he told you?'

'I had no choice. They had photographs of me accepting the money. It was do what they said, or . . . ' He made the slit-throat gesture with his finger.

'All right,' Caine said. 'Let's get down to details. Alexei told you to come to Marco Island?'

'He told me to apply for ten days' leave. Fly to Miami, stay one night at the Marriott, then drive out here. On the first day I had to go to a designated booth in the Island Plaza shopping centre, call a Miami number and say, 'Pimmit' — that's my codename — 'in place'. After that, he said I was to wait until I was contacted.'

'You were probably talking to a tape recorder,' Caine said. 'Or a hand-on phone.'

'What's that?' Eva said.

'Bookies use them. You can set up a telephone so when anyone calls that number, it hands the call on to another phone. If anybody traces the call, all they

get is a phone in an empty room. Obviously all they wanted was to put you in place. They set you up, Paul.'

'Why?' he said, hoarsely. 'I gave them everything they asked for. Always, everything.'

'You've served your purpose. The Comrades are through with you.'

'You . . . you mean they . . .'

'Look at it from their point of view. You're no use to them any more. What happens next will depend on how much you know about them. If it's more than they want the Office of Security to find out, they'll kill you. If not, they'll let OOS take care of you.'

Bogdanovich gulped noisily. 'There's a unit in Special Operations. They sometimes . . . If you've become an embarrassment to the Company, they take care of it. It's called incineration. You just disappear. All the records, everything. You don't know what they can do.'

'Oh, yes I do,' Caine assured him.

'Are you going to help me, Caine?'

'I'll try,' Caine said. 'If I can clear this thing up, I might be able to do

something. But you've got to help me first.'

'How?'

'I want you to write down everything you can remember giving them. Do you understand? Every single thing you can remember.'

'But . . . that would take hours!' he said. 'Hours!'

'Then sit up all night,' Caine said, unsympathetically. 'It's your life that's on the line, remember. Look, I need that information, Paul. If you come through, we'll get you out of this. Lynda will take you back to Miami. No one will look for you there.'

'Why do you want this Drosdow?'

'You know why.'

'I mean, why you? You're not CIA, you're not FBI. Why are you involved in this?'

'You know I can't tell you that,' Caine said. 'You're just going to have to trust me.'

'Trust,' Bogdanovich sighed. 'Who can you trust?'

'Will you do it?'

'I want you to take care of Eva,' Bogdanovich said. 'She didn't know about any of this. If anything happens to me . . .'

'We're going to try and make sure nothing happens to either of you,' Lynda said. 'Aren't we, Caine?'

'If Paul comes through for me,' Caine said.

'All right,' Bogdanovich said. 'I'll do it.'

'There's writing stuff in the cabin,' Caine said. 'Go below and get started. Hey, Hank! Valdes!'

'Yo!' Valdes said, from below.

'I think we might try some fishing now.'

'Great!' Valdes said. 'All of you?'

'Paul's got some writing to do,' Caine told him. 'But the ladies and I might take a crack at it. What do you say, Eva?'

Her smile was very bright and tight and brave.

'OK,' she said. 'OK.'

24

'I give up,' Harry Lloyd said, stubbing out his cigarette and lighting another. 'This whole damned take makes no sense at all!'

Caine's reappearance, especially with the Sanchez woman in tow, had thrown them. Apparently it had thrown Miami, too: Bensen's perplexity had been almost tangible. He had promised them he would get right on it and get back to them. Since when, silence. Bensen was probably waiting for instructions from Langley. Maybe Langley was waiting for word from God.

'One thing's for sure,' Balfour said. 'There's no honey trap going down here. My bet is that Caine is taking Bogdanovich someplace to meet Drosdow.'

'In a boat?'

'Maybe they want to be sure they're alone. Maybe they have to go to the same place every day and wait.'

'I don't buy that,' Forsyth said. 'Anyway, why would Drosdow put himself at risk to meet Bogdanovich? What could Bogdanovich know that would interest him?'

'Why are there more questions than answers, Grandpa?' Lloyd said, in a Mel Blanc voice.

'So, what are we supposed to do?' Balfour said.

'We wait,' Forsyth said. 'For Bensen.'

'What a nice change,' Lloyd remarked, savagely.

The unease simmered in Forsyth's mind like soup. Even though it had been he who first made the connection between Bogdanovich and David Caine, he still felt unhappy about it, NSA dossier and movements survey notwithstanding.

There was enough circumstantial evidence to point to Caine's being a Comrade: he'd had plenty of dealings with them while he was in army intelligence in Germany. They could easily have turned him then. His profile was close enough to what Avranilosa had heard. All the same, a few things still

bothered Forsyth. If Caine was the Comrade, how come the NSA could establish no link between him and Bogdanovich prior to their meeting on Marco Island? If Caine was supposed to be leading Bogdanovich into a honey trap, how come he'd let him bring his wife?

The thing that bothered him most of all was that Caine had run, which got him a Most Sought classification and made M-5 even more anxious to know what he was up to. Usually, if one of their agents was blown, the Comrades had him on an Aeroflot Tupolev to Sheremetyevo before you could say *Tovarishch*. In Forsyth's experience, a good agent never ran when he knew he was blown: a pro knew there was no place to hide. Yet Caine, who was if nothing else a pro, had run. And as if that were not enough, he had turned up at what he must have known, or at the very least suspected, was a surveillanced location.

The special link line to Miami gave its discreet bleep and Balfour picked up the handset. He grimaced, and put his hand

over the mouthpiece.

'Megacreep,' he announced.

'Yes,' Forsyth said into the phone.

'Anything new?' Bensen sounded aggrieved, as if all this had been done specifically to upset him. Caine had chartered a boat called *Sea Wind*, owned by a local man named Hank Valdes. Valdes had been checked out; he was clean. So why had Caine and the Sanchez woman gone cruising with Bogdanovich and his wife? Coastguard surveillance reported they hadn't landed anywhere, hadn't picked anyone up. What were they doing out there? They sure as hell weren't interested in fishing.

'Nothing.'

'No sign of Drosdow?'

'None. And none of anyone who might remotely be the swallow. What do we do, Donald?'

'Head Office says let go. Let them run.'

'What?'

'You heard me. Lift the surveillance. We're out of the picture, as of now.'

'Would you care to spend twenty seconds explaining why?'

'I'm just passing on the word. They say

we're to take no further interest, we take no further interest. Other arrangements are being made.'

'What other arrangements?'

'Negative. You don't need to know.'

That again, Forsyth thought, disgustedly. The old need-to-know principle. You weren't supposed to know more than was necessary to carry out your compartmentalized little function. You were a part of the Grand Design, but you weren't permitted to know what it was. The guy above you knew a little, but only a little more. And so on, all the way up the line.

'Jesus, what a waste,' Forsyth said.

'It's not my decision, Frank.'

'You fought like a lion, right?'

'What?'

'I want my protest logged.'

'I'll make a note of it,' Bensen said curtly, and hung up before Forsyth could say any more. Not that there was any more to be said. Someone up the line had made an Executive Decision. Good, bad or putrid, that was it.

'I've got bad news and bad news,' he said to Lloyd and Balfour as he put down

the phone. Lloyd shrugged.

'In that case, give us the bad news first.'

'The party's over. We're off this take.'

'You mean it?' Balfour said in disbelief. 'Bensen told you to drop it?'

'Right down the toilet,' Forsyth said. He walked out into the garden at the rear of the house on San Antonio Avenue they were using as a base. A soft breeze was coming in off Roberts Bay. He looked up and saw ibis flying overhead. He took a deep breath, then slowly let it out, letting his own tension dissipate with it.

There was no more he could do. All the unanswered questions were going to remain just that, unanswered, at least as far as he was concerned. Maybe one day he might learn what finally happened; more likely not. The price of freedom is eternal fuckups, he thought. He went indoors.

'You guys roll all this up, OK?' Forsyth said, putting on his jacket. 'I'll be back in a while.'

'I thought you said we're off this?' Lloyd remarked.

'You know how forgetful I am,' Forsyth said.

25

'Let me ask you a question, Mitch,' Drosdow said, leaning back in his chair. 'What would you do if you had a million dollars?'

They were alone in the big house. Kate was ostensibly visiting a friend in Baltimore. The servants had been given strict orders not to disturb them. The phones were switched off, the alarms switched on. Drosdow sipped his Rémy Martin and watched Butler Mitchell's face, as easy to read as a child's primer.

'First thing, I'd take early retirement,' Mitchell said. 'Then I'd take off. Round the world. A first-class suite on the QE2 to Southampton. London. A box at Ascot, Centre Court at Wimbledon, stay at the Connaught. Then on to Paris, the Ritz. Go to all those restaurants I've read about: Taillevent, Ledoyen, Lasserre, the Tour d'Argent. I'd buy a car, something fabulous, a Ferrari or a Lamborghini.

Drive to Nice, over to Florence, Rome. A suite at Hassler's, looking out over the Spanish Steps. Athens, Cairo, then Arusha in Tanzania. A safari to Kilimanjaro. I've always wanted to see Kilimanjaro, ever since I saw it in that movie, with Gregory Peck and Susan Hayward.'

'Ah, yes,' Drosdow said. 'Life can be beautiful when you've got money. Better than prison, Mitch?'

'Prison? Who's talking about prison?'

'It's an interesting subject,' Drosdow said.

'I can take it or leave it,' Mitchell said, uncomfortably, not liking the turn the conversation had taken. Drosdow smiled. He'd like it even less, presently.

'Lot of blacks in the prisons in this part of the world,' he said, ruminatively. 'That right, Mitch?'

'I expect so,' Mitchell said, with a shrug.

'Be pretty bad for a white man in there with all those blacks. I hear they do terrible things, gang rape, beatings.'

'What the hell is this, Fred? One minute we're having a pleasant conversation, the next you're talking about gang

rapes in black prisons.'

'Which would you prefer?'

'You're not making sense, Fred.'

'Indulge me,' Drosdow said. He got up and went across to his desk. He opened the drawer and took out a large manila envelope. From it he took a batch of documents, which he spread on the table. The red classification stamps looked like wounds: HANDLE VIA COMINT CHANNELS ONLY. TOP SECRET VIPAR.

Mitchell stared at them uncomprehendingly. He edged up to the table as if the documents were cobras that might strike him. He touched them gingerly.

'How in the name of God did you get these?' he whispered.

'Suppose I said I got them from you?'

'It would be a damned lie! I've never given you — '

'Of course not,' Drosdow said, briskly. 'You know that, and I know that. But suppose you had to try and convince M-5?' M-5 was the Office of Security at the NSA, the fiercest and most diligent security organization in government service.

'They'd believe me,' Mitchell said. 'They'd know I never — ' His voice tailed off as Drosdow's smile widened. He thought of the little 'favours' Drosdow had asked him to do over the few weeks that he'd known the man: first, the restricted directory, then items more sensitive — an organizational chart, a list of top-ranking NSA personnel. Never anything that seemed like . . . well, wrong.

'What's all this about, Fred?' he said, suddenly uneasy.

'My people are ready to move, and that means I have to give them what they want.'

Mitchell frowned. 'Your people?'

Drosdow sighed, as one might sigh at a child's inability to comprehend a nuance. He tossed a sheaf of cheques and receipts on the table.

'Your gambling debts,' he said. 'All paid off. The cheques were all drawn on an account at Manufacturers Hanover Trust, but deposits in those exact amounts came from the Narodny Bank — you know what that is, I assume?'

'You're . . . some sort of spy. Is that it?'

'An old-fashioned word,' Drosdow said. 'But it will do.'

Mitchell shook his head stubbornly. 'Whatever it is you want, I won't do it.'

'I was hoping not to have to go this far,' Drosdow said. He pushed a button by the side of his chair. A screen slid down from a slot above the fireplace. Drosdow pressed another button to dim the lights.

'What the hell is all this?' Mitchell said, making his tone belligerent. Drosdow made no reply. The screen lit up; the number nine in a circle appeared. Then the film started to run, counting down. The scene was a bedroom.

'Jesus Christ!' Mitchell whispered, recognizing it. The film ran on. The figures in the well-lit bedroom performed their predictable arabesques until their predictable conclusion. The screen went blank. Drosdow switched the lights back on. He looked at Mitchell. The man's face was stricken, colourless. His lips moved, but for a few seconds no sound came out.

'There are seven films altogether,' Drosdow said. 'Plus, of course, a great many still photographs.'

He gave it a moment to sink in. The bronze Ansonia Winter and Summer clock ticked softly in the silence.

'Kate . . . ?' Mitchell managed, hoarsely. 'Is she — ?'

'Kate knows nothing about my . . . loyalties,' Drosdow said briskly.

'You expect me to believe that?' Mitchell said, bitterly.

'Kate is a young woman in love. She thinks you're a wealthy man and that you'll probably marry her.' Drosdow watched the American closely. Mitchell wanted to believe it: he could see it in the man's eyes.

'You used her? Your own daughter? Why?' Mitchell said. 'Why?'

'Come, come, Mitch,' Drosdow said, impatiently, 'you're not as naïve as that.'

'You — ' Mitchell's colour came back. Anger lit his eyes. A vein throbbed in his temple. 'You bastard. Oh, you fucking bastard!'

'Spare me the gutter talk,' Drosdow snapped. 'You're facing the most important decision of your life. Don't let emotion cloud it.'

360

'No!' Mitchell said. 'A few favours, yes. I didn't mind that. But I won't be a spy. You hear me? I won't!'

'Just as you wish,' Drosdow said, pouring himself another cognac from the Waterford decanter on the sideboard. 'I trust you understand the implications of your refusal?'

'What do you mean?'

'Copies of everything here, the films, the documents, all of it, will be sent to your wife — oh, yes, we know all about Cathie, Mitch — and to the Director of the National Security Agency,' Drosdow said.

'I'll tell them about you,' Mitchell said. 'They'll see how you trapped me. All this.' He waved a hand to encompass the house, all of it.

'You have been removing secret materials from the National Security Agency,' Drosdow said, relentlessly. 'And you knew it. What difference if you go on doing it?'

Mitchell dumbly shook his head.

'Think carefully,' Drosdow said. 'One sight of this material and you'll be finished. Your wife will take you for every

penny you possess, and the NSA will break you, Mitch. They'll put you in the worst hellhole they can find and they'll throw away the key. You'll spend the rest of your life playing wife to some negro lifer.'

'I don't believe you. It wouldn't be just me. What about Kate? She'd go to prison, too.'

'That's right.'

'You bastard,' Mitchell groaned.

'You're repeating yourself,' Drosdow said, impatiently. 'You told me yourself you hated them, Mitch! You said they'd held you back for years, never given you the recognition you deserved. What loyalty do you owe people like that?'

'I wish I'd never laid eyes on you,' the big man said, putting his head in his hands. Dry, racking sobs burst out of him.

'Stop that!'

Drosdow's voice was like a pistol shot. Mitchell sat up, surprise and, for the first time, fear in his eyes. Drosdow nodded. At last the American realized just how deep was the water he was in.

'Is it really that hard a decision to make?' he said. 'What did the NSA ever do for you, anyway? I'm offering you a straight choice: a million dollars in your hand. Everything you've always wanted. All the good things: money, travel, clothes. And a beautiful woman to share them all with. Do it, Mitch. Do it, or I give you to M-5.'

'I . . . you've got to let me think,' Mitchell said. 'I've got to think.'

'No,' Drosdow said, grimly. 'You decide tonight.'

He let the silence lengthen. It didn't make any difference how Mitchell said it, as long as he said something. He waited.

'I . . . what would I . . . have to do?' Mitchell said. Drosdow smiled.

'Have a drink,' he said. 'You look as if you need one.'

26

By the time Valdes turned the *Sea Wind*
south into Marco Bay, Bogdanovich had
filled ten pages of a legal pad with his
sloping scrawl. Glancing through it,
Caine was astonished not so much by
what the Comrades had asked for as how
much Bogdanovich had been able to
supply. For all his lowgrade status, masses
of sensitive material passed through his
hands for pre-transmission coding.

Caine decided not to give Bogdanovich
and his wife any time to reconsider: he
insisted that instead of going back to the
house on Alamo Court, they should come
to the Marco Beach Marriott.

'We've got two rooms,' he told them.
'Paul and I can sleep in one, Lynda and
Eva in the other.'

'Why do we have to do that?'
Bogdanovich said, pettishly.

'I want you to finish those lists tonight,'
Caine told him. 'Then you'll be ready to

leave first thing in the morning.'

'Leave?' Eva said.

'I want you out of Marco tomorrow, Eva,' Caine said. 'In case whoever sent you down here decides it would be simpler to just remove you from the picture.'

Bogdanovich had that sick pallor again. 'You really think they'd do that?' he said, like someone who feels he has been unfairly treated.

'All I know is you're at risk. I want to get you someplace you won't be.'

'Like where?'

'I don't know yet. Maybe we can get Valdes to take us up the coast, Sanibel, Sarasota, Cedar Key. When we got there, you could jump ship. Lie low until I can clear this up.'

'Using what for money?'

'I could get some money to you,' Lynda said. 'Enough to live on.'

'Suppose I turned myself in?' Bogdanovich said. 'Told them all I know?'

'They already know all you know, Paul.'

Valdes brought the *Sea Wind* in towards her berth at the marina. Caine

could see people on the apron in front of the coffee shop, and wondered if Forsyth was among them. Maybe he'd been out looking for them in Gullivan Bay. It was a big bay.

They said so long to Valdes and walked down the jetty. Caine and Lynda stood watching as Paul and Eva Bogdanovich walked over to their Citation. Caine turned away as Bogdanovich got into the car and started the engine.

The explosion was flat and sudden.

He felt the warm movement of air past his head as he spun around, knowing what he would see before he saw it. The Citation was lying on its side, burning furiously. A thick, heavy pall of oily smoke lifted in the still air . . . *and he tried to get close enough to pull her out, screaming her name over and over, but they pulled him away, they dragged him kicking and fighting away from the burning Opel, his hands seared by burns he did not even feel . . .*

'Jesus!' he heard someone say in an awed voice. 'Did you see that?'

People were running into the parking

lot from the marina, shouting. A police car whooped past with all its lights flashing. The cops piled out, rushing to the blazing wreck with portable fire extinguishers.

'David?' Lynda said, very faintly.

He took her in his arms and she buried her face against his chest. He felt the shudders running through her body. He put his arm around her shoulder and walked her away. The chances of anyone being alive after that explosion were zero. He pushed through the crowd which had gathered, another unanswerable question going on and off in his brain like a neon sign. They had put a bomb in Paul Bogdanovich's car.

But who were they?

* * *

Nobody locked their cars on Marco Island, which made it childishly easy for Caine to hot-wire a Mercury Cougar and get the hell away from Towne Centre. Lynda's little Toyota could stay in the marina parking lot until Kingdom Come

as far as he was concerned: for all he knew there was a bomb under that, too. He glanced at her: she sat beside him, staring sightlessly at the road ahead of them, her arms folded tightly, her shoulders hunched. She had not spoken since saying that one word after the car blew up.

Caine drove over the bridge and north to Naples, reputed to have more millionaires to the acre than any other town in America. It was one of those places where they renovate hundred-year-old houses and call them monuments, all white clapboard and fretwork balconies. When they got there he checked into the Edgewater Beach Inn on Gulf Shore Boulevard. When they got to the room, she came into his arms, weeping.

'Hold me, David, hold me, hold me,' she sobbed.

He put his arms around her and held her tightly, intensely aware of the warm strength of her body against his own. After a while, the tremors ceased. She lifted her head and looked up at him, her eyes dark and unreadable. Her lips found

his fiercely, demanding. She kicked off her shoes. He picked her up and carried her across to the bed.

'Yes,' she said, throatily. 'Yes, yes, yes.'

Their lovemaking was urgent, eager, without tenderness, fuelled by a need deeper than love.

When it was over, she cried again, but more softly this time. He held her in his arms and said nothing. After a while, she stopped crying. She got up and went into the bathroom.

He heard water running. When she came out, she had washed her face and combed her hair. She looked pale and sad.

'I didn't expect this,' she said.

'Neither did I.'

'How do you feel about it?'

'Like in that Sondheim song: sorry-glad.'

'Yes,' she said. 'Yes.'

They were silent for a moment. He touched her bare shoulder.

'I'm sorry you had to see . . . what happened.'

'Who did it, David?'

He shook his head. 'I don't know.'

'It was so . . . brutal. So pointless. Would . . . our people have done something like that?'

'They do.'

'It's horrible.'

'Did you think it was some sort of game?' he said, more harshly than he had intended. He saw her flinch and was sorry for what he had said, but he did not apologize. Instead he went over to the telephone and had room service send up some food and a bottle of Jack Daniel's. They watched the late news as they ate, the TV creating a no-go zone into which they could both retreat without talking.

A Russian dissident was being exchanged at the Glieneckebrücke in Berlin. The commentator explained who all the people getting in and out of cars were. Russian soldiers stared stolidly at the cameras.

'Frederick the Great used to travel to his palace in Potsdam over that bridge,' Caine remarked. 'Not many people know that.'

'Have you ever been there?' Lynda asked.

'Yes,' he told her. 'About twelve years ago. We were bringing one of our agents out. Normally, civilians can't get within half a mile of it.'

In the background, Caine saw the gold Mercedes that belonged to Wolfgang Vogel, the East German lawyer who arranged such exchanges.

'Who's paying your fees, Wolfie?' he said to the flickering screen. And who, for that matter, was financing the return to Israel of the dissident, who had doubtless been ejected penniless from Russia by the KGB?

He took the lists Bogdanovich had written and spread them flat on the floor in front of the sofa. They watched the rest of the news. Among the agents being returned to the East were a Czech husband and wife who had spied for Prague while the man was a contract translator for the CIA. They had airline tickets to Zürich in their pockets when the FBI arrested them. They had sold their Manhattan apartment for $400,000, and had been planning to use the money to settle comfortably in Switzerland.

Their life would be somewhat less glamorous in Moscow, he thought.

He poured himself a healthy measure of Jack Daniel's and sipped it as he started reading Bogdanovich's notes. Lykov's shopping lists had included a predictably catholic range of requirements: they ranged from the very specific, indicating a formidable degree of existing intelligence, to the very vague, meaning the Comrades were trying to get a handle on something they knew very little about.

It was easy to understand why Lykov had asked for information about an air force general who'd been killed while testing a MiG-23 jet at Nellis air force base in Nevada; they wanted to know where the jet had come from, and what it was being tested for — or against. Lykov had also asked for any documents referring to the Aurora project, codename for the new B-1 Stealth bomber under development by Rockwell International; Bogdanovich had provided him with information about its stingray shape, and the revolutionary 'skin' which absorbed, rather than reflected, radar waves aimed

at the six hundred and twenty million dollar plane.

Bogdanovich's lists emphasized the Russian preoccupation with American high technology. There were requests for details of the hundred-million-dollar complex being built in New Mexico to test laserbeam weapons; for an update on the progress of phased-array radar; for information about the Goodyear radar satellite; for the specification of the Cryptag scrambler used on Company computers, and the new, speech-activated STU-II scrambler phones.

Equally predictable was the Kremlin's interest in the disposition of investigations into Russian espionage. Lykov had asked for information on the present where-abouts of the twenty-three Soviet bloc spies who had been exchanged in Berlin in June 1985. He asked for status reports on the all-in-the-family spy case involving Navy veteran John A. Walker, Jr, his brother Arthur, his son Michael, and his old navy crony, Jerry Whitworth. He wanted details of the case of Svetlana Ogorodnikova, who had involved an FBI

agent named Richard Miller in a classic honey trap recruitment, and Ludmilla Kondratjeva, who had testified against Miller and was found dead in her car in the surf near Malibu.

There had been a flurry of requests in August 1985, while the KGB defector Vitaly Yurchenko was in American hands, and a lot of other names which would have been familiar to anyone who read a weekly news magazine — Jonathan Pollard, Edward Howard, Ronald Pelton, and Larry Wu-Tai Chin, who killed himself by putting a plastic bag over his head while awaiting sentence. There were others Caine assumed were espionage suspects who had been arrested without a great deal of publicity. The last request Bogdanovich had received from Lykov had been for information on a KGB colonel named Viktor Gudarev who had defected with his son and a woman friend in Athens late in February 1986.

Caine looked up to find Lynda watching him. On television, Robert Mitchum was being driven somewhere by Jane Greer. It took Caine a moment or

two to remember the name of the film: *The Big Steal*. Mitchum is supposed to have stolen an army payroll. He's being hunted by William Bendix. What was the name of the suave guy who was supposed to be Greer's boyfriend? Knowles. Patric without a 'k' Knowles.

'Almost finished,' he said.

'This thing has gone a long way away from Tony Genevevo, hasn't it?'

'A long way.'

'Will whoever killed Paul and Eva try to kill us, too?'

'Quite possibly. If they find us.'

'I'm scared, David.'

'And I'm sorry I got you into this, Lynda.'

'It's not your fault. What happened.'

'In a way it is. In a way, everything that has happened is my fault.'

She was silent for a long moment, looking at him. It was as if she was making her mind up about something. He thought of the way he had embraced loneliness after Jenny died, and wondered if Lynda had done the same. She got up and came gracefully across the room,

bending down to kiss him on the lips, once, twice, her dark hair falling like soft rain around his face.

'What's that for?' he asked her.

'Openers,' she said.

27

'You sonofabitch!' Forsyth said.

Bensen blinked, swallowing noisily. 'That's enough, Forsyth. I'm not going to sit still while you call me names. As Chief — '

'Chief!' Forsyth fumed. 'You knew Special Ops was going to take Bogdanovich out, you bastard! You *knew*, and you didn't even see fit to tell me.'

'It was a policy decision. Langley — '

'Yeah, yeah,' Forsyth gibed. 'They had one of those seventh-floor brainstorm sessions where everyone talks integrated reciprocal mobility and ultimate logical necessity and shit like that. And you gave them the green light.'

'It was taken out of my hands,' Bensen said. 'The executive decision was maximal demotion. I told them Bogdanovich was our only lead to Drosdow. They said forget Drosdow. They told me to close the whole thing down.'

'The hell we will!'

Bensen shook his head wearily. 'Have you got anything I could use as an argument?'

'Nothing. Not a damned thing.'

'Then we leave the whole thing to the FBI, including Avranilosa and his little band of brothers.'

'Let them take them and welcome,' Forsyth said. 'That's small potatoes, Donald.'

'Oh, I wouldn't say that,' Bensen bridled.

No, you wouldn't, Forsyth thought. You wrote it up as the biggest espionage coup since we captured Major André. You can't unwrite it, even though the scalp-hunters were beginning to wonder if maybe Avranilosa was a plant after all.

'I want one more crack at Drosdow,' he said.

'Negative. How many times do I have to tell you? As of now the FBI has jurisdiction.'

'Donald,' Forsyth said, slowly, 'you are full of shit.'

Bensen blinked, like a priest encountering blasphemy. He buttoned his jacket,

then unbuttoned it again. He moved a piece of paper from one side of his desk to the other. Malice flickered in his eyes.

'You never learn, do you?' he hissed. 'All right. All *right*! I've taken all I'm going to take from you, Forsyth. I'm going to get your ass transferred out of here to somewhere so far away you'll have to use drums to get a message out.'

'Well, well,' Forsyth said. 'It bites.'

'You sour-tongued bastard, you think you're clever, don't you?' Bensen flared. 'You think you're a cut above the rest of us. You don't want to play by the rules. You want to strap on your sixguns and clean up, like the goddam Lone Ranger. Being nice to you doesn't work. So now I'm going to try it the other way, see how you like that. You are suspended from duty until further notice. Am I making myself clear?'

'Transparent,' Forsyth said.

'Then get the hell out of my office!' Bensen snapped.

'My pleasure,' Forsyth said. He got out of the Brickell Avenue building as fast as he could and went back downtown to the

Vanguard office, where he sat at his desk, smoking cigarette after unwanted cigarette, his face a furious mask of concentration.

Nobody spoke to him. The grapevine had already transmitted the news of his collision with Bensen, and people kept away from him, as if he had a communicable disease. Forsyth wasn't even aware of the atmosphere in the office. He had decided what he was going to do before he even got there.

No matter what Bensen did or didn't do, he was not about to give up on the Drosdow case. He wanted that turkey so badly it made his teeth ache.

But everything known about the man had been checked and double-checked, and they were still batting zero. Immigration had traced the forms filed by Drosdow when he landed at Miami International. They listed a false address in Bogotá as his home, and gave as his Miami address the Omni International. The hotel's records showed Drosdow had stayed there on four separate occasions, paying in cash. Nobody recalled anything

about him. Just another anonymous guest/room/service unit, processed through the machinery of the hotel as impersonally as a rivet in an assembly plant.

Avranilosa was no help. Never having seen the girl Drosdow was to meet in Key Largo, he was unable to give them a description that the dossier computers at Langley and Fort Meade could use. No trace of either Drosdow or the woman had been left at the Holiday Inn. Cross-checking of the date turned up only a Mr Smith and a Miss Jones, who had stayed in poolside rooms one night, and paid cash for their accommodation.

Subsequent to the events at Marco Island, every facet of Bogdanovich's life had been re-examined. His spot-check ratings had always been Alpha One; even the deep scans had failed to indicate anything untoward. Yet it was beginning to appear as if he had been passing classified material to the GRU for some time. Among the relevant documents he had handled was the dossier on ISS that Forsyth had requested after Genevevo's murder.

There was some kind of link there someplace, but no way could Forsyth put a finger on it. No trace of a link between this man Caine and the CIA analyst could be found. And since Bogdanovich was already selling classified material to the Comrades, the whole idea of honey-trapping him became ludicrous nonsense. Yet they had watched Caine establish contact with Bogdanovich, taking him out on the boat and — Forsyth guessed — pumping him. Then came the word: lay off. He saw why, now, of course. Those cold-eyed bastards in Langley had decided the simplest way of closing the case was to take Bogdanovich and Caine out of the picture. They'd taken care of Bogdanovich all right. Forsyth had been on his way into the parking lot at the Marina when the bomb went off. There had been no sign of Caine or the Sanchez woman since then.

He didn't buy the idea of Caine as a Comrade any more. He riffled through the ISS dossier again, as if somehow the information it contained on Caine would suggest a new approach. Of course it did

nothing of the sort. A good degree at Cambridge, straight into Army Intelligence. Service in England, Canada, Germany, Northern Ireland. Married to Jennifer Bruce, who had died in a car bombing in Berlin. Anything there? It might be worth checking. He made a note, then went on reading. Caine had resigned from government service in 1980, joined International Security Systems, transferred to America a year later. Home in Cherokee Triangle, no permanent female companion, bills paid on time. Clean as a whistle.

Forsyth ran a hand through his hair, yawned and rubbed the scratchy stubble on his chin. I need a shave, he thought. And a shower, and a clean shirt, and a large Black Label, not necessarily in that order. He lit another cigarette and doggedly went back to his digging. There had to be something, somewhere, even though everything he had fed into the magic box so far had come out zilch.

He tried cross-referencing names, ages, descriptions, locales, places of origin.

There were no common denominators for the computer to isolate. Drosdow didn't match up with any existing profile on the Langley, Fort Meade, or FBI computers, and neither did Caine and neither did anyone else. No one named Frederic Drosdow had flown on any commercial airline within the continental United States during the last thirty days. No credit card company had any record of him, nor could any bank account be traced. The payment for the house on Marco Island had been effected by a cashier's cheque, for cash paid into the Republic National Bank in Miami, using Avranilosa as a referee and his home as an address.

Dead end after dead end.

Come *on*, Forsyth told himself. His brain felt like a bowl of oatmeal. The lines of text on the computer monitor swam before his tired eyes. He knew what he ought to do was go right back to the beginning, start over. The thought was deadening. He got up and stretched. The office was emptying out as the day shift ended.

Three and a half hours later, he found what he had been looking for: the piece of information all the computer trawls had missed. Among the many visitors logged at Avranilosa's home was a well-dressed man of about fifty. He had dined with the Fat Man and Frederic Drosdow at a Key Biscayne restaurant that night. Not just any Key Biscayne restaurant, but the one managed by Lynda Sanchez. Avranilosa's guest caught an early plane next morning. It had been established that his name was Harold Percival, a realtor from Easton, Maryland. The appropriate checks were made: Percival's standing in his home town was impeccable. Since Genevevo had no knowledge then or later of Drosdow's intentions, Percival had been eliminated from the investigation.

Got you, you sonofabitch, he thought.

Something less than two hours later, showered, shaved, and wearing a fresh Sea Island cotton shirt and a dark blue Palm Beach suit from Jordan Marsh, Forsyth leaned back smiling in his seat as Eastern's flight EA198, a Boeing 737,

climbed like a homesick angel into the evening sky over Miami. For no reason he could think of, he found himself humming an old Bill Haley song: 'See You Later, Alligator'.

28

There was no mistaking the cold, alien feel of a gun muzzle against the back of the neck. Dick McClelland froze in the driver's seat of his Mercury Cougar, stifling a curse. Mugged outside my own apartment at nine thirty in the morning, he thought in disgust.

'All right,' he said. 'Don't do anything stupid. I'll hand you my wallet. Just take it easy, OK?'

'Do what I tell you. Drive!' an unnaturally hoarse voice commanded.

McClelland half turned, frowning, a protest forming in his throat. The man jammed the gun muzzle even harder against the base of his neck.

'Drive, I said!'

McClelland put the car in drive and moved off down Devonshire Place towards Connecticut Avenue. He stopped at the junction.

'Which way?'

'Drive into the zoo,' the man in the back said.

McClelland made a right and drove down the hill, and turned in through the gateway of the National Zoological Park.

'Head for the parking lot,' the man behind him said. 'Park off to one side someplace.'

There was nobody in sight. The zoo had opened only a few minutes earlier. McClelland silently cursed his bad luck as he coasted to a stop on the far side of the parking lot.

'Switch off and put the keys on the passenger seat,' the man said. 'Then turn around.'

McClelland did as he was bidden, turning warily. He let out his breath in a great gust of relief and anger.

'You!'

'I'm sorry, Dick,' Caine said with a wry grin. 'There wasn't any other way of doing it. I couldn't be sure how you'd have reacted if I just came up to you in the street.'

'You can put the gun away,' McClelland said, coldly. 'I'm not armed. What do you want?'

'I need some help, Dick.'

'You can say that again. Don't expect any from me.'

'Dick, you've known me for a long time,' Caine said. 'Give me a break. Trust me, just for a few minutes.'

'Give me one good reason why I should.'

'I will. Look, I'm going to put the gun away. Promise me you won't try anything.'

'Trust me,' McClelland said, sardonically. 'Just for a few minutes.'

'I want you to listen to my side of it,' Caine said. 'Will you?'

'Do I have a choice?'

'You called me a traitor. That day at the airport. Why?'

'You know the answer to that one.'

'Tell me anyway.'

'I'll tell you nothing.'

'You've got to give me a chance, Dick. I know you think I crossed over, but it's not true.'

'Then why did you run?'

'The moment you called me a traitor, I knew someone had fitted me up. Why,

how, didn't matter. I knew I wasn't going to find out sitting in a locked cell talking to a squad of dredgers.'

'Go on,' McClelland said. His training had reasserted itself after the first brief burst of anger. His feelings about Caine were not important. The first imperative was to listen and extract what he could from the situation.

'Tell me this,' Caine said. 'If I'm a spy or a defector, why am I still around?'

'If you aren't, why didn't you call Mother?'

'Nobody would have believed me,' Caine said. 'And anyway, I knew Kingly would change all the systems.'

McClelland neither confirmed nor denied the guess, although in fact it was true. Kingly had made swingeing changes in the wake of what was seen as Caine's defection, moving swiftly to render obsolete as much as possible of what Caine might be telling the Russians. These precautions taken, Kingly flew by Concorde to London for what were euphemistically referred to as 'urgent management consultations' but which everyone knew meant a security review.

London was paranoid about inside jobs, and nobody wanted another inquiry like the stringent review of the security services carried out in 1985 by Lord Bridge of Harwich.

When Kingly returned, signals flew thick and fast. The six remaining ISS consultants were recalled and replaced. McClelland, promoted to deputy Director, sent cleaning squads to each of the regions. Anyone who had been in active contact with Caine during the preceding year was debriefed. Close associates underwent polygraph tests and intensive interrogation. Every case in which he had been involved was reviewed. A completely new team was sent to replace the one Caine had led, the members of which were transferred to non-sensitive duties. Then, and only then, was Station Two returned to Active status.

'Tell me just one thing, Dick. Who said I was Red?'

'What difference does it make?'

'It was Avranilosa, wasn't it? Kingly expurgated the dossier before he gave it to me.'

'If you say so.'

'It had to be him. What I haven't figured out yet is why.'

'It couldn't perhaps be because it was true?'

'He lied to them, Dick. He was programmed to lie to them.'

'What reason would he have had to lie?'

'Let me put it another way: he was telling them what he believed to be the truth. So if they gave him polygraph tests, did all the business, he would come out clean. But he'd been programmed, Dick. By someone who wanted to be absolutely certain we were out of the picture.'

'And who was that?'

'Andrei Guchkov.'

'David,' McClelland said. 'Do you seriously expect me to believe all this?'

'All right, tell me; have they found him?'

'Why do you want to know?' The second imperative was to say as little as possible; let the man talk. Nod. Agree. Say only what had to be said. *Listen*.

'You remember I was going through his dossier that day, just before you drove me to National?'

'I remember,' McClelland said. And I also remember Kingly saying you probably pulled it so you could tell the Comrades what we knew about Guchkov, he thought.

'I knew it was him. Everything fitted: the descriptions, the timing of his arrival, everything.'

'Why didn't you say anything then?'

'Because I couldn't be sure.'

'Or because you preferred us not to make the same connection?'

'Let me run something past you,' Caine said. 'What if Guchkov's defection was a blind? Look what he gave us: a few small-time agents who'd probably served their purpose anyway. Look what he got in return: a conducted tour of Five and Six Operations, a breakdown of the Berlin station, a new legend, a bankroll. What if all that was part of a plan, right down to his disappearance?'

'It's a lot of what-ifs.'

'I'll offer you a bet,' Caine said. 'Guchkov flew from London to one of the European capitals. Rome would be good. Madrid or Lisbon would be even better.

From there he could get a flight to South America. Did they get a fix on him?'

McClelland hesitated. 'He took an Iberia flight to Madrid, then another out of Barajas to Montevideo. No sign of him after that.'

'He probably went to ground in the GRU *residenz* at Bogotá until he was ready to move. They gave him his new legend — Frederic Drosdow — and set up the connection in Miami with Avranilosa. The Fat Man is the go-between in the drug sale Guchkov used to finance his operation — the cynical bastard would enjoy that, it would amuse him. Then at the critical juncture, he discovered that Avranilosa was under surveillance.'

'By Genevevo.'

'Right. My guess is that, accidentally or otherwise, Genevevo got on to Guchkov or what Guchkov was really up to. Avranilosa, pushed by Guchkov, egged Saturnino Baca to take Genevevo out. His people spotted mine while they were setting up the hit, and Guchkov made a preemptive decision to take us all out. He didn't give a damn what happened. He'd

probably foreseen the possibility. Anyway, he was walking away from it. Nobody even knew he was there.'

'And what about the money?'

'It was to finance a honey trap. Guchkov told Avranilosa enough to make him — and us — believe it was on Marco Island. But it wasn't. The whole Marco Island setup was a decoy operation and it worked beautifully. We all homed in on another no-hoper, a Company coding clerk named Paul Bogdanovich who'd been selling secrets to the Comrades in Washington. Somebody put a couple of pounds of plastic explosive in Bogdanovich's car.'

'Which somebody?'

'I lean towards Langley.'

'You think the Company killed this Bogdanovich?'

'And his wife. Probably Domestic Operations' way of closing the file. Permanently. That way there'd be nothing to advertise the fact that they'd been operating on American soil.'

'They didn't try for you?'

'I don't know. I left my car where I

parked it. When they realize I'm not going to pick it up, they'll disarm it.'

'You don't even consider the possibility that Guchkov might have been behind it?'

'Why would he bother? While you've been chasing me, and I've been chasing Bogdanovich, and the boys from Domestic Ops have been chasing their tails, that bastard has been getting quietly on with whatever it is he really came to America to do.'

'Do you have any idea what that might be?'

'Yes,' Caine said. 'That's why I braced you, Dick. I need your help.'

'Suppose I were to entertain this . . . theory of yours,' McClelland said. 'Although there isn't one good reason on God's green earth why I should — what would you want?'

'What I want to know is on the computer somewhere, Dick,' Caine said. 'Somewhere in our surveillance reports on Genevevo, in Avranilosa's ITs, there's a name we haven't considered because it didn't seem germane. That name will tell us where to look for Guchkov.'

'That's it?' McClelland said. 'You don't know the name, you don't know where it is. But you want me to find it. Is that what you're saying?'

'It's the only thing I can think of,' Caine said.

'You could come in.'

'It would take too long,' Caine said. 'Even if I could make Kingly believe me.'

'What makes you think I believe you?'

Caine grinned. 'A woman knows these things,' he said. 'Will you do it?'

'How would I contact you?'

'You don't,' Caine replied. 'I'll find a way to contact you. It's safer that way. And Dick, don't let anyone at ISS know what you're doing, or why.'

'You must be joking,' McClelland said. 'If I were to report seeing you and taking no action, I'd be under security arrest before I finished saying it.'

Caine opened the rear door and got out. McClelland wound down his window.

'When will I hear from you?'

'Tomorrow. Between ten and noon. And . . . thanks, Dick.'

'Sure,' McClelland said, and drove off.

29

Red Centre was ready. Guchkov was ready. And so was Mitchell.

They had nursed him — correction, Kate had nursed him, pretending loving concern — through the cold-sweat coda that followed every freshman spy's first foray into espionage. Mitchell had been as jumpy as a kitten, walking into his office each day filled with the dread certainty of immediate apprehension.

Nothing happened. Guchkov would have been vastly surprised if anything had. Mitchell had been most carefully selected. The stuff he brought out was worthless, of course. The real reason Guchkov wanted it brought out was to prove to Mitchell that he could do it without being detected.

The next, equally predictable phase was euphoria. This was the point at which control became vital: over-confidence was far more dangerous than fear. They

nursed him through that, too; Guchkov with encouragement, Kate in other ways.

Mitchell had told her, of course. She handled it brilliantly. She made the man believe what Drosdow had already told him, that they would both go to prison for life if he balked, that he had to do it for their safety, for their future. She told him how fine he was, how brave. She made Mitchell feel strong, confident, daring. And he discovered the power in what he was doing: the power of knowing what others did not. He swung all the way from fear to a sort of elation. He was going to have a million dollars. He was going to ditch his wife and live with Kate. He really believed it.

Now Guchkov was ready for the kill. He smiled: an apt word, in the circumstances. Red Centre's laser satellite was at pre-launch status AOW: Awaiting Open Window. The final phase had begun.

He booked a table at the Tidewater Inn in Easton and, after drinks at Highfield, the three of them drove over there for dinner. Kate saw to it that Mitchell got most of the second bottle of Chardonnay

as Guchkov led the conversation around to computers.

They already had a good idea of the environment in which Mitchell worked; a question here, there, and it was not difficult to piece together from what he had told them and what they already knew. Beneath the NSA headquarters complex at Fort George Meade was an air-conditioned labyrinth, several city blocks long, housing the largest concentration of computer and data-analysis equipment in the world. Along aisle after gold-carpeted aisle ran serried rows of hardware: front-end interfaces, mass storage units, a brain so enormous that it could perform in nano-seconds calculations that would take an army of mathematicians decades.

Until recently, the biggest number-crunchers at the NSA had been Carillon and Loadstone. Built by Cray Research in Minnesota, Loadstone, which had provided only half the Agency's capacity, could transfer three hundred and twenty million words a second — say two thousand, five hundred books of three hundred pages each — and could accommodate

forty-eight disk storage units holding perhaps thirty billion words, each word retrievable within eighty-millionths of a second.

GRU knew most of this already, from published sources. What was important about the information was that Mitchell was telling it to them, further confirmation of Guchkov's control.

The other half of the NSA 'brain', Carillon, was made up of five quad-redundant IBM 3033s attached to laser printers that could produce hard copy at sixty thousand lines a minute. That was the state of the NSA art until 'Bubbles', the new Cray-2 supercomputer, came on line in June 1985. It was about this machine that Guchkov now encouraged Mitchell to talk.

'Astonishing though it is, Bubbles is only a stopgap machine,' the American told them. 'Seymour Cray is already working on an even bigger baby, which we expect to be online around 1988.'

To coincide with the inauguration of the Spacetrack system, no doubt, Guchkov thought, making a mental note.

'It doesn't seem possible,' he said. 'I read somewhere that the Cray-2 had a top speed of over a million flops a second.'

'It's a million, two, actually,' Mitchell said.

'Flops?' Kate frowned.

'Floating point operations,' Guchkov said, benevolently. 'Calculations. How much faster is it, Mitch?'

'Six to twelve times faster than Loadstone, forty to fifty thousand times faster than a business computer. What took a year to do in 1952, we can now do in a second. You should see that baby go, Fred!'

His enthusiasm was genuine. Like most computer people, he had an inbuilt conviction that the subject was ordinarily death to conversation. Fred and Kate were 'in the business', as it were, so he could assume a more informed interest on their part.

'How many of them are there?' Guchkov asked.

'There's one in the Agency think-tank at Princeton, another at NASA's Ames

Research Center.'

'That's the one in Mountain View, California?'

'That's the one.'

'How big a memory has this thing got?'

'Two billion bytes. The Cray-3 will have eight billion.'

'That's astonishing. It must be a hell of a thing to look at.'

'It doesn't look much like a computer, I'll give you that,' Mitchell smiled. 'It looks like a cross between a recreation-room bar and a fishtank. It's just . . . different from everything else, different the way a modern fighter is from a World War One biplane. There's a whole new area of thinking that goes with it. We're talking analog optical computers now, Fred. We're talking multiprocessing, light-sound interaction and charge-transfer devices. We're discussing achieving more than a quadrillion — that's one thousand million million — multiplications per second. They're into stuff at Chippewa Falls and New York University the man in the street has never heard of: cryogenics, optical logic, magnetic bubbles, laser recording,

kinetic activation. There are already machines that will convert the human voice into digital signals, others that will instantaneously transcribe spoken conversations . . . '

He was still going strong as they pulled to a stop in front of the house. Guchkov nodded and smiled, encouraging the man to talk himself dry.

'Come into the library and have a cognac,' Guchkov said. 'There are a few things I want to ask you about.'

'If you men are going to keep on talking about computers, I'm going to watch TV upstairs,' Kate said.

'I'm sorry, Kate!' Mitchell said, contritely. 'I just got so wound up, I forgot. Look, stay, we'll talk about something else.'

'No, no, you men have your brandy and cigars. I'll . . . see you later, yes?'

She kissed him lightly and went out, the fur wrap slung over her elegant shoulder like a bullfighter's cape. Mitchell beamed bemusedly at her as she closed the double doors behind her.

'Tell me about Platform,' Guchkov said, as if it were the most natural thing in

the world. He busied himself with the drinks so that he did not need to meet Mitchell's eyes.

'Went into operation at the end of '84,' Mitchell said, taking the glass from Guchkov and sitting down in one of the deep leather chairs in front of the fireplace. 'How did you know about it?'

Guchkov evaded the question by asking another of his own.

'Security?' Mitchell replied. 'Stringent. In fact, I'd go as far as to say Draconian. You know what DES stands for?'

'Data Encryption Standard. It's the national protection cipher system approved by the government for industry, banking and some of the federal agencies.'

'You do know your computers, don't you?' Mitchell said, admiringly. 'All right, if you know that, you know DES is based on what we call a 'key', an extra-long string of bits whose combination varies from user to user. Like the grooves in a doorkey, say. Same basic pattern for everyone, but each with different teeth and valleys. This key goes into a series of super-complex mathematical formulae

called S-Boxes. When they combine with the key, they encode the data into indecipherable bits, and reverse the procedure at the receiving end.'

'Difficult to break into,' Guchkov suggested.

'But not impossible. The process of ciphering includes something called intense validation. That means the cipher has been tested by being bombarded with sophisticated cryptanalytic attacks by a team of experts. It's called a brute force attack.'

'So you'd need super brute force to do what they couldn't.'

'Right,' Mitchell said. 'Say you could put together a machine with a million special-search chips, each capable of testing a million possible solutions a second. That gives you a testing capability of a trillion keys a second. You know the DES uses a fifty-six-bit key, so the number of possible combinations is about seventy quadrillion. So it would theoretically be possible for you to break into any DES cipher in about ten or twelve hours. Twenty, max. That's if you had the hardware, of course.'

'Could a machine like that be built?'

'All it takes is thirty, forty million dollars. The toughest trick is buying the technology without attracting attention. IBM and the NSA sleep in the same bed.'

'Could a machine like that break into the NSA system?'

'Nope. NSA uses a 128-bit key,' Mitchell said. 'You'd need more money than there is in the world to build a machine that could break into Bubbles.'

'What about intercept stations?' Guchkov asked, getting up and holding out his hand for Mitchell's glass. 'Do they have the same equipment?'

'In effect, yes,' Mitchell said. 'Most of the signals picked up by the intercept stations are too sophisticated to be attacked on receipt. So they bounce them off a DSP to us, and we analyse them. We're the host to fifty-two separate computer systems around the world.'

'What's a DSP?' Guchkov said, handing Mitchell another Rémy Martin.

'Defense Support Program. A type of satellite.'

He launched into a monologue about

the various types of communications satellites NSA used, and Guchkov nodded and smiled, only half listening. What was it Katja had said about the American? 'He gives new meaning to the word interminable,' she'd said, laughing that bitch's laugh. He wondered idly what she would do when all this was over. He'd grown to respect her in the time they'd been together: he admired professionalism above all else, and Katja Renis was a real pro.

While the American rambled on, Guchkov's mind slipped back to the day this operation had begun, so many months ago in Moscow. He remembered the day clearly, the pigeons foraging on the grass verges, the girls in their summer frocks smiling in the sunshine as he hurried through the city to the meeting of the Operations Executive at Znamenskaya Ulitza.

Of all the plans submitted to OE, his had been selected. That alone would have been a signal honour. To have been chosen to carry it out meant his reward would be even greater: a decoration, certainly; promotion perhaps as high as

Lieutenant-General, with the material rewards that accompanied it: a new car, possibly a European one, a *dacha* in the country or an apartment at one of the Black Sea resorts.

He remembered how nervous he had been, that first day, facing the bemedalled 'Grandfathers' seated around the shining table, their faces dour and unwelcoming. The meeting had been conducted by Colonel-General Ivashutin, head of GRU. Also present were his deputy, Pavlov; Drachev, Guchkov's superior, head of the Second Directorate; Goliakov, head of the Sixth, Electronic Intelligence; Professor Doctor Chebriakov, head of Space Projects; Zotov, head of Information.

'With your permission, Comrade General?'

Ivashutin had nodded.

'Proceed, Guchkov,' Pavlov interpreted.

'The initiative is to be known as Open Window,' Guchkov began. 'Its purpose is to secure, by or before this time next year, the successful covert launch of our assault satellite, *Smert Ptytsa.*'

'Yes, yes,' old Goliakov said. He was

famous for his impatience. 'We've all read your briefing paper. Ambitious. Perhaps too ambitious, young man.'

'We shall see,' Pavlov said, urbane as ever. He nodded to Guchkov, who unrolled his map, thumb-tacked it to an easel, and began his carefully prepared presentation.

'On Thursday, January 24, 1985, the United States Air Force launched its first secret space shuttle mission. Unlike all previous flights, which had been predominantly civilian, this one was controlled by the National Security Agency. None of the conversations between the crew and ground control was broadcast; all were heavily encoded. Even the actual takeoff time and the intended trajectory of the shuttle were kept secret.'

'Yes, yes, yes,' muttered Goliakov, testily. 'We all know that, man. Get on, get on!'

The reason for all this secrecy, Guchkov continued, was Challenger's payload: a thirteen and a half ton spy satellite, which the shuttle was to place in geostationary orbit 22,300 miles above the Equator, between the Indian Ocean

island of Diego Garcia and Singapore. From this thirty-degree segment of longitude, and only this segment, it was possible for satellites to 'see' the area in Russia used for space launches.

'The American satellite has processing capabilities greater than anything else in space,' Guchkov said. 'Its antennae are over a thousand feet in diameter. Any transmission on frequencies between one hundred megaherz and twenty gigaherz — a gigaherz is one hundred megaherz — whether it be radio, microwave or radar, can be picked up by its forward dish antenna and simultaneously relayed by its rear dish to the appropriate window, or intercept installation on earth, and from there onward to the NSA.'

'The satellite is called 'Big Bird',' Ivashutin interjected. 'It forms part of the American Spacetrack network. You will remember my mentioning it at our briefing in June. Although it is now their only spy-in-the-sky satellite, we cannot, must not, underestimate its capabilities. If we are to launch *Smert Ptytsa* undetected, we must neutralize that satellite.'

'And this officer has found a way?' Zotov asked, speaking for the first time. He rarely smiled. He was a squat, dark man whom his staff called *Gospodin Mrak*, Mr Gloom.

'Colonel Guchkov is one of our most outstanding officers,' Ivashutin said. 'His knowledge of the United States is encyclopaedic, unrivalled. He speaks their debased language as if he had been born there. He has studied their history and is an acknowledged authority on their military and defence systems. Go ahead, Guchkov. Tell them your idea.'

'Let us take a hypothetical case to begin with,' Guchkov said. 'We launch a satellite from Sary Shagan, or Kapustin Yar. Within a minute of lift-off, an American early-warning satellite spots the rocket plume and signals back to earth that a launch has taken place. The input is channelled via ADN — automatic digital network — to DEFSMAC at Fort Meade and simultaneously via the CRITICOM circuit to the White House situation rooms, the Pentagon, and NORAD in Colorado.'

'Perhaps it would be as well if you translated your acronyms as you go along, Guchkov,' Ivashutin said, concealing a smile. Zotov was glaring at the young officer, his face a mask of utter puzzlement that Ivashutin knew he would die before admitting.

'I am sorry. DEFSMAC is the Defense Special Missile and Astronautics Center at NSA. CRITICOM is the Critical Intelligence Communications circuit. And NORAD — '

'I think you could assume we know that one, Colonel,' Pavlov said.

'Yes, sir. NORAD — Air Defense Command at Cheyenne Mountain — tracks the missile's flight profile to make sure it is not on a threat azimuth. In due course, the satellite will send in telemetry intelligence that will inform the analysts what kind of rocket it was, how it was programmed, trajectory and so on.'

'So this spy satellite would detect our launch of the Death Bird within seconds, is that it?'

'Exactly,' Guchkov said. 'Let me ask Professor Doctor Chebriakov a question.

If we could black out the American satellite at the moment we launch *Smert Ptytsa*, what would the effect be?'

All eyes turned towards Professor Dr Chebriakov, in charge of the most important Russian space project of the last decade, and arguably the most important ever. The Death Bird, *Smert Ptytsa*, was a fifty-five foot long, thirty-seven thousand pound monster satellite packed with the most advanced laser weaponry yet developed. Laser technology was the one field where Russia was unquestionably ten years ahead of the West, and every bit of that technology had been incorporated into the design for the new 'bird'.

'Very simple,' Chebriakov said, jauntily. 'We would totally dominate space and there would be nothing anyone could do about it.'

If the satellite could be placed in orbit, he said, not only would Russia be able to neutralize every existing non-Soviet satellite in space, but she could also prevent any new ones from being placed in successful orbit.

There was a considering silence following this assertion. Complete Soviet domination of space would radically alter the balance of power between East and West. Every parameter of strike capability would have to be redefined. If the initiative was a success. But if it was not . . . Every one of them remembered the last time. Although not so much as a hint of the confrontation had reached the world's press, Soviet humiliation had been complete. The purges that followed were merciless. In their world, nobody ever forgave and nobody ever forgot.

'So we black out the American satellite,' Zotov said. 'And then?'

'Once our bird is up there, in orbit, the Americans will track her, of course, from space or from the ground,' Guchkov explained. 'They will wonder what she is. They may even ask us, but of course, we will not tell them. But from the day that she goes into orbit, the American space programme will be finished. Every time they make a launch, the Death Bird will destroy the payload. There will be no more spy satellites. Most importantly of

all, the Americans will never be able to put into space the hardware to effect what they call Star Wars.'

There was another considering silence. No one in the room needed to be reminded how much effort had already been expended, on the diplomatic as well as the espionage front, to sabotage in any and every way American progress with the machinery for the space-based Strategic Defense Initiative.

'The Americans are moving ahead very quickly with their research in SDI,' Guchkov said. 'The Pentagon has already constructed a 1200-million-dollar command centre at Falcon air force station, ten miles from Colorado Springs. Another 135-million-dollar Pentagon programme is in hand to develop Mimic — a gallium-arsenide microchip that will process electronic signals at five times the speed of silicon, with twice silicon's resistance to radiation. The Scientific Adviser to the President has stated publicly that they will be ready to test the pulse-laser system within three years. That is the real reason for Initiative Open Window, gentlemen.'

'No one here doubts the necessity, Colonel,' Zotov said. 'Are you going to enlighten us as to your methods for realizing it?'

'My plan proposes a series of set-pieces, each of which leads ineluctably to the next. I have prepared a dossier which enumerates those set-pieces if you wish to read it. The end proposition is to obtain access to the National Security Agency computer system.'

'You won't mind telling us how, I trust?' Drachev said, sardonically. He didn't like having his 'protectorate' taken out of his hands, especially by one of his junior staff. There was a dangerous precedent there. He had fought hard to gain control of Open Window, but Ivashutin had blocked every move he made.

'I spoke earlier of intercept stations,' Guchkov said, following the Chief's example and not allowing Drachev to rattle him. 'The Americans call them 'windows'. You see them on the map marked in red. The most valuable of them, at Kabkan in Iran, was abandoned

subsequent to the rise of the Ayatollah Khomeini. In 1980, the Americans entered into an agreement with the Chinese to build a new window in the Xinjang Ulghur Autonomous Region, close to our eastern borders; it is not yet operative. However, there are plenty of others, as you can see: at Asmara in Ethiopia, Sidi Yahia in Morocco, in Panama, in Puerto Rico, in Cyprus. The three most important windows however are those situated at Aurora, near Denver in the United States; at Menwith Hill, near Harrogate in England; and the least-known of them all, Pine Gap, near Alice Springs in Australia, in the heart of what is known as the Red Centre.'

There was an appreciative murmur of laughter as he took the spy-satellite photographs of the installation from the large artist's portfolio he had brought with him and pinned them to the board. Alongside them he thumb-tacked the enlarged colour photographs of the place taken by a GRU agent-in-place there.

With its radomes and supermarket-sized concrete buildings, Pine Gap looked

like a moon colony dropped by mistake on the spinifex-covered scrub. Eleven and a half miles south-west of Alice Springs, he told the 'grandfathers', on an unsign-posted road off the main highway, Pine Gap was not marked on any map. No tourist brochure, gazetteer or guide book so much as hinted at its existence. No visitors were permitted; no aircraft allowed to fly within two and a half miles of it. Operating under the name of the commonwealth of Australia Joint Defence Space Research Facility, the 500-million-dollar complex was the National Security Agency's most highly sophisticated inter-cept station.

'Since the Death Bird launch site at the Baikonur firing range is inside the field of vision of the new American satellite, the information would be relayed to this station, Pine Gap, and then onward by satellite to the NSA. It is this link we propose to interrupt.'

'All very well,' Zotov said, dourly. 'We've all read your paper, Colonel Guchkov. Very clever. But what's it all going to cost, eh? How much of my

budget is this going to gobble up?'

'The operation will show a profit of thirty million dollars,' Guchkov said. 'It is self-financing, Comrade General. I am following Lenin's dictum that the capitalists will sell us the rope we need to hang them. That is why it has been planned as it has: my 'defection' to the British, all of it.'

'Too many things to go wrong, if you ask me,' Zotov said, sourly. 'Far too many things to go wrong.'

'I, for one, think it is a remarkable piece of work,' Ivashutin said forcefully. 'Exceptional.'

'Couldn't agree more,' old Goliakov said, and banged his stick on the floor. To Guchkov's surprise, the others began applauding. Even Zotov joined in, although his face was taut with anxiety because of his *faux pas* . . .

★ ★ ★

By God, what a moment that had been, Guchkov thought. That night, after the formal adoption of his initiative, he had

gone out and got wildly, gloriously drunk. He picked up a woman in the Ukraina Hotel, a bosomy blonde on an Intourist package from Stockholm. She wasn't what he'd have called subtle, but she was willing, healthy and energetic. The next morning the silly cow had wanted to take his photograph on the Kalinin bridge.

'What are you smiling at?' Mitchell said. 'Did I say something funny?'

'I was thinking of something else,' Guchkov said. His expression changed to that of a cat stalking through long grass.

'Your new shift begins tomorrow.'

'That's right.'

'There is something I want you to do. This will be your last task for me.'

'What do you mean?'

'If you successfully complete your assignment, you will be paid that million dollars we once talked about.'

'What do you want me to bring out?'

'I don't want you to bring anything out. I want you to take something in.'

'I . . . don't quite understand.'

'Mitchell, you and I know that no single person could penetrate the NSA

421

computers from the outside. It would require a comprehensive knowledge of the system and its peripherals that no single person could have, even those with the highest security clearances. There is only one way to do it. A prepared program planted in the memory, to be triggered by an external command.'

'You . . . you've got such a program? What is it for?'

'The program is ready and waiting,' Guchkov said, ignoring Mitchell's question. 'I want it put into Bubbles. Tomorrow.'

Mitchell stared at him, dumbfounded. 'I can't do that,' he said, almost scornfully, like a child asked to do an adult task.

'You can,' Guchkov said. 'And you will. Bring proof to me tomorrow that you have done what I ask, and I will give you one million dollars in cash,' Guchkov said. 'You can go away with Kate, anywhere in the world. Live like a king.'

'I don't know,' Mitchell said, hoarsely. 'I don't know.'

You poor pathetic bastard, Guchkov

thought, without a shred of pity. All this time Mitchell had been psyching himself up to tell him that there were some secrets it just wasn't possible to bring out, only to find he was going to do the easiest thing there was: take something in. He had no doubt at all that Mitchell would do as he was bidden. There was no fight left in the man. He had been led by the cock to this point, drowning in greed and lust. There was no way out, none at all.

'Tomorrow,' Guchkov said, and left him there.

30

Come on, damn you, Caine thought. It was three hours since McClelland had gone into the ISS office at Aurora Heights. If anything was going to happen it had to happen soon. He hated the game he was playing, but he knew no other way to go. He had had plenty of time to think on the way back north from Florida, a lot of time to formulate the plan he set up before he waylaid McClelland outside his Woodley Park home.

The whole thing hung on his reading of McClelland. Loyal though he might still be to Caine, he was more loyal by far to the Service. He would do what Caine expected him to do: he would tell Kingly that Caine was around, and he would tell him about Guchkov. Meanwhile, all Caine could do was chew his fingernails and wait.

He wondered where Lynda was. He had hated to leave her, yet had known

that he must, from the moment he found Miles Kingly's name among those Stepan Lykov had instructed Bogdanovich to watch for in the Miami traffic. What he had to do now, he could best do alone. So he left her still sleeping, her dark hair tumbled across the pillow, wanting to waken her, knowing he would not.

Instead, he had written her a note, hoping she would understand. Maybe she would; more probably she would not. She would feel used, hurt. She would be angry and bewildered and justifiably unforgiving. It was quite possible that they would never meet again, in which case it was probably better for both of them if she came to think of him as someone who made a brief mark on her life, like a bruise that would fade and be forgotten. Hating to use her, knowing he must, he once again felt a pang of regret for the years he had courted loneliness after Jenny died. He wondered whether he had been a better agent or a worse because of it.

He was quite certain Lynda's apartment in Miami would be staked out.

425

When she reappeared, they would go on alert, waiting for him to put in an appearance. While they were expecting him down there, they wouldn't be looking for him in Washington. He looked across at the anonymous frontage of the ISS office. Come on, come on, he muttered.

The day preceding his encounter with McClelland, Caine travelled out to Takoma Park on the Metro and walked back to the Walter Reed Medical Center, where he took a Dodge Aries from the visitors' area of the parking lot. He drove it south on Georgia Avenue to the six-block sprawl of Howard University. It took less than ten minutes to exchange the plates from the Dodge for those of a beaten-up Volkswagen Kharmann Ghia convertible that looked as if it had been in its parking slot since Christmas. A quick visit to an army surplus store and a filling station accessory shop, and he was ready.

At 12.38 the doors of ISS opened and Miles Kingly came out. He was wearing a pale blue silk Giorgio Armani suit, a cream silk shirt, tasselled loafers and a narrow-brimmed straw hat. With him,

wearing a flowery summer dress, was Betty Torre. Kingly looked right and left, then walked briskly down the street, his hand at Betty's elbow gently guiding her along.

A hundred feet behind them Caine cut diagonally across the street. He was wearing a combat jacket, faded blue jeans, and a pair of Nikes. Like the Duracell tube bag slung over his shoulder, he had picked them up the day before at the surplus store. In addition, he had not shaved for a couple of days. As disguises went, it was perfunctory, but it was effective.

Kingly glanced at him and then away without any sign of recognition. Since the Vietnam Veterans Memorial near the Constitution Gardens pool had been dedicated in November 1982, combat jackets were a common sight on the streets of the capital. The veterans came in patient procession, ones, twos, dozens, coachloads, to see Maya Lin's black granite chevron, to reach out and touch the carved names of dead comrades. Caine looked like just another of them.

Kingly and Betty Torre stopped at the

corner of Court House and 14th, talking. Caine strolled by them on the opposite side of the street, heading for the Metro station. Even now, he kept on wishing he was wrong, but he knew he was not. Had he been wrong, the entire area would have been crawling with surveillance waiting for him to show. Their absence was further proof he no longer needed.

He watched as Kingly smiled, nodded and abruptly crossed the street towards the Metro. Caine moved into his wake. Anybody who'd seen *The French Connection* knew the best place to shake a tail was in the subway. How Kingly expected to succeed wearing a pale blue silk suit was another matter. He had no option: he had not known when he dressed that it would become necessary.

Kingly turned and turned again. He crossed and recrossed his own path several times until he ended up on the westbound platform. When the train came, Caine took a chance and got aboard, watching warily as Kingly waited until the very last minute to get on. At the next station, Clarendon, he jumped out,

and hurried across to the other side. Caine ducked behind a hoarding and when Kingly took the next train back to Court House, he still had him in sight.

At Court House, Kingly stood for several minutes near the ticket office, watching the passers-by until he felt sure no one had followed him. Then he hurried to a pay phone. When he had made his call he headed for the exit. Caine sighed, and made his move.

'Hello, Miles,' he said, falling into step alongside Kingly. Kingly stopped dead, his chubby face rigid with shock.

'I never saw you once,' he said, as cunning replaced the fear that had filled his eyes.

'That was the idea,' Caine said. 'Let's go, shall we?'

'Go where?'

Caine ignored the question. He took Kingly's elbow much as Kingly had taken Betty Torre's and steered him out of the station into the bright sunshine. Kingly's eyes flickered left, right, left again. He was getting his confidence back.

'What are you going to do, Caine?' he

said. 'Pull a gun on me? Even you can't be as stupid as that. All I've got to do is call a cop. You're wanted by every law-enforcement agency in America.'

'Shut up, Miles,' Caine said, wearily. There were lots of people on the street. Cars glided by. Kingly gave Caine a smile of feline challenge.

'I'm just going to walk away from you,' he said. 'And there's not a damned thing you can do about it.'

'Try it, Miles,' Caine said, 'and I will hurt you very badly.'

Kingly's confident smile dissolved, and fear washed the contempt from his eyes. Caine knew his weak spot. He was not just afraid, he was terrified of physical hurt. Caine pushed him forward, and Kingly flinched, as if anticipating a blow. Smiling all the way, as if they were two old friends who had met in the street, Caine steered him to the stolen Dodge and pushed him in. Kingly sat slackly in the seat, his eyes watchful, empty, as Caine switched on the Sony cassette recorder he'd bought and put it on the dashboard in front of them.

'What do you think this is going to achieve?' he said, pettishly.

'I want Guchkov, Miles. You just phoned him. Where is he?'

'You're crazy!'

'No,' Caine said. 'I was stupid. We all were. But not crazy. It had to be you, Miles. Nobody else could have done it.'

'I tell you I don't know what you're talking about,' Kingly protested.

'Just as you wish.'

Caine headed across Key bridge and up through Georgetown. He turned on to Wisconsin Avenue, driving around and then into the Naval Observatory. He parked in the campus-like grounds and turned off the engine. Kingly sat with his lips pressed together; he had not spoken during the entire journey.

'How long have you worked for them, Miles?' Caine asked. 'Since Berlin? Or before that, even?'

Kingly ignored the question. Caine shrugged.

'I think I always knew,' he said. 'The flash clothes you shouldn't have been able to afford. The access to information I

couldn't understand. It was a set-up, right from the start, wasn't it? That's why Guchkov was always so far ahead of us. You told him about Genevevo. They knew I was going to Miami before I did. We never made a move they didn't know about in advance. You let them kill our people. You were going to let them kill me, and when that didn't work, you fitted me up. You knew, of all people in the world, you knew if I saw the file on Viktor I'd make the connection. So you fitted me to look like a Comrade. You, all the time.'

'I always thought you were one of the brighter ones, Caine,' Kingly said. 'But you're out of your depth here.'

'We'll see. Where's Guchkov, Miles?'

'If you think for a second I'm going to tell you anything, you're a fool, like the rest of them.'

'That's the way you see it — we're all fools?'

'All you've got is a conclusion. You aren't going to get far with that.'

'You're right,' Caine said. 'That's why you're going to tell me everything you know.'

'If you believe that, you're an even

bigger fool than I thought, Caine. What are you going to do, kill me?'

'I've been giving it serious thought.'

'If you kill me, you will never find Guchkov. And if you don't, you're a dead man!'

He was so confident, so sure. Caine tried to suppress his anger. One part of him hated what he was going to do to Kingly; another part of him couldn't wait.

'Where is he, Miles?'

'Oh, go to hell,' Kingly said, contemptuously.

'Last chance.'

'Time is your enemy, Caine. And my friend. All I have to do is wait.'

'No, Miles,' Caine told him. 'You're not going to play Scheherazade with me.'

He got out of the car, opened the trunk, and took out a jerry-can. He unscrewed the cap and sloshed its contents all over Kingly, who recoiled in horror as the stink of gasoline filled the car. There was no way he could know that the liquid Caine had doused him with was water, with enough gasoline in it to smell but not to burn. He watched in

utter disbelief as Caine took a box of kitchen matches from his pocket.

'Jesus Christ, Caine!' he screeched, shrinking away but held in place by the seatbelt.

'Where's Guchkov?'

Kingly shook his head, whimpering. Caine struck a match and Kingly put his hands in front of his face, screaming with fear.

'No, don't, Christ, don't, don't!'

A heavy, faecal smell mingled with the gasoline fumes. Caine shook out the match, nostrils wrinkling with disgust: Kingly had fouled himself. It was as if he had collapsed inwardly. Gone was the urbane, well-dressed man of moments ago. In his place, enveloped in terror, was a blubbering baby in a wrecked silk suit.

Caine struck another match.

'Easton, Easton!' Kingly sobbed. 'He's bought a big house in Easton. Baltimore. Oh, Christ, put it out, put it out!'

'I want it all, Miles,' Caine said, remorselessly. This was even worse than he had expected, but he could not turn back now.

'Yes, yes, all right, yes, just don't
. . . don't burn me, Caine, David, please,
don't,' Kingly jabbered. Once he began, it
was as if he could not stop. Stinking,
crumpled, abject, Kingly told Caine
everything he knew about Open Window,
from the setting up of the cocaine deal in
Miami to the big house on the shore of
Chesapeake Bay. And as he did, the
parameters of his own treachery became
apparent.

'What's the name of the target officer
at NSA?' Caine demanded.

'I don't know.'

Caine shook the matchbox and Kingly
whinnied with fear.

'I don't know, I don't know!' he
whined. 'Oh, Christ, look at me, look at
the mess.'

'Get out!' Caine snapped. 'Get out of
the car!'

Kingly got out, eyes swimming in
shame and self-loathing. The pale blue
suit was ruined, wrinkled and stained
with his waste.

'Oh, Christ,' he wept. 'Oh, God.'

Caine opened the trunk of the big car.

He took Kingly's arm and pulled him around to the rear of the Dodge. The man stank. Before he knew what was happening, Caine stuck the stun-gun against Kingly's sternum and pulled the trigger. In the same moment, he grabbed Kingly's lapels in his left hand, so that when Kingly's knees buckled, he was able to thrust him backwards into the open luggage compartment. He slammed down the lid, got into the car, and drove back to Arlington with all the windows open.

He parked the Dodge on Calvert Street and walked up to the Court House, where he used a pay phone to call Dick McClelland. The ISS operator was unable to conceal her reaction when he told her his name. Caine allowed himself an unamused smile as he pictured the trace machinery being set into operation, the tape reels turning.

'Sorry to keep you waiting, sir,' the girl said. 'We're having a little difficulty locating Mr McClelland.'

'You've got ninety seconds before I hang up, Dick,' Caine said. 'Cut in or I'll do it now.'

'David?' McClelland's voice said. 'Is that you?'

'Listen carefully, Dick,' Caine said. 'I'm only going to say all this once. Kingly is the Comrade. He's told me everything. He'll do the same for you when you pick him up. And if he won't, you'll find a cassette on the back seat which says it all for him.'

'What in the name of God are you talking ab — ?'

'He's locked in the trunk of a dark blue Dodge Aries, Maryland plates, registration JJB-2689,' Caine said. 'The plates don't belong to the car, by the way.'

'Where is it?' he said. His voice had changed; now it was all business.

'Inside a one-mile radius of your office,' Caine said. 'If you send out the sweepers now, you ought to be able to find it in a couple of hours.'

'He's not . . . damaged?'

'Only his pride,' Caine said, harshly.

'You say he . . . confessed? How did you — ?'

'I threatened to set fire to him. He didn't know it was water mixed with petrol.'

'Jesus, David!'

'Save your sympathy,' Caine snapped. 'He's garbage. As you'll see when you pick him up.'

He hung up and walked away. The trunk of the Dodge had plenty of air in it. Kingly would survive until the sweepers found him, as long as he didn't choke on his own stench.

He took a Metro to Union Station, and in the men's room, he discarded the combat jacket and jeans, changing to the pale grey London Fog windbreaker, dark wool slacks, and dark brown Hush Puppies he'd been carrying in the Duracell bag. He spent another twenty minutes getting rid of his beard, then went out into the crowded reservation area to find a fat pigeon.

Half an hour later, driving a Ford LTD he'd hot-wired at a meter bay on New Jersey Avenue, Caine was driving past the Air Force Transmitting Station west of Bowie on the John Hanson Highway. In his inside pocket was a wallet containing a hundred and ninety-four dollars in cash, five hundred more in Amex

traveller's cheques, and a good selection of credit cards in the name of Desmond Briggs, a large, bespectacled man whom Caine had 'accidentally' jostled in the station newsstand. Beneath his left arm, snug in its Myres shoulder rig, hung the Smith & Wesson ASP Tom Crandon had given him in Miami.

With any luck, he thought, he'd be in Easton by four.

31

Forsyth stayed overnight at the Hyatt Regency on Capital Hill, which wasn't on Capitol Hill at all, but on New Jersey Avenue, opposite a Quality Inn motel. It was an unnecessary extravagance which he perversely enjoyed, a sort of the-hell-with-it gesture. And in a way, it wasn't entirely wasted, even if the dinner he bought his old friend Frank McCabe at Hugo's did nothing to alter his long-held prejudice that the better the view, the worse the restaurant's food. At least the meal provided him with the opportunity to ask for a favour to be repaid, and he was able to drive a fully equipped Company car out to Easton the following morning.

He got there shortly after ten. Traffic was light, lighter in the town itself. A tabby cat strolled haughtily across Washington Street, curling up on the steps of the Seven Stars Hotel, as he drove

through. With so few people about, the eighteenth-century façades gave the town an eerie, time-warped atmosphere.

Easton was Historic, with a capital letter, and Forsyth felt a surge of affection for it, and for the thousand places like it all over America, with their artsy-craftsy boutiques, the Puppens and Patchworks, the Little Rascals, the Country Punkins, the Lu-Evv Framing Shoppes. The prerevolutionary houses, taverns and museums would all be staffed by charming, knowledgeable middle-aged ladies who could not only tell you what George Washington ate for breakfast, but probably every secret in town. He smiled.

Life, liberty and the right to sell pomanders, leatherette bookmarks and spiral-bound souvenir jotters.

He parked the Cutlass and walked down Harrison Street to the offices of the Percival Realty Company, a block over from Magazine Alley. A bell tinkled as he pushed open the door. The outer office was light and airy, with enlarged photographs of splendid houses. At a desk facing the door sat a pretty young blonde

girl. Twenty-something, good figure, fresh complexion, bright smile. The sign on her desk said her name was Betty Adams. She made him feel a hundred years old.

'My name is Forsyth,' he said. 'I called from Washington.'

'Mr Forsyth,' a voice said. The door to the inner office had opened. In the doorway stood a tall, spare man with weatherbeaten skin and shrewd, bright, blue eyes. A light grey alpaca coat hung on his bony shoulders. He looked like he had just stepped out of a Norman Rockwell painting of canny old Yankees around a pot-bellied stove, but his voice was soft with Southern cadences. 'I'm Harold Percival. How may I help you, sir?'

'May I speak with you privately, Mr Percival?'

He noticed Betty Adams's sharp look of small-town curiosity. Percival hesitated for a moment, then made a gesture.

'Come in, come in,' he said.

His office was small and cluttered: a desk, a moquette-covered swivel chair, a couple of prints on the wall, a side table

with an old Underwood sit-up-and-beg typewriter on it, a filing cabinet and a set of shelves crammed with local directories, leaflets and maps.

'How can I assist you, Mr Forsyth?'

'Do you know a man named Frederic Drosdow?'

Percival frowned, unsuccessfully trying to conceal uneasy surprise. 'Drosdow?'

'Or Pedro Avranilosa?'

'I don't believe so. They certainly don't sound like local people. May I ask you why you want to know?'

'I'm a government agent, Mr Percival. I'm trying to trace Frederic Drosdow. Are you sure you don't know him?'

'Could I see some form of identification, Mr Forsyth?'

'The agency I work for prefers not to show ID, sir. Unless you insist.'

The unease he had discerned in Percival's eyes deepened. The old man looked at him and then away, out of the window. The prominent Adam's apple jiggled up and down as he swallowed.

Money, Forsyth thought sadly. They'd given him money to keep his mouth shut

and now he thought the tax inspector was on his trail.

'Mr Percival, this is a very serious matter,' he said slowly. No need to give the old boy a coronary. 'You do know Drosdow, don't you?'

'I . . . has he done something wrong?'

'You know him, then.'

'He made it a condition of our transaction that it remain completely secret. He was most insistent.'

'In other words, he paid you to keep your mouth shut.'

'See here — '

'Look, Mr Percival, I'm not interested in your finances. But it's imperative you tell me exactly what your dealings with Drosdow were. I promise you that what you tell me will not go beyond this room.'

'If I have your word of honour on that . . . ?'

'You have, sir.'

'A man called me. From Washington. Said he was acting on behalf of clients in Florida who wished to purchase a house in this area. They had a specific property in mind, and knew that I was the agent.'

'Who was this man?'

'He told me his name was Miles Kingly.'

'Go on.'

'The arrangements were . . . unusual. The client wished to purchase the property outright, for cash. I would be paid my standard commission. After three months, the house was to be put back on the market. When it was sold, I was to deduct a further commission and pay the balance into a nominated account at the First National Bank in Baltimore.'

'You didn't think that strange?'

'Strange? Yes, but perfectly legal.'

'Of course,' Forsyth said, and the old man flushed.

'They said if I would accept the commission, they would furnish first-class transportation to Miami, all expenses paid.'

'And?'

'I met Mr Drosdow in a house at Bal Harbor in Miami. The other man, too. What did you say his name was?'

'Avranilosa.'

'They signed all the papers. I remember thinking how perfunctory they were, as if the house itself were an irrelevancy.

445

Drosdow paid a deposit in cash. He gave me a briefcase with the money in it. They said the rest would be paid by banker's draft, and it was. I flew back to Washington, took care of the paperwork. That was it. The house was theirs.'

'And is Drosdow living there now?'

'I believe so. I haven't been out there.'

'Where is it?'

'It's on Route 333, about halfway between here and Oxford. A beautiful place, quite outstanding.'

'How much did it go for?'

'Four million.'

'Can you remember which bank the draft was drawn on?'

'Yes, of course. The Republic International Bank of Miami.'

'Have you got any photographs of the place?'

'Highfield? Yes, certainly.' Percival brought out an envelope from a rank of files in the middle drawer of his desk. He shook the pictures out and turned them so Forsyth could see them.

'Nice place,' Forsyth said. 'What about maps?'

'Of the estate? There are none.'

'Here's a pencil,' Forsyth said. 'Draw me one. And don't leave anything out.'

* * *

The dirt road ended at an ornate wrought-iron gate eight feet high, supported by twin stone pillars into which were chiselled the name of the house. A steel trapdoor on the right-hand one indicated the location of the recessed telephone connecting with the house.

Caine got out of the car and walked south along the six-foot-high stone wall. After about two hundred yards, it made a right angle down the gentle slope towards the river, and disappeared into a dense, cultivated thorn thicket. He walked back to the gate and then north. This stretch of wall was much longer, perhaps half a mile. As on the other side, the wall was topped with angled brackets supporting wicked German S-wire with closely set, razor-sharp rectangular blades. Porcelain carriers indicated the presence of an electrical current, or an alarm, or both.

Beyond the walls stood closely planted trees and rhododendron bushes. Through the gate he could see up the drive to where it bore right, into the trees. He could not see the house at all.

He walked back to the Ford and drove back up to the main road, and on to Oxford. Once the sister port-of-entry to Annapolis, the little town had boomed briefly before the First World War, then returned to its pre-revolutionary slumber. Today it was just a pretty residential village on an L-shaped spit of land pointing north into the Tred Avon river, with a couple of boatyards and a harbour used by watermen and weekend sailors.

He stopped at an Exxon station just outside town to buy a couple of things and get some directions. Following these, he drove to Applegarth's Marine Yard on Morris Street, picked up a couple more items there, then headed for Market Street. A sign outside the Waters United Methodist Church said Sunday worship was at eleven a.m. At the end of the street, fronting Town Creek, was a boatyard. A sign said *Shoreline Yacht*

Services. *Eli Johnson, prop.*'

Caine got out of the car and walked over to where a tall, weatherbeaten, skinny man of about sixty was hosing down a boat. He wore a faded denim coverall and a baseball cap that bore the legend '*Brinkman's: We're much more than an icecream store*'.

'Like to rent a boat for a couple of hours,' Caine told him.

'Plenty to choose from.'

'You Mr Johnson?'

'Eff I ain't, I better not be rentin you any my boats.'

He ambled on down the dock, and Caine followed him. He stood on the jetty and waved at one of the boats. 'Try the Glastron, there,' he said, gesturing towards a metallic-finished speedboat with a Mercruiser engine. 'Go ahead, start her up.'

Caine gave him a surprised look, then stepped down into the boat. He switched on the pumps to clear the bilges, then operated the power tilt to lower the propeller into the water. The engine started first time. The skinny old man on

the jetty grinned.

'Looks like you know what you're at,' he said. 'Switch her off and come up to the office. We'll do the paperwork.'

'Suppose I'd just switched her on?' Caine said as he followed the old man into the cluttered hut that served as his office. Johnson smiled mischievously.

'I was watchin you real close, son,' he said. 'I'd a stopped you.'

'And kicked me the hell out of your yard.'

'Somethin along those lines,' the old man said, with a wheezy chuckle. Switching on the engine before making sure there were no gasoline fumes in the bilges was an easy way to blow the stern right off a boat.

'Done much sailin in these parts, son?'

'First time,' Caine told him. 'Don't worry, though, I'm not going far. Just up the river a ways.'

'Only one thing you need to know, then,' Johnson told him. 'Where you see reeds, keep well offshore. You git your prop fouled, it's hell's own job gittin off. What you plannin to do, fish?'

Caine held up the Pentax eight by forty

BWCF wideangle binoculars he'd bought in town. The old man shrugged.

'Oh, you're one of them birdspotter fellers are you?' he said, like a man who couldn't quite believe any grown man would want to watch birds as a hobby.

'What time do you close?' Caine asked, as he pushed off.

'Round nine. If I'm gone, just tie her up and put the key through the mail slot.'

Caine took the boat out into Town Creek on quarter throttle and brought her bow around into the current. Then he eased the revs up till she was moving steadily through the water. Herring gulls wheeled overhead, watching his wake. At first, the shoreline was low and wooded, with strips of shingly beach fronting expanses of marshy grass. Nearer to Trippe Creek, it rose in sandy bluffs. Then he came around the headland and saw the big house sitting grandly on its low hill, terraced gardens sloping gently down to a natural inlet on the river with a jetty and a covered dock.

He hove to off the inlet. Using the binoculars he could see the hull of a

sleek-looking cruiser inside the covered dock. To the south, off to his right, stretched a strip of private beach with a barbecue pit and wooden bench-tables. Beyond and behind the beach lay open pasture, backed by tree-lined bridle paths. North of the dock lay formal gardens; beyond them the swimming pool glimmered in the late sunshine. Further back, a dovecote on what looked like a stable block poked up amidst the trees.

He checked his watch. About an hour till sundown.

$$\star \quad \star \quad \star$$

It took Butler Mitchell about an hour to drive out to Easton from Fort Meade. Apart from the usual holdups it was a pleasant drive. The Dodge 600 Turbo was still enough of a head-turner for it to be gratifying. He was looking forward to seeing Kate, glad all this was over. In the slim Prince Albert wallet in the inside breast pocket of his cream linen Gianni Versace suit were two open-dated first-class tickets to London and a draft of his

letter of resignation.

He did not know and resolutely refused to think about what the program he had planted was for. Let the specially trained Tiger Teams, whose job was to detect unauthorized entry into the mainframes, worry about that. He had done what Drosdow wanted; once he got the money he had been promised, their relationship would be ended, which would suit him just damned fine. There had been altogether too many espionage cases recently, and he didn't want to be another. He had not missed the significance of the Senate amendment to the defence authorization bill which mandated execution or life imprisonment without parole for anyone convicted of espionage.

He threw off the thought. What was done was done, and as of tonight he would be out of it. On the seat beside him was a Gucci document case stuffed full of travel brochures. As he drove along, carefully observing the speed limit and half-listening to his tape of Barbara Cook, he turned over in his mind some of the

things he planned to do when Drosdow finally paid off.

One million dollars. The thought of it hung in his imagination like a blimp over a football field. The interest alone would be more than a hundred and twenty thousand a year. Imagine never having to lift a finger again if you didn't want to. Imagine all the things you could buy, all the places you could go, all the things you could do.

Rich. What a word it was!

He swung around Easton on the bypass, following Route 333 across Peachblossom Creek, past the Country Club, paralleling the old Easton-Oxford railroad line as far as Trappe station. There, he turned right on a light-duty road that led down to Trippe Creek Lane, a dirt lane running down to the Tred Avon between thickets of gallberry, chokeberry, greenbrier and sand cherry. When he got to Highfield, he opened the metal trap and reported his arrival on the intercom.

After a few moments, the locked gates clunked open and swung back. Smiling, humming a tune, Mitchell drove in. Not

for so much as a second did it occur to him that anyone might be watching. Even had he been listening for it, it is doubtful he would have heard the *zizzz* of the motor drive on the Polaroid SLR 635 with which Frank Forsyth photographed him as he went by.

<p style="text-align:center">★ ★ ★</p>

While the Polaroid prints developed themselves, Forsyth fed the details of the Dodge 600 Turbo into the onboard computer fitted to the dash of the CIA Cutlass. He was immediately linked via Domestic Ops to the Department of Motor Vehicles' computer.

To obtain an operator's licence in the state of Maryland, an applicant was required to submit his name, address, licence number, thumbprint, restrictions (such as whether the driver wore glasses, or could only drive with automatic transmission), race, weight, height, signature, sex, birthdate and social security number. Photographs were optional, but usually supplied. The only information

not on the records was the colour of the applicant's hair and eyes which, with three good Polaroid shots blooming before his eyes, Forsyth hardly needed.

The DMV computer accepted his clearance and the readout came through in a matter of seconds.

'Rhett Butler Mitchell. *Rhett Butler*, for Christ's sake,' Forsyth muttered. 'What the hell kind of name is that?'

Born at Plymouth, Mass., on 2 January 1940, Mitchell lived at 2133 High Ridge Road, Laurel, Maryland. Licence number, as checked, RBM-7777, a Maryland vanity plate. Race, white; sex, male; weight, one hundred seventy-two; height, six feet, one inch. Social security number 228-74-9132. No traffic violations.

Next stop, Treasury Department. Forsyth knew, as any rookie cop did, that the records of the IRS were sacrosanct. Unlike the rookie cop, however, he knew that while *most* of them were, *all* of them were not. He tapped another question into the computer: *Provide employer and occupation Rhett Butler Mitchell Social Security Number 228-74-9132*. He waited.

After a while, the tiny screen blinked and the information zipped across it.

'Holy shit,' Forsyth breathed. The man who had just gone into Drosdow's house was a deputy chief in the Office of Communications Security at the National Security Agency.

★ ★ ★

Caine ran the Glastron towards the private beach below the house. She grounded gently, with a soft, grating sound. He jumped out and splashed ashore, lashing the painter to one of the picnic tables. The bluffs concealed him from the house.

He ran, crouching, towards the dock, the plastic bag containing the stuff he had bought in Oxford clutched in his hand. There was no one in sight. He went into the covered boat shed. Inside it was a thirty-one-foot Bertram Fly-bridge, white, handsome, glistening. He noted with satisfaction that there was a telephone on the wall, near the door. The lapping water sent flickering birds of light dancing across the walls.

Working swiftly but cautiously, Caine rolled an empty ten-gallon oil drum into the well of the Bertram. He prised off the lid and dropped it into the water. Next, he unrolled the ten yards of acetate curtain material and put it into the drum in an untidy pile, draping lengths over the sides of the drum and on to the decks of the cruiser. In a plastic bailing bucket he mixed coal oil and sawdust which he splashed on the curtains and on the decks. Then he soaked a roll of kitchen towels with methylated spirit and scattered them on top of the bunched curtains in the drum.

Across the top of the drum he now laid a length of plastic curtain rail. Taking a reel of cotton out of his pocket, he snapped off a two-foot length, tied one end to the rail and the other to a book of matches, the cheap, paper-covered kind. Nearly there.

He picked up the telephone and dialled 8222222. A nasal female voice squawked, 'Oxford Fire and Ambulance. Which service do you requi-er?'

'Fire,' he said.

When the Oxford Fire Department answered, he told them slowly and clearly that there was a fire at Highfield, on Trippe Creek Lane, and hung up before they could ask questions. All set.

He lit a cigarette. Carefully, deliberately, he opened the matchbook tied to the rod, wedged the unlit end of the cigarette behind the matchheads and closed the flap, thus anchoring the cigarette inside the matchbook with the lighted end outside. Very slowly, he lowered the matchbook so that it hung suspended inside the oil drum. Then he went below, took the cap off the Bertram's fuel tank, and stuffed one of his meths-soaked kitchen towels loosely into the aperture.

He ran out of the dock and up the path towards the formal gardens on the left. Twilight was falling; there were lights on in the big house up the hill. He edged along the path between the gardens and the kidney-shaped swimming pool. He reckoned it would take about five minutes until the cigarette burned down to the matchheads, igniting them and severing

the cotton so that the burning matchbook would fall into the incendiary mixture. Give the resulting fire two or three minutes to reach the open fuel tank. Say eight minutes in all.

In the event, he was thirty-eight seconds out.

32

'Well?'

'No word yet, Colonel-General,' his deputy chief reported.

Ivashutin made an impatient gesture. It was five a.m. Moscow time, but he felt no fatigue. He was nearly eighty, and sleep was no longer important to him. He looked at the clocks on the wall of his office: they showed London, Washington, Tokyo and Moscow time. It was nine p.m. in the American capital.

'You have spoken to Washington?'

'Yes, sir,' Pavlov said. 'They have heard nothing.'

'Damn the man!' Ivashutin said, irritably. 'He's done everything else perfectly. What's holding him up?'

'There's still time, sir. We still have three hours.'

'I know that, dammit!' Ivashutin growled. The American spy satellite routinely photographed the missile site

461

every twelve hours. With the missile on the pad, once that shutter clicked the fat would be in the fire.

'He'll come through, General. Do you want some coffee?'

'To hell with coffee,' Ivashutin said. 'Bring me some cognac. And tell them to get me Professor Doctor Chebriakov on the phone at Baikonur.'

Pavlov hurried away, leaving Ivashutin staring at the large-scale map of the world on the far wall of his office. Don't fall at the last fence, Guchkov, he thought. There is too much at stake. Far too much at stake.

He had come a long way for a boy who'd begun as a volunteer in the punitive formations of the Special Purpose Units. He'd been nineteen then. Twenty-two when he came into army intelligence. More than half a century; my God, where did the years go to? He was the last of a dying breed, the generation that had produced Brezhnev and Yuri Andropov, Chernenko, Kuznetzov. All gone now; there was a new breed in high office these days, pragmatic bargain-makers with university degrees who

worked for the system instead of making the system work for them. He didn't relish the thought of giving the grey men a chance to bring him down; he knew only too well with what zeal they would do it, and with what pleasure the Neighbours would assist them.

He looked around him. Unlike the strictly utilitarian cream-painted boxes most GRU officers worked out of, his office was ornately furnished, with oriental carpets and embroidered sofas. The walls were panelled in mahogany, and the high windows, looking out over the courtyard, had no bars on them. On his antique desk, once the property of a wealthy sugar merchant in Sverdlovsk, was a battery of telephones: a direct line to the Kremlin, another connecting to the principal GRU stations throughout Russia, still another to the Ministry of Defence, and so on. The sixth telephone, which was white, connected him directly with his deputy chiefs: Pavlov, Bekrenev, Zotov, Meshcheryakov, Kolodyazhny, Milstein and Sidorov.

The red scrambler phone purred; he picked it up.

'Is that you, Professor Doctor Chebria-kov?'

'At your command, General.'

'What is the present status of *Smert Ptytsa*?'

'She is on the launching pad, General. Everything is in readiness. We await only your clearance to commence countdown.'

'Countdown is twelve hours?'

'That is correct. Can you give me any indication when we will begin?'

'Not yet,' Ivashutin said, gruffly. 'We're all as anxious as you are to get started, Professor. But we can't give you a 'go' until we hear from our man in Washington.'

'I understand. You will forgive my question. My enthusiasm.'

'No apology necessary. We're all tense. It's only to be expected. I'm sorry to have disturbed your sleep.'

'I wasn't sleeping, General. I can't sleep. I won't sleep until our bird is flying.'

'Your dedication is commendable,' Ivashutin said. 'It will not be forgotten.'

'Thank you, General,' Chebriakov said,

thinking how true Ivashutin's words were. If everything went to plan, what he had done would not be forgotten. The same would be true if everything went wrong. The only difference would be who was doing the remembering.

'I'll call you as soon as we get word,' Ivashutin told him. 'Don't worry. It won't be long. I'm sure of it.'

I hope you're right, thought the scientist as he put down the telephone and looked out of his window. There on the featureless steppe, stark and ugly against the lightening sky, the F-2m launch vehicle with its huge payload stood within its mighty gantries, like an enormous modernistic skyscraper under construction. I hope you're right.

33

Guchkov detested guns.

Guns were for morons, assault groups, *boyeveya* squads, assassins. Brains were the most potent weapon, not firearms. Even so, he could not take the chance of encountering a situation where a weapon would make the difference; so he had chosen carefully. He wasted no time on the 5.45 PSM which was replacing the old 9mm Makarov throughout the Russian security services. Both guns were anyway a copy, and a poor one, of the German Walther PP. He gave serious thought to the 9mm fifteen-round Beretta selective-fire pistol which had replaced the old Colt .45 M1911 automatic in the US Army, but in the end, decided to go American because ammunition was so much easier to get.

There was a specialist firm in Wisconsin called Armament & Systems Procedures who made a very effective combat version of the Smith & Wesson M39 pistol. It

carried seven rounds of 9mm Parabellum, was very light — just under one and a half pounds loaded — and although hard to obtain, had much to recommend it. In the final analysis, however, he opted for fire-power and selected a .45 Detonics Combat Master Mark V, the one with the stainless steel finish. Slightly heavier than the ASP, and carrying one round less, the pistol was like a smaller, lighter version of the M1911, but with the same stopping power.

He held the pistol in his hand now as he pondered the best way of disposing of Mitchell. Guns were clumsy, noisy and far from reliable. Ricin would be much better.

The Technical Operations Department of the GRU, *Tyékhnecheskye Dyéystvye*, or *Tyé-Dyé* as it was known throughout the Service, had done enormous amounts of research into undetectable poisons: gly-colates, shellfish toxins, curare extracts. No one had yet come up with a better one than ricin, which was derived from the seeds of the castor oil plant, *Ricinus communis*. A slow-acting poison which took up to three days to kill, ricin induced car-diovascular collapse and all the external

symptoms of a genuine heart attack.

He went to the locked cupboard beneath the staircase to which only he had access. From it he took a long wooden box, and out of it lifted what looked like a target pistol. It was a 9mm Tokagypt, the Eyptian version of the Russian Tokarev TT33, extensively remodelled into what *Tyé-Dyé* called a non-discernible micro-bioinoculator — GRU jargonese for a battery-operated gun which fired a poison pellet without the target realizing he had been hit. The poison itself was carried in a tiny mercury phial which dispersed on impact, leaving the deadly poison slowly to find its way to the heart.

He looked at his watch. Six thirty. Mitchell would be arriving soon. He went into the huge circular foyer. As he did, Katja came down the stairs. She was wearing a Halston day dress and Magli sandals. Her golden hair was swept back in a style not unlike that of the English Princess Diana.

'What time is he due?' she asked, stopping at the foot of the ornate staircase like a model posing for a photographer.

'Any time now,' he said. He placed the Tokagypt poison gun between two books on a sofa table near the door and looked around.

'Are you ready?' he said.

'Yes. Everything is packed.'

'Good. We'll leave as soon as I have disposed of Mitchell.'

'With . . . that?' Katja inclined her head towards the hidden gun.

'Don't worry. He won't feel a thing.'

'How long will it take?'

'Twenty-four, forty-eight hours. More than long enough for you to ditch him.'

'Will I see you again?'

'It's a small world.'

'You're glad to be going back, aren't you, Andrei?'

'Yes,' he said. 'I am.'

He had already had more than enough of America. He detested its fat men and even fatter women, the pretentiousness of the architecture, the mindlessness of the television, the ghastly sameness of their food. He loathed the graffiti-defiled subways and the arrogant coloured youths with their ghetto-blasters, the filthy, littered

streets of the cities, the sidewalker hustlers who urged you to 'check it out', the blatant whores who walked up and touched your genitals, the illiterate cab drivers, the lurching panhandlers, the street crazies. Americans worshipped only two gods, money and success. They could not lead, and they refused to follow.

He remembered an SS captain he had once talked to in the Hofbrauhaus in Münich. Forty years after the end of the war, the man was still bitter about the fact that Germany had lost it, and bitterest of all that they had lost it to Americans.

'Man for man, they were not in our class,' he said, shaking his head at the memory. 'As an army, they were a rabble. The only reason they won was because there were so fucking many of them.'

Guchkov was looking forward to his return — triumphant return, he corrected himself — to the Motherland. All he had to do now was to confirm to Red Centre via the Washington Embassy that the 'logic bomb' was in place. As soon as that confirmation reached Moscow, the countdown to launch of *Smert Ptytsa* would

begin. At T minus 12, the massive assault on the American computer systems, orchestrated from the huge computer bunker beneath the Washington Embassy, would begin. Triggered by remote satellite controls, accurate to a microsecond, the program would turn the American satellite into so much junk orbiting in space, and simultaneously wreak havoc in the computers at Pine Gap in the Red Centre of Australia.

Long before then, Guchkov would have boarded the Aeroflot jet that would take him back to Moscow's Sheremetyevo airport and a welcome befitting a hero of the Soviet Union. There would be kisses from the Director, bear hugs from the Grandfathers, flowers from smiling children, a guard of honour. At the Aquarium, they would line up to shake his hand.

The GRU lieutenant who acted as a butler at Highfield came in and told him Mitchell was through the gate. Guchkov nodded and went to meet the American. The big Dodge came to a stop in front of the Palladian porch, tyres crunching on

the gravel. Mitchell got out, smiling. He was wearing a cream silk shirt, cream linen suit, and matching leather espadrilles. He looked, Guchkov thought, like a Harlem pimp.

'Well?'

Mitchell nodded.

'Let's go inside,' Guchkov said. 'I think this calls for a drink.'

'I won't be staying long,' Mitchell said. Guchkov smiled. How true, he thought. The sun was below the wooded bluffs across the river: he could see the lights of Bellevue, a mile away. Smoke lifted lazily into the air down at the dock; probably one of the servants burning trash.

'Kate's inside,' he said, leading the way towards the house. As he did the unmistakable sound of fire-engine sirens bored into the stillness of the evening, coming nearer. He frowned, sensing without knowing why that something was amiss. The sound of the sirens drew nearer. The wisp of smoke that he had noticed earlier had turned now into a roiling black pillar into which flickering fingers of orange flame lanced. He saw

one of the servants running down to the dock, shouting. Then a mighty explosion assaulted his eardrums like roaring thunder.

He watched, transfixed, as the entire dock erupted straight up like a volcano, massive chunks of metal and wood burning and turning against the soft, purpling sky. He felt the blast hit him like a hot hand, heard the chittering crash as two of the big drawing room windows were blown in. Oleg, the butler, came running out of the house.

'The fire department is at the gates, sir!' he yelled. 'What shall I do?'

'Let them in!' Guchkov shouted. There was no choice. Down at the dock a raging, leaping fire roared at the evening sky. He watched for a moment longer, stunned. Then he turned to see Mitchell standing in the doorway, gaping at the incredible scene.

'Get inside!' he snapped.

As he spoke, the fire department's huge red Mack truck roared past the house, churning up the gravel, gouging deep black tracks in the lawns as the driver

shortcut the distance to the dock. Men ran, shouting, hoses unsnaked, challenging the inferno at the jetty.

'Wait in the library!' he said to Mitchell. 'Go on, I'll be right there.' He hurried across to the telephone. It was dead. Cold fingers of unease touched his nerve ends. This was obviously hostile action, but who was the enemy? Kingly had said Caine was back in Washington. But how would he know where to find Guchkov? He looked up to see Katja watching him, a frown puckering the flawless brow.

'What is it?' she said. 'What has happened?'

He drew the Combat Master out of its shoulder holster and handed it to her. 'He's in the library,' he said. 'Kill him. I'll get the car.'

He went out of the front door and Katja walked into the library. Mitchell was pacing up and down, fear painted on his face.

'Kate!' he said, vast relief in his voice. 'What the hell's going on?'

'I don't know,' Kate said. 'It doesn't

474

matter. We have to get out of here. Is the program in place?'

'What about the money?'

'There's no time for that now. Is the program in place?'

'What program is that, Mitchell?' a voice interposed.

Katja swung around. A man had come into the room on soundless feet, a tall, well-built blond man wearing a grey windbreaker and dark slacks. Mitchell stared at him, a bewildered frown on his face.

'Who the hell are you?' he growled.

'It's Caine,' Katja said. 'Caine, isn't it?'

'And you're the swallow. Katja.'

She smiled and produced the gun that had been concealed by the folds of her dress. Mitchell gaped at her, paralysed, his jaw slack with shock.

'You know what happens now, Mitchell,' Caine said. 'She kills me, then she kills you. There's no payoff. There never was going to be one.'

'Kate?' Mitchell gasped.

'What did you do for them, Mitchell? What was the program she was talking about?'

'Kate?' Mitchell said again.

'Mitchell, they've double-crossed you,' Caine said, urgently. 'Tell me what you did.'

Mitchell shook his head. 'You wouldn't . . . Kate? You wouldn't do that?'

'You damned baby,' she said, and shot him through the heart. Mitchell cartwheeled backwards, crashing into the ornate fireplace. Like a tigress Katja swung around, turning the gun on Caine, but he was already diving to one side. Her first shot missed completely. She had pulled the trigger for her second shot when the bullet from Caine's ASP hit her on the bridge of her freckled nose. Her wild unaimed shot smashed into Caine's lower body and drove him back, yelling with pain, against the fine mahogany bookcase, the ASP skittering away.

Caine dragged himself to his feet. His body felt as if it was on fire. He could not see clearly, and his movements felt as if he was wading in treacle. After a moment's dizziness, his vision cleared. He saw Mitchell lying in front of the fireplace, the spattered blood on the walls. The man's

arm moved. Caine lurched across. Mitchell was staring up, his eyes drowning in agony.

'Pock,' he said. Blood came out with the word.

The cream linen suit was spattered with blood, a ghastly mess. Caine ripped the jacket open and took out Mitchell's wallet, shaking its contents on to the rug.

'What?' he shouted, shaking the dying man. 'What am I looking for?'

Mitchell tried to speak. Another gob of blood trickled from the writhing lips.

'God damn you, Mitchell, what?'

'Copy,' Mitchell said, clearly. Then he was dead.

Caine picked up a strip of card perhaps eight inches long and three wide. He knew enough about computers to know that the hieroglyphics on it were some kind of program. He put it into his pocket and lurched out into the hall. His hip felt as if someone was playing a blowtorch on it. He reeled and almost fell, bringing down a table near the door. A weapon clattered on the tile floor. He knew what it was: they'd taken poison guns off

Russian agents before. Grimly ignoring the searing rushes of pain driving through his entire body, he picked up the Tokagypt and staggered outside.

At the dock it looked as if the firemen were getting the blaze under control. He could see men walking up towards the house across the terraced formal gardens. He turned to his left and saw Guchkov in the Mercedes 380SEL convertible on the concrete washing apron in front of the garage, engine running.

Guchkov saw him in the same moment. He saw the Russian's startled expression, saw the car leap forward as Guchkov rammed his foot down. The car spat gravel and earth backwards as Guchkov swung the wheel to turn on to the drive. He missed it by a yard and the big car spun on to the grass, tyres whining as they sought purchase.

'Guchkov!' Caine screamed. Guchkov smacked the shift into reverse and came at him backwards, engine screaming. Caine fell out of the vehicle's path, lying helplessly on the ground as Guchkov swung the car side on, cursing, his face a

sweating mask of desperation. Caine pulled himself up to sitting position, bent his good right knee, and steadying both arms on it, fired the poison pistol. It made an insignificant sound: *bnfff!* Guchkov made a quick, irritated gesture like a man brushing away a wasp. In an instant that seemed like an eternity, Caine saw Guchkov look at the weapon in his hand, and knew that the Russian realized what had happened to him.

'That's for Berlin, you bastard!' Caine shouted. He had no idea whether Guchkov heard him.

Now he saw blue lights flashing among the trees bordering the main driveway. Guchkov saw them, too. He wrenched the Mercedes around, roaring away from the house in a flying shower of gravel, scouring extended S-grooves into the drive. He skidded off the drive between the huge oaks bordering it, sliding on the grass, fishtailing back on to the drive behind the police cars as they slammed to a stop. Down the drive the Mercedes roared as police officers piled out of their vehicles, firing wildly at the vanishing tail

lights. His face a rictus of frustration and terror, Guchkov raced towards the main gate. A telephone, a telephone: the thought hammered in his mind like a pulse. If he could reach a phone there was still a chance.

The gate loomed into view. He saw there was a police car standing in the road outside, and another one, an unmarked tan sedan, parked at right angles to it. Two patrolmen stood talking to a civilian. Guchkov jammed the gas pedal to the floor and the Mercedes powered forward, hurtling through the gateway like a juggernaut. The policemen leaped for safety as the Mercedes whiplashed past their Mustang with a smashing of grinding metal and glass, then slewed wildly on the grass verge on the far side of the road, tearing clods of earth out of the ground as Guchkov fought to control the car.

Over the roar of the engine, he heard the sound of shots, the spang of bullets hitting the coachwork of the car. He wrestled the Mercedes back on to the road, snatching a look in his mirror to see

the men running back towards their car. He roared up Trippe Creek Lane, heading for Route 333. Maybe there was still time to get through to Red Centre. Maybe they'd even be able to do something about the ricin.

Maybe.

34

When the four-vehicle motorcade bring-
ing the Sewer Squad arrived, Forsyth
came out of the house to meet them. The
Fire Department had gone; a pair of
Oxford P.D. Mustangs were still slewed in
the turning circle in front of the Palladian
porch, blue lights flashing, radios squawk-
ing. Down at the dock the blackened
wreck of the big Bertram lay on its side in
the water. The officer in charge of the
clean-up unit identified himself to For-
syth and looked around in wonderment.

'Hanrahan, Logistics Twelve,' he said.
'What the fuck went down here? It looks
like World War Three broke out.'

Forsyth shrugged and pointed with his
chin at the burly, grey-haired police
captain coming out of the house.
Hanrahan nodded and strode across to
confront the big policeman, whose ID
shield gave his name as Captain David
James. Hanrahan flipped open his own ID

wallet. The police chief stared at it for a moment, then spat on the ground.

'I might have known,' he said, disgustedly.

'Give me a rundown, chief,' Hanrahan said. 'What have we got here?'

'Out here we got that,' James said, with an angry gesture in the direction of the burned dock and the wrecked boat. 'Inside, we got a dead NSA officer, an unidentified woman with the top of her head blown off, and half a dozen servants who won't even tell us their names without talking to the Russian Embassy. That's what we've got. You want to tell me what it means?'

'You got an ID on the NSA man?'

'His name is Butler Mitchell,' Forsyth said, coming across to join them. 'I notified NSA as soon as I made him, coming in. They're sending an M-5 squad out. Should be here before long.'

'You'll find what was in his pockets on the table in the hall,' James said. 'The bodies are in the library. I sound like a goddamned Agatha Christie movie. On the physical evidence, somebody else was

wounded in there. We've got three different blood types. We've also got two guns, a .45 and a .38 ASP. Three shots fired from the .45. One of them killed the NSA man. The woman was killed with the ASP. Could be she wounded whoever killed her. You want to talk to the ME?'

'Maybe later,' Hanrahan said. 'Thanks a lot, chief. You can get your people out of here now. We'll take over.'

'What do you think, I'm just going to walk away from this?' James said. 'I've got TV people, newspapers banging on my door. My report . . . '

'Don't file it till you hear from us, chief,' Hanrahan said. 'OK?'

James looked at him for two long seconds, then decided against whatever it was he had been about to say. Hanrahan went into the house, and Forsyth followed him. The marble-floored foyer was circular, perhaps forty feet in diameter. Twin staircases bent upwards to a gallery. It looked like a set for *The Merry Widow*. They walked through to the library. Beautifully furnished, and lined with mahogany shelving, it was dominated at

the far end by a Victorian marble fireplace on which stood a gilded clock with two figures representing winter and summer. Above it hung a painting of a river scene. In front of the marble fireplace lay the body of Butler Mitchell, his cream linen suit incarnadined. The woman lay in an ugly sprawl about ten feet nearer the door, the Chinese carpet beneath her stiff with coagulating blood.

'Jesus!' Hanrahan said. Shaking his head, he crossed the long room, squatting on his haunches to examine the bloody smears on the bookcase and the floor where Caine had fallen. A chalked circle showed where a bullet had been dug out of the wood. Hanrahan made a mental note to collect it from the Oxford police.

'You gonna talk to the servants?' he asked Forsyth.

Forsyth shook his head. 'They'll all be Russians,' he said. 'We won't get a peep out of them, neither will M-5. They'll plead diplomatic immunity.'

'You're probably right,' Hanrahan said glumly. 'All right boys, come on in.'

A team of men in grey coveralls

appeared in the doorway. There was no change in their expressions as they saw what was waiting for them in the library. Like men who have worked together many times before, two of them went across to where Mitchell lay. They unrolled a heavy black plastic body bag, unzipped it, rolled the body in, and lugged it out of the room. Another pair did the same with the body of the woman. A trolley was wheeled in, stacked with cleaning solutions, pails, rolls of muslin, stain solvents — in fact, everything the team would need to remove every trace of what had happened in this room. For their pains, they were called the Sewer Squad.

'What's your reading of this, Forsyth?' Hanrahan asked. 'You think your Russkie friend was wounded?'

'He didn't drive as if he was.'

'He won't get far.'

He doesn't need to, Forsyth thought. Drosdow would only need to make one telephone call. His people would send out a team to pick him up and spirit him away to some Russian safe house. From

there they could put him on an Aeroflot plane or one of a dozen other airlines without anyone ever knowing he'd left the country. Or, if it was realized that his work had come to nothing, they might simply incinerate him.

'You got to report to the Director when you get back to town, Forsyth,' Hanrahan told him. 'I'll handle this end. You can take off any time you like.'

'Sure,' Forsyth said, allowing himself a grin at the thought of his impending interview with the chief. They wouldn't know whether to give him a medal or set fire to his ass.

He walked down to the dock and stood for a while staring at the wreckage, without really seeing it. It was almost dark. The lights of Bellevue looked pretty across the mile of water between. He played back the scenario he had constructed, testing it for flaws. Someone had got to Highfield by boat, probably rented in Oxford: they could check that easily enough. Beached it over yonder. Set fire to the dock and the boat in it. Cut the phone lines. Went in after Drosdow.

Who . . . what? Killed Mitchell and the girl, and wounded someone . . . someone else? Who?

Was it you, Caine? he wondered. And if it was, where the hell are you now?

35

The Central Medical Establishment doctor who dressed Caine's wound was a harassed-looking Scot with a tired smile. He had deft hands and a casual professional attitude that inspired confidence. He gave no name; nor did Caine ask for one. They both knew the rules.

The doctor told him he was in a private hospital. Although he was not supposed to, Caine knew that the Service maintained a maximum-security clinic on Old Court House Road, not far from Wolf Trap. The doctor told him that he'd lost a lot of blood before they got him there, and that the Service surgeons had to work hard, and fast, to save him. The heavy slug from Katja Renis's automatic had torn a hole in Caine's body low on the left-hand side, chipping a splinter out of his pelvis, burning past the large intestine and tearing apart the external oblique muscles. The doctor told him he was a

lucky man: he'd have his own built-in weather forecaster for the rest of his life.

'Every time there's rain in the air you'll have a wee twinge there, laddie,' he predicted. 'Probably get a job with the Meteorological Office when you retire.'

'How long have I been here?'

'Three days.'

Three days since the reckless race back towards Washington in Mitchell's car, fighting to stay conscious long enough to make the rendezvous in Annapolis.

'I can't remember meeting McClelland,' he said. 'But I suppose I must have.'

'You're here, aren't you?'

'Can I use the telephone?'

The doctor smiled and shook his head. 'Not till the dredgers are done with you, laddie,' he said. 'They'll be here tomorrow, so get some rest. You'll need it.'

The next day the debriefing officers from Station One arrived. They gave no names, either. One of them was about fifty, tall, thin, unsmiling, precise. He took all the notes. The other man, although much the same age, was positively tubby,

with dark hair, wide frank eyes, a ready smile and an ingratiating manner. He handled the Uher portable reel-to-reel recorder they brought with them and asked most of the questions. It was impossible to avoid thinking of them as Laurel and Hardy.

'Let's start at the beginning, shall we?' Laurel said, unsnapping the lock of his EIIR briefcase and taking out a Parker ballpoint. He was all business. Hardy smiled benevolently at Caine, as though to say, don't take it to heart, he's always like that. He radiated sympathy; he made you want to confide in him. Caine bet himself no money at all that they were the best dredging team in the Service.

'Bloody marvel, you are,' Hardy said, as if in admiration. 'One-man crime wave. Stolen cars, credit card fraud, interference with the US Mail. Then blowing up half of Easton. You've given us a lot of headaches, Caine. A lot of oil has had to be poured on a great deal of troubled water.'

'Costly, too,' Laurel put in. 'Very costly.'

'Are you going to tell me what happened?'

'All in good time, Caine,' Laurel said. 'All in good time.'

They spent three days with him, long, punishing twelve-hour days of questions and more questions, going over again and again every aspect of the Guchkov assignment, from Caine's initial involvement in Miami until the final moments at the big house in Easton. As Caine had thought, they were very professional and very, very thorough. He was glad he had nothing to hide from them.

As well as being professional and thorough, they were also fair: as the interrogation progressed, they told him more and more of what had happened subsequent to his getting the computer program to Dick McClelland that bloody night.

Immediately Caine handed over the program for the logic bomb, an ISS cover operation was set in motion. Caine was whisked away to the secret clinic near Wolf Trap. Mitchell's car, which he had appropriated to make the drive to the

492

rendezvous, was spirited away to a Service workshop from which it would emerge with a totally new identity. McClelland himself raced back to the ISS bureau in Arlington and spent the next half hour on the scrambler line to London.

At seven thirty the following morning, Sir James Bamford, the head of ISS, called a crisis meeting with the Joint Intelligence Chiefs, who concurred that their first priority was urgently to apprise NSA of the situation while at the same time concealing the role of ISS in uncovering it.

To ensure this, they decided to inform the Director of the National Security Agency that a British security officer named Kingly had been identified as a Soviet agent. Under interrogation he had revealed the existence of an ongoing Russian initiative codenamed Open Window whose purpose was to suborn and recruit a senior NSA officer named Butler Mitchell. Mitchell had been used by Russian military intelligence to plant a logic bomb inside the NSA computer network. A copy of the

program had been found in Kingly's possession, and this was transmitted to DIRNSA. His reaction to this intelligence was electric: within two hours of his receiving the program from Cheltenham, the logic bomb had been located and removed from the system.

Intensive analysis of the GRU program indicated that its function was to neutralize on command the American reconnaissance satellite known as Big Bird Three, in geostationary orbit above Diego Garcia in the Indian Ocean, and to trash reception and transmission from the tracking station at Pine Gap for a period of approximately fifteen minutes.

'What for?' Caine asked.

'We're coming to that,' Hardy said.

Crash program inspection of current satellite and aerial reconnaissance photographs showed unusual activity on the missile launch site at Baikonur. A new type of satellite, whose capabilities and functions were not known, was ready for launch into clandestine orbit.

'It was not unnaturally assumed that since the Soviets had gone to so much

trouble to effect a clandestine launch, the satellite's capabilities were inimical to our interests,' Laurel added, drily.

'So that was it,' Caine said. 'That was what bothered me. I couldn't figure out what Mitchell could possibly bring out of NSA that was worth so much money. But Guchkov didn't want him to bring anything out. He wanted him to take something in.'

'By George,' Laurel said, sardonically, 'I think he's got it.'

'What's happened to him? Is there any word yet?'

'No trace of him anywhere. He could have made it to the Kremlin in Washington,' Hardy said. 'If you're right and you hit him with that microbioinoculator, they'd have got him out — they couldn't take the risk of an autopsy. We're still checking.'

'Who was the girl?'

'Her name was Katja Renis. Czech refugee, been working in the School of Foreign Service at Georgetown University since 1973. Clean as a whistle until all this.'

'One way and another,' Hardy added, 'the Comrades are in some disarray. I suppose you get the credit for that, at least.'

Analysis of the logic bomb program also made it possible to establish the parameters within which the Soviet missile launch must take place to achieve optimum liftoff and orbit. These were projected as, respectively, within eighteen, forty-two, or sixty-six hours from the receipt of the signal activating the program. Acting on the premise that the countdown might commence almost at once, certain secret contingency plans involving air force pursuit planes carrying air-to-air missiles were immediately put into effect.

Then, less than six hours later, with the planes in the air and visible to Russian radar, the American Ambassador to Russia was admitted by his own urgent request to the presence of Secretary General Mikhail Gorbachev, to whom he presented a strongly-worded note from the President of the United States. With the letter came a copy of the GRU logic

bomb program that had been planted in the NSA computers by Butler Mitchell. The Presidential note stated unequivocally that if the launch planned by the Soviet Union were now to take place, the United States would feel itself at liberty to use all means at its disposal to destroy the missile.

Simultaneous with the destruction of the missile, all the details of the Russian initiative — with emphasis upon the GRU's role in smuggling sixty million dollars' worth of cocaine into the United States — would be released to the world press. This would indubitably result in a grave, and possibly permanent setback to plans for arms reduction talks at Geneva, and détente between East and West. The Secretary General's immediate response was requested.

'What happened?' Caine asked his interrogators.

'The launch has been indefinitely postponed.'

'So we win.'

'Win, lose, draw. They're only words. We do what we have to do. So do they.'

'You mean, no medal?'

'That's a good one,' Hardy said to Laurel. 'Eh?'

Laurel allowed himself a thin smile, as if he severely rationed them. 'It certainly is,' he said. Caine almost expected him to add 'Ollie'.

'What about Kingly?' Caine asked. Laurel's wispy smile disappeared, and his eyes became almost furtive.

'Of course,' Hardy said. 'You wouldn't have heard.'

'Heard what?'

'Hanged himself in his cell,' Hardy said. 'During interrogation.' The words did not match the evasiveness in his colleague's eyes. Caine did not pursue it. The British security services had their own equivalent of the CIA's 'maximal demotion'.

'Poor Miles.'

'Don't waste your sympathy on him, Caine,' Laurel said, stiffly. 'We still don't know how badly the treacherous bastard has compromised your organization.' It was the first time Caine had seen either of his interrogators show emotion. Laurel

obviously felt very strongly about treachery. Perhaps that was why he was such a good interrogator.

Caine got up and walked over to the window. He was still weak, but the wound was healing well. 'Have we got much more ground to cover?' he asked.

'Not much,' Hardy replied. 'We're nearly finished.'

'Any idea when I can return to active duty?'

'When you get out of here you'll be going back to London for redeployment,' Hardy told him. 'You've had much too high a profile to be any use here any more.'

'Will I have to fly straight back to London? Or would I be allowed to take a few days' leave first?'

'Where?'

'Miami?'

Laurel looked positively pained.

'I thought not,' Caine said. 'What about New York, then?'

'We'd have to get a reading on that,' Hardy said. 'Why do you want to go to New York?'

'To see a lady.'

'Mmmm,' Laurel frowned. 'That wouldn't be Lynda Sanchez, would it?'

'Tricky, Caine,' Hardy said. 'Having you back on the street so soon.'

'I could always resign,' Caine said, brightly. 'Then you wouldn't be able to stop me.'

'That's a good one,' Hardy beamed, looking at Laurel. 'Eh?'

They left soon afterwards. Caine ate, slept, ate, waited. For the first time, he was allowed to see the newspapers. One of them contained a brief item datelined Moscow that announced the unexpected retirement of General of the Army Pyotr I. Ivashutin and his replacement by a rising young star in Soviet military circles, Lieutenant-General, now Colonel-General, I. M. Drachev. The item went on to speculate that Ivashutin, known to be Director of Soviet Military Intelligence, had been relieved of his command for reasons not yet known in the West.

Time dragged by. Caine read a couple of the paperbacks that had been brought in for him, did his physiotherapy, and waited. Three days after his interrogation

a nurse came into the room pushing a trolley. On it was a phone.

'There's a call for you,' she said, and went out. Caine picked up the receiver. The remembered prim voice of Laurel came down the line.

'You're cleared for repatriation,' he said. 'Thought you'd like to know.'

'I'm accredited again?'

'With the not surprising exception of duty in the United States.'

'What about New York?'

'Sanctioned. Three days, no more.'

'Oooh, yer luvly,' Caine told him.

'Aren't I, though,' Laurel replied, drily. 'By the way, the Chief asked me to pass along some news. We finally found out what happened to your friend Guchkov. He's dead, Caine. Circulatory collapse on an Aeroflot flight from Washington to Moscow. Classic ricin poisoning symptoms. They made an emergency landing in Berlin, but he was dead before they touched down. So you did get him. I'm to tell you the Chief said 'well done'.'

Berlin: Caine smiled grimly at the irony. In his mind's eye he saw again

the desperation on the Russian's face as he wrestled with the wheel of the Mercedes, the sick certainty in his eyes at the moment of realization. Had he heard the words Caine shouted after him? It didn't matter one way or the other. The bastard was dead and that would have to do.

He got Lynda Sanchez's number from Information and called her. Her voice was guarded and anything but friendly.

'What do you want?'

'I want to see you, Lynda. To explain what happened.'

'I know what happened. And I don't plan to have it happen again,' she said.

'What about all the money I owe you?'

'Send me a cheque.'

'Lynda, Lynda, talk to me. Give me a chance to make it up to you.'

'Where are you calling from?'

'I'm in Washington. I'm taking the Amtrak to New York tonight. Why don't you fly up and join me?'

'Just like that?'

'I'll take you to every musical in town.'

'You walked out on me, Caine. You just disappeared.'

'I'll take you on that boat ride I promised you. All the way to Staten Island. How about it?'

'Look, you've got me flustered. I'm not used to that. Let me get back to you. Where are you staying?'

'Call me this time tomorrow at the Carlyle in New York.'

'The Carlyle? Are you rich, Caine?'

'Didn't I just tell you I'd take you for a ride on the ferry?' he said. 'The last of the big spenders, that's me. Come on, Lynda. Fly up here. It'll be my treat, the whole shmeer.'

Lynda Sanchez thought about that. 'It sounds terribly sinful.'

'Let's hope you're right,' he said.

He hung up, then sat for a long time looking at the telephone, surprised he had actually called her. She was the first woman he'd felt remotely attracted to since Jenny died. He thought back to the few days they had spent together, remembering Lynda's warmth and resource-fulness, her direct, no-nonsense approach to life. He remembered her walking across the parking lot in the Dadeland Mall.

Nothing noisy, but everything in the right places.

He pushed the button for the nurse. She went out and came back with a Samsonite softtop suitcase full of clothes, a wallet containing credit cards, a driving licence, and an acetate envelope containing ten twenty-dollar bills and two thousand dollars in traveller's cheques. As he got dressed, he thought about sharing New York with Lynda Sanchez. They would both have ghosts to exorcise there. It would be restorative; it might even turn out to be more. That was as much as anyone could hope for. In this business you only allowed yourself one dream at a time.

THE END

THE ECONOMICS OF HEALTH
AND HEALTH CARE

FIFTH EDITION

THE ECONOMICS OF HEALTH AND HEALTH CARE

Sherman Folland

Professor of Economics, Oakland University

Allen C. Goodman

Professor of Economics, Wayne State University

Miron Stano

Professor of Economics and Management, Oakland University

PEARSON

Prentice
Hall

Upper Saddle River, NJ 07458

Library of Congress Cataloging-in-Publication Data

Folland, Sherman.
 The economics of health and health care / Sherman Folland, Allen C. Goodman,
 Miron Stano.—5th ed.
 p. cm.
 Includes bibliographical references and index.
 ISBN 0-13-227942-8
 1. Medical economics. I. Goodman, Allen C. II. Stano, Miron. III. Title.

 RA410.F65 2007
 338.4'33621—dc22 2006044808

Acquisitions Editor: Jon Axelrod
Assistant Editor: Mary Kate Murray
AVP/Executive Editor: David Alexander
Editorial Director: Jeff Shelstad
Editorial Assistant: Michael Dittamo
Media Project Manager: Nancy Welcher
AVP/Executive Marketing Manager: Sharon Koch
Marketing Assistant: Patrick Barbera
Senior Managing Editor (Production): Cynthia Regan
Production Editor: Melissa Feimer
Permissions Supervisor: Charles Morris
Manufacturing Buyer: Diane Peirano
Cover Design: Kiwi Design
Cover Illustration/Photo: David McGlynn / Taxi / Getty Images
Composition/Full-Service Project Management: GGS Book Services

Credits and acknowledgments borrowed from other sources and reproduced, with
permission, in this textbook appear on appropriate page within text.

Pearson Education LTD. Pearson Education Australia PTY, Limited
Pearson Education Singapore, Pte. Ltd Pearson Education North Asia Ltd
Pearson Education, Canada, Ltd Pearson Educación de Mexico, S.A. de C.V.
Pearson Education–Japan Pearson Education Malaysia, Pte. Ltd

10 9 8 7 6 5 4 3 2
ISBN: 0-13-227942-8

Brief Contents

Contents

Preface

This is the fifth edition of a book that was conceived in 1990 and first published in 1993. To indicate how much the world of health economics has changed since 1993, we note that the first edition made but a single reference to "managed care."

From the beginning, we have sought to assist instructors in conveying a clear, step-by-step understanding of health economics to their students. We have also believed that it is important for instructors to demonstrate what health economics researchers are doing in theory and in empirical work. The book synthesizes contemporary developments around a set of economic principles including maximization of consumer utility and economic profit, and makes these principles accessible to undergraduate as well as to graduate students. Rather than organizing the book around the institutions specific to the health care economy, we have chosen to emphasize core economics themes as basic as supply and demand, as venerable as technology or labor issues, and as modern as the economics of information. We have constantly tried to improve accessibility to the book for the wide range of health services students and practitioners whose knowledge of economics may be more limited.

Students must have a working knowledge of the analytical tools of economics and econometrics to appreciate the field of health economics. Some students may be ready to plunge directly into "The Production of Health" (Chapter 5) upon completion of the introductory Chapter 1. However, Chapters 2 through 4 allow the students and their instructors to develop or to review needed analytical concepts before tackling the core subject matter. In Chapter 2, students with as little as one semester of microeconomics may review and study how economists analyze problems, using examples that are relevant to health economics. Chapter 3 provides a review of core statistical tools that characterize modern economic and health services analyses. Chapter 4 reviews the concept of economic efficiency, and shows how cost-benefit, and cost-effectiveness analyses fit into the general economic framework. As in our previous editions, no knowledge of calculus is needed in this part or elsewhere in the book.

Consistent with an emphasis on clarity of exposition, the book makes extensive use of graphs, tables, and charts. Discussion questions and exercises help students master the basics and prompt them to think about the issues. We also include features on up-to-date applications of theory and policy developments, as well as occasional tidbits containing purely background information.

We caution that some chapters, such as those on insurance, although devoid of advanced mathematics, will require considerable effort. No painless way is available to appreciate the scope of the contributions that scholars have made in recent years. More advanced students of the health care economy who seek further challenges can utilize a comprehensive references section, with over 900 sources, so that their (and our) work can be enriched through referral to the original sources.

What's Changed in the Fifth Edition?

The revised Chapter 4, "Economic Efficiency and Benefit Cost Analysis," now anchors our introductory section. This chapter reviews the concept of economic efficiency, and then builds on the framework to develop the main tools of program evaluation.

Our new Chapter 15, "The Physician's Practice," recognizes that physicians determine the content of hospital care, with hospitals often called the "doctors' workshops." However, doctors' information advantages over their patients lead some to question whether physicians are really "perfect," or true agents, or whether they induce patient demand in order to increase their incomes. We ask whether all doctors are well-informed regarding current best medical practice? Variations in surgery rates across small, seemingly identical geographic areas have caused many observers to be skeptics in this regard. Analyses of supplier-induced demand (SID) and small area variation (SAV) have been folded into this chapter.

Major changes have recently occurred in the U.S. Medicare program. The new Medicare Part D drug benefit has become a focus of U.S. health care policy and Chapter 21 provides details and careful analyses of this and other changes.

Finally, Chapter 24, "Epidemiology and Economics: HIV/AIDS in Africa" updates a popular chapter that we introduced in the previous edition that examines the economic consequences of epidemics. New to this edition is an estimate of the annual cost of the worldwide AIDS epidemic.

Additional Sources

The Internet now contains tables and charts that were once available only in book form, and then only after several years. We have chosen to focus on those sites that we believe to be both long lasting and reliable.

Bureau of the Census (www.census.gov)
Center for Disease Control (www.cdc.gov)
Centers for Medicare and Medicaid Services, formerly the Health Care Financing Administration, or HCFA (www.cms.hhs.gov)
Kaiser Family Foundation (www.kff.org), specializing in studies of health insurance.
National Institutes of Health (www.nih.gov)
Organization for Economic Cooperation and Development, for international data (www.oecd.org)
Social Security Administration (www.ssa.gov)

Health-related journals are increasingly accessible both in print and on the Internet. Most health economists make a point of browsing *Health Affairs*, an up-to-date policy journal. The *Journal of Health Economics* and *Health Economics* have emerged as the leading technical journals that specialize in health economics. As one can see from our reference section, there are also many other specialized journals to address readers' needs.

The *Handbook of Health Economics*, published in 2000, emerged as an invaluable source for specific topics, with more detail and more mathematic rigor than any text, including this one. Students and their teachers seeking research or dissertation topics should find this two-volume set to be most useful. However, the *Handbook* has not been updated, and we believe that our text provides a valuable supplement to *Handbook* topics.

Alternative Course Designs

The economics of health and health care encompasses an evolving literature, and there is no single "correct" order for the course design. U.S. economists typically organize topics through markets, with government roles coming much later. International economists and public health students and scholars often assign the governmental sector far more importance; it is "public" health, after all. Unfortunately, a text is necessarily linear in that one chapter has to follow another.

The *Economics of Health and Health Care* offers instructors considerable flexibility. We have divided the 24 chapters into six parts:

 I. Basic Economics Tools (Chapters 1–4)
 II. Supply and Demand (Chapters 5–9)
 III. Information and Insurance Markets (Chapters 10–13)
 IV. Key Players in the Health Care Sector (Chapters 14–17)
 V. Social Insurance (Chapters 18–22)
 VI. Special Topics (Chapters 23–24)

The categories are not entirely exclusive. Chapter 8, looking at the demand and supply of insurance, is as important to Part III on insurance as it is to Part II on demand and supply of goods.

From front to back, we follow an "economics" model in which consumers and firms are first analyzed in a world without government and governmental policies. As a result, explicit discussions of government policies do not come until Chapter 19, although regulation, licensing, and mandates are discussed in reference to other topics much earlier. Many economics instructors may wish to follow the chapters in the order of the book.

Instructors with public health or policy interests may wish to "tool up" on some of the earlier analyses, and then skip directly to Part V, in which we look at social insurance, health care regulation, and health care reform. After that, they may wish to browse selected topics. Although some analyses build on each other within chapters, we have sought to minimize cross-referencing among chapters.

Instructor's Material

Electronic Instructor's Manual with Solutions is available at the Instructor's Resource Center (IRC)

Instructors will be able to log on to www.prenhall.com/folland to access the Instructor's Resource Center (IRC). The Instructor's Manual will provide instructors with teaching hints, suggestions for discussion, and additional questions (with answers).

Acknowledgments

This book emerges from years of classroom and professional interaction, and we thank those students and colleagues who have discussed the economics of health and health care with us, and who have challenged our ideas. Annie Todd suggested the endeavor and introduced us to each other, and Tom McGuire convinced us that we could succeed. We have been blessed with outstanding editors—Jill Leckta, Leah Jewell, Rod Banister, Gladys Soto, Marie McHale, and, for this edition, Francesca Calogero and Michael Dittamo.

We have received outstanding support from our publishers, with John Travis, Maureen Wilson, and Kelly Warsak managing previous editions. Melissa Feimer is our most capable manager for this edition.

We are most grateful to instructors at over 300 universities in the United States, Canada, and abroad who have provided the market test for our work by adopting the book. Numerous professional colleagues generously offered their time and energy to read and critique various chapters. We thank:

Carson Bays, East Carolina University
James Burgess, Veterans Administration
Frank Chaloupka, University of Illinois–Chicago
Hope Corman, Rider College
Merton Finkler, Lawrence University
Howard Forman, Yale University
Andrew D. Foster, Brown University
Gary Fournier, Florida State University
H. E. Frech, III, University of California–Santa Barbara
Martin Gaynor, Carnegie Mellon University
John Goddeeris, Michigan State University
Warren Greenberg, George Washington University
Michael Grossman, City University of New York
Jack Hadley, Center for Health Policy Studies
James Hamilton, Wayne State University
Janet Hankin, Wayne State University
Govind Hariharan, Kennesaw State University
Ronald Horwitz, Oakland University
Harold Hotelling, Lawrence Technological University
Kathy A. Kelly, The University of Texas at Arlington
Paul Langley, University of Colorado
William Low, University of Northern British Columbia
Timothy McBride, St. Louis University
Tom McCarthy, National Economic Research Associates
Catherine McLaughlin, University of Michigan
Eleanor Nishiura, Wayne State University
Albert A. Okunade, University of Memphis
Martin Pernick, University of Michigan
Joann Richards, Oakland University
John Rizzo, Stoney Brook University
T. Paul Schultz, Yale University
Ya-chen Tina Shih, MEDTAP International, Inc.
Kosali Simon, Cornell University
John M. Tilford, University of Arkansas
Scott Vander Linde, Calvin College
Rob Verner, Kent State University
Kenneth Warner, University of Michigan
Gerard Wedig, University of Pennsylvania
Burton Weisbrod, Northwestern University
William White, Cornell University
Barbara Wolfe, University of Wisconsin–Madison
Michael Woolley, University of Southern California

We also thank the following colleagues who, with their classes, test-taught and test-learned parts of the text:

Randall Ellis, Boston University
Gail Jensen, Wayne State University
Thomas McGuire, Harvard University
Lee R. Mobley, Research Triangle Institute
Kathleen Possai, Wayne State University
Richard Scheffler, University of California–Berkeley
Nancy Wolff, Rutgers University

In the 16 years since we began this project, our wives have patiently supported our efforts and our young daughters have grown into talented young women. All have patiently watched their husbands and fathers learn about health economics. For all of this we are eternally grateful.

S.F.
Rochester, Michigan

A.C.G.
Detroit, Michigan

M.S.
Rochester, Michigan

CHAPTER

Introduction

The Relevance of Health Economics

Economic Methods and Examples of Analysis

Does Economics Apply to Health and Health Care?

Is Health Care Different?

New Challenges to Health Economists—Managed Care, Health Care Costs, and Health Insurance

Conclusions

Health and health care dominate the economic and political landscape in the United States and many other countries. Because most nations have experienced rapid increases in health care spending over the past 40 years, it is not surprising that health economics has emerged as a distinct specialty within economics. Health economics studies how resources are allocated to and within the health economy. The production of health care and its distribution across populations fall within this definition. Several examples will be introduced in this chapter to illustrate economic analysis of health care issues.

We also seek to demonstrate the magnitude and importance of the health sector. Various measures of size and growth will be used to establish the relevance of the health economy to both individual and national policy concerns.

The final goal of this chapter is to promote the theme that economics will help to explain how health care markets function. However, we will also stress the importance of recognizing features distinctive to health care markets so that appropriate modifications can be made to the economist's conventional analytical tools. Despite continuing controversy on major issues, health economists have been able to answer many questions of academic and policy interest.

The Relevance of Health Economics

The study of health economics is important and interesting in three related ways: (1) the size of the contribution of the health sector to the overall economy, (2) the national policy concerns resulting from the importance many people attach to the economic problems they face in pursuing and maintaining their health, and (3) the many health issues that have a substantial economic element.

1

The Size and Scope of the Health Economy

The health economy merits attention for its sheer size, constituting a large share of gross domestic product (GDP) in the United States, as well as other countries. It also represents a substantial capital investment and a large and growing share of the labor force.

Health Care's Share of GDP in the United States

More than $1 out of every $7 spent on final goods and services in the U.S. economy goes to the health sector. As recently as 1980, the share of GDP (the market value of final goods and services produced within the borders of a country in a year) devoted to health care was $1 in $11, and in 1960 it was just $1 in $20. Figure 1-1 tracks the health economy's share of GDP from 1960 to 2003. The conclusion? The health care sector is a large and growing portion of our economy.[1]

In calculating the *share* of GDP spent on health care, the effects of general inflation are netted out. Therefore, only three major possibilities exist to explain the substantially increased ratios shown in Figure 1-1:

1. People may be buying more health services. Patients may be consulting with health providers more frequently, doctors may be ordering more tests, or they may be prescribing more drugs.
2. People may be buying higher-quality health services, including products and services that previously were not available. Laser surgery, organ transplants, measles vaccines, and new treatments for burn victims have raised the quality of care since 1960. Economic theory suggests that people are willing to pay more for better quality.
3. Health care inflation may be higher than the general inflation rate. Higher incomes and the increased prevalence of insurance, including large government programs such as Medicare and Medicaid, may have led to increased health care prices over time.

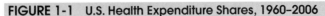

FIGURE 1-1 U.S. Health Expenditure Shares, 1960–2006

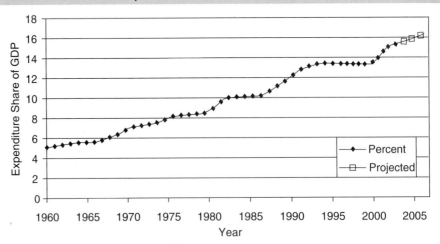

[1]In 2006, the Centers for Medicare and Medicaid Services announced slight changes in accounting methods that raised estimates of annual national health expenditures by 3 to 4 percent (Smith et al., 2006). Estimates of health shares of GDP correspondingly increased so that the 2003 ratio was revised from 15.3 percent to 15.9 percent. The 2004 share, the first year to rely exclusively on the new methods, was 16.0 percent. While these methods slightly change certain figures reported in this and later chapters, the new data reinforce the conclusion that health expenditures have continued to grow both absolutely and as shares of GDP.

We seek to understand these phenomena and their contributions to total spending. The study of demand, insurance, production, technology, and labor supply, among other topics, will help meet this challenge.

Health Care Spending in Other Countries

Examining the health economies of other countries enhances our understanding of the U.S. health economy. Many countries have large health care sectors and share the same major issues. Table 1-1 shows that in most countries the share of health care in the GDP grew rapidly between 1960 and 1980. However, the United States continued to grow into the 1990s, then slowed somewhat, before accelerating again around 2003. The data also indicate the relative size of the U.S. health economy compared to that of other countries. For example, the health care share of GDP in the United States is approximately twice as large as the share in the United Kingdom—a country with

TABLE 1-1 Health Expenditures as Percent of GDP in Selected OECD Countries

	1960	1970	1980	1990	2000	2003[a]
Australia	4.1	4.6	7.0	7.8	9.0	9.3
Austria	4.3	5.1	7.4	7.0	7.6	7.6
Belgium	3.4	4.0	6.4	7.4	8.7	9.6
Canada	5.4	7.0	7.1	9.0	8.9	9.9
Czech Republic			3.8	4.7	6.6	7.5
Denmark	3.6	8.0	9.1	8.5	8.4	9.0
Finland	3.8	5.6	6.4	7.8	6.7	7.4
France	3.8	5.4	7.1	8.6	9.3	10.1
Germany	4.8	6.2	8.7	8.5	10.6	11.1
Greece		6.1	6.6	7.4	9.9	9.9
Hungary				7.1	7.1	7.8
Iceland	3.0	4.7	6.2	8.0	9.3	10.5
Ireland	3.7	5.1	8.4	6.1	6.3	7.3
Italy				7.9	8.1	8.4
Japan	3.0	4.5	6.5	5.9	7.6	7.9
Korea			4.2	4.5	4.7	5.6
Luxembourg		3.6	5.9	6.1	5.5	6.1
Mexico				4.8	5.6	6.2
Netherlands		6.9	7.5	8.0	8.3	9.8
New Zealand	4.3	5.1	5.9	6.9	7.8	8.1
Norway	2.9	4.4	7.0	7.7	7.7	10.3
Poland				4.9	5.7	6.0
Portugal		2.6	5.6	6.2	9.2	9.6
Spain	1.5	3.6	5.4	6.7	7.4	7.7
Sweden	4.7	6.9	9.1	8.4	8.4	9.2
Switzerland	4.9	5.5	7.4	8.3	10.4	11.5
Turkey		2.4	3.3	3.6	6.6	6.6
United Kingdom	3.9	4.5	5.6	6.0	7.3	7.7
United States	5.0	6.9	8.7	11.9	13.1	15.0

[a]2003 or most recent year.

Source: Organization for Economic Cooperation and Development (OECD) Health Data 2005. Copyright OECD, 2005.

national health insurance. Is care costlier in the United States? Is it higher quality care, or is more simply being consumed?

Importance of the Health Economy in Personal Spending

Because it accounts for such a large share of the domestic product, the size of the health economy is also reflected through other key indicators. Two of these are especially easy to relate to at the personal level: (1) share of income spent on medical care and (2) number of jobs in the health economy.

Table 1-2 provides data on how U.S. consumers spend their disposable incomes. Table 1-2a shows that in 2004, consumers spent 17.1 percent of their budgets on medical care, as opposed to 13.8 percent on food and 14.9 percent on housing. When we add drug expenditures, we find that slightly more than $1 in $5 of consumption expenditures goes to medical care plus drugs and sundries. These figures represent a major shift in spending patterns. As recently as 1960, food represented about 25 percent of spending, housing about 15 percent, and medical care only 5 percent.

Importance of the Health Economy to the Labor Force

The flip side of spending is reflected through the jobs that have been created in the health economy. Table 1-3a shows that over 13.6 million people, almost 10 percent of the labor force, worked at various health service sites in 2003; almost 42 percent of them worked in hospitals.

TABLE 1-2 Total Personal Consumption Expenditures (in $ billions) by Type, 2004

	Total	*Percent of Total*
a. Personal Consumption Expenditures		
Total (in $ millions)	8214.3	100.0
Durable Goods	987.8	12.0
Nondurable Goods		
Food	1,134.7	13.8
Clothing and shoes	329.0	4.0
Gasoline, fuel oil, other energy	249.9	3.0
Services		
Housing	1,221.1	14.9
Household operation	446.2	5.4
Transportation	306.9	3.7
Medical care	**1,401.1**	**17.1**
Recreation	338.8	4.1
All other	1,798.8	21.9
b. Detailed Medical and Drug Expenditures		
Medical and Drug Expenditures	1,654.4	20.1
Physicians	323.3	3.9
Dentists	80.0	1.0
Other professional services	219.9	2.7
Hospitals and nursing homes	657.4	8.0
Health insurance	120.5	1.5
Drug preparations and sundries	253.3	3.1

TABLE 1-3A	Employed Civilians at Health Services Sites: 2003

Category	*Total Employment (in thousands)*
All Employed Civilians	137,736
All Health Services Sites	13,615
Hospitals	5,652
Nursing and care facilities	1,877
Home health care services	741
Outpatient care centers	873
Offices and clinics of physicians	1,673
Offices and clinics of dentists	771
Offices and clinics of chiropractors	142
Other health services sites	1,886

Source: U.S. Department of Health and Human Services, *Health United States, 2004,* Table 101.

TABLE 1-3B	Active Health Personnel and Number per 100,000 Population (in parentheses)			
Profession	*1970*	*1980*	*1990*	*2001*
Physicians	290,862 (143)	427,122 (190)	567,610 (230)	793,263 (274)
Dentists	95,700 (47)	121,900 (54)	147,500 (59)	168,000 (60)[b]
Optometrists	18,400 (9)	22,300 (10)	26,000 (10)	32,200 (11)[b]
Pharmacists	112,750 (55)	142,780 (63)	161,900 (64)	196,000 (70)
Podiatrists	7,110 (4)	7,000 (3)	10,600 (4)	12,424 (4)
Registered Nurses	750,000 (369)	1,272,900 (560)	1,789,600 (714)	2,201,800 (789)[a]

[a]1999 figure.
[b]2000 figure.
Source: U.S. Department of Health and Human Services, *Health United States, 2004,* Table 105.

Table 1-3b indicates the considerable growth in health care personnel since 1970 for selected professions. In 1970, there were 290,862 physicians, or 143 physicians per 100,000 people. By 2001, the number of physicians had more than doubled, and the number of registered nurses had almost tripled. The number of registered nurses per 100,000 people had also more than doubled from 369 to 789.

Reflecting the increases in spending, the health care sector serves increasingly as a source of employment. Thus, cutbacks in spending on health care will typically mean cutbacks in employment opportunities.

Capital Investment in the Health Economy

In addition to labor, a substantial amount of capital has been drawn to the U.S. health care system. The number of nursing home beds increased from about 1.3 million in 1976 to 1.8 million in 2002 (beds per person, however, decreased slightly). The number of beds in more than 6,000 short-stay hospitals peaked in the late 1970s, at almost 1.5 million, but the total number has leveled at approximately 975 thousand (in 2002). There are also considerable and growing amounts of other capital—such as diagnostic equipment—per bed.

Time—The Ultimate Resource

Data on health care expenses and labor and capital inputs reflect only some of the items used by people to produce health. Inputs that are not bought and sold in the marketplace are also important. These include peoples' own contributions of time and effort in producing health care and entail real costs to society.

For example, when people use their own time to produce better health for themselves, or for loved ones, as caregivers, the cost to the individuals and society is the value of the leisure that is foregone. Adults who are taking care of their elderly parents for two hours per day, seven days per week, provide care that might otherwise have to be purchased in the market for $10 per hour or more. In this simple illustration, the caregivers provide care worth over $7,000 per year. Though such examples are not necessarily the population norm, these time costs must be added to our measured health care costs.

We have stressed inputs, but the contribution of health resources to the economy is ultimately a measure of the value of the output—health itself. The value of improvements to our health is measured both in consumption and production. We value health both for its own sake and for its contribution to the production of other goods. The intrinsic value of being healthy is ultimately the value we attach to life and limb, which people commonly describe as infinite in certain circumstances and at least substantial in others. The value of health in the production of other goods is exemplified not just in reduced absenteeism rates but also in output per worker on the job. In both its consumption and production aspects, the output of the health sector makes a substantial contribution to the economy.

The Importance Attached to Economic Problems of Health Care Delivery

The health sector receives attention from policymakers because of its widely perceived problems. The substantial resources devoted to health care are reflected in a more meaningful way through the average level of this nation's spending for health care. Table 1-4 provides various measures of health care spending and its growth since 1960.

TABLE 1-4 National Health Expenditures (NHE) and Other Data for Selected Years, 1960 to 2006 ($ in billions)

Year	NHE	% Growth in NHE	GDP	NHE per capita	NHE % GDP	CPI	Price Indexes Hospital Rooms	Physician Services
1960	26.7		527	143	5.1	29.6	9.3	21.9
1970	73.1	10.6	1,040	348	7.0	38.8	23.6	34.5
1980	245.8	12.9	2,796	1,067	8.8	82.4	68.0	76.5
1990	696.0	11.0	5,803	2,738	12.0	130.7	175.4	160.8
1995	990.3	7.3	7,400	3,698	13.4	152.4	251.2	208.8
2000	1,309.9	7.2	9,817	4,560	13.3	172.2	N.A.	244.7
2003	1,678.9	7.7	11,094	5,670	15.3	184.0	N.A.	260.6
2004[a]	1,804.7	7.5	11,719	6,040	15.4			
2005[a]	1,936.5	7.3	12,376	6,423	15.6			
2006[a]	2,077.5	7.3	13,019	6,830	16.0			

[a]Projections from Heffler et al. (2005).

Source: Centers for Medicare & Medicaid Services, Office of the Actuary: Data from the National Health Statistics Group.

Table 1-4 shows how national health expenditures (NHE) grew from $27 billion in 1960 to $1,678.9 billion in 2003. During that period, the U.S. population grew by 59 percent from 186 million to 296 million. Thus, NHE per capita rose by a multiple of almost 40, from $143 in 1960 to $5,670 in 2003.

However, the real increase is what matters most. Prices, as measured by the broad-based consumer price index (CPI), rose 522 percent over the same period. After deflating by the CPI, we find that real expenditures per capita in 2003 were about 6.38 times the 1960 level—still a hefty increase.[2]

Inflation

Although we have deflated the spending values using the CPI, medical care prices have grown faster historically than prices overall. Table 1-4 also shows the pattern of health care inflation since 1960. Note that hospital and physician care prices have risen much faster than the CPI—a phenomenon that is typical of other health care services and commodities as well.

Growing costs are a common problem for maintaining health programs, and they have spurred numerous cost-containment efforts by the government in the past two decades. Understanding and evaluating the effects of such regulatory measures are important tasks for the health economist.

Access

For many, the rising costs significantly reduce accessibility to health care. Financial affordability influences demand for most goods and services, and there are many reasons why some people do not have health insurance. What is clear is that the number of uninsured has risen in the United States, and close to 45 million people now lack insurance. Many more are considered to have inadequate insurance. The problems of cost, inflation, and uninsured people have led to numerous proposals for some form of national health insurance. Later in this book, we will examine several broad groups of plans, as well as the national health insurance programs that exist in other countries.

Quality

Increases in the quality of care contribute to spending increases. Often, the focus is on ensuring quality through professional licensure and certification and, especially for hospitals, through quality-assurance programs. At the same time, concerns arise about access to high quality care for those without insurance or with minimal insurance. Some also are concerned that the quality of care in the United States is often excessive, especially for some forms of "high-tech" treatment. For such treatments, the costs of resources may exceed the benefits to patients. The interplay among insurance, technology, and consumption is of major interest to economists.

The Economic Side to Other Health Issues

Production, costs, and insurance are naturally issues that involve economics, but many other health issues have economic components, even though they may seem to be purely medical concerns. A few examples illustrate this point.

The choice of a health care treatment seems purely medical to many people, but physicians and other providers are increasingly aware that alternative treatments can be evaluated and compared on economic grounds. It is necessary to examine the costs

[2]The five-fold increase is determined by dividing $5,670 (2003 spending) by 1.840 (2003 CPI divided by 100) and dividing the result by the corresponding ratio for 1960. National health spending updates are available at the Centers for Medicare & Medicaid Services Web site (http://cms.hhs.gov).

of alternative techniques. Physicians are also increasingly sensitive to the economic side of the patient-physician relationship. The patient's preferences are considered valid in determining the appropriateness of a given treatment.

We also must explore the economic reasons behind people's health choices. People take care of themselves well at some times and poorly at other times. People's desired health status can be understood as a meaningful economic choice. Even addiction to a harmful substance can be understood better when analyzed as a possibly rational economic choice. Other health issues clearly have an economic aspect: What role should the government play in health? What health care investments should a developing country make? Should cigarette advertising be banned? Questions like these are not solely economic, but they have an economic side.

Economic Methods and Examples of Analysis

We have already provided a formal definition of health economics as "the study of the allocation of resources to and within the health economy." From another perspective, however, economics is what economists actually do and how they apply economics to health. Economists in practice use certain characteristic approaches to their analyses of the world.

Features of Economic Analysis

Many distinctive features of economics might be exhaustively identified, but we emphasize four:

1. Scarcity of societal resources
2. Assumption of rational decision making
3. Concept of marginal analysis
4. Use of economic models

Scarcity of Resources

Economic analysis is based on the premise that individuals must give up some of one resource in order to get some of another. At the national level, this means that increasing shares of GDP going to health care ultimately imply decreasing shares going for other uses. The "opportunity cost" of (what we give up to get) health care may be substantial.

While most people will recognize the money costs of goods and services, economists view time as the ultimate scarce resource. Individuals sell their time for wages, and many individuals will refuse overtime work even if offered more than their normal wage rate—because "it's not worth it." Similarly, many will pass up "free" health care because the travel and waiting time costs are too high.

Rational Decision Making

Economists typically approach problems of human economic behavior by assuming that the decision maker is a rational being. Rationality is effectively defined as "making choices that best further one's own ends given one's resource constraints." Some behaviors may appear irrational. However, when disputes over rationality arise, economists often attempt to point out, perhaps with some delight, that so-called irrational behavior often makes sense when the incentives facing the decision maker are properly understood.

Marginal Analysis

Mainstream economic analyses feature reasoning at the margin. To make an appropriate choice, decision makers must understand the cost as well as the benefit of the next, or marginal, unit. Marginal analysis often entails the mental experiment of trading off the incremental costs against the incremental benefits at the margin.

A prime example involves the purchase of brand-name drugs. Patients' decisions to buy brand-name drugs, particularly for elective treatments, may depend critically on whether they must pay $2 or $3 per pill, or, instead, a fraction of those amounts if prescription drug insurance is available.

Use of Models

Finally, economics characteristically develops models to depict its subject matter. The models may be described in words, graphs, or mathematics. This text features words and graphs. These models may be understood as metaphors for reality. We say, "This is the market for physician care," meaning "this is like the market for physician care." Any model can be pushed too far and must be tested against a sense of reality and ultimately against the facts. Nonetheless, they can be apt, and we can learn from them.

In economic analysis, the models are often abstract. Abstract models help to make sense of the world, in economics as in everyday life. A young child asking what the solar system is like will undoubtedly be shown the familiar drawing of the sun and planets in their orbits—an abstract model. The drawing is quickly grasped, yet no one supposes that the sky really looks like this.

Examples of Health Economics Analysis

What do economists do? Economists see, on the one hand, that physicians, clinics, and hospitals use labor and machines just like other segments of the economy. These health care providers charge prices for their services, and they hope to earn at least enough to keep themselves from wanting to switch to other types of work. In this sense, the economic theories that tell us what firms do and how they combine resources to maximize profits, provide insights into how the health care sector works.

On the other hand, the health sector is complicated. Consumers must often depend on health providers to tell them whether they are ill, and, if so, what they should do. Providers often prescribe treatments seemingly irrespective of their costs. Physicians may not only be entrepreneurs themselves, but they may also manage their own laboratories, control hospitals, or influence insurance companies that also affect the health care sector.

Some of the earliest work in health economics addressed several of these issues. Milton Friedman and Simon Kuznets, both of whom later became Nobel laureates, studied the so-called physician shortage of the 1930s. They discovered that although physicians earned 32 percent per year more than dentists, their training costs were 17 percent higher. The remaining difference was still large, however, and Friedman and Kuznets (1945) attributed part of the higher returns on investment enjoyed by physicians to barriers to entry into the medical profession. Barriers to entry tend to lower the supply of physicians, hence raising physicians' incomes and raising the rate of return on their investment in their own education. The situation also meant that the value to society of producing one more physician exceeded the costs of producing one more physician.

Reuben Kessel addressed the practice, common some years ago, for physicians to charge different fees to different patients. The practice was often interpreted as an act of charity, for it was thought that physicians were charging lower fees to poorer

patients. Kessel (1958) showed, however, that the practice of charging different fees might also be understood as a form of price discrimination that allowed physicians to increase their profits by charging more to those patients with greater ability to pay.

Kessel presented historical analysis supporting his case, arguing that physicians used the system of hospital privileges to perpetuate price discrimination. Physicians, in order to practice, are usually affiliated with hospitals. Historically, those who adopted competitive economic practices were often branded as "unethical" and could be denied membership in county medical societies, access to specialty certification, or hospital privileges.

These examples also illustrate two features of health economics. The first is the interdisciplinary nature of health research. Economists must know how health care is delivered. This information comes from health care providers, as well as from members of other disciplines, such as public health, sociology, and psychology, who study how organizations operate.

The second feature concerns the institutions in the health care system, including hospitals, insurers, or regulators. Examples of these include the following:

- relations of doctors to hospitals
- the organization and practices of the health insurance industry
- licensing and certification of health care providers

Such institutional concerns do not necessarily distinguish health economics from other forms of economic analysis, but the particular history and present form of health care institutions do set health economics apart from other fields. We must take care to describe the institutional characteristics of the health sector in order to devise appropriate models.

Does Economics Apply to Health and Health Care?

Many observers complain that economics is irrelevant to the study of health. This issue is raised often enough in serious contexts to require consideration. The complaint suggests a model of health care in which health is considered to be primarily a technical issue of medical science, better left to experts. One gets sick, and one sees a doctor who provides the medically appropriate treatment.

If economics studies how scarce resources are used to produce goods and services and then how these goods and services are distributed, then clearly economics applies. Certainly health care resources are scarce; in fact, it is their cost that concerns most people. There is no question that health care is produced and distributed.

Nevertheless, one can question whether the characteristic approaches of economics apply to health care. Are health care consumers rational? Do they calculate optimally at the margin? Imagine a loved one suffering cardiac arrest. Is there time or reasoning power left to calculate? Would anyone question the price of emergency services under such circumstances?

However, much of health care simply does not fit this emergency image. A considerable amount of health care is elective, meaning that patients have and will perceive some choice over whether and when to have the diagnostics or treatment involved. Much health care is even routine, involving problems such as upper respiratory infections, back pain, and diagnostic checkups. The patient often has prior experience with these concerns. Furthermore, even in a real emergency, the consumer has agents to make or help make decisions on his or her behalf. Traditionally the physician has served as the agent and more recently, the care manager has also entered the process. Thus, rational choices can be made.

FIGURE 1-2 Demand Response of Ambulatory Mental and Medical Care in the Rand Health Insurance Experiment

Source: Keeler, Manning, and Wells (1988) for mental health care; Keeler and Rolph (1988) for medical care.

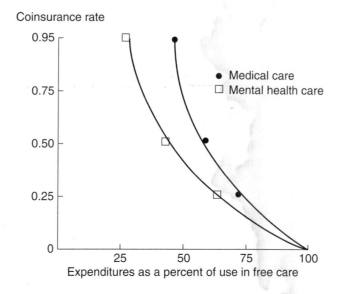

An Example: Does Price Matter?

Does price matter? Many have argued that health care is so different from other goods that consumers do not respond to financial incentives. These views have been justified by arguments that demand is based on need, or arguments that patients leave decisions entirely to their providers, who are concerned with their own interests rather than how much patients have to pay.

Data from the Rand Health Insurance Experiment give an unequivocal answer to this question: Yes, economic incentives matter. Figure 1-2 examines the use of ambulatory mental health and medical care where amounts of health care consumed are measured along the horizontal axis. These amounts are scaled in percentage terms from zero to 100 percent, where 100 percent reflects the average level of care consumed by the group that used the most care on average. This group, not surprisingly, is the group with "free" care. The vertical axis measures the economic incentives as indicated by the coinsurance rate—the percentage of the bill paid out directly by the consumer. Thus, a higher coinsurance rate reflects a higher price to the consumer.

The curve shown in Figure 1-2 is similar to an economist's demand curve in that it shows people consuming more care as the care becomes less costly to the consumer in terms of dollars paid out-of-pocket. More importantly, the curve demonstrates that economic incentives do matter. Those facing higher prices demand less care.

Is Health Care Different?

Although economics certainly applies to health care, it is more challenging to answer the question of how directly and simply it applies. Is economic theory so easily applicable that a special field of health economics is not even necessary? Is health care so special as to be unique? Or is the truth somewhere in between?

We argue that health care has many distinctive features, but that it is not unique in any of them. What is unique, perhaps, is the combination of features and even the sheer number of them. We review these distinctive features to alert students as to those

salient features of health care that require special attention. In each case where health is distinctive in economic terms, a body of economic theory and empirical work can be found that illuminates the issue.

Presence and Extent of Uncertainty

When Nobel laureate Kenneth Arrow (1963) directed his attention to the economics of health, he helped establish health economics as a field. He stressed the prevalence of uncertainty in health care, on both the demand side and the supply side. Consumers are uncertain of their health status and need for health care in any coming period. This means that the demand for health care is irregular in nature from the individual's perspective; likewise, the demand facing a health care firm is irregular.

Uncertainty is also prevalent on the supply side. Standard economic analysis often assumes that products, and the pleasures that they bring, are well understood by the purchasers. The purchase of steak, milk, new clothes, or a ticket to a basketball game provides expected well-being that is easily known and understood. In contrast, several cases of product uncertainty exist in the health field. Consumers often do not know the expected outcomes of various treatments without physicians' advice, and in many cases physicians themselves cannot predict the outcomes of treatments with certainty.

Arrow argued that uncertainty on both the supply and demand sides might lead to the result that insurance markets for various risks would often fail to arise. These factors suggested a role for government. Although others dispute the conclusion, the point stands that uncertainty is a prominent feature in the field of health, and the tools of economic analysis of uncertainty and risk will need to be used to analyze health issues fully. In a special 2001 edition of the *Journal of Health Politics, Policy, and Law* (Peterson, 2001), 27 health policy experts revisit Arrow's article to explore its impact on the evolution of health economics and health policy research.

Prominence of Insurance

Consumers purchase insurance to guard against this uncertainty and risk. Because of health insurance, neither most Americans nor citizens of other countries pay directly for the full costs of their health care. Rather, the costs are paid indirectly through coinsurance and through insurance premiums that are often, although not always, purchased through participation in the labor force.

Table 1-5 provides data on the sources of payment for personal health care services for selected years since 1960. In 1960, almost 52 percent of all personal health care expenditures were paid out-of-pocket, meaning that 48 percent was paid by third-party

TABLE 1-5 Health Service and Supplies ($ in billions) by Source of Payment

Year	Total	Out-of-Pocket	Private Health Insurance	Other Private	State/Local	Total Federal	Total Third Party	Percent Third Party
1960	25.0	12.9	5.9	0.6	3.4	2.2	12.1	48.3
1970	67.3	25.1	15.5	1.9	9.2	15.6	42.2	62.7
1980	233.5	58.2	68.2	9.4	31.5	66.1	175.2	75.1
1990	669.6	137.3	233.5	31.1	85.8	181.9	532.3	79.5
2000	1260.9	193.1	450.6	55.5	168.8	392.9	1067.8	84.7
2003	1614.2	230.5	600.6	61.5	214.2	507.5	1383.7	85.7

Source: Centers for Medicare & Medicaid Services Table NHE03. See http://www.cms.hhs.gov/NationalHealthExpendData.

payers (either private or government). In 2003, almost 86 percent was paid by third parties, with the increase due to the growth of both private insurance and public programs. Certainly, such separation from the direct payment must weaken some of the price effects that might be expected in standard economic analysis. Insurance changes the demand for care, and it potentially also changes the incentives of providers.

The changed provider incentives concern us more as the insurance portion of the bill increases. How the insurers pay the health care firm thus becomes a critical fact of economic life. Whether insurers cover a procedure, or a professional's services, may determine whether providers use the procedure. Furthermore, changes in insurance payment procedures can substantially change provider behavior and provider concerns. This was evidenced by Medicare's decision to change its hospital payment system during the 1980s to a system based on Diagnosis Related Groups (DRGs) in order to control costs more effectively.

Problems of Information

Uncertainty can in part be attributed to lack of information. Actual and potential information problems in health care markets raise many economic questions. Sometimes information is unavailable to all parties concerned. For example, neither gynecologists nor their patients may recognize the early stages of cervical cancer without a Pap smear. At other times, the information in question is known to some parties but not to all, and then it is the asymmetry of information that is problematic.

The problems of information mean that careful economic analysts must modify their methods. Standard analyses often assume that consumers have the necessary knowledge about the quality of the food or the clothing that they purchase. People purchase beef as opposed to fish, or cotton as opposed to nylon fabrics. They base their decisions on the characteristics of the goods, their prices, and their abilities to bring pleasure to the buyers.

The purchase of health goods and services departs substantively from this model. Consumers may not know which physicians or hospitals are good, capable, or even competent. They may not know whether they are ill or what should be done if they are. This lack of information often makes a consumer, sometimes referred to as the principal, dependent on the provider, as an agent, in a particular way. The provider offers both the information and the service, leading to the possibility of conflicting interests. Newhouse (2002), for example, speaks of a health care "quality chasm" that may be traced to both inadequate consumer information and to inadequate financial incentives. Health economics must address the provision of health services in this context.

Large Role of Nonprofit Firms

Economists often assume that firms maximize profits. Economic theory provides models that explain how businesses allocate resources in order to maximize profits. Yet many health providers, including many hospitals, insurers, and nursing homes, have nonprofit status.

What, then, motivates these nonprofit institutions if they cannot enjoy the profits of their endeavors? The economist must analyze the establishment and perpetuation of nonprofit institutions, and understand the differences in their behaviors from for-profit firms. This problem has recently emerged in the context of academic medical centers in the United States. Many current college students, and most certainly their parents and grandparents, are aware of the prominent role of great hospitals, affiliated with great universities such as Harvard or Johns Hopkins. The citizenry is aware of the hospitals as centers of health care—the larger medical community views them as research centers. Yet with the changing economics of the twenty-first century, both roles are open to question.

Restrictions on Competition

Economists and policymakers generally laud the competitive market because the entry of firms or providers in the face of high prices and/or profits will cause the other firms or providers to lower their prices. This entry and the resulting price reduction improve the well-being of consumers.

Nevertheless, the health sector has developed many practices that effectively restrict competition. These practices include licensure requirements for providers, restrictions on provider advertising, and standards of ethical behavior that enjoin providers from competing with each other. We must explain the forces that generated such practices and understand their potential benefits, but we must also understand their anticompetitive impacts and measure the magnitudes of the higher costs they may impose on society.

Regulation to promote quality or to curb costs also reduces the freedom of choice of providers and may influence competition. There is often substantial interest in regulating the health care sector. The causes as well as the impacts of the regulations require considerable attention. The pharmaceutical industry, for example, contends that patent protection is crucial for its financial stability. Economists must consider how regulations are developed, as well as who gains and who loses from them.

Other types of government interventions, particularly antitrust action, can serve to promote competition. Economic theory suggests that in the case of monopoly power, production may be reduced with a corresponding increase in price. Control of the monopolies or antitrust action to curb monopolistic practices may thus benefit the consumer.

Role of Equity and Need

Poor health of another human being often evokes a feeling of concern that distinguishes health care from many other goods and services. Many advocates express this feeling by saying that people ought to get the health care they need regardless of whether they can afford it. In practice, "need" is difficult to define, and distributing care under certain definitions of need may cause more economic harm than good. Yet the word signals a set of legitimate concerns for analysis.

Government Subsidies and Public Provision

In most countries, the government plays a major role in the provision of health services. In the United States programs such as Medicare and Medicaid inject the government into the financing of and payment for services. In addition, under many circumstances, governments provide health care services through clinics and hospitals. All told, government spending in the United States of $766 billion in 2003 accounted for over 45 percent of total national health care spending of $1,679 billion.

New Challenges to Health Economists—Managed Care, Health Care Costs, and Health Insurance

From the mid-1960s into the early 1990s, the U.S. health care system grew resolutely. As we saw in Figure 1-1, health expenditures went from 5.3 percent of the GDP in 1960 to 8.9 percent in 1980, 12.2 percent in 1990, and 15.3 percent in 2003. Buoyed by increased income, more generous insurance, and the availability of state-of-the-art technology and high-cost treatments, consumers and their insurers increased their health care spending dramatically.

The "fee-for-service" (FFS) system that fed this increase asked providers, mainly physicians and hospitals, how much they spent and then reimbursed them for their costs. The FFS system did not offer incentives for consumers to shop for less expensive

care, nor did it foster cost-cutting competition among providers. Particularly for those with health insurance, the health care system provided high-quality care (reflected by the frequent use of specialists and generously long hospital stays) at a high price.

In the 1980s, the atmosphere began to change. Facing increased expenditures in its Medicare program, the federal government initiated a payment scheme based on DRGs that told hospitals how much they would be paid and gave them the financial responsibility of cutting costs or losing money. This policy had a particularly strong impact on the length of hospitalization, which is one of the most expensive features of health care.

In addition, health maintenance organizations (HMOs), which had comprised only a small portion of the health care sector, were encouraged by federal legislation as alternative, lower-cost providers of health care. Through selective contracting with hospitals and physicians and stricter review of service utilization, these HMOs and their variants such as preferred provider organizations (PPOs) provided alternative forms of less expensive health care. Their enrollments burgeoned.

This emergence of such "managed care" plans has fueled a substantial and sometimes heated debate. Do the less expensive managed care plans wring the waste out of the health care system, or do they provide inadequate care? Are patients discharged from hospitals "quicker but sicker?" The popular press has covered the debate in great depth on television, in magazines, and in newspapers, extending even to the cartoon pages. Some readers may remember a puzzled Mike Doonesbury watching his physician and his insurance agent fighting over the proper diagnostic test on an injured knee.

Policy analysts and health care professionals have joined the debate. The journal *Health Affairs* periodically features predictions by analysts at the Centers for Medicare & Medicaid Services or CMS. Although health expenditure shares leveled off in the mid-1990s at about 13.5 percent of the GDP, the general public, and many analysts, were surprised to see the health expenditure share jump from 13.3 percent in 2000 to 15.3 percent by 2003. The particularly large jump in the health care share may have been caused more by a slowing economy (the denominator of the share of expenditures in GDP) than rising health spending (the numerator), but the sheer magnitude of the jump has raised concerns. One study suggests that health expenditure shares are likely to continue this upward trend, rising to 17.3 percent of GDP by 2010 and 18.7 percent by 2014 (see Heffler and colleagues, 2005). There are three major reasons:

1. **The changing impact of managed care.** The leveling off in the 1990s reflected the shift of a large portion of the population from FFS to the managed care sector, a change that provided a one-time decrease in expenditures. Managed care costs, however, grow at about the same rate as FFS costs. Hence, cost growth, which had been mitigated by a shift to lower-cost care, will resume because managed care costs grow also. Moreover, many consumers rebelled against highly publicized supposedly heavy-handed rationing tactics imposed by HMOs, and chose (most often through their employers) a "managed care light" variation with less stringent gate-keeping and fewer health care utilization controls. This lighter hand was almost certainly less effective in controlling costs.
2. **The demographic increase in older Americans who need more care.** Entering the second decade of the twenty-first century, the large baby boom population (born from the late 1940s to the mid-1960s) will be moving into the 55- to 64-age cohort. The higher costs that traditionally accompany this cohort will apply to an increasingly large portion of the population.
3. **Costly medical technology.** The continued availability and growth of state-of-the-art technology and high-cost treatments put additional upward pressure on health care costs. See Box 1-1 for an examination of this issue in an international perspective.

Technological Change and Health Care Costs—Why Rising Health Care Costs Affect All Nations

In a March 2005 speech to the National Association of Business Economics, Chairman of the Council of Economic Advisers, Harvey Rosen, noted that over the last several decades, the quality of health care has improved—diagnostic techniques, surgical procedures, and therapies for a wide range of medical problems have all continually improved. Treatment of a heart attack today is simply not the same "commodity" as treatment of a heart attack in 1970. Although innovations like coronary bypass surgery and cardiac catheterization have raised expenditures per heart patient, they have actually reduced the prices of obtaining various health outcomes, such as surviving hospitalization due to a heart attack.

Rosen noted that some improvements in medical technique are quite inexpensive. Prescribing aspirin for heart attack victims leads to a substantial improvement in their survival probabilities. But new medical technologies are often costly. For example, it costs about $2 million to acquire a PET (positron emission tomography) machine, which can detect changes in cells before they form a tumor large enough to be spotted by X-rays or MRI. Such costly improvements lead medical expenditures to grow.

This technology-based theory also helps explain why countries with different health care financing and delivery systems have all experienced increases in health care expenditures. Rosen argued that these societies have at least one thing in common—they have all been exposed to the same expensive innovations in technology. The technology-based explanation puts any debate over cost containment in a new light. Is it a bad thing if costs are rising mostly because of quality improvements? A key question in this context is whether people value these innovations at their incremental social cost. No one knows for sure, but economist Dana Goldman reiterates a provocative insight: "if you had the choice between buying 1960s medicine at 1960s prices or today's medicine at today's prices, which would you prefer?" A vote for today's medicine is validation of the improvement, and willingness to pay for improved quality!

SOURCES: Rosen, Harvey S. Chairman, Council of Economic Advisers, Comments on Health Care at the Conference of the National Association of Business Economics, March 21, 2005, www.whitehouse.gov/cea/nabe-healthcare032105.pdf; Goldman, Dana P., "Pressure from Rising Health-Care Costs: How Can Consumers Get Relief?" www.rand.org/commentary/102305PE.html.

Reasonable analysts have challenged these predictions. Although patients have resisted drastic restraints on health care utilization, nearly all insurance plans, including fee-for-service, face at least some form of utilization review. The challenges, then, rest on speculation regarding the continued nature of managed care cost reductions. Does managed care provide onetime cost reductions, or can it also reduce the rate of spending growth over time? Will employers (who provide a large portion of the health insurance) pay for the increasing costs, or will they try to influence providers to hold down the costs? Will the overall economy grow as quickly in the twenty-first century as it did in the last decade of the twentieth century?

Health care costs affect all economies. Other advanced countries, almost all of which have universal insurance, face upward cost pressures similar to the United States. In comparative perspective, economists may learn whether other countries can meet consumer demand, and continue to pay increasing costs, while maintaining universal coverage. Conversely, we must examine the cost impacts of extending health insurance to the one in seven Americans who does not fully enjoy the benefits of more and better health care, leading to improved health.

Conclusions

The features of the health economy are distinctive, but the health sector is not unique. Accounting for the features of the health sector falls well within the scope of economic inquiry. Uncertain events affect much of life, including automobile safety, household security, and the fortunes of most businesses. Insurance programs cover many of these instances, and every financial decision entails an element of risk.

Much of health care arguably finds the consumer relatively well-informed. In instances where the physician is asymmetrically better informed, the case is often not unlike the information deficit faced by the typical purchaser of other complex goods.

We commonly speak of needs for food and housing, and we have government programs to provide or subsidize the poor in these markets. Other professions are licensed in many states, and various industries are regulated. Nonprofit firms provide symphony music and college educations, as well as health care. Special tools of analysis are needed in all these cases, not just for health care.

Nevertheless, health and health care are unique in having this combination of distinctive features and perhaps in possessing the sheer number of them. It is unsurprising that a distinctive field of economic inquiry with a distinctive set of questions has arisen.

The relevance of health economics hinges on its ability to inform, and possibly influence, the decisions of those who make health care policy. In his January 1996 presidential address to the American Economic Association, distinguished health economist Victor Fuchs concluded:

> In the past three decades economics has made a positive contribution to health and medical care, and I believe that future contributions will be even greater. Now that the basic ideas of economics are gaining acceptance, it will be more important than ever for economists to master many of the intricacies of health care institutions and technologies. We will also have to consider the problems of dissemination in order to ensure that when we agree on research results, these results are understood and accepted by all relevant audiences including the media, politicians, and health professionals (Fuchs, 1996, p. 20).

Professor Fuchs's optimistic statement represents a useful conclusion to this introductory chapter and an important point of departure for the chapters that follow.

SUMMARY

1. Health care spending has grown rapidly in absolute and relative terms. It accounts for over one-seventh of the GDP in the United States, and its share of GDP is projected to continue to grow.
2. The growth in health care spending is attributable to more services, higher-quality services, and relative increases in the prices of health care services. Health economists seek to determine the underlying causes of these phenomena.
3. The size of the health economy is also reflected through other measures such as the number of jobs in health care professions and amount of capital.
4. Time spent obtaining and providing health care represents a key "unpriced" factor in the health economy.
5. The health economy is considerably larger in the United States than in other countries.
6. There are significant policy concerns not only with the growth of spending but also with access and quality.
7. Economists use models to explain economic behavior. The models are abstract simplifications of reality.
8. Health economists still disagree on some fundamental issues, such as the extent to which the competitive model applies to the health economy.

9. Health care services and the health economy possess a unique set of distinguishing features. The uniqueness of health care lies in the entire set rather than with individual distinctive features, such as the prevalence of uncertainty or insurance coverage.
10. Managed care has profoundly influenced the U.S. health care system. Analysts use economic models to predict its impact on health care spending.
11. Technological change through improved procedures, and new drugs, provides potential improvements in health care, but also possibilities of increasing costs, in all countries.

DISCUSSION QUESTIONS

1. Suggest several reasons why health care spending is higher in the United States than in other countries. Is the fact that the U.S. population spends more per capita on health care than people in any other developed country evidence of a failure of the U.S. system? What issues do you think are involved in answering the question?
2. Describe several key issues facing policymakers with regard to health care spending.
3. If greater health care spending leads to more jobs, why is there such concern about the rapid growth rates of spending?
4. Do consumers take the net price (including insurance and time) they face into consideration when choosing health care? What evidence suggests that price matters? Suggest real-life scenarios in which price may affect choices regarding health care.
5. Suppose that a woman works 40 hours per week with no opportunity for overtime. She also takes care of a sick parent. Can we say that her time has no value in providing this health care because she could not earn more at work?
6. What is meant by marginal analysis? Provide an example in which marginal analysis is useful in looking at policy questions.
7. Give three examples of quality of care in the provision of health services. Why might consumers be willing to pay more money to have each of them?
8. Describe the size of the health economy when measured by the quantities of capital and labor used to produce health care. What important inputs to the production of health are not being counted among these?

EXERCISES

1. Health care spending can be summarized by the following equation:

 $S = (\text{Population size}) \times (\text{health care quantity per person}) \times (\text{price per unit of health care})$

 a. Identify three factors that might lead to the rapid growth of health care spending.
 b. Compare health care spending to housing expenditures and to food expenditures. How are the sectors similar? How do they differ?
2. Identify five distinctive features of the health economy. Examine each one separately, and describe other commodities or sectors that share those features. Do any other commodities or sectors have all the features you listed?
3. In Table 1–1, calculate which country had the largest and smallest percentage increase in GDP share from 1960 to 1980. Compare these to similar calculations for the period 1980 to 2003. Discuss your results.
4. The United States, Canada, and the United Kingdom share the same language but have considerably different health care systems. Compare the three health shares of GDP from 1960 to 2003. What factors may explain the considerable differences among the three countries?
5. Table 1–4 provides indexes of the prices of health care inputs. Calculate the growth rates of the prices of hospital rooms and physician services. Compare them to the growth rate of the overall Consumer Price Index (CPI). Discuss your findings.
6. In Table 1–5, we see increases in out-of-pocket health expenditures by consumers, and in government expenditures. From year to year, which grew by a larger percentage? Over the entire period, which grew by a larger percentage?

7. Several Web sites provide useful information on health care and health resources use. Use a Web browser to find Web sites from:
 - Centers for Medicare & Medicaid Services (CMS)
 - National Institutes of Health (NIH)
 - Organization for Economic Cooperation and Development (OECD)
 - For students outside the United States, find governmental sites from your own country. Compare and contrast the data available from these sites.

8. The following chart shows health expenditures for the United States between 1960 and 2003.
 a. Calculate health expenditures per person for each year.
 b. Calculate percentage increases in health expenditures per person for each year.
 c. Can you find particular events in given years that might explain either small or large changes in the health expenditures per person or in the percentage changes?

Year	Population (in millions)	Health Expenditures ($ in billions)	Year	Population (in millions)	Health Expenditures ($ in billions)
1960	186.2	26.7	1982	235.1	321.0
1961	189.2	28.6	1983	237.4	353.5
1962	192.0	31.0	1984	239.6	390.1
1963	194.8	33.8	1985	241.9	426.8
1964	197.4	37.7	1986	244.2	457.2
1965	199.8	41.0	1987	246.5	498.0
1966	201.9	45.1	1988	248.9	558.1
1967	203.7	50.7	1989	251.4	622.7
1968	205.6	57.5	1990	254.3	696.0
1969	207.6	64.6	1991	257.7	761.8
1970	210.2	73.1	1992	261.3	827.0
1971	212.8	81.0	1993	264.8	888.1
1972	214.9	90.7	1994	268.0	937.1
1973	216.7	100.5	1995	271.3	990.2
1974	218.4	113.7	1996	274.3	1,039.9
1975	220.2	129.8	1997	277.6	1,093.1
1976	222.0	148.8	1998	280.8	1,150.9
1977	223.8	169.4	1999	284.1	1,222.2
1978	225.9	189.4	2000	287.3	1,309.9
1979	228.1	213.9	2001	290.3	1,426.4
1980	230.4	245.8	2002	293.2	1,559.0
1981	232.8	285.1	2003	296.1	1,678.9

CHAPTER 2

Microeconomic Tools for Health Economics

Scarcity and the Production Possibilities Frontier

Practice with Supply and Demand

Functions and Curves

Consumer Theory: Ideas Behind the Demand Curve

Individual and Market Demands

Elasticities

Production and Market Supply

The Firm Supply Curve Under Perfect Competition

Monopoly and Other Market Structures

Welfare Losses

Conclusions

This chapter provides an explanation of the microeconomic tools that are used in the text by reviewing material that may be encountered at the introductory and intermediate levels of learning. These tools are useful for a deeper understanding of ideas in health economics. This review does not substitute for an introductory course in the principles of economics, and a complete series of principles is necessary for a fuller understanding. Only by such study can one gain an understanding of the subtleties of the subject as well as the many large ideas that had to be reduced to make them palatable in a brief review. Although the material is presented in a way consistent with more detailed and rigorous treatments in a standard microeconomics course, the academic give-and-take of disputes over issues as well as much mathematical detail have been eliminated.

Please note also that the "Basic Economics Tools" chapters deal mainly with microeconomic issues; the macroeconomic issues are largely absent except in the sense that these subjects increasingly overlap. Microeconomic concerns involve individual decision makers such as households and providers, and specific industries such as the health insurance and hospital industries. The behavior of individual decision makers is the focus and subject of microeconomics. Health economics also addresses the problem of the efficient use of scarce resources, which too is a microeconomic issue.

This chapter starts with the concept of scarcity and reviews supply-and-demand analysis. After these introductory treatments of supply and demand, the chapter returns separately to demand first and then to supply, developing the underlying ideas behind these tools. We then combine them into models of market structures, emphasizing those featured in health economics.

Scarcity and the Production Possibilities Frontier

A fundamental idea in economics is that there is no such thing as a free lunch. The fact that little if anything is free implies that to get something, one must usually give up something else, such as time or other resources. A helpful theoretical tool that illustrates this idea is the production possibilities frontier (PPF).

The PPF is a curve drawn in a graph to illustrate the trade-offs between two categories of goods. The curve shows how our choices are constrained by the fact that we cannot have all of everything we want. The idea that we face resource constraints and must make trade-offs is central to the PPF, but similar ideas also apply to the individual firm or the individual consumer.

We begin the production possibilities problem with a table illustrating a classic dilemma concerning society's trade-off between guns and butter. Table 2-1 shows data on the amounts of guns or butter that a hypothetical society could produce with its resources. Guns and butter are meant metaphorically to refer to all goods and services with a military use versus those that have a domestic consumption use. The PPF could in principle also be drawn in many dimensions. What is essential is that the goods represented exhaustively account for all the goods in the economy.

Table 2-1 contains many numbers but illustrates two central ideas. Note first that as the number of guns increases, the number for butter falls, indicating that to produce more of one good we must give up some of the other. The amount of butter given up in order to produce an extra 100 units of guns is called the opportunity cost of 100 units of guns. Opportunity cost can be measured per 100 units of guns as here, but more commonly we are interested in the opportunity cost of the single next unit of guns, called the marginal unit. In either case, the opportunity cost represents what is given up.

The opportunity cost column reporting the costs of each 100 units of guns in terms of butter foregone illustrates a second idea—that of increasing opportunity costs. As the number of guns increases, the opportunity cost gets larger. If society is to increase its production of guns, say from 200 to 300 units, it must transfer the resources, labor, and capital previously used in butter production to gun production. The idea that this is

TABLE 2-1 Society's Trade-Off Between Guns and Butter

Point	Butter	Guns	*Opportunity Cost: Butter Given Up to Produce 100 Units of Guns*
A	936	0	
B	891	100	45
C	828	200	63
D	732	300	96
E	609	400	123
F	444	500	165
G	244	600	200
H	0	700	244

a frontier means that we are representing society's best possible production. Thus, when we first shift butter resources toward gun production, we can arbitrarily choose to shift those resources relatively best suited to gun production first. By choosing laborers who are handier at gun making than at butter making, we will gain the most guns per unit of butter we give up. As we shift more resources toward guns, we will have to dig deeper into our relatively good butter-producing resources, and hence give up greater quantities of butter. Increasing opportunity costs also illustrate the specialization of society's resources of labor and capital.

Graphing and its usefulness are illustrated by transferring the data in Table 2-1 into the graph in Figure 2-1. Note that if this society devotes all its labor and capital to butter production, the most butter it can produce is 936 units. The two numbers—936 units of butter and 0 units of guns—can be represented by point A in Figure 2-1. The other points are transferred in the same manner. We assume that the missing points between these data points will fit the same pattern, resulting in the PPF curve.

In the graph, the idea of no free lunch is illustrated by the downward slope of the PPF curve. In this example, increased gun production means we have to give up some butter production—hence, we get no free lunch. Second, the opportunity cost itself is illustrated in the slope of the curve. For example, the line between points B and C has a slope of 63 (the rise) over 100 (the run), and 63 units of butter per 100 units of guns is the opportunity cost we observed in the table.

The opportunity cost of one single unit of guns is virtually the slope of the PPF at a single point, which equals the slope of a line tangent at that point. Therefore, at point E the opportunity cost is identical to the slope of the tangent line to the PPF at E.

Finally, the idea of increasing opportunity cost is illustrated by the bowed-out shape of the PPF, showing its concavity to the origin. Recall that the slope is the opportunity cost. Thus, the slope becoming steeper means that the opportunity cost is increasing. Society could choose any point on the PPF, but society can be at only one point at a time. How society makes and achieves its choice are other matters to discuss, but at present we have merely illustrated the best possible practices of some hypothetical society. An interior point such as X means that the particular society is not doing the best it can; it is inefficient. A point such as Y is unattainable because of insufficient resources to produce the indicated amounts of both guns and butter.

FIGURE 2-1 Society's Trade-Off Between Guns and Butter. Point *X* Is Inefficient; Point *Y* Is Infeasible

BOX 2-1

There's Scarcity and Then There's Real Scarcity

Scarcity is clearly defined in economics; a good or service is "scarce" whenever it has a non-zero opportunity cost. So, goods and services generally are scarce, for the very rich even as much as they are for the very poor. The only question is whether one has so much as to have become satiated, at which point a good starts to become a "bad."

However, the way ordinary people use the word *scarce* is very clear, too. If money is scarce, that clearly means tough times. An American financial columnist some years ago wrote of an informal, non-scientific survey he had taken among people he met. He asked each of them "How difficult is it to make ends meet?" Those making over $80,000 often answered something like "Surprisingly it's not that easy, but we make it work." Those making in the $50,000s said something like: "We struggle at times, but we get by." And, those making in the $20,000s gave answers such as this: "It's a real struggle at times, but we manage." Apparently the phrases "making it

work," "struggle at times," and "we manage," as close as their meaning is in the official English lexicon, mean very different things in practice to different people.

Many American students, and perhaps many Canadian and European students as well, may be surprised to discover just how vast the differences among the world's countries are in terms of income, health, health expenditures, and the like. Germany and the United States are examples of the industrialized west; these populations experience nearly three to five times the material income as the Russian Federation or Brazil, and six to eight times that of either Albania or China. But, by far the most striking contrast is with the African countries of Nigeria and Ethiopia, who have little to spend on health care, and at the same time experience the largest health and health care deficit. Table 2-2 shows these and other data from a selection of countries across the globe.

TABLE 2-2 There Is a Strikingly Diverse Experience in Income, Health, and Health Care Across the World's Countries

Country	GDP per Capita	Health Expenditure per Capita	Life Expectancy	Average Years in Poor Health	Prevalence of HIV
Albania	3600	144	72	9.4	0.01
Bangladesh	1590	57	61	8.2	0.02
Brazil	7300	482	67	8.4	0.57
China	3920	176	70	7.4	0.07
Ethiopia	660	27	42	8.6	10.63
Germany	24920	2642	77	6.5	0.10
Nigeria	800	22	47	9.2	5.06
Russian Fed.	8010	368	66	6.6	0.18
United States	34100	4433	77	6.9	0.61

NOTES: GDP (for 2000) is via the purchasing power parity method; health care expenditures per capita were found by applying the 1990–98 average percentage of GDP spent on health care; life expectancy is estimated from birth; years spent in poor health and HIV are World Bank health risk indicators; HIV figures represent the percent of adults estimated to carry the virus.
SOURCE: World Bank website, www.worldbank.org/data/databytopic/class.htm, on April 29, 2002.

Practice with Supply and Demand

The most familiar ideas in economics are probably supply-and-demand curves. We will illustrate supply-and-demand analysis for a hypothetical market for apples.

The Demand Curve and Demand Shifters

In Figure 2-2A, a demand curve illustrates the demand for apples in a hypothetical market for a given period of time, say one week. The demand curve drawn shows a quantity demanded in this market for this time period for each possible price. For example, at a price of $5.25 per bushel, consumers would wish to buy a total of 345 bushels that week. The theory of demand suggests that quantity demanded would be less at higher prices—for example, 215 bushels at a price of $7.50. Some consumers may find that the price rise represents "the last straw" so that they buy none, while others may buy fewer apples than before, and yet others would not change their purchases. It is doubtful that anyone would use the occasion of a price rise as a reason to buy more.

This analysis is done *ceteris paribus*, meaning that we are assuming that all other things are held constant. The price of apples rises while people's tastes, perceptions, incomes, and so on stay the same. In life, it is common for two or more things to change at the same time. If, for example, the price of apples rises at the same time as tastes change, the result would be theoretically ambiguous, meaning that we cannot predict the direction of the change. In contrast, the demand curve depicts the behavior of consumers as price only changes.

As long as people buy less at higher prices, then the demand curve will be downward sloping. In statistical analysis, estimated demand curves are almost always downward sloping. The responsiveness of demand to price is measured by the elasticity. We will discuss elasticity in a later section. Other variables also will affect the demand for apples. For example, the amount of various foods that people buy may depend on their incomes; richer people tend to buy more. Demand may be affected by the price of other substitutable goods. When any other variable affects demand, its effect will be shown as a shift in the curve. For convenience, we call such variables demand shifters. A list of demand shifters includes the following.

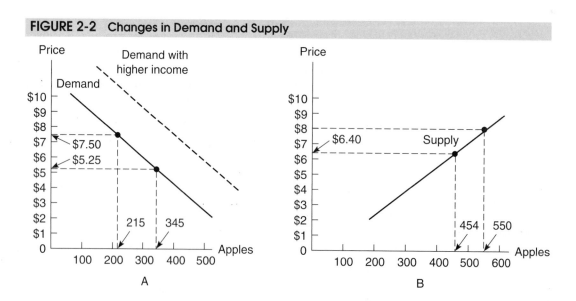

FIGURE 2-2 Changes in Demand and Supply

Income Generally, the quantity of a good that people wish to buy depends in part on their income. People with higher incomes tend to demand more of most goods. Such goods are called *normal* goods. But some goods, such as used clothing or generic brand goods, are purchased less often when people become richer. Such goods are called inferior goods. Let us assume that apples are normal goods. In Figure 2–2A, increased income in the community would tend to shift the demand curve outward.

Other Prices Prices of related goods also will affect demand. Related goods may be either substitutes or complements. If oranges are regarded as substitutes for apples, an increase in the price of oranges would cause the demand for apples to increase, shifting the demand curve to the right. In contrast, a complement is something that is used with apples, such as caramel. If the price of a complement rises, the demand for apples decreases or shifts left.

Insurance A variable that makes no sense for apples but that is essential on a list of demand shifters in health economics is insurance. Insurance reduces the price to the consumer at the point of service; given the lower price, a greater quantity of health care will be demanded. Although one can treat this as a movement down a given demand curve, we show in a later chapter that this is equivalent to a clockwise rotation in the original demand curve. Insurance plans have many complexities beyond changing the consumer's effective price, and these are also addressed in a later chapter.

Tastes Many other demand shifters may be grouped under the heading of tastes. Tastes can be literally what the word means, as when a new recipe increases interest in apples. The term can be less literal as well, as when we say that an older population has a greater demand for health care because it has a greater taste for health care.

The Supply Curve and Supply Shifters

Supply can be approached in a similar way. Figure 2–2B shows an upward-sloping supply curve for apples. It illustrates, for example, that apple growers would be willing to offer 454 bushels of apples for sale if the price were $6.40. At a higher price, say $8.00, more would be offered. Apple growers might be more willing to divert apples from cider production, to make greater efforts in harvest, or even to bring formerly unprofitable trees into production if the price were higher. Such reasons would suggest an upward-sloping supply curve such as the one shown.

We may likewise generate a list of supply shifters.

Technological Change As technology improves for producing a given product, the good becomes cheaper to produce. Certainly, technological changes that make products more costly without improving quality are ignored. As the product becomes cheaper to produce, suppliers are willing to offer more for sale at a given price. This increases supply, thus shifting the supply curve to the right.

Input Prices If the wages of apple pickers were to rise, this increase in an input cost would reduce suppliers' willingness to offer as much for sale at the original price. The supply would decrease, shifting the curve to the left.

Prices of Production-Related Goods The price of a good related in production, such as cider, also would be relevant. Because farmers can use raw apples for eating or for cider, generally a rise in cider prices will cause the apple supply to decrease, thus shifting the supply curve to the left.

Size of the Industry As more firms (in this case apple growers) enter a market, the supply of the product will be greater. Thus, entry of firms will cause supply to shift to the right.

Weather For a number of products, acts of God such as the weather will tend to affect production. The direction of the effect is obvious: Good weather increases supply.

Equilibrium

Under conditions of competition, the equilibrium in a market will be at the point where the demand and supply curves intersect. This is the point at which demanders' and suppliers' plans agree. In Figure 2-3, the equilibrium occurs at the price of $5.00 and at the quantity of 350 bushels. At higher prices, there will be excess supply, and suppliers who were unable to sell all their goods will be willing to bid prices down. At lower prices, there will be excess demand, and demanders who went undersupplied will be willing to pay more and will tend to bid prices up.

Comparative Statics

An equilibrium as depicted in Figure 2-3 is called a static equilibrium. It shows a picture of an unchanging equilibrium at a point in time. It is more interesting to assess how the equilibrium will change when the market is affected by some economic event. Figures 2-4A and B give two examples. Consider in Figure 2-4A what would happen to

FIGURE 2-3 Equilibrium Where Demand Equals Supply

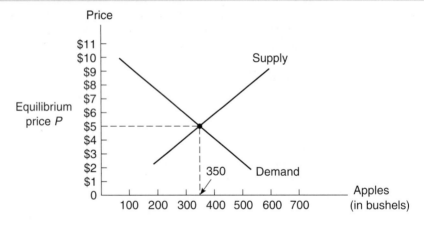

FIGURE 2-4 Market Effects of Supply-and-Demand Shifts

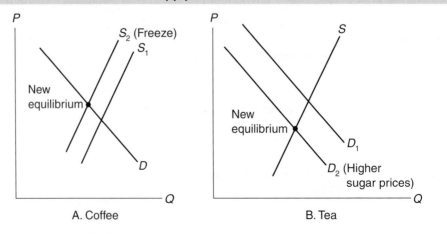

A. Coffee B. Tea

the market for coffee if there were a freeze in Brazil. This worsening of the weather would tend to shift supply to the left as shown. At the new equilibrium, the price of coffee is higher, and the quantity consumed is lower.

Similarly, in Figure 2-4B, consider what happens to the market for tea when the price of sugar rises. Because sugar is a complement, this event causes a shift to the left in the demand for tea as shown. The new equilibrium will have a lower price and a lower quantity.

A few exercises help to generate experience with comparative statistics and to demonstrate the applicability of this analysis:

1. A national health insurance proposal is passed that provides comprehensive health insurance to everyone. How would this affect the markets for health care in the short run?

Answer: The competitive model is probably robust enough to give some guidance. Insurance coverage will probably increase on average, causing the demand for health care to increase, shifting the curve to the right. This will increase the equilibrium price of care, as well as the quantity consumed. (The evidence suggests that an increase in medical prices did occur after the onset of the U.S. Medicare program for the elderly). The two results combined will increase the total money spent on health care. Among the many economists, many might offer alternative scenarios on this theme. For example, the analysis here is conducted *ceteris paribus*; if a successful cost control program were put into effect at the same time, the net result might be different.

2. A law is passed requiring that hospitals hire only nurses with baccalaureate degrees. How would this affect the market for hospital care?

Answer: Hospital markets are not perfectly competitive, but the predictions of the competitive model would probably give a good clue. Such a law would in effect increase an input price, thus shifting the supply of hospital care to the left. Under this interpretation, the equilibrium price of hospital care would tend to rise and quantity would fall.

3. Suppose the government lowers the reimbursement rates paid to physicians for Medicare patients. How would this affect the market for non-Medicare patients?

Answer: The government action probably serves as a supply shifter because Medicare patients are a production-related good. Physicians would shift more time and other inputs into non-Medicare patient production, shifting the supply to the right, lowering equilibrium price, and raising quantity.

Functions and Curves

Most economic discussions consider how two or more economic variables are related to each other. For example, consider what we have theorized about the relationship of the price to the quantity demanded. We say that the quantity demanded is a function of the price. Mathematically, a function is an arrangement whereby we plug in the value of the independent variable, here the price, and the function generates the value of the dependent variable, here the quantity demanded. Alternatively, we can say that quantity demanded depends on price.

Linear Functions

Before considering the writing of supply and demand in functional notation, consider the linear function. A linear function is that of a straight line and can be written as follows:

$$y = a + bx \tag{2.1}$$

where *y* is the dependent variable and *x* is the independent variable. A linear function, no matter what idea it represents, has characteristic features: an intercept and a slope, both of which are constants. The *y*-intercept is the value of the function evaluated when *x* equals zero. Here the intercept is *a*. The slope of a function is the increase in the vertical direction, or the "rise" divided by the increase in the horizontal direction, or the "run."

To determine the slope of this particular function, examine this function drawn as a curve in Figure 2-5. We use the word *curve* for all functions, including the straight line. As noted, the *y*-intercept is *a*. Similarly, the function crosses the *x*-axis at a value of zero for *y*. Setting *y* to zero and solving for *x* yields a value of $x = -a/b$. Now, to find the slope, divide the change in *y*, $-a$, by the change in *x*, $-a/b$, thus, generating a value for the slope of *b*, the slope of this linear function. The value of *b* in this case must be negative, as the slope is downward.

Demand Functions

The demand functions up to this point have been linear. In general, though, linear demand is only one special case. Even when demand is linear, there is a minor complication. Consider the following linear demand function:

$$Q_d = a - bP \tag{2.2}$$

where Q_d is quantity demanded and *P* is price.

A complication arises because economists customarily draw demand and supply curves with the independent variable, price, on the y-axis and the dependent variable, quantity demanded, on the x-axis. In standard mathematics, the dependent variable is usually drawn on the y-axis.

Most commonly, we will be considering cases where the dependent variable, such as quantity demanded, is a function of not one but several variables. For example, the quantity of spaghetti demanded, Q_d, may depend not only on the price of spaghetti, P_s, but also on the price of substitutes for spaghetti (such as other pastas), P_o, the individual's income, *Y*, and a taste factor, *Z*. Mathematically, using the general notation, the demand function for spaghetti would be written as follows:

$$Q_d = f(P_s, P_o, Y, Z) \tag{2.3}$$

Here the notation $Q_d = f(...)$ is read, "Quantity demanded is a function of P_s, P_o, *Y*, and *Z*." If the function in (2.3) also happens to be linear, its more specific form would have a characteristic linear look to it. Statisticians frequently use this case, and it

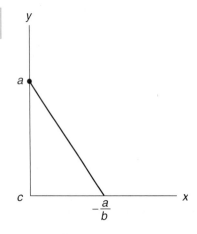

FIGURE 2-5 Graph of the Function *y* = *a* + *bx*

is useful to look at an example. A linear spaghetti demand function, for example, might look like this:

$$Q_d = 500 - 10P_s + 5P_o + 20Y + 40Z \qquad (2.4)$$

Linear equations with several independent variables have some things in common with the simple linear equation in (2.1). An intercept constant is calculated by setting all the independent variables equal to zero; here the intercept is 500. The slope values in such linear cases will be the coefficients of the independent variables in question. For example, the slope value for the income variable Y is 20. The slope gives information regarding the contributions of changes in the independent variables to the value of the dependent variable. Again, it is worthwhile emphasizing that functions in economics need not be linear. For example, the true spaghetti demand function might instead look like this:

$$Q_d = 7P_s^{-0.05}P_o^{0.002}Y^{0.8}Z^{0.01} \qquad (2.5)$$

which is not linear. Our theory says only a few things about a demand function: It is downward sloping in its own price, shifting rightward (leftward) with higher prices of substitutes (complements), shifting rightward (leftward) with income increases for normal (inferior) goods, and shifting rightward with a positive shift in tastes. Beyond these features, the demand function mathematically could take on many different forms.

Derived Demand

Demand by consumers for a final good or service may stimulate the provider of that service in turn to demand factors of production. There is no theoretical limit to how long this hierarchical chain can be, but in the health industry several good illustrations can be found. Individual consumers may wish to improve their health or the health of family members. They may demand exercise equipment, healthful foods, and visits to a physician. These consumers generate a derived demand for factors. Considering just a clinic, the manager purchases electronics, technical equipment, drugs, and labor services, as well as the physician's time. The physician and other medically trained personnel, in anticipation of this, had a derived demand for medical education.

Consumer Theory: Ideas Behind the Demand Curve

Consumer theory examines how rational individuals make consumption choices when faced with limited resources. The limited resources determine what options a consumer can afford. From among these options, the consumer attempts to pick the best one. The theory has two parts. One is a description of what the consumer prefers—what he or she thinks is best; for this description, we use the ideas of utility and of indifference curves. The second part is a description of what the consumer can afford; for this part, we use the idea of budget constraints. The use of indifference curves and budget constraints together constitutes indifference curve analysis.

Utility

Consider a consumer, Kathy Richards. Let us suppose she is an experienced consumer who knows what her tastes are for kinds of houses to live in, cars to drive, food to eat, and books to read. She can't afford everything she would like to have, but she knows what she would prefer if she could afford everything.

In summarizing this information about Kathy's preferences, we suppose that she has a utility function. Utility is a measure of her level of satisfaction with various combinations of consumer goods. It includes a market basket filled with a combination of housing, food, transportation, and so on, with perhaps many different types of each. Bundles preferred over other bundles are given a greater value of utility. Because more utility, thus defined, is always better, Kathy will logically seek to maximize her utility subject to the constraint of what is affordable to her.

Using functions, we say that Kathy's utility is a function of the goods and services she consumes. In practice, the level of detail we use will vary. On some occasions, we must specify most of the detailed consumption of Kathy's life. Then, we would describe her utility as a function of each good or service she buys, perhaps compiling hundreds of them. But in many cases, it is useful to abstract from this detail and describe Kathy's utility as a function of one or two goods of special interest, plus another general good representing all other goods she considers. At still other times, we will find it useful to describe Kathy's utility as a function of wealth. We will develop two examples in the following discussion. Theories using the idea of utility may propose that utility is either cardinal or ordinal. Cardinal utility means a metric measure, like a measure of weight or volume. It is characteristic of cardinal measures that the difference as well as the ratio between two measurements has meaning. One can meaningfully say, for example, that five quarts is three more than two quarts, and, for that matter, it is two and one-half times two quarts. Under ordinal utility, to the contrary, only the ranking has meaning. Examples of ordinal numbers are first, second, third, and so on.

It is preferable to theorize that consumers' utility is ordinal. It is safer to assume that consumers can rank their preferences than to assume that they can both rank and scale them. It seems safer to suppose someone can say that he or she is happy to have gotten a raise, but it seems questionable to suppose that he or she is 1.07 times as happy. Most theories of demand assume only ordinality. In a few cases, such as the theory of behavior under risk and insurance, some degree of cardinality is assumed. To illustrate ideas about utility, we should begin with the simplest case to draw. Figure 2-6 depicts Kathy's utility as a function of her wealth. The curve illustrates two ideas. First, the upward slope indicates that utility increases with wealth. Second, the bowed shape, concave from below, indicates that her utility increases with wealth at a decreasing rate.

Marginal utility is defined as the extra utility achieved by consuming one more unit of a good. Here, the only good is wealth so marginal utility is the extra utility

FIGURE 2-6 The Utility of Wealth

Kathy gets from one more dollar of wealth. An extra convenience of drawing the function graphically is that the marginal utility is the slope of the curve at a given point. Starting at any point on the curve and adding a single dollar to Kathy's wealth leads to extra utility for that dollar, which we have just defined as marginal utility (MU).

If we understand marginal utility as the slope, the marginal utility of wealth for Kathy gets smaller as she gets wealthier. That is, the slope gets flatter. An extra dollar means more to Kathy when she is poorer than when she is richer. Does this notion apply to most people? That it might apply seems plausible to most students, but the notion also introduces an element of cardinal utility.

Indifference Curves

Often, we wish to depict the consumer's preferences over two or more goods. The most convenient case to draw is when there are only two goods. To capture the sense of the real world in a two-good drawing, let one of the two goods represent all other goods generally, as if they were a conglomerate. Call this conglomerate OG, meaning Other Goods. Suppose that the good of special interest is Food. Figure 2-7 depicts a graph with these two goods, OG and Food, on the axes. Any point in the space, such as A, represents a consumer bundle. The bundle A includes the combination of 8 units of Food and 4 units of Other Goods. Other bundles that are labeled include B, C, D, E, F, and G, but any other point in the space is also a bundle.

Suppose we focus on bundle A and that we hypothetically ask Kathy to identify all other bundles as well that for her are indifferent to A (that is, points that give her the same utility as A). The entire set of such points is labeled U_1; as noted in the graph, any point along U_1 affords Kathy 112 utils (we will call the units of utility *utils*).

This curve is downward sloping, as well as bowed toward the origin. Notice, for example, that Kathy did not choose point C as being indifferent to A. This seems plausible because C represents more of both goods, and as long as she is not satiated with these two goods, then she would prefer C to A. Likewise, she has not picked point D as indifferent to A because D has less of both goods. Instead, she has picked points such as E, which has more Food but less OG. Presumably, at E she has just balanced the loss of OG against the gain in Food. These considerations suggest that it is understandable that the indifference curve through A is downward sloping.

FIGURE 2-7 Indifference Curves Between Food and Other Goods (OG)

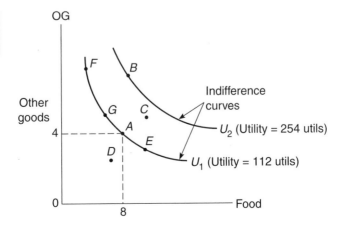

The curve is also convex to the origin. Consider that, at point *F*, Kathy has relatively a lot of OG and little Food. As Food is relatively scarce for her, she is willing to give up a lot of OG to get more Food. The rate at which she is willing to trade off the two goods is represented by the slope of the indifference curve, which is steep at point *F*. In contrast, as we move down the indifference curve, Kathy gains relatively more Food, and the more she gets, the less ready she is to give up still further OG to gain yet more Food. Thus, the curve becomes flatter.

Indifference curves for Kathy summarize and represent her preferences. Every possible combination of goods will lie on some indifference curve so that in principle there would be an infinite number of indifference curves in Figure 2-7, with higher curves representing greater satisfaction.

Budget Constraints

Indifference curve analysis uses preference maps and budget constraints. The budget constraint indicates the set of bundles the consumer can afford with a given income. Suppose that Kathy must allocate $30 of her family food budget per week between beef B and chicken C. If the price of beef is $2.00 per pound, and the price of chicken is $1.00 per pound, then she can afford any combination of B and C that costs less than or equal to $30, and her budget constraint is:

$$30.00 = 2.00B + 1.00C \qquad (2.6)$$

If we draw this constraint in Figure 2-8 with beef B on the vertical axis, then the budget constraint will start at 15 pounds of beef and proceed downward sloping to 30 pounds of chicken as the horizontal intercept. It is convenient to demonstrate this pattern by examining the mathematical function. Equation (2.6) can be transformed using algebra so that B appears on the left-hand side and all other terms are on the right. Thus, the equivalent budget constraint is:

$$B = \frac{30}{2} - \frac{1}{2}C = 15 - 0.5C \qquad (2.7)$$

FIGURE 2-8 Changes in Budget Constraints Due to Changes in Price or Income

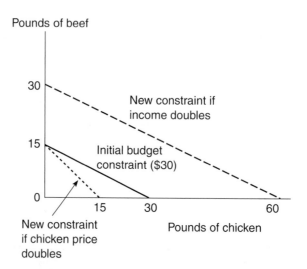

Pounds of beef

New constraint if income doubles

Initial budget constraint ($30)

New constraint if chicken price doubles

Pounds of chicken

a linear function with an intercept of 15 and a slope of –0.5. If, in Figure 2-8, the price of chicken rose, the amount that Kathy could buy, if she spent all $30 on chicken, would be less than before. If the price doubled, the chicken axis intercept would shift inward, permitting her to buy only 15 pounds of chicken rather than 30. The beef intercept is not affected when the price of chicken rises.

Consider instead an increase in the portion of her budget allocated to beef and chicken. A doubling to $60 would allow Kathy to increase the amount of beef from 15 to 30 pounds, or the amount of chicken from 30 to 60 pounds. As shown, the new budget constraint is parallel to the original budget constraint. Doubling the income in itself does not cause the prices to change. Because the slope of each budget constraint is the ratio of prices, the new constraint will be parallel. The intercepts will double.

Consumer Equilibrium

To maximize satisfaction given a budget constraint, the consumer will want to be on the highest attainable indifference curve. In Figure 2-9, the indifference curve U_1 is not the best possible, while the indifference curve U_3 is unattainable. Rejecting such alternatives, the consumer will find that she maximizes utility at a point of tangency, shown as point A in the figure. At this point, the rate at which the consumer is willing to trade beef for chicken, the slope of the indifference curve equals the rate at which the consumer is able to trade the two goods at market prices—the slope of the budget constraint.

One can derive the equilibrium for different prices and/or for different values of income. For example, in Figure 2-10A, as the price of chicken rises consecutively, Kathy consecutively chooses points A, B, C, and D. The collection of such points is called the price offer curve. The information from these data points along the price offer curve can be used to generate her demand curve. For example, point A in Figure 2-10A represents her best choice for a given budget and set of prices. Suppose the price of chicken for budget constraint MN is P_0. Then, plotting P_0 together with the quantity demanded at A, namely F_0, in the graph at right generates point A'. In the same manner, data on price P_1 and the quantity demanded F_1, at point B, generate point B' in the graph at right. Repeating this process generates the demand curve.

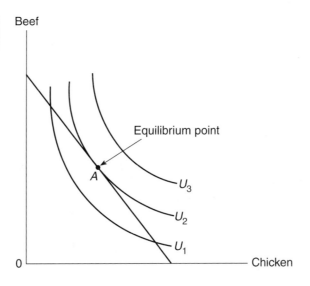

FIGURE 2-9 The Consumer's Equilibrium

FIGURE 2-10 Derivation of the Consumer's Demand Curve

A. Indifference Curves

B. Demand

FIGURE 2-11 Derivation of a Market Demand Curve

A. Mary

B. John

C. Market

Individual and Market Demands

The theory of consumer behavior focuses on the demand relationships of individual consumers. Many applications of demand theory, however, consider market demand. The extension from individual to market demand is straightforward. In Figure 2-11, health care demand is shown for two people who constitute a market for health care. For example, Mary demands 3 units at the price $p_H = 30$, and John demands 2 units. Market demand here at $p_H = 30$ is $(3 + 2)$ or 5 units. The market demand in panel C is derived by adding the quantities demanded at every price. The process can be extended to all of the consumers in the market, and it yields a market demand curve. If everyone's demand curve conforms to the law of demand, the market demand curve must also be downward sloping.

Finally, note that as with individual demand functions, other variables such as income and the prices of related goods (the shift variable we discussed earlier) affect

market demand. Thus, the market demand for some commodity X might be expressed in functional notation. Consider, for example

$$QD_x = f(P_x, Y, P_o, E)$$ (2.8)

where Y represents income, P_o represents the prices of other goods, and E represents a socioeconomic variable such as average educational attainment (in years of schooling).

Elasticities

We are often particularly interested in the responsiveness of the quantity demanded to other variables. For example, if the price of health care rises, will the quantity demanded fall by a large amount or a small amount? Economists use the term *elasticity* to describe the responsiveness of any term y (in this case, quantity demanded of health care) to changes in some other variable x (here, price of health care).

Elasticity is defined as the percent change in the dependent variable resulting from a 1 percent change in the independent variable under study.[1] In the case of the price elasticity of demand, it is as follows:

$$E_p = (\% \text{ change in quantity demanded}) \div (\% \text{ change in the price})$$

or

$$E_p = \frac{\Delta Q / Q}{\Delta P / P} = \frac{\Delta Q}{\Delta P}\left(\frac{P}{Q}\right)$$ (2.9)

where Δ refers to change in the variable. The price elasticity is always algebraically negative because an increase in price leads to a decrease in quantity demanded. Other elasticities, such as the income elasticity of demand, are derived similarly.

$$E_y = (\% \text{ change in quantity demanded}) \div (\% \text{ change in income})$$

or

$$E_y = \left(\frac{\Delta Q / Q}{\Delta Y / Y}\right) = \frac{\Delta Q}{\Delta Y}\left(\frac{Y}{Q}\right)$$ (2.10)

Income elasticity may be positive (if a normal good) or negative (if an inferior good). If a variable elicits no response at all, then elasticity is zero.

Numerical values for price elasticities are often reported in absolute values, eliminating the minus sign. Absolute values for price elasticities indicate the responsiveness of demand to price in that the greater the elasticity is the greater the responsiveness is. Absolute values greater than 1 are considered relatively responsive and are called elastic. Elasticities less than 1 in absolute value are called inelastic. In the limiting cases, zero price elasticity means that the demand curve is perfectly vertical, while infinite price elasticity means that the demand curve is perfectly flat.

The importance of price elasticity to policy questions can be illustrated with an example regarding cigarettes, which are clearly a health concern. Suppose that a state

[1] Percentages allow us to "standardize" our measure. In particular, the use of percentages eliminates problems comparing various goods that may be measured in pounds, liters, or meters. Here they are all measured in percent. For example, it becomes possible to compare demand elasticities for beef with automobiles, even though the price levels and quantities are different.

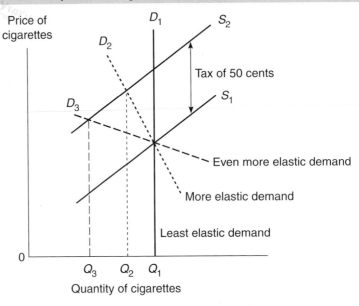

FIGURE 2-12 The Impact of a Cigarette Excise Tax

added 50 cents per pack to its tax on cigarettes. Together with supply-and-demand analysis, our elasticity concepts help us identify the main policy issues. Lawmakers are hopeful that such a tax increase will curb smoking and bring in tax revenue, but these tend to be contradictory goals. The exact effects will be difficult to predict unless reliable estimates are available of the cigarette price elasticity. If one discovered that demand is perfectly inelastic (D_1 in Figure 2-12), tax revenue would be at a maximum but with no effect on smoking or health. Alternative scenarios of increasingly elastic demand (D_2 and D_3) create bigger reductions in smoking but at the cost of decreasing tax revenues. Thus, the more elastic the response, the greater the effectiveness of an excise tax in inducing people to reduce their levels of smoking. Lewit and Coate (1982) indicate that teenagers, for example, are more responsive to cigarette prices than are adults. In such cases, taxes on cigarettes will be relatively more effective with teenagers.

Market demand elasticities vary by industry and by product. It is usually suggested that those goods and services that we call necessities tend to have elasticities less than one in absolute value, while luxuries are more elastic. Short-run elasticities are generally smaller in absolute value than long-run elasticities. It is further claimed that goods that cost only a tiny fraction of one's income motivate little or no "shopping around," hence making their demand elasticities very small in absolute value. Table 2-3 provides some common estimates of demand elasticities for a variety of products, and a reader can judge for oneself whether these patterns appear in practice.

Production and Market Supply

If market demand is one "blade of the scissors" in determining the price of a good, market supply by individual firms is the other. A typical firm will be faced with decisions on production levels, prices, production methods to be used, levels of advertising, and amounts of inputs to be purchased. The theory of the firm, much like the theory of

TABLE 2-3	Demand Price Elasticities for a Variety of Goods	
Good or Service	**Price Elasticity**	
Hospital Care[1]	–0.14 to –0.17	= melastic, neg. relationship
Physician Care[2]	0.16 to –0.35	
Apples (U.S.)[3]	–1.15	
Bread (U.K.)[3]	–0.26	
Gas, Short Run (Canada)[3]	–0.01 to –0.20	
Cigarettes (U.S.)[4]	–0.30 to –0.50	
Beer (U.S.)[5]	–0.20 to –0.40	
Beef (U.K.)[3]	–1.45	
Motion Picture Tickets[6]	–3.40	
Foreign Travel[6]	–3.10	

Notes: [1]Wedig (1988); [2]Manning (1987); [3]Mansfield et al. p. 103 (2002); [4]Keeler (1993); [5]Grossman (1998); [6]Ruffin & Gregory, p. 102 (1997).

consumer behavior for buyers, develops a framework for understanding how these choices are made.

The key assumption for most models of firm behavior is that the decision makers wish to maximize profits. It follows that the firm will try to minimize the costs of producing any given output and will undertake activities, such as advertising, only if they add to profits. Before examining such decisions, we will review production and cost relationships.

The Production Function

The production function shows the maximum sustainable output that can be obtained from all of the various possible combinations of inputs such as labor, materials, and machinery, with existing technology and know-how. It is useful to begin our discussion of production functions with a simple case—one in which there is just one input and one output. Suppose that food, perhaps in a hunter-gatherer society, were produced solely with labor. Let the production function be as shown in the top panel of Figure 2-13. The fact that the production function is rising indicates the idea that labor is productive; more labor means that more food is produced. The bowed shape of the curve illustrates a second idea—the law of diminishing returns.

It is understood in Figure 2-13 that the production takes place during a specified period of time. Thus, the output axis represents a flow of output per unit of time. Likewise, the labor input represents labor services applied during a specified period of time. The law of diminishing returns represents the idea that the marginal product (MP) of an input will eventually tend to fall as more is added. The MP (in this example, labor) is defined as the extra output that can be generated when one adds an additional hour of labor, holding all other inputs constant. In the figure, the food output increases from zero to 10 units when the first hour of labor is added. Thus, 10 units of food is the marginal product of the first unit of labor. When a second hour of labor is added, the output of food increases from 10 units to 16 units. The extra amount is 6 units, meaning that the marginal product of the second hour of labor is 6 units of food. The bottom panel of the graph illustrates the marginal product of consecutive hours of labor. The pattern of the MPs in this illustration is clear: They tend to get smaller as more labor is applied. This illustrates the law of diminishing returns. Notice that total output

FIGURE 2-13 Output and
Marginal Product of Labor

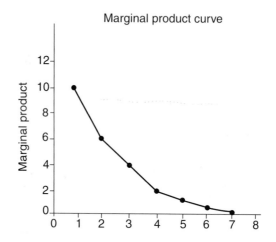

need never fall during diminishing returns. That is, the production curve itself never
turns downward in this illustration, although it may in some applications.

Production Functions

In practice, production processes may involve several different inputs, not just labor. It
is convenient to express the production relationship for a firm, or a unit of the firm, as
follows:

$$Q - f(X_1, X_2, \ldots, X_n) \tag{2.11}$$

Here Q represents output; $X_1, X_2,$ and so on are quantities of the various inputs.

The ultimate output of the health industry is health, and its related production
issues are termed the "production of health," a phrase that applies to larger popula-
tions but also to the consumer's production of his or her individual health. When
individuals seek to improve their family's health, they often purchase health care from
hospitals, clinics, nursing homes, home health agencies, and so on. One step removed
logically from health production, these elements of health care must themselves be
produced, and much economic research and concern are directed at this production
stage, too.

Consider, for example, the output of hospital X-ray services, which require the use
of labor by technicians, nurses, and radiologists, and machinery such as X-ray machines,
computers, and film. As with demand functions, production functions may take on

many different mathematical forms. The theory of production functions specifies only certain patterns for these functions.

One commonly applied functional form that fits the theoretical patterns for such functions is called the Cobb-Douglas form. Historically, it was one of the earliest production functional forms to be studied and applied to firms. It derives its name from the two authors who developed it, mathematician Charles Cobb, and economist (and later U.S. Senator) Paul Douglas. Many other functional forms of production have since been investigated, but this form is still commonly used in the classroom to illustrate the mathematics of the production process.

If the production of X-ray services just discussed fits the Cobb-Douglas form, and if inputs of all kinds are grouped into the categories of capital, K, and labor, L, the production function actually estimated might look like this:

$$Q = L^{0.8}K^{0.2} \qquad\qquad (2.12)$$

Here, as with any production function, there will be a unique level of maximum output for any combination of inputs. For example, Table 2-4 shows values of output corresponding to changes in L, holding K constant at 5 units. The change in output associated with a one-unit change in L is the marginal product of labor. More L (e.g., technicians) with the same amount of K will typically produce more Q (hence, a positive marginal product of labor), but as the machines become crowded or break down, the marginal product may fall as L increases. Hence, the marginal product in Table 2-4 diminishes. This decreasing marginal product again illustrates the law of diminishing returns. The average output or average product (AP) for each worker is Q/L, as shown in the last column.

Alternatively, we can derive various input combinations needed to produce a given output level. Table 2-5 illustrates several combinations that produce 10 units of output

TABLE 2-4 Production Schedule for X-ray Services

K	L	Q	MP	AP
5	0	0.00		
5	1	1.38	1.38	1.38
5	2	2.40	1.02	1.20
5	3	3.32	0.92	1.11
5	4	4.18	0.86	1.05
5	5	5.00	0.82	1.00
5	6	5.79	0.79	0.97
5	7	6.54	0.75	0.93

TABLE 2-5 An Isoquant Schedule

Q	L	K
10	1	100,000.00
10	5	160.00
10	7	41.60
10	8	24.40
10	10	10.00
10	11	6.80
10	13	3.50
10	20	0.63

<image_crop id="1" />

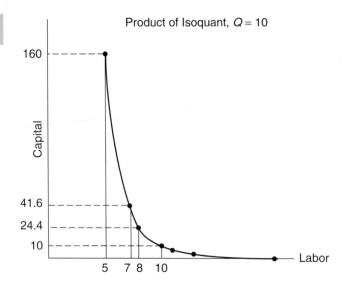

FIGURE 2-14 A Production Isoquant

for the production function represented by equation (2.12). This method closely parallels the indifference curve analyses introduced in an earlier section, except that we actually observe and measure the quantities produced (in contrast to the levels of utility that could only be ranked). Combinations of inputs producing equal output levels lie on an isoquant (literally, "the same quantity"). The isoquant in Table 2-5 is illustrated graphically in Figure 2-14. The isoquant map, representing all possible values of Q, would be the geometric representation of a production function.

The negative slope to an isoquant indicates the possibility of substituting inputs in the production process and of the positive marginal product of the inputs. Consider, again, the example of X-ray services. The numerical value of the isoquant slope, indicating how much capital (X-ray machines, film, computers) must be given up per unit increase in labor (nurses, technicians, radiologists), is called the marginal rate of technical substitution of labor for capital ($MRTS_{LK}$).

Is Substitution Possible in Practice? Empirical estimates reveal substantial substitution possibilities between physicians' assistants and physicians. Other studies reveal substitution between nurses and residents and between hospital capital and hospital staff. How can physical capital substitute for a human medical practitioner? Later chapters discuss these issues.

Isocost Curves

In order for the X-ray unit to maximize profits, the unit will want to minimize the cost of producing any given output. Letting TC represent total costs, w the price (wages, salaries, fringe benefits) of labor, and r the cost of buying or renting machines for the production period, the total cost is as follows:

$$TC = wL + rK \tag{2.13}$$

where L and K are the amounts of inputs used, labor and capital. For example, if $w = 50$, and $r = 20$, when the unit uses 30 hours of labor and 10 machines, $TC = 1,700 = (50 \times 30)+(20 \times 10)$. As with the consumer's budget problem, it is helpful to determine

all of the combinations of L and K that cost a given amount, such as \$1,000. The equation for this isocost curve is

$$1{,}000 = 50L + 20K \tag{2.14}$$

Again, as with the consumer example, we can rearrange the equation by placing capital (or labor) on the left-hand side, to yield

$$K = 50 - 2.5L \tag{2.15}$$

which is a linear equation as shown in Figure 2-15. The isocost curve for $TC = 686$ is also shown. More generally, equation (2.13) can be written as

$$K = TC/r - (w/r)L \tag{2.16}$$

Equation (2.16) shows the impacts of changes in wages and/or rental rates on the costs of purchasing various amounts of labor and/or machinery.

Cost Minimization or Output Maximization

In the example just given, the assumption that firms maximize profits requires that the X-ray unit select the least-cost method of producing its output. To produce Q^* units of output, the firm will wish to minimize the costs of that Q^* output, and hence be on the lowest possible isocost curve. The case where Q^* equals 10 units is illustrated in Figure 2-15. This will occur at point A, where the isocost curve is tangent to the isoquant representing 10 units of output. Higher isocost curves are unnecessarily wasteful; lower ones will not attain 10 units of output.

Suppose, on the other hand, that the firm has a budget of exactly \$686 and wishes to maximize its output. It is easy to see from Figure 2-15 that the same equilibrium condition will hold, and that the most the firm can produce is 10 units. Cost

FIGURE 2-15 Cost Minimization (Output Maximization) Determining Efficient Combinations of Labor and Capital

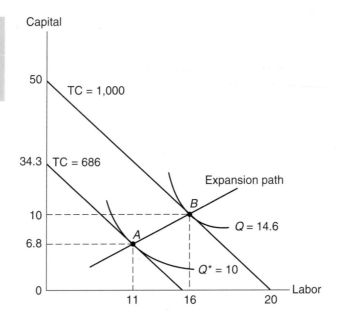

minimization and output maximization in the manner described lead to the same results.

LOOKING AT COSTS FROM A DIFFERENT VIEWPOINT Cost minimization can also be looked at from society's point of view. For example, hospitals may achieve cost minimization in applying hospital inputs, and home health care services may achieve cost minimization in applying home health care resources. But, for society as a whole to minimize its costs of care, we need to know which of these types of care is the most cost efficient for particular patients, home health care or inpatient hospital care, and we need to know if the quality of care is comparable.

Marginal and Average Cost Curves

By varying the production levels and finding the respective isocost curves, we can find the minimum cost of producing each output level. This is shown by the set of tangencies in Figure 2-15. The curve connecting these tangency points, *A* and *B*, is called the expansion path. Thus, the expansion path contains the information on the total cost and the average cost (cost/unit) of producing any output level.

If all inputs can be varied, then the long-run total cost and long-run average cost (LRAC) functions are generated. The LRAC curve is illustrated first in Figure 2-16. Total and average costs are related to the scale of the activity. If higher levels of production lead to improved ability to take advantage of specialization providing a better division of labor, it may be possible to reduce average costs; the case of decreasing long-run average costs is referred to as the case of economies of scale. If, on the other hand, the increased level of output leads to difficulties in managing and coordinating production activities, then long-run average costs may rise; this is referred to as the case of diseconomies of scale. Such issues are relevant for determining the optimal size for firms. For example, the socially optimal size and distribution of hospitals will depend on estimates of scale economies. As another example, it is clear that enough patient volume is needed to cover costs of such high-priced items as CAT scanners, a case of economies of scale. However, too many patients may lead to crowding of patients or to increased labor costs that could again increase costs, producing a case of diseconomies of scale.

In our specific Cobb-Douglas production function example, the LRAC will be a horizontal line reflecting constant average costs (about $68.60 per unit). This occurs simply because of the specific production function chosen as an example. Figure 2-16 shows the classical U-shaped relationship, which starts with economies of scale and

FIGURE 2-16 Long-Run Cost Curves for a Firm

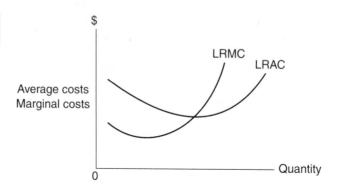

then yields to diseconomies of scale. The long-run marginal cost (LRMC) curve shows the cost of producing an incremental unit when all inputs (both machinery and labor) can be varied. It will go through the minimum point of the LRAC.

The short run corresponds to a period where at least one input (typically machinery or plant) cannot be changed. This form is particularly applicable to big-ticket machinery items in hospitals, for example. In such cases, there are some fixed costs (the machine costs or plant costs) that cannot be changed in the short run. The other costs are called variable costs (e.g., labor costs).

The Firm Supply Curve Under Perfect Competition

The cost curves we have reviewed can be used to develop a theory of the supply curve for a firm, but to do so we must know something about the demand curve for the firm's product. In our earlier practice with supply and demand, the demand curve represented the market demand for the product. The demand for a single firm's product may be different. To gain an idea of what a typical firm's demand curve will look like, we must know what type of market structure we are talking about.

Several market structures provide insights to an idealized world or applicability to the real world. One defining principle that distinguishes the various market structures is the degree of control that individual firms have over the price that they get paid. Two cases define the extreme forms of market structure: the competitive and the monopoly cases. We will look first at the competitive model, then discuss market structure more generally, and finally follow that discussion with the monopoly case.

The competitive model is rarely seen in the world in its idealized form. It requires several assumptions that ensure perfect competition. The assumptions are as follows:

1. A sufficient number of buyers and sellers of the good exist so that no single actor has any power over the price.
2. The good is homogeneous; that is, all producers produce the exact same good so that the market cannot be segmented on the basis of difference of goods.
3. Information is perfect. All buyers and sellers have information on all relevant variables such as prices and qualities.
4. No barriers to entry or exit are present. A producer starts producing, buying necessary machinery, patents, or anything else on terms that are equivalent to those already in the industry.

These assumptions ensure that a short-run market equilibrium can be represented by the price and the quantity at which demand and supply curves intersect. Figure 2-17 illustrates the model. Under the assumptions of competition, the demand curve facing the firm will be flat, as shown by the curve $D = MR = P$. To understand this point, consider a mental experiment. Suppose that the market for wheat was competitive and that it had determined, by the actions of market demand and supply, some equilibrium price for wheat, say $3.50 per unit, as shown. Suppose now that a single firm determined to raise its price above $3.50. Would anyone buy its product? They would not because they know (perfect information) that they can buy an identical product (homogeneous product) elsewhere for $3.50. In theory, at even a slightly higher price, the quantity demanded would slide horizontally to zero. On the other hand, suppose that the farmer wished to double the output. Would the farmer have to lower the price in order to sell it all? This would not be necessary because the farmer's output is small relative to the whole market (numerous buyers and sellers); hence, the farmer could sell as much as he or she wanted at the going price of $3.50.

FIGURE 2-17 The Competitive Firm's Supply Curve

The demand curve for this firm is labeled $D = MR = P$ indicating that it represents demand, as well as the marginal revenue for the firm and the going market price. It is worth noting that the market price is identical to the firm's marginal revenue. Marginal revenue is defined as the extra revenue obtained by selling one more unit of product. Because this firm can sell all it wants at the going market price, it can sell the marginal unit at that price, as well. Thus, marginal revenue equals price in the competitive model. It is only in cases where a firm has some monopoly power that marginal revenue will differ from price.

The profit-maximizing output for this competitive firm can now be deduced. The firm will maximize its profits at that output where marginal revenue (the price) equals marginal cost; this occurs in the figure at output Q^*. This output is called the firm's profit-maximizing output. The common sense of this seemingly technical proposition can be understood by examining a "wrong" output level—one that is not profit maximizing—for example, Q_1. Suppose a firm that is currently producing Q_1 units were to produce one more unit. The cost of this one extra unit would be A, by definition the point on the marginal cost curve at $Q = Q_1$. The revenue from this one extra unit would be B (which equals the price), the point on the marginal revenue curve at $Q = Q_1$.

The firm would increase its profits by producing that extra unit and would continue to increase its profits as long as the marginal revenue curve was above the marginal cost curve. Hence, maximum profits would occur only where $MR = MC$.

The supply curve for a firm shows the firm's profit-maximizing output at each possible price. The competitive firm is producing at the output where price equals marginal cost. If the market price were to rise in steps, the firm's adjustment steps would just be to follow the marginal cost curve on up.

The competitive firm's supply curve will be its marginal cost curve, as long as the price is sufficiently high to make it worthwhile to produce at all. Price must at least cover the firm's average variable cost (AVC).

The competitive market supply will be determined by the horizontal sum of the individual firm supply curves. This horizontal summing is done much in the manner in which we found market demand curves. The market supply curve in the competitive

case, the sum of firm marginal cost curves, will also represent the industry marginal costs of production. In general, under competition, the supply curve is the industry marginal cost curve.

What then determines the market price of a good? The answer is that combination of output and price at which market quantity demanded equals market quantity supplied, or the intersection of market demand and supply.

The assumption of free entry and exit, however, offers further insight into the workings of the competitive market. Suppose, for example, that the equilibrium price in the wheat market in the short run is high enough so that producers in the sector may earn attractive economic profits.[2] Any positive economic profit will be attractive to potential entrants. With perfect information and no barriers to entry, other suppliers will enter the market. This will increase market supply and drive down market prices. The entry process logically would continue in the long run until the prices have fallen enough to eliminate economic profits. In the long run, equilibrium profits will be zero, and price will be at the lowest point on each firm's long-run average cost curve.

However, if barriers to entry in the form of licensure or other restrictions exist, this adjustment process will be impeded. Sellers will be able to earn economic profits over long periods of time, perhaps indefinitely. Such a situation is not perfectly competitive even though the forces of demand and supply determine price at any moment. It is important to evaluate the extent to which all of the four conditions for competition stated at the beginning of this section are satisfied.

Monopoly and Other Market Structures

Firms in other market structures, unlike the perfect competitor, have market power, which is the ability to affect market price. These market structures entail the pure monopoly (and the natural monopoly version), monopolistic competition, and the several forms of oligopoly. In nearly all instances, the market power concept determines the characteristic of choice of optimal price or quantity. This concept is well illustrated by the pure monopolist.

A pure monopoly is an industry with a single seller who has no close substitutes. As such, the monopolist faces the whole market demand curve, which is usually downward sloping. Downward sloping demand and market power are synonymous concepts; this is because the monopolist, unlike the perfect competitor, will not lose all its customers when raising its price.

In health sectors, pharmaceutical firms that control patents for certain drugs may be pure monopolists. Individual physician practices are not pure monopolies, but because the numerous competitors of each are differentiated by reputation, patient loyalty, and patient/practice distance, each physician probably has some market power. Many economists treat physician markets as monopolistically competitive. Finally, when a town has only a few hospitals, each hospital also has some market power. There being few firms in that market, the hospitals would be considered an oligopoly.[3]

Equilibrium for the monopolist is illustrated in Figure 2-18. The demand curve facing the monopolistic firm is downward sloping because the monopolist faces the whole

[2]Economic profits represent profits after considering all costs including opportunity costs. A "normal" level of profits is necessary to keep firms in the market, and is a factor payment to the entrepreneur, just like a factor payment to workers or to owners of machines or materials.

[3]Degree of monopoly is a recurring theme in the discussion of market power and the need for regulation. We will return to this subject repeatedly.

FIGURE 2-18 The Monopolist's Equilibrium

downward sloping market demand curve. With a downward sloping demand curve, the incremental, or marginal revenue (MR) is less than the demand price. Why is this the case? Suppose the monopolist were selling Q_0 units at price P_0. Total revenue, TR_0, would be $P_0 Q_0$. The monopolist would be selling to everyone who is at least willing to pay the price P_0. In order to sell one more unit of the good, the monopolist would have to induce more consumers to buy by lowering the price. It may be impossible to lower the price to extra consumers without also lowering to all previous consumers. In this case, because the monopolist must lower the price to everyone else, the marginal revenue will be the price of the extra unit of the good sold minus the loss of revenue from everyone else who now pays less.

To maximize profit, the monopolist produces where $MC = MR$, at Q_0 in Figure 2-18. The corresponding price is P_0 and total profit is the rectangle $P_0 ACB$. If barriers to entry are persistent, the economic profits can be maintained and even increased through advertising, promotion, new product development, or other means.

The fact that the monopolist is earning excess profits suggests that the monopolist has reduced the amount produced from the competitive amount. The monopolist in the graph chooses point A on the demand curve. If the monopolist had acted like a competitor by setting a price equal to marginal cost (MC) it would have chosen point E, providing more output and charging a lower price. The induced scarcity caused by the monopolist necessarily raises the price to the consumer.

Welfare Losses

Economists seek to compare different economic situations or to examine the effects of different policies. In doing so, they often use the concept of allocative efficiency. One of the most widely used examples to illustrate the problem of inefficient resource allocation is found in the comparison of monopoly and competitive equilibria.

Consider once again the case of monopoly. Figure 2-19 shows the long-run marginal cost curve in an industry with constant marginal costs. With demand curve D, the competitive market equilibrium is at P_c and Q_c. Suppose, somehow, that the providers are able to form a monopoly. If so, it will be in their interest to raise prices by

BOX 2-2

Hospitals That Monopolize by Merger: Good or Bad? And, for Whom?

Monopolies or near monopolies are often created by mergers and acquisitions involving several firms. Bigness can be "good" when it enables firms to achieve economies of scale—provided they share this blessing with the public. The Federal Trade Commission, however, casts a skeptical eye on mergers when the monopolies so created cause "welfare losses" as described in this section.

U.S. hospitals went through a frenzy of mergers in the late 1990s, as is shown in the figure below. Did these create economic gains or welfare losses? Analysts try to answer this question by following up on the mergers, studying what happened afterward to hospital prices, availability, and accessibility of services.

But, there is now much more to the story. The American Civil Liberties Union (www.aclu.org, September 2005) is concerned that hospital mergers and takeovers by religious-affiliated groups means the reduction in the availability of reproductive health services. The complication creates challenging discussion questions: Is it right for the FTC to ignore religious beliefs about reproductive health services when assessing whether a hospital merger will curtail services? Is it right for those opposed to reproductive health to curtail such services via mergers and acquisitions?

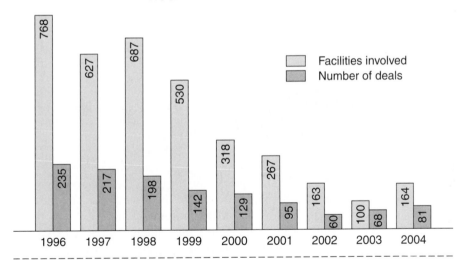

HOSPITAL MERGER ACTIVITY

Note: Includes deals completed or pending in the year noted. Includes mergers, acquisitions, joint ventures, long-term leases, and other partnerships.

Source: http://www.modernhealthcare.com/docs/03merge5.pdf

FIGURE 2-19 Welfare Loss of Monopoly

withholding services from the market. The resulting monopoly will produce at quantity Q_m, consistent with price P_m, where price is higher than marginal cost. The result reflects a loss to the consumer due to the monopoly. The total loss is indicated by the triangle ABC, called the welfare loss.

Welfare loss can be better understood if we think in terms of marginals. Consider first that the demand curve measures the highest price that people are willing to pay for an extra unit of the good. The price they are willing to pay measures their marginal benefit. Now consider what the consumer and society as a whole have to give up when they face a monopoly. The monopolist will choose output level Q_m. If we somehow could have produced one more unit of the good, the $(Q_m+1)^{th}$ unit, we would have made a net gain for society. The benefit of that extra unit is Q_mA in the graph because by marginal benefit (here equal to the height of the demand curve) we mean the benefit of the extra unit. Similarly, the cost to the monopolist, and thus to society as well, of the extra unit is Q_mB. Because the marginal benefit exceeds the marginal cost, the extra unit yields society a net gain of the rectangular shaded area.

Reasoning iteratively, another unit again yields another net gain to society, this time somewhat smaller than the first net gain. Net gains will continue to occur until we reach the output at which society's marginal benefit (demand) intersects its marginal costs, which occurs at C. The total net gain to society from increasing output up to the point at C equals the triangular area labeled ABC.

Conclusions

The microeconomic tools developed in this chapter consist of the production possibility frontier, demand-and-supply analysis, utility and indifference curve analysis, production and cost curves of a typical firm, firm behavior under competition and monopoly, and the measure of welfare loss. The economic tools used later in the text are direct applications or extensions of the tools developed here. By learning these ideas, you will gain an understanding of the terminology used in health economics, as well as an understanding of the type of reasoning used.

SUMMARY

1. The concept of scarcity underlies much economic thinking. Scarcity necessitates that decision makers make trade-off decisions at the margin. The production possibilities frontier represents these trade-offs, and its slope represents the opportunity cost of one good in terms of the other.
2. Supply-and-demand analysis of competitive markets is a basic tool of economics and provides insights that extend beyond the theoretical, perfectly competitive markets. Supply reflects sellers' offers as a function of price, and demand reflects buyers' offers as a function of price. The intersection of demand and supply describes the market equilibrium.
3. Comparative static analysis of demand and supply finds the new equilibrium after economic events shift either curve. Demand-increasing (-decreasing) events tend to raise (lower) equilibrium price, while supply-increasing (-decreasing) events tend to lower (raise) equilibrium price.
4. A relationship between one or more independent variables yielding a unique value for the dependent variable is called a function. The linear demand function, showing demand as a straight line, is only one special case of the many possibilities.
5. The utility function summarizes a consumer's preferences. Higher utility numbers are assigned to consumer bundles that provide higher levels of satisfaction, meaning that the consumer prefers these bundles.
6. Indifference curves are collections of points describing bundles that yield the same utility and hence the same level of satisfaction. Well-behaved indifference curves are downward sloping, continuous, and convex to the origin.
7. The budget constraint represents the combinations of goods that the consumer can afford given his or her budget. The budget constraint is downward sloping, and its slope is the negative of the ratio of prices.
8. In consumer theory, the consumer maximizes utility subject to a budget constraint. This means that the consumer picks the most preferred consumer bundle from among those he or she can afford. The equilibrium occurs at the tangency between the budget constraint and the highest attainable indifference curve.
9. Price elasticity depicts the responsiveness of demand to changes in price. It is defined as the ratio of the percentage change in quantity demanded to the percentage change in price. Each other elasticity also represents the ratio of a percentage change in a dependent variable to a percentage change in a given independent variable.
10. The production function describes the relationship of inputs to output. The marginal product of an input is the increase in output due to a one-unit increase in the input holding all others constant. That marginal product tends to decline as more input is added describes the law of diminishing marginal returns.
11. The average total cost curve of a firm shows the total cost per unit of output. The marginal cost curve shows the extra cost required to produce an additional unit of output.
12. The competitive firm in the short run produces that output where price equals marginal cost. The marginal cost curve is therefore the supply curve of the competitive firm.
13. In long-run equilibrium, entry by competing firms forces the typical competitive firm to produce an output level such that its price equals its minimum average cost. At this output, the competitive firm is producing the economically efficient output, and it is earning zero economic profits.
14. The pure monopolist faces the entire downward sloping market demand curve, and this implies that its marginal revenue lies below the demand curve. The monopolist restricts output, by comparison to the competitive case, and it charges a higher market price.
15. The pure monopoly case is one instance of a market in which a welfare loss occurs. A welfare loss, represented by an area under the demand curve and above the marginal cost curve, is an opportunity for mutual gains that is being foregone by the market.

DISCUSSION QUESTIONS

1. Explain the difference between cardinal and ordinal utility. Do you think that it is possible for researchers to find out which type of utility people actually have?

2. If a consumer always prefers more to less, can the indifference curves between the two goods be upward sloping? Explain. What if one of the "goods" is actually something unpleasant, like broccoli to a three year old?
3. The law of diminishing marginal returns states that eventually the marginal product of an input will tend to fall as more input is added. Describe real-life scenarios, explaining why this is likely to happen. For example, imagine a backyard garden of fixed size and all other inputs except labor also fixed; will adding a worker increase your output? Will adding another increase output by as much? Another?
4. If it makes sense that one type of labor can substitute for another in production, how can capital, a physical object, substitute for labor, a human being?
5. Describe the long-run equilibrium of the competitive firm. Conceptually remove a single assumption of perfect competition and analyze whether and how the process of long-run equilibrium would change? For example, if information were very imperfect, would the long-run equilibrium be achieved? If the firms' products were not exactly alike? If there were barriers to the entry of new competitors?
6. When a welfare loss occurs because of monopoly, what exactly is lost? Who loses it?
7. Resolve the following: "The price of ice cream increased in the summer, yet quantity also increased. Therefore, the law of demand does not apply to ice cream."
8. How is a production function affected by the invention of a new process related to it? Can this change result in lower prices to the consumer? What do you think? Do improvements in technological knowledge in the production of consumer goods necessarily reduce average family expenditures?

EXERCISES

1. Draw a production possibilities curve for an economy that produces two goods, health and entertainment. Show how this PPF would change if the technology for improving peoples' health was to improve. Show the change if there were an increase in the underlying available quantities of capital and labor.
2. Draw a production possibilities curve between health and all other goods. Insert a point in the drawing that illustrates an economy with an inefficient health system. Insert two additional points that illustrate two efficient economies but two that contrast in their relative emphasis on health care versus all other goods. Is there a cost to society of policies that lead to increases in health care? Explain.
3. Using a supply-and-demand graph and assuming competitive markets, show and explain the effect on equilibrium price and quantity of the following:
 a. A technological change that reduces the cost of producing X-rays on the market for physician clinic services.
 b. Increased graduations of new doctors on the market for physician services.
 c. The virtual elimination of smoking in the population on the market for hospital services.
 d. A price ceiling placed on physician fees in the market for physician services.
4. Graph the following demand functions:
 a. $Q_d = 110 - 3.3P$
 b. $Q_d = 100P^{-1.3}$
5. In a graph with OG on the vertical axis and Food on the horizontal, what is the Food-axis intercept? How does the budget constraint shift if the consumer's income level and the two prices all double?
6. Calculate the price elasticity for a $1 change in price at initial price level $300 for the demand function $Q_d = 1,500 - 1.5P$.
7. What is the slope of the isoquant described by the data in Table 2–5 when evaluated from a labor input of 7 to 8?
8. Assume that a monopoly firm has a linear demand curve and a constant marginal cost curve. Graph this firm's optimal output choice before and after a per-unit excise tax is placed on the output. Does the equilibrium price rise by as much as the tax?
9. Using equation (2.4), what is the demand equation as a function of P_s if the price of other pastas (P_o) is $2, the individual's income (Y) in thousands is $25, and tastes ($Z$) are represented by 20? What happens if the individual's income increases to $30?

CHAPTER

Statistical Tools for Health Economics

Hypothesis Testing

Difference of Means

Regression Analysis

Multiple Regression Analysis

Statistical Inference in the Sciences and Social Sciences

Conclusions

The ideas from economic theory must be tested and measured according to the standards of real-world data. Statistical techniques applied to economics are collectively called econometrics. In Chapter 2, we discussed supply and demand, as well as the importance of price and income elasticities. Economic theory predicts that demand curves will slope downward, but it does not predict the degree of responsiveness of demand to price and other variables; it is the task of statistical analysis to estimate these magnitudes. When close substitutes are available for a good, theory predicts that demand will be more sensitive to price than if no close substitutes are available. Yet it is hard to know whether a 1 percent increase in price will decrease the quantity demanded of the good by 10 percent, 1 percent, or 1/10 of a percent, yielding elasticities of −10.0, −1.0, or −0.1, respectively. Measurements of the economic behaviors of both people and firms may be crucial in analyzing whether drug companies raise drug prices, whether income subsidies will cause people to buy more drugs, or whether mandated levels of health care are economically efficient.

This chapter considers statistical methods that econometricians use to draw inferences from data that are collected. Many students with natural science backgrounds are familiar with laboratory experiments, where the environment is held as constant as possible and treatments are administered to experimental groups. The results are then compared to those of untreated control groups. One form of this design is called the dose-response model because the results or responses are generally related to the experimental treatment, or the dose.

Social science analysis of human behavior is rarely so fortunate as to find an experimental group that can be matched with a convenient control group. Social scientists, economists among them, must usually collect information from people doing day-to-day activities. Using statistical methods, they try to control for the confounding differences

among the people that they are analyzing. The more successful they are in controlling for such differences, the more reliable the analysis will be.

This chapter begins with discussions on how we form hypotheses. It then considers difference of means analysis as a way of introducing statistical inference. Most of the rest of the chapter concentrates on simple regression and multiple regression analyses that are most often used in economic and econometric analysis.

Hypothesis Testing

Economists who study health care have been confronted on occasion by statements that, while plausible, demand some validation:

"Twenty-year-old men have different cholesterol levels than 20-year-old women."
"Rich people spend more on health care than do poor people."
"Monopolists make more money than competitive firms."

These are all statements that either logic or casual observation would suggest to be true.

It would be useful, however, to have a rigorous method of determining whether the assertions are correct. Statistical methods suggest formulating these statements as hypotheses and collecting data to determine whether they are correct.

Take, for example, the first assertion about cholesterol levels for 20-year-olds. We state clearly both the hypothesis we wish to disprove (the null hypothesis), as well as the hypothesis the theory suggests to be the case (the alternative hypothesis). The null hypothesis, H_0, presently is:

Men's levels (c_m) equal women's levels (c_w), or

$$H_0 : c_m = c_w \tag{3.1}$$

against the alternative hypothesis H_1, that c_m does not equal c_w:

$$H_1 : c_m \neq c_w \tag{3.2}$$

To indicate that 20-year-old men's levels are, in fact, different from their counterpart women's levels, it is necessary to show convincing evidence that c_m is different from c_w. Hypotheses that are designed to test for equality among two or more items are sometimes called simple hypotheses.

Consider the second hypothesis, which asserts that rich people spend more on health care than do poor people. If we define health care expenditures of the rich (poor) as E_r (E_p), then the null hypothesis is:

$$H_0 : E_r = E_p \tag{3.3}$$

The alternative is:

$$H_1 : E_r > E_p \tag{3.4}$$

In this analysis, it may not be enough just to show that E_r is different from E_p. Certainly evidence that E_p is greater than E_r would not validate the hypothesis. Hypotheses that are used to test whether two or more items are greater (or less) than each other are sometimes called composite hypotheses. Having seen, then, how one might address the hypotheses in question, we now discuss how to test them.

Difference of Means

Let us return to the hypothesis about men's and women's cholesterol levels.[1] Some cholesterol is necessary to life; too much can be threatening, leading to coronary heart disease (CHD). Levels are measured in milligrams per deciliter (one-tenth of a liter). Levels typically range from 100 mg (extremely low) to 400 mg (extremely high). For individuals with levels between 240 mg and 300 mg, the likelihood of CHD is increased up to fourfold above that for individuals with levels below 200 mg.

Cholesterol levels depend on many factors. For example, those raised in more affluent families may have been better fed than those in poor families; poor children may have had diets higher in certain fats or starches. We would want to avoid bias in our results by making sure that our sample of women was not drawn primarily from one income level while the men were drawn from another.

We could attempt to avoid this sort of distortion by drawing our samples randomly from among all possible 20-year-olds, called the universe of data. Alternatively, we may try to choose samples of 20-year-old men and women from the same general income group. A sample of college sophomores, for example, from the same location and with similar socioeconomic status, may be a good group for holding many factors constant.

Even this example shows how difficult things may be to control. People of the same age (at the same college) may have had different prenatal care, birth weight, genetic composition, nutrition, vitamins, or exercise. The cholesterol level exhibited on a given test may depend on what the subject ate that morning (physicians often ask for a "fasting" cholesterol test to avoid this problem).

To compare men's and women's cholesterol levels, we need a test that can determine the differences between two distributions of continuous data. Continuous data are natural measures that in principle could take on different values for each observation. Examples include height, weight, income, or price. Categorical data refer to arbitrary categories such as gender (male or female), race (black, white, or other), or location (urban or rural). In this chapter, unless we specify categorical data, our methods will refer exclusively to the analysis of continuous data.

Suppose at this point that the econometrician tests one woman and finds her cholesterol level to be 180 ($c_w = 180$). The first man tested has a level of 150 ($c_m = 150$). This provides evidence that women have higher levels than men, because $c_w > c_m$, or $180 > 150$. It is not very convincing evidence, however. The man, or woman, or either, may not be typical of the entire group. What if a different man and/or woman had been selected? Would the answer have been different?

It seems logical to test several men and to compute the mean or average level by summing the levels and dividing them by the total number of men tested. Suppose, for example, that there were 30 men, and that the mean, or average level, \bar{c}_m, was 163.3. Suppose also that there were 30 women, and that the average level, \bar{c}_w, was 173.5. The difference, $d = \bar{c}_w - \bar{c}_m$, then, is 10.2.

The Variance of a Distribution

Although a difference of the two means is improved evidence, the econometrician desires a more rigorous criterion. It could be that the true level for both men and women is 170, but our sample randomly drew a higher average level for women (173.5) than for men (163.3). Figure 3-1 plots each observation. Although the mean levels differ (women have higher levels than men), some men have higher levels than some

[1]Sources for this discussion are U.S. Department of Health and Human Services (November 1990); and Rifkind et al. (1979).

FIGURE 3-1 Distribution of Cholesterol Levels for Women and Men

women. Statisticians have found the variance of a distribution to be a useful way to summarize its dispersion. To calculate the variance of women's levels, we subtract each observation from the mean (173.5), square that term, sum the total, and divide that total by the number of observations, N. Hence, variance, V, equals:

$$V_w = \frac{(110 - 173.5)^2 + (125 - 173.5)^2 + \ldots + (215 - 173.5)^2}{30} \quad \text{(3.5)}$$

This term reflects the variance of any individual term in the distribution. If V is large, then the dispersion around the mean is wide and another woman tested might be far from our mean. If V is small, then the dispersion around the mean is narrow and another observation might be close to the mean.

Standard Error of the Mean

The variance is often deflated by taking the square root to get the standard deviation, s, yielding:

$$s = \sqrt{V} \quad \text{(3.6)}$$

As with V, a large (small) value of s indicates a large (small) dispersion around the mean. Statisticians have shown that we can calculate the standard error of the mean itself by dividing s by the square root of the number of observations. Suppose, then, that the women's variance, V_w, equaled 587, so the standard deviation would equal the

square root of 587, or 24.2. The standard error of the mean would then equal s_w divided by the square root of 30, or (24.2 ÷ 5.5), which equals 4.4.[2]

A powerful theorem in statistics, the Central Limit Theorem, states that no matter what the underlying distribution, the means of that distribution are distributed like a normal, or bell-shaped, curve. Hence, we can plot the normal distribution of means of women's levels with a mean of 173.5 and a standard error of 4.4.

Statisticians have also shown that a little more than 68 percent of the area under the curve would be within one standard error, or between levels of 169.1 (173.5 – 4.4) and 177.9 (173.5 + 4.4), and that 95.4 percent would be within two standard errors. This means that we could be about 95 percent sure that the true mean cholesterol level for 20-year-old women was between 164.7, [173.5 – (2 × 4.4)], and 182.3, [173.5 + (2 × 4.4)].

A similar calculation can be done for men, yielding a similar measurement. Intuitively, the further apart the means and the smaller the dispersions (standard errors), the more likely we are to determine that the average level for men is smaller than that for women. To test the hypothesis formally, we then construct a "difference of means" test. We wish to compare the measurement $d = \bar{c}_w - \bar{c}_m$, to zero, which was the original hypothesis.

Here $d = 10.2$. The variance of the difference is defined as the sum of the variances of the standard errors. If the standard error for women was 4.4 as we calculated it, and the standard error for men given the sample in Figure 3-2A was 4.1, then the standard error of the difference would be:

FIGURE 3-2 Cholesterol Levels

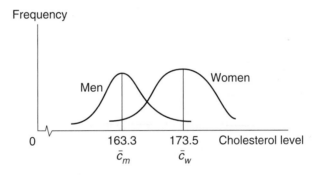

A. Means of Cholesterol Level

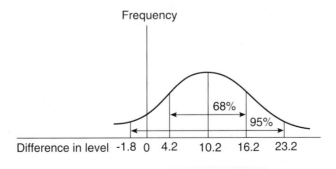

B. Difference of Means

[2]Formally, in a sample, we calculate the standard error by dividing by $n-1$. All calculations are rounded to the nearest tenth.

$$s_d = \sqrt{4.4^2 + 4.1^2} = \sqrt{19.36 + 16.81} = \sqrt{36.17} = 6.02 \qquad \textbf{(3.7)}$$

The difference and its distribution also can be plotted.

The most probable value of the difference, as noted in Figure 3-2B, is 10.2. About 68 percent of the distribution lies between 4.18 (i.e., $10.2 - 1 \times 6.02$) and 16.22 (i.e., $10.2 + 1 \times 6.02$). About 95.4 percent of the distribution lies between -1.84 (i.e., $10.2 - 2 \times 6.02$) and 22.24 (i.e., $10.2 + 2 \times 6.02$).

This experiment would find good, although not absolutely conclusive, evidence that 20-year-old women have higher cholesterol levels than 20-year-old men. The probability that the difference of 10.2 would have been found, when the true difference is 0, is certainly less than 32 percent (100 percent less than the 68 percent figure); however, it is greater than 4.6 percent (100 percent less the 95.4 percent figure).

Alternatively, the t-statistic, comparing the numbers 10.2 and 0.0, equals $10.2 \div 6.02$, or approximately 1.69. Statisticians calculate tables of t-statistics, whose critical values are related to the size of the sample. With a sample of 30, a t-statistic of 1.69 is statistically significant at about the 90 percent level. Still another way of phrasing this is to say that there is not more than a 10 percent chance that this difference of 10.2 between women and men was the result of a random draw from two distributions that have the *same* means.[3]

Hypotheses and Inferences

This process illustrates the steps that are necessary to test hypotheses appropriately. The econometrician must do the following:

1. State the hypotheses clearly: $c_m = c_w$, against $c_m \neq c_w$.
2. Choose a sample that is suitable to the task of testing: a matched sample of men and women of the same age, in the same location.
3. Calculate the appropriate measures of central tendency and dispersion: the mean and the standard error of the mean for both men and women, leading to the difference of the two means.
4. Draw the appropriate inferences: 20-year-old men have different cholesterol levels than 20-year-old women, if we accept inferences at a 10 percent confidence level (although economists often use more rigorous 5 percent or even 1 percent confidence levels).

No matter how sophisticated the method used, good statistical analysis depends on the ability to address these four criteria and stands (or falls) on the success in fulfilling them. Box 3-1 provides a particularly good example of how analysts have examined the impacts of electromagnetic fields (EMFs) on children living near power lines.

There are, of course, measures of central tendency other than the mean. Analysts may worry that someone with a particularly high cholesterol count may influence the mean. A different measure, the median, calculates a statistic such that half of the observations are greater than the median and half are less. Thus, a median cholesterol level of 173.5 would imply that half of the sample was higher than 173.5, and half lower. The median is less sensitive to extreme values in the data (e.g., someone with a count of 400 would have no more effect on a median of 173.5 than does another with a count of 300). However, the median presents some mathematical problems in hypothesis testing. Simple formulae for standard errors of medians are not available, so hypothesis testing is difficult.

[3]The difference in this example is approximately the difference found in Rifkind et al. (1979). The standard errors in the Rifkind article are smaller because they come from analyses using larger samples.

BOX 3-1

No Link Between Childhood Cancer and Electromagnetic Fields

In 1979, Dr. Nancy Wertheimer and her assistant, Ed Leeper, reported that children who lived near power lines had twice the normal incidence of leukemia. The study was criticized because it was small and relied on indirect evidence rather than direct measurements of exposure to electromagnetic fields (EMFs). However, the report and its findings had major impacts. Parents of children with cancer sued power companies. Owners near power lines saw reductions in the values of their homes.

Scientists began to examine the issue. While the studies tended to be small, and sometimes inferred exposure many years after the children had developed cancer, some did find associations between power lines and cancer.

In 1997, a new collaborative study between scientists at the National Cancer Institute and specialists from the nation's leading medical centers reported that there was no evidence showing that electric power lines cause leukemia in children. The study compared 636 children with acute lymphoblastic leukemia, the most common childhood cancer, to 620 healthy children who were matched to the cancer patients by race, age, and residential neighborhood. The researchers asked, "Did the children who developed leukemia have a higher exposure to magnetic fields produced by power lines?"

To answer the question, the researchers assessed the children's exposure to magnetic fields produced by power lines in their current and past residences, as well as where the mothers lived when they were pregnant. They measured the fields in the children's yards, schools, and day care centers and also had the children walk around with measurement devices. Investigators did not know which children had had cancer.

The research team, headed by Dr. Martha S. Linet of the National Cancer Institute, found that the children living in houses with the highest EMFs were about 24 percent more likely to develop leukemia than children in houses with the lowest EMFs. However, this difference was not statistically significant. Nonetheless, the fact that positive relationships exist over some range of the data is often misinterpreted as proof that definitive relationships exist.

Dr. Linet's group tested the hypothesis by relating the differences in means among groups, which were relatively small, to their variation, which was relatively large. This indicated that their measured effect was probably due to chance, rather than reflecting systematic differences. Their statistical test implied that they could not confidently reject the null—that the true rates of leukemia were equal and unrelated to the level of EMFs.

SOURCE: Martha S. Linet, Elizabeth E. Hatch, Ruth A. Kleinerman, et al., "Residential Magnetic Field Exposures and Childhood Acute Lymphoblastic Leukemia," *New England Journal of Medicine 337* (July 3, 1997): 1–7.

Regression Analysis

The difference of means analysis is extremely useful in treating continuous data that can be broken up by categories, such as gender, race, or location.[4] Yet many interesting economic variables occur naturally as continuous variables. Health care expenses, physician visits, firm profits, as well as prices and/or incomes could take large numbers of values naturally, and are grouped into categories only with serious loss of information. If we have information on income, in terms of dollars per year, we can distinguish among households with incomes of $10,000, $20,000, $30,000, and so on. If we were to

[4]Although difference of means considers only two categories, analysis of variance methods allow the consideration of three or more categories. Newbold (1995) presents good discussions on this and other statistical topics.

define high income as greater than $40,000, for example, separating all of the different incomes into two categories, we would then have no way of distinguishing between households with incomes of $10,000 and $20,000 (or, for that matter, between households with incomes of $50,000 and $100,000).

Regression analysis allows the econometrician to fit a straight line through a set of data points. How might this be used for policy analyses? Economists and health policy makers alike have long sought to determine how responsive cigarette consumption is to excise taxes. Recognizing that cigarette smoking is a dangerous habit, economists have reasoned that if the price is raised by taxes, consumption is likely to decline, but the question is "how much?"

Cigarettes are produced nationally and are subject to the same federal taxes, but excise tax rates vary from a few cents per pack in some states to well over $1 per pack in others. In 2001 and 2002, the National Institute of Health, as part of a larger study called NESARC, interviewed almost 10,000 individuals across the United States who had smoked within the past 12 months.[5] These subjects were asked their average daily cigarette consumption over the past 12 months. They were also asked a wide range of questions focusing on addictive behaviors, including smoking, drinking, legal, and illegal drugs, as well as numerous questions about occupation, education, and income. Because the state of residence was known, an analyst could append readily available data on state level excise taxes.

Suppose that we wish to relate the amount of cigarettes smoked per day to the tax price of the cigarettes. Since cigarettes must be purchased in order to be consumed, we would like to know how responsive the quantity demanded is to the tax price (the tax price elasticity). Recall that the price elasticity relates the percent change in quantity to the percent change in price. It would be useful to draw a straight line that would summarize the relationship.

Ordinary Least Squares (OLS) Regressions

Two rules are commonly used to determine this line. The first rule is that the deviations (unless the line fits perfectly) from the line must sum to zero. Positive deviations must be offset by negative deviations. We can show, however (see Figure 3-3), that many lines have this characteristic. For example, dashed lines R_1 and R_2 both have zero net deviations. It is necessary to have a second criterion by which to distinguish among the large number of lines where the sum of the deviations equals zero.

The second criterion is to minimize the sum of the squared deviations of the actual data points from the line that is fitted. Even though the sum of the deviations equals zero, the sum of the squared deviations must be positive (any number multiplied by itself is either zero or positive). Hence, one can choose among the many lines that have sums of zero deviations by picking the one line with the minimum or least sum of the squared deviations. Such analyses are called ordinary least squares (OLS) analyses.

The resulting equation would have the following form:

$$Q = a + bP + \varepsilon \tag{3.8}$$

where P and Q refer to price and quantity, and a and b are the parameters to be estimated. Parameter a is sometimes referred to as the constant, or the intercept. It might refer to the demand for Q in the unlikely event that the tax price of cigarettes was zero. Parameter b refers to the slope of the line and shows the direction and magnitude of

[5]The NESARC (National Epidemiologic Survey on Alcohol and Related Conditions) is among many publicly available databases that can be acquired without charge on the Internet. At this time, it is located at http://niaaa.census.gov/ (accessed July 21, 2005).

the impact of a change in P on the quantity demanded. Because we expect a higher level of P to decrease the amount of cigarettes purchased (assuming that the subjects purchase the cigarettes that they smoke), we expect b to be negative.

The last parameter is the error term ε. No regression analysis will fit the data exactly. Errors are likely and may reflect several causes. We may have omitted a variable, such as age (older people may smoke more) or education (more educated people may be more aware of the dangers of smoking). We may have measured one or more of the explanatory variables or the dependent variable (the amount of cigarettes) inaccurately. All of these may stand in the way of our predicting the amount demanded exactly. In advanced econometric work, understanding ε is crucial for ensuring that the estimated parameters are accurate. Our exposition here will assume that ε obeys the rules to allow us to make appropriate inferences with OLS analyses. We will examine some exceptions later in the chapter.

A Demand Regression

Table 3-1 shows the result of a simple regression of cigarette consumption against the tax price of cigarettes.

$$Q = 17.02 - 3.75* \textit{tax per} \text{ pack, } R^2 = 0.01 \qquad \textbf{(3.9)}$$
$$(0.34)$$

This equation indicates that a \$1 increase in the tax price P of a pack of cigarettes leads to a decrease in quantity demand of 3.75 fewer cigarettes per day among those who smoke. The standard error of estimate for the coefficient of price, P, is 0.34. This term is similar to the standard error of the estimated mean in the example of men's and women's cholesterol levels earlier in the chapter. As before, the smaller the standard error is relative to the estimated value of b (in this case, −3.75), the better the estimate.

In this regression, the standard error of 0.34 is relatively small compared to the coefficient, −3.75; hence, the coefficient is significantly different from zero. The expression R^2 is used to measure the fraction of the variation of the quantity of cigarettes explained by the price alone. An R^2 of 0.01 implies that about 1 percent of the variation was explained.

It is useful to examine this simple regression in detail because it has many features that occur in more complex analyses. Consider the following hypothesis:

H_0: Tax price doesn't matter; that is, $b = 0$

against the alternative hypothesis, which is:

H_1: Tax price is inversely related to quantity consumed; that is, $b < 0$.

The test of the hypothesis is similar to a difference of means test. In particular, we are testing the difference between −3.75 (estimated with standard error 0.34) and 0. Remember that because demand is downward sloping, the coefficient will be negative. The t-statistic here is 10.9; that is, the value of the coefficient, 3.75, divided by the standard error of 0.34. The value of 10.9 suggests that we can be more than 95 percent sure that the tax price has an effect on quantity of cigarettes consumed. This term is statistically significant in its difference from zero.

If 1 percent of the variation of the quantity of cigarette demand is explained, then 99 percent is unexplained. In part, this occurs because the regression does not include some variables that are likely to be important. We have noted earlier that there are several other variables that might help to explain the consumption of cigarettes. If these are included in the analysis, we are likely to explain more of the variation in cigarette consumption. The inclusion of more variables in a *multiple regression* is explained later.

This example illustrates cross-sectional analysis, which provides snapshots of a slice of the population at one period in time. Because we do not follow the people in the sample over time, we may not be aware of continuing health problems, changes in wealth or income, or systematic differences in ability that cannot be measured and which cross-sectional models treat as "random noise." As a result, cross-sectional regressions often explain less variance than panel data, which follow households over time, or time-series data, which calculate aggregates over time.

Estimating Elasticities

Regressions also are used to estimate elasticities. Recall that the definition of the price elasticity of demand (E_p) is the percentage change in quantity demanded, elicited by a 1 percent change in price. This is written as:

$$E_p = \frac{\%\ \text{change in quantity}}{\%\ \text{change in price}} = \frac{\Delta Q\ /Q}{\Delta P\ /P}, \text{or } E_p = \frac{\Delta Q}{\Delta P}\left(\frac{P}{Q}\right)$$

The term ΔP stands for a one-unit change in the price, while the term ΔQ represents the resulting change in the quantity demanded. It follows that $\Delta Q/Q$ is a measure of the percentage change in quantity, whereas $\Delta P/P$ is a measure of the percentage change in price. In rearranging terms at the right, the term $\Delta Q/\Delta P$ represents the ratio of changes and is the reciprocal of the slope of the demand curve. With a linear function as in this case, this is the coefficient of price; that is, −3.75.

In calculating an elasticity from the coefficients estimated in a regression, a different elasticity may be calculated for each different starting price that is assumed. Therefore, it is also necessary to have reference values for P and Q, and the mean (or average) values are often used. In our sample, the mean number of cigarettes smoked per day is 15.3 (about three-quarters of a pack), and the mean tax price is $0.454 (about $.45 per pack).

Hence, calculated at the mean,

$$E_p = -3.75 \times (0.45 \div 15.3), \text{ or } -0.11 \tag{3.10}$$

This says that a 10 percent increase in the tax price of cigarettes would lead to a 1.1 percent decrease in quantity demanded. Does this make sense? Cigarettes, after all, are an addictive substance, and many people find it difficult to reduce their demand. Yet, there is clearly a negative effect, and one could also argue that doubling the tax (say from $.50 per pack to $1 per pack— a 100% increase) could reduce demand by 11.1%, a sizable amount.

Multiple Regression Analysis

Students of economics are aware that real-world relationships are seldom two-dimensional, as useful as this situation would be in drawing graphs. As noted, demand for cigarettes may be related not only to the price, but to income, Y. Older people (variable A for age) may smoke more, having been addicted for longer, and more educated people, E, may recognize the dangers of smoking and smoke less. In addition, women have traditionally smoked less, and various groups, variable G, may have differing tastes toward smoking cigarettes. Indeed, the omission of important variables may lead to particular behavior in the error term, ε.

If each relationship could be graphed, assuming that nothing else was changing, then simple regression would work fine. Fortunately, the mathematics necessary to estimate the appropriate relationship can accommodate more than two dimensions. It is easy to write the following multiple regression:

$$Q = a + bP + cY + dA + eE + fG + \varepsilon \qquad \textbf{(3.11)}$$

Although the example presented in Table 3–1 will use eight dimensions now rather than two dimensions, we use exactly the same least squares criteria as before. The interpretation of the coefficients is similar to before but is done with more confidence. With the simple regression, relating Q only to P, the econometrician would not know whether income, Y, or age, or education, was varying as well. Including them in this regression allows us to "hold constant" these other variables and reduce the error. As a result, elasticities can now be calculated under the condition that "all else is equal."

The R^2 measure of variation explained earlier also is available here. R^2 will always rise with more variables. (If you add variables, you can't explain less of the variation!) Several methods can be used to interpret R^2, and some statisticians wish to maximize R^2; that is, to explain as much variation as possible.[6] While this may be desirable, most econometricians are at least as interested in the values of the parameters that are estimated.

Interpreting Regression Coefficients

Table 3-1 shows both the original simple regression (A), and a more complex multiple regression (B) where the standard errors of the coefficients and the t-statistics are also included. This multiple regression shows that a $1 increase in the tax price of cigarettes, P, implies a decrease in quantity of tax demanded of 2.77 cigarettes per day. Income, measured in thousands of dollars per year, has a slightly negative effect, but

[6]Often, R^2 is adjusted for the number of explanatory variables and the number of observations, and is termed as the adjusted R^2 or \bar{R}^2. Its relation to R^2 is:

$$1 - \bar{R}^2 = \frac{n-1}{n-k-1}\left(1 - R^2\right)$$

where n is the number of observations and k is the number of explanatory variables. Adding more variables, k will always raise R^2 but will not necessarily raise \bar{R}^2.

TABLE 3-1 Excise Taxes and Cigarette Demand

Variable	A. Simple Regression			B. Multiple Regression			C. Interactive		
	Coefficient	Std. Error	t Value	Coefficient	Std. Error	t Value	Coefficient	Std. Error	t Value
Intercept	17.02	0.19	89.79	17.46	0.62	28.11	17.39	0.62	27.96
Excise Tax	−3.75	0.34	−10.89	−2.77	0.33	−8.38	−2.78	0.33	−8.42
Income (in $ × 1,000)				−0.0019	0.0025	−0.78	−0.0020	0.0025	−0.82
Gender (1 if male)				2.17	0.21	10.58	2.33	0.22	10.71
Race (1 if African American)				−5.06	0.33	−15.26	−4.30	0.48	−8.95
Age (in years)				0.13	0.01	18.59	0.13	0.01	18.58
Educational Level				−0.65	0.05	−12.20	−0.65	0.05	−12.19
Hispanic (1 if Hispanic)				−6.41	0.37	−17.48	−6.42	0.37	−17.52
African American and Male							−1.44	0.66	−2.18
R^2	0.0119			0.1114			0.1118		
Excise Tax Elasticity	−0.1114			−0.0822			−0.0826		
Number of Observations	9,810			9,810			9,810		

Source: Computations from NESARC by A. Goodman, 2005.

that effect does not differ statistically from zero. Older people smoke slightly more, and more educated people smoke slightly less. Women, African Americans, and Hispanics all smoke significantly fewer cigarettes than do white males.

As was done with the simple regression, predicted values of the dependent variable and values of the elasticities can be computed. As before, hypotheses can be tested. The addition of more variables leads to a fall in the price elasticity from about −0.11 to about −0.08, but still statistically significant.

Most often, again, econometricians are interested in whether coefficients are positive or negative and whether they differ significantly from zero. In the cigarette example, excise tax increases clearly accompanied decreases in cigarette consumption. In a now famous example, Box 3-2 presents the surprising results of a detailed multivariate analysis looking at the impacts of hormone replacement therapy on postmenopausal women.

Dummy Variables

In health care research, econometricians often are interested in whether particular groups of patients or subjects differ from others. For example, Table 3-1 denoted women, African Americans, and Hispanics, by using 1 if the person was a member of such a group, and zero otherwise. These groups were indicated by using binary, or dummy, variables. For example, an econometrician may wish to indicate whether a household is white (white = 1), or not (white = 0), or whether it is headed by a woman (female = 1) or not (female = 0).

Figure 3-4 shows how the estimated coefficients of these two variables could be treated, using the regression from Table 3-1. The northwest box indicates an observation for which both male and African American equal 0. If male = 1, then the coefficient b_m for both lower boxes indicates whether the person smokes more or less (and whether

BOX 3-2

Hormone Replacement Therapy—Rigorous Statistics Reveal Surprising Results

As of July 2002, approximately 38 percent of post-menopausal women in the United States used hormone replacement therapy (HRT). While the U.S. Food and Drug Administration–approved indications for HRT include relief of menopausal symptoms (hot flashes, night sweats, and vaginal dryness) and prevention of osteoporosis, long-term use has been common to prevent a range of chronic conditions, especially heart disease. Advertisements by drug companies urged women to take HRT so they would stay "forever feminine."

Although widely used, many scientists had expressed concern that studies finding benefits of HRT were based on nonrandom samples of women who sought out the hormone therapy. The users of HRT were better educated and healthier than postmenopausal women who did not take HRT. Thus, some researchers felt that "selection bias" could account for the effectiveness of HRT because those women for whom it was not effective and those who found the side effects bothersome or harmful, as well as less educated and sicker women, were not included in the studies.

Between 1993 and 1998, a randomized clinical trial called the Women's Health Initiative (WHI) studied 16,608 postmenopausal women aged 50 to 79. Roughly half of the participants were randomly assigned to the experimental group and received HRT, a daily tablet containing conjugated equine estrogen and medroxy progesterone acetate (progestin). The other half was randomly assigned to the control group and received a placebo (an inert pill with no medical properties). Study participants were contacted by telephone six weeks after randomization to assess symptoms and reinforce adherence. Follow-up for clinical events occurred every six months with annual in-clinic visits required. A multitude of health outcomes were measured related to cardiovascular disease, stroke, cancer, fractures, and death. The statistical analysis was complex and compared the health outcomes for the experimental group who took the estrogen/progestin tablet to the control group who took the placebo.

Formal monitoring began in the fall of 1997, with the expectation of final analysis in 2005 after an average of approximately 8.5 years of follow-up. An independent data and safety monitoring board (DSMB) examined interim results to determine whether the trial should be stopped early, in particular if the treatment proved either significantly beneficial or harmful to the experimental group, relative to the control group.

By May 2002, an average of 5.2 years into the analysis (recall that women had entered the study over a five-year period), the DSMB determined that there were significantly higher risks of breast cancer, coronary heart disease, stroke, and pulmonary embolism in the experimental group, and that these increased probabilities outweighed some evidence of reduced risk of fractures and colon cancer. Therefore, the DSMB recommended an early stopping of the estrogen plus progestin component of the trial because it would be unethical to put more women at risk for adverse events by continuing HRT. The results were released in the *Journal of the American Medical Association*, and due to the sheer number of women being treated and the surprising findings, the results made front-page headlines and led off the nightly news for several weeks. A treatment that had been taken for granted as beneficial in reducing menopausal symptoms and preventing heart disease had been subjected to a carefully designed randomized clinical trial. The results sent shock waves through the medical system.

SOURCES: Writing Group for the Women's Health Initiative Investigators, "Risks and Benefits of Estrogen Plus Progestin in Healthy Postmenopausal Women," *Journal of the American Medical Association* 288 (3) (2002): 321–333; Suzanne W. Fletcher and Graham A. Colditz, "Failure of Estrogen Plus Progestin Therapy for Prevention," *Journal of the American Medical Association* 288 (3) (2002): 366–368.

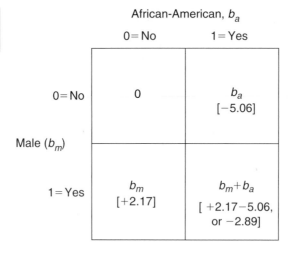

FIGURE 3-4 Interpreting the Effects of Dummy Variables

In Table 3-1, coefficient b_a = –5.06, and coefficient b_m = +2.06. We see that African American women ("northeast box") smoke 5.06 fewer cigarettes than white women. White men smoke 2.17 more cigarettes than white women. Finally African American men smoke 2.89 = (–5.06 + 2.17) fewer cigarettes per day than white women.

this is significant). This is a row effect. If African American = 1, then the coefficient b_a indicates whether white households purchase more or less cigarettes (and whether that is significant). This is a column effect. If the household is both white and female-headed, then the combined effect is $(b_m + b_a)$.

In fact, if one felt that black males may have particular attitudes or preferences for smoking, one could estimate a coefficient that addresses the interaction of the two effects (1 if African American and male, 0 otherwise). This would be coefficient b_{am}. Here, the impact of being black and male would be $(b_a + b_m + b_{am})$. This is noted in the Interactive Model of Table 3-1. Compared with white women (the "northwest" quadrant of the diagram), white men smoke 2.33 more cigarettes, African American women smoke 4.30 fewer cigarettes, and African American men smoke (2.33 + 4.30 – 1.44), or 3.41 fewer cigarettes.

Statistical Inference in the Sciences and Social Sciences

Natural scientists attempt, not always successfully, to control experimentally for all of the other possible sorts of variation other than the relation being studied. By contrast, econometricians are seldom so fortunate. Occasionally, experimental economic studies are done, but such projects are expensive. One such study was the multimillion-dollar health insurance experiment of the late 1970s and early 1980s, funded by the federal government. We discuss parts of that study in several later sections of the book.[7] Even with the careful planning that went into the experimental design, this study could not avoid some major analytical issues.

Other fields have similar problems. A 1988 report from the Panel of the Institute of Mathematical Statistics referred to analytical problems in chemistry:

The data are frequently complex with a large number of dimensions, may sometimes have a time element, and can be further complicated because of missing values. In some instances, standard multivariate or time series methods

[7]There are excellent reviews by Manning and his collaborators (1987) and Newhouse et al. (1993).

may suffice for analysis, but, more commonly, novel developments are required, for example, to handle the problem of multivariate calibration ... (Olkin and Sacks, 1988, p. II-1)

Econometricians must most often use natural experiments and must seek ways to account for the other variations. Because many policies, such as the provision of public health services or the regulation of the prescription drug industry, depend on accurate measurement of economic phenomena, it is essential that the measurements be accomplished carefully and scientifically.

Conclusions

This chapter has provided a "taste" of the statistical methods necessary to address questions that occur in health economics and to clarify the analyses where statistical material is presented later in the text. To understand the text, it is important to be able to formulate questions in terms of hypotheses, read statistical test results to determine if the result is significant, understand statistical significance, and interpret reported regression results.

The emphasis on problems to watch for in statistical analysis is not meant to generate undue skepticism over the statistical data to be reported. On the contrary, the discussion is meant to help distinguish the better studies where confidence can best be placed. Statistics applied to health economics may provide important information even though individual statistical analyses may be flawed by the use of improper techniques. A lab dish may be chipped, but one does not conclude that it is impossible to prove anything through laboratory experimentation.

SUMMARY

1. Economists usually must collect information from people doing day-to-day activities and use statistical methods to control for the confounding differences among the people that they are analyzing. The more successful they are in controlling for such differences, the more reliable the analysis will be.
2. Statistical methods suggest formulating economic assertions as hypotheses, and collecting data to determine whether the hypotheses are correct.
3. Hypotheses that are designed to test for equality among two or more items are called simple hypotheses. Hypotheses that are used to test whether two or more items are greater (or less) than each other are called composite hypotheses.
4. Several steps are necessary to test hypotheses appropriately. The econometrician must:
 - state the hypotheses clearly,
 - choose a sample that is suitable to the task of testing,
 - calculate the appropriate measures of central tendency and dispersion, and
 - draw the appropriate inferences.
5. Regression analysis allows the econometrician to fit a straight line through a set of data points. In ordinary least squares regression, the sum of the squared deviations of the actual data points from the line is minimized.
6. R^2 measures the proportion of the total variation explained by the regression model. While it may be desirable to maximize R^2, most econometricians are at least as interested in the values of the parameters that are estimated.
7. Identification is the problem of estimating the underlying functions (structural relations) within the context of a joint (simultaneous) relationship, such as demand and supply.
8. Important skills in statistical analysis include:
 - understanding statistical significance,
 - interpreting reported statistical results, and
 - detecting problems in reported statistical findings.

DISCUSSION QUESTIONS

1. List at least three ways in which natural experiments differ from laboratory experiments.
2. What is the difference between a simple hypothesis and a composite hypothesis? Why might economists choose one over another?
3. In considering the difference in cholesterol levels between men and women, what is the null hypothesis? What is the alternative hypothesis? Is the alternative hypothesis simple or composite?
4. Suppose that we wish to compare the health status of two groups of people. What variable might we use to measure the status? What variables might we wish to control in order to draw the appropriate inferences?
5. If someone reports that the mean weight for fourth-grade boys is 80 pounds and for fourth-grade girls is 78 pounds, what must you know to test hypotheses using the difference of means?
6. If we are trying to relate output to labor inputs and capital inputs using regression analysis, would we expect the coefficients of the regressions to be positive or negative? Why?
7. What are dummy variables? How are they useful in identifying differences among groups?
8. Suppose that you used regression methods to estimate the demand curve for physician visits and found a positive relationship; that is, you found that the higher the price is, the more visits are demanded. What problem has likely arisen? Explain the problem in words. Why might it make statistical inference difficult?
9. Rich people consume more health care services than poor people. Explain two ways one might test this hypothesis.

EXERCISES

(For students with access to spreadsheet computer programs.) Consider the following data for a cross section of individuals in the population, in which

Q = Quantity (in 100s) purchased in a year
P = Average price of aspirin in that year
Y = Annual income
A = Age of buyer

OBS	Q	P	Y	A	OBS	Q	P	Y	A
1	1	1.5	20	25	16	1	4	15	25
2	2	1.5	40	20	17	8	2	15	55
3	4	1	12	25	18	9	1	40	50
4	2	1	10	30	19	1	4	10	45
5	2	1	8	30	20	10	1.5	30	55
6	3	2	30	35	21	6	1.5	35	60
7	3.5	1.5	30	40	22	2	1	30	40
8	4	2	20	40	23	3	1	25	40
9	7	1	20	45	24	3	2	20	35
10	1	3	15	40	25	3	2	15	35
11	2	2	18	30	26	4	3	20	35
12	3	2	20	32	27	1	4	20	25
13	3.5	2	15	36	28	1	4	25	30
14	4	2	10	30	29	2	5	28	30
15	2	3	25	20	30	3	1	30	32

Now consider questions 1 to 4:

1. If we divide the population into two groups, up to age 35 and over age 35, which group purchases more aspirin?

2. If we divide the population into three groups—up to age 30, over 30 and up to 45, and over 45—do the purchases vary by age?

3. What is the relationship in a regression analysis between Q and P? Between Q and Y? Between Q and A?

4. Calculate the multiple regression that relates Q with P, Y, and A. Which variables are statistically significant? What is the elasticity of Q with respect to P, to Y, and/or to A?

5. From Table 3–1, column b, suppose income is $20,000, the excise tax on cigarettes is $1, and the person is a 40-year-old white, non-Hispanic male who completed high school (education level = 9). Calculate the elasticities of demand for aspirin with respect to excise tax, income, and age.

6. Consider demand curves for aspirin, estimated for two different sets of consumers:

$$\text{(a) } Q = 20 - 5P + 0.2Y$$

$$\text{(b) } Q = 30 - 5P + 0.2Y$$

If $Y = \$20$ and $P = \$1$, calculate the price and income elasticities for group (a) and group (b). Whose elasticities will be higher? Why?

7. Given the regression estimate of the demand equation of

$$Q_x = 1{,}000 - 3.3P_x + 0.001Y$$

where Y is income, what is the change in demand if price rises by $1, holding income constant? What is the percentage change in demand if price rises by $1 from an initial price of $P_x = \$200$ given $Y = \$10{,}000$? What is the effect on demand of a $1 increase in income, holding price constant?

8. Consider the estimated demand equation of

$$Q_x = 1{,}000 - 3.3P_x + 0.2P_z + 0.001Y$$
$$\qquad\quad (3.5) \quad\ (2.1) \quad\ (0.5)$$

with t values in parentheses, where P_z is the price of another good Z, and Y is income, is good Z a substitute or a complement? Can we say confidently whether good X is a normal good or an inferior good?

4

Economic Efficiency and Cost Benefit Analysis

In health economics, policy concerns require that we frequently and systematically evaluate alternatives. Just as rational individuals want to make the best choices given resource constraints, governments, too, face choices constrained by resource availability. For example, legislators and other policymakers must decide whether to spend more on preventive care versus giving more support to acute care facilities, or perhaps versus medical research. When government regulates, its own expenditures may be relatively small. The economic consequences of its regulation can be very large, however, and corresponding care must be taken in evaluating the alternative scenarios. Economists base such decisions on the concept of efficiency. In developing the microeconomic tools for this textbook, we explained the "welfare loss" caused by a monopoly restricting quantity of production by charging too high a price. The nature of this welfare loss is that it describes an inefficiency—society has foregone opportunities for mutual gain. Efficiency, however, applies to a broader range of phenomena than just monopoly, and we will begin here by developing the concept more fully.

Economic Efficiency

Economic efficiency exists when the economy has squeezed out every opportunity for net benefits possible through voluntary means. Consider a single market, such as a local market for apples. Consumers' preferences for the apples can be measured

by their willingness to pay for them; each person might have a different amount of money in mind. Likewise the opportunity costs to society of an apple can be measured by the marginal cost of production. In some cases, there will be extra or "external" costs or benefits involved, but for the moment, let's assume that all the benefits and costs are the private willingness to pay net of marginal costs. An efficient result for society will require that the wants of consumers, as reflected in their demand, be gauged against the costs to society of the required production.

Economists use the tools of demand and supply analysis to define the efficient allocation of resources in competitive markets, and this idealized sort of market is convenient to explain the concepts. The competitive market is a market form that functions "properly." We will also see that for markets that do not function properly, or for cases where markets do not exist at all, the underlying benefit and cost concepts often still apply.

The demand curve for apples represents consumers' willingness to pay for various amounts of apples. Marginal willingness to pay is another way of representing the demand function relating the quantity of apples demanded to the price of apples. Imagine, for example, that individual consumers are lined up left to right in descending order on the willingness to pay for one apple. At small total quantities (along the market demand curve), the marginal willingness to pay is high, as only those who place considerable value on getting an apple are willing to pay for it. At larger quantities, the consumer's marginal willingness to pay is lower; additional consumers would not buy unless the price was lower.

At price P_1, in Figure 4-1, consumers together spend amount P_1Q_1. This is part of the measure of what the apples are worth to the consumers, and this much is also paid out by them. The total value of the apples to the consumers, however, also includes the additional shaded area under the demand curve, which is referred to as the consumers' surplus triangle. The consumers would have been willing to pay more than P_1, but did not have to do so. To see this, reconsider the example. Each consumer who buys an apple is willing to pay the price on the demand curve. That price reflects his or her

FIGURE 4-1 Consumers' Surplus

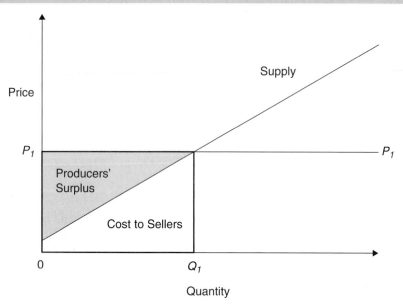

FIGURE 4-2 Producers' Surplus

benefit, but one must subtract the market price to get the net benefit. The shaded area then is simply the sum of the net benefits of each individual buyer.

Alternatively, we say that the consumers' surplus at Q_1 equals the total value to consumers (the area under the demand curve up to Q_1) minus the amount that they must spend, P_1Q_1.

Figure 4-2 presents a supply curve, which in the competitive market case measures the marginal costs for producers to bring apples to market—the higher the market price offered to them, the higher marginal cost they are willing to bear. Suppose that the market price of apples was $10 per bushel, but that some of the producers would supply apples even if the price was only $5. The $10 per bushel that they receive constitutes a surplus of $5 per bushel in excess of the price that is necessary to induce them to transfer resources from other uses to producing apples. Total consumer expenditures P_1Q_1 are apportioned into the resource cost to the sellers (the white area), plus the shaded area showing *producers' surplus*.

The economic criterion for maximizing well-being is to maximize the sum of the consumer and the producer surplus. Combining the supply and demand diagrams in Figure 4-3, we see that the gains to consumers plus the gains to producers (the total net benefits to society) are given by the total shaded area. We calculate total "welfare" of the community in this market by using this equation: Total Welfare = Consumers' Surplus + Producers' Surplus.

Figure 4-3 shows that the sum of the surpluses is maximized at quantity Q_1 where demand equals supply. If quantity was less than Q_1, we could increase both consumers' and producers' surplus (the shaded areas) by increasing Q. If quantity exceeded Q_1, we could increase the surpluses by reducing Q because the incremental quantity (beyond Q_1) costs more (the supply curve), than it is worth to the consumers (the demand curve).

Understand that efficiency requires that the optimal quantity be brought to market. In several places in this textbook we find that monopolies are economically

FIGURE 4-3 Efficient Quantity

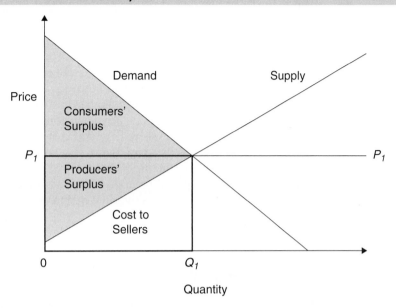

inefficient by bringing too few goods to market. In contrast, polluters generally produce too many goods whose by-products impose costs on society that exceed the goods' market prices.

In competitive markets, supply and demand provide the efficient quantities of goods to the market—prices ration supply and demand according to consumer preferences and producer costs. However, there is a wide range of goods for which such market signals are not readily available. These include bridges, parks, water purification systems, or mandated clean air. Decisions on whether to screen for certain types of cancers, or whether to provide vaccines to the public, for example, must also be evaluated on criteria that do not easily lend themselves to market tests.

With absent or incomplete markets, various evaluation tools have been developed to measure and compare project costs and benefits. Characterized in general as *cost-benefit* analysis, these tools seek to determine the appropriate quantity by measuring incremental or total costs and incremental or total benefits. We address these methods in the following section.

Cost-Benefit Analysis: Background

Cost-benefit analysis (CBA) provides one good method for evaluating proposed public projects. Early forms of CBA were introduced a century ago by the U.S. Army Corps of Engineers to evaluate flood control and other water systems. With the large public works projects during the Depression of the 1930s, the need to justify expensive programs became readily apparent. In 1950, a Congressional subcommittee recommended procedures for using the benefit/cost ratio to compare projects. The introduction of Medicare and Medicaid in 1965 led health economists to focus more on CBA. The federal government continued to improve and standardize methods, and since 1981, all new federal regulations must undergo CBA.

CBA measures the benefits and costs of projects in money terms. This often requires that we place dollar values on years of life or improvements in health and well-being. These challenges have led to the development of new ideas, and health analysts now use the general term economic evaluation to represent the entire collection of tools. Throughout the discussion, we will take the perspective of society as a whole rather than the narrower focus of the individual or firm. This is the appropriate perspective for public projects. The logic, however, can be applied to the investment decisions of a single hospital deciding whether to invest in a PET scanner or even to the decision problem of a young man or woman considering a career in medicine.

Cost-effectiveness analysis (CEA) and cost-utility analysis (CUA) have emerged as the principal alternatives to CBA. CEA applies to problems where the goal is accepted at the start and the problem is only to find the best, most efficient, means to achieve it. CUA is a special form of CEA that introduces measures of benefits that reflect individuals' preferences over the health consequences of alternative programs that affect them.[1]

Cost-Benefit Analysis: Basic Principles

The basic idea of cost-benefit analysis is reflected in the measurement problems that it addresses. For example, CBA evaluates public investment costs, including those that have no market, to determine their prices. These may entail benefits or costs over many periods. Public choices involving either benefits or costs that are external to the market they came from are also addressed by CBA. Projects, such as putting a dam across a river or reconsidering the efficiency of a congressional program, are controversial. Within health economics, controversies over the wisdom of immunization programs, patient screening, or heart transplants, for example, invoke many problems and criticisms that cost-benefit thinking must address.

CBA rests on the premise that a project or policy will improve social welfare if the benefits associated with it exceed the costs. The benefits and costs that are counted must include not only those directly attributed to the project but also any indirect benefits or costs through externalities or other third-party effects. Thus, where B represents all the benefits and C represents all of these costs, a project is deemed worthwhile if $B - C > 0$. Also, projects are commonly ranked according to the benefit to cost (B/C) ratio; thus, a higher B/C ratio generally indicates a project that will deliver greater social benefits for a given dollar of costs.

Measuring Costs

As in standard economic theory, costs are measured as opportunity costs. The most common difference between public and private project evaluation is that public projects often have opportunity costs that have no market to serve as a guide for pricing. On the one hand, a dam project can destroy habitat for animal life, cover historical landmarks under water, and force whole towns to close down. On the other hand, it can provide people who fish with new territory, attract waterfowl, and provide campsites and swimming areas for recreation. None of these examples is either a cost or a benefit that can ordinarily be bought and sold in markets. Much of the controversy of CBA derives from the imprecise task of placing dollar values on these difficult to evaluate

[1]Excellent collections of articles providing comprehensive analyses of many of the issues raised in this chapter are found in Gold et al. (1996) and Drummond et al. (1997). C. Goodman (1998) provides a concise summary of the literature as well as a practical guide to the evaluation process.

costs and benefits. In some cases, the required values can be inferred. For example, the benefits of a newly created lake view might be inferred by observing how much the market values of nearby homes increase. For many cases, however, there is no easy answer.

The previous example also mentions a second problem. Public investments may have side effects that impose additional measurement difficulties. Consider a public immunization program that would offer protection against the flu to a wide cross-section of Americans and is especially concentrated on the elderly and the ill. The costs of materials and manpower can be measured directly, and the benefits to those immunized can be estimated fairly easily. The program, however, also benefits people who never get immunized by reducing the number of infected carriers, thus, reducing their exposure to the flu. These external benefits must be counted in the CBA, yet accurate estimation may prove difficult.

A pollution clean-up program raises similar questions of how to treat externalities. For example, factories that discharge contaminants into the air or water create external costs by damaging the environment and adversely affecting third parties. Conversely, pollution abatement creates external benefits to others (e.g., boaters and home owners) who are not directly involved in the firm's decisions. They typically do not pay for the benefits they receive.

Risk Equity Versus Equality of Marginal Costs per Life Saved

Calamitous events often engage public sympathy to support rescue programs and emergency health care. These programs, in the abstract sense, seek to reduce health risks to the victims—for example, the risk of catching an infectious disease. It is sometimes said that society ought to apply public resources so that health risks are shared equitably across the population. Perhaps equalizing life risks is impossible, but suppose that it were possible. Would it be the best choice for the use of society's resources? Viscusi (2000) explains why such a plan would cause society to fall short of its welfare potential. Contrast a plan that follows sound economic principles. Were we instead to distribute public investments so that the marginal cost of a life saved were equalized across publicly funded programs, we would maximize lives saved for a given overall budget. The idea is simply that each next dollar spent should be placed where it does the most good (marginal analysis in CBA is discussed in detail later in this chapter). Does U.S. spending follow this cost efficiency standard? In Box 4-1, Tengs reports on estimated costs of a life-year saved in 13 categories of programs. These cost figures are certainly far from equal!

Marginal Analysis in CBA

Figure 4-4 illustrates the marginal analysis principle applied to CBA. The marginal social benefits curve, representing the sum of all beneficial effects from increasing the abatement program by one unit, is shown as the downward-sloping MSB curve. The marginal social costs, representing at each point the sum of all costs of increasing the program by one unit, is shown as the MSC curve. For many pollutants, the marginal social benefits will include the benefits to the public of improved health. As an example, the incidence of cancer and respiratory disease has been linked to various forms of air pollution.

Society's net benefit will be maximized where marginal social benefits equal marginal social costs. CBA represents an attempt to get the information with which to make the assessment. To illustrate the logic, suppose the current level of discharge at Q_2 can be observed and that a project or legislation requiring Q_3 is proposed. If MSB and MSC are properly measured, valid estimates of the project benefits are given by

BOX 4-1

The Cost of Saving Lives

The need to encourage rational social choice has been forcefully made by Harvard University's Center for Risk Analysis. After reviewing publicly available studies of life-saving interventions, the Center found enough data to compute the cost per life-year saved for 587 interventions representing an unprecedented range of both health and nonhealth programs. Estimates for selective interventions include:

Resource savings are subtracted from costs. Thus, some programs, such as childhood immunizations and prenatal care, have negative net costs because the costs of the programs are more than offset by the subsequent savings from lower health care costs.

It is clear from such extraordinarily large variations in the cost per life-year that reallocations within and across the two categories of interventions can produce considerable savings in dollars, lives, or both. The estimates also demonstrate the clear need for an ongoing effort of this kind to help policymakers select programs that best use society's limited resources.

Intervention	Cost per Life-Year ($1993)
Medical	
Childhood immunizations	less than 0
Prenatal care for pregnant women	less than 0
Influenza vaccine for all citizens	140
Mammography for women age 50	810
Annual mammography for women ages 40–49	95,000
Intensive care for ill patients undergoing major vascular operations	850,000
Nonmedical	
Random motor vehicle inspections	1,500
Water chlorination	4,200
Pneumonia vaccination	12,000
Construction safety rules	38,000
Home radon control	141,000
Ban of asbestos in roof coatings	5.2 million
Strengthening of buildings in earthquake-prone areas	18 million

Source: Reprinted from *Risk Analysis*, Tengs, Tammy O. et al. "Five-Hundred Life-Saving Interventions and Their Cost-Effectiveness," *Risk Analysis 15* (1995): 369–384, Elsevier Science, with kind permission from the author and Springer Science and Business Media.

the area under the MSB curve between Q_2 and Q_3, and similarly for costs by the area under the MSC curve. The net benefit is equal to area A.

Discounting

For projects that last more than one period, the future costs and benefits must be discounted to put them on an equal basis with present values. This necessity arises from one of two basic reasons, both of which suggest that future dollars usually are not worth as much to people as present-day dollars. First, a dollar today has opportunities other than the project of study. That dollar could have been invested in an interest-bearing instrument, such as a bond, and then it would have been worth the dollar plus the interest in next period's dollars. Conversely, next period's dollar must be discounted at the market rate of interest to discover its present value.

Second, people have a tendency to prefer the present when allocating spending. Which would you prefer, a dollar right now, or the same dollar 10 years from now? Many of us would choose the dollar now. One consequence of this time preference is that the equilibrium interest rate will be positive, rewarding those who wait and exacting a cost on those who can't wait or simply don't wish to.

FIGURE 4-4 **Efficient Use of Resources Where Marginal Benefits Equal Marginal Costs**

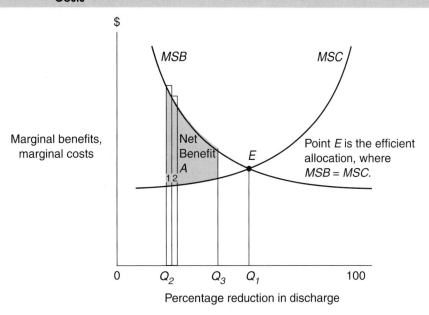

Together, the time preference and the potential foregone interest from dollars spent on a project help to explain why we discount future money values. Having accepted discounting[2] as a necessity, the most commonly used method is relatively simple, even though the complexity of the underlying issues may be oversimplified by this approach (Frederick, Loewenstein, and O'Donoghue, 2002). Each period's costs and benefits are divided by a "discount factor" raised to the power, t, the number of the time period, counting from the present as zero. The discount factor is $(1 + d)$, where d is the social discount rate, which for the present we assume is the market rate of interest. The present value equation is then

$$PV = \sum_{t=1}^{T} \frac{(B_t - C_t)}{(1+d)^t} \qquad \text{(4.1)}$$

where t is zero for the initial period and increases up to the period T in which the project ends. For example, in period one, the next period after the project starts, the discount factor is raised to the power one, and the net of benefit over cost in this future period is divided by $(1 + d)$. If a market interest rate of 6 percent were used for d, then the denominator would become (1.06).

Notice also that the denominator in (4.1) becomes larger as t grows larger. This assumes that we discount the more distant future more heavily. This fact of discounting has raised difficult quandaries for both health care and environmental projects: Should those living in the present so disregard future generations? At first glance, time discounting may seem to guarantee that we will bequeath an unhealthful and polluted condition of life to the future generations. For reasons like these, some analysts

[2]A simple introduction to discounting is provided in the appendix to this chapter.

propose that the social rate of discount, d, be set at a lower level than the current market interest rate or that we apply discount rate patterns that decline over time. It is clear in (4.1) that the lower the chosen value of d the greater is the emphasis placed on the future.

Is the market rate of interest the appropriate social discount rate? In the riskless, perfectly competitive, perfect information world, there is a single interest rate equal to the rate of return on private investment. This rate is also equal to the rate earned by savers. It reflects the rate at which they are willing to give up current consumption for future consumption. Economists usually argue that the appropriate discount rate for both private and public investment decisions would be this single interest rate for models like this one in which a constant social discount rate is assumed.[3] Research continues, however, on discounting theory, and, as we have suggested, some variations on the model propose nonconstant patterns of the discount rate over time (Cairns and Pol, 1997).

There are two ideas that help to clarify why most economists prefer to use the market rate of interest in the present context. First, economists often temper the claims some people make on behalf of future generations with the knowledge that all human valuations must ultimately come from people living in the present. In a sense, we all speak for future generations through our actions in the capital markets. Second, using market interest rates also has the advantage of measuring what people actually do as opposed to their responses to more hypothetical questions.

Perhaps the most troublesome issues about using market interest rates for project evaluation lie in the areas of equity and justice. Inequities in discounting may arise when low- and high-income groups differ in their patterns of time preference, but it might be more keenly felt by people with a life-limiting disease who favor long-term medical research applicable to them.

In conclusion, there are sound economic reasons why people often prefer present dollars to future dollars, and these require, in most cases, some form of discounting of future benefits and costs. To serve this purpose, the market rate of interest is commonly applied as the social discount rate. However, there continue to be many theoretical controversies over the issue, and health economists are active participants in these debates.

Risk Adjustment and CBA

Having chosen to apply the market interest rate, however, we must recognize that there are many market interest rates. Chief among the reasons that these differ is that projects that are relatively more risky tend to have relatively higher rates of interest. Often evaluators will adjust the social rate of discount to reflect the riskiness of the public project. Even this is conceptually not an easy task, however. Private markets for capital projects have private bidders and sellers, and they naturally are capable of assessing perceived riskiness to themselves of adopting a prospective project. In contrast, public projects in principle represent the public at large, whose view of the project's risk might be difficult to discern. Nobel laureate Joseph Stiglitz has recommended that a relatively lower social discount rate better reflects the public's role (Stiglitz, 1988).

Stiglitz also proposes certainty equivalents to eliminate the biases that can result from including a risk-adjustment factor in the discount rate. Under the certainty equivalent method, the uncertain net benefit in any period, often represented by a probability

[3]Baumol (1968) is often credited with providing the clearest rationale for this view.

distribution over project outcomes, is replaced by its equivalent (the decision makers are indifferent between the risky set of outcomes and a value to be received with certainty). The more risky a project, the lower will be the certainty equivalent to someone who is risk averse. The cost-benefit criterion represented by equation (4.1) is then applied using the certainty equivalents for each period.

Distributional Adjustments

Although cost-benefit analysis is intended primarily to improve efficiency, as some of these examples have shown, changes in the income distribution often result from a project. In cases of narrowly focused projects, the tendency is to have a relatively small number of large gainers and perhaps many small losers. To the extent that society is concerned about equity, the distribution of the gainers and losers by income group should be a consideration. At the practical level, after projects are ranked according to their net benefits, decision makers could invoke informal judgments as to the relative effects on the distribution of income and then adjust their rankings. More formally, Stiglitz proposes distributional weights through which the net benefits or losses of lower-income groups are given more weight than other groups. Of course, the method still will be subjective in that the weights themselves will necessarily reflect the judgments of the decision makers.

Inflation

Another concern deals with the treatment of inflation. Conceptually, macroeconomic inflation is not a problem. Because estimates of the inflation rate often turn out to be incorrect, it is best to measure both benefits and cost in current or real terms and then discount at the real (inflation-free) discount rate. If an inflation factor is introduced, then the discount rate should be increased by that inflation rate to get the nominal rate. It is important, though, that the discount rate reflect that inflation factor and not some other rate.

Valuing Human Life

One of the most difficult but often unavoidable tasks in health care CBA is to place a value on human life (for George Bernard Shaw's perspective, see Box 4-2). Several approaches are widely used. The first, known as the human capital approach, estimates the present value of an individual's future earnings. This approach has been especially favored in legal applications that require estimates of damages. It also measures the loss of national output from mortality and morbidity or the production gains from saving and extending life. In other ways, however, the human capital approach is flawed as a welfare measure in that it does not directly measure an individual's willingness to pay to avoid risks of death, injury, or illness, nor does it measure what an individual is willing to accept as compensation for taking on such risks.

Willingness to pay is exemplified in many everyday questions, such as "How much are you willing to pay for the reduction in risks provided by new locks on your door?" The flip side of this concept is the compensation you would require to accept an additional risk to life and limb. As in the previous case, the willingness to accept method has many everyday examples. In fact, its theoretical basis is found in the economic thought regarding the compensating differentials paid to laborers across various lines of work, a line of thought that dates back to the foundations of modern economics.

One of Adam Smith's successes in *The Wealth of Nations* was to explain why the wages of workers differed across jobs—explanations that still resonate well with modern economic theory. The wages of work differ across jobs, said Smith, according to its

BOX 4-2

The Price of Everything

The famous Irish playwright, George Bernard Shaw, once said, "An economist is someone who knows the price of everything and the value of nothing." Did Shaw hit the nail on the head in the case of value-of-life measurement?

There are in fact both technical and philosophical issues that raise concern. One technical question has already been asked. Have "all other things" truly been held constant during and across the analyses, such other things as the psychic rewards one receives from work? Consider someone interested in becoming a firefighter, clearly a risky job. Will the extra risk be just offset by the extra salary (assuming the fire department pays better than alternative jobs) so as to give an accurate reading of his or her value of life? Not likely, especially when high-risk professionals like firefighters feel pride in the protection they provide to the community. The earned sense of honor is a "psychic" reward that may, in their own eyes, overcome a shortfall in their

differential compensation in wages. A firefighter might even conceivably accept the job at less pay than is available elsewhere.

There remains, however, a bigger question than such technical issues because there is a larger sense to life than economists have intended to capture. The nature, meaning, and ultimate value of life are fundamental mysteries to economists, just as they are to humanity in general.

Yet on an everyday basis, humans must make choices about everyday risks, and most of us desire to trade and share these risks. We may do so to feel safer or simply to handle those consequences that can be planned for. When someone is buying insurance for a life risk or when a courtroom is deciding a just compensation to a widow, value-of-life assessments are being made. The economic approach we have described in this chapter helps in the making of such assessments, and, in this way, it helps people to share the risks of life.

difficulty, the effort required to learn it, the "agreeableness" of the work, among other features. To Smith "agreeableness" meant both the pleasantries and perquisites of employment but also its risks and dangers.

In the modern theory of compensating differentials (Rosen, 1986), the worker is seen to offer labor services to the employer but also to purchase employment characteristics. Jobs may provide psychic benefits or psychic costs aside from their monetary compensations. Thus, the health economist's focus on the worker's implied valuation of his life can in principle be discovered by methods that separate the several influences on compensating monetary differentials.

We can observe, for example, that structural iron workers earn a higher salary than they could have earned in their next best alternative in a safer occupation. To accurately infer the iron workers' valuations of life, we need to assess more than the observed wage differential but also those other aspects that they "purchase" by taking the job. These might include added prestige, the perquisites of the employment, and other benefits. In addition, modern theory accounts for the other offers of the firm that are provided with the employment, such as expenses toward improving the safety features of the iron workers' job experience.

The two methods we have described—willingness to accept, deriving from labor economic theory of compensating differentials, and willingness to pay, deriving from consumer purchasing behavior for risk-reducing devices—are nearly two sides of the same coin. A basic difference, however, is that purchasing behavior is limited by a person's budget; we can only afford to pay so much to reduce our risks. In contrast, the willingness to accept has no theoretical limit.

Researchers in health economics and other disciplines have applied both approaches. Table 4-1 illustrates the wide range of estimates that investigators have

TABLE 4-1 How Much Is One Life Worth?

Range of implied values of a human life extrapolated from what people pay for various products, services, or regulations that can change the risk of death.

Basis for Calculation	Value of Life ($1990, in millions)
Labor Market Studies	
Leigh (1987)	$10.4
Moore & Viscusi (1987)	$2.5–$7.3
Kneiser & Leeth (1991)	$7.6
Gegax, Gerking, & Schultz (1991)	$1.6
Outside of Labor Market Studies	
Fire fatality risks	
Garbacz (1989)	$2.0
Automobile accident risks	
Atkinson and Halvorsen (1990)	$4.0
Cigarette smoking	
Ippolito and Ippolito	$0.7
Air pollution	
Portney (1981)	$0.8

Source: Viscusi (1993), various tables.

found from various applications. The wide range calls for explanations. Do households underestimate or overestimate risks for some activities? Are there inadequacies in the underlying data and methods? Until such questions are answered, the valuation of benefits will remain problematic and will limit the role of CBA.

Cost-Benefit Analyses of Disease-Screening Programs

Notwithstanding the difficulties of CBA, one finds excellent examples in the literature.[4] To illustrate, we examine a CBA of various screening tests used to detect gonorrhea in asymptomatic women (Goddeeris and Bronken, 1985). Screening for various forms of cancer, sexually transmitted diseases, and other conditions is commonly endorsed or proposed by medical authorities.

Screening results in four possibilities: true positive, true negative, false positive, and false negative. Individuals testing positive will return for treatment, which for some will produce adverse reactions. The study measured the expected net benefit per individual screened. The costs include screening costs, time costs, and treatment costs, including those for adverse reactions. The benefits consist of improvements in treatment resulting from early detection, the value of reassurance from negative test results, and the external benefit that detection has in limiting the spread of the disease.

Furthermore, some future medical costs can be avoided by early detection. Table 4-2 shows the per-case net benefits of three alternatives for the estimated values of the parameters. Only the TM test, the most common test, produced positive net benefits per patient screened at the baseline parameter values. Thus, the authors concluded that TM is both worthwhile and superior to the alternatives considered.

The analysis in Table 4-2 reflects a larger policy debate with respect to disease screening. The major categories of positive benefits from screening programs accrue

[4]See also Weisbrod (1971) for an early, but classic, cost-benefit study involving research on poliomyelitis.

TABLE 4-2 Net Benefits of Gonorrhea Screening

	Screening Alternative		
	TM	*Gonozyme Fast*	*Gonozyme Slow*
Dollar values			
S (screening cost)	10	20	13
T (treatment cost)	28.5	21	28.5
R (reassurance)	10	10	10
B (benefit from early treatment)	2,869	2,869	2,869
A (adverse reaction cost)	15	15	15
F (false positive cost)	4,500	4,500	4,500
Net Benefits V	18.6	−124.7	−118.7

Source: Reprinted from *Medical Care*, John H. Goddeeris and Thomas P. Bronken, "Benefit-Cost Analysis of Screening." *Medical Care 23* (1985), 1242–1255, with permission from Lippincott Williams & Wilkins.

from the treatment of disease for people who were unaware that they had a disease. This is directly related to the prevalence of the disease. The major costs of the screening program are related to the unneeded treatments that accrue to patients who are incorrectly judged to have a disease, reflected by the false positive rate.

Russell (1994) looks at three major screening initiatives: (1) the Pap smear for cervical cancer (for women), (2) screening tests for prostate cancer (for men), and (3) high blood cholesterol. She notes that in many cases, the probability of a false positive result from the screen (yielding major costs) is greater than the probability of disease prevalence (for which treatment provides major benefits). Thus, cost-benefit analysis of screening programs in which false positive rates are high may indicate net economic losses due to the unnecessary treatment, even though the diseases that they address may be life-threatening.

Cost-Effectiveness Analysis

Given the difficulties of placing monetary values on life and health, as well as valuing other intangible benefits, CEA sometimes provides a more practical approach to decision making than CBA (Garber and Phelps, 1997). CEA compares the costs of achieving a particular nonmonetary objective, such as lives saved. In cost-effectiveness analysis, one assumes that the objective is desirable even if the benefits have not been evaluated in monetary terms (strictly speaking, each of the projects might yield negative net benefits were it feasible to compute those net benefits). Though the valuation of benefits is avoided, the problems of determining costs remain.

The proper comparison of costs per output in CEA is based on the ratio of incremental costs to incremental output. Let the change in social costs incurred due to a particular project be $C_1 - C_0$, and let the gain in health output be $E_1 - E_0$. Then the various projects are compared by the ratio:

$$\text{CEA ratio} = \frac{C_1 - C_0}{E_1 - E_0} \tag{4.2}$$

The costs as usual are in dollars, while the outputs are the chosen health status measure. It can be seen that to compare projects with this method, the outputs must be measured in the same units across all projects considered.

Advantages of CEA

The task under CEA is conceptually similar to the production decision of the firm, which is to produce a chosen level of output from among alternative production methods at the lowest possible cost. Also, as in the firm-production decision, the objective must be quantifiable and measured in the same units across projects. Otherwise, a clear relationship between costs and output cannot be determined.

For example, cost-effectiveness analysis has been applied widely by the Department of Defense to determine the most cost-efficient means of achieving a particular level of military preparedness. Objectives can be quantified, in terms of ability to deploy forces, and the most efficient means of achieving the objectives is estimated. Note that CBA is not feasible in such cases because the benefits of the military capability cannot readily be evaluated in monetary terms. As another example, many communities are currently interested in recycling to the point where mandatory recycling is becoming more widespread. Assuming that a community has decided on the goal of reducing garbage mass, cost-effectiveness analysis can be used to compare recycling with incineration and other waste-management strategies.

Finally, CEA can be a useful first step toward undertaking a cost-benefit study. If the analysts run into significant problems in undertaking a CEA, it is unlikely that a CBA will be feasible. Conversely, good progress in developing a CEA can often determine whether it is possible to take the next step and extend the CEA into a cost-benefit study.

Cost-Utility Analysis, QALYs, and DALYs

The pressing and frequent need for cost-effectiveness analyses of health projects might account for the development of practical variations of the technique, which together can be described as cost-utility analysis. Principal among these is the QALY; under this variation, each project is evaluated on the basis of its incremental costs per extra QALY delivered to the patients or other subjects (Garber and Phelps, 1997; Ried, 1998).

The QALY is a weighting system that assigns a value, q, ranging from 1 (perfect health) to 0 (death) to represent quality of life for each year. The details of QALY construction can be found elsewhere (Gold et al., 1996; Torrance, 1997). In its welfare economic version, the weights for QALYs are in principle derived by eliciting the individuals' preferences for different states of health. In practice, the QALYs are often summed over groups of people. In this case, the procedure departs from standard welfare economics by its comparison and in some cases imposing of interpersonal "utilities" across people summed in a cardinal manner, practices that welfare economists generally avoid. However, once the weights are agreed upon and the QALYs are acceptably calibrated, then the measure becomes:

$$QALY = \sum_{i=1}^{\text{maximum duration}} F_i q_i / (1+d)^i \tag{4.3}$$

where F_i is the probability that the person is still alive at age i; d is the time discount factor; and the value q_i is the quality weight, between 0 and 1, assigned to each year of the person's remaining life (Garber, 2000).

Suppose, for example, that a patient has the opportunity for a treatment that will extend life by one year with a probability of ($F_1 = 0.9$) and by two years with a probability of 0.5 ($F_2 = 0.5$). The patient will die with certainty after two years. Quality weight

q_1 is 0.8 in year 1 and q_2 is 0.6 in year 2. The discount rate is 0.05 per year. Thus, using equation (4.3) the QALY computation is:

$$QALY = (0.9 \times 0.8 \div 1.05) + (0.5 \times 0.6 \div 1.05^2) = 0.96$$

indicating that the expected effectiveness of the treatment is 0.96 QALYs. This serves as the denominator for equation 4.2. Costs per QALY can then be used to compare alternative interventions

An Ace Inhibitor Application of Cost Effectiveness Analysis

An ACE inhibitor is a medical treatment that can improve the life course of a patient with juvenile onset diabetes (Type 1). The issue for investigators Dong and his colleagues (2004) was whether there is an advantage for the patient to be treated with this drug at the conventional time, at the onset of a condition called microalbuninura, or whether to treat right away when the diabetes is diagnosed. They chose as their standard of health outcome, the quality-adjusted life year (QALY). Their goal was to identify the cost per life-year saved by switching to the earlier treatment plan. They chose the tools of cost-effectiveness analysis to do this.

These researchers investigated two other dimensions of analysis: patient age and blood category. These are studied for patients ages 20, 25, and 30 years, and for three patient blood categories, two of which are shown in the Table 4-3 (HbA1c = 7% and HbA1c = 9%). These blood categories matter for the length of time for which treatment can be maintained, but we identify them here merely as two medically relevant patient categories. Costs included treatment and related exam costs as well as changes in costs to treat common disorders that affect diabetics during the course of their lives. All costs were discounted at a discount rate of 3 percent. Note that ACE Inhibitor treatment done immediately at the time of the diabetes diagnosis is indicated as "Early" whereas treatment at the conventional time is indicated as "Standard." The "QALYs" are the patient's remaining quality-adjusted life years, discounted at the 3 percent rate; this QALY figure should not be confused with life expectancy of the patient.

The "Difference" is positive in every case, showing that Early treatment costs more, but achieves more life-years, QALYs. Is the switch to early treatment cost effective? The cost-effectiveness ratio, the one needed to determine which treatment method delivers the incremental QALY at least cost, requires data for the baseline QALY for each

TABLE 4-3 Cost Effectiveness Tools Applied to Study of Two Treatments

		Blood Category					
		HbA1c = 7%			HbA1c = 9%		
Age	*Treatment*	*Total Costs*	*QALYs*	*$/QALY*	*Total Costs*	*QALYs*	*$/QALY*
20 yrs	Early	125,169	21.603		142,588	20.455	
20 yrs	Standard	121,614	21.496		140,488	20.303	
20 yrs	Difference	3,555	0.108	32,972	2,100	0.152	13,814
25 yrs	Early	122,234	20.998		137,970	19.941	
25 yrs	Standard	118,894	20.914		135,847	19.801	
25 yrs	Difference	3,341	0.085	39,530	2,124	0.140	15,169
30 yrs	Early	118,158	20.255		132,095	19.290	
30 yrs	Standard	114,739	20.170		130,053	19.175	
30 yrs	Difference	3,419	0.086	39,912	2,042	0.115	17,778

Source: Dong et al. (2004), with permission from ADIS.

age/blood category. It is common, however, that such data may be unavailable and it may even be unethical to generate data for untreated populations. The baseline QALY levels do matter, for example, for blood category HbA1c = 7%. Numerical experiments will show that cost-effective choice depends on the baseline QALY level.

Not having baseline QALY data, these authors, as is seen in Table 4-3, focused on other questions: (1) at what age is early treatment most effective and (2) for which blood group is early treatment most effective? To investigate these questions, the authors have calculated the incremental cost between treatments in ratio to the incremental QALYs. Their data are very useful for this purpose, and they conclude that early treatment is most cost effective for the youngest age groups, and that blood category HbA1c = 9% achieves the most cost-effective gains.

Is CUA Consistent with CBA?

The cost-benefit analysis, CBA, is based on the central economic standard of efficiency, the Pareto Principle, which states that if an option of society improves the well-being of some people while harming no one then that option enhances welfare. Put simply, CBA has been developed to be the standard of modern welfare economics. To say that CUA is consistent with CBA, would be to say that cost-utility analysis, too, chooses the very best efficiency options for society; in the jargon of welfare economics, it would be "first best."

Recent work (Garber and Phelps, 1997; Bleichrodt and Quiggin, 1999) casts doubt; these findings conclude that very restrictive underlying conditions would be required in theory to cause cost-utility analysis to attain the welfare economic standard. Yet more recent is Blomqvist's (2002) finding that CUA cannot, as typically applied, attain the first best result just described. One important insight in these works can be stated simply. When individuals are asked about their comparisons of treatment options, outcomes and costs in developing CUA valuations, they generally consider these options in isolation. That is, they are not taking into account the overall health system and population. The resulting option chosen could be very valuable, but by restricting the more global thinking inherent in standard welfare economics, it cannot be considered first best.

Extra-Welfarism

Can a standard outside of standard welfare economics, one perhaps based on very different principles, give us a better world? Standards making this claim are called "extra-welfarist." Does it matter if we have two different approaches to health care project evaluation, one based within welfare economics and one outside of it?

Health economists often argue (e.g., Bala and Zarkin, 2000) that consistency with welfare economics is a valuable attribute to an evaluation in that the fundamentals of welfare economic analysis describe the conditions under which a project will generate a net improvement in social welfare. Similarly, it is pointed out that the welfare basis of CBA, the willingness-to-pay principal, is appropriately broader than extra-welfarist approaches. Besides counting patients' willingness to pay for extended life years, it includes their willingness to pay for side benefits to recreation and family life made possible by the treatment (Olsen and Smith, 2001).

The extra-welfarists point to inadequacies in the standard economic welfare framework. As this framework is applied, it is commonly said that it counts up individual utilities without recognizing the interdependencies between people or their identification with the whole. Furthermore, the extra welfarist approach using QALYs avoids a problem of willingness to pay; it avoids inequities that can be caused by an inequitable income distribution. Ability to pay is an important determinant of willingness to pay

(Weinstein and Manning, 1997). Finally, many who apply QALYs simply argue that it is a practical "decision-maker's approach" (Brouwer and Koopmanschap, 2000).

The Ageism Critique of QALYs

It has long been known and pointed out that health policy based on QALYs tends to place a reduced value on older people when considering a medical intervention. This happens because a successful treatment of an old patient saves fewer life-years, those years are already limited by nature. The policy question is simply "Is this view of the elderly fair?"

The issue is made much deeper with the philosophical assertion of Williams (2001) who asked a stronger question: Is an extra life year to be valued the same if an older person versus one younger receives it? The "fair innings" approach argues that the younger person merits more concern. We are each entitled according to this view, to our "fair innings," a normal human number of years (see also Daniels, 1985). Note that in this version, the old person's shorter life expectancy is not the main issue, even an equal gain in QALYs is no longer assumed to have the same value between young and old.

An alternative approach, DALYs, or disability-adjusted life years, points out that we humans tend to be dependent on the middle age groups when we are very young or very old. To the adherents of this view, the greater social-related weights should be placed on people in the middle age groups. The DALY theory provides a "hump"-shaped set of weights favoring the age groups in the middle.

That these philosophical issues are unresolved is made clear by Eric Nord's position (2001). He argues that the value each of us attaches to our own lives depends on our point of view as situated in our time and place, that is, as we see it at our given age. Nord's view is more consistent with standard economic methods of assessing value of life, which emphasize either the person's willingness to pay for health or willingness to accept risks. Nord, in effect, raises the question of whether public valuation of an old person's life should differ from the person's own perception.

In any case, public perceptions of people's worth offers a complexity of values. Proposals in Oregon or the United Kingdom to ration service by curbing service to the older patients have been controversial. While the debate helps to clarify the policy issue, a clearly correct consensus view continues to elude us.

Conclusions

The evaluation of prospective health projects has generated substantial interest among health economists in both the theory and the practical means to conduct evaluations so as to improve the society's well-being. Cost-benefit analysis has a long history in both theory and application. It requires the measuring of all benefits and costs attributable to the project both directly and indirectly. The need to identify external effects and to assign values to them in the absence of guidance from active markets poses both difficulty and controversy in practice. Future costs and benefits must also be adjusted to offset their differences from present values. Methods of discounting to accomplish this task are open to debate in that projects whose benefits are achieved only in the more distant future tend to benefit from lower rates of social discount. The most difficult task of all for CBA is probably that of attaching dollar values to human life. The willingness-to-pay principle, stemming from standard welfare economics, is viewed as unsatisfactory by those health economists who prefer an "extra-welfarist" approach.

Cost-effectiveness offers a lesser but perhaps more practical evaluation result. By avoiding the assignment of dollar values to human life outcomes, the CEA focuses on providing useful guidance to the decision maker. The problems of measuring costs still

apply, but the most arbitrary and controversial steps are avoided. The CEA approach requires that the output of the various projects be described in common terms. Several methods of output measurement and various discounting techniques have led to variations on CEA as a group called cost-utility analyses.

Most prominent among cost-utility analyses is to measure health output as quality-adjusted life years, QALYs, or disability-adjusted life years, DALYs. These methods, and the debate over health economic evaluation in general, are aimed at improving health policy for society. At its simplest level, economic evaluation recommends projects that achieve net positive benefits to society and prioritizes among these by their relative efficiency in doing so. Health and health care, however, provide some of the toughest applications and have helped to reveal the natural complexity of the seeming common sense behind the rules of thumb we apply to projects aimed at saving life and limb.

Despite its potential, CBA applications in health care still are less prevalent than one would expect. Difficulties in evaluating benefits, especially the value of life and improved quality of life, place limits on CBA and its usefulness to decision makers. As a result, cost-effectiveness analysis using QALYs has emerged as the principal tool for program evaluation.[5]

In 1993, the U.S. Public Health Service convened a panel of experts to help resolve controversies, standardize methods for cost-effectiveness studies, and develop consensus-based recommendations.[6] The panel recommended that these evaluative studies should take a societal perspective and that analysts should try to measure consequences through QALYs. Most importantly, the panel cautioned against decisions based solely on cost-effectiveness measures. Equity and other considerations also should be examined.

SUMMARY

1. Economic efficiency requires the maximization of total welfare, with the optimum quantity reflecting the sum of consumers' and producers' surpluses.
2. Unlike private decisions made in the marketplace, (social) cost-benefit analysis (CBA) involves evaluation of social benefits and social costs in public project analysis. Often, markets do not exist to evaluate the benefits and costs of such projects.
3. CBA rests on the principle that society's welfare will be improved whenever the benefits of a project exceed its costs.
4. CBA represents an example of marginal analysis. The social optimum is achieved when marginal social benefit is equal to marginal social cost.
5. Though in principle CBA appears simple, it can be difficult to apply. The difficulties include identifying all the relevant costs and benefits, including third-party effects, assigning monetary values, and making projections over many years for projects with long lives.
6. The monetary values of future net benefits must be discounted. The choice of the appropriate discount rate remains controversial.
7. Health care projects must often value human life. The human capital approach and the willingness-to-pay approach have been the most widely applied methods.
8. Cost-effectiveness analysis can be used when it is difficult to place a monetary value on the benefits of a project. CEA is used to compare the costs under alternative projects of achieving some desired and quantifiable nonmonetary objective, such as the cost of detecting a case of cancer or the cost of a life-year saved.
9. Cost-utility analysis (CUA) is a special case of CEA in which the objective is measured in Quality-Adjusted Life Years (QALYs) or some other indicator, such as DALYs, that takes into account individuals' preferences for health.

[5]Comprehensive bibliographies of CBA and CEA studies are found in Elixhauser (1993) and Elixhauser et al. (1998).

[6]Details are found in Gold et al. (1996) and a series of articles in the *Journal of the American Medical Association*. See Russell et al. (1996), Weinstein et al. (1996), and Siegel et al. (1996).

DISCUSSION QUESTIONS

1. Would the concept of consumers' surplus be a sound welfare measure if the income distribution were deemed inequitable? If so, in what way?
2. In what ways is social cost-benefit analysis similar to a consumer's decision about allocating resources or to a firm's investment decision? In what ways is it different?
3. What external benefits or costs would you expect from a project designed to develop sanitary waste product disposal in a third-world village? Why do these need to be considered as part of a CBA of the project?
4. Why are jobs that are created as a result of a social project not normally considered as a benefit?
5. Some suggest that a dollar value cannot be placed on life; that is, life is priceless. Explain how the dilemma to social decision created by this view might be resolved.
6. Does it matter whether a higher or lower discount rate is applied to the CBA of a social project? If so, why?
7. Discuss possible reasons why the estimates of the value of life presented in Table 4-1 differ so much.
8. How does the willingness-to-pay principle of welfare economics differ from the valuation of an extra life-year in applying QALYs?
9. Distinguish between cost-benefit analysis (CBA) and cost-effectiveness analysis (CEA). Can CEA replace CBA in all cases? If not, why not?
10. In the example of the ACE Inhibitor, what decision issue is the marginal cost relevant to? The extra QALYs?
11. Consider the information provided in Box 4-1, "The Cost of Saving Lives." If a society has a fixed budget that it can devote to all interventions, formulate a prioritizing rule that would save the greatest number of years of life for a given budget.

EXERCISES

1. Using Figure 4-3, explain why a pollution abatement program that reduces discharge beyond Q_1 is inefficient.
2. Consider the following two projects. Both have costs of $5,000 in Year 1. Project 1 provides benefits of $2,000 in each of the first four years only. The second provides benefits of $2,000 for each of Years 6 to 10 only. Compute the net benefits using a discount rate of 6 percent. Repeat using a discount rate of 12 percent. What can you conclude from this exercise?
3. Consider the following table of costs and benefits from a governmental policy to clean the water in a local area.

Level of Abatement	Total Costs	Total Benefits
0%	$0	$0
10	10	80
20	22	150
30	40	200
40	70	240
50	105	280
60	150	320
70	210	350
80	280	375
90	350	385
100	420	390

a. What level of abatement is most efficient by general economic criteria?
b. Would a 70 percent level of abatement pass a cost-benefit test? Is it efficient?
c. How would you respond to those who argue for 100 percent abatement?

4. Consider a project that costs $10,000 today. It will provide benefits of $4,000 at the end of Year 1, $3,500 at the end of Year 2, and $3,500 at the end of Year 3. If the discount rate is 6 percent, will this project be approved using cost-benefit analysis? Would your answer change if the discount rate is:
a. 5 percent
b. 4 percent

5. Consider a hypothetical three-stage screening test for a cancer with the following rates of detection and costs:

	Number of Cases	
Stage	Detected	Total Costs
1	100	$200,000
2	105	260,000
3	106	300,000

a. Calculate the average cost per cancer detected in the three stages.
b. Calculate the marginal cost per cancer detected in the three stages.
c. Suppose that the marginal benefit per treated case is $12,000 per person. What would be the optimal screening, given the costs?

6. In the diagram below, calculate
a. Total consumer expenditures.
b. Total cost to sellers.
c. Total consumers' surplus.
d. Total producers' surplus.
e. The sum of the consumers' and the producers' surplus.

7. Suppose that producers need to have licenses to sell apples, and that only 90 units of apples are licensed (i.e., Q is limited to 90). Calculate
a. The sum of the consumer surplus and producer surplus.
b. The reduction in consumer well-being because of the licensing.

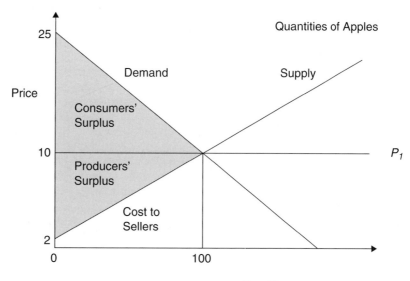

Appendix

Discounting is used in many applications involving comparisons of different streams of returns and/or costs over a number of periods. For example, an analyst might be asked to compare Investment A, which provides $20 at the end of Year 1 and $20 at the end of Year 2, with Investment B, which provides $12 at the end of Year 1 and $29 at the end of Year 2. Although Investment B returns $41 over the 2 years compared to $40 for Investment A, most of the return on Investment B comes later, at the end of Year 2. It is often necessary to compare the investments with a criterion that considers the timing of the returns. The analytical tool used for such comparisons is usually referred to as *discounting*.

Suppose George is offered the opportunity to buy a bond that will return $1, one year from now. How much is he willing to pay now? George always has the option to keep his money and earn interest rate r. He will buy the bond if he can pay a price far enough below the $1 return next year such that that price, multiplied by one plus the interest rate, equals $1. Algebraically, if the rate of interest is r and the unknown amount is x_1, then:

$$x_1(1+r) = 1$$

The value for x_1, then, can be solved as:

$$x_1 = \frac{1}{(1+r)}$$

If the rate of interest is 5 percent (or 0.05), then x_1, the discounted value of $1, one year hence, equals 1/1.05, or 95.24 cents.

Similarly, the discounted value of $1, two years hence, is:

$$x_2(1+r)^2 = 1$$

The value for x_2, then, can be solved as:

$$x_2 = \frac{1}{(1+r)^2}$$

If, again, the interest rate is 5 percent, then x_2 equals $1/1.05^2$, or 90.70 cents.

Returning to the preceding example, we can calculate that the present value (the sum of x_1 and x_2), or PV, for Investment A will equal $37.19, or ($20/1.05 + $20/1.05^2$). The PV of Investment B is $37.73. Thus, George will prefer Investment B.

In summation notation, the present value of a stream of returns R and costs C, over time, is given by:

$$PV = \sum_{t=1}^{t=T} \frac{(R_t - C_t)}{(1+r)^t}$$

It is easy to demonstrate that the relative PVs of Investments A and B may depend on the interest rate (or in evaluation studies, sometimes referred to as discount rate d) chosen for the analysis. If an interest rate of 15 percent were used instead of 5 percent in the previous example, the PV for Investment A would be $32.51, compared to $32.36 for Investment B. Intuitively, the higher interest rate gives the larger but later return in Investment B less weight.

CHAPTER

The Production of Health

The production of health is a central concern to the health economist and to public policy. Consider that the role of health care in society, including medical care provided by physicians, is ultimately a production question. What is the contribution of health care to the health status of the population? We can then ask what is the best way to produce and distribute health care?

In medical terms, this chapter concerns the efficacy and effectiveness of all those features of life, not only medical care, that plausibly contribute to our health. Unlike the typical doctor in practice, however, we look for evidence of the response of a "treatment" in the change in the health status of populations, as opposed to the treatment response of a medicine for the individual patient in the hospital. We will see that the two approaches must remain in harmony and that both are fundamentally searches for causal relationships.

The Production Function of Health

A production function summarizes the relationship between inputs and outputs. The study of the production of health function requires that we inquire about the relationship between health care inputs and health. The answers that economists and medical historians offer to this question surprise many people. First, the contribution of practitioner-provided health care to the historical downward trends in population mortality rates was probably negligible at least until well into the twentieth century. Second, while the total contribution of health care is substantial in the modern day, its marginal contribution in some cases may be small.

This distinction between total and marginal contributions is crucial to understanding these issues. To illustrate this distinction, consider Figure 5-1A, which exhibits a theoretical health status production function for the population. Set aside the difficulties of measuring health status in populations, and assume that an adequate health

89

FIGURE 5-1 Production of Health

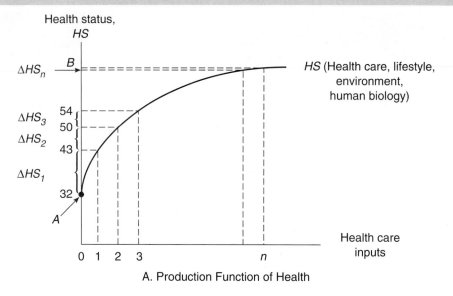

A. Production Function of Health

B. Marginal Product of Health Care

status (*HS*) measure has been agreed on. Health status is shown here to be an increasing function of health care. Also, to avoid a perspective that is too narrowly focused on health care, we specify further that health status depends at least upon the population's biological endowment, environment, and lifestyle.[1] Thus, $HS = f$(Health Care, Lifestyle, Environment, Human Biology). Improvements in any of these latter three factors will shift the curve upward.

A production function describes the relationship of flows of inputs and flows of outputs over a specified time period so the inputs and output in Figure 5-1A are

[1]This categorization of groups of inputs is not the only reasonable one, but it illustrates the main issues, and it has an excellent history. It was developed by the Canadian government for its pioneering work begun three decades ago (LaLonde, 1974).

measured over an implied period of time, such as a year. In practice, we might use the number of healthy days experienced by the population per capita, mortality rates, or disability days, to indicate health status.

To simplify the depiction, we have reduced all health care inputs into one scale called Health Care. In reality, health care consists of many different health care inputs. Many of them include types of medical care provided by doctors of medicine or osteopathy, but many are also provided by other health care professionals. Conceptually, the health care measure, HC, may be thought of as an aggregate of all these types of health care, the aggregation being based on dollar values.

The marginal contribution of health care is its marginal product, meaning the increment to health caused by one extra unit of Health Care, holding all other inputs constant. Increasing Health Care from zero to one unit in Figure 5-1A improves health status by ΔHS_1, the first unit's marginal product. Numerically, this first unit of Health Care has increased the health status index from 32 to 43; $\Delta HS_1 = 11$ Health Status units. The next unit of medical care delivers a marginal product of $\Delta HS_2 = 7$, and so on. These marginal products are diminishing in size, illustrating the law of diminishing marginal returns. If society employs a total of n units of Health Care, then the total contribution of Health Care is the sum of the marginal products of each of the n units. This total contribution as shown, AB, may be substantial. However, the marginal product of the nth unit of medical care is ΔHS_n, and it is small. In fact, we are nearly on the "flat of the curve." Marginal product is graphed on Figure 5-1B.

We have drawn the health production function as a rising curve that flattens out at higher levels of health care but never bends downward. Would the health production function eventually bend downward? Is it possible to get too much health care so that the health of the population is harmed? This is a logical possibility under at least two scenarios. *Iatrogenic* (meaning provider-caused) disease is an inevitable by-product of many medical interventions. For example, each surgery has its risks. Combinations of drugs may have unforeseen and adverse interactions. If the rate of iatrogenic disease does not fall while diminishing returns sets in, it is possible for the balance of help and harm from health care to be a net harm.

Medical scientists, such as Cochrane (1972), have pressed the case that much medical care as often practiced has only weak scientific basis, making iatrogenesis a real probability. Writing for the public audience, Dubos (1960) and Illich (1976) once warned of a medical "nemesis" taking away our abilities to face the natural hardships of life by "medicalizing" these problems. Illich argued that this medicalization would lead to less personal effort to preserve health and less personal determination to persevere; the result becomes a decline in the health of the population, and thus a negative marginal product for medical care.[2]

Return to the distinction between total product and marginal product. Often, it is the marginals that are relevant to policy propositions, not the totals. For example, no one seriously recommends that society eliminate all health care spending. However, it is reasonable to ask whether society would be better off if it could reduce health care expenditures by $1 billion and invest those funds in another productive use, such as housing, education, transportation, defense, or other consumption. We could even reasonably ask if health itself could be improved by transferring the marginal $1 billion to environmental or lifestyle improvements.

[2]The medicalization argument was reinforced by Thomas McKeown's (1976) research showing that medical care warranted little credit for the historical declines in mortality rates in England and Wales. The works by McKeown and by Cochrane remain the reference points for the continuing debate within medicine and the social sciences over the role of medicine (Alvarez-Dardet and Ruiz, 1993; Farmer and Nardell, 1998; Frenk, 1998).

Many of our government programs are designed to encourage health care use in certain population groups, such as the poor and elderly. Other programs, such as tax preferences for health insurance, benefit people who are neither poor nor elderly and encourage their consumption of health care. The theoretical issues raised here suggest that we question the wisdom of each of our programs. The theoretical questions can be investigated with data of several kinds either directly or indirectly relevant to the production of health issue. It is useful to begin with the historical role of medicine, which indirectly bears on the issue of health production. After providing an overview of these efforts, largely the work of medical and economic historians, we then turn to econometric studies of the modern day production function.

The Historical Role of Medicine and Health Care

Many medical historians agree that practitioner-provided medical interventions played only a small, perhaps negligible, role in the historical decline in population mortality rates. Effective medicine is a fairly recent phenomenon, and the delivery of effective medical interventions on a scale sufficient to affect population health indicators most likely appeared only well into the twentieth century. Though the magnitudes of other causes of mortality declines are still disputed, it is clear that a larger role, one of the most significant ones, might be attributed to public health measures and the spread of knowledge of the sources of disease. However, a number of scholars in this field attribute the largest share of the credit to improvements in environment, particularly to the greatly increased supply of foodstuffs that became available due to the agricultural and industrial revolutions.

The Rising Population and the Role of Medicine

The notion that medicine played a relatively minor historical role is certainly not new, and it has been asserted by researchers of various ideologies. This point of view is associated with the work of Thomas McKeown (1976), who focused on the dramatic rise in population in England and Wales from 1750 to the modern day.

The pattern of world population growth, including population growth in England and Wales, has interested many scholars including McKeown. World population is hard to estimate for the distant past, but research by the United Nations (1996) and others show that something extraordinary happened during the last 300 years. In the first century the population was roughly 300 million. For a thousand years thereafter, until the era of Viking ships, little or no change occurred. By the Age of Enlightenment, starting just before 1700, the population may have risen to 600 million. Then things began to change rapidly. Within a single century, the world population passed 1 billion people. The next 5 billion arrived within a mere 200 years. Figure 5-2, based on United Nations data, reveals this startling pattern.

Returning to the history of England and Wales, the large rise in their populations in the period following 1750 is to a large degree a story of the population's health. Population increase comes from increased birth rates, reduced mortality, or increased net in-migration. Migration was not an important source of population increase in England and Wales; when accurate birth rate and death rate data became available from 1841, these data alone proved able to account for the population change. Likewise, fertility probably did not account for the change because recorded birth rates have declined during the period since data has become available. Declines in birth rates are a common finding in countries undergoing industrialization and modernization. In contrast, recorded mortality rates did decline substantially.

FIGURE 5-2 World Population from 10,000 B.C. to the Modern Day

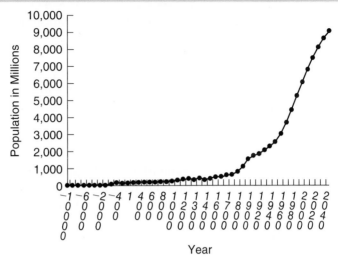

Source: World Population Resources Institute for Mimetic Research. FuturesEdge.org, accessed June 10, 2002.

McKeown began by investigating which diseases contributed to the decline in death rates. Mortality data are very limited prior to the mid-1800s, but the records revealed an emerging picture. Table 5-1 shows death rates by disease category for three different time periods. The table shows that airborne infectious diseases account for the largest single portion of mortality reduction, and waterborne infectious diseases also make up a substantial portion of known causes. Regarding the airborne diseases, other data suggest that the main airborne diseases showing a decline in mortality include tuberculosis, bronchitis, pneumonia, and influenza.

TABLE 5-1 Death Rates* (per million) in 1848–1854, 1901, and 1907

	1848–1854	1901	1971	*Percentage of Reduction (1848–1854 to 1971) Attributable to Each Category*	*For Each Category, Percentage of Reduction (1848–1854 to 1971) That Occurred Before 1901*
I. Conditions attributable to microorganisms:					
1. Airborne diseases	7,259	5,122	619	39	32
2. Water- and foodborne diseases	3,562	1,931	35	21	46
3. Other Conditions	2,144	1,415	60	12	35
Total	12,965	8,468	714	72	37
II. Conditions not attributable to microorganisms	8,891	8,490	4,070	28	8
All diseases	21,856	16,958	5,384	100	29

*Standardized to the age/sex distribution of the 1901 population.
Source: Reprinted from McKeown, Thomas, *The Modem Rise of Population.* New York: Academic Press. 197A (p. 54).

BOX 5-1

Feature: Tuberculosis and the Magic Mountain

Thanks to the efforts of writers such as Nobelist Thomas Mann, the tuberculosis (TB) sanitarium of 100 years ago has found a permanent place in literature. Mann's novel, *The Magic Mountain*, describes with a mastery of medical detail, often admired by physicians, the character's struggle with the deadly disease. Mann's incomparable development of character and dialog bring a reality to the society unique to this sanitarium, representing one he had himself visited. Hans Castorp, a young German engineer, is smitten with Clavida Chauchat, a young woman at the "good" Russian table. The Italian Settembrini's intellectual arguments with Naptha can only result in a duel. We grieve when Hans's cousin

Joachim, a good, simple military man, succumbs to TB and his body is sledded down the mountain. Hans survives to return to the lands below.

Though effective chemical interventions were not available until after 1940, doctors did treat TB prior to 1940, notably with the widespread use of sanatoria, such as the one in *The Magic Mountain*. Declines in TB mortality during the period studied by McKeown represented perhaps the single most important example of declines in the mortality rate. Can we credit the sanatoria for this progress? This is unlikely because it is unlikely that their capacity was ever large enough to affect the pattern of mortality in populations. For an account of the retreat of tuberculosis, see Smith (1988).

What Caused the Mortality Rate Declines?

Many presume that the declines in the mortality rates were due to improvements in medical science provided to the public through medical practice, but counterarguments to this proposition bring it into question. In most cases, an effective specific medical intervention was not available until late in the period, well after the greater part of the mortality decline had occurred.

The argument can be illustrated for the cases of respiratory tuberculosis and a group of three upper respiratory diseases—bronchitis, pneumonia, and influenza. Mortality rates for these diseases fell to relatively low levels prior to the availability of effective medical interventions, whose availability occurred respectively after 1930, and for some cases well into the 1950s and 1960s. The picture is shared by waterborne diseases. About 95 percent of the mortality declines in cholera, diarrhea, and dysentery occurred prior to the 1930s when intravenous therapies became available. Likewise, typhoid and typhus mortality already had fallen to low levels by the beginning of the twentieth century. The pattern McKeown found for England and Wales also can be illustrated for the United States. McKinlay and McKinlay (1977) provided data for the United States from 1900 to 1973. Figure 5-3 shows these patterns for several infectious diseases. In most cases, as is shown, the availability of the effective medical intervention occurs well after the majority of the mortality declines.

One of the most important changes in mortality in the twentieth century was the decline in infant mortality. Does this type of mortality follow the same pattern? A highly readable account of the modern historical pattern of infant mortality is offered in Victor Fuchs's *Who Shall Live?* (1974). Fuchs noted that infant mortality rates in New York City improved markedly from 1900 to 1930 and that this decline was due to declines in deaths from "pneumonia-diarrhea" complex. Fuchs concluded: "It is important to realize that medical care played almost no role in this decline. While we do not know the precise causes, it is believed that rising living standards, the spread of literacy and education, and a substantial fall in the birth rate all played a part" (p. 32).

FIGURE 5-3 Fall in the Standardized Death Rate per 1,000 Population for Four Common Infectious Diseases in Relation to Specific Medical Measures for the United States

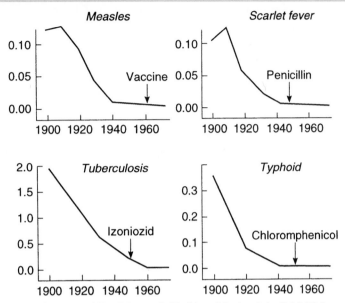

Reprinted from *Millbank Memorial Fund Quarterly/Health and Society,* John B. McKinlay and Sonja M. McKinlay, "The Questionable Contribution of Medical Measures to the Decline of Mortality in the United States in the Twentieth Century, *Millbank Memorial Fund Quarterly/Health and Society* 55 (1977): 405–428, with the permission of Blackwell Publishers.

In the 1930s, antimicrobial drugs were introduced. Between 1935 and 1950, the fall in infant death rates accelerated. Fuchs proposed that during this period "both medical advances and rising living standards contributed to the reduction in infant deaths" (p. 32). Declines in infant deaths flattened somewhat beginning about 1950 but resumed a stronger decline about 1965. If specific effective curative medicines were not largely responsible for mortality declines, is it nevertheless possible that other tools in the physician's black bag were effective? Unfortunately, this, too, is unlikely. The problem is that there probably were few effective tools available until well into the twentieth century. Even a clear knowledge of what caused disease was not widespread until the 1900s.

On the Role of Public Health and Nutrition

If medicine cannot be credited with the large declines in population mortality rates after 1750, what then can be credited? Other candidate causes appear sufficient to explain the decline: reduction in exposure to infection and improvement in the human host's ability to resist infection. Of these two, reduction in exposure was the primary method through which public health measures could be effective. The role of public health measures is of interest in itself.

Some studies strongly emphasize the importance of public health. During the industrial revolution, urban areas developed faster than cities could accommodate. The poor condition of sanitation, the tons of animal dung, the ever-present chimney smoke, and the inadequacy of fire protection and water purity must have accounted for a good share of the urban health deficit during the industrial revolution. Data throughout much of the 1800s record significantly (approximately 20 percent) higher crude death

rates in the cities and some historians claim that the urban deficit continued well into the twentieth century. Notably, Woods and Hinde (1987) demonstrated that improvements in urban mortality rates in England and Wales during these years narrowed the gap between urban and rural areas. Changes in diet between urban and rural populations were probably less important than improvements in public health efforts.

Available evidence establishes that public health contributed significantly to mortality declines; however, it can be disputed that public health was the major contributor. McKeown, for example, argued that while public health was effective for many diseases, it affected primarily the exposure to waterborne and foodborne disease organisms; thus, it cannot account for the large decline in airborne infectious disease mortality.

Public health measures include immunizations, quarantines, standards for sanitary water supplies and sewage systems, and sanitary handling and treatment of foodstuffs. During the era of study, its most important influence appears to be on the waterborne and foodborne diseases, notably the improvement of water supplies.

However, these public health measures came into widespread use late in the era of mortality declines. Among foods carrying pathogens, milk was most important because it became more widely available and consumed by the nineteenth century, and it was a notorious carrier of microorganisms for such diseases as dysentery, typhoid, streptococcal sore throat, and infantile gastroenteritis. Commercial pasteurization was developed, and it was widely used only in the twentieth century.

Control of water purity and sewage systems came into play in the latter part of the nineteenth century, and these changes surely had a positive effect. McKeown argued:

> From the evidence it is clear that the death rate from water- and food-borne diseases declined continuously from the second half of the nineteenth century. . . . There is no doubt that [this decline] was due to reduced exposure brought about by improvements in hygiene . . . and their decline coincided with advances in hygiene, particularly, in the nineteenth century, purification of water and sewage disposal. (p. 121)

Are developing countries today going through a similar transition in public health measures? We can get a closer look at the role of sanitation and clean water supply in determining a population's health. Bangladesh and Bukidnon, in the Philippines, provided a third world "laboratory" for a study of this kind (Lee, Rosenzweig, and Pitt, 1997). These researchers examined econometrically 385 households in 15 Bengali villages, while the Philippine sample examined 448 households over four time intervals. The results, however, were cautionary: "Neither variation in water sources nor improvements in sanitation facilities appeared to significantly affect child survival." In contrast, two measures that did prove to be important predictors of healthier children were the parent's wealth and education, two subjects to which we will return shortly.

Nevertheless, McKeown's argument for the central role of nutrition has credibility among scholars. The introduction of two American foods—corn and potatoes—may alone have made a significant contribution. Agriculture experienced large advances, including new crops, crop rotation, seed production, winter feeding, and improvements in farm implements.

The connection between improved nutrition and infectious diseases is fairly clear. Infectious disease creates a relationship between the host and the agent of the disease. While control of the agent is directly helpful in reducing disease incidence, the condition of the host helps determine its resistance to disease. A person who is better housed, better rested, and—with emphasis here—better fed will be more resistant and less likely to die subsequent to exposure.

What do we know of the role of nutrition in fact versus theory? Do the improvements in health result from better nutrition, as McKeown hypothesized? Some scholars dispute the claim for nutrition, and contradictions can be found. Wealthy aristocrats in England, people who could afford as much food as desired, suffered about the same death rates as the working class until well into the eighteenth century. Even after this time, they had substantially worse mortality than average Americans, including farmers.

The puzzle and its potential importance intrigued the Nobelist economic historian Robert Fogel (1986): "The decline in mortality rates since 1700 is one of the greatest events in human history" (p. 105). His work suggests that about 40 percent of the historical decline in mortality rates was due to improved nutrition, a figure he noted is ". . . neither inconsequential nor everything." The biggest rewards went to the infants, he argued, and neither a high-caloric diet nor the ability to afford one were necessarily improvements in nutrition. The healthy American farmers probably had better protein in their diets than the English of either social class.

What Lessons Are Learned from the Medical Historian?

The study of historical declines in mortality rates thus reflect controversy over the relative importance of public health measures versus nutrition and other environmental factors. The consensus is fairly clear over the minor role of medical practice. What conclusions for modern health policy can be drawn?

First, we cannot conclude that medical research is unimportant in history or in the present day. Medical research contributes not only through improvements to medical practice, but also through its influence on health-enhancing practices.

Typhoid provides a good example. As we have seen, mortality from typhoid declined substantially well before the arrival by 1950 of chloramphenicol. Medical research, however, contributed to our understanding of the cause and transmission of typhoid and generated public health measures such as filtering public water supplies, chlorination of water supplies, and establishment of drinking water standards. All of these factors occurred historically in time to have a major effect on mortality.[3] Selma Mushkin's (1979) estimates on the contribution of medical research to mortality experience tend to confirm this idea. She estimates that medical research accounted for almost one-third of the cost savings to society from reduction in sickness or death rates in the United States from 1900 to 1975. The period 1900 to 1930 accounts for half the value of medical research effects, even though it came largely before the specific effective medical practice interventions.

The idea that investments in medical research play a major role in our health and well-being is drawn most strongly by Murphy and Topel (2005). They seek to value medical research based on the evidence of what people are willing to pay for extensions to their lives. What value should we place on the advances to medical knowledge that provided kidney dialysis and extended the lives of victims of renal failure? Observation of people's willingness to pay for such care is the appropriate measure of its value, say these researchers. Health economists, who generally cite advancements in technology as the prime cause of the costliness of today's health care, do not find it surprising that Murphy and Topel's approach estimates a huge contribution from medical research. Given their estimate of mortality reductions from 1970 to 2000, increased

[3]The ideas in this paragraph come from Schneyer, Landefeld, and Sandifer (1981). Vehorn, Landefeld, and Wagner (1982) estimated the contribution of medical research to mortality reductions in the United States over the period 1930 to 1978. From 23 to 48 percent of the mortality improvements were attributed to medical research, which they concluded is a cost-beneficial investment.

longevity added $3.2 trillion to national wealth. Since 1970, reductions in heart disease mortality alone have been worth about $1.5 trillion. The medical research share of these gains, even if this amounted to only 10 percent of the total, easily compensates for the $36 billion we invest in it annually.

Second, the question of whether a given medical intervention works with afflicted patients requires a different numerator and a different denominator. If we wish to assess the effectiveness of a given treatment for a particular form of cancer, the numerator should be the mortality not in the general population, but of patients who have cancer. Likewise, the denominator should be the number of afflicted patients, not the general population.

Finally, the argument regarding the role of medicine is a historical one. Successful medical intervention came late in the period, but it did come. Today, the arguments must be different. For example, we might be called on to advise a developing country on the best strategy for investment in health care relative to investment in industry or education.

If the inferences from history are sometimes overdrawn or even invalid, what have we learned from history that we can apply to modern policy? Perhaps the best result of this overview is a healthy skepticism toward the effectiveness of any given medical practice, and more importantly, to its significance and benefit to the population. It is in this spirit that the U.S. government has increasingly come to fund outcome studies. Outcome studies seek to address the effectiveness and appropriateness of specific medical practices on patient outcomes. The studies attempt to reduce the prevalent uncertainties in medical practice, and they offer important inquiries into the wisdom of using the marginal billion dollars on medical care delivery, particularly in terms of costs and benefits to the population as a whole. In the same spirit, "evidence-based medicine" aims to close the gap between outcomes research and physician practice.

What Does Health Care Contribute?

As we discussed earlier, the contribution of health care or any other health input can be seen in two ways. On the one hand we take interest in the total contribution of health care, while on the other hand economic decisions require us to measure the marginal contributions. In the next section we will examine the production function of health. The focus is primarily on the marginal contribution. Yet a needed perspective would be lacking if we did not also examine the total contribution of health as do Bunker, Frazier, and Mosteller (1994).

These authors analyzed dozens of studies on the effectiveness of health care in each area to which it is applied, they are able to estimate and sum the total contribution of health care to health. First they find preventive health care is still somewhat disappointing. Screening programs and many immunization programs extend life typically by only a week or two (immunization for diphtheria is a standout success in comparison to the group). Clinical curative services, in contrast, have a strong beneficial effect in several cases; among these the largest contribution comes from improved treatment of heart disease (this measured as 1.2 years extension to life). The authors sum up by saying that health care offers "an estimated gain in life expectancy of about five years and a potential for adding one and a half or two more years, all derived from therapies already known to be efficacious" (p. 238).

Finally, they demonstrate that health care is often effective in treating depression, pain, and discomfort, and the gains to quality of life and well-being are probably substantial. Pain, including pain from migraine headaches, terminal cancer, heart treatment, and many more cases can be effectively reduced and sometimes eliminated. Adding the effective treatment of myopia and dental disease suggests a substantial

contribution to quality of life. So, in examining health care's effect on the margin in the next section, we can recall the evidence just described and keep in mind that the contribution of health care in total has been substantial in recent decades.

The Production of Health in the Modern Day

The investigation of the modern health production function requires econometric techniques. An understanding of the strengths and limitations of these contributions requires attention to the underlying conceptual issues.

Preliminary Issues

Two conceptual issues bear on our interpretation of the results. These two issues can be posed as questions faced by every researcher: (1) how to measure health, the dependent variable in these studies and (2) how to eliminate biases in the estimates.

How to Measure Health

Consider the measurement of health. We desire a measure of population health status that must capture the aspects of health status that are meaningful to us and must be measurable with adequate precision. It is difficult to attain both of these goals. We are most confident in the accuracy of mortality rate data, but mortality rates do not adequately capture several meaningful aspects of health status, such as reduction in pain and suffering and other improvements in the quality of life. The approach of past research in this field is understandable. Mortality data have necessarily been emphasized because of their accuracy, as well as because of their importance in the public mind. However, other indicators of health status, such as morbidity (illness) rates and disability days, have also been used. In discussing the empirical literature, we begin with the mortality studies and then consider studies of morbidity.

Eliminating Biases?—Reduced Form Versus Structural Equations

Consider that the statistical estimates are properly based on data for the availability of some health care inputs in the population, not on the amounts of all inputs actually used. In the process, bias can enter those estimating equations that mistakenly include influences beyond those of the health inputs. Reduced form equations include all these influences, but introduce bias that will understate the true contributions of health care. To eliminate this bias, the researcher's goal is to estimate the structural equations, where such extraneous factors have been removed.[4]

The Contribution of Health Care to Population Health: The Modern Era

Health economists inevitably use different study designs and data sources to estimate the marginal product of health care. The resulting numbers need to be converted to a common basis, and for this we use the elasticity of health with respect to expenditure on health care inputs: percentage change in health ÷ percentage increase in health care expenditures.

Table 5-2 reports the elasticities from several studies of the production of health. Each study applies econometric methods to analyze survey data; these range from

[4]For further discussion of this issue and method, see Rosenzweig and Schultz (1983); Grossman and Joyce (1990); and Atkinson and Crocker (1992).

| TABLE 5-2 Measuring the Contribution of Health Care to Population Health ||||
Study Cited	*Date of Study*	*Health Care Elasticity**	*Significant?*
Hadley	1982	0.12 to 0.17	Yes
Hadley	1988	0.20 to 1.00	Yes
Sickles and Yazbeck	1998	0.03 to 0.05	Yes

*This is the elasticity of health with respect to health care expenditure.

statewide data to data on county groups (Hadley, 1982, 1988) to data on individuals (Sickles and Yazbeck, 1998). Though not shown in the table, recent investigations (Cremieux, Oulette and Pilon, 1999) confirm a significant contribution of health spending to reduce infant mortality (in Canada).

The several studies offer insights because of their differences. They suggest that lifestyle and environment expenditures could provide more benefits per dollar of cost than health care; and efforts to improve schooling or reduce cigarette smoking offered appealing trade-offs with health care spending. The Hadley studies helped to establish that health care spending makes a statistically significant contribution to health and argues that health care passes benefit cost criteria at the margin. The latest study follows its subjects through time.

Is Health Care Worth It?

We find that health care is a statistically significant contributor to health on the margin, but that its marginal effect on health is small. In contrast, we find that the most important factors influencing mortality are related to socioeconomic status and lifestyle (Thornton, 2002). Health care matters, but we are nearly "on the flat of the curve." Does this mean that it is logical now to cut back on investment in health care technology? Does it mean that health care provides little benefit? Anyone who believes these things needs to recall first the economic difference between marginal benefits and total benefits. Our calculations of marginal benefits are based on a production function with a given technology. Let us first look at how important technological improvements have been, assuming against fact that the marginal benefit were zero, by then reconsidering the past two or three decades.

Murphy and Topel (2005), as we have seen, estimate that the American gains in life expectancy from 1970 to 2000, based on willingness to pay principles, are worth over $3 trillion. We invest a small fraction of that in health technology research. Much of the gains is probably due to health care. Similarly Cutler (2004) ties 40 percent of the gains in life expectancy between 1950 and 2000 to medical improvements in just two categories: low-weight infant care and cardiovascular disease treatment. Again, based on willingness to pay, the life gains are worth the extra costs of medical care overall—not even counting the benefits from other forms of health care.

But now let's recall that the marginal benefit of health care (technology held constant) is small, but not zero. We have earlier suggested that the elasticity of health care on the margin is about 0.10. To illustrate the issue, suppose that 0.10 were the true production elasticity of health care, and let the U.S. Congress reallocate $100 billion from other programs to health care expenditure. In 1997, the United States was spending $1 trillion on health care. This $100 billion transfer would have increased health care expenditure by 10 percent. We would extrapolate the improvement in health to be $10 \times 0.10 = 1$ percent. If "health" were defined as average life expectancy, a 1 percent gain would mean an increased average life expectancy of $76 \times 0.01 = 0.76$ years, provided

this increased expenditure was maintained indefinitely. Spread over the population (for a life span), however, the 0.76 years of life could prove fairly cheap, leading to incremental benefits that exceed the incremental costs.

Issues of Race and Gender

Hadley's data show that health care affects different subpopulations differently. Table 5-3 reports the health care production elasticity for Medicare (65 or over) populations, and it splits the data into subpopulations. Reading across the row labeled "Medicare Expenses," higher elasticities for females (as opposed to males of the same race) and higher elasticities for blacks (as opposed to whites of the same gender) suggest that blacks and females benefited from health care relatively more at the margin. Hadley (1988) confirmed the pattern that the health of blacks responded more strongly to health care at the margin.

Prenatal Care Works

The importance of population subgroups is reinforced by neonate mortality studies. (Corman and Grossman, 1985; and Corman, Joyce, and Grossman, 1987 are the starting points for these paragraphs.) A neonate is an infant one month old or younger. Thus, the neonate mortality rate refers to deaths to neonates per 1,000 live births. What can be done to reduce these deaths? The early studies observed counties in the United States and identified several factors that seemed to cause higher neonate mortality rates. Table 5-4 displays the production of neonate mortality study by Corman, Joyce, and Grossman (1987).

The table presents their estimates of the contribution of each measured factor to the reported mortality rate decline. Use of medical services—both for neonatal intensive care and for prenatal care—is included. The WIC program is the shortened name for the governmental program designed to provide improved nutrition for women, infants, and children; it is a means-tested program, meaning that it is directed to the poor. The BCHS variable is the authors' measure combining various Bureau of Community Health Services projects, including maternal and infant care, as well as community health centers.

TABLE 5-3 The Production Elasticity of Health Care, Education, Income, and Cigarette Consumption, Medicare Populations, 1970 County Group Data

	Independent Variable	White Males 65+	Black Males 65+	White Females 65+
Medicare Expenses	0.123[b]	0.163[b]	0.141[b]	0.173[b]
Education	0.128[b]	0.060	0.025[b]	0.106
Income	0.020	0.012	NS	0.011
Cigarette Sales	−0.053[b]	−0.134	0.110[a]	0.045[a]

Medicare Expenses = Medicare expenditures per Medicare enrollee: Education = average number of highest education year attained; Income = total family income and other unearned income; Cigarette Sales = cigarette sales per capita.

NS = coefficient is not significant and rounds to zero.

[a]Significant at the 5 percent level.

[b]Significant at the 1 percent level.

Source: Reprinted from Jack Hadley, *More Medical Care, Better Health?* Washington, DC: Urban Institute, 1982, pp. 61–62, with permission from the publisher.

TABLE 5-4 Contribution of Selected Factors to Reductions in Neonate mortality Rates, 1964–1977

Factor	Whites Total Effect	Blacks Total Effect
Organized family planning	0.084	0.526
WIC	0.425	1.330
BCHS	0.002	0.030
Neonatal intensive care	0.140	0.534
Abortion	0.824	2.109
Prenatal care	0.434	1.949
Total explained reduction	1.9	6.5
Total reduction	7.5	11.5
Percentage explained	25.3	56.5

Note: Figures record estimates of the reduction in deaths per 1,000 live births predicted to have been caused by various factors.

Source: Reprinted from *Journal of Human Resources*, Hope Corman, Theodore J. Joyce, and Michael Grossman, "Birth Outcome Production Function in the United States," *Journal of Human Resources 22* (1987): 339–360. Reprinted by permission from The University of Wisconsin Press.

The data recorded in Table 5-4 indicate that of the total reduction in neonate mortality for whites during the period, 1.9 deaths per 1,000 live births, or 25.3 percent, can be explained by the observed factors, whereas for blacks a greater amount, 6.5 or 56.5 percent, can be explained. The table is read as follows: During the period studied, the WIC program resulted in a reduction of white neonate mortality rates of 0.425 deaths per 1,000 live births, while for blacks WIC reduced neonate mortality by 1.330 deaths per 1,000 live births.[5]

A novel experiment (Williams and Lien, 2005) reinforces the value of prenatal care. When public transportation workers in Alleghany County, Pennsylvania went on strike in 1992, prenatal visits among the poor were sharply curtailed. The results were significant reductions in the quality of birth outcomes, especially for those affected during the early stages of pregnancy.

The World's Pharmacies

While we examine the breakdown of medical care by important subpopulations, note also the role of pharmaceutical availability in determining population health. Recent research (Shaw, Horrace, and Vogel, 2005; Miller and Frech, 2004) finds that OECD countries with higher drug consumption have greater life expectancies. The magnitude of the effect is on a par with the effects of reduced cigarette consumption and increases of fruit and vegetables in the diet.

Morbidity Studies

Data on mortality rates are an important part of the story. However, mortality rates tell only part of the story, and for many people who use health care, it may not be the most important part. Other measures of health also should be examined. These include morbidity data and other indicators of health. Work also is being done on developing a

[5]Currie and Gruber (1996) showed general Medicaid eligibility to improve birth outcomes in a study across states in the United States. (This is distinguished from the particular Medicaid spending directed to prenatal care). These authors, however, raised issues about the cost-effectiveness of improvements in Medicaid eligibility.

measure of the quality of life, and quality of life may become the subject of production studies.

How Does Health Care Affect Other Measures of Health?

The Rand Health Insurance Experiment (RHIE), one of the largest, randomly controlled economic experiments ever conducted, provided the best opportunity to verify those early results. It was designed to test the effect of alternative health insurance policies on the demand for health care and on the health status of a large and closely watched group of people from all walks of life.

Our interest in this chapter is derived from a big side effect of that experiment. Rand researchers discovered that the greater the portion of their health care bill that individuals are required to pay, the less health care they choose to purchase. While this should not have been surprising, what did surprise most health economists was how great the difference was; the fully insured purchased roughly 40 percent more health care than those who had to pay their own bills. This provides a great opportunity to ask: "Were the people with 40 percent more health care also 40 percent more healthy?" It is a serendipitous, but perfectly valid, way to test the real contribution of health care to people's health within the context of a scientifically controlled experiment.

Fortunately, RHIE analysts kept detailed records on each subject, including a dozen or more measurements under each category of physical health, mental health, social health, and general health index. They also examined their subjects' dental health, persistence of symptoms, health habits, and disability days. The results are easy to summarize. For dozens of items, virtually no differences were found between the groups studied.

A simple example from the RHIE illustrates the point well. Table 5-5 provides detail on work loss days per employed person per year—a measure of health status and morbidity that some economic researchers like to use because it ties directly to both health and productivity. This table separates the Rand subjects into four groups, which differ by type of health insurance policy. Some subjects pay nothing out-of-pocket for their health care/health insurance package; some pay 25 percent to 50 percent of their bill themselves; others pay all of their health care bills up to a certain amount, called a deductible. The subject's out-of-pocket cost ranges from zero (free) to about 95 percent of the bill. Newhouse et al. (1993) summarizes: "Our results show that the 40 percent increase in services on the free-care plan had little or no effect on health status for the average adult."

The effects on children showed a somewhat similar pattern. Valdez et al. (1985) examined data for 1,844 children in the Rand study—children who differed primarily by the type of insurance plan their families obtained. Children under the cost-sharing plans consumed up to one-third less care. However, the reduction in care was not significantly related to health status measures. It appears clear that while free provision of

TABLE 5-5 Work Loss Days per Employed Person per Year, by Plan

Plan	*Mean*	*Standard Error of Mean*	*95% Confidence Interval*	*Number of Persons*
Free	5.47	0.42	4.65–6.29	1,136
Intermediate (25%, 50%)	4.82	0.37	4.09–5.55	983
Individual Deductible	4.54	0.36	3.83–5.25	787
Family Deductible (95%)	4.82	0.53	3.78–5.86	600

Source: Reprinted by permission of the publisher from *Free for All? Lessons from the RAND Health Insurance Experiment* by Joseph P. Newhouse, Cambridge, MA: Harvard University Press, 1993. Copyright © 1993 by the RAND Corporation.

health care to children might be justified on equity grounds, it may not be justifiable on the basis of benefits to health (Newhouse et al., 1993).

On the Importance of Lifestyle and Environment

The importance of lifestyle and environment for a population's health is illustrated by Barbara Wolfe (1986). She investigated the trends in health status in several industrialized countries, and looked at trends in medical expenditures and lifestyle factors, such as cigarette and alcohol consumption. Previous international studies indicated little or no significant effect of medical expenditures, but by controlling for lifestyle, she demonstrated a positive relationship between health care and health in several countries. Later work (Hitiris and Posnett, 1992) corroborated this finding: Nations that have better health care in comparison with other nations have healthier citizens. However, what about lifestyle and environment, whose importance was revealed indirectly? Didn't we always know that much of our health depends on the wisdom of our own choices?

The role of lifestyle was best illustrated by Victor Fuchs in his book *Who Shall Live?* (1974). He compared average death rates in Nevada and Utah for 1959 to 1961 and 1966 to 1968. These two states are contiguous, and they share "about the same levels of income and medical care and are alike in many other respects" (p. 52). Nevertheless, average death rates in Nevada are greater than those in Utah. Table 5-6 shows the results of Fuchs's work. Fuchs argued that the explanation for these substantial differences surely lies in lifestyle.

> Utah was, and remains, inhabited primarily by Mormons, whose influence is strong throughout the state. Devout Mormons do not use tobacco or alcohol and in general lead stable, quiet lives. Nevada, on the other hand, is a state with high rates of cigarette and alcohol consumption and very high indexes of marital and geographical instability. (p. 53)

Inasmuch as Fuchs's illustration lends support to his point regardless of the time period, it may not appear necessary to see how Utah is doing today. However, it is hard not to be curious. The age-adjusted death rate per 100,000 resident population is a good, rough tool to measure average health. In 2002, Utah, with its low age-adjusted death rates, was a national leader in health (this death rate equaled 566.2), similar to Hawaii (707.0), while Nevada's rate was much higher (778.8), but significantly lower than the national average (847.2). Before concluding that a simple life and plenty of sun are the tickets to good health in and of themselves, consider that many of the top

TABLE 5-6	**Excess of Death Rates in Nevada Compared with Utah, Average for 1959–1961 and 1966–1968**	
Age Group	*Males (%)*	*Females (%)*
Less than 1	42	35
1–19	16	26
20–39	44	42
40–49	54	69
50–59	38	28
60–69	26	17
70–79	20	6

Source: Reprinted from Victor R. Fuchs, *Who Shall Live? Health, Economics, and Social Choice,* Expanded Edition, Singapore: World Scientific Publishing Company, 1995, p. 52, with permission from the author and World Scientific Publishing.

10 healthful states, while they may be sunny, are known to be chilly: Minnesota (767.2), New Hampshire (772.8), Idaho (729.0), and Colorado (648.0). Yet Fuchs's point rings true; what we do for ourselves often matters the most for our health.

Cigarettes and Health

Many have chosen to quit smoking (or to avoid becoming addicted to cigarette smoking in the first place). Americans know that heart disease and cancer are the two leading killers, but most do not realize how substantial of a part is played by smoking-related deaths. Using the category "malignant neoplasms of the respiratory system" (the category for lung cancer), we find that the 2002 death rate (54.7) is twice as high as that for any of the following: breast cancer (14.5), prostate cancer (10.6), pneumonia and influenza (22.8), diabetes mellitus (25.4), HIV (4.9), or motor vehicle–related injuries (15.7).[6] We already have seen the negative health production elasticity of cigarettes, which makes it clear that cigarette smoking affects the average health of the community and is statistically significant at that level.

While smoking certainly causes ill health, it is pleasurable as well, and one's degree of health can affect the decision to quit. For example, a healthy individual may be more likely to quit as a preventive measure; on the other hand, a critically ill individual may quit as a curative measure (Jones, 1996). Folland (2006) interprets the role of family and community in a manner similar to this preventive motive. Individuals may acquire better health and be willing to take fewer life-risks, such as smoking, upon adding to family or community social capital.

The Family as Producer of Health

Women have long been warned to avoid cigarettes and alcohol while pregnant. Are such lifestyle factors important enough to be included as factors in the production of newborn health? The answer is yes. In the production of newborn birth weight (an important guide to infant health outcomes), maternal cigarette smoking has a significant negative effect (Rosenzweig and Schultz, 1983; Rosenzweig and Wolpin, 1995). Data on maternal smoking now show that taxing cigarettes leads to improved birth outcomes via its effect on smoking behaviors of expectant mothers (Evans and Ringel, 1999).

Maternal behavior also can have strong and tragic consequences in the case of drug use. Joyce, Racine, and Mocan (1992) found that the alarming increase in low birth weight births in New York City, particularly among blacks, was due in large part to an epidemic of illicit substance abuse by pregnant women. The explosion of cocaine use had horrible consequences for these babies. Other research by Kaestner, Joyce, and Wehbeh (1996) cautions that the ever-present problem of getting honest and accurate self-reports of drug use will cause the researcher to overstate somewhat the harm done to newborn health. The issue, however, is only one of degree; maternal drug use causes significant harm to newborns.

Looking at this at a more abstract level, a study from Sweden (Bolin, Jacobsen, and Lindgren, 2002) develops the theory of how parents make health investments in themselves and their children. If parents individually make these decisions strategically—in response to the expected decisions of the others—these decisions together will not be optimal for the family. Even more significant health investment problems will occur, they warn, where parents split up in divorce because the non-caregiver may lose some incentives to invest in the child's health. The parent's incentive to invest in their children's health is clearly a critical factor in child health.

[6]These death rates are age-adjusted deaths per 100,000 resident population, based on data from the National Vital Statistics System.

Environmental Pollution

It is well known that pollution causes ill health and death in individuals, and that the elderly and people with respiratory diseases are more susceptible. The degree to which reductions in pollution will improve the health of populations is somewhat less clearly defined. That pollution effects on health are sizable and statistically significant can be shown in both industrialized and lesser-developed countries (Cropper et al., 1997). Based on levels of total suspended particulates (TSP) in New Delhi between 1991 and 1994, the average pollution level was five times the limit recommended by the World Health Organization (WHO). Variations in deaths in New Delhi responded statistically to the variations in pollution; if these estimates prove true, then a reduction of pollution levels of about one-third would reduce deaths by more than 2 percent.

A similar study by Schwartz and Dockery (1992) in Philadelphia suggests that reducing the pollution level there by the same 100 micrograms per cubic meter would reduce deaths by more than 6 percent in the general population and nearly 10 percent for the elderly. This is because with our generally better health status in the United States, more people live long enough to become part of the population most sensitive to respiratory problems from pollution.

Income and Health

While we know that good health during the years when an individual is forming a career can be a big boost to that person's income later in life (James Smith, 1998), we also know that being rich does not necessarily cause one to choose to live and eat wisely. Even programs designed to raise the income of poor families, such as (pre-welfare reform) Aid to Families with Dependent Children in the United States, did not always correlate with good health habits among the recipients (Currie and Cole, 1993; Currie and Gruber, 1996).

Though some earlier work did suggest that being richer in America was generally better for one's health, research by Deaton and Paxson (2001) brings that conclusion into question. Examining in detail both U.S. and British data over time, they find the relation of income and health to be complex and contradictory. There was a substantial decline in mortality since 1950, but rather than growing incomes as the cause, they conclude that "a more plausible account of the data, is that, over time, declines in mortality are driven by technological advances, or the emergence of new infectious diseases, such as AIDS" (p. 29).

Part of our problem thus far in researching the contribution of income to health in the industrialized world is that incomes do not vary greatly enough to detect the larger patterns. Pritchett and Summers (1996) leave little doubt that extremely low incomes have a strong effect on people's health. Though they treated the econometric challenges with great respect in establishing their conclusion, the most persuasive arguments may be those provided by simple graphs fitting various health statistics to per capita income data. These curves fit well and reveal that "modern" standards of good health are enjoyed solely by the industrialized countries with mortality experience turning sharply worse with lower income levels, conditions common in the underdeveloped world.

The Role of Schooling

What of education? Since education includes both formal and informal training (such as experience or on-the-job training), some portion of education is impossible to measure accurately. Most often health economists focus on schooling as measured by years of schooling, or academic accomplishments such as diplomas or degrees. Health status

is significantly correlated with schooling as we have seen.[7] If the marginal product of health care is truly small ("we are on the flat of the curve"), then perhaps we should reduce public health expenditures on health care at the margin and transfer the expenditures to education. However, the wisdom of such a policy depends on which of the two theories is correct.

Two Different Theories About the Role of Schooling

The ideas and work of two health economists serve to develop and contrast the two theories. First, Michael Grossman's (1972a, 1972b) theory of demand entails a central role for education. Grossman contends that better-educated persons tend to be economically more efficient producers of health status. Better-educated people understand the technology or have the know-how needed to stay healthy. They also know better how to use medical and other market inputs and their own time to produce health. Under this view, the marginal transfer of resources makes good sense.

Much of the available research concentrates on formal schooling. Other health economists have put forward hypotheses under which schooling and health status are correlated only because they are both related to one or more other factors. The problem can be seen as the familiar self-selection problem. Do people who choose higher levels of schooling have unobserved characteristics that also make them likely to be healthier?

Victor Fuchs (1982) has suggested a theory that involves certain microeconomic aspects of time discounting, that is, comparing the future to the present. Decision makers must discount future benefits and costs of a social investment to make them comparable in terms of present values (see Chapter 4 for details). A decision maker with a high discount rate will tend to prefer projects with immediate payoffs versus long-term projects. Now consider individuals facing a possible investment in education. Because education requires current costs to gain distant payoffs, individuals with relatively low discount rates will be more likely to invest in education. Similarly, health investments require substantial current outlays to gain distant payoffs because the payoffs may be extended years toward the end of life. It follows that individuals with long time horizons will tend to invest in both education and health. This will cause health status to be correlated with education, but further increments to education will not cause improvements in health status.[8]

Empirical Studies on the Role of Schooling in Health

Health economists investigated the reasons why schooling is associated with better health. Berger and Leigh (1989) examined data on thousands of individuals in two samples. One, the Health and Nutrition Examination Survey, used blood pressure as a measure of health status. The other, the National Longitudinal Survey of Young Men, used measures of functional limitations and disability. The authors first observed the individual's choice of schooling using standard statistical techniques. They found that years of schooling is related to several demographic characteristics, such as age, race, ethnic background, family characteristics, and IQ. They also developed a measure of the effect of unobserved factors, which include factors such as personal time preference. They then posed the question: Do such unobserved self-selection factors affect

[7]Hadley (1982) found education a significant contributor to population health at the small area level of analysis. Education also contributes significantly in studies within developing countries (Pitt, 1997).

[8]Fuchs (1982) proposed as well the alternative related hypothesis that schooling tends to effect a change in the people's time preferences. Both the Fuchs hypothesis and the Grossman hypothesis would imply the observed positive correlation between schooling and health.

health status or does schooling directly improve health status? Their results are consistent for both samples and for all measures of health status. Schooling directly improves health status measures, but no significant effect results from unobservables, such as time preference. This result is consistent with the view that schooling improves one's ability to produce health.

The issue of schooling and health is also important in developing countries. Studies of families in Nicaragua by Jere Behrman and Barbara Wolfe are relevant. Behrman and Wolfe (1989) posed the question: "Does more schooling make women better nourished and healthier?" They took steps to control for the influence of other factors that affect both schooling and health by accounting for the women's childhood background factors. They concluded that "the estimated positive health impact of the woman's schooling is largely representing schooling per se rather than unobserved fixed endowments so that . . . the woman's schooling does seem to make the woman healthier" (p. 660).

If a woman's schooling makes her a more efficient producer of health, then we also should expect that it will improve her children's health. Standard estimates of the effect of a woman's schooling on her children's health indeed show this effect. However, other work by Wolfe and Behrman (1987) casts serious doubt. The two authors collected data for sisters in Nicaragua. This allowed them to compare the health status of the children of the more educated using econometric techniques. Because the sisters had essentially the same childhood background, these data and methods allowed them to control for unobserved elements in childhood background. Their results were clear: Once childhood background is controlled for, a mother's education has no significant effect on her children's health status.

If it seemed difficult to distinguish the precise role for education in health, that it has a role is made clear in a recent study by Lleras-Muney (2002), who approached the problem in a unique way. Knowing that compulsory education laws came into being in various places at various times in the twentieth century, she reasoned that the related birth cohorts from that era would have experienced different levels of education but would have been similar in many other respects. This formed a natural experiment in which she could analyze the survival patterns of these people to detect a pure influence of education on health. Furthermore, the education laws could not have been directly manipulated by the study subject so they were good "instruments" for education. By this approach, she was able to conclude that education has a clear, causal, and positive effect on health. By 1960, the early century education experience appeared to have increased life years by 1.7 years, a substantial increase and one not due to time preferences of the subjects.

Conclusions

In this chapter, we investigated many topics related both directly and indirectly to the production of health. The health production function exhibits the law of diminishing marginal returns. While the total contribution of health care is substantial, the marginal product is often small. Historically, we found that much of the decline in mortality rates occurred prior to the introduction of specific, effective medical interventions. Thus, historically both the marginal and the total contributions of health care, at least as provided by the health practitioner, were probably small until well into the twentieth century. The small, modern-day marginal product of health care is statistically significant. However, in the major, controlled health insurance experiment, the better insured exhibited little or no health gain from the extra health care they consumed. Health care benefits people differentially and is generally more productive on the margin for women and blacks. Similarly, certain categories of health care have greater marginal

effects on the population than others; prenatal care programs are examples of the more productive categories.

Whether schooling or health care is the better investment toward improving health depends on which alternative theory is correct: Does schooling improve one's own health production skill, or do some individuals select for both schooling and health because of other factors? Recent research has shown an effect of education on health, though it does not rule out a role for the alternative theories. The production of health will continue to stimulate both theoretical and empirical research.

SUMMARY

1. The production function for health exhibits diminishing marginal returns. In developed countries, the total product of health care is probably substantial at the same time that the marginal product is relatively small.
2. The historical declines in mortality rates in representative industrial countries were substantially responsible for the large growth of populations.
3. The historical declines in population mortality rates were not due to medical interventions because effective medical interventions became available to populations largely after the mortality had declined. Instead, public health, improved environment, and improved nutrition probably played substantial roles.
4. The marginal product of health care in the United States is small. Recent studies find elasticities in a narrow range around 0.10.
5. Nevertheless, the total contribution of investment in health care technology over the past several decades is probably in the trillions of dollars; much of the improvement in life expectancy in this period can be attributed to health care improvements.
6. The Rand Health Insurance Experiment found that increased use of health care has little effect on the illness rates of the study population.
7. Lifestyle and environment are major and statistically significant determinants of population health status.
8. Health care contributes more substantially to health for subgroups of the population, including infants and also certain ethnic minority groups.
9. Education, as measured by years of schooling, is positively related to population health. One theory proposes that schooling improves the efficiency by which to produce one's own health. Other theories suggest that both schooling and health are linked to other unobserved variables.

DISCUSSION QUESTIONS

1. Assume that health production is subject to diminishing returns and that each unit of health care employed entails a constant rate of iatrogenic (medically caused) disease. Would the production of health function eventually bend downward? Explain.
2. What evidence is there to suggest that the United States is on the "flat of the curve" in health production? Is a typical developing country likely to be on the flat of its health production function? Discuss the differences.
3. Which of the following are important in explaining the modern rise in population in England and Wales: birth rates, death rates, and net migration rates? Describe the evidence.
4. "Medical interventions were not important in the historical declines in mortality rates, but that does not imply that medical research was unimportant." Explain this viewpoint.
5. What role did public health play in the historical decline in mortality rates?
6. Suppose you were hired as an adviser to a developing country and you were versed in the theory of production, the historical role of medicine, and the modern-day health production

function studies. Their government seeks advice on the wisdom of a relative emphasis on health and health investment versus other forms of economic investment. What would be your advice?

7. Someone says the following: "Lifestyle may be the most important determinant of health status, but changing lifestyles may not be the least costly way to improve population health status." Explain the circumstances under which this opinion could be true. Is it likely to be true in reality? What does the evidence on lifestyle suggest about government policies to improve the public's overall health?

8. Summarize the two theories on how schooling is correlated with health status. Which of the two theories does the evidence support?

9. Research shows that the returns for prenatal health care are high, whereas it may cost hundreds of thousands of dollars to keep an acutely ill, elderly person alive. What does this suggest about the appropriate allocation of resources among members of society?

10. What is the total contribution of health care to health as estimated by researchers? What parts of health care are most effective in this regard?

EXERCISES

1. Graph the production of health function $HS = 10HC^{0.5}E^{0.3}LS^{0.4}HB^{0.2}$ in a graph with axes HS and HC, assuming $E = 10$, $LS = 5$, and $HB = 7$. Graph the marginal product of health inputs. Is it increasing or decreasing? Show how the curve changes when E is increased to 15.

2. Which factors in Table 5-4 were important in explaining improvements in black neonate mortality rates? White neonate mortality rates? Speculate on why some of these factors may have been more important for blacks.

3. What are the differences between mortality and morbidity? Would you expect the two variables to be related to each other? If so, how?

4. We know that correlations never explain; it is our theories that provide explanations. Reexamine Table 5-4 and draft theories to explain why WIC has a larger contribution than Organized Family Planning. Why do the contributions differ between blacks and whites on WIC, abortion, and prenatal care?

5. Pritchett and Summers argue that income per capita is strongly and positively related to health status when viewed across the world. From data in Table 2-2, which you will find in Chapter 2 of this text, plot a graph of GDP per capita against life expectancy for the countries shown. Does your plot confirm the Pritchett and Summers finding?

6

The Production, Cost, and Technology of Health Care

Production and the Possibilities for Substitution

Costs in Theory and Practice

Technical and Allocative Inefficiency

Technological Changes and Costs

Diffusion of New Health Care Technologies

Conclusions

Recognizing that health is the ultimate output in the health sector, we understandably find considerable policy interest directed toward the production and cost of the intermediate output, health care. Despite exceptions, both politicians and consumers seeking lower health costs do not seek cuts in "necessary" health care—only that which is "purely wasteful." Yet, health care, even when needed, inevitably "costs too much."

This chapter addresses production, cost, technology, and efficiency of health care. We investigate first the question of what degree of flexibility the manager or the public policymaker can find in the production process in order to make improvements. Must physicians always be called for certain tasks, or can nurses and other less expensive inputs be substituted? Can managers safely vary the mix of types of nurses employed? These questions reduce to one: To what degree can health care inputs substitute for one another?

Second, the study of cost functions can provide further clues to finding efficiency gains. Economists find that economies of scale and scope exist in many industries, and society would be better off if firms were to choose the size that minimizes average costs. Theory states that the perfectly competitive industry achieves this in the long run without outside interference. Health care firms are generally not perfectly competitive nor necessarily perfectly managed, and health economists inquire into the extent of any excess costs.

The next issue of the chapter is the technical and allocative efficiency of health care firms. These types of efficiency and the inefficiency they define articulate in economic terms the central research issue of the American consumer's complaint: "I am paying an arm and a leg for my family's health expenses. Am I really getting my money's worth?"

We then examine how greatly the picture changes as technology, the major mover in the health care industry, changes. We will see that even when new health technology

improves our lives, it can also make life more expensive. Insurance plays an important role as a shifter of demand, though probably its greater influence is through its effect on technological innovations.

Finally, we study the economics of how and why new health care technology diffuses through the health system and forms a "logistic" pattern. The diffusion can be rapid, although it may be slowed by regulatory or institutional realities.

Production and the Possibilities for Substitution

Economists often note that there is more than one way "to skin a cat," that different techniques are available to produce the same product. A single technique is one recipe for production, meaning one specific combination of inputs. When multiple techniques are available, one can choose a relatively capital-intensive (labor-intensive) technique during times when capital (labor) is relatively cheap. It also means the ability to use cheaper forms of labor in substitution for more expensive forms.

While multiple techniques are common in many industries, health practitioners often argue that there is basically only one correct way of treating a given illness. The belief that only a single technique is possible or wise is what Victor Fuchs has called the "monotechnic view." If such a view correctly described production processes, cost-saving substitutions would be difficult if not impossible without reducing either output or quality. A more flexible production process permits cost-saving improvements that may be beneficial to consumers. Economists investigate this question using the concept of substitution.

Substitution

Flexibility means the ability to substitute one input, such as capital, for another input, such as labor, while maintaining the level and quality of output. This does not mean that the two inputs are equivalent, but only that alternative combinations are possible. Figure 6-1 illustrates a case with no input substitution and a case where an infinite

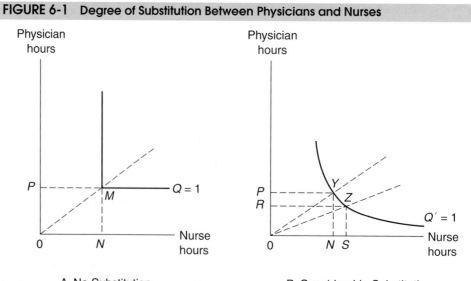

FIGURE 6-1 Degree of Substitution Between Physicians and Nurses

A. No Substitution

B. Considerable Substitution

number of techniques are available. In panel A, the isoquant shows the possible combinations of nurse hours and physician hours required to treat one patient case in a hospital; the isoquant is labeled $Q = 1$. Given this situation, only one sensible production technique combines the two inputs. Physicians and nurses must be combined in the ratio given by *0P/0N*, the ratio of inputs used at the corner point *M*. Notice that *0P/0N* is also the slope of line segment *0M*.

What does this mean? In panel A, *0P* physician hours are required to produce one case, and the addition of nursing hours beyond *0N* will not add to output unless physician hours also are increased. This applies to a production problem where patient care requires certain professional tasks that only a physician is trained and competent to perform. To use nurses to perform any "physician tasks" would result in less care or at least lower-quality care.

The figure shows that if *0N* nursing hours are required to treat one case, the addition of physician hours will not replace these nursing hours. The fact that the isoquant is flat when moving to the right from *M* means that adding nurses beyond the required combination produces no more output (i.e., they would be wasted). Likewise, the fact that the isoquant is vertical when moving upward from *M* means that additional physician hours beyond the required ratio combination are simply wasted resources. How would an isoquant look if substitution were possible? Panel B illustrates this. Again, a unit isoquant is depicted, but a smooth downward-sloping convex curve illustrates that many different combinations of inputs could be chosen without being wasteful. For example, one case can be treated with the (*0P, 0N*) combination of inputs or equivalently with the (*0R, 0S*) combination. Each point on the isoquant represents a different technique. The slope of any isoquant, such as the isoquant labeled $Q' = 1$, is called the marginal rate of technical substitution (see Chapter 2), and it represents the rate at which nurse and physician hours can be exchanged while still maintaining output.

It should be reemphasized that even though substitution is available in panel B, nurses and physicians are not equivalent. It is not even true that a fixed number of nurses always can replace a physician. Moving along the curve from point *Y* to point *Z*, the rate of substitution changes; that is, the slope becomes flatter, indicating a diminishing marginal rate of technical substitution. To replace one hour of physician time at point *Y* requires some number of nursing hours; however, at point *Z*, where fewer physician hours are being used, it requires a much greater number of nursing hours. That is, as physician time grows scarcer relative to nursing hours, it becomes more difficult to replace. This retains the idea that while substitution is possible, it may be difficult, expensive, or unsafe to have nurses do certain physician tasks, and vice versa. The curve may even become flat at some point, indicating that a minimum of required physician time has been reached.

What Degree of Substitution Is Possible?

The graphs in Figure 6-1 define terms, but they do not tell us which of the two cases is true of the health care world. From the 1970s on, economists addressed the question of whether physician extenders (as noted in Box 6-1) could substitute for physicians. *Physician extenders* is an umbrella term referring to specially trained physician assistants or nurse practitioners who are utilized to perform certain tasks, including some that formerly were performed by the physician.

The estimates obtained are equivalent to the measurement of a few points along an isoquant, such as the ones just depicted. This work suggested that substitution could be substantial. Depending on the number of physician hours employed, one physician extender could substitute for 25 percent to more than 50 percent of a physician's services. Since physician extenders have a much lower training cost, this degree of

BOX 6-1

Health Care Professionals: Expanding the Possibilities

The greater amount of health manpower research tends to focus on physicians, dentists, and managers. Yet each researcher is aware that a large share of "getting better" depends on the allied health professions. These professionals, besides often providing a human touch to care, can significantly improve the health production process.

First, the variety of specializations among allied health labor provides the benefits of Adam Smith's "division of labor." The theory explains how a focus by each expert on his or her specialized task yields greater output for the whole than were one to insist that each person be a generalist. Imagine a hospital where every professional was a generalist. This health professional then keeps the electronic records, prepares patients, sees patients, draws blood, takes X-rays, and so on. With present-day complex technologies this is not even possible, let alone efficient. Office managers, registered nurses, medical technicians, X-ray technicians, physicians, and medical records specialists together solve this economic problem as a team.

Second, the availability of other health professionals enhances the possibilities for substitution in production. Nurse practitioners and physician's assistants can substitute for physician time and, if used wisely, can expand output by freeing physicians for tasks more directly suited to their training (Brown, 1988). A similar ability has been found between physicians and non-physician services in producing mental health services (Deb and Holmes, 1998). Expanded functions for dental assistants and dental hygienists have offered lower dental care prices without loss of quality (Liang and Ogur, 1987). Likewise, research suggests possibilities for substitution between registered pharmacists and pharmacy technicians (Okunade and Suraratdecha, 1998).

Nurse anesthetists are already generally accepted in practice, and while midwives are often limited by law, they have a long history of being called upon to deliver babies. Finally, a stronger general emphasis on providing information to patients has made a wide variety of caregivers into information providers as well.

substitutability could result in substantial savings. Reportedly, the observed physicians were not employing sufficient numbers of assistants to make the practice fully profitable to the physicians.

Elasticity of Substitution

The hospital has provided a related focus of production studies. One study presents evidence of substitution among various categories of hospital inputs. It also illustrates a second and more convenient way to measure the possibilities for substitution between inputs, the elasticity of substitution (E_S), which measures the responsiveness of a cost-minimizing firm to changes in relative input prices. It is defined as follows:

$$E_s = \frac{\text{Percentage change in factor input ratio}}{\text{Percentage change in factor price ratio}}$$

What does this elasticity mean? If a firm were a cost minimizer, then it would be responsive to changes in input prices, and it would tend to respond by shifting away from the now costlier input to the now relatively cheaper input. Suppose that a hospital is currently at combination *Y* in panel B of Figure 6-1 using *0P* physician hours and *0N* nursing hours to treat one case. Suppose also that physicians are paid $200,000 per year and nurses are paid $40,000 per year. Suppose, finally, that the hospital employs

100 physicians and 100 nurses. As a result of a 10 percent increase in the relative wage rate of physicians (from $200,000 to $220,000), the cost-minimizing hospital moves to combination *Z*, which substitutes *NS* nursing hours for *PR* physician hours. The relative physician input ratio decreases from the one shown by the slope of the line segment *0Y* to the one shown by the slope of *0Z*.

Assume that the decrease in the slopes (i.e., the ratio of factor inputs) is 6 percent. The elasticity of substitution, E_s, has a value of 0.6, indicating that every 1 percent change in relative factor prices leads to a 0.6 percent change in the relative use of those factor inputs. Whereas the ratio of physicians to nurses was previously 1.00, a 10 percent increase in relative physician wages (from 5 to 5.5 times nurses' wages) would change the input ratio to 0.94 (a 6 percent decrease). This would represent the replacement of one physician ($220,000) with five nurses ($200,000), hence lowering costs by $20,000.[1] We will report E_s in absolute value as positive numbers, even though it is understood that the firm's response is to decrease the relative use of a more expensive input.

The minimum value of E_s is zero, and a firm with isoquants represented by the one shown in panel A of Figure 6-1 will have an elasticity of substitution equal to zero because it always will use the same input combination to produce a given level of output regardless of relative factor prices. Higher values of E_s indicate a greater potential for substitutability.

Estimates for Hospital Care

Physicians are important to productivity of all hospital inputs (Pauly, 1980; Bays, 1980), and Jensen and Morrisey (1986) incorporated this fact into their analysis of the elasticity of substitution between hospital inputs. They estimated a production function for hospital care and generated the isoquants and estimated the elasticities of substitution. Patterns of input use were observed in the process across a large number of hospitals.

Table 6-1 shows the estimates of elasticities of substitution between pairs of inputs. For example, a 1 percent increase in the price of medical staff relative to nurses would result in a 0.547 percent decrease in the ratio of medical staff to nurses.

How are we to judge the estimated degree of substitutability? Are these numbers large or small? The elasticities reported are at least sufficient to show that some substitutability exists between virtually all pairs of hospital inputs. In fact, the authors conclude that "all inputs in both teaching and nonteaching hospitals are substitutes for each other." The smallest values for substitution reported here are between beds and categories of labor. It may seem nonsensical that one can substitute people for beds; but "beds" here represent a convenient measure of the various and often complex capital inputs used by a hospital. The data suggest that even in hospital care production, for which labor is undoubtedly the critical input, capital can be substituted on the margin for labor.

We note that Custer and Willke (1991) and Lehner and Burgess (1995) have shown these results to be sensitive to the particular definition of the physician's input. Even so, most health economists probably would agree that while substitution possibilities exist among many health care inputs, their range is still uncertain.

Recent studies have shown that home health care can substitute for hospital care, and this provides a different and broader level of analysis of substitution. Is the "home hospital" as good? Is it less costly? Illife and Shepperd (2002) report that studies of randomized trials of home versus hospital care find little difference in mortality outcomes or in costs.

[1]The new ratio is 99 physicians to 105 nurses, or 0.94.

TABLE 6-1 Substitution Elasticities for Teaching and Nonteaching Hospitals Evaluated at the Mean

Input Pair	Nonteaching Case-Mix Adjusted Admissions	Teaching Case-Mix Adjusted Admissions
1. Medical Staff with Nurses	0.547	0.159
2. Medical Staff with Beds	0.175	0.155
3. Nurses with Beds	0.124	0.211
4. Nurses with Residents	—	2.127
5. Medical Staff with Residents	—	0.292

Source: Jensen and Morrisey (1986). Copyright © 1986 MIT Press Journals. All rights reserved.

Costs in Theory and Practice

The production function, its isoquants, and the elasticities of substitution have consequences for costs. We will show how the cost function is derived and explain the technical terms *economies of scale* and *economies of scope*.

Deriving the Cost Function

As we noted, the production function describes the input/output relationships, and the cost function describes the cost/output relation. The two are closely related, and under the right conditions the two functions can be derived one from another. The closeness of this relationship is illustrated in Figure 6-2.

Panel A, which depicts several isoquants, illustrates the production function, let's say for a physician practice. An infinite number of isoquants exist in principle, and we have chosen to show only three. The lowest isoquant shows that many different points (or combinations) of capital and labor that are capable of producing the 100 physician office visits. Higher isoquants, of course, produce more, 150 and 200 visits, respectively.

Imagine that Figure 6-2, panel A, had no straight, slanted lines (*AB* and so on). The lines you have "removed" identify the cost consequences of the firm's input choices. Without them, the graph would characterize a firm that knows "only half of the story," only the output consequences of its input choices. Do firms exist that would simply ignore the cost inputs? Would they say: "We wish to help people get well regardless of what it costs and economics is not an appropriate consideration."

In reality, health care firms, like all others, must meet their creditors or close their doors—they must at least break even. A tougher question for economists, however, is whether the many nonprofit firms strive to minimize costs. And then we must further ask, how well do they achieve this goal? But, you may ask: Why must we fuss over such technicalities? The reason is that economic theory derives the cost function only if the firm in question seeks to minimize its costs. Before showing how the derivation works, consider that Ellis (1993) makes a good case that we are "safe" in this regard. Ellis addresses this question: If a community hospital board discovered that it could treat 1,000 patients with proper care and still permit a waste of resources worth $20,000, then some board member could sensibly suggest: "Eliminate the waste and we could treat even more patients." We will assume that health care firms reason in this way.

Cost Minimization

While isoquants show the many combinations of inputs to produce a given output; they do not by themselves describe the cheapest combination of inputs to produce the given output. The firm minimizes costs of producing a given level of output with

FIGURE 6-2 Production Function for a Hypothetical Physician Practice

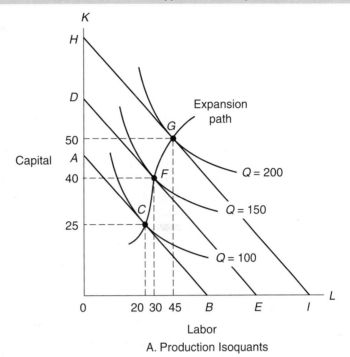

A. Production Isoquants

B. Derived Total Cost Function

the aid of a second tool—the isocost curve, the downward-sloping straight lines in Figure 6-2.

An isocost curve is the collection of all combinations of capital and labor that together cost a given amount. Let the level of total cost being considered be, TC, this money can buy many combinations of capital and labor, K and L, in fact any combination whose costs add up to $TC = rK + wL$, where r is the rental price of capital and w is

the wage rate of labor. The "rental price of capital" means the cost to the firm of using the capital for one period, regardless of whether it actually rents the capital or owns it. This particular isocost equation can be transformed algebraically so that K appears on the left-hand side and all other terms appear on the right, yielding the equivalent equation, $K = TC/r - (w/r)L$, which is an isocost line.

The firm wishing to produce a given output level, say 100 visits, will minimize its costs by choosing the lowest isocost curve that is tangent to the 100-visit isoquant. In the figure, least-cost production of 100 visits occurs at input combination $L = 20, K = 25$ at point C on isocost curve AB. Given knowledge of the input prices, we can calculate the output cost. For example, let $r = \$1,200$ and $w = \$1,000$; then, least-cost production of 100 visits will cost \$50,000. Alternatively, if the firm wishes to produce 150 visits, the least-cost production would occur at point F, which entails 30 units of labor and 40 units of capital for a total cost of \$78,000. In this fashion, the combination of the production function represented by the isoquants and the cost requirements represented by the isocost curves generates a set of outcomes, or points C, F, and G. The set of all possible points of tangency, such as these, is called the *expansion path*.

The expansion path supplies the information that associates a given output with its minimum cost. When these cost and output data are recorded in a graph, as in panel B, the result is the firm's total cost function. The cost function has a lazy S-shape, a pattern that is thought to be typical of many firms in practice. It also goes through the origin, indicating that if this firm produces nothing, it will incur no costs, meaning that the firm has no fixed costs. Economists refer to a period of time long enough for the firm to alter or avoid any of its commitments to input suppliers as the long run. Thus, the implication is that the cost function shown is depicting the firm in the long run.

This cost function is a "frontier" in that it represents the minimum possible cost of producing a given output. Actual firms may operate somewhat inefficiently, and we will observe cost levels above the frontier. It is a contradiction to say that one could observe a cost level *below* the cost frontier. Analysts often wish to determine whether health care firms are operating on or above their cost frontier, and we will return to this efficiency issue later. At present, we address a different issue—whether a firm is operating at an economical point on the frontier from the point of view of society as a whole.

Economies of Scale and Scope

To simplify the exposition, we separate the issues of economies of scale and scope, treating scale economies first. Consider a physician firm such as the one depicted in Figure 6-2. The long-run total cost function as shown in panel B can be transformed to express information about economies of scale. The average costs for this firm can be calculated by dividing the given cost level by the corresponding number of physician visits. The resulting long-run average cost ($LRAC$) function is shown in Figure 6-3. A firm is said to experience economies of scale when its long-run average cost is declining as output increases. Thus, the firm depicted exhibits economies of scale in region AB. Conversely, the firm experiences diseconomies of scale if and only if the long-run average cost is increasing as output increases, such as occurs in the region BC.

What output level would a profit-maximizing firm choose in this case? It is tempting to suppose it would choose output Q_B, at which its average costs are lowest (AC_B), but this is not necessarily the case. A firm is not in the business of minimizing its average costs and would do so only if, coincidentally, the output that minimized costs also maximized profits.

A related concept is economies of scope. By definition, economies of scope are possible only for a multi-product firm and because many health care firms are multi-product in nature, the concept is highly relevant. Economies of scope occur

FIGURE 6-3 The Long-Run Average Cost Function

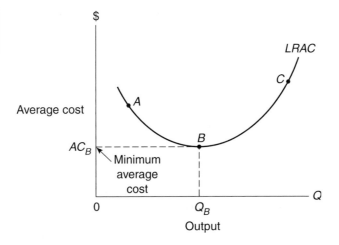

whenever it is possible to produce two or more different goods jointly more cheaply than they can be produced separately. As an illustration, consider the provision of pediatric hospital care (for children) and geriatric hospital care (for the elderly). Suppose there were two hospitals in town—one that provided only pediatric care and one that provided only geriatric care. Would the total cost of pediatric plus geriatric care be lower if one single hospital provided both? It may be cheaper to combine the two hospitals and achieve scale economies, but that is not the point at present. However, it might still be cheaper to combine them when the inputs needed for both types of care interact well together. Perhaps things learned in pediatrics have applications in geriatrics and perhaps the two could support each other so that the result would be lower total costs. If so, by producing the two different outputs jointly, we achieve economies of scope.

Economies of scope are illustrated by equation (6.1). Here, a cost function is depicted in mathematical notation. Two different outputs are shown, Q_1 and Q_2. For example, Q_1 may represent pediatric care and Q_2 may represent geriatric care. The example in equation (6.1) concerns the attempt to produce output levels $Q_1 = 100$ and $Q_2 = 150$ either jointly or separately. Economies of scope exist if the cost of producing the two outputs jointly, that is,

$$TC(Q_1 = 100, Q_2 = 150)$$

is less than the sum of the costs of producing each quantity separately, that is,

$$TC(Q_1 = 100, Q_2 = 0) + TC(Q_1 = 0, Q_2 = 150)$$

In summary, economies of scope occur in this example if the following inequality holds:

$$TC(Q_1 = 100, Q_2 = 150) < TC(Q_1 = 100, Q_2 = 0) + TC(Q_1 = 0, Q_2 = 150) \qquad \textbf{(6.1)}$$

Why Would Economies of Scale and Scope Be Important?

The concepts of economies of scale and scope are of considerable interest to both public policy and to managerial policy. We will illustrate their significance using the idea of economies of scale, but we can use similar arguments to show the importance of economies of scope.

Recall that a profit-maximizing firm wishes to do just that, maximize profits. It has no intrinsic interest in producing at that level of output at which average costs are at a minimum unless that output also coincidentally maximized profit, but this is not generally the case. Consumers would like for firms to minimize average costs as long as these cost savings are passed on to the public. One of the reasons that economists promote the theory of perfect competition is that competition forces the firm in the long run to operate so that it minimizes average costs. The competitive firm is guided by competition, as if by an invisible hand, to serve society's interests in keeping costs low.

Most health care firms, such as hospitals and physician practices, do not operate in perfectly competitive markets. Therefore, competitive pressures will not necessarily force them to operate at the most efficient scale of operation. There may conceivably be too few or too many providers. If there are too many, existing hospitals may be smaller than is required for the efficient scale; small hospitals may be forgoing the profit-maximizing opportunities available through greater economies of scale.

Historically, area-wide health planning, promoted by various government programs since the 1940s, encouraged the reduction of "excess beds." These programs also promoted the "rationalization" of geographic patterns of critical and expensive diagnostic equipment, such as CT scanners. The programs expressly aimed at reducing the growth in health expenditures, would make more sense to economic thinking if the health care were either unnecessary or if the rationalization were expected to take advantage of economies of scale.

Present-day hospital mergers also raise questions about economies of scale: "To what degree are hospital mergers justified by the existence of economies of scale?" Sinjay and Campbell (1995) ask. They offer theory and evidence to support the idea that mergers can be motivated by the desire for scale economies. For example, suppose two neighboring hospitals are both so large that they are operating at outputs achieving well above minimum average costs. Resistance by physicians and nurses within each hospital makes the needed trimming impossible. Let Mercy Hospital merge with St. Boniface and the combined management might gain the muscle to make the needed reductions.

The gain to society from exploiting economies of scale also illustrates the natural monopoly. The essential idea can be seen from a simple example. Figure 6-4 shows a health care unit (perhaps a hospital) that provides the diagnostic services of an MRI scanner. If many such firms are in the market area, then perhaps no single MRI scanner is operating at an output level at which it achieves the lowest long-run average cost. Because of its competition, the hospital unit depicted operates at point D, where

FIGURE 6-4 Gains from Exploiting Scale Economies

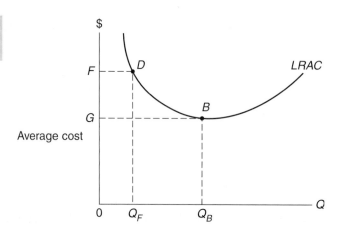

average costs are *0F*. If society had fewer MRI scanners, the remaining ones could operate at a higher capacity, say at point *B*, with lower average costs of *0G*.

These arguments depend on finding empirical results showing that further advantages from economies of scale at the level of the firm are available to society as a whole. The average cost curve in Figure 6-4 records only the costs incurred by the hospital unit. From society's broader perspective, the costs incurred by the patients and their visiting families and friends also are relevant. To see the point more clearly, draw the MRI scan example to its extreme. Suppose the minimal average cost occurs when one scanner serves a rural region of 400 miles in radius. Would residents of this region be better off building only one centrally located scanner? Or would the necessarily large travel costs make such a plan foolish in the extreme?

Empirical Cost-Function Studies

Once the theoretical ideas are understood, the fundamental questions become empirical. Are there, in fact, economies of scale and scope available to be exploited in real-world health care firms? At what level of output and for what combinations of outputs are these economies achieved?

Differences Among Hospital Cost Studies

Two themes occur often and represent differences in approach. We will describe long-run versus short-run studies, and behavioral versus structural cost functions.

Long-Run Versus Short-Run Studies

Economies of scale, as we have seen, are defined by the shape of the long-run average cost curve. The difference between the long run and the short run is well-defined in economics. The long run is a period of time sufficiently long for the hospital to end any fixed commitments and to make any cost-saving adjustments that are possible. The short run is a period of time during which the hospital still has some fixed commitments, that is, some inputs that cannot be varied. An example is the number of beds set up for service.

Although the distinction is clear in theory, it is difficult to determine which case is represented by the data. Are hospitals that are being observed in cross sectional analyses (at a given point in time) all achieving long-run cost minimization? Have they all adjusted their levels of capital, equipment, and other fixed commitments to their desired long-run levels? These assumptions seem doubtful, particularly during times when our health system is in flux. Conversely, are the currently observed hospitals using capital and equipment levels that were determined without reference to the current state of their markets? This, too, seems an extreme view.

Structural Versus Behavioral Cost Functions

Economic and health service analysts frequently distinguish between structural and behavioral cost functions. By structural cost function, we mean a cost function that is derived in a consistent manner from economic theory, just as we have derived it in the previous section. That is, the production isoquants and the isocost curves are used to derive the cost-minimizing level of costs for each possible level of output.

In contrast, behavioral cost functions (Evans, 1971) are derived from analyses of the patterns in costs in actual data across hospitals. Variables are included that distinguish real-world differences between hospitals. The variables matter for costs but often do not have a clear role in the theory of cost functions. Sometimes behavioral cost functions omit variables, like factor costs such as employee wage rates or equipment

rental rates, that are difficult to measure in the real world but that are theoretically important.[2]

Difficulties Faced by All Hospital Cost Studies

What do hospitals produce? The difficulty of measuring the heterogeneous hospital output trips up nearly all hospital cost studies. First, hospitals differ by type of cases they treat; this is the "case-mix problem." Medicare's Diagnosis Related Group (DRG) payment system identifies 506 groups of cases, so the hospital is a multi-product firm to an unusual degree. Some studies have virtually neglected the problem, others have used multi-product cost functions with adjustments for case mix and related variables. Although the multi-product approach is superior, even multi-product methods rarely incorporate more than four or five hospital output categories. Even the question of whether sufficiently refined hospital cost estimates are achievable in principle has not gained a consensus among health economists.[3]

A related problem is how to treat quality. Unobserved or incorrectly measured variations in quality between hospitals may lead to errors in research examining economies or diseconomies of scale. Research to measure quality continues, and much of our understanding of hospital costs may be amended when better quality measures are incorporated into cost studies.

The case-mix issue is illustrated in Figure 6-5, and the quality issue, though not illustrated explicitly in the figure, is similar. The figure illustrates a situation where the true, long-run average cost function is flat, exhibiting neither economies nor diseconomies of scale. The three cost curves shown represent three hospitals, each with a distinct case mix. In order of ascending costs, these are Hospital 1, which treats uncomplicated medical cases; Hospital 2, which treats more complicated surgical cases; and Hospital 3, which treats the most highly complex level or tertiary cases.

FIGURE 6-5 The Case-Mix Issue

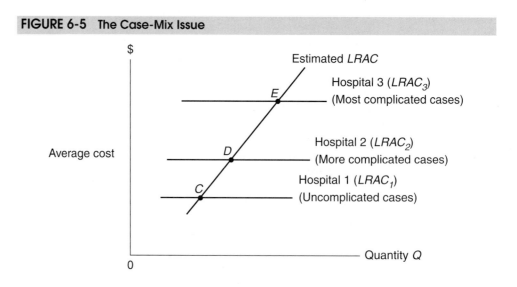

[2]Cowing, Holtmann, and Powers (1983) have argued that omitting input prices is equivalent to the dubious assumption that there are no substitution possibilities between inputs. Omitted variable bias in general is discussed in Cremieux and Ouellette (2001).

[3]Work by Olesen and Petersen (2002) promises to provide ways to incorporate large numbers of hospital outputs into fewer output measures.

Suppose that points C, D, and E represent the data observations available to the researcher for each hospital type for a given statistical study. The researcher may mistake the unobserved case-mix differences for diseconomies of scale, that is, mistakenly believe that the long-run average cost curve is rising as shown by the connecting line. This case is illustrative only because the underlying patterns of case mix, quality, and size of output could yield errors in either direction. Alternative approaches to treating the case-mix problem have been investigated extensively.[4] These studies show that case-mix differences between hospitals are materially important when estimating scale economies and cannot be overlooked.

Researchers may lack reliable measures of hospital input prices. The cost of capital or the starting registered nurse's wage may seem simple data to collect (a matter of contacting an executive in the finance office), but they are often difficult to define adequately. Unfortunately, errors in measurement of hospital input prices have substantial consequences for the results.

Finally, most hospital cost-function studies omit physicians' input prices entirely. Physicians are not under hospital control, and this independence, as well as the accounting and the physician practice of billing the patient separately become problems. Physician costs are properly part of production costs, and their omission results in biased econometric estimates of hospital costs. Early research experience with hospital costs (Bays, 1980; Pauly, 1980) established that physicians do matter.

We have developed cost theory and explained differences in empirical approaches to teach concepts but also to identify the messy looking reality of this research. Consider the very basic issue of scale phenomena. Of those who chose the theoretically most consistent "structural" approach, some (Conrad and Strauss, 1983) found economies of scale, some (Cowing and Holtman, 1983) found constant returns to scale, yet others (Vita, 1990) reported diseconomies of scale. Researchers who applied the behavioral cost-function approach (Granneman, Brown, and Pauly, 1986) found economies of scale for the emergency department. Yet others (Vita, 1990; Fournier and Mitchell, 1992) demonstrated that results also differ depending on the investigator's assumption of a long-run versus a short-run equilibrium. These studies establish that the difficulties in hospital costs center on the problems of measuring output in a multi-product firm where quality matters a great deal.

In examining "short-run" versus "long run" costs consider how "too much capital to be consistent with the long run" comes to be measured, and why it is inconsistent with long-run equilibrium? In the short run, capital is fixed, and it may be inconsistent with long run cost minimization. A manager who could magically change this capital could probably improve the firm's profits. In contrast, the long run is defined as a long enough time to enable the manager to have selected the appropriate level of capital to achieve the highest profits.

We are all stuck with the short-run reality, but the econometrician may assess what might have been, if capital had been variable in the short run. Thus, by measuring the simulated response of profits to an increase in capital, the researcher can infer the long-run versus short-run answer: No change in profits implies the long run, while an increase in profits implies the short run. Things get more complicated, however, because it is also possible for firms to choose their long-run capital level inefficiently. Bilodeau and colleagues (2002) recently conducted a cost-function study indicating that the U. S. hospital system is overcapitalized.

[4]Hornbrook and Monheit (1985) study the importance of case mix. From data for 380 hospitals, they found that larger-scale hospitals in their sample tended to admit case mixes with relatively shorter lengths of stay.

Summarizing Cost Studies

What can we conclude from this discussion of cost-function analysis? At the end of the 1970s, a consensus seemed to emerge that hospitals exhibited economies of scale with a moderate ideal size of about 250 beds. Instead of polishing this consensus and affirming it, the succeeding work brought it into question. The results spanned the gamut from scale economies to diseconomies.

We have so far focused on hospitals, but a study of nursing homes also highlights the quality issue. When quality was ignored, Gertler and Waldman (1992) found scale economies. However, a quality-adjusted model showed scale economies only for low-quality nursing homes. Average-quality homes had constant costs, while high-quality homes were associated with diseconomies of scale.

Technical and Allocative Inefficiency

In addition to issues of scale, efficiency can be measured in two other ways, each also of great concern to health care firms and policy makers. Economists refer to these as technical and allocative efficiency.

Technical Inefficiency

Technical inefficiency is illustrated in Figure 6-6, panels A and B. Panel A depicts a production process with one input, while panel B depicts a production process using two inputs, capital and labor. Technical inefficiency implies that the producer is not achieving a maximum output from a given input combination. It is as if workers or machines were misused, not working at full capacity, or not cooperating well.

In both panels, each firm's actual experience is indicated by a firm number. A technically inefficient firm falls off its frontier. In panel A, the production frontier is shown as the production function labeled $f(L)$. Firms 4 and 5 are shown to be on the frontier; that is, they are currently technically efficient. In contrast, Firms 1, 2, and 3 are off the frontier and thus are currently technically inefficient. In panel A, the firm inefficiencies

FIGURE 6-6 Technical Efficiency and Inefficiency at the Firm Level

A. One Input

B. Two Inputs

are measured as relative distances from the frontier. The distance focused on may be the output (vertical) distance—what output could have been achieved with these inputs—or the input (horizontal) distance—how many fewer inputs could have achieved this output? Generally, these alternative approaches to inefficiency measurement will yield somewhat different results.

Panel B shows an isoquant representing frontier practice treating for 100 cases. Suppose that the actual current output of all firms depicted in panel B is known to be 100 cases. Firms 6 and 7 in the panel are on the isoquant for 100 cases and thus are currently representing frontier practice and are technically efficient. Firms 8, 9, and 10 are off the isoquant, indicating that they have employed more input quantities than technically efficient production requires. As was the case in panel A, both output and input distance functions can be used as measures of inefficiency.

Allocative Inefficiency

Technical efficiency applies conceptually to production within a given firm. By contrast, allocative efficiency requires the efficient allocation of inputs between firms and between outputs. Essentially, it requires that each type of capital and labor be put to its most rewarding use in society. Economic theorists have shown that allocative efficiency in production will result if each firm buys or hires inputs in competitive markets and if each firm minimizes production costs. Assuming competitive input markets—and thus fixed input prices common to all firms—permits us to describe allocative efficiency at the firm level. Here, allocative efficiency requires that each firm respond optimally to input prices; correspondingly, allocative inefficiency implies choosing an inappropriate combination of inputs in the sense that input prices have not been appropriately considered.

To illustrate, consider Figure 6-7. In this figure, the isoquant for 100 cases is illustrated as the curve labeled $Q = 100$. Assume that the firm being examined is currently producing its desired level of output, and that the desired level happens to be 100 cases. Two isocost curves also are depicted, one indicating a cost level of $50,000 and the other a cost level of $42,000. Suppose that the firm in question was observed operating at a point A. Because this firm is treating 100 cases using an input combination on the 100 cases isoquant, we can say this firm is technically efficient. However, it is not allocatively efficient.

FIGURE 6-7 Technical Allocative Efficiency

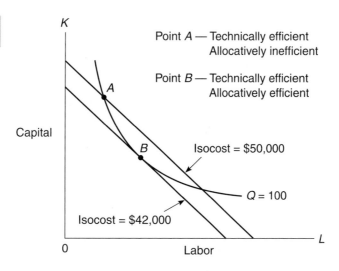

To confirm this idea, consider that the firm in question alternatively could have produced 100 cases at point *B*. As point *B* lies on a lower and thus less costly isocost curve, the firm at *B* would reduce costs from $50,000 to $42,000 by moving from point *A* to point *B*. Point *B* entails a tangency of the desired isoquant with the lowest feasible isocost curve. A tangency implies an equality of the ratio of input prices to the ratio of marginal products for the inputs (the equality of marginal output per dollar for each input). This is the firm's appropriate response to input prices, and its key condition for allocative efficiency.

Though the conditions for efficiency of both types are well-defined, several different empirical techniques have appeared to address them. These techniques can be grouped into two categories: nonfrontier and frontier studies. In the nonfrontier studies, actual outputs or cost experiences for two or more groups of firms are compared while attempting to control for the effect of extraneous variables. In frontier studies, actual outputs or firm costs are compared to the best possible experience. We emphasize frontier studies because they are conceptually closer to the definitions of technical and allocative efficiency.

Two types of empirical frontier analysis have emerged. One, data envelopment analysis (DEA), was developed earlier and has been used most often in hospital studies. The other, the stochastic frontier method (SFA), was developed in 1977, with applications in health care proliferating in the late 1980s.

Frontier Analysis

The Data Envelopment Analysis (DEA) Approach

DEA is illustrated in Figure 6-8. The frontier production, initially unknown to the researcher, is revealed as more firms are observed. A few such firms are represented by the points labeled 1 through 10. The data envelopment method finds the frontier isoquant for a selected level of output (for example, $Q = 100$) by forming an envelope of the data. Researchers use linear programming to construct this efficient outer shell of the data points. Given the estimated frontier, technical inefficiency then is measured as a relative distance from the frontier.[5]

FIGURE 6-8 The Data Envelopment Method

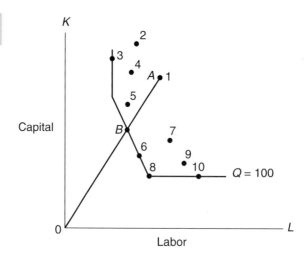

[5]See Fare and Lovell (1978) for economic applications of the DEA approach.

DEA attracts researchers and research readers because it imposes no assumptions about the parameters of the underlying distribution of inefficiency. Analysts refer to this as "nonparametric." Its cousin SFA, contrasts with DEA because researchers must guess in advance the statistical distribution of the inefficiencies. Those who prefer SFA argue that DEA assumes that all firms lying distant from the frontier are inefficient. Suppose that during a given year, the Huron Hospital nurses go on strike. Suppose further that the hospital is measured as experiencing substantial inefficiency; the hospital was operating at a substantial distance off the frontier for similar hospitals. Was the hospital really inefficient or only apparently so? Should the researcher charge the entire shortfall in output to management error or should an adjustment be made (a "handicap" frontier) reflecting its special difficulties?

The Stochastic Frontier Analysis (SFA) Approach

SFA treats each firm uniquely by assuming it to be affected by a potential shock to its ability to produce care. Consider a hospital that is managed with perfect technical and allocative efficiency. Suppose this hospital discovers that its long-time major supplier has gone bankrupt. It takes months before comparable prices, qualities, and reliability are restored with new suppliers. Regardless of management's response to these events, the hospital's cost and output data for the year will differ from other apparently similar hospitals having standard experiences. This will be true even if the management is "perfect," a model for other managers.

If each firm is randomly shocked during the period in ways that affect its production and cost performance, the firm's best possible practice, its frontier, will be randomly shifted. When the frontier function is partly random, the result is a "stochastic process"—hence, the name stochastic frontier.

Techniques developed by Aigner, Lovell, and Schmidt (1977) make it possible to estimate both the individual firm's expected frontier and the firm's inefficiency. The stochastic frontier concept is illustrated in Figure 6-9, an example that focuses on average costs. The mean average cost frontier is the dark curve. The individual firm's frontier is shifted by random shocks whose distribution must be assumed by the researcher from among known, parametric distributions. Thus, each hospital has a unique frontier and inefficiency distance from its frontier.

FIGURE 6-9 The Stochastic Frontier Method

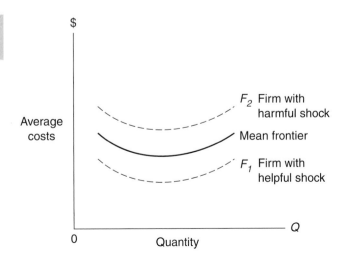

Many health economists recognize pluses and minuses to both approaches and treat them as complementary tools (Kooreman, 1994a, b). Meanwhile, the work of theoreticians in econometrics moved the approaches toward each other. Work with "panel data"—gathered as a sample of hospitals followed for many periods—suggests how the SFA method can be used without imposing the strong parameter assumptions (Lee and Schmidt, 1993). We look at two empirical questions as examples of DEA and SFA:

1. How efficient are U.S. hospitals on average?
2. Are for-profit hospitals more or less efficient than nonprofits?

Valdmanis (1990) applied the DEA technique to two groups of hospitals in 1982, one representing 33 nonprofits and the other 8 public hospitals in Michigan. Her measures indicated that the nonprofits achieved, on average, 86.6 percent of technically efficient use of inputs, while the public hospitals performed better, achieving 98.5 percent or near frontier efficiency. These high-efficiency levels via DEA conform to the several other U.S. results as well as to figures reported from Norway (Magnusson, 1996). Stochastic frontier studies (Zukerman, Hadley, Iezzoni, 1994; Sloan, 2001) also report fairly modest levels of inefficiency.

The efficiency differences among for-profit and public hospitals in the Valdmanis DEA study favored the public hospitals, though the difference was small; the pattern also was noted again a few years later (Ozcan et al., 1992). More recent DEA studies show even smaller differences between for-profit and other hospitals, causing two researchers to describe the pattern plainly: "We find no evidence that differences in ownership structure affect technical efficiency after controlling for other factors" (Burgess and Wilson, 1998, p. 100). The SFA studies generally also found minimal differences between the organizational types.[6]

In addition to comparisons of hospital groups, successful frontier techniques might identify and rank hospitals to assist hospital managers and public policy makers in steering health care production toward greater efficiency. Errors in measuring efficiency may "average out" when groups are compared, for example, nonprofits versus for-profits, but it appears doubtful as yet whether individual hospital estimates are robust and error-free enough to be useful in practice. Recent research on this question suggests that skepticism is warranted (Folland and Hofler, 2001; Street, 2003; Cremieux and Ouellette, 2001).

Technological Changes and Costs

The rapid pace of technological change in the health care industry raises economic questions about the effects these changes will have. Technological change may reduce costs when it improves the productivity of health care resources, or it may increase costs when it improves the quality of care or introduces new and costlier products. Because it often raises costs in the health sector, many researchers hypothesize technological change to be the major contributor to health sector inflation. Deep and widespread insurance coverage in the health sector may induce technological innovations of the type that increase costs. The effects on costs and the improvements to quality of care will depend on the diffusion of these new technologies to providers. Thus, patterns of diffusion have also become a critical subject of study. We investigate these issues in the remaining sections of this chapter.

[6]Psychiatric hospitals (Mark, 1996), nursing homes (Kooreman, 1994a; Vitaliano and Toren, 1994); group homes (van Lear and Fowler, 1997), physician clinics (Defelice and Bradford, 1997; Gaynor and Pauly, 1990) and physicians working in hospitals (Chilingerian, 1995) also have been studied.

Technological Change: Cost Increasing or Decreasing?

Technological change necessarily entails an improvement either by providing less costly production methods for standard "old" products, or alternatively by providing new or improved products. In either case, cost experience is improved in the sense that it will be less expensive to produce a given output, holding quality constant. However, the mix of products and services sold may change in directions that raise the average cost of a patient day, a case treated, or a physician visit. Consequently, the total health care expenditure per capita may rise.

These concepts are illustrated in Figure 6-10. In panel A, we hold quality of care constant and illustrate the isoquants representing 100 cases before and after a technological change. The technological improvement in panel A shifts the isoquant inward. The firm chooses an efficient combination of inputs at point E and after the change at point E'. This change results in the attainment of a lower isocost curve for treating the 100 cases.

Panel B illustrates the introduction of a new technology that makes it possible to treat 100 cases with better health status outcomes, thus providing a higher quality of care. Improvements entailing new products or, as shown in panel B, an improved quality of care are beneficial to the consumer, but they may be more costly. This is illustrated by a shift outward of the 100-case isoquant, resulting in production on a higher and costlier isocost curve. The typical patient treated will pay more for care. In some cases where patients are heavily insured, we may question whether the change is worth it to patients when they pay increased insurance premiums, or to society as a whole.

Health Care Price Increases When Technological Change Occurs

How do we measure the cost of a treatment when the treatment changes radically over a mere one or two decades? For example, heart attack treatment (myocardial infarction) changed substantially from 1975 to 1995. Some new effective inputs proved extremely inexpensive (see the feature on aspirin in Box 6-2). Some materials did not exist in 1975, such as the intraortic balloon pump. Treatment practices changed; the

FIGURE 6-10 Cost-Decreasing and Cost-Increasing Technological Changes

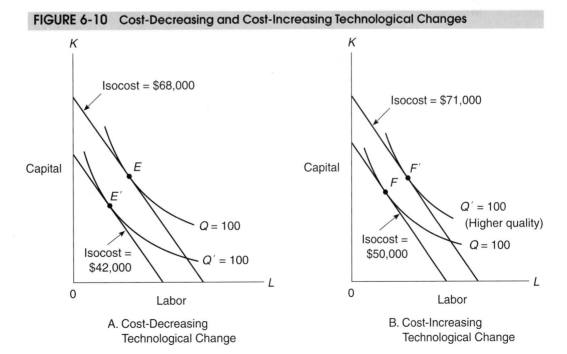

A. Cost-Decreasing
Technological Change

B. Cost-Increasing
Technological Change

average length of a hospital stay is now much shorter. Most important to the patient, the treatments are now more effective and have improved the length and quality of life for heart attack victims.

Treatment effectiveness improved, and in some cases less expensive inputs become available. Sometimes newly designed inputs were more costly than the ones they replaced. To see whether heart attack treatment in 1995 was more expensive per episode than in 1975, we must hold quality constant within the analysis.

These are the essential problems of any price index. Consumers are familiar with the Consumer Price Index (CPI) used to measure inflation. A subset of this index focuses on medical care. In this case, the multi-product character of hospital care can be confusing.

Until recently hospital prices were each defined into selected components of hospital care. Room charge, nursing, lab, and other service centers were each given a price index and then the results were combined into a hospital price index. Though useful, this approach often distorted the cost picture. For many years the room charge was weighted heavily, and unfortunately room charges soared. The index therefore tended to exaggerate hospital price inflation. Even more confounding, hospital average length of stay declined rapidly in the United States, and the old price index neglected this savings. Although patients paid much more per day, it was offset in part by shorter stays. Political debate centered on these price indexes, causing considerable misunderstanding. The DRG legislation that Medicare installed in 1983 was partly a reflection of wide public concern that health care inflation was out of control.

Recognizing that this problem revolved around technological change, Scitovsky (1985) proposed that health economists analyze a number of specific illnesses, that is study the cost of treatment for specific illnesses. One should collect data on the number of and charges for specific services used in treating these conditions. The analysts should then compare average charges for treating at different points in time.

Gathering data on clinic care in Palo Alto, California, she applied this approach to myocardial infarction (heart attack) and several other diseases. Her data covered

BOX 6-2

Aspirin, the Wonder Drug at a Bargain

References to prototypes of aspirin date back to the works of the Greek physician, Galen. These references mentioned salicylate-containing plants, such as willow bark and wintergreen. We today usually attribute aspirin to the Bayer Company in Germany in the latter 1800s. Throughout its history, professionals praised aspirin for its excellent powers to relieve pain and fever (Andermann, 1996).

We think of this humble product as a cheap, "over-the-counter" drug that is widely available at a few pennies per dose. While fairly safe, it can have serious side effects with overdosing. Physicians, for many decades, said that "if aspirin had been proposed now as a new drug it would probably require a prescription." While it is

doubtless that it will remain an over-the-counter drug, it now seems like a new product. Because of new discoveries of its benefits to heart patients, its influence continues to expand.

This is reflected in various treatment regimens on heart outcomes. David Cutler found that the basic three regimens—intensive technologies, non-acute pharmaceuticals, and behavioral change—have approximately equal contributions to improved outcomes. The non-acute drugs (pharmaceuticals) include those to control hypertension, reduce cholesterol, treat pain, dissolve clotting, and thin the blood. Aspirin is an effective blood thinner and is now regularly prescribed as a preventative measure as well as to reduce the recurrence of heart attacks (Cutler, 2001).

three decades, beginning in 1951, and they showed a mixed pattern. The treatment cost for earaches in children declined, but the treatment cost for appendicitis in children rose. Often, the trend for a specific treatment depended on the decade. Heart attack treatment costs inflated sharply from 1964 to 1971 but declined somewhat from 1971 to 1981.

Aside from mixed results, Scitovsky's approach omitted measures of quality, which surely had improved over the years. Health economists prefer that quality be defined in terms of the ultimate output—the patient's health. If a heart attack victim treated today stays alive longer and lives more fully than a patient treated 20 years ago, then we must adjust for this.

A good example of making the needed adjustment is a study done by Cutler and colleagues (1999). They developed two myocardial infarction treatment price indexes that measure patient gains in quality-adjusted life years (QALYs). They evaluated these gains in dollar terms, and allowing for errors, particularly in valuing life years, these authors proposed a range of price inflation estimates. Their research shows clearly that

1. technological change makes a difference in patient lives.
2. the fact that substantial quality improvement had previously been omitted meant that previous estimates of inflation in health care needed to be reduced.

How well are their ideas corroborated by the data? Table 6-2 indicates that technological change has improved the quality of heart attack treatment and that this quality adjustment can turn what at first looks like price inflation into one of price deflation. Their further research suggests that the true decline in the heart attack treatment price might be much larger than these figures.

TABLE 6-2 Comparing the Unadjusted Approach with a Quality-Adjusted Measure of Price Increases of Treatment of Myocardial Infarction (1983–1994)

Index	Average Annual Price Changes
Unadjusted Indexes	
Official Medical Care CPI	3.4%
• Hospital component	6.2
• Room	6.0
• Other inpatient services	5.7
Heart attack unadjusted episode approach[a]	2.8
Quality Adjusted Indexes	
Quality (extra years of life)	−1.5
Quality (extra QALYs)[b]	−1.7

[a]Experts recognize that several alternatives are applied when selecting for analysis the market basket of goods and services whose inflation is to be measured. The table reports a fixed-basket method; the patient is assumed to purchase essentially the same combination of medical goods in each year studied. Chain indexes allow for the representative market basket to change over time, and it therefore adds realism. But, how frequently should the basket be recalibrated? When a 6-year calculation of the basket is used, the average annual percentage change becomes 2.1 percent; with an annual recalculation, it becomes 0.7 percent.

[b]QALYs are quality-adjusted life years. This quality of treatment is the same as the previous one except for the additional consideration of the degree to which the patient is able to lead a full, active life in the years after treatment.

Source: Adopted from Cutler et al. (2001). Reprinted by permission of the University of Chicago Press.

Diffusion of New Health Care Technologies

It takes time for a new product innovation to be widely adopted by providers. Some firms adopt rapidly, some slowly, and some not at all.

Who Adopts and Why?

Students of innovation adoption of health technologies have found at least two basic principles that guide adopters: the profit principle and information channels. The first posits that physicians, for example, tend to adopt a new surgical technique if they expect to increase their revenues—this could happen through enhancing their prestige or by improving the well-being of their patients. The second is a compatible principle deriving originally from sociology, and it emphasizes the role of friends, colleagues, journals, and conferences at informing and encouraging the adoption decision.

Escarce (1996) emphasized the "information externalities" inherent in adoption by the first physician to adopt. An externality is the uncompensated, beneficial effect on a third person caused by the actions of a market, in this case, the actions of the first adopter. By adopting a technology, the physician communicates to friends and colleagues the expectation that the new product will benefit his or her patients and practice. The adopter paves the way for new infrastructure, new seminars, and library materials that reduce the cost of adoption for colleagues. The process tends to build on itself, perhaps at an increasing rate, until all the main body of potential adopters has acted, only then slowing the increase in total adopters until the community's maximum potential is reached.

The data are consistent with this process; in many industries, adoption occurs slowly at first, then at an increasing rate that continues at a decreasing rate asymptotically approaching its limit. Compare this description in words with Figure 6-11, which illustrates the classic pattern of diffusion as a logistic curve. A new data set is tested empirically by estimating the logistic function where P is the proportion of individuals or firms adopting, the maximum potential proportion of adopters is K, with parameters a and b to be estimated:

$$P_1 = K/(1 + e^{-(a + bt)}) \tag{6.2}$$

FIGURE 6-11 The Diffusion of a New Technology

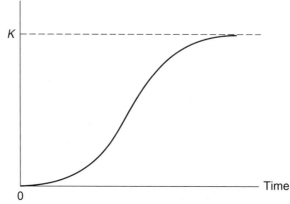

Proportion of potential users adopting the new technology

K

Time

0

Escarce's data fit this time pattern quite well. He studied a new surgical procedure, laparoscopic cholecystectomy, introduced in 1989, which is a minimally invasive technique to remove diseased gall bladders. He found the diffusion curve to fit the logistic pattern common to diffusion studies. He then examined the differences between those who adopted and those who did not. Adopting surgeons were more likely to be younger, male, board-certified, U.S. medical school graduates, and urban-located. Younger individuals are more likely adopters. In fact, in one study older physicians proved less likely to adopt even though their expected gains in profit were much higher than for their younger counterparts (Rizzo and Zeckhauser, 1992). Finally, Escarce's data showed little difference between managed care and fee for service; there was no clear winner in the race between these two to adopt the newest technology.

Other Factors That May Affect Adoption Rates

The economic theory of innovation sheds some additional light on these issues (Kamien and Schwartz, 1982, and Scherer, 1984). As we have described, the firm will tend to adopt an innovation when the present value of future profits due to the innovation is positive. Waiting too long may provide competitors with an advantageous share of the market, which may be permanently sustained. However, waiting has benefits in that one may take advantage of future advances and learn from the experience of others. Waiting may reduce risks so more risk-averse firms may choose to wait somewhat longer. Small firms, which are less able to diversify, may tend to be more risk averse (see Sloan et al., 1986), partially explaining the slower rate of adoption among small hospitals. A study in Norway shows further that the profit principle matters (Klausen et al., 1994).

Sloan and colleagues (1986) found that mandatory rate-setting programs retard diffusion of technology in some cases, particularly in the instances of coronary bypass surgery, morbid obesity surgery, and intraocular lens implants. However, the degree of slowing tended to be small. Teplensky et al. (1995) conclude that restrictive rate-setting programs tend to retard significantly the adoption of new technology. Also, Caudill et al. (1995) report a slowing of the adoption of new blood dialysis technology when faced with restrictions on health care capital investment imposed by Certificate-of-Need legislation (CON). CON laws, which are generally applied at the state level, require hospitals to gain approval from planning agencies when they wish to expand their size or to make a major capital purchase.

Diffusion of Technology and Managed Care

Managed care arrived with hopes that it would control health care expenditure increases by removing the financial incentives for physicians to overprescribe, overtreat, and overhospitalize their patients. The same flattening of incentives—no extra money for extra treatment—potentially dampens the physician's interest in cost-increasing technological change. As we have seen throughout this chapter, the flattening of financial incentive must be expected to slow innovation and the adoption of innovative technologies. Although we address the ultimate effect of managed care on health care inflation elsewhere in this text, it is appropriate here to ask: "Does a higher penetration of managed care into the health system tend to slow the growth in availability of new technologies?"

The answers seem to be "yes" for some technologies and "no" for others. Baker (2001) compared penetration of HMOs with adoptions of a new technology, magnetic resonance imaging (MRI); he found a slowing of adoptions associated with

HMOs. Hill and Wolfe (1997) examine a managed care–like system in Wisconsin. These authors reported time trends of adoptions for selected technologies, and the data suggest a retardation of several of the technologies but continued growth of several others. Friedman and Steiner (1999) investigated the availability of intensive care units and found no difference in admission rates under managed care versus fee-for-service care.

Conclusions

This chapter examined issues on the supply side of health care. Health care is fundamentally a production process, and it shares many characteristics with economic production generally. The production function, which summarizes the relationship of inputs and outputs, also embodies the technology. Technology that permits substitution between inputs provides better flexibility to the manager. The neoclassical cost function derives from the theory of production together with the theory of profit-maximizing behavior. Cost estimation describes the cost curves, which identify the economies of scale and scope. Health care firms may fail to achieve allocative or technical efficiency, or both. These analyses are used to search for differences between for-profit, not-for-profit, and other kinds of firms.

Health firms may differ in technology because the adoption of new technologies differ among firms and is never instantaneous. Technology improvements in health care production may either increase or decrease costs depending on their effect on quality. Both market structure and regulation can affect the speed at which innovations are adopted.

SUMMARY

1. Health care goods and services can frequently be produced in different ways in the sense that they use different combinations of factor inputs.
2. The elasticity of substitution is used to measure substitution. It represents the percentage change in the ratio of factor inputs resulting from a 1 percent change in relative factor prices.
3. Economists have found some substitution not only among different kinds of medical staff but even between hospital beds and medical staff.
4. The principles of cost minimization, as represented by the locus of tangencies between the firm's isoquants and isocost curves, are used to derive the cost curves (total and average). Economies of scale refer to a declining long-run average cost. Economies of scope represent situations where the cost of producing goods jointly is less than the sum of the costs of separate production.
5. Early empirical work on hospitals found evidence of economies of scale and an optimum size of about 250 beds. Several recent contributions suggest no economies of scale past very small hospitals, and perhaps even some diseconomies of scale for larger ones.
6. Technical inefficiency occurs when a firm fails to achieve the maximum potential output from a given set of inputs. It can be measured as a relative distance from the frontier production function or correspondingly as a distance from the isoquants of the frontier production function. Allocative inefficiency arises in the case of competitive input markets when a firm fails to purchase inputs, given their prices, in a manner that minimizes costs.
7. Efficiency can be measured by recently developed frontier methods of two types. The data envelopment method estimates the frontier by statistically forming an envelope of data points representing production data. The stochastic frontier method estimates simultaneously a randomly shifting frontier and the firm's distance from that frontier.

8. Technological change in health care may reduce costs if it improves production technology of existing products or increase costs if it emphasizes new products and higher-quality versions of old products.
9. New health care technologies are adopted gradually in an industry, and the pattern of adoption fits the logistic curve. Adoption patterns are influenced by regulation, age of the adopter, profitability, and channels of communication.

DISCUSSION QUESTIONS

1. Explain whether there is any difference between goals in maximizing output for a given cost or minimizing the cost of producing a given level of output.
2. What are cross-sectional data? Why do economists find it so critical to control for case mix in studying health care cost functions? What are the analytical dangers if they do not?
3. How do legal restrictions on practice for nurses and physicians tend to affect the observed elasticities of substitution? Would they tend to be higher if legal restrictions were removed? Would quality of care be affected?
4. Given the cost function and economies of scale and scope information reviewed in this chapter, does a policy encouraging large, centralized hospitals seem wise? Will market forces tend to reward centralization of hospital services?
5. Speculate on what types of services are more appropriate to large, regional hospitals, and what types of services are more appropriate to small, local hospitals.
6. Economists define the elasticity of substitution as the percentage change in the capital/labor ratio elicited by a 1 percent change in the factor price (wages/capital costs, for example) ratio. Would you expect the elasticity of substitution to be positive or negative? What would be the elasticity of substitution of a set of right-angled isoquants? Why?
7. Contrast technical and allocative efficiency. How can technical and allocative inefficiency in health care firms affect patient welfare?
8. What does stochastic mean in stochastic frontier efficiency estimation? Give several real-life examples of events that could shift the production frontier.
9. Which of the following types of technological change in health care are likely to be cost increasing: (A) threats of malpractice suits that cause physicians to order more diagnostic tests on average for a given set of patient symptoms; (B) a new computer-assisted scanning device that enables physicians to take much more detailed pictures of the brain; (C) the introduction of penicillin earlier in this century; (D) greater emphasis on preventive care? Discuss.
10. As technologies diffuse, why do some firms adopt them before others? What types of technologies would you expect to be adopted most quickly? Most slowly? What factors can slow the rate of diffusion of new medical technologies?

EXERCISES

1. Draw an isoquant that shows relatively little substitution between two factor inputs and one that shows relatively large substitution. Let the vertical axis represent capital and let the horizontal axis represent labor.
2. Draw isocost curves that are tangent to your isoquants in exercise 1 and that have the same slope. Mark the points of tangency and note the capital/labor. Draw new, flatter isocost curves that are tangent, again each having the same new slope. Mark the points of tangency and note the capital/labor ratio. In which case is the change in the capital/labor ratio greater? Which will have a higher elasticity of substitution?
3. Determine the elasticity of substitution in the case of the isoquant in panel A of Figure 6-1.

4. Suppose a firm has the following production technology for Goods 1 and 2.

Good 1		Good 2		Both		
Q1	Cost	Q2	Cost	Q1	Q2	Cost
10	50	10	60	10	10	100
20	100	20	100	20	20	180
30	150	30	130	30	30	250

 a. Does Good 1 indicate economies of scale? Why?
 b. Does Good 2 indicate economies of scale? Why?
 c. Do the two goods indicate economies of scope? Why?

5. If any firm's price of labor and capital each double, what will happen to the expansion path (i.e., locus of tangencies between the isoquants and isocost curves)? What will happen to the firm's average cost curve?

6. Figure 6-6, panel A, illustrates technical inefficiency for firms with a one-input production function. It was explained that inefficiency could be measured by output distance or, alternatively, input reduction distance. Sketch and explain the comparable measures for the two-input production function.

7. In Escarce's account of diffusion, do improved "channels of information" matter regardless of the information content? Does all information increase the adoption rate? If not, what information does?

8. Calculate the average costs at points *C*, *F*, and *G* in Figure 6-2. Do they imply increasing or decreasing returns to scale? Why?

CHAPTER 7

Demand for Health Capital

Chapter 5 considered the production of health in the aggregate by looking at the impacts of various factors on health for society as a whole. Here, we show how individuals allocate their resources to produce health.

Economists' understanding of this decision has been deepened by the important work of Michael Grossman. His model has enabled us to understand thoroughly the role of several variables, such as age, education, health status, and income in the production of health through the demand for health capital.

The Demand for Health

The Consumer as Health Producer

Grossman (1972a, 1972b) used the theory of human capital to explain the demand for health and health care. His research became a standard beginning point for much subsequent work. According to human capital theory, individuals invest in themselves through education, training, and health to increase their earnings. Grossman shows the way in which many important aspects of health demand differ from the traditional approach to demand:

1. It is not medical care as such that the consumer wants, but rather health. People want health; they demand medical care inputs to produce it.
2. The consumer does not merely purchase health passively from the market. Instead, the consumer produces health, combining time devoted to health-improving efforts with purchased medical inputs.

137

3. Health lasts for more than one period. It does not depreciate instantly, and can be analyzed like a capital good.
4. Perhaps, most importantly, health can be treated both as a consumption good and an investment good. As a consumption good, health is desired because it makes people feel better. As an investment good, health is desired because it increases the number of healthy days available to work and to earn income.

Figure 7-1 provides a simple schematic diagram that explains the concept of health capital. Just as one thinks of a car or a refrigerator as a capital good (or "stock of capital") that provides a stream of services over time, one can conceive of a person's stock of health capital that provides the ultimate output of "healthy days." One might measure the stream of output(s) as a single dimension of healthy days, or in several dimensions of physical health, mental health, and limited activity, e.g. one can no longer play "singles" in tennis.

Consumers apply sets of health inputs, which might include market inputs of health care, but also diet, exercise, and time, to their physical make-up, thus making investments in health capital. These investments maintain or improve the consumers' stocks of health, which in turn provide them with healthy days. Over time, the health stock may grow, remain constant, or decline (again, like a car or a refrigerator), either slowly with age, or more precipitously with illness or injury.

From Figure 7-1, and the accompanying discussion, we see how the end goal, "healthy days," guides consumer decisions as to how much time and money to invest in health stock. We will see that the prices of health care, the peoples' wage rates, and their productivities in producing health, will dictate how resources are to be allocated among health capital, and other goods and services that people buy.

Consider a consumer, Ed Kramer, who buys market inputs (e.g., medical care, food, clothing), and combines them with his own time to produce the stock of health capital that produces services that increase his utility. Ed uses market inputs and personal time both to invest in his stock of health and to produce other things that he likes.

These other items include virtually all other things that Ed does. They include time spent watching television, reading, playing with and teaching his children, preparing meals, baking bread, or watching the sun set, a composite of other things people do with leisure time. We shall call this composite home good *B*.

FIGURE 7-1 Investing in Health Capital

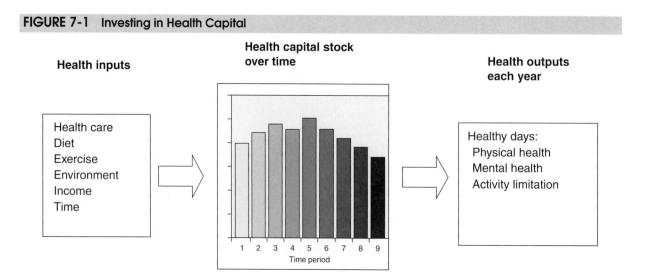

Time Spent Producing Health

An increment to capital stock, such as health, is called an investment. During each period, Ed produces an investment in health, *I*. Health investment, *I*, is produced by time spent improving health, T_H, and market health inputs (providers' services, drugs), *M*. Likewise, home good *B* is produced with time, T_B, and market-purchased goods, *X*. If, for example, we considered good *B* as baking bread, the market goods might include flour, yeast, kitchen appliances, and gas, water, and/or electricity. Thus, Ed is using money to buy health care inputs, *M*, or home good inputs, *X*. He is using leisure time either for health care (T_H) or for producing the home good (T_B).

Using functional notation:

$$I = I(M, T_H) \qquad (7.1)$$

$$B = B(X, T_B) \qquad (7.2)$$

These functions indicate that increased amounts of *M* and T_H increase *I*, and that increased amounts of *X* and T_B increase *B*.

In this model, Ed's ultimate resource is his own time. Treat each period of analysis as being a year in length, and assume that Ed has 365 days available in the year. To buy market goods such as medical care, *M*, or other goods, *X*, he must trade some of this time for income; that is, he must work at a job. Call his time devoted to work T_W. Because our focus is on the health aspects of living, we realize that some of his time during each year will be taken over by ill health, or T_L. Thus, we account for his total time in the following manner:

$$\text{Total time} = T = 365 \text{ days} = T_H \text{ (improving health)} + T_B \text{ (producing home goods)}$$
$$+ T_L \text{ (lost to illness)} + T_W \text{ (working)} \qquad (7.3)$$

Recall that his leisure time is spent either improving his health or producing home goods.

Labor-Leisure Trade-Offs

The potential uses of Ed's time are illustrated by the labor-leisure trade-off. Our variation on this analysis also helps illustrate the investment aspects of health demand.

Trading Leisure for Wages

In Figure 7-2, the x-axis represents Ed's work and leisure time. Suppose that he considers his time spent creating health investment to be "health-improvement time" and that he calls T_B his leisure. In reality, he may do some health-improving activities at work, may obtain some enjoyment or satisfaction from healthful time, and so on, but assume here that these categories are exclusive. Assume further that the number of days lost to ill health and the number of days spent on health-enhancing activity are fixed (we relax this assumption later). Variables T_{L0} and T_{H0} refer to time lost and time spent on healthy activities, respectively. The maximum amount of time that he has available to use either for work, T_W, or leisure, T_B, is thus $365 - T_{H0} - T_{L0}$, so:

$$\text{Time Available for Work or Leisure} = 365 - T_{H0} - T_{L0} = T_W + T_B \qquad (7.4)$$

Leisure time, T_B, is measured toward the right while time spent at work, T_W, is measured toward the left. For example, if Ed chooses leisure time, *OA*, then he has simultaneously chosen the amount of time at work indicated by *AS*. These are indicated in Figure 7-2.

FIGURE 7-2 Labor-Leisure Trade-Off

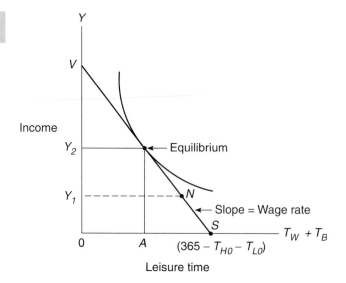

Recall that Ed's total amount of time available for either work or leisure is given by point S. If he were to choose point S for the period, he would be choosing to spend all this available time in leisure; that is, in the pursuit of the pleasures of life (albeit without the wage income to produce them). The y-axis represents income, which can be obtained through work. This income can be used to purchase either market health goods or other market goods. Thus, if he chooses point S, he will not be able to purchase market goods because he has no wage income.[1]

If, beginning at S, Ed gives up one day of leisure by spending that day at work, to point N, he will generate income equal to OY_1, which represents his daily wage. In economic terms, this quantity represents income divided by days worked—that is, the daily wage. The slope of the line VS depicting the labor-leisure trade-off reflects the wage rate.

Preferences Between Leisure and Income

Consumers have preferences regarding income and leisure, just as they had among other goods in Chapter 2. As before, Ed would like more income and more leisure so the indifference curve map is shaped normally. In Figure 7-2, in equilibrium, Ed's trade-off of leisure and income is the same as the market trade-off, which is the wage rate. Here, he takes amount OA of leisure and trades amount AS of leisure for income, OY_2.

In Figure 7-3, Ed has made a different choice with respect to time spent investing in health status. To illustrate, suppose that time spent on health-producing activities, T_H, is increased from T_{H0} to T_{H1}. Correspondingly, suppose that the number of days lost to ill health has been reduced from T_{L0} to T_{L1}. What effect will this have on the horizontal intercept, which is the total time remaining for work or leisure? On the one hand, time spent producing health reduces time available for other activities. Time spent on health investment increases health stock and, in turn, reduces time lost to illness.

[1]We ignore income that is earned through non-work efforts—for example, through returns to financial investments.

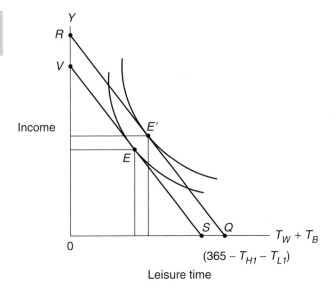

FIGURE 7-3 Increased Amount of Healthy Time Due to Investment

If the net effect is a gain in available time, then this illustrates the pure investment aspect of health demand. The health investments "pay off" in terms that not only add to potential leisure but that also increase the potential income, shifting the income-leisure line outward from VS to RQ. The expenditure of time (and medical care, too) for health-producing activities may later improve Ed's available hours (because he is sick less) of productive activity.

As a result of his investment, Ed can increase his utility, moving from point E to point E'. Not only does investment in health lead to his feeling better, but it also leads to more future income and may lead to more leisure, as well.

The improvement in health status also might increase Ed's productivity at work, perhaps resulting in a higher wage and a steeper income-leisure curve. In any case, it is clear that Ed might wish to engage in activities to improve his health, even if the only value of health is its effect on his ability to earn future income.

The Investment/Consumption Aspects of Health

The Grossman model describes how consumers simultaneously make choices over many periods or years. It is also instructive, on occasion, to represent a whole life span as a single period. This can show the dual nature of health as both an investment good and a consumption good.

Production of Healthy Days

For our purposes, we will view health as a productive good that produces a single output, healthy days. This production function relationship is illustrated in Figure 7-4. The horizontal axis measures health stock in a given period. The greater one's stock of health, the greater the number of healthy days, up to a natural maximum of 365 days. The bowed shape of the curve illustrates the law of diminishing marginal returns (additional resources have decreasing marginal impacts on the output). Note also the concept of a health stock minimum shown as H_{min}. At this point, production of healthy days drops to zero, indicating death.

FIGURE 7-4 Relationship of Healthy Days to Health Stock

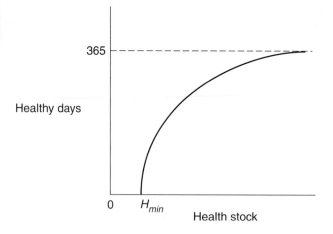

Production of Health and Home Goods

Consider the possibilities for producing health, H, and home good, B, given the total amount of time available. Figure 7-5 shows the production possibilities trade-off. Note that the curve differs from the usual production possibilities curve in several respects. First, from point A to point C, health improvements increase the amounts of the home good, B, and health, H, attainable. It is necessary to increase health beyond H_{min} in order to obtain income and leisure time from which to produce B.

Moving along the production possibilities curve, Ed shifts his uses of available time and distributes his purchases of market goods. The move from E to C indicates that he has made more time available for health and that this move has reaped the side benefit (increased leisure time) of increasing the availability of market goods and time used to increase production of the home good, baking bread.

Suppose that Ed desires health solely for its effect on the ability to produce income and the leisure time to produce the home good bread, B. This would imply that his indifference curves between H and B would be vertical lines. (Ed places no intrinsic value on H, so he would not trade any B to get additional health.) In such a case, he would maximize his utility by producing as much B as possible. The utility-maximizing choice would

FIGURE 7-5 Allocation of Resources Between Health and Bread

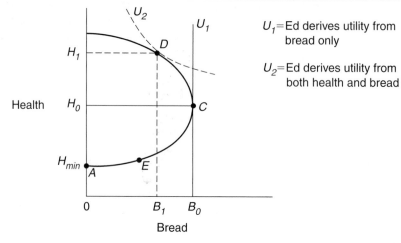

U_1 = Ed derives utility from bread only

U_2 = Ed derives utility from both health and bread

be at point *C*, a point of tangency between indifference curve U_1 and the production possibilities curve. He produces amount B_0 of the home good, and H_0 of health.

Now assume instead that Ed achieves utility not only from producing *B*, but also directly from health itself (he likes feeling better). In this case, his indifference curve, U_2, has the more familiar curved shape in Figure 7-4, sloping downward from left to right. It is more realistic to say that he values health both as a consumption good, as is shown in Figure 7-4, and as an investment in productive capacity. The former suggests that he enjoys feeling healthy; the latter, that feeling healthy makes him more productive, thus allowing him to earn more. In general, by including Ed's "feeling healthy" in this consumption feature of the model, he will choose a higher health stock than under the pure investment model. In Figure 7-4, health stock, H_1, exceeds H_0. The cost of this increase in *H* is some of the home good, such that B_1 is less than B_0.[2]

Investment over Time

The Cost of Capital

People make choices for the many periods over their life cycles, rather than just for one representative period. As a beginning point for each analysis, we feature the pure investment version of the model (point *C* in Figure 7-5). We then discuss the analytical changes when consumers, in addition, value health intrinsically (point *D* in Figure 7-5).

We demand health capital because it helps us earn more and feel better. What does it cost? By analogy, a health clinic, for example, purchases thousands of dollars of X-ray equipment. The return to the X-ray equipment is in the future earnings that ownership of the equipment can provide.

Suppose that an X-ray machine costs $100,000, and that its price does not change over time. Suppose that the annual income attributable to the use of the X-ray machine is $20,000. Is purchasing the machine a good investment? Consider the alternative: Instead of purchasing the X-ray machine, the clinic could have put the $100,000 in a savings account, at 5 percent interest, yielding the following:

$$100,000 \times 1.05 = 105,000 \text{ at the end of Year 1}$$
$$105,000 \times 1.05 = 110,250 \text{ at the end of Year 2}$$
$$110,250 \times 1.05 = 115,763 \text{ at the end of Year 3}$$
$$115,763 \times 1.05 = 121,551 \text{ at the end of Year 4}$$
$$121,551 \times 1.05 = 127,629 \text{ at the end of Year 5}$$

For the investment in an X-ray machine to be desirable by these criteria, it should provide at least $27,629 in incremental revenue over the five years.

The problem is more complicated, however, because capital goods depreciate over time. Most students recognize that a five-year-old personal computer, for example, is worth almost nothing. Even though it may do everything it ever did, new programs may not work on it, new equipment may not hook up to it properly, and it may be relatively slow compared to new machines. If the machine originally cost $2,000, and the firm has not budgeted $2,000 for replacement, they may find themselves without a working computer!

Similarly, suppose that the clinic knows that the X-ray machine will wear out (or depreciate), so that it will be worth only half its original value in five years. The clinic

[2]Goodman, Stano and Tilford (1999) provide a more detailed model addressing the production of health and home goods.

must earn enough not only to cover the opportunity cost from the bank, but also to maintain the value of the machine. For an investment in an X-ray machine to be worthwhile, then, it must not only earn the competitive 5 percent return each year, but it also must provide enough return to cover depreciation. This suggests that the cost of holding this capital good for any one year, as well as over time, will equal the opportunity cost of the capital (interest foregone) plus the depreciation (deterioration of value). In this example, the depreciation cost is $50,000, or half of the $100,000 original cost.

The Demand for Health Capital

Conventional economic analysis provides a powerful conceptual apparatus by which to analyze the demand for a capital good. The cost of capital, in terms of foregone resources (for health capital, both time and money), is a supply concept. The other needed tool is the concept of the marginal efficiency of investment (*MEI*) a demand concept that relates the return to investment to the amount of resources invested.

Marginal Efficiency of Investment (*MEI*) and Rate of Return

The *MEI* can be described in terms of the X-ray machine example. A busy clinic may wish to own more than one X-ray machine. But how many? The clinic management may logically consider them in sequence. The first machine purchased (if they were to buy only one) would yield a return as we have discussed. Suppose that return each year were $20,000.

We also can calculate the rate of return, which would be $20,000 ÷ $100,000, or 20 percent per year. The management would buy this machine if the incremental revenue brought in covered its opportunity cost of capital and the depreciation. In terms of rates, management would choose to own the first X-ray machine as long as the rate of return, 20 percent, were greater than the interest rate (the opportunity cost of capital) plus the depreciation rate.

If management considered owning two machines, it would discover that the rate of return on the second X-ray machine would probably be less than the first. This is best understood by recognizing that a clinic buying only one X-ray machine would assign it to the highest-priority uses, those with the highest rate of return. If the clinic were to add a second X-ray machine, then logically it could be assigned only to lesser-priority uses (and might be idle on occasion). Thus, the second machine would have a lower rate of return than the first. The clinic would then purchase the second machine only if its rate of return were still higher than interest plus depreciation.

The Decreasing *MEI*

Other machines probably could be added at successively lower rates of return. In Figure 7-6, the marginal efficiency of investment curve, *MEI*, describes the pattern of rates of return, declining as the amount of investment (measured on the horizontal axis) increases. The cost of capital (that is, the interest rate, r, plus the depreciation rate, δ_0) is shown as the horizontal line labeled $r + \delta_0$. The optimum amount of capital demanded is thus H_0, which represents the amount of capital at which the marginal efficiency of investment just equals the cost of capital. This equilibrium occurs at point A.

Like the marginal efficiency of investment curve in this example, the *MEI* curve for investments in health also would be downward sloping. This occurs because the

FIGURE 7-6 Optimal Health Stock

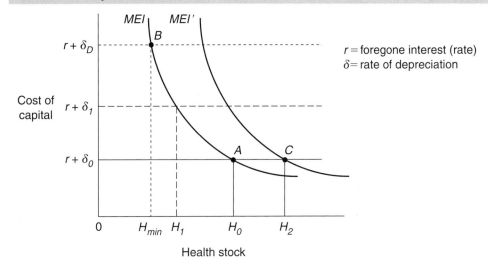

production function for healthy days (see Figure 7-4) exhibits diminishing marginal returns. The cost of capital for health would similarly reflect the interest rate plus the rate of depreciation in health. Understand that a person's health, like any capital good, also will depreciate over time. Thus, the optimal demand for health is likewise given at the intersection of the *MEI* curve and the cost of capital curve ($r + \delta_0$).

Changes in Equilibrium: Age, Wage, Education, and Uncertainty

Return to Ed Kramer and to Figure 7-1. Based on the analyses thus far, Ed has chosen an equilibrium level of health stock, by deciding how much to work, how much time to spend on health, what kind of diet, and how much exercise to do. He allocates his resources such that every year he maintains a constant level of health stock, and this provides him with an equilibrium level of healthy days per year. How does his investment in health change in response to changes in age, wage, and education? The model depicted in Figure 7-6 provides a useful way to investigate several important model implications. Consider age first.

Age

How does Ed's optimal stock of health vary over a lifetime? In this model, the person's death itself is endogenous, meaning that the age of death is determined as part of the model. Ed chooses his optimal life span, a life span that is not infinite. By this model, all of us, at some time, will optimally allow our health stock to dissipate to H_{min}. This feature depends in a critical way on how the depreciation rate (a cost factor) varies with age, as well as how long the person expects to live (and enjoy the benefits of good health).

Looking first at costs, Ed's health stock may depreciate faster during some periods of life and more slowly during others. Eventually, as he ages, the depreciation rate is likely to increase. In other words, the health of older people is likely to deteriorate faster than the health of younger people.

Consider then the effect of aging on Ed's optimal health stock. Return to Figure 7-6. We assume that the wage and other features determining the *MEI* are not substantially altered by this aging. However, by hypothesis, the depreciation rate, δ, increases with age from δ_0 to δ_I and ultimately to δ_D. These assumptions imply that the optimal health stock decreases with age.

This situation is shown in Figure 7-6 by the fact that the optimal health at the younger age, H_0, is greater than H_I, the optimal stock at the older age. Higher depreciation rates increase the cost of holding health capital stock. We adjust to this by holding a greater amount of health capital in periods when health is less costly. In old age, health depreciation rates are extremely high, δ_D, and optimal health stock falls to H_{min} at point B.

This conclusion is consistent with the observation that elderly people purchase a greater amount of medical care, even as their health deteriorates. Grossman explains the phenomenon:

> Gross investment's life cycle profile would not, in general, simply mirror that of health capital . . . This follows because a rise in the rate of depreciation not only reduces the amount of health capital demanded by consumers but also reduces the amount of capital supplied to them by a given amount of gross investment. (p. 238)

Turning to the returns from investment, consider by way of analogy a consumer who has two cars, the same models, built by the same maker. One is 2 years old, with 20,000 miles of wear; the other is 12 years old, with 120,000 miles of wear. Each car has had the "bumps" and "bruises" that accompany driving in a major city. Suppose that the 2-year-old car is damaged in the parking lot with cosmetic damages that will cost $2,000 to repair. The decision is obvious. However, would the owner incur the same level of costs to repair the 12-year-old car that is most likely near the end of its useful life?

The analogy to individual health is immediate. A younger person may choose complicated surgery to replace knees or hips, to maintain earning capability or quality of life. An older person may choose not to do so. In Figure 7-6, this suggests, that as the expected length of life decreases, the *MEI* curve shifts to the left, because the returns from an investment will last for a shorter period of time. This will tend to reinforce the decrease in investment that occurs due to increased depreciation.

Other features of the model suggest that people will increase their gross investment (the amount of dollars spent) in health as they age. This suggests, in turn, that the elderly would demand more medical care than the young, as we frequently note to be the case.

Thus, the pure investment model generates the prediction that optimal health will decline as the person ages. Will this prediction change when we assume more realistically that an individual also will value health for consumption reasons (good health makes one feel better)? The issue relies on whether older persons get more or less direct utility from the enjoyment of healthy days. If people increase their valuation of healthy days as they age, this somewhat offsets the predicted health stock decline.

Wage Rate

Figure 7-6 illustrates the effect of a change in the wage rate on Ed's optimal level of investment. Increased wage rates increase the returns obtained from healthy days (8 hours' work will bring in $160 rather than $120 if the wage rate increases to $20 from $15). Thus, higher wages imply a higher *MEI* curve, or *MEI'*.

Assume now that the original *MEI* curve describes the lower-wage case and yields optimal health stock, H_0. *MEI'*, above *MEI*, shows the marginal efficiency of investment

for someone with higher wages. At new equilibrium point C, the higher wage will imply a higher optimal level of health stock, H_2, in this pure investment model. The rewards of being healthy are greater for higher-wage workers, so increased wages will tend to increase their optimal capital stock.[3]

The model illustrates one more implication of the wage factor. Consider that when Ed retires, his wage effectively drops to zero. The pure investment version implies that he would change his optimal health stock to H_{min} upon retirement. Once he retires, he would make no further investment in health, but instead would allow health to depreciate until death.

How would the analysis be amended by considering the consumption aspects of health—that good health makes people feel good? First, Ed would presumably continue to obtain utility directly from healthy days. Thus, optimal health stock would not necessarily drop to H_{min} directly upon Ed's retirement, but it would do so only when depreciation rates became sufficiently severe.

Second, if retirees and those who are still working obtain utility directly from healthy days, then the only significant change upon retirement would be the pure investment aspects. Therefore, even when we include the consumption aspects of health, we would expect people to reduce their health stock upon retirement.

Education

Education is of special interest in the demand for health. Higher education is most often related to better health, and most economists believe that education may improve the efficiency with which one can produce investments to health and the home good. Examples of improved efficiency may include improved ability to follow instruction regarding medicines or better knowledge of harmful effects of smoking, drinking, or addictive drugs, to name just a few.

The effect of education is illustrated in Figure 7-6. Here, the *MEI* curve illustrates the marginal efficiency of investment for the consumer with a low level of education (measured, for example, by years of schooling), while the *MEI'* curve illustrates the same person with a higher level of education. This model indicates that because education raises the marginal product of the direct inputs, it reduces the quantity of these inputs required to produce a given amount of gross investment.

It follows that given investments in health can be generated at less cost for educated people, and thus they experience higher rates of return to a given stock of health. The result, as shown, is that the more educated people will choose higher optimal health stocks, H_2, than the less educated, who will choose H_0.

This explains the widely observed correlation between health status and education. Educated people tend to be significantly healthier. However, this explains only the correlation of health status and education from the supply side in that it considers only the increased efficiency with which we produce health. One also might wish to explain education from the demand side.

Educated people are also likely to recognize the benefits of improved health. They may enjoy eating nutritious food or doing physical exercise. They may recognize the dangers of smoking and the long-term problems of overexposure to the sun. They may enjoy feeling and looking good. As such, all else equal, they would have a greater taste for health relative to other goods.

[3]This result may be ambiguous. Although the increased wage rate potentially increases the return to investment, it also represents an increased opportunity cost of time in producing health investment. Hence, the *MEI* curve may shift downward, and it is possible that the equilibrium demand for health investment will fall.

The demand for health due to education is difficult to separate from the supply effect of education, which implies more productivity in producing health. Clearly, however, both exist and both are important.

Uncertainty

The Grossman model starts with the assumption of perfect certainty as to future outcomes, but outcomes are not always certain.[4] What impact does uncertainty have on the optimal level of health investment and health capital? In a given year, Ed must choose how much to invest in health care. He may choose to consume his resources or he may choose to invest in a nonhealth financial asset, which by assumption is less risky than a health investment.

Chang (1996) treats the investment in health as a potentially risky venture. By contrast, the income from savings is risk-free if the market interest rate is assumed constant. In Chang's model Ed Kramer is an investor who is evaluating a portfolio selection between a risky asset and a risk-free asset. Following Chang's analysis, two effects can occur.

Suppose that Ed's earnings depend on his health. If he were to fall ill next year, his ability to work and his earnings (the return on his next year's health capital) would fall, and Ed is concerned about that risk. An additional dollar of investment in health capital this year will help insure against that loss by increasing his health capital stock and, hence, his earnings and consumption next year. This first effect—the improvement of future earnings—would shift his *MEI* curve outward, and would lead Ed to increase his investment in health capital to reduce his risk.

However, Figure 7-6 shows that the marginal efficiency of investment is downward sloping. This second effect means that unless changes occur in productivity, increased health investment moves Ed down his *MEI* curve. Therefore, if the increased investment this year has no impact on Ed's ability to earn income next year (Ed gets headaches, but he still can work a full day for a full day's pay), then increased risk would affect health investment negatively by lowering the return on the health investment.

Ed evaluates the two impacts. If the first effect is larger than the second, increased risk will lead him to invest more in health capital. If the second is larger than the first, Ed either will choose current consumption rather than health investment or alternatively will invest in a financial asset that, by assumption, is less risky than health investment.

Empirical Analyses Using Grossman's Model

In the last several years, many researchers have examined health production using Grossman's model. The resulting literature examines the separable impacts of age and education. It also looks at the various time components of health investment within families. The analytical methods and insights from the Grossman model permit researchers to examine the impacts of health status on the demand for health and health care. Box 7-1 shows how the model addresses addictive behavior.

Sickles and Yazbeck (1998) developed and estimated a structural model of health production that looks at the demand for leisure and the demand for consumption for elderly males. Measuring health production is a difficult problem. The authors use a

[4]The role of physician uncertainty with regard to treatment outcomes is central to the study of small area variations, which is discussed further in Chapter 15.

BOX 7-1

Rational Addiction

Economists Gary Becker and Kevin Murphy (1988) provide an interesting perspective on addictive behavior and describe conditions under which rational people choose to consume addictive goods. Their work challenges our common moral concepts and attitudes toward addiction. It also offers similarities and contrasts with Grossman's model of the demand for health.

Becker and Murphy argue that addictive behavior (as most current or former smokers would agree) must provide some pleasure or people would not pursue it. For a good to be addictive, in their model, past consumption (of the good) must increase the marginal utility of current consumption. Becker and Murphy describe past consumption as contributing to "consumption capital" of the good in question. Smoking cigarettes presently may entail a learning experience in the sense that future consumption of an additional cigarette becomes more enjoyable. This important feature also applies to many goods and services and does not necessarily separate those goods that society has made taboo or bad. For example, listening to Mozart presently also may entail a learning experience. Mozart symphonies may become more enjoyable in the future as this learning experience continues.

Many addictions, however, are harmful. Harmful, in the Becker and Murphy context, means that the capital good—that is, the consumption capital—has harmful effects similar to a reduction in health status in the Grossman model. Smoking cigarettes may reduce healthy days, and may reduce income. Such harmful effects are part of what Becker and Murphy call the "full price" of the addictive good.

In the model, a good is potentially addictive to the consumer if the effects of present consumption of the good tend to increase future marginal utility more than they increase future full price. This pattern is called *adjacent complementarity*.

For example, the potential cigarette smoker would choose to start smoking, even knowing that it is addictive, if smoking tends to increase future enjoyment from smoking more than it

increases future harmful effects from smoking. This dynamic model explains why a rational person may choose to ingest a harmful substance, knowing fully its harmful effects.

A permanent increase in the tax on cigarettes may reduce consumption by a considerable extent, even though smokers are addicted. Estimates of the price elasticity of cigarettes are usually thought to be between -0.2 and -0.7, with some estimates higher (toward -1.0). This evidence suggests that addictive consumption patterns for cigarettes do respond rationally to economic stimuli. How individuals value the present relative to the future determines how reactive they will be to the imposition of such a tax.

Researchers use such models to study the implications of public health policies on addictive behavior. Chaloupka (1991) and Cameron (1997), among others, apply rational addiction models to the impacts of cigarette prices and taxes. Chaloupka, looking at the United States, finds support for the models. Cameron, examining Greek smokers, does not.

Baltagi and Griffin (2001) reexamine the econometric estimation of rational-addiction cigarette consumption models considered by Becker, Grossman, and Murphy (BGM). Using a panel data set of 46 states over the period 1963 to 1992, the authors' findings support the rational addiction hypothesis and provide "more plausible" (according to the authors) estimates than BGM's original results.

Gruber and Koszegi (2001) argue that smokers' preferences are time inconsistent, with individuals both not recognizing the true difficulty of quitting and searching for self-control devices to help them quit. Their analysis suggests that optimal government policy must depend not only on the externalities that smokers impose on others but also on the "internalities" imposed by smokers on themselves. Because of these internalities, the authors estimate that the optimal tax per pack of cigarettes should be at least $1 higher than is calculated using the rational addiction analyses.

(See Chapter 23 for a more detailed discussion of rational addiction.)

Quality of Well-Being (QWB) scale, developed by Kaplan and Anderson (1988), based on mobility, physical activity, social activity, and physical symptoms and problems.

They find that both health care and leisure consumption tend to improve health. A 1 percent increase in health-related consumption improves health by 0.03 to 0.05 percent. Depending on the technique used, a 1 percent increase in leisure increases health by 0.25 to 0.65 percent.

Demand for health is estimated by Gerdtham and Johannesson (1999) based on a Swedish sample of over 5,000 adults. Health capital is measured by a categorical measure of overall health status. The results are consistent with the theoretical predictions and show that the demand for health increases with income and education and decreases with age, urbanization, being overweight, and being single.

Strauss et al. (1993) examine the depreciation of health capital by using indicators of adult health for men and women in Malaysia, Jamaica, Bangladesh, and the United States. They find that activity limitation increases with age; in Grossman's terms, this implies that health decreases. Furthermore, this activity limitation tends to occur more frequently for women than for men. They also find that increased education leads to improved health, but that the impact of education decreases for older people.

We can study health investment by looking at the demand for preventive care. Kenkel (1994) estimates the determinants of women's purchases of medical screening services, designed for the early detection of breast and cervical cancer. Annual use of these screening tests decreases with age, a result consistent with women rationally reducing care as the payoff period shortens over the life cycle and as the depreciation rate rises. Furthermore, increased schooling tends to increase the use of the screening services, implying more efficiency in producing health.

Mullahy and Sindelar (1993) examine the relationships among alcoholism, income, and working. Poor health may reduce income either by reducing productivity, which results in lower wages, or by reducing labor market participation (whether and/or how much one is working). Alcoholism is an illness that reduces people's health capital. Mullahy and Sindelar find the labor market participation effects are more powerful than the wage (productivity) effects in reducing earnings, and hence reducing the return to health. By these criteria, successful alcoholism treatment would appear to have significantly positive economic returns.

In a retrospective essay on research achievements and directions in the 30 years after Grossman's pioneering analysis, Leibowitz (2004) finds that increases in the parents' valuations of time will also affect the relative costs of alternative inputs to children's health. As a result, mothers who work outside the home may employ substitutes for their own time that are less effective in producing child health. For example, working mothers can substitute prepared foods for their own time in producing meals for their children. However, these prepared foods are often high calorie and high fat, perhaps leading to less nutritious diets for their children (Leibowitz, 2003; Anderson et al., 2003).

In yet another application, Borisova and Goodman (2004) examine the importance of time in the compliance of drug abusers with methadone treatment, as a substitute for heroin. Because most drug abuse treatment comes at only nominal or zero cost, the time spent traveling to, and receiving, the daily treatment becomes critical. The authors find, as expected, that increased travel and treatment time significantly reduce treatment compliance.

In short, Grossman's model has yielded considerable insight into the determinants of health and into the allocation of resources (both time and money) into health-creating activities. It has crossed fields of economics, including labor and development economics, and has provided fruitful results in cross-disciplinary demographic and sociological research as well.

Conclusions

This chapter has addressed the demand for health and medical services from an individual perspective. It has treated health as a good that is produced like all others, using market inputs as well as an individual's time. People benefit from health in four important ways:

1. They feel better when well.
2. They lose less time to illness, and hence can work more.
3. They are more productive when they work and can earn more for each hour they work.
4. They may live longer.

By analyzing the demand for health in this way, we recognize that the demands for health care inputs—from physicians' services, to drugs, to therapy—are demands that are derived from the demand for health itself. Consumers, jointly with providers, allocate resources among health care inputs based on the demand for health. We address the specific demand for health inputs in Chapter 9.

SUMMARY

1. It is not medical care per se that consumers want, but rather health itself. Medical care demand is a derived demand for an input that is used to produce health.
2. Consumers do not merely purchase health passively from the market, but instead produce it, spending time on health-improving efforts in addition to purchasing medical inputs.
3. Health lasts for more than one period. It does not depreciate instantly, and thus can be treated as a capital good.
4. Demand for health has pure consumption aspects; health is desired because it makes people feel better.
5. Demand for health also has pure investment aspects; health is desired because it increases the number of healthy days available to work and thus earn income.
6. Consumers prefer more income and more leisure so indifference curves between income and leisure are negatively sloped. The slope of the line depicting the labor-leisure tradeoff is the wage rate.
7. Because health is a capital good, the cost of holding health for any one year, as well as over time, will equal the opportunity cost of the capital (interest foregone) plus the depreciation (deterioration of value).
8. The *MEI* curve for investments in health is downward sloping. This occurs because the production function for healthy days exhibits diminishing marginal returns. Thus, the optimal demand for health is likewise given at the intersection of the *MEI* curve and the cost of capital curve $(r + \delta)$.
9. The pure investment model generates the prediction that optimal health will decline as the person ages if the depreciation rate of health increases as a person ages.
10. The rewards of being healthy are generally greater for higher-wage workers so those with increasing wages will generally tend to increase their optimal health stock.
11. Health can be generated at less cost for more highly educated people, resulting in a higher optimal health stock than for less educated people.

DISCUSSION QUESTIONS

1. Why do we treat leisure and earnings as ordinary utility-increasing goods?
2. Describe the aspects of health that make it a consumption good. Describe those that make it an investment good.
3. Give examples of how health is produced from market and nonmarket goods.

4. Why is the depreciation of a capital good a cost to society? In what ways does a person's health depreciate?
5. Why might older people's health care expenditures increase in the Grossman model even though their desired health stock may be lower?
6. List at least three factors that might increase an individual's marginal efficiency of investment in health capital.
7. Suppose that a young woman goes on to medical school and becomes a physician. Would you expect her expenditures on medical goods for her own health to be higher or lower than a nonphysician? Why?
8. From your experience, do you think the typical person becomes less healthy upon, or shortly after, retirement? What does the Grossman model predict?
9. People who earn a higher salary can afford more goods, including health care. However, according to Grossman, they will choose a higher desired health stock. Why is this so according to the model?

EXERCISES

1. Draw an isoquant between medical inputs and other inputs in the production of a given amount of health investment. What does the isoquant mean? How would the isoquant look if substitution was limited? If a high degree of substitution was possible?
2. Suppose that no amount of other goods can compensate for a loss in health. How would the individual's indifference curves look? Is this a reasonable assumption in terms of what we actually see taking place?
3. Suppose that John Smith gets promoted to a job that causes two changes to occur simultaneously: John earns a higher wage, and a safer environment causes his health to depreciate less rapidly. How would these two changes together affect John's desired health capital?
4. Suppose that John could work 365 days per year and could earn $200 per day for each day he worked. Draw his budget line with respect to his labor-leisure choice.
5. Suppose that John chooses to work 200 days per year. Draw the appropriate indifference curve, and note his equilibrium wage income and labor-leisure choices.
6. Suppose, in exercise 5, that John's wage rises from $200 to $210 per day. Show how his equilibrium level of income and labor-leisure will change.
7. Suppose that John is ill 10 days per year. Draw the impact of this illness on the equilibrium defined in exercise 5. How will it change his equilibrium allocation of earnings and labor-leisure?
8. Answer the following.
 a. Depict Sara's optimal stock of health capital at age 18, with a high school diploma and a wage of $6 per hour.
 b. Suppose that she invests in a college education, expecting to get a better and higher-wage job. Show how her optimal stock of health capital changes by the age of 30 due to the increased wage. Then, show how her education would affect her optimal health stock if education also made her a more efficient producer of health.
 c. Suppose that after age 30 her wage stays the same. As she ages, show what happens to her optimal stock of health capital, assuming that the depreciation rate of health increases with age.

CHAPTER 8

Demand and Supply of Health Insurance

Health insurance is critical to any discussion of the health economy. Most Americans, and indeed most citizens of other countries, do not pay directly for their health care. Rather, insurance companies or other programs indirectly pay for much of the care, with the consumer paying directly only a portion of the bill. The patient's portion is sometimes called coinsurance. Insurance coverage is provided through the payment of premiums (in privately financed systems) or taxes (when insurance is provided publicly). The premiums are often, although not always, purchased through the consumer's participation in the labor force.

Health care expenses are uncertain. Many illnesses occur rarely and seemingly at random. When they do, they may cost a great deal, and they can be financially troublesome, if not ruinous, to households. Costs could be so high that without financial help treatment might not be available.

Because insurance is so important to the demand and supply of health care, as well as the government's role in allocating health resources, we introduce several fundamental factors relating to the demand and supply of insurance. This provides a set of tools for addressing issues such as the demand for and supply of health care, the role of information in health care markets, and the variation of health care among various markets. We return to insurance issues in Chapter 11, which will look at the operation of insurance markets.

What Is Insurance?

For a clear picture of what insurance is, consider the demand for insurance without all of the detailed trappings (deductibles, premiums, coinsurance, etc.) that accompany modern insurance plans. Consider a club with 100 members. The members are about the

same age, and they have about the same lifestyles. It seems that about once a year one of the 100 members gets sick and incurs health care costs of $2,000. The incidence of illness seems to be random, not necessarily striking men, women, the old, or the young in any systematic fashion. Club members, worried about potential losses due to illness, decide to collect $20 from each member and put the $2,000 in the bank for safekeeping and to earn a little interest. If a member becomes ill, the fund is used to pay for the treatment. This, in a nutshell, is insurance. The members have paid $20 to avoid the risk or uncertainty, however small, of having to pay $2,000. The "firm" collects the money, tries to maintain and/or increase its value through investment, and pays claims when asked.

This example illustrates several desirable characteristics of an insurance arrangement.

1. The number of insured should be large, and they should be independently exposed to the potential loss.
2. The losses covered should be definite in time, place, and amount.
3. The chance of loss should be measurable.
4. The loss should be accidental from the viewpoint of the person who is insured.

In general, insurance reduces the variability of the incomes of those insured by pooling a large number of people and operating on the principle of the law of large numbers. That is, although outlays for a health event may be highly variable for any given person in the insurance pool, the average outlays for the group can be predicted fairly well. The law of large numbers shows that for a given probability of illness, the distribution of the average rate of illness in the group will collapse around the probability of illness as the group size increases.

This chapter considers the theory and practice of health care insurance. It is necessary to quantify the idea of risk, as well as attitudes toward risk. With those ideas, it is then possible to consider the structure of insurance policies and how markets evolve to provide them.

Insurance Versus Social Insurance

It is useful to distinguish between insurance, as provided through the pooling of risk, and government programs (often referred to as social insurance), such as Social Security, Medicare, and Medicaid in the United States. Insurance is provided through markets in which buyers protect themselves against rare events with probabilities that can be estimated statistically. The government programs are insurance programs with the government as insurer and are distinguished by two features:

1. Premiums (the amounts paid by purchasers) are heavily, and often completely (as in the case of Medicaid), subsidized.
2. Participation is constrained according to government-set eligibility rules.

In addition, government insurance programs often transfer income from one segment of society to another. Given the importance of such social insurance programs, we devote an entire chapter (Chapter 21) to them later in the text.

Insurance Terminology

It is helpful to consider some terms that are used to discuss insurance. Although much of the analysis that we will perform uses the standard economic language of prices and quantities, the insurance industry has developed a particular set of definitions. These include:

Premium, Coverage When people buy insurance policies, they typically pay a given premium for a given amount of coverage should the event occur.

Coinsurance and Copayment Many insurance policies, particularly in the health insurance industry, require that when events occur, the insured person share the loss through copayments. This percentage paid by the insured person is the coinsurance rate. With a 20 percent coinsurance rate, an insured person, for example, would be liable (out-of-pocket) for a $10 copayment out of a $50 charge. The insurance company would pay the remainder, or 80 percent. Thus, coinsurance refers to the percentage paid by the insured; copayment refers to the amount paid by the insured (such as a fixed payment for a prescription).

Deductible With many policies, some amount of the cost of health care is paid by the insured person in the form of a deductible, irrespective of coinsurance. In a sense, the insurance does not apply until the consumer pays the deductible. Deductibles may be applied toward individual claims, or, often in the case of health insurance, they may be applied only to a certain amount of total charges in any given year.

Coinsurance and deductibles often are used together. For example, an insurance policy may require that John pay the first $100 of his medical expenses out-of-pocket each year. It may then require that he pay 20 percent of each additional dollar in charges. This policy would be said to have a deductible of $100 and a coinsurance rate of 20 percent.

Many feel that deductibles and coinsurance are simply ways that insurance companies gouge consumers to make extra money. Economists, in contrast, have found that deductibles and coinsurance may be used to design policies that lead to desirable economic consequences. The requirement of a copayment makes consumers more alert to differences in the true costs of the treatment they are purchasing. The charging of deductibles discourages frivolous claims or visits, and also makes insured people more aware of the results of their actions. Both may serve to avoid claims and to reduce costs.

Finally, there are a few other terms that describe various features of insurance:

Exclusions Services or conditions not covered by the insurance policy, such as cosmetic or experimental treatments.

Limitations Maximum coverages provided by insurance policies. For example, a policy may provide a maximum of $2 million lifetime coverage.

Pre-Existing Conditions Medical problems not covered if the problems existed prior to issuance of insurance policy. Examples here might include pregnancy or cancer.

Pure Premiums The actuarial losses associated with the events being insured.

Loading Fees General costs associated with the insurance company doing business, such as sales, advertising, or profit.

With these in mind, we turn to a more formal analysis of risk and insurance.

Risk and Insurance

To this point we have assumed that all decisions occur under conditions of certainty; that is, consumers know what the prices, incomes, and tastes are and will be. Clearly, however, many decisions are made in which the outcome is risky or uncertain.

We begin by considering the insurance coverage of an event that occurs with the known probability, p, leading to a predictable loss and/or payment. This assumption will be used to characterize peoples' choices under uncertainty. We will then extend the

general characterization to health insurance, which differs because the payment may be affected by the insurance. We address this difference once the basic points regarding risk are developed.

Expected Value

Suppose John considers playing a game in which a coin will be flipped. If it comes up heads, John will win $1; if it comes up tails, John will win nothing. How much would John be willing to pay in order to play this game? Analysts rely on the concept of expected value for the answer. With an honest coin, the probability of heads is one-half (0.5), as is the probability of tails. The expected value, sometimes called the expected return, is:

$$E(\text{heads is called}) = (\text{probability of heads}) \times (\text{return if heads, i.e., } \$1) \\ + (\text{probability of tails}) \times (\text{return if tails, } \$0) \quad \textbf{(8.1)}$$

The expected value is $0.50; that is $(1/2 \times 1) + (1/2 \times 0)$. If he uses the decision criterion that he will play the game if the expected return exceeds the expected cost, John will play (pass) if it costs him less (more) than $0.50. More generally, with n outcomes, expected value E is written as:

$$E = p_1 R_1 + p_2 R_2 + \ldots + p_n R_n$$

where p_i is the probability of outcome i, (that is p_1 or p_2 through p_n) and R_i is the return if outcome i occurs. The sum of the probabilities p_i equals 1.

The special case where the price of the gamble is exactly $0.50 and is equal to the expected return is analogous to a situation in insurance in which the expected benefits paid out by the insurance company are equal to the premiums taken in by the company. This equality of expected benefit payments and premiums is called an actuarially fair insurance policy. In reality, insurance companies must also cover additional administration and transaction costs to break even, but the definition of an actuarially fair policy provides a benchmark in talking about insurance.

Marginal Utility of Wealth and Risk Aversion

The foregoing example implies that John is indifferent to risk. That is, for him the incremental pleasure of winning $0.50 (the gain of $1 less the $0.50 he paid to play) is exactly balanced by the incremental displeasure of losing $0.50 (the gain of zero less the $0.50 paid to play). Suppose, however, the sizes of the bets were changed so that the coin flip would now yield $100, or nothing, and that John was now asked to bet $50 to play. John may now think a little harder. He may now refuse an actuarially fair bet—$50—on the grounds that he cannot afford to risk the $50 loss if the coin lands tails. This suggests that the disutility of losing money is larger than is the utility of winning a similar amount. This would be true, for example, if he felt that the utility of an extra dollar of wealth were worth more when he is relatively poorer than the utility of an extra dollar of wealth is worth when he is relatively richer. The utility from an extra dollar is called the marginal utility of wealth.[1]

It is important to incorporate the individual's utility of wealth function into the analysis. In Chapter 2, we assumed that consumers could only rank bundles but could not (and need not) compare magnitudes of satisfaction. To understand the utility model of risk behavior, however, we must further assume that consumers can rank alternatives and compare their magnitudes.

[1]Wealth refers to the sum of the consumer's net assets in money terms. It is related to income, which is the flow of funds in any given period. We refer to one or the other for some discussions, but the substance of the insurance analysis refers to both.

FIGURE 8-1 Total Utility of Wealth and the Impact of Insurance

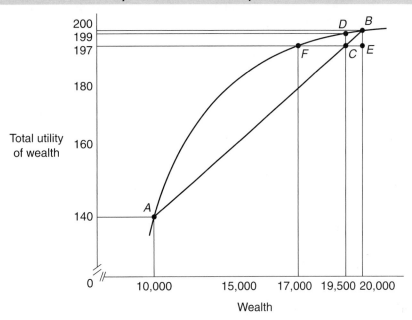

Consider Figure 8-1. Suppose that John's wealth is $10,000. That wealth gives him a utility level of $U_1 = 140$ and allows him to buy some basic necessities of life. This can be denoted as point A. Suppose his wealth rises to $20,000. Will his utility double? While it is hard to know for certain, it is likely that the next $10,000 may not bring him the incremental utility that the first $10,000 brought. Thus, U_2 is likely to be less than twice U_1. Suppose, for example, that $U_2 = 200$. This is denoted as point B.

Do all of the points on the utility function between U_1 and U_2 lie on a straight line? If they do, this is equivalent to saying that the utility from the 10,001st dollar is equal to the utility from the 19,999th dollar, and hence the marginal utility is constant. This also is unlikely. Because the marginal utility of earlier dollars is likely to be larger than that of later dollars, the utility curve is likely to be bowed out, or concave, to the x-axis.

The marginal utility of wealth refers to the amount by which utility increases when wealth goes up by $1. This rise in utility, divided by the $1 increase in wealth, is thus the slope of the utility function. The bowed shape of the utility function shows a slope that is getting smaller or flatter as wealth rises; thus, the marginal utility of wealth is diminishing.

Suppose that John's wealth increases to $20,000. He understands, however, that if he becomes ill, which may occur with probability 0.05, his expenses will cause his wealth to decline to $10,000. If this occurs, he can calculate his expected wealth, $E(W)$,

$$E(W) = \text{(prob. well)} \times (\textbf{wealth if well}) + \text{(prob. ill)} \times (\textbf{wealth if ill})$$
$$0.95 \times (\$20{,}000) + 0.05 \times (\$10{,}000) = \$19{,}500 \tag{8.2a}$$

and expected utility, $E(U)$:

$$E(U) = \text{(prob. well)} \times (\textbf{utility if well}) + \text{(prob. ill)} \times (\textbf{utility if ill})$$
$$0.95 \times (\text{utility of } \$20{,}000) + 0.05 \times (\text{utility of } \$10{,}000) \tag{8.2b}$$
$$0.95 \times (200) + 0.05 \times (140) = 197$$

Thus, the expected utility $E(U)$ is 197 or point C because of the risk of illness. Geometrically, this is the line segment between points A and B, evaluated at wealth level $E(W) = \$19{,}500$. The expected utility due to risk must be compared to the utility

of 199 (point *D*), corresponding to the utility that he would receive if he could purchase insurance at an actuarially fair rate. As drawn, the risk leads to a loss of 2 units (199 to 197) of utility.

Purchasing Insurance

Suppose that John can buy an insurance policy costing $500 per year that will maintain his wealth irrespective of his health. Is it a good buy? We see that at a net wealth of $19,500, which equals his initial wealth minus the insurance premium, his certainty utility is 199. John is better off at point *D* than at point *C*, as shown by the fact that point *D* gives the higher utility. If insuring to get a certain wealth rather than facing the risky prospect makes John better off, he will insure.

We can, in fact, use Figure 8-1 to calculate the maximum amount that John would be willing to pay for the insurance by moving southwest down the utility function to the level of *U* = 197 and reading the level of wealth (off the x-axis) to which it corresponds, or point *F*. The distance *FC* reflects John's aversion to risk. At point *F*, John would be willing to pay up to $3,000 (that is, initial wealth of $20,000, less $17,000 at point *F*) for insurance and still be as well off as if he had remained uninsured. If, for example, he were able to purchase the insurance for $2,500, he would get $500 in consumer surplus.

This analysis illustrates several facts:

1. Insurance can be sold only in circumstances where there is diminishing marginal utility of wealth or income—that is, when the consumer is risk averse. By examining Figure 8-1, we can see that if marginal utility were constant, a requirement that John pay an actuarially fair premium for insurance would leave him no better off than if he were uninsured.

2. Expected utility is an average measure; John either wins or loses the bet. If exposed to risk, he will have wealth, and hence utility, of either $20,000 (with utility of 200), or $10,000 (with utility of 140), with a risky expected wealth of $19,500. Insurance will guarantee his wealth to be $19,500. If he does not fall ill, his wealth will be $20,000 less the $500 insurance premium; if he falls ill, his wealth will be $10,000 plus the $10,000 payment for the loss of health, minus the $500 premium—again $19,500.

3. If insurance companies charge more than the actuarially fair premium, people will have less expected wealth from insuring than from not insuring. Even though people will have less wealth as a result of their purchases of insurance, the increased well-being comes from the elimination of risk.

The Demand for Insurance

If risk-averse people will purchase insurance, how much will they purchase? The next two sections present a classic model introduced by Mark Pauly in 1968 to consider the fundamental demand and supply decisions regarding insurance.

How Much Insurance?

We have discussed why John would choose to buy insurance so we now consider how much insurance he would choose. Recall that John's expected utility involves his wealth when ill, with a probability of 0.05, or when healthy, with a probability of 0.95. If ill, his wealth will fall from $20,000 to $10,000.

We address John's optimal purchase by using the concepts of marginal benefits and marginal costs. Consider first a policy that provides insurance covering losses up to

$500. Although it would hardly seem worth buying a $500 insurance policy when John loses $10,000 if he is ill, it is a useful place to start.

The goal of maximizing total net benefits provides the framework for understanding his health insurance choice. He benefits from health insurance only in the case when he is ill and receives the insurance benefit payments. He still pays the insurance premiums when ill, but he gains financially net of those premiums. When well, only the premium applies to him; it is thus a net cost.

In turn, the marginal benefits when well will decline as additional insurance coverage is purchased; this is understood by applying the law of diminishing marginal utility. In contrast, the marginal costs when well will rise as additional insurance is purchased. John's solution is to purchase so that the marginal benefits equal the marginal costs.

Suppose that he must pay a 10 percent premium ($50) for his insurance, or $1 for every $10 of coverage that he purchases. The following worksheet describes his wealth if he gets sick.

		Insurance Worksheet—$500 coverage—Wealth if Ill
	Original wealth	$20,000
less	Loss	$10,000
	Remainder	$10,000
plus	Insurance	500
	Sum	$10,500
less	Premium	50
or	**New** wealth	$10,450

For the initial coverage, John's wealth, if well, is $20,000 less the $50 premium, or $19,950. His marginal benefit from the $500 from insurance is the expected marginal utility that the additional $450 brings. His marginal cost is the expected marginal utility that the $50 premium costs. We describe these benefits and costs in Figure 8-2. If John is averse to risk, the marginal benefit (point A) of this insurance policy exceeds its marginal cost (point A').

Should John increase his coverage from $500 to $1,000? He must compare the marginal benefits of this next $500 increment to its marginal costs. Because John is slightly wealthier than before, if ill (starting at $10,450 rather than $10,000) the marginal utility from an additional $450 of wealth (calculated as before) will be slightly smaller than before. Hence, the marginal benefits from the second $500 increment will be slightly smaller than for the first $500 increment. His marginal benefit curve, MB_1, is downward sloping, with his new marginal benefit at point B.

Similarly, because he is a little less wealthy than before if well, an additional $50 in premiums will cost a little more in foregone (marginal) utility of wealth than the first increment at point B'. Thus, his marginal cost curve, MC_1, is upward sloping.

By reiterating this process, we can see that John will adjust the amount of insurance, q, that he purchases to the point at which the marginal benefits equal the marginal cost. The quantity, q^*, at which they are equal (point X) is John's optimum insurance purchase.

Changes in Premiums

How will his insurance decision change if premiums change? Consider first the impact of a higher premium, say 15 percent rather than the 10 percent used earlier. With the

FIGURE 8-2 The Optimal Amount of Insurance

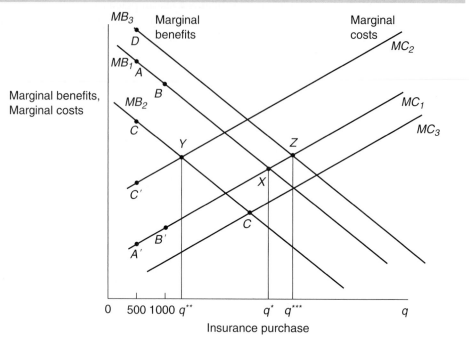

15 percent premium ($75), John faces the following calculation regarding a policy that provides $500 worth of coverage:

	Insurance Worksheet—Higher Premium Wealth if Ill	
	Original wealth	$20,000
less	Loss	$10,000
	Remainder	$10,000
plus	Insurance	500
	Sum	$10,500
less	*New premium*	75
or	**New** wealth	$10,425

If he stays well, his wealth is $20,000 less the $75 premium, or $19,925. John's marginal benefit from the $500 from insurance is now $425 rather than the previous value of $450, so point C lies on curve MB_2 below the previous marginal benefit curve, MB_1. We can fill in additional points on this curve, which reflect the higher premium.

Similarly, John's marginal cost is the expected marginal utility that the (new) $75 premium costs him. This exceeds the previous cost in terms of foregone utility, so point C lies on curve MC_2 above the previous marginal cost curve, MC_1. Again, we can fill in additional points on this curve and find the intersection of MB_2 and MC_2 at point Y. The resulting analysis suggests that consumers react rationally to higher premiums by reducing their optimum coverage from q^* to q^{**}.

Changes in Expected Loss

How will the insurance decision be affected by changes in expected losses? Returning to the original example with a premium of 10 percent, suppose that instead of $10,000, John expected to lose $15,000 if ill. Consider again the first $500 of insurance coverage. His wealth, if healthy, is $19,950, so nothing changes with respect to marginal cost. John remains on curve MC_1 at point A'. The marginal benefit calculation, however, does change:

	Insurance Worksheet—Higher Expected Loss Wealth if Ill	
	Original wealth	$20,000
less	*New loss*	$15,000
	Remainder	$ 5,000
plus	Insurance	500
	Sum	$5,500
less	Premium	50
or	**New** wealth	$5,450

As before, the insurance gives him a net benefit of $450. However, this net benefit increments a wealth of $5,000 rather than $10,000. If we assume that an additional dollar gives more marginal benefit from a base of $5,000 than from a base of $10,000, then the marginal benefit curve shifts upward because of the increased expected loss. This provides point D on curve MB_3 in Figure 8-2. It follows that in equilibrium, an increase in the expected loss will increase the amount of insurance purchased at point Z, or q^{***}.

Changes in Wealth

Finally, consider the impact of changes in an individual's initial wealth. Suppose John was starting with a wealth of $25,000 instead of $20,000. Again, assume a premium rate of 10 percent.

	Insurance Worksheet—Increased Wealth Wealth if Ill	
	Increased wealth	$25,000
less	Loss	$10,000
	Remainder	$15,000
plus	Insurance	500
	Sum	$15,500
less	Premium	50
or	**New** wealth	$15,450

At the higher level of wealth, the same insurance policy provides a smaller increment in utility, so the marginal benefit curve shifts down from MB_1 to MB_2. However (for the same expected loss), the $50 premium costs less in foregone marginal utility relative to the increased wealth, a downward shift of MC_1 to MC_3. As a result of both downward shifts, the new equilibrium value of q at point W may be higher or lower than the original value of q^* (as drawn in Figure 8-2, it is lower). If, however, increased wealth is accompanied by increased losses, then the MB curve may shift down less; if so, the amount of insurance may increase because increased expected losses would make increased insurance more desirable.

The Supply of Insurance

In the last example, we assumed a 10 percent premium rate, but to determine the amount of coverage someone will buy, we must know how insurers determine the premium. To do this, we develop a model of the insurance market, beginning again with the club that insures its members against illness. The officers of the club do not know, nor necessarily care, who will file a claim.[2] All that is necessary for the club to function as an insurer is that revenues cover costs. In practice, insurance companies will also incur administrative and other expenses that also must be covered by premiums.

Competition and Normal Profits

Let's return to John's insurance problem from the previous section. John is buying insurance in a competitive market, and under perfect competition, all firms earn zero excess profits. Recall that John faced a potential illness with a probability of 0.05 (1 in 20). He sought to buy insurance in blocks of $500, and at the outset, his insurer, Asteroid Insurance, was charging him $50 for each block of coverage, or an insurance premium of 0.10 ($50 as a fraction of $500). Assume also that it costs the insurer $5 to process each insurance application. Asteroid's profits per policy are:

$$\text{Profits} = \text{Total revenue} - \text{Total costs}$$

Revenues are $50 per policy. What are Asteroid's costs? For 95 percent of the policies, the costs are $5 because the insured does not get sick and does not collect insurance. The only costs are the $5 processing costs per policy. The costs for the other 5 percent of the policies are $505, consisting of the $500 payment to those who are ill plus the processing costs of $5.

Thus, the profits per policy for Asteroid are:

$$\begin{aligned}
\text{Profits} &= \$50 - (\text{Probability of illness} \times \text{Costs if ill}) \\
&\quad - (\text{Probability of no illness} \times \text{Costs if no illness}) \qquad \textbf{(8.3)} \\
\text{Profits} &= \$50 - (0.05 \times \$505) - (0.95 \times \$5) \\
\text{Profits} &= \$50 - \$25.25 - \$4.75 \\
\text{Profits (premium} = 10\%) &= \$50 \,(\text{revenues}) - \$30 \,(\text{costs}) = \$20
\end{aligned}$$

These are positive profits, and they imply that another firm (also incurring costs of $5 to process each policy) might enter the market and charge a lower premium, say, 8 percent, to attract clients. The cost side of the equation would remain the same, but the revenues, which equal the premium fraction multiplied by the amount of insurance, would fall to $40. Hence, profits fall to:

$$\text{Profits (premium} = 8 \text{ percent)} = \$40 \,(\text{revenues}) - \$30 \,(\text{costs}) = \$10$$

which is still positive. It is easy to see that entry will continue into this industry until the premium has fallen to $0.06 per dollar of insurance, or 6 percent, which would provide revenues of $30, offset by the $30 in costs, to give zero profits.

A little algebra can verify that the 6 percent (or 0.06) premiums must be tied directly to the probability of the claim (0.05). Quite simply, for Asteroid, the revenue per policy is aq, where a is the premium, in fractional terms. The cost per policy in terms of payout is the probability of payout, p, multiplied by the amount of payout, q, plus

[2]Insurers must recognize whether they are getting nonrepresentative slices of the risk distribution. Analysts refer to this as *adverse selection*, and it can lead to financial losses for the insurer.

a processing cost, *t*, which is unrelated to the size of the policy (assuming it costs no more to administer a $10,000 policy than a $500 policy). So:

$$\text{Profit} = \text{Revenue} - \text{Payout} = aq - (pq + t) = aq - pq - t \qquad (8.4)$$

With perfect competition, profits = 0, so:

$$0 = aq - pq - t$$

We can solve for the competitive premium *a* as:

$$a = p + (t/q) \qquad (8.5)$$

This expression shows that the competitive value of *a* equals the probability of illness, *p*, plus the processing (or *loading*) costs as a percentage of policy value, *q*, or *t/q*. If loading costs are 10 percent of the policy value, *q*, then $(t/q) = 0.10$. Hence, in equilibrium $a = (0.05 + 0.10) = 0.15$. The premium for each dollar of insurance, *q*, is $0.15. If insurers charge less, they will not have enough money to pay claims. If they charge more, firms like Asteroid will have excess profits, and other firms will bid down rates in perfectly competitive markets.

Previously, in the discussion on the bearing of risk, we considered insurance policies that would compensate the individual against the loss based solely on the probability of the event's occurring, although Box 8-1 shows a case where the probability itself may actually change. Such rates are referred to as actuarially fair rates. The actuarially fair rates correspond to the rates in which the loading costs, *t*, as a percentage of insurance coverage, *q* (that is *t/q*), approach 0, hence:

$$a = p + (t/q) = p + 0 = p \qquad (8.6)$$

Knowing that premium *a* equals *p* under perfect competition (with no loading costs), we can now solve for the optimal coverage against any expected loss. It can be shown that to maximize utility, John will add coverage up to the point where his expected wealth will be the same whether he is ill or well. In the earliest example, the particular illness occurred with a probability of 0.05 and incurred a loss of $10,000. In a competitive insurance market (ignoring loading costs), John's wealth, if well, will be:

$$\text{Wealth (if well)} = \$20,000 - \text{cost of insurance, or:}$$
$$\$20,000 - (\text{premium } a) \times (\text{coverage } q)$$

His wealth, if ill, will be:

$$\text{Wealth (if ill)} = \$20,000 - \text{loss} + \text{insurance reimbursement} - \text{insurance premium or:}$$
$$\$20,000 - \$10,000 \text{ loss} + \text{coverage } q - (\text{premium } a) \times (\text{coverage } q)$$

To maximize the expected utility we equate the wealth if well with the wealth if ill:

$$[\textbf{Wealth (if well)} = \$20,000 - aq] = [\$20,000 - \$10,000 + q - aq = \textbf{Wealth (if ill)}] \quad (8.7)$$

Subtracting $20,000 − *aq* from both sides and rearranging terms yields:

$$q^{opt} = \$10,000$$

<interim_title>chronicle insurance text</interim_title><interim>

<interim_title>page 164 Supply and Demand</interim_title>

<interim>

<interim_title>page 164, Box 8-1</interim_title>

</interim>

<interim_title>page 164</interim_title>

<interim_title>Box 8-1 Viatical</interim_title>

BOX 8-1

"Viatical" and Accelerated Benefits—Market Reponses to Certain Death

Thus far, we have shown that an insurance market will function if the insurers and the insured can predict the probability that the adverse event will occur. Insurers who underestimate the probability or the timing of an event may lose money.

In 1997, Laura Casteneda of the *San Francisco Chronicle* wrote about problems in the "viatical" insurance market. The term *viatical* comes from ancient Rome, where travelers embarking on a difficult journey prepared a package of supplies and money called a viaticum. With viatical settlements, insurance holders would immediately receive lump sums from 50 to 85 percent of the face values of the policies, depending on how long they are expected to live. The shorter the time until the expected death, the larger the percentage that was paid to the insured.

Starting in the late 1980s, viatical brokers provided settlements to people with AIDS. With an almost certain probability of death, often in a short time, brokers could calculate the probabilities of death and provide funds to ailing patients so the patients could have cash assets during the last few years of their lives.

The success of a potent combination of drugs called protease inhibitors extended the lives of many AIDS patients. Although the inhibitors are good news for the AIDS patients, they were bad for business for many viatical companies. Suppose a broker paid an AIDS patient 80 percent of the face value of a $100,000 policy, based on the expectation that the patient would live for two more years. The economic cost to the broker would be the $80,000 payment plus the interest rate that represents the opportunity cost of carrying the debt. Suppose, however, that the improved treatment enables patients to live for four or five years rather than for two years. What had seemed to be a good "buy" for the broker would become a money-losing proposition.

Viatical settlements are still available, but the insurance market has responded as well. The Illinois Division of Insurance reports that some life insurance policies now provide an accelerated death benefits (ADB) option. The insurance company will pay a percentage of the policy's face value, minus any outstanding policy loans, if the life insurance policy has this feature. This enables the insured to deal with his or her insurance broker, rather than a different agent.

ADB options usually pay 50 percent to 80 percent of the face value of the policy. Those insured may be able to choose between a lump sum or monthly payments, and state laws may also let life insurance companies pay up to 75 percent of the policy's face value for some specific medical conditions, such as heart attack, Alzheimer's disease, or major organ transplant.

SOURCES: San Francisco Chronicle, March 10, 1997, p. E2; www.ins.state.il.us/Life_Annuities/viatical.htm (accessed June 20, 2005).

John's optimal level of coverage for a loss of $10,000 in the absence of transactions costs is $10,000! It is more realistic of course to assume that transactions costs *t* will be positive; in fact, loading charges are often substantial. John's best choice is to insure for less than the full health expense. This standard result from the mathematics of health insurance is often contrasted with the propensity of consumers to seek full coverage.

The Case of Moral Hazard

To this point, we have discussed the theory of risk, as well as the demand and supply of insurance when the events and the losses are random. The insurance policies discussed thus far represent indemnity policies, in which the insurer's liability is determined by

a fixed, predetermined amount for a covered event. Indeed, the term *indemnity* comes from the Latin *indemnis*, meaning "unhurt." Insurance renders the insured party financially unhurt by the random event.

In the previous section, we showed that the optimal insurance policy covers the entire loss when there is no transaction cost, and less than the full loss in the more realistic case when transactions costs are positive. We now address the effects of the price system on the provision of insurance.

Thus far, we have assumed that the amount of the loss was fixed—that it did not change merely because people bought insurance. However, in many cases, buying insurance lowers the price per unit of service at the time that the services are purchased. If people purchase more service due to insurance, then many of the insurance propositions just presented must be modified.

Demand for Care and Moral Hazard

Suppose John faces the probability $1 - p = 0.5$ that he will not be sick during a given time period and so will demand no medical care. He also faces probability, p, also equal to 0.5, that he will contract an illness that requires medical care. John fears that he will contract diabetes—if so, without insulin he will die. In Figure 8-3, panel A, we assume that his demand for insulin is perfectly inelastic, that is, unresponsive to its price. We saw earlier (ignoring the transactions costs) that John would be willing to pay insurance to cover expenditures P_1Q_1, his expenditures should he need care. An actuarially fair insurance policy would then charge John $0.5P_1Q_1$, and he would purchase the policy because it insured him against the risk of diabetes.

Consider, instead, John's demand for dermatological care (skin care for conditions such as acne or psoriasis). John's demand curve for these elective treatments may very well respond to price; that is, the quantity demanded may vary inversely with price. This is noted in Figure 8-3, panel B. If he purchases insurance that pays his entire loss, then this insurance makes treatment (ignoring time costs) free. Because the marginal price to John is zero, he would demand Q_2 units of care for a total cost of care of P_1Q_2,

FIGURE 8-3 Demand for Care and Moral Hazard

With *inelastic* demand, insurance has no impact on quantity demanded.

With *elastic* demand, insurance increases quantity demanded. This is moral hazard.

A. Inelastic demand

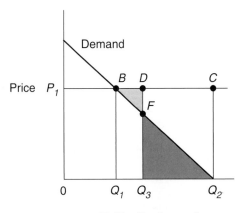

B. Elastic demand

shown as rectangle $0P_1CQ_2$, which is obviously larger than rectangle $0P_1BQ_1$. Why only Q_2 units when the care is "free?" Even free care entails time costs that keep the full price from equaling zero.

This response to economic stimuli leads to one of two possibilities that was not a problem either in the abstract or for a condition like diabetes:

1. If the insurance company charges the premium $0.5P_1Q_1$ (where 0.5 refers to the probability of illness) for the insurance, the company will lose money. This occurs because the expected payments would be $0.5P_1Q_2$. Amount P_1Q_2 exceeds P_1Q_1 because the induced demand leads John to consume more care (Q_2) with insurance than he would have consumed (Q_1) without insurance.
2. If the insurance company charges the appropriate premium, $0.5P_1Q_2$, for the insurance, John may not buy insurance. This amount may exceed the medical expenses that he would have spent on average had he chosen to put away money on his own, or to "self-insure." While John may be willing to pay more than $0.5P_1Q_1$ to avoid the risk, he may not be willing to pay as much as $0.5P_1Q_2$.

This rational response to economic incentives brought about by the elasticity of demand to the price of care is often termed *moral hazard*. Moral hazard refers here to the increased usage of services when the pooling of risks leads to decreased marginal costs for the services. More generally, moral hazard relates to any change in behavior that occurs in response to a contractual arrangement (here, the decision to insure). Failure to protect oneself from disease, because one has health insurance, would be another form of moral hazard. Our analysis gives a simple measure of the costs of moral hazard—netting out the costs of servicing the insurance (which do not reflect increased use of services), the excess of premiums over John's expected outlays had he not purchased insurance.

Thus, John's insurance premium has two components. The first is the premium for protection against risk, assuming that no moral hazard exists. The second is the extra resource cost due to moral hazard. As before, John chooses insurance coverage q^* by weighing marginal costs against marginal returns, whereas before the returns were the utility gains when John was ill. The twist here is that the costs now have two dimensions— the pure premium and the moral hazard. For some categories of care, the second may be important.

This analysis helps predict the types of insurance likely to be provided. It is clear that the optimal level of insurance is likely to increase relative to the expected loss as the degree of moral hazard decreases. Suppose we use demand price elasticity as an indicator of the potential for moral hazard. Theory then suggests the following:

1. Deeper (more complete) coverage for services with more inelastic demand.
2. Development of insurance first for those services with the most inelastic demand, and only later for those with more elastic demand.

Data on current insurance coverage by area of service support the first hypothesis, and historical data support the second.

Effects of Coinsurance and Deductibles

This analysis also provides insight into the impacts of deductible provisions and coinsurance in insurance policies. Returning to Figure 8-3, panel B, suppose that Q_1 reflects $500 of expenses (rectangle $0P_1BQ_1$) and that Q_2 is three times Q_1 (rectangle $0P_1CQ_2$), which reflects $1,500 of expenses. If the insurance contains a deductible, John

BOX 8-2

What's the Opposite of a Moral Hazard?

We have noted that there are many forms of moral hazard, economic responses to contractual arrangements. Blogger Nick Owen reported a 2004 study that found that the use of cameras, a "contract" to fine motorists who run red lights, actually increased the number of accidents at those intersections. While there are fewer "T–bone" collisions, there are more rear-end collisions.

The study, funded by the Federal Highway Administration and presented in January 2005, confirmed that right-angle crashes decrease and rear-end crashes increase once the cameras are installed. There are almost always signs indicating that cameras are present. This leads to more rear-end accidents at camera locations because motorists abruptly stop before the intersections, and fewer right-angle accidents at camera locations because drivers are speeding into intersections on the red lights. However, the study dug deeper and found that the red light cameras saved money— $39,000 to $50,000 annually for each intersection—because the rear-end collisions were less expensive than broadsides.

Blogger Owen proposes yet another option: "Don't tell the motorists that the cameras are there. They would know that the city has them, but not necessarily which intersection . . . or perhaps a city could buy a limited number of movable cameras." This would minimize what he terms the "immoral hazard," or whatever one would call the opposite of a moral hazard.

SOURCES: Web log: www.wikidsystems.com/WiKIDBlog/13 posted by Nick Owen; Michael Laris, "Hitting Brakes on Red Light Cameras," *Washington Post,* February 18, 2005, Page B05, www.washingtonpost.com/wp-dyn/articles/A33271-2005Feb17.html, accessed August 22, 2005.

will compare the position he would attain if he covered the deductible and received level Q_2 free with the position he would attain if he paid the market price for all the medical care he consumed.

Assume again that the probability of illness, p, equals 0.5. Consider first a policy containing a deductible, which requires John to pay the risk premium plus the first $500 of his medical care (rectangle $0P_1BQ_1$), after which all additional care is free. John will buy this policy because it protects him from risk and allows him to purchase Q_2 units of medical care for $500. His gain is the area under the demand curve, Q_1BQ_2.

Suppose now that the insurance company raises the deductible from $500 to $700. Will John continue to buy the insurance? Recall that without insurance, John would have purchased amount Q_1 of health services; the $700 deductible yields amount Q_3. When ill, John is paying more for the amount $(Q_3 - Q_1)$ of incremental health care than he believes the value of incremental care to be. The incremental costs are rectangle Q_1BDQ_3; the incremental benefits are the area under his demand curve (trapezoid Q_1BFQ_3). The difference is triangle BDF, and this represents a welfare loss to John.

However, after paying the deductible, he can get as much additional health care as he wants at zero cost, and he will buy quantity Q_2. This yields welfare gain triangle Q_3FQ_2 (incremental benefits less zero incremental costs). If Q_3FQ_2 (his welfare gain) is larger than BDF (his welfare loss), he buys the insurance, even with the $700 deductible. If BDF is larger than Q_3FQ_2, the loss exceeds the gain, and John is better off self-insuring and spending P_1Q_1 (in this example, $500) with probability 0.5.

Hence, the deductible has two possible impacts. A relatively small deductible will have no effect on individual usage, here Q_2. A large deductible makes it more likely that individuals will self-insure and consume the amount of care they would have purchased with no insurance, here Q_1.

A wide range of coinsurance coverage has been developed. Many analysts have considered how they may be formulated to lead to more economically efficient outcomes. We turn to that analysis next.

Health Insurance and the Efficient Allocation of Resources

This section examines the impact of health insurance on health care demand. Economists often wish to examine the efficient allocation of resources, which occurs when the incremental cost of bringing the resources to market (marginal cost) equals the valuation in the market to those who buy the resources (marginal benefit). If the marginal benefit is greater (less) than the marginal cost, one could improve society's welfare by allocating more (fewer) resources to the sector or individual, and less (more) resources to other sectors.

Consider Figure 8-4, which shows the marginal cost of care and the demand for care by a consumer under alternative conditions of insurance. If this consumer is not insured, then the optimal choice of health care is Q_0 units. The price (including travel time, parking, and the cost of bringing the service to market) reflects the cost to society of bringing the entire package to the market. Based on the consumer's (and the physician's) preferences, the marginal benefit, as described through the demand curve, equals the marginal cost. In economic terminology, this is an efficient allocation.

The Impact of Coinsurance

Consider now what happens when John pays only a fraction of the bill, say, at a 20 percent coinsurance rate. If, for example, P_0 was \$50 for an office visit, John must now only pay P_1, or \$10, so his demand will increase. A new demand curve (labeled with 20 percent coinsurance) is generated as the original demand curve rotates outward, and a new equilibrium is reached with the new quantity demanded Q_1. The cost of bringing services to market has remained the same, P_0. Services valued at P_0Q_0 are now being provided. The incremental amount spent (incremental cost) is $P_0 \times (Q_1 - Q_0)$, or the rectangle ABQ_1Q_0.

FIGURE 8-4 Health Care Demand with Insurance

The incremental benefit can be measured by the area under John's original demand curve, ACQ_1Q_0. The remaining triangle ABC represents the loss in well-being that occurs because John is purchasing more health care than is optimal. It is a loss in well-being because the incremental resource cost ABQ_1Q_0 exceeds the incremental benefits ACQ_1Q_0 by triangle ABC.

What exactly does this mean? It means that John is led by insurance to act as if he was not aware of the true resource costs of the care he consumes. It also means that the insurance implicitly subsidizes insured types of care (organized health care settings, prescription drugs) relative to other types of health care (e.g., good nutrition, exercise, over-the-counter drugs, uninsured types of care) that may be just as effective. It also subsidizes insured types of care relative to nonhealth goods. The degree of this distortion depends on the exact specification of the policy (that is, deductibles, maximum payments, rates of coinsurance), but it is apparent that insurance can distort the allocation of resources among health care and other goods.

An interesting example of moral hazard impacts comes through interactions between primary and secondary insurance coverages. This type of interaction concerns so-called "Medigap" plans, which provide additional coverage to the elderly above the amount paid by Medicare. Another example involves insured employees who have secondary coverage through their spouse's insurance. Moral hazard problems in these cases may be magnified.

John's employer, General National, provides health insurance to all its workers, with policies that pay 60 percent of all medical expenditures. Many of General National's workers also are covered under their spouse's insurance plans, but General's plan is considered the primary insurer for these dually covered workers. The secondary policies cover 60 percent of the expenses left uncovered by General's plan.

Figure 8-5 shows a demand curve for visits for the typical General National family if they had no insurance. The family would purchase 12 visits per year, at a price of $50, spending $600. If General National is the primary insurer, the out-of-pocket price to its insured will fall by 60 percent to $20 per visit. As drawn, the lower "out-of-pocket" price to patients increases quantity demanded to 24 visits. General National will pay $720, or 60 percent of the $1,200 total cost; its employees will pay $480.

Consider, however, the impact of secondary insurance. By paying 60 percent of the remainder, the secondary insurers reduce the out-of-pocket cost to the employees by another 60 percent, from $20 per visit to $8 per visit. Not surprisingly, the quantity of visits demanded increases again, this time from 24 to 29 visits. The secondary insurers pay $12 per visit, or $348 for the 29 visits. Moreover, the primary insurer, General National, faces increased claims due to demand induced by the coverage of the secondary insurers. General's liability increases from 60 percent of the original $1,200 in expenditures to 60 percent of $1,450 in expenditures—the higher level resulting from the secondary coverage.

A combination of coverages, while providing additional employee benefits, exacerbates the moral hazard problem brought on in general by health insurance. The inefficiencies and welfare losses that occur when decisions of one firm increase the health care costs facing another pose a difficult problem for policy makers.

Losses may be even more significant in the market context than in the individual context, as described by Figure 8-6. Clearly, as before, more services are used than are optimal. This has elements of both a redistribution of resources (from consumers and insurers to providers) and a deadweight loss (referring to a loss that comes from the misallocation of resources between types of goods). At the original price, P_0, and quantity, Q_0, producers were being paid the marginal cost to bring the products to market.

FIGURE 8-5 Impact of Secondary Insurance on Primary Coverage and Utilization

FIGURE 8-6 The Effect of Insurance Cost Sharing with Upward Sloping Supply

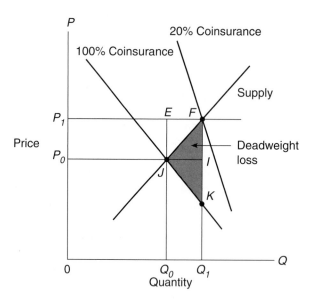

Moving from Q_0 to Q_1 leads to an increase in total expenditures from P_0Q_0 (rectangle $0P_0JQ_0$) to P_1Q_1 (rectangle $0P_1FQ_1$).

The deadweight loss comes from a misallocation of resources among goods (i.e., more health care is provided than should be, according to consumer preferences). Incremental benefits induced by the establishment of a coinsurance regime (i.e., the area under the original demand curve) are measured by the trapezoid Q_0JKQ_1.

Similarly, the additional resource costs of bringing the treatment level $(Q_1 - Q_0)$ to society is trapezoid $Q_0 JFQ_1$. The deadweight loss from the insurance induced overproduction of health services can be summarized as the difference in areas between the two trapezoids, or triangle *FKJ*.

The Demand for Insurance and the Price of Care

Martin Feldstein (1973) has shown that the demand for insurance and the moral hazard brought on by insurance may interact to increase health care prices even more than either one alone. Insurance is related to the expected loss; in health care, this is related in part to the price of care. Increased price of care is related to an increased demand for insurance, as noted in the upward sloping *I* curve in Figure 8-7.

The second impact is that of insurance on the price of care. More generous insurance and the induced demand in the market due to moral hazard lead consumers to purchase more health care. Curve P_1 shows that if the supply curve for health care is horizontal, then increased insurance will not increase the price of care above PC_1. The equilibrium is at point *A*, with health care price PC_1 and insurance quantity Q_1.

If, however, the product supply curve is less than perfectly elastic (the product supply curve rises), more generous insurance causes market price to increase. This impact is traced as curve P_2. Start at point *A*. We see here that the increased product price (the vertical arrow) due to the moral hazard brought on by insurance leads to an increased demand for insurance (the horizontal arrow), which again feeds back on price of care and so on. The moral hazard together with the upward-sloping product supply curve leads to a new equilibrium, *B*, with higher price of care, PC_2, and higher quantity of insurance, Q_2. The combination of factors leads to a higher price of health care and a higher demand for insurance than would have occurred were there no insurance.

FIGURE 8-7 The Interaction of Insurance and Price of Care

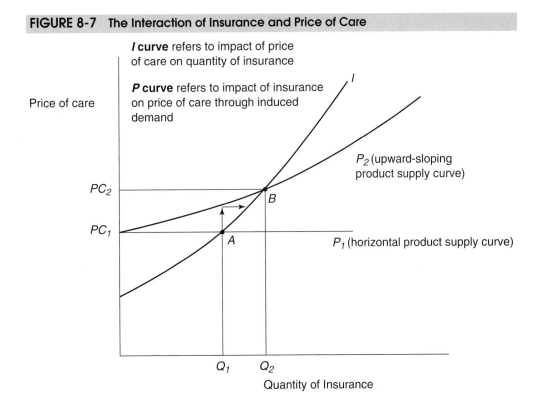

The Welfare Loss of Excess Health Insurance

From the preceding discussion, one would ask why society would support policies that seem only to result in misallocations of resources. In fact, the foregoing analyses concentrate only on the costs. It is important to emphasize that people buy insurance, willingly taking on additional costs to themselves, to protect against the risk of (possibly substantial) losses.[3] This protection provides major benefits through the protection against risk; the benefits from protection against risk offset the losses discussed here.

Many researchers have attempted to calculate the welfare losses of excess health insurance. One of the earliest and most prominent of the researchers was Feldstein (1973). The researcher measures the cost of the excess insurance by measuring the demand for health care and the coinsurance rate, and calculating the size of the loss polygons in Figure 8-6.

Measuring the benefits also is straightforward conceptually. One can use Figure 8-1 to measure the horizontal difference between John's expected utility and his actual utility. This represents the dollar amount that he would have been willing to pay for insurance over and above the amount that he was charged. Provision of insurance to John at the actuarially fair rate provides a utility gain to John through the reduction of uncertainty. Adding these gains across individuals provides a measure of net benefits to be compared to the costs of the excess insurance.

In plain terms, insurance policies impose increased costs on society because they lead to increased health services expenditures. These increased expenditures may occur in several ways:

- increased quantity of services purchased due to decreases in out-of-pocket costs for services that are already being purchased;
- increased prices for the services that are already being purchased;
- increased quantities and prices for services that would not be purchased unless they were covered by insurance; or
- increased quality in the services purchased, including expensive, technology-intensive services that might not be purchased unless covered by insurance.

Any procedures that raise the coinsurance rate will tend to reduce the costs of excess insurance but also will reduce the benefits from decreased risk bearing. Feldstein found that the average coinsurance rate was about one-third, or 0.33; that is, people paid $0.33 of every $1 of costs out of their own pockets. Raising the coinsurance to 0.50 or to 0.67 would cut the amount of insurance purchased, reducing the excess insurance, but also increasing the amount of risk borne by the clients.

The welfare gains from changed coinsurance, then, are:

$$\text{Welfare gains} = \text{Change in benefits} - \text{Change in costs} \qquad \textbf{(8.8)}$$

Feldstein's analysis considers the welfare gains from increasing the average coinsurance rate from 0.33 to 0.67. He discovers that the costs fall much more than do the benefits as coinsurance rates rise. He estimates the welfare gains to be approximately $27.8 billion per year (in 1984 dollars) under the "most likely" parameter values.

Feldman and Dowd (1991) updated Feldstein's 1960s estimates with 1980s parameters from the Rand Health Insurance Experiment regarding both price elasticity of the demand curve and attitudes toward risk. They calculate a lower bound for losses of

[3]Students might ask about people whose employers pay the entire insurance bill. Most economists believe that employees choose the insurance in lieu of a compensating take-home wage, thus paying for insurance themselves.

approximately $33 billion per year (in 1984 dollars) and an upper bound as high as $109 billion. For perspective, the upper and lower bounds constituted between 8.9 and 29.1 percent of all 1984 health expenditures.

Manning and Marquis (1996) seek to calculate the coinsurance rate that balances the marginal gain from increased protection against risk against the marginal loss from increased moral hazard, and find a coinsurance rate of about 45 percent to be optimal. Although the impacts of proposed changes depend crucially on the underlying econometric estimates (see Nyman, 1999, for further discussion), the fact that current coinsurance rates are far lower than 45 percent suggests an important role for restructuring insurance to reduce excess health care expenditures.

Conclusions

This chapter has concentrated on the unique role of insurance in the health care economy. No other good in people's day-to-day budgets is so explicitly tied to the arrangements for insurance as is health care. Such arrangements affect not only expenditures for serious illnesses and injuries, but also plans for more routine expenditures, such as children's well-care visits (for infants and toddlers) and eye and dental care.

We have characterized risk and have shown why individuals will pay to insure against it. The result, under most insurance arrangements, is the purchase of more or different services than might otherwise have been desired by consumers and/or their health care providers. Considerable health care policy debate focuses on how insurance policies can be structured in order to reduce purchases and minimize insurance costs without compromising the health of the insured.

SUMMARY

1. Many illnesses occur rarely and seemingly at random, but when they do, they entail substantial costs.
2. Insurance reduces variability of people's assets by pooling a large number of units and operating on the principle of the law of large numbers. Although outlays for a health event may be highly variable for any given unit in the pool, average outlays for the group are fairly predictable.
3. One should distinguish between insurance, as is provided through the pooling of risk, and government programs, such as Social Security, Medicare, and Medicaid, which also redistribute wealth.
4. Insurance can be sold only in circumstances where there is diminishing marginal utility of wealth or income (i.e., when the consumer is risk averse). With constant marginal utility, requiring that individuals pay actuarially fair premiums would leave them no better off than if they were uninsured.
5. Expected utility is an average measure; the individual either wins or loses the bet.
6. If insurance companies charge more than the actuarially fair premium, people will have less expected wealth through insuring than through not insuring. Even though people will be less wealthy by purchasing insurance, the increased well-being comes from the elimination of risk.
7. In theory, the optimal amount of insurance in the absence of loading costs is to fully insure against the expected loss. With loading costs, the optimal coverage is less than the expected loss.
8. Moral hazard refers to the increased usage of services when the pooling of risks leads to decreased marginal price for the services. This suggests:
 - more complete coverage for price inelastic services, and
 - earlier development of insurance for services that are most inelastic.

9. Insurance policies lead to increased costs to society because they lead to increased expenditures on health services. They provide increased benefits through the reduction of risks.
10. Losses due to excess insurance are estimated at between 8.9 and 29.1 percent of all health expenditures. This suggests the importance of restructuring insurance to reduce excess health care expenditures.

DISCUSSION QUESTIONS

1. Discuss the difference between cardinal and ordinal utility. Why is cardinal utility necessary for the analysis of risk and insurance?
2. What does the term moral hazard mean? Give examples.
3. The deductible feature of an insurance policy can affect the impact of moral hazard. Explain this in the context either of probability of treatment and/or amount of treatment demanded.
4. Describe the benefits to society from purchasing insurance. Describe the costs. Define and discuss the welfare gains from changes in insurance coverage.
5. If only risk-averse people will buy health insurance, why do many people who buy health insurance also buy lottery tickets (an activity more consistent with risk taking)? Speculate on the differences and similarities.
6. Is it ethical for viatical brokers to offer settlements to people with terminal diseases? Is it ethical for them to offer settlements to elderly people simply because they may die soon?
7. Because health insurance tends inevitably to cause moral hazard, will the population necessarily be overinsured (in the sense that a reduction in insurance would improve welfare)? Are there beneficial factors that balance against the costs of welfare loss?

EXERCISES

1. Suppose that Nathan's employer provides a health insurance policy that pays 80 percent of $1 over the first $100 spent. If Nathan incurs $1,000 in expenses, how much will he pay out-of-pocket? What percentage of his expenses will this be?
2. Suppose that rather than flipping a coin, one rolls a die. If the value is 1, 2, 3, or 4, the player wins $1. If it is 5 or 6, the player loses $1. Calculate the expected return.
3. A standard roulette wheel has an array of numbered compartments referred to as "pockets." The pockets are red, black, or green. The numbers 1 through 36 are evenly split between red and black, while 0 and 00 are green pockets. For every $1 that one bets on red, one wins $1 if the roulette ball lands on red, and loses if it lands otherwise. Similarly for black. What is the expected return to a red or a black bet? Why?
4. a. Draw a utility of wealth curve similar to Figure 8-1 for consumers who are not risk averse. How would its shape differ from Figure 8-1?
 b. Draw a utility of wealth curve similar to Figure 8-1 for "risk lovers." How would its shape differ from Figure 8-1?
5. a. Show the gains from insurance, if any, in exercise 4a.
 b. (Difficult) Show the cost of insurance in exercise 4b.
6. We have discussed the role of utility functions in the purchase of insurance.
 a. Suppose Edward's utility function can be written as:

 $$U = 20Y \text{ where } U \text{ is utility and } Y \text{ is income per month.}$$

 What is his marginal utility if income is $1,000 per month? $2,000 per month? Is Edward likely to insure against loss of income? Why?
 b. Suppose instead that Edward's utility function can be written as $U = 200Y^{0.5}$. What is his marginal utility if income is $1,000 per month? $2,000 per month? Is Edward likely to buy insurance against loss of income? Why?
7. Suppose, if ill, that Fred's demand for health services is summarized by the demand curve $Q = 50 - 2P$, where P is the price of services. How many services does he buy at a price of

$20? Suppose that Fred's probability of illness is 0.25. What is the actuarially fair price of health insurance for Fred with a zero coinsurance rate?

8. In exercise 7, if the insurance company pays Fred's entire loss, what will Fred's expenses be? How much will the company pay? Will it continue to offer him insurance at the actuarially fair rate? Why?

9. Suppose that the market demand for medical care is summarized by the demand function:

$$Q_d = 100 - 2p$$

and the market supply is summarized by the supply function:

$$Q_s = 20 + 2p$$

 a. Calculate the equilibrium quantity and price, assuming no health insurance is available.
 b. Suppose that health insurance is made available that provides for a 20 percent coinsurance rate. Calculate the new equilibrium price and quantity. (Hint: How does the demand curve shift?)
 c. Calculate the deadweight loss due to this insurance.

10. Suppose, in exercise 9, that the coinsurance rate was raised to 50 percent.
 a. Calculate the new equilibrium price and quantity. (Hint: How does the demand curve shift?)
 b. Calculate the deadweight loss due to this insurance.
 c. How does your answer compare to the deadweight loss in exercise 9?

Consumer Choice and Demand

- Applying The Standard Budget Constraint Model
- Two Additional Demand Shifters—Time and Coinsurance
- Issues in Measuring Health Care Demand
- Empirical Measurements of Demand Elasticities
- Impacts of Insurance on Aggregate Expenditures
- Other Variables Affecting Demand
- Conclusions

We have described health capital investment as a choice made by the consumer who values health but who also values the home good, which involves all the good things made possible by using income and time. These ultimate goods, health capital and the home good, are produced by the consumer by allocating a portion of time to each, as well as a portion of income to those marketed goods, such as medical care, M, and various other goods, OG, that are used in the production process.

Figure 9-1 helps illustrate this transformation from one model (see Chapter 7) to the other—the conventional analysis of choice over marketable goods—which is the focus of this chapter. The production possibilities frontier in the figure illustrates the consumer's trade-off between health investment and the home good. Choosing these optimal quantities, I^* and B^*, the consumer also implicitly chooses an allocation of time available for these production tasks, to work that provides income, and to leisure. The final step in understanding this process is to see how that income will be used to buy those marketable goods, such as medical care, that will in turn help the consumer produce health investment and the home good. The consumer faces a trade-off in the marketplace between the use of income to purchase medical care and the use of the money to purchase other goods. This trade-off is the budget constraint of standard consumer theory and is the focus of this chapter.

Applying the Standard Budget Constraint Model

As with the demand for health capital model, standard indifference curve analysis of consumer choice under a budget constraint describes the consumer with fairly strong assumptions. We assume that the consumer is rational and perfectly informed, that

FIGURE 9-1 Demand for Health Capital Determines the Optimal Amounts of the Home Goods and Health Capital Investment

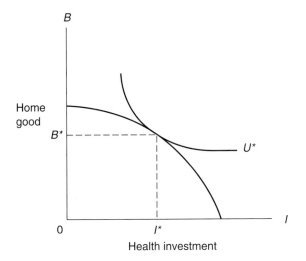

there is no uncertainty about the future, and that important decisions are made as if the future were known with certainty. Although we will later relax some of these assumptions, this model produces many reliable predictions on consumer behavior related to health.

Many might object to this approach at the start, believing that we have few choices when we need health care, at least for the urgently ill. If you are lying on the pavement and the ambulance arrives, do you ask for a list of prices and providers?

Nevertheless, a theory of rational choice over health care and other goods is defended on several grounds. First, many health care options leave room for some thoughtful consideration or at least some planning. Second, the physician serves as an agent for patient-consumers and can make rational choices on their behalf even in urgent situations.[1] Finally, the ultimate test of any theory is whether it predicts well, and we will show empirically that people, as consumers of health care, do respond to economic incentives.

In economic theory, the logic of consumer choice is straightforward. It indicates that consumers can choose any affordable combination or bundle of goods, and from among these affordable bundles, they will choose the one preferred. The depiction of this choice requires two elements:

- The consumer's preferences—described by a set of indifference curves
- The consumer's budget constraint—described by the straight budget line

To make the graphical depiction possible, we abstract from the many goods available in the real world and assume instead that only two goods are available. The results for this two-good world generally hold when the model is extended to many goods. Let one of these two goods represent a composite of other goods, and call this good Other Goods, or *OG*. Assume that the health care good is physician office visits consumed during a year, or VISITS. The consumer's name is Ellen Anderson.

[1]Problems may occur in describing a relationship where the provider, acting as an agent for the patient, helps to determine the amount of care. This is known as supplier-induced demand, and it is explained in Chapter 15.

The Consumer's Equilibrium

Figure 9-2 depicts these elements of the choice problem. The indifference curves labeled U_1, U_2, and U_3 represent some of Ellen's indifference curves (not all are depicted), and together the indifference curves describe her preferences. The indifference curve U_1, for example, represents all points—that is, bundles of OG and VISITS—that provide her with utility level U_1. Utility is an index of preferences that can most easily be understood as a measure of satisfaction. Because OG and VISITS are both goods to the consumer, it follows that indifference curve U_2 is preferred to U_1 and so on; that is, "higher" indifference curves are preferred.

Let Ellen's budget be Y dollars for the period. If the price of other goods, OG, is P_{OG} and the price of VISITS is P_V, then the sum of her expenditures, $P_{OG} \times OG$ plus $P_V \times$ VISITS, cannot exceed her income, Y. To spend all her income means to be on the budget line, which is given by the equation:

$$Y = P_{OG} \times OG + P_V \times \text{VISITS}$$

Point M represents the amount of other goods consumed if no visits occur. Point N represents the amount of visits if no other goods are purchased. The budget line is shown as line MN in Figure 9-2, and its slope will be given by $-P_V/P_{OG}$, which is the negative of the ratio of prices.

The consumer equilibrium is shown as point E in Figure 9-2, a point of tangency between the highest indifference curve attainable, U_2, and the budget line. In contrast, all points on indifference curve U_3 are unattainable, and points on U_1 are not chosen because the consumer can afford points she prefers to these. The equilibrium point E is a point of tangency, meaning that the slope of the indifference curve equals the slope of the budget line at this point.

The slope of the indifference curve is called the marginal rate of substitution (MRS). It tells the rate at which Ellen is willing to trade other goods for physician visits. Recall that the slope of the budget line is the negative of the ratio of prices. This is the rate at which she is able to trade other goods for physician visits at current market prices. An equilibrium is reached only if the rate at which she is willing to

FIGURE 9-2 Consumer Equilibrium Analysis

U_3 provides a higher level of utility than does U_2, which provides a higher level than U_1

Consumer optimizes at point E

trade the two goods, the MRS, is equal to the rate at which she is able to trade the two goods, $-P_V/P_{OG}$. This will have the result that in equilibrium, a dollar's worth of *OG* will yield the same extra utility as a dollar's worth of VISITS.

Demand Shifters

Ellen's response to price changes can be determined by examining the new equilibria that would occur as the price of *V* varies. Figure 9-3 shows the effects of changes in prices at constant income *Y*, dropping from the highest price, P_V^1, to a lower price, P_V^2, to the lowest price, P_V^3.

At the highest price, P_V^1, income *Y* buys V_1 visits at equilibrium point E_1. At the lower price, P_V^2, Ellen chooses equilibrium point E_2 (with V_2 visits), and at the lowest price, P_V^3, Ellen chooses equilibrium point E_3 (with V_3 visits). The number of visits, *V*, increases because visits have become less expensive relative to other goods.

Figure 9-4 plots a demand curve relating the price of visits to equilibrium quantity demanded. The data come from Figure 9-3. Point E_1 from Figure 9-3 corresponds to point *A* in Figure 9-4, and similarly points E_2 and E_3 correspond to points *B* and *C*. The demand curve summarizes Ellen's response to price changes, holding income and preferences constant.

The responsiveness of the consumer's demand to price is measured by the price elasticity. Price elasticity, E_p, is the ratio of the percentage change in quantity demanded to the percentage change in price. Algebraically, it is:

$$\text{Elasticity} = E_p = \frac{(\Delta Q/Q)}{(\Delta P/P)} \tag{9.1}$$

FIGURE 9-3 Change in Number of Visits as Visit Price and/or Income Changes

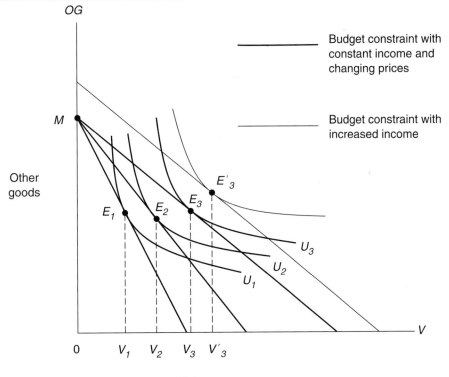

FIGURE 9-4 Demand Curve Derived from Figure 9-3

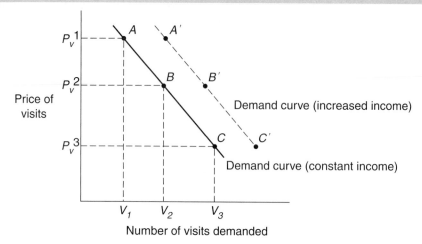

Here, the numerator is the change in quantity divided by the initial quantity level; that is, the numerator is the percentage change in quantity. Because the demand curve is downward sloping, the percentage change in quantity (the numerator) will always be negative in response to an increase in price. Likewise, the denominator is the percentage change in price. The higher the elasticity is in absolute value (the farther away from 0), the more responsive the consumer is to price. Note that equation (9.1) also can be written as:

$$\text{Elasticity} = E_p = \left(\frac{\Delta Q}{\Delta P}\right)\left(\frac{P}{Q}\right)$$

A similar analysis develops the consumer's response to changes in income. Returning to Figure 9-3, recall that point E_3 is determined by income, preferences, and price, P_V^3. Suppose that Ellen's income now increases. Because the relative prices are not changed by the income increase, the slope of the budget line is not changed, but Ellen can now buy more of both visits and other goods. Her new equilibrium point is E_3'. This is translated in Figure 9-4 to point C'. We can similarly draw points A' and B' on Figure 9-4 to indicate the impacts of an income change and prices, P_V^1 (new point A') and P_V^2 (new point B').

The responsiveness of demand to changes in income is measured by the income elasticity. Income elasticity, E_Y, is the percentage change in quantity demanded divided by the percentage change in income:

$$\text{Income elasticity} = E_Y = (\Delta Q / Q)/(\Delta Y / Y), \text{ or}$$

$$E_Y = \frac{\Delta Q}{\Delta Y}\left(\frac{Y}{Q}\right) \tag{9.2}$$

Finally, although two-dimensional indifference curves are not well suited to the handling of larger numbers of substitute and complement goods, the effects of changes in the prices of other goods can be analyzed. One would expect that increases in the prices of substitutes to physician visits (hospital outpatient services, visits to other providers) would increase the demand for office visits. In other words, an increase in the price of a substitute will shift the demand curve to the right in Figure 9-4. Increases in the prices of complements (diagnostic services) would reduce demand for office visits.

FIGURE 9-5 Changed Preferences Due to Illness

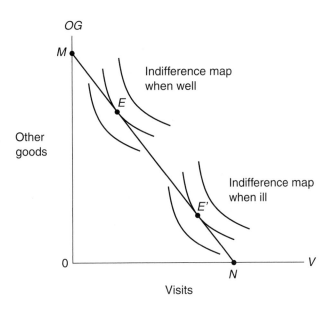

Health Status and Demand

Figure 9-5 illustrates how differences in patient health status can be handled. Suppose that Ellen is viewed in two different time periods in which her situation is the same in all economic respects except her health status. In Period 1 (equilibrium point E), she is fairly healthy. In Period 2, her overall health status is lower because she is ill. The change in health status will affect Ellen's preferences (often referred to as tastes) over VISITS and OG as reflected by different sets of indifference curves and changed levels of physician care, here point E'.

Note that although Ellen consumes more visits in Figure 9-5 when she is ill, in both cases she has the same MRS of visits for other goods at the equilibrium. Indeed, as long as the prices of the two goods do not change, all consumers in equilibrium will adjust to the prices until all consumers have the same MRS.

The analysis thus far suggests that price, income level, tastes, health status, and other circumstances influence the consumption of physician services. Other considerations, the roles of insurance and of time, cannot be overlooked.

Two Additional Demand Shifters—Time and Coinsurance

Two demand-shifting variables "look" like changes in the price: time price and coinsurance. First, Ellen's time price, the value of the time she must give up for a physician visit, can represent a significant portion of her full price. Second, insurance causes Ellen's effective price, the price paid "out-of-pocket," to be reduced below the market price.

The Role of Time

Recall from Chapter 7 that time is an important element in the demand for health. The consumption of health care services requires considerable time for some services and procedures. Economic observation suggests that people value their time. Many turn down additional work, even at increased wages. Still others decline to drive across

town to save $5 or $10 on an item, even though the cost of driving is far less than the $5 or $10. These choices probably occurred because the additional time spent wasn't worth it to the consumer.

Given the opportunity cost of time, a focus on the money costs of health care ignores a substantial portion of the economic costs. The discrepancy between the total economic costs and the money costs will be especially large for low-priced services, for services where patient copayments are small, and for patients with high opportunity costs of time.

As an example of time cost effects, suppose that Ellen must go to the doctor for a 10-minute visit. It will take her 15 minutes to travel each way (30 minutes in all), 20 minutes to wait in the office, and 10 minutes with the doctor. Suppose further that the money cost of the visit is $25, and that she values her time at $10 per hour. Traveling and parking cost $5 total. The full price of each visit is then $40:

- One hour of time valued at $10
- One visit priced at $25
- Travel and parking costs at $5

Figure 9-6 illustrates that Ellen demands six visits when her full price is $40. A money price increase of $5 causes the new full price to be $45, at which she demands five visits. Restating the price elasticity formula from equation (9.1), we find that the elasticity with respect to the full price is

$$E_p = \frac{(\Delta Q / Q)}{(\Delta P / P)} = \frac{(-1/5.5)}{(+5/42.5)} = -1.545$$

As appropriate, we use "arc elasticity" to evaluate the price at the midpoint (42.5) between the beginning (40) and the ending (45) price, and similarly for quantity.

Here, P represents the full price; that is, $P = P_M + P_T$. The full price is the sum of money price and time price. In contrast, the money price elasticity in this case is:

$$E_{pM} = \frac{(\Delta Q / Q)}{(\Delta P / P)} = \frac{(-1/5.5)}{(+5/27.5)} = -1.000$$

FIGURE 9-6 Demand and Time Price for Physician Visits

In general, the money price elasticity is smaller than the full price elasticity by the same proportion as the money price is smaller than the full price. To make sense of this, try comparing the ratio:

$$P_M \div (P_M + P_T) = 27.5 \div 42.5 = 0.647$$

to the ratio:

$$E_{pM} \div E_P = -1.000 \div (-1.545) = 0.647$$

How might this apply? Assuming that the poor have a lower opportunity cost of time than the well-to-do, one would predict that they would more likely tolerate or endure long waiting times in clinics or physician offices. At the same time, even those poor whose physician fees are subsidized (e.g., by Medicaid) must pay their time price. Wishing to increase physician visits among the poor, we might choose to reduce the time price by building nearby clinics and expanding outreach programs, a strategy that has been developed in many localities.

In practice, does time price affect demand? In pioneering work on time price, Acton (1975, 1976) examines the effects of travel times, waiting times, and other variables on quantity demanded of outpatient visits and physician care. Table 9-1 reports his elasticity estimates. For example, outpatient care, T_{Out}, is the own-time price, and T_{Phys} refers to the other good (cross-time price). The own-time price elasticity for outpatient visits, –0.958, nearly reaches unity, and the own-time price elasticity for physician visits, though small, also shows the importance of time. The positive cross-elasticities suggest that outpatient and physician visits are substitutes.

Subsequent work usually supports an important role for time. Coffey (1983) finds time price also relevant to the decision to seek care initially, as well as the quantity consumed, though her estimates are small (with the exception of public provider care). Mueller and Monheit (1988) find time-price elasticities for dental care to significantly affect the quantity of dental care consumed. Likewise, the National Health Service in the United Kingdom, which has eliminated most price constraints on the use of health care resources, finds the remaining waiting time price to be an important rationing factor (Blundell and Windmeijer, 2000). Does time-price affect health care demand? Yes. It makes sense in theory, and it matters in practice.

The Role of Coinsurance

Building on our study of insurance in Chapter 8, we see coinsurance as a demand shifter that works by modifying the effective price. When a third party, such as an insurance company, pays a portion of the hospital bill, the remaining portion paid by the consumer is called coinsurance rate r. Thus, more insurance means a lower r.

Effects of Reduced Coinsurance on the Individual Consumer

Suppose Ellen has no health insurance and pays all her health care bills out of pocket. Figure 9-7 shows Ellen's demand for health care as D_0. Because she is uninsured, the market price also is always Ellen's effective (out-of-pocket) price. At a market price of P_1, her quantity demanded is Q_1. A simple thought experiment reveals the issue. Suppose Ellen is given a health insurance policy at no charge (that is, with no impact on the rest of her

TABLE 9-1 Acton's Time Valuation Equations

Dependent Variable	Outpatient Visits	Physician Visits
Elasticity with respect to T_{Out}	–0.958	0.640
Elasticity with respect to T_{Phys}	0.332	–0.252

disposable income) that pays 50 percent of each of her bills, giving her a coinsurance rate of $r = 0.5$. The market price, P_1, is no longer the effective price; the effective price becomes $0.5 \times P_1 = P_1'$. Using her demand curve, D_0, as our guide, we see her now demanding Q_1'. This develops a first principle—her quantity demanded under coinsurance can be found along the out-of-pocket demand curve, provided we identify and apply the effective price.

It is more useful to identify her demand curve with respect to the market price. Ellen acted as though her health care demand had shifted, and this "rotating shift" can be shown to be equivalent to the previous analysis. In Figure 9-7, let us reverse the question and ask: If Ellen demands Q_1' when she has 50 percent insurance coverage and faces an effective price of P_1', then what market price is she apparently willing to pay (part paid by her out-of-pocket and part paid by her through her insurance company)? The answer is P_1, and the resulting combination of quantity demanded and market price is Point E in Figure 9-7. By plotting such points (not forgetting the case where $P = P' = 0$), we trace the demand curve with respect to the market price, D_1. Ellen, by receiving the insurance, will act just like an uninsured Ellen whose health care demand curve rotated to the right, hinged at Point B.

The exercise makes two theoretical facts clearer: insurance will increase Ellen's demand for health care, and insurance will make Ellen's demand for health care less elastic. Suppose Ellen's coinsurance rate were zero, meaning she pays nothing for health care. Would her demand be even less elastic? Most health economists would predict that her demand curve would become vertical, hence perfectly inelastic. Since she pays nothing, her demand is totally unresponsive to money price.

Market Effects

The effect of a reduced coinsurance alone, for Ellen, is an increase in the quantity demanded. Ellen does not demand enough care to influence market prices. Individual consumers are price takers; their individual actions have no effect on the price so they face essentially a horizontal supply curve. Suppose, however, that the coinsurance rate changes for many consumers in the market. For the market as a whole, the relevant supply curve slopes upward, indicating that higher prices might be required to motivate producers to offer greater market quantities.

FIGURE 9-8 Market Impact of Coinsurance

D_0 = Market demand without insurance

D_1 = Market demand with coinsurance

Figure 9-8 shows an equilibrium of price and quantity with an upward-sloping supply curve. The original market equilibrium price is P_0 and the equilibrium utilization is V_0. In this case, if coinsurance rates are generally reduced, the increased market demand will raise market quantity demanded to V_1 and the market price to P_1. Total health care expenditures will rise from P_0V_0 to P_1V_1. Many economists feel that such effects are major reasons for the increases in health care costs in the United States.

Issues in Measuring Health Care Demand

With the current concern about health care expenditures, reliable estimates of demand elasticity become essential. Recall that elasticity measures the responsiveness of demand to a change in a related variable. Price elasticity helps determine the effects of health insurance practices and policies. The effect of public policies to improve the accessibility of health care will depend on the money and the time price elasticities.

Prices, incomes, time prices, and coinsurance rates do matter. Increased prices and coinsurance rates reduce demand for services. Raising income increases the demand for services. "Economic" factors are not consumers' only considerations, but they matter.

In this section, we focus on variables of interest to science and public policy. We examine how health care demand responds to money price, insurance coverage, and time price. In addition, we examine the effects on market demand of income and other variables. Each study attempts to apply econometrics to estimate a demand function statistically; all variables relevant to demand are considered simultaneously. For ease in exposition, we consider the important variables separately.

Reviewing the difficulties faced by researchers and the differences between studies can be helpful to understanding the results. In effect, we ask the question: Why do the reported elasticities vary so often from one study to another? In most cases, the differences arise because of the different choices the researcher made in the face of problems common to research in this field. We identify five issues.

Individual and Market Demand Functions

Our analysis so far has focused on the individual. It suggested the following type of demand function for physician visits, referred to as V:

$$V = f(P, r, t, P_0, Y, \text{HS}, \text{AGE}, \text{ED}, \ldots)$$

where P is price per visit, r is the patient's coinsurance rate, P_0 is the price of other goods, Y is a measure of income, t is a time price, HS is the patient's health status, and AGE and ED stand for variables such as age and education to reflect other need and taste factors. This functional notation shows that certain variables are likely to affect V, but it does not specify the relation exactly.[2]

Often, however, economists are interested in market demand functions. Care is needed to move from individual to market demand. Even the measure of utilization poses a challenge. For example, most studies will use the number of visits per person (rather than the total quantity of visits) as the dependent variable. They then attempt to control for the size of the market by considering total population. This leads to serious problems in the interpretation of results.

Measurement and Definitions

Unlike the carpenter's simpler problem of measuring the length of a wall, there are alternative definitions of health care quantities, as well as many alternative measuring tools. Investigators often measure the quantity of services in dollar expenditures. One problem is that expenditures reflect a complex combination of price of care, quantities of care, and qualities of care.

Alternative measures include quantity of visits, patient days, or cases treated, yet these do not necessarily measure the intensity of care. One person may spend five days in the hospital for observation; another may spend five days for brain surgery. Consequently, the literature contains a variety of measures and a variety of reported elasticities.

A related problem is to define the price of services. Because of the prevalence of health insurance, most patients do not pay the full price for their treatments. Moreover, the price per unit of service that they pay may be related to the *size* of the bill because of deductibles, coinsurance, or limits. A $50 treatment, for example, may cost $50 if it occurs before the deductible limit is reached, or $10 (assuming 20 percent coinsurance) if it occurs after the deductible limit has been reached. The statistical problems in this case are fairly complicated, but it should suffice here to note that the resulting price elasticities may vary.

Differences in the Study Populations

Different researchers, naturally, use different samples or populations. Elasticities will differ between populations and even within populations at different points in time. For example, many health economists believe that income elasticities for health care have become smaller over the years in the United States, presumably because of the effects of programs like Medicare and Medicaid.

Furthermore, it is possible, in theory, for Californians to have a different price elasticity for physician services than Minnesotans. People in one state may be older (for

[2]Econometricians often use the OLS method discussed in Chapter 3. In this case, the regression is:

$$V = b_0 + b_1 P + b_2 r + b_3 t + b_4 P_0 + b_5 Y + b_6 \text{HS} + b_7 \text{AGE} + b_8 \text{ED} + \varepsilon$$

with the variables defined as before, and ε is the error term.

example, Florida) or have better access to larger varieties of health providers. It is theo-retically possible that people will exhibit different price elasticities for dental care than for pediatric care. Thus, some variation in reported elasticities is inevitable even when one uses the "same" measures, definitions, and techniques.

Data Sources

Populations differ between studies, and the sources of data may differ in ways that result in different elasticity estimates. For example, a common source of health care data is the insurance claim. Claims data, however, are limited to services covered by insurance and used by the insured. Furthermore, claims data often lack detail on individuals' characteristics, such as education and income. In contrast, health interview survey data often incorporate personal data, but their accuracy depends on the recall ability of the people being interviewed.

Experimental and Nonexperimental Data

Much of health care demand research used nonexperimental data, and thus the researcher could not control the environment or assure that other extraneous variables were held constant. These data typically represent samples across individuals or markets—that is, a slice of experience. If the necessary assumptions hold, then available statistical techniques can provide valuable analytical insights.

A useful alternative involving the natural experiment is sometimes possible. A natural experiment, for example, may occur when a given area changes its health insurance plan (see Box 9-1, which looks at changes in rural Arkansas). The change enables one to observe differences in health care utilization before and after. We presume that only the policy changes; all other factors are held constant. Unfortunately, other demand-related factors often change also.

BOX 9-1

A Natural Experiment in the Mississippi Delta

New national legislation, and the local changes it brought, provided a natural experiment for researcher John Tilford and his colleagues (1999). They studied the response of previously uninsured school children in the Mississippi Delta region of Arkansas to the provision of health insurance. The straightforward "before-and-after" design is typical of research using natural experiments.

What would the children (or really their parents) do when they suddenly had coverage? Would we find "pent-up" demand, showing health expenditures greater than normal until old problems had been cared for and cured where possible? Or would we find lower than average use, showing perhaps that the same reasons their parents had chosen to remain uninsured were still in operation?

These researchers gathered four years of insurance claims data and analyzed the children's pattern of health care use. Contrary to the "pent-up" hypothesis, their health care use increased in the four years following the introduction of insurance; at the end of the study period, these children were consuming health care fairly typical of other insured children. This actual pattern suggested more that the children took some time to change old patterns of use or even nonuse of health care.

The authors warn that this local experiment may not be easily generalized to other areas across the country. It does, however, give us a clear incentive to look for this pattern of response by the newly insured elsewhere.

In a controlled experiment, subjects are randomly assigned to treatment and control groups to measure responses directly to changes in the levels of demand-related variables. Such experiments, however, are costly to perform and are not without their own difficulties.

Empirical Measurements of Demand Elasticities

Price Elasticities

The focus of health care demand studies is on price elasticity. Table 9-2 reports a selection of estimates by type of care. The dependent variable in each case is the quantity demanded. In some cases, it is a market aggregate, such as admissions per capita; in other cases, the unit of observation is the individual consumer. Most reported elasticities range between 0.0 and –1.0, indicating that consumers, while responsive to price, are not responsive to a substantial degree. Suppose that the price elasticity for physician services was between –0.08 and –0.20, and physicians raised their prices by 10 percent. This would reduce consumption by 0.8 to 2.0 percent.

A further distinction among studies should be made. The price elasticities reported in Table 9-2 measure the individual consumer's or the market's response to price changes. That is, they are not firm specific but represent the demand for the health care good or service in general.

TABLE 9-2 Price Elasticities from Selected Studies

Study	Dependent Variable	Price Elasticity
All Expenditures:		
Rosett and Huang (1973)	Expenditures for hospital and physician services	–0.35 to –1.5[a]
Manning et al. (1987)	All expenditures	–0.17 to –0.22
Physician Services:		
Fuchs and Kramer (1972)	Physician visits per capita	–0.15 to –0.20
Newhouse and Phelps (1976)	Physician office visits	–0.08
Cromwell and Mitchell (1986)	Surgical services	–0.14 to –0.18
Wedig (1988)		
Health perceived excellent/good	Physician visits	–0.35
Health perceived fair/poor	Physician visits	–0.16
Hospital Services:		
Feldstein (1971)	Hospital admissions per capita	–0.63
Newhouse and Phelps (1976)	Hospital length of stay	–0.06
Manning et al. (1987)	Hospital admissions	–0.14 to –0.17
Nursing Homes:		
Chiswick (1976)	Nursing home residents per elderly population	–0.69 to –2.40
Lamberton et al. (1986)	Nursing home patient days per capita elderly	–0.69 to –0.76

[a]Rosett and Huang report that price elasticity varies by level of coinsurance. Elasticities reported range from –0.35 for 20 percent coinsurance to –1.5 for 80 percent coinsurance. Wedig reported estimates based on the National Medical Care Utilization and Expenditure Survey (NMCUES) for 1980 and separated 5,322 observations on adults into subsamples by perceived health status.

TABLE 9-3 Firm-Specific Price Elasticities

Study	Dependent Variable	Price Elasticity
Physician Services:		
Lee and Hadley (1981)	Physician price	−2.8 to −5.1
McCarthy (1985)	Physician visits	−3.1 to −3.3
Hospital Services:		
Feldman and Dowd (1986)	Hospital patient days	−0.7 to −0.8
	Hospital admissions	−1.1
Gaynor and Voght (2003)	Hospital discharges	−4.9
Nursing Homes:		
Mukamel and Spector (2002)	Case-mix adjusted days	−3.5 to −3.9

The demand for physician care in general will be less elastic than the demand for the services of a particular physician. For example, suppose a medical symptom is worrisome, and the patient chooses to see a physician. The more worrisome the symptom, the less responsive he or she is likely to be to market price. Which physician to see is a completely different question. The consumer who knows the quality and price of each physician would choose the lowest-priced physician among those of equal quality. The point is that there are few substitutes for physician care, but there are many substitutes among individual physicians. Thus, firm (physician)-specific demand will be more price responsive than overall demand.

This is illustrated in Table 9-3, which reports studies of firm-specific demand elasticities. As we observe, these elasticities tend to be considerably higher in absolute value than most of the elasticities reported previously in Table 9-2.

The firm-specific elasticities have further significance. They indicate the degree of competition in the health services market. Under perfect competition, firm-specific elasticities will approach negative infinity. The reported physician care elasticities may be large enough that competition is a reasonable approximation. In contrast, the smaller estimates for hospitals suggest considerable market power.

Individual Income Elasticities

Economic theory suggests that increased income causes increased purchases for most goods. Most goods have positive income elasticities and are referred to as normal goods. Those with negative elasticities are referred to as inferior goods. Table 9-4 reports estimated income elasticities for a selection of studies by type of health care. In most cases, the magnitudes are small. This indicates that while health care is generally a normal good, the response is relatively small; that is, inelastic.

Income elasticities also help define when goods are necessities or luxuries. We call goods "necessities" when the income elasticity is between 0 and +1. When income elasticities exceed +1, goods are called "luxuries." From the properties of elasticities, a 1 percent rise in income increases the budget share devoted to a luxury and decreases the budget share devoted to a necessity. From Table 9-4, the results are not surprising; people commonly perceive health care to be a necessity.[3] Box 9-2 examines "concierge medicine" an explicitly luxury form of health service provision.

[3]Issues also arise regarding the appropriate definition of income, particularly with respect to short-term versus long-term (or permanent) income. Those interested should examine Goodman (1989).

TABLE 9-4 Income Elasticities from Selected Studies

Study	Dependent Variable	Income Elasticity
All Expenditures:		
Silver (1970)	Expenditures	1.2
Rosett and Huang (1973)	Expenditures	0.25 to 0.45
Hospital Services:		
Newhouse and Phelps (1976)	Admissions	0.02 to 0.04
Dental Services:		
Silver (1970)	Expenditures	2.40 to 3.20
Anderson and Benham (1970)	Expenditures	0.61 to 0.83
Physician Services:		
Silver (1970)	Expenditures	0.85
Anderson and Benham (1970)	Expenditures	0.22 to 0.41
Fuchs and Kramer (1972)	Visits per capita	0.20 to 0.57
Newhouse and Phelps (1976)	Visits	0.01 to 0.04
Nursing Homes:		
Chiswick (1976)	Residents per elderly population	0.60 to 0.90

BOX 9-2

Concierge Medicine

Patient preferences are nowhere more visible and controversial than in an arrangement known as concierge medicine. Some patients are willing to pay additional amounts ranging from $1,500 to $20,000 annually for very personalized attention and higher levels of service from their physicians. The concierge contract will often include longer office examinations, no waiting times, and other privileges. The *New York Times* estimated that about 250 physicians have established concierge practices, but that the number seems to be growing rapidly in some parts of the country. Critics call this type of practice elitist and caution that concierge medicine is completely unregulated.

SOURCE: Amy Zipkin, "The Concierge Doctor Is Available (at a Price)," *New York Times*, July 31, 2005 (www.nytimes.com/2005/07/31/business/your_money/31doctor).

Income Elasticities Across Countries

Given these findings, it may be surprising that studies of aggregate health expenditures across countries report substantially higher income elasticities. Often the magnitudes exceed unity. An early cross-national study was published by Newhouse (1977) who regressed per capita medical expenditures for 13 developed countries on a variable representing per capita income. From the estimated coefficient of this equation, he then calculated the implied income elasticity for various levels of income. The elasticity estimates ranged from 1.15 to 1.31. He concluded that despite within-country results showing health care to be a necessity, health care in fact is a luxury good.

Parkin and colleagues (1987) pointed out several potential weaknesses in most existing cross-national studies, but despite their objections, offered improved results

that tended to support the finding of cross-national income elasticities greater than 1.0.[4] Gerdtham et al. (1992) and Getzen and Poullier (1992) also lend support to the result.

Is it inconsistent that within-country health care income elasticities are small, while cross-national estimates exceed 1.0? Can health care be a necessity at the individual and market levels but a luxury at the country level? A hypothetical example illustrates that income elasticity results at the national aggregate level do not necessarily apply to individual or market level. Suppose that two countries, one rich and one poor, each provided free health care to their citizens irrespective of income. Then within-country income elasticities might be small if not zero. Yet the richer country might provide greater quantities, higher technology, and better qualities of health care to each of its citizens. Thus, the cross-country income elasticities could be high.

These and related ideas are more fully developed by Getzen (2000), who shows that the individual's response to more income is different than the nation's response to more income. He also notes that symptoms of illness and pain are often more important reasons we as individuals seek out the doctor, while the available health care resources and technologies at the national level often reflect the nation's economic well-being.

The results of this small but well-established line of research have been challenged by two Canadian researchers, Blomquist and Carter (1997). By studying a large set of countries over time, observing time patterns and country-specific effects, they tentatively concluded that health spending grows about 2 percent faster than income in a manner suggesting the role of technological progress. But what about the original research goal; are the income elasticities for health spending greater than 1.0? Of 18 countries studied, they find that 11 income elasticities were either less than 1.0 or so close to 1.0 that the null hypothesis (that the elasticities equaled 1.0) could not be ruled out. Whatever direction this line of research work takes in the future, researchers are gaining increasingly sophisticated understanding of the methods and challenges of performing cross-national studies.

Insurance Elasticities

Consumer responses to changes in insurance are important because insurance coverage has grown dramatically in the past 30 to 40 years and because we frequently must consider possible changes in social insurance. While the issue of insurance effects must be treated separately from price effects, they are closely intertwined with the issue of price elasticities.

Consider a health insurance policy where the consumer pays a fixed percentage of the bill—that is, a fixed coinsurance rate, r. In such a case, the net price that the consumer pays would be a simple multiple of the market price, P:

$$\text{Net price} = rP$$

When the market price increases by 1 percent, so does the net price; that is:

$$1.01 \times \text{Net price} = r(1.01P)$$

Under such an insurance plan, the coinsurance elasticity would be the same as the price elasticity.

However, most health insurance plans are not so simple. In practice, they include deductibles and maximum dollar expenditure (MDE) limits in addition to the coinsurance rate. The result is that the effective coinsurance rate depends in part on the size of the bill. In practice, price and coinsurance elasticities will differ somewhat.

[4]Three of these arguments are especially noteworthy. First, highly aggregated data such as national income or national health care expenditures do not necessarily imply individual behavior. Second, most studies use exchange rates to convert foreign country values to U.S. dollars, but exchange rates may not accurately reflect the purchasing power of the currency. Finally, the results are sensitive to the functional form (econometric method) used.

A further difficulty arises because most studies have been performed on nonexperimental data. One of the major concerns with nonexperimental data is that the groups compared are not always randomly selected. For example, suppose that a company allows its employees to enroll in either a high-coverage plan or a low-coverage plan. Some people may choose to work for the company because it offers the high-coverage insurance plan. Others who expect to use large (low) amounts of services will naturally enroll in the high- (low-) coverage plan. Still others, if sufficient insurance is not available from the company, will purchase more generous insurance privately. If the demand analysis proceeds by comparing these groups, the results may misstate the true effect of coinsurance. This is because the major decision was made in deciding which group to join. The behavior is known in economics as *adverse selection*.

The Rand Corporation, funded by the United States Public Health Service, mounted an experiment beginning in 1974. Households at six sites across the nation were randomly assigned to groups that had different levels of cost sharing, ranging from free care to care with 95 percent coinsurance and including a maximum dollar expenditure limit. The families were paid a lump-sum payment to be sure that no family was made worse off by the experiment. Because the assignment was random, adverse selection could be minimized, and the random assignment of coinsurance also allowed researchers to investigate the effects of coinsurance on expenditures.

They observed family health care use and expense experience over a period that varied from three to five years for various experimental groups. This intensive and expensive experiment improved our understanding of the response of health care consumers to economic incentives. Table 9-5 summarizes some of the key results of the Rand Health Insurance Experiment.

We note that coinsurance has a considerable effect on the level of average medical expenditures. From an extreme of a 95 percent coinsurance to the opposite extreme of free care, or zero coinsurance, the average family's medical expenses increase by nearly 50 percent, from $679 to $982. Even hospitalization rates are responsive, increasing from 7.9 percent of those in the 95 percent coinsurance group to 10.3 percent in the free care group, representing an increase of about 30 percent. We must conclude from the Rand experimental data and analysis that both price and insurance do matter considerably.

TABLE 9-5 A Summary of the Effects of Coinsurance on Mean Annual Use of Medical Services in the Rand Health Insurance Experiment

Plan	*Likelihood of Any Use (%)*	*One or More Admissions (%)*	*Total Expenses (1991 $)*
Free	86.8	10.3	982
	(0.8)	(0.5)	(50.7)
Family Pay			
25 Percent	78.8	8.4	831
	(1.4)	(0.6)	(69.2)
50 Percent	77.2	7.2	884
	(2.3)	(0.8)	(189.1)
95 Percent	67.7	7.9	679
	(1.8)	(0.6)	(58.7)
Individual Deductible	72.3	9.6	797
	(1.5)	(0.6)	(60.3)

Source: Reprinted by permission of the publisher from *Free for All?: Lessons from the RAND Health Insurance Experiment* by Joseph P. Newhouse, Cambridge, MA: Harvard University Press, Copyright © 1993 by the RAND Corporation.

Newhouse and colleagues (1993) conclude:

> All types of service—physician visits, hospital admission, prescriptions, dental visits, and mental health service use—fell with cost sharing. There were no striking differences among these services in how their use responded to plan. Another partial exception was demand for mental health services—which, the results indicate, would have been more responsive than other services to cost sharing had there been no cap on out-of-pocket expenditure. (pp. 338–339)

The Rand study, which has proved very valuable, was not designed to track the effects of insurance on the elderly. Other researchers, however, find that the elderly consume more health care when they are more fully insured. The elderly, who are automatically eligible for Medicare hospital insurance, may opt for additional coverage via Medicare Part B or via private insurance. A confounding factor, one which the randomized experimental approach of the Rand study eliminates, is the possibility that those who buy the extra insurance might be those who expect to be more ill, another form of adverse selection. Hurd and McGarry (1997) separated out this confounding issue, and they conclude that the insurance effect among the elderly is due primarily to the way in which insurance changes the economic incentives that accompany illness rather than adverse selection.

Impacts of Insurance on Aggregate Expenditures

Rand researchers, estimating coinsurance and income elasticities to be approximately 0.2, sought to calculate the demand-related portion of the sevenfold post-World War II real increase in U.S. health expenditures due to the spread of health insurance. The answer was "not much"—only 10 percent of the increase. All else being equal, the spread of health insurance would have increased health expenditures by 70 percentage points, rather than the 700 percent measured.

Income tripled over the period. Positing an income elasticity of 1.0, this would have increased expenditures by only 60 percentage points. The income elasticity estimate was, in fact, 0.2, according to Rand, indicating that only $0.6 = 3 \times 0.2$, or 60 percentage points of the 700 percent increase, could be explained by increased income. Adding 60 percent to the 70 percent attributed to insurance still yields only a 130 percentage point increase, or less than one-fifth of the entire increase of 700 percent.

Other Variables Affecting Demand

The studies we have reviewed often incorporate many other variables of interest in the demand function estimates, and considerable information relevant to policy issues has been obtained.

Ethnicity and Gender

Many studies of demand examine the influence of race, and find that blacks tend to consume less medical care than the other large, self-identified ethnic groups when other factors are held constant.[5] Although the majority of studies of ethnic differences in health care have focused on the experience of blacks and Hispanics, other ethnic

[5]For blacks, see Anderson and Benham (1970) and Newhouse and Phelps (1976). For females, see Newhouse and Phelps (1976), Silver (1970), and Scheffler (1984). Scheffler found that although females have increased probabilities of entering a hospital, mean hospital expenditures thereafter tend to be lower.

differences also have been noted, often when a given disease, for example Tay-Sachs disease, appears predominantly within one group—in this case, Jews of Eastern European origin.

Part of the differences may be of social origin; for example, blacks and other ethnic groups may be reluctant to seek care or may be treated differently by white physicians. However, ethnic differences, more broadly understood, may help explain geographic patterns across the United States. For example, westerners tend to rely less on hospitals and physicians, while residents of the more snowbound north central states rely more heavily on nursing home care for the elderly than other areas on a per capita basis.

Females differ from males most clearly in their time pattern of medical care usage. During childbearing years, women are relatively heavy users of health care, but women are healthier in the long run and they predominate in the numbers of the elderly. Thus, they are predominant among physicians' older patients. Though a great deal of public attention and concern in the past decade has turned to the science of treating diseases prominent among women, death rates for cancers are often as high or higher among men as among women. For example, mortality rates from prostate do not differ much from mortality rates from breast cancer. Myocardial infarction (heart attack) is a notorious killer of men, though women's rates have been increasing.

Thus, researchers will continue to study the differences in medical demand between the sexes, and the many differences among ethnic and cultural groups. These include not just differences among skin color groups but among the many subcultures and local cultures within these larger groups. These differences may offer the explanation for demand variations not accounted for by the usual demand variables and may yet help identify and explain many health demand questions that have remained unanswered.

Variations in sexual behavior have proved tremendously important in explaining variations in the pattern of infections with HIV and mortality due to AIDS. Homosexuals in the United States were long the major group at risk and most prominent among deaths with intravenous drug users are second in numbers. Though much public effort was addressed to the prevention of a feared epidemic among heterosexuals, especially youth, the pattern has remained steady. In contrast, the world's attention is turned more toward Africa, where transmission of the disease is primarily heterosexual, and the size of the epidemic forms a crisis for world public health efforts.

Urban Versus Rural

Studies sometimes find differences in health care usage due to rural status. If rural residents use less care, the reasons why are not necessarily clear. Rural dwellers may differ culturally, and some analysts argue that this factor is more important to one's perception of life than ethnicity is. Whether born to rural life or to have adopted it, it may become linked to tastes, health status, and relative reluctance to seek out a physician. The lesser health demand by westerners, already identified previously, could be understood in this view as an artifact of the predominance of rural areas in the region.

The contrasting argument is made that it is the greater travel distances required to obtain health care in rural areas rather than rural culture or tastes that account for the demand patterns. Thus, studies of geographical patterns of health care demand must take special care to measure the full price of physician or hospital care, that is, to include the travel time price.

Education

Education is strongly associated with better health. If you are a college student, the odds are very good that you are healthier than your noncollege counterparts. As in the demand for health capital model, this may be because you are a more efficient producer

of health, you are less likely to smoke, and you are more likely to eat a healthful diet. Or it may be that you are the sort of person with a long-term goal, and to meet that goal you have identified the need to take proper care of yourself. For the researcher sorting out such questions, the complexity of the issue is multiplied by confounding factors, especially income. Educated people tend to earn more, a fact not lost on most college students. We then must determine whether education improves one's health, or whether the income it brings affords a healthier life.

Age, Health Status, and Uncertainty

Older people consume three to four times more health care than the younger population. Though the relationship is no surprise, Grossman's theory of this pattern makes the issue more intriguing to the research community. If we invest in our health each period and yet our health depreciates somewhat during each period, why do we necessarily buy greater quantities of health care as we get older? Very plausibly, as Grossman assumed, the depreciation rate gets larger as we age, thus greater inputs of our own time and health care are required to restore our health. This makes the correlation of health demand and age appear logical. Yet our own goals for our health may decline as we age, which, at some point, may work in the opposite direction.[6] Perhaps more interesting is the relationship of health status to the price elasticity of health care demand. Theory is not clear on this point, but it is plausible that sicker people will tend to be less sensitive to price.

Wedig (1988) finds that the price elasticity of the decision to seek health care tends to be lower in absolute value for those with poorer health status, regardless of which measure is used to record health status. However, no clear pattern over health status can be determined with respect to level of care—that is, the amount of health care consumed given that the consumer has chosen to seek health care.

Finally, uncertainty will affect health care demand. When a consumer, worried about a future health risk, seeks advice or preventive treatment, we call this a precautionary demand (Picone, Uribe, and Wilson, 1998). Elderly patients, for example, may smooth their utility over time by spending now to avoid sharp drops in well-being and mobility in the future. Some empirical evidence suggests that older people have somewhat less tolerance for risk and that one's degree of risk tolerance influences one's decision whether to buy health insurance.

Conclusions

The importance of price and income for many consumers has been limited by the spread of managed care, a development that has led to a greater research focus on quality and other health care issues. Nevertheless, demand theory continues to be relevant. The substantial increases in out-of-pocket costs for prescription products experienced by many patients have affected utilization of drugs in the expected direction (see Chapter 17 for specifics). Hospitals and other providers continue to compete for patients as well as for contracts with managed care organizations. The more recent estimates of price elasticities for hospitals and nursing homes shown in Table 9-3 indicate that the demand facing both types of providers is even more sensitive to price than prior studies have shown. Time and distance can also be important as theory suggests. In a dramatic demonstration, Currie and Reagan (2005) found that each additional mile to the nearest hospital reduces the probability that central-city black children will

[6]See, for example, Andersen and Benham (1970), and Cromwell and Mitchell (1986).

have a check-up by 3 percentage points, regardless of whether they are privately or publicly insured.

A good understanding of the standard theory of demand is also important because it serves as the rationale for market-based, consumer-driven approaches to health care delivery. Over 3 million households were enrolled in consumer-driven health plans (CDHPs) in 2005, and their numbers were increasing rapidly. Described more fully in Chapter 19, the consumer-driven strategy typically involves high-deductible catastrophic insurance and other features, including a health savings account, that enable consumers to take greater control over their spending decisions. By empowering consumers, supporters of this strategy envision a more competitive health care system in which cost-conscious patients restrain the power of providers to reduce questionable services and to keep fees low. Evidence on the impact of CDHPs at this time is largely anecdotal, but their growth will undoubtedly create new opportunities for more current applications of demand theory.

SUMMARY

1. The theory of rational choice over health care and other goods helps explain our decisions because many health care options are not urgent, leaving room for thoughtful consideration or at least some planning.
2. In addition, physicians serve as the patient-consumer's agents and can make rational choices even in urgent situations.
3. Depicting the consumer's choice requires knowing preferences, as described by a set of indifference curves, and resource constraints, described by the budget line indicating income and market prices.
4. Consumer equilibrium occurs only if the rate at which they are willing to trade two goods, or MRS, equals the price ratio at which they are able to trade the two goods. In equilibrium, a dollar buys the same marginal utility from all goods.
5. Price elasticity, E_p, is the ratio of the percent change in quantity demanded to the percent change in price. Income elasticity, E_Y, is the percent change in quantity demanded divided by the percent change in income.
6. The time spent acquiring services constitutes a substantial portion of the economic costs. The discrepancy between the total economic prices (including time) and the money prices will be especially large for low-priced services, services with small patient copayments, and for patients with high time costs.
7. Insurance plays a major role in health services demand. Many health care purchases are at least partially covered by health insurance so that a portion is paid for by someone other than the consumer.
8. The impact of coinsurance depends critically on the price elasticity of demand for health care. If consumers do not respond to price changes in the absence of insurance, changes in coinsurance will have no impact on quantity of services demanded.
9. Coinsurance makes the demand curve for health services less responsive (less elastic) with respect to the price.
10. Quantity of services is often measured by dollar expenditures. One problem is that expenditures reflect a combination of price of care, quantity of care, and quality of care. Alternatively, quantity may be measured in numbers of visits, patient days, or cases treated.
11. It is often difficult to define prices of services since insured patients usually do not pay the full price. Moreover, the net price paid by consumers is influenced by deductibles, coinsurance, or other limits.
12. Most reported price elasticities indicate that consumers respond to price changes. However, these elasticities (between 0.0 and −1.0) are not large compared to many other goods and services.
13. In most cases, income elasticities are low. While health care is a normal good, since its demand increases with income, the response is relatively small. However at aggregate levels, across countries income elasticities often exceed +1.0.

14. Coinsurance has a considerable effect on the level of average medical expenditures. Both price and insurance matter.
15. Income and insurance changes since World War II may explain approximately 130 percentage points of the 700 percent increase in U.S. health expenditures, through increased demand for services. Researchers attribute the remainder to increased costs brought on by technological change.

DISCUSSION QUESTIONS

1. Discuss how time costs affect health care demand, and speculate on this and possible other reasons for the lower observed per capita demand for health care in the western United States.
2. Define *price elasticity of demand*. How does an increase in the coinsurance rate affect the consumer's price elasticity?
3. Why are firm-specific demand price elasticities higher than elasticities for demand in general? Why does a high elasticity indicate a very competitive market?
4. For the following pairs of services, which of the two services would you expect to be more income elastic? More price elastic?
 a. Surgical services versus allergist services
 b. Heart surgery versus cosmetic surgery
5. It has been discovered that countries with higher per capita incomes spend more than proportionally as much on health care. What does this imply about the cross-national income elasticities? Why might this occur, even though individual income elasticities seem to be quite low?
6. The frequencies of health care visits are often used to measure service demand. Many, however, criticize the use of this variable. What are some pros and cons of the use of visits?
7. We often speak of how price rations goods. What are other rationing measures in clinics in which free care is provided?
8. Explain or show why the impact of changes in coinsurance rates on demand depends on the elasticity of demand. What sorts of health care goods or services will be responsive to changes in coinsurance rates? What sorts will tend to be relatively less responsive?
9. A profit-maximizing firm finding that its demand is inelastic will necessarily find it profitable to increase its price; therefore, its equilibrium price elasticity will necessarily be greater than 1.0 in absolute value. Are the market- and firm-specific elasticity data reported here consistent with this theory?
10. The consumer's indifference curves in Figure 9-2 indicate substitutability between visits and other goods. What will the indifference curves look like if the consumer perceives no substitutability? What will happen to the elasticity of demand in this case?

EXERCISES

1. Suppose that Martha's income is $40,000 per year. She can spend it on health care visits, which cost $80 per visit, or on groceries (standing for all other goods), which cost $100 per bag of groceries. Draw Martha's budget constraint. Using indifference curves, show Martha's optimum if she buys 300 bags of groceries per year.
2. Suppose that Martha's income rises to $42,000 per year, and that she increases her consumption of health care visits by five visits. Using the graphs for exercise 1, draw the new equilibrium. What is her income elasticity of demand for health care visits?
3. Consider the following information on Alfred's demand for visits per year to his health clinic, if his health insurance does not cover (100 percent coinsurance) clinic visits.
 a. Alfred has been paying $30 per visit. How many visits does he make per year? Draw his demand curve.
 b. What happens to his demand curve if the insurance company institutes a 40 percent coinsurance feature (Alfred pays 40 percent of the price of each visit)? What is his new equilibrium demand?

P	Q
5	9
10	9
15	9
20	8
25	7
30	6
35	5
40	4

4. Suppose that a consumer makes V_0 physician visits each year at a price of P_0. If the price elasticity is –0.4, what will happen to the number of visits if the price increases by 10 percent? What will happen to total physician expenditures? Why?

5. If the price elasticity of demand is –0.5 and the income elasticity is +0.3, then what will be the effect of a simultaneous 10 percent increase in price and a 10 percent increase in income on health expenditures?

6. Draw a diagram for hospital care that reflects the income-elasticity estimates found empirically. As income increases, what happens to the proportion of income spent on hospital care?

7. Would the opportunity cost of waiting time be higher for higher-income people or lower-income people? Given your answer, for which income group would money price tend to be a smaller portion of the full price?

8. Explain how the demand for health insurance is related to the demand for health care. Would the demand for health care then depend also on whether the person paid for the insurance or alternatively was provided the insurance at a subsidized cost?

CHAPTER

Asymmetric Information and Agency

Overview of Information Issues

Asymmetric Information

Application of the Lemons Principle: Health Insurance

The Agency Relationship

Consumer Information, Prices, and Quality

Conclusions

The traditional theory of demand, as we have seen, begins with the assumption that individuals are fully informed about prices, quantities, and the relationships of medical care and other inputs to their levels of health. We examined decision making within a model that assumed perfect information. Depending upon the purpose of the model, such an assumption may be justified even if it is not realistic. However, a more complete understanding of the health economy requires particular insight into the effects of various informational problems in health care markets.[1]

Though imperfect information has long been regarded as a feature of the health economy, insight into its specific effects was not well understood until the economics of information emerged as a distinct specialty. The development of tools to study asymmetric information and agency relationships has greatly enhanced the field of health economics. Asymmetric information encompasses situations where buyers and sellers have different levels of information; agency concerns situations where, for lack of information, buyers or sellers rely on other parties to help make decisions.

[1]The emergence of health economics as a distinct field is often traced to Kenneth J. Arrow's (1963) seminal article, "Uncertainty and the Welfare Economics of Medical Care." Arrow emphasized the role of imperfect information and uncertainty, especially the features of health care markets due to the "imperfect market-ability of information." McGuire (2000) provides a comprehensive review of the relevant literature. See also a special issue of the *Journal of Health Politics, Policy and Law* (October 2001) that examines Arrow's contribution within a contemporary context. In that issue, Robinson (2001) downplays often-repeated claims that asymmetric and imperfect information are responsible for the unique organization and institutional features of health care markets.

Overview of Information Issues

The markets for many health care services and for insurance in particular are marked by significant degrees of asymmetric information and agency relationships. For example, adverse selection, a phenomenon in which insurance attracts patients who are likely to use services at a higher than average rate, results from asymmetric information. Most analysts agree that potential beneficiaries have better information than the insurer about their health status and their expected demand for health care. As a result, premiums for higher-risk patients will be underpriced, encouraging such patients to overinsure, whereas the opposite holds true for lower-risk patients. Adverse selection reduces the efficiency of health insurance markets while redistributing income from the healthy to poorer risks.

Information and agency problems account for many other important characteristics of health care markets. The possible preference for health care delivery by nonprofit hospitals and nursing homes (Chapter 13) has been attributed to patients' lack of information and inability to discern quality. For some patients, a nonprofit status might be taken as reassurance of higher quality because decisions are made independent of a profit motive. Lack of quality information also is an important motive for licensure and other regulatory measures.

The present chapter has three goals. First, we introduce information asymmetry, describe its relative prevalence, and determine its consequences, especially for insurance markets. It will quickly become clear that adverse selection in insurance is only one consequence of asymmetric information.

Asymmetric information, as when a patient is less well-informed about appropriate treatments than the attending physician, typically leads to an agency relationship between the patient and provider. The second goal of this chapter is to describe the agency relationship and examine some of the problems arising in health care markets from imperfect agency. The special and controversial case of supplier-induced demand (SID) is revealed as an assymetric information/agency problem in Chapter 15.

Our final goal is to examine the effects of imperfect consumer information on the price and quality of health care services. Despite consumers' informational disadvantages, they often influence markets in predictable ways. Here and throughout the chapter, we identify arrangements that commonly evolve to reduce the disadvantages for the less well-informed parties. Thus, the ultimate consequences of asymmetric information and imperfect agency on the efficient functioning of markets are often not as severe as one might initially assume.

Asymmetric Information

Basic microeconomic theory usually includes an assumption that the market being analyzed exhibits perfect information. Under conditions of perfect information, all consumers and producers have complete information on all prices, as well as the quality of any good or service available in the market. Consumers also will be as well informed about the product as the seller.

Although information is never perfect in the real world, perfect information serves as a useful starting point because the properties and predictions of the standard models relying on this assumption are so well understood. Also, as students of economics are repeatedly taught, the relevant issue is whether the predictions derived from standard models apply to real-world markets. In many cases, the predictions derived from these models hold up reasonably well.

Cases do arise, however, where imperfect information does seem to matter. During the past four decades, economists have developed new insights into the effects of imperfect and asymmetric information. This section examines some of that work, including contributions by health economists to the specific problems of the health sector.

On the Extent of Information Problems in the Health Sector

Before investigating several contributions to the economic theory of information, we begin by asking how prevalent information problems are in the health sector. It is obvious not only that information is imperfect in health care markets, but also that information is asymmetric. Levels of information will differ among participants, such as between physicians and patients in many transactions. Often the patient is poorly informed compared to the provider about his or her condition, the treatment available, expected outcomes, and prices charged by other providers. Furthermore, we presume that the information problems that exist in the health sector are prominent enough to require the special analysis of the economics of information.

Although we can agree that information problems arise in health care markets, we must avoid the temptation to overemphasize this point. To say that information problems exist in the health sector does not mean that these problems are necessarily worse than in any other market. Markets for insurance, other professional services, automobile and appliance repairs, and many other goods and services also exhibit asymmetries. We should not necessarily conclude that information asymmetries in health care markets make it impossible for corrective institutions, practices, or products to evolve; nor do they necessarily preclude the possibility of competition.

Why? Pauly (1978) noted that half or more of physician visits customarily are made for services, such as general checkups or chronic care, for which the patient has some if not considerable experience. From data on the portion of medical expenditures attributable to ambulatory physician care, we can estimate that if half of this care is reasonably well-informed, then about 8 percent of total medical care is informed. Reasoning in this manner about all sorts of medical care and products, Pauly concluded that plausibly "one-fourth or more of total personal health-care expenditures might be regarded as 'reasonably informed'" (p. 16). By adding nursing home services and chronic conditions, Pauly (1988a) subsequently argued that this ratio is about one-third.

Further, for several medical care issues, the provider shares in the information gap with the patient. As we will emphasize when describing the "small area variations" literature in Chapter 15, the provider often is uncertain if not uninformed about the outcomes of many medical procedures. In such cases, information asymmetry does not necessarily arise even though it may be correct that the patient is ill-informed.

Finally, economic analysts of information asymmetry problems have been able to show that markets may perform well in the face of some degree of information asymmetry provided a sufficient portion of the consumers are reasonably well-informed. Perhaps a majority of consumers who use personal computers are relatively poorly informed about their technical aspects and relative qualities and prices. However, a significant minority of consumers tends to be highly informed. In markets like this, the informed minority may be sufficient to provide the economic discipline it takes to make the market perform well so that the rest of us will find that the higher-priced computers also tend to be of higher quality.

We conclude this section by summarizing its main point. Certainly information gaps and asymmetries exist in the health sector. They are perhaps more serious for

health care than for other goods that are important in household budgets. This makes it useful for the student of health economics to investigate the theory of information asymmetries and its application to health care. However, one should not assert that information gaps preclude the possibility of having a high degree of competition. In particular, mechanisms to deal with information gaps should not be overlooked. These mechanisms include licensure, certification, accreditation, threat of malpractice suits, the physician-patient relationship, ethical constraints, and the presence of informed consumers.

Will a state of relative consumer ignorance preclude high levels of competition? Will health care markets be characterized by a high degree of price dispersion and the provision of unnecessary care or care that is not in the patient's best interests? Can some of the characteristics of health care markets and the evolution of their institutional arrangements be related to asymmetric information? The following sections address these and other questions by beginning with the pioneering work on asymmetric information.

Asymmetric Information in the Used-Car Market: The Lemons Principle

Nobel Laureate George Akerlof (1970) is often credited with introducing the idea of asymmetric information through an analysis of the used-car market. Though seemingly unrelated to health care, his classic article is worth studying for two reasons. First, it tells us much about adverse selection and the potential unraveling of health insurance markets. Adverse selection provides a key to our understanding of some major contemporary issues, such as the reasons that some may remain uninsured, or the performance of health maintenance organizations or other delivery systems. Second, Akerlof's example leads right into the issue of agency.

In Akerlof's example, used cars available for sale vary in quality, from those cars that are still in mint condition to some that are complete lemons. Information asymmetry arises if, as is plausible, the sellers know better the true quality of their cars than do the potential buyers. Akerlof devised an example that showed that cases may arise where such information asymmetry causes the market for used cars to perform poorly or even to disappear entirely.

To illustrate the nature of the used-car example, consider a somewhat simpler example, but one that retains the essential features. Suppose that nine used cars are to be sold (potentially) that vary in quality from 0, meaning a lemon, to a high of 2, meaning a mint-condition used car, a "cream puff". In fact, suppose that the nine cars have respectively quality levels (Q) given by the cardinally measured index values of $0, \frac{1}{4}, \frac{1}{2}, \frac{3}{4}, 1, 1\frac{1}{4}, 1\frac{1}{2}, 1\frac{3}{4}$, and 2. Under a cardinal index, a car with a value of 1 has twice the quality of a car with an index of $\frac{1}{2}$. The distribution of these cars is shown in Figure 10-1, where the horizontal axis shows the quality level and the vertical axis shows the uniform probability, in this case, of randomly picking a car of each given quality.

Suppose further that the owner of a car knows its quality level exactly but that the potential buyers know only the distribution of quality. It is known that the owners have a reserve value on their cars, so that reserve value to the seller = $1,000 × Q$. That is, the owners would sell their cars only if they could get at least $1,000 for every unit of quality that the car has. On the other hand, the nonowners are more eager for used cars and value them so that the value to nonowners = $1,500 × Q$. To make this experiment a complete market, suppose that an auctioneer is hired to call out market prices; sales take place when the auctioneer finds a price that successfully equates quantity demanded with quantity supplied.

FIGURE 10-1 The Availability of Products of Different Quality (Uniform Probability of Picking Each Car)

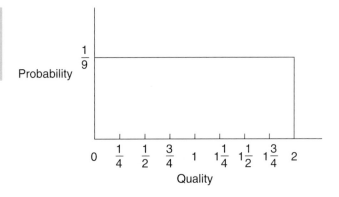

Does a Market Exist?

Consider what would happen under asymmetric information. Suppose the auctioneer calls out an initial price of $2,000 per car. At this price, all owners know it is worthwhile to sell their cars, so all nine cars will be supplied. However, nonowners, knowing only the distribution of quality but not the quality of each individual car, will make a best guess that a given car is of average quality; that, is $Q = 1$. They would not buy any cars at a price of $2,000 because they are willing to pay only $1,500 per unit of quality. They guess that all cars have a quality of 1, for a product of $1,500 \times 1 = \$1,500$, which is less than the $2,000 asked. They would be willing to buy cars only if the price were less than or equal to $1,500.

So the auctioneer, perhaps trying to accommodate the potential buyers, tries a lower price, say $1,500. Unfortunately, at this price, the owners of the two best cars will withdraw from the market. Why? The owner of the car with two units of quality is receiving only $1,500 \div 2$, or $750 per unit of quality; the owner of the car with $1\frac{3}{4}$ units will act the same way. The withdrawal of the two best cars causes the average quality of the seven remaining cars to fall. With nine cars, the average of the distribution was $Q = 1$. Now at a price of $1,500 per car, the best car offered will have a quality level of 3/2, and the average quality will be $\frac{3}{4}$. Potential buyers would now be willing to pay only $1,500 per unit of quality $\times \frac{3}{4}$ unit of quality per average car, or $1,125 for any car. Just as the previous price of $2,000 per car was too high, the new price of $1,500 is too high for buyers.

Will an equilibrium price ever be found? Surprisingly, in this example, no equilibrium that satisfies both buyers and sellers will be found. The reader can discern this by trying several successively lower prices. In the end, the cars will not be sold even though nonowners value the cars considerably more than their current owners. Akerlof saw the problem this way: When potential buyers know only the average quality of used cars, then market prices will tend to be lower than the true value of the top-quality cars. Owners of the top-quality cars will tend to withhold their cars from sale. In a sense, the good cars are driven out of the market by the lemons. Under what has become known as the Lemons Principle, the bad drives out the good until, as in some cases such as this one, no market is left.

Imperfect Versus Asymmetric Information

To see that the problem is asymmetric rather than imperfect information for both buyers and sellers, consider what would have occurred if information had been symmetric. Suppose that both owners and nonowners were uncertain of the quality, that they

knew only the average quality of used cars on the market. Again, let the auctioneer start with a price of $2,000 per car. All owners, at their best guess, may presume that their car is of average quality, and that the average will again be $Q = 1$. Thus, at a price of $2,000 per car, all nine cars would be offered for sale. However, the nonowners would be willing to pay, at most, $1,500 based on their guess that a given car is of average quality (that is, $1,500 per unit of quality, multiplied by expected quality of $Q = 1$). Again, suppose the auctioneer tries to accommodate the potential buyers by offering a lower trial price, say $1,500. If the owners have imperfect information rather than better information, they will guess that their cars are of average quality, and thus worth (to them) $1,000 per unit of quality, multiplied by the average quality of 1. So the owners are willing to supply nine cars at a market price of $1,500, and the buyers are willing to purchase them at that price. The market thus exists, and clears (supply equals demand) if the information is symmetric—in this case, equally bad on both sides.

This example is extreme in several respects. The assumption of an auctioneer, the assumption that there is only one price for the used cars, the implicit assumption that the parties are not influenced by risk, and even the assumption that the quality of the cars is exogenously given could each be modified to add more realism. Since the lemons example was published, several analysts have worked on models that modify these assumptions. In some cases, this changes the result significantly. However, Akerlof's main point remains illuminating.

Application of the Lemons Principle: Health Insurance

Adverse selection applies to markets involving health insurance and to analyses of the relative merits of alternative health care provider arrangements. The application of the Lemons Principle to health insurance can be seen directly with the help of the previous example, a mirror image of the insurance problem. In Figure 10-2, let the horizontal axis measure the expected health expenditure levels of a population of n potentially insured people, instead of measuring the quality of used cars. Assume that they have the same demographic characteristics and that their expected health expenditure levels for the insured period range from a low of $0 up to an expenditure level of M. The vertical axis represents the probability with a uniform distribution (so that the probability of any level of spending is $1/n$). The insurer must at least break even, which means that the premium (or price) received from each insured must cover the insured population's average expenditure and other expenses (including marketing and overhead).

FIGURE 10-2 Uniform Probability of Expenditure (Expected Health Expenditure Levels)

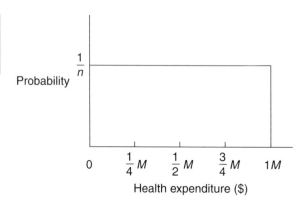

Information asymmetry will likely occur because the potential insureds know more about their expected health expenditures in the coming period than does the insurance company. To illustrate, assume a potential insured knows his or her future expenditure exactly but that the insurance company knows only the distribution of expenditures for all insured persons.

Again, use the device of the auctioneer to illustrate the point. Suppose this time that the auctioneer attempts a first trial price of $0! All potential beneficiaries would certainly demand coverage at this price. Just as certainly, the insurance company, expecting an average expenditure of $\$\frac{1}{2}M$, would require a premium of at least $\$\frac{1}{2}M$.

Following Akerlof's analysis, suppose the auctioneer tries a higher price, say $\$\frac{1}{2}M$, hoping that this will clear the market. In this case, all potential beneficiaries who expect an expenditure level below $\$\frac{1}{2}M$ will choose to self-insure, that is, leave the insurance market altogether, because this premium is higher than their privately known levels of health expenditure. When these healthier people leave the market, the average expected expenditure level of the remaining insured persons, those with expected expenditures from $\$\frac{1}{2}M$ to $\$M$, rises to $\$\frac{3}{4}M$. Thus, the higher health risks tend to drive out the lower health risk people, and a functioning market may even fail to appear at all for some otherwise-insurable health care risks.

Observe again that it is the asymmetry of information rather than the problem of incomplete information that leads to this result. If patients were no better at predicting their health expenditures in our example than the insurer, adverse selection would not take place. That is, all potential beneficiaries would have expected expenditures of $\$\frac{1}{2}M$ and would be willing to purchase insurance at the premium of $\$\frac{1}{2}M$.

Inefficiencies of Adverse Selection

This example illustrates the effects of adverse selection. Analysts of the health insurance industry recognize that even in its less extreme forms, adverse selection will appear. Even if functioning health insurance markets do evolve in the presence of information asymmetry of this kind, the resulting adverse selection leads to economic inefficiencies.

What are the inefficiencies? Unlike the example, few people can know exactly their future level of expenditures. Risk is the main reason for insurance. However, if the lower risks are grouped with higher risks and all pay the same premium, the lower risks face an unfavorable rate and will tend to underinsure. They sustain a welfare loss by not being able to purchase insurance at rates appropriate to their risk. Conversely, the higher risks will face a favorable premium and therefore overinsure; that is, they will insure against risks that they would not otherwise insure against. This, too, is inefficient. In addition to inefficiency, income will be redistributed from consumers who are lower risks to those who are higher risks.

Is adverse selection merely a theoretical prediction or a serious problem? Evidence of adverse selection has been found in markets for supplemental Medicare insurance (Wolfe and Goddeeris, 1991) and individual (nongroup) insurance (Browne and Doerpinghaus, 1993). In more recent work with a sample of single, employed persons, Cardon and Hendel (2001) found that those who were insured spent about 50 percent more on health care than the uninsured. Although this gap appears to support the existence of adverse selection, it could also be due to two other reasons. First, by lowering the price of health care to the patient, the consumption of additional health care is encouraged, that is, moral hazard occurs. Second, the insured may have different observable characteristics, such as age, that are associated with higher spending. However, insurers could incorporate observable characteristics in setting premiums. It is the unobservable characteristics that are the source of asymmetric information, and

hence adverse selection. Cardon and Hendel found only a small and statistically insignificant effect of unobservables in explaining the spending gap.

As this study suggests, if information asymmetry threatens to lead to inefficiency and even to the elimination of functioning markets in some cases, we would expect consumers, providers, and insurers to resort to other economic devices and institutions to help mitigate the problem. To illustrate, while the lemons problem in used-car markets is real, a buyer may hire a mechanic to examine the car of interest, the seller may offer a warranty, and agencies or consumer unions may arise to provide quality information. In health insurance markets, beneficiaries often are not covered for preexisting conditions. Premiums for individual policies may be based on other information that insurers use to predict expenditures. They may consider factors such as age, employment status, and occupation.

Experience Rating and Adverse Selection

Group insurance can be a more useful mechanism to reduce adverse selection. Most employees and their families in the United States are insured through employer group plans rather than through individual policies. Group plans enable insurers to implement experience rating, a practice where premiums are based on the past experience of the group, or other risk-rating systems to project expenditures. Because employees usually have limited choices both within and among plans, they cannot fully capitalize on their information advantage. Box 10-1 examines the practice of "reunderwriting" premiums based on new information.

Although experience rating can reduce adverse selection, it has come under increasing attack with the rapid growth of managed care plans such as health maintenance organizations (HMOs). HMOs receive a predetermined premium to provide the contracted health care for their enrollees. In contrast to traditional insurance where providers are independent of insurers, HMOs integrate insurance with the provision of health care.

HMOs and other managed care organizations have been promoted heavily on the belief that they have a powerful self-interest in eliminating the inappropriate care that might be recommended by agents in traditional fee-for-service systems. However, the intense competition to enroll healthy populations in managed care plans, known as "cream skimming" or "cherry picking," has led to concerns that insurers are more interested in finding favorable groups than providing quality care. Experience rating also redistributes income toward healthy populations, and the perceived inequity of such redistributions has become a public issue.

To deal with these concerns, several states have introduced some degree of mandated community rating—a practice in which an insurer charges all groups within an area the same premium. In a less rigid form, upper and lower limits on premiums are established through rate bands. The effects of these changes have not yet been determined, but Goldman et al. (1997) predict some serious redistributional consequences of the community rating schemes considered for California. In particular, because health care spending in wealthy, urban areas is relatively high, their model predicts large regional transfers of income from poorer, rural communities to those areas.

The Agency Relationship

An agency relationship is formed whenever a *principal* (for example, a patient) delegates decision-making authority to another party, the *agent*. In the physician-patient relationship, the patient (principal) delegates authority to the physician (agent), who in

BOX 10-1

Reunderwriting: Is Health Insurance Different?

Insurers evaluate medical histories to set premiums for those who are not covered by their employer's group health plans and decide to buy individual policies. This process is called underwriting. Usually, and unlike automobile insurance, it is done only once, at the time a person applies for coverage. In contrast, some insurers engage in reunderwriting, a process under which policyholders' claims are evaluated every year. Much like premiums for drivers who have infractions or accidents, reunderwriting can result in dramatic rate increases for those who file claims, especially when they are for serious conditions. State regulations limit the practice of reunderwriting, but consider the many ramifications on consumer behavior (e.g., emphasis on health promotion) and insurance markets (e.g., the kind of insurance, if any, to buy) if such policies were the norm.

SOURCE: Chad Terhune, "Insurer's Tactic: If You Get Sick, the Premium Rises," *Wall Street Journal* (April 9, 2002): A1.

many cases also will be the provider of the recommended services. The motive behind this delegation of authority is that the principals recognize that they are relatively uninformed about the most appropriate decisions to be made and that the deficiency is best resolved by having an informed agent. Thus, asymmetric information and agency are closely related phenomena.

Agency and Health Care

What would the perfect agent do? The perfect agent physician is one who chooses as the patients themselves would choose if only the patients possessed the information that the physician does. This is in line with the medical code of ethics to the extent that the patient's own interest focuses on his or her health. When any conflict arises, the perfect agent focuses on the patient's preferences, not his or her own.

The problem for the principal is to determine and ensure that the agent is acting in the principal's best interests. Unfortunately, the interests may diverge, and it may be difficult to introduce arrangements or contracts that eliminate conflicts of interest.

As an example, Dranove and White (1987) ask why physicians are not reimbursed on the basis of improvements in patient health. More simply, why are they not reimbursed only if the patient is cured? It would appear that such a contract would arise naturally to merge the interests of both principal and patient. The authors suggest that such contracts do not exist because of the problem of asymmetric information, although in this case it is the physician who may lack information about the patient's well-being.

To illustrate, consider patients with low back pain. Regardless of their improvement, the patients have financial incentives to understate the extent of their improvement. The provider also has an incentive to overstate the difficulty in treating the patients and in improving their health in order to increase the payment (which, let us assume, is based on the difficulty of the case). Further, it is these information problems and not other special characteristics of health care delivery that preclude payment based on the degree of improvement of the patients' conditions.

Dranove and White further apply agency theory to explain other features in the organization of health care delivery. Patients often establish a long-term relationship

with a physician and pay that physician on a fee-for-service basis. As discussed earlier, such an arrangement would appear prone to lead to conflict between patient and provider. It is thus natural to ask the following questions: Why does this particular physician-patient arrangement arise and why is it so common?

Dranove and White argue that a continuous relationship between patient and physician provides the patient with increasing information with which to monitor the physician. This information places constraints on the extent to which the provider is able to deviate from an agency responsibility. Monitoring also encourages the physician to make appropriate referrals to other providers when he or she is unable to provide the services alone.

We can add to their argument by pointing out that a continuous relationship reduces the cost of transferring information about medical history, circumstances, and preferences from patient to provider. These advantages of the usual physician-patient relationship would be eroded if patients and providers were to switch to limited-period contracts under which providers are reimbursed on a different basis.

Consumer Information, Prices, and Quality

We next examine the effects of imperfect information on the price and quality of medical services. Would relatively poor consumer information reduce the competitiveness of markets? Does increasing physician availability increase competition and lower prices as traditional economics suggests? What happens to quality? How do consumers obtain and use information? Several studies provide helpful insight.

Consumer Information and Prices

Satterthwaite (1979) and Pauly and Satterthwaite (1981) introduced one of the most novel approaches to handle issues involving consumer information and competition. The authors identify primary medical care as a reputation good—a good for which consumers rely on the information provided by friends, neighbors, and others to select from the various services available in the market. Physicians are not identical and do not offer identical services. Because of this product differentiation, the market can be characterized as monopolistically competitive.

Reputation Goods

Under these conditions, the authors show that an increase in the number of providers can increase prices. The reasoning behind this surprising prediction is logical. Recall that a typical consumer relies on other consumers for information regarding their experiences with physicians. Thus, when physicians become numerous, the average number of friends who see any provider diminishes; this, in turn, diminishes the average level of information available. The consumer's responsiveness to prices and other practice characteristics depends on his or her knowledge of—that is, information about—the available alternatives. Thus, this reduced information reduces the price responsiveness (i.e., the elasticity) of the firm demand curves, causing the equilibrium prices to rise. The economic idea is that reduced information tends to give each firm some additional monopoly power.

That reduced information enhances monopoly power and reduces the elasticity of the firm demand curves is consistent with standard theory. That such a situation may arise as the number of sellers increases is an unconventional and counterintuitive idea.

The authors have, however, provided empirical support for their theory, and the interested reader is referred to their work for further study.

The Role of Informed Buyers

The degree to which imperfect price information contributes to monopoly power should not be overemphasized. Recall that it is not necessary for every buyer of a commodity to have perfect price information to elicit relatively competitive pricing conditions. Realistically, most consumers lack complete price information about many of the goods and services they buy (they don't know what alternative sellers are charging). Yet, despite variations in the prices of individual items among, for example, grocery stores, the average charges for a set of items across similar types of stores are likely to be similar and close to competitive pricing. A growing body of literature shows that it is sufficient to have enough buyers who are sensitive to price differentials to exert discipline over the marketplace. This will likely hold especially where the damaging threat exists of having any systematic differentials publicized by consumer organizations or the low-priced merchants themselves.

These arguments suggest that while imperfect price information will likely produce higher prices, this phenomenon may be substantially limited. In health care markets, where many services are fully or partially covered by insurance, there are added considerations. While a patient may become less sensitive to price levels and price differentials in the choice of providers, third-party payers, such as insurers, have assumed a monitoring function. Through selective contracting and other fee agreements, the actual reimbursement is often lower than the provider's charges.

Price Dispersion

The distinction between the effective transaction price and a provider's charge also obscures evidence of dispersion of fees as distinct from the average level of fees. Under conditions of imperfect consumer information, Nobel Laureate George Stigler (1961) argued that variation in prices will increase.

Building on Stigler's insight, Gaynor and Polachek (1994) developed measures of the degree of both buyer and provider ignorance by using frontier regression methods. These authors separated price dispersion into measures of incomplete buyer information, incomplete seller information, and random noise. They found that both patients and physicians exhibited incomplete information with the measure of ignorance being one and one-half times larger for patients than for physicians.

In addition, Juba (1979) found that the variations in physician fees appear to be larger than those found in other relatively competitive markets. It is not clear, though, that variations in effective transactions pricing resulting from insurance agreements lie outside of competitive norms.

Consumer Information and Quality

Because consumers cannot easily monitor quality, the search for information regarding quality can be costly. At the same time, the consequences of poor quality care can be severe. (Box 10-2 describes the effects family visits can make on quality by reducing information asymmetries in nursing home care.) Thus, as previous discussion suggested, despite asymmetric information, patients rely on a variety of countervailing arrangements that are intended to reduce their search costs. These include licensure and certification, the threat of malpractice suits, codes of ethics, and various quality

BOX 10-2

Asymmetric Information and Quality of Nursing Home Care

As previously described, the lack of a clear profit motive may make nonprofit organizations more attractive to patients when they cannot easily observe or determine quality. Although this argument seems plausible, empirical support for it had been lacking until Chou (2002) developed a novel application to quality of care in nursing homes (where nearly two-thirds are for-profits). Because many nursing home patients are too cognitively or physically incapacitated to be able to monitor and evaluate their care, Chou used the absence of visits by a spouse or children (the

patient's representatives) within one month of admission as an indicator of information asymmetry. There were no significant differences between for-profits and nonprofits when asymmetric information was not present. With asymmetric information, a very different picture emerged. For-profits had higher mortality rates as well as higher rates of decubitus ulcers, dehydration, and urinary tract infection. Chou concluded that for-profits "have more incentive to compromise on those aspects of quality of care which are hard to monitor."

assurance schemes that are either mandated or voluntary. The Internet is also becoming a major source of information despite widespread concerns about the accuracy of online information.

At this point, we pursue the consumer's direct role through the Dranove and White argument that the physician-patient relationship enables patients to monitor providers and to encourage physicians to make appropriate referrals. To the extent that many specialists rely on referred patients, these specialists would seem to have incentives to maintain quality. Are they also rewarded with higher prices when they provide higher-quality services? Theory suggests that if consumers have the ability to distinguish between quality, then the demand for higher-quality providers and thus price should be greater than for lower-quality providers. Haas-Wilson (1990) examined this proposition using data from the psychotherapy services market. She investigated whether the prevalence of referrals from informed sources affects the price of social workers' psychotherapy services. Informed sources include other health providers and other professionals, such as school counselors and clergy.

Regression analysis of a sample of social workers' fees indicated that fees are positively and significantly affected by the percentage of clients who were obtained through informed referrals. The evidence shows that patients rely on informed sources (agents) for information and that higher quality, as measured by informed referrals, is rewarded by higher fees.

Other Quality Indicators

With the increasing dominance of HMOs and other managed care organizations, the availability of information to help consumers select among plans, and how consumers respond to the information, have become major issues. The National Committee for Quality Assurance (NCQA), a private accreditation body for HMOs, issues report cards based on about 50 standardized measures of a plan's performance (such as childhood immunization rates, breast cancer screening, and asthma inpatient admission rates). *Newsweek*, *U.S. News & World Report*, and various consumer groups also regularly rate HMOs. A key assumption behind these efforts is that information about quality will, like price information, help discipline providers through patient choices.

Low-quality HMOs will not survive or at least they will not be able to charge high-quality prices. Initial evidence on the intended effects of plan performance ratings brings the report card strategy into question. Tumlinson et al. (1997) found that independent plan ratings are relatively unimportant to consumer choices. Only 17 percent of respondents indicated that such ratings are essential, compared with 72 percent for specific plan benefits and 62 percent for out-of-pocket costs. Chernew and Scanlon (1998), employing multivariate statistical methods on consumer choice of plans, confirm that "employees do not appear to respond strongly to plan performance measures, even when the labeling and dissemination were intended to facilitate their use" (p. 19).

In subsequent work, Scanlon and colleagues (2002) examined a flexible benefits system introduced by General Motors (GM) in 1996 and 1997 under which employees and retirees received a fixed amount of dollars that could be spent across a variety of fringe benefits categories. Any excess in spending over the allotted "flex dollars" are paid out of pocket. GM developed ratings (e.g., superior performance, below expected performance) for six performance categories (e.g., preventive care, access, patient satisfaction) to help those who wanted to select an HMO choose among the available plans (typically two to six depending on the employees' geographic area). As expected, the study found that higher out-of-pocket prices imply lower enrollments. Also as expected, employees tended to avoid plans with many below average ratings. However, plans with many above average ratings were not much more successful in attracting enrollees relative to plans with many average ratings.

Together with other results on plan switching (Beaulieu, 2002), we can conclude that the provision of quality information does influence consumers, particularly when the quality ratings are negative. Nevertheless, it is clear that much more work is needed regarding quality indicators and patients' perceptions of quality. Box 10-3 provides a provocative example indicating that lower cost care may, in some cases, provide higher quality.

Finally, despite health plan report cards, licensure requirements, and many other mechanisms to promote quality, a series of influential reports released by the Institute of Medicine (1999, 2001) suggested that as many as 98,000 deaths and a million excess injuries annually in the United States can be attributed to problems with quality and safety in hospitals. By calling for a fundamental overhaul of the U.S. health care system, the reports raise troubling questions about existing safeguards as well as patients' perceptions of quality and their ability to monitor it.

Conclusions

There is little doubt that information gaps, asymmetric information, and agency problems are prevalent in provider-patient transactions. However, for some health care services, the problems are not necessarily greater or larger than those for other goods. Patients are likely to be relatively poorly informed about treatment for conditions that they have not previously experienced and about care involving newer technologies. The informational asymmetries and reliance on provider-agents are likely to be most pronounced in these situations.

Although there is a potential lack of competition, even wide information gaps do not necessarily lead to market failure. Leaving aside the role of licensure and regulation, arrangements have evolved to enable patients or their insurers to monitor the

BOX 10-3

Quality and Cost: Is There a Free Lunch?

Persistent claims of inefficiency and waste in hospital care pose a major challenge to the policy maker as well as to the health economist. If higher hospital costs do not improve health outcomes, the potential to better control health care spending without harming patients is obvious. Solberg et al. (2002) examined the relationship between cost and quality across 18 integrated health care delivery systems in Minnesota over the late 1990s. Standardized cost values were applied to the services provided by each care system to obtain a measure of resources used rather than premiums actually charged by the 18 systems to employers and their employees. These standardized costs were also adjusted for case mix to eliminate the effects, for example, of systems with older and sicker patients. To represent quality, the study focused on quality indicators for three common chronic diseases (asthma, dia-

betes mellitus, and depression) and five preventive services, such as cholesterol tests and mammograms. Relative quality of individual care systems varied widely across the conditions. More importantly, the results did "not support the common assumption that higher cost means higher quality. In fact, there is some evidence to the contrary, since a number of lower cost care systems also had higher measures of quality attainment" (p. 420).

The Solberg findings have yet to be corroborated. Using a national sample of Medicare beneficiaries with similar conditions, Picone et al. (2003) found that a more intense (more services) hospital stay improved patient survival and functional status among those who survived. However, *longer* hospital stays did not improve either outcome's measure.

quality and prices of providers. Furthermore, higher-quality producers are rewarded by greater demand and higher prices. Evidence suggests that the variation in physician fees exceeds what is found in more competitive markets. Price dispersion data indicate some ignorance on the parts of both physicians and patients, with the patients being the lesser informed. Nevertheless, because of the use of referrals, accreditation, and other arrangements, the provider's ability to raise prices above those charged by others and to sell low-quality services at high-quality prices is significantly constrained.

SUMMARY

1. Health care markets tend to be characterized by both imperfect information and asymmetric information. Asymmetric information describes a situation in which those on one side of a transaction have better information than those on the other side.
2. Often, providers are relatively well-informed (e.g., about the patient's illness and possible treatments). In other cases, buyers are relatively well-informed (e.g., the purchaser of insurance knows more about his or her health status and pertinent habits than the insurer does).
3. The extent of consumer information problems should not be exaggerated. Consumers are reasonably well-informed on about one-fourth to one-third of their health care spending.
4. One possible consequence of asymmetric information is that a market will not exist. Even if it exists, a general reduction may occur in the quality of goods available (the "Lemons Principle").
5. The Lemons Principle appears as the problem of adverse selection in health insurance and other health care markets.
6. Adverse selection results from asymmetric information, not equally imperfect information. Adverse selection in insurance results in inefficiencies through higher-risk consumers overinsuring, relative to the amounts they would purchase at actuarially fair rates, and lower risks correspondingly underinsuring.

7. An agency relationship tends to be formed when a party (principal) delegates decision making to another party (agent). The problem for the principal is to develop a contract or relationship to ensure that the agent is acting in the principal's best interests.

8. Various agency relationships have evolved to mitigate the problems associated with asymmetric information between patient and provider. These include the continuous physician-patient relationship and the health maintenance organization.

9. Other constraints, such as licensure and accreditation, codes of ethics, and the threat of litigation, limit the ability of providers to deviate from their agency responsibilities.

10. Many health care services are reputation goods. In markets for reputation goods, an increase in the number of providers can lead to an increase in monopoly power and higher prices.

11. The existence of informed buyers helps exert discipline over the market by limiting price increases and price differentials among sellers.

12. Higher quality tends to be rewarded with higher prices. Patients also respond to quality indicators in selecting a hospital. However, they rely only modestly on objective plan ratings in their selection of HMOs. Negative ratings have a greater impact on consumer decisions than positive ratings.

Discussion Questions

1. The market for higher education is another example where a high degree of information asymmetry is likely. What mechanisms have evolved to help students in their choice of schools and classes within schools? Do you have confidence that higher-priced institutions provide higher-quality education?

2. The situation in which an individual is interviewing for a job also exhibits information asymmetry. Explain why. How does the relatively poorly informed party deal with this?

3. The use of professional and independent buyer-agents to help individuals purchase automobiles or houses is becoming a more common phenomenon. Given the conflict of interest facing the physician-agent, why do we not see greater use of a buyer-agent who is retained by the patient?

4. The used-car market has publications that provide information on the quality and prices of used cars. Are similar avenues of information available to health consumers? What kind of information do they provide? Is it more or less effective than the information available on used cars? How would you, as a patient, find information about a provider's quality or prices? How would you assess the confidence you have in that information?

5. What is a reputation good? What are examples of reputation goods outside the health care sector? Show what Pauly and Satterthwaite predict will happen to the demand curve for health services as a result of an increase in the number of providers.

6. Stigler argued that the variation in fees increases as buyer information decreases. Suppose you observe that each seller in a market is charging the identical price. What potentially conflicting inferences can you draw?

7. Why don't physicians guarantee their work as do many auto repair shops?

8. Various commentators have suggested that only 15 to 20 percent of all health care services have been subject to rigorous, controlled investigation, that is, care based on what is commonly called "evidence-based medicine." Assume that this statement is correct. What are some implications for efficiency of health care delivery?

9. Refer to the "Quality and Cost" feature (Box 10-3). How is it possible to have a situation where higher costs, as measured by the resources used to provide care, do not produce higher quality?

Exercises

1. Suppose that in the Akerlof example, there are only eight cars ranging in quality from $\frac{1}{4}$ to 2 (i.e., there is no complete lemon). Hence, the mean quality level is 1.125. Determine whether the market disappears completely, and, if not, how many cars will be sold.

2. Consider the agency relationship in malpractice cases under a contingency fee system. The plaintiff (party that sues) typically pays his or her attorney about one-third of any monetary damages that are awarded (and nothing if the case is lost). Supporters of this system claim that client and attorney share a common goal of maximizing the award. Is there, however, an inherent conflict between attorney and client in the amount of attorney time and other resources that are devoted to the case?

3. Give three examples of asymmetric information in which the health consumer has information that is unavailable to the health provider. Give three concrete examples in which the health provider has information that is unavailable to the health consumer.

4. In the Akerlof example, the individuals are treated as indifferent to risk. What would you expect to see in these markets if individuals wanted to avoid risk? What if there were some "risk lovers?"

The Organization of Health Insurance Markets

Chapter 8 introduced the concept of insurance with a primary focus on health insurance. Insurance is an arrangement that allows risk-averse people to reduce or eliminate the risks they face. Consumers buy insurance to replace the uncertainty of a large loss or major expenditure with the more certain prospect of regular premiums. Profit-seeking firms supply insurance. In an idealized insurance market, the premium (as a percentage of the potential loss) will approach the probability of the event occurring.

In previous chapters, we concentrated on the impact of insurance on individuals. In this chapter, we focus on the insurance market and the behaviors of firms within that market. Within the context of the employer-provided health insurance that is common in the United States, we establish who pays for health insurance. We continue with an examination of employer-provided insurance and job mobility. We then look at the traditional community-rated health insurance (where individuals or groups all pay the same premium) and show how that market has changed, and we follow with an analysis of the uninsured. We finish the chapter by examining linkages among insurance, technological change, and health cost inflation.

Loading Costs and the Behavior of Insurance Firms

Consumers can improve their well-being by sacrificing a (relatively) small, certain, premium to insure against the probability of a considerably larger loss. It is important now to demonstrate how the policies will be offered to specific groups and why, in fact, some groups will find it difficult to get insurance at all.

215

We have referred to the model of a competitive industry, in which the firms will compete to where economic profits become zero, or normal. If profits are higher (lower), firms will enter (leave) the market. Only when profits have become zero, or normal, will entry and exit cease. In this model, the insurance carriers would collect money during the year and pay some of it out. In good years, carriers would pay out less than collected; in bad years, they would pay out more. Economic analysis would suggest that the good (and bad) years will be random. Systematically good (bad) years suggest excess profits (losses), and the probability of entry into (exit from) the industry by other firms.

We also have previously shown how moral hazard can lead firms to offer certain types of coverage and not others. In particular, firms would be reluctant to cover conditions that are accompanied by price-elastic demands for services.

Impacts of Loading Costs

Insurance firms have costs of doing business that are added to the claims payouts. These loading costs are largely related to the numbers and types of customers and claims processed. Even in perfect competition, these costs must be passed on to consumers, or else the insurers will not be able to cover all costs and will be forced to leave the market. The incidence of these costs suggests that insurers will shy away from covering events that are almost certain to occur, or those that seldom occur.

Consider consumers who behave as though they have a utility of wealth (W) function exhibiting diminishing marginal utility of wealth. In Figure 11-1, the amount the consumer would be willing to pay over the actuarially fair amount (also interpreted as consumer surplus) is shown by the horizontal distance between the expected utility line and the (curved) utility function, measured in dollars. For example, at point F, this horizontal distance is FG. Clearly, the horizontal distance between the expected utility line and the utility function is zero if the event never occurs (i.e., if we are at point A). It increases up to some point as we move in a southwest direction, with increased probability of illness, and then decreases, as the illness becomes more certain, toward point B.

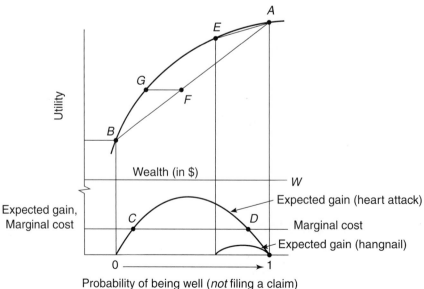

FIGURE 11-1 Impacts of Loading Costs on Availability of Insurance

This means that the extra premium people are willing to pay to avoid risk is smallest either for rare events or for almost certain events.

Because insurance is taken against risk, as the probability of the uncertain event approaches either 0 or 1, insurance becomes less desirable. Near point *A*, the expected loss—that is, the probability of the event—multiplied by the loss if the event occurs is not large enough for the consumer to bother to insure. Near point *B*—because the event is almost certain—the consumer might as well set the money aside and avoid the trouble of dealing with the insurer. Most people do not seek insurance against losses due to common colds.

Figure 11-1 addresses this issue graphically. The top portion of Figure 11-1 shows the utility function we have just discussed. Moving southwest from the initial wealth (point *A*), we see that the gain from insurance increases initially, then eventually falls back to zero when the probability of illness becomes 1. Below this graph, we plot the probability of the event on the x-axis and the expected gain on the y-axis. The lower x-axis is best understood as the probability of being well, which decreases from 1 (under point *A* where the event never occurs) to 0 (under point *B* where the event always occurs). Thus, at $p = 0$ (at *A* where there is no loss) or at $p = 1$ (at *B* where a loss is certain), the expected gain from insurance is zero. Because the marginal benefits are positive in between, the marginal benefit curve has a hump in the middle.

Insurance for Heart Attacks and Hangnails

In comparing types of losses, at any value of *p*, the larger the expected loss, the larger the gain from the insurance. This is easily seen by comparing the distances between the expected utility line and the utility curve for a small loss (line segment *EA*) and for a large loss (line segment *BA*). Segment *EA* shows a small distance; segment *BA*, a larger one. Hence, if the consumer has equal probabilities of a hangnail (small loss) and a heart attack (large loss), the expected gain from insurance for major (heart attack) coverage will be larger than for minor (hangnail) coverage.

Consider now the firms' decisions in providing insurance. If the event is almost certain, the firms' costs of administering the policy may exceed the benefits to the consumers. For simplicity, we have drawn these costs as constant marginal costs—a horizontal line.[1]

From probability 0 to point *C*, it will not pay to insure claims because the firms' marginal costs exceed the expected consumers' marginal benefits. Between points *C* and *D*, expected marginal benefits exceed marginal costs. To the right of point *D*, again the marginal costs exceed the expected marginal benefits, and no insurance will be provided. As the diagram is drawn, no firm could afford to offer hangnail coverage.

Loading Costs and the Uninsured

The analysis provides one avenue for addressing the problem of the uninsured. Health insurance in the United States is largely available through participation in the labor market. Those who do not participate in the labor market, and indeed those who are employed by small businesses, self-employed, or sporadically employed, may find it difficult to get insurance.

Many explanations have been proposed, but it is apparent that the per-person costs of processing information and claims of those individuals who are outside larger organizations (either companies or unions) may be higher. This would result in an

[1] It is likely that the higher the probability of claims, the more administration time is needed (forms filled out or verification). Hence, with more claims or more complicated claims, the marginal cost of processing the claims may rise.

increase in the firms' marginal costs relative to the consumer's marginal benefits and would reduce or eliminate the range of services that may be offered.

The analysis also helps address the impacts of entry and exit in the insurance market. More efficient processing and information handling presumably will lower the premiums that must be paid by customers in the market. If we again address Figure 11-1, we recognize that improved information handling and processing would not only lead to lower prices, but also would permit firms to offer services (based on probability of occurrence) that had not previously been offered.

Consider points C or D, where the expected marginal benefit was previously just equal to (or possibly just below) the marginal cost. The ability of an insurer to lower costs would allow that insurer to offer coverage for types of events that previously were uncovered. Conversely, increased costs, either due to market forces or often due to mandated types of coverage, would force firms to cut back coverage on events for which the limited amount of consumer surplus would not allow the firms to pass the increased costs on to the customers.

Employer Provision of Health Insurance: Who Pays?

The largest segment of the American population acquires health insurance through the workplace, and this began almost by accident. During World War II a booming economy coupled with wartime shortages left consumer goods in short supply, so wage and price controls were imposed as anti-inflationary devices. Predictably, compensation needed to be changed in order to attract workers because wage controls in a full-employment economy prevented companies from raiding each other for workers. Fringe benefits were not legally considered as part of the wage package, but they were used to provide flexibility in worker compensation, and to improve the allocation of workers among sectors of the economy. One of these fringe benefits was health insurance.

Economists start their analyses of the impact of health insurance by looking at the labor market. We assume that a lower market money wage rate leads an employer to hire more workers for two reasons: (1) the employer can substitute labor for more expensive equipment; and (2) the employer can sell more products at lower prices, hence requiring more workers. Assume at the outset there is no health insurance benefit, and that the market wage is $20 per hour. Employers will hire workers as long as the incremental (marginal) revenue from the goods those workers produce exceeds the $20 per hour wage. To begin, assume that the employer hires 1,000 workers, at an equilibrium money wage of $20 per hour.

Suppose that workers negotiate a health insurance benefit worth $1 per hour, and costing exactly $1 for the employer to provide. The employer, who was previously willing to pay $20, will now be willing to pay $20 less the $1 cost to provide the benefit. Other points on the employer's demand schedule, showing the number of workers it would hire at different wages, will also change by the $1 cost of the benefit.

The workers of course would prefer to get the $1 benefit on top of the previous $20 wage, but if they were previously willing to accept a wage of $20, they will now be willing to supply their labor for $1 less, because they value the benefit at $1. In the resulting equilibrium, the net wage (money wage + the value of the benefit) remains unchanged at $20, but the equilibrium money wage falls to $19, or by exactly the amount of the benefit. Workers accept lower money wages, and the same 1,000 workers are employed at the same net wage, $19 in money wages plus the $1 benefit. The workers are no worse off at a wage of $19 with the health insurance than at $20 without the health insurance because the insurance is worth the $1 that it cost in reduced wages.

Following Lee (1996), consider a labor market with a typically downward-sloping demand for labor, D, and a typically upward-sloping supply of labor, S, as noted in Figure 11-2. The demand for labor is related to the marginal productivity of workers. The supply of workers is related to the wage in this industry relative to the wage in other industries. Workers will choose to work in this industry as long as the wage they can earn exceeds their opportunities in other jobs. In Figure 11-2, at equilibrium point b, the equilibrium wage is W_1 and the equilibrium quantity of labor demanded and supplied is L_1.

Suppose that workers in the market negotiate a health insurance benefit worth $z/hour at that margin, and it costs employers exactly $z/hour to provide. What happens? Employers who were previously willing to pay W_1 per hour for workers will now pay W_1 less $z. Other points on the demand curve will shift downward in a similar manner so the demand curve will shift downward by exactly $z to D'.

What will happen to the supply curve? Because the workers were willing to supply various amounts of labor at various wage rates according to the supply curve before, now that they are receiving a benefit worth $z they will offer their labor for $z less. Hence, the supply curve will shift downward by exactly $z to S'.

What is the result? As before, the net wage remains the same, but the money wage falls by $z. The equilibrium wage has fallen to W_2 at point b', or by exactly the amount of the benefit. Workers have taken their benefits in lower money wages, and the same number of workers, L_1, is employed at the same net wage. For a real-world example of who pays, see Box 11-1.

By assuming that the marginal benefit was worth exactly what it cost to provide, the previous example ignored the moral hazard involved in health insurance. Recall from Chapter 8 that for many types of health care, fractional coinsurance leads consumers to consume health care past the point at which marginal benefits equal marginal costs. This provides benefits that on average may be worth less to the workers than what they cost to provide.

Suppose, as is common, that workers negotiate subsidized coverage for prescription drugs. This benefit might induce workers to purchase drugs beyond the point at which marginal benefits equal marginal costs (for example, some workers may have no need to

FIGURE 11-2 Interaction of Health Insurance and Employee Wages

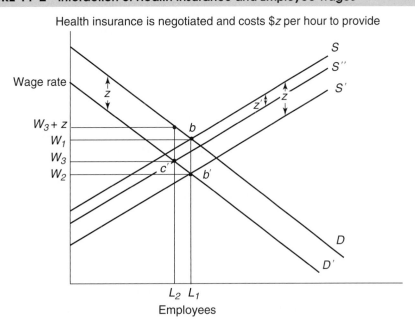

Health insurance is negotiated and costs $z per hour to provide

BOX 11-1

Who Pays? BART, Unions Clash on Wages and Health Benefits

Trade-offs between health benefits and wages are increasingly occurring in very public negotiations. In mid-2005, northern California's Bay Area Rapid Transit (BART) and its workers were nearing the end of a four-year contract that had provided 22 percent wage increases. *San Francisco Chronicle* reporter Patrick Hoge wrote that in addition, all of BART's nearly 3,200 employees, including managers and other nonunion employees, enjoyed health coverage for which they paid $25 per month to cover an entire family.

BART was also funding an in-perpetuity health benefit for retirees that had been started between 1993 and 1996. Like many public agencies, BART has not set aside enough money to pay for the benefit in the future, and with health care costs and the number of retirees rising, BART predicted that costs would mushroom.

A national change in government accounting standards scheduled for July 2007 will require BART to show such "unfunded liabilities'" on its balance sheets. BART was afraid that doing so would hurt the agency's bond rating—its ability to borrow money in the future.

BART management's first 2005 offer was a zero wage increase over four years. Not surprisingly, the unions found this to be unacceptable, and a strike threatened to strand more than 300,000 daily commuters.

Leaders of BART's two largest unions and the transit system came to a contract agreement three hours after a strike deadline. Management and the unions agreed to wage increases, but they were much less than four years earlier, and they came at a cost of increased monthly healthcare payments.

The four-year contract proposal would give workers a $300 payment the first year but no raise, a 2 percent raise the second year and third year, and a 3 percent pay hike for the final year, or 7 percent over 4 years, compared to 22 percent in the previous four years. Meanwhile, their monthly healthcare costs would triple to $75 a month.

BART officials said the new contract would help trim a projected $100 million budget deficit without any fare increases in addition to those already announced.

SOURCES: Patrick Hoge, "BART, Unions Clash on Health Benefits," *San Francisco Chronicle*, June 26, 2005. <http://sfgate.com/cgi-bin/article.cgi?f=/c/a/2005/06/26/BART.TMP>, accessed August 1, 2005, <http://www.kron.com/Global/story.asp?S=3612064>, accessed August 1, 2005.

use prescription drugs). If the average benefit is worth z'/hour, or less to the workers than the z/hour that it costs to provide, then the new supply of labor curve, S'', will have fallen by less than the demand for labor (still D', reflecting what it costs to provide the benefit).

Spousal Coverage: Who Pays?

An analysis derived from Mark Pauly (1997) helps to examine the issue of spousal insurance coverage. What happens if the husband has family insurance coverage where he works, and the wife chooses not to take coverage where she works? Who pays in this case? The subtleties of the analysis may be surprising.

Suppose that employees in a town can work in either Alpha or Beta types of employers. Alpha employers employ only married men; half of the spouses do not work, and half of the spouses work in the Beta sector. Half of the Beta employers' employees are spouses of the men in the Alpha sector and half are single. At the outset, no health insurance is provided and the "pure" wage (W_1 from Figure 11-2) for each employee in both the Alpha and Beta sectors is $50,000 per year. Assume that whatever health insurance is implemented, all employees of each firm are given the same take-home pay regardless of insurance cost.

Suppose now that the Alpha firms (employing only married men) offer to buy family coverage for their employees worth $4,000 per year. The Beta firms

(half spouses; half single) offer to pay $2,000 per year per person for their employees, as long as those who elect coverage pay an additional $10 per month, or $120 per year. In this situation, all Alpha workers will choose family coverage; it is a better buy because the employee is covering himself, his spouse, and his children for $4,000. As a result of market processes, money wages for Alpha workers fall by $4,000 to $46,000. In the Beta sector, wages per worker will fall by $1,000 to $49,000 (because half of the workers use coverage that costs $2,000 per person). Who pays?

- Two-worker families covered through Alpha firms pay $5,000 for $4,000 in coverage. This occurs because wages have fallen by $4,000 in the Alpha sector (where the men work) and by $1,000 where their spouses work.
- Single-worker families covered through Alpha firms pay $4,000 for $4,000 in coverage, again because wages have fallen by $4,000 in the Alpha sector.
- Single-worker families covered through Beta firms pay $1,120 (reduced wages of $1,000 + $120 from the monthly payments) for $2,120 ($2,000 + $120 from the monthly payments) in coverage.

Are the Beta firms better off because they don't pay for the health care for half of their employees? No, because they are still paying a net wage of $50,000 for the labor services that they use. Are the Alpha firms worse off because they are paying benefits for people who don't work for them? No, they too are still paying a net wage of $50,000 for the labor services that they use. Single workers at the Beta firms benefit because they receive $1,000 more in coverage than they are paying for—a transfer from married households, which receive $1,000 less in coverage than they are paying for!

How the Tax System Influences Health Insurance Demand

One of the most important factors in the increased demand for health insurance in the post-World War II era has been the tax treatment of health insurance. Suppose John earns $1,000 per week and would like to buy health insurance. Ignoring state and local taxes, assume that he is in the 28 percent marginal tax bracket, so his take-home pay is $720 per week. Suppose further that health insurance would cost him $60 per week. His net take-home pay would then be $660 per week.

Suppose, instead, that John's employer purchases insurance for him, also at a price of $60 per week. This fringe benefit is exempt from income taxation, as it has been since World War II. Although John's total compensation is still $1,000 per week, he is taxed only on the wage portion, or $940. His take-home pay will now be 72 percent of $940, or $677 per week. His $17 improvement in well-being occurs because he does not pay $17 in tax on the $60 insurance benefit. The $677 in net compensation with insurance is clearly superior to the $660 net take-home pay without insurance

If marginal tax rates increase, consumers have incentives to increase employer health expenditures. Employers also benefit from this arrangement because their levels of Social Security taxes will fall. Currently, both employees and employers pay 6.20 percent for the Social Security portion and 1.45 percent for the Medicare portion. Because insurance is an expense to the employer rather than a wage (on which Social Security and Medicare taxes must be paid), it is exempt from Social Security and Medicare taxes. In the 1950s, U.S. federal marginal rates went as high as 91 percent, and even today many people pay marginal (federal plus state) tax rates approaching 40 percent.

The allocative problem within the economy is that health expenditures have been chosen for special treatment. Consider Figure 11-3. This figure shows an entire wage package consisting of the sum of wages, W, and insurance, I. Intercept M on the y-axis shows the amount of wages if no insurance is in the package. Similarly, intercept N on

FIGURE 11-3 Impacts of Preferential Treatment of Employee Insurance

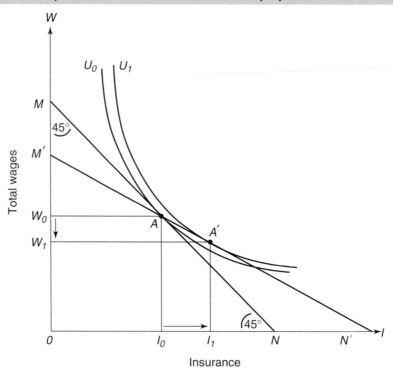

the x-axis shows the amount of insurance in the unlikely case that John received his entire compensation as insurance benefits. If no special tax treatment is given, then the line has a 45° relationship to the x- and y-axes, a slope of −1.0. In other words, $1 of insurance trades for $1 in wages, and the initial allocation is at point A, with wages W_0 and insurance I_0.

The subsidy of health insurance through the government policies lowers the price of $1 of insurance relative to $1 of wage remuneration. Suppose that the employees even recognize the subsidy and are prepared to give up some wages for an insurance subsidy. The "give back" rotates the x-intercept down to M', but the subsidy causes the budget constraint line to rotate to point N' on the x-axis. Hence, $1 of wages actually buys more than $1 of insurance. Figure 11-3 shows that without special tax treatment, John is consuming package A of I_0 and W_0. Even if the "give back" left John unchanged at point A, the changed relative prices will now make it more attractive to move to a more insurance-rich package. Thus, the tax system leads John to choose combination A', with more insurance at the expense of lower wages, and increased utility at U_1. Not only will John buy more insurance, but the tax subsidy may encourage him to insure for the kinds of low- or high-probability events (e.g., routine dental care) that might otherwise be left uninsured.

Who Pays—Empirical Tests

The trade-off between wages and insurance is important enough to merit serious empirical investigation. Morrisey (2001a) notes that most empirical studies thus far associate health insurance with higher, rather than lower, wages. Because compensation (wages plus insurance) is based on productivity, employers spend considerable effort identifying workers who are better motivated, more dependable, more highly

skilled, and better able to interact with clients and customers. Most researchers have only age or schooling measures to capture productivity, and other attributes of more or less productive workers are unobserved. Because more productive workers get both higher wages and more health insurance, the substitution between wages and insurance may be swamped by the productivity effect.

Gruber and Krueger (1992) examine workers' compensation insurance, and Gruber (1994) looks at mandated maternity benefits coverage. Both studies confirm the existence of "group specific" average wage adjustments. That is, those groups that were paid more in benefits received lower wages.

Jensen and Morrisey (2001) use 1994 and 1998 data from the Health and Retirement Survey (HRS) to examine the wage-coverage tradeoff for workers born between 1931 and 1941. The HRS provides information on wages, health insurance coverage, demographic characteristics, and health status measures for workers and their spouses. The authors used the health status of spouses as an indicator of the demand for health insurance.

They found evidence of compensating differentials for older workers. Other things equal, those workers with health insurance were estimated to have annual wages that were approximately $6,300 lower. Since annual family health insurance coverage provided through an employer often costs $6,000 to $7,000 per year, the evidence suggests that workers do pay for their health insurance through lower wages.

Adams (2004) looks at the impacts on smaller firms of the imposition of pure community rating in New York in the small group market in 1993. Community rating prevents carriers from charging different premiums based on age. If smaller firms had been cutting wages of older workers prior to pure community rating to offset their higher health care costs, then one would have expected the reform to lead to higher relative wages for older workers at these firms. The reform did increase the relative wages for older workers, both in relation to older workers in other states and in relation to older workers at large firms within the state.

Other Impacts of Employer Provision of Health Insurance

Employer provision of health insurance has other impacts as well. Because the employer is a large, single buyer of coverage, the purchase of insurance through the employer provides scale economies of dealing with insurance providers that single purchasers could never enjoy. This tends to lower the effective price of coverage to the employees.

In addition, group purchase by employers addresses the problem of adverse selection in the provision of insurance. Recall that in Chapter 8, we considered a club whose members participated in an insurance arrangement. The arrangement worked well because the contract provided a necessary service to the members. In particular, the probability of a claim was a random event that could be calculated, and that was independent of the actions of the members.

Central to this result is the proposition that the probability of usage is independent of the insurance plan. Suppose that the consumer knows that the probability of a claim is not the 5 percent that was assumed by the insurance company, but rather 10 percent. If able to convince an insurer that he or she indeed belonged to the less risky (5 percent) category, the consumer would be able to buy insurance much cheaper than the actuarially fair premium. This consumer would get a bargain; the insurer would lose money. The inability to identify probabilities, and hence their impacts on the insurance market, is often referred to as adverse selection.

As an example, consider an insurance plan that offers major hospitalization coverage. Consider also that many heavy smokers may recognize their higher probabilities of lip, throat, or lung cancer and heart disease. If they can prevent the insurer from

finding out about their smoking, then they can purchase much cheaper insurance than the appropriate premium, given their prior conditions.

It can be argued that the purchase of insurance by employers minimizes adverse selection by providing a more appropriate pool for the fixing of insurance rates. This is because most groups contain a broad mix of risks, by virtue of having been formed for some purpose other than insurance.

Employer-Based Health Insurance and Labor Supply

Because most private health insurance is obtained through employment and is typically not portable to different employers, researchers have sought to determine the extent to which health insurance may affect labor supply. The two major impacts relate to retirement age and job mobility.

Health Insurance and Retirement

Aging workers face a dilemma. Gruber and Madrian (2002) show that compared with those age 35 to 44, those age 55 to 64 are:

- twice as likely to report themselves in fair health and four times as likely to report themselves in poor health,
- seven times as likely to have had a heart attack and five times as likely to have heart disease, and
- forty percent more likely to have a prescribed medicine (with twice as many medicines if receiving a prescription).

As a result, their medical spending is almost twice as large and twice as variable as the younger group.

While declining health makes retirement more attractive, it also makes employer-provided insurance more attractive, especially for those younger than 65 years of age, at which time Medicare would provide insurance for a large portion of the care. Thus, individuals face an incentive to postpone retirement until they are eligible for Medicare at age 65.

Researchers have generally focused on the impact of retiree health insurance on retirement behavior. Gruber and Madrian summarize 16 studies, and report that the availability of retiree health insurance raises the odds of retirement by between 30 and 80 percent.

Health Insurance and Mobility

Health insurance may also affect worker mobility between jobs. Employees may fear losing coverage for preexisting conditions, which are generally defined as any medical problem that has been treated or diagnosed within the past six months to two years. This job lock may have several economic effects:

- Less productive workers may stay at jobs for insurance reasons only, leading to decreased economic output because they would not be replaced by more productive workers.
- Even if all workers are equally productive, some workers may stay in jobs for fear of losing the health insurance benefits to the exclusion of those who would otherwise fill the jobs.

- Those who do change jobs may be denied coverage, face higher premiums, or only obtain insurance subject to a waiver that excludes coverage of their health condition.

Both Cooper and Monheit (1993) and Madrian (1994) address the issue. We look more closely at Madrian's presentation.

Madrian uses a simple matrix of the probability of job mobility to consider the impact of job lock. Because job lock is caused by the potential loss of health insurance coverage with changing jobs, one would not expect those with coverage through both their own employment and an outside job to face job lock.

	Employer-Provided Health Insurance	
	No	Yes
No other health insurance	*a*	*b*
Other health insurance	*c*	*d*

Madrian tests for the magnitude of job lock by examining whether those workers with employer-provided health insurance and other coverage are more likely to change jobs than those without alternative coverage, or:

$$(\text{cell } d) - (\text{cell } b) > 0$$

However, if a man is in cell *d*, it may be due to the insurance provided by his wife, who may be providing income as well; all else being equal, the additional income could lead to increased mobility. Hence, Madrian derives a second test: Whether having other health insurance increases mobility more for those who have employment-based insurance than for those who do not, or:

$$(d - b) - (c - a) > 0$$

This test is referred to as difference-in-difference, the difference between $(d - b)$ and $(c - a)$.

Madrian's most general model looks at the probability of turnover of married men. The data come from the 1987 National Medical Expenditure Survey (NMES), which collected detailed information for 1987 about health insurance and medical care utilization, with several questions about employment, for approximately 14,000 households. She estimates a probit model where the dependent variable is whether the married man changed jobs (1 if he did; 0 if he did not) during the 15-month survey period. The coefficients of a probit model determine the probabilities of job change.

We insert predicted job turnover probabilities into Madrian's matrix Table 11-1. The raw estimate indicates that the mobility rate under job lock (cell *b*) is 0.085, or 26 percent lower than cell *d*, which shows a mobility rate of 0.115. The difference-in-difference estimates, attempting to account for any independent effect of other health insurance on mobility, give an alternative estimate of 31.1 percent.

These results are consistent with anecdotal evidence of job lock as an unintended consequence of the system of employment-related coverage in the United States. It could be addressed through changes that are broadly consistent with prudent insurance practices. These include elimination of preexisting condition clauses and the development of health insurance pooling mechanisms in local labor markets that might promote continuity of coverage across employers. Job lock also must be considered as a consequence of mandated approaches to health insurance benefits, both at state and national levels.

TABLE 11-1 Predicted Job Turnover Probabilities Under the Possibility of Job Lock

| | Employer-Provided Health Insurance | |
	No	Yes
No other health insurance	0.256	0.085
Other health insurance	0.244	0.115
Estimates of job lock		
$(d-b)$	26.1% (13.8%)	
$(d-b)-(c-a)$	31.1% (17.7%)	

Note: Standard errors are in parentheses.
Source: Madrian (1994). Copyright © 1994 MIT Press Journals. All rights reserved.

The Market for Insurance

Although we have discussed the provision of insurance in theory, we now consider some institutional features of the market for health insurance. Such a discussion must address the roles of the Blue Cross insurers, which were originally nonprofit firms, and the commercial insurers, which were typically for-profit. With increased competition in the health care sector, many distinctions have blurred. Nonetheless, to understand the current insurance market, it is helpful to consider how it has developed over time.

The Market for Private Insurance

The number of those privately insured in the United States has burgeoned since the pre–World War II period. From a base of 12 million insured in 1940, it increased by a factor of more than six by 1950 (to 76.6 million), and doubled again (to 158.8 million) by 1970. By 1980, over 187 million residents of the United States had private health insurance.

Well into the 1970s, most of the coverage was provided either by insurance companies (usually in group settings) or by Blue Cross and Blue Shield plans. Since the late 1970s, use of other plans has increased, with declines in both the shares and the absolute numbers of those covered by both the insurance companies and the "Blues." This reflects the movement toward self-insurance by large firms, as well as toward various arrangements through HMOs, preferred provider organizations (PPOs), point-of-service (POS) providers, and other forms of managed care.

Table 11-2 provides more recent health insurance coverage status, as well as type of coverage. The largest portion of the population has private coverage, and the largest portion of that comes through the workplace. In 2004, slightly more than 198 million people had private coverage, with almost 88 percent (over 174 million) getting the coverage from the workplace. Over 79 million had health insurance through the government—some (particularly those with Medicare) were dually covered by both the private market and the government. Based on these government estimates, the number of uninsured increased from about 39 million in 1999 to almost 46 million in 2004.

Insurance Practices

At least two organizational and practice issues characterize the health insurance industry and link it to the emerging issues of managed health care, which will be considered in more depth in Chapter 12. The first issue is a conflict between insurers and the insured (most often represented by the health care providers) regarding the amounts of claims, and indeed whether the claims should be paid at all. From the earliest

TABLE 11-2 Health Insurance Coverage Status and Type of Coverage, 1987–2004 (shown in thousands)

| Year | Total People | Covered by Private or Government Health Insurance | | | | | | | Not Covered |
| | | Private Health Ins. | | | Government Health Ins. | | | | |
		Total	Total	Emp.-based	Total	Medicaid	Medicare	Military	
1987	241,187	210,161	182,160	149,739	56,282	20,211	30,458	10,542	31,026
1990	248,886	214,167	182,135	150,215	60,965	24,261	32,260	9,922	34,719
1995	264,314	223,733	185,881	161,453	69,776	31,877	34,655	9,375	40,582
1996	266,792	225,077	187,395	163,221	69,000	31,451	35,227	8,712	41,716
1997	269,094	225,646	188,532	165,091	66,685	28,956	35,590	8,527	43,448
1998	271,743	227,462	190,861	168,576	66,087	27,854	35,887	8,747	44,281
1999	274,087	234,807	197,523	174,093	66,582	28,221	36,109	8,564	39,280
2000	276,540	237,857	200,249	177,286	66,935	28,613	37,028	8,334	38,683
2001	282,082	240,875	199,860	176,551	71,295	31,601	38,043	9,552	41,207
2002	285,933	242,360	198,973	175,296	73,624	33,246	38,448	10,063	43,574
2003	288,280	243,320	197,869	174,020	76,755	35,647	39,456	9,979	44,961
2004	291,155	245,335	198,262	174,174	79,086	37,514	39,745	10,680	45,820

Source: U.S. Census Bureau, *Current Population Survey*, March 1988–2005.

instances of health insurance, providers, most particularly physicians, have argued that their judgments must not be questioned on cost grounds. Insurers, in contrast, have felt that they could increase their profits and reduce premiums by judiciously questioning treatments and costs.

Why would providers ever consent to having someone second-guess their decisions? Goldberg and Greenberg (1977) traced the growth of health insurance in Oregon in the 1930s. At that time, physicians shared in the Great Depression with the larger population, and they saw acceptance of health insurance, even with its accompanying oversight, as a way of increasing earnings. Although insurance was attractive when times were difficult, considerable opposition arose from physicians' groups, such as the Oregon State Medical Society. They threatened to expel physicians who participated in the plans and to establish their own plans. The plans established by the physicians tended to be less strict in their cost reviews.

Blue Cross and Blue Shield plans were started by medical providers, with Blue Cross providing hospital payment and Blue Shield providing physician payment. The Blues typically offered more complete and more comprehensive coverage, and they paid participating providers directly. They also were usually generous in the payment of hospital care. The development and success of large hospitals in the post-World War II United States was at least in part supported by the generosity of Blue Cross and Blue Shield reimbursement of hospital stays on per-diem bases. The fiscal distress facing many large hospitals in the last fifteen years may be traced to the changes in financing that have accompanied the demise of Blue Cross and Blue Shield leadership in the provision of health insurance, in part related to the strictures placed by Diagnosis Related Group (DRG) controls. DRGs were introduced through Medicare to provide prospective fixed payments for specific diagnoses. These payments induced cost-containment measures that often resulted in reduced hospital stays.

The second organizational pattern that has characterized the industry is the change in "rating" clients. Insurers must pool their clienteles to determine risk premiums based on their experiences with the groups. Blue Cross plans began with a method called community rating. All subscribers in a given location, irrespective of age or

health experience, were charged the same premium. This contrasts with experience rating, or risk rating, in which the insurer charges group premiums (to a company or to a fraternal or service organization) based on its experience with the group.

Community rating provides a fundamental information problem. Low-risk clients are overcharged, and their premiums are transferred to higher-risk clients in the same pool. Advocates of community rating argue that this allows high-risk and low-income clients to buy insurance that would otherwise have been unavailable.

However, if an insurer can identify groups with low risk, it may offer members of these groups lower-cost insurance, or "pick off" these segments of the market. Alternatively, many large firms choose alternative carriers who, again, will charge lower premiums than the community-rated Blue plans. The large firms may in fact choose to self-insure. This "cream skimming" practice may leave the plans that continue to community rate their clienteles with risk pools that are so risky they require almost prohibitively high premiums. Clearly, the extent to which community rating can survive is related to the amount of competition in the health insurance market.

The Past 20 Years

The shift toward managed health care through HMOs and PPOs in the past 20 years has induced a change in philosophy among Blue Cross and Blue Shield insurance plans. The typical Blue Cross and Blue Shield system was facing stiff competition from smaller organizations that were peeling off supposedly more desirable clients from the community-rated system. This would suggest higher costs for those who remained in the system.

One explicit response to the changing marketplace was the 1994 approval of a change in organizational status. Blue Cross plans now can become for-profit firms or establish for-profit subsidiaries. An important example of this occurred in California, where Blue Cross sought to go "for profit". By California law, if such a conversion occurs, the value that has been created in the process must be earmarked for charitable purposes.

Why change? One fundamental reason involves the ability to raise capital. Nonprofit organizations must generate funds through their revenues, whereas for-profit firms may sell stock. With more competition in the marketplace and renewed emphases on lowering premiums and costs of care, the option to sell stock became more attractive.

In a wide-ranging interview (Iglehart, 1995), Blue Cross of California Chief Executive Leonard Schaeffer offered three reasons for the changes in the Blue Cross system:

1. Most Blues plans were big, and had not reacted quickly to marketplace changes.
2. The Blues were successful for a long period of time, and traditional operations got "embedded." This led to a resistance to change.
3. The national association was made up of an "unwieldy" national association with 69 independent plans.

At the time, Schaeffer envisioned that there would be "30, perhaps even 20" associations, organized on a regional basis.

It is useful to evaluate these conversions a decade later. Hall and Conover (2003) note that although the Blues no longer held the overwhelming market shares of 50 years earlier (more than two-thirds of the commercial market), their 2003 share was still considerable. Blue Cross controlled at least half the individual market in 33 states, and more than one-third of the group market in 29 states.

The authors find that conversion created pressures to increase profitability leading to both positive and negative changes. They find little evidence, however, of price increases that differ from overall trends or of dramatic changes in medical underwriting practices. Providers have been most profoundly affected by conversions because converted Blue Cross plans have forced them to offer deep discounts. Hall and Conover conclude that although the evidence is imperfect, there is little indication of harm to the affordability and accessibility of health care at the state level. They caution, however, that each conversion and each state contains unique elements so that proposed future conversions should be assessed on their own terms.

The Uninsured: An Analytical Framework

With the high costs of health care and the inevitability to most of incurring at least some expenses, it has become crucial for individuals to have access to health insurance. In the United States, health insurance availability has been linked to the workplace. Yet surveys have shown that well over 40 million Americans have no health insurance at any moment in time (see Box 11-2), that the number has been climbing recently, and that a large fraction of these people are employed.

Table 11-3 shows that not all people get health insurance through the workplace, and that the problem is particularly severe for small firms and for certain age groups. In 2003, of the 141.8 million nonelderly working Americans (the elderly are covered through Medicare), 26.5 million, or 18.7 percent, were uninsured. The problem was particularly severe for individuals and families getting coverage through small employers. Of the 29.7 million people working in firms with 25 or fewer employees, about 9.7 million people (or 27.4 percent) were uninsured. Contrast this to workers in firms with 1,000 or more employees. A total of 39.3 million workers are in this category, with

BOX 11-2

Counting the Uninsured

Many readers might be surprised to learn that estimates of the uninsured are generally done by survey methods, in samples of the population who are interviewed, rather than by censuses, in which all are counted. Most estimates of the uninsured come from the National Health Interview Survey (NHIS), the March supplement to the Current Population Survey (CPS), the Medical Expenditure Panel Survey (MEPS), and the Survey of Income and Program Participation (SIPP).

The CPS identifies individuals as uninsured if they have lacked coverage for the entire previous calendar year (although many analysts believe that respondents incorrectly provide information about their current insurance status). The SIPP identifies individuals who are uninsured for each month of a four-month reference period. The NHIS identifies individuals as uninsured if they lacked coverage in the month prior to the survey. The MEPS data count as uninsured those without coverage for the entire interview round (an average of three to five months).

Surveys, unlike censuses, do not count every person. Instead, they look at large samples and extrapolate the results to the entire population. As a result, varying counts from varying sources lead to slightly different estimates. The 2002 estimate, using the NHIS, was 40.6 million; using the MEPS it was 45.9 million. The 2004 estimate, using the MEPS, was 48.1 million uninsured.

SOURCE: U.S. Department of Health and Human Services, *Understanding Estimates of the Uninsured: Putting the Differences in Context,* http://aspe.os.dhhs.gov/health/reports/hiestimates.htm, accessed April 13, 2006.

TABLE 11-3 Health Insurance of Workers by Employer Size, 2003

Business Size (# of Workers)	Non-elderly (in millions)	Private		Public		Uninsured
		Employer	Individual	Medicaid	Other	
Total	141.8	100.3	7.9	5.4	1.6	26.5
		70.7%	5.6%	3.8%	1.1%	18.7%
Self-employed	12.8	6.2	2.5	0.3	0.2	3.5
		48.6%	19.6%	2.7%	1.8%	27.4%
Less than 25 workers	29.7	15.8	2.2	1.6	0.4	9.7
		53.3%	7.3%	5.4%	1.4%	32.6%
25 to 99 workers	17.2	12.0	0.8	0.8	0.2	3.5
		69.8%	4.5%	4.5%	0.9%	20.5%
100 to 400 workers	16.3	12.6	0.5	0.6	0.1	2.5
		77.0%	2.9%	3.7%	0.7%	15.6%
500 to 900 workers	6.1	4.8	0.2	0.2	0.1	0.8
		78.0%	3.7%	3.3%	1.1%	13.9%
Over 1000 workers	39.3	31.2	13	1.5	0.4	5.0
		79.4%	3.2%	3.7%	0.9%	12.8%
Public Sectors	20.1	17.6	0.6	0.5	0.3	1.4
		86.4%	2.7%	2.3%	1.5%	7.1%

Source: Catherine Hoffman, Alicia Carbaugh, and Allison Cook, *Health Insurance Coverage in America*, 2003 Data Update, Kaiser Family Foundation, November 2004, Table 7, with permission.

5.0 million (or 12.8 percent) uninsured. Box 11-3 addresses several common misperceptions about the numbers and motivations of the uninsured.

Under any circumstance, it is important to examine the reasons that some individuals lack insurance. As noted, insurers must be able to lower the loading factors, which are the costs of determining probabilities of claims and processing claims. The ability to insure through the workplace gives the opportunity to improve the experience rating. In principle, private insurers can insure those outside the workplace, and many do, particularly with relation to affinity groups, such as organizations and clubs, or in terms of insuring the elderly. If high costs lead to onerous payments, then the problem may be poverty rather than high prices. This would suggest the need for governmental subsidies in a social insurance scheme.

Table 11-4 examines the percentages of the uninsured by age and finds considerably higher, and generally growing (over time), percentages of uninsured persons in age categories 25 to 34 (23.8 percent in 2002) and 35 to 44 (17.8 percent in 2002). Holahan and Prohl (2002) note that from 1994 to 2000 the percentage of those who were uninsured was essentially unchanged. During a time of economic prosperity, the rate of employer-sponsored insurance increased sharply, so that more people had employer coverage. However, these increases were offset by reductions in other forms of coverage, particularly Medicaid and state-sponsored insurance and private non-group coverage, so the overall rate of "uninsurance" did not change.

The Working Uninsured

Consider now the working uninsured. Employees' remuneration may be considered as net wage, w_n, an hourly sum that equals the sum of money wage, w, plus insurance, i_0:

$$w_n = w + i_0 \tag{11.1}$$

BOX 11-3

Some Myths About the Uninsured

Myth: **The uninsured go without coverage because they believe they do not need it or don't want it.**

Fact: Only 7 percent of the uninsured report the main reason they lack insurance is because they don't think they need it. The majority of the uninsured (52 percent) say the main reason they don't have health insurance is because it is too expensive. The next most common reason is not being eligible for their job's health benefits (11 percent).

Myth: **Most of the uninsured do not have health insurance because they are not working and so don't have access to health benefits through an employer.**

Fact: Eight in ten uninsured Americans come from working families; even at lower income levels, the majority of the uninsured have workers in their families. However, 81 percent of uninsured workers are employed by firms who do not sponsor health benefits or are not eligible for their employer's plan. Few workers, even low-wage workers, turn down health benefits when available.

Myth: **The uninsured often receive health services for free or at reduced charge.**

Fact: Less than a quarter of families with at least one uninsured member report having received care for free or at reduced rates—in part, because the uninsured frequently go without needed care. Charges for services may actually be higher for the uninsured in comparison to fees negotiated by managed care organizations or set by public payers.

Myth: **The uninsured can get the care they need when they really need it and are able to avoid serious health problems.**

Fact: Over one-third of the uninsured report needing care in the previous year but not getting it and nearly half of the uninsured report postponing care—rates at least three times higher than those with insurance. Studies repeatedly bear out that the uninsured are less likely than those with insurance to receive services for major health conditions, including traumatic injuries, heart attacks, pregnancy, and cancer.

Myth: **Buying health insurance coverage on your own is always an option.**

Fact: When job-based health benefits are not offered or affordable, the purchaser of an individual policy faces a wide variety of covered services and prices, when healthy enough to qualify. The average annual cost of a family policy purchased in the individual market is about $3,300, in contrast to the average cost of $2,700 that an employee pays out-of-pocket towards group coverage. Since a person pays the entire premium costs for an individual plan, it is an even less viable option for the low-income uninsured. Beside these premium differences, deductibles and other cost-sharing requirements are often much higher in the individual insurance market.

SOURCE: www.kff.org/uninsured/upload/Myths-about-the-Uninsured-Fact-Sheet.pdf, with permission, accessed August 17, 2005.

Figure 11-4 shows the equilibrium employment point A for the profit-maximizing firm, where the value of the marginal product equals the net wage, w_n, that must be paid for benefit level i_0. At this equilibrium, L_0 workers are employed.

The literature suggests that many businesses, especially small businesses, may have limited experience ratings; as a result, their loading costs may be high, as much as 10 to 40 percent higher than those paid by large firms. If the loading costs are high, then the small firms may be able to afford to pay only small, or zero, i. To compete with other firms, they must match the w_n ; hence, it may be necessary that their w be larger than the wage level for other firms.

McLaughlin and Zellers (1994) summarize three major types of barriers to small business provision of health benefits. The first, affordability, is a price-related barrier

TABLE 11-4 Percentage of Population Under Age 65 Not Covered by Insurance

Age Category	1984	1989	1995	2000	2002
Under 6	14.9	15.1	11.8	11.7	9.1
Ages 6–17	13.4	14.5	14.3	12.8	11.5
Ages 18–24	25.0	27.1	28.0	29.7	28.2
Ages 25–34	16.2	18.3	21.1	22.7	23.8
Ages 35–44	11.2	12.3	15.1	16.8	17.8
Ages 45–54	10.5	11.0	11.6	12.8	14.1
Ages 55–64	8.7	10.0	9.9	12.5	11.6

Source: U.S. Department of Health and Human Services, *Health United States* (2004), Table 131.

FIGURE 11-4 Impact of Mandated Benefits on Employment

and is summarized in Figure 11-4, leading to increased net wage, w_n. Particularly in low-wage industries, a combination of low profit margins, low wages, and high premiums may make it difficult to provide health benefits.

There are two other broad categories of nonprice-related barriers to the offering of health benefits. Insurance redlining or preexisting-condition clauses may exclude specific individuals, or companies that employ them, from insurance coverage. The authors note that redlined industries typically employ older workers (over age 55), have high employee turnover, seasonal workforces, or workforces paid by commission or on the basis of other contractual terms. Lawyers' offices may be redlined because of fears of litigation, and physicians' offices because of fears of high utilization of health care services.

In the late 1980s and early 1990s a particular confluence of such factors occurred in the case of beauty shops, which had great difficulty buying group insurance for their employees (McLaughlin, 1993). Compared with the general population, three large groups of beauty shop employees were costly to insure:

1. Workers who worked only intermittently. Evidence showed that some workers enter the labor force when they need health care. Such adverse selection of the insured pool may lead to high costs for insurers.

2. Young women of childbearing age who were likely to have children. This again led to high insurance costs.

3. An apparently large homosexual workforce whose members were at higher risk of exposure to HIV/AIDS.

In short, many nonprice barriers are placed before certain groups, including preexisting condition clauses, long delays in processing applications, and, if the would-be client is persistent, extraordinarily high premiums, which make enrollment prohibitively expensive. As a result, many small businesses simply cannot obtain insurance.

A third barrier to the provision of coverage may be termed attitudes. Many firms are uninterested in offering insurance. Sometimes a large number of their employees can piggyback on health plans of spouses' or partners' employers. In such cases, employees prefer to be compensated in higher wages rather than in benefits.

Feldman and colleagues (1998) analyze a 1993 survey of Minnesota small employers. One of the problems with this type of research is that the costs of premiums are available for those firms that do buy insurance, but they are not for those that do not. (Consider asking people who did not buy cars how much they didn't spend!) The researchers carefully assigned insurance premiums to those who did not buy, and found that a $1 decrease in the price of individual insurance increased the probability of coverage from 0.610 to 0.627. This seemingly small change implies that a 1 percent decrease in insurance premium leads to a substantial 3.91 percentage point increase in small firm demand for insurance (an elasticity of −3.91).

In contrast, Kronick and colleagues (2004) found much smaller responses in a trial in which they randomly assigned small businesses to experimental treatments which varied by how much employers and employees were required to pay for coverage. A treatment which reduced the price of insurance from $145 to $60, or 57 percent, was estimated to raise the total offering rate from 73 to 79 percent of San Diego businesses, an elasticity of −0.14. They concluded:

- The small employer market is a smaller target than is sometimes thought.
- Even very substantial subsidies have limited effect on employer decisions.
- Programs that subsidize insurance for small businesses are unlikely to have a substantial effect in reducing the number of uninsured.

The Impacts of Mandated Coverage

Many groups have advocated that the federal government or individual states mandate some, more, or particular types of coverage. Returning to Figure 11-4, if such coverage is provided through employer insurance, the mandates would raise the amount of i, as well as its costs. Firm responses to the increased marginal costs may result in two adverse impacts. The first is for the company to stop offering insurance entirely because it is too expensive. Thus, rather than having modest health coverage with the benefits of whatever experience rating may exist within the workplace, there may be no coverage at all. (Alternatively, play-or-pay proposals might require firms to provide a minimal level of insurance or to pay into an insurance pool that would insure the uninsured). The firm then may have to raise the wage to keep employees, who would have to buy their own insurance. This may allow for employee choice, but it also denies the employee workplace-related experience rating.

The second adverse impact also may be understood by examining Figure 11-4. The equilibrium of value of marginal product and net wage at point *A* represents a labor force of the appropriate size to maximize profits for the producer. To the extent that mandated coverage reflects increased worker benefits—that is, to the extent that i_1

exceeds i_0—it must either increase net wage, w_n, or decrease base wage, w. If net wage w_n rises, marginal workers now cost more than they are worth in terms of marginal productivity, and if firms are acting to maximize profits, some workers may be let go, leading to the new equilibrium point B. By this analysis, the result of mandated coverage, similar to the result of a binding minimum wage, is likely to be some additional unemployment amount $(L_0 - L_1)$, which, of course, means sharply curtailed insurance benefits.[2] How much the employment falls is related to the elasticity (or responsiveness) of the labor demand curve to the increased gross wage.

Alternatively, if base wage, w, falls to maintain net wage, w_n, in the face of increased benefits, the workers have less money to spend on other goods; insurance has effectively crowded out other expenditures. Furthermore, the firm may lose workers to other firms that are willing to pay the increased w_n as a result of the mandated coverage.

Mandated insurance benefits have become most popular at the state level. States mandate provider, benefit, and coverage extensions. Coverage mandates as of 2001 included chiropractors (44 states), optometrists (38 states), and dentists (36 states). Benefit mandates included mammography screening (49 states), alcoholism treatment (43 states), and maternity length of stay (50 states + Washington DC). Thirty-seven states mandated continuation of coverage to employees, and 36 states mandated coverage for handicapped dependents.

Jensen and Morrisey (1999) found that smaller firms were affected disproportionately by mandates in part because they were less likely than larger firms to be able to avoid the costs of mandates by self-insuring. This implied that because health insurance would be more expensive for smaller firms (because they must include the mandated benefit), they would be less likely to offer coverage to employees.

Insurance, Technological Change, and Higher Costs

We have seen that increased insurance coverage increases health care demand, and we know that increased demand raises price levels. However, health insurance also can induce innovations, which may be either cost decreasing or cost increasing. Furthermore, as Weisbrod (1991) has explained, a two-way relationship can exist between insurance and innovation as new health products also may stimulate the demand for insurance.

The Cost-Increasing Bias Hypothesis

Intuitively, because increased health insurance usually reduces the out-of-pocket portion of the bill, the patient may be willing to spend considerably more when insured. Consumers may realize that premiums will tend to rise if all patients act likewise, but they will make use of the best, new, expensive technology to the maximum extent affordable, generally beyond the point where the marginal benefits equal the full marginal costs. Consequently, the payoff to owning a patent to new, costly health care technology increases.

Process innovations (improvements to existing treatment processes that make them less costly) and product innovations (improvements through the introduction of new products, which could make the treatment more costly even when lowering the cost of improvements to the patient's well-being) may be affected differently.

[2]Although a minimum wage may be in place, if employers must pay more due to local market conditions, then an increase in the minimum wage may have no impact on employment. Similarly, if employers are already offering more than the mandated coverage, broadening the mandates may have little or no impact.

Insurance can encourage new products and influence innovations toward those that increase costs.

The Goddeeris Model

By its very definition, technology involves innovative change over time. As a result the model we use will be looking at changes in health expenditure Δm on the x-axis and changes in health care Δh on the y-axis. These elements of the relationship between insurance and innovation are made more explicit by a model formulated by John Goddeeris (1984a). Consider providers who currently offer levels of health care h_0, which is paid for by medical expenditures m_0. Ignoring inflation, if there are no changes in health technology, change Δh will be zero, as will be the change in expenditures Δm. We denote that point as the origin of the graph, or point 0.

Providers may choose innovations to improve health care if they lead to increased profits. Some innovations are "cost reducing" (negative values of Δm), and some may provide better health, but at higher cost levels (entailing positive values of Δm). The curve in Figure 11-5 $\Delta h(\Delta m)$ shows the theoretical impacts of increased medical expenditures Δm on improvements in health, Δh. Goddeeris hypothesizes that innovations that tend toward cost-increasing change (higher values of Δm) also yield greater improvements in health (higher values of Δh). Under what circumstances will innovations be chosen?

Consumers are commonly insured such that they pay only a fraction, z, of the provider's bill out-of-pocket. Potential innovations have consequences for the equilibrium health of the consumers and for the costs of treatment. Looking at the function, $\Delta h(\Delta m)$, an innovation may raise health by Δh_1 and reduce treatment costs by Δm_1; this example results in point D_1 in panel A. An alternative innovation may increase treatment costs, say by m_2, but substantially increase health, say by Δh_2, the outcome of which is shown by point D_2 in panel A.

By investing in a given innovation, providers seek to increase profits. Their extra profit obtained through the innovation equals the extra revenue minus the extra costs. If patients value each additional unit of health at a constant rate of \$1, then they are

FIGURE 11-5 The Impact of Increased Innovation Expenditures on Health

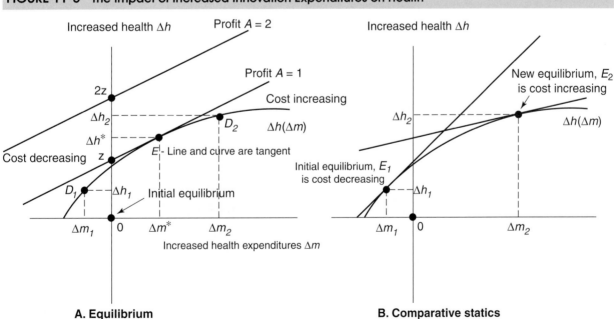

A. Equilibrium **B. Comparative statics**

willing at most to pay $1 for $1 improvement in health status. However, the providers can charge a full price per unit of $\Delta h/z$ for the innovation. In other words, suppose that consumers have a 10 percent coinsurance rate. Providers could charge up to $9.99 for an improvement worth $1 to the consumer, because the consumer would be paying less than $1 $(0.1 \times \$9.99)$ out-of pocket for the improvements.

Providers evaluate innovations by comparing extra revenues to extra costs. In Figure 11-5A, we represent profits by the isoprofit lines, defined as a collection of points that yields a constant profit level. The isoprofit equation for profit level A is thus:

$$\text{Extra profits } (A) = \text{Change in Revenues} - \text{Change in Costs} = \Delta h/z - \Delta m \quad \textbf{(11.2)}$$

If we algebraically rearrange terms, the isoprofit equation can be written treating the dependent variable, Δh, as a function of the remaining terms. That is, the isoprofit equation is:

$$\Delta h = z(A + \Delta m) = zA + z\Delta m$$

This is a linear (straight line) equation with intercept zA and slope z. Thus, the lower the coinsurance rate (the more comprehensive the insurance), the smaller the slope of the line.

Two isoprofit lines are shown in panel A. The isoprofit line for extra profit level $2 is so labeled in the graph. Its intercept is found by setting Δm equal to zero in the function $\Delta h = z \times 2 + z\Delta m$; thus, the intercept is $2z$. Similarly, the $1 isoprofit line has an intercept of z. In general, higher isoprofit lines yield higher extra profit levels. In panel A, the isoprofit line 2 is unattainable given the function $\Delta h(\Delta m)$ shown. In contrast, isoprofit line 1 is just attainable. The equilibrium choice will be a point of tangency between the $\Delta h(\Delta m)$ function and the highest isoprofit curve attainable. Under the circumstances shown in panel A, the equilibrium will be at point E, with change in medical expenditure Δm^*, and corresponding change in health Δh^*, which is slightly higher than vertical intercept z.

Compare the profit-maximizing equilibria for two values of z, let's say a 20 percent coinsurance rate and a 10 percent coinsurance rate. From equation (11.2) the larger the value of z, then the steeper is the isoprofit line. In panel B, innovators find their optimal choices to have changed when the isoprofit curves became flatter. Assume that if the initial coinsurance rate is 20 percent (or 0.2), the optimal choice initially is point E_1, a point of tangency. When the insurance coverage becomes more generous, coinsurance rate z falls to 0.1, implying that the highest extra profit will be attained at a new equilibrium, in this case at point E_2 in panel B. We can conclude that the more generous insurance coverage induces a higher level of Δm than for the initial equilibrium. The innovator has switched from an emphasis on cost-reducing (because equilibrium Δm_1 is negative) innovations, such as at point E_1, to cost-increasing innovations (because equilibrium Δm_2 is positive) such as at point E_2.

Evidence on Insurance, Technological Change, and Inflation

Newhouse (1978b, 1988) set out the basic empirical models designed to test the underlying hypotheses and measure the contribution of health insurance to health care inflation. First, the conventional view emphasized the role of insurance as a demand shifter; this is measured by the variable "change in insurance." Second, the level of health insurance (indicated by the average coinsurance rate) was hypothesized to induce innovations, thus causing inflation indirectly through cost-increasing technological

change. By 1988, Newhouse had found, though somewhat tentatively, evidence that supported the induced-innovation hypothesis, leaving uncertain whether any role at all existed for the conventional demand-shifting avenue.

Investigating a larger data series and providing more testing of underlying econometric issues, Peden and Freeland (1998) helped resolve the remaining questions. They studied the coinsurance level, the level of noncommercial research spending, and the annual change in average coinsurance from 1963 to 1993, during which time real per capita health spending grew by 373 percent. About half of this expenditure increase was due to the level of coinsurance, giving support to the induced-innovation hypothesis. In contrast, their data offered little support for the demand-shifting effect of reduced coinsurance. Personal income growth over the period contributed more than 20 percent of the inflation, which was more than previously thought.

Does Induced Technological Change Make the Patient Better Off?

A troubling aspect of the relationship of insurance coverage to innovation was pointed out by Goddeeris (1984b). Health insurance coverage, which reduces the fraction of the bill paid by the patient out-of-pocket, may induce many patients to use new health technologies that are not worth their full cost. The average patient pays the full cost of new technologies through an increase in insurance premiums in addition to out-of-pocket costs. Goddeeris showed that the average patient may be worse off after the new technology is introduced than before it was invented; however, this issue of potential welfare gains or losses from innovation is complex to pursue.

One problem is that the current insurance system tends to provide the consumer with incentives such that what is good for an individual is bad for society. Patients may understand fully that if everyone used the new, expensive health technology, then costs would increase substantially for all. However, individuals may receive significant personal benefits and correctly ascertain that their personal contributions to higher premiums are small.

A second problem is that alternative insurance schemes with better incentive structures may never arise. Goddeeris shows that if insurance plans paid a flat lump sum per given diagnosis instead of a fraction of the charges, then the problem of "harmful" innovations would not arise, but that such policies are not likely to be implemented. Although his analysis does not prove that the recent pattern of technological change in health care has harmed patient welfare in net, it explains the possibility. It also shows that the possibility for harmful patterns of innovation is consistent with the existing incentive structure of insurance coverage.

Conclusions

Chapter 8 introduced readers to the concept of insurance and to the specific issue of health insurance for individuals. In this chapter, we focused on the insurance market and the behaviors of firms within that market. We established that in a market setting, insurance constitutes an important part of the wage package, and to the extent that it is valuable to the workforce, higher insurance is reflected in lower money wages. This market result occurs irrespective of who contractually pays for the insurance.

We've shown how many of the trappings of the U.S. health care system are related to the employer base of the health insurance. The system of tax deductibility pushes employees to ask for higher proportions of untaxed insurance relative to taxed wage benefits. The linkage of insurance to the workplace also tends to lock employees into certain jobs, constraining mobility. We continued with a brief discussion of the evolution of the health insurance industry. This industry was formerly defined by the Blues

(Blue Cross and Blue Shield) with their nonprofit status, community rating, and predilection for hospital care. The decline in the primacy of the Blues in the late 1980s and 1990s has led to profound changes in the provision of health insurance and the delivery of care.

The chapter also included several implications about the uninsured. These are often people who are not working, and hence are uninsured. There are others whose health, employment, or lifestyle statuses may not permit commercial insurers to provide insurance profitably. Government mandates to employers that they insure everyone, if they insure anyone, often cause employers to drop insurance plans entirely, thus leaving larger numbers at risk. A safety net for those who are difficult to insure requires a social contract that only the government can provide. We finished the chapter by looking at the impact of insurance on cost-increasing technological change. Having looked at the structure of the insurance industry, we turn next to issues of managed care.

SUMMARY

1. In theory, individual health insurance trades off a guaranteed reduction in wealth (the insurance premium) for a reduction in uncertainty due to ill health through the pooling of risk. The organization and cost conditions in some health insurance markets, however, suggest that some contingencies may not be insurable.

2. The economies of scale in processing information suggest that smaller firms or unions may see marginal insurance costs relative to marginal benefits levels. These higher costs may reduce or eliminate the range of services that they offer.

3. If health insurance is valued by the workers in an industry, then competitive pressures mean that increased health benefits are offset by reduced money wages.

4. Subsidizing health insurance through government tax policies lowers the price of $1 of insurance premium relative to $1 of wage remuneration. This leads employees to purchase more health insurance relative to wages than would otherwise occur.

5. Health insurance is a key determinant in the decision to retire. Studies suggest that the availability of retiree health insurance raises the odds of retirement by between 30 and 80 percent.

6. Employer-provided health insurance may inhibit worker mobility between firms, thus locking employees into jobs. Researchers find this job lock to be responsible for 25 to 31 percent reductions in employee mobility.

7. Much of the American health insurance environment has been defined by Blue Cross and Blue Shield plans, which as nonprofit firms were typically exempted from profits taxes, property taxes, and federal and state corporate taxes. Analysts once felt that such tax treatments gave the Blues considerable competitive advantages, but over the past 15 years, the Blues have been subjected to considerable competition.

8. Many groups have advocated that the federal government or individual states mandate either more coverage or various types of coverage. In reaction:
 • Companies may stop offering insurance entirely because it is too expensive.
 • Marginal workers may now cost more than they are worth, and some of them will be let go.

9. The Goddeeris model shows how technological change can be influenced by insurance coverage. Greater insurance coverage increases the relative profitability of cost-increasing technological innovations versus cost-reducing ones.

DISCUSSION QUESTIONS

1. Suppose each person's health expenditures can be predicted with certainty by both the insured and the insurer. What are the implications for insurance markets? Explain the prevalence of insurance for highly predictable events, such as routine dental services.

2. In 1986, the U.S. federal income tax system changed marginal tax rates so that the top marginal rate fell from 50 to 33 percent. Given the way that fringe benefits are negotiated, what would you expect to happen to the demand for health insurance as a fringe benefit? Why?

3. Suppose, as a worker, your health insurance currently allows you to buy whatever prescription drugs you wish for $2 per prescription. In contract negotiations it is proposed to change this benefit to "10–20," that is, you pay $10 for generic drugs and $20 for brand name drugs. What would your reaction be? What would economic analysis predict?
4. Suppose that a company pays its workers $20 per hour and provides an additional $2 per hour worth of fringe benefits, including a basic health insurance policy. Discuss the firm's reaction to a state mandate that requires it to expand the items covered in the health care policy. What is likely to happen to the number of people employed?
5. Blue Cross plans typically have practiced community rating. If other insurance firms are seeking healthier patients at reduced rates, what impact will this have on Blue Cross net revenues? Why?
6. It often is advocated that health insurers be prevented from denying insurance to those with preexisting conditions, such as cancer or AIDS, at "reasonable" rates. Analyze the impacts of such regulations on insurance markets.
7. What is job lock? Would you expect job lock to increase or decrease if employer-based health insurance were to be replaced by government-provided health insurance?
8. Suppose a household does not carry health insurance. Can we conclude that this reflects failure of insurance markets? Why or why not?

EXERCISES

1. Using Figure 11-1, illustrate the probability that someone will obtain insurance for treatment for:
 - A hangnail
 - A broken arm
 - A "bad hair" day
 - Viral meningitis
2. Using Figure 11-2:
 - Calculate an initial labor market equilibrium (wages and employment) determined by the demand and supply of labor.
 - Indicate the wage and employment impacts of a health insurance policy that costs $2 per hour to employers and is worth $1.50 per hour to the workers.
 - Indicate the wage and employment impacts of a health insurance policy that costs $1.50 per hour to employers and is worth $2 per hour to the workers.
3. Using Figure 11-2, consider an insurance policy that provides free "purple aspirin" to all workers. This benefit provides no conceivable advantage (workers don't care whether their aspirin is purple or white) but comes with cost z. Show the new labor market equilibrium indicating the wage and employment impacts.
4. Using Figure 11-2, indicate the wage and employment impacts of a health insurance policy that costs $2 per hour to the workers and is worth exactly $3 per hour to the workers. Why do your answers to exercises 2, 3, and 4 differ?
5. Consider the market demand for labor L_D and the supply of labor L_S, where W is the market wage.

$$\text{Demand: } L_D = 1,000 - 20W$$
$$\text{Supply: } L_S = -200 + 40W$$

 a. What is the equilibrium market wage? What is the equilibrium employment level?
 b. Calculate the equilibrium market wage and employment level if the workers negotiate a benefit worth $1 that costs the employers $2.
 c. Calculate the equilibrium market wage and employment level if the workers negotiate a benefit worth $2 that costs the employers $1.
6. Consider two workers, Ralph and Steve. Both of them work for the same employer, and each earns $15 per hour. Ralph is taxed at the 15 percent marginal rate. However, Steve is married, and due to his wife's income, he is taxed at the 28 percent marginal rate. Using Figure 11-3, indicate which one would be expected to seek more health insurance and why.

7. Suppose that Charlie's Pizzeria in Kalamazoo, Michigan, employs 10 employees at a wage level of $8 per person. All other costs (ovens, rent, advertising, return to capital) total $40 per hour, and the pizzeria sells 12 pizzas per hour at a cost of $10 per pizza. Suppose the state of Michigan mandates health coverage that can only be covered at a cost of $1 per hour, if it is offered at all. Charlie finds that if he offers insurance, he could maintain production by letting one worker go and running his pizza ovens a little hotter, leading to costs of $45 per hour.
 a. What are Charlie's original profits?
 b. What is Charlie's elasticity of demand for labor? How is this calculated?
 c. What will happen to Charlie's profits in the short run if he chooses to pay for mandated insurance?
 d. What will Charlie's long-run decision be? Why?

8. In the Goddeeris model in Figure 11-5, how would the equilibrium change in expenditure, Δm, be affected if there were a vertical parallel shift in the $\Delta h(\Delta m)$ curve, say caused by increased support of medical technological research? Show graphically the alternative possibility if support for research tended to emphasize cost-reducing innovations.

CHAPTER 12

Managed Care

Health insurance will generally increase consumers' health care consumption. People who are insured consider the out-of-pocket cost of care rather than the true full cost at the point of service. This means that they purchase inpatient days, outpatient visits, or prescription drugs, for example, beyond the point at which the marginal benefit of the care equals its marginal cost. For insurance to provide a net benefit to society, the costs of this increased consumption must be overcome by the benefits of reduced patient risk. Even with these risk-reduction benefits, improved insurance coverage leads to increased costs to society.

A simple analogy may help address the dilemma. Suppose that rather than health care insurance, employers provided food and clothing (F&C) insurance for their workers. A "fee-for-service" F&C plan would allow the consumers to purchase their food and clothing at any merchant they choose, and would reimburse the consumers subject to coinsurance rates and deductibles. A consumer facing a 20 percent coinsurance rate could purchase filet mignon for $20 per pound and have the insurer pay $16 per pound, or 80 percent of the price. Another consumer could purchase designer athletic shoes for $200 and have the insurer pay $160, again 80 percent of the price. Consumers would likely buy more (or more expensive) filet mignon or athletic shoes than if they had to pay the full amount themselves. The market effect of such plans would likely cause consumers and their insurers to worry about F&C cost and expenditure inflation.

Suppose that in response to the perceived high costs of food and clothing, a group of consumers and their employers organized and offered a "managed F&C" plan. In this plan, members (consumers and the employers) would pay a fixed amount per person per month into the plan for food and clothing, presumably less than they were paying (together) under the fee-for-service plan. In return for this reduced cost plan, the consumers would be limited to shopping at a single shopping center with which plan managers had negotiated lower prices for food and clothing. Moreover, the plan managers could limit the types of goods purchased (no filet mignon) and might attempt to curb total consumer expenditures. It is likely that at least some consumers would find such a plan attractive due to its lower costs.

Analysis of this "managed care" F&C arrangement raises a host of questions. For individual consumers, one might ask:

- Are they getting the same quality of goods as before?
- Are they being denied goods that they "should" be getting?
- Are their expenditures reduced?
- Are they less well-fed, less healthy, or less well-dressed than before?

At the market level, one might ask:

- Do aggregate F&C expenditures decrease or does their growth rate decrease?
- Do the managed F&C plans meet consumer preferences?
- Can the merchants earn sufficient returns to stay in business?
- Is there competition in the managed care F&C market, and do the managed care F&C plans influence the fee-for-service F&C plans in terms of the prices or selection of goods?

With this in mind, we turn to the issue of managed health care. One might argue that physician practice must be managed in order to address high health care costs. This suggests that networks of providers, including HMOs, PPOs, and independent practice associations (IPAs), are widely seen as means to restore competition to the health care sector and as means to control expanding heath care costs. We devote this chapter to managed care with particular attention to the distinctive combination of insurance and care exemplified by HMOs and similar organizations. Unless distinguishing the individual types of institutions, we will refer to them as managed care. The HMO receives special attention in this chapter for its pioneering role and for the fact that much of the scholarly and policy research has focused on HMOs.

HMOs appear to overcome the information problems inherent in fee-for-service (FFS) health care markets that may be exacerbated by ordinary insurance coverage. Under FFS, the provider provides health care and advises the consumer on how much is needed. At first glance, it appears that the consumer's imperfect information about health care, when combined with FFS remuneration, may create the incentives for substantial overconsumption. The HMO organizational form appears to eliminate the overconsumption incentives and replace them with cost-control incentives and even possibly incentives toward underconsumption.

We begin this chapter by describing managed care and its cost-cutting potential. We then turn to HMOs as a form of health care organization in which the functions of insurance and the provision of care are combined. We describe the HMO and its organizational relatives, and we assess the theory and evidence on their effects. We then turn to the market effects of managed care on providers, insurers, and the adoption of new health care technology.

What Is the Organizational Structure?

It is instructive to provide a general description of managed care, leading to a more specific discussion of HMOs, while recognizing that the concept of managed care is undergoing constant changes. Analysts speak of an organized delivery system as a network of organizations (for example, hospitals, physicians, clinics, and hospices) that provides or arranges to provide a coordinated continuum (from well care to emergency surgery) of services to a defined population. This system is held clinically and fiscally accountable for the outcomes and the health status of the population served. It is tied together by its clinical (treatment) and fiscal (financial) accountability for the defined population. Often the organized delivery system is defined by its association with an insurance product.

In principle, managed care creates incentives for keeping people well by emphasizing prevention and health promotion practices and by treating those who become ill at the most cost effective location in the continuum of care. Through a more centralized management of services, the goal is to provide additional quality-enhancing features for a given price or to provide a given set of quality attributes or outcomes for a lower price. A primary provider typically serves as the patient's gatekeeper to help ensure appropriate care and limit overutilization.

Two features characterize the contemporary managed care organization (MCO). The first is the extensive reliance on health care information systems. Initially, these systems were developed mainly to replace clerical functions, such as billing and record keeping. Indeed, the "embryonic" development of clinical information systems constituted a fundamental barrier to the success of managed care organizations. In the 1990s, large health centers budgeted millions of dollars per year to integrate systems that often were developed separately and almost never "talked to each other" (Shortell et al., 1994). A major challenge facing managed care is the design of information networks that provide direct clinical support to improve the process of care.

A second feature of MCOs is a studied de-emphasis of the acute care hospital. Hospitals provide expensive care, and moving toward cost-effective systems necessarily moves away from hospitals. As noted earlier, primary care physicians are often the gatekeepers of managed care systems, directing patients to appropriate (i.e., cost-effective) treatment settings. If they "feed" patients into the hospital instead, this leads to increased costs. Managed care seeks a vertical integration of what had previously been a generally unintegrated system of health care treatment. Through coordination of care and improved information, such integration has the potential to address the health care costs in a manner that would appear to address criteria of economic efficiency. Yet the integration is costly, and the quality of the resulting care may not match all consumer preferences. Some also claim that managed care systems have incentives to underuse services, which may be harmful to patients.

The HMO represents a prime example of managed care on which there has been considerable research. We begin by describing HMOs and continue with their history and the rationale for a government policy that has promoted their development.

What Are the Economic Characteristics?

Managed care features a health care delivery structure involving the integration of insurers, payment mechanisms, and a host of providers, including physicians and hospitals. What distinguishes managed care from the fee-for-service care that also might plausibly attempt to integrate the various health care system parts?

Analysts identify three particular mechanisms by which health insurance plans seek to contain costs and/or improve quality of care:

1. Selective contracting, in which payers negotiate prices and contract selectively with local providers such as physicians and hospitals.
2. Steering of enrollees to the selected providers.
3. Utilization review of the appropriateness of provider practices. This utilization review may be prospective (in advance), concurrent (at the same time), or retrospective (looking back).

Of the three, most analysts find selective contracting to be most important. Dranove, Simon, and White (1998) point out that contracts may be awarded on the basis of the providers' willingness to accept particular payment plans and monitoring of treatment styles and quality of care. Morrisey (2001b) notes that under selective contracting (unlike fee-for-service care), some providers get contracts and some do not. Service price becomes important in managed care system negotiations with providers.

The selective contracting and the steering distinguish managed care from the more standard fee-for-service care. Although the press concentrates on utilization reviews attributed to managed care, Morrisey argues that indemnity plans that include pre-hospital admission certification would be classified as managed care plans under this definition. Almost everyone now reviews utilization, so utilization review in itself is not helpful in discussing managed care.

How, then, might we distinguish MCOs and FFS? Cutler, McClellan, and Newhouse (2000) provide a useful conceptual model that asks how much a patient would have to be compensated to move from FFS to MCO coverage. The compensation presumably would be related to the patient's difference in utility (satisfaction) between FFS and MCO coverage. If an MCO and an FFS plan were identical, the compensation would be zero; if the MCO leads to less (more) utility, compensation must be positive (negative) to make the client indifferent.

Three differences between MCOs and FFS might affect compensation:

1. *Difference in health*. If the MCO provides reduced health (relative to FFS) due to reduced treatment, then the compensation must be positive for those who choose the MCO. This positive compensation might be offset if the MCO is better at managing the overall care process or at providing "well-care."
2. *Cost savings*. If, holding health constant, the MCO provides savings due either to less treatment or cheaper treatment, then the compensation must be negative, because the MCO is saving money for its clients.
3. *Financial risk from different out-of-pocket payments*. Clients may prefer an MCO if it insures them from having to make large out-of-pocket payments. If so, the compensation will be negative because payment variability is reduced. The size of the compensation would depend on the MCO's cost-sharing provisions, as well as reimbursement for out-of-plan use.

This framework suggests that one must measure the differences between managed care and fee-for-service along several dimensions: health, price of care, and quality of care. In fact, patients who value health less (or other things more) may choose less health and/or health care by choosing an MCO, or possibly even no insurance, rather than FFS care.

It does not necessarily tell us which mechanism provides the appropriate level of care at which marginal benefits equal marginal costs. Recall that under FFS, with fractional coinsurance, clients may overuse services. Under MCO, they may use fewer services and possibly not enough services, but it is not clear whether they will use the efficient amount.

With this framework established, we can look at the emergence of managed care plans and what the market for managed care will look like. We also can look at the differences in health, price, or quality of care, recognizing that consumers and employers, acting on their behalf, will evaluate all of these dimensions in spending their health insurance dollars.

The Emergence of Managed Care Plans

Managed care describes a variety of arrangements with the following common features. First, much, if not all, of the patient's care is provided through a specific network of hospitals, physicians, and other health care providers. Second, considerable centralized oversight of resource use, often referred to as utilization review, occurs within the network. Here, we provide a brief overview of the types of managed care plans and the extent to which physicians and hospitals now contract with insurers under capitation arrangements.

Employer-Sponsored Managed Care

Managed care accounted for 97 percent of the enrollment of employer-sponsored health insurance in 2005, with traditional FFS plans making up the rest. Figure 12-1 shows the historic and remarkable shift to managed care from just 27 percent of enrollment in 1988. Figure 12-1 also shows the proportions enrolled in the three main types of employer-sponsored managed care plans.

Health maintenance organizations (HMOs) provide relatively comprehensive health care, entail few out-of-pocket expenses, but generally require that all care be delivered through the plan's network, and that the primary care physician authorize most services provided. Each subscriber is assigned a primary care physician upon joining the HMO. If health care services are provided but not authorized by the primary

FIGURE 12-1 Health Plan Enrollment for Covered Workers, by Plan Type, Selected Years

Source: Kaiser Family Foundation/Health Research and Educational Trust, *Employer Health Benefits, 2005 Annual Survey*, Chart #6. Available at www.kff.org/insurance.

care physician, then the HMO does not cover the services. The subscriber is personally liable for payment of the nonauthorized services. HMOs that directly employ physicians are called staff model plans. In the simplest characterization, these physicians are paid salaries by the HMO, although some HMOs do base payments on factors such as patient load. Alternatively, plans that set up their network by contracting with physicians in geographically spread out, independent solo or small group practices are called independent practice associations (IPAs). Both types assign primary care physicians as gatekeepers for covered services. IPAs are more common than staff model HMOs and constitute the fastest-growing type of HMO.

Preferred provider organizations (PPOs) give subscribers two distinct tiers of coverage. When subscribers use the PPO's preferred provider network, the required cost sharing with deductibles or coinsurance is lower than when they use nonnetwork providers. Although a network is formed, PPOs have no physician gatekeepers. Rather, patients simply must pay more out of pocket if they choose to go outside the network. In this way, PPOs create financial incentives for subscribers to use network providers rather than go outside the network for care.

PPO contracts with physicians and hospitals generally address the prices providers will charge the PPO. In return for promising to charge a lower than average price, selected providers become part of the PPO's preferred network. No guarantee is given that the provider will see patients under the plan, but if the network is not too large and the PPO's cost-sharing provisions for subscribers are network-favorable, then the provider may enjoy a large increase in patient care business by joining the network. Prompt payment for services is another advantage.

Providers often agree to submit themselves to some form of utilization review under the contract. Most PPOs require preadmission certification for a hospital stay and concurrent utilization review for such stays. About half require a mandatory second opinion for a recommendation of surgery.

Point-of-service (POS) plans are a hybrid of HMOs and PPOs. Like PPOs, POS plans offer two tiers of insurance benefits. Coverage is greater (out-of-pocket costs are lower) when members use network providers and less generous (out-of-pocket costs are higher) when they use nonnetwork providers. Like HMOs, however, POS plans assign each member a physician gatekeeper, who must authorize in-network care in order for the care to be covered on in-network terms. Most POS plans do not require authorization for a member to use out-of-network services, but such care is covered on less-generous terms.

Table 12-1 categorizes the organizational structures. The matrix rows indicate whether an organized provider network is formed. The columns indicate whether a gatekeeper is part of the arrangement. The gatekeeper and the provider network represent two particular forms of health system control. HMOs provide both, while FFS plans provide neither.

Medicaid Managed Care Plans

In the last few years, many states have adopted managed care models for the Medicaid coverage they provide to families with dependent children and pregnant women who meet their low-income criteria for Medicaid eligibility. They believe that managed

TABLE 12-1 Different Health System Organizational Structures

		Gatekeeper	
		No	*Yes*
Provider	*No*	Fee-for-service (FFS)	Point-of-service (POS)
Network	*Yes*	Preferred provider organization (PPO)	Health maintenance organization (HMO)

care may help contain program costs, which are major parts of most states' budgets. As of 2004, 26.9 million Medicaid beneficiaries nationwide were enrolled in some form of managed care. This represents a sharp increase from the 2.7 million as recently as 1991.

As with employer plans, Medicaid managed care plans vary considerably. In some areas, states have contracted directly with HMOs that already exist in local markets. In others, states have created their own loosely structured provider networks, which contract with selected providers for discounted services and use physician gatekeeping to control utilization. Some Medicaid programs use a combination of the two approaches.

Managed Care Contracts with Physicians

Managed care contracts with physicians vary considerably. Most HMO and POS plans pay their network physicians on a capitation basis. Under capitation, the plan pays the physician's practice a fixed fee, generally an actuarial per-member-per-month (PMPM) dollar amount, in return for the treatments provided to members of the insurance plan. Physicians also may be responsible for the costs of referrals, laboratory tests, and hospital services. Thus, HMO and POS plans shift the costs of care, as well as the risk associated with those costs, directly onto physician practices. In so doing, these contracts put physician earnings at risk. If care provided under such arrangements turns out to cost less than the fixed-dollar plan payment, the practice makes a profit. If instead care costs more than the payment, the practice must take a loss.

In contrast, PPO contracts with physicians rarely involve capitation. Instead, they specify the discounted fees for various services that the plan will pay in exchange for the privilege of being in that plan's network. If a physician joins the PPO's network and happens to provide services to one of that plan's subscribers, the practice must accept the prenegotiated fees as payment in full. "Balance billing" of the patient (for the remainder of a higher bill) is not allowed.

Utilization review procedures are commonly covered in managed care contracts, whether they are HMO, PPO, or POS plans. Physicians must follow particular care-review procedures. Most managed care contracts also require a certain degree of physician record keeping on their enrollees (e.g., plan-specific patient encounter forms may have to be filed with the insurer each time care is provided).

Medicaid managed care contracts with physicians parallel those of private managed care plans, although specific service packages are determined heavily by the state's policies. In states that have set up their own Medicaid provider networks, the state contracts directly with individual gatekeeper physicians, agreeing to pay them a small fixed fee (e.g., $3 per month) for each Medicaid enrollee under their jurisdiction. In return for this payment, the physician serves as the gatekeeper for Medicaid-covered services.

While 88 percent of physicians had managed care contracts in 2001, only 32 percent of all physicians had capitation contracts (Kaiser Family Foundation, 2004, Exhibit 6.2). Primary care physicians exhibited higher prevalence of capitation contracts than did specialists because the primary care physicians serve more often as gatekeepers in HMO and POS plans. Primary care physicians with capitation contracts include general family practitioners (47 percent), general internists (48 percent), and pediatricians (54 percent).

Some physicians limit the risk associated with capitation by obtaining stop-loss provisions in their contracts or by purchasing reinsurance against large losses. A stop-loss provision limits the physician's liability per enrollee under the plan to, for example, $25,000 per year for any single enrollee. Once the cost of services provided to any one patient reaches the threshold, the insurer would cover all additional expenses. Reinsurance works the same way, although the coverage need not be part of the explicit contract with the insurer; it may be purchased separately from a reinsurance company. Reinsurance for physician practices may specify either a stop-loss threshold

per patient or a stop-loss for all patients (collectively) with that insurer. The reinsurer would pay all or most of any additional expenses once incurred expenses reach the specified threshold.

Managed Care Contracts with Hospitals

HMO and PPO plans contract with only a subset of the providers (physicians and hospitals) in the areas that they serve. This key feature of the managed care sector allows plans to promote price competition among hospitals that might otherwise lose plan business.

As recently as the early 1980s, less than 20 percent of the insured population was enrolled in managed care plans, with most in Kaiser-model HMOs (named after the Kaiser-Permanente HMO system) where the HMO owned the hospitals that its members used. In the 1980s, many states passed "selective contracting" laws, which provided insurers with greater flexibility to develop alternative health plans and to test different design features. These laws led to growth in PPOs and allowed more flexibility than the "closed-system" HMOs, such as Kaiser.

By 2004, the estimated proportion of hospitals reporting revenue from capitated contracts had increased to 41 percent (from 30 percent in 1998). Hospitals in urban areas, and particularly inner-city facilities, are more likely to report capitation revenues than are rural hospitals (Kaiser Family Foundation, 2004, Exhibit 6.7).

The probability and characteristics of contracts between individual managed care organizations and hospitals appear to depend on three sets of factors:

1. Plan characteristics, including whether it was a PPO or an HMO (and possibly what type of HMO), plan size, whether the plan serves several localities, and how old the plan is
2. Hospital characteristics, including size, ownership (including for-profit versus nonprofit status), location (city versus suburb), teaching status, and cost structure (reflecting prices)
3. Market characteristics, generally measured at the metropolitan area level, including the penetration and rate of growth of managed care plans

Research has found equivocal results, most often on the important issue of hospital costs, which are used to reflect prices to the plans. Early studies found that before managed care plans became popular, more competitive markets had higher hospital costs. This occurred because under cost-reimbursement fee-for-service systems, hospitals could (and did) compete on the basis of services and quality rather than price. More recent research has suggested that competition in hospital markets can lead to lower costs when the insurance market includes sufficient managed care penetration.

Zwanziger and Meirowitz (1998) examine the determinants of plan contracts with hospitals in a study that looks at the three categories. For HMOs and PPOs in 13 large, metropolitan statistical areas (MSAs), they report:

- Managed care plans prefer to contract with nonprofit hospitals, preferring even public hospitals to for-profit ones.
- Plans will more likely contract with large hospitals compared with medium-sized hospitals, and more likely with medium-sized hospitals compared with small hospitals.
- Hospital cost factors (which reflect hospital prices) do not significantly affect contracts.

It is useful to elaborate on a couple of the findings. The authors suggest that for-profit hospitals may be less willing to agree to managed care plan concessions than

nonprofit hospitals. Alternatively, plan choice may reflect consumer demand, and consumers might prefer nonprofit hospitals, using the nonprofit status to indicate a higher quality of care.

The insignificant role of costs, reflecting prices, indicates a need for further analysis. The authors believe that the price of services ought to matter in the decision to affiliate, particularly when one has controlled for other factors. They conclude that their cost terms may not reflect the prices, as they believed they would. Alternatively, it is possible that managed care plans may use costs as quality proxies, or alternatively that the public correlates low costs with perceived lower quality.

Development and Growth of Managed Care: Why Did It Take So Long?

Why did it take managed care so long to become a force in the marketplace? A variety of institutional, economic, and political forces have influenced its development and growth. Above all, the story of managed care in the United States requires an account of the strenuous historical opposition from organized medicine. Early on, organized medicine fiercely opposed alternatives to free patient choice and particularly alternatives to FFS. These alternatives posed a threat to a physician's ability to earn excess profits (known as economic profits or rents). Kessel (1958) described the historic political actions of organized medicine and proposed the thesis that FFS enabled physicians to charge some patients a higher fee than others for essentially the same service, a pattern known as price discrimination. Such price discrimination is difficult or impossible under the contracts that characterize prepayment-based organizations. First, providers will find it difficult to determine how much individual consumers value the services. Second, the prepayment-based organization may be able to shop among providers, thus limiting the providers' monopoly power.

Organized medicine also has created other barriers to managed care development. For example, it opposed physicians' participation in plans and organizations that were not controlled by physicians and/or that were not offering a free choice of physician. Such restrictions were successfully challenged by the Federal Trade Commission in the 1970s.

Federal Policy and the Growth of Managed Care

The HMO Act of 1973 represented a turning point in federal policy in promoting the development of alternative delivery systems as a cornerstone of a cost-containment strategy. The act enabled HMOs to become federally qualified if they provided enrollees with comprehensive benefits and met various other requirements. Loan guarantees and grants for startup costs were made available, but the main advantage accruing to a federally qualified HMO was that it could require firms in its area with 25 or more employees to offer the HMO as an option. Other regulatory barriers subsequently were reduced.

Despite these changes, the numbers of HMOs and HMO enrollees did not accelerate until the 1980s. When incentives to enroll Medicare and Medicaid recipients were improved, the entry of for-profit HMOs led to growth from 235 in 1980 to 623 in 1986. Growth slowed in the late 1980s and some consolidation occurred in the number of HMOs, but the upward trend in enrollment resumed in the 1990s. While the number of plans declined slightly from 1990 to 2000, total enrollment increased from 33 million to 81 million persons. Since then, HMO enrollments and the number of plans have decreased, but the gap has been filled by the growth of PPOs, which offer more flexibility in choosing providers. PPOs have grown rapidly in recent years. As noted in

Figure 12-1, HMO and PPO memberships in employer-sponsored plans were roughly equal in 1996. By 2005, 61 percent of the covered workers chose PPO coverage, compared to 21 percent choosing HMOs.

Although percentage enrollments are highest in the Northeast and the West (California alone accounts for 25 percent of national HMO enrollment), HMOs and PPOs have increased their market penetration in other areas. The most recent figures regarding the industry structure indicate that mixed and IPA models dominate HMO membership. Table 12-2 provides additional information on the characteristics of HMOs and their enrollees.

The Economics of Managed Care

The erosion of barriers to prepaid plans, coupled with some provider markets that are characterized by economic profits, gives us the key elements to understanding the rationale for managed care. Figure 12-2 starts with consumer demand D_f under fee-for-service insurance. Assuming that the price is constant at P_f, total expenditures, $P_f Q_f$, are represented by the larger rectangle. These total expenditures also would represent the expected insurance component of the individual's wage package.

A managed care option by constraining choice of provider as well as various coverages is viable only if it reduces expenditures. By exerting market power over suppliers, HMO managers may lower prices from P_f to P_m. A price reduction is possible when providers have been earning economic profits.[1] In effect, managed care reduces or eliminates those economic profits.

Demand also may be reduced from D_f to D_m by reducing inpatient care, by limiting length of stay, minimizing supplier induced demand, and, in general, by encouraging

TABLE 12-2 Number of HMOs and HMO Enrollment by Selected Characteristics, 2004

Characteristics	Plans Number	Plans Percent	Enrollments Number	Enrollments Percent
All plans	412	100.0	68.8	100.0
Model type				
IPA	176	42.7	24.6	35.8
Group	96	23.3	15.3	22.2
Mixed	140	34.0	28.9	42.0

Geographic Region	Number	Percent	Percent of Regional Population
Total	412	100.0	
Northeast	77	18.7	30.1
Midwest	126	30.6	18.7
South	126	30.6	16.0
West	83	20.1	34.4

Source: U.S. Department of Health and Human Services, *Health United States 2005*, Table 137.

[1] From a provider's perspective (e.g., a physician or hospital treating both FFS and MCO patients), its pricing decision is very similar to one involving price discrimination. Chapter 17 formally covers price discrimination within the context of pharmaceutical products. Here, the provider's demand from the MCO market is likely to be far more elastic than its demand from the FFS market because the MCO can contract with other doctors or hospitals if the provider tries to raise rates for the MCO's enrollees. As shown in Chapter 17, price will be lower in the market with a more elastic demand.

FIGURE 12-2 Treatment and Expenditures Under Managed Care

more cost-effective care through the use of information technology and financial incentives to providers. The resulting expenditures are shown by the smaller rectangle representing total expenditures, $P_m Q_m$.

It follows that managed care trades some constraint of consumer choices for lower per unit prices for care. As drawn in Figure 12-2, both decreased price per unit of care and decreased quantity of care contribute to decreased expenditures. Note, however, that a natural response to decreased prices is to increase quantity demanded. Total consumer expenditures will fall as long as the price decreases are not fully offset by increased quantity demanded.

Modeling Managed Care

The changed incentives from managed care have caused many to predict success in constraining utilization and cost of care. The underlying logic behind this proposition is intuitive. When providers agree to handle all patients' health care needs for fixed, prearranged fees, the providers accept and bear a substantial part of the financial risk. By bearing the risk of delivering services at a fixed premium, managed care plans have strong incentives to reduce excessive care. The fixed premiums would also seem to provide incentives to offer forms of preventive care that are cost-effective from the care managers' perspectives. Such preventive care could decrease the need for more subsequent (expensive) curative care.

Will managed care plans provide enough care or the right types of care? The following analyses, derived by Goodman and Stano (2000), treat managed care plans as staff model HMOs where physicians are HMO employees.

Modeling Individual HMOs

Individual HMOs wish to determine the number of consumers to serve, or quantity, and the level of service to provide, or quality. One might compare them to urban suburbs, which set the qualities of public schools and the sizes of the police forces by the preferences of their residents and by the costs of providing them. Just as suburbs provide menus of public services, HMOs provide menus of care in inpatient and outpatient settings. To keep things

simple, we will assume that HMOs provide only one type of service (visits), and that the HMOs are differentiated in quality by how many visits each offers.

We assume that HMO treatment costs are related to member health status, which is a function of care received at the HMO and elsewhere, as well as other factors including diet, environment, and lifestyle. People's long-term health relates in part to short-term decisions about how much care to provide. This follows directly from the long-term nature of human capital, most particularly health capital. Thus, because patients live for many years, treatment decisions at one HMO may affect treatment costs at other HMOs. Moreover, HMOs have the dual incentives of keeping people healthy and attracting healthy people.

An HMO's total annual costs are higher if it provides more services per enrollee (quality) or if it has more members (quantity). Having healthier members lowers HMO costs. Assume that health care works—that health is related positively to the level of services by all providers. Because at any time in the future these individuals may be members of a given HMO, average health status of the population is related to the level of treatment of the whole population by all providers. This will affect the costs for these providers in that better health will *lower* costs.

How Much Care?

The previous section indicated that profit-maximizing HMOs might not recognize the system-wide impact of health services on consumers' health. Although an individual HMO seeks to maintain the health of its own clientele, it does not recognize that its decisions may affect the costs of other HMOs. We call this an externality because it is a benefit that affects others but is not considered by any individual HMO.

Suppose instead that an HMO has clinics at a number of locations throughout several states, referred to as HMO_1, HMO_2, and so on. Although HMO_1, for example, may not account for this possibility, the HMO entrepreneur, to maximize profits, must consider the impacts of health services on the health of others elsewhere.

This is easily shown in Figure 12-3. Without the externality, HMO_1 optimizes at point A, providing quality level x_1^{mkt}. Level x_1^{mkt} is economically inefficient, however, because it does not account for the fact that improved treatment at HMO_1 lowers costs throughout the system.

FIGURE 12-3 Externality Model of HMO

The optimal quality level of x_1 is at point B, or x_1^{opt}. This occurs by recognizing the downward shift in the marginal cost curve by a factor that reflects the effect of the health externality on the costs facing HMO_2, HMO_3 and so on, as well as HMO_1. Level x_1^{mkt} indicates an inefficiently small level of HMO services, and by implication a substitution of non-HMO and/or nonhealth care inputs (such as the patient's own time) for the HMO care.

Although the potential loss of patients may influence treatment decisions of fee-for-service providers as well as HMOs, the capitation method of payment to HMOs makes the disenrollment problem particularly important. Fee-for-service providers are paid for each unit of care. Aside from uncollectible bills, they do not risk losses on services provided currently or in the future.

In contrast, by integrating insurance with the provision of health care, the HMO receives a fixed payment per enrollee to cover costs in the current period, and over time, for those who remain enrolled. Unlike fee-for-service care, where payment in every period is likely to cover costs, the HMO must consider the timing of expenditures and the financial losses of overspending on patients who may disenroll. One way for an HMO to self-insure against long-term losses attributable to disenrollment is to economize on care for those currently enrolled.

What Types of Care?

In this section, we consider the long-term consequences of potential movement among HMOs on decisions among treatment practices. If an HMO receives constant revenue per patient each period, its goal is to minimize costs. Patients stay in the HMO for two periods, which might be considered as early and late in their lives. The HMO may offer:

- High-tech, possibly capital-intensive procedures leading to high Period 1 costs and zero Period 2 costs
- Low-tech, less capital-intensive procedures, leading to low costs in both periods

Because the revenues are the same with either high-tech or low-tech care, the HMO's problem is to minimize costs, using the cheaper (over time) of the two procedures.

Suppose that increased competition through increased choice raises disenrollment rates. With higher disenrollment rates, low-tech continuing care becomes the more financially viable option, even if the present discounted values are equal and even if high-tech treatment is more economically efficient in producing health. Here, HMOs self-insure against future disenrollment by reducing current costs through (low-cost) continuing care rather than high-tech treatment.

In evaluating how much and what types of care are offered by HMOs, we see that the HMO faces an economic externality because it cannot capture fully the gains of its treatment over time. As a result, it will offer less care and lower-tech care than FFS plans. As noted, if the HMO were to merge with others forming a larger network, the larger firm might internalize this positive externality, because the network owners could expect that clients who leave one HMO might join another HMO within the network. The receiving HMO would then take advantage of the now-healthier clients who had benefited from their earlier treatment.

Framework for Prediction

Clearly, this model simplifies the situation because many forms of managed care exist providing a myriad of services. It provides a framework, however, for addressing possible HMO cost savings relative to FFS plans. FFS plans encourage overutilization to the point where marginal private benefits can be far less than marginal costs. HMOs are

widely believed to discourage this deadweight loss and other forms of overutilization, such as supplier-induced demand. To evaluate utilization, however, one must control for the health of the client population, which might be impacted by HMO "cream skimming" of the healthier clientele.

This simple model provides predictions that are consistent with the rising conflict between HMOs and their members. The popular press reports stories about inadequate levels of services and the unavailability of expensive, high-tech treatment options.

Where Managed Care Differs from FFS—Dumping, Creaming, and Skimping

We recognize that one of the key differences between HMOs and FFS plans involves the form of payment. Hospitals and other FFS providers are paid for each treatment in order to cover costs. HMOs are paid fixed rates per person irrespective of the amount of treatment used. These differences have led to discussions within the medical and policy communities regarding three purported practices.

1. *Dumping.* Refusing to treat less healthy patients who might use services in excess of their premiums.
2. *Creaming.* Seeking to attract more healthy patients who will use services costing less than their premiums
3. *Skimping.* Providing less than the optimal quantity of services for any given condition in a given time period.

Because the HMO's costs relate to the average health of its clientele, practices such as dumping (unhealthy patients) and creaming (healthy patients) may occur. If the HMO can identify and dump patients who are sicker, it can improve the average health of its clientele and hence lower its costs. As noted in Ellis (1998), the patient and the public at large may not notice this decision. The HMO may honestly say that it is not equipped for this kind of case and that the patient would be better served elsewhere. This behavior contrasts with cost-based FFS care. Inasmuch as every penny spent on even the most severe case theoretically is paid back to the hospital, the cost-based hospital will not dump anyone.

Creaming is the practice of seeking out or emphasizing low-severity patients. The HMO benefits from creaming because all patients of sufficiently low-case severity require few hospital services, so that premium exceeds patient costs. Some patients believe that their malady is so mild that the hospital care is hardly worth the trip; these patients correspond in practice to the young, vigorous, and healthy people that HMOs prefer to have in their service populations. The FFS provider also creams because its reimbursement covers costs for each of its patients.

Skimping involves cutting back on services to the point that patients' welfare is reduced. FFS providers will not skimp because each nursing hour, electronic instrument, and surgery that they employ will be reimbursed. In contrast, skimping provides the opportunity for the HMO to increase profits. Because the HMO has been paid the premium in advance, reducing the amount of services will lower costs and may raise profits. The uncertainty regarding profits occurs because reducing the benefits for a given severity of illness may cause the HMO to lose some patients to FFS plans or to other HMOs.

Equilibrium and Adverse Selection in a Market with HMOs

Providers may have incentives for seeking patients, but patients also may select themselves into particular types of care. Cutler and Reber (1998) demonstrate the potential adverse selection of sicker consumers toward FFS care and healthier patients toward

HMOs. This work also explains how HMO penetration can respond strongly to small changes in relative pricing.

Suppose Jeff has just graduated from college and landed a job with Sante Fe Futons. The firm offers its employees a choice of membership in one of two health plans—an HMO that charges a flat, prearranged price, P_{HMO}, or a deluxe care FFS plan with deductible, D, and co-insurance rate, r. Letting the severity of illness, s, be measured by the expenditures required to treat at the FFS level, Jeff calculates the extra cost E of FFS to be:

$$E = \text{FFS cost} - \text{HMO cost} = (\text{Deductibles} + \text{FFS copay}) - \text{HMO price}$$
$$E = (D + rs) - P_{HMO} \tag{12.1}$$

Is the extra cost E to use FSS worth it, or should Jeff use HMO care instead?

To evaluate Jeff's decision, we must find market values for the parameters in equation (12.1) and then compare them to the value received. Under perfect competition, both FFS and HMO providers earn zero profits. For the FFS providers, profit for the average patient is written as:

$$\pi_F = D + \overline{rs}_F - \overline{s}_F = 0$$

indicating that the firm collects patient deductibles, D, and patient copayments, \overline{rs}_f, and spends \overline{s}_F for treatment (with the "bars" indicating sector averages). Rearranging terms, this means that the market deductible is:

$$D = (1 - \overline{r})\overline{s}_F$$

For the HMO parameters, we again assume that in the long run, competition will drive profits to zero. Hence, premium, P_{HMO}, must cover average payments for $\alpha \overline{s}_H$ condition s_H:

$$\pi_H = P_{HMO} - \alpha \overline{s}_H = 0$$

Parameter α reflects Cutler and Reber's assumption that HMOs achieve efficiencies in providing care, as well as restricting the amount of hospital care provided, reducing the cost of care. With no cost reductions, α would equal 1; Cutler and Reber assert that the real-world value of α is about 0.9.

Substituting these terms into (12.1) provides the following expression for Jeff:

$$E = [(1 - \overline{r})\overline{s}_F - \alpha \overline{s}_H] + rs \tag{12.2}$$

Thus, E is comprised of a market-determined constant (in brackets) plus an increment of expenditures rs, depending on the severity of the condition. It is reasonable to assume that the market-determined term is positive so E is the upward-sloping line in Figure 12-4.

How much does Jeff value health care? Assume that he values each unit of s equally. Then, he values $100 worth of care at $100, $200 worth of care at $200, and so on. In other words, we can draw a 45° line for his valuation, V, of FFS care.

Let's start at expected level of care, $s = 0$. Jeff is young, healthy, and doesn't expect to use much service. If he were to join the FFS plan, however, he would have to pay the average FFS client expenditure, which is more than the average HMO fee, plus his share, r, of the services that he uses. Because the extra FFS costs are higher than the

FIGURE 12-4 Selection into HMO and FFS Settings

value that he puts on them (the *E* curve is above the *V* curve), Jeff chooses to join the HMO. If Jeff has a chronic condition requiring ongoing treatment, he recognizes that each unit of ongoing treatment is subsidized by the FFS plan at rate $(1 - r)$. With increasing treatment, FFS becomes a more attractive option as *V* exceeds *E*.

At severity level s', Jeff would be indifferent between the HMO and FFS plans because the extra value of FFS just equals the extra cost. If all consumers were similar to Jeff in everything except their health, consumers with expected severity less than s' would join the HMO, while those expecting severity greater than s' would choose FFS.

Suppose the FFS plan increased its coinsurance rate, *r*. Then, the FFS plan becomes less attractive; this can be seen by rotating the *E* line counterclockwise to E_2. Consumers who were previously indifferent between HMO and FFS plans will shift to the HMOs. The younger and healthier HMO patrons are now joined by some of the (not as young and not as healthy) former FFS patrons. Hence, the healthiest among the former FFS patrons become the sickest HMO members. As a result, the average severity in both plans increases.

How Does Managed Care Differ?—Empirical Results

Economic and organizational theories have suggested that managed care will differ from more traditional fee-for-service plans. One might predict that managed care organizations will spend less per member, reducing health care costs. Theory would also predict, however, that if fewer resources are used, quality of care may also suffer. Policymakers have considerable interest in whether this theoretical proposition is true. From early on, it was reported that total costs—that is, the sum of premiums and out-of-pocket expenses—were from 10 to 40 percent lower for HMOs. The cost differences were attributed largely to lower hospitalization rates, not to lower ambulatory care-use rates.

Methodological Issues—Selection Bias and Quality of Care

Conceptually, it would seem fairly simple to compare health care costs in managed care and fee-for-service plans. Researchers would collect data on cost of care across a wide spectrum of the population. Controlling for items, such as patient age (older people have higher costs) and existing health status (sicker people have higher costs), one could use multiple regression statistical methods to compare costs.

Two major issues complicate the comparison—selection bias and quality of care. The methods previously discussed work only if patients are randomly assigned to either HMO or FFS treatment. Analysts worry that this random assignment does not exist in the real world. On the one hand, HMOs offer comprehensive benefits and so they may attract and retain sicker members. If this is not addressed, studies may make HMOs look more expensive than they really are. On the other hand, HMOs may attract disproportionately younger members and families who tend to be healthier and for whom the costs of care tend to be relatively lower—studies that ignore this problem may make HMOs look less expensive.

Does managed care offer quality of care that is comparable to care under FFS? Managed care provides incentives to reduce the costs of care. Does it also provide incentives to cut corners by reducing the quality of care? Although some consumers may choose to pay less for lower quality care (just as some buy cheaper tires or cheaper cuts of meat), it is essential both to measure quality and to control for quality differentials in evaluating differences in health care costs.

The definition of quality is by no means obvious. Cutting health care quality would likely lower costs in the short term, but it might increase the longer-term costs if patients required additional services later. Furthermore, if information about quality were available to consumers, lowering quality would tend to erode demand. Despite the importance of quality-of-care issues to health care analysis in general and to analysis of managed care in particular, quality issues are difficult to resolve.

Quality may range from consumer perceptions of the provider-patient relationship to the outcome effects of health care on health status. Donabedian (1980) provides three general descriptors:

1. *Structure*. The quality and appropriateness of the available inputs and their organization
2. *Process*. The quality of the delivery of care
3. *Outcome*. The ultimate quality of care but the most difficult to measure scientifically

Comparative Utilization and Costs

Due to the evolving nature of both managed care and fee-for-service provision, some of the earlier studies are more interesting for their historical perspective than for their current applicability. Luft (1978, 1981) found that HMO enrollees, especially prepaid group practice members, had lower hospitalization rates. No clear evidence showed that these lower rates were attributable to reductions in the less important, discretionary procedures. Furthermore, the evidence at hand could not dismiss the possibilities that biased self-selection of HMO membership or underutilization in HMOs was responsible for the observed differences.

Arnould and colleagues (1984) confirmed Luft's conclusion that length of stay is not significantly different between the HMO and the FFS patients. They also found that the use of surgeon visits, as well as lab charges, per patient were lower for the HMO users (significantly lower for hysterectomy and appendectomy), although total hospital charges were significantly lower for the HMO patients only in the case of appendectomies. Thus, although differences occur in costs of elements of hospital care, no strong case could be made to conclude that HMOs produce hospital care more cheaply overall.

The Rand Study: A Randomized Experiment

In the Rand Health Insurance Experiment, patients were assigned randomly to different plans in a controlled experiment, thus apparently eliminating selection bias. Would HMO costs still be lower under such circumstances?

The Rand study (Manning et al., 1984) compared HMO and FFS patients in the Puget Sound area where 1,580 individuals were assigned randomly to either an FFS physician of their choice or to the Group Health Cooperative (GHC) of Puget Sound— an HMO in Seattle, Washington. The 431 FFS individuals were in one of four groups:

1. Free care
2. 25 percent of expenses up to a maximum out-of-pocket liability of $1,000 per family
3. 95 percent of expenses up to a maximum out-of-pocket liability of $1,000 per family
4. 95 percent coinsurance on outpatient services, up to a limit of $150 per person ($450 per family)

In addition to the experimental GHC group of 1,149 persons, a control group consisted of a random sample of 733 GHC members who had previously been enrolled for at least one year.

Total expenditures per person were $439 for the experimental group, including out-of-plan use (which may be substantial), compared to $609 for the free care FFS group (group 1). As seen from Table 12-3, ambulatory utilization, as indicated in the columns labeled "Face-to-Face Visits" and "Preventive Visits," was about the same. Thus, the 39 percent increased spending for FFS members (or 28 percent reduction for GHC) was due largely to a much higher admission rate and increased hospital days per person. The study could not pinpoint the reasons for GHC's lower hospital use.

To put the potential cost savings into better perspective, note that the use rates for the experimental HMO patients did not differ materially from the last two categories of FFS, the categories on "95 percent" coinsurance (group 3) and "Individual deductible" (group 4). Thus, for some population groups, a shift to HMOs would not lead to savings, although the cost savings for other population groups might conceivably be important.

TABLE 12-3 Annual Rates of Admission and Face-to-Face Visits

Plan	Admission Rate	Hospital Days	Face-to-Face Visits	Preventive Visits
	Per 100 Persons		Per Person	
GHC experimental	8.4	49	4.3	0.55
	(0.67)	(9.6)	(0.14)	(0.02)
GHC control	8.3	38	4.7	0.60
	(1.01)	(9.0)	(0.17)	(0.02)
Fee for service				
Free	13.8	83	4.2	0.41
	(1.51)	(26)	(0.25)	(0.03)
25%	10.0	87	3.5	0.32
	(1.43)	(28)	(0.35)	(0.03)
95%	10.5	46	2.9	0.29
	(1.68)	(9.9)	(0.34)	(0.04)
Individual deductible	8.8	28	3.3	0.27
	(1.20)	(5.1)	(0.33)	(0.03)

Note: Standard errors are in parentheses.

Source: Manning et al. (1984). Copyright © 1984, Massachusetts Medical Society. All rights reserved.

The Most Recent Evidence

In a series of studies, Miller and Luft (1994, 1997, 2002) have summarized findings regarding quality of care, utilization, and customer satisfaction. In the late 1980s and early 1990s, managed care (compared to FFS) enrollees received more preventive tests, procedures, and examinations (such as cancer screening; pelvic, rectal, and general physical examinations).[2] Outcomes on a wide range of conditions (including congestive heart failure, colorectal cancer, diabetes, and hypertension) were better or equivalent to those using FFS plans. HMO enrollees were less satisfied with quality of care and physician-patient interactions but more satisfied with costs.

Their 1997 article found that HMO plans and providers cut hospitalization and use of more costly tests and procedures, often with little visible effect on quality of care "given the high prices of the indemnity insurance/fee-for-service system." However, simply carrying out the same clinical processes but with fewer resources can negatively affect quality of care in some cases, such as Medicare home health care.

In their 2002 review, which covered the period 1997 to 2001, Miller and Luft included HMOs and some mixed models, but excluded studies purely on PPOs. Table 12-4 summarizes their analysis along six dimensions: (1) quality of care, (2) access to care, (3) satisfaction, (4) prevention, (5) length of stay, and (6) use of expensive resources. In the first line, for example, 14 studies showed better (HMO) quality, 15 showed worse quality, and 18 were in the middle. The overall results summarized in Table 12-4 are similar to those in the two previous articles. Compared with non-HMOs, HMOs had similar quality of care, more prevention activities, less use of hospital days and other expensive resources, and lower access and satisfaction ratings. Together with other studies (see Box 12-1), we now have a much better understanding of the performance and role of HMOs.[3]

Growth in Spending

Analysts believe that managed care reduces utilization, especially of hospital care. A different but related question is whether managed care organizations also have lower growth rates in spending. If they do, a continued shift toward managed care will

TABLE 12-4 HMO Plan Performance Update: An Analysis of Published Literature: 1997–2001

Indicator	Favorable to HMOs	Mixed	Unfavorable to HMOs	Total
Quality of care	14	18	15	47
Access to care	2	4	4	10
Satisfaction	0	3	8	11
Prevention	7	3	0	10
Length of stay	5	5	0	10
Expensive resources	8	7	0	15

Source: Miller and Luft (2002).

[2]Rizzo (2005) recently verified that HMO patients get substantially more preventive care than FFS patients, and that this is not due to a selection effect where patients/physicians with preferences for preventive care are more likely to choose HMOs.

[3]Glied (2000) summarizes many articles that examine impacts of managed care on costs and on utilization. Her tables discuss the populations, comparison groups, controls for differences in patient characteristics, and impacts on treatment aspects, such as charges and length of stay.

BOX 12-1

What Do HMOs Actually Do?

There seems to be little doubt that HMO expenditures per member are substantially lower—sometimes 30 to 40 percent lower—than expenditures in traditional indemnity plans. Are these reductions achieved mainly by managing access and utilization, and lowering payments to providers that reduce their economic profits? What is the role of risk selection and quality? The early literature on HMOs focused on hospitalization rates, but several recent contributions provide new insights into these challenging questions.

Using methods described earlier in this chapter to decompose differences between FFS and HMOs, Cutler, McClellan, and Newhouse (2000) focused on Massachusetts patients with newly diagnosed heart disease, both those with heart attacks (acute myocardial infarction), which are relatively expensive to treat, and those with less severe forms of ischemic heart disease. By selecting one condition, the authors avoid some of the problems associated with aggregation across conditions. By studying heart disease, risk selection is minimized because even if a patient chose a plan based on some expectation of heart disease, the choice would not likely be based on expectations regarding the severity of the disease.

The study results are very clear and powerful: "Essentially all of the differences in reimbursement. . . [result from] differences in the prices paid for particular services, rather than differences in quantity or quality of services received" (p. 327). The authors caution about generalizing findings based on life-threatening conditions, such as a heart attack, where insurance status may have little effect on treatment. They also suggest that cardiac care is well-known for providing sizable economic rents to both hospitals and cardiologists. Thus, the price effect may not be as large for other kinds of services.

Polsky and Nicholson (2004) also decompose the differences between HMOs and non-HMOs into differences in risk selection, utilization, and prices. They use a national sample for overall expenditures, which were $188 (9.3 percent) lower for HMO members. Consistent with the Cutler study, lower prices paid by HMOs were the main determinant of expenditure differences. Prices were actually $269 less for the HMOs, or more than the expenditure difference because their utilization was $81 higher. Risk selection accounted for only $35 of this amount.

With their consistent results, the two studies provide a clearer picture of the role of HMOs. HMOs are quite successful in using their leverage to negotiate lower fees, and they do this without obvious reductions in quantity or quality. Risk selection also is not a major factor. However, it must come as a disappointment to many proponents of managed care that there is no indication that HMOs have been able to fulfill their promise and potential of applying information technology and better management to *improve* the process of health care delivery.

As such, HMOs and other MCOs are constantly evolving and introducing new managerial solutions. The current focus is on pay-for-performance (P4P) plans. These are incentive plans in which physicians are given cash bonuses to meet guidelines for quality care and to implement evidence-based medicine. In 2005, there were numerous employer-initiated P4P programs, and the Centers for Medicare and Medicaid Services also launched a major demonstration. Preliminary results from the largest effort, known as the Rewarding Results program, indicated that financial incentives can motivate change if the rewards are substantial. Overall, P4P can raise quality, but such programs are difficult to implement, and they should not be seen as "magic pills" that both lower costs and improve health care delivery.

result not only in reductions in spending levels, but also in the long-term rate of increase.

It is important to provide a framework for discussing the relationship among FFS, MCOs, and total costs, particularly because terminology can be confusing. Suppose we are concerned about costs per person for treating a particular illness over three periods.

Let us assume that people use either FFS or managed care and that the population is fixed. We can calculate the total treatment costs as:

$$\text{Total treatment costs} = (\text{Number in FFS}) \times (\text{FFS costs/FFS enrollee})$$
$$+ (\text{Number in MCO}) \times (\text{MCO costs/MCO enrollee}) \quad \text{(12.3)}$$

Dividing both sides by the total population, we get:

$$\text{Treatment costs/Person} = (\text{Fraction of population in FFS})$$
$$\times (\text{FFS costs/FFS enrollee})$$
$$+ (\text{Fraction of population in MCO}) \quad \text{(12.4)}$$
$$\times (\text{MCO costs/MCO enrollee})$$

Suppose, in Period 1, that FFS treatment costs $2,000, MCO treatment costs $1,000, and that 60 percent use FFS and that 40 percent use MCO care. The treatment costs per person will be:

$$\text{Treatment costs/Person} = (0.6) \times \$2,000 + (0.4) \times \$1,000$$
$$= \$1,200 + \$400 = \$1,600$$

This is noted in column 1 of Table 12-5 as Period 1.

If FFS and MCO costs were to stay constant and patients were to switch from the more expensive FFS to the less expensive MCO, costs per person would fall. As noted in Table 12-5, if a 10 percentage-point movement occurs from FFS to MCO, treatment costs per person would fall because 1 in 10 people would be substituting a (MCO) treatment that is half the price of the other (FFS) treatment. As calculated in Table 12-5, the total costs per person would fall by $100, or 6.25 percent.

What is less obvious is that unless the population shift from FFS to managed care continues, cost reduction and cost containment may be difficult. Suppose that in Period 3 the percentage in FFS remains at 50 percent, but the costs of both FFS and MCO increase by 10 percent. The total cost per person accordingly increases by 10 percent from $1,500 to $1,650. If total costs per enrollee in each sector were to continue to increase by 10 percent and no change occurred in the MCO market share, the total costs per person on aggregate also would increase by 10 percent. This occurs irrespective of the fact that a larger proportion of the population (Period 3) is now being treated in managed care settings than was being treated in Period 1.

This analysis provides important insights into the impacts of managed care plans on health care costs and health care cost increases. To the extent that large shifts of insureds into managed care have led to lower-cost treatments, there may have been

TABLE 12-5 Managed Care and Cost Containment: An Example

	Period 1	Period 2	Percent Increase	Period 3	Percent Increase
Fraction of population MCO	0.4	0.5		0.5	
FFS costs per enrollee	2,000	2,000	0.00	2,200	10.00
MCO costs per enrollee	1,000	1,000	0.00	1,100	10.00
Total costs per person	1,600	1,500	−6.25	1,650	10.00

one-time cost decreases relative to what they would have been. However, if managed care and FFS plans face the same cost inflation for the services that they offer apart from the one-time decreases, overall cost inflation is unlikely to abate.

Early studies by Luft (1981) and Newhouse and colleagues (1985) found the growth rate of HMO spending to be roughly the same as the growth rate under FFS, and recent studies have not contradicted those findings. Policymakers have relied on shifts into managed care to reduce health care costs and health care growth rates. However, if the shifts do not continue, costs will continue to inflate, albeit from lower bases.

Competitive Effects

Up to this point, we have concentrated on the direct effects of managed care and managed care organizations. We have asked what managed care organizations look like, whether they provide less costly care, and whether they provide different quality care. In this section, we address the indirect effects of managed care through the market mechanism. By indirect, we mean that existing health providers must respond to competition from the managed care sector.

After discussing some of the theoretical concerns, we will evaluate the impact of competition in three ways. We will look at the impact of managed care on hospital markets, on insurance markets, and finally on the adoption of technological change.[4]

Theoretical Issues

The spread of alternative delivery systems can elicit substantially greater competition in other sectors only if competition is absent at the start. Otherwise, both providers and insurers would be operating at, or close to, their minimum costs of production. Although there is bound to be disagreement on the extent of the degree of market imperfections, most would agree that the insurance and provider markets are less than highly competitive.

Consider the consequences of having a larger number of products and competitors to an existing monopolistic seller. In Figure 12-5, D_1 is the current market demand and P_1 is the monopoly profit-maximizing price (where marginal revenue MR_1 equals marginal cost MC) for each firm (average cost is omitted for clarity). The entry of other firms will have the following effects on each individual firm:

- Shift the demand curve to the left to D_2
- Shift the marginal revenue curve to the left to MR_2
- Increase the elasticity of demand at any price because there are now more competitors

With the same costs facing each firm, the new profit-maximizing price (where marginal revenue MR_2 equals marginal cost) for each is reduced to P_2. If the decrease in firm demand is sufficiently large, it is possible that an individual firm will no longer be able to earn a competitive return at Q_2. This would occur if the demand curve shifts (due to the entry of competitors) so that it is everywhere below the firm's average cost curve.

[4]Competition can also affect quality and other dimensions of care. Scanlon and colleagues (2005) found that lower levels of HMO competition, as measured by the Herfindahl-Hirschman Index, actually produce better results on several quality dimensions. Higher HMO penetration was associated with higher quality. The study also found that plans that publicly report their data have higher quality than those that do not.

FIGURE 12-5 Impact of Entry of Alternate Providers into a Monopolistic Market

The existing firm also may respond in other ways. It may attempt to reduce its administrative costs. More importantly, it may try to court customers by attempting to market plans that limit utilization of services, and hence the costs of the services, through various devices. These include utilization review and the adoption of health care plans with increased cost sharing. Of course, it could establish its own HMOs and PPOs, further increasing competition. It also could improve the quality of its service. Further, it may embrace forms of emerging nonprice competition, such as advertising and marketing.

Is this theoretical scenario applicable? Many items are likely to be affected by the spread of HMOs and PPOs. These include the provider and health insurance markets, the phenomenon of biased selection, the roles of employers, and the rate of innovation and diffusion of technology. To focus our discussion, we will limit it to three areas: (1) the impact of HMOs/PPOs on hospital markets, (2) their impact on insurance markets, and (3) the impact on the adoption of technological change.

Managed Care Competition in Hospital Markets

A first step in looking at the impacts of managed care penetration is to examine the determinants of the penetration itself. What is it about particular markets that lend themselves to high levels of HMO activity? Dranove, Simon, and White (1998) use a supply-demand framework to address this question.

What are the demand characteristics? The authors view employers as the primary health insurance shoppers. Serving as agents for their employees, they seek the best deals.

What are the supply characteristics? The authors seek to identify market features that would reduce costs of payers to contract with providers. They expect that the supply of managed care will be higher in markets where the managed care organizations can negotiate with and monitor the providers more cheaply. They also expect that excess hospital capacity may make hospitals more amenable to negotiation.

Regarding demand, higher managed care penetration accompanies more educated and more urbanized populations. Regarding supply, higher managed care penetration is related to lower percentages of physicians in solo practice, hospital market concentrations, and hospital occupancy. In short, managed care comes in where large numbers of half-filled hospitals are found. The authors express concern that the low rate of managed care penetration in more concentrated markets may imply anticompetitive behaviors, meriting antitrust considerations.

Early work viewed the hospital as competing for patients, physicians, or both. It was argued that widespread health insurance allowed individual consumers and their physician-agents to be much less concerned about the price of care. Hospitals would compete on the basis of services and amenities rather than price, a so-called "medical arms race." McLaughlin (1988, p. 207) argues that the "providers are responding not with classical cost-containing price competition but, instead, with cost-increasing rivalry, characterized by increased expenditures to promote actual or perceived product differentiation."

Feldman and colleagues (1990) examined the Minneapolis/St. Paul area, addressing the degree of competitive bidding for HMO contracts, whether HMOs can get discounts, and whether HMOs tend to rely on low-price hospitals. They found that HMOs generally did not extract major discounts. In fact, price did not seem to be the major HMO consideration in the selection of hospitals with whom to affiliate. Rather, it was hospital location and the range of services that the hospital offered. There was no indication as to whether HMOs tend to affiliate with lower-priced hospitals.

Melnick and colleagues (1992) obtained hospital transactions prices negotiated by a large California PPO in 1987. Their regression analysis controlled for hospital characteristics, such as ownership, teaching, Medicare and Medicaid demand, and market structure. Four key findings emerged from the analysis.

1. Controlling for other factors, the PPO paid a higher price to hospitals located in less competitive markets.
2. If the PPO had a larger share of the hospital's business, it was able to negotiate a lower price.
3. The more dependent the PPO was on a hospital, the higher price the PPO paid.
4. Hospitals with high occupancy located in markets with high average occupancy charged the PPO higher prices.

Morrisey (2001b) terms the Melnick research as "a watershed," demonstrating that traditional concepts of competition could apply to hospital markets and potentially to other health care markets as well.

Managed Care Competition in Insurance Markets

Commensurate with the spread of HMOs, PPOs, and various forms of managed care, the health insurance industry is changing rapidly. Many have noted that health insurers were previously lethargic in introducing innovative insurance products and in their cost-containment efforts. In addition, we consider the historic opposition by organized medicine, tax advantages and provider control of the Blues, and the constraints imposed by state regulation and antitrust laws, all of which previously inhibited change in the insurance market.

Frech and Ginsburg (1988) identified the dramatic changes that occurred after 1977 when the insurance market was divided about equally between the Blues and commercial insurers. The growth of HMOs and PPOs was accompanied by substantial increases in patient cost sharing, increased utilization review, and self-insurance by many large firms.

Under self-insurance, a Blue Cross and Blue Shield or another organization will act only as a third party in processing claims. More competition is introduced because self-insured firms have more control over their health plans and more direct interest in cost-containment measures.

Baker and Corts (1995, 1996) identify two conflicting effects of increased HMO activity on conventional insurance premiums:

1. *Market discipline*. HMO competition may limit insurers' ability to exercise market power, thus driving down prices, a standard competitive argument.
2. *Market segmentation*. HMOs may skim the healthiest patients from the pool, thus driving insurers' costs and prices up.

Their model suggests that if increased HMO penetration does lower the premium levels, the market discipline effect becomes relatively less important, so at higher levels of penetration, the market segmentation effect may raise premiums. Their empirical work verifies this hypothesis: Across metropolitan areas, market penetration up to 14 percent decreases premiums, but market penetration beyond that point raises them. Wickizer and Feldstein (1995) find comparable market discipline effects, although they do not investigate market segmentation effects.

Joesch, Wickizer, and Feldstein (1998) investigated nonprice impacts of HMO market competition. They found that increased HMO penetration reduced insurers' likelihood of increasing insurance deductibles, or "stop-loss" levels (the levels limiting losses to those insured). Moreover, groups located in markets with higher HMO enrollments were more likely to adopt utilization management or PPO options.

Managed Care and Technological Change

The impact of managed care on technological change is potentially significant in controlling health care costs, as well. Increased incomes and changed coinsurance rates are insufficient to explain the increases in health care costs over the past 50 years. Most analysts attribute a major role to the advances in high-cost technologies that were fed by payment mechanisms that were at best indifferent to controlling costs. To the extent that managed care plans explicitly seek cost containment, one would expect careful monitoring of attention directed toward high-cost technologies.

Baker and Spetz (2000) compiled an index using 18 technologies available in 1983, including cardiac catheterization and neonatal intensive care units. They then aggregated hospitals within metropolitan areas and compared metropolitan areas on the basis of degree of HMO market shares. Fundamentally, they found that HMO market shares did not matter. Although modest variations were found, no substantive differences were seen in technology at given points in time or in the dispersion of technologies over time.

Managed care plans, through their emphases on cost containment, would seem to be important vehicles for reining in the usage of high-cost-high-technology procedures and facilities, but research has not (yet) proved this. Medical facilities and medical practice styles change slowly, and it may be too early to see changes induced by the recent market penetration of managed care plans. Or it may be that the public demands high (and costly) technology, irrespective of who provides it.

Conclusions

This chapter has considered HMOs and other managed care health delivery systems that combine the functions of insuring patients and providing their care. We began by describing managed care and providing the rationale for a government policy that promotes it.

Our discussion has emphasized that HMOs and other care managers have incentives to curtail costs because they serve as both insurers and providers (see Box 12-2

BOX 12-2

DRIVE-THROUGH DELIVERIES—MANAGED CARE AND MANDATES

One of the heated issues regarding managed care has involved the movement toward one-night hospital stays for mothers expecting normal (or non-Cesarean deliveries) childbirth. Fueled by stories of instances where children died shortly after the mother's release, there has been an enormous public outcry to require managed care plans to provide at least a second night of hospital care.[5] Jensen and Goodman (1999) examine the economics of the analysis.

As recently as 1980, nearly 70 percent of mothers experiencing vaginal delivery had hospital stays of 3 days or more (Gillum, Graves, and Wood, 1998, Table R). Inpatient care was very costly, yet as long as hospitals were reimbursed for what they charged, they had no incentive to send the new mother home earlier. Almost certainly, the marginal benefits to the woman of being in the hospital for a third day did not measure up to the costs of keeping her there.

This became apparent to care managers. Pressure to reduce the stay was considerable, and by 1995, the average length of stay for a mother with a vaginal delivery was 1.7 days, with 46.8 percent of all mothers staying 1 day or less. For the vast majority, home care (starting the second day) along with appropriate outpatient follow-up has become the alternative. Home care carries its own costs, requiring the woman's time and probably assistance from family, friends, or hired caregivers. Nonetheless, it generally provides an appropriate level of care at a far lower cost than the inpatient care that it replaces.

The key phrase is "normal" childbirth. Medical care is not exact and mistakes are made. Managed care opponents have seized on cases where a baby who was sent home the second day after birth developed an ailment and needed to return to the hospital or, worse still, died. Keeping the baby an extra day, they argue, would prevent these problems.

In many states legislation has required insurers to guarantee at least 2 nights of hospital stay to all mothers with normal deliveries. Maryland's 1996 Early Discharge of Mothers and Babies Bill guaranteed that mothers and babies have coverage in the hospital for 48 hours for a normal vaginal delivery and 96 hours for a normal Cesarean delivery.

Liu, Dow, and Norton (2004) analyze the impacts of state "length of stay" mandates in 32 states, comparing the costs of the increased length of stay to the estimated health benefit, relying on infant mortality estimates that one infant life could be saved for each 1,400 normal newborns moved from early discharge (less than 30 hours) to longer lengths of stay. They find that for normal vaginal deliveries the average state law decreased early discharge (less than two-night stays) by 16 percentage points and increased average hospital charges, implying a $1,281 cost per early discharge averted by the law. This could be converted to a crude estimate of $1.79 million per life saved. They characterize their estimate as neither "highly cost-effective [n]or hugely cost-ineffective relative to estimates of the value of a life (often in the range of US$ 1–10 million)."

[5]In the late 1990s, the "drive-through delivery" and other restrictions became fodder for late-night talk-show jokes and ridicule of HMOs. Did consumers respond to the managed care backlash by "voting with their feet"? Marquis and colleagues (2004/2005) examined HMO market penetration in two periods, 1994 to 1998 and 1998 to 2001, with the former representing the pre-backlash period. There was little evidence of substantial consumer exit and plan switching even in markets where consumers had more options.

for a particular example relating to normal childbirths). Thus, the incentives for additional, less essential procedures are reduced, and we can show that system-wide even less care may be given than would be economically efficient. One key finding is that managed care organizations tend to reduce hospitalization—one of the most expensive of the health care services. While other findings are mixed, little evidence suggests that the quality of the care provided in HMOs is inferior to FFS care. Another key finding is that MCOs have been able to reduce fees paid to providers.

In the 1990s, cost pressures moved more users into managed care. By 2005, fee-for-service (FFS) health care enrollment for covered workers had fallen to 3 percent, from 73 percent less than two decades earlier. Yet customers also rebelled against the more stringent cost controls of HMO plans, preferring what some analysts refer to as "managed care light"—care brought forward by PPO or POS plans. These less stringent controls were palatable with the deceleration of health care costs in the late 1990s. However, with costs increasing again at double-digit rates in the first years of the twenty-first century, consumers and policy analysts will be forced to reexamine the types of care management they are willing to accept.

SUMMARY

1. Managed care seeks to integrate what previously had been an unintegrated system of health care treatment. Such integration has the potential to reduce health care costs, but the integration is costly and may limit choice of provider.

2. In HMOs, PPOs, and other MCOs, the functions of insurance and the provision of care are combined. In return for a prepaid premium, MCOs agree to provide enrollees with comprehensive health care over a given period of time.

3. By agreeing to handle all of a patient's health care needs for a fixed, prearranged fee, a provider is bearing a substantial part of the financial risk. By bearing such a risk, the managed care organization has a strong incentive to develop strategies for reducing excessive care and minimizing other inefficiencies.

4. HMOs control utilization and costs by imposing physician gatekeepers and requiring treatment within defined provider networks. PPO plans maintain the provider networks but do not require physician gatekeepers. Point-of-service (POS) plans maintain the physician gatekeeper role but do not require treatment within defined provider networks.

5. There has been a dramatic shift from FFS to managed care in employer-sponsored plans. By 2005, 97 percent of these workers were in managed care plans with 61 percent selecting PPOs.

6. A theoretical model of the structure of the managed care market shows that different-sized providers may be offering different levels (qualities) of care. Due to the impact of potential disenrollment that is not faced in the fee-for-service sector, one might expect inefficiently low levels of care in the managed care sector.

7. If providers can charge different consumers different amounts, the providers can earn additional profits. Price discrimination is difficult or impossible under the contracts characterizing prepayment-based organizations because:
 - Providers will find it difficult to determine how much individual consumers value the services.
 - Prepayment-based organizations may be able to shop among providers, thus limiting the providers' monopoly power.

8. Managed care organizations typically provide comprehensive sets of ambulatory and inpatient services, including routine office visits and preventive care, generally without coinsurance or a deductible. Paperwork is reduced, and uncertainty over coverage is minimal. These features make membership attractive to consumers, especially to some who are concerned about out-of-pocket costs.

9. In contrast to FFS arrangements, the managed care enrollee's choices of providers and access to hospitals (aside from emergency care) are limited. Also, direct access to specialists may require referral from the patient's gatekeeper—the primary care physician.

10. The consensus is strong that managed care reduces utilization, especially of hospital care, but there is little evidence that the quality of care is inferior to that in an FFS system.
11. Recent evidence indicates that the lower expenditures per enrollee under managed care are associated largely with the lower fees they are able to negotiate with some providers. Risk selection is not a major factor.
12. In addition to individual cost-related impacts of managed care organizations, there are also competitive impacts. Although market penetration does not always lead to lower hospital prices, it does appear to reduce insurance premiums.
13. Managed care plans, through their emphasis on cost containment, would seem to provide important opportunities for reining in the usage of high-cost-high-technology procedures and facilities. Research findings to date have not supported this hypothesis.

DISCUSSION QUESTIONS

1. What are the key elements that distinguish managed care from FFS plans?
2. What are the principal differences among HMO, PPO, and POS plans?
3. How do the economic profits (rents) that may be earned by some groups of providers enable MCOs to limit expenditures? What role does the price elasticity of demand play in this process?
4. Why is selection bias such an important issue in measuring HMO performance?
5. Discuss ways that managed care organizations may be able to reduce costs of care to their clientele.
6. Why do some critics argue that managed care organizations provide lower-quality care than FFS plans? Evaluate this possibility from a societal perspective.
7. After a large increase in membership, HMO enrollments flattened in the late 1980s and many HMOs suffered financial difficulties. How might this be explained according to what is known about the supply and demand for HMOs?
8. If everyone chose to join an HMO, would average HMO expenditures per case tend to rise or fall? Would national health expenditures tend to rise or fall?
9. What features of managed care organizations tend to inhibit or discourage people from joining? What features tend to attract people? Discuss the advantages and disadvantages of managed care enrollment.
10. Why is the growth of managed care plans a relatively recent phenomenon? Describe governmental policies and practices that have encouraged managed care organizations and inhibited them.
11. If traditional FFS leads to demand inducement, what constrains the HMO from underproviding care?
12. Explain how the availability of alternative delivery systems is expected to produce competitive effects throughout the health economy.
13. Discuss the ways that managed care organizations can influence the adoption of new technologies.

EXERCISES

1. Consider an HMO with a demand curve of the following form: $Q = 100 - 2P$. Suppose that its marginal and average costs were \$20. If the firm maximizes profits, determine its price, output, and profits.
2. In exercise 1, if the firm must act as a perfect competitor, in the long run what will happen to equilibrium price and equilibrium output?
3. Consistent with Figure 12-2, assume that the FFS price was \$100 per visit and the average patient made eight visits per year. A competing managed care organization came in and charged \$80 per visit, providing seven visits per year.
 a. Calculate the change in total expenditures.
 b. Graph the FFS and the managed care market equilibria as was done in Figure 12-2. What do our findings suggest about demand for managed care compared to demand for FFS care?

4. Consider the discussion on adverse selection into HMOs and FFS care, as noted through equation (12.2) and Figure 12-4. Suppose that, on average, FFS clients bought $2,000 in services ($\bar{s}_F = 2,000$) and HMO clients bought $1,500 in services ($\bar{s}_H = 1,500$), with an efficiency factor of 0.9. The FFS plan charges a 10 percent coinsurance rate.
 a. Set up this problem graphically, labeling the E and V curves.
 b. If a client expects to spend $250 on care, will he or she choose an HMO or an FFS plan? Why?
 c. At which value of s would the client expect to be indifferent between an HMO and an FFS plan? Why?
 d. How would your answer to parts (b) and (c) change if the HMO adopted a 20 percent coinsurance rate?
5. Assume that in Figure 12-5, so many providers entered the health care market that individual demand curves fell below the average cost curves. Draw the new equilibrium. What would happen to short-run profits in the health care market?
6. Exercise 5 discusses a short-run equilibrium in the health care market. With entry and exit into and from the market, graph and discuss the long-run equilibrium.
7. In Table 12-5, the market penetration for managed care rises from 40 percent to 50 percent between Periods 1 and 2 and stays at 50 percent. Suppose, instead, that it fell from 40 percent to 30 percent and stayed at 30 percent.
 a. What would happen to total costs and to rates of cost increase?
 b. How do your results compare to the discussion regarding Table 12-5? Why?

CHAPTER 13

Nonprofit Firms

Nonprofit firms account for only 5 percent of the GDP, but they make up a significant portion of the health care sector. The 60 percent of community hospitals that are non-profit provide nearly 70 percent of the beds and treat a similar proportion of the nation's hospital patients. Nonprofit firms also offer 30 percent of nursing home care and half of the inpatient specialty mental health and substance abuse treatment. We also see nonprofits providing education, collecting and providing blood, operating symphony orchestras and opera companies, and facilitating the conservation of land.

Inasmuch as nonprofits are prominent in health care, especially in the important hospital industry, they pose questions of considerable interest. Will the economic behavior of nonprofits be distinctly different from that of the more common for-profit firm or from government enterprise? A growing body of literature addresses such questions and adds to our understanding of nonprofit firms in general. Studies within health economics contribute to both the general theory of nonprofit firms and the understanding of vital issues of the health economy.

An Introduction to Nonprofits

What is the nonprofit firm? People commonly assume that nonprofits are firms organized to provide charitable goods or community services and that they obtain their revenues largely from donations. While many fit this category, the definition does not serve well conceptually, nor does it make an important economic distinction. On one hand, many profit-making firms provide important goods and services to the community, and many provide basic goods, such as food and housing to the poor. On the other hand, many nonprofit firms serve the well-to-do, and many serve in competition with for-profits. Many obtain the lion's share of their revenues from the sale of goods and services at prices similar to their for-profit competitors. Health care nonprofits obtain more than 90 percent of their revenues from "sales and receipts."

In economic language, the important distinction of the nonprofit is the *nondistribution* constraint. This means that no one has a legal claim on the nonprofit's residual, the difference between the revenues and its costs, or what an ordinary firm would call its profits. Because there is no residual claimant, it is possible that the nonprofit's objectives will differ from profit making. Two secondary distinctions between nonprofits and for-profits are also consequential. First, nonprofits are exempt from corporate income taxes and often from property and sales taxes. Second, donations to nonprofits receive favorable tax treatment. These distinctions make the nonprofit a potentially different economic entity, but is it?[1]

Why Nonprofits Exist and Why They Are Prevalent in Health Care

In any economy like that of the United States, three types of firms can be found: private profit making, government, and voluntary nonprofit enterprises. Why do each of these types of firms exist? Society's economic institutions are not created at random. They must reflect some basic economic incentives and unmet needs that the firms and the laws establishing them were created to satisfy.

Nonprofits as Providers of Unmet Demands for Public Goods

Burton Weisbrod's analysis (1975) guides the following exposition. In the United States and other Western economies, economists view a perfectly competitive industry under certain circumstances as economically efficient, and empirical data suggest that competition often fosters growth. Government enterprises under this account are needed only in cases where competitive markets fail. As this theory unfolds, nonprofits are needed, in turn, in cases where government enterprise also fails. We begin by reviewing the standard explanation of the role of government enterprise, and we then introduce Weisbrod's explanation in which the nonprofit firm satisfies demands for public goods unmet either by private markets or the government.

Under the standard economic explanation, government enterprise might possibly—though not necessarily—have a role in improving market efficiency in cases where competitive markets tend to fail. The most prominent cases of market failure involve externalities and public goods. Two examples will clarify these issues.

Market Failure: Externalities

Most consumer goods provide private benefits and little or no externalities. An externality is an uncompensated direct effect of the production or consumption of a good on persons other than the producers or consumers. Consider a good with no externality. When one enjoys a hamburger at a local restaurant, the pleasure is primarily private, and the benefit goes to the one who consumes. There is no effect on parties external to the market, other than the producer or consumer. However, consider the case where one purchases a vaccination for influenza. This good entails a private benefit: The purchaser will less likely suffer from influenza. In addition, there is an external benefit to others because the purchaser will be less likely to infect others.

Free markets tend to underproduce goods for which there exist significant external benefits. For example, the purchasers of vaccinations will tend to consider primarily the private benefits and will ignore the external benefits to the community. The benefit to society is the sum of the private benefits and the external benefits to the

[1]For further discussion on the nature of nonprofit firms, see Weisbrod (1988).

community. Because demand will represent only the private benefits, it will understate society's benefits and give a false or inadequate signal to the market. The market then produces less than the amount that would maximize net social benefits. This is economically inefficient, and we call this situation a case of market failure.

Generally, economists recognize both beneficial and detrimental externalities, but they argue over their relative importance and the appropriate remedy. The existence of a significantly large externality raises the possibility of a role for government. This is only a possibility because inefficiencies entailed in governmental activity might offset the potential gains. If we recognize that markets may fail, we must recognize that governments too may fail to act efficiently. The mainstream approach, however, usually recognizes that in some cases governmental activity will improve the net benefits to society.

Market Failure: Public Goods

The vaccination is a private good with an external benefit. The external benefit of this good itself entails certain public good aspects. To understand this fully, consider first the case of a pure public good, defined as a good that is both nonexcludable and nonrival. *Nonexcludable* means that people cannot be economically excluded from consuming the good even if they refuse to pay for it. *Nonrival* means that one person can consume the good without depleting it for others. Our hamburger is an example of a private good, not a public good. The hamburger is excludable because McDonald's can easily refuse the hamburger to someone who refuses to pay. Likewise, the hamburger is a rival good because the act of one person's consuming the burger causes it to be depleted in that it is eaten up.

Contrast the hamburger with a classic example of a pure public good, national defense. Imagine an antimissile system that effectively puts a defensive umbrella over a country. This defense system would be nonexcludable because any person living in the country would benefit even if he or she individually refused to pay for it. It would be impossible, let alone costly, to allow the nonpayer alone to be subject to an enemy missile strike. Likewise, the defense system is nonrival because the protection one individual receives does not diminish the defense enjoyed by others in the country.

Public goods like this are often provided by government enterprise. Private enterprise may provide too little of a public good or even none at all, if hypothetically it were given the responsibility. Remember that a public good, such as defense, is nonexcludable. Therefore, if private enterprise were to attempt to provide defense, it could well find many or most citizens choosing to be *free riders*. A free rider is a person who consumes the public good but refuses to pay. Private enterprise does not have the power to tax or otherwise force consumers to pay. It cannot refuse or exclude the service of the public good to nonpayers.

The Public Good–Private Good Aspect of Donations

Now consider an example of a public good that is conceptually more challenging, charitable donations. A charitable donation to the health of others in the community has the characteristics of both a public good and a private good. The need for both concepts becomes clear in Richard Steinberg's (1986, 1987) work, which argues that donations to public goods motivate the donor as both private and public goods. If you donate a parcel of wetland to a land conservancy, this dedicated land can be enjoyed by anyone, because your enjoyment does not diminish the enjoyment of the same property for others. The dedicated land is a public good. At the same time, you can enjoy the

act of giving, which some describe as providing you, the donor, with a warm glow you get from doing (and perhaps from being known to have done) a good thing (Arrow, 1975; Andreoni, 1990).

Now consider a case where the government provides a public good. This case will enable one to understand Weisbrod's explanation of the kind of government failure that provides a rationale for the existence of nonprofits. In Figure 13-1, let the curves D_1 through D_5 represent the demand curves of five different voting individuals for a public good to be provided by the government. Let the demand curves represent the external benefits to these different groups of taxpayers. These demand curves represent the marginal benefits to the taxpayer donors.

To pay for this public good, assume that these five different taxpayers are to be equally taxed at a per-unit tax rate of MT, which is the marginal tax. Because the five individuals are being equally taxed, the marginal tax for each will be exactly one-fifth of the marginal cost to society. Thus, if the government were to provide output $0C$, then each of the five taxpayers would be charged $0C \times MT$, and the total tax receipts would exactly pay for the project. If the output were $0B$, then $0B \times MT$ would be collected from each individual, and so on.

The government must choose a single level of output. What level will government choose to provide if the outcome is left to the democratic political process? Economists find it convenient to imagine an elected manager whose continued term in office is determined by the ability to provide the "right" level. If level $0A$ is proposed, four of the five voters would prefer more (why?) and would vote against it. If level $0B$ is proposed, three of the five would prefer more and would vote against that level. In contrast, level $0D$ would provide too much public good for three of the five voters, and similarly for level $0E$. Only level $0C$ will gain a majority vote. This majority is made up of Voter 3, who is exactly satisfied because her marginal benefits equal the marginal tax, and Voters 4 and 5, who would like to see more but are satisfied with level $0C$. Suppose the manager proposed just a little more than $0C$. This is too much for Voter 3, who now votes against the manager in favor of someone else who would reduce the public good level back to $0C$.

FIGURE 13-1 The Median Voter Model of Public Goods

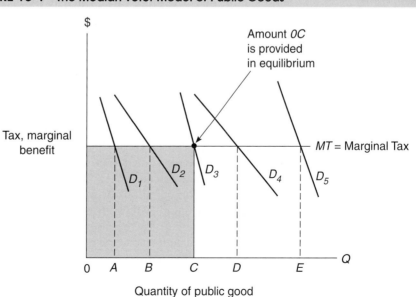

Weisbrod's point is illustrated in this example. The government enterprise level chosen entails dissatisfied voters on the margin, whose demands are not exactly satisfied. The marginal tax rate is perfectly tailored only to Voter 3, the median person. For this person, the marginal benefit just equals the marginal tax rate at the provided output. It is theoretically possible to design a tax system so that for each person the marginal tax equals his or her marginal benefit, but it is difficult to accomplish this in practice. Without such a tax system, some voters will prefer less of the public good and some will prefer more of it. The government enterprise will have failed to satisfy the demands of those who would prefer more. Such unsatisfied voters will have the incentive to form a nonprofit enterprise and provide the good themselves.

It follows from Weisbrod's theory that nonprofits arise because private profit-motivated markets will tend to underproduce goods or services entailing beneficial externalities. In turn, the government also may underprovide such goods and services in the eyes of a significant minority of voters. These citizens will tend to include those who perceive the external benefit to the community most keenly. Such citizens (here, Voters 4 and 5) establish nonprofit corporations.

Weisbrod's analysis applies to health care when it is not a pure private good. The health care provided to the indigent is itself private because the indigent person could have been excluded had we wished. The care is also rival, as it is consumed by the recipient. Nevertheless, the health care provided to the indigent entails a beneficial externality to any charitably-minded person. It is this external benefit that is a public good, and it is in this sense that health care is not a pure private good.

Relevance to Health Care Markets

Hospital services, nursing home services, and kidney dialysis services are probably not pure private goods. The Weisbrod analysis will apply in principle to any such services that provide external benefits to the community at large. Thus, nonprofit health care enterprises may arise where a sufficient minority of voters are dissatisfied with the quantity or quality of such services provided by the for-profit sector or government. The theory provides a plausible account of the historical rise of non-profit hospitals. Hospitals in the United States and in many countries often began as charitable institutions, providing care primarily to the poor and relying heavily on donations.[2]

Furthermore, the theory encompasses a broader range of external benefits than are involved in the provision of indigent, uncompensated care. High-quality, prestigious hospitals may enhance a community's sense of pride and well-being. They may indirectly provide benefits to local businesses. Their excess capacity also provides insurance for the currently healthy citizens that a bed will be available should they need one.

However, the purely charitable aspects of hospital care have become less important. Improvements in medical technology transformed hospitals into workshops for doctors—places for treating all patients, both rich and poor. By 1996, donations accounted for less than 3 percent of average hospital revenues, and only about 3 percent of patients relied on donations or welfare as their principle source of payment. Hospital finance departments wrote off unpaid patient bills, but these accounted for less than 1 percent of billings. The demise of hospital donations has been attributed to the growth of hospital insurance coverage, especially since the advent of Medicare and Medicaid. The decline in donations is consistent with the Weisbrod theory. Individual

[2]The history of hospitals and the relative importance of nonprofit versus for-profit status are further explored in Bays (1983), Frech (1990), and Temin (1988).

demands have stayed fairly stable while increases in public sector provision or financing have occurred.

With the decline in cash donations, other forms of donations as well as other forms of nonprofit hospital advantages have become relatively more important. Donations of time and energy for board members and other individuals may now be relatively more important. To be sure, cash donations still play an important role in certain capital fund drives, but in the present day, the financial advantages enjoyed by nonprofit hospitals stem more importantly from the subsidization of nonprofits by the government through tax exemptions. Generally, nonprofits do not pay corporate, property, or sales taxes although for-profits do. The only tax advantage enjoyed by for-profits is the ability to write off losses during bad years.

Nonprofits as a Response to Contract Failure

A related theory with early origins complements Weisbrod's ideas. Arrow (1963) suggested that the prevalence of nonprofits is due to the uncertainty of identifying quality of care. Hansmann (1980) expanded this idea and theorized that the nonprofit sector helps to repair the problems of contract failure that occur when the quantity or quality of output is difficult to observe. Thus, asymmetry of information between the firm and the buyer of services becomes important (as noted in Chapter 10) in explaining the nonprofit role.[3]

A classic example of the contract failure illustrates the problem. Suppose you wish to contribute food and clothing to suffering people in Ethiopia. You can find a firm to deliver the care. However, it would be prohibitively costly to verify that the firm actually is delivering the desired goods to the designated population. You would hardly fly to Ethiopia just to check on this. Under these circumstances, you may prefer to employ a nonprofit firm.

As a deliverer of the aid packages, a for-profit firm will be perceived to have a conflict of interest. Such a firm could increase its profits by reneging on its promise. The nonprofit cannot distribute its residual so it would have less incentive to renege. In this case, the nonprofit, by better serving the donor's interests, also serves the market more efficiently.

Applications of Contract Failure to Nursing Home Care

Contract failure is not confined to the issues of donated goods and services, as it can exist even when the purchaser is close at hand. Contrast the management of hotels and nursing homes. Hotels are profit-seeking enterprises that provide rooms and suites along with housekeeping services, dining, and recreation to travelers and residents. Nursing homes also provide rooms and suites, dining, and recreation along with housekeeping services and, of course, specialized nursing services largely for an older and often infirm population. In fact, many nursing homes began as hotels.

What is the difference? Hotel patrons are assumed to be utility-maximizing consumers who compare benefits and costs in deciding whether to stay at the hotel. Nursing home patients may not be able to assess the quality of the facility and the care they receive accurately, perhaps because of their health impairments. Relatives or friends may obtain only limited impressions upon visiting and may not be sophisticated assessors of the quality of long-term care. A for-profit home, in contrast to a for-profit hotel, may appear to have a conflict of interest in the eyes of some demanders.

Do for-profit nursing homes in practice provide lower quality? The measurement of quality is itself an issue of dispute. Outcome measures, such as changes in patient

[3]The essential idea was developed further in a model by Easley and O'Hara (1983).

health status, are best in principle, but reliable outcome measures are difficult to obtain. Analysts must often rely on input data, such as the number of registered nurses per patient, but these data, although more readily available, can be easily misinterpreted. For example, does a nursing home with more nurses per patient provide higher quality or is it simply less efficient?

Hirth (1999) demonstrated a related and confounding issue in theory. Studies have often neglected the market structural environment that the nonprofit experiences and the effect of the nonprofit on that environment. Under plausible conditions, an influx of nonprofit homes will drive up the average quality in the market, making the nonprofit a productive agent for change whether or not it exhibits a higher quality itself. This research also shows that the nonprofits can be expected to give market signals of higher quality and that they will tend toward the high end of the quality spectrum.

Much of the available evidence suggests that there is an apparent for-profit advantage in cost without apparently lower quality. Quality, however, is difficult to assess and other reports disagree with the earlier view. In practice, nursing homes with more personnel per patient tend to have better patient outcomes, but it is difficult to sort out efficiency and quality. Gertler (1989) addressed these problems and found a higher quality level in nonprofit homes.[4]

Relevance of Contract Failure to Hospitals and Other Firms

If contract failure theory applies to nursing home care, it does not appear appropriate for hospitals, a point noted by Hansmann (1980). Hospital patients are under the close supervision of physicians acting as the patients' agents. Physicians have little incentive to misinform patients by overstating the quality of care. More likely, the physicians' incentives would cause them to encourage patients to choose the highest quality available. Thus, physicians as agents of the patients may eliminate the potential contract failure.

Sloan (1988) further suggests that a double standard frequently is applied by those who favor the contract failure theory. The field of physician services, which are nearly all provided on a for-profit basis in the United States, seems ripe for the application of contract theory. Consumers would find it just as hard to assess the quality of physician care as they would hospital care, so why do nonprofit firms not take over the physician care sector?

The Role of Physicians in the Hospital Industry

The theories so far account for the presence of nonprofit institutions in general. Bays (1983) adds a special theory to account for the rise of nonprofit hospitals. His is called an interest group theory.

Bays notes that nineteenth century U.S. hospitals were charitable institutions where physicians largely donated their time. Notably, medical technology had not yet developed to the point where hospitals were important to the physician either technologically or economically. With rapid population growth and hospital expansion in the early twentieth century, for-profit hospitals flourished, accounting for about half of existing hospitals in 1910 and reaching their zenith by 1930. These for-profit hospitals were generally small.

As medical technology advanced, hospitals became the workshops of doctors. Holding admitting privileges at one or more hospitals was crucial to a physician's practice. Hospitals also grew rapidly in size. With greater interest in the operation of hospitals, physicians increasingly developed and used their influence as an interest group to

[4]For further study, see Cohen and Spector (1996) and Davis (1991).

exert some control over them. By controlling hospital admitting privileges, organized physicians gained a degree of market power, including the ability to exercise discipline over physicians whose practices tended to erode the market power of the organized group. For example, the affiliation by some physicians with prepaid group practice was treated as "unprofessional conduct."

Under this theory, physicians prefer nonprofit hospitals because they have greater power within them. Power over decision making permits the physician to enhance personal income. Physicians can order hospital services complementary to their own services, perhaps well past the extent that would be profitable to the hospital. This account, Bays points out, is consistent with the policy stand of the AMA in support of Hill-Burton, a 1946 federal act that provided construction aid and loan subsidies to nonprofit hospitals. Furthermore, the favored tax treatment and subsidies to nonprofit hospitals arise in part through physicians' political support—support that ultimately benefits the physician through the provision of lower-cost complementary hospital inputs.

How then can we account for public acquiescence in supporting the nonprofit mode? The tax relief and dollar subsidies to nonprofit hospitals take resources from the general public majority to support the narrower interests of the physician minority. To account for this anomaly, Bays appeals to interest group theory.

Under interest group theory, small groups may gain power when their interests are highly concentrated and their membership is homogeneous. It will be worthwhile in such cases for physicians to support lobbying on behalf of measures that result in significant benefits to them, whereas the loss to the general public is diffused. While the individual consumer may benefit by challenging the status quo, the personal gains are small relative to the personal costs. The theoretical situation depicted by Bays, a situation that substantially and lopsidedly favors the physician at the expense of the general public, may nevertheless represent a regulatory equilibrium.

Financial Matters and the Nonprofit

Lacking the ability to distribute net revenues, the nonprofits do not issue equity stock and lack this avenue for raising capital. Although this is a disadvantage if it needs to respond to changing market conditions, the nonprofit also has some financial advantages. It is exempt from corporate, property, and sales taxes, and its bonds are generally tax-exempt as well. It may also have market advantages, such as the responsiveness and loyalty generated by the consumer's response to nonprofits under the contract failure situation. Finally, it is more likely to attract donations than is the for-profit.

What is the bottom line when all advantages and disadvantages of the nonprofit are considered? Which ownership form can respond to a rapidly expanding demand the quickest? Past research generally indicated that rapid demand change favored the for-profit as measured by changes in their market share. Hansmann, Kessler, and McClellan (2002) recently determined that over the past 20 years, the for-profit hospital form has been the most responsive to demand change in an era of declining hospital demand.

Summary of the Reasons for the Prevalence of Nonprofits

Several theories explain the existence of nonprofits. In some cases, these theories are complementary, while in other cases, there are sharp contrasts. Weisbrod accounts for the existence of nonprofit firms in an economy with three sectors: for-profits, government, and nonprofits. In his view, nonprofits arise to provide for unmet demands for public goods, most notably in cases where there are significant external benefits to the provision of a good.

Hansmann's view is complementary to this account, emphasizing the special role for nonprofit firms in cases of contract failure (cases where it is difficult to observe the good's provision or quality). These two theories provide insights into the prevalence of nonprofit firms in the provision of hospital care and nursing home care. Under either of these two accounts, the public deference to nonprofit firms (including favorable tax treatment) makes some sense.

In contrast, Bays offers an interest group theory under which physicians prefer nonprofits and use their influence to further the role of nonprofits out of interest for personal gain. Under Bays's account, favored treatment of nonprofit hospitals is not so clearly in the public interest. This multiplicity of theories regarding the existence of nonprofit firms, particularly of hospitals, is mirrored in a multiplicity of theories of hospital behavior.

Models of Nonprofit Hospital Behavior

Health economics offers many descriptions of hospital behavior. We begin with a nonprofit model that applies in principle to an entire class of nonprofit firms. We then follow with two theories that are specific to hospitals.

The Quality-Quantity Nonprofit Theory

When economists study nonprofit hospital responses to policy change, they begin by positing an objective of the hospital decision makers. Most frequently, they choose either a utility-maximization or a profit-maximization type of model. The first and most prominent model of the utility-maximizing hospital was proposed by Joseph Newhouse (1970) and applied to nonprofit firms in general. For Newhouse, the hospital's objective was to maximize the utility of the decision makers. Utility of the firm reflects an index of the decision maker's preferences and can be thought of as a measure of satisfaction, similar to the utility of a consumer.

The special difficulty for the case of hospitals is to describe the complex elements and interactions of the set of hospital decision makers. Nonprofit hospitals in the United States tend to have three parties with considerable decision-making authority. The trustees are nominally in charge of the hospital, but boards of trustees may include people with widely varying backgrounds, knowledge of health care, and management expertise. The trustees' decision-making agent is the hospital administrator or CEO. This manager may have varying degrees of actual power and authority. Finally, the arbiters of medical decision making are the physician staff. The physicians also may exercise considerable decision-making authority. We assume that this complex decision-making apparatus resolves into a single utility function and describes a set of well-behaved indifference curves.

The Utility Function

In Newhouse's model, the hospital's preferences are defined over quantity and quality of output. Quantity of output could be measured in several ways, but we assume that it is measured by the number of cases treated by the hospital over a given time period. We further assume that there is only one type of case to be treated, though there could be hundreds. Output quality can entail many different characteristics of the care provided. Some top decision makers may value the quality or beauty of the hospital structure, and others may emphasize expertise of the physician or nursing staff. Still others may emphasize prestige in the medical community, and yet others may stress the quality of the tender loving care provided. Graphically, we shall suppose that just one index of quality exists.

This conception of the nonprofit hospital is consistent with the external-benefits account of the role of nonprofit firms. The utility derived from producing quantity and quality might arise because care to these patients entails an external benefit to the community at large and to the hospital decision makers in particular. The external benefit could take on many forms, being purely charitable in some cases or purely concerned with personal prestige and influence in others. Nevertheless, the hospital's objective could be construed as maximizing the external benefit.

The Quantity-Quality Frontier

The hospital does not simply maximize quantity or maximize quality, but instead selects a combination of quantity and quality that maximizes utility. It faces a budget constraint, as it must pay its bills and cannot run negative net revenue as a general rule. Furthermore, the nondistribution constraint on all nonprofits entails that this hospital has no incentive to choose positive net revenues as a general rule. Thus, the budget constraint effectively requires that the sum of patient-generated revenues plus donations equal the hospital's costs.

Following Newhouse, assume that all revenue sources, which are primarily patient-generated revenues, are summarized in an average revenue curve labeled $D(q_1)$ in Figure 13-2. This curve is the demand curve facing the hospital. This demand curve would generally depend on the level of quality, q_1, and higher quality of care would translate into a higher demand for care. For example, $D(q_2)$ would represent the demand curve for a higher-quality level of care. Quality is costly to produce so we can assume that higher-quality levels will entail higher average costs. For example, average cost curve $AC(q_2)$ represents the average cost curve for quality level 2, a higher-quality level than for average cost curve $AC(q_1)$, the average cost curve for quality level 1.

The budget constraint requires that the hospital produce where average revenue equals average cost. For example, output Q_1 satisfies the budget constraint for quality level 1. If consumers place a higher marginal valuation on the incremental quality than it costs to produce, then $D(q_2)$ will shift up by more than will $AC(q_2)$, and incremental

FIGURE 13-2 Hospital Average Cost Curves

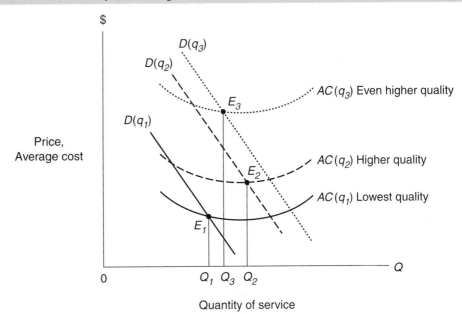

Quantity of service

FIGURE 13-3 Hospital Quality-Quantity Trade-Offs

quality will be accompanied by incremental quantity. Eventually, however, it is likely that the cost of incremental quality will increase by more than consumers' willingness to pay for it. In other words, $AC(q_3)$ constitutes a much bigger increase than $D(q_3)$. When this happens, incremental quality comes at the expense of quantity of services (fewer people can afford the higher-quality services). Although Q_2 exceeded Q_1, quantity Q_3 (and all further quantities) represents decreases in equilibrium quantity as trade-offs with increased quality.

Examining the pattern of equilibrium points reveals a quality/quantity frontier (such as is depicted in Figure 13-3). From E_1 to E_2, quality and quantity increase together. In contrast, from E_2 to E_3, the equilibria follow a trade-off between rising quality and a declining quantity. The curve q^*Q^* in Figure 13-3 is intended to represent the overall pattern.

Maximization of Utility

Given the possibility frontier, the hospital decision makers choose the point that maximizes utility. The constrained utility maximization point occurs at a point of tangency between the frontier and the highest indifference curve attainable. In Figure 13–3, utility maximization occurs at point A.

On the one hand, let the hospital preferences place sole weight on quantity. Then, the hospital would behave like a constrained quantity maximizer and produce at point B. On the other hand, let the hospital primarily value quality, and further let quality as perceived by the top decision makers be primarily the prestige of the hospital as compared to its peers. It would produce at point C. This special case is similar to a model of the hospital as a conspicuous producer as proposed by Lee (1971). A unique feature of Lee's approach, however, is that the hospital chooses production technologies that are conspicuously prestigious, such as for open heart surgery or transplants. The hospital's search for prestige may lead to socially inefficient production technologies or output qualities.

The Hospital as a Physicians' Cooperative

A different account of the nonprofit hospital is provided in theories that believe that hospitals maximize the pecuniary gain to the decisive set of decision makers. Mark Pauly and Michael Redisch (1973) describe the nonprofit hospital as a "physicians'

cooperative," assuming that the hospital is controlled by a physician staff who operate the hospital so as to maximize their net incomes.

This view of the hospital focuses on the "full price" of the hospital care, meaning the total charges to the patient by both the hospital and the physician. Assume that the patient pays a single bill representing the full price of the care and let donations be zero. The full price of care will be determined by consumer demand and depends on the total quantity of care offered by the physicians' cooperative. The amount of care produced and offered to patients depends, in turn, on the quantity of inputs chosen by the top decision makers, here the physicians. Summarize hospital inputs as capital, K, and labor, L. Let the physician input be M, which is fixed if the hospital selects a "closed staff."

Maximizing Net Revenue per Physician

The hospital is then run so as to maximize the net revenue (NR) per physician (M), or NR/M. The net revenue is the sum of all of the revenue less factor payments to non-physician labor and payments to capital. The net revenue per physician divides that revenue over the total number of physicians, M. An increase in the number of physicians, M, initially increases revenues per physician. Eventually, revenues per physician must fall because (due to the fixed levels of nonphysician labor and capital) the percent increase in revenues (in the numerator) will be smaller than the percent change in number of physicians (in the denominator).

Figure 13-4 shows the optimal staff size if the physicians can limit the size of the staff, or "close" the staff. Here dollar values are on the vertical axis and the number of physicians on staff, M, is on the horizontal axis. The curve N denotes average physician income. The N curve starts at the origin point A (no revenue), rises to a maximum at point B, and then falls. Curve s depicts the supply curve of physicians, which is infinitely elastic, plausibly representing a case in an urban, physician-dense environment. For physicians who are on the staff, the optimal staff size would be M^*, where curve N reaches its maximum.

In contrast, if the hospital has an open staff, physicians are free to enter as long as their resulting average income, N, equals or exceeds their supply price, s. The open-staff equilibrium occurs at point C, where net revenue (the demand for physicians) equals supply, s, with M_0 physicians hired. Regardless of the number of physicians on

FIGURE 13-4 Maximizing Net Average Physician Revenue in Hospital

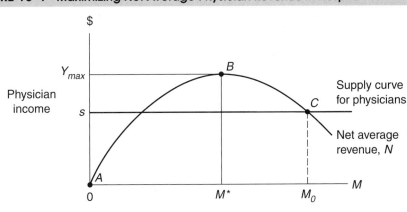

Number of staff physicians

staff (either a closed-staff or an open-staff equilibrium), the hospital inputs are chosen to maximize residual income for the medical staff. If the Newhouse model is viewed as resulting from the maximization of external benefit perceived to accrue to the community, then the Pauly-Redisch objective is the complete opposite.

A Comparison of the Quantity-Quality and the Physicians' Cooperative Theories

It is useful to contrast the two models by comparing them on the same graph. To do so, we represent combined (physician and hospital) revenues as a single function:

$$R = R(K, L, M_0)$$

The combined revenues depend on the quantity and quality of care produced, which in turn depend on the amounts of the inputs used. Like Newhouse, assume that the hospital/physician care is produced efficiently so that a higher quality of care requires necessarily a higher level and hence cost of inputs. The hospital may receive additional revenues in the form of donations, D_0, and government subsidies, G_0. Let physician supply be perfectly elastic at a constant supply price, s. Constant input prices, r for capital and w for labor, complete the description. Finally, define the hospital residual, HR, revenues as the following equation:

$$HR = R(K, L, M_0) - wL - rK - sM_0 + D_0 + G_0 \qquad \textbf{(13.1)}$$

Under the Pauly-Redisch model, the hospital residual, HR, is usurped by the physicians on the staff. For a given level of physicians on the staff, M_0, the physicians will maximize their average incomes by maximizing HR itself.

In contrast, the Newhouse hospital will maximize utility of quantity, Q, and quality, q, subject to the constraint that the hospital residual is zero; that is, the hospital breaks even. To simplify the graphical representation, let the hospital residual function, HR, form a rounded hill, following Spence (1973). The contours of that hill are shown in Figure 13-5 in a graph with quantity and quality of care on the axes. The contours are analogous to contour lines on a topographical map. For example, the contour line labeled $HR = 1$ represents the collection of all combinations of quality and quantity of

FIGURE 13-5 Hospital Quantity-Quality Contours and Hospital Residual

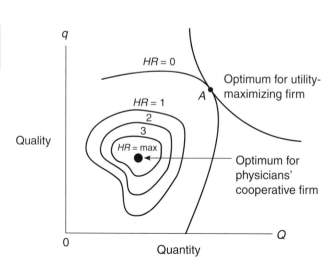

care that yield a hospital residual of $1 million. Contours farther away from the maximum residual point, $HR = HR_{max}$, yield successively lower levels of hospital residual. The contour curve labeled $HR = 0$ indicates the combinations of quality and quantity that yield a zero residual.

Quantity-Quality Contours and Hospital Residual

Begin with the Pauly-Redisch analysis of a closed hospital staff. Let the hospital physician staff be fixed at some level, M_0. The Pauly-Redisch hospital chooses the quantity-quality combination that maximizes the hospital residual, point $HR = HR_{max}$. The hospital residual then goes to the staff physicians, and these physicians will thus have maximized their average incomes. In contrast, the Newhouse hospital maximizes utility at point A, the point of tangency between the $HR = 0$ contour, representing the Newhouse budget constraint, and the highest indifference curve attainable. Thus, in the closed-staff case, the models yield very different results. As depicted, the Newhouse hospital tends to produce more quantity and quality of care. Under the Pauly-Redisch behavior however, the physicians indirectly usurp the hospital care residual, and this includes the donations and government subsidy as well. It is as if the nonprofit hospital is a for-profit firm in disguise. If we believed that the nonprofit hospitals behaved like this, we would likely call for an end to government tax exemptions for this nonprofit status (Clark, 1980).

Effects of Increased Competition

Before leaving the comparison of models, examine an effect of increased competition in the hospital sector. If entry were free, then all potential firms that may want to compete for hospital care patients are free to do so. Potential competitors could include alternative delivery systems as well as other hospitals. As more competitors enter the market and compete for business, the demand for care at any existing hospital will tend to fall. For our purposes, this means that competition will tend to shrink the hospital residual hill in size.

Figure 13-6 depicts a case where competition has continued until the maximum hospital residual attainable is zero. As we move away from the top of the hospital residual hill in any direction, the contours reflect negative and successively more negative residuals. The result is that the Newhouse and the Pauly-Redisch nonprofit hospital in this end result will converge in their choices of quantity and quality.

FIGURE 13-6
Convergence of Hospital Models in Long-Run Equilibrium Under Free Entry

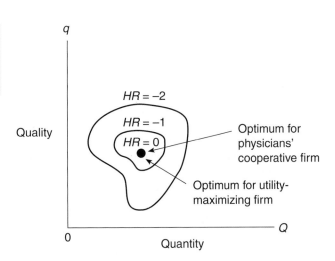

The hospital industry has experienced increasing competition in the last 25 years. Especially noteworthy are the competition from alternative delivery systems and the competitive incentives introduced under Medicare's prospective payment system. A tendency for nonprofit hospitals to converge toward for-profit-like behavior has long been noted in theory (Newhouse, 1970), and more recently it has been proposed as a probable result of hospital competition.

The Evidence: Do Nonprofit Hospitals Differ from For-Profit Hospitals?

Since the physicians' cooperative would choose nonphysician inputs and outputs much like a pure profit-oriented firm, we look at empirical comparisons of nonprofit and for-profit hospitals. Despite what appears to be a big difference in orientation, only a few behavioral differences are clear in theory. Sloan and colleagues (1998), in fact, conclude that there is not a "dime's worth of difference," basing this conclusion on studies of quality, cost, and efficiency of hospitals by ownership type.

Theoretically the nonprofit will produce at a higher quality, a higher quantity, or both. The Newhouse nonprofit could be very quantity oriented; it may strive to provide large quantities of basic hospital care to a deserving, perhaps destitute, population. Yet another nonprofit hospital might strive single-mindedly for the highest quality of care possible (Newhouse argued that there would be a bias toward quality). These (potentially) different types of nonprofits make comparisons of average quality of all nonprofits versus for-profits difficult to interpret. Thus, lack of quality differences on average is consistent with theory.

Clearly the orientation of the two ownership types is designed to be different, but are there differences in practice? Beginning with quality, McClellan and Staiger (1999) find higher mortality rates for the elderly in for-profit hospitals overall, but the small difference on average masked substantial variation with a number of markets showing quality superiority in the for-profit hospitals.

Who provides the most charity care? Norton and Staiger (1994) measured differences in care provided to the uninsured by nonprofit and for-profit hospitals. They found that hospitals in the same market area tend to serve the same number of uninsured. It may be possible, nevertheless, to encourage nonprofit hospital markets to increase their charity care. This could occur if the financial incentives of tax-exempt status encourage development of nonprofit hospitals, which according to Hassan and colleagues (2000), "are forced to provide higher levels of charity as a condition for gaining access to the tax exempt [bond] market."

Several studies investigate potential differences in managerial practices. Ballou and Weisbrod (2003) find substantial differences among religious, secular nonprofit, and government hospitals in patterns of CEO compensation. However, Brickley, van Horn, and Lawrence (2002) find for a large sample of nonprofit hospitals that compensation incentives for CEOs are significantly related to financial performance, and also they found little evidence that nonprofit hospitals provide "explicit incentives for their CEOs to focus on altruistic activities."

Several studies found other specific differences. Hoerger (1991) has suggested a test that avoids the indeterminacy; it can be understood using Figure 13-5. Again, consider that increased competition shifts the nonprofit's break-even profit contour, $HR = 0$, inward toward the origin; with this shift, the nonprofit optimum also moves toward the origin. At the same time, the for-profit's profit level falls, whereas the nonprofit's profit level is more or less fixed at breakeven. Hoerger concluded that the for-profit hospital would exhibit greater variability in its profit level, and the argument also suggested that the for-profit would show less variability in its quality/quantity response to changes in the economic environment.

Hoerger supported his hypothesis by studying a large, national sample of hospitals from 1983 to 1988, finding that for-profit hospital profits were significantly more variable than those of the nonprofit hospitals. Devising a crucial test, however, is complicated by the fact that for-profit hospitals also sort themselves geographically in distinctive patterns (for example, they are more urban than nonprofits). Mobley and Bradford (1997) show that once these geographical choices are incorporated into the analysis, differences in the variability of profits cannot be distinguished with confidence.

Several technical issues have shown the differences between for-profit and non-profit hospitals more clearly. As we discussed, Hansmann et al. (2002) found the for-profit to be quicker in adjusting to market demand changes, presumably due to better access to the capital markets. Hirth et al. (2000) studied the responses of firms providing dialysis care during a period of decreasing dialysis payments. The nonprofits tended to maintain quality and offset the dollar losses by cutting back on amenities, while the for-profits took the reverse route.

Finally, Silverman and Skinner (2001) found different patterns of DRG "creep" in which hospitals may "upcode" or recategorize patients into a more profitable Diagnosis Related Group (DRG) used to determine Medicare payments. The authors compared the DRGs of "pneumonia" and "respiratory illness"—where the line between the two DRG categories is fuzzy for many patients. The authors found generally that hospitals facing tougher financial conditions tended to upcode patients into the more profitable DRGs. The upcoding response, however, was greater for the for-profit than for the nonprofit hospitals, and greatest for hospitals that had just recently converted to for-profit status.

The Harris Model

The two hospital models strongly contrast the roles of the two principal power groups in the modern hospital, the physician staff group and the trustee-administrator group. The utility-maximizing models posit this power distribution to be resolved somehow into a coherent utility function, and it is tempting to view the utility function as representing the top management as constrained by the realities of physician behavior. The Pauly-Redisch model posits the de facto control by the physicians. In either case, there is presumably a resolution of power that occurs, perhaps even harmoniously. The hospital theory proposed by Jeffrey Harris (1977) represents an entirely different approach. The hospital, under Harris's account, is the scene of continual conflict within an organization inherently split into two parts—what Harris describes as a noncooperative oligopoly game.

The Harris model is noteworthy for two additional reasons. Harris is a physician with a Ph.D. in economics and he devised his account after experience as a physician in an urban hospital. As an economist, he is trained in complex economic organizational theories, but he presents his work in words and images describing experience within a hospital.

The Hospital as Two Firms

Harris proposes that the hospital's internal organization is really two separate firms interacting in a complex way. The hospital's structure has two main parts: the trustee-administrator group that serves as the supplier of inputs, and the physician staff that serves as the demanders. Like an automobile parts-and-service shop, the hospital has technical experts providing the actual service and requesting supplies from the organization. Unlike the auto shop, the physician's loyalties lie almost entirely with the patient. The physician is the patient's "hired gun."

Rather than having a predictable technological and inventory problem, the administrator has the problem of providing inputs to the physician-agent during a complicated, uncertain sequence of events. Consider Harris's account of a hypothetical case history:

> Mr. X comes to Dr. A with a fever and a cough. A chest X-ray reveals a density. He is hospitalized. Penicillin is administered. Although the fever subsides with this treatment, a repeat X-ray shows that the density has not disappeared. A sputum cytological examination is performed and lung cancer is diagnosed. Further studies suggest that the cancer can be removed surgically. An operation is performed. Unfortunately, massive postoperative bleeding occurs. Matched whole blood is administered. Despite this treatment, a cardiac arrest ensues and an emergency resuscitation (code call) is announced. Mr. X is transferred to Intensive Care with chest tubes and a respirator. A special contrast study (angiogram) reveals the site of bleeding. A repeat operation is performed. (p. 469)

The moral of this account is that rather than being a predictable assembly-line procedure, the hospital service is unique and customized for each patient and it plays out in an unpredictable way. The physician hurries to various supply centers, demanding services on behalf of his patient. The administrator supplies these services. Under the circumstances, market-like negotiations between the supplier and demander are impossible, as are lengthy determinations of an exact price for the patient prior to treatment. The problem is not merely that the patient is usually heavily insured, but instead, the unusual agency relationship that requires the physician to make noneconomic decisions on the patient's behalf. As Harris states,

> There is a special negative externality in an arrangement in which one makes repeated marginal decisions about life and death. This externality is so important that the physician's participation in the "market" for angiograms and code calls is explicitly foreclosed. Whether or not it is justified, this notion has an important influence on the way the hospital is organized. (p. 473)

The hospital, according to Harris, solves the rationing problem with a variety of nonprice-related decision rules. "There are loosely enforced standards, rules of thumb, side bargains, cajoling, negotiations, special contingency plans, and in some cases literally shouting and screaming" (p. 478).

Implications

Harris's model provides three implications. First, given the role of physicians, we can expect that the hospital's preferences for new technology will be driven by the preferences of the physician demanders. The physician-agent will tend to prefer technologies that are complementary to existing capacity and that are thus quality enhancing. Second, hospital regulation aimed primarily at the trustee-administrator group may have little effect. That is, regulation to limit hospital costs must establish incentives for and constraints on the physician-agent as well as the administrator. Third, reorganization of the hospital along product lines might make it a more effective organization. For example, reorganizing departments by cardiology, neurology, and so on may better help to integrate the physician into the decision-making apparatus.

Summary of Models of Hospital Behavior

While many theories of nonprofit hospital behavior exist, we have described three main types. Most commonly, hospitals are depicted in research as being either utility maximizers or profit maximizers. Of the utility-maximizing type, the Newhouse model

is a prominent example, and it depicts the top hospital decision makers as choosing the best combination of quantity and quality of care. Of the profit-maximizing models, the Pauly-Redisch physicians' cooperative version is perhaps most prominent. This approach depicts the nonprofit hospital as effectively making choices that serve to maximize the pecuniary gain to physicians—the decisive set of decision makers. The Harris model forms a distinctive alternative, describing the hospital as two separate firms representing opposing interests that interact in what professional economists would term a *noncooperative oligopolistic* game.

The continued attempts to distinguish the theoretical models will remain a serious interest for policy if only for the importance of this issue to the nonprofit's favored status. For example, would we continue to extend tax-exempt status to the Pauly-Redisch type of nonprofit? Ironically, if we become successful in identifying nonprofit hospitals by behavioral type, we may find that hospitals of all types coexist.

What Causes Conversion of Nonprofits into For-Profits?

About 7 percent of nonprofit hospitals converted to for-profits between 1970 and 1995, and the conversion rate has been increasing in recent years. Usually, conversion means the sale of the hospital assets to a profit-oriented corporation and the use of the proceeds to fund a nonprofit foundation. Several ideas recur in this new literature. Lakdawalla and Philipson (1998) explain that if hospital decision makers value profit goals and output goals, then increases in consumer demand that improve profitability will induce some nonprofits to convert. In such cases, shedding the nonprofit constraint has become more attractive. Others make essentially the same observation in noting that the secular decline in the importance of donations to nonprofit hospitals makes continued nonprofit status less important to many decision makers. A reduction of tax benefits can also erode loyalty to the nonprofit status; the data show that tax rate changes have the corresponding effect on nonprofit market share.[5]

More idiosyncratic, individual motives may be just as important. Conversion is frequently motivated in part by financial distress, and the new management often succeeds in relieving the distress by providing new cash and by streamlining operations. However, case studies reveal that personal financial benefits sometimes accrue to the nonprofit decision makers who agree to the conversion. In cases when the nonprofit management goals stay in place after conversion, the conversion may be motivated by the desire to gain greater access to capital; raising equity capital is possible for for-profits but violates the nondistribution constraint for nonprofits.[6]

The question of whether society gains a net benefit from these increasing conversions has come to interest health economists. At least two possible efficiency gains have been suggested. Dynamic efficiency involves better access to capital enabling the rapid development of needed facilities, and efficiency of operation. Efficiency of operation may occur if new management and control eliminate entrenched practices and streamline operations. In addition, this type of efficiency difference should be observable in cost-efficiency studies that compare nonprofit hospitals with for-profits, a subject to which we return shortly.

The experience with conversion provides another opportunity to test the implications of ownership status. Picone, Chou, and Sloan (2002) find that conversion from nonprofit into for-profit status is typically followed by a short-term decline in quality

[5]Gully and Santerre (1993) and Hansmann (1987) examine the effects of tax rates on nonprofit market shares.

[6]For further investigation of conversions, see also Mark (1999), Cutler and Horwitz (1998), and Goddeeris and Weisbrod (1998).

as measured using mortality rates. Santerre and Vernon (2005) warn that conversion, by altering the nonprofit/for-profit mix in a market area, has implications for market-level economic efficiency. They suggest that the typical U.S. hospital market has an inefficiently large number of nonprofits.

The Relative Efficiency of Nonprofits Versus For-Profits

Economic efficiency takes on several meanings. The "social efficiency" of a market structure requires that total social benefits net of opportunity costs be maximized. The early criticism of nonprofit market structure pointed to its tendency to overproduce—to produce to the extent that marginal cost exceeds marginal benefit. However, the gains from the provision of underprovided public goods, the benefits from mending "contract failure," can overcome this drawback.

Other types of efficiency—scale, technical, and allocative (discussed in Chapter 6)—are provided by the perfectly competitive industry under for-profit ownership. Beginning with the work of Harvey Leibenstein (1966), economists have taken more interest in whether for-profit firms always maximize and always attain complete technical and allocative efficiency? The pursuit of such issues has been furthered by the corresponding development of econometric tools to estimate whether and how far firms fall short of best practice or frontier production. Many economists now recognize that real for-profit firms may fall short of perfection. The relative efficiency of for-profits versus nonprofits must be decided by the evidence.

There are several varieties of nonprofit hospitals. They often will be efficient in the production of hospital output, meaning cases treated. However, these hospitals cannot control the other inputs into the community's health production, such as exercise and diets. Ellis (1993) contends that the combination of nonprofit hospital care and the community's other health production inputs will most probably produce community health inefficiently.

The Newhouse hospital produces the chosen quantity/quality combination efficiently but it may choose a quality in excess of its worth in the production of community health. The Pauly-Redisch hospital produces the hospital service side of care efficiently, but the physicians in control employ excessive amounts of hospital service in the production of patient care. The Harris hospital's internal competition and cross-subsidization may, despite appearances to the contrary, restore social efficiency in a previously imperfect health economy.

Property Rights Theory and Its Application to Nonprofits

Frech (1976) argues that an essential economic problem arises because of the nondistribution constraint. Because "profit" cannot be taken out of the nonprofit firm, the opportunity cost of nonpecuniary benefits is lowered, making them more attractive to the manager.

Private property rights are important to the for profit firm. This is evident as former Soviet Union and other former Eastern Bloc countries struggle toward market economies. The key property rights entail the right of the owner to decide on the employment of the firm's resources, the right to keep the residual, and the right to sell the value of any gains (that is, to sell the property rights). The firm's wealth is the market value of its assets. In theory, the market value of a firm's assets will equal the present value of all future dividends.

In any for-profit firm, the day-to-day managers will make decisions for the owners. These agents for the owners probably acquire some independence and have the

opportunity to act as imperfect agents. It is costly for the owners to monitor the managers perfectly, and the owners may accept some degree of departure from pure profit-maximizing behavior. The manager may find it rewarding to seek nonpecuniary gains as well as profits in any given period.

Nonpecuniary benefits could include anything other than money rewards that the manager enjoys, including pleasant office space, extra staff, the firm's prestige, or even the prestige of producing high-quality and high-quantity output. Because profit making is what creates firm wealth, this behavior means that the firm will behave as if the top decision makers valued two goals, wealth and nonpecuniary benefits. Thus, the firm is a utility maximizer, but here the indifference curves are described over firm wealth and nonpecuniary benefits. The curves U_1 and U_2 in Figure 13-7 represent examples of these indifference curves for the top decision makers of the firm.

The production of nonpecuniary benefits will affect the wealth attainable by the firm. For example, if the hospital introduces an unprofitable open heart surgery capability for prestige reasons, it will find that its current profits and hence its wealth are reduced. This idea suggests that the firm will face a constraint on its choices, the constraint being the trade-off between maximum possible wealth and the level of nonpecuniary benefits. This wealth-benefits possibility frontier is shown in Figure 13-7 as curve *FF*.

The For-Profit and Nonprofit Equilibria

The for-profit firm, as managed by the top decision makers, is really a utility maximizer over wealth and nonpecuniary benefits. The utility will be maximized in a manner common to all constrained maximization problems at a solution where the highest attainable indifference curve is reached. The for-profit utility maximization occurs in Figure 13-7 at the point of tangency labeled *A*.

The nonprofit firm experiences a radical attenuation of property rights. There is no property right attaching to the residual and hence to wealth. Only the manager or administrator, and perhaps some other employees, are in a position to attach or usurp the firm's wealth by funneling this wealth to themselves in subtler forms. When this occurs in money terms, we can term the payments a form of salary. Nonprofits in any industry usually are limited in the degree of salary that can be paid to managers, so that unreasonably large salaries are discouraged by regulatory agents. Thus, the most wealth a nonprofit firm can or will accrue is limited to the present value of this implied

FIGURE 13-7
Optimization Between Wealth and Nonpecuniary Benefits

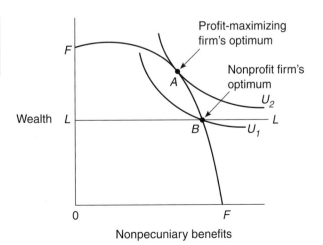

salary limit. In graphical terms, the nonprofit faces a second constraint in that wealth may not exceed that salary limit, *LL*, in Figure 13-7.

A nonprofit firm with similar preferences as the for-profit firm depicted will therefore maximize utility at the point labeled *B*. Note that at *B*, the nonprofit reaches the highest indifference curve attainable given its constraints—that is, indifference curve U_1. The implication of Frech's analysis is that the nonprofit will tend to choose a higher level of nonpecuniary benefits than the for-profit. If these nonpecuniary benefits entail items that are not productive, then the nonprofit will tend to be a more costly and inefficient producer than the for-profit firm.

Are Nonprofit Health Care Firms Less Efficient?—Hospital and Nursing Home Studies

Cost-efficiency has been compared frequently between nonprofit and for-profit hospitals, and the studies are generally of two types: nonfrontier and frontier studies. Before the frontier techniques described in Chapter 6 became widely available, comparisons of hospital performance by ownership essentially compared actual costs after adjusting for confounding factors. These nonfrontier studies matched hospitals pair-wise or compared carefully selected groups of hospitals. These studies usually found little, if any, cost efficiency differences between the nonprofits and the for-profits; occasionally, the results ran opposite to accepted theory so that the nonprofits evidenced higher efficiency levels. Sloan (2000) provides a full review of the evidence.

More recently, Kessler and McClellan (2001) examined longitudinal data on hospital treatment of elderly Medicare beneficiaries suffering new heart attacks. They found the for-profit hospitals could treat this type of patient at somewhat less expense (2.4 percent less) without reduction in quality of care. Frontier approaches attempt to identify the best possible practices. A firm is observed to be inefficient when it falls short of the best possible production practice frontier or above the cost frontier. Wilson and Jadlow (1982) compared nuclear medicine services in nonprofit and for-profit hospitals and found for-profits more efficient.

Frontier studies are conducted either by data envelopment analysis (DEA) or by stochastic frontier analysis (SFA). Though an earlier comparison study using DEA (Ozcan et al., 1992) had suggested small differences, more recent work (Folland and Hofler, 2001; Burgess and Wilson, 1998) concludes that no significant difference in efficiency can be found between nonprofit and for-profit hospitals.

This general finding in DEA studies is supported by the SFA studies. Zuckerman et al. (1994), addressing both method and empirical issues, found no differences between for-profit and nonprofit hospitals in their "whole sample" method results, though a small yet significant difference favoring the for-profits was observed in their "split sample." Later studies have thus far shown no significant difference.[7]

Such a conclusion does not warrant rejection of property rights theory or of the Frech hypothesis, but it does raise the question of the theory's applicability to the hospital sector. The possibility that nonprofit hospitals are of the Pauly-Redisch type is sufficient to account for this result. Cost efficiency in production may be the somewhat ironic side benefit of de facto physician control. However, if the theory does not appear to apply to nonprofit hospitals, it is nevertheless natural to ask in turn whether for-profit nursing homes differ in cost-efficiency from nonprofit homes.

[7]See also Vitaliano and Toren (1996).

BOX 13-1

Why Are RN's Wages Higher in Nonprofit Nursing Homes?

Holtmann and Idson (1993) provide recent evidence to explain why registered nurses (RNs) are paid higher wages by nonprofit than by for-profit nursing homes. As described previously, nonprofits are formed in response to patients' informational limitations in assessing quality. Specifically, because of patients' difficulties in distinguishing among nursing homes of varying quality, the market will fail to produce high-quality nursing homes.

Holtmann and Idson observe, as have others, the differentially higher wages that RNs receive in the nonprofit nursing home sector. Earlier studies (for example, Borjas, Frech, and Ginsburg, 1983) attributed these differentials to the premise that because nonprofits do not distribute the residuals (the revenues less the costs), they are less interested in minimizing the costs. Holtmann and Idson propose an alternative hypothesis that nonprofits pay nurses higher wages to get higher quality.

Using sophisticated econometric analyses, the authors discover that the differential wages reflect quality-enhancing characteristics of the nurses, such as years of experience and length of tenure on the current job. Both of these reflect higher quality of care because the provision of such care may require more stable employment relationships.

The authors then compare the quality and the property rights hypotheses. According to the property rights hypothesis, employees in nonprofit homes are paid higher wages than they could command in for-profit homes; this implies a higher return to their productivity-related attributes than in for-profit homes. However, the authors' methods show that workers in nonprofit facilities generally are compensated at a lower rate for their productivity-related attributes, and it is the fact that they have more of these attributes that leads to the wage differences. They view these distinctions as "strong evidence against the property-rights hypothesis that nonprofits are paying wasteful, inefficient wage premiums" (p. 73).

Nursing homes provide another test for nonprofit efficiency. Do nonprofit homes sometimes appear to be less efficient merely because they are offering a higher quality of care (see Box 13-1 for a discussion). Under the theory of "contract failure," nonprofit nursing homes naturally should tend toward higher quality of care. For example, we know (Nyman and Bricker, 1989) that high occupancy rates are a significant indicator of high efficiency scores. We don't know, however, how occupancy rates are related to quality of care, and how they affect the length of waiting lists for those elderly who would like nursing care near their natural home, another aspect of quality.

Conclusions

This chapter has examined the nonprofit firm in the health care sector. We began with a description of the nonprofit firm, noting the importance of the nonprofit constraint. We then asked why nonprofit firms exist? We found three principal accounts. Weisbrod explained how nonprofit firms might arise to provide public goods that are neglected by the private markets and the government. Hansmann explained how nonprofit firms might be formed to reduce or eliminate a contract failure that arises because consumers may not trust the profit-motivated firm to perform faithfully certain functions, often charitable ones. Finally, Bays explained that the reason the nonprofit form might take over the hospital industry is because an interest group, the physicians, finds greater financial rewards under the nonprofit system. Under these theories, the nonprofits

can improve the well-being of the community, overcoming the for-profit firm's tendency to underproduce in the presence of beneficial externalities.

We then investigated three models of nonprofit hospital behavior. The Newhouse hospital model is motivated by the desire to provide service to the community, often the quality of care being as important as the quantity. In contrast, the Pauly-Redisch hospital model is really under the physicians' control, who use it to maximize the average physician's income. We contrasted these two hospitals as polar opposites in that the Newhouse hospital model may be interpreted as motivated by the good of the community, whereas the Pauly-Redisch model does not vary from monetary gain. We showed the irony that under pressure of competition, these differently motivated firms may behave essentially the same. The Harris hospital model casts a different and illuminating picture of what a nonprofit hospital looks like on the inside to a physician/economist at work in the hospital.

Finally, the nonprofit and for-profit health care firms were contrasted regarding cost efficiency. Frech's theory makes a strong claim for the relative efficiency of for-profit firms with the nondistribution constraint of the nonprofit firms effects lowering the opportunity cost of nonpecuniary benefits, the "perks" that tempt managers to make inefficient choices. The data from recent efficiency studies offer little support regarding hospitals, which generally have found little, if any, significant difference.

The first half of the twentieth century saw radical changes in the structure of the health care industry, particularly in the prevalence of nonprofit firms. Since then we have gained a better understanding of the economic factors that make nonprofits attractive, and we are beginning to understand what can make them disappear.

Summary

1. The defining characteristic of a nonprofit firm is the nondistribution constraint. Furthermore, nonprofits are typically tax exempt, and donations to nonprofit firms receive favorable tax treatment.

2. The Weisbrod theory for the existence of nonprofits proposes that nonprofit firms arise to fulfill unmet demands for public goods.

3. The contract failure theory for the existence of nonprofits proposes that nonprofit firms are advantageous under circumstances where it is difficult or impossible for the purchaser of the good to verify the delivery and the quality of the good.

4. The interest group theory for the existence of nonprofit hospitals proposes that physicians favor the nonprofit hospital organizations because they can exercise greater economic control within them.

5. Utility-maximizing models of nonprofit firms are exemplified by the Newhouse model, in which the hospital decision makers choose preferred combinations of quality and quantity of care subject to a break-even constraint.

6. The physicians' cooperative model depicts the hospital under de facto physician control exercised so as to maximize average physician income.

7. The Harris hospital model is distinct from both the utility-maximizing type and the income-maximizing type. Harris depicts the nonprofit hospital as the outcome of two noncooperative interacting firms represented by administrators on one side and physicians on the other. These groups often must employ nonmarket decision making in life-or-death situations.

8. Under property rights theory, the nonprofit health care firm is less efficient than its for-profit counterpart because the incentive to maximize firm wealth is attenuated by the nondistribution constraint.

9. Evidence suggests that nonprofit hospitals in the United States are not very different in economic efficiency from for-profit hospitals.

Discussion Questions

1. What is the nondistribution constraint? In what way is the nondistribution constraint circumvented in the Pauly-Redisch model? What implication does this have for the efficiency of the Pauly-Redisch nonprofit hospital?
2. If the delivery and quality of care by health care firms could be cheaply and accurately monitored by a monitoring agency, would there be any contract failure in health care remaining? Would there be any need for nonprofits in health care? Would any arise?
3. If the interest group theory applies to hospitals, why doesn't it also apply to nursing homes? Would a doctor-owned, for-profit hospital be as attractive to physicians as a nonprofit hospital?
4. Suppose that population growth expands the quality-quantity frontier of a Newhouse utility-maximizing nonprofit hospital. How would its choice of quantity and quality change? In your view, is a for-profit hospital likely to respond more quickly to population growth? Discuss.
5. Under which of the three models of hospital behavior described in this chapter does the tax-exempt status of nonprofit hospitals make the most sense? Under which the least?
6. Can we say which are the most efficient hospitals—nonprofits or for-profits? Which are the most efficient nursing homes? What qualifications apply to our present knowledge in each case? What is your view?
7. Why might information problems lead to consumer preferences for nonprofit provision of some goods and services? Reconcile your answer with the observation that most physician care, drug products, and many other services are provided by for-profit firms.
8. In what sense do nonprofits earn "profits" and need to earn "profits" to survive?
9. What are some cost advantages that nonprofits have over for-profits? Are there any disadvantages?
10. Explain the logic behind the argument that donations have characteristics of a public good.
11. Weisbrod, Bays, and Hansmann present three different theories on the existence of nonprofit organizations. Compare and contrast them in regard to the types of firms and the ways they are financed.

Exercises

1. In Figure 13-1, if two additional voters had demand curves equal to D_5, what amount of the public good would tend to be provided by the democratic government? Which voters would be unlikely to promote a nonprofit? Which likely?
2. In Figure 13-1, suppose that Voter 5 comes to value the public good even more than before. Will there be an increase in the amount provided through the median voter model of the voting process? Why or why not? Suppose that Voter 5 can bribe one of the other voters to change his or her preferences. Which one will Voter 5 approach?
3. Under the physicians' cooperative model, if the supply price of physicians were to rise, how would this affect the equilibrium staff size in the open-staff case? How would it affect the optimal staff size in the closed-staff case?
4. Of the Newhouse and the physicians' cooperative models, which nonprofit hospital is likely to produce more quantity and quality in equilibrium with barriers to entry? In long-run equilibrium, with free entry and exit?
5. In the property rights model graph in Figure 13-7, if strenuous regulatory activity were to lower the maximum salary level, LL, of nonprofits, how would this affect the nonprofit efficiency level?
6. Consider Figure 13-2 and 13-3. Suppose that technological improvements allow hospitals to produce quality at lower average costs. What will happen to the average cost curves in Figure 13-2? What will happen to equilibrium quality and quantity in Figure 13-3?

CHAPTER

Hospitals and Long-Term Care

Background and Overview of Hospitals

Hospital Utilization and Costs

Nursing Homes

Hospice, Home Health, and Informal Care

Conclusions

In 2002, there were 5,794 hospitals with close to one million beds in the United States (Table 14-1). Of the 13.6 million persons employed at all health service sites in 2003, 5.7 million were employed at hospitals. Hospital care is the most visible component of total health care spending, and the hospital remains at the center of an evolving health economy. At the same time, the aging of the population has created a major challenge for the adequate provision of long-term care. This chapter provides an overview of the hospital and long-term care sectors. It also examines several controversies including the "medical arms race" and cost shifting for hospitals, and various quality, demand, and cost issues for nursing homes.

Background and Overview of Hospitals

We distinguish among the many types of hospitals by using four criteria: length of stay, type, ownership, and size. Hospitals are categorized as short stay (usually less than 30 days) or long term (usually more than 30 days). The community hospital is the type with which the general public is most familiar, consisting of all nonfederal general hospitals that provide acute, short-term care.[1]

Many community hospitals are also teaching hospitals, with residency programs approved by the Accreditation Council for Graduate Medical Education. Other hospital types are mental, including those treating alcoholism and other chemical dependencies; tuberculosis and other respiratory diseases; and other specialties (e.g., maternity, orthopedic, and rehabilitation).

Hospital ownership can be private or public (federal, state, county, or local). Private hospitals are either nonprofit or proprietary (for-profit) hospitals. Table 14-1

[1]More extensive discussions of many of the topics in this section are found in Starr (1982), Temin (1988), and Raffel and Raffel (1994).

TABLE 14-1 Hospital Data

	1980	1990	2000	2002
All hospitals	6,965 (1,365)[a]	6,649 (1,213)	5,810 (984)	5,794 (976)
Federal hospitals	359 (117)	337 (98)	245 (53)	240 (50)
Nonfederal hospitals	6,606 (1,248)	6,312 (1,113)	5,565 (931)	5,554 (926)
Community	5,830 (988)	5,384 (927)	4,915 (824)	4,927 (821)
Nonprofit	3,322 (692)	3,191 (657)	3,003 (583)	3,025 (582)
For-profit	730 (87)	749 (102)	749 (110)	766 (108)
State-local government	1,778 (209)	1,578 (169)	1,163 (131)	1,136 (130)
Psychiatric and other long-term	702 (256)	892 (183)	631 (105)	605 (103)
Community hospitals (size)				
6–199 beds	4,120 (341)	3,730 (314)	3,489 (290)	3,514 (287)
200–499 beds	1,393 (430)	1,369 (417)	1,179 (358)	1,157 (353)
500 or more beds	317 (218)	285 (196)	247 (176)	256 (180)
Occupancy rate[b]	75.6	66.8	66.1	67.8
Admissions (per 1,000 pop.)	159	125	120	120
Average length of stay (days)	7.6	7.2	5.8	5.7
Outpatient visits (per 1,000 pop.)	890	1,208	1,894	1,932

[a]Numbers in parentheses are beds in thousands.

[b]Percent of beds occupied.

Sources: U.S. Department of Commerce, *Statistical Abstract of the United States* (2004 and earlier issues); and U.S. Department of Health and Human Services, *Health, United States* (2004–05 and earlier issues).

indicates that there were 1,136 public short-stay hospitals in 2002, mainly state or local. Nonprofits dominate the remainder.

Hospital size is generally measured by number of beds. This does not mean that one doubles hospital size by putting a second bed in each room, but rather that the support services, types of equipment, and to some extent administrative staff, are related to the number of people that the hospital can house, and hence the number of beds.

Most short-stay hospitals are relatively small with fewer than 200 beds. However, the categories consisting of hospitals that have more than 200 beds account for 65 percent of all beds. The largest hospitals usually are affiliated with university medical schools and provide tertiary care in addition to primary and secondary care. Tertiary care consists of the most complex procedures such as organ transplant surgery and open-heart procedures. The typical community hospital is limited to secondary care consisting of the more common surgical and medical procedures. Primary care consists of the kinds of preventive and curative care received by patients who are not hospitalized.

History

Hospitals date back to ancient Egypt and Greece. Since then, places of healing in many countries were organized by religious establishments. Illness was closely associated with a lack of faith or superstition, and priests often administered care. Even today, it is not unusual for the afflicted to believe that they are being punished or cursed, and in some parts of the world, shamans and other "medicine men" are called upon to exorcise evil spirits.

Early hospitals in the United States were associated with the poor or with mental and infectious diseases, and medicine was practiced mainly at the home. This picture changed as more effective surgery became possible following scientific and technological

advances in the last half of the nineteenth century. The modern U.S. hospital emerged at the turn of the twentieth century. In particular, important advances in antisepsis to help fight off infections greatly increased the probability of surgical success. Major advances in anesthesia, anatomy, and physiology and the invention of the X-ray also contributed.

Two nonscientific factors helped accelerate the process. One was the rapid pace of urbanization resulting from industrialization. Rural areas could not support sophisticated hospitals because of transportation problems and low population densities. Urbanization also created health problems, such as outbreaks of infectious disease that were much less common in rural areas and that required hospitalization.

The second factor was a financial one. Early hospitals relied on philanthropic contributions or state and local government funds. These alone would have been inadequate to support the growing numbers and costs associated with the modern hospital. Urbanization created wealth, and the rise of an urban middle class led to a greater ability to pay, as well as third-party payment through private insurance and workers' compensation, which originated in the early 1900s.

The opening of The Johns Hopkins Hospital in Baltimore in 1885 was a significant milestone. Though few other hospitals would ultimately be able to emulate or compete with its international reputation, The Johns Hopkins Hospital introduced the latest advances in medical technology and hospital design. Through its affiliation with The Johns Hopkins University, it became a model of the teaching and research hospital.

Organization

The typical nonprofit community hospital is governed by a board of trustees that selects the president and approves most major decisions. Traditionally, board members were often leading members of the community known for their ability to contribute or raise funds. In recent years, the increasing financial complexity of decisions facing the modern hospital has made a strong business background an extremely important qualification.

The hospital's decision-making power rests with the medical staff rather than the administrators or the board. To appreciate the significance of this phenomenon, consider that the medical staff in most hospitals is composed of admitting physicians who are not hospital employees. Physicians apply for staff privileges to admit patients and perform certain procedures. Because physicians often have admitting privileges at several hospitals and bring patients to the hospital, admitting physicians have considerable influence on hospital decision making by serving on many committees relating to hospital governance and patient care. As such, the hospital has been referred to as the physician's "rent-free workshop" where the physician can direct substantial resources for patient care but is not held directly accountable for those resources. Physicians also bill separately for their services.

To deal with the conflicts and cost pressures created by the traditional system, more hospitals now rely on permanent physician-employees who are paid salaries or combinations of salaries and bonuses, the latter driven by various incentives. As these staff physicians are no longer the driving force to admit patients, hospitals with permanent staff physicians must have other means to attract patients. The source of patients for such hospitals is often affiliation with or ownership of HMOs. Hospitals also advertise directly through the broadcast or print media or purchase physician practices to gain new patients.

The hospital industry has undergone major change. Due to declining inpatient utilization, many smaller hospitals have closed while others have merged or reorganized. Hospitals face considerable pressure to join networks of providers in order to participate in managed care plans and to become diversified health care centers with

expanded primary care facilities. Many hospitals have concentrated resources on freestanding outpatient surgery units and other outpatient programs, such as cardiac rehabilitation. Table 14-1 reveals the extent of these changes. Inpatient admissions per capita dropped 25 percent from 1980 to 2002, and the occupancy rate dropped from 76 to 68 percent. Over the same period, the number of outpatient visits per capita more than doubled.

Despite this dramatic shift to outpatient care, hospitals will continue to face challenges, especially as Medicare and Medicaid budgets tighten. Governments provide nearly 60 percent of hospital revenues, although this figure can exceed 75 percent for many urban and small hospitals that rely heavily on poor and elderly patients. Proposals to reform Medicare and Medicaid also tend to reduce hospital spending and reimbursement rates. Thus, hospitals that disproportionately depend on Medicare and Medicaid are especially vulnerable. Nevertheless, in an increasingly competitive, cost-conscious environment, all hospitals are under considerable pressure to respond quickly to new incentives and opportunities.

Regulation and Accreditation

Hospitals are subject to a wide variety of state and federal regulations over quality, costs, and reimbursement. Hospitals are licensed at the state level, although licensure is often focused on the adequacy of the hospital's physical plant and other inputs. Hospitals have their own quality assurance programs but federal legislation established professional standards review organizations (PSROs) in 1971 to monitor quality while limiting utilization. After considerable controversy regarding their effectiveness, PSROs were replaced in 1984 by peer review organizations (PROs) that performed case-by-case peer review and monitored Medicare utilization in hospitals and other facilities. PROs were often dominated by physicians and hospitals and their impact was questioned. In the mid-1990s, the Centers for Medicare and Medicaid Services (CMS) adopted the position that case-by-case inspection brings only marginal improvements in quality. In 2002, PROs were replaced by quality improvement organizations (QIOs), intended to monitor and improve care.

Hospitals also are subject to numerous other regulations and requirements. Many of these relate to reimbursement, such as Medicare's prospective payments system (PPS), and various forms of state rate regulation. Certificate-of-need (CON) laws limit capital spending, and hospitals are subject to antitrust laws intended to promote competition.

In addition to meeting licensure and regulatory requirements, most hospitals and many other health care facilities seek accreditation from the Joint Commission on the Accreditation of Healthcare Organizations (JCAHO). The JCAHO is a private, non-profit organization that was founded in 1952 and has a board dominated by representatives from physician and hospital associations. It sets standards for patient safety and quality of care. Hospitals seeking accreditation are evaluated by a visitation team, which examines hospital compliance with JCAHO standards. To maintain accreditation, the hospital must undergo an on-site review every three years.

Many third-party payers reimburse only for care provided in accredited hospitals. Although hospitals can be evaluated by federal inspectors to qualify for Medicare and Medicaid reimbursement, JCAHO accreditation also satisfies the federal requirement. The JCAHO is clearly a powerful organization and the potential for conflict between professional self-interests and public interests is evident. The influence of the JCAHO can be used to limit hospital competition and to protect physicians against other groups of providers, such as chiropractors and doctors of osteopathy, by denying them access to hospitals or influence within hospitals.

Hospital Utilization and Costs

The relentless growth of hospital costs has served as the impetus for many forms of regulation and other policy initiatives. Table 14-2 shows the increases in total hospital costs, as well as costs per day and costs per admission. Hospital costs account for 31.4 percent of national health expenditures and have increased at an annual rate of 10.1 percent since 1960. Table 14-2 also shows that a small and dwindling share has been paid out-of-pocket, especially after Medicare and Medicaid were introduced in 1965. Governments now pay for 59 percent of all hospital costs compared to 38 percent in 1965. Despite a growing and aging population, the cost increases do not result from more inpatient admissions. The number of hospital beds has been declining for many years (Table 14-1), and occupancy rates for community hospitals have rebounded only slightly from the 62 percent bottom reached in 1997. Rather, the cost per day and cost per admission and the shift to outpatient services, leaving hospitals with high fixed costs, are the main driving forces. The influence of these determinants of hospital costs is intertwined closely with numerous features of health care markets including changes

TABLE 14-2 Hospital and Nursing Home Costs

	1960	1970	1980	1990	2000	2002
National health care spending ($ billions)[a]	27	73	246	696	1,300	1,553
Hospital care ($ billions)	9.2	28	102	254	413	487
Percent of total health spending	34.1	38.4	39.2	36.5	31.7	31.4
Percent of hospital care paid by						
Out of pocket	20.8	9.1	5.2	4.4	3.2	3.0
Private health insurance and other private	37.0	36.0	40.5	42.4	32.5	33.9
Government	42.5	55.0	54.3	53.2	59.0	58.9
Medicare	—	19.4	26.0	26.7	30.5	30.7
Medicaid	—	9.6	10.4	10.9	16.9	17.1
Other government[b]	42.5	26.0	17.9	15.6	11.6	11.1
Average hospital cost ($)						
Per day	—	—	245	687	1,149	1,290
Per stay	—	—	1,851	4,947	6,649	7,355
Nursing home care ($ billions)	0.8	4.2	18	53	92	103
Percent of total health spending	3.2	5.8	7.1	7.6	7.1	6.6
Percent of nursing home paid by						
Out of pocket	77.9	53.6	40.0	37.5	27.0	25.1
Private health insurance and other private	6.3	5.1	5.7	13.3	12.4	10.9
Government	15.7	41.2	54.2	49.2	60.6	64.0
Medicare	—	3.4	1.7	3.2	10.3	12.5
Medicaid	—	22.3	50.2	43.9	48.1	49.3
Other government	15.7	15.5	2.3	2.1	2.2	2.2

[a]All monetary values are in nominal dollars.

[b]Includes the Department of Veterans Affairs and state and local spending.

Sources: U.S. Department of Health and Human Services, *Health, United States* (2004–2005 and earlier issues); and U.S. Department of Commerce, *Statistical Abstract of the United States* (2004 and earlier issues).

in technology and reimbursement methods. We develop these issues and many others relating to hospital costs and health care system reform in other chapters. In this section, we address two of the many other concerns relevant to the growth of hospital costs. The first concerns the effect of competition on costs, and the second deals with cost shifting.

Competition and Costs

Increased competition is generally welcomed by consumers as a driver of lower prices, greater availability, and improved innovation and quality. Whether increased competition among hospitals provides similar benefits is of considerable policy and academic interest. Such concerns are interesting and unique. With the exception of natural monopolies resulting from economies of scale, economists usually endorse competition as being in the best interest of consumers. Evidence is substantial that higher levels of seller concentration in most markets lead to higher prices and reduced choices. Indeed, this is the premise behind federal and state antitrust laws.

Even though hospitals enjoy only limited economies of scale (Chapter 6), some analysts suggest that the hospital market is an exception to the standard paradigm. They argue that hospital competition has encouraged an unproductive and costly medical arms race (MAR), as described in Box 14-1, with unnecessary duplication of expensive capital equipment as well as unnecessary expenditures on advertising in order to attract patients. Competition also may create pressure to fill beds through questionable admissions.

Why should hospital care be different? The answer lies with the reimbursement mechanisms traditionally used by insurers, which paid hospitals on a retrospective cost basis. Higher costs generally meant higher payments to hospitals. Unlike other industries, where sellers must compete on the basis of price for customers, retrospective reimbursement meant that hospitals were largely immune from the discipline exerted by the competitive process.

This situation has changed in recent years. Hospitals as well as insurance companies must compete for their managed care business through price and quality. Hospitals also are now reimbursed by many major third-party payers on a prospective basis at rates that are independent of their actual costs. It would appear that hospitals have a strong financial stake in being efficient and in avoiding capital investments that are not profitable.

Kessler and McClellan (2000) examined the effects of hospital competition on the costs and outcomes for Medicare beneficiaries who incurred heart attacks. They found that, prior to 1991, competition improved outcomes in some cases, but also raised costs. After 1990, there were substantial decreases in costs and substantial improvements in outcomes. A part of the welfare improvement resulted from the higher HMO enrollments over this period.

Elsewhere, Zwanziger and Mooney (2005) studied HMOs in New York State which until 1996 regulated the rates (determined largely by historical costs) private insurers were required to pay for inpatient care. After the 1996 reforms, HMOs were able to negotiate lower prices with hospitals that were located in more competitive markets.

Finally, we observe other effects of managed care, including its role in the large decline in the number of hospitals and beds since 1980. Dranove and colleagues (2002) describe the financial pressures created by managed care for hospital consolidation and improved efficiency. Their work demonstrates the substantial impact associated with the growth of managed care. For the average market, the consolidation between 1981 and 1994 attributable to managed care represented the equivalent of a decrease to 6.5 equal-sized hospitals from 10.4 such hospitals.

Game Theory and the Medical Arms Race (MAR)

The 2002 Academy Award-winning movie, *A Beautiful Mind*, brought considerable public attention to John Nash and his contributions to game theory. Game theory is a powerful analytical tool used increasingly in economics and many other disciplines. It can be used, for example, to show why it may be in the best interests for each hospital to engage in an MAR even when hospitals as a whole are negatively affected. Game theory begins with a payoff matrix of the type shown in Figure 14-1. Suppose there are two large hospitals, A and B, in a market, each facing the decision of whether to add an expensive heart transplant unit without knowing what its rival will do. The payoff matrix shows the total profit for each hospital (with values for A's profit shown first) resulting from the four combinations of strategies. For example, if both adopt (the "northwest" cell), each hospital will have a total annual profit of $100 (million). If A alone adopts (the "northeast" cell), assume that it will have a significant advantage resulting in a profit of $200 (million), while B loses $50 (million).

Game theory tries to predict a solution, that is, the strategy chosen by each participant. It is clear that both hospitals with a combined profit of $300 (million) will be better off if neither introduces the unit. However, if the hospitals cannot agree (for example, they may not trust each other or they may believe that antitrust laws preclude cooperation), game theory predicts a solution in which each hospital will adopt the unit and combined profits will be $200 (million). Why? Given the payoff matrix, each hospital has a dominant strategy. That is, regardless of what Hospital B does, A will always have a higher profit by adopting rather than not adopting, that is, $100 (million) versus -$50 (million) if B adopts and $200 (million) versus $150 (million) if B does not adopt. Similarly B's dominant strategy is to adopt, and, hence, a scenario results consistent with the MAR hypothesis.

Students of game theory will recognize this as an example of the prisoner's dilemma and the solution as a Nash equilibrium. McKay (1994) and Calem and Rizzo (1995) provide other applications of game theory to other decisions including hospital quality and specialty mix. In addition to decisions involving the acquisition of technology and introduction of new services, game theory can provide insight into hospital advertising and other forms of nonprice competition.

FIGURE 14-1 Payoff Matrix (millions of dollars)

		Hospital B	
		Adopt	Do Not Adopt
Hospital A	Adopt	100, 100	200, −50
	Do not adopt	−50, 200	150, 150

Hospital Cost Shifting

For various legal and ethical reasons, hospitals provide substantial amounts of uncompensated care. Most of this care is provided to uninsured indigents, but uncollectibles from incompletely insured patients are also considerable. In addition, many third-party payers place stringent limits on reimbursement rates, and proposals to reduce Medicare and Medicaid expenditures typically call for further reductions. After an initial period of generous payments under PPS, by 1993 Medicare paid only 89 percent of hospitals' costs to treat its patients, compared to 93 percent for Medicaid and 129 percent for private patients.[2]

[2]Prospective Payment Assessment Commission (1995, Tables 1–8).

Are the costs of uncompensated care and "discounts" to some third-party payers passed on by hospitals to other patients as is often claimed? If Medicare and Medicaid cuts are passed on to others, there would be no savings to society but merely a shifting of the hospital cost burden. Similar shifting would occur if the number of uninsured or poorly insured increases because of an increase in part-time employment in the services sector and cutbacks in fringe benefits by some employers.

Intuition suggests that these costs are shifted. After all, services must be paid for and it stands to reason that the burden for nonpayers must be picked up by others. However, the issue may not be as simple as it first appears. To see why, we develop a model of hospital fee determination.

We examined a variety of hospital behavior models in Chapter 13, but for simplicity assume that hospitals maximize profits (or the undistributed residual in the case of nonprofits). Suppose also for simplicity that there are just two groups of patients: private (insured or self-pay) and Medicare. The downward-sloping demand curve for the private sector and the constant Medicare hospital reimbursement rate (R_1) per patient are shown in Figure 14-2. The private demand curve (panel A) is negatively sloped because at least some patients economize or substitute other services as their out-of-pocket obligations increase, and hospitals that raise fees lose patients to other hospitals. Assume further that R_1 covers the average variable cost (C_1) for a fixed number of Medicare patients seeking admission (i.e., Q_2 Medicare patients in panel B) but that the rate does not necessarily cover all costs. Finally, assume that the hospital is operating below capacity, as is the case for many hospitals, and that C_1 is constant over the relevant range and equal to marginal cost.

If the hospital is unable to price discriminate in the private sector, it will accept Q_1 private patients (the quantity where marginal revenue equals marginal cost) and charge the price, P_1. It also will accept all Medicare patients (Q_2) at the Medicare rate[3]

FIGURE 14-2 Analysis of Changes in the Medicare Hospital Reimbursement Rate

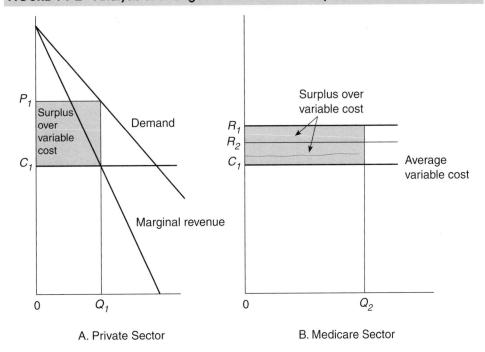

A. Private Sector B. Medicare Sector

[3] With capacity limitations, it will first raise the price to eliminate those private patients whose marginal revenue is below the Medicare rate.

so that the hospital treats a total of $(Q_1 + Q_2)$ patients. Total revenues of $(P_1Q_1 + R_1Q_2)$ produce a surplus over variable costs equal to $(P_1 - C_1)Q_1 + (R_1 - C_1)Q_2$.

Suppose that the Medicare reimbursement rate is lowered to R_2, but that the rate still covers the average variable and marginal costs so that the hospital continues to accept Q_2 Medicare patients. Contrary to intuition, it makes no sense to increase prices in the private sector. Hospital surpluses diminish at prices above P_1 because the hospital will lose private-sector patients whose marginal revenue exceeds marginal cost. The optimal private rate remains at P_1 for the Q_1 private patients, and no cost shifting occurs.[4]

This is not the end of the story because the hospital's revenues are reduced. In the long run, revenues must cover all costs, or else the hospital cannot survive. If revenues exceed costs for the hospital in Figure 14-2 after the lower Medicare rate, then the private rate may be unaffected in the long run, as well. Suppose, however, that the hospital's revenues now fall short of total costs. If it cannot reduce costs, the hospital and others in the same situation may be forced out of business or forced to merge. As this happens, demand will increase for the remaining hospitals and, as a result, the private rate also could rise.

Determining the burden of lower public reimbursement is complex. The burden ultimately can be borne by many groups through reductions in the number of hospitals, lower compensation to hospital employees as the demand for their services diminishes, reduced access to care for those with public insurance or those receiving uncompensated care, and higher fees to the private paying groups.

A review of the evidence on cost shifting by Morrisey (1995) indicates that cost shifting through higher prices has taken place but that it is far from complete. One study included in his review shows that California hospitals reduced the amount of uncompensated care by $0.53 for every $1 decrease in their discounts to third parties. This would have been unnecessary if the hospitals could have shifted the costs to others. Other studies showed partial cost shifting through higher fees.

Closures, Mergers, and Restructuring in the Hospital Industry

We have already referred to some of the dramatic changes affecting hospitals. The growth of managed care and the introduction of reimbursement methods that discourage inpatient care and long lengths of stay have contributed to declining inpatient utilization. In response, capacity has been reduced through the sharp drop since 1980 in the number of hospitals and beds (Table 14-1). Even so, with occupancy running at just 68 percent in 2002, excess capacity remains one of the most visible and significant characteristics of the hospital industry.

Although hospital closures can be painful to a community, the restructuring of the hospital industry should be viewed as a market response to cost-containment efforts. Nevertheless, it remains important to determine just how well the market works for this sector, and, in particular, whether inefficient hospitals are more likely to close.

Cleverly (1993) examined 160 community hospitals that closed between 1989 and 1991. Most were small, located in rural areas, and had sustained progressively larger losses for several years before closing. High costs and high prices, low utilization, and little investment in new technology were common features. From the characteristics of failed hospitals, Cleverly describes the road to failure. High prices and lack of investment in technology drive patients away. With lower utilization, costs per patient increase and cash flows become negative. The deteriorating liquidity ultimately leads to closure.

The relatively large number of small, rural hospital closings has challenged policy makers to maintain access for rural populations. To prepare for unexpected influxes of

[4]Cost shifting could arise if the hospital was not previously maximizing profit and was accepting "unprofitable" patients. The lower Medicare rate would encourage the hospital to reduce the number of these unprofitable patients by raising the private rate.

patients, small hospitals have higher rates of excess capacity and, hence, lower occupancy rates than larger hospitals. Various federal programs provide subsidies to these hospitals. Nevertheless, rural hospitals can increase their chances of survival by practicing good management and responding to competitive pressures. Succi and colleagues (1997) found that rural hospitals gain an advantage and reduce the threat of competition by differentiating their services. Those that offer more basic services and high-tech services compared to the market average are less likely to close.

With the continued growth of managed care in the 1990s and hospitals' increased reliance on managed care patients, the pace of hospital restructuring accelerated. Nearly every hospital was facing serious financial and competitive challenges. Hospitals responded by merging, participating in multi-hospital systems, and by forming various strategic alliances with other hospitals and physician practices. There are two intended effects of these activities. First, by downsizing administrative units, eliminating duplication, and taking advantage of economies of scale through integration, hospitals seek to become more efficient and, therefore, more successful in competing for managed care contracts. Jantzen and Loubeau (2000) found that price and hospital participation in networks are very important to managed care organizations in awarding contracts. Second, hospitals and hospital systems, through their size and partnerships, seek to counter the pricing pressure and other demands that have been placed on them by managed care organizations.

In an emerging literature on these developments (Olden et al., 2002), health economists seek a better understanding of the two principal effects of the restructuring, whether hospital care is being produced at lower costs than would otherwise have been observed, and whether prices have risen as a result of less competition among hospitals. There is some evidence supporting the first effect (Sprang et al., 2001), a consequence that is beneficial to society as well as to the hospitals. However, there is also evidence indicating that merged hospitals charge higher fees than otherwise, especially when the merging hospitals gain substantial market shares (Krishnan, 2001). Because the latter is an undesired effect from society's perspective, regulators and policy makers must remain vigilant in monitoring and assessing the restructuring efforts that continue in the hospital sector.

Nursing Homes

The rapid growth of the elderly population in many countries has led to considerable interest in the problems associated with long-term care. Long-term care encompasses a wide variety of services and arrangements used to care for the elderly and others with serious functional impairments.

In this section, we concentrate on the nursing home. Numerous economic issues have been investigated in the nursing home literature (Norton, 2000). Following some background information, we will focus on issues involving quality, cost shifting, and financing the care.

Background and Costs

The elderly have traditionally been cared for until death by their families so the nursing home is a relatively recent phenomenon. Raffel and Raffel (1994) trace its origins. The first "nursing homes" in the United States were the county poorhouses of the eighteenth and nineteenth centuries, established for invalids and those without families. Most of the patients were elderly, and the conditions were dreadful. Other state and local facilities evolved and some, usually with higher standards, were sponsored by religious and fraternal groups. The Social Security Act of 1935 provided funds for patients

in private nursing homes, but the major increase in funding and nursing industry growth came after the 1965 passage of Medicare and Medicaid.

In 1960, nursing home care amounted to less than $1 billion, with 78 percent coming out-of-pocket (Table 14-2). Twenty years later, in 1980, spending reached $18 billion, with Medicaid's share at 50 percent and only 40 percent coming out-of-pocket. By 2002, spending had grown to $103 billion, with Medicaid contributing 49 percent (another 13 percent came from Medicare) and patients or their families paying just 25 percent. Between 1963 and 2000, the nursing home population over age 65 grew from 446,000 to 1.47 million. About two-thirds are in for-profit facilities.

BOX 14-2

Hospital Quality: Does Your Hospital Deserve a Passing Grade?

Quality of care has emerged as a national policy priority. Through a variety of voluntary and mandated mechanisms, hospitals are constantly being evaluated for quality of care on the premise that publicly available report cards will encourage improvements. If embarrassment about poor performance is not a sufficient motivator, hospitals have a major financial stake in raising quality to secure managed care contracts and to attract the growing numbers of patients that are choosing consumer-driven health plans.

Two reports published in the July 21, 2005, *New England Journal of Medicine* provide unprecedented insight into the quality of hospital care and the impact of public reporting. One (Williams, et al., 2005) evaluated an initiative implemented by JCAHO in 2002 that required most accredited hospitals to report 18 standardized performance indicators for several common conditions. Seventeen indicators assessed processes of care; one was mortality. Analysis of quarterly data for heart attacks, congestive heart failure, and pneumonia indicated substantial gains in 15 of the 18 measures over the two-year study period. The gains were greatest for hospitals that had been the worst performers at the start of the evaluation period.

A second report (Jha et al., 2005) examined 10 quality indicators for patients discharged at 3,558 hospitals in 2004, also for heart attacks, congestive heart failure, and pneumonia. Mean performance scores (representing proportions of patients who satisfied the criteria) were 89 percent for heart attacks, 81 percent for congestive heart failure, and 71 percent for pneumonia.

Performance varied substantially among hospitals and many failed to provide patients with broadly accepted treatments at surprisingly high rates. It is possible that the scores reflect, in part, record keeping omissions rather than failure to provide treatment, but such omissions themselves would indicate a quality problem.

Regional variations are also startling. Among the 40 largest hospital regions, Boston led the way in treating heart attacks, with a performance score of 95 percent. San Bernardino was at the bottom with 83 percent. Overall, hospitals in the Midwest and Northeast outperformed those in the South and West.

Quality has not been ignored in economic analyses. Tay (2003) examined the impact of quality and distance on (non-HMO) Medicare patients admitted to a hospital for heart attacks. Medicare patients who are not enrolled in managed care plans have a wide range of hospital choices, and price is not an issue to them. Consistent with economic theory, Tay found that distance has a significant negative impact on demand, while quality, measured by various input and health outcomes measures, has a significant positive impact. Remarkably, some patients are willing to travel much further for higher quality, even for conditions where a small delay to treatment can have a big impact on outcomes. The bottom line is that quality matters a great deal to patients who can now find hospital performance ratings under the Centers for Medicare and Medicaid Hospital Quality Initiative at: www.cms.hhs.gov/quality/hospitals.

The burgeoning nursing home population and the growth of costs are connected closely to Medicare and Medicaid. Medicare typically covers beneficiaries who are discharged from hospitals and who require skilled nursing care to help recover from an acute illness. A skilled nursing facility provides round-the-clock nursing care and other medical supervision. Historically, Medicare reimbursed on a cost basis, but the Balanced Budget Act of 1997 mandated a shift to prospective reimbursement with fixed per diem payments determined by the category in which a patient is placed. The goal of this change was to shift the financial risk to nursing homes.

Medicaid, in contrast, pays for the long-term care of the poor including the nonelderly as well as elderly. It covers both skilled nursing care and intermediate (custodial) care. Because Medicaid is administered by the states subject to federal requirements, eligibility requirements and payment methods can vary widely. In the 1980s, many states phased in prospective payment systems that distinguished only between patients in skilled and intermediate care facilities. The rates were often set too low for heavy-care patients, discouraging nursing homes from admitting them. To provide better incentives, states increasingly are adopting case-mix reimbursement systems where payment depends on a more comprehensive classification of patient types.

A 1987 legislative change created new standards that drove costs higher. All nursing homes participating in federal programs, including Medicaid-only facilities, must now meet the same standards as Medicare's skilled nursing facilities. Also, nursing homes participating in federal programs must evaluate each resident's needs and "provide services and activities to attain or maintain the 'highest practicable level' of function (physical, mental, and psychosocial well-being)." These requirements led to large increases in staffing and the use of rehabilitation services.

Quality of Care

Despite increasingly stringent state and federal requirements, the public cares most about quality. To many, nursing homes evoke powerful images of neglected and poorly treated patients. It is natural that health economists and other scholars have concentrated their efforts on nursing home quality.

As we have seen from those chapters that deal with quality issues, researchers seek ways to define and measure quality. Regulatory standards for nursing homes tend to focus on structure, measured by the quantity and categories of inputs used to provide care, rather than evaluating how the care is delivered (process), or monitoring outcome indicators such as patients' satisfaction or their quality of life.

It follows that the most comprehensive and readily available information on nursing homes and other health care institutions comes from input data—their types and costs. Scholars have used these data to examine the relationship among quality and nursing home size, ownership, expenditures, and source of payment.

One would expect some positive association between size and quality as a result of economies of scale and scope. If such economies occur over some range of output, larger institutions would be able to provide the same quality of care at a lower cost, or a higher quality of care for a given level of spending per patient. Davis's (1991) review of a large number of studies, including those that used process and structure measures of quality, suggests that no clear relationship exists.

A more important issue involves quality and cost or expenditure per patient. Do "you get what you pay for" in nursing care? Using structure measures of quality, not surprisingly, most analysts find a positive relationship, but these results are not meaningful. If inputs represent quality, one expects a close relationship between various measures of input and quality. Of the 18 process and outcome studies included in Davis's literature review, only 6 indicate a positive relationship between quality and

FIGURE 14-3 Analysis of Changes in the Medicaid Nursing Home Reimbursement Rate

cost or inputs, while the results in 11 are insignificant (1 is negative).[5] The failure to find positive relationships consistently is troubling. It indicates that improvements are needed in measuring quality as well as in formulating the statistical models used to estimate the relationships.

A third area of interest is in the relationship between type of ownership and quality. The previous chapter discussed the concept of contract failure within the context of nursing homes. Put simply, contract failure arises when quality is not easily observable. In the case of nursing homes, patients may believe that nonprofit organizations are more likely to serve their interests than ones motivated by profits. Is this view justified by the evidence? Nursing home costs per patient are higher for nonprofits so that structure measures are clear on this point. However, because analysts have not been able to detect an unambiguous positive relationship between quality and costs, it follows that they would have great difficulty in detecting any relationship between type of ownership and process or outcome measures of quality. Davis's review confirms this conclusion.

Finally, Davis also reviews the literature on quality and the proportion of public pay (Medicaid) patients. Many believe that nursing homes dominated by Medicaid patients are inferior. Expenditures per resident are lower in homes with higher proportions of Medicaid patients so that structure measures unequivocally support a negative relationship between quality and the proportion of Medicaid residents in a nursing home. However, with few studies that have used process or outcome measures, further work is needed to help settle the issue.

Excess Demand

For many years, nursing home observers have characterized the nursing home industry as having excess demand, and have argued that excess demand is one of the reasons for the allegedly inferior quality of care provided to public pay patients. Economists are

[5]In one of the largest studies of long-term outcomes, Porell and colleagues (1998) found little relationship between quality and facility characteristics, such as size and ownership type. They likewise found that higher RN staffing levels do not improve outcomes. Except for nursing homes at the highest staffing levels, Schnelle et al. (2004) also found few differences. Those with the highest staffing levels (top 10 percent) scored significantly higher on 13 of 16 care processes measured by the study.

naturally intrigued by, and at the same time skeptical of, claims of persistent shortages of any commodity. Put simply, they believe that prices, and ultimately supply, will increase to eliminate the excess demand. To examine the possibility of excess demand for nursing home care, Figure 14-3 introduces a variant of an approach originally developed by Scanlon (1980). It shows the demand and cost conditions for a representative nursing home. The demand curve reflects only the private demand (self-pay or insured), while R_1 represents the Medicaid reimbursement rate. The segment AC along R_1 shows the number of Medicaid patients seeking admission. For simplicity, assume a constant (horizontal) marginal and average variable cost (C_1) up to the capacity level (Q_c patients) where it becomes vertical.

Under the conditions represented here, the profit-maximizing nursing home will first select all private patients whose marginal revenue exceeds R_1 and then fill the remainder of beds with Medicaid patients. The nursing home admits Q_1 private patients paying a price, P_1, and ($Q_c - Q_1$) Medicaid patients, leaving an excess demand of BC Medicaid patients.

The shortage can be reduced or even eliminated by raising the Medicaid rate. At R_2, nursing homes will raise the private fee to P_2 and substitute $A'D'$ Medicaid for AD private patients. The excess demand is reduced to $B'C'$ from BC.[6] Conversely, reductions in the Medicaid rate will lower Medicaid admissions and the private fee but increase the excess demand. Similarly, an increase in private demand resulting from higher incomes or more prevalent private long-term insurance will reduce Medicaid admissions and increase the excess demand.

One additional aspect should be considered. If the nursing home industry is profitable, and evidence suggests that it is, one would expect entry of additional nursing homes to reduce the excess demand. However, nursing homes also are subject to certificate-of-need (CON) regulations, and it has been argued that legislators have intentionally used CON and other restrictions to limit nursing home entry as a way of limiting Medicaid spending.[7] There is a similar theme of legislative aversion to policies that would raise the Medicaid rate which, as shown earlier, increases public spending while squeezing out private patients.

Various tests have been proposed for the shortage hypothesis. For example, in our model, changes in reimbursement rates do not affect total utilization, just the composition between private and Medicaid patients. Any new beds will more likely be filled by Medicaid than by private patients because that is the population for which there is excess demand. Using national data for 1969 and 1973, Scanlon's empirical tests indicate considerable excess demand for Medicaid patients. However, states may vary widely in their willingness to fund public patients, and changes may have taken place in more recent years to reduce the shortages. For example, Nyman's (1993) estimates for 1988 for Minnesota, Oregon, and Wisconsin generally do not support the shortage hypothesis.

Financing Long-Term Care

The continuous growth of the population that will need long-term care (LTC), the requirement that patients must meet income and asset tests to qualify for nursing home benefits under Medicaid, and the budgetary problems created by the growth of

[6]The rate that would eliminate the Medicaid excess demand is found by sliding the segment $A'C'$ further up the marginal revenue curve until the quantities such as $B'C'$ are eliminated. Clearly, the rate must be above R_2.

[7]CON regulations require health care providers to obtain approval from state planning agencies for capital expenditures exceeding a threshold level such as $500,000. CON was federally mandated until 1987 and then left to the states.

Medicaid spending have led to many proposals to reform Medicaid. The need to deplete one's assets is especially irksome to the middle class. The sore point is that after paying a lifetime of taxes to support Medicaid and other welfare programs, one must become poor ("spend down") to qualify for Medicaid. A variety of proposals have been introduced ranging from those allowing individuals to have higher incomes and retain a higher proportion of their wealth to qualify for public assistance, to those that would cover everyone who meets certain medical requirements.

Short and Kemper (1994) estimate the effects of a variety of plans. The least costly would create a front-end entitlement covering everyone for a limited period, for example, three to six months of care. Back-end entitlements that cover everyone after a certain waiting period of, say, one or two years of nursing home care, are more costly. The most expensive are proposals without limitations even if they have cost-sharing provisions. Short and Kemper estimate that full entitlement with a 30 percent coinsurance rate would increase overall nursing home expenditures by nearly 20 percent and public expenditures by about 80 percent (due to the overall increase in utilization and the substitution of public spending for private spending).

The alternative to greater public spending, especially in an era when many government programs are being downsized, is a strategy to encourage more private long-term coverage or home care. The market for such insurance is growing and subsidies or tax incentives could be used to encourage further growth. Allowing for tax-deductible contributions to LTC accounts, similar to retirement plans, is one of the ideas that has been advanced.

Federal policy to contain public spending centers on two strategies: Encourage home care and other potentially less costly substitutes for nursing home care, and encourage more private coverage for LTC. The market for private LTC insurance is growing, and legislation passed in 1996 allows employers 100 percent deductions on their contributions to group plans. The legislation also provides some tax relief to individuals who itemize their returns and purchase tax-qualified policies. Nevertheless, only 5 to 7 percent of the elderly have LTC coverage. Similarly, only 5 percent of firms with more than 1,000 workers offer a group benefit for LTC to their employees. Of those that do, the employee participation rate is low—on the order of 6 percent (Jones, 1999).

What are the barriers to growth of private LTC insurance? They include confusion over the benefits provided by Medicare and private health plans, perceptions that such insurance is unaffordable, and perceptions that governments will somehow meet LTC needs. The low probability (about 1 percent) that employed workers will need LTC before they retire, coupled with uncertainty over future premiums and medical technology, increase the difficulty of selling LTC insurance to the working population. To overcome these barriers, some analysts propose additional tax incentives by allowing all taxpayers a 100 percent tax deduction for premiums or allowing tax-deductible LTC accounts, similar to retirement accounts. The new Medicare drug bill, effective in 2004, allows individuals to create health savings accounts that can be used to pay for qualified LTC insurance premiums.

The more visible strategy to contain public spending is the federal government's emphasis on alternatives to nursing home care. Nursing home residents have constituted a decreasing share of a growing elderly population. Between 1985 and 1995 the elderly population grew nearly 18 percent and the number of nursing home residents over age 65 also increased, but Bishop (1999) estimated that had 1995 nursing home shares remained at 1985 levels, a quarter of a million additional elders would have been in nursing homes. Where have all these patients gone? The high rates of growth of home health care and other LTC arrangements may provide an answer.

Hospice, Home Health, and Informal Care

The budgetary pressure of caring for the growing elderly population in hospitals and nursing homes has promoted interest in other less costly arrangements. Hospice and home health programs are perceived to be cost-effective and are heavily funded at the federal level.

Hospice care is intended for the terminally ill. Most hospice patients receive care in their own homes, but the use of special facilities is becoming more prevalent. In hospice, an interdisciplinary team of health professionals provides individualized care that emphasizes patients' physical and emotional comfort (i.e., palliative as opposed to curative care), as well as support for family members. Hospices strive for improved quality of life in a patient's final days and death with dignity.

Medicare introduced hospice benefits in 1983, but higher reimbursement rates in 1989 accelerated growth in the number of hospices. Higher reimbursement rates will increase significantly the number of Medicare-certified providers, improving access for Medicare beneficiaries. Hamilton (1993) estimated that every dollar increase in the daily rate raises the probability of certification by 1.7 percent. There were about 106,000 hospice patients at any time during 2000. With evidence that hospice programs offer savings, many private insurers also have added coverage for hospice care.

Home health care, the larger and more important program, provides care to patients with acute and long-term needs, including those with disabilities, those recuperating from a hospital stay, and even the terminally ill. The home-care benefit was included in the initial Medicare legislation of 1965 that was extended in 1973 to certain disabled persons under 65. By 1996, about 2.4 million home health care patients were on the rolls of agencies at any time, and their numbers were growing rapidly. With a doubling of patients in just four years between 1992 and 1996, home health care became one of the fastest-growing components of total spending. Between 1992 and 1996, Medicare spending for home health care grew from $7.7 to $18.1 billion. Medicare spending, however, fell to $7.6 billion by 1999 following the Balanced Budget Act of 1997. As with nursing home care, the act mandated a shift from a cost-based to a prospective-based system of reimbursement, and installed an interim system of payment limits over the intervening period. By 2000, there were only 1.4 million home health care patients at any time.

The rationale for public funding for home health care rests on the premise that it is much less expensive than either hospital or nursing home care. Even though a home health visit is unquestionably far less costly than a day spent in an institution, the effect on total health spending is not entirely clear. The principal issue is the extent to which home health substitutes for "unpaid" care by family members and other caregivers, or for institutional care.[8] Policy makers are concerned that more generous public funding for home care will substitute for previously "unpaid" care without significantly increasing the overall care for patients. Yoo and colleagues (2004) have shown that formal and informal LTC are close substitutes. From data for 15 OECD countries, they estimated that the availability of a spouse caregiver, measured by the male-female ratio, reduces LTC spending by $29,000 (in $1995), a figure that exceeded the annual Medicaid payment to an intermediate care facility.

The substitutability of informal care with LTC is confirmed by Van Houtven and Norton (2004), who introduce a utility-maximizing framework to analyze the informal care decisions by children and their elderly parents. Children select the optimal amounts

[8]An extensive literature is available on the impact of home care on hospital utilization. Hughes's (1997) meta-analysis found that home care unambiguously reduces hospital days for the terminally ill. For others, the effect on hospital days is negative though not overwhelmingly large.

of consumption, leisure and informal care, subject to their budget constraints. The utility function includes the parent's health status. The utility functions maximized by parents include consumption, formal medical care, and the informal care available from their children. The simultaneous maximization process predicts that informal care could be either a substitute or complement to formal care, and that the substitute or complement effects may vary with the type of formal care consumed (e.g., substitute for LTC and complement to inpatient/outpatient hospital care). The results of their empirical estimation indicate that informal care provided by children is a net substitute for both LTC and hospital care and physician visits. It is a complement to outpatient surgery.

The policy and cost implications of the significant substitutability of informal care for LTC are substantial. Social changes that reduce children's abilities or commitments to care for their parents would further strain private and public budgets. Conversely, well-designed programs that provide incentives for children or other family members, especially those who are not in the labor force, to care for parents could lead to substantial government savings.

Conclusions

Following a discussion of the history and organization of hospitals and hospital costs, we examined two economic and policy issues—the medical arms race hypothesis and cost shifting. Careful analysis indicates that both issues are far more complex than they first appear.

The existing literature confirms this analysis by indicating that the common perceptions of a wasteful MAR and complete cost shifting do not accurately represent how hospital markets function. We also examined restructuring in the hospital industry and some issues relating to hospital quality.

In the long-term care sector, we focused on nursing homes, emphasizing three issues: quality, especially for Medicaid patients; shortages; and financing nursing home care. We found that economic theory and empirical evidence can provide useful and sometimes surprising results. For example, no clear relationship exists between costs and quality. It is also possible to have a persistent shortage of nursing home beds without any mechanism, such as price, that would alleviate the shortage.

Finally, we examined potentially less costly alternatives to nursing homes and the role of informal care. Home health care represents one of the fastest-growing components of health care spending.. Informal care and LTC are close substitutes so that policies that encourage informal care could substantially reduce public spending for LTC.

SUMMARY

1. The modern hospital evolved at the turn of the twentieth century following the invention of the X-ray and significant advances in antisepsis, anesthesia, and the biological sciences.
2. Hospital spending has grown rapidly in recent decades as a result of the growth of private and public insurance and other factors. It accounts for about 31 percent of health expenditures.
3. The hospital industry has experienced rapid change, including reductions in the number of hospital beds and inpatient utilization and significant growth of outpatient services. Hospitals are facing competitive pressure to restructure through mergers, participation in hospital networks, and other partnerships.
4. Hospitals are licensed and subject to a wide range of state and federal regulation.
5. Many analysts believe that the hospital industry is in a medical arms race resulting in unnecessary duplication of expensive technology. The limited empirical evidence does not support this view.
6. Intuitive reasoning suggests that the costs of discounts or uncompensated care to some patient groups must be passed on to other paying groups. More formal analysis leads to a

richer set of results including situations where costs cannot be shifted. The empirical literature indicates that cost shifting is far from complete.

7. Improvements in the quality of hospital care, and the role of publicly available performance indicators, have emerged as major policy and research themes.

8. The nursing home population has grown dramatically since the introduction of Medicare and Medicaid. Governments pay 64 percent of all nursing home costs.

9. Nursing home quality has been examined through structure, process, and outcome indicators. Surprisingly, no conclusive evidence relates cost to quality or supports the view that nursing homes with higher proportions of Medicaid patients produce lower-quality care.

10. A familiar theme in the nursing home literature is one of persistent excess demand by Medicaid patients. A model of chronic excess demand is plausible, although recent evidence indicates that excess demand is not a universal phenomenon.

11. Financing LTC for the growing elderly population is a great social challenge. The nursing home population is leveling off. Home health care and other alternatives are growing rapidly in number of patients and costs. They can be cost-effective alternatives to hospital and nursing home care.

12. Informal care and long-term care are close substitutes. By encouraging or discouraging informal care, policies have significant budgetary implications for Medicare and Medicaid.

Discussion Questions

1. Explain why it is often claimed that hospitals compete for doctors rather than patients. What are some of the implications of this phenomenon, assuming that it is true?

2. Even nonprofit hospitals must earn a "profit." Evaluate this statement.

3. What is the medical arms race (MAR) hypothesis? What features of hospital markets make the presence of an unproductive MAR possible?

4. Suppose that the Medicare rate of hospital reimbursement is reduced. Explain why the costs may not be shifted to other patients in the short run.

5. Explain why only about 5 percent of adults buy long-term care coverage.

6. Hospital costs have grown following the growth of private and public insurance. Describe other factors that could account for some of the growth.

7. The title of an August 21, 2005, article in the *New York Times* was "It's the Simple Things, but Some Hospitals Don't Do Them." Use Box 14-2 to discuss and explain why hospitals may fail to provide some simple and effective life-saving procedures.

8. Explain how excess demand for nursing home beds may persist over long periods of time. How can the hypothesis be tested?

9. Nonprofits are dominant in the hospital industry while for-profits dominate the nursing home industry. Develop some possible explanations for this difference.

10. Informal care provided by children and other family members are good substitutes for LTC for parents. Describe some potential social and demographic changes that may reduce the availability of such informal care. Develop policies that may help take advantage of the substitutability to delay entry of the elderly into LTC facilities.

Exercises

1. What is a dominant strategy in game theory? Using Figure 14-1, replace the entry in the first row and second column with (125, −50). Does A have a dominant strategy? Does B? What is the solution to this game?

2. Assume that there are three groups of hospital patients (instead of two as shown in Figure 14-2): private, Medicare, and Medicaid (which has a lower fixed rate of reimbursement than Medicare). Explain how a hospital would select patients in order to maximize profits.

3. Suppose that the Medicaid reimbursement rate does not cover the variable costs of patient care. Will a profit-maximizing hospital accept Medicaid patients? If not, under what circumstances will the hospital accept such patients?

4. Assume that a patient's health can be improved by home care or institutional care. Use isoquants and isocost curves to determine the condition for efficient utilization of these two forms of care. Under what circumstances will an insurance program promote or fail to promote efficiency?

5. Consider Figure 14-2. Suppose that a hospital has the ability to be a perfect price discriminator in the private market, that is, it can charge every private patient the maximum that the patient is willing to pay. Explain how this will affect the number of private patients the hospital will take and the impact on the hospital's profits.

CHAPTER

The Physician's Practice

A Benchmark Model of the Physician's Practice

Supplier-Induced Demand (SID)

Small Area Variations (SAV)

Other Physician Issues and Policy Puzzles

Conclusions

Physicians both provide important labor in medical care production and make key decisions in the health system. In Chapter 16, we examine the characteristics of physicians as labor in the production of health, including the investment decisions they must make to become physicians. In this chapter, we focus on the physician as decision maker, whether in solo practice or in a group practice. Since the physician largely controls and directs the use of medical inputs as an agent for the patient, physician practice decisions heavily influence the quantity, quality, and cost of the health care system.

Physician practice behaviors, however, pose many challenges for economic understanding. Physicians make decisions that determine the content of hospital care and these hospitals are often called the "doctors' workshops" (Pauly, 1980). As agents for the patients, physicians potentially neglect their roles as representatives of the community. The doctor's large information advantage over the patient leads researchers to question whether the typical physician is really a "perfect" agent, or perhaps, at times, even induces patient demand in order to increase income.

Patients expect medical practice to be scientifically based, and this raises yet another information question: Is each doctor well informed regarding current best medical practice? Variations in surgery rates across small, seemingly identical, geographic areas have caused many observers to be skeptics in this regard.

With so many departures from the usual economic model of the firm, health economists have offered a variety of physician practice models to capture these departures. Instead of a review of these models and variants, we first develop a "benchmark model." This model is quite general and will be used to show the important hypotheses as special cases.

A Benchmark Model of the Physician's Practice

The following model, introduced by McGuire and Pauly (1991), captures most of the observed physician behaviors as special cases of a utility-maximizing physician decision maker. Describing a physician as a utility maximizer just means that the physician

values other items besides profit. The profit-maximizing firm in the conventional theory can be thought of as a utility maximizer who emphasizes profits far beyond other goals. In this benchmark model, the physician gets utility from (1) net income and (2) leisure, and disutility from (3) inducement, the physician's own efforts to induce patients to buy more care than appears medically necessary. This last factor introduces the supplier-induced demand (SID) controversy into the model. As we will see, the question regarding SID is whether physicians use their knowledge advantage to abuse their agency role for monetary gain.

Let the physician's utility function be:

$$(1)\ U = U(\pi, L, I)$$

where π is the net income from the practice; L is the physician's leisure time, and I is the degree of inducement. The physician can choose any amount of labor and inducement effort consistent with the profit level that is implied by these choices.

With three variables to consider, the physician must consider the willingness to trade off between three pairs of goals:

Net income π and Leisure L;
Leisure L and Inducement I;
Net income π and Inducement I.

The overall decision involves all three variables, but a good understanding of the model can be acquired by focusing on two pairs.

First, consider the tradeoff between income and leisure. In Panel A, Figure 15-1, assume that the work hours return a constant revenue, w, for each hour worked. As depicted, a physician's "wage," w, determines the slope of this labor/leisure tradeoff. Starting from the maximum possible leisure (the horizontal intercept in the graph) each hour worked represents one hour less leisure. Corresponding to this, income rises by w, the net payment per hour worked. It follows that higher wage levels $w_2 > w_1$, and then $w_3 > w_2$ will result in steeper rising income lines. The optimal points on each

FIGURE 15-1 Supply of Physician Labor

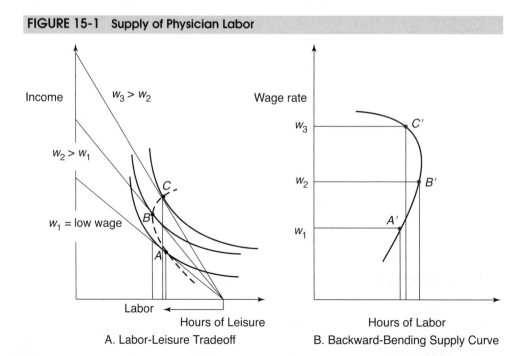

A. Labor-Leisure Tradeoff

B. Backward-Bending Supply Curve

income line are chosen by the physician; the indifference curves shown in Figure 15-1 illustrate this process.

Note that the path of optimal points—from *A* to *B* to *C*—at first heads to the northwest and then bends back and upward to the right. This pattern is recast in Panel B where wage levels (w_1, w_2, and w_3) and labor are on the axes, in this case forming the "backward bending labor supply curve". As conventionally explained, in the region from *A'* to *B'*, the physician is primarily motivated by higher wages to substitute labor for leisure; but, in the region from *B'* to *C'*, the physician's income effect dominates this substitution effect. The physician becomes rich enough to wish to spend more time enjoying the income.

These graphs show that the physician's income and especially the income effect play critical roles in determining how much he or she is willing to work. In Panel B, suppose a physician is at point *C'* and then the wage rate falls. The physician shown would move along the curves toward point *B'*. This implies a wish to compensate for lost income by working more. Later in this chapter we will consider whether and how the physician would be able to find the additional patients. But notice now that a rise or fall in income, for any reason, will cause the physician to reevaluate the choice about how much to work.

Consider next the tradeoff between net income π and inducement *I*. The model proposes that physicians dislike inducing patient demand. With each unit of induced patient care, the physician experiences a decline in utility that must be offset by the extra utility gained from the extra income that inducement brings. Figure 15-2 represents the process of choosing levels of net income π and inducement, *I*. The indifference curves represent the physician's preferences. The indifference curves slope upward because one of the two "goods," *I*, is really a "bad." To remain on the same indifference curve, the physician must gain additional net income to offset the disutility of engaging in a higher level of *I*. As is the usual case, however, higher curves are preferred.

In Figure 15-2, net income π with zero inducement is shown at point *A*. This point represents mQ_o, where *m* is the assumed profit rate (related to, but not necessarily identical to the physician's wage) from each unit of patient care, and Q_o is the amount of patient care with zero inducement. Net income π increases by rate *m* with each unit

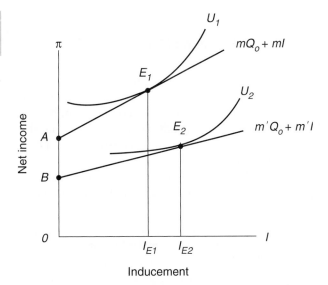

FIGURE 15-2 Physician's Response to Reduced Rate of Profit

of inducement I along the income line $mQ_o + mI$. The physician's initial equilibrium is determined by the tangency of the net income line and the indifference curve, shown at E_1, where the physician induces OI_{E1} of extra patient care.

If there is a lower profit rate m', the net income line becomes flatter and lower, or line $m'Q_o + m'I$. The physician now chooses equilibrium point E_2. In this case, it results in OI_{E2}, a higher level of inducement than OI_{E1}, even though doctor had a higher profit at E_1.

We will apply the model to explain the economic controversies over the nature of physician practice. The model's economic novelty is the assertion that physicians can induce demand but that they dislike doing so. To see its applicability, consider two of the most prominently discussed controversies surrounding physician behavior: Supplier-Induced Demand and Small Area Variations.

Supplier-Induced Demand (SID)

On becoming ill, consumers hire health care professionals to act as their agents. A physician, however, is not merely an agent, but also a provider and the seller of the care. In this situation some physicians might potentially misuse their agency powers to their own advantage.

Reconsider Figure 15-2 and note that the physician depicted at equilibrium E_1 has chosen to induce demand by OI_{E1}. If such inducement is very common, it may be very difficult to detect because when everyone induces, it becomes normal. Economists have focused instead on identifying changes in consumer demand caused by a reduction in the physician's profit rate, usually stemming from increased competition. In this case the theory explains the increased inducement in that physicians seek to recover lost revenue by promoting procedures to patients. It also provides a test to detect inducement.

In Figure 15-2, assume that new competition brings the initial profit rate m down to m'. As seen, the physician's response is to increase inducement from OI_{E1} to OI_{E2}. Thus, we predict that physicians will increase their inducement of demand in response to more competition.[1] Testing for changes ignores the underlying question: "At what level was the physician inducing demand to begin with?" Empirical studies invariably test for changes in inducement, leaving the underlying level unknown (Phelps, 1997).

The Supply and Demand Model

Notice that if all physicians in the market behaved like our individual physician, an increase in the supply of physicians would lead to an increased aggregate quantity of care. Note, however, that one need not assume SID to predict aggregate demand increases in response to increased competition. A simple market supply and demand model also predicts this. From Figure 15-3, we note that an increase in supply from S_1 to S_2 implies an increased quantity consumed from Q_1 to Q_2, and a decreased price (or fee) from P_1 to P_2.

Uwe Reinhardt proposed a "fee test" to address this confusion, claiming that a rise in physician fees to a level higher than before the supply increase could only be caused

[1]This response, however, is not a necessary outcome given the assumptions of the theory. Students can experiment with alternative shapes of well behaved indifference curves to find instances where physicians reduce inducement instead.

FIGURE 15-3 The Supply and Demand Model of SID

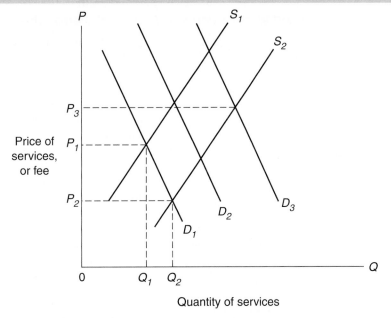

Quantity of services

The Supply and Demand model shows quantity increases resulting from a supply increase. The Reinhardt Fee test argues that SID is identified when demand increases sufficiently to cause the price (fee) to rise.

by inducement. This is an interpretation of the shift in demand D_3, which is sufficient to cause fees to rise from P_1 to P_3. However, Feldman and Sloan (1988) have also shown that a model incorporating quality as a demand determinant can explain the same phenomenon. If physicians respond to competition by increasing their quality, and if that higher quality earns a higher price, then SID is again not needed for an explanation.

The Target Income Hypothesis

Economists who first proposed the SID criticism of physician behavior formulated the "target income hypothesis" (Evans, 1974). This argues that physicians have desired incomes that they strive to achieve or to restore whenever actual income falls below the targets. This target income model is a special case of the benchmark model, though a relatively extreme one.

Target income behavior suggests that for the physicians in question, income becomes not merely the main thing but the only thing. This extreme focus on an income target, as well as the disinterest in further income in excess of the target, constitute features that have caused many health economists to question the target income idea.

Would physicians adjust their price and quantity decisions if their target income changed? Suppose we asked physicians their desired income. Do physicians who express levels much higher than their current income choose different and more profitable price and quantity combinations than others? Evidence (Rizzo and Blumenthal, 1996; Rizzo and Zeckhauser, 2003) suggests that they do. Furthermore, physicians appear to change their price and quantity choices when they make gains in income from sources unrelated to their practices (for example, stocks and bonds). For one physician's perspective, see Box 15-1.

BOX 15-1

SID and Target Income: A Physician's Perspective

The models of SID and target income necessarily abstract from the care process rendered by skilled professionals who are seeking to provide the most appropriate treatment for their patient. This personal perspective comes from an assignment in a health economics course at a local university. The writer is a physician who is director of pulmonary critical care at a large hospital.

I would, however, agree that physician behavior does and will change in response to income fluctuation but I would lend some insight into the current thought process. Recall, always, that the physician does not determine charges or the criteria for reimbursement for inpatient or outpatient services. The physician does not "approve" of the levels of service for an inpatient or the criteria to an MRI, CT, or PET scan. Insurance companies and Medicare determine all these rules. By and large, most physicians attempt to provide the best available care, but now being cognizant of the myriad of work needed to support a claim.

Let me give an example of how this works in my private practice. I am asked to see a patient in consultation. The patient may have been post-op with respiratory failure. Without regard to patient insurance, I provide care and dutifully document my activities with the patient. After the patient recovers, I post a billing, let's say to Medicare. There was

an initial consult and 10 days of care in the ICU and step-down unit. Based on my provider ID number (PIN) my claim is categorized. Routinely, I get 10–15 percent rejection due perhaps to incomplete data transmission or another doctor who also billed a similar "category" code. I then must use my staff to copy the progress notes in medical record and provide these documents to the payer. The delay is now perhaps 90–120 days.

Have I put my income interest above the patient's best interest and welfare? A resounding No!! However, what physicians are actively pursuing is the details and methodology to code and document properly so as to receive payment for what has been actually done . . . I favor full prosecution of fraudulent behavior, but there is a distinct philosophical difference between billing what was actually performed and understanding the nuances of the billing coding, reimbursement world as contrasted to a doctor that would purposely "up-code" billing for services not rendered and deliberately mislead a patient. Institutions are also working aggressively to accurately document patient care and co-morbidity to increase (read legally!) reimbursement and document a higher case-mix index. Continued efforts by payers to monitor services, prescription patterns, and key benchmark care points will not only help rein in any outliers but also improve patient care and safety by eliminating wasteful care.

The Benchmark Model as a Synthesis

An approach toward merging the various SID models can be seen using the benchmark model. Figure 15-4 compares target income behavior in panel A with profit-maximizing behavior in panel B. In panel A, once competition forces the profit rate m to a lower level, m', the new equilibrium is tangency point E_2. This much is identical to the graph in Figure 15-2. Now examine the broken line drawn parallel to line $mQ_o + mI$ (the original budget line) and just tangent to the lower indifference curve, U_2, at point E_2'.

The broken line identifies the physician's changed inducement in a different way. It hypothetically removes income from the physician who is at E_1 until the physician attains the equivalent utility to E_2. The change in inducement caused by the "removal" of income is called the income effect and it is measured in this case as $I_{E1}I_{E2}'$.

Panel B shows the contrasting profit-maximizing behavior. Notice that the income effect in this case is zero; we see this in panel B because the equilibrium inducement does not change when income is removed. Similar to the previous analysis, the broken line shows this tangency at E_2', which equals the inducement level at E_1. Why is a zero income effect like the profit maximizer? The profit maximizer gains utility only by the net dollars brought in so he or she values inducement as long as it brings more net income. As a result, the profit maximizer's income effect will always be zero. Notice in

FIGURE 15-4 The McGuire-Pauly Synthesis of SID Benchmark Models

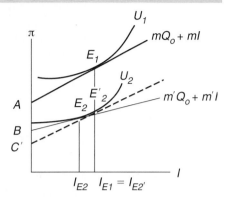

A. Physician responds to lowered profit rate m' by increasing influence on patient demand.

B. When there is no income effect, as in profit-maximizing behavior, then the model predicts a decline in supplier influence will follow a decrease in the profit rate.

addition that the physician in panel B would reduce inducement when faced with greater competition and a lower m. The new equilibrium is at E_2.

The McGuire-Pauly synthesis tells us that the size of the income effect is critical to understanding and identifying SID behavior. A lower profit rate, m, has two offsetting effects on inducement:

> *Substitution effect*: If inducement is less profitable (smaller m), providers would do less inducement, that is, substitute away from it.
> *Income effect*: Decreased income would make inducement more desirable.

For inducement to increase, a positive income effect on inducement must be large enough to overcome the negative income effect on inducement. This fact led analysts to search for evidence of a substantial positive income effect.

The Parallel Between Inducement and Advertising

Analysts have found it easy to confuse inducement with one or more of the many marketing practices common to virtually all firms. Promotion practices can include advertising but could also include quality enhancements, provision of information, enhancements of the practice surroundings, and greater time spent with the patient. Unfortunately, it can also contain misinformation, and it could be narrowly self-interested or even fraudulent. The research problem is that it is difficult to distinguish socially harmful SID from the more benign forms of the marketing practices. Even advertising, which is often criticized by the public, can be beneficial when it provides information (Nelson, 1974), or at least benign when it is complementary to the advertised product (Becker and Murphy, 1991).

Stano (1987) argued that an influx of new competition (which reduces the physician's profit rate) may lead physicians to induce more, or less, depending on the cost structure of the firm's production and its advertising. Stano felt that if the physician's SID is analogous to advertising/inducement, then inducement would usually decline in an increasingly competitive market. This view reveals the possibility that the physician's response to increased competition may be socially benign or even beneficial.

What Do the Data Say About Supplier-Induced Demand?

Two criticisms were raised about much of the earlier SID work. First, many of those studies could not distinguish between the SID model and the conventional supply and demand model. Second, many estimates of the SID effect proved to be statistically flawed, meaning that the econometric coefficient that was thought to be evidence of SID could not be disentangled from other coefficients. In Box 15-2 Dranove and Wehner provide an example of such flaws by looking at the "supplier-induced pregnancies."

Physician Fees, Fee Tests, and Fee Controls

Reexamining the competitive model in Figure 15-3, we see that with a sufficient degree of SID the physician's fee level can rise in response to greater competition. Recall the Reinhardt fee test for SID, which suggests that the SID availability effects might alternatively be tested via their effects on physician fees. Figure 15-3 applies precisely only to the perfectly competitive market structure. It may be more realistic to describe physician markets as monopolistically competitive. McGuire (2000) showed that the implications of availability on fees in that case are not so clear. In addition, if physicians can adjust their quality in response to increased competition, then higher fees could result even when there is no inducement (Feldman and Sloan, 1988).

A more promising approach has been to identify physicians' desired income. Rizzo and Blumenthal (1996) use surveys of physicians to compare their desired incomes to their actual current incomes. Physicians with greater "gaps" were found to make greater price increases. Evidence like this supports the target income model of SID most directly.

BOX 15-2

Supplier-Induced Pregnancies

Dranove and Wehner (1994) challenged the accuracy of standard statistical methods used by health economists to test for SID in an unusual and revealing way. They deliberately assumed—counter to all logic—that obstetricians have the power to influence demand for the delivery of babies. They further "assumed" that an increase in obstetricians per capita will lower the expected incomes of these obstetricians and impel them to use their superior knowledge vis-à-vis the patient to induce demand for childbirths. The two then applied a typical SID approach to investigate.

First they showed that availability of obstetricians and gynecologists per capita and childbirths per capita were positively correlated, an interesting result but one consistent with the ordinary long-run operations of supply and demand. They then measured the "pure SID" effect. Their estimated SID elasticity for obstetricians per capita was 8 percent and significant. Using this figure in their further calculations they found that a one standard deviation influx of obstetricians will induce an additional 7 percent in childbirths per capita. Can we conclude that the obstetrician newcomers were, let's say, socially very active? Hardly.

Gruber and Owings (1996) also applied the fact that pregnancies are determined by parents and not by the doctors. Reasoning that the fall in fertility among U.S. women was unrelated to their model of obstetrical care, they measured the change in Caesarian deliveries relative to vaginal deliveries, C-sections being more lucrative for obstetricians. They concluded that the drop in fertility and consequent effects on physician income led to an increase in C-sections. Physicians were able to recoup about 10 percent of their income drop by encouraging the C-sections.

Cases where the physicians lack the power to choose their prices provide another useful thread of research on SID. Rice (1983) studied changes in Medicare fee levels in Colorado. The imposed uniform fee was higher than the fee physicians previously received in some areas and lower in others. He found that a higher fee tended to elicit a lower amount of services per case, that is, it lowered the intensity of care. In contrast, a lower fee tended to increase the intensity, that is, the amount of services per case. By selling more services to each patient on average, physicians appeared to be compensating for lost income. In a similar design, Nguyen and Derrick (1997) found that Medicare fee reductions led to increased volumes of care for the physicians in their sample who incurred the greatest fee reduction. Yip (1998) likewise found that Medicare fee reductions (in New York State) led to increased volumes.

Elsewhere, Grytten and Sorenson (1995) distinguished between patient and primary physician-initiated visits under the fixed-fee schedule of Norway's public health care system. The investigators did not find any evidence of either SID or rationing of physician-initiated visits, though there was some indication of inducement for laboratory tests. More recently, Sorenson and Grytten (1999) studied the effects of increased competition in Norway. Increases in the number of physicians in an area, as expected, reduced the number of patients seen by a typical physician. However, contrary to the SID hypothesis, Norwegian physicians did not compensate for their falling incomes by increasing services for patients who remained.

As we have modeled the physician practice, SID potentially breaks the trust between physician and patient. This "imperfect agency" can harm patient welfare when compared to the perfect physician/agent. Patients who incur surgeries, medicines, tests, and other procedures solely in response to the physicians' changed income positions, would be experiencing care that is at least wasteful and very possibly harmful to their health.

How does one measure the patient's utility? If we rely on patient self-reports, we get another provocative contrast. Carlsen and Grytten (2000) find that patients in Norway report *greater* consumer satisfaction after increases in the market area's availability of physicians. Plausibly, each physician has a somewhat smaller workload and makes up for this in part by spending more time with each patient. The two authors reason that if patient utility is adequately gauged by their reported consumer satisfaction, then SID may not matter to patient welfare.

Small Area Variations (SAV)

We have seen that what patients don't know can hurt them, and their relative lack of knowledge is especially worrisome because of the physician's dual role as provider and agent. But are physicians themselves always well informed? Do they know the true productivities of the medical procedures they provide? For health conditions where alternative treatments could be used and where substantial uncertainty prevails regarding productivities, physicians may vary in their preferred treatment practice styles. Are the substantial variations in medical and surgical use rates per capita across small geographic areas caused by these information problems?

Economists took interest in the study of small area variations (SAV) upon recognizing its significance for social welfare. Whereas SID stems from the information gap between physicians and patients, SAV probably occurs because of the physician's uncertainty and lack of knowledge. In this case, even if all physicians acted as perfect agents for their patients, their own lack of knowledge of the true productivities of available procedures would create welfare losses for the patient, an economic problem stemming from the inadequate diffusion of medical information (Phelps, 2000).

Modern SAV research stems from the pioneering work of John Wennberg and colleagues who studied New England hospital markets. Their evidence of wide variations across small service markets was corroborated by later studies. Why did women in one New England town undergo hysterectomies at more than twice the rate of another apparently similar New England town? Understandably the variations proved worrisome, and many researchers focused on discovering their sources.

The favored measures of small area variations have been the coefficient of variation (CV) and the systematic component of variation (SCV). The coefficient of variation relates the standard deviation of observed medical use rate to the mean of the same measure. Dividing this by the mean, the researcher adjusts for the size of the rate being studied. For example, the unadjusted rate for treatment of Guillain-Barré syndrome (a relatively rare disorder, afflicting only about 1 person in 100,000) will be much smaller than the rate for treatment of the common flu. Division by the mean rate of each serves to put these on a common basis.

The SCV is a twist on this theme. Here, the researcher first removes from the observed treatment rate that portion of its variation that can be attributed to the random nature of the disease. The remaining portion then becomes a better measure of the effects of systematic factors, such as physician practice styles, and supply and demand factors.

Table 15-1 excerpts data from a study by Wennberg (1990) featuring the CV statistic. Phelps (1997) suggests that a CV in range 0.00 to 0.10 indicates low variation, 0.10 to 0.20 is moderate, while over 0.20 is high. Of the 10 ailments reported, most of these procedures would be considered highly variable based on the size of their CV statistic. The extremal ratio, also reported in the table, while not as reliable a measure of variation, is easier to visualize. It is the ratio of the largest rate observed across the small areas to the smallest. Thus, the rate of mastoidectomy across the study areas varies by a factor of over four.

Contributions to These Variations

Researchers have investigated these variations. Much of the SAV work focuses on the contribution of socioeconomic characteristics of the population and the role of the availability of supplies of hospital and physician services (see Alexander et al., 1999). The studies together reached two conclusions: (1) Supply variables are important and demand characteristics play a somewhat lesser role though both are statistically and

TABLE 15-1 Variations by Medical Procedure Category

Surgical Procedure	No. of Cases	Coefficient of Variation	Extremal Ratio
Colectomy	3,190	.116	1.47
Open heart surgery	1,439	.232	2.29
Appendectomy	5,381	.305	2.86
Thyroidectomy	949	.342	3.35
Total hip replacement	1,717	.353	2.99
Diaphragmatic hernia	2,178	.369	3.45
Coronary bypass surgery	3,744	.383	3.62
Mastoidectomy	569	.461	4.03
Spinal fusion w/wo disc excision	1,234	.520	5.20
Total knee replacement	998	.525	7.42

Source: Wennberg (1990).

materially significant; and (2) such variables do not seem to suffice, as much variation is left unexplained (Folland and Stano, 1990).

The Physician Practice Style Hypothesis

Wennberg (1984) argued that much of the observed variation is closely related to the degree of physician uncertainty with respect to diagnosis and treatment. When there is little consensus about the effect and value of a medical procedure, a wide range of physician treatment choices lies within the bounds of accepted practice. The physician's habits of treatment choices, beliefs about efficacies, and patterns of practice are seen as "style." Some suggest further that physicians in a given market tend to "follow the pack" and eventually share a common set of beliefs. These beliefs, and consequently their practice styles and use rates, often differ across markets.

Practice style probably varies among physicians due to an incomplete diffusion of information on medical technologies. The true production function may not be widely known. Some physicians may be optimistic about the good effect of a given procedure, yet others pessimistic.

Furthermore, as medical science uncovers better information about the true production function, efforts to disseminate this information will help reduce unnecessary surgery. The practice style hypothesis also suggests problems in distinguishing SID from SAV. Areas with high proportions of "optimistic" providers will have high surgery rates, tempting some observers to conclude that SID is prevalent, whereas the true source could be practice style. Physicians in these high utilization areas might even be acting as perfect agents, informing their patients honestly and supporting their patients' preferences regarding treatments.

Checking the Practice Style Hypothesis Against the Data

How well does the practice style hypothesis hold up empirically? Unfortunately there is no direct and objective measure of practice style. Physicians' beliefs are at best only indirectly revealed through their practice patterns. Indirect evidence is available, however, and it comes from several sources.

Education, Feedback, and Surveillance

Studies show that information programs directed at physicians can alter their behaviors and thus presumably their practice styles. One study found that an informational program significantly affected the tonsillectomy rates in 13 New England areas. Another found that the rate of "unjustified" hysterectomies dropped by two-thirds subsequent to a review program introduced in the Canadian health system.

Comparing Utilization Rates in Homogeneous Areas

A second empirical approach was developed in an influential study by Wennberg and Fowler (1977). The authors studied use rates and population characteristics for six areas in Vermont. After finding that morbidity and many socioeconomic variables were not sufficient in explaining the variations in this region, they concluded that variations in use rates probably are due largely to practice style differences across the small areas.

Though practice style in principle can determine the observed variations across small areas, it is invalid to simply infer that a given set of observed inter-area differences is necessarily due to practice style. For example, Green and Becker (1994) studied small areas in Michigan where acute cardiac ischemia (ACI) discharge rates ranged from high to low by a factor of three. The large variations proved to be mainly due to

differences in the underlying rate at which patients chose to use the hospital emergency room rather than to differences in physician decision making. They concluded that area variation does not necessarily mean variation in practice style.

Multiple Regression Approaches

It may be best to approach the problem with multivariate techniques. As more variables are added to the analysis, one learns better how much of the observed variation can be explained by standard socioeconomic variables without resorting to the practice style hypothesis. The residual unexplained variation from the regression then represents an upper bound on the contribution of practice style (Folland and Stano, 1989).

Multiple regression studies using standard socioeconomic variables explain substantial amounts of the inter-area variations, especially when they focus on aggregated utilization rates (commonly represented by a weighted average of many procedures) in larger geographic areas. Multiple regression analysis of individual procedures, as opposed to aggregates of procedures, is generally less successful in explaining the variations. Phelps and Parente (1990) found that standard demand and supply variables typically account for between 40 and 75 percent of the variation in their study of 134 separate diagnostic categories.

Elsewhere, Escarce (1993) found that 43 percent of the variation in cataract surgery rates for the Medicare population is explained by socioeconomic variables. This still leaves a potential 57 percent that may be due to practice style. However, it is clear that the influence of practice style is well below Escarce's upper bound. He could identify several nonpractice style influences. After purging the surgery rates of any possible practice style influence, Escarce found that the variation in cataract surgery rates was reduced by only a small amount.

These contributions indicate that practice style could be important for many procedures, but the contribution of the many standard variables cannot safely be overlooked. Surely the inadequately informed physician is out there, but the question of "to what degree?" has proved more difficult to answer, and that degree could be small.

SAV and the Social Cost of Inappropriate Utilization

The most important yet controversial issue in the SAV literature is the proposition that substantial variation in utilization rates is an indication of inappropriate care. The potential savings from improving the quality of care and reducing excessive utilization has led to a national focus on research into patient outcomes. Indicative of this priority, the U.S. Congress in 1989 created the Agency for Health Care Policy and Research "to determine what works and to develop practice guidelines and standards."

The economic cost of physician misinformation can be theoretically identified in Figure 15-5. Suppose that the marginal benefit curve MB^* represents the true patient benefit given full information; then the efficient quantity of services is R_2. If physician lack of knowledge led them to believe that MB_1 represented the true benefits, then the area, A, would describe the value of the patients' foregone opportunity, their welfare loss. This area represents the inefficiency or welfare loss to society from underutilization; the patient's true willingness to pay (represented by MB^*) exceeds marginal cost for each unit of care from R_1 to R_2. In a similar fashion, one can measure the welfare loss of inefficiently excessive utilization at rate R_3 by triangle B.

Despite the simple and direct application of consumers' surplus concepts to the welfare losses of practice variations, it has proved difficult to generate reliable estimates of these costs. Phelps and Parente (1990) and Phelps and Mooney (1992) approached the problem by using regression analysis to estimate true marginal benefit

FIGURE 15-5 The Inefficiency of Misinformation About the Marginal Benefit of Health Care

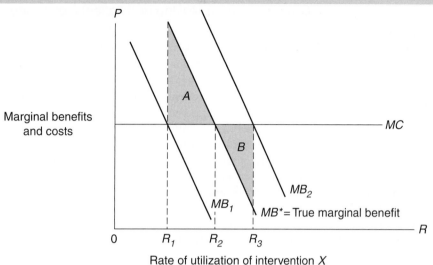

Rate of utilization of intervention *X*

curves. However, the approach has drawn criticism in several respects. Regression always predicts the dependent variable imperfectly, leaving a residual. How much of the residual is due to inappropriate use and how much to legitimate omitted factors, such as patient preferences, can never be known with certainty.

Furthermore, Dranove (1995) has pointed out that patients also make errors when predicting the true value that medical care will actually deliver. This additional "noise" also disturbs our estimates. Most economists studying the issue probably would agree that while inappropriate use occurs commonly and is often costly, we do not yet have confident estimates of the total costs of inappropriate care.

Despite the empirical challenges, many researchers in the medical community now recognize the importance of using an economic concept of benefits, as opposed to benefit measures determined strictly by medical science, and they urge physicians to involve patients in treatment decisions (see Box 15-3). Differences between economists and medical researchers over SAV, practice style, and appropriate care thus appear to be narrowing. In particular, the consensus is growing in the health services literature that cost-effectiveness analysis and other forms of program evaluation (Chapter 4) are the best means to identify and rank treatments through their effects on social welfare.

SAV Analysis in Other Applications

Another common usage of SAV is to study inequalities in environment and in health care availabilities. Wheeler (2004) provides an example of the SAV framework used to study inequalities in environmental hazards and finds that environmental hazards affect disproportionately those who are materially less well off. Folland's (2005) study of East European economies in transition (from a 1988 baseline) provides a SAV example focused on inequalities of health care across small areas of command systems. There were larger variations in health care availability across small areas in the command systems compared to U.S. reference regions but larger variation in the U.S. regions for mortality rates.

BOX 15-3

Clinical Decision Making and Patient Preferences

David Eddy is a pioneer in studying the role of information, medical science, and preferences in clinical decision making. Eddy (1990) breaks the treatment decision into two main components—evaluating the outcome of the alternatives and then comparing and choosing from among the options. The first component is largely a scientific one determined primarily through clinical studies of patient outcomes. However, for many patient conditions, even a fully informed physician will face the problem of inadequate scientific information.

The second component, comparing the alternatives, involves judgment and patient preferences. Eddy emphasizes that "it is the patient's preferences that should determine the decision" (p. 442). A failure to make appropriate decisions can arise from failures in both stages. Clearly, physicians' inadequacies in education and training,

as well as deliberate attempts to misrepresent outcomes (e.g., to engage in SID), will distort information needed at the second step. Similarly, if patients misrepresent their preferences or physicians misinterpret their preferences, or if inadequate information is communicated to patients, the second step will be flawed.

The medical community is increasingly being alerted to the role of the patient through the development of information technology to improve the decision-making process. For example, Barry et al. (1995) have developed an interactive videodisc that helps patients with prostate cancer choose from among several treatment options. To help with the decision, patients answer questions designed to measure their attitude toward risk and their ability to tolerate discomfort.

Other Physician Issues and Policy Puzzles

Physician Pricing and Price Discrimination

As physician payment mechanisms have evolved with the growth of private and public insurance and the spread of managed care, physician decisions on pricing, accepting publicly insured patients, and entering into managed care contracts have become extremely complex. Many of these issues are taken up in other chapters, especially those on managed care and government regulation. Here, we examine price discrimination, one aspect of physician pricing that received a great deal of attention in the early literature.

There is widespread agreement that physicians in private practice have at least some degree of monopoly power. That is, physicians are not generally price takers and do not face horizontal demand curves. By raising prices, they will lose some but not all of their patients. With relatively low barriers to entry in regional markets for those who are already licensed physicians, it sometimes is useful to characterize physicians as monopolistic competitors with highly elastic demand curves. In many applications that do not directly involve entry and exit, however, it is easier and more useful to apply the monopoly profit-maximizing model to the physician firm. Here the marginal revenue curve lies below the demand curve because lowering the price to one customer requires lowering the price to all other customers. Hence, marginal revenue is less than price.

In a simple monopoly model, as described by Figure 15-6, the physician produces quantity, C, at which the marginal cost curve, MC, intersects marginal revenue curve, MR, or point F. At quantity C, the demand curve indicates that price A can be charged, and the total revenues equal $0ABC$. The physician's profits equal total revenues less total costs, which are indicated by the average costs and quantity C, or box $0CDE$. Hence, profits are equal to the remainder, or box $ABDE$.

An important feature of the pricing policies of the medical profession is the ability of the physician to discriminate among customers. In economic terms, discrimination

FIGURE 15-6 Profit Maximization and Price Discrimination by a Monopoly

means treating different customers differently. Consider a storekeeper who sells candy. The storekeeper likes adults more than teenagers, and charges the adults less for boxes of candy than he charges teenagers. Can this practice persist?

Certainly not over time! Teenagers who wish to have the candy simply will ask adults to buy the candy for them. Alternatively, adults who buy candy could resell the candy to teenagers for at least the price they paid. Competition among adults, in this example, would bid down the price of the candy to where the adults would be making normal, or zero, profits in selling the candy at the same price that it was sold to them.

Health services cannot be resold in this manner. Suppose a rich person needs knee surgery, and the physician knows that the rich person could pay considerably more than a poor person for the surgery. The rich person cannot have a poor person buy knee surgery and resell it to him. This simple example suggests the considerable leeway that physicians have to charge different prices to different customers.

Returning to Figure 15-6, even after the physician has chosen to charge fee A for the service, there is still room for price discrimination. Suppose that one more customer, who was not willing to pay price A but instead is willing to pay $(A-1)$, comes to the office. The marginal cost (MC) of providing patient care, although higher than at point F, is less than price $(A-1)$. Thus, the physician can increase profits by the amount of the shaded area. In principle, the physician can continue and attract yet additional patients by charging them even less than $(A-1)$. As long as the price paid by those patients exceeds MC, the physician's profits will increase.

Paying for Outcomes

When a customer gets a car fixed, the mechanic usually guarantees the work, and if the outcome is not satisfactory the customer can go back and have the mechanic make things right. Why can't we do the same with physicians?

Dranove and White (1987) have argued that the common physician form of contract stems from both the difficulty of evaluating the health status of the returning patient as well as to the fact that unobservable patient behavior is very important to

the outcome. How can one tell if the patient's claim of pain is true, and how can one be sure that the patient has followed the treatment regime faithfully including taking his medicine as prescribed?

Leonard and Zivin (2005) note that outcome-based contracts are most likely to be successful when both the patient and the practitioner play important complementary roles. This means that they must work together (the provider in diagnosis and the patient in compliance with treatment regimens) in managing or treating diseases, such as diabetes, asthma, or HIV infections. Effort-contingent contracts are likely to be successful when either the patient's or the provider's effort is necessary, but not both; surgery is a good example.

The authors take advantage of a unique opportunity to observe patient choices between fee-for-service and fee-for-outcome of care in Cameroon, investigating patients who chose between the two types of payments. Payment by outcome is rare among physicians in the developed world, but it is common among traditional healers in many African countries. In rural Cameroon, patients may choose mission-based physicians who are compensated by physician effort or may choose traditional healers who are compensated by patient outcomes, with both types of providers covering a variety of illnesses. Leonard and Zivin find that when illness requires large amounts of effort by *both* patients and providers, the patients are more likely to seek treatment from traditional healers who are paid based on outcomes. When the disease is not particularly responsive to one of the two types (physician or patient) of effort, patients visit effort-compensated physicians.

Conclusions

Our benchmark model depicts the physician as one who values positively net income, and leisure, and dislikes inducing patient demand. It shows that a physician may respond to increased competition by greater effort at inducement. The model also shows that for the supplier-induced demand (SID) hypothesis to be supported, the physician's income effect must be positive and substantial.

Small area variations can be understood as a result of uneven diffusion of medical information to these same physicians. The evidence indicates that substantial variation in physician practice style exists even after accounting for the standard supply and demand variables. Physician practice also responds to new information. Removing all practice style variation that it is possible to remove may create improvements to social welfare, although it is not clear how large they will be.

Some independent issues close the chapter. Price discrimination enables a physician with some monopoly power to increase his or her profits. Though payment by outcome is rare in physician practice, it is observed among traditional healers in Africa, where it is found to be beneficial for patient cases that require the complementary effort of both physician and patient.

SUMMARY

1. A benchmark model describing the physician as seeking to maximize utility over income, leisure, and inducement, captures most observed physician behavior.
2. In the benchmark model, the physician faces tradeoffs with income and leisure but also with income and the disutility of inducement.
3. Supplier-induced demand (SID) usually refers to physicians' deviating from their agency responsibilities to provide care to their self-interest rather than their patients' interests.
4. Inducement behavior can be understood as the physicians' having strong income effects in response to reduced practice profitability.

5. The target income hypothesis suggests that physicians use their discretionary advantage to achieve a target level of income or an improvement in their relative income.
6. One profit maximization approach develops the analogy between inducement and advertising. It predicts that inducement will diminish as competition reduces the gap between a physician's marginal revenue and marginal cost.
7. Small area variations (SAV) refer to the frequently wide inter-area variations in the per capita use rates found for many medical and surgical procedures. Such variations have been found in the United States and many other countries.
8. The practice style hypothesis, which refers to physician uncertainty in diagnosis and treatment, has been proposed as the major explanatory factor for small area variation.
9. Practice style can be modeled as an information problem based on the physician's incomplete knowledge of the productivities of his or her treatment alternatives.
10. Most of the evidence for the practice style hypothesis is indirect, coming from studies showing the following:
 - Changes in practice patterns following physician education and monitoring
 - Wide variations in utilization rates across small, homogeneous areas
 - High, unexplained residuals in multiple regression analyses of inter-area utilization rates.
11. SAV is generally interpreted to suggest that there is considerable unnecessary or inappropriate care being provided. There is no way to infer, however, whether a particular area provides too much care or just the right amount.
12. Price discrimination by physicians may increase their profits, in part because health care can not generally be resold by recipients.

Discussion Questions

1. Suppose that insurers monitored all health care payments to determine whether the services were appropriate. Would you expect to see more or less tendency toward SID?
2. Figure 15-2 shows how increased competition can lead to a higher degree of inducement at point E_2. This suggests that providers try to induce more usage to compensate for lower profit margins. Suppose, however, that the physician ends up at a point where there is less inducement. What types of preferences would lead to reduced inducement in response to less profits?
3. If physician fees are fixed so that they do not adjust to changes in supply, explain how SID can be manifested.
4. What are some criticisms of the target income approach to SID? In the target income model, what determines the physician's target income? Would target incomes differ between physicians in practice? Would some physicians choose instead to be income maximizers?
5. What forces limit a provider's ability and willingness to engage in SID? In the profit-maximizing model of SID, what are the costs to the physician of inducement? Give examples of inducement costs.
6. Assuming that SID is prevalent and substantial, what are the implications for policy? A policy to reduce Medicare payment rates? A policy to increase the number of medical school graduates?
7. What is SAV? What are some economic forces that can help explain SAV? What are some demographic and other considerations? How might physician uncertainty lead to SAV? What evidence supports the practice style hypothesis?
8. Do high utilization rates necessarily indicate the provision of unnecessary care? If not, why not?
9. If the cause of SAV is lack of information about the productivities of various procedures, would you expect SAV to have increased, decreased, or stayed the same over time? Why?
10. As new technologies become available more rapidly for given procedures, would you expect an increased or decreased amount of SAV?
11. Suppose large variations occur in use rates within a typical small area, as well as among small areas. What would this mean for the practice style hypothesis?

EXERCISES

1. Explain why the indifference curves in Figure 15-2 are positively sloped.
2. In Figure 15-2, suppose that the initial profit is $1 per unit of inducement ($m = 1$). Suppose then, that increased competition lowers m from 1 to 0.5.
 a. Draw the new profit line $\pi = mQ_0 + mI$.
 b. Demonstrate the case where the change in profit increases the level of inducement.
 c. Demonstrate the case where the change in profit decreases the level of inducement.
3. In comparing SAV among diseases and diagnoses, would more complicated diseases suggest greater or lesser variation?
4. Consider the approximation of the welfare loss due to inter-area deviations from the correct rate of care. All else equal, which procedures would yield the largest welfare losses—those with low-price elasticities or those with high-price elasticities? Why is this the case?
5. In Figure 15-5, suppose for each patient that marginal cost = $100, that $R_1 = 1$, $R_2 = 2$, and $R_3 = 3$. Suppose also that one-third of the physicians use treatment levels R_1, R_2, and R_3 each. What would be the "cost per patient" of SAV, if all of the demand curves have slopes of –50? (Hint: Use the parameters above, to figure out the sizes of triangles A and B).

16

Health Care Labor Markets and Professional Training

The Demand for and Supply of Health Care Labor

Factor Productivity and Substitution Among Factors

Health Manpower Availability and the Meaning of Shortages

Medical Education Issues and the Question of Control

Licensure and Monopoly Rents

Other Physician Labor Issues

Conclusions

Commensurate with its high share of GDP and the labor-intensive nature of its output, the health care economy employs a large number of workers. We use the term *labor* here in the general economic sense of an input in production that is distinct from capital and that is provided by human beings. Like other goods and services, the production of health services requires both labor and capital.

While many health sector workers are relatively unskilled, the health sector also requires large numbers of highly trained professionals. Most physician specialists obtain years of postgraduate education past their medical school education. This chapter addresses labor issues that range from general supply and demand principles that can be applied to all health care occupations, to specialized topics involving shortages of doctors and registered nurses, medical education and licensure, and various practice decisions of physicians.

The Demand for and Supply of Health Care Labor

Table 1-3a in Chapter 1 shows the magnitude and variety of health care occupations, and the importance of labor not only to the health sector, but to the overall economy. In 2003, 13.6 million people, nearly 10 percent of all employed civilians, were employed at health services sites. These data do not include millions of other workers in the pharmaceutical and health insurance industries, as well as those in industries providing supplies, capital goods, and services for people providing direct patient care. Workers in some other health-related occupations, such as pharmacists employed in drugstores, also are not shown.

Many of these numbers have increased substantially with the growth of the health economy. Between 1970 and 2003, the number of active physicians rose from 291,000 to 793,000, an increase of 173 percent; the number of registered nurses nearly tripled from 750,000 to over 2.2 million. Table 1-3b also indicates that the per capita ratios have grown substantially since 1970 for the major health care occupations.

How labor is used—and how it is combined with other factors of production—helps determine both the amount of health care provided and the wages and salaries of the providers. The productivity and training of health care providers are important to the working of labor markets and to the demands and supplies of labor.

We begin by describing the factors that determine labor demand. Demand for a factor of production, either labor or capital, is derived from the demand for health. We demand health care providers because we demand health care, and we, in turn, demand health care because we demand health.

Production Functions and Isoquants

Recall that the production function describes the relationship of factors of production (the inputs) to the resulting goods and services produced (the outputs). Under the existing technology and know-how, it shows the maximum sustainable output that can be obtained from all possible combinations of inputs, such as labor, materials, buildings, and equipment.

Economists often simplify the production relationship as follows:

$$Q = f(L, K) \tag{16.1}$$

where Q represents output over a period of time, and L and K represent the quantities of labor and capital inputs over the period. Many features of a production function can be illustrated graphically through isoquants. Recall also that an isoquant represents all combinations of inputs (e.g., labor and capital) that result in a given level of output. Figure 16-1 (panels A and B) describes isoquants for two different situations.

In panel A, the isoquant shows a technology in which labor and capital are fairly good substitutes for each other so that labor and capital can be combined in many different proportions to produce output. The budget line, AB, reflects the trade-off of the costs of capital and labor, and point X is the location at which the costs of producing Q^* units of output are minimized.

With the given set of input prices (wages and payments to capital) the optimum (cost-minimizing) capital-labor ratio $(K/L)_0$ is the slope of a ray from the origin

FIGURE 16-1 Production with Varying Rates of Substitution

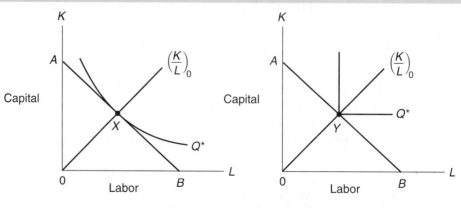

A. Elastic substitution

B. No substitution

through point X. Due to the curvature of the isoquant, a change in relative input prices changes the optimum capital-labor ratio. In panel A, labor and capital are good substitutes as we move along a given isoquant. Lower prices of labor (i.e., a flatter budget line) will lead to a relatively large substitution of labor for capital, and vice versa.

In contrast, panel B shows a technology in which labor and capital are not good substitutes; as drawn, they must be used in fixed proportions to one another. Although point Y represents the same ratio (K/L) as point X, changes in the factor prices will not change the capital-labor ratio. Specialized surgeries, for example, may require specific ratios of labor to capital with little substitution available. The degree to which substitution among inputs is possible, either between health care labor and capital, or among different types of health care labor, is a key issue in manpower planning and in determining the efficiency of production exhibited by health care firms.

The demand for any type of health care labor depends in part on these substitution possibilities. The demand for a factor of production also depends on the price of the output. Consider an example. Suppose you were working as a skilled worker in a bicycle manufacturing plant, and suppose that bicycle riding was becoming more popular. The increase in demand would result, at least temporarily, in a higher price for bicycles. More bicycle workers would be demanded as a consequence.

Marginal Productivity of Labor

Consider that the demand for an input, and consequently the wage paid to the input will depend at least in part on the input's productivity. This is one explanation as to why college-educated workers earn more money than others. If college-educated workers are more productive than others, then the demand for them will be greater. Although this is only one theory that explains the earnings advantage of college graduates, it illustrates the premise that more productive laborers are in greater demand.

Reconsider the idea of marginal product—the increase in output when an input is increased by one unit. Suppose that labor in equation (16.1) represents the number of laboratory technicians employed. If we add one lab technician to the production process, holding the available lab equipment and materials (i.e., K) constant, we probably would increase lab output. This increase is the marginal product of lab technicians.

Although additional lab technicians in the production process are likely to increase output, they likely will add incrementally less output. As we increase an input, holding all others constant, output will tend to increase but at a decreasing rate. This illustrates the law of diminishing returns.

The number of lab technicians that one should hire depends also on the price of output. Suppose that lab tests sell for $50 per unit. Suppose also that an additional technician would increase output by four tests per day. If these tests sell for $50 each, the technician is bringing in an additional $200 in revenue. The extra revenue generated is called the marginal revenue product (MRP).

Would it pay to hire this extra technician? Clearly the answer depends on the wage per day. If technicians earn $100 per day, the technician nets the hospital a $100 gain ($200 marginal revenue product less $100 wage), and thus it pays to hire another one. It always pays to hire laborers whose marginal revenue products exceed their wage.

Would it pay to hire still another technician with a marginal product of three tests per day? Because output (the tests) sells for $50 each, this next technician is netting the hospital $50 because the marginal revenue product, $150 in this case, exceeds the wage, $100. It will pay the firm to continue to hire more workers up until the point where the marginal revenue product equals the wage.

Figure 16-2 represents the marginal revenue product curve for lab technicians. The curve is downward sloping, reflecting the law of diminishing returns. In competitive

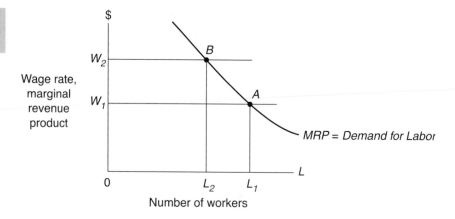

FIGURE 16-2 Firm Hiring Decisions at Different Wage Levels

markets, the MRP curve in Figure 16-2 is found by multiplying the marginal product curve (not shown) by the price of output. The optimal number of lab technicians depends on the wage rate. At wage W_1, the optimal input demand at point A is L_1. At a higher wage, W_2, the firm would demand fewer technicians, L_2, at point B.

This analysis shows that the demand for labor is precisely the marginal revenue product of the labor curve. Through the marginal product, this curve is closely related to the production function for the laboratory test and to the price of the output laboratory tests. If the price of the lab tests increases, the marginal revenue product increases, and more labor is demanded. If better machines are made available so that lab technicians become more productive, the demand for their services will also increase.

Factor Substitution and Labor Demand

At this point, recall the meaning and importance of the substitutability of one input for another. Suppose, for example, a newly invented machine allows lab technicians to perform certain functions that were formerly done by radiologists. This makes technicians better substitutes for radiologists. As a result, the demand for technicians will tend to increase. This change will also tend to shift the demand for radiologists and probably make it more elastic—that is, flatter and more responsive to the wage rate. As a result, if the firm finds it can substitute more easily between inputs, it will tend to become more resistant to input price changes, replacing increasingly expensive inputs with cheaper substitutes.

In recent decades, firms and policy makers have become especially interested in substitution possibilities in their efforts to control health care costs. To the extent that nonphysician providers can substitute for physicians, firms can hire lower-cost workers, hence cutting costs and possibly increasing the amount of the service provided. We address this issue in more detail later in the chapter.

The market demand for various occupations is determined by horizontally summing the demands of the individual firms. We see the market demand for laboratory technicians in Figure 16-3 as the downward-sloping curve labeled D_1. Under competitive conditions, the labor market equilibrium, and consequently the equilibrium wage, depends on the interaction of both demand and supply.

The Supply of Labor

The supply of labor tends to slope upward, implying that the higher the wage rate in a given market, the more workers or labor time will be forthcoming. First, those workers currently employed may choose to work more hours if higher wages are offered.

FIGURE 16-3 Market Demand and Supply for Laboratory Technicians

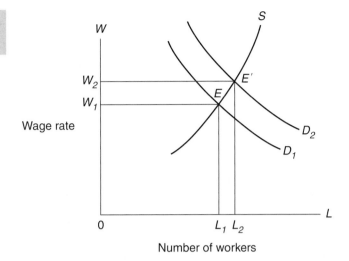

Second, similar workers may be attracted into the market from elsewhere. The labor supply curve for lab technicians is shown in Figure 16-3 as S.

The equilibrium market wage, W_1, for technicians, along with the market-clearing number of technicians, L_1, is determined by the intersection of the supply and demand curves. Consider that the market equilibrium wage will tend to increase in response to any demand-increasing event. These events include increases in the firms' desires to substitute lab technicians for other laborers, increased productivity of the technicians, and increases in the price of the lab outputs. Here, demand increases to D_2, increasing the equilibrium wage to W_2 and employment to L_2.

Similarly, the market wage will tend to fall in response to events that increase the labor supply. These include increased graduations of trained technicians or influxes of technicians into the market from other professions or other locations.

Changes in supply can take place relatively quickly for those health care occupations requiring minimal education or training. For physician specialists and others requiring the highest levels of education and training, the number of new professionals is determined by the admission decisions of medical schools as well as the decisions of applicants made many years earlier. Physicians must be licensed by a state in order to practice in that state. Requirements for licensure include graduation from an accredited medical school, passing a licensure examination, and completing one to two years of internship or residency in an accredited graduate medical education program. Many graduates, nevertheless, complete three- to four-year residency programs. Many physicians also become board-certified specialists. The requirements typically include advanced residency training for periods of three to six years, practice in the specialty, and passing the board examination.

Through education and training, medical students make investments in their human capital. Economists treat the decision to invest in human capital with the same tools used to analyze investments made by businesses in physical capital. The decision maker will consider the revenues associated with investment along with all costs, including any opportunity costs. For medical students, the foregone earnings associated with the time it takes to complete their medical education is an important opportunity cost, but monetary values must also be imputed to nonpecuniary gains, such as the satisfaction from helping the ill and the prestige associated with being a physician. The internal rate of return is defined as the rate that equates the present value of revenues with the present value of costs (see the Appendix to Chapter 4 for a discussion of discounting). Prospective medical students, in principle, will compare the return from

medical education with those of other possible occupational choices and select the highest one.

Information regarding the rate of return to a medical education also is useful to the policy analyst. Suppose we discovered that the average rate of return to medical education is high and rising. This information might mean that physicians are becoming increasingly scarce, suggesting a shortage. Numerous studies have attempted to estimate the rate of return to a medical education, and some of these will be described later in this chapter.

Factor Productivity and Substitution Among Factors

The supply of health services, and consequently health care prices, depends on the number of workers. However, productivity of labor inputs represents a critical determinant of supply. Productivity improvements increase output. Alternatively, the same output can be produced with fewer inputs. In a macroeconomic sense, general improvements in productivity represent a major source of economic growth and rising standards of living. At a microeconomic level, productivity gains in an industry can lead to lower prices for the goods and services produced in that industry and possibly to higher rates of remuneration for workers.

The productivity of a factor of production can be measured as the average product of the factor—that is, the ratio of total output (Q) to the amount of a particular labor input (L):

$$\text{Average product of labor} = Q/L \qquad \textbf{(16.2)}$$

This definition corresponds to the concept of average product used in microeconomics and is distinguished from marginal product, which is defined as the change in output associated with a one-unit increase in the input, holding all others constant.

Despite the simplicity of the concept of average product, difficult problems occur in measuring it. Output may be heterogeneous, consisting of many different outputs. In such cases, one often uses the dollar value of output for the numerator, Q. Similarly, many different kinds of labor are used in the production process. In such cases, a weighted sum of related inputs often is used in the denominator term, L.

Measurement of Physician Productivity

Reinhardt (1972) undertook a classic study of physician productivity. He examined general practitioners in private practice for three measures of output: total patient visits, office visits, and patient billings. In addition to physician time, he considered the use of various auxiliary personnel. Reinhardt estimated the marginal product of physician time—the increment to output resulting when one extra hour of physician time is added to the production process.

He found that the marginal product tended to increase up until the point where the physician is working a total of about 25 hours per week; the marginal product eventually declines to zero at about 110 hours per week. He found that starting from a base of 60 hours per week, a 1.0 percent increase of physician input would result in an increase of 0.8 percent in the number of patient visits produced.

In addition to studying the physician's productivity, Reinhardt examined the substitution possibilities between physician and other labor inputs. Consider physician aides. The aides' marginal products were highest when about one aide was present per physician. Physicians could improve productivity of their practices and increase profits

if they doubled the number of aides from two aides per physician (the average he found) to four aides per physician.

The Efficient Utilization of Physician Assistants: Substitution Among Inputs

The possibility that physicians were underutilizing aides was a provocative one. In 1988, Brown refined Reinhardt's work. Brown's marginal product estimates of physician time and other inputs, calculated at mean values of the variables, are shown in Table 16-1. The marginal products of auxiliary workers are shown in the columns labeled *MP* for data from physician offices of various categories. These include all physicians, solo physicians, and group practice physicians.

By dividing *MP* by the wage rate (*W*) of each input to get the marginal product per dollar spent on each factor, we can draw inferences about whether physicians are underutilizing or overutilizing various categories of workers. The marginal product per dollar is the relevant measure when determining which input to increase. To increase profits, one should hire the extra input that has the greatest *MP/W*. If this marginal product per dollar is not equal for each category of worker, the firm can save money by trading lower-producing workers per dollar (low *MP/W*) for higher-producing ones (high *MP/W*).

Brown concluded that physicians were underutilizing nursing inputs. Consider, for example, the data for practical nurses in all physicians' offices. These practical nurses have a higher marginal product per dollar, 0.129, than do physicians, 0.114 so the offices would become more profitable if one substituted practical nurses for physicians.

In addition, Brown found that physicians in group practices were on average 22 percent more productive than those in solo practices. He suggested that this figure, much higher than the 5 percent estimated by Reinhardt, resulted from advantages that group practices have in employing physician assistants. From Table 16-1, we can see that the marginal product of physician assistants (PAs) for solo practices was estimated to be negative. In contrast, PAs are productive on the margin in group practices. Even so, group practices are underutilizing PAs.

Other work provides considerable evidence on the extent of the substitutability between physician time and other labor inputs. Escarce and Pauly (1998) found that each hour of time for an office-based internist substitutes for $60 in nonphysician costs or vice versa. Elsewhere, the growth of managed care organizations has heightened interest in PAs and nurse practitioners (NPs) to improve productivity and lower costs. Jacobson and colleagues (1998/1999) report that PAs/NPs can perform 50 to 90 percent

TABLE 16-1 Marginal Products and Efficiency of Input Use

Input	All Physicians		Solo Physicians		Group Physicians	
	MP	MP/W	MP	MP/W	MP	MP/W
Physician	2.967	0.114	2.686	0.102	2.793	0.110
Secretary	0.192	0.043	0.253	0.058	0.105	0.023
Registered nurse	0.585	0.104	0.628	0.109	0.625	0.114
Practical nurse	0.542	0.129	0.533	0.132	0.485	0.109
Technician	0.320	0.067	0.321	0.059	0.278	0.057
Physician assistant	0.231	0.040	−0.014	−0.003	1.082	0.192

Note: MP = Marginal product
MP/W = Marginal product per dollar wages spent on input

Source: Reprinted from *Journal of Human Resources*, Douglas M. Brown, "Do Physicians Underutilize Aides?" *Journal of Human Resources* 23 (1988): 342–55 with permission from the University of Wisconsin Press.

of the tasks of primary care physicians without compromising quality when they work collaboratively with physicians. They also found that PAs/NPs have greater scope of practice and autonomy as the proportion of managed care patients in a health care organization increases. Despite legal impediments and other limits on the use of PAs/NPs, the delivery of primary care is likely to rely increasingly on these skilled physician substitutes as organizations try to move toward their optimal input mix.

Health Manpower Availability and the Meaning of Shortages

Table 1-3b presented data on a selection of health manpower groups.[1] In each category, the total number of professionals has increased, often substantially, since 1970. The population of ordinary citizens (the potential consumers) also increased during the period. Except for podiatrists however, Table 1-3b made clear that the number of professionals has been increasing more rapidly so the number of professionals per 100,000 population also has increased. In fact, the rate of increase for physicians and registered nurses per capita has been sharp.

Despite these increases, a recurrent policy concern has been the availability of various critical categories of health manpower. The issue usually hangs on whether we have or will have enough of these professionals; that is, whether as discussed in Box 16-1, there will be shortages or surpluses.

Availability of Physicians

Manpower analysis often focuses on the availability of personnel to provide needed or demanded patient care. Many federal physicians (approximately 20,000, or 2 percent of the total) provide services only to the portion of the population eligible, such as veterans. Furthermore, many physicians do not provide care for patients. Because the portion providing office-based patient care to the public has not changed much over recent decades, the rapid increase in physicians per capita also has meant a greater number of patient care physicians per capita.

Of the 748,000 active, nonfederal medical doctors (MDs) in the United States in 2002, 658,000 provided direct patient care (Table 16-2). Of those, slightly over three-fourths were office based and the rest were hospital based, including residents. As we noted previously, the pattern of the portion of physicians available for patient care has not been changing rapidly.[2]

Physicians form a large number of specialties rather than a homogeneous group. About 50 percent of office-based physicians practice in primary care, and 20 percent are in general surgery or the surgical specialties, with the remainder having other specialties. Concerns about specialization as well as about uneven distributions between rural and urban areas have long been heard in the United States.

Planners and policy makers often worry about having adequate quantities of health manpower and avoiding serious shortages, especially of physicians. In the mid-twentieth century, a need-based method, based entirely on medical considerations, became the dominant approach to determining health manpower requirements. As illustrated by

[1]Although regrettably sexist, the term *manpower* has evolved as the standard term for planning health care needs.

[2]There were 49,000 doctors of osteopathy (DOs) in 2002. Although we often combine DOs with MDs when considering physician supply and access to physician care, there have been major differences in the historical development and organization of the two groups. Unless otherwise indicated, our discussion will focus specifically on MDs.

BOX 16-1

Is There a Shortage or Surplus of Physicians?

For most of the 1960s and 1970s, policy makers feared the possibility of severe physician shortages. Following an increase in government support for medical training and residency programs, and the subsequent rapid growth of managed care, large surpluses of physicians, especially specialists, were projected by the turn of the century (Weiner, 1994). HMOs and other managed care organizations are under intense pressure to control costs by eliminating unnecessary care and encouraging improvements in physician productivity.

Despite some softening in market conditions facing new physicians in the 1990s (Miller et al., 1996), these large surpluses failed to materialize. On the contrary, newspapers and professional publications were teeming with warnings of impending shortages. In contrast to the micro-level detail associated with manpower planning models, a highly publicized study by Cooper and colleagues (2002) examined macro trends in income per capita, population, and demographic changes. They also considered supply shifters, such as the decline that has taken place in physician work effort as well as substitution of non-physician clinicians for physicians. With the medical educational system currently in place,

their model projects a shortage of 50,000 physicians by 2010 and a much larger shortage of 200,000, or more than 20 percent of projected demand, by 2020.

Others have reacted to this study by pointing to the difficulty in making long-term projections when so many factors influence both demand and supply. The ability of market forces and institutional adjustments to prevent health care labor markets from becoming seriously out of balance should also not be ignored.

Economists often see manpower shortages very differently from accounts in the media. Nevertheless, the issues were widely debated by the medical establishment, and in 2004 a number of influential organizations concluded that there would be significant and persistent shortages of physicians. The Council on Graduate Medical Education and the Association of American Medical Colleges recommended 15 percent increases in medical school enrollments and entry-level residency positions by 2015. In 2005, the American Medical Association, which had predicted surpluses and sought for many years to limit first-year enrollments at medical schools to 17,000, announced its support for expanded enrollments and residency training positions.

SOURCE: USA Today, "USA Today Examines National Physician Shortage," March 4, 2005, www.medicalnewstoday.com/medicalnews.

TABLE 16-2 Physicians by Type of Practice: 1980–2002

Type of Practice	Number (in thousands)			Percent		
	1980	1990	2002	1980	1990	2002
All physicians	487	646	902	100	100	100
Medical doctors (MDs)	468	615	853	95	95	95
Active nonfederal	418	540	748	86	84	83
Patient care	362	488	658	74	76	73
Other	56	52	90	11	8	10
Federal	18	21	20	4	3	2
Inactive/Unknown address	32	55	85	7	9	9
Doctors of osteopathy (DOs)	19	31	49	4	5	5

Source: U.S. Department of Commerce, *Statistical Abstract of the United States (2004–05)*, Table 149.

the classic study of Lee and Jones (1933), under this approach, the number of physicians required to serve in a given market area was calculated from the needed number of procedures that, in turn, was based on the incidence of morbidity (illness) in the population. Under what Fuchs (1974) has criticized as the monotechnic approach, it was assumed that a fixed single technique that includes a fixed amount of physician time is required to treat each particular type of illness. Total physician time, or physician equivalents, was determined by aggregating over a broad range of medical conditions. Economic considerations, such as the potential substitution of other inputs for physician time, changes in technology, differences in patients' preferences, and even costs were generally ignored.

Economic Definitions of Shortages of Health Professionals

Economic definitions of manpower shortages usually differ from those based solely on medical grounds. Economists usually apply definitions based on considerations of how characteristics of a given market for professionals deviate from those that would be found in an ideal, highly competitive market. As a result, several approaches for determining shortages are found in the literature.

Excess Demand

Begin with the conventional economic definition of a shortage: the excess of the quantity demanded over the quantity supplied at market prices. Figure 16-4 depicts a shortage defined in this way: The health manpower shortage at the wage W_1 is equal to $L_{d1} - L_{s1}$. If the wage instead had been W_2, no shortage would exist. This is because at the higher wage, less labor services would have been demanded and more would have been supplied.[3]

FIGURE 16-4 An Economic Shortage

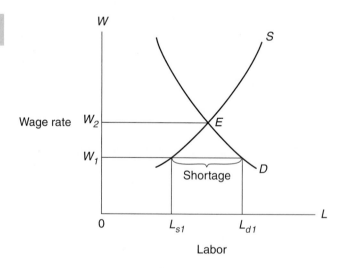

[3]Lane and Gohmann (1995) provide a dramatic example of the difference between the economic approach to nursing shortages and a noneconomic need-based approach developed by the Office of Shortage Designations. The Office identifies counties with shortages by using the ratio of full-time equivalent nurses in short-term general hospitals to the average daily number of patients. The economic model identified 423 counties (out of 1,880) as shortage areas, whereas the noneconomic approach designated 565 counties. Notably, the two models agreed on only 133 cases of shortage.

This definition, though valid, raises critical questions in the case of health manpower. Why didn't the wage rise to equilibrium, thus, automatically eliminating the shortage? The usual case of persistent excess demand is associated with stickiness in wages or prices imposed by law or regulation. A common example in many American and European cities is legally enforced rent control in the housing market.

What would cause wage stickiness in health manpower markets? It seems doubtful that health manpower wages are sticky in the sense of administered rents or prices, or that health manpower shortages in terms of excess demand are a serious policy problem. Some analysts have argued that excess demand shortages are not serious concerns for most categories of professionals.

Relatively Rapid Increases in Wages: Dynamic Shortages

An unnecessary focus on excess demand also obscures the fact that economically meaningful shortages of professionals may well exist even when supply and demand are in short-term equilibrium. In particular, a shortage may occur when demand and supply conditions change over time. Suppose, for example, that demand for a category of health professionals expands over time, and that the supply of these professionals is slow to respond or even perhaps faces barriers in responding. The result may be a large rise in wages relative to the wage gains of other professionals.

To illustrate, consider Figure 16-5, which depicts the demand for physicians at two points in time: an initial Period 1 and a subsequent Period 2. We compare the equilibrium quantity in Period 1 with that in Period 2. The wage increase from W_1 to W_2 may indicate a shortage, even though quantity supplied equals quantity demanded (at L_1 and L_2) in both periods. We would say a shortage exists if the relative wage of physicians has risen sharply relative to that of other professionals. The measure of shortage under this approach is the relative wage and the direction of its movement.

Several variations on this general approach have been described. The pattern of wages over time may be more complex than the movement described from equilibrium at W_1 to an equilibrium at W_2. We might find, for example, that the initial market response to increased demand for the professionals would be to raise wages to W_2. Only after these high wages had induced the expansion of supply to S_2 would we observe market wages adjusting to W_3 (and quantity supplied to L_3). Under this scenario, the professional's wage for a time falls, here from W_2 to W_3. Thus, a decline in

FIGURE 16-5 Changes in Equilibrium over Time Depending on Supply Adjustments

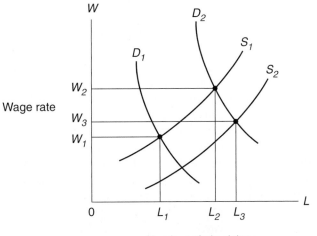

Number of physicians

relative wage during a given period may reflect a long-run adjustment offsetting a shortage and not necessarily an indication of excess supply.

Relative Rates of Return

How should we measure the monetary gains from professional training? Hansen (1964) provides a classic measurement approach that is both plausible and consistent with theory. He proposes that the relevant measure of monetary gains to a given health professional group must take into account the various opportunity costs incurred by professionals in obtaining their training. The internal rate of return is a measure that attempts to accomplish this conceptual task.

The internal rate of return is the discount rate that equates the present value of the stream of costs to the stream of revenues from education. The higher the rate of return, the greater the financial rewards are to investment in the human capital attained through education. To determine whether a given health professional group is in relatively short supply, we can compare the rate of return to that of other professionals and examine these comparative data over time.

High, even excessive, rates of return may occur whenever the supply of labor fails to respond quickly to changes in demand. In some instances, the underlying reason for this slowness in response may be barriers to entry faced by potential health professionals. A barrier to entry exists, in this case, when a potential health professional faces higher entry costs than incumbents faced.

This definition includes cases where potential entrants are completely barred from entry. Such barriers would occur if controls on slots in health professional schools limited entry. They also occur to some degree whenever entry to the profession is limited by licensure laws. The issue of licensure laws is of special interest here because it is common in the health professions. Because of this connection, we treat the empirical literature on rates of return to physician education in the discussion of licensure in a later section of this chapter.

The Role of Monopsony Power: Shortages of Registered Nurses

Practitioners who describe health manpower availability often rely on reported percentages of unfilled, budgeted positions. One explanation of this measure (using Figure 16-4) is excess demand. Excess demand, however, is generally temporary; as long as prices are not rigid, price increases will tend to cure the problem. More plausibly, the analyst will focus on changes in the percentage of unfilled, budgeted positions, analogous to dynamic definitions of manpower shortages. First, however, we must address the problem of interpreting reported data for markets that are monopsonistic.

Monopsonistic Labor Markets

A monopsony is a market that in theory has only one buyer; for example, a monopsony would be one hospital that hires virtually all registered nurses in the market. Under monopsony, a firm may report unfilled, budgeted positions, for example, for registered nurses, even when the firm is actually in equilibrium. The paradox is that such a monopsony firm may announce that it wishes to hire more nurses even though it is unlikely to take the necessary steps to do so.

The paradox is explained by the monopsony firm's upward-sloping supply curve. Because it is a big employer, it has the power to influence nurses' wages and, thus, to induce more nurses to work by raising the average nurse wage level. The monopsony firm is willing to hire more nurses at the current wage, but it has no intention of paying a higher wage in order to hire more nurses.

These ideas can be illustrated with the help of Figure 16-6. Imagine that one hospital is the only demander of nurse labor in the market. The hospital's demand curve for

FIGURE 16-6 Nurse Shortage Under Monopsony Conditions

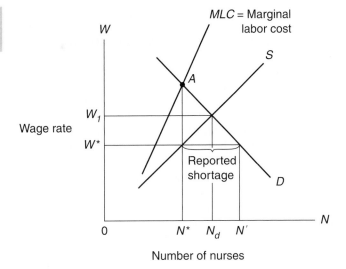

Number of nurses

nurse labor, labeled D, represents the marginal revenue product curve for nurses employed at that hospital.

Under monopsony the supply curve for labor will no longer represent the marginal labor cost, MLC, to this hospital. If this hospital had been a competitive hirer, competition would have meant that the hospital could have hired as many nurses as it wanted at any given wage. In a competitive market, N_d workers will be hired at wage W_1.

Consider the monopsonist's marginal labor cost curve, MLC. When the monopsonist hospital seeks to add one nurse to its labor force, it must pay a higher wage than before in order to induce this marginal (extra) nurse to work. But it then must pay all of its employed nurses a higher wage. The problem arises entirely because the labor supply curve faced by this firm is rising as is typical under monopsony, instead of being flat as is typical under competition.

The extra (marginal) labor cost incurred for that one nurse is not just the wage it pays. It also includes the extra wages it must pay all its other nurses. As a result, the marginal labor cost curve, MLC, will lie above the labor supply curve, S. The monopsonist will hire fewer and at a lower wage than will the competitor.[4]

Reported Shortages

Suppose now that the hospital acts to maximize its profits. It would find it profitable to hire an additional nurse as long as the extra revenue the new nurse brought in, the marginal revenue product, exceeds the extra cost of the nurse to the hospital, the marginal labor cost. Thus, as long as the demand curve (the marginal revenue product) lies above the marginal labor cost curve for a given level of nurse employment, it always will pay to hire more nurses. The hospital achieves its profit-maximizing complement of nurses where $D = MLC$, an employment level of N^* nurses in Figure 16-6. The equilibrium wage is found on the corresponding point of the labor supply curve; here it is W^*.

[4]Early evidence indicated that nursing markets were monopsonistic. Sullivan (1989) found the typical hospital's labor to be upward sloping to a degree that suggested monopsony power in the nursing labor markets. However, Hirsch and Schumacher (1995) note that an upward-sloping labor supply curve for nurses is a necessary but insufficient condition for monopsony effects. In examining RNs' wages relative to wages for females with a college degree across a large number of markets, they find that relative wages were not related positively to the number of hospitals per square mile as predicted by the monopsony model. The same authors (1998) also show that unionization is not a countervailing force to hospital monopsony power. More recently (2005), they found very modest decreases in RN wages in response to increases in hospital concentration, but that this effect cannot be sustained over the long run due to the relatively high mobility of nurses.

BOX 16-2

Extreme Regulation? California's Staffing Ratios Law

In response to a perceived erosion of patient care standards and quality of hospital care, as well as strong lobbying by the California Nurses Association, California became the first state to establish minimum nurse-to-patient ratios for general acute care hospitals. Although the legislation was passed in 1999, the specific ratios were not finalized until late 2003. The law took effect in January 2004.

Critics of this law argued that it would exacerbate California's nursing shortage, limit a hospital's ability to admit patients, and significantly raise health care costs. Four months after the ratios were implemented, the vast majority of hospitals reported that they could not meet the "at-all-times" requirement, which mandated that a substitute nurse cover for a nurse who is on break or leaves the unit for other reasons. The hospital industry was fighting against the higher staffing ratios that were scheduled for future years.

The California initiative is being monitored carefully in other states for its effects on quality, access, and costs. It is still too early to reach any clear conclusions about the effects of such an unprecedented regulation, but preliminary findings from a study of 68 hospitals found a 21 percent increase in RN hours of care per patient day with an 18 percent decrease in the number of patients per RN. However, there were no significant improvements, as measured by lower rates in two commonly used measures of quality: patient falls and bedsores.

SOURCES: "First Evaluation of California's Much-Watched Ratios Law," *Medical Study News*, August 9, 2005; and Donaldson et al. (2005).

At this equilibrium wage, W^*, the hospital would desire to hire N' nurses. It may well budget for these nurses and effectively report a shortage of $(N' - N^*)$. The hospital acts as if it did not realize that if it wants more nurses to work, it must pay its nurses more. At any rate, a shortage in this case has a limited meaning; it only means additional nurses are desired at the current wage level.

This theoretical point suggests the hazards of interpreting data on unfilled budget positions. The possibility of monopsony power in labor markets suggests that unfilled positions data may overstate the problems of nursing availability. The problem is somewhat mitigated by the fact that these data typically represent unfilled budgeted positions because a hospital is unlikely to budget for all the positions it might desire at the current wage. Furthermore, the analyst might in any case be interested in changes in the percentage of unfilled budgeted positions. If the number of unfilled positions were rising rapidly, it would suggest an increasingly relative scarcity of nurses.

Medical Education Issues and the Question of Control

From their authority in treatment decisions, physicians are the dominant providers in the health economy. Most other health care workers carry out their tasks under the direction of physicians. As a result, economists have concentrated on the training and practice of physicians even though they represent a minority of workers providing patient care. Many professions require a considerable length of time for education and training, but the time period for formal training of physicians is among the longest. In addition, medical education poses the question of who has control. Does the medical profession itself exercise control over access to medical education in order to improve its own profitability? It is helpful to study medical schools and their funding, as well as information about the supply of potential medical students.

Sources of Medical School Revenues

Medical school education is subsidized heavily by the government. This situation is an outcome of public concern for the adequacy of the supply of physician labor. The rapid growth in medical school enrollments did not arise by accident. Several actions by Congress, beginning with the Health Professions Educational Assistance Act in 1963, provided grants to medical schools and financial assistance to students. Some of this federal support hinged on enrollment increases. In 1971, however, federal support to medical schools was increased substantially and came in the form of capitation grants, which were grants that rewarded the medical schools for expanding their enrollments by giving money on a per-student basis, initially about $3,000 per year per student. With fears of physician surpluses emerging by the late 1970s, assistance under the Health Professions Educational Assistance Act was phased out, and enrollments stabilized.

Nevertheless, medical education is still subsidized heavily. Tuition represents a relatively small source (about 4 percent) of medical school revenues so the student pays only a small portion of the true cost of the investment in education. Governmental support for operating revenues and through grants and contracts is typically about 30 percent of total revenues. The largest share (about 50 percent) comes from reimbursements for health services provided to patients (Jones et al., 1998).

Capital Market Imperfections Justify Subsidies

The policy that students pay for a relatively small share of their training raises questions in light of the fact that physicians earn high incomes and receive relatively high rates of return on their investment. However, at least part of this subsidy can be understood as a policy that attempts to overcome imperfections in capital markets where potential medical students would have to go to get the loans needed to pay for their education. The economic imperfections stem from the students' difficulties in getting these markets to lend up to the full value of the investment.

Even though there is a perception that a medical education pays off handsomely, it is difficult for a potential lender to secure the loan adequately. The investment in education is an investment in human capital. Human capital cannot be bought and sold in the same way that physical capital can be.

Most plainly, one cannot repossess a human being. Although the bank knows that the typical medical graduate easily can afford to repay the loan, it is difficult to guarantee this repayment in an individual case, and potential medical students may not get the needed loans even though the investment is worthwhile. From society's point of view, this problem may result in insufficient numbers of medical students.

Leffler and Lindsay (1981) conclude that with such capital market imperfections, reliance on private markets leads to an underinvestment in medical education. Thus, government support can be justified on economic grounds. These authors estimated that an optimal level of support would be about 36 percent of the costs of medical education, which is a substantial figure.

Teaching Hospitals, Medical Schools, and Joint Production

Medical education is a good example of joint production. That is, medical schools produce at least three products jointly:

- Medical education
- Patient care
- Research

TABLE 16-3	Hypothetical Example of Joint Production at a Medical School	
		(in millions of dollars)
Total cost of school		60
Cost if school produced only patient care		30
Cost if school produced only education		50
"Pure" cost of education[a]		30
"Pure" cost of patient care[a]		10
Joint costs[a]		20

[a]The pure cost of education is total cost (60) less the cost of producing only patient care (30). The pure cost of patient care is total cost (60) less the cost of producing only education (50). Joint costs are total costs (60) less all pure costs (30 + 10).
Source: Newhouse (1978a).

To reimburse for patient care or to fund medical education appropriately, it is necessary to determine the pure costs and the joint costs of these activities. An example taken from Newhouse (1978a) illustrates these terms.

In Table 16-3, the total annual cost for a medical school that produces only education and patient care is shown to be $60 million. If the school produced only education with only the minimum patient care needed to do this, its costs would be $50 million. If it produced only its present volume of patient care and no medical education, its costs would be $30 million.

Incrementally, the cost of patient care raises the school's budget from $50 million to $60 million. Thus, the pure cost of patient care is the extra $10 million. Reasoning in a similar fashion, adding education to the cost of patient care raises the budget from $30 million to $60 million. Thus, the pure cost of education is $30 million.

Notice that the difference between total cost of this hypothetical medical school and all the pure costs is $20 million. This $20 million is called the joint cost. It follows that if the school were reimbursed only for pure costs, it would run a deficit. Much of the controversy with respect to funding revolves around the problem of who will pay for the joint costs.

The issue of joint production has centered on the teaching hospital, which also jointly produces patient care and medical education by providing internship, residency, and medical research. In particular, with the substantial cost differences between teaching and nonteaching hospitals, third-party payers are concerned about whether they are unnecessarily subsidizing medical education. The conventional wisdom in the 1970s was that the cost of education and affiliation with a medical school was substantial.

An examination of the cost differences between teaching and nonteaching hospitals shows that nonphysician costs per day are 21 percent higher in teaching hospitals. However, sorting out the causes for cost differences and making appropriate statistical adjustments refine these data. After this is done, nonphysician costs, though still higher in teaching hospitals, show a difference that is typically less than 10 percent (Sloan, Feldman, and Steinwald, 1983).

Foreign Medical School Graduates (FMGs)

Physician supply in the United States depends to a significant degree on foreign medical school graduates (FMGs), and reliance on them continues to grow. As a proportion of the total number of active physicians, FMGs increased from less than 14 percent of the total in 1963 to 25 percent in 2003. Critics are concerned that the United States and other rich nations are draining valuable talent from many poor countries that have inadequate health care systems.

Nevertheless, the availability of physicians from other countries can have important policy and planning implications. Foreign national FMGs can increase the responsiveness of physician supply in the United States to changes in the physician wage.

Rapid increases in physician wages send a market signal to potential physicians, increasing the estimated rate of return to an investment in medical education. It takes a long time, however, for new applicants among American college graduates to get to medical school, be trained, and enter practice. As a result, the supply of new American physicians will respond slowly to the wage signal. Foreign national FMGs, already trained but currently practicing elsewhere, can respond more quickly so the availability of foreign national FMGs makes total physician supply in the United States, in principle, more elastic.

These facts about FMGs can be used by policy makers during periods of shortages and increasing fees. Immigration policy can be relaxed to admit more foreign national FMGs during periods of physician shortages, and vice versa during periods of perceived physician surpluses. This happened during the 1960s, when preferential treatment was given to foreign national FMGs. Requirements subsequently were tightened by a 1976 act once shortages were no longer perceived.

In addition to immigration policy, the number of FMGs, including U.S. graduates of foreign medical schools, is influenced by certification and licensure requirements. All FMGs must take certification examinations required for admission into an approved graduate medical education program. The 1976 act also placed restrictions on the access of FMGs to graduate medical education.

A frequent concern about FMGs is quality of care. Arguments for tightening standards for FMGs usually are justified by claims that these graduates are inferior in quality to those educated in U.S. and Canadian medical schools. The conclusions are based on comparisons of examination performance and other measures of the credentials and personal attributes of FMGs and their U.S. counterparts.

Studies of the quality of care provided by FMGs, however, find little difference between the two groups. Some have argued that differences are more likely to arise in ambulatory care settings because there is less organizational control than in hospital settings. A study that examined more than 14,000 patient episodes by nearly 1,200 physicians in three specialty groups found little difference in performance. FMGs, in fact, sometimes outperformed U.S. medical school graduates (Rhee et al., 1986).

The Control of Medical Education

In 1974, Victor Fuchs wrote that "most economists believe that part [of physicians' high incomes] represents a 'monopoly' return to physicians resulting from restrictions on entry to the profession and other barriers to competition" (p. 58). Fuchs refers to the claim that physicians restrict entry to their profession in order to drive up prices for their services and make larger incomes for themselves.

Do physicians control entry to their profession in order to earn above-normal returns on their investment? This question can be asked in two steps, taking first the issue of whether physicians do, in fact, earn above-normal returns. Historically, physicians often have earned above-normal returns. Distinguished economists found this to be the case using data from early in this century, and it was suggested that control of entry was the cause. Subsequent studies found high returns in at least some more recent historical periods.[5]

How is it that physicians could control entry? Our present ideas and beliefs about the role of organized medicine in controlling entry owe much to Kessel (1958), who

[5]See Burstein and Cromwell (1985). For earlier work, see Friedman and Kuznets (1945) and Leffler (1978).

argued that monopoly power was attained by organized medicine through the licensure of physicians and the control of access to medical education. The first, licensure, is explored later in this chapter. At present, consider Kessel's account of the control over medical education exerted by physicians primarily through the American Medical Association.

Control over Entry

Shortly after the founding of the American Medical Association (AMA) in 1847, the organization campaigned state by state to get the medical profession controlled through licensure. Having largely achieved this goal by the turn of the century, the AMA turned its attention to the control of medical schools, which had proliferated in number. In 1906, the Council on Medical Education of the AMA inspected the 160 medical schools existing at that time, declaring only slightly more than half of them to be acceptable. The council sought support for this position through the Carnegie Foundation, which in 1910 issued the Flexner Report calling for substantial reductions in the number of medical schools and control on their quality. Kessel argued:

> If impact on public policy is the criterion of importance, the Flexner Report must be regarded as one of the most important reports ever written. It convinced legislators that only the graduates of first class medical schools ought to be permitted to practice medicine and led to the delegation to the AMA of the task of determining what was and what was not a first class medical school. (p. 28)

Following this report, the number of medical schools fell to 85 by 1920 and to 69 by 1944. Kessel pointed out that giving the AMA charge over determining the supply of physicians was like "giving the American Iron and Steel Institute the power to determine the output of steel" (p. 29). The AMA also was able to gain control over the internship/residency process through its ability to certify hospitals for such training. It also maintained control over the process through which physicians become board certified. The picture is one of significant power and means to control entry.

The AMA also was able to exercise control over substitute providers (e.g., optometrists, podiatrists, chiropractors) by influencing licensure to limit their scope of practice and later to limit third-party reimbursement for their services. Starr (1982) wrote of a survey of 9,000 families conducted between 1928 and 1931, which found that nonphysician providers treated only 5.1 percent of all attended cases of illness. He concluded that "physicians had medical practice pretty much to themselves" (p. 127).

Kessel's argument is historical and written nearly 50 years ago, yet many analysts point to anomalies in recent medical school data as continuing evidence of control of entry by the medical profession. The large excess demand for medical school slots by qualified applicants to medical schools has been used to support the claims. Over time, large fractions of medical school applicants in the United States have been rejected; that is, there appears to be a substantial excess demand for medical school slots. Is this evidence of monopolizing control by the medical profession? Kessel's view certainly suggests that it is.

Another View: The Donor Preference Hypothesis

This simple story of professional control can be challenged. Hall and Lindsay (1980) argue that medical schools do not take larger proportions of applicants and medical school enrollments respond only partially to applicant demand because the administrators of medical schools are responding rationally to their economic incentives. As we have seen, medical school revenues come not so much from tuition paid by students but from "donors"—that is, sources such as government agencies, alumni, businesses,

research organizations, and so on. For the most part, it is these donors who are the true demanders of the output of medical schools—trained physicians.

The donors, however, often are interested only in some of the many potential graduates—those with specific attributes in terms of personal characteristics and performance and professional goals. For example, medical schools discriminate among applicants by test scores, and they also discriminate among applicants by selecting younger ones, those with specific specialization interests, and those who indicate a willingness to return to shortage areas. These attributes reflect the preferences of the donors. In other words, to ensure that donations and financial support continue, medical schools establish a selection process to recruit the "appropriately qualified" students. Thus, the data on excess medical school applicants should not be viewed as true excess demand when we see that the true demander is the medical school donor.

In addition to providing an explanation for the apparent excess demand for medical school slots, Hall and Lindsay show that medical school enrollments rise in response to both applicant demand and the more important demand for trained physician graduates by the donors. These results tend to contradict the view that medical school enrollments are controlled by the AMA to maximize the returns to its members.

Other evidence also supports this new view. If medical schools are artificially keeping their enrollments small to benefit organized medicine, then why don't these schools also raise their tuition charges to clear the market? The fact that tuition is only a small fraction of the true cost of education tends to support the Hall and Lindsay hypothesis.

In summary, we may say that organized medicine historically exerted considerable influence over the supply of trained physicians. Such influence is consistent with a view of the profession as one seeking above-normal returns by trying to control entry of new physicians. However, data in recent decades indicate that medical school enrollments are responsive to market forces. These data further suggest that continuing to view medical education as controlled by a monolithic or conspiratorial medical profession is somewhat implausible.

Licensure and Monopoly Rents

Licensure is not unique to the health care professions. However, licensure of physicians has received unparalleled attention. The first licensure requirements (though they had little effect and were minimally enforced) for prospective doctors were passed in New York City in 1760.[6] Subsequently, many states introduced licensing, often through state medical societies. After the 1820s, however, many of the same states modified or abolished licensure. It was not until after the founding of the AMA in 1847 and the last decades of the nineteenth century that stronger licensure laws were widely promulgated.

The primary controversies with respect to licensure relate to its role in limiting competition and the role of professional societies on state licensure boards. The conventional view held by many economists is that organized medicine has used control of licensure for self-interest by limiting entry (and by influencing the licensure requirements of potential competitor providers to the advantage of physicians). Some, however, have advanced a public interest argument for licensure—that is, as a result of information imperfections, the public demands quality controls. Licensure and certification help fill these information gaps.

[6]Starr (1982, p. 44). Starr provides a fascinating history of licensure legislation in the United States.

Many economists believe that licensure and professional control over medical education ensure that physicians earn economic rents, which are payments to factors over and above those necessary to induce them to provide their services. These views were heavily influenced by the early work of Friedman and Kuznets (1945) and Kessel (1958). Friedman and Kuznets examined the relative return of physicians and dentists. After adjusting for training differentials, they estimated that about half of the 33 percent excess earnings of physicians between 1928 and 1934 represented economic rents.

Much has changed in the health industry since these earlier articles. However, the broader issues of monopoly rents and motivation for licensure remain controversial. Despite other empirical estimates supporting the rent hypotheses, several critiques of these studies have appeared. Leffler (1978) argued that many earlier studies failed to take into account some important economic considerations that tend to reduce estimates of the return. These adjustments include the high number of hours worked by physicians, their expected mortality rates, and the progressive income tax structure.[7]

A subsequent study undertaken by Burstein and Cromwell (1985) compared the internal rates of return of physicians to dentists and lawyers. The authors incorporate many adjustments into their estimates, including length of physician training, length of working life, and the earnings of medical residents. The rates of return were high compared to lawyers; for example, 12.1 percent versus 7.2 percent in 1980, the last year included in the study. The returns were high also for specialization based on board-certification requirements. This was true despite the rapid growth in physician supplies and the constraints imposed by third-party payers to contain costs over the study period. The authors concluded that "the conventional picture of medicine as a financially attractive profession is strongly confirmed" (p. 76).

This strong conclusion is further supported by a more recent and direct test of physician pricing. Seldon and colleagues (1998) examined physicians' price-cost margins, defined as $(P - MC)/P$ where P represents price and MC represents costs. Under highly competitive conditions and marginal cost pricing (i.e., where P approaches MC), the price-cost margin is zero. If physicians have monopoly power and the ability to maintain price above marginal cost, the margin will be positive. The researchers estimated the margin at 23 percent overall (and from 13 to 54 percent across the nine regional markets in the study). These estimates indicate "nontrivial" levels of monopoly power that produced a welfare loss to the U.S. economy of about $8 billion in 1996 dollars.

Public Interest or Self-Interest

The specific issue of licensure is but a part of the broader issue of regulation reflecting the two competing theories: public interest versus self-interest motives.

Public Interest and Self-Interest Theories of Regulation

The public interest motive is based on theories of market failure, such as information failure. According to the public interest view, the demand for regulatory measures, such as licensure, is due to the limited information patients have about quality and the relatively high costs of obtaining information. Drawing on Akerlof's lemons model introduced in Chapter 10, Leffler (1978) argued that asymmetric information will lower quality. Thus, a "state-enforced minimum quality standard is claimed to be an efficient response to costly quality information" (p. 173).

[7]In addition to the adjustments suggested by Leffler, Headen (1990) separated the labor from entrepreneurial returns for self-employed physicians in family practice. He found that about 16 percent of the reported incomes are associated with their entrepreneurship.

In contrast, the self-interest motives for licensure and other forms of regulation to reduce competition have long been accepted in economics but only relatively recently have been formalized (Stigler, 1971; Peltzman, 1976). In this theory, discussed in more detail in Chapter 19, regulation is a return to special interests that provide financial and political support in return for favored legislation. Thus, a demand for political favors arises from the rent-seeking behavior of special interest groups. The effort and amount of resources expended by a special interest group are limited by the rents that would accrue from the favored legislation.

Evidence of Public Interests Versus Self-Interests

Paul (1984) tested the public interest versus self-interest theories using data on the initial decisions by states to license physicians, and he rejected the public interest theory. His findings show a strong negative association between the year of initial licensure and the number of AMA-associated physicians in a state per capita.

Graddy (1991) also tested the competing hypotheses by estimating the probability (and type) of regulation by states of six health care professions. Variables representing the public interest view included the profession's educational requirements in years (to capture the complexity of the service) and professional liability insurance rates (to represent the potential risk to consumers in the absence of regulation). The legislative environment was represented by variables, such as the strength of the majority party and the rates of turnover of legislators. Variables, such as the size of the occupation and its proportion of members belonging to a professional association, represented private interests.

The statistical approach was made possible through the fact that licensure practices for many professions vary substantially across states. The professions and type of regulation across the states are summarized in Table 16-4. Graddy found important roles for each of the categories of explanatory variables in determining the kinds of regulation. She found a higher probability of a stricter form of regulation as the profession's educational requirements are higher—a finding consistent with a public interest motive. The overriding conclusion, though, is that no single dominant motive can be found for regulation. Legislators respond to organized interests, the public interest, and their own legislative environments.

Licensure and Quality

The Graddy evidence supports, in part, a public demand for regulation. We also know that physician board certification, or even board eligibility, increases remuneration,

TABLE 16-4 Number of States Regulating Occupations by Type of Regulation, 1984

Occupation	*Unregulated*	*Registration*	*Certification*	*Licensure*
Dietician	40	0	4	6
Occupational therapist	23	0	0	27
Psychologist	0	0	5	45
Social worker	17	5	3	25
Physician assistant	5	14	28	3
Nurse-midwife	8	0	17	25

Source: Reprinted from *Journal of Health Politics, Policy and Law.* Elizabeth Graddy, "Interest Groups or the Public Interest—Why Do We Regulate Health Occupations?" *Journal of Health Politics, Policy and Law 16* (1991): 25–49, with permission from Duke University.

meaning consumers are willing to pay more for those with additional training and credentials.[8]

Does licensure actually improve the quality of care? Gaumer's (1984) review of the empirical evidence questions whether the goals of protecting the public and ensuring minimal standards of competency are being achieved. He found that (1) in spite of licensure, a substantial amount of deficient care is being rendered; (2) quality of care would not be impaired if the scope of practice of secondary (nonphysician/dentist) providers were increased; (3) the licensing process may "not accurately assess the practice competence of applicants" (p. 397); and (4) fees and provider incomes are higher in states with more restrictive licensure requirements (supporting the self-interests motive for regulation).

More specifically, with respect to the quality of physician care, he cites studies indicating that 5 percent of physicians are "unfit to practice," 8 to 22 percent of obstetrics patients and 61 to 65 percent of well-care patients received deficient care, and that 7.5 percent of all cases in two hospitals indicated physician-inflicted injury (p. 395).

Brennan and colleagues (1991) provide additional evidence on the quality of medical care in hospitals. Licensure is just one of many regulatory requirements intended to ensure that standards are being met. From a large number of randomly selected admissions, the researchers found that nearly 4 percent produced "adverse events," defined as injuries caused by medical management. Nearly 14 percent of these injuries led to death. The authors concluded that "there is a substantial amount of injury to patients from medical management, and many injuries are the result of substandard care" (p. 370).

Though no one is suggesting that eliminating licensure and other requirements will reduce such negative outcomes, it is clear that regulation does not ensure quality care. The condemnation of current levels of health care quality by the Institute of Medicine (2001), and the positive reaction of both policy makers and health care leaders to it, is a clear example of the limits of regulation. Nevertheless, one could still ask whether tighter regulation would help. From his review, Gaumer concludes as follows:

> Research evidence does not inspire confidence that wide-ranging systems for regulating health professionals have served the public interest. Though researchers have not been able to observe the consequences of a totally unregulated environment, observation of incremental variations in regulatory practices generally supports the view that tighter controls do not lead to improvements in quality of service. (p. 406)

As a result of the questionable effects of licensure on quality, changes in the health care environment, and the anticompetitive effects of restrictions on entry and restrictions on the scope of practice of potential competitors (e.g., podiatrists, nurse practitioners), the benefits of licensure are being reexamined. Svorny (1992) suggests that the benefits have been weakened by, among other things, the added liability that courts have placed on hospitals and HMOs for the negligent conduct of independent physicians and by the increased use of salaried physicians. In a stronger attack, Safriet (1994) concludes:

> Clearly these barriers serve no useful purpose, and in fact contribute to our health care problems by preventing the full deployment of competent and cost-effective providers who can meet the needs of a substantial number of consumers. (p. 315)

[8]See Wilensky and Rossiter (1983).

Other Physician Labor Issues

The prominence of physicians and their dominating role in treatment decisions have led to important research on a variety of labor issues. Many are associated with physician earnings, and we examine two of these issues below.

Specialization

Studies of physician specialty selection are especially important because of widespread beliefs that quality health care requires access to an appropriate mix of specialists. Policy effort in recent years has also been directed toward encouraging more physicians to go into primary care, especially in underserved areas. Some medical schools have responded to the challenge by favoring applicants who are committed to primary care.

Economists recognize the role that nonpecuniary rewards, such as status and social responsibility, may play in decisions to specialize. Nevertheless, the economic focus is usually on the degree to which physicians respond to financial incentives. Decisions to specialize are normally made early in the physician's education and training career so Nicholson (2005) was curious about medical students and their knowledge of physician incomes. He examined surveys of first- and fourth-year students conducted annually by large medical schools and found systematic biases in the responses. The students overestimated incomes in the 1970s but underestimated incomes by about 25 percent in more recent years. The study also showed a significant learning pattern with estimates that were much more accurate for fourth-year students than for those in their first year. The estimates were also more accurate for a specialty that a student was more likely to select.

How strong is the response to earnings potential, especially in light of the wide income variations by specialty? For 2002, the U.S. Department of Labor reported average earnings of $307,000 for anesthesiologists and $255,000 for general surgeons, compared to $153,000 for pediatricians and $150,000 for family practitioners. Economic theory suggests that a rational decision ought to be based on expected lifetime income, not simply the current earnings within a specialty, and several studies indicate substantial responsiveness. Estimated elasticities of entry into specialties with respect to changes in expected lifetime earnings are usually greater than one, leaving little doubt that physicians respond to income when making their specialty decisions. Nevertheless, a recent study of specialty choice provides some unique results on differences in specialty earnings.

Bhattacharya (2005) describes four possible explanations for the wide income disparities across specializations: (1) differences in hours worked, (2) differences in length of residency and other required training, (3) difference in the attributes and skills needed to perform in a specialty, and (4) barriers to entry into some specialties. The first three possibilities which reflect competitive labor market forces account for only one-half the observed differences in lifetime earnings. He concluded that the remainder of the differences results from differential entry barriers, suggesting that some specialist fees are excessive relative to competitive fees. From a policy perspective, a strong case can be made to pressure those specialty boards that impose relatively high entry barriers in order to increase their number of residency slots.

Physician Income by Gender

Women now account for about one-half of new medical school graduates. They also represented 26 percent of professionally active physicians in 2002 compared to just 11 percent in 1980. This dramatic shift toward gender balance is likely to continue, and sociologists have eagerly studied a wide range of phenomena including the female

physician's approach to patient care relative to the male physician. Economists have focused more narrowly on labor market issues, such as differences in earnings, job status, and hours worked.

Female physicians earn less than male physicians. An annual survey conducted by *Medical Economics* indicated that female physicians earned $55,000 less than males in 2002. Among the usual reasons for the gender gap is that women are more likely to choose the lower paying specialties, and to work fewer hours than male physicians due to disproportionate burdens in raising a family. In a recent study, Sasser (2005) describes several mechanisms through which family responsibilities affect the gender gap. These include the fewer number of years in active practice that female physicians may anticipate and, thus, a reduced willingness by the female physician or her employer to invest in human capital. Greater household responsibilities could affect specialty selected and characteristics of the job environment that are sought. After controlling for specialty, practice setting, demographic and professional characteristics, Sasser finds that female physicians "earn 11 percent less for being married plus 14 percent less for having one child and 22 percent less for having more than one child." The main determinant of these earnings differences are personal choices to reduce working hours sharply upon marriage and having children.

Despite Sasser's strong conclusions, the story of the gender earnings gap remains incomplete and complex. Timothy Hoff (2004) provides a rich example using hospitalists, a relatively new specialty consisting of hospital-based general physicians who focus on the care of hospitalized patients. He found that female hospitalists earn significantly less per year than their male counterparts even after controlling for demographic, professional, and job-related characteristics. Hoff also controlled for marital status and children. Furthermore, male and female hospitalists worked similar schedules and had similar levels of commitment. Thus, he concluded that the pay gap, at least in this new specialization, is real and not due mainly to personal and career choices. Hoff urges the medical establishment and policy makers to take pay inequality seriously and to develop mechanisms to address the problem.

Conclusions

We used some basic economic tools to provide important insights into a variety of health care labor issues, including the demand and supply of labor, optimal input decisions and factor substitution and labor shortages. We examined two earnings issues as they related to specialization and the gender gap. This chapter has also addressed several aspects of medical education. In particular, we have tried to examine whether various characteristics of physician training and licensure are designed to increase barriers to entry into the profession, so as to produce higher-than-normal rates of return.

We caution that rapid restructuring of the U.S. health care system, especially through managed care and post-managed care initiatives, is creating profound changes. As previously noted, physicians are increasingly organized in or affiliated with large groups that compete for managed care contracts. The widespread purchase of physician practices by hospitals, a strategy that many hospitals have come to regret, provides another example of a dramatic change. The adoption of pay-for-performance and growth of consumer-driven health plans are other recent innovations that may have major effects on health care delivery. As a result of these developments, the economic power and professional influence of physicians have undoubtedly been affected in ways that are still largely unknown. Clearly, these represent new challenges for the health economist.

SUMMARY

1. In 2003, 13.6 million people, nearly 10 percent of all employed civilians, worked at health services sites.
2. The demand for labor is precisely the marginal revenue product of labor curve. It is closely related to the production function and is directly related to the price of the output.
3. The supply of labor tends to slope upward, implying that the higher the wage rate is in a given market, the more laborers will be forthcoming. Workers currently employed may choose to work more hours if higher wages are offered; other workers may be attracted from elsewhere by the higher wages.
4. There are basically two types of shortages: need shortages and economic shortages. Need shortages use a nonmarket, or noneconomic, definition of shortage.
5. One definition of an economic shortage is the excess of quantity demanded over the quantity supplied at the market wage rate. Stickiness in wages helps explain why the wage does not rise to equilibrium, thus, automatically eliminating the shortage.
6. Meaningful shortages of professionals may exist even when supply and demand are in short-term equilibrium. If demand for a category of health professional expands over time and supply is slow to respond, the result may be a wage increase that is large relative to wage gains of other professionals.
7. Under labor monopsony conditions, a firm may report unfilled, budgeted positions, for example, for registered nurses, even when the firm is in equilibrium. A monopsony firm may announce that it wishes to hire more nurses even though it is unlikely to take the necessary steps to do so.
8. Medical education is heavily subsidized. Tuition is a relatively small source of revenues; thus, the student pays only a small portion of the true costs of the investment in education.
9. Medical education is a good example of joint production. Medical schools produce medical education, patient care, and research.
10. Kessel argued that monopoly power was attained by organized medicine through licensure of physicians and control of access to medical education.
11. According to an alternative view of medical education, the donor-preference hypothesis, medical school revenues come not so much from tuition paid by students but from donors, such as government agencies, alumni, businesses, and research organizations. For the most part, it is these donors who demand and control the output of medical schools: trained physicians.
12. Licensure is a prominent example of the controversy of self-interest versus public interest views of regulation.
13. It is generally believed that licensure has given physicians economic rents. Licensure has not led to obvious improvements in quality.
14. There are wide differences in the earnings across physician specialties. Usual labor market explanations account for only one-half the variations, suggesting differences in barriers to entry among specialties.
15. There are also substantial gender differences in earnings. It is not yet clear whether these differences can be fully explained by the personal and professional decisions made by female physicians.

DISCUSSION QUESTIONS

1. Give examples of ways in which labor and capital can be substituted for each other in the production of health services.
2. In the text, we considered only forgone income and tuition as costs of going to medical school. Enumerate other monetary and nonmonetary opportunity costs. Why are these opportunity costs relevant?
3. Why might demand for nurse labor by hospitals or other organized health providers be monopsonistic?

4. What is the marginal product of an input? Marginal revenue product? Why does the demand for a factor correspond to the marginal revenue product curve? What will determine whether the demand for a factor will be elastic or inelastic?

5. Why will a profit-maximizing physician firm want to equalize the marginal product per dollar spent across all inputs?

6. What is meant by the term *barriers to entry*? What are some entry barriers for someone who wants to be an obstetrician? For someone who wants to be a nursing assistant?

7. If barriers to entry into a profession were absolute so that entry would not be possible, what would the supply curve look like? What would the supply curve look like if entry into an occupation were free and easy? Thus, what role do barriers to entry play in explaining relative rates of return to an occupation?

8. Define *monopsony* and *marginal labor cost*. Why is the marginal labor cost in the case of monopsony above the supply (average labor cost) curve? What is the nature of the inefficiency or misallocation associated with monopsony power? Is there any inefficiency when the supply curve facing the monopsonist is perfectly elastic?

9. It is argued that imperfect capital markets constitute one reason for subsidizing medical education. Discuss why the market for human capital differs from, say, the market for housing capital (that is, buying a house).

10. If there were no subsidies for medical education, would classes be larger or smaller? Would the return to medical education be larger or smaller? If physician education was not subsidized, would the economically warranted supply of physicians tend to emerge?

11. What are the social benefits and costs behind regulating the number of medical schools?

12. What is joint production? What does the term *joint production costs* mean? Given that medical schools engage in joint production of education, patient care, and research, what inferences can be drawn about the economies of scope in producing these three outputs?

13. In contrast to medical education, numerous night and part-time law schools have been established. Compare and contrast the various aspects of training that have led to these different educational systems.

14. What are some factors that help explain earnings differences across specialties? Why might the earnings differences persist over long periods of time?

15. The rate of return on investment in medical education exceeds that for other professions. What are arguments for and against government subsidies?

16. Female physicians earn considerably less than their male counterparts. Discuss some of the reasons that account for the differences? What kind of evidence would lead one to conclude that at least some of the difference is due to bias or discrimination?

EXERCISES

1. Consider the firm's demand (MRP) for labor, such as in Figure 16–2. If the demand elasticity is –0.5, what will be the effect of increased wages on total labor earnings?

2. Using Figure 16–3, graph and analyze the impact of an increase in the price of lab tests on the labor market.

3. Consider the market for highly skilled laboratory technicians. Graph the impacts on market wages if limitations on immigration were lifted. Would more or fewer services be provided? What would happen to the price?

4. In this chapter, we discuss how physicians' marginal products rise up to 25 hours and then slowly fall to zero at 110 hours. Graph both marginal and total products from this statement.

5. Using supply-and-demand analysis, model the equilibrium level of physicians' incomes. What would be the impact on physicians' incomes of more stringent policies on the employment of foreign medical school graduates?

6. Suppose that a medical school provides three outputs—patient care, education, and research—and that the total cost of the school is $100 million per year. If the school produced only education, its costs would be $60 million. If the school produced only patient care, its

costs would be $30 million. If it produced only research, the costs would be $20 million. Joint costs for each pair would be $10 million.

a. What are the pure costs of education, patient care, and research?

b. What are the joint costs?

7. Suppose that the licensure requirements for health care providers were eliminated. Use supply-and demand analysis to predict what may happen to the price and quantity of health care services. Are there other considerations—in particular, mechanisms—that could evolve to replace licensure?

CHAPTER 17

The Pharmaceutical Industry

Prescription drugs and the pharmaceutical industry occupy increasingly important places in the health economy. Drug therapies traditionally have supplemented nutrition, sanitation, and medical care as methods for preserving health. Vaccinations for diseases such as smallpox represented early public health initiatives that saved many lives. Insulin, developed in the 1920s, prevented the certain deaths that once accompanied diabetes, and a world without antibiotics, introduced in the 1940s, or the polio vaccination, in the 1950s, would be unthinkable.

Today, drugs are used to treat many diseases and conditions. Examples include chemotherapy for cancer, steroids for skin diseases, psychotropic drugs for mental health problems, beta-blockers for heart disease, clot busters for stroke, and protease inhibitors for AIDS. Some of these drugs represent alternatives to more invasive surgical procedures. Others are used in conjunction with surgical and radiation treatments. Still others provide treatment for conditions where no treatment was available previously.

Despite these successes, the U.S. pharmaceutical industry has come under intense media and legislative scrutiny. Pharmaceutical firms are among the largest and most profitable businesses in the United States. Led by Pfizer, with sales of $52.9 billion, five pharmaceutical firms ranked in the top 100 on the *Fortune* list of largest firms in 2004. The profit performance of the pharmaceutical industry is even more striking. As recently as 2001, it ranked first in rates of return on revenues, assets, and stockholders' equity. Despite negative publicity, litigation problems, widespread efforts to contain drug spending, and loss of patent protection for several major drugs since then (see Box 17-1), pharmaceuticals in 2004 still ranked third, twelfth, and thirteenth, respectively, among *Fortune*'s 47 industry groupings on these three measures of financial performance.

With prescription drug spending rising more quickly than spending for other health care products, the industry is a convenient target for the budgetary challenges

facing patients and insurers. The introduction of new and expensive drugs, increasingly promoted through direct marketing to consumers, has only added to the expenditure burden and heightened criticism of the industry.

This burden becomes especially severe for those who suffer disproportionately from chronic and other conditions that fuel the use of drugs. Policies to deal with these pressures include the recent expansion of Medicare (Part D) to include outpatient prescription drug benefits (see Chapter 21), and proposals to regulate prices as well as to permit the reimportation of drugs from Canada and other countries. Private insurance initiatives include higher patient copayments, increased emphasis on generic products, and new strategies, such as the development of drug formularies. Formularies, approved lists of drugs, were adopted by most managed care plans by the late 1990s. The patient may have difficulty in obtaining reimbursement for any drugs that are not on the list.

BOX 17-1

An Image Crisis: Does the Pharmaceutical Industry Need an Extreme Makeover?

The pharmaceutical industry has a long history of superior financial performance, but are the good times coming to an end? The industry appears to be suffering from a serious credibility gap associated with the withdrawal of Merck's painkiller Vioxx and from controversies regarding the safety and efficacy of widely used antidepressants and other products including hormonal replacement therapies for menopausal women.

All this could not be coming at a worse time for the industry. Third-party payers are renewing efforts to promote generics or to substantially increase copayments for brand-name products. In an extreme example of the changes that are taking place, state workers in Georgia face copays of $100 for certain brand-name products, such as the antidepressant Zoloft. By 2007, patent protection will expire for some leading sellers, including Zocor and Provachol, the widely prescribed cholesterol-lowering drugs, and Norvasc, a blood pressure medication. These three drugs alone generate nearly $10 billion in annual sales.

In the current climate of suspicion, it may be more difficult to find new "blockbusters" to replace existing best sellers. The FDA appears less likely to approve new products if there are significant side effects and if there are current therapies that are good. Also, with growing perceptions that drug makers have not been forthcoming about the risks of their products, some experts suggest that direct-to-consumer advertising no longer has the kind of sales impact that it once had.

As a result of the diminished outlook for future earnings, share prices for many of the top firms dropped on average about 25 percent between 2000 and 2005. Several companies announced layoffs as well as cuts in their research budgets. Merck, which was hit especially hard, unveiled plans in 2005 to reduce its worldwide labor force by 11 percent and to close or sell 5 of its 31 manufacturing facilities. But can Merck and the industry rebound? The *New York Times* interviewed an industry spokesperson who argued that it was "addressing its image crisis by being more careful with its advertising, by pledging more disclosure of clinical trial results and by working to make low-priced drugs available to poor and uninsured Americans." With enormous resources and lobbying clout (consider the absence of price controls in the recent Medicare drug benefit legislation), the industry's ability to rebound should not be underestimated.

SOURCES: Alex Berenson, "Big Drug Makers See Sales Decline with Their Image," *New York Times*, November 14, 2005, www.nytimes.com/2005/11/14/business/14pharma.html; Leila Abboud, "Stung by Public Distrust, Drug Makers Seek to Heal Image," *Wall Street Journal*, August 26, 2005, p. B1; Barbara Martinez, "Drug Co-Pays Hit $100," *Wall Street Journal*, June 27, 2005, p. D1.

Pharmacoeconomics, which includes cost-benefit, cost-effectiveness, and cost-utility analyses, plays an increasingly important role in pharmaceutical decisions, but policy must address other questions. Of the many possible issues, this chapter selects several of more general interest to health economists. After describing the structure and regulation of the pharmaceutical industry, we focus on the following areas:

1. The role of pharmaceutical products in the production of health, patient choices of drugs under various insurance schemes, and the effects of technological change on the use of drugs
2. Drug pricing issues, including price discrimination by sellers and price regulation by the government
3. Pharmaceutical research and the determinants of innovation
4. Cost containment through use of generic products and other measures

We conclude with recent evidence on the effects of drugs on health derived from international comparisons on drug utilization.

Structure and Regulation

In 2003, spending on prescription drugs amounted to $179 billion or 10.7 percent of national health expenditures, up from 8.5 percent just four years earlier and 4.9 percent in 1980 (Smith et al., 2005). The growth rate in prescription drug spending in 2003 was also 10.7 percent. Although this was the lowest growth rate since 1997, it marked the ninth consecutive year of double-digit increases. Consumers' out-of-pocket costs for drugs represented 30 percent of total spending on drugs, and accounted for 23 percent of all out-of-pocket costs—more than any other health spending category. With their growing share of a growing total amount, some large third-party payers have reported that their reimbursements for drugs exceed their reimbursements for physician services. Even though most of the increases in drug spending have been due to greater use of drugs and to new products rather than to higher prices of existing products, these spending increases help create public perceptions that something is seriously wrong with the conduct of pharmaceutical firms, and that stiff measures are needed to contain drug costs.

With its long history of relatively high profits and rich set of features—patent protection, high research and development spending, intense product promotion, and heavy regulation—the pharmaceutical industry always has drawn the attention of economists in the field of industrial organization. Scholars describe levels of competition in an industry; how the competitive environment influences decisions on prices and other decision variables, such as advertising, research and development (R&D), and quality; and the consequences of these decisions for socially efficient allocations of resources.

Competition

The level of competition usually holds the key to firm and industry behavior. Economists measure competition within the standard industrial classification (SIC) developed by the U.S. Department of Commerce to categorize firms into meaningful industry and product groups. The SIC codes range from two to seven digits, with each successive digit representing a finer degree of classification. The "pharmaceutical preparations" industry, Code 2834, is formally defined as "establishments primarily engaged in manufacturing, fabricating, or processing drugs in pharmaceutical preparations for human or veterinary use."

TABLE 17-1 Concentration in Selected Manufacturing Industries: 1992

SIC	Industry	C_4	C_8	HHI	N	Shipments (in $ billions)
2834	Pharmaceutical preparations	26	42	341	583	50.4
2043	Cereal breakfast foods	85	98	2,253	42	9.8
2841	Soaps and detergents	63	77	1,584	635	14.8
2851	Paints	29	43	305	1,129	15.0
2911	Petroleum refining	30	49	414	131	136.6
3571	Computer and office equipment	45	59	680	803	38.2
3674	Semiconductors	41	58	541	823	32.1
3711	Passenger cars	84	91	2,676	398	151.7
3721	Aircraft and parts	79	93	2,717	151	62.9
3861	Photographic equipment	78	83	2,408	832	22.1

Source: U.S. Bureau of the Census, "Concentration Ratios in Manufacturing," *1992 Census of Manufacturers*, Report MC92-S-2.

The four-firm (C_4) and eight-firm (C_8) concentration ratios for any selected four-digit SIC codes indicate the share of industry output produced by the four or eight largest firms. Analysts use these concentration ratios, shown in Table 17-1 for pharmaceuticals and several other industries, to gauge competition. The pharmaceutical industry is one of the largest and most rapidly growing manufacturing industries. As measured by concentration ratios, it also appears to be much more competitive than many industries.

Another method used to measure competition is the Herfindahl-Hirschman Index (HHI). Compare an industry with four firms, each with 25 percent of the market, to a second industry, also with four firms, but where one firm has 85 percent of the market and the other three each have 5 percent. Both industries have a four-firm concentration ratio of 100 percent. However, one might guess that the one in which the leading firm has 85 percent of the market is more monopolized. The HHI incorporates differences in the size distribution of firms by squaring the market shares of each and adding them together so that the lowest value approaches 0 (thousands of tiny firms) and the highest value approaches 10,000 (with a pure monopoly). In the previous example, the respective HHIs are 2,500 and 7,300.

Table 17-1 shows that compared to other well-known industries, in addition to relatively low concentration ratios, there are a relatively large number of firms (N) and the HHI is relatively low. Do these data indicate substantial competition? Most analysts would argue that for pharmaceuticals they could be especially misleading. Drugs in different therapeutic categories usually are not substitutes for each other. Concentration ratios for narrower drug classes are better indicators. When such data are available, they still can show considerable competition. In many cases, however, the concentration ratios will be higher, sometimes much higher. Schweitzer (1996) illustrates this with a class of drugs used to control hypertension. The top four firms controlled 91 percent of the market in 1992. Why? Patents and other barriers to entry often restrict competition.

Barriers to Entry

A barrier to entry is any factor that impedes the entry of new firms into an industry or product market. Patent protection granted by government represents a classic example. To gain further protection, pharmaceutical firms adopt a common business strategy of surrounding a product with patents on many variations of that product.

A patent forms a legal barrier. Advertising and promotion also can create economic barriers when they successfully increase brand loyalty. Pharmaceutical promotion differs from that of typical consumer goods because pharmaceutical firms direct much of their marketing at physicians rather than patients, the end users through "detailers" who directly visit physicians' offices. Critics of this practice believe that detailing may lead to questionable financial arrangements that encourage the physician to prescribe a particular product, possibly in place of a cheaper drug or nondrug substitutes.

Pharmaceutical firms also reach physicians by distributing samples, by direct mail, and by advertising in medical journals. Following the FDA's relaxation of rules governing advertisements through the media in 1997, the industry responded by increasing advertising in newspapers, on radio, on television, and even on freeway billboards, all aimed directly at patients. It is too early to evaluate the effects of these forms of promotion, but some physicians have raised questions about the misinformation and confusion created by the ads.

As a last example of protection from competition, the regulation of drugs itself can create entry barriers. The Food and Drug Administration (FDA) approval process for a new drug is costly and time-consuming. A new firm will find it difficult to marshal the financial and expert resources needed to go through the process and especially to have a portfolio of products under development to spread risks. Only 1 of about 5,000 to 10,000 chemical compounds screened ultimately is approved as a drug, and of those reaching the market stage, only 3 of 10 products ever become profitable.[1] Not surprisingly, such odds (3 in 50,000–100,000 chemical compounds) create formidable deterrence to new drug development, and new pharmaceutical firms often concentrate on generic products.

Regulation

The pharmaceutical industry is one of the most heavily regulated of all industries. Governments regulate most firms for worker safety and health concerns, but pharmaceutical products are subject to further oversight by the FDA. Following a public scandal over adulterated food products and dangerous medicines with unknown contents, the federal government introduced the Food and Drug Act of 1906. The act did nothing to prevent the public from dangerous medicines. It did not even require formal testing but dealt mainly with labeling. Requirements for testing and safety were introduced with the Federal Food, Drug, and Cosmetic Act of 1938. However, these requirements were left mainly to the drug companies.

Two events accelerated regulatory change. Exposure of questionable drug industry practices in hearings held by Senator Kefauver in 1959 was soon followed by the thalidomide tragedy. Thalidomide, a tranquilizer widely used in Europe to treat morning sickness in pregnancy, was discovered to cause severe defects in babies, who were sometimes born with deformed, flipper-like limbs. The drug was available on an experimental basis in the United States at the time. Fortunately for the United States, the number of thalidomide babies was relatively small. The FDA delayed approval, and the distributor withdrew the product quickly after reports of the European experience.[2]

Although the thalidomide tragedy was averted in the United States, Congress nonetheless approved amendments in 1962 giving the FDA considerably more control over the introduction of new products. The new legislation required much more testing

[1] See PhRMA (2005) and Grabowski and Vernon (1994).

[2] Thalidomide still is marketed with a warning on pregnancy. Interest is growing in its use to treat bone cancer, inflammatory diseases, and autoimmune disorders for patients with advanced AIDS.

and extended the FDA's authority to regulate premarket testing (including generic drugs). Equally important, the legislation for the first time required evidence of efficacy.[3]

FDA review has become a lengthy, complex process. Following the discovery stage during which new chemicals are synthesized, the firm conducts preclinical animal studies involving short-term toxicity and safety tests. The drug firm next must file an application with the FDA to conduct clinical trials. If approved, the trials are conducted in three phases. Phase I begins with small groups of healthy volunteers and focuses on safety and dosage. Phase II trials involve a larger number of subjects, often several hundred, who have the targeted condition, and concentrates on the drug's efficacy.[4] Stage III trials usually are conducted on thousands of patients in different settings so that safety and efficacy can be determined more precisely.

If these trials indicate safety and efficacy, and the drug's safety is supported by long-term animal studies, the company submits a New Drug Application (NDA) containing all the data and results to the FDA. The FDA review usually takes more than a year. Total development time for a new product stands at about 14 years, nearly double the eight-year period in the 1960s (DiMasi, 2001).

These requirements provoke considerable controversy and provide obvious trade-offs between the goals of protecting the consumer and rapid innovation. The economic approach is to weigh the gains in safety and efficacy against the cost of delaying patients from utilizing useful products. Economists also are concerned about the potential stifling of innovation caused by regulation and its adverse effects on competition.

In a classic study of the 1962 amendments, Peltzman (1974) found a sharp decline in new product development, especially of innovative drugs, after 1962, as well as higher prices from the decreased competition. These consequences far outweighed the benefits of reduced spending on ineffective drugs, creating a net welfare loss of about 6 percent of total drug sales.

The FDA recognized these problems and in the mid-1970s developed policies to accelerate the review of "important" drugs. Dranove and Meltzer (1994) found that important drugs reach the market about three years sooner than other drugs. Thus, they argue that the losses resulting from delays in the approval process have been overestimated. A 1984 act also eliminated the full range of tests for generic products that were required by the 1962 amendments.[5]

The Production of Health and Substitutability

We have seen that spending on prescription drugs is increasing rapidly and that drug firms have some monopoly power. Before examining how that power is exercised, we turn to the role of prescription drugs in producing health and their relationship to other medical inputs using the concept of a health production function.

Recall that the patient's demand for health leads to a demand for health inputs such as drugs and medical care. Consider the following production function for a

[3]The legislation also gave the FDA authority over the manufacturing process and extended testing requirements to include generic drugs and drugs that are similar to available products ("me-too" drugs). It also transferred regulation of drug advertising for prescription products from the Federal Trade Commission to the FDA.

[4]The terms *efficacy* or *effective*, as used by the FDA, mean that a drug has positive effects compared to a placebo. Efficacy does not imply that the product is cost-effective or that it meets other economic criteria for efficiency.

[5]To expedite the review process, 1992 legislation and the Modernization Act of 1997 provide the FDA with additional resources derived from user fees levied on the industry. This has considerably reduced approval times.

patient with chronic and severe low-back pain—one of the most common reasons for physician office visits and hospitalization:

$$HS = f(D, M) \qquad (17.1)$$

where HS represents the individual's health status in the current period, D represents prescription drugs, and M represents all other medical inputs in this period, given existing technology and medical know-how. If no drugs or medical inputs are applied, the patient might experience considerable pain and be unable to perform many normal tasks, including work.

Assume that this patient's health can be improved by medical intervention. Suppose an individual consumes the amount of drugs, D_1, and the amount of other medical inputs, M_1, as noted at point E of Figure 17-1. How do the drugs and the medical inputs substitute for each other?

Figure 17-1 shows three different effects of drug products and their relationship to other medical inputs. Isoquant 1 shows that drugs (e.g., narcotic analgesics or muscle relaxants) must be used in a fixed proportion to other inputs (e.g., physical therapy, counseling, and surgery in some cases). Here, inputs D and M are perfect complements with no substitutability between them.

At the other extreme, Isoquant 2 reflects a production function where inputs are perfect substitutes: The marginal rate of technical substitution (MRTS) is constant, meaning that drugs substitute for the other inputs at a constant rate. (Depending on the prices of each, a patient would use one or the other, but not both.) Finally, the solid portion of Isoquant 3 reflects an intermediate situation where D and M can substitute for each other, but where the MRTS is diminishing. Fewer and fewer amounts of M are needed to substitute for a unit increase in D as more drugs are used.

It seems unlikely that D and M are either perfect complements or perfect substitutes. Many conditions are likely to involve some substitutability, although its extent

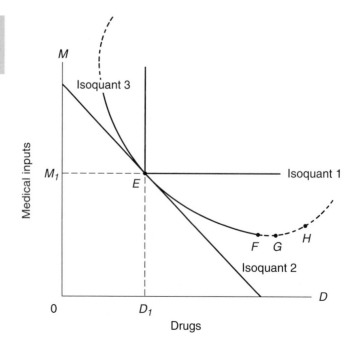

FIGURE 17-1
Substitution Between Drugs and Other Medical Inputs

may vary widely among conditions and even patients. Pharmacological and other clinical studies must determine not only substitutability, but also the "uneconomic" portions of an isoquant, meaning those combinations that never should be selected.

Such combinations arise when additions of D over some range (e.g., dashed segment FG) will not benefit or harm the patient. Here, the marginal product of D is zero and the isoquant becomes horizontal. It is also possible that increases in D beyond some point may harm the patient and require more medical intervention to maintain the same health status. In this region (arc GH), the isoquant will become positively sloped. Similar logic may apply to the vertical portion of an isoquant with increases in M. Patients will not want to be in the regions shown by the dashed segments.

Least-Cost Production

How will the patients and their providers choose? To abstract from the many possible levels of health that might be attained, as well as the inherent uncertainty of medical practice, assume that the patient/provider believes that it is reasonable to attain HS_1 in Figure 17-2. The rational patient seeks to find the combination of D and M on HS_1 that minimizes spending. Without insurance coverage for either D or M, the total cost (C) of care can be written as:

$$C = P_D D + P_M M$$

or,

$$M = C/P_M - (P_D/P_M)D \qquad\qquad \textbf{(17.2)}$$

where D and M are quantities of drugs and other inputs, and P_D and P_M are their respective prices. If, for example, $P_D = \$50$ and $P_M = \$100$, the slope of the budget line in equation (17.2) is -0.5.

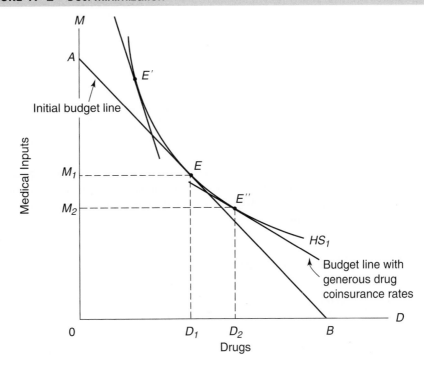

FIGURE 17-2 Cost Minimization

The cost-minimizing combination is shown at E, where the isoquant, HS_1, is tangent to the budget line, AB. The optimal inputs are shown by D_1 and M_1, and total spending is given by these quantities multiplied by their respective prices. At E, the numerical slope of the budget ($P_D/P_M = 0.5$) equals the MRTS, the slope of the isoquant. Suppose, for example, that $D_1 = 4$ and $M_1 = 6$, so total costs for HS_1 equal:

$$\text{Costs} = \$50 \times 4 + \$100 \times 6 = \$800$$

If prescription prices increase above $50, the budget line will become steeper and the rational patient will try to substitute more medical care by moving to the left on the isoquant to a point such as E' (and vice versa to E'' if medical care prices increase).

Insurance and Substitutability

Assume now that like most Americans the patient has insurance coverage. Begin with a policy that covers a constant proportion (e.g., 80 percent) of spending on either D or M. Out-of-pocket patient costs are $10 for each prescription (20 percent of $50) and $20 for a medical visit (20 percent of $100). Because the slope of the patient's budget line does not change, the optimal choice remains at point E, and the patient continues to buy four units of drugs and six visits. Total drug costs will continue to be minimized with the patient paying 20 percent ($160) and the insurer paying 80 percent ($640) of the $800 total bill.

However, D and M often are not treated uniformly under traditional health insurance. Consider a policy that pays 80 percent of medical costs but requires a deductible of only $5 (copayment) for each prescription. The patient's drug price is the $5 deductible regardless of the actual price of the medication. If the patient's out-of-pocket drug costs diminish, the numerical slope of the cost-minimizing budget line diminishes (in our example, it is now $5 \div \$20 = 0.25$). The patient will have an incentive to substitute D for M at E''. Continuing the example, let D_2 increase from 4 to 5, and M_2 fall from 6 to 5.75.

The patient's cost burden diminishes from $160 to $140 or:

$$(5.75 \text{ visits} \times \$100/\text{visit} \times 0.2 \text{ coinsurance rate}) + (5 \text{ units of drugs} \times \$5/\text{unit})$$

However, the total cost of care (patient plus insurer) increases from $800 to $825. We know this is true because we already determined that E is the least costly combination to provide HS_1. Similarly, if prescription prices (to the insurer) increase, say to $100, the patient still pays $5 and will remain at E'' with the insurer picking up the increased drug costs. Patients have no incentive to economize by making substitutions and moving toward E. The higher the prescription price, the greater the distortion.

A similar distortion toward excessive levels of M and greater total costs is created when the patient's coverage excludes or limits drug benefits. Here, the savings from the reduced M will more than offset the additional drug spending from improved drug coverage.

Technological Change

A new category of experimental drugs, blood vessel inhibitors, is generating extraordinary excitement in the medical community by fighting both cancer and heart disease. Technology often is associated with such major breakthroughs. More often, however, new drugs are similar to existing drugs, but they may produce somewhat better outcomes (if only for some patients) or reduced side effects.

FIGURE 17-3 Technological Change

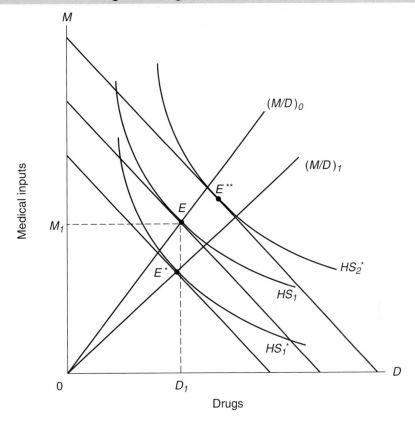

With technological improvements fewer inputs are needed to produce a given health outcome, or outcomes that were previously unattainable are now attainable. For example, begin with HS_1 in Figure 17-3 and let HS_1^* represent all combinations of inputs with a new drug that led to the same health status as HS_1. If the cost-minimizing ratio of inputs at a given price ratio remains unchanged, so that it lies along the ray OE (denoted $(M/D)_0$), the innovation would represent a neutral technological change. As drawn, the new drug saves a relatively high amount of the medical input at any given price ratio. That is, drug utilization increases relative to medical care as the patient moves to E^* and substitutes D for M. As noted in the figure, the lower ratio of M to D is reflected in the less steeply sloped ray, $(M/D)_1$.

New technology can increase costs for two reasons. First, it can routinely provide health levels that were unattainable previously (e.g., HS_2^* at point E^{**}). It may require much more drug use and possibly increased use of M, as well. When health improvements are dramatic or when drugs treat serious conditions that were not treatable previously, cost concerns are likely to be far less troublesome than those leading to only marginal improvements in health.

The second cost pressure comes from insurance. As we have seen, a patient with a constant copayment will be insulated from any price increases of the new drug. Assume that the slope of the budget line in Figure 17-3 reflects the patient's copayment of $5 and the patient moves from E to E^*. If the price of the new drug is high enough, the total cost of care at E^* could be substantially higher than total costs at the original equilibrium at E.

For conventional goods, where the consumer pays the entire price out-of-pocket, such technological changes will not be introduced because they will not be demanded. With insurance, the determination and elimination of cost-inefficient technology are far more difficult. A cost-inefficient drug might be marketed successfully simply because it is more convenient for the patient to reduce other services and take more medications at E^*.

Drug Pricing and Profits

Drug pricing and profitability undoubtedly generate the strongest reactions among the public and the media. News reports paint pharmaceutical companies as exploiting patients through patents and other strategies that reduce competition. Many studies have found that pharmaceutical profits, as reported in financial statements, are consistently among the highest of all industries. Table 17-2 illustrates a study that compared 14 major industry groups. The pharmaceutical industry had the highest rate of return on equity—double the average—during the period 1980 to 1993.

This dramatic difference often is attributed to monopoly power, but the profit picture is far less clear. Conventional accounting methods treat R&D and advertising and promotion as current expenses even though, like physical investment, they provide returns in future years. Expensing can be thought of as an extreme form of accelerated depreciation in that all of the "R&D capital" is used up in one year. It raises rates of return by reducing taxes. When Clarkson made adjustments to capitalize and depreciate these "investments," the industry's return remained higher than average (13.3 percent versus 10.2 percent) as shown in Table 17-2, but it was well below the highest (22.5 percent for computer software).

TABLE 17-2 Accounting and Corrected Rates of Return on Equity for Selected Industries, 1980–1993

Industry	Accounting	Corrected
Foods	17.58	14.95
Paper	9.20	8.92
Chemicals	13.43	8.46
Pharmaceuticals	24.37	13.27
Petroleum	22.03	15.81
Rubber products	12.45	9.05
Ferrous metals	−6.77	−2.91
Engines	9.22	8.26
Office machines	3.57	7.47
Electrical machines	12.26	9.93
Motor vehicles	0.07	1.54
Aerospace	10.65	9.06
Computer software	22.05	22.56
Entertainment	5.49	5.66
Average	12.32	10.19

Source: Kenneth W. Clarkson, "The Effects of Research and Promotion on Rates of Return" in Robert B. Helms (ed.) *Competitive Strategies in the Pharmaceutical Industry*, Washington, DC: AEI Press, 1996, with permission.

Others argue that if drug R&D is riskier than other types of investments, a higher rate of return is needed to attract capital into the industry. Without trying to sort through all the measurement nuances, it seems reasonable to conclude that pharmaceutical firms earn above normal rates of return but that their profitability has been exaggerated by simple accounting comparisons.

Monopoly Pricing

We begin with a firm selling a single product (or a composite of products) at a uniform price to all buyers. Figure 17-4 shows the demand and cost conditions facing the firm. Demand is a negatively sloped curve for several reasons. Even though patients with fixed copayments are insulated from higher prices and will have a perfectly inelastic demand, others have more limited coverage or no drug coverage at all. Patients with limited (or no) coverage will likely substitute generic or over-the-counter products as a drug's price increases. Some may reduce utilization by not complying with the medication regimen. The firm also must consider purchasing decisions by managed care organizations and other large buyers, such as hospitals, which can be sensitive to price changes.

On the cost side, the marginal cost of manufacturing and distributing the product is usually relatively low—about half the total cost. R&D and various promotion costs are substantial. In Figure 17-4, we show the marginal cost (MC) as constant and the average cost (AC), due to high fixed costs of R&D and promotion, as a downward-sloping curve. The profit-maximizing output occurs where MC equals MR, resulting in P_M and

FIGURE 17-4 Drug Pricing

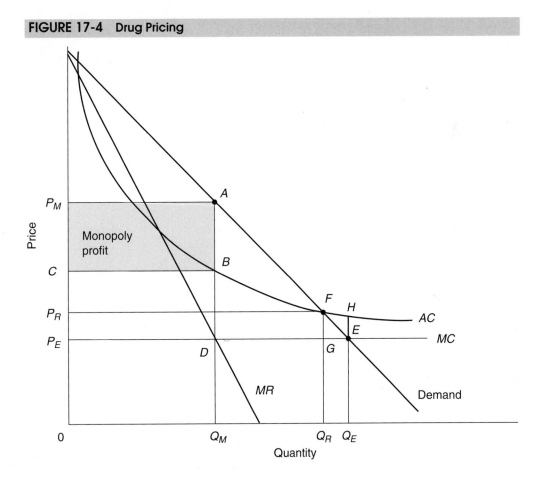

Q_M. Assuming that economic profits are earned, the price must lie above average cost. Economic profits are shown by the shaded rectangle P_MABC. Consistent with the hypothesized demand and cost structures, the gap between price and the low marginal cost will be large.

The profit-maximizing model also predicts that the difference between price and marginal cost will vary inversely with the elasticity of demand. Lu and Comanor (1998) examined pricing decisions on new products, and their findings support profit-maximization. Initial (launch) prices are considerably higher for products that represent large, therapeutic gains than prices for new "me-too" drugs that are similar to available products. Why? Demand will be relatively inelastic for a product that provides significant benefits as compared to other products. Launch prices are also much higher when few branded substitutes exist. This factor similarly reduces a product's demand elasticity and requires a higher price for profit maximization.

Price Discrimination

A firm may be able to increase profits beyond the level described in Figure 17-4. One of the most interesting features of the pharmaceutical industry is third-degree price discrimination or market segmentation where different groups of buyers are charged different prices. News stories abound about Americans flocking to Mexico, where prices are much lower, to buy drugs. Hospitals or managed care groups often are charged less than retail pharmacies, and prices for drugs used in veterinary medicine can be much lower than prices for similar products packaged for human use.

What accounts for the wide variations in price? One explanation is straightforward. If a firm can distinguish between markets with different demand characteristics and limit arbitrage (third-party resale at lower prices in higher-priced markets), it can increase profits by charging different prices. Assume, for simplicity, that the firm described in Figure 17-4 sells only in the United States and Mexico. In Figure 17-5, its total demand is separated into the U.S. and Mexican demands. With higher incomes and better insurance, the demand is relatively inelastic in the United States. Assume

FIGURE 17-5 Price Discrimination

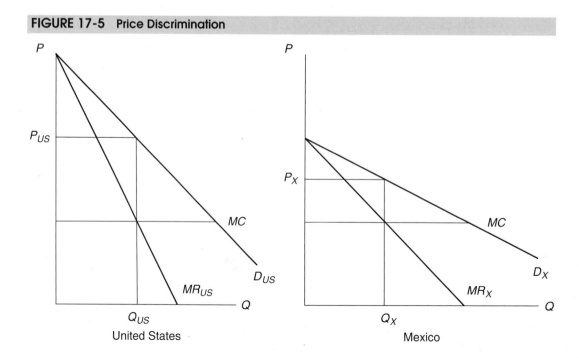

further that the marginal costs of production and distribution remain constant and are equal in both countries, and that prices are not regulated in either market.

Profit maximization occurs where *MR* equals *MC* in each market, resulting in quantities Q_{US} and Q_X. Even though marginal revenue will be equal in the United States and Mexico, the price is higher in the market with the less-elastic demand (United States). Total profits must be greater than those obtained under uniform pricing.[6]

Behavior Other Than Profit-Maximizing Behavior

Pharmaceutical firms sometimes face constraints, including governments that regulate prices or rates of return and large buyers with market power to negotiate quantity discounts (as described later). However, even in the absence of such constraints, a firm will not always try to maximize profits, at least in the short run. Despite patent protection and high development costs, an extraordinary return on a product may encourage other firms to try to develop a better or less expensive substitute. An incumbent producer will recognize this incentive and sometimes engage in strategies to deter entry. Under limit pricing, a firm reduces its price to a level that makes it less attractive for a potential entrant.

The negative publicity associated with unusually high prices also may temper a firm's behavior. A prominent case involved the public outcry over the prices charged by Burroughs Wellcome (now part of GlaxoSmithKline) for AZT—the first promising treatment for AIDS. Because full-blown AIDS cases cause almost-certain death, the demand curve for an AIDS cure would be very price-inelastic. Hence, our earlier analyses suggest that a profit-maximizing firm could charge a considerable markup over marginal cost. Following considerable pressure from activist organizations, Burroughs Wellcome reduced prices below the $8,000 needed for a year's treatment (Hansen, 1996). Nevertheless, the firm put itself and the pricing practices of the entire pharmaceutical research industry under a spotlight. Critics proposed price caps, using AZT and other new drug treatments costing thousands of dollars as symbols of greed. As noted in Chapter 24, competition from generic drugs in 2000 and 2001 reduced prices to less than $1,000.

Monopsony Pricing and Price Controls

Price discrimination is not the only possible explanation for price differentials. Prices in some foreign countries can be lower because their governments regulate prices or their national health plan serves as a monopsony buyer. Continuing with Figure 17-5, suppose that the Mexican government imposes price controls. Conceptually, it can drive price as low as the marginal cost, further increasing the price differential with the United States. Critics charge that by failing to control prices in a similar manner, consumers in the United States bear the burden of the development costs and that the United States subsidizes other countries.

Proposals have been made to limit prices in the United States or even to treat pharmaceutical firms as regulated utilities. Return to Figure 17-4. It is theoretically possible to reduce price to P_R, raising quantity to Q_R, and enabling the firm to just

[6]A convenient formula for profit maximization is:

$$P = \frac{MC}{\left[1 + \dfrac{1}{E_p}\right]}$$

where E_p is the algebraic value of the price elasticity of demand. With the same *MC* in both markets, price must be higher when demand is less elastic (e.g., -2 versus -4).

cover its costs and earn a normal rate of return. However, the administrative complexity of regulating prices of multiproduct firms that are continuously introducing new products is enormous. Consider just the variations of a single product available in different strengths, forms (tablet, liquid), and delivery systems (oral, intravenous, patch, inhaler). In addition, Abbott (1995) found that pharmaceutical firms often set much higher introductory prices under regulation.

The complexity and potential perverse effects of regulation prompt many analysts to conclude that cost containment is better left to private initiatives. They also worry about the damaging effects of price or rate-of-return controls on innovation. Both topics will be covered later in this chapter.

Competition and Generic Entry

Once a patent expires, other firms can enter the market. Entry barriers are considerably lower than those for new product development, and the 1984 Drug Price Competition and Patent Restoration Act further eased requirements. The act replaced the safety and efficacy testing under the 1962 amendments with much less costly bioequivalence tests. If approved, the FDA certifies a generic as "therapeutically equivalent" to the branded version. The new legislation has greatly increased generic applications, and as one would expect, firms target those markets with the greatest opportunities. These are large markets and those where drugs are used to treat chronic conditions (Bae, 1997).

What happens to prices and market shares after generic entry? Wiggins and Maness (2004) recently estimated an 83 percent drop in prices of anti-infectives (e.g., penicillins, tetracyclines) as the number of sellers increases from 1 to between 6 and 15, with further drops in price as more firms enter the market. This conventional finding on the impact of entry runs counter to a more complex story that had been developed for pharmaceutical pricing. Previously, Grabowski and Vernon (1992) examined 18 drugs that first experienced generic competition after the 1984 act. Generics captured one-half of their markets within two years. Surprisingly, though, as generic prices were falling, brand producers were raising theirs and widening the price gap over time. This phenomenon, corroborated by Frank and Salkever (1997), suggested that generics are not viewed as close substitutes by some patients or their providers. Pioneer firms can retain some monopoly power by capitalizing on the brand loyalty and relatively inelastic demand of this group. That is, as generics siphon off price-sensitive patients, the price-insensitive ones are left. The pioneer takes advantage of this market segmentation by raising brand-name prices for its loyal customers. (Pioneers can even introduce their own generic versions to compete in the generic segment.) We will return to the demand for generic substitutes in the section on cost containment.

R&D and Innovation

Domestic R&D expenditures for research-based pharmaceutical firms rose from $1.5 billion in 1980 to nearly $31 billion in 2004 (PhRMA, 2005). Another $8.2 billion was spent abroad. Over the same period, the share of domestic sales devoted to domestic R&D increased from 13.1 to 18.8 percent, the highest ratio among all major industries. Firms would not undertake these investments unless they could gain protection for their work. The patent system provides one method for providing protection.

A patent gives the holder the right "to exclude others from making, using, or selling the invention." The usual term for a patent is 20 years, but there are exceptions for drug products. To partially offset the delays posed by the long testing and regulatory

review period, the Drug Price Competition and Patent Restoration Act of 1984 allows extensions for up to 5 years so long as the total effective patent life does not exceed 14 years. A year earlier, Congress also passed the Orphan Drug Act, permitting extensions (and providing other benefits) for drugs designed to treat rare conditions that might otherwise not be profitable.[7]

On the one hand, patents and other legal protections, such as trademarks and copyrights, can lead to monopoly power, which is not in the public interest. On the other hand, a firm would be much less willing to spend millions of dollars on research if others can become free riders by mimicking its innovations. By being first, firms still would invest in R&D but at reduced levels. The question of just how much less is clearly an empirical issue.

Mansfield (1986) found that 60 percent of pharmaceutical drugs between 1981 and 1983 would not have been developed without patent protection. This figure is especially dramatic compared to the 11 other industries he sampled. The chemical industry was the only other industry with a substantial impact (30 percent).

Although the effects of the patent system are small in most industries, it is critical to pharmaceutical innovation. We, therefore, turn our attention to the determinants of pharmaceutical R&D and a conceptual framework to examine the effects of FDA regulations and patent law on innovations.

Investment Decisions

Net present value analysis provides a simple yet powerful approach to investment decisions. Letting R_t and C_t represent the revenues and costs in time, t, the net present value, NPV, of a project is given by:

$$NPV = \sum_{t-1}^{t=T}(R_t - C_t)/(1+r)^t \qquad (17.3)$$

where r is the discount rate or cost of capital and T is the life of the project. Following some of the discussion in the Appendix to Chapter 4, under the standard decision rule, a project is accepted if the net present value is positive.

Several characteristics of pharmaceutical R&D become apparent if we break NPV into three components representing:

a. The research, testing, and review period (m years)
b. The effective period of patent protection (n years) after the product is launched,
c. The period following patent expiration (s years, where $m + n + s = T$)

$$NPV = \underbrace{\sum_{t=1}^{t=m}(R_t - C_t)/(1+r)^t}_{\textbf{a.}} + \underbrace{\sum_{t=m+1}^{t=m+n}(R_t - C_t)/(1+r)^t}_{\textbf{b.}} + \underbrace{\sum_{t=m+n+1}^{t=m+n+s}(R_t - C_t)/(1+r)^t}_{\textbf{c.}} \quad (17.4)$$

In the first component listed, **a**, the firm will not have any revenue and there will be large, negative net cash flows reflecting the high R&D costs. To offset these costs, a successful project will require even larger positive net cash flows in later years, particularly over the period represented by the second component, **b**, the effective patent life.

[7]Schweitzer (1996) describes the incentives provided by the act and how they have led to a large number of products that have been given orphan status. He argues, however, that the act does little to help populations in developing countries who suffer from diseases that are rare in the developed world. Together with the high cost of many existing drugs, the responsibilities of industrialized nations and the pharmaceutical industry to poorer nations are becoming major social and political issues.

Despite potential competition from generics and significant erosion of sales, products still may capitalize on brand recognition, marketing efforts, and new uses to remain successful after patent expiration, the last component, **c**.

This framework further tells us that regulations and testing procedures that increase costs in the first component reduce *NPV* and make an investment less attractive. Similarly, *NPV* is reduced by an increase in the length of the research, testing, and review period, because it must reduce the length of the patent protection period, **b**. Conversely, changes such as reduced regulation or fast-track laws to lower initial costs and speed up the review process as well as extensions of patent rights each serve to increase *NPV*.

Finally, the risks are important. Projects with higher risks should be discounted at a higher rate or, put another way, high-risk projects need a high rate of return to be viable. To the extent that a firm can reduce risks, for example, by supporting a portfolio of diverse projects or sharing risks through joint ventures with other firms, the discount rate, *r*, diminishes and the likelihood of investment is increased. This also suggests that large firms have an advantage over smaller firms in R&D.

R&D Spending

We have noted that total industry R&D spending is substantial and rising. Despite the spending, the 17 new chemical entities approved by the FDA in 2002 was the lowest total since 1983. Cockburn (2004) notes that the development pipeline is full and that an increase in new drugs entering the market is likely to be seen over the next 3 to 10 years. He also attributes the substantial growth in R&D costs to the rise of the biotechnology sector and changes in the structure of the pharmaceutical industry. The latter includes consolidation within the industry and competition from the biotechnology-based sector, which have led to a "vertical disintegration" of the R&D process.

Analyses of R&D at the firm level provide some startling figures on costs and their recent growth rates. Focusing on the more significant innovations, DiMasi and colleagues (1991) estimated total costs, computed as capitalized expected costs and discounted at 9 percent, at $231 million in 1987 dollars per new chemical entity that was marketed. Because there is substantial attrition as projects move to successive stages of development, about two-thirds of the cost is attributable to the preclinical phase. In a controversial update covering the late 1990s, DiMasi, Hansen, and Grabowski (2003) estimate average out-of-pocket R&D costs for new chemical entities at $403 million (in year 2000 dollars). This figure reaches $802 million when capitalized at 11 percent.[8]

How do firms recover these formidable amounts? Our understanding of the returns to investment has been aided greatly by the work of Grabowski and Vernon (1994, 1996), which follows sales over the life cycle of a product. Grabowski and Vernon found that a product has an effective patent life of about 9 to 13 years and a market life of about 20 years. Cash flows do not become positive until the third year

[8]Although the high quality of the study is supported in an accompanying editorial by Frank (2003), DiMasi's findings were attacked even prior to their formal publication. Two former editors of the prestigious *New England Journal of Medicine* (Relman and Angell, 2002) raised serious questions about the innovativeness of the pharmaceutical industry and many of its marketing practices. They further argue that DiMasi misrepresents R&D costs for new drugs in that new chemical entities represent a minority of drugs that are newly approved. In more recent criticism, Light and Warburton (2005) voice concern about biases and other limitations of the proprietary and confidential survey data used by DiMasi. The accuracy and consistency of such data cannot be independently verified—an important caveat if one believes that pharmaceutical firms have an incentive to overstate development costs. See also DiMasi and colleagues (2005) for their response to these concerns.

after launch, and sales peak in the tenth or eleventh year. The most significant finding is that a substantial portion of a company's revenue and profits are derived from a few big winners. Only the top 20 percent of new drugs have an *NPV* that is substantially positive; the *NPV* of the representative new drug is actually negative. This highly skewed distribution reinforces the firm's need for diversification by having a large number of drugs under development to reduce risks. It also suggests difficulties for smaller firms that cannot sustain a large R&D program.

Firm Size and Innovation

Henderson and Cockburn (1996) ask the question: "Are the research efforts of larger firms more productive than those of smaller rivals, and if so, why?" They search for evidence of the effects of size on "important" patents granted and find that the returns to size are significant. This result is not surprising, but their contribution lies in distinguishing between "economies of scale" and "economies of scope." Recall that a firm experiences economies of scale when its long-run average costs decrease with higher output. It has economies of scope if the cost of producing two or more different products is less than the costs of separate production. Earlier work, which did not distinguish between these effects, showed mixed results on the effects of firm size on innovation.

For innovation, these concepts need clarification in that output is not easily or uniquely measured. One approach measures output through patents. Economies of scale arise if patents granted increase more rapidly than the size of an R&D program. Economies of scope will be realized if a joint program to develop different drugs is more productive than with distinct programs.

The industry also is responding in other ways to the growing cost of R&D and conducting clinical trials. Strategic alliances have risen sharply. The alliances, often between a pharmaceutical and a biotech firm, are designed to pool efforts to innovate or bring products to the market more successfully. As part of this process, less pharmaceutical R&D is being conducted "in house" as firms look for R&D partners to reduce costs and spread risks. These partners include contract research organizations that are used to conduct clinical trials and, in some cases, to provide a broad range of drug-development services.

Henderson and Cockburn found that size is important and that larger programs are more productive. However, it is due more to economies of scope than to economies of scale. Little gain is achieved in increasing the size of an individual program beyond some minimal threshold level. Economies of scope arise when different research activities can share inputs, thus, lowering cost. More important, spillovers of knowledge among projects raise overall productivity. The authors also found significant spillovers of information among firms.

Cost Containment

The rapid growth in drug expenditures has led to great policy interest in cost containment. President Clinton's 1993 health care reform plan included a mechanism to regulate prices through caps geared to prices in other countries and to producer costs. Despite questionable methods, a series of General Accounting Office reports in the early 1990s, indicating that U.S. prices were higher than prices in Canada and the United Kingdom, intensified interest in drug price controls.

We already have addressed some of the difficulties of regulating prices for large numbers of constantly changing products. We also have addressed the problems of recovering common costs. If prices are driven toward marginal costs, R&D investment

BOX 17-2

Are There Other Ways to Promote Innovation While Keeping Drug Prices Low?

As we have seen, research and development costs and their role in drug pricing remain controversial. We have also seen through Figure 17-4 that the monopoly power that results from patent protection for new drugs can result in a large gap between price and marginal cost. For efficiency reasons, economists favor policies that set prices equal to marginal cost. With low marginal costs for most drugs, access to drugs would increase for those who currently face a price barrier.

Are there mechanisms other than patent protection that encourage innovation but still allow for the benefits associated with marginal cost pricing? This question is not a new one, but it has become increasingly relevant with the rapid growth of drug spending and the recent dearth of breakthrough innovations. Despite the pharmaceutical industry's large budget for R&D, only 20 percent of the drugs introduced in the past decade are considered major breakthroughs by the FDA.

Several alternatives have been proposed. Each involves substantial federal government involvement. One would expand the government's already large role in basic scientific research to include the research currently undertaken by pharmaceutical firms. This proposal represents a major restructuring with pharmaceutical companies serving mainly as manufacturers, marketers and distributors of drugs. A more creative alternative that would leave the pharmaceutical R&D infrastructure intact would have the government buy patents for potentially important and/or widely used products from drug companies at a premium, and then place the drugs in the public domain where they would be treated and priced like generics. A variant of this idea calls for the government to pay pharmaceutical firms for their innovations based on the benefits they provide over existing treatments. In addition to lower prices and greater access, the goal of these proposals is to encourage significant inventions rather than the marginal improvements associated with "me-too" drugs.

The pharmaceutical industry, not surprisingly, strongly opposes these changes. The proposals are tantamount to a government takeover or, at a minimum, to substantial government control of pharmaceutical R&D. One can also question whether any of them will improve the efficiency of research spending, when levels of funding and priorities are determined through a political process.

SOURCE: Eduardo Porter, "Do New Drugs Always have to Cost So Much?" *New York Times*, November 14, 2004, Section 3, p. 5.

and the resulting innovation may decrease, to the detriment of the public's welfare. (Box 17-2 describes several conceptual proposals intended to promote marginal cost pricing while maintaining high rates of innovation.) Many countries have introduced various forms of regulation to rein in spending. Western European countries tend to control either producers' prices or reimbursement rates while England has a profit control system (Huttin, 1999). In the United States, Medicaid programs "discount" prices and impose restrictions on utilization. The federal government also discounts prices for drugs purchased by the Department of Veterans Affairs and other federal agencies.

Most outpatient drug purchases in the United States are paid by users out-of-pocket or by private insurance (Medicare's coverage for outpatient prescriptions started only in 2006). We, therefore, turn to the cost-containment efforts of the private sector, especially those introduced through managed care. These efforts include price discounting and the exercise of monopsony power, much like their public insurance

counterparts. To narrow our discussion, we will describe three other strategies: higher copayments, use of generic drugs, and the adoption of drug formularies.

Copayments

A higher copayment seems simple and straightforward. It is intended to shift a larger share of the cost burden to the patient and to decrease consumption of marginally beneficial drugs. Moreover, under many current copayment plans, prescription drugs cost only a fraction of their over-the-counter substitutes.

However, a higher copayment may lead to other results. Recall from Figure 17-2 that an increase in the out-of-pocket cost of a drug will decrease its use as patients substitute other inputs for drugs.

With no substitutability, use of drugs remains unchanged; only the distribution of the costs between patients and insurers is affected. As we noted earlier in the chapter, if significant substitutability among treatments is possible, the total health care cost could increase as inefficient cost-minimization combinations are selected.

However, when generic substitutes are available (multiple-source drugs), strategies involving differential copayments for brand products offer the potential for substantial shifts toward lower-priced generics without affecting overall utilization. Managed care plans have introduced tiered copayment systems where the patient pays, for example, $5 for a generic drug, $10 to $15 for a brand-name product on an approved list (formulary), and more if it is not found on the formulary. Patients and providers who consider the generic a close substitute will choose the generic.

The key question is whether there will be a large substitution toward generics. Motheral and Henderson (1999) examined two plans with tiered systems that increased brand-name copayments more than copayments for generics. They found little effect on total drug utilization. However, utilization of brand-name products decreased about 18 percent relative to a control group that had no price increases. This substitution produced substantial savings to the health plans.

Other evidence for a wider set of drug benefit arrangements is even more revealing. From a sample of over 400,000 working-age adults, Joyce and colleagues (2002) found that doubling copayments for all drugs from $5 to $10 reduced average drug spending by 22 percent, and by about one-third when copayments were doubled in two-tier plans. Adding a second $20 tier for brand-name drugs that previously had a $10 copayment for all drug purchases reduced spending by 19 percent. As a final illustration, drug spending was reduced by 8 percent in two-tier plans that mandated generic substitution as compared to those that did not mandate such substitution.

Finally, we caution that higher copayments and other cost-sharing schemes not only reduce costs, but also change treatment. Goldman et al. (2004) found substantial decreases in utilization within the most common drug classes from a doubling of copayments. Reductions ranged from a low of 25 percent for antidiabetics to highs of 44 percent for antihistamines and 45 percent for nonsteroidal anti-inflammatory drugs (NSAIDS). Utilization for those with chronic illnesses was less responsive to the copay increases. Nevertheless, the authors were concerned about the health effects of the large reductions, especially for patients with diabetes.

This concern is reinforced by a recent review of the cost-sharing literature. Gibson and colleagues (2005) concluded that these arrangements generally work as intended—by encouraging generic use and limiting overuse. But their study also found reports that higher cost sharing can also disrupt treatment through lower levels of adherence, lower use of essential medicines, and, in some cases, drug discontinuation. The authors suggested that a "one-size-fits-all approach could be replaced with targeted incentives for

patients and providers to use the right medications at levels of use that are appropriate for their health conditions."

Generic Substitutes

About 70 percent of prescriptions are written for multiple-source drugs (Hellerstein, 1998), and the vast majority of the top-selling drugs have generics. With generic prices considerably below their brand-name counterparts and FDA certification of their therapeutic equivalence, one would expect little resistance to generic versions from physicians and their patients. This has not been so.

Interest in promoting generic products has a long history. Antisubstitution laws were passed by most states after World War II, prohibiting pharmacists from substituting a generic for a prescribed brand, but mounting cost pressures led to reforms. In 1970, Massachusetts became the first state to legalize drug product selection and, by the end of the decade, most others followed. Despite the potential for cost saving, an early study of Michigan's substitution laws was revealing (Goldberg et al., 1979). After 1974, substitution by a pharmacist was allowed unless the doctor wrote "dispense as written" or "DAW." Relatively few prescriptions were written with this restriction. However, substitutions were given for less than 2 percent of all multiple-source prescriptions.

Substitution has increased well beyond the levels of the 1970s, and generics' share of the prescription drug market was about 50 percent in 2003, in large part due to the Hatch-Waxman Act of 1984 (which allows a generic producer to file an abbreviated new drug application and to use the pioneer company's clinical research). Nevertheless, physicians continue to write the trade name for most prescriptions. Using 1989 survey data, Hellerstein (1998) examined multiple-source prescriptions for the eight largest drug classes. Only 29 percent of the prescriptions were written for generics. Why? Hellerstein explains with information and agency theory. Because physicians do not gain from any cost savings, they have little incentive to invest in the information about availability of generics or their effectiveness and prices. In his empirical model, Hellerstein found that patient characteristics are not important in prescription decisions. Physician characteristics are important. In particular, physicians with a larger share of HMO and prepaid plan patients will more likely write generic prescriptions.

Drug Formularies

Managed care's strong financial interest in cost containment has led to policies that go well beyond the promotion of generics by monitoring physicians and requiring substitution. Many use pharmacy benefit managers to negotiate discounts and improve the efficiency of their claims-processing and pharmacy operations. They are increasingly adopting other methods, such as drug-utilization review programs and lower cost, mail-order sources for prescriptions. One of the most ambitious and controversial strategies, however, involves the use of formulary committees to develop a list of approved drugs. A positive formulary restricts the choice of drugs to those on the list. A negative formulary excludes drugs on a list.

The formulary review and approval process can be elaborate, dealing not only with generic substitution but also with recommendations of different drugs that can be used to treat a condition. Ideally, the review committee will periodically review all drugs in each therapeutic class for their clinical effectiveness, safety, and cost. Mather (1999) observes that, when properly implemented, the formulary can be an effective and well-accepted tool. If drug-product decisions are based largely on cost instead of clinical outcomes, Mather suggests that "the health system may experience higher overall costs

and the pharmacy benefit may be sharply criticized by health plan providers, enrollees, and suppliers wishing to see their products on the list" (p. 277).

The widespread adoption of formularies has elevated the importance of pharmacoeconomic analyses. Pharmaceutical firms face strong pressure to provide clinical and economic data that justify their inclusion in the formulary. Formulary committee members require the skills to compare, interpret, and analyze data from many different sources and to justify their decisions. They are under especially great pressure from both patients and providers when new and improved drugs come onto the market.

Conclusions

Our overview of the pharmaceutical industry focused on individual provider and patient decisions, firm pricing and investment decisions, and public policy issues in regulation and cost containment. Throughout, we have emphasized the use of basic economic tools to simplify and make sense of complex problems. We have neglected, however, to place some of the issues within a global context, and we will conclude with insights from international data.

It might appear from the material presented that drug spending in the United States has gone beyond any level that could be considered reasonable or efficient. If so, then the United States is not alone among developed countries. As measured by the percent of health spending devoted to drugs (see Table 22-1), the United States actually ranks near the bottom among industrial countries (though it is the biggest spender in absolute dollars). Many factors account for the wide variations in shares across countries in addition to price differences. These include differences in physician practice patterns, cultural attitudes toward drugs, licensure laws, and insurance and other financial arrangements (physicians are permitted to dispense drugs in some countries). All nations are dealing with the same pressures and the need to find mechanisms to promote cost-efficient use of drugs and other health care inputs. After all, the most important economic question is the value of drugs in producing health.

Fortunately, recent work is providing new and surprising results. Frech and Miller (1999) took advantage of the wide differences in drug utilization and health status across 21 OECD countries to investigate the productivity of drugs, other medical inputs, wealth, and lifestyle. They used regression analysis with alternative measures of a nation's health status as the dependent variable. Independent variables included a country's wealth, pharmaceutical spending per capita, other health spending per capita, and various lifestyle indicators.

Some of the findings are consistent with our analyses in previous chapters. Wealth, measured by GDP per capita, showed significant and positive effects on life expectancy. A doubling of GDP increases life expectancy by 6 percent at age 40 and by 9 percent at age 60. Lifestyle (measured by smoking, alcohol, and consumption of animal fat) also has important effects. In particular, the consumption of animal fat, the most important lifestyle variable, has positive effects on life expectancy at birth, age 40, and age 60 up to certain levels of consumption (92, 78, and 70 grams per day, respectively). Nonpharmaceutical inputs showed no statistically significant effects at any of the three age levels.

The most interesting and surprising results relate to pharmaceutical spending per capita, with strong positive effects on life expectancy at ages 40 and 60. A doubling of drug spending increases life expectancy by 2 percent and 4 percent, respectively, at these age levels. The study also estimated the lifetime pharmaceutical cost of extending life by one year. For the United States, these costs for males and females at age 40 are

$21,000 and $23,000, and about $17,000 and $19,000 at age 60. Analyses of infant mortality show that drug consumption has a small, positive (harmful), but statistically insignificant effect. The consumption of animal fat, with a negative (beneficial) impact, is the most important variable.

These international comparisons support views that pharmaceuticals are extremely productive, especially as compared to other health care inputs. Pharmaceutical companies and their profits are highly visible, and they make convenient targets. Although economists usually lead the charge in developing strategies to reduce inefficiencies, Frech and Miller's findings warn of the danger in focusing disproportionately on policies and measures that contain drug spending.

SUMMARY

1. Spending on prescription drugs has grown at double-digit rates for nearly a decade. In 2003, prescription drug spending accounted for 10.7 percent of national health care spending, up from 8.5 percent in 1999 and 4.9 percent in 1980.
2. The pharmaceutical industry is characterized by significant barriers to entry and substantial regulation. The industry has been regulated since 1906, but 1962 legislation had the most profound effects.
3. Pharmaceuticals substitute for health and nonhealth inputs in the production of health. A rational patient will select least-cost input combinations. Relative changes in a patient's out-of-pocket costs resulting from insurance will lead to substitution of drugs for other health care inputs or vice versa.
4. Technological change, even when the benefits are marginal, is often cost-increasing due to insurance.
5. Pharmaceutical firms earn higher than normal profits, but the extent of their profits is exaggerated greatly by conventional accounting data.
6. Opportunities are substantial for price discrimination. Markets, or groups of buyers, with inelastic demand will pay higher prices.
7. Generic products often capture a significant share of the market following patent expiration. Nevertheless, through effective marketing and promotion, trade names still can retain a monopoly premium.
8. R&D spending is substantial, and a firm's profits often depend on a few big winners. Firms need to earn substantial amounts over the effective life of a patent to justify the risks.
9. Larger R&D programs are more productive than smaller programs. Economies of scope play an important role.
10. Price, rate-of-return regulation, and national formularies are used in other countries to contain costs. In the United States, higher copayments, the promotion of generic substitutes, and other managed-care strategies, such as drug formularies, have been adopted.
11. Higher copayments encourage substitution toward generics as well as a decrease in overall utilization. In some cases, they may also lead to disruptions in treatment.
12. Spending on drugs in the United States is not out of line as compared to other developed countries.
13. Drugs are highly productive in improving health compared to other medical inputs.

DISCUSSION QUESTIONS

1. Explain and distinguish between the "concentration ratio" and the "HHI." What are the limitations of these measures within the context of the pharmaceutical industry?
2. Direct-to-consumer (DTC) advertising of prescription drugs is growing rapidly. List several products with which you have become familiar as a result of such advertising. Discuss the pros and cons of DTC advertising from the perspective of physicians and patients.
3. Use Figure 17-1 to explain how an isoquant can be positively sloped. Under what circumstances may a patient actually end up in the positively sloped region (e.g., at point *H*)?

4. Regulation is often proposed (and widely used in other countries) to limit prices or profits. Discuss possible adverse effects of regulating prescription prices. In light of your discussion, what accounts for the strong pressure in many countries, including the United States, to regulate prices?
5. What are barriers to entry? Describe three potential barriers in the pharmaceutical industry. What are some consequences of these barriers?
6. In 2004, Congressman Dennis Kucinich proposed the Free Market Drug Act. This legislation would have removed patent protection on drugs developed with public funds and given control over pharmaceutical R&D to the National Institutes of Health (NIH). Evaluate this type of proposal in terms of the effects on price, competition, and level of innovation.
7. There are wide differences across countries in the share of health resources spent on drugs. Describe possible economic and noneconomic factors that may contribute to the variation.
8. Direct-to-consumer (DTC) advertising has been criticized for possibly misleading patients and for increasing spending on drugs. Discuss the benefits and costs of DTC advertising.

EXERCISES

1. Use Figure 17-2 to explain why cost minimization through a tangency between an isoquant and a budget line does not apply in cases where D and M are either perfect complements or perfect substitutes. Describe the cost-minimization process and the effects of changes in the relative prices of D and M in these special cases.
2. Assume that a patient has 80 percent coverage for medical services but no coverage for prescription drugs. An 80 percent drug benefit is added. Show graphically what will happen to the relative utilization of M and D, and total spending on health care, to attain a given health status. What happens to the amount spent on drugs (insurance plus patient amounts)? Why will total spending on health care diminish when the 80 percent drug benefit is added?
3. A pharmaceutical firm faces the following monthly demands in the U.S. and Mexican markets for one of its patented drugs:

$$Q_{US} = 300,000 - 5,000P_{US} \text{ and } Q_X = 240,000 - 8,000P_X$$

where quantities represent the number of prescriptions. Assume that resale or arbitrage among markets is impossible and that marginal cost is constant at $2 per prescription in both markets. Monthly fixed costs are $1 million in the United States and $500,000 in Mexico.
 a. Draw the demand, marginal revenue, and marginal cost curves for each market. Estimate the profit-maximizing prices and quantities graphically and/or determine the solutions algebraically. What are the firm's total profits?
 b. Determine the quantity in each market and maximum possible total profits if the firm engages in perfect (first degree) price discrimination. Is this behavior possible?
4. Assume that the firm in exercise 3 cannot prevent resale and is forced to set the same price in both markets. Find the price graphically and/or algebraically and show that total profits are less than those from part 3a.
5. For your answer in 3a:
 a. Calculate the price elasticity of demand in each market at the optimal price.
 b. Verify that the prices and elasticities are consistent with the profit-maximizing formula given in footnote 6.
 c. Why are both elasticities fairly close to unity? (Hint: Think about the requirement for profit maximization when marginal cost is zero.)
 d. If a firm finds that its price elasticity is numerically less than 1, what advice would you have?
6. Consider only the U.S. market from exercise 3. Graph solutions to parts 6a and 6b using the demand, average cost, and marginal cost curves. Also try to develop the answers algebraically.

 a. Price regulation is proposed. Find the regulated price that enables the firm to cover all its costs. Caution! There are two mathematical solutions. Which one will regulators prefer?

 b. Find also the economically efficient price (i.e., one that is consistent with marginal cost pricing). What subsidy per prescription is required to enable the firm to cover all its costs?

7. Compare your results in exercises 6a and 6b with the profit-maximizing solution for the United States obtained in exercise 3a. Explain which of the three alternatives you would prefer if you were responsible for public policy. Be sure to consider some of the problems of regulating prices.

8. Many insurance companies increased premiums by 15 percent or even more in the first years of this decade, blaming soaring pharmaceutical costs for their premium increases. Evaluate the validity of this justification. (Hint: Consider spending on pharmaceuticals as a share of national health expenditures.)

CHAPTER

Equity, Efficiency, and Need

Are health care markets healthy? Are they efficient, and do they provide the care that people need? These questions occupy the minds of the many people who study health care. Efficiency questions arise because of the high costs that people must pay for health care. Are these costs too high? Likewise, equity questions are raised because many people, certainly including the uninsured, face barriers in obtaining health care.

Compared to Canadians and Europeans, Americans will more likely find experts who favor competitive market solutions to health care system problems, though most here (as elsewhere) will argue that this approach is often ill-suited to the nature of health care markets. Canadians and Europeans are more willing to use government interventions, such as social insurance programs to address health care equity problems. The Clinton proposal to expand comprehensive social health care insurance to the general population died in Congress in the United States in 1994. However, Medicare reform and access for the uninsured remain centrally important, and many Americans find equity and efficiency in the health care system to be the fundamental issues.

A solid background in these issues requires a study of the economics of efficiency, the departures of many health care markets from the competitive model, the role of equity concerns, and issues of social justice theory. Because of the central role of "need" in health equity discussions, it also requires that we investigate the meaning of health care need. These subjects are the themes of the present chapter.

The chapter is primarily based on welfare economics, which is defined as the study of normative issues that bear on economics. "Normative issues" deal with how people

believe the economic world *should be*, as opposed to "positive issues" that deal with how the world of economics functions *in practice*.

So, welfare economics defined as "the study of normative economic issues" would encompass those that are critical of existing markets and question the distribution of goods and services. This understanding, however, is itself disputed by some health economists (Hurley, 2000; Culyer, 1989) who argue that an "extra-welfarist" viewpoint is required, rejecting some or all of the philosophical principles on which welfare economics is based. Yet other theorists attempt, within welfare economics, to rework our understanding of the previously accepted conception of welfare and efficiency (Absolo and Tsuchiya, 2004).

While we focus on standard welfare economic theory, we will point to sources where students can explore the extra-welfarist view more fully. We describe the standard results for competitive markets, but also the many market flaws that cause markets to deviate from competition, causing many competitive efficiency propositions to fail. We will also explain and describe the role of need and need-based distributions in the health economy. Finally, we will present theories of social justice and explain why welfare economic claims must be grounded in a philosophical position on justice.[1]

Efficiency and Competitive Markets

The meaning of economic efficiency can be made fairly clear within the context of the Edgeworth box for exchange. This approach shows theorems that are developed in more sophisticated mathematical models. The analysis here generates the First Fundamental Theorem of Welfare Economics and illustrates the Second Fundamental Theorem as well. The First Theorem demonstrates that competitive markets under certain conditions are economically efficient. The Second Theorem establishes that a society can achieve any desired economically efficient outcome by competitive markets if it starts from the appropriate initial endowments.

The Concept of Pareto Efficiency (Optimality)

A century ago, the economist Vilfredo Pareto defined the concept of efficiency most frequently used by economists today. According to Pareto, an economically efficient (optimal) outcome in society is one under which it is impossible to improve the lot of any person without hurting someone else. Pareto efficiency also implies that no further exchanges would be found that could improve the lot of everyone to some degree. An efficient economy necessarily would have exhausted all means for mutual gains.

The Edgeworth box, using a hypothetical two-person economy and showing exchanges between these two people, provides a context in which to make the idea of Pareto efficiency clear. The box also is convenient for describing the mutual gains from trade and for defining the Pareto concept of efficiency.

Suppose that persons A and B, say Abner and Belinda, inhabit a desert island, forming a two-person economy. Further suppose that only two goods are available on the island. Food, F, is gathered and is available in a fixed total amount, F_0, and medicine, M, is likewise available in a fixed amount, M_0.

To form the Edgeworth box, consider Figure 18-1. Abner's preference map (indifference curves) is illustrated in the southwest corner. There is no reason to draw the axes out further than M_0 and F_0, which represent the total amounts of medicine and

[1]For an excellent alternative exposition of welfare economic issues, see Williams and Cookson (2000).

FIGURE 18-1 Edgeworth Box for Exchange; Pareto Efficient Points Lie on the Contract Curve

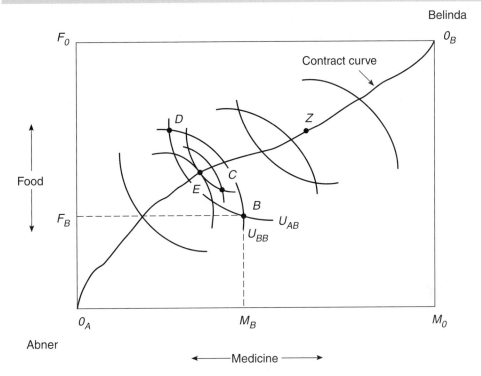

food available on the island. Belinda's preference map is similar to Abner's except that it starts at the northeast corner. It is also constrained by amounts M_0 and F_0.

Any point in the box represents a complete and exhaustive distribution of the island's endowment of food and medicine. For example, point B represents a distribution in which Abner has M_B units of medicine and Belinda has $M_0 - M_B$ units of medicine. Similarly, at B, Abner has F_B units of food and Belinda has $F_0 - F_B$ units of food. With this orientation, we ask whether point B is an economically efficient distribution.

The answer to this question must be no. To see this fact, examine by comparison point C. Point C lies on an indifference curve that is above (to the northeast of) indifference curve U_{AB} and, therefore, C is superior to B in Abner's view. Similarly, point C lies on an indifference curve that is above (to the southwest of) indifference curve U_{BB} and, therefore, C is superior to B from Belinda's view. Because point C is attainable and improves the lot of both persons while harming neither, it follows that the original point B is not economically efficient.

Geometrically, the analysis just completed regarding point B can be repeated for any point that forms a "lens" from the indifference curves passing through it. A lens is formed by the indifference curves U_{AB} and U_{BB} from point B to point D. Whenever such a lens can be found, it will be possible to identify one or more other points superior to the initial point. Reapplying this reasoning, point C is also not Pareto efficient. Pareto superior moves, where the welfare of both improves, can be made from point C. In contrast, a Pareto efficient point in the box is a point of tangency between two indifference curves, such as point E. It is impossible to move from a point of tangency without harming the lot of one of the two persons.

Each of Abner's indifference curves will have a point of tangency with one of Belinda's indifference curves. The collection of all Pareto efficient points in the box is

called the *contract curve*, which is so labeled in the figure. For example, at point O_A, Belinda has all of both goods, and even if many or most people consider this inequitable, it is Pareto efficient.

Trading Along the Budget Line

Having defined efficiency in the context of the Edgeworth box, we next ask whether the competitive market generates an efficient equilibrium in exchange. In a competitive market, each person treats prices as given and responds to prices by choosing the utility-maximizing bundle subject to his or her resource constraint. The resource constraint depends on the person's initial endowment of food and medical care. Let the initial endowment for this two-person economy be represented by V in Figure 18-2. Either person may trade away from his or her initial endowment at the market prices. Thus, Abner's resource constraint will be represented by a budget line that passes through point V. As with any budget line, the slope of this line is the negative of the ratio of the price of medical care to food.

The slope of the budget line represents the rate at which one can trade one good for another at market prices. The steeper the budget line is in Figure 18-2, the greater the price is of medical care relative to food. For example, budget line AB represents a relatively lower price of medical care relative to food than does budget line CD.

The Competitive Equilibrium

To find the competitive equilibrium, we must identify how much each would be willing to trade. Abner's offer curve, for example, is the collection of points representing his offer for trade at each possible set of prices. Start at point V. Given budget line AB, Abner stays at point V, the point of tangency between budget line AB and the highest indifference curve that is attainable.

FIGURE 18-2 The Intersection of Offer Curves Determines the Competitive Equilibrium

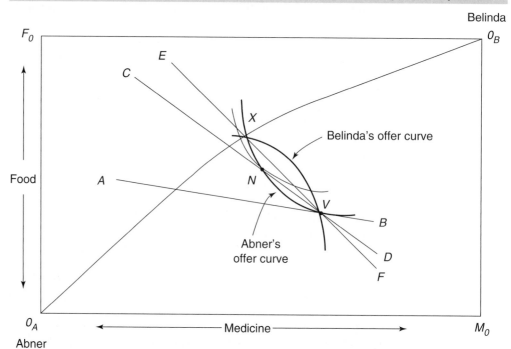

Suppose the price of medical care were higher relative to food, leading to the steeper budget line *CD*. Given budget line *CD*, Abner would trade some medicine for some food to go from point *V* to point *N*. With budget line *EF*, Abner would trade to point *X*. Connecting all such points generates Abner's offer curve.

The figure also shows Belinda's offer curve, beginning at endowment point *V*. The two heavily shaded offer curves represent voluntary trades for the two parties. For trade, as in a competitive market, to be mutually voluntary, the offers of the two persons must agree. The offer curves agree only at their point of intersection, labeled point *X* in the figure. Point *X* thus constitutes the competitive market equilibrium in exchange for this two-person economy, starting with the endowment of *V*.

The First Fundamental Theorem of Welfare Economics

Is the competitive equilibrium, *X*, Pareto efficient? Yes, and there are two reasons that it must be so for every competitive equilibrium. The intersection of two offer curves is reached by a single price line from point *V*. Each person is at a point of tangency between the budget line and the highest attainable indifference curve. At point *X*, Abner's indifference curve (not shown) is tangent to the budget line. Likewise, at point *X*, Belinda's indifference curve (also not shown) is tangent to the budget line. Because these indifference curves are tangent to the same budget line at the same point, they must be tangent to each other. Because they are tangent to each other at point *X*, this point is Pareto efficient. The same argument applies for any competitive equilibrium; therefore, we have shown the First Fundamental Theorem in this context, namely that the perfectly competitive market equilibrium is Pareto efficient.

The theorem makes the competitive market solution attractive. If perfect competition can be achieved, then the market forces left to their own workings will generate an efficient outcome—an invisible hand solution. However, the theorem evokes several serious questions: Can competitive markets be achieved in health care? Is the context of this theorem appropriate for health care? Would the competitive market solution be equitable or would it leave too many people without adequate health care? We will address each of these questions. However, we begin this process by exploring the issue of equity within the context of the Second Fundamental Theorem.

Redistribution of the Endowment

The applicability of the First Fundamental Theorem is extended by the Second Fundamental Theorem, which states that given an appropriate endowment, any Pareto efficient outcome can in principle be achieved by a competitive market. Figure 18-3 illustrates the significance of this theorem.

In Figure 18-3, suppose that the initial endowment is *V*, and suppose that this endowment results in the competitive outcome represented by point *E*. Point *E* is only one of an infinite number of Pareto efficient points. It may be an outcome that is viewed as inequitable by some members of the society, here either Abner or Belinda, or both. In real life, the society may have millions of members, and this market outcome may even be perceived as inequitable by a majority of people.

The Second Theorem, however, defines a central role for competitive markets, even in cases where some competitive outcomes are considered inequitable. This idea is illustrated in the figure. Suppose, for example, that society prefers outcomes in the vicinity of point *F* to outcome *E*. By the Second Theorem, a competitive market can achieve the desired outcome, but it requires a different initial endowment from point *V*. As shown, the endowment point *W* is a suitable point from which to achieve an equitable market outcome, point *F*. Seen this way, redistribution combined with

FIGURE 18-3 A Preferred Efficient Outcome May Be Achieved by an Initial Redistribution of Resources

competitive markets generates an efficient and equitable outcome. This contrasts with command systems that reject free markets, as well as with alternative schemes, such as price discrimination.

Price Discrimination

An alternative method often proposed for achieving a more equitable outcome is to provide certain services to the poor at reduced, subsidized prices. It may be surprising to learn that such systems are not consistent with Pareto efficiency. Consider the proof of the efficiency of competitive markets. It was crucial that both parties achieve a point of tangency to the same budget line. If different prices for medical care are charged to the poor than to the rich, then the two face different slopes of their budget lines. The result would be a position such as point S in Figure 18-3, a point that is not Pareto efficient. For an intuitive argument, consider a situation where the poor are subsidized in purchasing bread. The poor would adapt to the subsidized price until the rate at which they were willing to trade bread for other goods was equal to the rate at which they could exchange the goods at the subsidized price. The result is that the poor would undervalue bread in comparison to the wealthy. It would be more efficient for the poor to buy up bread and sell it to the rich. Such a side market, which would improve efficiency in the bread example, is not possible for medical care, which is not easily transferable. Thus, subsidized prices for medical care would generate an inefficient equilibrium.

The two theorems, along with the inefficiency of price discrimination, suggest the superiority of income transfers as a solution to equity problems in health care markets.

In Figure 18-3, the following situation takes place: By transferring initial resources between the two persons, the market is allowed to achieve an efficient outcome within the equitable range.

Trade-offs Between Equity and Efficiency

The theoretical superiority of redistribution of income to programs, such as price subsidies, has led many analysts to favor income maintenance programs as policy tools to offset the problems of poverty, including the problems of access to health care. Income maintenance programs are government programs designed to provide cash subsidies to the poor so as to maintain their incomes at or above a preset floor. Despite continuing interest in such programs, policy makers often have hesitated to use large-scale income redistribution.

Economists explain a major criticism of income maintenance by appealing to Arthur Okun's (1975) analogy of the leaky bucket. The act of transferring wealth from one group to another in society may generate disincentives that discourage productive effort. The tax-paying group incurs a tax burden that may reduce work incentives, and the recipient group receives subsidies that may reduce incentives to work and to self-help. By analogy, when we transfer income, our task is similar to transferring water in a leaky bucket. The amount of income available to be redistributed may decline as a result.

Rebecca Blank (2002) challenges the equity-efficiency trade-off idea, arguing that situations exist where the efficiency costs of improving equity may be very small, such as when the group receiving the benefit is unlikely to change its behaviors. She further posits that in some cases equity and efficiency are complementary.

In past decades, the federal government sponsored large-scale experiments to investigate the degree of work loss induced by the incentives inherent in income maintenance programs. These experiments reported reductions in work effort on average of between 5 and 10 percent. However, the work reduction estimates were considerably higher for certain subgroups, such as "male nonheads" (meaning nonheads of families) and women. Also, results generated in an experimental situation make it difficult to predict the results if the program were to become universal and permanent.

Deviations from the Competitive Model in the Health Care Sector

Another major criticism of the applicability of our theoretical analysis concerns the question of whether health care markets are sufficiently competitive or whether they can be made to be sufficiently competitive for competitive outcomes to be obtained. Substantial differences exist between most health care markets and the theoretical model of competition. For the results to hold, several assumptions must apply.

The Assumptions Under Perfect Competition

The First and Second Theorems apply to competitive markets. For a market to be perfectly competitive, it must have free entry and exit, perfect information, a homogeneous product, and numerous buyers and sellers each with no power over price. Furthermore, the efficiency of competitive markets is derived under conditions where

no significant externalities, public goods, or natural monopolies exist. Finally, the actors in the competitive markets are alternatively consumers maximizing their utility or producers maximizing their profits.

Many have criticized the applicability of the theorems to the health care sector, claiming that health care markets are typically not perfectly competitive. Most of these criticisms are valid, and they have frequently been recognized in health economics writing. The health care markets depart from competition in several ways:

1. Barriers to entry exist in health care markets. Such barriers include licensure laws and health planning controls on prices and facility construction.
2. There are often few enough firms that those in the market have some degree of monopoly power.
3. Health care services are not uniform in quality or other characteristics.
4. Motivations other than pure profit are common in health care.
5. The model depicts the operation of markets under conditions of certainty. However, health events entail a considerable degree of uncertainty.
6. Information problems exist.
7. Externalities are prevalent in health care.

Several of the seven listed deviations need little further explanation. However, we consider three for extended discussion: the role of uncertainty, the role of information, and the role of externalities.

The Role of Uncertainty

The uncertain nature of health status gives rise to the demand for insurance coverage among persons who are risk averse. In the present context, insurance creates problems for the efficient functioning of health care markets. Four issues should be noted:

1. Insurance changes the price of care to the insured person, which in turn leads to the distortions described under price discrimination.
2. Insurance causes the price paid to suppliers to differ from the price paid by the consumer, and this distorts the efficient matching of production to consumption.
3. Large insurance companies and government programs negotiate payment rates, thus removing price determination, at least in part, from the market.
4. In some health care markets, insurance coverage is so complete as to distort the health care producer's incentives to be efficient.

The Role of Information

The efficiency results for competitive markets depend on all parties having complete information available. As we have shown elsewhere, it is particularly problematic for markets to function when information is imperfect and asymmetrically available to the parties in the market. Potential problems of information and efficiency arise either when the physician is much more informed about the appropriateness and effectiveness of treatments and techniques than the consumer is, or when the consumer has more knowledge of his or her health status and health habits than the potential insurer does.

The Role of Externalities

Finally, health care markets are subject to prevalent externalities. A prominent externality will occur whenever participants in the market are significantly concerned about the health care received by others, not just their own health care. This externality may

be difficult to internalize in private charity markets, and it arguably causes health care markets to be inefficient. Because some analysts have identified externalities as the most important efficiency argument for social insurance programs in health care, we develop an extended discussion later in this chapter.

Promoting Competition in the Health Care Sector

If we could manipulate real-world markets as easily as we can change the assumptions of theory, then it would follow from our theoretical discussion that we should promote competition in health care markets whenever possible. Often the promotion of competitive elements in health care markets will prove useful. However, further theoretical grounds exist to qualify our statements.

The Theorem of the Second Best

One qualification involves the Theorem of the Second Best in welfare economics. Consider an economy in which there is more than one departure from the conditions of perfect competition. Consider further any policy that corrects one or more of these departures from perfect competition but does not correct all of them. It has been shown under the Theorem of the Second Best that such a policy may not necessarily improve society's welfare.

An intuitive understanding of why this result is obtained can be gained by considering a market where there exists a pure monopolist (a departure from the conditions of perfect competition) who is also a polluter (a departure from the conditions under which competition is efficient). Basic theory shows that a monopolist will produce less output than a competitive industry would have under otherwise similar conditions. A policy that hypothetically converts the industry to perfect competition would resolve one discrepancy but not both because both output and pollution would increase. Societal valuations of the extra output versus the extra pollution could in principle determine whether the change worsened society's well-being. Thus, correcting some economic "wrongs" but not all of them may not necessarily improve welfare.

This classic example of the monopolist polluter illustrates the idea of the theorem, but it does not make clear its applicability to the health sector. Consider a somewhat more controversial health-related example. Physician licensure laws grant licensed physicians a degree of monopoly power, a distortion from the competitive conditions. At the same time, however, health consumers have imperfect information on therapies and prices and are less informed than the physicians. This, too, is a departure from competitive conditions. If one eliminated the imperfection caused by licensure but did not simultaneously address the information problem, patient welfare could be worsened. This could happen because, without licensure restrictions on physicians, poorly informed consumers could be fooled by quacks and possibly dangerous treatments. This example also illustrates the Theory of the Second Best.

It would be a misapplication of the Theorem of the Second Best to conclude that all health care policies that improve competitive elements are incorrect. More properly, the theorem states that we cannot assume competitive policies will improve welfare. We necessarily operate in the world of second best because it will be impossible to convert all health care markets into the model of perfect competition. A competitive policy may improve the functioning of health care markets in a manner that improves society's well-being. Each policy must be considered on its own merits, not solely on the grounds that it promotes competition. Thomas Rice provides a separate critique of the competitive model in Box 18-1.

BOX 18-1

The Rice Critique

Welfare economics warns that the benefits of competition require many assumptions that do not hold for the health economy. To fix one of these flaws by itself does not necessarily help society. Understanding these caveats, we noted that most health economists favor competitive markets when they do improve welfare. Thomas Rice (1998), however, makes the stronger case that too often health economists promote competition but fail to acknowledge the many market flaws.

His line of reasoning is essentially the same—that many needed assumptions are violated. However, his more extensive list illuminates additional basic issues:

1. The law of diminishing marginal returns may not hold.
2. Consumer utility may depend on factors other than goods and services.
3. Consumer tastes are not fixed but are often learned.
4. Consumers may not be rational.
5. Individuals may not be the best judges of their own well-being.
6. The social welfare function depends on more than individual consumption.

These issues, recognizable to economists, could raise serious questions for the analysis we have described. For example, if the assumption of rationality fails to approximate behavior, then most microeconomic theory needs to be reevaluated.

Items 5 and 6 further show how thorny the underlying normative issues are. U.S. society often makes choices that imply that individuals are not the best judges of their own well-being. Examples include motorcycle helmet laws, criminalization of drugs, and mandatory retirement contributions. Wide acceptance of these limitations suggests that Rice is correct on item 5 and possibly item 6. However, controversy always arises over where to draw the line.

A particular debate arises regarding those who are uninsured. Mark Pauly (1996) suggests that voters could probably be convinced that the value of certain reforms aimed at reducing the rate of uninsurance is worth the costs. However, he asserts that, "If we cannot convince the decisive voters of the value of what we value, then I think we need to accept the verdict of democracy" (p. 14). Uwe Reinhardt (1996) responds:

> I, for one, believe that, if this nation is ever to have truly universal health insurance coverage and a truly humane safety net all around, an elite espousing those goals would have to impose that state of affairs on a generally confused plebs that has quite unstable, often logically inconsistent and utterly malleable preferences on the matter (p. 24).

Reinhardt echoes the frustration of many health economists on this point, but many also question Rice's items 5 and 6 in the process. *Plebs* here means the general populace, but it shares the same root with the word *plebiscite*, a vote of the general populace. Would health policy "impose(d) . . . on a generally confused plebs" pass a plebiscite?

An Economic Efficiency Rationale for Health Care Programs Based on Externalities

An externality occurs when someone external to the market transaction—that is, someone who is neither the buyer nor the seller—is affected directly by the transaction and not compensated. A common example in health care occurs in the case of immunization for contagious diseases. Here, people outside the market transaction—people who are not presently being immunized—are affected by the immunization because the immunized person is less likely to become a carrier of the disease. This situation is an example of a beneficial consumption externality.

In the presence of a beneficial externality, the competitive market will tend to produce an inefficiently low level of output. The Pareto efficiency definition can be transformed in terms of a single market as the condition that marginal benefits equal marginal costs in equilibrium. Individuals in a well-functioning, perfectly competitive market in theory will use medical care until the marginal benefits, measured through the demand curve, equal marginal costs, which in equilibrium will equal the price. In Figure 18-4, this leads to an efficient level of consumption, Q_m, in the absence of externalities.

A marginal external benefit to people in society must be added to the marginal private benefit, which is measured by the demand curve, leading to the marginal social benefit. In Figure 18-4, the marginal external benefit curve is shown as *MEB*. The marginal benefit to society as a whole is the vertical sum of the *MEB* curve and the demand curve. The result is the marginal social benefit curve, *MSB*. Efficiency for society occurs at output level Q_{opt}, whereas the market would achieve an inefficiently low level of output, Q_m. Thus, on efficiency grounds alone, society may be justified in subsidizing immunizations.

Although immunization for contagious diseases illustrates the logic and role of beneficial consumption externalities in justifying subsidies for (or possibly public provision of) care, such as the polio immunizations of the 1950s and 1960s, it represents a fairly minor problem and could not in itself be used to justify large social insurance programs. However, an alternative health care externality, one that we have identified elsewhere as a charitable externality, can in principle be sufficiently important to justify such programs.

This externality would occur, for example, whenever people feel that some segment of society is receiving insufficient care in the sense that the charitably minded person would be willing to pay to help these people get care. Willing to pay here means that they would pay if it were so arranged that their contribution would be perceived as helping the poor to acquire health care. Such charitable feelings are probably widespread in most societies. As Pauly (1971) argued:

> The desire to eliminate the diseconomy that the presence of curable but uncured disease or injury may exert on others does appear, in general terms, to be a common characteristic of human beings. At least at some levels, most of us would be willing to give up some of our income to help a suffering fellow.

FIGURE 18-4 The Socially Efficient Equilibrium in the Presence of a Beneficial Externality

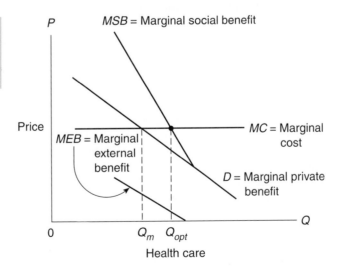

Some may, of course, be immune to such feelings, but individuals may also be immune to contagious disease, and this should cause no insurmountable theoretical problems. (pp. 10–11)

This externality has a different source than the case of immunization and is probably more important, but the economic argument is of the same form. In Figure 18-4, consider the curve *MEB* to measure this charitable externality. Then, as before, the efficient level of output, Q_{opt}, is greater than the market output, Q_m. Under certain circumstances, this efficiency may be sufficient grounds to intervene, for example, by providing a program of social insurance.

Need and Need-Based Distributions

Even if we can identify accurately the efficient allocation of health care, we nevertheless may find many people in society dissatisfied with the outcome because many people will not get the health care they need. If an efficient market cannot be created, the same concern will still exist in most people's minds. That is, there will be additional concerns, over and above efficiency concerns, regarding equity. In the health care literature, the concerns for equity most often center on the question of whether people are getting the health care they need. Thus, health care needs must be addressed.

Unfortunately health care need is often either undefined or variously defined. The definitions employed may take either extreme, need being defined maximally or minimally. For example, Culyer and Wagstaff (1993) review several definitions of health care need; they conclude that a maximal need definition is superior, defining need as:

> the expenditure required to effect the maximum possible health improvement or, equivalently, the expenditure required to reduce the individual's capacity to benefit to zero. (p. 436)

In contrast, some analysts or policy makers treat health care need as a minimal requirement or standard of adequacy. Federal health planning efforts in the 1970s sought to control the perceived proliferation of health care in order to control costs. Health planners at the time, as well as most health cost control advocates in any era, argued implicitly that consumers were getting more health care than they really needed.

Often the discussion of needs gets disconnected from the fact that the output of health care and the distribution of health care to meet people's needs are chosen in the context of society's choices of all its public goals. We present a construction of need that brings this to mind. Let health care needs be defined within the context of the choice of society's goals for population health status as well as in the contexts of other goals, such as education and defense. To illustrate, we identify in Figure 18-5 the production function for health defined over the levels of a variable input, health care, given the conditions of environment, E; lifestyle, LS; and human biological endowment, HB. Here the technically maximal health status is HS_{max}. To achieve this health status level, a health care level of HC_{max} is needed. However, society may choose a lesser health status goal than the maximum achievable, using the savings to further other goals. For example, if society through its choice processes selects health status goal HS_0, then health care level HC_0 is needed.[2]

The choice of a health goal implies a needed level of health care, that is, a level of health care "utilization." In the early 1990s, economists debated the issue of whether

[2]The exposition of need focuses on the consequences; Hurley (2000) describes this interpretation as strongly "consequentialist" and further describes alternative views.

FIGURE 18-5 The Production Function for Health

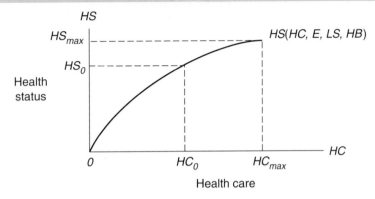

utilization or "access" was the superior choice for defining needs. The words *equity of access*, which frequently appear in public documents in various countries, suggest an equal opportunity, especially a financial opportunity (Mooney et al., 1992). For many health economists, however, *access* is difficult to define. While health care utilization is more easily measured, it is usually also the ultimate reason for our concern about access (Culyer, van Doorslaer, and Wagstaff, 1992a, 1992b).

Health Care Needs and the Social Welfare Function

How, then, is the health status goal selected? We depict this choice using the concept of a social welfare function.

The Utility-Possibility Frontier

The Edgeworth box shows the efficient choices available to society in allocating resources among people. Yet it is also apparent that at many points on the contract curve, Abner or Belinda may be allocated few or no resources. These points are unquestionably economically efficient, yet they may be indefensible within any definition of a humane society.

Economic theory suggests that a social welfare function reflecting society's overall preferences is necessary to determine which of the efficient points is chosen. We can trace out a utility-possibility frontier, *UU*, from the points in the Edgeworth box in Figure 18-1. Begin at the allocation where Belinda has everything and Abner has nothing. In Figure 18-6, we can assign Abner a utility of zero and evaluate Belinda's utility as the intercept of the vertical axis.

We can then draw a *UU* curve by reallocating resources to Abner from Belinda as we move along the contract curve in Figure 18-1. Recall that the fundamental property of Pareto efficient distributions is that Abner's utility can come only at the expense of Belinda's utility. Therefore, the *UU* curve in Figure 18-6 must be downward sloping. The horizontal axis intercept summarizes the point at which Abner has all of the resources.

The Social Welfare Function

It is now up to society to decide which point on *UU* to choose. This decision must be made according to the rules by which societies operate, through debate, consensus, and maybe even dictatorial power. Economists define this as a social welfare function. Consider a society in which the consensus was that everyone's utility level should be exactly the same, with no variations tolerated. We would recognize this as a set of right-angled social indifference curves along a 45-degree line from the origin. The optimum

FIGURE 18-6 The Utility–Possibility Frontier and Social Welfare Maximization: Egalitarian Preferences

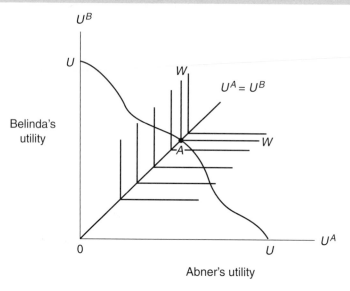

allocation would be at point A, which is a tangency between the WW curve and the UU curve. This would indicate equal utility levels for Abner and Belinda. From point A, we can then return to the one point on the contract curve in Figure 18-1 in which the utility levels are equal, denoted Z. Selecting this point leads to the unique allocation of the two goods to Abner and Belinda (although not necessarily the same amounts to each, as shown in Figure 18-1).

Many would argue that the specific social welfare function (with equal levels of utility) discussed previously would be highly questionable. Humane societies might agree that everyone should be provided with enough resources for at least a minimal standard of living; for Abner this would be U^A_{min}, and for Belinda this would be U^B_{min}. This can be characterized as two constraints on the UU curve in Figure 18-7. Such societies would consider no social welfare function that would provide Abner with less utility than U^A_{min}; this would be similar for Belinda regarding U^B_{min}. Even here, however, the answer depends on the exact social welfare function chosen. Societies in which people like Belinda are most influential may have social welfare functions with social indifference curves like $W'W'$. In this case, people like Belinda would get larger shares of the resources than people like Abner. The optimum at point B, although providing subsistence living for citizens like Abner, would leave citizens like Belinda better off than the optimum in Figure 18-6.

The Social Welfare Function and Health Care Needs

Within this framework, we now discuss the various social choice processes that scholars and policy makers have proposed for the equitable provision of health care. Let the social welfare function of society (SW) represent the preferences of society as a whole. The function in a commonly used form:

$$SW = f(U_1, U_2 \ldots, U_n) \tag{18.1}$$

where social welfare is characterized as a function of the utility levels of each of the n persons in the society. Utility for each person as usual depends on his or her consumption

FIGURE 18-7 The Utility Frontier and Social Welfare Maximization: Preferences Favoring Belinda

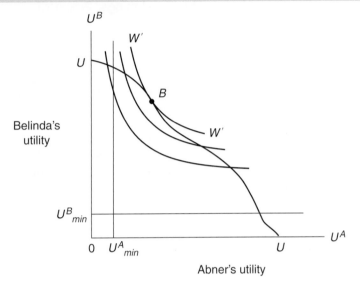

of the available goods in society, including health care. In addition, we may suppose that each individual to some degree perceives an external benefit from the consumption of health care by others.

Society may be perceived to be efficient when it acts as if it were choosing among its variables to maximize the social welfare function. The choice process may be conceived graphically in Figure 18-7 as choosing the highest social indifference curve attainable given the utility possibility frontier. The level of health care needed can be defined within this context. The health care needed by each person in society is that which maximizes *SW*. Social welfare will be maximized when society chooses its optimal health status goals in conjunction with optimal levels of other goals. One example of a societal choice process is Williams's "fair innings" proposal in Box 18-2.

The social welfare function has proved flexible within health economics because it can be used to formulate other conceptions of health equity. Some health economists propose that society's health goal should be the maximization of community health and propose that the quality-adjusted life years (QALYs) that remain in the life expectancy of the community be used as the measure of health. Wagstaff (1991) showed how this concept, as well as equity adjustment factors, can be incorporated into the social welfare function framework. Bleichrodt (1997) attempted to make the QALY approach more concrete by demonstrating mathematical assumptions that give the utility of the QALY interpersonal comparability, making the social welfare function a matter of simply adding up all individual utilities. This is a return to utilitarianism of the eighteenth century, but also a novel use of the social welfare function framework.

Norman Daniels's Concept of Health Care Need

To assume that health care need is determined by the same social choice mechanism by which society makes all its choices of social goals is to treat health status like all other goals. Some analysts argue that health is special and that health care needs have a more objective independent basis. Others argue that the standard economic conception of

BOX 18-2

The "Fair Innings" Proposal

Alan Williams (1997) proposes that people would generally agree to the principle that everyone is entitled to a normal span of life at a reasonable level of quality. The Williams metaphor fits on both sides of the Atlantic: Cricket has one or two innings and baseball has nine innings—generally that is all anyone gets—but everyone should get that much. This idea applies with most force to trade-offs in life years between the old and the young; in this context, it implies a rationing by age.

Consider two individuals, each of whom stands to gain eight good quality extra years of life after being "rescued" from a lethal disease by medical technology costing $100,000. Let one of

these people be 80 years of age and the other 30 years of age. If resources are scarce, which individual should get the treatment? The "fair innings" concept would clearly require the treatment go to the younger person since the 80-year-old person has had his or her fair innings already.

Valuations by society in this fair innings scheme are generally not so simple. This central issue lies in how much society prefers to help the one versus the other. If we agree that the elderly facing illness and the young facing illness are not equal, then the question for Williams becomes "to what degree are we as a community averse to this inequality?"

society's well-being is flawed. Its dependence on the individual's conception of his own well-being, its reliance on the Pareto principle, and its usual insistence that social choice issues depend solely on individual utilities have been criticized as "welfarism." Those making the criticism include recent Nobel economist Amartya Sen. To address the special role of health, the philosopher Norman Daniels (1985) has developed a health care needs definition, and we provide an outline of his approach here.

1. *Health care is special.* Under this view, health care can be separated from other goals. To make this separation plausible, health care must be viewed as a primary good that is special because it is central to the task of attaining or restoring a fair equality of opportunity. In this sense, it comes prior to other considerations.
2. *Species-typical functioning.* It is further argued that the human species has a range of functioning that is typical and appropriate to it. Disease here means the absence of health; health is defined as the ability to attain a functioning level typical to the species.
3. *Fair equality of opportunity.* Given the nature of society and the human species, there is a range of behavior opportunity that every person in society should have available. The range will vary somewhat from person to person inasmuch as we each have different endowments of skills and abilities, but all are entitled to their fair share.

To use the fair equality of opportunity standard of health care need, we must imagine that there is a degree of objectivity behind its construction, and that need so constructed would be observable in common by most people. We do not solve this matter here, but instead point out what Daniels's project entails. If Daniels's view was accepted as correct, then health care need could be identified separately from the context in which other goals for society are chosen. We leave as a discussion question the issue of whether this is possible.[3]

[3]The issue can be pursued further with Daniels's stimulating and controversial book (1985) and articles (1981, 1982).

Economic Criticisms of Need-Based Distributions

The ideas of mainstream economics often clash with need-based conceptions of the appropriate distribution of health care resources. The economic criticisms are directed to particular conceptions of need and can be understood as saying "if by need you mean X, then the following criticism applies. . . ." Several criticisms of this sort are found in the literature.

1. *The bottomless pit.* Health is undoubtedly subject to diminishing marginal returns in production. Thus, if the technical maximum health status goal is chosen, the marginal unit of health care will have nearly zero effect on health status. Because it is doubtful that all societal goals can be attained maximally, social welfare generally would be improved if society would reduce health care use somewhat and use the freed resources for other goals. For that matter, health care needs at or close to the technical maximum also could exhaust most of society's resources and thus constitute a bottomless pit.

2. *Needs should not be chosen independent of costs.* Society's health status goals should depend in part on the costs of health and thus on the price of health care. This is so because the costs of health care resources determine the amounts of other goods that must be given up to attain health goals. No society is wealthy enough to attain the maximum amounts of all goals, and health has opportunity costs.

3. *The role of scientific medicine in determining needs.* From similar reasoning, it follows that health needs cannot be determined solely on the basis of scientific medical knowledge. The role of medical experts is critical in needs analysis, inasmuch as scientific data are required to determine the medical inputs needed to attain a given health goal. However, the appropriate health status goals themselves must be chosen with knowledge of society's economic constraints and its values. In some form, the political process is required to identify the trade-offs that society is willing to incur to attain any given goal.

4. *Monotechnic needs.* Finally, Fuchs (1974) has pointed out that when needs analyses are stated in terms of needed health resources per capita, they often implicitly falsely assume that only one available technique exists for pursuing a health status goal. More plausibly, many opportunities exist for substitution, not only among health care inputs but also among health care inputs and other inputs into the production function of health.

Horizontal Equity and Need

Health care need is also a central focus in attempts to answer questions about the equitable treatment of people with equal needs. Equal treatment of equals is known as horizontal equity. To understand the issues and findings, we draw on the work of van Doorslaer and Wagstaff (1992). These authors define inequity by beginning with the following equations:

$$m_1 = a_p + b_p h_i, \qquad \text{if poor} \tag{18.2}$$

$$m_1 = a_r + b_r h_i, \qquad \text{if rich} \tag{18.3}$$

In these equations, m is medical expenditure; a_p and a_r are constant levels of expenditure when healthy for the poor and the rich, respectively; b_p and b_r are constant coefficients of health status, h_i, which equals 0 when the person is healthy and 1 when sick.

Horizontal equity occurs when $a_p = a_r$ and $b_p = b_r$; that is, when the expected average spending of the rich and poor are equal both when well ($h_i = 0$) and when sick ($h_i = 1$). Does this square with your own sense of what equity means?[4]

Comparing Horizontal Equity Among Countries

To generate a measure of the degree of inequity, the authors then calculate the standardized expenditure shares, based on equation (18.2), which are the groups' shares of total expenditure reflected by their spending. The final result is described graphically in Figure 18-8. Here, the curve labeled *g* measures the cumulative standardized shares against the cumulative population arranged by income level. As shown in this hypothetical example, the poorest 20 percent of the population accounts for about 5 percent of medical expenditure, the poorest 40 percent accounts for about 11 percent of the expenditure, and so on. If spending favors the rich, the curve will lie below the diagonal, as in this case. When spending favors the poor, the curve will lie above the diagonal. The degree of inequality is measured as the ratio of the area of the ellipsoid *A* to the total area under the diagonal.[5]

The Results

The van Doorslaer and Wagstaff results for inequity across countries are shown in Table 18-1. These data suggest that unequal use by people and income groups given health status is the common rule, not the exception. However, the negative numbers in the table show countries where the estimated inequality is in favor of the poorer people. Only in the Netherlands, Spain, the United Kingdom, and the United States does

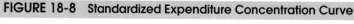

FIGURE 18-8 Standardized Expenditure Concentration Curve

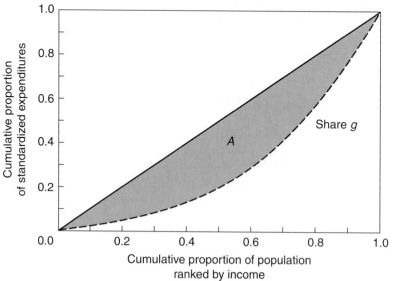

[4]Mooney et al. (1991, 1992) question whether equity means equal expenditure. An individual may differ from another because of different preferences, so even with equal access, the amount of expenditures on care will differ. Culyer, van Doorslaer, and Wagstaff (1992a, b) respond to this objection.

[5]If the curve lies above the diagonal, then the inequality is measured as the ratio of the negative area of the ellipsoid to the total area under the diagonal.

TABLE 18-1 Tests of Inequality Across Countries

Country	Measure of Inequality[a]	Statistically Significant
Denmark	−0.055	Yes
Ireland	−0.077	Yes
Italy	−0.036	Yes
Netherlands	0.025	No
Spain	0.146	Yes
Switzerland	−0.043	No
United Kingdom	0.013	Yes
United States	0.028	Yes

[a]Measured at the 1 percent level of statistical significance.

Source: Reprinted from *Journal of Health Economics*, Eddy van Doorslaer and Adam Wagstaff, "Equity in the Delivery of Health Care: Some International Comparisons." *Journal of Health Economics 11* (1992): 389–411, with permission from Elsevier Science.

the distribution tend to favor the rich, although in the Netherlands the result is not statistically significant. When the elderly are left out of consideration in the United States, then the distribution even in the United States favors the poor. Although measurement and definition issues of horizontal equity may elicit disagreement, these numbers representing unequal use for a given health status across income groups are clearly defined and tell an important part of the story.

Theories of Social Justice

Inevitably, a treatment of what health care distribution is equitable and what health care needs should be met in a society depends on ethical theory. An ethical theory serves to identify a context and reasoning to determine what ought to be done, as opposed to mere positive analysis of what is the case. Ethical theories that serve to determine a fair or just distribution of economic resources are sometimes called theories of social justice. Seen this way, any notion of equity or need in health care, to be complete, must be connected to an ethical theory or perhaps to a theory of social justice.

Several theories of social justice have been proposed. It cannot be said that we have a consensus-accepted theory of social justice. Even without a consensus, however, theories of social justice help to illuminate the issues that must be addressed if a consensus is to be achieved. We offer a brief overview of three social justice theories, along with a selection of criticisms of each theory.

Utilitarianism

Utilitarianism became prominent in the nineteenth century and is still current in modified forms. It can be understood as the greatest good for the greatest number. In its classical form, it identified the social optimum coincident with maximization of the sum of utilities of all persons in society. Classical utilitarianism in effect defines the social welfare function as the sum of individual utilities.

In the form of utilitarianism promoted by Jeremy Bentham in the eighteenth and nineteenth centuries, an individual's utility was conceived of as cardinally measurable, at least in principle, and comparable among individuals. The utilitarian ethic originally was conceived somewhat literally as maximization of society's total satisfaction level.

Utilitarianism captures the idea of trade-offs among goals. Under this construction, society may choose to accept some harm for a few members in return for a greater good for the many. As such, it avoids the bottomless pit criticisms mentioned earlier. Health status would not generally be maximized for every individual in society under this view.

Some Criticisms of Utilitarianism

Classical utilitarianism came to be criticized within the economics profession early in the twentieth century. Economists generally rejected the idea that utility could be cardinally measurable and comparable among people. It is viewed as unscientific to suppose that one individual's level of satisfaction could somehow be added to that of another person. Modern social welfare theory in economics has proceeded along ordinal utility lines. Utility in these theories retains the role of ranking preferences among alternatives, but the notion of a fixed quantitative measure of happiness was discarded in most modern theory.

Two other criticisms of utilitarianism illustrate some of the weaknesses identified in the theory. One is the question of domain—that is, whose utilities are to count? Utilitarianism does not itself identify where to draw the boundaries of membership in the society. Are foreign people or noncitizens to count? If not, why not? Are animals to count? Unborn future generations? Is the utility of the fetus to count or only that of the already born?

A second criticism raised by Robert Nozick (1974) poses a similar question regarding possibly malevolent individuals in society. For example, suppose an individual, because of bigotry or sheer malevolence, gets satisfaction out of the suffering of some other group in society. Is the malevolent utility of such a person also to count?

Rawls and Justice as Fairness

John Rawls (1971) approached the concept of social justice from a different viewpoint. Here, a primary principle of justice is that social choices must be fair. Rawls views it as unfair for social choices to be dominated by people with economic or political power who often have vested interests because of their circumstances in society. Instead, to be fair, we should make our choices from a position divorced from arbitrary special interestedness. Such a position, it is proposed, is one from behind the "veil of ignorance."[6]

The Rawlsian veil of ignorance is a hypothetical situation in which we can think rationally but for which our particularities of self and economic situation are as yet unknown. It is as if we could somehow contemplate life in society before we are born and before we know whether we will be rich or poor, black or white, male or female, tall or short, and so on. Rawls's idea is that, so divorced from our vested interests of life, we would generally come to a consensus about principles of social justice, and specifically we would agree to the Rawlsian maximin principle.

Under the maximin principle, we would each reason that without knowing who we were to become in society, we would presume that we could be the person worst off. Under such circumstances, we would agree, argues Rawls, only to a system of justice in society that maximized the position of the worst off. This need not result in complete equality of incomes and resources including health care, but departures from equality would be permitted only if the lot of the worst off would improve. Health care under a

[6]Olsen (1997) notes that Rawls's maximin principle is the most prominent of a class of egalitarian social justice principles. Olsen's exposition offers a diagrammatic depiction of each social justice theory prominent in health economics.

Rawlsian system of social justice would presumably also be provided if the needs of the worst off were regarded as a priority.

Some Criticisms of Rawlsian Justice

Rawls's theory of justice also has drawn criticism, and we illustrate some of these criticisms. It has been pointed out that Rawls assumes that each of us behind the veil of ignorance is extremely risk averse. Suppose that an alternative situation, A, offered everyone an income of $10,000, while alternative B offered one person $9,000 but everyone else $100,000. Under the maximin principle, persons behind the veil would choose alternative A, the alternative with the higher income for the worst off. Would people really be so risk averse as to forgo even extremely good odds of a large gain?

The Rawlsian theory of justice also appears subject to the bottomless pit argument. The instance of health care provides a good example of the problem in the views of Arrow (1973):

> Thus there could easily exist medical procedures which serve to keep people barely alive but with little satisfaction and which are yet so expensive as to reduce the rest of the population to poverty. (p. 251)

Despite the criticisms, Rawlsian justice provides a prominent example of a theory of social justice that entails a strong presumption in favor of equality—a presumption that permits inequalities to arise only if they contribute to the lot of the worst off.

Liberalism, Classical and Modern

Classical liberalism refers to the political philosophy developed largely during the Age of Enlightenment, which centers on the eighteenth century. Led by the principles of John Locke (1660), it emphasizes the rights of the individual to his property and to himself. In this view, a person enters the state voluntarily, and he is free to choose what he deems best for himself and his family. The tradition was the intellectual guide to the American Constitution, as is well-known to American school children. These "classical liberals" also included Adam Smith and, later, John Stuart Mill and Friedrich Hayek. Liberty in this tradition was largely a matter of emphasis as opposed to a fixed constraint. These philosophers largely supported taxation and often mentioned favorably things, such as government programs, to improve the well-being of the community; Locke (1697, p. 4), for example, favored government aid to the poor, Smith favored public schooling for working class children (1976, p. III, II, 303), Mill applied a utilitarian calculus to public issues (1975), and Hayek, whose life spanned the creation of the New Deal, spoke favorably of social health insurance itself (1960, p. 298). Would classical liberals, in sum, support for example a modern universal social health insurance? Folland (2005) reasons that they might do so.

In contrast to the older, verbal tradition of these economic philosophers, the modern libertarian, Robert Nozick (1974), departs both in analytical style and by drawing stronger implications. Nozick asserts that government must limit itself to maintaining only the necessary services: the "minimal state."

Nozick proposes that natural rights suggest the necessity for a *libertarian constraint*. By a libertarian constraint, he means that any system of social organization should prohibit the coercion of others, and people are entitled to keep any property received through a voluntary transaction. From these principles, Nozick justifies the existence of a minimal state. He argues that these principles of justice necessarily limit the role of the state, and in consequence, social programs beyond the minimal functions of government in providing public police protection services would not be warranted.

It follows that social programs providing for health care also would not be warranted, and the health care needs of one person would not place obligations on any other person other than for what he or she voluntarily is willing to accept.

Some Criticisms of the Modern Libertarian Theory

A central focus of criticism is the assumed libertarian constraint itself. For those who do not accept the constraint as an implication or necessity of natural rights, it will be hard to see why we are not free to trade off some degree of liberty in order to make gains in efficiency. For example, the Food and Drug Administration restrictions on the availability of certain drugs represent restrictions on liberty, but at least, in some cases, they may be supportable on efficiency grounds. Pauly (1978) has argued that if the costs of conveying information to the public are sufficiently large, substantial efficiency gains may accrue simply by restricting access to a potentially dangerous drug. The restriction of access may in some cases require a physician's prescription; in other cases, it may require banning the drug from the market.

Members of society frequently accept rules that restrict liberty somewhat but that are expected to improve outcomes. Wittman (1982) has discussed the potential efficiency of simple rules in day-to-day life and in sports. A traffic light restricts liberty but promotes the efficient and safe flow of traffic. If we accept the principle that liberties can be traded off to gain certain efficiencies, this raises the question of whether we must accept the libertarian constraint.

Conclusions

The three theories of social justice described here attempt to ground our understanding of the distribution of goods and services—including health care—in a system of ethics. The brief review of these theories cannot account for all arguments and rebuttals nor is it an exhaustive coverage of the many normative models available. Those interested in ethics, as it concerns economic distribution, should consult the original sources. The theories, however, serve to show how widely people's understanding of appropriate distributions of health care differ, and their consideration suggests that we have as yet no consensus. Nevertheless, these issues of justice are raised whenever society wishes to modify the distribution of health resources on grounds of need and equity. The issues are no less important because there is disagreement.

The meaning of efficiency is more sharply defined. Here the issues of controversy involve the degree of efficiency attainable either with existing health care markets or with health care markets as modified by new policies. The theoretical model of perfect competition generates a Pareto efficient outcome. Health care markets in practice, however, differ in many respects from those that have perfect competition. Perhaps the most notable discrepancies of actual health care markets from the theoretical model arise because of the role of uncertainty, the problems of information, and the presence of externalities.

Perfection in either direction is not attainable. We must inevitably accept approaches to health care distribution that are second best, evaluating each proposal on its merits. While perfect competition is unattainable, proposals that improve the degree of competition in health care markets may nevertheless improve society's well-being. On the other hand, proposals for providing social insurance programs to at least some segments of the population can be supported in principle on efficiency grounds whenever substantial charitable externalities are present. Alternatively, social insurance programs may be justified on the basis of one or more systems of social justice.

SUMMARY

1. Pareto efficiency defines a situation where it is no longer possible to make mutually beneficial changes. It is Pareto efficient to exhaust all avenues for gains that benefit someone and harm no one.

2. Under theoretical conditions of perfect competition, the competitive market is Pareto efficient. In the Edgeworth box for exchange, regardless of the initial endowment position, a competitive free exchange will lead to a Pareto efficient point, a point on the contract curve. This is the First Fundamental Theorem of Welfare Economics.

3. The Second Fundamental Theorem of Welfare Economics also is illustrated by the Edgeworth box for exchange. The theorem holds that any Pareto efficient outcome can, in principle, be achieved by a competitive market, given a suitable initial distribution of resources.

4. Price discrimination is Pareto inefficient. This result includes that form of price discrimination arising when a favored segment of the population is provided reduced prices for health care so as to improve access.

5. The health care sector deviates from the conditions of perfect competition in many respects. These include major issues of the role of uncertainty, the role of information, and the role of externalities.

6. The Theorem of the Second Best suggests that promoting competitive features in health care markets is not welfare enhancing per se. Nevertheless, many competitive proposals in practice may be welfare enhancing.

7. Social programs for the subsidization or provision of health care can be theoretically rationalized on grounds of efficiency as well as equity. The usual efficiency argument posits the existence of a charitable externality in health care. The presence of externalities may, in principle, justify market interventions.

8. Need-based distributions of health care resources tend to be based on equity grounds and usually imply a rejection of market outcomes. Health care need may be understood as health care resources required to attain a given health goal chosen by society.

9. Society's optimal choice of goals may be summarized by the social welfare function, defined over all possible combinations of the individual utilities of society members. This leads to the optimal choice by selecting the point on the utility-possibility frontier that maximizes social welfare.

10. Norman Daniels's concept of health care need is based on the fair equality of opportunity. It argues that health care needs may be identified separately from other social decisions.

11. Several need-based distributions can be criticized on economic grounds. These grounds argue that health care needs should not be (1) the technical maximum, (2) independent of cost, (3) chosen solely on technical medical criteria, or (4) monotechnic.

12. A philosophical theory of justice is needed to provide an ethical grounding for a proposed distribution. There is no present consensus on such a theory of justice.

DISCUSSION QUESTIONS

1. At point 0_A in Figure 18-1, Belinda has all of both goods. Is this point Pareto efficient? Is it equitable? Discuss.

2. If society could clearly choose an equitable point reflecting a distribution of the two goods, is this point inevitably going to lie on the contract curve?

3. Choose an example of a health care market and identify ways in which it differs from the perfectly competitive model. Do you think that these deviations from competition could each be repaired by appropriate policies? Discuss.

4. We describe several economic criticisms of need-based distributions. Do any of these criticisms apply to Norman Daniels's conception of health care need?

5. Speculate on how each of the three described theories of social justice would view government programs designed to provide infant and child care to the poor using tax dollars.

6. Under utilitarianism, one maximizes the total utility of society. What does this imply about the marginal utility for each person? What does it imply about the total utility for each person?
7. Suppose society determined that it must provide a minimal sustained level of health to everyone. What would this imply regarding society's expenditures on health?
8. Insufficient health care for some often is seen as a problem of insufficient income to purchase health care. Discuss two alternatives to social programs that provide health care.

EXERCISES

1. Prove that point B in Figure 18-1 is not Pareto efficient.
2. Draw an Edgeworth box like the one in Figure 18-2 but with only these details inside: the point V and budget line AB through V. Using indifference curves, depict the utility-maximizing choice for Abner. Now let the budget line rotate to CD, drawn to reflect a higher relative price of medical care. Again identify the utility-maximizing choice for Abner.
3. Is it possible to find a point on the contract curve that is not a competitive equilibrium?
4. Let Q_{opt} in Figure 18-4 represent the optimal level of health care in society under the external benefits rationale for social health care programs. Would members of society necessarily view Q_{opt} as the equitable amount of health care?
5. If all tax-paying members of society became "hard hearted," feeling no external benefit in the health care provided to others, then what would be the optimal health care output under the external benefit rationale in Figure 18-4?
6. In Figure 18-7, which depicts the utility-possibility frontier, would society ever choose an inefficient point (inside UU) as the optimal point?
7. Suppose Fred has an income of $5,000 per year, and Harry has an income of $105,000 per year. If we tax $50,000 from Harry to give to Fred, will this represent a Pareto improvement for society? Why or why not? Would this improve society under some other criteria?

CHAPTER

Government Intervention in Health Care Markets

Economic Rationale for Government Intervention

Forms of Government Intervention

Government Involvement in Health Care Markets

Government Failure

Competitive Strategies

Conclusions

Previous chapters have revealed the scope of government involvement in health care delivery. We have seen that (1) government spending accounts for a substantial portion of all health care spending, (2) governments are deeply involved in producing as well as financing health care services, and (3) governments regulate the health care industries. Also, we have found that governments are at the center of most contemporary health care issues. These include major policy issues, such as national health insurance and initiatives intended to control costs and increase access to care, and also less publicized issues, such as those involving federal government support for education and research.

The purpose of this chapter is to provide a framework for assessing the role of governments in health care markets. We begin with the conventional approach favored by economists, which emphasizes market failure as the rationale for government intervention. This is followed by a historical review, including examples of federal, state, and local involvement in the health economy. We continue with a discussion of government failure to identify impediments in developing effective programs. As an alternative to regulation, we also address competitive strategies to improve health care delivery and to meet this nation's policy goals.

Economic Rationale for Government Intervention

As we have seen, efficiency is one common standard for evaluating the desirability of economic allocations. Inefficient allocations are associated with various distortions that lead to market failure. The previous chapter introduced the distortion resulting from beneficial externalities as one justification for social programs in health care.

Monopoly Power

Monopoly power provides the classic example of market failure. A profit-maximizing monopolist produces to the level at which marginal revenue equals marginal cost. Because the marginal revenue lies below the demand curve, the monopolist will reduce production below competitive levels, and the price charged by the monopolist will exceed the marginal cost of production. The reduced production and the price–marginal cost gap together create the welfare loss.

Figure 19-1 summarizes these standard results. With a perfectly elastic competitive supply in the long run, which also represents the industry's average costs (AC) and marginal costs (MC), the competitive price and quantity are P_C and Q_C. If this industry is monopolized and no changes occur in demand or costs, the profit-maximizing output is given by Q_M, where $MR = MC$. The higher monopoly price is P_M, and the welfare loss is represented by triangle ABC.

However, monopoly power need not be associated solely with pure monopoly. The monopoly model is applied commonly to markets in which one or a small number of sellers are dominant. Several health care markets seem to hold a potential for the exercise of monopoly power. Examples include hospital services in markets with few hospitals, pharmaceutical products that are protected by patents, and some health insurance markets dominated by Blue Cross and Blue Shield associations.

The potential for monopoly power exists even in markets characterized by a large number of sellers, as in the markets for doctor and dental services. Licensure laws and other forms of regulation restrict entry into some professions. Furthermore, professional associations may be able to reduce price competition by setting minimum fee schedules or by inhibiting the flow of information to buyers.

Several issues arise regarding monopoly power. First, some barriers to entry result from government intervention itself. These include licensure and patent laws. Licensure is intended to ensure minimal standards of quality; patent laws are intended to promote innovative activity.

FIGURE 19-1 Welfare Loss of Monopoly

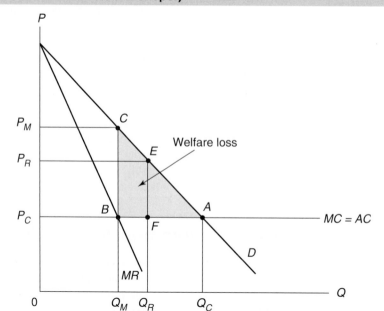

Second, monopoly power may be inevitable in some situations and does not necessarily lead to economic profits. In a small market, for example, demand may be sufficient for only one hospital to survive while it just covers costs. If demand were to diminish, even the one existing hospital might not be able to survive unless it either received subsidies or donations, or cut its costs.

Third, the proposed cure to monopoly inefficiencies may be worse than the problems posed by the existence and exercise of monopoly power. Some have argued that direct intervention through public provision or price controls could worsen the situation because of government failure. These critics suggest that countervailing forces and other constraints on the full exercise of monopoly power will tend to arise in private markets, especially where antitrust laws are enforced vigorously.

In the simplest case and in the absence of government failure, price controls can theoretically reduce the welfare loss caused by monopoly. In Figure 19-1, suppose a maximum fee control of P_R is established. The monopolist's marginal revenue is constant, equal to the price, P_R, up to an output of Q_R. Because marginal revenue exceeds marginal cost up until output Q_R, the monopolist will produce at least to Q_R. Beyond Q_R, the marginal revenue is found from the usual *MR* curve because the monopolist would have to lower prices to attract more buyers. Marginal revenue then will be below marginal cost and eventually will become negative. The profit-maximizing output is Q_R, and the welfare loss is now reduced from area *ABC* to area *AEF*. While it appears in this case that price regulation can be an effective instrument in reducing prices, monopoly profits, and welfare losses, consider that a typical hospital or physician provider may produce many different services. Consider also that demand and technology change constantly and that it may be difficult to monitor quality. As we will discuss later, price regulation under such circumstances becomes far more difficult.

Public Goods

A public good should not be confused with the public provision of a good. The postal service and garbage collection service are examples of public provision of private goods. Such goods may be provided by government because of natural monopoly or a desire to subsidize certain users (e.g., rural postal customers). In contrast, a pure public good is one for which consumption is nonrival (i.e., consumption by one individual does not reduce someone else's consumption) and nonexcludable (i.e., a consumer cannot be excluded from consuming the good either by having to pay or through some other mechanism). National defense is used often as an example of a pure public good. Other examples of goods having some degree of "publicness" include highways, bridges, and parks.

Market failure arises because an inefficiently small quantity of pure public goods typically will be provided without government intervention. Figure 19-2 develops this proposition. Begin with a simple case involving two persons whose demands and marginal benefits for a public good are represented by D_A and D_B. By definition, a public good is nonrival and nonexcludable. Each person must consume the identical quantity that he or she buys or that is made available. Thus, the marginal social benefits (*MSB*) are the sum of the two individuals' marginal private benefits. Since, unlike private goods, each will get the same amount of the public good, the combined willingness of the two consumers to pay for the public good, the *MSB*, is the vertical summation of D_A and D_B.

Assuming constant costs, the efficient quantity is Q_E, where *MSB* equal the marginal costs of production, *MC*. Will the efficient quantity become available without government intervention? Knowing that their contributions are important, the two consumers may decide to cooperate by making voluntary contributions to fund at least

FIGURE 19-2 The Optimal Quantity of a Public Good

some of the good. In fact, if each contributes according to his or her marginal private benefit at Q_E by paying P_A and P_B, respectively for every unit, enough money will be collected to cover the cost of providing the optimal quantity Q_E. It is not certain, however, whether this solution will be reached.

More realistically, public goods usually involve a large number of individuals. In principle, determining the optimal quantity, using a vertically summed marginal social benefit curve, follows the two-person example. The major difference is that these people are unlikely to cooperate to fund substantial amounts of the public good through voluntary contributions. Instead, more are likely to become free riders (i.e., make no contributions) because they cannot be excluded from consuming the good and because any voluntary contribution one makes to the provision of the good will have a negligible impact on the good's availability. The predicted undersupply of public goods in private markets has led many to conclude that governments should be responsible for making them available.

Are health care services public goods? Health services provided to one person are not at the same time consumed by others. Also, those who do not pay can be excluded from receiving care. Therefore, health care services are private goods even though they may involve public provision (e.g., through the Veterans Administration) or public financing (e.g., through Medicare and Medicaid). Thus, the public goods rationale for government provision of health care is not immediately apparent.

Despite this caveat, economic theories of public goods are highly relevant to certain health care issues. Consider the following cases:

Information

Information can be thought of as an economic good with a large public content. One consumer obtaining information does not reduce the information available to another. Although those who do not pay often can be excluded from receiving information, the

marginal cost of providing information to another individual is often relatively small. It can be argued that information will be underproduced in private markets and that government intervention is needed to increase its availability.

The government may take on two distinct roles. The first is to help disseminate existing knowledge to the public. This can be achieved either through direct provision or through subsidizing private sector activities. Second, governments may expand the stock of knowledge by taking an active role in scientific research, again by direct provision or through subsidizing private sector research. The federal government has pursued both strategies.

Redistribution

Voluntary giving also has a public goods dimension. Donations help to raise lower-income persons' standards of consumption, including their consumption of health care. By letting others donate and knowing that one's contribution will have little impact on total contributions, individuals often become free riders. To help offset this effect, it can be argued that mandatory programs are needed to correct the undersupply of voluntary giving.

However, considerable disagreement can arise over the form of the redistribution. Should it be done through cash transfers to let recipients spend their additional incomes as they see fit? Or should some programs take the form of in-kind transfers (e.g., Medicaid) where the transfers must be used to purchase health care services? The many issues relating to equity and mechanisms for redistributing income are discussed in Chapters 18 ("Equity, Efficiency, and Need") and 21 ("Social Insurance").

Externalities

In contrast to pure or nearly pure public goods, another group is composed of those goods that have third-party effects, also known as externalities. Recall that externalities arise when a third party is affected by another party's consumption or production of a good. If a neighbor's loud music or smoke from leaves burning bothers you, a negative externality has been created.

Moreover, to be considered an externality, the effects must be transmitted outside the price system. A situation where an increase in demand for lower-cholesterol meats raises their prices, adversely affecting consumers of these products, is not an externality. The higher prices ration the supply of low-cholesterol products.

The major problem is that many negative or positive externalities may not be reflected fully in the prices of the goods and services with which they are associated. Thus, even when competitive forces drive prices to the marginal private cost of production, social efficiency requires that marginal social benefits equal the marginal social costs. Marginal social benefits sum the marginal private benefits and any marginal external benefits that might exist, while marginal social costs similarly sum the marginal private costs and any marginal external costs.

When a negative externality, such as pollution, creates a marginal external cost, a competitive market tends to overproduce the polluting good relative to the socially efficient quantity. The market price will not reflect the external cost. Conversely, competitive markets tend to undersupply goods that create beneficial (positive) externalities. Marginal social benefits exceed the price at the competitive output. Positive externalities can be important in health care, as when a charitably minded person derives satisfaction from knowing that the sick, poor, or uninsured consume more health care. More tangible externalities are created when others are inoculated against communicable diseases.

Positive externalities should not be confused with health benefits that are largely private. Subsidies that lead to improved health are often supported on the grounds that recipients will benefit society by being more productive. However, the gains from an individual's increased productivity are largely private. Thus, the effects of the consumption of health care on productivity are not externalities.

Other Rationales for Government Intervention

Several other arguments favor government intervention. An important responsibility of the federal government is to stabilize the economy through macroeconomic policies. Although macroeconomics does not usually focus on specific sectors of the economy, changes in monetary, fiscal, and debt policy can have major effects on federal and state health care programs, as well as on private health care spending through changes in taxes and interest rates.

Another distinct category involves government's role in promoting the consumption of merit goods. Merit goods are commodities thought to be good for someone regardless of the person's own preferences. Support for the arts, compulsory education, and mandated consumption of other goods are in part supported by arguments that individuals do not always know what is in their best interests. Undoubtedly, to some extent, public policy with respect to public health interventions, such as seat belts and alcohol, tobacco, and drug use, has reflected the merit goods idea.

A final role for government involves incomplete markets which occur when private markets fail to meet an existing demand. Certain insurance markets, such as those for patients with cancer, AIDS, or other preexisting conditions who seek new insurance, are sometimes suggested as examples of incomplete markets in the sense that such patients may not be able to buy insurance at any price. It has been proposed that government has a role in filling these gaps by providing insurance or requiring insurers to do so.

It is important to determine, however, whether some of these markets are truly incomplete. Is there sufficient demand by those willing to pay actuarially fair rates so that a market would emerge? Because premiums would, on average, match insurance payments, they would be very high. Are such patients seeking subsidies by having legislation guaranteeing access to insurance at lower than actuarially fair rates?

Forms of Government Intervention

Governments can adopt a variety of policies and instruments to influence the allocation of resources or the distribution of income. The principal categories relevant to health care are selective commodity taxes and subsidies, public provision of health care, transfer programs, and regulation.

Commodity Taxes and Subsidies

We already have established that a competitive market is inefficient when beneficial (positive) externalities result from the consumption of a commodity. Using inoculations against infectious disease as an example, we extend our previous work to show how taxes and subsidies can, in principle, correct for the externality.

Let demand, D, and supply, S, in Figure 19-3 reflect the marginal private benefits (MPB) and marginal private costs (MPC) of inoculations. MPB equals MPC at the equilibrium quantity, Q_1. However, the competitive allocation is inefficient when those

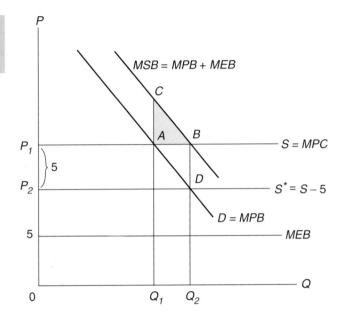

FIGURE 19-3 Using Commodity Subsidies to Correct for Positive Externalities

who are inoculated confer a marginal external benefit (*MEB*) on others. Too little is produced at Q_1 because marginal social benefit, the vertical sum of the *MPB* and *MEB*, exceeds marginal social costs (here equal to *MPC* because there are no external costs). Pareto efficiency and the elimination of the welfare loss shown by triangle *ABC* require output Q_2 where *MSB* equals *MPC*.

The imposition of a commodity tax or subsidy provides a method of correcting for the externality. Assume for simplicity that the marginal external benefit is constant at $5 per inoculation. To correct for the externality, Congress can provide producers with a subsidy[1] of $5. The supply curve facing consumers will shift down by the amount of the subsidy to S^* because producers will need to receive $5 less than before from consumers to produce the quantities shown along the original supply, *S*. With the new supply, the equilibrium price paid by patients decreases to P_2, and the equilibrium quantity rises to the optimum Q_2. Governments pay producers $5Q_2$, or rectangle P_1BDP_2.

This simple example illustrates several important features of a commodity subsidy. First, the price paid by consumers will fall by the full amount of the subsidy only when the supply is perfectly elastic, as in Figure 19-3, or when the demand is perfectly inelastic. In other cases, as with a positively sloped supply, the price paid by consumers will not fall by $5. Including the subsidy, producers will receive a higher price than before. Both consumers and producers share the benefits of the subsidy even though it is paid to producers.

As the elasticity of demand increases, or elasticity of supply decreases, the equilibrium price falls by smaller amounts, and the equilibrium quantity increases by larger amounts. In the long run, the competitive market supply will be highly elastic (perfectly elastic in a constant-cost industry). Thus, the benefits of a subsidy will accrue mainly to consumers in competitive markets.

[1] A $5 subsidy to the consumer will shift the demand curve up by the $5 so that the new demand mirrors *MSB* and passes through point *B*. The solution remains the same. Consumers buy quantity Q_2 at price P_1, paying P_2 net of the subsidy. It will generally be easier to administer commodity taxes and subsidies through producers than consumers.

Second, to achieve efficiency, decision makers need accurate estimates of both the monetary value of the externality and elasticities of demand and supply. The costs of administering taxes and the difficulties of accurate estimation are strong arguments against the use of a corrective subsidy unless the positive externality is substantial.

Finally, we note that policy makers can achieve the results described in Figure 19-3 by taxing those who are not inoculated rather than subsidizing those who are (see exercise 4). By imposing a cost on those who refuse inoculations, the opportunity cost of an inoculation is its price minus the tax. The lower effective price increases quantity. The administrative complexity of monitoring those who are or are not inoculated argues against this approach.

When consumption of a good, such as smoking, leads to harmful (negative) externalities, the marginal external cost must be added to the marginal private cost to determine the efficient solution. The competitive output will be greater than the optimum. To reduce consumption, price must be raised. A price increase can be achieved either through a corrective tax to shift the supply curve up or through a subsidy to nonsmokers that raises the effective price of smoking.

Public Provision

Roads, education, water, and police and fire protection are just a few examples of the many goods and services provided by governments. Most of these goods are not pure public goods. Although national defense often serves as an example of a good that is both nonrival (my use does not prevent your use) and nonexcludable (I cannot keep you from enjoying the good even if you don't pay for it) the same cannot be said of water, education, and most health care services. Inoculations are rival and excludable even though they may generate substantial positive externalities.

Public provision of health care is a complex process requiring a decision for each of the three basic economic questions (what? how? and for whom?) faced by every society. The "what" question relates to the types of health care to be provided (e.g., limited services, such as inoculations or comprehensive health care) as well as their quantity and quality. Whether governments themselves produce the services and how they do it, or whether they contract with the private sector, is a part of the "how" question. The "who" question deals with the financing and distribution of the services. Will the program be created as a universal entitlement, as an entitlement for some groups, or as one with other eligibility requirements? Furthermore, should the program be "free" at the point of service and funded mainly by tax revenues or should user fees be charged? The funding mechanism could have large impacts on the resources allocated to health and on the possible redistributions as from rich to poor and young to old.

Transfer Programs

Cash transfer programs usually are intended to meet society's equity concerns by redistributing income, with recipients free to spend their income in any way they want. Social Security for the elderly and some disabled is the principal example, but income supports also are provided for the poor. Cash transfers to the poor include Temporary Assistance to Needy Families (TANF), which is funded by the federal government and administered by the states.

In-kind transfers (benefits other than cash) also redistribute income, but their main purpose is to increase a recipient's consumption of specific goods or services. Important in-kind transfers include Medicare for the elderly, food stamps, housing, and

Medicaid for the poor who pass means tests. Medicare and Medicaid are described in detail in Chapter 21.

Regulation

Governments influence the allocation of resources by establishing rules and regulations. In the extreme, governments can prohibit certain goods or activities entirely, such as the production and consumption of illicit drugs. More commonly, governments regulate the form or terms under which goods are produced or consumed. Regulation may appeal to legislators because it appears to tackle problems without incurring substantial government spending in the process. For example, regulating managed care to prevent "drive-through" deliveries appears to respond to a public concern at little direct cost to government. However, as described in Chapter 12, the legislation imposes significant costs on others.

Regulation in health care markets can take many forms: licensure laws; mandates; and regulation of price, quality, and quantity of services. Several examples of regulation are provided in the following sections. Chapter 20 will focus exclusively on the principal regulatory mechanisms in health care markets.

Government Involvement in Health Care Markets

Hardly any economic activity is free of government intervention. Intervention comes mainly through three activities: provision of goods and services, redistribution, and regulation. Governments have pursued each of these activities in the health economy. Through public hospitals, the Veterans Administration, and other programs, they provide substantial amounts of health care, though this activity is overshadowed by social insurance programs for the elderly and many poor. The provision of health care and of health insurance is also the major means used to redistribute income to lower-income groups from higher-income groups. Less obvious to many is government's role as a regulator. At the federal level, the Securities and Exchange Commission (SEC), the Environmental Protection Agency (EPA), and the Occupational Safety and Health Administration (OSHA) are among the numerous regulatory agencies that affect

BOX 19-1

What Is HIPPA?

The Health Insurance Portability and Accountability Act (HIPPA), passed in 1996 and taking effect in April 2003, is the most far-reaching health care regulatory measure ever approved. A principal goal of HIPPA is to protect workers for loss of coverage when they change jobs, especially to reduce "job lock" for those with preexisting conditions. It also prohibits discrimination by insurers based on health status. Among other goals, including standards for electronic data interchange, the Act also was intended to guarantee the security and privacy of patient health data. Patients must be able to access their records and know how their personal information will be used. HIPPA requirements are complex, and the penalties for failure to comply are stiff. As a result, a cottage industry consisting of legal experts, information specialists, and consultants has emerged to help physicians, hospitals, insurers, and other providers to become and maintain HIPPA compliance The economic effects of HIPPA, in terms of costs and consequences, have not yet been evaluated, but they are likely to be substantial.

nearly every business and working individual. In addition, various state and local requirements, such as those governing building and safety codes, may have to be met.

However, when economists and others speak of regulating or deregulating the health care industries, they are not referring to the kinds of social and commercial controls cited earlier but rather to regulations that are targeted specifically at the health care industries. Government involvement in the health economy takes on many forms, some of which are developed elsewhere in this text. Here we provide examples to highlight the variety and scope of government intervention in health care markets.

Support of Hospitals

As described in Chapter 14, the modern hospital did not begin to emerge until the confluence of several developments in the late nineteenth century, such as major improvements in anesthesia, antisepsis, and in the invention of X-rays. Temin (1988) characterizes hospitals prior to this period as being more like municipal almshouses funded by taxes or voluntary contributions. Hospitals "existed for the care of marginal members of society, whether old, poor, or medically or psychologically deviant" (pp. 78–79).

In retrospect, one can argue that public support for hospitals was based on a redistribution motive and by a desire to deal with the negative externalities associated with the insane and those harboring communicable diseases, such as tuberculosis. With the improvements in physicians' abilities to diagnose and to treat patients surgically, hospitals grew rapidly in the first decades of the twentieth century. Public hospitals continued to serve the poor but also focused their attention on the growing middle classes. Ultimately, patient payments and insurance became the primary sources of funds for many of these institutions.

The Hill-Burton Act

Federal support for private hospitals was minimal until the passage of the Hill-Burton Act in 1946. The program was designed to expand rural health facilities by providing for matching grants to nonprofit institutions. Temin found that the Hill-Burton program contributed substantially to the rise in hospital beds per capita between 1947 and 1970.

The Hill-Burton Act, however, also required states "to survey its hospital needs, to develop a statewide plan for the construction of public hospitals and health centers, and, finally, to construct needed hospitals and health centers." This process of planning was carried a step further with the enactment of other health-planning legislation. As governments increasingly emphasized cost issues in the late 1960s, the health planning agencies that were created turned to capital expenditures controls to limit hospital growth and costs. The resulting *Certificate-of-Need*, or CON, requirements represented a major turning point toward an increasingly regulated health care system.

The Veterans Administration and CHAMPUS

In addition to direct subsidies for hospital construction, governments are also major providers of health care. State, county, and municipal hospitals account for approximately twenty percent of total hospital beds in the United States. The largest public provider is the Veterans Administration (VA). In 2003, the VA spent $25.6 billion for providing, among other services, hospital care for 588,000 patients and almost 50 million outpatient visits. The ostensible purpose of the VA is to provide care for service-related injuries through institutions that specialize in providing and undertaking research for such care. However, a veteran may be treated for other conditions unrelated to service injuries if facilities are available and the veteran indicates

an inability to afford treatment from other sources. As a result, most patients in VA hospitals are lower-income people treated for conditions not related to their military injuries.

In addition to direct care provided by the VA, the federal government finances care for retired military personnel and dependents of active-duty, deceased, and retired military personnel through the Civilian Health and Medical Program for the Uniformed Services (CHAMPUS). The program has a large number of potential beneficiaries and is similar in its scope of service coverage and administration to Medicare. Because beneficiaries are encouraged to use on-base facilities with low charges, CHAMPUS finances only a relatively small portion of care for eligible beneficiaries.

Food and Drug Administration

As noted in Chapter 17, various pieces of drug legislation have been passed, beginning with the Food and Drug Act of 1906. Legislation adopted in 1962 required increased testing and evidence of efficacy and gave the Food and Drug Administration (FDA) considerably more control over the introduction of new products than previously. The pharmaceutical industry believes that regulatory requirements lengthen the period to FDA approval to about 10 to 14 years and raise the cost of introducing new drug products, estimated by DiMasi and colleagues (2003) to be as high as $800 million to the point of marketing. The economic issues of drug regulation pit the relative gains in drug safety and efficacy against the discouragement to innovation and the delays in availability attributable to the approval process.

Mandated Health Insurance Benefits

The insurance industry is regulated mainly at the state level. The state's traditional role is to ensure financial solvency of insurance companies. However, in both auto and health insurance, the states have expanded their roles considerably. One relatively recent phenomenon in health insurance is exhibited by the proliferation of mandated insurance benefits. Such laws had grown from 48 in 1970 to about 1,000 in 1991. By 1997, over 600 new mandates had been introduced across the United States, ranging from acupuncture to massage therapy. They often pass after lobbying by special interest groups who traditionally have been excluded, or after highly publicized cases involving persons who find they are not covered for heart transplants or certain expensive experimental therapies.

Gabel and Jensen (1989) found that these requirements prevent insurers from offering lower-cost alternatives that exclude the mandated benefits. This effect could be substantial for many lower-income individuals who have been priced out of the market.

Tax Policy

Federal and state governments provide substantial tax subsidies for the consumption of health care and purchases of insurance. In particular, employer contributions to group health plans are not included in an individual's taxable income (escaping federal, state, and Social Security taxes). Individual payments for health insurance as well as many health care expenses can be itemized if they exceed threshold levels (7.5 percent of adjusted gross income in 2005).

Some have argued that the substantial reductions in the after-tax prices of insurance and health care represent a major reason for the growth of insurance and consequent growth of health care spending that began in the 1960s and 1970s. Thus, a

proposed cost-containment strategy is to reduce such subsidies. Without discussing the merits of this argument here, we wish only to point out that there seems to be little justification for the extensive tax subsidies. Ironically, the tax advantages are greatest to those in the highest marginal tax rates, meaning that the subsidies do not promote equity.

Public Health

We have thus far focused largely on the study of personal health and health care decisions. Public health, in contrast, deals with communicable diseases, epidemics, environmental health issues, and other activities with significant third-party health effects, such as smoking and the use of drugs and alcohol.

Until the latter part of the nineteenth century, public health was a state and local responsibility. However, in 1878, the U.S. government created the Marine Hospital Service, which became the U.S. Public Health Service in 1912. Despite the federal responsibilities, state and local governments spent over $46 billion in 2003. Odin Anderson (1990) provides an excellent history of public health in the United States.

Other Government Programs

Numerous other channels for government involvement exist. Some are apparent—such as support for medical education and medical schools, which will influence the supply of providers. Similarly, support for health care research undertaken directly by a government agency, such as the National Cancer Institutes or undertaken by other public and private organizations, can have a substantial impact on the spread of technology and the direction of the health care system. For example, critics of the U.S. system claim that it has placed excessive emphasis on high-tech medicine at the expense of preventive medicine and that this bias stems in part from the kinds of research projects that are supported.

Other forms of intervention are less obvious. Changes in immigration policy can affect the supply of health care personnel. Also easily overlooked is the role of the federal government as the nation's largest employer in providing fringe benefits to its employees. The Federal Employees Health Benefits Program (FEHBP) offers numerous insurance options to employees and their dependents. Because of its size and its ability to experiment with alternatives, the FEHBP has the potential to influence and serve as a model for the private sector.

To summarize, governments at all levels have intervened heavily in the health care sector. The intervention has taken the forms of direct provision of care, financing of health insurance (especially of Medicare and Medicaid), subsidizing of medical education and the construction of health facilities, subsidizing of purchases of health insurance through the tax structure, and the regulation of health care industries. This intervention has major effects on the total resources devoted to health care as well as on the distribution of resources within the health care industries.

Table 19-1 indicates the scope of public spending in 2003, overall as well as across health care industries. Public spending ($766 billion) accounts for nearly 46 percent of total health care spending of $1,679 billion, and is concentrated on expenditures on hospital, physician, and nursing home care. However, these amounts understate the impact of public programs. By influencing levels of competition, purchases of health insurance, and the innovation and spread of technology, government activities also have substantial effects on private spending.

TABLE 19-1 National Health Expenditures, by Source of Funds and Type of Expenditure, 2003

Type of Expenditure	Total	Private					Public		
		All Private Funds	Consumer			Other	Total	Federal	State and Local
			Total	Out-of-Pocket	Private Insurance				
Amount in Billions									
National health expenditures	**$1,678.9**	**$913.2**	**$831.1**	**$230.5**	**$600.6**	**$82.1**	**$765.7**	**$541.7**	**$224.0**
Health services and supplies	1,614.2	892.6	831.1	230.5	600.6	61.5	721.7	507.5	214.2
Personal health care	1,440.8	809.2	749.2	230.5	518.7	60.0	631.5	479.8	151.7
Hospital care	515.9	215.1	193.7	16.3	177.4	21.3	300.8	242.1	58.7
Professional services	542.0	356.0	322.7	83.8	238.9	33.3	186.1	139.3	46.7
Physician and clinical services	369.7	246.8	221.2	37.6	183.6	25.5	123.0	101.3	21.7
Dental services	74.3	69.4	69.4	32.9	36.5	0.0	4.9	2.9	1.9
Other professional services	48.5	34.9	32.1	13.3	18.8	2.8	13.6	8.8	4.8
Other personal health	49.5	4.9	—	—	—	4.9	44.6	26.3	18.3
Nursing home and home health	150.8	58.6	53.5	37.5	15.7	5.4	92.2	64.1	28.1
Home health care	40.0	15.1	13.9	6.6	7.3	1.2	24.9	18.6	6.3
Nursing home care	110.8	43.5	39.4	30.9	8.5	4.2	67.3	45.5	21.8
Retail outlet sales, medical products	232.1	179.6	179.6	92.9	86.7	—	52.5	34.3	18.2
Prescription drugs	179.2	136.0	136.0	53.2	82.9	—	43.2	25.2	18.0
Other medical products	52.9	43.5	43.5	39.7	3.8	—	7.2	9.1	0.2
Durable medical equipment	20.4	12.8	12.8	9.0	3.8	—	7.6	7.4	0.2
Other nondurable medical products	32.5	30.7	30.7	30.7	—	—	1.7	1.7	—
Government administration and net cost of private health insurance	119.7	83.3	81.9	—	81.9	1.5	36.4	20.2	16.2
Government public health activities	53.8	—	—	—	—	—	53.8	7.4	46.3
Investment	64.6	20.6	—	—	—	20.6	44.0	34.2	9.8
Research	40.2	2.5	—	—	—	2.5	37.6	33.3	4.3
Construction	24.5	18.1	—	—	—	18.1	6.4	0.9	5.5

Source: Centers for Medicare & Medicaid Services, Office of the Actuary, National Health Statistics Group, http://cms.hhs.gov/statistics/nhe/historical/t3.asp. Accessed September 1, 2005.

419

Government Failure

Market failure and concerns about the distribution of income can be seen as necessary conditions for government intervention. We have to ask whether government can improve efficiency and better meet society's equity objectives. Many might argue that this question has already been answered. Governments in each of the 30 countries that belong to the Organization for Economic Cooperation and Development (OECD) are heavily involved in their health economies, to the point where nearly all have universal health care coverage. The United States, with 25 percent of the population receiving coverage through publicly financed or publicly administered insurance schemes in 2000, has by far the lowest rate (followed by Mexico and Turkey with 50 and 66 percent respectively). But even in the United States, the federal, state, and local governments account for nearly 46 percent of national health care spending.[2]

The real issues are the extent and forms of government involvement. The difficulties of agreeing on objectives, choosing from many different policy instruments, and selecting the correct values of these instruments create many opportunities for "government failure." Jan Tinbergen, who shared the first Nobel Prize in Economics in 1969 with Ragnar Frisch, dealt with the process of choosing an optimum policy. In a major contribution, Tinbergen (1952) formulated relationships between a government's policy instruments and its targets. His analysis highlights the interdependence of the different sectors of an economy and points to the inherent deficiency of uncoordinated policy (agricultural, trade, health, and so on) decisions.

In more contemporary work, the literature on public choice illustrates many of the problems in developing and implementing policy. Public choice attempts to model how decisions are made through the political process. Many models of public choice have been created. We limit our discussion to two features that are relevant to efficiency: special interest groups and bureaucratic behavior.

Who Does the Regulator Represent?

In this chapter and elsewhere that we have addressed regulatory activities such as licensure or other quality controls, we have assumed that the regulator knows the right actions to take. Most often we treat the regulator as representing an omniscient but benevolent despot who knows what is good for the economy and regulates accordingly. Yet students of railroad regulation might argue that the railroads played major roles in influencing their regulators. Likewise, some observers believe that the American Medical Association has influenced laws on licensure and legislation on Medicare. Can the theory of regulation address issues such as these?

It can. An influential school of economists often associated with the University of Chicago has argued that the regulation process, like many others that we have examined, is a "maximizing" process, in which a regulator seeks "votes" from a group of potential beneficiaries. These votes would allow the transfer of wealth, such as monopoly profits, from those who are regulated to those who benefit from the regulations.

In this model formulated by Peltzman (1976), the regulator seeks supporters by imposing a percentage "tax" (rate t) on those who are regulated, with the tax receipts (tax rate, t, multiplied by the wealth of those being taxed) being transferred to the beneficiaries. A higher tax rate on those who are regulated (more stringent regulation) may

[2]Using OECD data, the proportion for the United States was 44.2 percent in 2000, compared to the OECD average of 72.2 percent (Docteur and Oxley, 2003). Private health insurance for basic services dominates only in the United States and Switzerland, and accounts for a substantial minority in Germany and the Netherlands. In several countries, such as Canada, private insurance fills gaps in the public coverage.

win more supporters, but it also may mobilize more opponents. The successful regulator seeks a certain transfer of wealth while gathering votes to effect this transfer efficiently.

Suppose the regulator starts with a modest tax. The imposition and increase of this tax yields favorable votes for two reasons:

1. The revenues increase the probability of support from the potential beneficiaries.
2. The revenues increase the value of the transfer to the beneficiaries.

Opposition also will be heard. Those who would be regulated will oppose a transfer because it is coming from them. Their opposition will grow the higher the tax is (the more stringent the regulation is), that is, the more that is being taken from them.

The regulator's optimal tax rate occurs where the marginal benefits from regulation equal the marginal cost, or:

$$\begin{array}{ccccc} \text{marginal} & & \text{marginal} & & \\ \text{increase in} & & \text{revenue} & & \text{marginal} \\ \text{probability of} & \times & \text{product from} & = & \text{opposition from} \\ \text{support} & & \text{those regulated} & & \text{increased taxes} \\ [1] & & [2] & & [3] \end{array} \qquad \textbf{(19.1)}$$

This is easily seen in Figure 19-4. The initial incremental, or marginal, benefits are high because of the high number of potential beneficiaries (term 1), and because considerable wealth is available to be transferred (term 2). The initial opposition, measured in dollar terms, may be small because the taxes are small; that is, the regulation is not onerous.

As the tax rate rises, the marginal benefits fall for two reasons. There may be fewer supporters to attract (term 1), and the taxation or regulation may be reducing the wealth left for the beneficiaries to tax (term 2). At the same time, opposition to the tax (regulation) grows because of the increased tax level. The regulator's optimum occurs where the marginal benefits from increasing the tax equal the marginal costs at tax rate t^* and expected marginal revenue, R^*.

Note that as long as the left-hand side of equation 19.1 is positive, the expected marginal transfer from those who are regulated to the beneficiaries increases (up to the point t_{max} in Figure 19-4). However, the successful regulator will stop short of t_{max}, because "excessive" regulation may compromise his or her majority.

FIGURE 19-4 The Regulator's Optimum Level of Regulation

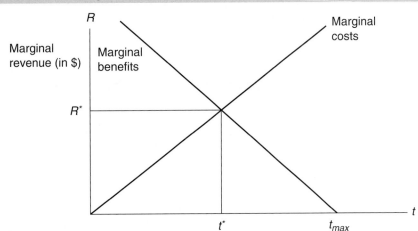

Remember, also, that the potential beneficiaries seek transfers of wealth. The two terms on the left-hand side of equation 19.1 suggest that regulation will be sought if there is a large group of supporters (term 1) or if there is a smaller, well-organized group that perceives large expected gains (term 2). Thus, one may see regulations imposed that benefit relatively small but well-organized groups of potential gainers.

While this analysis does not negate the economic arguments in favor of regulation, it provides sobering insights into how regulations may be implemented. Regulators may respond to similar economic incentives as do other economic men and women. The resulting regulations, although possibly addressing issues of economic efficiency, most likely will reflect the particular preferences of the beneficiaries, moderated by the opposition of those who stand to lose under the regulations.

Bureaucracy and Efficiency

Lawmakers pass legislation, but government bureaucrats are responsible for implementing programs. Do bureaucrats try to minimize the costs of their activities? Relatively little is known about the technical efficiency of the bureaucracy, but it is clear that government operations do not face the discipline of the marketplace. No income statements, balance sheets, and stock market prices are available to evaluate the success of a government program and motivate the bureaucracy, even though it is not completely immune from oversight (from legislatures, public watchdogs, and even government agencies, such as the General Accounting Office). Nevertheless, the hypothesis that governments operate at lower levels of technical efficiency than the private sector is a plausible one.

Aside from the inefficiency associated with failure to minimize costs, government programs are also subject to allocative inefficiencies. That is, there may be too little or too much of a program. This problem is illustrated in Figure 19-5, which shows the true marginal social benefits (*MSB*) and marginal social costs (*MSC*) of a government program to provide home health visits. The social optimum is at Q_1 visits where *MSB* = *MSC*. However, this allocation may not be attained for several reasons. Supporters of the program (lobbyists, legislators who support it, top bureaucrats who will run it) will

FIGURE 19-5
Overexpansion of a
Government Program

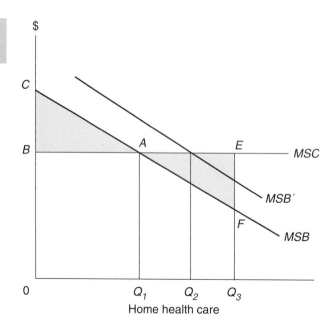

be motivated by self-interests to overstate the benefits (and understate the costs). If benefits are inflated to MSB', the perceived optimum is an inefficiently large program at Q_2.

A model of bureaucratic behavior developed by Niskanen (1971) is consistent with this result, but for a different reason. There is a welfare gain, or consumer surplus, shown by triangle ABC at the efficient quantity Q_1. This means that total social benefits are greater than total social costs at Q_1. Niskanen reasoned that power and prestige motivate bureaucrats to push for large programs potentially to the point where total social benefits equal total social costs. In this limiting case, the program is expanded to Q_3 where the welfare gain at the efficient level (triangle ABC) is exactly offset by the welfare loss (triangle AEF) from the inefficient expansion.

These arguments warn us against the danger of concluding that social welfare is necessarily improved by government intervention when there is market failure. Equally serious government failure can result from inappropriate policies and high levels of technical and allocative inefficiencies.

Competitive Strategies

Regardless of any changes in the direction of U.S. health care policy, governments will remain heavily involved in the financing and delivery of health care. The battle is over the superiority of (1) increased government involvement through both expanded regulation and additional government programs to provide or finance health care, or (2) an increased emphasis on market mechanisms and market forces with corresponding decreases in the use of regulatory instruments.

This controversy is not new to the academic and policy-making communities, where it is referred to as the debate over competition versus regulation. Those who deny the applicability of the competitive framework are most likely to favor regulatory strategies. Proponents of further regulation tend to argue that information imperfections, flawed agency relationships, and other distortions cannot be readily corrected by attempts to promote partial forms of competition. Proponents of regulation also have been strongly influenced by the rapid growth in overall health spending and in spending on Medicare, Medicaid, and other public programs. The spending record in the United States, as compared to other more highly regulated systems, has reinforced beliefs among many that health care markets do not work like most other markets. Many believe that increases in supplies of hospital beds and physicians increase utilization of marginally necessary or even unnecessary services. There are widespread views that physicians can and do create demand and that empty beds in hospitals will be filled through physicians' discretionary decisions to admit patients.

Those who share these views advocate controls limiting hospital capacity and physician supplies, and increasing the monitoring of services being provided. We have outlined the general forms of these controls. What is competition in health care? Pauly (1988a) defines competition through the conditions of "free entry and potential entrants willing[ness] to offer goods and services to consumers, with no one firm large enough to have an important influence on levels of and quality" (p. 35).

From this definition, in a competitive health care industry we would expect (1) price-elastic demands facing providers; (2) a tendency toward marginal cost pricing; (3) efficiency in production—allocative as well as technical efficiency; and (4) the availability of alternatives in terms of price, quality, and form of delivery.

Others see competition in a more limited way, largely through the form of government policy rather than the structure or performance of health care markets. A competitive

health care policy is one that relies primarily on financial incentives rather than controls to achieve goals. Those supporting this approach believe that market participants respond to changes in prices in a predictable and substantial way. Supporters of competitive approaches also argue that even imperfections in their strategies are preferable to the distortions caused by imperfect regulation.

Under either view of competition, forms of government intervention, such as CON laws, utilization review, and mandated benefits, are anticompetitive—they compel. To be more specific in the distinction between competition and regulation, consider the uninsured. From the competitive point of view, many of the uninsured are seen largely as having insufficient income to purchase insurance. Their dilemma is aggravated by mandated benefits and other requirements that drive up insurance prices. A competitive solution is to subsidize purchases of insurance for lower-income uninsureds through tax credits, and to deregulate insurers so that lower-priced options become available. In contrast, programs that would provide insurance for the uninsured are seen as lacking in incentives for efficient consumer search. Bearing in mind these distinctions, we turn to several broad competitive strategies for reforming the U.S. health care system.

Increased Cost Sharing

Martin Feldstein was the earliest and the best-known advocate of using increased cost sharing to overcome the incentives to overinsure. He also argued that the prevalence of "first-dollar insurance" up to certain limits (which are often inadequate for catastrophic events) is the result of the tax preferences described previously for purchases of insurance, especially of employer-provided group insurance. He and others have advocated a variety of plans that would involve reducing the tax subsidies and increasing patients' out-of-pocket costs. This would be achieved through high coinsurance rates on initial health care expenditures, but with declining coinsurance until the maximum out-of-pocket liability is reached.

The effects of coinsurance on moral hazard and demand elasticities have been described in the chapters on demand and insurance. Findings from the Rand Health Insurance Experiment support the hypotheses that consumers respond in a significant and substantial way to changes in their share of costs.

Development of Alternative Delivery Systems

The dominant competitive strategy, which evolved in the 1970s, has been the promotion of delivery systems that can provide an alternative to traditional fee-for-service with its comprehensive first-dollar insurance coverage. The cornerstone of this strategy has been the promotion of health maintenance organizations (HMOs), preferred provider organizations (PPOs), and other forms of managed care.

As described in Chapter 12, HMOs and other managed care health plans provide comprehensive sets of services for fixed monthly premiums. Typically, there is minimal (or no) cost sharing for covered services. In exchange for expanded coverage, a patient's choice is restricted to specific providers and hospitals. Furthermore, the patient's primary care physician serves as the gatekeeper in that this physician's approval is required for referral to most specialists and nonemergency hospital admissions.

Expansion of the population covered by managed care has been a major policy goal. The primary motive behind the managed care strategy is the view among many policy makers that the traditional form of health care delivery was the primary culprit in rising costs and unnecessary care.

Managed care has reduced costs by lowering the rate of hospitalization and lower payments to providers. However, the rates of managed care cost increases have paralleled the rates of increase elsewhere, limiting the overall potential for cost containment. Nevertheless, federal policy continues to emphasize the managed care strategy by proposing expanded incentives for those who select prepaid, managed care systems, especially Medicare and Medicaid beneficiaries.

Consumer-Driven Health Plans and Health Savings Accounts

According to some analysts, consumer-driven health plans (CDHPs) paired with health savings accounts (HSAs) represent the most dramatic change in the private health insurance market since the spread of managed care. They believe that the consumer-driven approach represents a novel strategy that could revolutionize health care delivery. Or, could CDHPs just be a passing fad? To understand current developments, we need to consider earlier proposals for medical savings accounts (Stano, 1981; Pauly, 1994b; Pauly and Goodman, 1995). Employers or public payers would make contributions to what was termed an individual's Medical Savings Account (MSA), an IRA-type of account. The account would allow purchase of relatively low-cost catastrophic insurance with high deductibles. Balances in an MSA can then be used to pay out-of-pocket costs, or the unused portion can be distributed to the individual at the end of a designated period or at retirement.

Advocates of MSAs argued that comprehensive, tax-subsidized insurance creates substantial moral hazard and ineffective incentives for efficient consumption of care. In contrast, the lure of potential distributions from an MSA, like spending one's own dollars, provides the individual with an incentive to become a prudent user of care. In principle, patients will be less likely to consume unnecessary or marginally beneficial care, and stronger market forces will help restrain prices.

After years of debate, the 1996 HIPPA legislation included a provision for a demonstration with up to 750,000 MSAs to be made available to the self-employed and small firms with 50 or fewer employees. Individuals would choose plans with high deductibles and other cost-sharing features. They were allowed to put a certain percentage of the deductible into a tax-free savings account to pay for out-of-pocket expenses or future health care needs including long-term care. Withdrawals for non-medical purposes were taxed and penalized for those under age 65.

Some analysts projected considerable savings from more efficient levels of utilization (Ozanne, 1996; Heffley and Miceli, 1998). However, few people adopted MSAs relative to the 750,000 that were authorized, and new enrollees into MSAs are no longer allowed.

Since then, several significant developments have put the MSA approach back into the spotlight. In 2002, the Internal Revenue Service authorized the Health Reimbursement Arrangement (HRA)—a restrictive scheme that is completely employer-controlled. More significant, the HSA legislation was passed in 2003 as part of the Medicare prescription drug act. The HSA is a less restrictive MSA, owned by the employee, and open to anyone enrolled in a high deductible health plan and not already covered by public or private insurance. For an individual, the deductible must be between $1,000 and $5,000 ($2,000 and $10,000 for a family plan).

The CDHP movement that included President Bush (it was a major health theme in his 2004 reelection campaign) was a driving force behind these legislative expansions. In most cases, a CDHP features a high deductible health plan combined with an HRA or HSA. The motive for the CDHP is the desire to create highly informed consumers and to give them the incentives and the tools so that they take charge of

BOX 19-2

What Do Doctors Really Charge?

If consumers are to become savvy price-comparison shoppers for health care, they must first know what providers really charge. The current situation is similar to the one facing new car buyers who are looking at sticker prices and knowing very little about the discount they could get. For the most part, patients do not have access to the kind of information that lets them know the "discounts" from charges that many health insurance plans negotiate with physicians and other providers. In 2005, Aetna, a major insurer made the fees it negotiated with physicians in the Cincinnati area available to enrollees in all its plans. In one example of the differences reported by *The Wall Street Journal*, the fee for an office visit for a new patient with moderate to severe problems at one internist was $161.32, compared to $132.23 at another. Such data were made available for 600 procedures. Advocates of CDHPs believe that patients armed with this type of information will offer consumers more choices and help keep prices in check.

SOURCE: Vanessa Fuhrman, "Insurer Reveals What Doctors Really Charge," *The Wall Street Journal*, August 18, 2005, p. D1.

their health care decisions (see Box 19-2 for an example). Their search for price and quality would counter the power of medical providers and the inefficiencies in the current marketplace. In this sense, the CDHP contrasts sharply with managed care under which the patient is a more passive participant and where the managed care plan administrators take responsibility for prices and quality. There were over 3 million enrollees in CDHPs in 2005, and their numbers were growing rapidly.

Evidence on CDHPs and HSAs is still largely anecdotal.[3] Any enthusiasm must be tempered by the undesired consequences that may result from a system that depends on voluntary enrollments. Healthier individuals are more likely to be attracted to high-deductible health plans. They may be able to purchase catastrophic coverage at relatively low rates and will be more likely than others to have funds left over in their HSA accounts. There is a justifiable concern that this selection phenomenon will lead to escalating premiums for the sicker populations who remain in managed care and conventional plans so that the net effect could turn out to be largely a redistribution of income toward the healthy.[4]

Health care reforms introduced in Singapore in 1984 provide an example where theory, for the case of a mandated MSA system, has been put to a stronger test. Singapore requires all workers and the self-employed to contribute a portion of earnings to Medisave accounts (Massaro and Wong, 1995). The Medisave account is used to pay for hospital care and a limited amount of outpatient care (the remainder is paid out-of-pocket). Once Medisave balances reach a certain level, funds can be transferred for other approved uses. At death, balances become part of the deceased's estate.

[3]See Clancy and Gauthier (2004) for an excellent collection of articles on CDHPs that include discussions of adverse selection.

[4]There are two other serious problems associated with HSAs and high deductible policies. First, patients in these plans may be tempted to scrimp on preventive health care measures, which are often among the most cost-effective. Second, a small proportion of individuals with serious chronic and acute conditions account for a large share of annual health care spending. These patients will have exceeded their maximum out-of-pocket requirements and may not have a strong incentive to economize on their use of health care. See Cogan, Hubbard and Kessler (2005) for a well-crafted defense of HSAs and other market-based reforms.

**FIGURE 19-6 The
Intended Effects of
Competitive Strategies
on Demand and Supply**

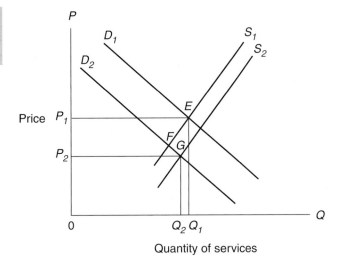

Evidence indicates that hospitals have become more productive and efficient and that patients are satisfied with the quality of care. The record on cost containment is unclear.

Representation of the Competitive Approach

The shortcomings of the existing system of health care delivery, together with the goals of the competitive approach, can be illustrated with the help of Figure 19-6. At the risk of neglecting the various market imperfections and resulting inefficiencies that we have studied, we rely on the simplicity of the demand-supply paradigm. Let S_1 and D_1 represent the existing demand and supply curves for health care. The equilibrium quantity is Q_1, and total spending is represented by the rectangle $0P_1EQ_1$.

Competitive strategies have two broad goals. The first is to reduce demand by increasing the number of patients in managed care settings who are sensitive to price and the diminishing marginal benefit associated with health care. By encouraging the use of managed care and reducing the tax subsidy for employer-provided health insurance, it is expected that demand for health services, especially the relatively less beneficial services, will diminish to D_2. The equilibrium quantity will decrease, as will prices and expenditures, though the price effect will be small where the elasticity of supply is large.

However, there is another important role for competitive strategies, which operates through effects on the supply side. Here, a relaxation of regulatory, entry, and capacity controls is seen as reducing producer costs and increasing the supply of providers. At the same time, competitive pressure introduced through consumer search will push providers to become more efficient producers of care so that any given quantity of care can be provided at lower cost. These effects are represented by a rightward shift in supply to S_2.

The combined effects, if substantial, would lead to large decreases (from $0P_1EQ_1$ to $0P_2GQ_2$) in health care spending, as illustrated in Figure 19-6, or to reduced growth rates in spending. Of course, the predicted effects must materialize. Otherwise, the strategies would be ineffective and might even backfire. For instance, if supply does increase but prices remain rigid and large amounts of supplier-induced demand (SID) follow, then both demand and supply may increase, thereby aggravating the utilization and spending problems. For this reason, the issues of SID and the existence of independent demands that are responsive to financial incentives are seen by some economists as being at the heart of the controversy.

Conclusions

This chapter emphasizes market failure as the economic rationale for government intervention. Monopoly power provides the classic example, but public goods and externalities are two additional categories that are relevant to health care. Government policies, in principle, can correct misallocations resulting from market failure. To do so, governments can use specific commodity taxes and subsidies, public provision of goods and services, transfer programs, and regulation.

Through a wide variety of programs, governments at all levels have become major players in the health economy, accounting for 46 percent of national health expenditures. However, government activities also are associated with government failure. Information deficiencies, the efforts of special interest groups, and bureaucratic behavior can lead to socially undesirable programs or inefficient levels of these programs. Nonetheless, despite concerns about the effectiveness of government programs, governments will almost certainly continue to dominate the health economy through their various spending programs and heavy regulation.

At the same time, the United States has prompted competitive strategies to deal especially with the cost and access concerns. The emphasis in this policy has been on an expansion of health care delivery by various forms of managed care. With the strong political pressure to downsize the role of government, there is likely also to be continuing interest in market-driven changes to Medicare and Medicaid, through HSAs and other measures. It remains to be seen whether such changes can break the "stalemate between halfway competition and ineffective regulation" (Altman and Rodwin, 1988, p. 323) to bring meaningful reforms to the health economy.

SUMMARY

1. Government spending accounts for about 46 percent of total health care expenditures.
2. The traditional rationale for government intervention is market failure. Sources of market failure include monopoly power, externalities, and public goods.
3. There is a public goods aspect to information and redistribution that can be used to justify a role for government in health care.
4. Commodity taxes and subsidies, public provision, transfer programs, and regulation are the principal policy instruments used by governments.
5. Regulation refers to the use of nonmarket means to affect the quality, price, or quantity of a good or service. The principal categories of regulation include fee controls and rate regulation, quantity and capacity controls, and quality controls.
6. Governments have been involved in a wide variety of activities, including the direct provision of health care, subsidizing the production of health care, the provision of social insurance, public health, and regulation of health care products and providers.
7. Traditional economic descriptions depict regulation as a process in which the optimal policy is determined and imposed by an omniscient regulator. Alternative theories suggest that regulations result from political processes. Thus, the regulations will reflect the particular preferences of the beneficiaries, moderated by the opposition of those who stand to lose if the regulations are imposed.
8. The past two decades have witnessed a major debate over whether to rely increasingly on regulatory strategies to achieve health policy objectives or to rely increasingly on competitive strategies.
9. Competitive strategies include increased cost sharing, the promotion of alternative delivery systems, more aggressive enforcement of antitrust laws, and the promotion of consumer-driven health plans built around various forms of health savings accounts.

DISCUSSION QUESTIONS

1. What is meant by market failure? What is the potential role of government in each instance of market failure found in the health care sector?
2. In what sense can information and redistribution be thought of as public goods? Explain whether private markets will oversupply or undersupply these goods.
3. What are some examples of government providing health care? Of subsidizing the production or consumption of health care? Of providing insurance for health care? Of regulating health care markets?
4. Why is government needed to provide a public good? Under what circumstances might the voluntary contribution model described in Figure 19-2 work reasonably well?
5. The standard monopoly-competition comparison describes the welfare loss. Develop arguments to support the view that in the real world:
 a. the welfare loss is exaggerated.
 b. the welfare loss is understated.
6. Why does air pollution represent a public health externality? How do regulations operate in addressing the air pollution? How do markets operate?
7. What are the major competitive strategies proposed by economists? How, for example, would elimination of the tax subsidy for employer-provided health insurance reduce spending on health care?
8. Discuss some key arguments against competitive strategies from an American perspective. From a European perspective.
9. What are Health Savings Accounts (HSAs)? Why might HSAs decrease health care spending? What are some problems with the HSA concept? Consider an Aetna enrollee in a CDHP with a high deductible HSA who is choosing between the two physicians described in Box 19-2. How might the fee information influence her to choose the lower priced physician? Why might the patient still choose the higher priced one?
10. The pharmaceutical industry has been subject to considerable regulation in bringing drugs to the marketplace. Discuss the benefits and costs to society from such a policy.

EXERCISES

1. What is meant by the welfare loss of monopoly? Who bears this loss? Determine the regulated price in Figure 19-1 that will eliminate the welfare loss. Why will it be difficult in practice to adopt this solution?
2. Suppose that the public good in Figure 19-2 is associated with increasing costs of production (i.e., where the *AC* is positively sloped). Will the two individuals be able to fund the optimal amount if each pays according to marginal benefits? Repeat if there are decreasing costs of production.
3. Assume a positively sloped, short-run supply curve in Figure 19-3 and a constant $5 per unit marginal external benefit. Show what happens with a $5 subsidy given to producers. Who gains the benefits of this policy?
4. Using Figure 19-3, explain how a $5 tax on those who are not inoculated will result in the efficient output. Why is this approach unlikely to work in practice?
5. Take a commodity, such as cigarettes, that is associated with negative externalities. Assume that the marginal private cost of production and the marginal external cost per unit are both constant. Graph the actual and efficient quantities. Show how a tax on producers (or consumers) can result in the efficient output. Explain whether it is possible to attain efficiency with a subsidy.
6. Instead of using *MSB* and *MSC* in Figure 19-5 to deal with problems of government failure, show the optimal and Niskanen results using a graph with total social benefits and total social costs.
7. Using the demand-supply framework in Figure 19-6, explain how increased cost sharing could lead to lower utilization and spending on health care.

20

Government Regulation: Principal Regulatory Mechanisms

Do the Laws of Supply and Demand Apply?

Objectives of Regulation

Regulation of the Hospital Sector

Prospective Payment

The Theory of Yardstick Competition and DRGs

Prospective Payment: Recent Evidence

Regulation of Physician Payment

Antitrust

Conclusions

We have demonstrated that conventional economic tools can play a powerful role in explaining how health care markets work. While we must account for the special features of the health economy and modify the analysis where appropriate, we have found considerable empirical evidence attesting to the rationality of decision makers. Such considerations guide the evaluation of principal regulatory mechanisms applied to the health care economy.

Do the Laws of Supply and Demand Apply?

Supporters of competitive strategies believe in the power of market forces to allocate resources to their best uses regarding health care, but it would be unwise to ignore concerns about the strength of market forces. Consider this article taken from *The Wall Street Journal*, a publication known for its strong resistance to government intervention in the marketplace.

In a conventional market, a high-cost, low-quality producer would be doomed, or, at least, worried. But the laws of economics have been repealed in the health business. Consumers don't comparison shop and often lack the information to do so. Many hospitals compete to buy the latest technology rather

than provide the lowest-cost quality care. And providers resist outsiders' attempts to gauge quality. The result: a seemingly unstoppable increase in the cost of health care. ("Laws of Economics Often Don't Apply in Health Care Field," *The Wall Street Journal*, January 22, 1992)

To support this argument, the article compared cost and outcome data for coronary bypass surgery at two Pennsylvania hospitals located 38 miles apart. One hospital charged about 50 percent more than the other in 1989, but its death rate considerably exceeded the expected death rate as determined by the age and health of the patients; in other words it performed worse than it should have. The death rate at the lower-priced hospital was below the expected rate (it performed better). A lack of access to such information about price and quality, lack of incentives to patients, and provider resistance to releasing mortality data were singled out as culprits.

We have established that most health care providers (hospitals, clinics, physicians) face portions of downward demand curves; that is, they have some monopoly power. When this happens, the desirable outcomes of competitive markets become much more difficult to achieve. Using competitive markets as a comparison group, one can classify policies into three major categories:

1. Policies that recognize monopoly power and try to control it. These policies include some traditional features, such as utilization review, capital controls, or rate controls.
2. Policies that try to make monopolistic firms act like competitors. These policies include prospective payment plans for physicians and hospitals.
3. Policies that attempt to prevent the accumulation of monopoly power. Most antitrust policies fall into this category.

As we saw in Chapter 19, the fundamental story regarding regulation relates to monopoly power. In Figure 19-1, the provider faced a downward-sloping demand curve and a constant marginal cost curve. In equilibrium, price exceeded marginal cost. As a result, at least some consumers who would have willingly paid more than it cost to produce the health care service were unable to get it. The shaded triangle *ABC* in Figure 19-1 represented the loss to society from monopoly.

The consequences of real-world monopoly and production are more complex. We have ignored the possibility of quality degradation under monopoly and also the possibility that technological innovation may be retarded if producers are not provided the monopoly power of a patent. Nevertheless, Figure 19-1 illustrates that competitive markets often will be more efficient than markets in which firms have monopoly power.

Objectives of Regulation

Early regulation in the United States focused on the transportation and utilities sectors. Concern with excessive monopoly power and natural monopoly arising from economies of scale and high capital expenditures led to the 1888 establishment of the Interstate Commerce Commission, which regulated railroads and shipping. Subsequently, other federal and state regulatory commissions came to regulate a variety of commodities (some of which have since been deregulated) including electricity, gas, telephone service, oil pipelines, airlines, and broadcasting. The overriding objective in regulation was, and continues to be, rate setting. Its primary goal is to limit the high price-cost margins that would otherwise be expected.

Despite concerns with possible abuse of monopoly power in certain health care markets, those favoring increased regulation do not rely on the traditional monopoly

power argument. They focus on the absence of discipline in markets brought on by a lack of consumer information and the prevalence of comprehensive insurance.

Lack of consumer information, as discussed elsewhere, has been used to justify licensure and other quality controls as means to ensure minimal standards of care. Similarly, the role of insurance as a source of market failure was discussed earlier, emphasizing the lack of incentives to both patient and provider to shop around or otherwise conserve resources. Perhaps more importantly, we emphasized the role of traditional forms of insurance in contributing to moral hazard. Unlike other sources of market failure, market failure associated with insurance has led to regulation of fees and also to regulation of hospital revenues and costs.

Regulatory Policy

Regulation refers to the use of nonmarket means to address the quantity, price, or quality of the good brought to market. Because regulations typically address the quantity of services used, the quality of the services, or the amount that payers (either individuals or insurers) are charged, consider total expenditures in a given health care market.

By definition, expenditures, E, equal the price of health care, P, multiplied by the quantity of services, Q, or $E = PQ$. Price of care, P, also depends on quality of care, q. Quality of care in this framework can be thought of as any aspect of a service for which someone is willing to pay extra. An example may be a private rather than a shared hospital room. Under many circumstances, the private room does not make the patient recover more quickly. However, the patient may be more comfortable with the privacy, and hence be willing to pay more for it.

The key feature of this framework is the idea that within the health economy, regulation uses nonmarket means to affect P, Q, or q, or combinations. For example, licensure requirements may raise quality, which is likely to increase price. If they also restrict the supply of providers, they are *further* likely to increase price. Other regulations, such as the Medicare Prospective Payment System, may tend to decrease the amount of services used, lowering expenditures. We will address these aspects elsewhere in this chapter. The point here is that most regulations are directed toward changing price, quantity, or quality.

However, the objective of regulation is not merely to reduce spending; otherwise, rationing or even prohibiting certain services may meet this objective successfully. Rather, its goals are to promote minimal quality levels while eliminating the inefficient components of spending.

Regulatory Instruments in Health Care

A variety of price, quantity, and quality controls have been introduced. Here, we provide a brief overview of these controls, leaving more detailed analyses of hospital regulation for the next section.

Fee Controls and Rate Regulation

The hospital sector has been the main object of rate regulation. In an early review of this subject, Sloan (1983, p. 195) defines rate regulation as establishing "the terms under which public and/or private insurers pay hospitals." In the 1960s and 1970s, many states adopted various mandatory or advisory forms of regulation. State approval of rate changes was generally based on hospital costs per day or per admission, or on a hospital's overall costs.

Reimbursement for hospital care was usually on a retrospective basis, determined by allowable costs that were incurred. A number of states, however, adopted prospective forms of reimbursements beginning in the 1970s. Some have been mandated at the

state level while other programs are voluntary. The goal of these arrangements is to remove the disincentives hospitals have to be efficient producers under cost-based retrospective reimbursement and to limit the amount of care they provide patients who are hospitalized. Dranove (2000) and Salkever (2000) provide good descriptions of the development and implementation of such arrangements.

Prospective reimbursement, especially once it was adopted by Medicare in 1983, marked an important turning point in regulatory efforts to contain the growth of hospital costs. Medicare's Prospective Payment System (PPS) limits hospital revenues per Medicare patient. Under PPS, hospitals are reimbursed a fixed amount per admission, determined by the patient's diagnostic condition, regardless of the hospital's actual costs. The strategy behind PPS is simple. By limiting revenues, it provides hospitals with strong disincentives to extend lengths of stay and provide unnecessary or marginal care. A detailed discussion of PPS and its effects is found later in this chapter.

Quantity and Capacity Controls

The controls on quantity tend to be indirect rather than direct, with the most prominent example being Certificate of Need (CON) laws. These laws require hospitals to obtain approval from planning agencies for capital expenditures in excess of various threshold levels. The operational premise is that unnecessary duplication of facilities as well as the mere availability of facilities leads to higher costs (i.e., fixed costs spread out over fewer users) and to higher rates of utilization (due to access and/or physician discretion).

Utilization review (UR), although primarily directed at quality, also has been supported on the basis of its expected negative effects on quantity. To the extent that third parties choose not to reimburse for services determined to be inappropriate, UR could have a deterrent effect on the provision of questionable services.

Regulation of the Hospital Sector

Given the hospital industry's large share of the U.S. health economy, policy makers have addressed cost inflation through regulation, primarily at the state level. In this section, we focus on the three major forms of hospital regulation: rate regulation, utilization review, and certificate of need.

Rate Regulation, Utilization Review, and Certificate of Need

As described previously, rate regulation defines the terms under which hospitals are reimbursed. The underlying premise has been that, due to market power, hospitals may charge rates that vary from the cost of providing the services. Prospective forms of reimbursement also are intended to deal with hospital inefficiency and incentives to overprovide care.

Rate regulation (RR) may occur on a daily (or per-diem basis) or on a per-patient or per-admission basis. The goal of rate regulation is to lower costs or at least to reduce the rate of hospital cost inflation.

UR programs seek to determine whether specific services are medically necessary and whether they are delivered at an appropriate level of intensity and cost. Ermann (1988) identifies three general types of utilization review:

1. Preadmission review examines the necessity of hospital admission before admission occurs to determine if inpatient care is necessary.
2. Concurrent review ascertains whether patients need continuing care by means of record review.
3. Retrospective review attempts to identify questionable patterns of care.

Another form of UR is second-opinion surgery review. This either requires or encourages patients who are contemplating elective surgery to seek advice from a second physician. One of the key questions in analyzing the impacts of any form of utilization review is the extent to which "truly" unnecessary procedures are eliminated as opposed to the extent that the quality of care suffers.

CON regulation addresses capital expenditure (either beds or other expensive hospital equipment). The general aim is to reduce excess capacity or to eliminate costly duplication of resources. An unintended impact occurs, however, if this review process reduces competition in the provision of the services. This reduction of competition, of course, could lead to increased monopoly power and to higher prices.

Empirical Findings on Regulation

Utilization Review

Utilization review seeks to reduce unnecessary costs without adversely affecting patient health, but its results have been mixed. A large body of research reviewed the Professional Standards Review Organizations (PSROs) that were established at local levels under federal laws in 1972. Two factors led to difficulties in evaluation. First, there was a wide variation among PSROs. Some may have been quite effective, while others were not. Looking across a whole group may not provide much guidance. Second, the PSRO program had two mandates. Cost was to be contained, and quality was to be ensured. It is clear that if quality-related aspects of health care provision cost money, then these two goals may conflict with each other. Not surprisingly, empirical results were generally inconclusive.

Wickizer, Wheeler, and Feldstein (1989) subsequently found that UR reduced admissions by 13 percent, inpatient days by 11 percent, expenditures on routine hospital inpatient service by 7 percent, expenditures on hospital ancillary services by 9 percent, and total medical expenditures by 6 percent. The same authors (1991) also found that the adoption of UR implies substitution effects (approximately $9 per insured person per year) suggesting a limited, although measurable, effect.

As for concerns that patients will get less care and with less certain (and possibly less positive) outcomes, Ermann (1988) cites the lack of conclusive evidence. There is a general consensus that UR may cut costs, but that it is less likely to impact the quality of the health care product either positively or negatively.

Rate Regulation

Much of the early research investigating the impact of RR centered on Connecticut, Massachusetts, New Jersey, New York, Maryland, and Washington, which either had or adopted RR through the 1970s and early 1980s. Studies investigating the impacts of RR looked at costs or changes in costs in these states, or in hospitals within these states. The typical method estimated a regression such that:

$$log\ C_t - log\ C_{t-1} = b(X_t - X_{t-1}) + dD + \varepsilon$$

where the left-hand side reflects the change in the logarithm of hospital expenses (or the logarithm of the percent change in expenses) as a function of changes in explanatory variables, X, and imposition of rate regulation, D. If coefficient d is negative, then all else being equal, the imposition of regulation D reduces the growth in costs.

Dranove and Cone (1985) carefully discuss the impacts of rate regulation. They examine the possibility of regression to the mean. Suppose at a given point some states have unusually high or unusually low costs. If these differences are transient due to jumps in energy or insurance costs, for example, then total costs would be expected to

return to the mean as the transient events disappear. Laws enacted in high-cost states may appear successful because the effects attributed to the laws really are caused by regression of the state to the overall mean of all states. The reverse, of course, also is possible. States that were below the mean could see rising costs, even with effective regulation.

The authors seek to explain (1) expenses per admission, (2) expenses per day, and (3) expenses per person, with the following explanatory variables:

Income—median family income
Education—population percentage with high school diploma
Age—population percentage over age 65
Insurance—population percentage insured against physician expenses
Metro—population percentage living in an urban area
Union—population percentage who are union members

and the following policy variable:

Law—number of years the law has been in effect

The regression results are presented in Table 20-1. Multiplying each coefficient of the law variable by 100 approximates (due to the logarithmic transformation of the dependent variable) the law's percentage impact. For example, those states with a regulation law exhibited approximately a 1.32 percent smaller increase in expenses per admission than other states, a 1.41 percent smaller increase in expenses per day, and a 1.04 percent smaller increase in expenses per person. Dranove and Cone suggest that mean regression made laws in New York and Massachusetts look more effective than they were (costs would have decreased anyhow). Conversely, mean regression made laws in Connecticut, New Jersey, and Washington look less effective. Adjusting for regression to the mean moved New Jersey from 4 percentage points worse than the average rate-setting state to 4 percentage points better.

TABLE 20-1 Percentage Change in Hospital Cost			
Variable	*Expenses per Admission*	*Expenses per Day*	*Expenses per Person*
Constant	0.70[a]	0.72[a]	0.46[a]
Income	0.66[a]	1.13[a]	0.79[a]
Education	−0.63[b]	−0.69[b]	0.30
Age	0.35[b]	0.28	0.83[a]
Insurance	−0.094	−0.26[b]	−0.67
Metro	−0.016	−0.70[b]	−0.33
Union	−0.11	−0.33[a]	−0.57
Law	**−0.0132[a]**	**−0.0141[a]**	**−0.0104[b]**
Adjustment	−0.20[b]	−0.005	−0.333[a]
Adjusted R^2	0.46	0.50	0.52

[a]Significant at 1 percent level.

[b]Significant at 10 percent level.

Source: Reprinted from *Journal of Health Economics.* David Dranove and Kenneth Cone, "Do State Rate Setting Regulations Really Lower Hospital Expenses?" *Journal of Health Economics 4* (1985): 159–165, with permission from Elsevier Science.

Certificate of Need

CON legislation has been studied in a variety of contexts. Salkever and Bice (1979) provided early and useful analyses of the programs. Their methods predicted costs using binary variables to represent the presence, comprehensiveness, and maturity of programs designed to regulate capital formation. Almost all of the studies found essentially no impact of CON on total expenditures.

Nevertheless, it is plausible to expect that other hospital inputs may increase to substitute for limits on capital expenditures. Salkever and Bice note that hospitals appear to have substituted investment for new services in place of investment in beds. Sloan and Steinwald (1980) reported similar results, as well as increased ratios of registered nurses and licensed practical nurses per bed.

Recognizing the problem of characterizing CON across states, Mayo and McFarland (1989, 1991) examine hospital costs over time in Tennessee. CON seeks to reduce capital expenditures, thus, preventing costly duplication of facilities. One can posit three impacts:

1. The intended impact on capital costs, which reduces cost by reducing capital expenditures.
2. The substitution effect in which the hospitals substitute nonregulated inputs for the regulated ones. This may offset capital cost reductions.[1]
3. The increased monopoly power of existing hospitals. If competitors cannot engage in capital expenditures, then existing hospitals gain monopoly power. Incentives to innovate, and hence lower production costs, may be lost if competition is lessened.

Mayo and McFarland find the direct effects of CON to lower hospital costs, and the indirect substitution and market concentration effects to raise them. While many studies in other states indicate no significant effect of CON, newer models suggest the importance of modeling cost-containment policies at the hospital rather than at the regional level. Hospitals react to cost-containment policies not only by changing the costs of the services, but also by adjusting the amounts of the services and the inputs into the services.

The 1990s brought new perspective to the evaluation of the traditional regulatory mechanisms. With the emergence of managed care, utilization review has become a common feature of almost all health care systems. The general concern about health care costs has made CON regulations somewhat outdated. Existing hospitals are addressing hard questions, such as whether to close units rather than planning new ones. More competitive market mechanisms are impacting the physician and the hospital sector.

Conover and Sloan (1998) assess the impact of CON regulation on hospital spending per capita, hospital supply, diffusion of technology, and hospital industry organization for the years 1976 through 1993. Long-term CON programs were associated with what they termed a "modest (5 percent)" long-term reduction in acute care spending per capita, but not with significant reduction in total spending per capita. The authors doubt that CON regulations have had much effect (either positive or negative) on quality of care.

Antel and colleagues (1995) address two major issues in measuring the impacts of the regulations over the contiguous 48 United States for the years 1968 to 1990. First, if factors like high wage rates persist over time, they might affect state-level hospital

[1]Mayo and McFarland's 1989 article does not address this issue. Responding to Keith Anderson (1991), they reestimate their cost equation. Our discussion uses the reestimated 1991 equation.

BOX 20-1

CON in Michigan: Costs or Competition?

Like many areas, metropolitan Detroit's hospital beds are in the wrong places. Large numbers of empty beds are located in the city of Detroit, whose population has fallen by half to about 900,000, in the last 40 years. At the same time, many of Detroit's suburban areas, with a combined population of over 3 million, argue that they do not have enough beds. The following narrative shows how CON legislation entered into an attempt by two area hospitals to move beds into growing areas.

Henry Ford and St. John Hospitals, two of Detroit's very large hospitals, also have suburban facilities. Each hospital claimed to provide about $100 million a year in uncompensated care, mostly in Detroit. The hospitals insisted that to remain viable, they must improve their "payer mix" by shifting hospital beds to places with more wealthy and well-insured people.

Oakland County, one of the wealthiest counties in the United States, with a population of 1 million, lies just north and west of Detroit. Although developed later than Detroit, even in this suburban county population shifts have led to uneven coverage with respect to hospital beds. Providence Hospital (a subsidiary of St. John Health) sought to transfer 200 licensed beds from locations in eastern Oakland County, close to Detroit, about 20 miles further west in the same county. Henry Ford sought to transfer 300 beds from Detroit about 25 miles away into the southwest part of Oakland County.

Michigan's CON program has the following regulatory power over hospital beds:

Three facility types must receive a certificate of need on the basis of bed need: acute care hospitals, psychiatric hospitals, including specialized programs for child/adolescents; and, long-term care facilities. Any entity that seeks to increase the number of licensed beds, physically relocate beds from one licensed site to another...replace beds, or acquire a hospital, psychiatric hospital or long-term care facility must receive a CON to do so.

Expansion opponents argued that the proposed additions would drive up costs and wait times in the county. Some also said that moving beds out of Detroit would worsen the city's dire health care crisis. Expansion supporters believed the opponents feared they would lose patients — and income — to the new hospitals.

In fall 2002, the Michigan State Legislature passed a law exempting the Henry Ford and St. John plans from the CON requirement. That exemption could be withdrawn if 7 of 11 CON commission members decided that those plans might harm access and delivery of health care. In June 2003, the Commission declined to overrule the exemption. The opponents sued.

In March 2005, The Michigan Court of Appeals ruled in favor of allowing the two area hospital groups to move ahead. The three-judge court unanimously affirmed a lower court's decision that the plaintiffs — Trinity Health and William Beaumont Hospitals — did not have legal standing to prevent the other hospitals from adding beds.

It may reinforce analysts' cynicism about the regulatory process to recognize that in this particular instance CON, originally derived to address costs, had little to do with costs, and everything to do with hospital competition and profitability.

SOURCE: Tom Walsh, "Hospital Fight Is Heading to West Oakland County," *Detroit Free Press*, May 23, 2003, www.freep.com/money/business/walsh23_20030523.htm, accessed August 25, 2005; Carol Hopkins, "Appeals Court Allows Hospitals to Expand," *Oakland Press*, March 24, 2005, www.theoaklandpress.com/stories/032405/loc_20050324011.shtml, accessed August 25, 2005.

costs and influence the states' regulatory decisions. If these factors are not accounted for properly in the analyses, it is difficult to measure the regulatory impacts accurately. Second, regulations may interact with each other. For example, hospital responses to the Medicare PPS may raise costs; rate regulation may limit the cost-increasing effects of the Medicare system.

The researchers model six regulatory instruments. If regulation were effective, each of these instruments would be expected to lower costs.

1. Proportion of hospital revenue affected by mandatory state rate-setting regulation
2. CON programs passed by the states in the 1960s and 1970s
3. 1970s legislation that denied Medicare and Medicaid cost reimbursement to hospitals that were expanding capacity without prior approval by local planning agencies
4. Professional Standards Review Organization to control hospital services utilization
5. Medicare prospective payment, beginning in 1984
6. Price controls under the Economic Stabilization Act from 1971 through 1974

They examine costs per day, costs per admission, and costs per person. The "simple" impacts, without interaction among them, indicate that rate regulation and economic stabilization policies had substantive impacts; the other instruments did not. However, more complex models indicate that rate regulation, which seemed effective in the simple models, appeared unable, alone, to control per-day, per-admission, or per-person hospital costs. Nor was there any evidence that federal utilization controls or state and federal hospital investment restrictions lowered hospital costs.

Interestingly, the authors found the Nixon-era price regulations to have been effective in lowering costs. They conjecture that this occurred because the controls covered hospital wages and other input prices. Also, because the controls were temporary, hospitals may have had less incentive to adjust or to evade them.

Finally, there are political issues. One can conjecture as to whether CON rules, as they have evolved, pertain to costs, or whether they have other impacts. Box 20-1 provides a case study of how CON rules were used to attempt to prevent hospital expansion, in a setting in which hospital costs appeared to have little to do with the issue.

Prospective Payment

The enactment of Medicare and Medicaid involved the federal government to a large degree in the reimbursement of services. Program costs have increased substantially over the years, and as costs have grown, so has interest in cost-containment policies.

In this section, we focus on the Medicare program that converted the financing of Medicare hospital care to a prospective payment system based on Diagnosis Related Groups (DRGs). We discuss the system in the present context because its widespread use stems from its adoption by the Medicare program. However, the PPS under DRGs has wider significance to other segments of the health sector, as well as to the regulation of industry in general.

Description of PPS

Prospective payment is best seen in contrast to the former retrospective reimbursement system under Medicare. Under retrospective payment, a hospital submitted its bill to Medicare after the care has been given, and the costs to the hospital were known. Retrospective payment allowed the hospitals to recover their expenses, as allowed by Medicare rules, regardless of whether these expenses were high or low, excessive or efficient. Under retrospective reimbursement, incentives to control costs were questionable.

Prospective payment sets payment rates prior to the period for which care is given. By setting a fixed reimbursement level per admission, prospective payment provides economic incentives to conserve on the use of input resources. Hospitals that use more

resources than covered by the flat rate lose the difference. Those with costs below that rate retain the difference.

As of 2005, Medicare's payment systems could be grouped as follows:

1. Inpatient acute care in short-term hospitals and psychiatric facilities
2. Ambulatory care furnished by physicians, hospital outpatient departments, ambulatory surgical centers, and clinical laboratories
3. Post-acute care furnished by skilled nursing facilities, home health agencies, inpatient rehabilitation facilities, and long-term care hospitals
4. Dialysis services furnished in outpatient centers and hospice care
5. Ambulance services and products furnished by durable medical equipment suppliers
6. Services furnished by private health plans under the Medicare Advantage program

In 2000, program payments plus payments by beneficiaries (or third-party payers on their behalf) for inpatient acute care in short-term hospitals, physician services, and managed care plans, all paid by prospective payment methods, accounted for 70 percent of Medicare spending.

DRGs define one of the primary mechanisms for prospective payment. Under PPS, patients are admitted according to their condition under one of 504 applicable DRGs. Each DRG attempts to represent a case type that identifies patients with similar conditions and processes of care. Table 20-2a gives an example of both some of the most complex procedures, as indicated by DRG weight, as well as some of the least complex.

Each DRG is given a flat payment rate calculated in part on the basis of costs incurred for that DRG nationally. These rates are modified somewhat in practice to account for differences in local wages, urban versus rural location, and other factors such as whether the hospital is a teaching hospital. For example, based on Table 20-2a, a heart transplant is about 1.87 (i.e., 19.82/10.61) times as costly as a liver transplant, and about 130 (i.e., 19.82/0.15) times as costly as a normal newborn. The rates are flat in

TABLE 20-2a DRGs by Weight—Five Highest and Five Lowest

DRG	DRG Title	Weights	Mean Length of Stay
Highest Weights			
103	Heart transplant	19.8195	57.5
483	Tracheostomy except for face, mouth & neck diagnoses	15.2827	41.0
504	Extensive third degree burns w/skin graft	13.8097	33.6
480	Liver transplant	10.6132	22.8
495	Lung transplant	8.8879	16.2
Lowest Weights			
33	Concussion, age 0–17	0.2075	1.6
382	False labor	0.1607	1.3
343	Circumcision, age 0–17	0.1533	1.7
391	Normal newborn	0.1519	3.1
448	Allergic reactions, age 0–17	0.0970	2.9

Source: www.cms.hhs.gov/researchers/pubs/datacompendium/2003/03pg4243.Zip, accessed August 26, 2005.

TABLE 20-2b Five Most Common DRGs by Number of Discharges—2001

DRG	Description	Total Payments (thousands)	Average Payments ($)	Number of Discharges	Average Total Days
127	Heart failure and shock	$3,603,784	5,045	686,830	5.3
089	Simple pneumonia and pleurisy, age greater than 17 with complications or comorbidity	2,968,699	5,494	506,410	5.9
088	Chronic obstructive pulmonary disease	1,829,334	4,431	399,849	5.1
209	Major joint and limb reattachment procedures of lower extremity	3,797,007	9,204	373,905	5.0
116	Other permanent cardiac pacemaker implants	4,534,966	10,964	368,837	3.6

Source: www.cms.hhs.gov/researchers/pubs/datacompendium/2003/03pg4243.pdf, accessed August 26, 2005.

the important sense that they are not varied or softened for hospitals that spend more than the rate, or for that matter less. Some of the most common DRGs, based on hospital discharges, are shown in Table 20-2b, with by far the largest number of discharges related to heart failure and shock.

The Theory of Yardstick Competition and DRGs

Shleifer (1985) has described the theory of yardstick competition, which is a close approximation to PPS under DRGs. We can think of yardstick competition as the ideal form of such a system, while the actual Medicare payment system is a real-life approximation.

Shleifer describes yardstick competition in the context of markets where firms have at least some monopoly power. Most medical providers face downward-sloping demand curves so they possess some degree of monopoly power.

Recall that compared with competitive firms monopolistic firms reduce outputs and correspondingly charge higher prices. Moreover, secure monopolistic firms lack some of the incentives to be cost efficient that rigorous competition would provide. In US hospital markets prior to PPS, one of the most serious cost-efficiency disincentives was the retrospective payment system already discussed. Shleifer's yardstick competition describes a regulatory scheme, much like Medicare's PPS, that restores cost-consciousness incentives.

Consider Figure 20-1 in which the hospital faces demand curve D, and where marginal and average costs equal C_0. As we have seen before, the monopoly hospital will provide Q_0 units of output and charge P_0 indicated by point M. In contrast, with retrospective reimbursement, the hospital will be paid C_0, and will produce at the intersection of demand D with C_0, at point R.

Suppose the hospital knows that it could produce at lower cost if it would hire a team (a fixed cost that is unrelated to output) of efficiency experts and carry out its advice (also a fixed cost). Recall that efficiency requires a firm to produce a quantity at which marginal cost (value in production) equals the market price (value in consumption). The problem for yardstick competition is to set up a payment scheme so that these firms have the incentives to spend just the right amount of money and effort on reducing production costs.

FIGURE 20-1 The Impact of Yardstick Competition

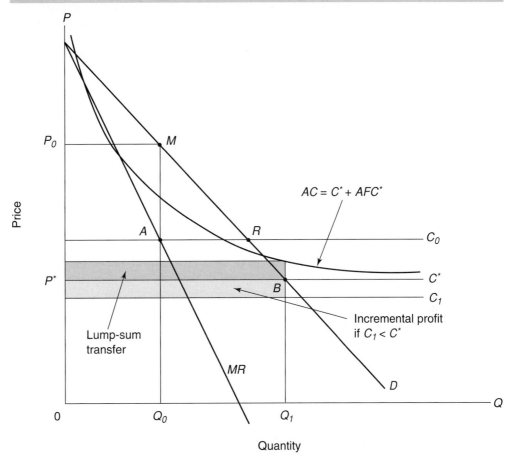

What is just the right amount of expense to incur in the effort to reduce production costs? Suppose the hospital discovers that it could reduce its marginal costs of production by $100 per case treated if it were to spend $150,000 on cost-reduction efforts. Suppose the hospital treats 5,000 cases per year. Would the cost-reduction effort be worth it? The example is shown in the first line of the following schedule.

	Marginal Cost of Efficiency Effort		*Marginal Revenue Generated*
Step (1)	$150,000	<	$100 × 5,000 = 500,000
Step (2)	$270,000	<	$100 × 5,000
Step (3)	$490,000	<	$100 × 5,000
Step (4)	$750,000	>	$100 × 5,000

Step (1) represents the first of four possible steps in cost reduction. Each step will reduce costs per case by $100. With step (1), reducing per-unit costs by $100 costs a total of $150,000 in cost-efficiency efforts. The extra $1 saved for every case treated generates $500,000 in extra revenue.

Clearly, this step of cost saving is worthwhile because it costs less ($150,000) than it saves ($500,000). By similar reasoning, one more step of cost saving also would be

worthwhile, costing $270,000, but saving another $500,000. Step (3) is worthwhile, too, but that is where we would stop. Unregulated monopolists or retrospectively reimbursed firms may not have the incentives to take these three steps. It would be good to have a payment system that would induce them to do so.

How does yardstick competition provide this inducement? Return to Figure 20-1. With yardstick competition, prices at which the hospital is reimbursed are set beforehand at fixed rates. These rates—that is, these regulated prices—are set equal to the averages of the marginal costs of all other hospitals in the market.

Suppose the regulator is able to determine the marginal cost of each hospital. Consider Hospital 1. Recall that the cost-reduction efforts represent a fixed cost to the hospital, and the average fixed cost (graphed in Figure 20-1) must be covered by additional revenues. Hospital 1 is assigned service price C^*, equal to the average marginal cost of all of its competitors, Hospitals 2 through N, and a break-even subsidy (dark shaded area), again equal to the average of all of its competitors. With its revenue per patient now fixed prospectively, Hospital 1's incentive is to invest in cost-cutting technologies or practices.

Recall what the "yardstick competition" does. It induces the hospital to reduce its marginal costs from C_0 to some lower level and to price its output at the "average" marginal cost of its competitors. We treat the cost-cutting innovation as a fixed cost for the hospital output. As a result, the hospital's new average cost curve AC is the sum of the (now-lower) marginal cost C^* and the optimum average fixed cost, AFC^*. The new output occurs where C^* is equal to the demand price, or point B. The optimal output becomes Q_1, and the price falls to P^*, which equals C^*.

Suppose, fortuitously, that the hospital's new marginal cost equals C^*. Under yardstick competition, it will lose an amount equal to the fixed costs of reducing its marginal costs, or the dark shaded area in Figure 20-1. The yardstick pricing scheme provides a lump-sum subsidy to the hospital, allowing it to "break even" despite incurring the fixed costs required for its cost-reducing efforts.

If the hospital has succeeded in lowering its marginal costs to C_1, which is less than C^*, then it will earn a profit equal to $Q_1 (C^* - C_1)$, the lightly shaded area. If the hospital cannot lower its costs to C^*, then it will lose money. In either case, because the hospital's actual costs do not enter into the price that it receives, and because the hospital can earn a profit if it reduces costs, the hospital has a considerable incentive to reduce its costs.

In this yardstick model, hospitals are not subsidized for inefficient behavior. Hospitals compete, and this competition leads to an optimum solution discussed earlier. The competition, known as a "Nash equilibrium" (after Nobel Laureate John Nash), refers to a market solution in which each firm does the best that it can, given the decision of others. It is an equilibrium because once the choices are made, no firm has any motive to change its action. Shleifer notes it is

> ... essential for the regulator to commit himself not to pay attention to the firms' complaints and to be prepared to let the firms go bankrupt if they choose inefficient cost levels. Unless the regulator can credibly threaten to make inefficient firms lose money ... cost reduction cannot be enforced. (p. 327)

The model implicitly assumes that all hospitals are the same, but Shleifer, shows how to construct a statistical multiple regression that would generate a solution in the more realistic case where hospitals differ from each other. Furthermore, he demonstrates a closely related scheme of pricing based on average industry costs that leads to virtually the same results in the realistic case where the theoretically needed lump-sum subsidies would be difficult to calculate or difficult to pass politically.

Returning now to DRGs as practiced, consistent with Shleifer's formulation, a hospital's actual costs do not enter into the formula for its payment rate. As a result, the hospital must become a price taker in the strictest sense. If it costs the hospital more to provide the service than the DRGs allow, the hospital either loses money on the service and is forced to stop offering it, or it is forced to cross-subsidize the service from other services that may be produced at costs lower than their DRGs. Thus, the cost-cutting incentives are strong.

Although yardstick competition applies to the hospital, many of the costs reflect orders from physicians who are generally not even employees of the hospitals. Box 20-2 provides an example of how physicians and hospitals might align incentives.

BOX 20-2

The Alignment of Provider and Hospital Incentives

Kathryn Stewart notes that most physicians do not see direct connections between their local hospital's financial position and their everyday actions in managing inpatients. They hear hospital executives "fussing" about saving money and assume it is the hospitals' problem, not theirs. Dr. Stewart offers several ways for physicians to help their hospitals address costs.

1. Change your mind-set about the use of acute-care hospitals. An acute-care hospital is for patients who are unstable in terms of vital signs or mental status, who require complicated surgery or procedures, who might suffer death or severe morbidity without 24-hour-a-day monitoring, or who require a rapid diagnosis to prevent death or severe morbidity. Problems that are less severe can be handled on an outpatient basis.

2. Don't include the kitchen sink. When a patient needs to be admitted to the hospital, make every attempt to limit care to the reason for admission. If another, unexpected problem surfaces while the patient is in the hospital, ask, "Would I admit this patient to the hospital for this problem if I saw him or her in the office?" If the answer is no, then don't treat the problem while the patient is in the hospital.

3. Use other levels of care. Numerous hospital alternatives did not exist even a decade ago. Patients can receive physical and occupational therapy, get X-rays and lab work, and even receive intravenous (IV) drugs and total parenteral (through a vein) nutrition at home or in skilled-care nursing homes. Once stabilized and with a treatment plan, the patient can be moved out of the acute-care hospital to another place to finish treatment. It is simply too expensive today to use acute-care hospitals for these purposes.

4. Bring costs down. General rules include:

- *Pay attention to medication costs.* If a medication can be given by mouth (e.g., it is formulated that way and the patient has a functional gastrointestinal tract), then give it by mouth as soon as possible. Many drugs work as well or better that way. Intravenous drugs are expensive so change from IV to oral as soon as possible, but don't simply choose the cheapest drug on the market. An expensive once-a-day IV antibiotic may be less expensive than a cheaper twice-a-day antibiotic once staff costs of administering the drugs are factored in.

- *Don't do a test in the hospital that will not be used to make decisions about the rest of the patient's stay.* If a test is not directly related to the reason for admission and it will not change the course of the hospital diagnosis and treatment plan, don't do it in the hospital.

- *Remember, most hospitals count their census at midnight.* If the patient is in that bed at midnight, you have just added another day to the length of stay. Consider sending the patient home tonight unless there is something critical to be done in the morning.

Aligning provider and hospital incentives saves money. A careful examination of the recommendations suggests that it may also improve quality of care!

SOURCE: Kathryn Stewart, "Seven Ways to Help Your Hospital Stay in Business," www.aafp.org/fpm/20030500/27seve.html, accessed November 11, 2005.

How accurate are the yardstick payments generated for DRGs? Although DRGs are designed to elicit cost-cutting behavior, they would be expected, on average, to equal provider costs. Ginsburg and Grossman (2005) report that Medicare and other payers have found it difficult to devise payment rates that closely follow relative costs for different services. Medicare prospective payment for inpatient care, which is based on DRGs, determines the relative payment for each DRG on the basis of average charges for patients in that DRG across all hospitals. To the degree that the pattern of charges systematically diverges from the pattern of unit costs, then relative payments for different DRGs will not reflect relative costs. As a result, patients in some DRGs are more profitable than others.

A recent MedPAC analysis estimated that DRG 107, coronary artery bypass graft with catheterization, is systematically 9 percent more profitable than the average DRG, while DRG 127, heart failure and shock, is 6 percent less profitable than the average (MedPAC, March 2005, Table 10). Few Medicare systems are based on actual cost data, and Medicare's hospital reimbursement rates are based on 1982 costs, which are then inflated annually.

As a result, charges for services with the most rapidly advancing technology tend over time to have the largest markups over costs. Ginsburg and Grossman note that this is probably the reason that DRG 517 (percutaneous transluminal coronary angioplasty stent without acute myocardial infarction) is 16 percent more profitable than the average Medicare case. Higher markups for services that use advancing technology result from increasing productivity that comes from experience in designing and manufacturing equipment and devices and in providing services.

Newer models of equipment are often more productive or have lower costs than what they replace. For example, recent advances in CT scanning equipment have reduced the time it takes to do a scan, meaning that a machine and technician staff can perform more scans per day. Similarly, the physician time required to perform many cardiovascular surgical procedures has fallen over time as the technology has evolved. In addition, as new services are provided to more patients, equipment and dedicated space and personnel are used at a higher capacity, which is another factor behind productivity gains over time. For some supplies, such as prepackaged instruments and supplies that physician practices purchase for certain procedures, entry by additional manufacturers leads to lower prices. These declines in costs often mean that payment rates that are not revised frequently soon become out of date, leading to profit margins that are higher than those for services not experiencing these trends.

On the Effects of Medicare's Prospective Payment System

Yardstick competition in theory and the actual Medicare PPS in practice change firms' economic incentives considerably. Results to date show some clear impacts, as well as some remaining ambiguities. We examine briefly several categories of possible effects.

Average Hospital Length of Stay

One method of cutting costs available to hospitals in theory is to reduce the number of days of care taken to treat a patient case. Average length of stay did drop after the advent of PPS, 9 percent in the first year, and a total of 14.6 percent between 1982 and 1985. Hodgkin and McGuire (1994) develop a model in which the prospective payment level affects the hospital's choice of intensity of care, which affects the demand for admissions. The model suggests that both the average payment level and the incentives created by changes in the marginal rate affect hospital utilization. The effect of PPS on length of stay is plausible and clearly established in the data.

Subsequent data have shown the decreases to be pervasive and long lasting. MedPAC data tracing hospital length of stay have shown continual decreases. Length of stay for all hospitals fell by 32.2 percent from 1989 to 1999, with annual declines exceeding 5 percent from 1993 to 1996. The rate of decline fell below 2 percent per year after 1998, and was reported as 1.3 percent in 2003 (MedPAC, *2005 Annual Report to Congress*, Figure 2A–5).

Access and Quality

DesHarnais and colleagues (1988) found no evidence of quality reductions for a sample of 646 U.S. hospitals. Also relevant to quality issues, Carroll and Erwin (1987) showed no significant difference in several major health status measures for patients being transferred from hospitals to nursing homes before and after PPS. In surveying the evidence as of 1991, Feinglass and Holloway (1991) conclude that while evidence can be found of individual instances where access or quality has been limited because of PPS, there was little direct, generalizable evidence that PPS had reduced the quality of care for Medicare patients.

MedPAC (2000, p. 61) reports that from 1990 through 1999 there had been a net reduction of 340 short-term acute care hospitals (440 closing; 100 opening or reopening). The reduction in total capacity was much smaller than the 6.5 percent decline in hospitals because the closed hospitals were generally small and had low occupancy rates and very low volumes.

The most recent MedPAC analyses provide mixed results regarding quality of care. In-hospital mortality declined from 1998 to 2003 for eight conditions or procedures; rates for coronary artery bypass graft, congestive heart failure, and gastrointestinal hemorrhage fell by more than 20 percent. The 30-day mortality rate decreased for six measures from 1998 to 2003 but increased slightly for two, pneumonia and stroke. The 30-day rate reflects not only the in-hospital experience but often care experienced in post-acute and outpatient settings. Data from the Quality Improvement Organization (QIO) program on the clinical effectiveness and appropriateness of care in hospitals show improvement for 18 of 25 measures. They note that many beneficiaries still are not receiving clinically indicated services.

Further MedPAC analyses indicated that the rate of adverse events increased for 9 of 13 measures analyzed from 1998 to 2003. The most common is decubitus ulcer (bedsores), for which the rate increased over the period. The second most common, failure to rescue, results in death. MedPAC indicates concern about the trends for some measures, particularly the patient safety indicators, but argues that none of these measures provide "compelling" evidence that payments are, or are not, adequate.

Severity of the Case Mix

Another observed change following the onset of Medicare's PPS has been the increase in common case-mix indexes. A case-mix index is a numerical measure of the assortment of patient cases treated by a given hospital so that a higher index value indicates a greater average degree of complexity of the cases and consequently a greater need for input resources. Some of the increase in the indexes has probably occurred because hospitals are being more careful about which diagnosis they choose (for patients with multiple diagnoses) to categorize the patient for Medicare payment purposes. This maneuver is sometimes called "DRG creep."

Many analysts have expressed concern that the PPS under DRGs would induce hospitals to save on costs by cutting corners, reducing quality, refusing to treat costly patients, or closing treatment units. That is, the system would reduce access to care and the quality of care. Research has addressed these issues to some extent.

Sloan, Morrisey, and Valvona (1988a) found that use of intensive care units did not fall after PPS, allaying fears about access to needed care. Use of many diagnostic and treatment technologies did fall after PPS started, but these also fell for non-Medicare patients. DesHarnais and colleagues (1988) used statistical techniques to estimate quality changes in a sample of 729 U.S. short-term general care hospitals following Medicare's PPS. The results were negative, meaning that no evidence of quality reduction was found.

Through the late 1980s it was difficult to distinguish this as the cause of increased case complexity, but it seemed clear that hospital treatment practice patterns changed following PPS. Also, average severity of the cases treated on an inpatient basis in hospitals increased subsequent to PPS suggesting that less severe cases are now assigned to outpatient treatment.

A recent study revisits the DRG creep issue. Silverman and Skinner (2004) found that between 1989 and 1996, the percentage point share of the most generous DRG for pneumonia and respiratory infections rose by 10 points among not-for-profit hospitals, 23 points among for-profit hospitals, and 37 points in hospitals converting to for-profit status. After 1996, however, there was a dramatic decline in upcoding ratios, with the greatest drop among for-profit hospitals.

Why did this occur? Differential upcoding by for-profits was not because of sicker patients or attenuation in "downcoding" caused by more efficient billing systems. A variety of other audits conducted by the government and by nongovernment researchers have found ex post that chart data could not support the severity of disease actually billed for. Upcoding took the form of presumptive diagnosis; while there was no documentation that the patient actually had the disease, it could not definitely be ruled out.

In explaining the higher propensity of for-profits to upcode, the authors appeal to the Pauly and Redisch's (1973) distinction, as noted in Chapter 13 between for-profit hospitals, where physicians either share residual hospital revenue or received salaries, and not-for-profit hospitals, where "no administrator can afford to incur the displeasure of the medical staff . . ." (p. 89). For upcoding to occur, administrators must be willing to engage in ex ante risky but potentially profitable behavior, and physicians must acquiesce by approving (and until 1995, signing) the DRG claims submitted by the hospital to Medicare.

Hospitals' Financial Condition

Most agree that PPS puts a degree of financial stress on hospitals, particularly on those that have higher than usual costs. This, after all, is the way in which PPS alters financial incentives. However, hospitals run on the principles of yardstick competition might well increase their wealth positions subsequent to PPS. In any case, at the beginning of Medicare's PPS, the fixed-payment rates proved sufficiently generous that average operating margins of hospitals were substantial, thus reducing the cost-saving incentives. Payment rates did not subsequently keep up with inflation, perhaps due to Congressional concern about windfall profits, and operating margins fell steadily. By the late 1980s and extending through the early 1990s, average operating margins for the Medicare segment of patients tended to be negative.

More recent data create an overall margin that combines both inpatient and outpatient margins. Table 20-3 reports 2003 margins of −1.9 percent for all hospitals, ranging from −6.2 percent for rural hospitals to +5.8 percent for major teaching hospitals. MedPAC predicts a convergence of the margins for 2005. MedPAC notes (MedPAC 2005, pp. 59–60) that hospitals with consistently negative margins tended to perform

TABLE 20-3 Overall Medicare Margin by Hospital Group

Hospital Group	2000	2001	2002	2003	2005[a]
All hospitals	5.2%	5.0%	2.3%	–1.9%	–1.5%
Urban	6.2	5.8	3.0	–1.3	–1.3
Rural	–2.6	–1.3	–3.3	–6.2	–3.1
Major teaching	14.2	13.4	11.5	5.8	5.0
Other teaching	5.0	4.5	2.0	–1.9	–1.7
Nonteaching	0.3	0.6	–2.6	–5.8	–4.7

[a]Projections that reflect the effects of policy changes.
Source: MedPAC (2005), Table 2A–4, p. 51.

poorer on two key cost-influencing factors compared with hospitals that consistently perform well under Medicare—namely occupancy rate and length of stay. The negative margin group had much lower occupancy rates, which would translate into higher unit costs because fixed costs (such as plant and equipment) are spread over fewer units of output. Similarly, Medicare length of stay dropped more for the positive margin group than for the negative margin group, resulting in lower costs per discharge because the drop in days of care reduces variable costs, such as nursing time and meals.

Early Evidence of Effects on Costs

Medicare's goal was to control costs. So the ultimate question is whether PPS succeeded. This question, however, can be addressed from at least three perspectives. First, did individual hospitals respond by reducing their expenditures? Evidence indicates that they did so, at least in the first year. Zwanziger and Melnick (1988) observed that for a sample of California hospitals, those under the strongest pressure from PPS responded by reducing expenditures.

Second, did PPS reduce expenditures in Medicare's budget? Hospital savings seem likely. Medicare outlays for hospital care increased at an annual rate of 3.5 percent from 1984 to 1987, compared to 7.1 percent from 1977 to 1982, and hospital care fell as a proportion of the Medicare budget from 70 percent to 57 percent by 1988. Subsequently, PPS payments per case rose only slightly faster than the consumer price index so that by 1993, after the first 10 years of PPS, Medicare's share of hospital payments remained at 28 percent despite a 23 percent growth in Medicare enrollments.

Lastly, did per-capita expenditures for society as a whole fall as a result of Medicare's PPS? This is a much more difficult question to answer. Feinglass and Holloway (1991) argue that the savings from PPS were one-time-only events, occurring in the early years of PPS. This possibility is evidenced by increasing late 1980s inflation rates for U.S. health care expenditures, which in real terms were outstripping the inflation rates of 1980 to 1985.

In a statistical study of the issue, Sloan, Morrisey, and Valvona (1988a) find a significant reduction in hospital patient-generated revenues per capita subsequent to PPS, but they note that the savings are found primarily in reductions in admissions, a category PPS does not provide specific incentives to reduce. They note the possibility that utilization review under peer review organizations (PROs)—a utilization review effort begun along with Medicare's PPS—could conceivably be the source of per-capita cost reductions for hospital care. Shifts to outpatient care, which similarly do not provide specific cost-reduction incentives, also may occur.

Prospective Payment: Recent Evidence

PPS was developed at least in part to address perceived cost increases in the health care sector, but early analyses indicated that its effectiveness was at best mixed. We examine here analyses provided by MedPAC. Costs per inpatient stay, indicated by discharge data, can be rewritten as the following equation:

$$(\text{cost/discharge}) = (\text{days/discharge}) \times (\text{service intensity/day}) \times (\text{cost/service unit})$$

So, a hospital stay that lasts eight days, with two treatments per day at a cost of $100 per treatment, will cost:

$$(\text{cost/discharge}) = (8 \text{ days}) \times (2 \text{ treatments}) \times (\$100), \text{ or } \$1,600.$$

It is easy to apply this formula to changes over time. Some manipulation leads to:

$$\% \text{ Change in (cost/discharge)} = \% \text{ Change in (days/discharge)} + \% \text{ Change in (services/day)} + \% \text{ Change in (cost/service)}$$

Table 20-4 provides results of the formula. Costs are measured relative to general price inflation, so the table suggests, for example, that costs increased by 2.5 percent more per year than goods outside the hospital sector from 1985 to 1989. During that period, the most important variable was length-of-stay reduction, which went from an increasing factor (0.8 percent per year) to substantial decreases of −1.3 percent per year from 1989 to 1992 and −3.3 percent per year from 1992 to 1996. This was somewhat offset by increased services per day, although overall services per discharge (the sum of percentage changes in days/discharge and services/day) appear to have dropped.

Other MedPAC analyses indicate that from 1993 through 1999, on average, the annual increase in cost per discharge was only +0.8 percent, more than 2 percentage points a year below the increase in the hospital "market basket." One of the hospital industry's key tools for cutting costs was reducing length of stay, largely by discharging patients to various forms of post-acute care earlier in their stays. But they also cut costs in other ways, such as reducing staffing levels, providing smaller increases in compensation, and substituting less-skilled workers (such as nurse aides for RNs).

In 2000, private payer payments to hospitals once again began rising faster than costs. The payment-to-cost ratio for private payers rose 1.3 percentage points per year through 2003—almost as rapidly as in the late 1980s—and hospitals' profits from privately insured patients rose by 6 percentage points. Health plans continue to negotiate prices with hospitals, but many providers gained the upper hand in these negotiations. Payers' primary leverage in price negotiations is the threat of selective contracting, but their use of this tool was limited by both hospital consolidation and consumers'

TABLE 20-4 Average Annual Hospital Cost Changes

Years	Cost/Discharge	=	Days/Discharge	+	Services/Day	+	Costs/Service
	Average Annual Changes (%)						
1985 to 1989	2.5		0.8		2.2		−0.3
1989 to 1992	1.3		−1.3		1.4		1.3
1992 to 1996	−2.7		−3.3		0.9		−0.3

Source: MedPAC (March 1999), Appendix D, Table D–1.

reluctance to accept limitations on their choice of providers, preferences for so-called "managed care light." Pressure from private payers has waned considerably (Nichols et al., 2004). These factors lessened the financial pressure from private payers over the next three years, and the rate of hospital cost growth climbed back to levels not seen since the early 1990s, once again exceeding growth in the market basket, on average, by more than 3 percentage points a year.

Regulation of Physician Payment

Traditionally, physicians in the United States have been paid on a fee-for-service (FFS) basis. Under FFS, each physician has a schedule of fees and expects to be reimbursed for each unit of service provided.

As commercial insurance proliferated following World War II, benefit schedules generally were used to determine reimbursement. These schedules contained the maximum amounts that the insurers would pay for a particular service. If the provider charged less, the lower amount would be paid. Typically, also, individuals paid the providers' charges and were reimbursed (indemnified) by insurers according to the benefit schedule. Indemnity plans are still common in the for-profit insurance market.

UCR Reimbursement, Assignment, and Alternative Payment Mechanisms

Following the introduction of Medicare in 1965, another system for reimbursing providers became more prevalent. It uses fee screens and is commonly called the usual, customary, and reasonable (UCR) payment mechanism.

The fee screens are determined by the maximum of the doctor's median charge (i.e., usual charge) and the customary fees charged by the other physicians in the area. Some criterion, such as the eightieth percentile of the distribution of charges, may be selected for this cutoff. In addition, higher charges may be allowed if they are deemed reasonable in light of any unusual circumstances that would justify the higher payment. Under UCR, the maximum reimbursement is the lowest of the actual charge or the two fee screens.

Clearly, the UCR method is far more complicated and difficult to administer than the benefit schedule because it involves data collection on every provider. Supporters of this approach argue, however, that it is flexible and fair because it allows for differences across different specialty groups and market areas. Once Medicare adopted the UCR, the Blues and many other third-party payers followed.

However, several concerns with UCR soon became apparent. Many critics argued that UCR is inflationary. Providers have incentives to raise their charges, thus increasing the usual and customary screens and resulting in increased future payments. Furthermore, there is no incentive to compete by charging less than the screens. To deal with this problem, Medicare and many Blue Shield plans introduced various mechanisms to limit the increases in the screens.

Relative Value Scales

Relative value scales (RVSs) were developed by state medical societies and other organizations (the California RVS, developed in 1969, was one of the most widely used). An RVS establishes a weight (or multiple) for each procedure. The weight may reflect the time needed to perform a procedure and its complexity. Although the RVS

does not provide fee information, if providers adhere to the guide, the price they set for any one procedure will determine the prices charged for all other procedures.

One must recognize that any system of relative value scales depends on a set of given technologies. When, for example, the method of treating heart disease changes, the RVS for that category also must change in order to remain valid. If the technological advance causes the treatment to become cheaper, the treatment may become more profitable to the provider as long as the treatment retains its old place in the relative value scale.

Over the years, perceived inequities in Medicare's UCR system between primary care and surgical specialties led to attempts to change Medicare's physician payment system. Harvard University researchers, led by William Hsiao, undertook the task of developing a "resource-based" RVS, or RBRVS, as an alternative method of reimbursing physicians. As a result of their work, a new Medicare payment system, based on RBRVS, was phased in over a five-year period beginning in 1992.

The RBRVS (MedPAC, 1999) has three components, corresponding to three different types of resources used to provide physicians' services:

1. *Physician work*, including the time, intensity of effort, skill, and risk to the patient associated with each service. On average, this accounts for 52 percent of the fee.
2. *Practice expenses*, including the cost of nonphysician staff, office space, equipment, and supplies. This accounts for 44 percent of the fee.
3. *Professional liability insurance*, accounting for 4 percent of the fee (for some services this amount is higher; in the late 1990s insurance accounted for 12.1 percent of the total relative value unit for spinal laminectomy—surgery).

The system introduced a major restructuring of fees away from specialists and toward primary care providers, through conversion factors that reflect resources used. The conversion factors are updated under the so-called sustainable growth rate (SGR) system, in which CMS (Medicare and Medicaid) must target a rate of growth. Target expenditures for each year equal target expenditures from the previous year increased by the SGR, a formula specified in the statute comprising the following four factors: (1) the estimated percentage change in fees for physicians' services, (2) the estimated change in the average number of Medicare fee-for-service beneficiaries, (3) the estimated 10-year average annual growth in real gross domestic product (GDP) per capita, and (4) the estimated change in expenditures due to changes in law or regulations.

The SGR system addresses only input price inflation and productivity growth and, therefore, does not fully account for changes in the cost of providing physician services. Moreover, annual updates penalize spending above the target and reward spending below the target, thus, leading to payments that diverge from the costs of efficiently provided care. Recent rapid growth in the volume and intensity of physicians' services per beneficiary is driving the growth in Medicare physician spending and resulting in the consistently negative annual updates.

Regulators are finding it difficult to set an appropriate target for overall spending on physician care. Such spending is influenced by patient and provider preferences, the diffusion of technology, and the location of care. In testimony to Congress in July 2005, CMS Administrator Mark McClellan noted:

> Presently, we project a negative 4.3 percent update to physician payment rates for 2006 and additional negative updates *for the following six years* [emphasis added]. The current system eventually corrects the discrepancy and under our latest projections results in positive updates after 2012. CMS is fully cognizant of the potential implications of seven years of negative physician updates,

remains concerned, and is closely monitoring physicians' participation in the Medicare program and beneficiaries access.[2]

Antitrust

We have addressed the issues of regulating monopolistic firms, as well as trying to make them act like competitors. A third form of regulation attempts to keep monopolies from forming. This is typically referred to as antitrust policy. A discussion of federal antitrust law in the United States appropriately begins with the Sherman Act. This act was passed in 1890 and followed widespread perceptions of abuse of consumers in several industries as a result of trust arrangements. In a trust, a central board votes all the stock of the members of the trust. The best known, Standard Oil Trust, was able to monopolize the markets for crude and refined oil, achieving a 90 percent share by combining more than 100 firms into the trust.

The Sherman Act has two main sections. Section 1 specifies that "every contract, combination in the form of a trust or otherwise, or conspiracy, in restraint of trade . . . is declared to be illegal." The main target of Section 1 is price fixing and market division. Under Section 2, "every person who shall monopolize, or attempt to monopolize, . . . shall be deemed guilty of a felony."

Because enforcement of the Sherman Act was a problem, and specific antitrust practices were not stated, two additional actions by Congress strengthened the antitrust laws. The Clayton Act, first passed in 1914, addressed practices such as price discrimination (when the price discrimination restrains trade), interlocking directorates, mergers, and joint ventures. The Federal Trade Commission Act, also passed in 1914, created an independent agency to help enforce the laws. The act also addressed "unfair" methods of competition and "unfair" practices, such as false advertising. The Robinson-Patman Act of 1936 modified the price discrimination provision of the Clayton Act. The 1950 Celler-Kefauver Antimerger Amendment focused on vertical mergers (for example, when a firm merges with its input suppliers).

Enforcement

The federal antitrust laws are enforced by two agencies. The Antitrust Division of the Department of Justice (DOJ) was formed in 1903. The DOJ alone has the power to seek criminal charges. Shortly after its creation, it launched a major wave of "trust-busting," culminating with the breakup of the Standard Oil and American Tobacco companies following court decisions in 1911.

The second agency, the Federal Trade Commission (FTC), is an independent agency with exclusive jurisdiction over the FTC Act. Because the two agencies are small, they are selective about the cases they pursue, seeking to deter anticompetitive behavior and to clarify the application of antitrust laws with precedent-setting reviews.

Exemptions

It is well-known that professional baseball and labor unions have received special exemptions from federal antitrust laws. Many other industries are at least partially exempt. These include agriculture, fishing, the many regulated industries, and national defense contractors. In addition, there are some important limits relevant to the health industries.

[2]www.cms.hhs.gov/media/press/testimony.asp?Counter=1509, accessed August 27, 2005.

First, federal antitrust applies only to entities involved in interstate or foreign commerce; so many firms are excluded. It would seem that many health care providers, such as hospitals and physicians, are immune from federal antitrust because their activities affect mainly local, within-state markets. However, the courts have ruled that it is sufficient to show that the seller is receiving substantial reimbursement from Medicare (or other out-of-state payers) or purchasing supplies from out-of-state vendors. As a result of this interpretation, there is a broad applicability of federal antitrust laws to health care markets (the relevant case is *Summit Health, Ltd. v. Pinhas*, 59 U.S.L.W.4493).

Nevertheless, two important exemptions, though not unique to health care, are particularly important in health care antitrust. The McCarran-Ferguson Act of 1945 exempts the insurance industry to the extent that the industry is regulated by state law. With the monopsony power enjoyed by Blue Cross and Blue Shield in many states, a broad interpretation of this exemption would give the Blues and other insurers a free hand in exercising that power. The courts, however, have narrowed this exemption by carefully defining insurance activities and eliminating antitrust protection for the many noninsurance activities that may be undertaken by insurance companies.

The second exemption is referred to as the Noerr-Pennington doctrine. Through two decisions handed down by the Supreme Court, private parties and professional organizations have broad immunity from antitrust for lobbying activities, even where those lobbying activities lead to anticompetitive legislation. For example, lobbying efforts designed to tighten licensure requirements or limit the scope of practice allowed for other groups of providers could be protected under Noerr-Pennington even though the legislation reduces competition. This doctrine is especially important in health care as a result of the intense political lobbying by professional and trade associations. It is also worthwhile to note that the Noerr-Pennington doctrine is based on First Amendment constitutional law, which provides for guarantees to freedom of speech. The link to constitutional grounds gives the doctrine even more force than is usually the case regarding antitrust law. First Amendment protection also has been extended to professional advertising so that advertising freedoms have a force beyond antitrust and competitive grounds.

Because the basic premise of antitrust policy points toward competition with its result of pricing at marginal cost, it is useful to address a potential criticism that relates to health insurance. Figure 20-2 revisits the issue of insurance-induced moral hazard. The optimal quantity of health care is purchased where demand D equals marginal cost MC or quantity Q^*. If coinsurance rate r lowers the price facing the consumers from P_2 to rP_2, then the demand curve rotates clockwise to D_1 and quantity demanded increases to Q_2, leading to a welfare loss equal to the sum of areas $(A + B)$. It would appear that if providers have monopoly power, and charge a higher price, say P_1, consumers would demand less care, here Q_1, thus reducing the welfare loss from area $(A + B)$ to area A. It would follow that forcing providers to charge the lower price P_2, corresponding to the marginal cost of providing care, would actually increase the welfare loss of excess consumption to area $(A + B)$.

Gaynor, Haas-Wilson, and Vogt (2002) expose a potential flaw in this "conventional" analysis, which assumes that the coinsurance rate is constant at all prices of care. They show that a competitive insurance industry will adjust the coinsurance rate depending on the price of the medical services, rather than leave it fixed. Lower medical service prices will lead to lower coinsurance rates with both leading to increased purchases. Curve D_{true} represents the quantity that would be demanded if insurance companies were to adjust coinsurance rates at all prices. D_{true} is bowed inward because decreases in price from P_1 allows the consumer increasingly larger amounts of services at lower out-of-pocket prices and coinsurance rates.

FIGURE 20-2 Welfare Optimum in the Presence of Insurance and Regulation

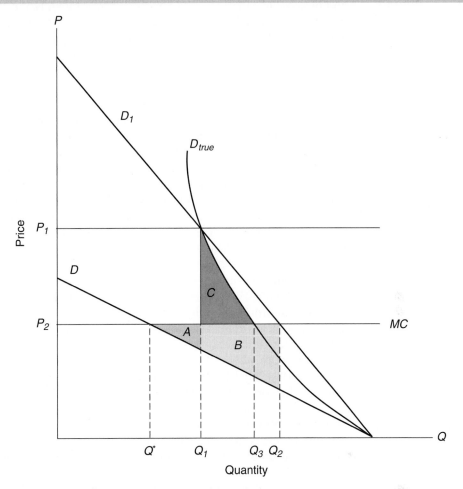

With this coinsurance rate flexibility, demand schedule D_1 is not relevant for evaluating welfare, and areas A and B are not relevant to calculating welfare losses. Using D_{true}, decreasing price from P_1 to marginal cost MC will result in welfare gain C. If insurers set the premiums competitively, reducing the price of medical services toward marginal cost improves consumers' well-being!

Measuring Monopoly Power

Perhaps the most natural measure of monopoly power, yet the most difficult to implement, is a direct comparison of the price to the marginal cost. The eminent economist Abba Lerner (1943) proposed the following measure, d, of monopoly power.

$$d = \frac{P - MC}{P} = 1 - \frac{MC}{P}$$

where P = market price and MC = marginal cost. Clearly, in the theoretical limit under perfect competition, $d = 0$ because price equals marginal cost. Because MC is in theory less than price when monopoly exists, then d will increase and will approach 1 if MC is low relative to price.

Lerner's measure is elegant, and it captures the essence of monopolistic behavior and its economic inefficiencies very well. Unfortunately, it is difficult if not impossible in many cases to measure marginal cost, especially for the modern multiproduct firm with its complicated production processes. Consequently, economists also have developed other measures that may indicate market power.

Measures of Concentration

Chapter 17 introduced measures of concentration for the pharmaceutical industry. The concentration ratio describes the percentage of total industry sales accounted for by the largest firms in an industry. The logic behind this approach is the premise that the greater the market share held by a few firms, the more likely it is that firms are colluding. The concentration ratio itself does not indicate inefficiency (as does a gap between price and marginal cost), but high concentration ratios offer a greater possibility that firms collude to engage in anticompetitive behavior. The maximum value for a concentration ratio is 100 in the case of a monopoly, and often the four-firm concentration ratio (i.e., share accounted for by the four largest firms) is used. A four-firm concentration ratio of 80 percent indicates more monopoly power than a four-firm concentration ratio of 20 percent.

A second measure of market monopolization, the Herfindahl-Hirschman Index (HHI), calculates the sum of the squares of the market shares, expressed as a percent, held by each firm in an industry. The maximum value is 10,000 (i.e., 100^2), and the minimum approaches zero. As noted in Chapter 17, the HHI is considered superior to the concentration ratio because it captures the size distribution of firms in that larger firms are given more weight. Under the *Merger Guidelines* issued by the Department of Justice in 1984, a market with an HHI value above 1,800 is considered "highly concentrated," while one below 1,000 is considered "unconcentrated."

Many economists argue that the concentration ratio and HHI concepts say little about competitive behavior. Some industries with few firms may compete vigorously, whereas others with many firms may not. It is also critical to define the relevant geographic and product markets carefully. One may see many hospitals in a given state, implying a low concentration ratio. However, if they are separated geographically, they may have monopoly power in the relevant geographic area or in the market for a particular service if it is impractical to receive that care elsewhere. We will see later in this chapter how the definition of the relevant market is crucial in the practice of antitrust policy.

Antitrust Procedures

Gaynor and Vogt (1999) show that in deciding whether anticompetitive behavior should be addressed under the Clayton or Sherman Acts, the courts and the enforcement agencies go through a fairly routine sequence of steps. Using hospital mergers as an example, the steps (Miles, 1998) are:

1. Defining the relevant product market
2. Defining the relevant geographic market
3. Identifying the competitors in the relevant product/geographic market
4. Calculating the market shares of the competitors and HHI
5. Calculating the merging firms' post-merger share and the post-merger HHI, and determining the likely competitive effect of the merger
6. Considering any factors that mitigate or exacerbate anticompetitive effects

In defining the relevant market, analysts must find the smallest group of products for which no close substitutes exist. A product is to be included in the relevant market

if buyers easily could find a substitute for it in response to a price increase of the merging firms. In addition, a supplier is to be included in the relevant market if it does produce the same product or does not produce the relevant product currently but could easily come to produce it. DOJ's 1984 *Merger Guidelines* say that the relevant market, both product and geographic, is the smallest market in which the sellers, acting as a cartel, could implement profitably a "small but significant and nontransitory price increase." They later go on to say that, most often, this means a 5 percent increase for a period of at least one year. Box 20-3 provides a DOJ review of a proposed hospital merger.

Defining the relative geographic market has become critical. If a market is defined too narrowly, the true impact of a merger on market concentration will be overestimated. Conversely, a market that is defined too broadly will lead to an underestimate of the impact on the concentration of a merger.

The relevant geographic area for antitrust purposes, then, is the smallest area in which buyers could not switch easily to providers elsewhere in order to escape

BOX 20-3

How the Department of Justice Works: A Marin County Consolidation

The DOJ reviews proposed hospital mergers and publishes findings on a Web site. This 1997 example provides the economic reasoning used to evaluate mergers for potential antitrust violations.

Marin County, California, is across the Golden Gate Bridge directly north of San Francisco. Two hospitals, Marin General and Ross, proposed to consolidate their inpatient mental health services. While the two hospitals compete in providing inpatient and other psychiatric care to adults, Marin General does not provide the chemical dependency programs and the inpatient psychiatric services for children and adolescents that Ross provides. The hospitals stated that they would continue to compete in the sale of the consolidated services and would not jointly determine prices for the consolidated services, other than for Medicaid and indigent patients covered under the county's program Joint pricing for Medicaid and county program patients will not eliminate competition, however, since the hospitals do not compete for that business.

The DOJ approved the consolidation. Note the explicit economic analyses and considerations. The approval has been quoted verbatim, with the particular features numbered to clarify the specific issues.

APPROVED:

1. The proposed consolidation will not result in *per se* illegal conduct, and under a rule-of-reason analysis the Department is not prepared to say that the consolidation is likely to have a net anticompetitive effect. While these are the only hospitals in Marin County providing inpatient psychiatric care, the venture explicitly preserves the potential for price competition between the hospitals and includes protections against the unnecessary sharing of confidential business information.

2. The venture may lower the cost of adult mental health services by eliminating duplicative costs and spreading fixed costs over a larger population. The consolidation may thus permit the hospitals to offer competitive rates for the care of Medicaid patients and indigent patients covered by a Marin County program.

3. On the other hand, the venture has significant potential for eliminating competition in quality of care or other nonprice areas, and joint pricing for Medicaid patients could facilitate collusion on the pricing for other patients.

4. On balance, and on the facts presented, the Department does not have a present intention to challenge the venture, but that view could change depending on how the venture actually operates.

SOURCE: www.usdoj.gov/atr/public/health_care/9950.htm, accessed August 2, 2005.

attempts to exercise monopoly power. In effect, this definition revolves around the ability of producers to raise prices above competitive levels. This ability may be best measured with the demand price elasticity of facing the producers. Relatively low price elasticities increase the ability of producers to raise prices. Reliable measures, or even indirect evidence, of elasticity are often not available so the courts will look at a variety of approaches.

The Elzinga-Hogarty (EH) Criterion

One common standard for determining market areas involves measurements of product flows into and out of an area—an approach consistent with the economic concept of a market. Here, the work of Elzinga and Hogarty (1978) has been influential. The authors define a geographic market as one in which the outflow of goods to other areas is relatively small and the inflow (imports) from elsewhere is also relatively small.

The logic is simple. If producers exported significant amounts elsewhere, they could not raise prices without jeopardizing their external markets. Thus, those external markets must be included. Similarly, if imports are substantial, price increases would result in users substituting more imports. Therefore, the geographic markets supplying the imports must be included. Criteria of 75 percent and 90 percent were suggested; that is, both imports and exports must be less than 25 percent (10 percent) of the product flows. To satisfy the 90 percent criterion, hospitals must provide at least 90 percent of their services to patients residing in the market, and patients residing in the market must receive no more than 10 percent of their care from hospitals located in other market areas.

Despite advances made by economists in defining markets, court decisions in merger cases have been contradictory. Some cases have accepted the EH method, while others have relied on various methods including ad hoc approaches, such as defining markets by the 15-mile radius around a hospital. Thus, the law remains unsettled on this important issue.

Much of the analysis has involved hospital mergers. Consider a proposed merger of two neighboring hospitals. Antitrust analysts look at two fundamental concerns:

1. Hospital services technology involves large fixed costs (we see very few 10-bed hospitals), which must be spread out over a large demand.
2. Without a merger, one or both might go bankrupt, leaving a monopoly anyhow.

To demonstrate the economics behind the rules and practices, consider Figure 20-3. Curve AC reflects average costs, and the representative hospital's service demand is D_h. If each representative hospital equates marginal revenues and marginal costs at point A, it loses money, because P_h (determined by the demand curve) is less than average cost AC_h. The loss for each hospital is indicated by the (darker shaded) box with height $(AC_h - P_h)$.

If the hospitals are allowed to merge, the demand curve facing the single new entity shifts to the right because there are more people to serve. It also becomes less elastic because the number of competitors is reduced. As drawn, the merged hospital equates marginal revenues and marginal costs at point B and earns a profit indicated by the box with height $(P_m - AC_m)$. Note, however, that this is achieved with a higher price, because P_m exceeds P_h, and Q_m of services provided by the newly monopolized hospital is far less than the amount $(2Q_h)$ that was provided by the two hospitals. Antitrust policy makers must address issues such as these.

FIGURE 20-3 Potential Impacts of Hospital Mergers

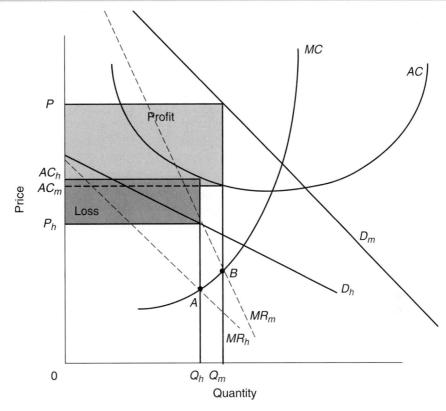

Conclusions

This chapter discusses and analyzes specific regulatory mechanisms that have been introduced into the health care economy. Early regulatory mechanisms, including rate regulation, utilization review, and Certificate-of-Need programs, sought to control markets that seemed otherwise impervious to competitive forces. Rate regulation was somewhat effective in reducing expenses per admission, per day, and per capita; CON regulation (addressing capital expenses) was largely ineffective; and utilization review was somewhat effective in reducing admissions, inpatient days, and expenditures. With the growth of managed care throughout the economy in the 1990s, utilization review has come to characterize almost all health delivery systems, whether they are formally regulated or not.

The imposition of PPS in the 1980s can be interpreted as a form of regulation that promotes competition. We see how payment by DRG promotes a form of yardstick competition among monopolistic firms. Medicare's PPS has reduced length of stay in hospitals subject to the regulation but has not led to reduced quality of care or access to care. With the particular limitations on inpatient care, many large U.S. hospitals have come to face major financial challenges, and analysts will be monitoring governmental responses to the considerable political pressure to adjust reimbursement rates.

With the challenges facing hospitals, interest in antitrust approaches toward regulation was renewed. Regulators continue to face the trade-off between the potentially increased efficiency of larger-scale firms, at the potential cost of decreased competition and higher prices for the delivered services.

SUMMARY

1. Economists feel that regulation often is needed when competitive market pressures are not present. One can categorize the policies as those that:
 - Recognize the monopoly power and try to control it.
 - Try to make monopolistic firms act like competitors.
 - Attempt to prevent the accumulation of monopoly power.
2. Regulation refers to the use of nonmarket means to affect the quality, price, or quantity of a good or service. Principal categories of regulation include fee controls and rate regulation, quantity and capacity controls, and quality controls.
3. Empirical findings on utilization review have tended to be inconclusive, although Wickizer, Wheeler, and Feldstein find that utilization review reduces admissions, inpatient days, and expenditures.
4. Studies of rate regulation suggest that this regulatory device is effective in reducing expenses per admission, per day, and per capita.
5. Studies of CON tended to find it ineffective. Mayo and McFarland, in contrast, find that CON significantly lowered the number of beds and consequently costs in a single state.
6. The Medicare Prospective Payment System (PPS) based on DRGs predetermines a flat fee per case. Hospitals that exceed this rate suffer losses, while hospitals with case costs below the rate receive profits.
7. Medicare's PPS approximates yardstick competition. By setting the payment rates according to industry average marginal costs, yardstick competition induces the firms to choose the socially efficient level of cost-containment expenditure.
8. Medicare's PPS has reduced length of stay in hospitals subject to the regulation. It is doubtful that the regulation has led to reduced quality of care or access to care. Case-mix severity has increased post-PPS. Finally, while it is likely that the system has helped control Medicare's budget, it is unclear whether a reduction has occurred in per capita costs.
9. Relative value scales (RVSs) originally were developed by state medical societies and other organizations as guides in establishing physician fees and reimbursement rates. The weights under the resource-based RVS (RBRVS) introduced under Medicare's physician payment reforms are determined by the inputs needed to provide procedures, including physician work, practice expenses, and professional liability insurance.
10. Antitrust refers to the use of government policy or legislation aimed at deterring collusive arrangements and certain other practices that restrict competition.
11. If insurers set the premiums competitively, moving the price of medical services toward the marginal cost improves consumers' well-being.
12. The Lerner index is a measure of a firm's monopoly power. Concentration ratios and the HHI often are used to measure market monopolization.

DISCUSSION QUESTIONS

1. Describe the major regulatory strategies that have been adopted in the United States.
2. How does prospective payment change the incentive to hospitals as compared to retrospective reimbursement? What predictions would one make as a result of the adoption of reimbursement based on DRGs?
3. Some argue that controls on some payers lead to a shift in cost to other payers (and that a one-payer system is needed). What evidence would suggest cost shifting to other third-party payers? What evidence suggests that not all the costs are shifted?
4. What is regression to the mean? How might this affect our evaluation of the efficacy of rate regulation?
5. CON legislation is designed to control costs by limiting capital expenditures. However, CON also may influence competition in the hospital market. Discuss at least two ways in which this might occur.

6. Under Shleifer's theory of yardstick competition, why does the firm have an incentive to reduce its costs? If all firms respond by reducing their costs, will the payment rate also subsequently fall?
7. What is the Medicare PPS program under DRGs? How has the Medicare PPS payment under DRGs affected hospital practices? Length of stay? Quality of care? Financial condition?
8. Does the Medicare PPS payment under DRGs reduce costs? Discuss.
9. Market power means that providers face downward-sloping demand curves. Give three examples of health services providers who have considerable market power. Give three examples of health services providers who have little or no market power.
10. Why is the determination of relevant markets so important to antitrust cases? Why will plaintiffs want narrow definitions and defendants want broad definitions?
11. Consider the location where you live or go to school. Have there been hospital mergers or closings in the last several years? How would you explain them in the context of material presented in this chapter?

EXERCISES

1. In Figure 19-1, suppose the demand for the good was summarized by the equation:

$$P = 100 - 0.5Q$$

$$MR = 100 - Q$$

and that the marginal cost equals the average costs at $10 per unit.
 a. Calculate the optimum market quantity in a competitive market. (Hint: Set price equal to marginal cost.)
 b. Calculate the quantity brought to market by the monopolist.
 c. Calculate the monopolist's profit.
 d. Calculate the deadweight loss to society from the monopoly.
2. Suppose that a hospital has a production function of the type:

$$\log Q = a \log S + b \log B$$

where Q is quantity of output, S is level of services, and B is number of beds, with a and b as parameters. The hospital buys S at price p_s and B at price p_b.
 a. If regulators force the hospital to decrease the amount of B by 10 percent, what must the hospital do to maintain quantity Q?
 b. If the hospital maintains quantity Q, what will be the effect of the regulation on total hospital expenditures? Why?
3. Suppose that Hospitals A through E have the following marginal costs for a given procedure:
 Hospital A — $2,000
 Hospital B — $2,200
 Hospital C — $1,800
 Hospital D — $2,700
 Hospital E — $2,300
 Calculate the yardstick price that would be assigned to each hospital. Which two hospitals will be assigned yardstick prices that do not cover their current marginal costs?
4. Examine the analysis in Figure 20-1. Suppose that the hospital's initial equilibrium price, P_0, is $10,000, the initial equilibrium quantity is 1,000 procedures, and the initial marginal cost per procedure is $5,000.
 a. What is the initial profit level for the hospital?
 b. If it costs $500,000 in fixed costs to bring in a consultant who will reduce marginal costs to $4,500, what does the new average cost curve look like?

c. Suppose that the hospital is given a yardstick price of $4,600, and it raises its production to 2,000 procedures. Calculate the following:

 i. Lump sum break-even transfer

 ii. Hospital's profit or loss

 iii. Increase in consumer surplus brought about by the imposition of yardstick pricing

5. Suppose that the town of Greenville has three hospitals. Hospital A has a 30 percent market share, Hospital B has a 35 percent market share, and Hospital C has a 35 percent market share. Hospital A and Hospital B have proposed to merge. The government argues that the merger would constitute monopoly power, but the two hospitals disagree.

 a. Provide a clear argument in favor of the hospitals' position.

 b. Provide a clear argument in favor of the antitrust position.

6. Consider an industry with six firms with the following market shares.

 Firm A — 38 percent

 Firm B — 28 percent

 Firm C — 13 percent

 Firm D — 11 percent

 Firm E — 6 percent

 Firm F — 4 percent

 a. Compute the four-firm concentration ratio. What is the value of the HHI?

 b. Suppose Firm D proposes to merge with Firm E. Calculate the new four-firm ratio and the new HHI.

7. Consider the equation for costs per hospital discharge:

$$\text{cost/discharge} = (\text{days/discharge}) \times (\text{service intensity/day}) \times (\text{cost/service unit})$$

 a. Suppose that cost/service unit increased by 10 percent and days/discharge stayed constant. If we know that cost/discharge increased by 15 percent, then what happened to the service intensity? Why?

 b. In part a, what can we say about quality of care?

 c. Can we be sure that if we reduced the number of days per discharge that costs would fall? Why or why not?

21

Social Insurance

Throughout this book, we have emphasized the role that markets can play in providing health care. We have also generally used economic efficiency, provided in theory by perfectly competitive markets, as a standard against which to judge the costs and benefits of policies. In this chapter, we address instead the issues that arise when a society considers providing for health care by offering health insurance, to some significant degree, at the public's expense. Such insurance programs provided through taxes or regulations are called *social insurance programs*. Having provided an overview of the rationales for social insurance in health care, we now turn to an examination of social insurance. We begin by considering the history of health care social insurance throughout the world, with some emphasis on the United States. We then examine Medicaid and Medicare and their effects, and close by examining prospects and issues for the future.

Social Insurance Policies and Social Programs

Social insurance programs can be broken down into five categories. While not mutually exclusive, programs of the following five types exist in the United States and in other countries.

1. **Poverty:** Poor people lack purchasing power to buy the amounts of goods that are considered necessary to provide the minimal standards of decent life. Programs directed toward persons experiencing poverty involve either cash or more often goods "in kind," such as rent vouchers or food stamps.
2. **Old Age:** The elderly have attained a certain age, generally coinciding with retirement from active employment. Programs include income maintenance, such

as Social Security, as well as services and considerations (such as old-age housing or Meals-on-Wheels) that may address the generally decreased mobility of the elderly.

3. **Disability:** The disabled have either temporary or permanent inability to work because of illness or work-related injuries. Programs generally provide cash benefits. Disability programs were among the earliest social insurance programs available.

4. **Health:** Programs cover illness or well-care financing and/or provide facilities for various groups. In the United States, most programs are addressed to the elderly and/or poor, with the government financing the individual's health care either entirely or in part. In other countries, governments have more direct involvement in the financing and delivery of health services for larger segments (or all) of the population.

5. **Unemployment:** The unemployed receive assistance due to a temporary loss of work. While unemployment-related programs generally provide short-term cash benefits, in many countries, longer-term unemployment may lead into poverty-related welfare programs.

Several other definitions are useful in considering social insurance programs. Some programs, termed *entitlements*, are available to all who qualify. Food stamps, for example, are available to all households whose incomes fall below specified levels, related in part to income, family size, and geographic location. Medicaid, or financed health care for the poor (to be discussed in considerable detail later in this chapter), is also an entitlement program for some. Housing programs in the United States, in contrast, are not entitlements. Only limited numbers of subsidized units (on the supply side) or vouchers (on the demand side) are available.

Many programs are *means-tested*; that is, they are available only to individuals or households who meet certain income criteria. Households who receive aid for poverty-related problems may lose some or all of the aid if their incomes pass certain levels. This reduction in aid may have the unintended effect of discouraging efforts by low-income households to find jobs. This effect may occur because if poverty-related aid is reduced by $1 for each $1 earned on the job, the job earnings are potentially taxed at rates approaching 100 percent.

Finally, aid may take various forms. Often, it is tied to the purchase of certain items, such as food or housing. This procedure ensures that the people use the aid to buy items that the legislators have deemed important. Under certain circumstances, it may be more efficient to provide a cash subsidy rather than one in kind. Economists have long felt that it is cheaper, and therefore more efficient, to provide cash instead. Generally, such cash programs would make the recipients better off in their own eyes: Which would you prefer, $100 in cash or $100 worth of physician care? Most people would answer "$100 in cash!" Legislators and the voting public, however, often seem to prefer that the subsidies be made in kind rather than in cash to control the purchases of those receiving the subsidies.

Program Features

We discuss certain common features to characterize health-related social insurance programs in the United States and elsewhere:

1. Contributions—taxes, deductibles, and coinsurance
2. Benefits—how much, who is included, and what types of treatment are included
3. Length of coverage

4. Means of reimbursement to providers
5. Methods of determining payment levels to providers

The first three items describe the receipt of care. The last two describe the provision of care, as well as the political problems involved in initiating plans.

Although supported by government, most social insurance plans are not without cost to the recipients. Many are funded by tax collections, and recipients of care often are also taxpayers. In some cases, the taxes in question may be regressive. A regressive tax is one for which lower income people pay higher portions of their incomes to the tax than do richer people. In contrast, a progressive tax is one in which lower-income people pay lower portions of their incomes to the tax than do richer people.

In the United States tax payments into the Social Security program have been somewhat regressive. Since its beginning in 1935, the tax has been a constant percentage of wage income, up to a ceiling at which the marginal tax rate becomes zero. This means that on average, people in higher-income groups pay a smaller proportion of their income in payroll taxes; thus, the tax is regressive. For 2005, the wage base for Social Security was 6.20 percent on a base salary of $90,000. Since workers with wages of $100,000 pay the same amount, 6.20 percent of $90,000, or $5,580, the tax percentage for the more affluent is 5.58 percent, rather than 6.20 percent below the $90,000 cap. The effective tax rate obviously falls as wage income rises. In contrast, the Medicare tax rate is now 1.45 percent of *all* wage income, a constant percentage.

To determine whether a social insurance program is redistributive in net—whether it in net causes a transfer of money from the rich to the poor—one must consider not just the tax payments made but also the benefits received. For example, data for the Social Security program in the United States tend to show that Social Security is redistributive—that the poorer people in a given age group tend to gain more in net than do the rich.

In addition to tax payments, eligible recipients often must pay deductibles or coinsurance. Time costs with respect to paperwork, or waiting time for appointments or treatment, also must be considered.

Levels of benefits and length of coverage are fairly similar to the workings of private insurance. Given the equity considerations of social insurance, political considerations may affect both. Determining who and which treatments are covered is also important. Coverage of individuals may involve children and spouses. Coverage of treatments may mandate coverage of certain diseases (i.e., end-stage kidney disease) and exclude others (i.e., optometric or chiropractic services).

Health-related social insurance also has supply-related characteristics. Some expenses may be paid directly by the patient and may be reimbursed; others may be paid directly by the government to the provider. In some countries, all physicians who participate in the national health care program are government employees.

Historical Roots of Social Insurance

European Beginnings

The United States is often characterized as the only industrialized country lacking a comprehensive health-related social insurance system. Experts date the pioneering legislation for a system of compulsory national health insurance to Germany in 1883. National health insurance spread to other European countries at the end of the nineteenth and the early part of the twentieth centuries.

The German system and the other European systems were extensions of already-existing voluntary associations, which were often guild or mutual aid groups whose

benefits to members included the pooling of insurable risks. The political impetus for converting or merging voluntary local groups in a system of national coverage was often its usefulness as a stabilizing influence:

> Political discontent precipitated the introduction of social insurance in both Germany and England. . . . In Germany, Bismarck introduced social rights to avoid granting wider political rights; in Britain, Lloyd George sought social rights within the context of existing rights to political participation. But both were basically defensive efforts to stabilize the political order. . . . (Starr, 1982, p. 239)

The German laws of 1883 set up a highly decentralized program that covered workers in mining, transportation, construction, manufacturing, mechanical trades, and establishments using power machinery. Other countries followed. Austria (1888), Hungary (1891), Sweden (1891), Denmark (1892), and Belgium (1894) were early adopters of health insurance. With Spain's adoption of a plan in 1929, nearly every European country had enacted health insurance laws. Some were compulsory, as in Germany, but other countries, such as Belgium, Denmark, Sweden, and Switzerland, provided government subsidies to voluntary mutual insurance funds.

The United Kingdom established its first social health insurance system in 1911. The 1911 legislation creating social insurance in Britain is of special interest because it helped to prepare for the British National Health Service that was adopted in 1946. Governmental provision of health care through a national health service system is most prominently exemplified in the Western countries by the United Kingdom. Government provision was common in Eastern European countries and the former Soviet Union, which began its system in 1926.

Early Experience in the United States

Compared with the European countries, the United States came late to social insurance, and to governmental health insurance in particular. In the late nineteenth century and early twentieth century, the American experience was similar to that of Europe in that voluntary group purchasing arrangements, mutual benefit associations, and the like were common. However, in the United States, the funding of these voluntary societies was not taken up by government and from the advent of the German system in 1883 to the beginnings of the British system in 1911, governmental compulsory insurance for health care was not really an issue in the United States.

In the early years of the twentieth century, health insurance plans began to gain supporters. The American Association for Labor Legislation supported such a plan, and the American Medical Association initially responded positively to health insurance proposals. Political consensus was lacking, however; for example, Samuel Gompers, president of the American Federation of Labor, opposed compulsory health insurance.

The major advance of social insurance legislation in the United States occurred with the establishment of the Social Security program in 1935. Despite the social insurance thrust of the program and the reform-minded support for it, the legislation made concessions to political opposition to the New Deal, including the omission of governmental health insurance. The omission of health insurance from the Social Security Act was by no means the Act's only conservative feature. It relied on a regressive tax and gave no coverage to some of the very poor, such as farm laborers and domestics.

Proponents of compulsory health insurance plans were no more successful through the 1940s and 1950s. President Truman proposed "a single health insurance

system that would include all classes of the society, even those . . . not covered by Social Security" (Starr, p. 282). During the public debate over these issues, compulsory health insurance often was called socialized medicine, a term that greatly weakened its support during the political climate of the early years of the Cold War. Though Truman won the election in 1948, his success was never translated into a health insurance program.

The Establishment of Medicare and Medicaid

The social insurance debate in the United States often ranged between those who believed in voluntarism and voluntary insurance, as won in negotiations between self-reliant industries and unions, and those who believed that only a compulsory insurance program would provide the insurance that was necessary for the larger population. The major social insurance programs for health care in the United States, Medicare and Medicaid, passed in 1965. President Lyndon Johnson had supported health care for the aged, and by winning a landslide victory in the 1964 election, he was able to push for these programs. The political climate also had shifted somewhat in favor of such programs. Even so, the 1965 passage of the Medicare bill, in a form apparently more extensive than the President had even initially asked for, is a story of individuals interacting in a complex way.

The resolution of the debate in the form of Medicare and Medicaid has achieved widespread political support since the 1960s. However, the fundamental concerns about Medicare and Medicaid stem from their rising costs. By the mid-1990s, with growing elderly and poor populations as well as continual health care cost inflation, the total costs of the social insurance programs were perceived by many to have grown out of control. Politicians sought to ensure that Medicare would have a sufficient trust fund to meet future needs, while balancing these needs against the increased taxes and payments for services necessary to support them.

The wider issue of social health insurance for the population as a whole has not yet been decided. The experience of 1993 and 1994 with the Clinton health plan, however, was a "massive political upheaval" (Skocpol, 1995). President Clinton was elected in 1992 with a campaign promising health system reform. There had been signs of growing interest among the electorate in health system reform including social health insurance. The Clinton plan was drafted during January through May 1993 by a large task force of government officials, health policy experts, congressional staffers, and others. With many perceiving the task force to be secretive, plan supporters were unable to develop a coalition of interests around clearly defined features of reform, while substantial interests, such as insurers, lobbied and advertised against the plan. During 1994, the plan was reworked to respond to critics. The public, however, came to believe that Clinton's plan would entail considerable government bureaucracy, cost, and inefficiency. By the end of the summer of 1994, the plan had failed. Box 21-1 discusses the failures and successes of the Clinton health care policy in more detail.

Medicare and Medicaid in the United States

As mentioned previously, Medicare and Medicaid were enacted in 1965. Medicare is a national program that primarily provides compulsory hospital insurance to the elderly plus optional medical coverage to which nearly all elderly subscribe. In contrast, Medicaid is a program operated by the states with matching federal dollars. It primarily provides health care coverage to people who are considered poor.

BOX 21-1

Health Policy in the Clinton Era: Once Bitten, Twice Shy

Americans will recall the Clinton Administration's spectacular 1993 and 1994 failure to pass the Health Security Act, a comprehensive health plan. Economists David Cutler and Jonathan Gruber (both of whom took part in the Administration) offer viewpoints as to what went wrong . . . and what went right.

What went wrong? Cutler and Gruber identify both political and economic factors. Political processes, both within the "Hillary Commission" (led by the President's wife), which formulated the plan, and in interactions with Congress, led to fierce opposition both from health care trade groups and from the Republican Party.

The authors note that the proposed plan, as any universal coverage effort, involved significant redistribution by income, by geography, by family type, and between firms providing and firms not providing insurance. Income redistribution was probably the most important. The primary beneficiaries were to be lower-income groups that did not have access to either Medicaid or to employer-sponsored insurance.

With the exception of an increase in the cigarette excise tax, money for subsidies was to come from reduced growth rates of health insurance premiums, but this revenue source was "not convincing." First, most of the public did not believe that these savings (from the premiums) would materialize and expected that a future tax increase would be necessary. Second, they believed that the plan would pay for health care for the poor by rationing others' use of health services. In September 1993, three in five of those earning $20,000 to $30,000 (the middle class, whose support was essential) supported the Clinton plan; by April 1994 only two in five did so. After a lengthy congressional debate, the proposal was pulled in 1994 when it became clear that it would lose.

What went right? After having tried (and failed) to formulate a comprehensive policy, the Administration pursued a "bite-size" policy. The authors view the bite-size policy as being very successful, expanding coverage for children, improving long-term care and care for the disabled, and dramatically changing the public's view of cigarettes. They note that the "record looks small only in comparison to what might have been, not in comparison to past Administrations."

SOURCE: David Cutler and Jonathan Gruber, "Health Policy in the Clinton Era: Once Bitten, Twice Shy," in Peter R. Orszag and Jeffrey A. Frankel (eds.) *American Economic Policy in the 1990s*, MIT Press: Cambridge, MA, 2002.

Medicare[1]

Medicare has traditionally consisted of two parts: Hospital Insurance (HI), also known as Part A, and Supplementary Medical Insurance (SMI), also known as Part B. A third part of Medicare, sometimes known as Part C, the Medicare Advantage program, was established as the Medicare + Choice program by the Balanced Budget Act (BBA) of 1997 (Public Law 105-33) and subsequently renamed and modified by the Medicare Prescription Drug, Improvement, and Modernization Act (MMA) of 2003 (Public Law 108-173). The Medicare Advantage program expands beneficiaries' options for participation in private-sector health care plans.

The MMA also established a fourth part of Medicare: a new prescription drug benefit, also known as Part D. Part D activities are handled within the SMI trust fund, but in an account separate from Part B. The traditional treatment of SMI and Part B as

[1]These summaries of Medicare and Medicaid are necessarily simplified and abridged. For more detail, go to www.cms.hhs.gov/publications/overview-medicare-medicaid/MedicareMedicaidSummaries2005.pdf (accessed November 17, 2005).

FIGURE 21-1 Number of Medicare Beneficiaries, 1966–2004

Note: ESRD is end-stage renal disease.
Source: Centers for Medicare and Medicaid Services data Compendium, 2003 (data through 2000); 2004 and 2005 Annual Reports of the Boards of Trustees of the Federal Hospital Insurance and Federal Supplementary Medical Insurance Trust Funds (data for 2003 and 2004); Juliette Cubanski et al., *Medicare Chartbook*, 3rd ed., The Henry J. Kaiser Family Foundation, Summer 2005 with permission.

synonymous is no longer accurate since SMI now consists of both Parts B and D. There are two separate accounts within the SMI trust fund to ensure that funds from one part are not used to finance the other.

When Medicare began on July 1, 1966, approximately 19 million people enrolled. In 2004, almost 42 million people were enrolled in one or both of Parts A and B of the Medicare program, and about 5 million of them have chosen to participate in a Medicare Advantage plan. Figure 21-1 displays the growth of the Medicare program since its inception.

Medicare Coverage

Part A generally is provided automatically to persons age 65 and over who are entitled to Social Security or Railroad Retirement Board benefits. Similarly, those who have received such benefits based on their disability for at least 24 months also are entitled to Part A benefits. In 2004, Part A provided protection against the costs of hospital and specific other medical care to about 41 million people (35 million aged and 6 million disabled enrollees). Part A benefit payments totaled $167.6 billion in 2004.

Medicare's Part A coverage includes:

- Inpatient hospital care coverage, requiring an initial deductible payment, plus copayments for all hospital days following day 60 within a benefit period
- Skilled nursing facility (SNF) care, which generally is covered by Part A only if it is within 30 days of a hospitalization of three or more days and certified as medically necessary
- Home Health Agency (HHA) care, including care provided by a home health aide
- Hospice, which is provided to those terminally ill persons with a life expectancy of six months or less and who elect to forgo standard Medicare benefits and receive only hospice care

SMI (Part B) benefits are available to almost all resident citizens age 65 and over. Part B coverage is optional and requires payment of a monthly premium. Part B covers

- Physicians' and surgeons' services (in both hospital and nonhospital settings)
- Some covered services furnished by chiropractors, podiatrists, dentists, and optometrists
- Services in an emergency room or outpatient clinic, including same-day surgery, and ambulance services

Part B also covers other services including clinical laboratory tests, X-rays, diagnostic tests, ambulance services, and blood that are not supplied by Part A. Almost all persons entitled to Part A also choose to enroll in Part B. In 2004, the Part B program provided benefits of $135.4 billion to about 39 million people (33 million aged and 6 million disabled).

While all Medicare beneficiaries can receive their benefits through the original fee-for-service program, most beneficiaries enrolled in both Part A and Part B can choose different forms of service delivery by participating in a Medicare Advantage (Part C) plan instead. Organizations that seek to contract as Medicare Advantage plans must meet specific organizational, financial, and other requirements. Following are the primary Medicare Advantage plans:

- Coordinated care plans, which include HMOs, PSOs, PPOs, and other certified coordinated care plans and entities that meet the standards set forth in the law.
- Private, unrestricted fee-for-service plans, which allow beneficiaries to select certain private providers. For those providers who agree to accept the plan's payment terms and conditions, this option does not place the providers at risk, nor does it vary payment rates based on utilization.

These Medicare Advantage plans are required to provide at least the current Medicare benefit package, excluding hospice services. Plans may offer additional covered services and are required to do so (or return excess payments) if plan costs are lower than the Medicare payments received by the plan.

Some health care services are not covered by Medicare. Noncovered services include long-term nursing care, custodial care, and certain other health care needs, such as dentures and dental care, eyeglasses, and hearing aids. These services are not a part of the Medicare program unless they are a part of a private health plan under the Medicare Advantage program.

Beginning in 2006, Part D provides subsidized access to prescription drug insurance coverage on a voluntary basis, upon payment of a premium, to individuals entitled to Part A or enrolled in Part B, with premium and cost-sharing subsidies for low-income enrollees. Part D coverage includes most FDA-approved prescription drugs and biologicals. (The specific drugs currently covered in Parts A and B will remain covered there.) For an additional premium, plans may also offer supplemental coverage exceeding the value of basic coverage. To encourage employer and union plans to continue to offer prescription drug coverage to Medicare retirees, Part D provides for certain subsidies to those plans that meet specific criteria.

Figure 21-2 analyzes features of the Part D coverage. Annual premiums are estimated to start at $450 in 2006, and there will be a $250 deductible. After the deductible, Part D will cover 75 percent of all incremental expenditures up to $2,250. Between $2,250 and $5,100, the insured will pay for his or her drugs on a dollar-for-dollar basis. Above $5,100 per year ($425 per month), Part D will pay 95 percent of all expenses over the $5,100 benchmark.

FIGURE 21-2 Medicare Part D Prescription Drug Benefit

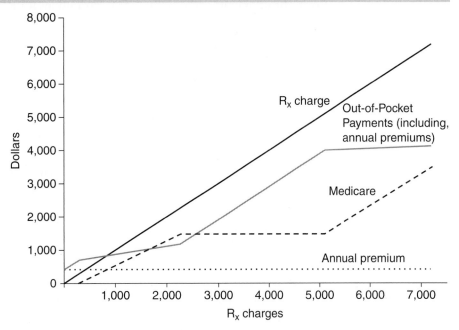

The particular financing plan leaves open conjecture as to who will participate. The break-even point where the participant is no worse off than not participating (that is, premium + out-of-pocket expenditures equal total charges), occurs at a value of $850 per year (about $70 per month). The program appears to be generous for people with small levels of expenditures (up to about $200 per month) or large levels of expenditures (over $425 per month), but participants in the middle will derive no benefit as charges rise between $200 and $425 per month). Program participation will depend on the distribution of drug expenditures and the availability of alternative coverage by those who are eligible.

Program Financing

The Medicare Part A program is financed primarily through a mandatory payroll deduction (FICA tax). The FICA tax is 1.45 percent of earnings (paid by each employee and also by the employer) or 2.90 percent for self-employed persons. This tax is paid on all covered wages and self-employment income without limit.

The SMI trust fund differs fundamentally from the HI trust fund with regard to financing. SMI is now composed of two parts, Part B and Part D, each with its own separate account within the SMI trust fund. The nature of the financing for both parts of SMI is similar, in that both parts are primarily financed by beneficiary premiums and contributions from the general fund of the U.S. Treasury.

Part B is financed through premium payments ($88.50 per beneficiary per month in 2006) and contributions from the general fund of the U.S. Treasury. Beneficiary premiums are generally set at a level that covers 25 percent of the average expenditures for aged beneficiaries. Therefore, the contributions from the general fund of the U.S. Treasury are the largest source of Part B income.

Similarly, Part D will be financed primarily through premium payments and contributions from the Treasury general fund, with general fund contributions accounting for the largest source of Part D income, since beneficiary premiums are to represent,

on average, 25.5 percent of the cost of standard coverage (as described in the next section). The premiums and general fund contributions for Part D will be determined separately from those for Part B.

Beneficiary Payment Liabilities

Parts A and B beneficiaries are responsible for charges not covered by Medicare and for various cost-sharing features of the plans. These liabilities may be paid by the beneficiary, by a third party, such as a private "medigap" insurance policy purchased by the beneficiary, or by Medicaid if the person is eligible. Medigap refers to private health insurance that, within limits, pays most of the health care service charges not covered by Parts A and B of Medicare.

For hospital care covered under Part A, the beneficiary's payment share includes a onetime deductible at the beginning of each benefit period ($952 in 2006). This covers the beneficiary's part of the first 60 days of each spell of inpatient hospital care. If continued inpatient care is needed beyond the 60 days, additional coinsurance payments ($238 per day in 2006) are required through the ninetieth day of a benefit period.

For Part B, the beneficiary's payment share includes the following: one annual deductible ($124 in 2006), the monthly premiums, the coinsurance payments for Part B services (usually 20 percent of the medically allowed charges), a deductible for blood, certain charges above the Medicare-allowed charge (for claims not on assignment), and payment for any services that are not covered by Medicare. For outpatient mental health treatment services, the beneficiary is liable for 50 percent of the approved charges.

Provider Payments

Before 1983, HI payments to providers were made on a "reasonable cost" basis. Since 1983 Medicare payments for most inpatient hospital services have been made under PPS. As discussed in Chapter 20, under PPS a specific predetermined amount is paid for each inpatient hospital stay, based on each stay's DRG classification. In some cases, the payment the hospital receives is less than its actual cost for providing the HI-covered inpatient hospital services for the stay; in other cases it is more. The hospital absorbs the loss or makes a profit. Certain payment adjustments exist for extraordinarily costly inpatient hospital stays, and payments for skilled nursing care and home health care are rehabilitation and psychiatric care are currently reimbursed on a reasonable cost basis, but prospective payment systems are expected in the near future.

Before 1992 for SMI, physicians were paid on the basis of "reasonable charge," initially defined as the lowest of (1) the physician's actual charge, (2) the physician's customary charge, or (3) the prevailing charge for similar services in that locality. Beginning in 1992, allowed charges were defined as the lesser of (1) the submitted charges, or (2) the amount determined by a fee schedule based on a relative value scale (RVS). Most hospital outpatient services are reimbursed on a prospective payment system, and home health care is reimbursed under the same prospective payment system as Part A.

Doctors or suppliers who agree to accept the Medicare-approved rate as payment in full ("take assignment") may not request any added payments, or "balance bill" (beyond the initial annual deductible and coinsurance) from the beneficiary or insurer. If the provider does not take assignment, the beneficiary will be charged for the excess (which may be paid by medigap insurance). Limits now exist on the excess that doctors or suppliers can charge. Physicians are "participating physicians" if they agree before the beginning of the year to accept assignment for all Medicare services they furnish during the year. Since Medicare beneficiaries may select their doctors, they have the option to choose those who participate.

Medicare Summary

The Medicare program covers 95 percent of our nation's aged population, as well as many people who are on Social Security because of disability. In 2004, Part A covered about 41 million enrollees with benefit payments of $167.6 billion, and Part B covered about 39 million enrollees with benefit payments of $135.4 billion. Administrative costs for both Parts A and B were under 2 percent of disbursements in 2003. Total 2004 disbursements for Medicare were $208.9 billion.

Medicaid Overview

Medicaid, referring to Title XIX of the Social Security Act, is a federal-state matching entitlement program that pays for medical assistance for certain vulnerable and needy individuals and families with low incomes and resources. This program is the largest source of funding for medical and health-related services for America's poorest people. In 2003, it provided health care assistance to more than 41 million persons and total expenditures for fiscal year 2003 were $223 billion.

Gruber (2002) notes that Medicaid comprises four public insurance programs in one. The first provides coverage of most medical expenses for low-income women and children families; this function absorbs only about one-quarter of program dollars but encompasses two-thirds of program enrollees. The second provides public insurance for the portions of medical expenditures not covered by Medicare for the low-income elderly, and the third covers most medical expenses for the low-income disabled. The fourth pays the nursing home expenditures of many of the institutionalized elderly. The last three functions apply to only one-third of beneficiaries but use three-quarters of program dollars.

Within broad national guidelines established by federal statutes, regulations, and policies, each state (1) establishes its own eligibility standards; (2) determines the type, amount, duration, and scope of services; (3) sets the rate of payment for services; and (4) administers its own program. Medicaid policies for eligibility, services, and payment vary considerably even among similar-sized and/or adjacent states, and the services provided by one state may differ considerably in amount, duration, or scope from services provided in a neighboring state.

Medicaid Eligibility

Medicaid does not provide medical assistance for all poor persons. Even under the broadest provisions of the federal statute, it does not provide health care services even for very poor persons unless they are in one of the designated groups. Low income is only one test for Medicaid eligibility for those within these groups; their resources also are tested against threshold levels (as determined by each state within federal guidelines).

States generally have broad discretion in determining which groups their Medicaid programs will cover and the financial criteria for Medicaid eligibility. To be eligible for federal funds, however, states must provide Medicaid coverage for certain individuals who receive federally assisted income-maintenance payments, as well as for related groups not receiving cash payments. Although there is a long list, Medicaid "categorically needy" eligibility groups for which federal matching funds are provided to states include:

- Those meeting the requirements for the Aid to Families with Dependent Children (AFDC) program in effect in their state on July 16, 1996, or—at state option—more liberal criteria

- Children under age six or pregnant women whose family income is at or below 133 percent of the federal poverty level (FPL)
- All children born after September 30, 1983, who are under age 19, in families with incomes at or below the FPL

The Scope and Duration of Medicaid Services

The Medicaid program allows considerable flexibility within the states' Medicaid plans (see Box 21-2 for a particular example related to the state of Oregon). Indeed, some analysts compare state programs to determine how differing program features might work. However, a state's Medicaid program must offer medical assistance for certain basic services to most categorically needy populations, including inpatient hospital services, outpatient hospital services, prenatal care, vaccines for children, physician services, nursing facility services for persons age 21 or older, and family planning services and supplies.

Within broad federal guidelines and certain limitations, states determine the amount and duration of services offered under their Medicaid programs. States may limit, for example, the number of days of hospital care or the number of physician vis-

BOX 21-2

Oregon Medicaid's Doctor-Assisted Suicide

Perhaps nowhere is the state-level autonomy in the U.S. Medicaid system more apparent than in the items that the various states choose to cover. In late February 1998, the state of Oregon's Health Services Commission voted 10 to 1 to include doctor-assisted suicide on the list of "treatments" covered for Medicaid patients, reported Peter Steinfels of the *New York Times*. This decision joined doctor-assisted suicide to other forms of "comfort care" for any "terminal illness, regardless of diagnosis."

Residents of Oregon voted twice, in 1994 and again in 1997, to legalize doctor-assisted suicide. However, neither vote dealt with the public financing of the procedure.

Dr. Alan Bates, who headed the commission, acknowledged the divisive nature of the decision. He noted, however, that if dying people with private insurance could pay for medical help in taking their own lives, why should poor people be deprived of the same opportunity?

The federal government bars all federal support, direct or indirect, for assisted suicide. That means that Oregon must segregate carefully the medical services involved in assisting suicide and pay for them with the state's own dollars. Reporter Steinfels noted that in effect, the federal government is saying that taxpayers throughout the country should be spared "moral complicity" in Oregon's innovation.

The issue continued to be controversial. In 2002, U.S. Attorney General John Ashcroft went to court to challenge Oregon's practices. After numerous appeals, the U.S. Supreme Court agreed to hear the case, and in January 2006 ruled, in a 6-3 vote, that a federal drug law could not be used to prosecute Oregon doctors who prescribed overdoses intended to facilitate the deaths of terminally ill patients. Writing for the majority, Justice Anthony Kennedy noted "He [Ashcroft and his successor, Alberto Gonzales] is not authorized to make a rule declaring illegitimate a medical standard for care and treatment of patients that is specifically authorized under state law."

SOURCES: Steinfels, Peter, "Oregon Medicaid's Doctor-Assisted Suicide," *New York Times,* March 7, 1998, National/Metro Section., http://www.foxnews.com/story/0,2933,181881,00.html, accessed April 26, 2006.

its covered. States must provide sufficient levels of services to achieve the purpose of the benefits, and benefit limits may not discriminate among beneficiaries based on medical diagnosis or condition.

Payment for Medicaid Services

Under Medicaid, states may pay health care providers directly on a fee-for-service basis or through various prepayment arrangements, such as HMOs. Each state has broad discretion in determining the payment methodology and payment rate for services. Generally, payment rates must be sufficient to enlist enough providers so that covered services are available at least to the extent that comparable care and services are available to the general population within that geographic area. Providers participating in Medicaid must accept Medicaid payment rates as payment in full. States must make additional payments to qualified hospitals that provide inpatient services to a disproportionate number of Medicaid beneficiaries and/or to other low-income or uninsured persons under what is known as the "disproportionate share hospital" (DSH) adjustment.

States may impose nominal deductibles, coinsurance, or copayments on some Medicaid recipients for certain services, but certain Medicaid recipients, including pregnant women and children under age 18, are excluded from cost sharing. All Medicaid recipients must be exempt from copayments for emergency services and family planning services.

Medicaid is a cost-sharing partnership between the federal government and the states. The federal government pays a share of the medical assistance expenditures under each state's Medicaid program. That share, known as the Federal Medical Assistance Percentage (FMAP), is determined annually by a formula that compares the state's average per-capita income level with the national income average. States with higher per-capita income levels are reimbursed smaller shares of their costs. By law, the FMAP cannot be lower than 50 percent or higher than 83 percent. In 2004, the FMAPs varied from 50 percent (10 states) to 77.1 percent (Mississippi), with the average federal share among all states being 60 percent.

Medicaid Summary

Initially, Medicaid was formulated as a medical care extension of federally funded programs providing cash income assistance for the poor, with an emphasis on dependent children and their mothers, the disabled, and the elderly. Legislation in the late 1980s assured Medicaid coverage to an expanded number of low-income pregnant women, poor children, and some Medicare beneficiaries who are not eligible for any cash assistance program. Legislative changes also focused on increased access, better quality of care, specific benefits, enhanced outreach programs, and fewer limits on services.

Most Medicaid recipients require relatively small average expenditures per person each year. The 2002 data indicate that Medicaid payments for 25.5 million children (constituting 49 percent of all Medicaid recipients) averaged about $1,470 per child. For 13.2 million adults, average payments were $1,865 per person.

Medicaid pays for over 40 percent of the total cost of nursing facility or home health services care; 2002 data show that Medicaid payments for nursing facility and home health care totaled $39.3 billion for more than 1.8 million recipients of these services—an average expenditure of almost $22,245 per nursing home beneficiary. The national data also show that Medicaid payments for home health services totaled $3.9 billion for more than 1.1 million beneficiaries—an average expenditure of $3,685 per

home health care beneficiary. With the elderly or disabled percentage of the population increasing faster than the younger groups, the need for long-term care is expected to increase.

The Medicaid-Medicare Relationship

The Medicare and Medicaid programs work jointly for many beneficiaries. The Centers for Medicare & Medicaid Services estimates that Medicaid currently provides some level of supplemental health coverage for about 6.5 million Medicare beneficiaries. Medicare beneficiaries who have low incomes and limited resources also may receive help from the Medicaid program. For those eligible for full Medicaid coverage, the Medicare health care coverage is supplemented by services that are available under their state's Medicaid program, according to eligibility category. These additional services may include, for example, nursing facility care beyond the 100-day limit covered by Medicare, prescription drugs, eyeglasses, and hearing aids. For persons enrolled in both programs, any services covered by Medicare are paid for by the Medicare program before any payments are made by the Medicaid program because Medicaid is always the "payer of last resort."

The Medicare prescription drug benefit, started in 2006, includes those who also receive coverage from Medicaid. In addition, individuals eligible for both Medicare and Medicaid will also receive the low-income subsidy for both the Medicare drug plan premium and assistance with cost sharing for prescriptions. Medicaid will no longer provide drug benefits for Medicare beneficiaries.

State Children's Health Insurance Program

The State Children's Health Insurance Program (SCHIP) was established in the Balanced Budget Act of 1997. SCHIP was designed as a federal-state partnership, similar to Medicaid, with the goal of expanding health insurance to children whose families earn too much money to be eligible for Medicaid, but not enough money to purchase private insurance. SCHIP is the single largest expansion of health insurance coverage for children since the initiation of Medicaid in the mid-1960s.

SCHIP is designed to provide coverage to "targeted low-income children." A "targeted low-income child" is one who resides in a family with income below 200 percent of the FPL or whose family has an income 50 percent higher than the state's Medicaid eligibility threshold. Some states have expanded SCHIP eligibility beyond the 200 percent FPL limit, and others are covering entire families and not just children.

If a state elects to establish an expanded Medicaid program using SCHIP, the eligibility rules of Medicaid apply, and the services provided under SCHIP mirror the Medicaid services provided by that state. Regardless of the type of health benefits coverage provided by a state, they must provide coverage for well-baby and well-child care, immunizations, and emergency services.

Public Insurance and Health

How does public insurance affect health? In part, this depends on how effective the public insurance programs are in reaching their targeted populations. Janet Currie (2004) argues that countries with universal programs seek to maintain a minimum level of service for all individuals, at a reasonable cost to government. In the United States, the goal is to maintain such a standard for selected groups of vulnerable or "deserving" individuals, such as children, the elderly, and the disabled. One of the problems is that targeting will always be imperfect. Some of those who take up benefits will

not "deserve" them, and some of those who are eligible for benefits will not take them up. If take-up by eligible individuals is low, then the program may fail to reach its main goal of helping the targeted group. If take-up by ineligibles is too high, then government revenues will be diverted from other productive uses.

Researchers have identified two categories of impediments to program take-up. The first is program *stigma*, the premise that some people are embarrassed or afraid to apply for programs, even though they might benefit greatly. Second, individuals face costs of learning about, and applying for programs, and these costs may deter some from using them. Moreover, the costs may be highest for precisely those individuals in greatest need, and in cases where the beneficiaries are young children or infirm adults, the costs may be borne by individuals other than the beneficiaries. The costs that these impediments impose on would-be participants may be sufficiently large to prevent them from enrolling in potentially beneficial programs.

Gruber (2002) traces the potential effects of a Medicaid improvement in Figure 21-3. With the adoption or enhancement of a program, such as Medicaid, depending on the population characteristics, there will be increased eligibility of the poor or the young. Some of them may have been previously uninsured. To the extent that they find the public insurance attractive, they take up coverage. For those who were previously insured by

FIGURE 21-3 **Analyzing the Impacts of Improved Medicaid Coverage**

Source: Adapted from Gruber (2002).

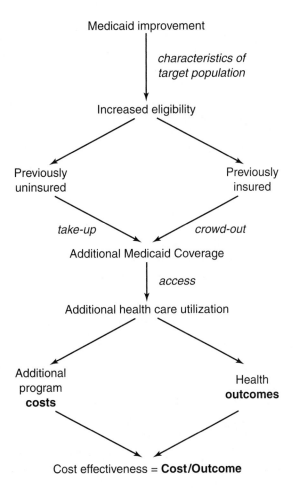

other means, some may choose to substitute the public insurance. In the literature, this impact is referred to as "crowd-out" since the public insurance has replaced the private insurance. Either one of these will have some measurable impact on Medicaid coverage.

The increased coverage would be expected to impact health care utilization. Analysts have found that this impact depends on access to the health care, which may relate to the availability of providers and the distance, cost, or convenience of dealing with the providers. Increased utilization increases costs and presumably improves outcomes, which are typically measured in terms of reduced morbidity (illness) or mortality (death). The incremental cost per unit of outcome is often summarized in terms of costs per illness day prevented, or costs per death prevented—measures of the program's cost efficiency.

Cutler and Gruber (1996) examine the economics of crowd-out. Consider a household that is choosing between health insurance and all other goods, and assume that more generous plans offer a greater range of providers or cover a wider set of services. As noted in Figure 21-4, households valuing insurance highly (for example, those demanding the highest quality providers) will exhibit utility function V_m (more services), and select point D. Those valuing insurance less highly will exhibit utility function V_l (less services), and select point E.

Suppose the government introduces free public insurance with generosity M. It may have a lower value relative to the private policies for a couple of reasons. Because of low Medicaid reimbursement rates, some providers may be reluctant to treat Medicaid patients. Some households may prefer to avoid public programs because of the stigma of being enrolled. Households cannot purchase a supplement to Medicaid; if they want higher insurance, they must return to the original budget constraint. Hence, the budget constraint is the kinked set of segments $ABMC$. Responding to the public coverage, people with low values of private insurance, such as those at point E,

FIGURE 21-4 **Analyzing the Economics of Crowd-Out**

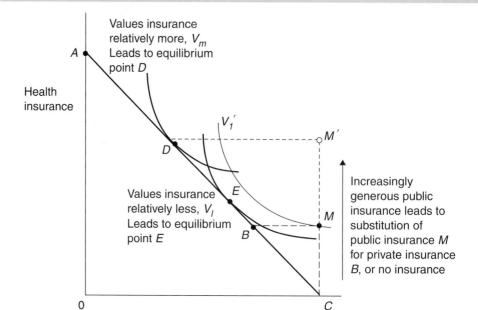

will enroll in the public sector, because utility level V_l' (passing through point M) is higher than V_l. Households with a high valuation of insurance will retain their private insurance at point D. As the value of the public insurance (point M) rises (say to M'), the households are more likely to drop private insurance and enroll in Medicaid.

To the extent that the Medicaid coverage provides insurance where none has been available, one observes take-up; to the extent that it replaces existing insurance, one observes crowd-out. Cutler and Gruber estimate that under Medicaid expansions about half of the increase in Medicaid eligibility has been associated with a reduction in private insurance coverage (crowd-out), with the remainder representing take-up by those who were previously uninsured.

The Effects of Medicare and Medicaid

Though we can be certain about the provisions of Medicare and Medicaid, we are necessarily less certain about their effects. We consider here a selection of findings on what is known about the effects of Medicare and Medicaid on:

- Health care costs
- Access to health care
- Health status

Costs and Inflation

The implementation of Medicare and Medicaid coincided with a considerable increase in health care costs in the United States. While health care costs had been rising before 1965, both in simple percentage terms and in comparison to the general rate of inflation, the hospital care inflation rate increased somewhat after the implementation of Medicare and Medicaid.

The expenditure levels of the two programs increased much more rapidly than most people had expected. Figure 21-5 shows the pattern of expenditures over time. In

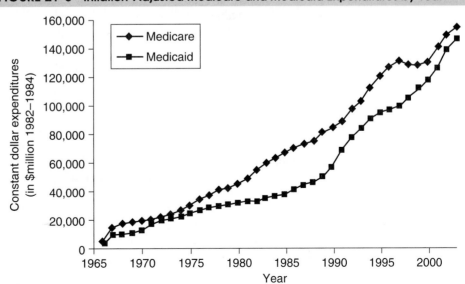

FIGURE 21-5 Inflation-Adjusted Medicare and Medicaid Expenditures by Year

monetary terms, percentage increases in expenditures on both programs were in double digits for most of the years. Even accounting for the substantial rate of inflation since the late 1960s, Medicare outlays increased by a factor of 7.8 from 1970 to 2003, and Medicaid outlays by a factor of 10.6 over the same period.

The populations at risk also grew for both Medicare and Medicaid. From 1970 to 2003, the number of Medicare enrollees grew at a compounded rate of about 2 percent—included disabled enrollees beginning in 1973. This rate exceeded population growth and can be attributed in part to the aging of the population. Growth in the enrollee population often is cited as the primary reason for growth in Medicaid payments. Responding to the availability of Medicaid, which provided cost sharing for many programs, many states changed their needs standards for several types of programs, allowing more families to qualify for cash assistance.

Why Spending Has Risen: Increased Coverage, Technological Improvement, and Increased Inefficiency

The increase in the population that is eligible and covered by Medicare and Medicaid clearly helps explain why program expenditures have risen, but it does not fully account for the inflationary effects that these programs could have. Newhouse (1978a) suggests three ways through which insurance programs, such as these, could affect prices and costs, even without growth in the population served.

First, Medicare and Medicaid both tended to increase the insurance coverage of the populations eligible. An increase in insurance has expansionary effects on the demand for care.

Newhouse explains, however, that these social insurance programs may have additional effects. Insurance coverage may induce technological improvements. If more costly technological improvements are induced by these social insurance programs, then the cost per unit of care may rise.

Finally, Newhouse proposes a third theory for the effect of insurance on costs and quantity used. This may be called the "increased inefficiency" theory. The idea is that when insurance covers a substantial portion of the health care bill, institutions, such as hospitals, have less incentive to control costs. It is not clear from this theory that the advent of Medicare and Medicaid, for example, would cause the level of inefficiency in hospitals to increase over time, but such a pattern is at least consistent with the theory.

The Evidence

What do we know about the patterns of health expenditure inflation subsequent to the adoption of Medicare and Medicaid, and what do we know about the sources of this inflation? One approach to these questions is to partition the observed rise in expenditures into its logical components: changes in population, in quantity per capita, and in the nature of services provided per visit or per admission.

Cutler and Meara (1997) find a dramatic change in medical spending over time, and disproportionately so for the very young (those less than 1 year old) and the old (those age 65 or over). From 1963 through 1987, per-person spending on infants increased by 9.8 percent per year, and per-person spending on the elderly increased by 8.0 percent per year (compared to 4.7 percent per year for the others).

Moreover, they find that essentially all of the disproportionate growth of spending for the very young and the old was accounted for by high-cost users within those groups, and that a substantial amount of high-cost medical use is associated with the increasing technological capabilities of medicine. Among infants, high-cost users are premature

babies with substantial respiratory or other acute conditions. For the elderly, high-cost users are generally patients with severe cardiovascular problems or cancer.

These data are consistent with the Newhouse theories, but they do not address the theories directly (see Newhouse's 1988 econometric study for more detail). It seems likely that technological change has played a substantial role. However, the evidence is not precise, and while we have a fairly clear understanding of how social insurance programs like these could affect price and use rates, we are not equally certain about the magnitudes of the effects.

Irrespective of the considerable costs, the predominant evidence seems to suggest that both Medicare and Medicaid have succeeded in addressing the problems of access to which they have been directed. That there was a change in health care use rates among the lower-income groups and the elderly following the beginning of Medicare and Medicaid is evident from the data.

Table 21-1 investigates two dimensions of health care access and utilization: the interval since the last physician contact and the number of hospital discharges per 1,000 population. In 1964, just prior to the passage of Medicare and Medicaid, 69.7 percent of those aged 65 and older had seen a physician within the past year. This was 4.2 percent higher than the general population and 8.1 percent higher than the group aged

TABLE 21-1 Indirect Impacts of Medicare and Medicaid

A. Age Comparisons

Interval since last physician contact

	Percent Less than One Year			Age 65+ Relative to:		
	1964	*1990*	*1995*	*1964*	*1990*	*1995*
Total	66.9	78.2	79.5	1.042	1.114	1.132
Age 45–64	64.5	77.3	79.9	1.081	1.127	1.126
Age 65+	69.7	87.1	90.0			

Hospital discharges per 1,000

	1964	*1990*	*1995*	*1964*	*1990*	*1995*
Total	109.1	91.0	86.2	1.742	2.734	3.096
Age 45–64	146.2	135.7	122.4	1.300	1.833	2.181
Age 65+	190.0	248.8	266.9			

B. Income Comparisons

Interval since last physician contact

	Percent Less than One Year			Income < $15,000 Relative to:		
	1964	*1990*	*1995*	*1964*	*1990*	*1995*
Total	66.9	78.2	79.5	0.876	0.988	0.984
Income < $15,000	58.6	77.3	78.2			
Income > $50,000	73.6	81.7	83.5	0.796	0.946	0.937

Hospital discharges per 1,000

	1964	*1990*	*1995*	*1964*	*1990*	*1995*
Total	109.1	91.0	86.2	0.939	1.563	1.632
Income < $15,000	102.4	142.2	140.7			
Income > $50,000	110.7	72.5	61.6	0.925	1.961	2.284

Source: Derived from *Health United States* (1998), Tables 77 and 87.

45 to 64. By 1990, those aged 65 and older were 11.4 and 12.7 percent more likely than the respective comparison groups to have seen a physician within a year.

Another measure of access for the elderly involves hospital discharges per 1,000 population. In 1964, those aged 65 and older had 190.0 compared with 146.2 for the group aged 45 to 64, or a 30 percent differential. By 1990, the differential had grown to 83.3 percent, and by 1995 to 118.1 percent.

Similar comparisons are appropriate when comparing the less affluent to the more affluent. In 1964, those with incomes less than $15,000 were 79.6 percent as likely to have seen a physician in the past year as those with incomes higher than $50,000. By 1990, they were 94.6 percent as likely.

In 1964, those with incomes less than $15,000 had 102.4 hospital discharges per 1,000, compared with 110.7 discharges for those with incomes higher than $50,000, or only 92.5 percent as many. By 1990, the lower-income people had 96.1 percent more discharges per 1,000 people, and by 1995 they had 128.4 percent as many.

Clearly, many other factors in the health care system have changed since the enactment of Medicare and Medicaid. One might ask whether the poor overuse inpatient care, seeking hospital emergency care instead of more appropriate outpatient care. Nonetheless, by these gross measures, the poor and the elderly have improved their access dramatically since 1965, with a boost from Medicare and Medicaid.

We also can learn something about the effects of the two programs by examining data on the out-of-pocket expenditures of eligible recipients. Table 21-2 reports these figures, comparing 1966 (pre-Medicare and Medicaid) and 1984. As shown in Subtable A, out-of-pocket expenditures were reduced sharply after the programs as a percentage of total expenditure. However, expenditures out-of-pocket by persons age 65 or older as a percentage of income and beneficiary liabilities as a share of

TABLE 21-2 Two Measures of Health Care Expenditure Burden for the Elderly Under Medicare

Subtable A: Personal Health Care Expenditures for Persons 65 Years or Older per Capita, by Source of Funds: Fiscal Year 1966 and Calendar Year 1984

	1966		1984	
Source of Funds	*Amount*	*Percent*	*Amount*	*Percent*
Per Capita	$445	100.0	$4,202	100.0
Out-of-Pocket	237	53.2	1,059	25.2
Private Insurance	71	15.9	304	7.2
Other Private	5	1.1	16	0.4
Medicare	—	—	2,051	48.8
Medicaid	—	—	536	12.8
Other Government	133	29.8	236	5.6

Subtable B: Mean Out-of-Pocket Health Costs as a Percent of Income for Persons 65 Years of Age or Older, Selected Years, 1966–1984

	Mean Out-of-Pocket Expenditures	*Mean Personal Incomes*	*Out-of-Pocket as a Percent Year of Income*
1966	$300	$2,000	15
1977	690	5,592	12
1981	1,187	8,639	14
1984	1,575	10,615	15

Source: Gornick et al. (1985).

total health expenditures stayed fairly constant since the beginning of the programs (Subtable B).

These data on use rates and financial access to care, however, leave at least one question unanswered. Would we find that these social insurance programs increased access to care in a study that controlled, among other things, for the level of health status or health care need, rather than just comparing data before and after the event?

The answer appears to be yes. Davis and Reynolds (1976) examine the effect of access to these public assistance programs in a statistical context that controls for other factors. For people with the same health status, they compare average health care use by those eligible for assistance with those low-income people not receiving assistance. Examine Table 21-3 excerpted from their study. These data indicate a fairly strong impact of improved financial access on care.

These data, however, do not resolve a perhaps more important question: Have the inequalities in use rates between the low-income and high-income groups been reduced? The difficulty in assessing inequalities in use rates between the low-income and high-income groups lies in the fact that lower-income groups tend to be sicker. Are use rates equal after adjusting for health status?

This issue is disputed in the literature, but the relevant evidence has been reviewed by Starr (1986, pp. 117–118). He concludes that the poor show significantly lower levels of physician use at comparable levels of health and disability, and that the age-adjusted number of physician visits per 100 bed-disability days proved to be 80 percent higher among higher-income whites than among whites below the poverty level.

Before concluding the discussion on access to health care, we identify a characteristic of access specific to the Medicaid program. Because Medicaid is state operated, as we have noted, characteristics vary somewhat across the nation. As recently as 1987, Medicaid was fundamentally restricted to children in very low-income, single-parent families. Since then, a series of legislative initiatives has extended Medicaid more broadly among children. By 1996, all pregnant women and all children under age 6 who had family incomes below 133 percent of the poverty line, and all children age 13 and younger with family incomes below 100 percent of the poverty line, were eligible for Medicaid. Coverage is being phased in for all children born after September 1983 until poor children of all ages are covered.

The net result is that the proportion of the child population enrolled in Medicaid increased from 15.7 percent in 1989 to 23.2 percent in 1995. For children under the age of 6, the percentage grew from 20.3 to 29.6. Interestingly, at the same time that Medicaid eligibility increased, there was a reduction in children's private insurance coverage. There are two plausible reasons. First, the 1990s saw a leveling off in the

TABLE 21-3 Annual Predicted Utilization for Low-Income Persons by Health Status and Welfare Eligibility, Adjusted for Other Characteristics, 1969

| | Health Status | | | | | |
| | Public Assistance Recipients | | | Other Low-Income Persons | | |
	Good	Average	Poor	Good	Average	Poor
Physician Visits	4.09	4.95	7.10	2.29	3.36	5.12
Hospital Admissions	0.14	0.16	0.21	0.09	0.11	0.15
Hospital Days	2.40	2.72	3.47	1.18	1.42	2.04

Source: Karen Davis and Roger Reynolds, "The Impact of Medicare and Medicaid on Access to Medical Care" in Rossett (ed.) *The Role of Health Insurance in the Health Services Sector*, New York: Neal Watson, 1976 with permission.

variety and generosity of employer-provided health insurance, affecting both low- and high-income households. To the extent that lower-income households have been affected disproportionately by changes in job-related insurance, they may have substituted Medicaid. Second, newly eligible families may have voluntarily dropped private insurance coverage in order to enroll in Medicaid.

Coincident with the expansion of Medicaid since the late 1980s, analysts have seen an increase in physician contacts for the poorest segment of the population. Table 21-4 shows the access to physicians over a six-year period. Those in good or excellent health increased their average number of contacts by 11.1 percent, and those in fair or poor health increased their average number of contacts by 31.5 percent. Although increased federal coverage under Medicaid comes with increased state matches, Medicaid scholars have noted that unlike cash assistance welfare, health care is viewed as a "positive good" that everyone should receive. Holahan, Wiener, and Wallin (1998, p. 58) note "declining Medicaid caseloads are matters of concern for state officials while falling cash welfare caseloads are matters of pride."

Health Status

The ultimate question regarding Medicare and Medicaid is whether or not these programs improve the health status of the eligible populations. This question is a specific application of the production function of health. Early econometric studies of the effects of health care on mortality rates suggested small and insignificant effects. The Rand Health Insurance Experiment with its randomized format, found little or no effect on health status in most cases for increased health care consumed by people with better insurance coverage. Into the mid-1980s, the evidence seemed to weigh against the belief that health care made a significant difference in the health status of populations generally, and the insured populations in particular. However, studies from the mid-1980s on have found important evidence to the contrary.

Hadley's studies (1982, 1988) focus on the role of Medicare expenditures. He finds a significant impact of Medicare on mortality rates, and this health care provides incremental benefits that exceed the incremental costs (i.e., it is cost beneficial). Hadley also finds a stronger impact of Medicare expenditures for population subgroups including blacks whose lower-than-average health status has been of public concern.

Other researchers also have evaluated the impacts of selected Medicaid programs. Reichman and Florio (1996) use a health production framework to evaluate race-specific effects of participation in New Jersey's HealthStart (Medicaid) program on birth weight and on newborn hospitalization costs in 1990. The results were mixed. Black participants had increased birth weights and lower hospitalization costs, but no evidence was found of improved birth outcomes or lower costs for whites.

TABLE 21-4 Average Number of Physician Contacts in Last Year for Children Under Age 15

Family Income	Good/Excellent Health			Fair/Poor Health		
	1987–1989	*1993–1995*	*Percent Change*	*1987–1989*	*1993–1995*	*Percent Change*
Below Poverty Line	3.6	4.0	11.11	10.8	14.2	31.48
Poverty Line to Twice Poverty Line	3.8	3.9	2.63	15.2	16.2	6.58
Above Twice Poverty Line	5.0	4.9	−2.00	22.6	20.7	−8.41

Source: Derived from Table 3-7, *Economic Report of the President* (1998).

Favorable impacts also must be measured against their incremental costs. Currie and Gruber (1996) measure the impacts of increased Medicaid eligibility (throughout the United States) for pregnant women between 1979 and 1992. Certain groups saw substantial improvements. For example, a 30 percentage point increase in eligibility among 15- to 44-year-old women was associated with a decrease in infant mortality of 8.5 percent. However, even the most carefully targeted changes in Medicaid eligibility cost the Medicaid program $840,000 per infant life saved, raising important questions of cost effectiveness. In a similar study, Joyce (1999) finds reductions in newborn costs associated with Medicaid participation (this time in New York) to be between $100 and $300 per recipient, insufficient to offset program expenditures.

Medicare: Recent Changes and Future Prospects
Recent Changes

In 1996, trustees of the Hospital Insurance (Part A) Fund predicted that the Part A Trust Fund would have a zero balance by 2001. With little appetite for increased payroll taxes, the U.S. Congress chose to make major changes in how Medicare paid health care providers through the BBA of 1997.

Joseph Newhouse served for many years as a member of the Medicare Payment Advisory Commission (MedPAC). He provides valuable insights on the features and impacts of the BBA, tracing the mid-1990s problems to four major factors (Newhouse, 2001):

1. Reimbursement that was [still, even with hospital DRGs] primarily cost-based
2. Generous reimbursement of new entrants into the health care industry
3. An incentive that the PPS (DRGs) gave to "unbundle" inpatient hospital services (which were controlled) to post-acute sites (which were not)
4. For home health services, an ill-defined criterion for eligibility for benefits

According to Newhouse, the BBA (as well as some major anti-abuse and antifraud efforts in the Medicare program that were instituted at the same time) "almost certainly" reduced Medicare outlays, by increasing the incentives for efficient production by mandating the development of prospective reimbursement systems for post-acute care. For hospital outpatient departments, it ended cost-based reimbursement. These two changes virtually ended cost-based reimbursement throughout the Medicare system. Payment formulas for new entrants and for home health services were adjusted downward, and the BBA reduced physician payments.

Representatives of hospitals and physicians argued that the measures were unexpectedly harsh. Since the low Medicare outlays in 1998 and 1999 were well below projected outlays, Congress provided givebacks amounting to about 3 percent of Medicare spending, a figure that Newhouse characterizes as "small."

Future Prospects

Despite these major changes, it is apparent that the U.S. Medicare system will become much larger over the next quarter century. Figure 21–6 displays projections of the Medicare-eligible population, starting in 2010. Projections into the future can be risky, but this one is a fairly safe bet. All of the people who will be 65 years of age in 2040 are already 30 years old. To project future populations, demographers statistically "age" the various population cohorts by predicting deaths between now and then. Immigration and emigration generally provide only small adjustments at the national level.

FIGURE 21-6 Medicare Enrollment Projections over the Next 30 Years

Source: MedPAC Analysis of the Social Security Administration 2004 Trustees Report Intermediate Assumptions; U. S. Department of Health and Human Services, Medicare Payment Advisory Commission, *Healthcare Spending and the Medicare Program: A Data Book*, Washington, DC, June 2005.

Any way that one looks at things, Medicare will grow. The population in the 65-plus age category will increase to 80 million, the result of the baby boom starting in the late 1940s and extending through the early 1960s, an increase of 147.3 percent. The total population, in contrast, is projected to increase by only 34.5 percent.

Projections of future spending must always be treated with caution, but the aging population and expected increases in health care costs suggest a major increase in the Medicare share of the GDP. Figure 21–7 shows how Medicare spending, 2.7 percent of GDP in 2005, is expected to jump to 6.8 percent of GDP by 2030. The addition of the prescription drug benefit (Part D) in 2006 accounts for more than one-third of the 5.1 percentage point increase, but even without Part D, whose impacts must be considered speculative, the percentage would be expected almost double, from 2.7 to 5.1 percent.

Victor Fuchs (2000), a long-time student of Medicare, has argued that we could understand the future Medicare problem better if we could dispel three "myths."

Myth 1. The rapid growth in Medicare expenditures results primarily from demographic change. While it is true that the population over age 65 is growing rapidly, and is expected to accelerate through 2020, the rate of growth of real per capita health care expenditures for each age-gender group over 65 has been over 4.0 percent per year. Most of this growth reflects increases in the quantity and quality of medical care, largely associated with the introduction and diffusion of new medical technology.

Myth 2. The long-run rate of increase of Medicare spending can be significantly slowed without reducing services to the elderly. Start with the expenditure identity:

$$\text{Expenditures} = \text{Input price} \times \text{Input quantity} \qquad \textbf{(21.1)}$$

FIGURE 21-7 Projected Medicare Spending as a Percent of Gross Domestic Product (GDP), 2000–2030

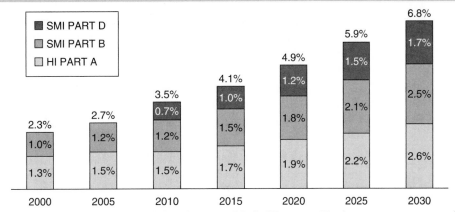

Note: HI is Hospital Insurance. SMI is Supplementary Medical Insurance. Numbers may not sum to total due to rounding.

Source: 2005 Annual Report of the Boards of Trustees of the Federal Hospital Insurance and Federal Supplementary Medical Insurance Trust Funds; Juliette Cubanski et al., *Medicare Chartbook*, 3rd ed., The Henry J. Kaiser Family Foundation, Summer 2005, Figure 1-1.

This can be rewritten as:

$$\text{Expenditures} = \left[\text{Input Price}\right] \times \left[\frac{\text{Input quantity}}{\text{Output quantity}}\right] \times \left[\text{Output quantity}\right]$$

and converted to:

$$\%\,\Delta \text{ in expenditures} = \left[\begin{array}{c}\%\,\Delta \text{ in}\\ \text{input price}\end{array}\right] + \left[\%\,\Delta \text{ in }\frac{\text{Input quantity}}{\text{output quantity}}\right] + \left[\begin{array}{c}\%\,\Delta \text{ in}\\ \text{output quantity}\end{array}\right]$$

where Δ refers to change. Quite simply, expenditure growth can be reduced only by (1) reductions in growth of input prices—what we pay our physicians, hospitals, or drug companies; (2) reductions in growth of levels of inputs per level of output—or increased productivity; or (3) reductions in growth of services. Fuchs argues that items (1) and (2) may produce only limited impacts—the necessary reductions may be in outputs (services).

Myth 3. Means-tested Medicare benefits will not have adverse effects on work or savings incentives because most Medicare beneficiaries are out of the workforce and are not savers. Fuchs observes that such means tests may impose very high implicit marginal tax rates. While the currently elderly may not react to these rates, younger Americans might choose the rational action of working less hard and saving less in their younger years, rather than face very high implicit taxes after the age of 65. This will reduce the amount of resources available for those currently over age 65, as well as the amount of savings for those under 65 to finance their retirement.

Fuchs provides three responses to the crisis implicit in elderly health spending projections.

1. Slow the growth rate of health expenditures. As previously noted, this may not be desirable or feasible: undesirable because many medical advances have improved quality of life for the elderly; infeasible because the elderly want all of the care that might do them some good.

2. Impose higher taxes on the young. Fuchs views such tax hikes as highly unlikely, as they will add to an already high burden of support that the young are asked to pay in support of the elderly.

3. Provide more of their own income by increases in work and saving. Fuchs (1999) examined elderly retirement savings, concluding that, "most low income elderly could have saved more prior to age 65."

Criticisms of the U.S. Health Care System

Critics of the Medicare and Medicaid delivery systems have expressed concerns about the sizable personal liabilities involved for individuals entering hospitals under Medicare. Here are some examples of uncovered expenditures under Medicare and Medicaid. In 2006, the inpatient hospital deductible under Medicare was $952 for a stay of 1 to 60 days. Patients were required to pay $238 per day for days 61 to 90, $456 per day for days 91 to 150, and all costs for each day beyond 150 days.

Subscribers to Medicare Part B were required to pay the following:

* A monthly premium of $88.50 in 2006
* A $124 annual deductible. As of January 1, 2006, the deductible is indexed to the increase in the average cost of Part B services for aged beneficiaries.
* Coinsurance payments of 20 percent of the Medicare-approved charge
* 50 percent for most outpatient mental health

Overall, beneficiaries have been liable for substantial portions of the Medicare community–based population's total spending on medical care (16.2 percent, or one in $6, according to MedPAC, 2004). Services, such as drugs, dental care, eyeglasses, and most long-term care, are not covered (although most Medicare patients' out-of-pocket liabilities are reduced by private supplemental insurance or various forms of public assistance). Are these personal liabilities under Medicare too burdensome? Certainly, some Americans think so.

Because Medicaid refers to 51 separate programs, there are numerous variations in coverage. Holahan and Liska (1997) find that a major source of variation in Medicaid spending among states comes from their differences in coverage of their low-income populations. In 1994, less than half (46 percent) of all Americans below 150 percent of the poverty line were covered by Medicaid.

Gruber (2002) follows Medicaid program take-up in the 1980s and 1990s. He notes that take-up was close to full in the early 1980s, but fell over time as Medicaid expanded. By 1996, 31 percent of children were eligible for Medicaid, but only 22.6 were enrolled, for an average take-up rate of 73 percent, but a marginal rate that was much lower. Eligibility varied substantially among the states; from 1983 to 1996 eligibility rose by over 50 percent in New Mexico, by 45 percent in Hawaii, and by 39 percent in Arizona, but by only 1 percent in Utah and 6 percent in Rhode Island, and it actually fell by 2 percent in Alaska. There are no estimates of eligibility for Medicaid and take-up of the program by the elderly and disabled. These would be complicated

TABLE 21-5 Average Annual Changes in Medicaid Enrollment and Spending, by Group and per Person, 2000–2003

Group	Enrollment (in millions)			Spending Per Enrollee ($)			Total Spending ($ billions)		
	2000	*2003*	*% Change/Yr.*	*2000*	*2003*	*% Change/Yr.*	*2000*	*2003*	*% Change/Yr.*
Aged and Disabled	9.9	10.8	2.9	11,879	14,122	5.9	117.3	151.9	9.0
Families	22.3	29.8	10.1	1,988	2,403	6.5	44.4	71.6	17.3
All Enrollees	32.2	40.6	8.0	5,023	5,512	3.1	161.4	223.5	11.4

Source: John Holahan and Arunabh Ghosh, "Understanding The Recent Growth In Medicaid Spending, 2000–2003," *Health Affairs Web Exclusive*, Exhibit 6, DOI 10.1377/hlthaff.W5.52; ©*2005 Project HOPE—The People-to-People Health Foundation, Inc.*, with permission http://content.healthaffairs.org/cgi/content/full/hlthaff.w5.52/DC1, accessed August 30, 2005.

because many elderly or disabled who are not currently eligible could become eligible by spending down enough of their resources to qualify.

Aside from these gaps in the Medicare and Medicaid programs, many critics of the American system characterize its main weakness as the problem of the uninsured. Approximately 45 million people at any point in time go without health insurance. While this does not mean that they go entirely without care, the uninsured consume only half as much health care on average as those who are insured.

Holahan and Ghosh (2005) argue that without Medicaid the numbers of uninsured might have been much higher. As noted in Table 21–5 Medicaid spending increased by about one-third between 2000 and 2003, largely driven by enrollment growth. The program saw rapid increases in enrollment of children and nondisabled adults. Many more Americans were covered by Medicaid at the end of the period than at the beginning, even though there were few expansions of and even some reductions in eligibility standards. Thus, the growth in enrollment was largely due to the economic downturn, which led to declines in incomes and made more people eligible under existing eligibility standards.

The large increase in Medicaid and SCHIP enrollment for children offset the decline in enrollment in employer-sponsored insurance. As a result, the number of uninsured children declined slightly. Medicaid enrollment among adults also rose, but the increase only partially offset the decline in employer-sponsored coverage, and there was a large increase in the number of uninsured adults.

Health spending per Medicaid enrollee grew at a rate below that experienced in the private sector, in part because states made policy choices that affected benefits and provider reimbursement rates. The large growth in Medicaid spending, 10.2 percent per year, nonetheless represented fairly rapid growth. Medicaid played its role as a safety net, providing coverage to those facing economic declines and loss of employer-sponsored coverage, but the result was a sharp increase in program costs.

Conclusions

In this chapter, we have presented a general discussion of social insurance and its application to the health care sector. Almost all modern industrialized countries provide fairly comprehensive health care social insurance, and we have reviewed the history of these developments and the pattern in the United States.

Today, the major health care social insurance programs in the United States are Medicare and Medicaid. These programs increase costs in theory and have been

increasingly costly in practice. It is clear that they have had a beneficial effect on access to care among the elderly and low-income groups, and recent studies suggest that they have a beneficial effect on health status. They leave, however, a fairly large number of the poor or uninsured without health care coverage.

Whether or not the United States should move to a national health insurance program must reflect the values of the public. Comprehensive social insurance for health care in the United States would directly address and presumably solve the widely perceived problem of providing for the uninsured, a group that often includes people in the poverty, near-poverty, and other lower-income groups.

These problems can be addressed in many ways. We have noted the salient policy features or decision issues in the plans considered by Congress in 1993 through 1994 and since. What can economics say about these features, whose ultimate choice or the choice of no change depends on the values of the voting public? There are areas of theory and evidence in economics that shed light on these questions. It is also useful, however, to look at health reform beyond the borders of the United States. We begin by comparing the features of health systems across countries in the next chapter.

SUMMARY

1. Several different types of social insurance policies and social programs exist. They are usefully grouped into poverty programs, old-age assistance, disability, health, and unemployment.
2. Social program features include contributions, benefits, length of coverage, means of reimbursement to providers, and methods of determining payment levels to providers.
3. Social insurance originated in nineteenth-century Europe. Groups in the United States have supported health care social insurance programs throughout the twentieth century. This history led to the adoption of Medicare and Medicaid in 1965. Since then, however, the United States remains one of the few developed countries that has not adopted a comprehensive health care social insurance program.
4. Medicare is a national program that provides hospital insurance to the elderly, along with optional supplemental physician care insurance. The Balanced Budget Act of 1997 established several new categories of Medicare options, and prescription drug coverage (Part D) was approved in 2003, and started in 2006.
5. Medicaid programs are funded through matching state and federal funds and run by the states. They provide health care to certain categories of the needy and are the primary providers of nursing home aid.
6. Medicare and Medicaid expenditures have increased rapidly since the programs began, due to increased medical care prices, population covered, and quantity of care per capita consumed by the population, as well as due to changes in the nature of the services provided.
7. Medicare and Medicaid accompanied clear improvement in access to care by the lower-income population, as evidenced by increased utilization rates by lower-income groups, both absolutely and relatively, to the higher-income groups.
8. With the aging of the baby boom cohort and the improvements in health care technologies in the early twenty-first century, Medicare must determine how best to structure, provide, and finance the benefits that it is providing to this growing segment of the population.

DISCUSSION QUESTIONS

1. In what ways does social insurance differ from private insurance?
2. Of the five types of social insurance programs described, which types describe Medicare? Which types describe Medicaid?
3. What are the similarities between Medicare and Medicaid? What are the differences?
4. What factors contributed to the historical growth in Medicare spending?

5. Describe how Medicare has affected access to care for the elderly.
6. Is health status affected by the access to health care provided through social insurance programs? Discuss the evidence.
7. What are some possible reasons that other industrially advanced countries have far more comprehensive social insurance programs for health care than does the United States?
8. Historically in the United States, what groups have supported social insurance for health care, and what groups have opposed it? Why do you think this is the case?

EXERCISES

1. Calculate the average tax rate for Social Security at incomes of $25,000, $50,000, $75,000, and $100,000. Do the same for Medicare. (Hint: You may choose to do each graphically.) Characterize each tax as being progressive, regressive, or neutral.
2. Figure 21-2 describes the Medicare Part D prescription drug benefit. Look at the website referenced and determine the marginal coinsurance rates, applicable in each segment. Then calculate the average amount spent at the following levels of charges: $1,500, $3,500, $5,500, and $7,500. Discuss the "burden" of payments under this schedule.
3. Consider Currie's discussion of take-up of social programs, where the x-axis is program enrollment and the y-axis refers to monetary costs and benefits.

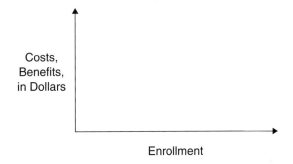

 a. If we measure the number of people enrolling in a program on the x-axis, why would the "demand" for these programs be downward sloping? Draw a demand curve.
 b. Why would the costs of establishing a program be upward sloping? Draw a supply curve.
 c. What does the equilibrium where supply equals demand, mean?
 d. How can one model program "stigma" and what does it do to equilibrium enrollment? Why?
4. Figure 21-3 traces the economics of take-up and crowd-out. Suppose you had a population of 1,000 families: 200 had Medicaid insurance, 700 had some other type of insurance, and 100 were uninsured. Suppose now that Medicaid increases eligibility rules that would allow an additional 100 families to get coverage. After one year, 250 families now have Medicaid, 675 now have some other type of insurance, and 75 are uninsured.
 a. Calculate the average take-up and crowd-out both in numbers of families and in rates.
 b. Calculate the marginal take-up rates occurring due to the eligibility change.
 c. Has insurance coverage for the population increased? Why or why not?
 d. Has insurance coverage for all families increased? Why or why not?
5. Consider the analysis described in Figure 21–4. Tom and Dick each earn $15,000 per year. Tom has a spouse and two children, and Dick is unmarried. Health insurance and other goods trade off dollar for dollar (there is no tax advantage to health insurance).
 a. Where would each of the two be located on the budget constraint, and why?
 b. Which of the two would more likely take up a health insurance program, such as Medicaid?
 c. How would your answers to the first two parts change if health insurance were subsidized (as it is) relative to all other goods?

6. Table 21-4 shows the effect of enhanced Medicaid programs on children who are below the poverty line. The table shows how physician utilization has increased for the poor children.
 a. Compare the levels of utilization between children who are below the poverty line and children who are above twice the poverty line. Who had more care in 1987? In 1993? Who is likely to be sicker?
 b. Compare the relative amount of utilization between the two groups. What happened to these measures from 1987 to 1993? Discuss your answer.

7. Fuchs's analysis (p. 485) examines determinants of Medicare spending.
 a. How is (input/output) related to health care productivity?
 b. If input prices rise by 4 percent, and output rises by 3 percent, what must happen to keep the percentage increase in expenditures no higher than 2 percent? Why?

Comparative Health Care Systems and Health System Reform

We now consider the experiences of other countries in providing large-scale health care. We do so for two reasons. First, many other countries have constructed programs that predate U.S. programs by decades. There are rich variations in programs and experiences that are themselves worth discovering. Second, and more importantly, the U.S. system has some gaping holes compared with the coverage extended by many other systems. Understanding the approaches used by other countries may provide important clues to assessing our own system.

Contemporary Health Care Systems

Many industrialized countries either provide health care directly through the government or provide publicly funded health insurance with comprehensive coverage. Rather than describing details about the health care programs of dozens of countries, we will characterize the basic types of systems employed and to develop a few examples in greater detail.[1]

A Typology of Contemporary Health Care Systems

Consider a broad framework for describing different approaches. For this purpose, Gordon (1988) developed a useful typology of four health benefit systems. We note countries that fall into each category.

[1]The Social Security system maintains an archive called *Social Security Statistics Throughout the World*, in which it describes the health, unemployment, and poverty programs of more than 100 countries. It is located at www.ssa.gov/policy/docs/progdesc/ssptw, accessed August 13, 2005.

1. **Traditional sickness insurance** is fundamentally a private insurance market approach with a state subsidy—for example, Germany.
2. **National health insurance** involves a national-level health insurance system—for example, Canada.
3. **National health services** have the state providing the health care—for example, the United Kingdom.
4. **Mixed systems** contain elements of both traditional sickness insurance and national health coverage—for example, the United States.

In comparing economic data across countries, Table 22-1 shows per capita health expenditures expressed in U.S. dollars in many countries for 2002. These figures have been adjusted by the purchasing powers of the local currencies (known as purchasing power parity). Other columns show each country's health care spending as a percent of GDP for selected years.

The countries vary substantially. Other countries (e.g., Denmark, France, Italy, the Netherlands, and Switzerland) spend larger percentages on inpatient care than does the United States. It may surprise readers to discover that in percentage terms, for 2002, the U.S. pharmaceutical expenditures were among the lowest.

Several countries (including Canada) have lower rates of infant mortality (measured in deaths per 1,000 live births) than the United States figure of 6.8 deaths per 1,000 live births. Several countries also have higher life expectancies at birth. The United States has the largest expenditures per capita ($5,267). It is also the biggest spender as a share of GDP (14.6 percent by OECD figures). These figures, as well as concerns about access to health care, are the sorts of indicators that have led many to question what Americans are getting for their spending. However, high expenditures may have three meanings:

1. High average level of services
2. High resource costs for services
3. Inefficient provision of services

In examining cross-country differences, we keep these points in mind. A high level of services reflects at least the possibility that populations have chosen to spend their incomes in this fashion. We have noted previously that higher income levels are reflected in higher consumption levels of all normal goods, including health care. Cross-national studies indicate a substantial responsiveness of health care expenditures to increased income (relatively large income elasticity). U.S. expenditure levels reflect, in part, the higher per-capita income level in the United States.

National Health Programs: United Kingdom and Germany

In this section, we examine the national health systems of the United Kingdom and Germany in detail. In the next section, we will contrast Canada's plan, a national health insurance system, with that of the United States, an example of a mixed system.

As shown by the comparative data in Table 22-2, the resources available across systems can vary widely. The United States has 26 percent fewer hospital beds per capita than the United Kingdom, but it has 20 percent more physicians. The United States has fewer nurses per 1,000 than does Germany. Germany, by comparison, has two-thirds more physicians per capita than the United Kingdom. Korea has smaller staffs of physicians and nurses than do the other countries, and Hungary has larger ones.

TABLE 22-1 Health Care Spending and Outcomes in Selected Industrial Countries, 2002

	Macro-econ. References GDP/ Capita, US$ PPP	Total Exp. on Health/ Capita, US$ PPP	Expenditure In-pat. Care Tot. Exp. In-patient % THE (2002)	Tot. Pharm. & Other Exp. % THE (2002)	% of GDP Spent on Health Care			Deaths per 1,000 Live Births (2002)	Life Expectancy at Birth, 2002	
					1970	1990	2002		Female	Male
Australia	28,168	2,504[b]	40.2[b]	13.8[b]	4.9	7.8	9.1[b]	5.0	82.6	77.4
Austria	28,842	2,220	38.2	16.1	4.3	7.1	7.7	4.1	81.7	75.8
Belgium	27,652	2,515			4.0	7.4	9.1	4.9	81.1	75.1
Canada	30,429	2,931	28.8[c]	16.7[c]	7.0	9.0	9.6	5.2[b]	82.2[b]	77.1[b]
Czech Republic	15,098	1,118	37.8	22.6			7.4	4.2	78.7	72.1
Denmark	29,228	2,583	50.7[c]	9.8[c]	8.0	8.5	9.0[c]	4.4	79.5	74.8
Finland	26,616	1,943	39.2	15.9	5.6	7.9	7.3	3.0	81.5	74.9
France	28,094	2,736	41.3	20.8	6.3	8.6	9.7	4.1[c]	82.9[c]	75.8[c]
Germany	25,843	2,817	36.1	14.5		8.7	10.9	4.3	81.3[b]	75.6[b]
Greece	19,041	1,814		15.3	6.1	7.5	9.5	5.9	80.7	75.4
Hungary	13,891	1,079	29.0	27.6			7.8	7.2	76.7	68.4
Iceland	28,404	2,807	54.6[b]	14.0[b]	5.1		9.9	2.2	82.3	78.5
Ireland	32,571	2,367		11.0		6.6	7.3	5.1	80.3	75.2
Italy	25,569	2,166	41.8[c]	21.9[c]		8.0	8.5[c]	4.7	82.9	76.8
Japan	26,860	2,077[b]	38.9[b]	18.8[b]	4.5	5.9	7.8[b]	3.0	85.2	78.3
Korea	19,524	996	21.5	25.6		4.8	5.1		80.0[b]	72.8[b]
Luxembourg	49,207	3,065	40.3	11.6			6.2	5.1	81.5	74.9
Mexico	9,026	553	33.2	21.4			6.1	21.4	77.4[c]	72.4[c]
Netherlands	28,983	2,643	40.8	10.4	6.9	8.0	9.1	5.0	80.7	76.0
New Zealand	21,943	1,857			5.1	6.9	8.5	6.3[a]	80.9[b]	76.0[b]
Norway	35,531	3,409	49.0[b]	9.2[b]	4.4	7.8	10.0[c]	3.9[b]	81.5	76.4
Poland	10,804	654					6.1	7.5	78.7	70.4
Portugal	18,376	1,702					9.3	5.0	80.5	73.8
Slovak Republic	12,256	698	35.0	37.3			5.7	7.6	77.8	69.9
Spain	21,592	1,646	27.6	21.5	3.6	6.6	7.6	3.4	83.1	75.7
Sweden	27,255	2,517	31.2	13.1	6.9	8.5	9.2	2.8	82.1	77.7
Switzerland	30,725	3,446	48.0	10.3	5.6	8.5	11.2	4.5	83.0	77.8
Turkey	6,448	446[a]		24.8[a]			6.6[a]	38.3	71.0[c]	66.4[c]
United Kingdom	27,959	2,160			4.5	6.0	7.7	5.3	80.4[b]	75.7[b]
United States	36,006	5,267	27.6	12.8	6.9	11.9	14.6	6.8	79.8[b]	74.4[b]

Source: Copyright OECD Health Data 2004, 3rd ed.; [a]2001; [b]2001; [c]2003.

TABLE 22-2 Health Care Resources

	Acute Inpatient Beds/1000 (2001)	% of U.S.	Practicing Physicians/ 1,000 (2001)	Practicing % of U.S.	Nurses/ 1000 (2001)	% of U.S.
Canada	3.2	110.3	2.1	87.5	10.0	126.6
France	4.0	137.9	3.3	137.5	7.0	88.6
Germany			3.3	137.5	9.7	122.8
Hungary	6.0	206.9	3.2	133.3	8.3	105.1
Korea	5.2	179.3	1.5	62.5	1.6	20.3
United Kingdom	3.9	134.5	2.0	83.3	9.0	113.9
United States	2.9		2.4		7.9	

Source: Copyright *OECD Health Data 2004*, 3rd ed.

The United Kingdom: The National Health Service

Great Britain's National Health Service (NHS) was established in 1946 and provides health care to all British residents. It is financed largely (about 83 percent) through general revenues, with capital and current budget filtering from the national level down to the regional and then to the district level. The plan pays general practitioners on a capitation basis and hospital physicians largely on a salaried basis. In addition to the NHS, there is also a private-sector health system. About 10 percent of Britons purchase private health insurance.

Services are not entirely free. As of 2004, patients paid 80 percent of the cost of any dental work up to £372 (about $681 at the September 2005 exchange rate of $1.83 per £). Patients paid £6.30 (about $11.50) for each prescription. Those receiving means-tested benefits and their adult dependents, children under age 16 (under age 19 if a student), pregnant women, and nursing mothers are exempt from dental and prescription charges. People over the state pension age and certain other groups are exempt from prescription charges.

The general practitioner (GP) serves as the gatekeeper to the health care system. GPs are not government employees. Rather, they are self-employed and receive about half their incomes from capitation contracts. They typically treat routine conditions and will refer patients to hospitals for more specialized care. The referral usually will be to a district hospital. Once at the hospital, the patients are under the care of physicians (consultants) who are allocated staffed beds and junior hospital staff to work under their direction.

Table 22-1 shows that U.K. spending per capita ($2,160) in 2002 was just 41.0 percent of the U.S. level ($5,267) and a little more than half, when expressed as a ratio to GDP (7.7 percent as opposed to 14.6 percent). How does the United Kingdom keep its health care expenditures this much lower while providing universal access to health care? Though patients have relatively easy access to primary and emergency care, specialty care is rationed through waiting lists and limits on the availability of new technologies. A relatively simple model is useful to illustrate this phenomenon.

A Model of Rationed Health Care and Private Markets

We can examine the practices of an NHS-type of organization diagrammatically. In panel A of Figure 22-1, we treat the supply of health services as totally price inelastic. Why? The supply curve, being a reflection of what is provided by the government, is a vertical line. This indicates that the quantity supplied is not responsive to the price of the services.

Furthermore, the money price of the services is set by the government at P^*, which is less than the market clearing price of P_c. Predictably, there is excess demand ($Q^* - Q_0$)

at the administered price, P^*. Because most health care cannot be bought and resold, other forms of rationing, largely time related, become important. There are many ailments for which the waiting period for treatment by the NHS is months or even years. Table 22-3 shows examples for numerous specialties in the London region in 2001.

FIGURE 22-1 Prices and Quantities in a Controlled Market

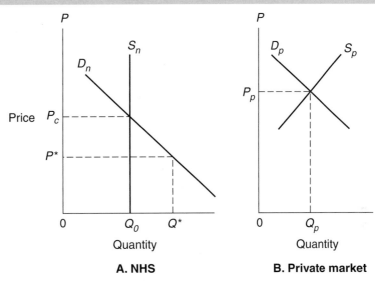

A. NHS

B. Private market

TABLE 22-3 Inpatients Waiting Six Months or More—London Region, 2000–2001

Health Authority	Inpatients Waiting 6 Months or More as % of the Total Number of Inpatients Waiting	Inpatients Waiting 6 Months or More as % of the Total Number of Inpatients Waiting for Each Specialty		
	All Specialties	Trauma & Orthopedics	Urology	Ear, Nose, and Throat
Barking & Havering	28.5	36.8	19.1	33.5
Barnet	24.9	32.8	22.5	31.4
Bexley & Greenwich	27.8	37.5	18.8	40.5
Brent & Harrow	27.0	32.8	26.0	32.0
Bromley	30.5	39.1	16.7	22.5
Camden & Islington	21.8	30.4	16.7	24.8
Croydon	32.8	51.8	30.6	10.9
Ealing, Hammersmith & Hounslow	25.4	34.7	23.9	41.7
East London and the City	25.5	29.0	19.4	38.7
Enfield & Haringey	32.5	37.1	25.0	38.5
Hillingdon	25.7	34.0	18.4	29.2
Kensington, Chelsea & Westminster	19.5	24.0	16.9	26.3
Kingston & Richmond	23.9	35.5	15.2	41.6
Lambeth, Southwark & Lewisham	34.0	36.5	28.5	42.9
Merton, Sutton & Wandworth	25.9	36.2	6.7	34.6
Redbridge & Waltham Forest	34.5	48.2	35.9	35.9

Source: Report by the Comptroller and Auditor General, HC 221, Session 2001–2002, 26 July 2001.

Again, as might be predicted, a private market for services has developed for those who choose to enter the private market without governmental aid, either due to strong preferences for private care or due to the ability to pay more than the NHS price. Because there is excess demand at P^*, that excess demand represents in part people who are queued and who may wish to pay in the private sector to avoid the long waits. Those who participate in the private market, shown in panel B, will pay P_p for the quantity of services, Q_p.

Performance Under the NHS and More Recent Reforms

On the one hand, a system, such as the NHS, that depends on queuing for access to care often leads participants to postpone or simply not purchase certain services. On the other hand, the NHS devotes considerable resources to such high-return services as prenatal and infant care. To these populations served, and to the larger public concerned with equitable provision of care to these segments of the population, the universal nature of the service is particularly beneficial.

In addition, although the United Kingdom has spent considerably less on health care than the United States and many other countries, by most measures of mortality and morbidity the United Kingdom does about as well. Certainly, many nonmedical factors are involved in determining disease and death rates in a population, and these factors also will vary across countries.

Despite universal access to care in the United Kingdom, historically there have been considerable regional disparities in funding and in the use of health care. Evidence shows that upper-class patients have received substantially more care for a given illness than have lower-class patients (Maynard, 1990). Thus, even where access is universal, the results are not necessarily equal (note again the differences within various areas of the London region in Table 22-3).

The NHS has been extremely popular with the public. Nevertheless, 1991 reforms were introduced by Conservative party Prime Minister Margaret Thatcher. The reforms replaced the centralized, hierarchical NHS bureaucracy with a quasi-market mechanism. A purchaser/provider split was created where "purchasers" of health care, regional health authorities and general practice fund holders, are allocated budgets to purchase services for their populations. These purchasers are distinct from providers—mainly hospitals. The incentives for efficiency and a responsive system come as providers compete for contracts with purchasers.

Julian Le Grand (2002) notes that following Tony Blair's Labour party victory in 1997, the government remained committed to the purchaser/provider split, but emphasized "cooperative" rather than competitive arrangements. As a last resort, purchasers could still shift their purchasing away from providers. According to Le Grand:

> The quasi-market was largely abolished and market-based competitive pressures mostly eliminated. Despite an ostensible commitment to collaboration and the introduction of some measures designed to foster it, central control was maintained and indeed, as illustrated by the proliferation of central agencies and control instruments, greatly increased. (p. 121)

Despite the changes in direction, one can still ask whether the system changes since the early 1990s were effective. Waiting lists fell for a time from 1997 through 2001, although they began to rise thereafter. Waiting times fell, with an 8.5 percent drop in the numbers waiting more than 12 months for treatment and a 13.3 percent drop in the number waiting more than 15 months, as compared with the previous year. Le Grand also calculates an efficiency index (Table 22-4) of health activities per unit inputs used. There appear to have been some early efficiency gains under the quasi-markets,

TABLE 22-4 Efficiency in England's Hospital and Community Health Services

Year	Cost-Weighted Activity Index	Expenditures	Efficiency Index	Efficiency Increase (%)
1988–89	100.0	100.0	100.0	
1989–90	102.2	101.7	100.5	0.5
1990–91	103.5	102.7	100.8	0.3
1991–92	108.9	105.4	103.3	2.5
1992–93	112.3	108.6	103.4	0.1
1993–94	116.8	110.4	105.8	2.3
1994–95	121.7	111.9	108.8	2.8
1995–96	126.5	113.9	111.1	2.1
1996–97	128.6	115.5	111.3	0.2
1997–98	130.9	118.1	110.8	−0.4
1998–99	133.6	121.6	109.9	−0.8

Source: Julian Le Grand, "Further Tales from the British National Health Service," *Health Affairs 21* (3) (2002): 116–128. Reprinted by permission of The People-to-People Health Foundation.

although these seemed to attenuate in the late 1990s (in the first years of Labour government).

Recently there have been two major problems. The first has related to capacity constraints—shortages of doctors and nurses, as well as relatively small levels of acute hospital beds. Also, a shortage of nursing home beds has meant difficulties discharging elderly patients from the hospital, preventing hospitals from taking on new admissions.

Second, incentive problems pervaded the system. NHS providers were paid salaries to work 11 sessions per week in the NHS. If NHS providers were willing to work (and be paid) for only 10 of the 11 sessions, they were allowed to work as much as they like in the private sector—where they were paid on a fee-for-service basis. The longest NHS waiting lists occurred in the specialties in which specialists had the highest private earnings.

In response to some of the indicators in Table 22-3, the NHS made major efforts to reduce patient waiting times. In 2005, the Healthcare Commission reported that overall satisfaction of patients with most NHS services was high. The number of people waiting more than six months for admission as inpatients in England decreased by 85 percent from March 2000 to March 2005. There has also been a significant drop in the number of people waiting more than 13 weeks for an appointment as outpatients—down by 92 percent over the same period. For specialties with high inpatient death rates, the number waiting less than six months increased by 8 percent between 1999 and 2005.[2]

More than 50 percent of people with heart attacks now receive clot busting drugs within an hour of a call for help, and 84 percent receive them within 30 minutes of arrival at hospital. In Wales, the target to reduce the amount of time people wait for cardiac surgery from 10 months to 8 months has been met.

The impacts have been mixed, however. While recent British government figures show that performance goals in meeting the 48-hour target for booking appointments with GPs are being met, people in some areas are now finding it increasingly difficult to book appointments in advance or see a GP outside normal working hours. Patient surveys, carried out in 2004 to 2005, found that around a quarter of people were waiting

[2]See Commission for Healthcare Audit and Inspection, *State of Healthcare 2005*, www.healthcarecommission. org.uk/NationalFindings/StateOfHealthcare/fs/en?CONTENT_ID=4006361&chk=sNVkqk, accessed November 15, 2005.

more than two days for an appointment and a third of general practices would not book appointments more than two weeks in advance. Many people also experience problems gaining access to NHS dentists, with 58 percent of dental practices not taking on new NHS patients (up 40 percent from 2001).

The experience of the NHS in the area of cost containment seems clear. Rationed care cuts money costs, and even with increased expenditures from the health care reforms, total U.K. expenditures were expected to be well below the European Union and the United States.

Germany

The German health care system is rooted in the programs laid out by Bismarck in 1883. Legislation required workers in various occupations to enroll in sickness insurance funds. The original legislation covered only a small fraction of the population. Nevertheless, the basic approach of mandatory enrollment in autonomous sickness funds, financed by payroll taxes, was expanded and today lies at the heart of the German social insurance program.

Policy analysts sometimes characterize the German health care system by the "three *Ss*"—solidarity, subsidiarity (decentralization to public and private organizations), and self-governance. Solidarity, a sense that all citizens are concerned with the provision of equal access to health care, is at the heart of the German health system. Although many Americans support such a goal, the base of support is not similar. American analyst Uwe Reinhardt (1994) has characterized Germany's system as "not the American way" (p. 22). See Box 22-1 for one particularly interesting difference.

BOX 22-1

Are People in All Nations the Same?

Is convergence of the world's many health systems desirable? An academic recently returned from a German sabbatical with this story:

> My wife and I became good friends with a German couple named Joachim and Marlene. At some point they told us, half humorously, that theirs was a "mixed marriage." Joachim came from Baden, while Marlene was from Schwaben, two neighboring areas that few foreigners could tell apart.

Cultural differences may motivate health care consumers, and three cases suggest large consequences from such differences. U.S. patients demand the latest health technologies when a serious illness occurs or threatens. Correspondingly, high-tech scanners and other new diagnostic equipment are much more common in the United States, and their use has significant cost consequences. Are costs that are inflated for this reason to be considered inefficiencies, or merely questions of taste?

Similarly, medical anthropologists argue that cultural differences among countries influence both the diagnosis and treatment of common mental illnesses. Historically, U.S. physicians apply the diagnosis of schizophrenia to patients much more commonly than do European physicians. Furthermore, the patients' approaches to mental illness depend in important ways on their culture.

Finally, a number of European health systems reflect European perceptions of illness and the human need for recuperation. Joachim and Marlene told of visiting the health spa, "the Kur," prescribed by a physician and fully covered by the health insurance system. Daily regimens require vigorous and healthful activities, yet a proposal in the United States to offer universal access to basic health care, including access to the health spa when needed, would hardly be treated seriously.

Structure of the System

In the German system, all working persons must have health insurance with costs divided between employer and employee.[3] Employees' shares are collected as payroll taxes at rates proportional to their gross wages. The average contribution rate to sickness funds in 2003 was 14.3 percent. Individuals with incomes beyond a given ceiling are eligible to choose the private health system. Approximately 88 percent of Germans have social health insurance, 10 percent have private insurance, and the remaining 2 percent are covered by other, sector-specific governmental schemes (including military, police, social welfare, and assistance for immigrants seeking asylum).

The social insurance component is organized around 292 sickness funds. These funds are independent and self-regulating. Contributions toward the sickness funds constitute the major system of financing health care. The sickness funds are responsible for collecting contributions, purchasing benefits on an in-kind basis and paying providers. Sickness fund membership is mandatory for employees whose gross income does not exceed € 3,862 (about $4,866 at 2006 exchange rates of $1.26 per €) per month in 2004.

The sickness funds pay providers directly for services provided to their members at rates negotiated with individual hospitals. Regional groups of funds negotiate with regional doctors' and dentists' associations for payments for ambulatory and dental care.

Only recently (the late 1990s) have members of the Statutory Health Insurance (SHI) system been allowed to choose which sickness fund they wished to join—previously, membership was determined by occupational status. Altenstetter (2002) notes that the bulk of membership changes moved from the general sickness funds (with the highest number of the elderly) to the "enterprise funds," which offer lower payroll taxes.

The sickness funds are required by law to provide a comprehensive set of benefits. These include physician ambulatory care provided by physicians in private practice, hospital care, home nursing care, and a wide range of preventive services. The funds, like disability insurance, also provide additional cash payments to those who are unemployed as a result of illness.

As for reimbursement, ambulatory providers are paid on a fee-for-service basis, hospitals on a prospective basis. Both public and private (including for-profit) hospitals exist, with the public hospitals accounting for about half the beds. Hospitals tend to use salaried physicians, and, unlike the United States, physicians in private practice generally do not have admitting privileges. Thus, many doctors have invested in elaborately equipped clinics to compete with hospitals by being able to perform a wide range of procedures.

The German experience is especially relevant to the United States. Coverage and delivery are provided through a number of independent plans, similar to the United States where, for the most part, large numbers of employee groups, independent insurers, and providers reach agreements without direct government intervention. Germany relies on a mandated approach for the working uninsured, where coverage for certain conditions is required by law. Germany has also introduced cost controls similar in principle to prospective payment under the United States DRG mechanism, alt' full implementation has been delayed until 2009.

[3]The material on the German system, with some updates, is based on Altenstetter (2002), Riesberg (2004), and Altenstetter and Busse (2005).

The Role of Government
Each level of government has specific responsibilities in the German system.

- The *central government* passes legislation on policy and jurisdiction.
- *State governments* are responsible for hospital planning, managing state hospitals, and supervising the sickness funds and physician associations.
- *Local governments* manage local hospitals and public health programs.

This framework is relatively decentralized. As we have noted, the sickness funds and physicians' associations enjoy considerable administrative autonomy.

The SHI Modernization Act (2003)
Although there have been numerous reforms in the last 30 or more years, the passage of the SHI Modernization Act in 2003 sought to address increasing expenditure of the SHI contribution rates (on average from 13.6 percent of gross income in 2001 to 14.4 percent in 2003) and perceived deficiencies in the quality of health care. Its stated objectives were to improve the efficiency and quality of health care, and to stabilize SHI contribution rates in order to avoid disincentives for employers to invest in job-creating activities without rationing.

The legislation seeks to generate substantial savings for SHI from an expected € 9.8 billion in 2004 (about 7 percent of the expected sickness funds expenditures) to € 23 billion by 2007. In 2004, the bulk of expected savings (4 percent of current SHI expenditures) was to be achieved by shifting costs to users and the SHI insured. In comparison, the anticipated savings from measures targeting health care providers and the pharmaceutical industry total € 1.5 billion in 2004, rising to € 3 billion in 2007.

The main elements for savings or cost-shifts are:

- Exclusion of some benefits, especially over-the-counter drugs.
- Restructuring of copayments by (1) introducing new copayments; (2) standardizing copayment levels across sectors; (3) while children under age 18, antenatal care, and preventive services are still exempt from copayments, abolishing the general exemption of poor people.
- Annual copayments are now limited for every SHI insured to 2 percent of annual gross household income at the (documented) request of the insured; for the chronically ill, the annual financial burden of copayments is limited to 1 percent. Deductions for spouses and children apply. See Table 22-5 for more detail.

TABLE 22-5 Selected German Copayments in Euros (2004–2005)

Prescription drugs	10%, with minimum 5€ and maximum 10€
Conservative dental treatment	10€ per dentist consulted per quarter except referrals
Ambulatory medical treatment	10€ per physician consulted per quarter except referrals
Transportation (e.g., ambulance)	10%, with minimum 5€ and maximum 10€
Hospital stay and inpatient rehabilitation after a hospital stay	10€ per day
Preventive spa or inpatient rehabilitation unrelated to hospital stay	10€ per day

Note: As of May 2006, 1€ = $1.26.
Source: Busse and Reisberg (2004, Table 12).

In 2006, a "special" contribution of 0.5 percent of contribution will be levied on all SHI members (but not employers). As a result, the longstanding fifty-fifty parity in financing will change to approximately 46–54 for employers versus members.

Performance

Despite the frequent calls for reform in Germany, as well as the recurrent complaints that the system is in crisis, the German health system has been relatively successful at controlling costs. Before the 1970 to 1977 reforms, spending increased at a 14.4 percent annual rate, but this dropped to 6.5 percent from 1977 to 1983 and to 5.1 percent from 1983 to 1989.

For a better perspective of the relative success of various health systems in controlling inflation, examine Figure 22-2. One notices that the upward trends in expenditures continued into the early 1990s for the United States, but the rate of increase was more modest in the other systems.

Although the absolute share of German health care expenditure increased from 9.9 percent in 1996 to 10.9 percent in 2002 the real annual growth rate was lower than most of the other OECD countries. Furthermore, SHI expenditures remained relatively stable, increasing from 6.14 percent of the GDP in 1992 to 6.32 percent in 2002. This occurred because it primarily sought to prevent sickness fund expenditure from increasing faster than the income. This goal has led to efforts to contain costs and the policy of income-oriented expenditure, with the aim of stabilizing contribution rates.

In addition, health and health care inequities between the former East Germany and West Germany have been reduced substantially since reunification. Most of the relative East German deficits in equipment, building and maintenance standards, and

FIGURE 22-2 Health Expenditures as Percentage of GDP, 1960–2002

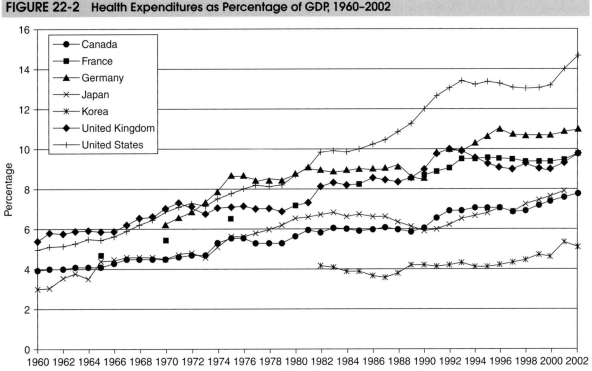

Source: Copyright *OECD Health Data 2004,* 3rd ed.

nursing home capacities have been addressed. Staff capacity and reimbursement have also been increased close to western levels.

The World Health Organization's *World Health Report 2000* showed Germany to rank twenty-fifth, compared to France (first) and the United Kingdom (eighteenth)—regarding performance, cost-effectiveness, and underemphasis on health promotion and disease prevention. Although the report elicited some methodological criticisms, many German observers viewed the general conclusion to be valid. Altenstetter and Busse (2005) argue that change will be difficult without a new alliance of stakeholders with the political will to redefine the allocation of financial burdens, establish a new balance in the relationship between SHI and private health insurance, and secure patient access to medical innovations for all Germans.

Busse and Reisberg (2004) identify several issues facing the German health care system in the near future.

Cost-containment and reimbursement. The gap between expenditures and income of sickness funds and the future viability of the pay-as-you-go principle are major political concerns. Germany has the highest health care expenditure share in the European Union. Unification of East and West Germany was accompanied by a sharp increase from 9.3 percent of GDP in 1990 to 10.4 percent in 1995, most of which can be explained through a lower level of income in the former East Germany (similar expenditures in the numerator, but a smaller income in the denominator). While cost-containment was successful in stabilizing expenditures in ambulatory medical and dental care and also hospital care after 1998, spending on care provided by allied health professionals, medical devices, and transport/emergency services was less effectively curbed. Expenditure on pharmaceuticals increased rapidly in the early 1990s, was effectively controlled through budgets until 2000, but began to increase again.

The impact of the prospective payment system for hospitals and ambulatory physicians. As in other countries, such systems are expected to lead to complicated interplay of incentives across levels of care.

Strengthening the revenue basis. Expected problems on the revenue side match some on the expenditure side. First, the high unemployment rate (over 10 percent) has narrowed the financial basis of SHI contributions. Second, labor is responsible for an ever-decreasing share of the national income, while the share of capital is increasing. Third, civil servants and the self-employed are currently not covered by statutory health insurance. Also, like the United States, the share of elderly people in the population is increasing while the relative number of people of working-age to support them is decreasing.

In short, analysts have found that the German system has put considerable emphasis on free choice, ready access, high numbers of providers, and technological equipment, and rather less emphasis on cost effectiveness or cost containment (in spite of numerous cost-containment acts). Formal waiting lists and explicit rationing decisions are virtually unknown. The public has supported these priorities, and if they are used as criteria for assessment, the health care system appears to work well. Many of the problems are similar to those that have been identified in the United States.

The Canadian Health Care System

As a result of the rapid increases in U.S. health care costs and growing concern over the large number of uninsured, many in the United States look at Canada's health system as a possible model for reform in this country. The widespread perception in the

United States is that Canada has successfully developed a comprehensive and universal national health insurance program that is cost-effective and highly popular.

Background

The Canadian system of financing and delivering health care is known as Medicare, not to be confused with the U.S. Medicare program for the elderly. In Canada, each of the 10 provinces and 3 territories administers a comprehensive and universal program that is partially supported by grants from the federal government. Various criteria established by the federal government with respect to coverage must be met. Coverage must be universal, comprehensive, and portable, meaning that individuals can transfer their coverage to other provinces as they migrate across the country. There are no financial barriers to access, and patients have free choice in the selection of providers.

Canada's Medicare should also be distinguished from Britain's NHS. Most Canadian physicians are in private practice and have hospital admitting privileges. They are reimbursed by the provinces on a fee-for-service basis under fee schedules negotiated by the provinces and physician organizations. Hospitals are also private institutions, although their budgets are approved and largely funded by the provinces.

The Canadian system originated in the 1930s when compulsory health insurance programs were introduced by some provinces.[4] The main impetus, however, came from the federal legislation adopted in 1957 that provided cost sharing for inpatient hospital services, and the Medical Care Act of 1966 that provided cost sharing for physician care. Since 1972, every province and territory has provided universal coverage for hospital and physician care.

The extraordinary U.S. interest in Canada's approach is attributable to the fact that Canada and the United States share a long border and similar heritage in terms of language, culture, and economic institutions. The health care systems evolved similarly until the 1960s. Even as recently as 1971, both countries spent approximately 7.5 percent of their GDPs on health care.

Since 1971, however, the health care systems have moved in different directions. While Canada has had publicly funded national health insurance, the United States has relied largely on private financing and delivery (although governments have been heavily involved through Medicare, Medicaid, and numerous regulatory programs). During this period, spending in the United States has grown much more rapidly despite large groups that are either uninsured or minimally insured.

The Canada Health Act of 1984 defines the criteria and conditions for the provinces and territories to satisfy in order to qualify for their full share of the federal transfers under the Canada Health Transfer (CHT) cash contribution.

1. **Public administration:** The administration of the health care insurance plan must be carried out on a nonprofit basis by a public authority;
2. **Comprehensiveness:** All medically necessary services provided by hospitals and doctors must be insured;
3. **Universality:** All insured persons must be entitled to public health insurance coverage on uniform terms and conditions;
4. **Portability:** Coverage for insured services must be maintained when an insured person moves or travels within Canada or travels outside the country; and

[4]There was considerable support for national health insurance in both the United States and Canada up to the late 1940s, with much of it coming from organized labor. Organized medicine in both countries strongly opposed the proposals, but the AMA in the United States was more successful than its Canadian counterpart in linking national health insurance to "socialized medicine" and preventing its adoption. Maioni (1995) provides further discussion of this fascinating history.

5. Accessibility: Reasonable access by insured persons to medically necessary hospital and physician services must be unimpeded by financial or other barriers.

Two key provisions of the Act guide Canada's Medicare:

1. No extra-billing by medical practitioners or dentists for insured health services under the terms of the health care insurance plan;
2. No user charges for insured health services by hospitals or other providers under the terms of the health care insurance plan.

The provinces and territories also provide coverage to certain groups of people (e.g., seniors, children, and social assistance recipients) for health services that are not generally covered under the publicly funded health care system. These supplementary health benefits often include prescription drugs, dental care, vision care, medical equipment and appliances (prostheses, wheelchairs, etc.), independent living, and the services of podiatrists and chiropractors. The level of coverage varies across the country. Many Canadians have supplemental private insurance coverage, through group plans, which covers the cost of these supplementary services.

Table 22-6 provides comparative data on the two countries. Canada is geographically larger than the United States but has only slightly more than one-tenth the U.S. population. Although a wealthy country, its GDP per capita is only about 79 percent of the U.S. level. With a national health system providing universal coverage, public funds

TABLE 22-6 Comparative Data—Canada and the United States

	Canada	*United States*
Population—2005 in millions	32.8	295.7
Population over 65 (2002, %)	12.7	12.3
GDP—2004 (billions of 2004 $US)	1,023	11,750
GDP per capita—2004 ($2004)	31,500	40,100
Public expenditures as % of GDP (2001)	41.7	34.9
Health spending per capita—2002	2,931	5,267
Health spending—2002 (% of GDP)	9.6	14.6
Percent of health spending (2002):		
Public expenditures	69.9	44.9
Inpatient care	28.8	27.6
Outpatient care	28.5	43.7
Pharmaceuticals	16.6	12.8
Acute care inpatient beds/1,000 population (2001)	3.2	2.9
Average length of stay in days (2001)	7.3	5.1
Uninsured population in percent	0.0	15.3
Out-of-pocket payments per capita ($US)—2002	445	737
Private insurance % expenditure on health—2002	12.7	36.2
Tobacco (% population)—2001	18.0	18.4
Alcohol consumption (liters/capita)—2001	7.8	8.3
Life expectancy (in years) at birth—females (2001)	82.2	79.8
Life expectancy (in years) at birth—males (2001)	77.1	74.4

Sources: GDP, Personal Income and Productivity Trends: Canada v. United States, www.cia.gov/cia/publications/factbook, accessed August 20, 2005; Health, *OECD Health Data 2004*, 3rd ed.

account for more than two-thirds of total health spending. Canada has maintained substantially lower health spending and share of GDP per capita than the United States, despite its higher bed-population ratio and longer lengths of stay.

Canada's physician-population ratio is 12 percent lower and its nurse staffing level 27 percent higher than the U.S. level (Table 22-2). In all, Americans spend 80 percent more per capita on health care ($5,267 versus $2,931), although about 15 percent of the U.S. population goes without insurance coverage at any time. Canadians drink a little less alcohol and smoke a little less than Americans. Despite lower spending, Table 22-6 shows that commonly compared health status indicators—such as life expectancy (about 2.4 years longer for women and 2.7 years longer for both men)—are more favorable in Canada than in the United States. Finally, public opinion polls indicate that Canadians support their system more than Americans support theirs and are concerned about any threats to it.

Given the Canadian record, health care scholars, policy makers, and politicians have shown great interest in determining the sources for its apparent success. In particular, health researchers have focused on the sources of the savings under the Canadian plan. One comparative study of spending per capita is especially revealing.

Physician Fees and Quantity

Fuchs and Hahn (1990) provide a detailed breakdown of Canadian and U.S. expenditures by specific services, while separating their price and quantity components. They also compare the U.S. state of Iowa with the Canadian province of Manitoba. Both jurisdictions have a few large cities and large rural areas with relatively homogeneous populations. The data have again been adjusted to reflect purchasing power parity. Fuchs and Hahn estimated that spending on health care per capita was 38 percent higher in the United States in 1985. More striking was the disparity in spending on physician services; it was 72 percent higher in the United States, and 178 percent higher for the procedures component. (The relative ratios of Iowa to Manitoba were slightly lower.)

Because spending is the product of prices and quantities, it seems logical to pursue differences in fees (prices) and utilization per capita (quantities). Overall, fees were 239 percent higher in the United States for 1985. Though there were variations in the ratios across service categories, U.S. fees were considerably higher in each category. The net incomes of U.S. doctors were also substantially higher than were their Canadian counterparts.

Perhaps more surprising than the fee differentials are estimates of the service volume. Despite the much higher spending per capita for physician care, the quantity of care per capita was considerably lower in the United States. Thus, the savings in Canada, at least for physician care, do not come from reduced volume of care.

Why Are Fees and Hospital Costs Lower in Canada?

Patients in Canada have longer lengths of stay, in part because of the greater use of Canadian hospitals for chronic long-term care. Nonetheless, after adjusting for differences in case mix between the two countries, Newhouse, Anderson, and Roos (1988) found that the cost per case-mix adjusted unit was roughly 50 percent higher in the United States. Several reasons can be proposed for this phenomenon.

In Canada, unlike the United States, physician fees result from negotiation between physicians' organizations and the provincial governments, as well as from other limits on total spending. Physicians cannot evade the fee controls by charging extra (sometimes called balance billing) to patients who can afford it.

Hospital costs are similarly regulated by the provinces through approval of hospital budgets. Hospitals and provinces negotiate operating budgets financed by the provincial governments. The capital budget may include other sources of funding, but provinces still must approve capital expenditures. Thus, a centralized mechanism allocates resources to the hospital sector and determines the distribution of resources among hospitals.

Occupancy rates are higher in Canadian hospitals. Also, the provinces have limited the capital costs associated with expensive new technologies.

Table 22-7 provides comparisons on several relatively recent and expensive technologies among Canada, the United States, the United Kingdom, and Germany, with some other OECD countries available for comparison. Analyses from the 1980s indicated that the United States has greater availability of many of the technologies, but data for 2002 suggest that other countries are catching up.

Administrative Costs

The centralized system of health care control in Canada has led to theories about the possible economies associated with administrative and other overhead expenses. Almost all patients in the United States are familiar with extensive paperwork and complex billing practices. For providers and third-party payers, the paperwork is more than an inconvenience; it involves major administrative expenses.

In a 2005 article, Woolhandler, Campbell, and Himmelstein (WCH) compared 1999 Canadian and United States administrative costs and calculated U.S. excess per capita administrative costs of $752, or $209 billion in aggregate. This implied that a single-payer, Canadian-style health system for the United States would save $0.71 cents out of every $1 of administrative costs.

Reexamining their data, Aaron (2005) argues that looking at per capita expenditures overstates the difference because it depends on arbitrary assumptions relating to currency values and wage rates. Aaron's preferred comparison observes that administrative costs in the United States accounted for about 31 percent of total health care spending compared to 16.7 percent in Canada. This 14.3 percentage point differential, if applied to the United States, would save 46.1% (i.e. 14.3 divided by 31) of U.S. administrative costs (compared to WCH's 71%), or $489 per capita. However, even this more conservative calculation points to excess spending of $159 billion per year!

A Comparison

The foregoing data suggest that the Canadian system is more effective than the U.S. system in several respects. Costs are lower, more services are provided, financial barriers do not exist, and health status as measured by mortality rates is superior. Canadians have longer life expectancies and lower infant mortality rates than do U.S. residents.

However, the comparisons do not tell the whole story, nor do they necessarily imply that the United States should adopt the Canadian approach. In particular, many Canadians are no longer confident that the provinces will be able to afford their current systems. As a result of unprecedented federal deficits in the 1990s, the Canadian government substantially reduced its cash transfers to the provinces. Despite considerable improvement in the federal government's fiscal health in recent years, resulting in larger transfers to the provinces, the provincial governments are faced with the following options to cope with their increased burdens: find new sources of tax revenue, impose more stringent fee and budgetary controls on health providers, find ways to increase efficiency in health care delivery, scale back on benefits by no longer insuring some previously covered services, and impose user fees.

TABLE 22-7 Availability of Selected Technologies, 2003

	MRI Units		CAT Scanners		Radiation Therapy		Lithotripsy		Hemodialysis		Mammographs	
	Number	Per Million	Number	Per Million	Number	Per Million	Number	Per Million	Number	Per Million	Number	Per Million
United States	2,342[b]	8.2	3,660[b]	12.8	1,155[b]	4.0	893[b]	3.1	1,138[b]	4.0	3,394[b]	11.9
Canada	147	4.2	326	9.7			13[b]	0.4	2,736[b]	87.9	600[b]	19.3
Germany	451[b]	5.5	1,096[b]	13.3	875[b]	10.6	268[c]	3.3				
United Kingdom	210	3.5	326	5.8	190	3.3			3,189[b]	53.8	472	8.0
Austria	110	13.4	221	27.3	36	4.5	19	1.6	715[c]	88.8		
Czech Rep.	22[c]	2.2	123[c]	12.1	94[c]	9.2	33[c]	3.2	1,268	124.3	135[c]	13.2
Finland			73	13.3	47	8.8	2	0.4			206	39.6
France	141[b]	2.4	531[b]	9.0	359[c]	6.0	47[c]	0.8	12,146[b]	205.2	2,524[c]	42.4
Hungary	25[c]	2.5	69[c]	6.8					898[b]	88.4	110[a]	10.8
Iceland	5	17.4	7	20.9	4	13.9	1	3.5			5	17.4
Italy	605[c]	10.4	1,336[c]	23.0	218[b]	3.8	1		1,736[b]	202.7		
Japan	4,501[c]	35.3	11,803[c]	92.6	837[c]	6.6	814[c]	6.4				
Korea	430	7.9	1,526	30.9	220	4.5	325	6.0	7,313	139.8	1,186	19.4
Luxembourg	5	4.5	12	24.7	3	4.5	1	2.4			10	22.4
New Zealand	15	3.8	46	11.2	29	8.1	2	0.5			90	25.1
Portugal	41	4.0	134	13.1	35	3.4	15	1.4	2,000	183.6	121	11.1
Spain	258[c]	6.2	535[c]	12.8	152[c]	3.6	73[c]	1.7				
Switzerland	103[c]	14.1	131[c]	18.0	77[c]	10.6	31[c]	4.3	38	5.2		

Sources: Copyright *OECD Health Data 2004*, 3rd ed.; [a]2000; [b]2001; [c]2002.

Similar to the shift we have seen for the United States, the provinces have forced large reductions in hospital capacity with a corresponding substitution of outpatient care for inpatient care. However, with the exception of Ontario, the movement toward regionalization or "devolution" is their most conspicuous reaction to the fiscal constraint imposed by the federal cutbacks. Regional boards with budgetary authority have replaced centralized provincial departments. The goals of this reorganization are similar to those expected from managed care: develop an efficient, coordinated, and accountable system for the regional population. Unlike the United States, however, this goal is to be accomplished by planning rather than through competition.

It is clear that Canada, like many other countries, faces difficult choices in finding a balance between quality and cost while maintaining the principles of its universal health care system. Canada has been able to limit spending and health care's share of GDP despite sluggish recent growth of its economy. To deal with the fiscal constraints, Canada is taking a different approach than one involving market reforms, and it is too early to evaluate its success. Additionally, there are serious economic considerations that we have not addressed.

Critics of the Canadian system charge that health care is rationed in the sense that all the care that patients demand, or would be provided to meet their best interests, cannot be supplied on a timely basis. As noted in the model on the British NHS, rationing below market price leaves some people, who would be willing to pay more, unable to purchase any of the good at all. Box 22-2 shows that until 2005, with the landmark *Chaoulli v. Quebec* lawsuit, and its finding in favor of the plaintiff, Canadian laws made it exceedingly difficult to buy rationed goods in the private market.

Though specific estimates of such shortages are not available, the consensus is that the limits on capacity and on new technology result in longer waiting periods for hospital services. The "safety valve" of a private system, as in the United Kingdom, for those who are willing to pay more is not readily available, although some Canadians (particularly those near large U.S. border cities such as Buffalo and Detroit) use the U.S. facilities for this purpose.

Defenders of the U.S. approach claim that the waiting and queues found in Canada would be unacceptable to many U.S. patients. There is a greater level of amenities in the United States, and the greater availability of specialized care, together with high-tech medicine, often is viewed as an indicator of superior quality.

Furthermore, some analysts believe that the difference in health care spending between the two countries is not nearly as great as it appears. Krasny and Ferrier (1991) suggest that the following three factors represent much of the gap:

1. The failure to account for capital costs in Canadian hospitals
2. The larger proportion of elderly in the United States
3. The higher level of spending on research and development in the United States

Different Systems: The Public's Evaluation

Decisions about health care systems ultimately reflect the attitudes of the public with regard to satisfaction, cost of care, and quality of care. Schoen and colleagues (2005) surveyed citizens of Australia, Canada, Germany, New Zealand, the United Kingdom, and the United States who had had recent experience with their countries' health care systems, regarding general satisfaction, access to care, cost of care, and quality of care. Recall Gordon's typology and note that Germany has traditional sickness insurance; Canada national health insurance; New Zealand and the United Kingdom, national health services; and Australia and the United States, mixed systems. Comparative

BOX 22-2

Chaoulli v. Quebec: The Future of Private Health Insurance in Canada

Georges Zeliotis, a 70-year old salesman and a resident of the province of Quebec, had suffered from several health conditions requiring that he undergo medical treatment, including heart surgery, and several hip operations. He was placed on a hospital waiting list in Montreal for hip surgery for nearly a year before he was able to receive his treatment. While on the waiting list, Zeliotis sought to determine if he could pay to obtain hip surgery through a private health care facility. He also wanted to purchase private health care insurance in the event that he should require similar treatment in the future, but both obtaining hip surgery by means of a private facility and purchasing private health care insurance were prohibited by Quebec law.

Jacques Chaoulli, a physician in Quebec, has provided medical services to many of his patients at their homes. Chaoulli appealed to the government of Quebec to cover the costs of the home medical treatment offered to his patients, and requested that the province grant him the right to establish a private and autonomous hospital. The province denied both of Chaoulli's requests.

Zeliotis and Chaoulli challenged specific sections of Quebec's laws. They challenged Article 15 of Quebec's Health Insurance Act, which prohibited private insurance for services covered by the government's insurance plan. Article 15 did not, however, prohibit private insurance completely. It only prohibited private insurance for medical treatments, such as basic medical services and surgeries that were already insured under the government's public insurance plan. Accordingly, for basic medical treatment, patients could only purchase government insurance. For all other health services, they could choose from different private insurance plans, or no insurance at all.

They also challenged Article 11, which prohibited private contracting for medical services in hospitals by physicians who were nonparticipants in the government insurance plan. Whereas the first law concerned patients and how they could pay for medical services, Article 11 concerned

doctors and how they could charge for medical services. It prohibited those doctors who chose not to participate in the government's public insurance plan from setting up private hospitals and then charging directly for their medical services.

Zeliotis and Chaoulli believed that patients should be free to purchase private health insurance or to receive medical services through private health providers, should they choose, but the matter of private versus public delivery of health care services constituted only one issue. The second issue focused on whether it was appropriate for governments to prohibit private medicine when many patients face long delays for medical treatment in the public health system.

In June 2005, after a lengthy court battle, the Canada's Supreme Court ruled:

> The evidence in this case shows that delays in the public health care system are widespread, and that, in some serious cases, patients die as a result of waiting lists for public health care. The evidence also demonstrates that the prohibition against private health insurance and its consequence of denying people vital health care result in physical and psychological suffering that meets a threshold test of seriousness.
>
> Where lack of timely health care can result in death . . . where it can result in serious psychological and physical suffering, the . . . protection of security of the person is triggered. In this case, the government has prohibited private health insurance that would permit ordinary Quebeckers to access private health care while failing to deliver health care in a reasonable manner, thereby increasing the risk of complications and death. In so doing, it has interfered with the interests protected by . . . the Canadian Charter.
>
> *Section 11 HOIA and s. 15 HEIA are arbitrary, and the consequent deprivation of the interests protected by s. 7 [of the Canadian Charter] is therefore not in accordance with the principles of fundamental justice (italics added).*

The Court found that restricting access to private medical services was illegal vis-à-vis the significance of waiting lists for treatment under Quebec's public health system. It set off fierce debate about the future of health care in Canada.

SOURCES: www.mapleleafweb.com/features/medicare/charter-health-care/background-chaoulli.html, accessed August 14, 2005; Supreme Court of Canada, Citation: *Chaoulli v. Quebec (Attorney General)*, 2005 SCC 35 Date: 20050609, Docket: 29272.

TABLE 22-8 Health System Views and Experiences Among Sicker Adults in Six Countries, 2005

	Australia	*Canada*	*New Zealand*	*United Kingdom*	*United States*	*Germany*
Unweighted Sample Size	702	751	704	1,770	1,527	1,503
Overall System View (in %)						
Only minor changes needed	23	21	27	30	23	16
Fundamental change needed	48	61	52	52	44	54
System needs to be completely rebuilt	26	17	20	14	30	31

Source: Cathy Schoen et al., "Taking the Pulse of Health Care Systems: Experiences of Patients with Health Problems in Six Countries," *Health Affairs Web Exclusive*, November 3, 2005, W509–525, Exhibit 7. Reprinted by permission of The People-to-People Health Foundation.

studies are fraught with methodological problems, and this study takes special care to use similar methods and questionnaires across the six countries.

Table 22-8 compares attitudes. When asked to rate their country's care system overall, the majority of sicker adults (66 to 85 percent) in all countries saw room for improvement. Sicker adults in Germany and the United States were most negative, and those in the United Kingdom and Canada least negative.

With respect to quality of care and access to care, the study team asked several questions relating to:

- Waiting time for specialist appointments or for elective surgery
- Cost-related reasons for:

 Not filling a prescription
 Not visiting a doctor when ill
 Not getting a recommended test, treatment, or follow-up care
 Out-of-pocket expenses for medical bills

Table 22-9 presents several of these "quality of care" measures. German and U.S. patients reported similar rapid access, with other countries lagging behind as they have in past surveys. Those surveyed in the United States reported considerably higher financial burdens on patients and in forgoing care because of costs. Half of the sicker adults in the United States said that they had had some access problems in the previous two years because of cost. Moreover the percentage of U.S. sicker adults forgoing care was much higher on all three indicators compared with a comparable 2002 study by Blendon and colleagues (Blendon 2003). One-third of U.S. patients spent more than $1,000 out-of-pocket in the past year, a much higher percentage than any other country, and U.S. patients were also the most likely to pay $100 or more each month for medications.

Differences in Health Care Spending Across Countries

We have noted that different countries have different incentive systems, and, in fact, have differing shares of national product in the health care sector. Having described the systems, and having examined briefly the shares of national product in the health sector, it is appropriate now to explore why the shares differ.

TABLE 22-9 Access, Waiting Times, and Costs Among Sicker Adults in Six Countries, 2005

	Australia	*Canada*	*New Zealand*	*United Kingdom*	*United States*	*Germany*
Wait for Specialist Appointment	552	592	552	1,207	1,179	1,181
Among Those Needing to See a Specialist						
Less than 1 week (%)	11	10	17	11	20	27
More than 4 weeks	46	57	40	60	23	22
Wait for Elective Surgery	179	165	181	231	352	235
Less than 1 month (%)	48	15	32	25	53	59
4 months or more	19	33	20	41	8	6
Access Problems Because of Cost in Past 2 Years (%)						
Did not fill prescription	22	20	19	8	40	14
Did not visit doctor when sick	18	7	29	4	34	15
Did not get recommended test or follow-up	20	12	21	5	33	14
Any access problems due to cost	34	26	38	13	51	28
Out-of-Pocket Expenses in Last 2 Years						
None	10	22	9	65	15	5
More than $1,000	14	14	8	4	34	8

Source: Cathy Schoen et al., "Taking the Pulse of Health Care Systems: Experiences of Patients with Health Problems in Six Countries," *Health Affairs Web Exclusive*, November 3, 2005, W509–525, Exhibit 6. Reprinted by permission of The People-to-People Health Foundation.

A Simple Model of Health Expenditures Shares

Consider a model of health expenditures. Let us call total expenditures on health care E. By definition, these expenditures equal the price of health care multiplied by the quantity of health care consumed, or $E = PQ$. Defining the share of national income spent on health care as s, we calculate s as the ratio of E to national income, Y, or:

$$s = PQ/Y \tag{22.1}$$

The share, s, can increase because either the price or quantity has increased, or because the national income has decreased. In fact, mathematically it can be shown that:

$$(\% \text{ Change } s) = (\% \text{ Change } P) + (\% \text{ Change } Q) - (\% \text{ Change } Y) \tag{22.2}$$

The preceding expression is an identity, mathematically true by definition. Even so, it can provide useful insights. If the price of health care, P, increases by the same rate as the price of all other goods, so that Y increases at that same rate, then the health care share of national income does not change.

Applying the Model

Rather than looking just at the percentage changes that occur, we try to examine why they occur. Consider, for example, that prices of health care may be related to the kind of health system the country has or to the social insurance scheme. Also consider that

the quantity of health care used, Q, tends to increase when national income, Y, increases. Note also that the quantity of health care, Q, tends to be negatively related to the price of health care, P, through the demand relationship.

Consider several ideas, in turn:

1. An increase in the price of health care would increase the share if there were no consumer response. The extent to which consumers reduce quantity demanded (in response to price changes) will offset the increase in prices.
2. An increase in the number of people in the population who use health care would tend to increase health care expenditures.
3. An increase in national income, Y, that is unaccompanied by an increase in demand for health care would decrease the share. However, this effect would be offset to the degree that increased national income leads to increased demand; the effect depends on the income elasticity of demand. If, in fact, a 1 percent increase in national income leads to a 1 percent increase in expenditures (that is, the income elasticity at the national level is +1.0), then the share will be constant.

It is important to examine the differences among countries with respect to payment mechanism. Economists often implicitly view expenditures in the context of perfectly competitive markets. If this is valid, as noted in Figure 22-3a, then total health expenditures (the numerator of fraction of GDP going to health care, indicated by the box with bold outlines) accurately reflects the resource costs P^* of health care at the margin. Anderson and colleagues (2003), however, note that the markets for the health workforce (especially physicians) are still largely national and even local within countries. Moreover, many markets related to health care within localities do not satisfy the rigorous conditions of the textbook model of competition.

We find varying degrees of monopoly power on the "sell" side of the market and varying degrees of monopsony power on the "buy" side. Because monopolists (Figure 22-3b) equate marginal costs to marginal revenues, they are able to raise prices above those they would obtain in perfectly competitive markets, thus, earning "rents," defined as the excess of the prices actually received by sellers above the minimum prices the sellers would have to be paid to sell into the market. Figure 22-3b shows that the

FIGURE 22-3 Health Expenditures by Market Structure

A. Competitive B. Monopolistic C. Monopsonistic

resource costs (the box defined by the supply curve) are considerably less than the total expenditures (the sum of the resource costs and the monopoly rents), with the difference going as rents to providers. Q_b is also less than Q^*, under competitive markets.

Countries differ in the degree to which they try to whittle away at the rent earned on the supply side through the creation of market power on the buy (monopsony) side of the market. A single-payer system would be called a "pure monopsony." Because a pure monopsonist (Figure 22-3c) must pay increased resource costs to all supply factors, the monopsonist faces a market marginal cost curve, not unlike the monopolist's marginal revenue curve. Here, the producer provides quantity Q_c, but expenditures are much smaller than in Figure 22-3b.

Note again that in each case, the quantity of services provided falls short of the optimum Q^*. Quantities Q_b and Q_c are intentionally drawn to be identical, but in the monopolistic case, extra resources are transferred from the buyers to the sellers.

In the United States, the huge federal Medicare program and the federal-state Medicaid programs do possess some monopsonistic purchasing power, and large private insurers may enjoy some degree of monopsony power in some localities, but the highly fragmented buy side of the U.S. health system is relatively weak by international standards. This is one factor, among others, that might explain the relatively high prices paid for health care and for health professionals in the United States.

In comparison, the government-controlled health systems of Canada, Europe, and Japan allocate considerably more market power to the buy side. In each of the Canadian provinces, for example, the health insurance plans operated by the provincial governments constitute pure monopsonies: They purchase (pay for) all of the health services that are covered by the provincial health plan and used by the province's residents. While even pure monopsonists are ultimately constrained by market forces on the supply side—that is, by the minimally acceptable prices of the providers of health care below which they will not supply their goods or services, monopsonistic buyers enjoy enough market clout to drive down the prices paid for health care and health care inputs fairly close to those reservation prices.

For the United States, most measures of aggregate utilization, such as physician visits per capita and hospital days per capita, typically lag below the medians of other Western countries. Since spending is a product of both the goods and services used and their prices, this implies that much higher prices are paid in the United States than in other countries. But U.S. policy makers need to reflect on what Americans are getting for their greater health spending. The authors conclude that the answer lies in the higher prices paid by U.S. health consumers.

In a follow-up analysis, Anderson and colleagues (2005) revisit the high level of U.S. health expenditures, examining two commonly proposed explanations: (1) that other countries have constrained the supply of health care resources, particularly for elective services, which has led to waiting lists and lower spending; (2) the threat of malpractice litigation and the resulting defensive medicine in the United States adds to malpractice premiums and, more importantly, the practice of defensive medicine, hence increasing costs.

If, in fact, consumers in other countries must wait for procedures that U.S. consumers can get immediately, then the international consumers are bearing waiting time costs that do not enter national accounts. The researchers argue however, that the procedures for which waiting lists exist in some countries represent a small part of total health spending. Using U.S. survey data, they calculated the amount of U.S. health spending accounted for by the 15 procedures that account for most of the waiting lists in Australia, Canada, and the United Kingdom. Total spending for these procedures in 2001 was $21.9 billion, or only 3 percent of U.S. health spending in that year.

For the impacts of malpractice litigation, the authors examined data on numbers of malpractice claims against physicians and the awards resulting from those claims in the United States, Canada, Australia, and the United Kingdom. All four countries manage malpractice claims through a British-style tort system. The evidence that such litigation differentially affects the United States was modest. In all four countries, malpractice litigation costs for claims against physicians were small ($16 per person in the United States, $4 in Canada, $12 in the United Kingdom, and $10 in Australia) compared with total health spending. Increased use of services because of defensive medicine probably contributed more to health spending than the actual costs of litigation, but it was difficult to establish how much care was attributable to defensive medicine in the United States or elsewhere.

National Health Insurance

Return now to the question of broader social insurance for health care. We have noted that the United States has no comprehensive social insurance program for health care. Should the United States adopt national health insurance? It would seem that this issue is dead with the demise of the 1993–1994 Clinton plan. Nevertheless, health system reform is still on the agenda in the United States and many other countries. It is wise to be acquainted with the possible features of such plans.

Different Kinds of National Health Insurance (NHI) Plans

An NHI plan should possess several desirable aspects. It should:

- provide a health "safety net" for all residents, irrespective of age or employment status.
- provide choice for providers and patients.
- provide market incentives for cost containment.
- be relatively easy to administer.

There is considerable room for controversy even within this list of presumably noncontroversial goals. To illustrate, the *Journal of the American Medical Association* (May 1991) asked health care experts to formulate plans for health insurance reform. More than 80 proposals were submitted, and after rigorous review, the journal published 13 of them. During the 1993–1994 national debate on health reform, at least as many plans and versions of plans came before Congress.

Particular bills at particular times will vary considerably, especially when one considers the options across countries. Several features of the bills considered by Congress in 1993–1994 address questions posed by most reform efforts. Policy makers faced a dilemma as to whether to fund NHI coverage by individual mandate, employer-employee mandate, or general revenues. An individual mandate is a law that requires individuals to buy health insurance for themselves, with subsidies for those who can't afford it. The subsidies usually would be funded out of general revenues. The employer-employee mandates would require taxes on wages for the employee's share. The employer's share may fall on the employee in the form of lower wages. Subsidies out of general revenues would provide for the unemployed.

People advocating a Canadian-style system seek a single-payer system with government revenues providing all of the NHI. A final alternative is the medical savings accounts method of payment that would allow people to set up a tax-free savings account out of which they can pay the out-of-pocket costs of their health care. Usually, these systems entail health insurance with high deductibles and coinsurance.

BOX 22-3

American Attitudes Toward Health Care Issues

In Spring 2002, National Public Radio, the Kaiser Family Foundation, and the Kennedy School at Harvard University surveyed over 1,200 respondents on attitudes toward health care. The survey reported that the vast majority of people in the top income categories have very few problems getting health care or paying for it. On the bottom, however, many are burdened by such problems, and when they are, the problems may be serious. When asked to name the two most important health care issues for the government to address, access to health care and insurance issues (54 percent) received the most mention. The accompanying chart indicates responses to several alternatives.

Survey authors note that although this survey did not ask respondents to choose among the various options, other surveys have consistently shown that a majority of the American public favors no single option. They conjecture that this fact, combined with the cost and winners and losers involved in any proposal, helps explain why consensus is often hard to reach in expanding health coverage.

A national health plan, financed by taxpayers, in which all Americans would get their insurance from a single government plan	40%
Offering uninsured Americans income tax deductions, tax credits or other financial assistance to help them purchase private health insurance on their own	73%
Requiring businesses to offer private health insurance for their employees	76%
Expanding neighborhood health clinics	80%
Expanding state government programs for low-income people, such as Medicaid and the Children's Health Insurance Program, to provide coverage for people without health insurance	84%

SOURCE: www.npr.org/news/specials/healthcarepoll/healthgraphs.pdf, Chart 19, accessed August 6, 2002.

Some plans would define a minimum acceptable level of insurance, with people allowed to purchase more extensive coverage if desired and if they can afford it. Others would define one plan to fit all. At the beginning of the debates, many plans featured universal coverage. As support for universal coverage waned in Congress, more plans offered lesser goals for reaching the population. Box 22-3 examines Americans' attitudes from a 2002 survey.

The Costs of NHI

National health insurance programs certainly cost a great deal of money, but it is important to distinguish which costs are incremental. In other words, what are the additional costs to society from the imposition of NHI?

From society's point of view, the incremental cost of NHI in the United States is the extra total expenditure on health care that would be incurred if we switched to national health insurance. Inasmuch as most people already are insured for almost all hospital care and most physician care, the extra cost of NHI would be much smaller than many people expect.

The truly incremental costs stem from several sources. First, the major reason for switching to an NHI plan is to extend coverage to the 45 million uninsured. It should be understood that the uninsured already consume health care. Zero insurance does not necessarily mean zero care.

Using data from surveys of individuals, providers, and government programs, Hadley and Holahan (2003a) estimated that uninsured Americans received $35 billion

worth of uncompensated health care in 2001. Governments picked up $30.6 billion of the cost, while physicians' and hospitals' forgone time, profits, and philanthropy were responsible for between $7.5 to $9.8 billion worth of care for uninsured Americans.

Hadley and Holahan (2003b) then projected that it would cost between $33.9 billion and $68.7 billion to cover the uninsured. The lower cost would be under a government program, which would likely pay providers less, while the higher cost assumes the uninsured are enrolled in private-sector insurance plans that pay providers more. Increases in medical spending of this range would increase total health care spending by 3 to 6 percent and would raise health care's share of GDP by less than one percentage point.

Second, the insured population will incur some incremental cost to the extent that an NHI plan provides greater typical coverage than people already choose to buy or have provided to them by other sources. Third, any tax-supported system of financing care necessarily entails a deadweight loss to society. This is true even if the program is of the employer-mandated type because a law forcing employers to incur expense is really a tax. The deadweight losses that accompany taxes mean that some efficiency loss will result, caused by the disincentives to work and invest.

These sources of incremental costs to society are probably the most significant. In one sense, the incremental costs are the real costs to society, whereas differences in financing methods are not as economically meaningful. It may be politically more palatable to choose a plan that does not greatly expand the government budget; employment-mandated plans may be attractive politically for this reason. Nonetheless, society incurs the cost irrespective of whether it is financed through the government or mandated to employers by law.

Ensuring Access to Care

In this section, we group reforms by their two main motivations: the desire to see that people who are sick get health care and the desire to control the rising cost of health care.

Employer Versus Individual Mandates

The country that wishes to provide universal coverage for health care must choose one scheme or another to extract tax payments from its households. Schemes for employers or government to pay the bills are only mechanisms by which households ultimately pay. In the U.S. debate, two mechanisms have been featured and contrasted prominently in proposals: employer versus individual mandates.

Employer mandates form the backbone of the health systems in Europe, Latin America, and Asia (Krueger and Reinhardt, 1994). Under the employer mandate, the employer must procure health insurance for its employees and their dependents. Although the employer writes the check, the firm undoubtedly will pass on as much of this cost as it can to customers in the form of higher prices or to employees in the form of lower wages. Under the individual mandate, workers are obligated to purchase health insurance for themselves and their families, either from private insurance (individually purchased) or through a group, such as a work group, professional organization, or religious group. The poor are subsidized in their purchases through government taxation of the relatively well-to-do.

In Chapter 11, we showed that a lower market money wage rate leads an employer to hire more workers. Assuming at the outset that there are no benefits, and that the market wage is $20 per hour, employers will hire workers as long as the marginal

revenue from the goods those workers produce exceeds the $20 per hour wage. To begin, assume that the employer hires 1,000 workers.

If a health benefit is mandated that is worth $1 per hour, and costs exactly $1 for the employer to provide, employers who were previously willing to pay $20 will now pay $20 less the $1 cost to provide the mandated benefit. Other points on the demand schedule will also change by the $1 cost of the benefit.

Workers previously willing to accept a wage of $20 will now be willing to supply their labor for $1 less since they value the mandated benefit at $1. The net wage (money wage + the value of the benefit) remains unchanged at $20, but the equilibrium money wage falls to $19, or by exactly the amount of the benefit. Workers accept lower money wages, and the same 1,000 workers are employed at the same net wage, $19 in money wages plus the $1 benefit. The workers are no worse off at a wage of $19 with the mandated benefit than at $20 without the mandated benefit because the benefit is worth the $1 that it cost in reduced wages.

Business leaders often complain that employer mandates either will reduce profits or force firms out of business (see Box 22-4). Such responses often seem to be made, however, under the assumption that only the one firm is affected by the mandate. If all firms were made to bear the same labor costs, it is doubtful that closings would result. In the short run, firms would pay workers less, take less in profits, and raise prices to consumers. "Economists are convinced, however, that in the longer run more and more of the cost of the employer mandate would likely be shifted backward to employees . . . through smaller real (inflation-adjusted) increases in wages than would have been warranted by long-run productivity gain" (Krueger and Reinhardt, 1994, p. 44).

BOX 22-4

Curbing Health Care Costs Key to Michigan's Growth! Or Is It?

This editorial appeared on June 9, 2002, in the *Detroit News*. Students may note how little the arguments have changed since then!

Health insurance costs rose 15 percent last year in Michigan and are expected to climb by even more this year. Michigan employers who provide health insurance for workers are begging for relief as soaring premiums eat into profits. They warn that if insurance costs continue to rise unchecked, *they'll have to cut off benefits and won't be able to make crucial investments in their businesses* [emphasis added].

The *News* argued that the main reason why rising insurance costs had not cost Michigan employees their medical benefits was the strong presence of organized labor. Unions locked the Big Three automakers and other unionized industries into long-term contracts that prevent them from reducing these benefits. The union presence,

they argued, forced even nonunionized companies to maintain union-level benefits to compete for workers. The *News* concluded that generous and secure health care coverage had helped make Michigan an expensive place in which to do business, and that it had cost Michigan job growth.

Is this logic valid? Who pays the costs? And do the costs represent worker preferences? Economists would disagree with the newspaper's "conventional wisdom."

Do the high health insurance benefits cost Michigan's residents jobs or impede economic growth? Montagne (2002) notes that unions generally seek richer benefit packages than would otherwise be negotiated. Rather than increasing employer costs, economists would argue that these benefits simply represent a different way that Michigan residents have chosen to take their wages.

SOURCE: www.detroitnews.com/2002/editorial/0206/10/a14-509813.htm, accessed June 10, 2002.

If the labor supply curve is very unresponsive to the wage rate, or inelastic, the employer's extra health benefit costs are offset by lower wage expenditures regardless of whether the laborers value the benefit highly or not at all. Most economists who study the issue probably would agree that the aggregate labor supply, at least in the long run, is nearly vertical for men and also highly inelastic for women. In this scenario, the mandate has little effect on producers, their competitive position, or their customers. Whether the program helps or harms the well-being of society under conventional economic analysis depends to a large extent simply on whether workers value their health insurance as much as or more than they did their foregone wages.

On appearances, the individual mandate provides the same result with a clearer pathway. The cost falls on the one to whom it is assessed. Pauly (1994b, 1997) describes an individual mandate, enforced by employers and subsidized for the poor, requiring all individuals to purchase a minimum health plan or better. He argues that this approach is desirable so that people can relate their taxes to what they are paying to obtain benefits.

During the U.S. debate of 1993–1994, disputes arose frequently over the fraction that the employer pays versus the fraction paid by the individual. The presumption in these arguments is that the chosen fraction reflects the burden. Economists, however, tend to agree that the fraction chosen does not matter. Some argue that it is a political necessity to overlook the economics, yet others insist that an open public discussion of the genuine issues would improve the quality of national debate.

Separation of Health Insurance from Employment

In redesigning a health system, a good argument can be made for revising or replacing the prevailing system of employer-provided insurance. Change can be accomplished by either a single-payer system or an individual mandate. The benefits of employer provision are partly the result of a deception, which may be well meant but causes economic distortions.

During World War II, the U.S. government froze prices and wages. Competing for workers, firms expanded their fringe benefits, which were not subject to the freeze. In postwar years, employer contributions to health insurance were and continue to be tax exempt, providing workers with a substantial discount and inviting inefficiencies of overinsurance. Meanwhile, many of the unemployed, as well as many low-wage employed, go without health insurance.

Health insurance problems also occur when workers change jobs. When leaving their old company's health coverage behind them, workers have little choice but to buy an individual policy or do without insurance entirely. Individual policies are often more expensive, sometimes pose administrative problems, and sometimes are a lower financial priority for people out of work. Workers have often found preexisting conditions to be uninsurable.

To deal with these and other distortions, some economists recommend radical changes in the tax system to remove the tax subsidy that effectively ties health insurance to the workplace. Fuchs (1994, p. 11) argues: "... that if government imposes enough mandates, enough subsidies, enough surcharges, and enough controls and regulations, the tie to employment can be severed. However, such a complex system invites evasion, gaming, and litigation." At that time, Fuchs recommended a value-added tax to finance universal coverage of health insurance. It is not without controversy, but it does suggest an alternative system in which health insurance is not tied to the job.

Single Payer Versus Multiple Insurers

A move in the United States toward universal coverage also entails the option of a single insurer, presumably the federal government. The option of multiple insurers retains part of the status quo in the United States, where many private insurance companies

provide the majority of insurance, with government providing about 40 percent. The most prominent single-payer proposal discussed in the U.S. debates has been the Canadian Medicare system.

In principle, costs can be reduced by consolidating insurers if there are economies of scale in administration or if gains can be made from pooling those insured. Assuming that administrative savings can be achieved by switching to a government single-payer system is somewhat risky, however. The same administrative technology is available to the private sector, and if further economies were possible, it is likely that surviving private firms would be those who merged to take advantage of the economies, provided the existing firms were not earning monopoly profits. In addition, the profits that private insurers gain are not a waste to the economy, but rather are a payment for capital that government also must incur.

In an example of the theory, the single-payer system reduces costs by eliminating the multiple forms and policy rules that face hospitals, clinics, and nursing homes. With hundreds of different health insurers, the difficulty of coordinating many different policies falls on hospitals and physicians; it is external to the insurance company. Nevertheless, it is a real economic cost to society, and it could be reduced if the government as single payer offers fewer forms and some standardization. These are costs that increase with decentralization.

The operation of the government enterprise also raises issues of incentives. Government may fail to reduce costs because government, in most cases, lacks the profit incentive and the discipline of market competition.

In any case, the switch to a single-payer system would largely eliminate the health insurance industry. Do the problems of the health care system warrant this type of change? More modest reforms may address specific problems. For example, the problem of the uninsured can be addressed by mandated coverage including subsidies for the poor. The problem of providing coverage for people with preexisting conditions can be solved through the individual mandates and, without using mandates, was addressed by recent "continuation of benefits" or COBRA legislation.

A potential benefit of the single-payer system lies with the possibility of common coverage. We may worry now that some insured people have inadequate policies in terms of the depth and breadth of coverage. In contrast, the single payer could offer one policy or just a few, regulated so that each one is deemed adequate by policy makers representing the public. In contrast, the availability of many policies from many companies offers variety, tailoring policies to the individual preferences for cost-sharing features and coverage.

Would employer-based universal health insurance make the United States uncompetitive internationally? Industry executives often respond as did Red Polling, then chairman of Ford Motor at a 1992 staff meeting of President-elect Clinton:

> . . . health care costs give Japanese automakers an advantage over Ford of $500 per car. Ford spends as much on health care as it does on steel. Health care providers are our biggest suppliers. (Pauly, 1997, p. 28)

Economists point out two features of employer-based universal health insurance that contradict such analyses: (1) health insurance is part of the total labor compensation package, and (2) the incidence of the implied tax falls primarily on the worker. The workers demand health insurance as well as money as part of their compensation. When they bargain for it, their bargaining indicates that they feel buying health insurance as a tax-preferred fringe benefit is worth the inevitable reduction in wages. Understood as such, the workers' purchase of health insurance through the employer is just a different way of purchasing a consumption good. It is essentially the same, in

this respect, as the purchase of food or housing with wages. Yet industry executives rarely complain that the high U.S. cost of food or housing makes them uncompetitive internationally, nor do they claim conversely that the high cost of housing in Japan gives Ford a big advantage in exporting cars to that country.

Health Care Reform and International Competitiveness

When health insurance costs increase or employer-based universal coverage is mandated, the adjustments will come to wages, profits, or prices (e.g., cars). The degree to which it falls on reduced wages in theory depends on the elasticities of the labor supply and demand. We will discuss that side shortly, but first suppose that it fell entirely on the employer. To consider the ability of the firm to pass along this cost to the buyer, panels A and B of Figure 22-4 depict the demand, marginal revenue, and marginal cost curves for the firm under the alternative assumptions that A, it has some monopoly power, and B, it faces considerable competition.

In panel A, the demand curve is downward sloping and the marginal revenue curve lies below the demand curve. If health costs cause the firm's wage bill to increase, this will affect the marginal cost of producing cars, shifting curve MC upward to MC'. In response, the equilibrium price will increase from P_0 to P_1. In this sense, part of the increase in marginal costs has been passed on to the consumer. However, suppose that the firm faces substantial competition from other U.S. car companies and from abroad so that its demand curve is flatter. The more elastic demand curve implies that the firm will lose substantial business if it raises its price. In this case, the demand curve and marginal revenue are close together. The limiting case in Panel B shows them to be identical. Now note that as marginal cost increases, the price of cars does not increase. The equilibria to compare are points K and L.

These analyses indicate that the ability of the firm to pass its health costs on to the consumer depends on its elasticity of demand. If the increased car price includes hundreds of dollars of increased health costs, it is only because the firm had the power to pass these increased costs on to the consumers. The more vulnerable our firms are to competition, the less ability they have to pass extra costs along to consumers. If not consumers, then who pays for them?

FIGURE 22-4 The Effect of a Rise in Marginal Cost on the Price of Cars

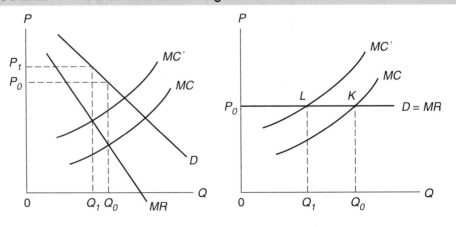

A. Some monopoly power B. Under perfect competition

As we discussed earlier in this chapter, to the extent to which the laborers value a health insurance fringe benefit (at its cost in this case), the labor supply shifts downward, with the entire cost of the benefit falling on the laborers. If the supply curve is nearly vertical, as is likely in the aggregate, then the incidence will inevitably and entirely fall on the workers. The general implication of the analysis is that health insurance costs or employer-mandated health benefits become a national tax borne by workers, which will have little effect on the competitiveness of our products internationally.

Conclusions

In this chapter, we have examined a variety of health care systems found elsewhere. Variations exist in terms of financing, provider payment mechanisms, and the role of government, including the degree of centralization. The United States stands out as the country with the highest expenditures on health care.

Systems that ration their care by government provision or government insurance incur lower per-capita costs. On the other hand, in the largely private U.S. system, waiting times tend to be shorter than in rationed systems, a conclusion that follows from theory as well as from observation. Americans have been more dissatisfied with their health system than Canadians or Europeans have been with theirs. The study of comparative systems suggests several features of other systems that may be worth adopting. It also suggests that cultural differences among countries may dictate that systems tailored to the local culture be different even in the long run.

Health reforms can be grouped into two broad categories: assuring access to health care and controlling health care costs. European systems generally provide universal, employer-based coverage. Reform in the United States has considered mandates to increase access, and we have examined the theory behind mandates.

We also found that the incidence of health premiums under employer-based systems does not depend on the fraction paid by the employer. This implies that much of the national debate on this issue has been focused on issues that most economists think irrelevant. Single-payer plans, such as that in Canada, offer theoretical economies of administration, but in practice it is more difficult to identify whether the observed cost advantages in Canada are likely to survive the translation into a reformed U.S. system. Because the incidence of the implied tax under a U.S. employer-based social insurance system is likely to fall largely on the worker, the reform has little or no theoretical effect on the economy's competitiveness and is no different from the individual mandate in this respect.

Countries have sought to control costs in a variety of ways. Strategies include a global budget, increased cost sharing, and various market incentives. The United States has fundamentally left cost containment to managed care. Although managed care achieves cost savings and may have contributed to the decline in the U.S. health cost growth rate, its potential will be limited to the extent that employers fail to offer true financial advantages to consumers who choose the low-cost health plans. American-style HMOs, the classic example of managed care, probably will not transfer unchanged to other countries because of cultural and system structure differences. In short, economics can evaluate what it will cost to extend health insurance universally, but only a national consensus can determine whether it should be done.

SUMMARY

1. A useful typology of health benefit systems provides four categories:
 - Traditional sickness insurance: the private insurance market approach, with state subsidy
 - National health insurance: the state establishes a national-level health insurance system

- National health service: the state provides the health care
- Mixed system: mixed elements of the previous

2. Among all countries, the United States is by far the biggest spender in absolute per-capita terms. It is also the biggest spender as a share of GDP.

3. The United Kingdom's NHS provides relatively easy access to primary and emergency care, while elective services are rationed either through long waiting lists or by limiting the availability of new technologies. The NHS devotes considerable resources to high return services, such as prenatal and infant care.

4. The United Kingdom reformed its health system in 1991 to include elements of competition. The United States has fewer hospital beds per capita than the United Kingdom and fewer nurses per bed as well. Health care spending per capita in the United Kingdom, however, is only 41 percent of the U.S. level.

5. Germany manages to provide a health system that delivers universal health insurance while avoiding the queues that often trouble governmental systems. However, costs per capita have been increasing faster than the incomes per capita, a problem leading to a series of reforms, most recently in 2004.

6. Compared to the U.S. system, the Canadian system has lower costs, more services, universal access to health care without financial barriers, and superior health status. Canadians have longer life expectancies and lower infant mortality rates than do U.S. residents.

7. Canada's single-payer system appears to have substantially lower administrative cost burden than the United States. Some of the general cost differences between the two countries may be overstated due to failure to account for Canadian hospitals' capital costs, and higher levels of spending on research and development in the United States.

8. National health systems appear to reduce health spending. However, careful analysis across alternative systems must impute the additional time costs, as well as differential quality of care in NHS systems, before deciding conclusively on the full costs of alternative systems.

9. National health insurance (NHI) proposals include compulsory private insurance programs through employers and tax credits for the purchase of private insurance, as well as proposals for an all-government system.

10. From society's viewpoint, the cost of NHI is the incremental cost of additional health care purchased by people due to improved insurance coverage. Savings from successful cost controls may offset these costs.

11. Switching from the current U.S. health system to a single-payer system may save money by saving administrative work.

12. For the entire country, labor supply is inelastic. Assuming inelastic supply, the incidence of a mandated health insurance program falls mainly on workers. International competitiveness in product markets is not affected.

13. Some recommend the separation of health insurance from employment in order to eliminate the inefficiency caused by the tax-exempt status of employer-provided health insurance.

DISCUSSION QUESTIONS

1. Discuss the factors that may lead one nation to spend more per person on health care than another nation. What are the implications of finding health care to be income elastic in cross-national studies? When health care is income elastic, will richer countries tend to have a higher or lower proportion of GDP spent on health care?

2. In countries in which there is nonprice rationing for care, waiting time costs may be substantial. How could you evaluate the economic costs of the waiting time?

3. Create a table comparing the British, German, and Canadian health care systems with respect to financing, availability, and costs of care. How do they compare with the system in the United States?

4. Suppose that the price of health care services rises and the quantity demanded falls. Under what conditions might the health care share of GDP fall? Rise?

5. It is important to compare items under the rubric of "all else equal." What are some of the crucial factors that must be adjusted when comparing health expenditures across countries?

6. Distinguish between an NHI system and an NHS. Provide examples of each. What kind of a system does the United States have?
7. As noted in Table 22-8, levels of satisfaction in health care systems seem to have converged in the last 15 years. Are these measures useful indicators of the performance of health care systems?
8. A common thesis in economics is that markets are efficient unless characteristics are present that lead to market failure. What sorts of market failure in the health economy can be used to justify adoption of universal NHI? What kinds of government failure can be used to argue against this proposal?
9. Do countries with more comprehensive national programs for the provision of health care tend to have lower average costs than the United States? Do they have lower rates of growth in costs? Discuss.
10. Speculate about the level of technology available across countries. Do you think that better health care is available in the United States than in Canada? Do international health indices suggest this? What are the complicating issues?
11. Would individual mandates for health insurance be more burdensome to the poor than employer mandates? Would lower-income groups be wise to favor one plan over the other?
12. If the national labor supply curve were elastic instead of very inelastic, how would an employer-mandated health insurance plan affect the country's international competitiveness?
13. How could a single-insurer health insurance system provide cost savings over a multiple-insurer system like that in the United States?
14. What ideas discussed in this chapter would be suitable to recommend to a country just now revising its health system? To pursue equity? To pursue cost containment?

EXERCISES

1. Consider the allocation of services in the United Kingdom's NHS, as noted in Figure 22-1. If the government raises the administered price up from P^*, trace what would happen to expenditures in the NHS and in the private sectors.
2. Define income elasticity of health care demand. If income increases by 1 percent and the income elasticity of health care demand is 0.5, does the share of income going to health care increase or decrease? Why?
3. Suppose the price elasticity of health services is –0.5. What will happen to the share of health care expenditures, given a 10 percent decrease in health care prices?
4. For more advanced students, Table 22-1 provides data for at least rudimentary estimates of income elasticity of health care expenditures. Estimate a regression equation of the following form:

$$\text{Log (Expenditures per capita)} = a + b \log (\text{GDP per capita})$$

What is the implied income elasticity of expenditures across countries?

5. From the data in Table 22-1, estimate a regression equation of the following form:

$$\text{Log (Infant deaths per 1,000)} = c + d \log (\text{Expenditures per capita})$$

What does your resulting equation say about the "effectiveness" of expenditures per capita (without adjusting for any other factors)?

6. Suppose that a firm faces a downward-sloping demand curve and offers no health insurance to its employees. Let an employer mandate for health insurance be enacted. If this causes the firm's marginal costs to increase, will the firm pay the full cost of the health insurance out of profits? Is the mandate likely to increase the firm's marginal costs?

7. Suppose that a monopolist faced the following demand curve for its goods. Its marginal cost per unit of production is 50, and it faces no fixed costs.

Price	Quantity
100	100
90	200
85	250
80	300
70	400
60	500
55	550
50	600
40	700
30	800
20	900
10	1,000
0	1,100

 a. Calculate the profit-maximizing output and price.
 b. Suppose the workers negotiate a health insurance benefit increase that increases marginal cost per unit from 50 to 60. Calculate the new profit-maximizing output and price.
 c. Who bears the costs of the benefit increase? Why?
8. Figure 22-3 shows various types of national health insurance systems.
 a. Compare the total expenditures in panels a and b. Which is larger? What determines which will be larger? Why?
 b. Compare the total expenditures in panels b and c. Which is larger? In which are resource costs larger? Why?
 c. If the demand curves truly reflect consumer preferences, which of the three panels is economically efficient? Show the economic losses and the transfers for those panels that are not economically efficient.
9. The Organization for Economic Cooperation and Development (OECD) provides some of the best data available for comparative international work. Its website is www.oecd.org. Use the OECD data to examine the health care system of Mexico along the following dimensions:
 • financing
 • expenditure
 • technology
 • coverage

CHAPTER 23

The Health Economics of Bads

An Introduction to Bads

Models of Addiction

Rationales for Public Intervention

Advertising Restrictions on Cigarettes and Alcohol

Excise Taxes and Consumption of Cigarettes and Alcohol

Conclusions

No discussion of the health economy can be complete without addressing one of the most prominent and controversial issues—the consumption of health bads. In a market economy, the consumer's sovereignty usually is regarded as given, that is, the consumer is "free to choose." However, we can find many exceptions any society—cases where society encourages or discourages desired choices. We encourage and promote use of motorcycle helmets, automobile emissions-control devices, old-age pensions, and good prenatal care. We often discourage the purchase of alcohol, street drugs, and cigarettes.

The reason to intervene in private decisions could be paternalistic, but it also could appeal to economic efficiency. Cigarette smoking affects not merely the cigarette buyer and seller—effects that are internal to the cigarette market—but also the health of nonsmokers nearby, an external cost. Since many health insurers do not distinguish between smokers and nonsmokers, perhaps because of high monitoring costs, nonsmokers may pay higher premiums than warranted by their actual health risks. The personal hazards of excessive alcohol consumption are also serious, including disability due to alcoholism and fatality due to liver disease. The external costs include possible harm to family or neighbors as well as the excessive, dangerous, and often-fatal traffic accidents due to drunk driving. Finally, when smokers and drinkers underestimate the probabilities of ill health due to their consumption, the imperfect information provides an efficiency rationale for measures, such as taxes, that tend to curb the behaviors.

Economists as citizens may choose one side or the other of these controversies because their values are not determined by their being economists, but economists as scientists can illuminate the issues that are of interest to the public. For many, the question is not whether to intervene in private decisions to smoke or drink, but how to do so more effectively and unobtrusively. This hinges on many issues although two economic questions are central. First, what is the relationship of price to demand? Second, what is the relationship of product advertising to total consumption?

An Introduction to Bads

Economic reasoning is helpful for any approach to the analysis of bads, such as cigarette smoking and excessive alcohol consumption. Box 23-1 shows how consumption of alcohol and tobacco varies across countries. Economic models of addiction as well as market failure help determine whether intervention is justified on efficiency grounds. Alternatively, models of consumption, advertising, price, and taxation help provide relatively unobtrusive and cost-effective means to intervene, once intervention is chosen.

BOX 23-1

Who Smokes and Who Drinks? Cultures and Behaviors

It is common enough to find families who drink wine with dinner, or groups of people who smoke together. A comparison of the consumption across countries gives some perspective. It may surprise some Americans that U.S. consumption per capita of both "bads" is relatively low among the developed countries shown. In Cruz-Smith's popular novel, *Gorky Park*, the Russian central character, Arkady is asked, "Why didn't you ever go to America?" Arkady answered, "If I went to America, I would have had to quit smoking." Alcohol consumption data are from the STAKES (2002) health group in Finland; the cigarette consumption data are from an Australian health group from OECD, World Bank, and individual sources.

Consumption of Alchohol in 1998

as 100% alcohol per inhabitant, litres

(Bar chart, countries top to bottom: Portugal, France, Ireland, Germany, Czech Republic, Spain, Denmark, Hungary, Austria, Greece, Belgium, Netherlands, Russia, Italy, Great Britain, Finland, Latvia, USA, Japan, Sweden, Norway, Iceland, Estonia. X-axis: 0, 4, 8, 12. Legend: Spirits, Wine and beer)

Country	% Males	% Females	Consumption
Japan	57.5	14.2	3,180
Greece	46.0	28.0	2,500
Singapore	29.0	2.0	2,500
Netherlands	40.9	31.2	2,300
Denmark	36.0	36.0	2,170
Spain	43.5	24.5	2,100
France	38.0	20.0	2,010
Switzerland	30.1	24.1	2,000
Canada	30.0	28.0	1,800
Germany	35.6	21.5	1,800
Ireland	29.0	28.0	1,800
United States	28.6	24.6	1,800
Sweden	21.6	23.8	1,710
Italy	38.0	26.0	1,600
Norway	34.0	33.0	1,550
Australia	27.1	23.2	1,480
New Zealand	27.0	26.0	1,420
UK	28.0	26.0	1,400

Prevalence and Consumption Per Capita in Grams of Tobacco

Source: International Health, *How Australia Compares*, www.aihw.gov.au/publications/health/ihhac, accessed (2002).

That cigarettes qualify as bads follows from the high death rates attributed to cigarette smoking. Deaths per capita from respiratory cancers rank highest among national death rates from malignancies and second only to categories of heart disease overall. Motor vehicle deaths are less than half this rate, and only a handful of states have HIV/AIDS death rates that exceed one-half of the respiratory cancer rate. Cigarette smoking is known to affect other disease categories as well, such as emphysema and heart disease. There is little doubt that getting successive generations of youth to choose never to smoke would lower average population age-adjusted mortality rates substantially. Econometric studies of health production commonly find cigarette consumption to be a significant and materially important predictor of mortality rates.

In contrast to smoking, moderate alcohol consumption does not harm many groups of people and is reported to benefit some. Yet, substantial harm occurs with excessive consumption and inappropriate related behaviors, such as drunk driving.[1] Applying a novel means to identify the effect of drinking on traffic fatalities, Leavitt and Porter (2000) found that drivers with "alcohol in the blood" are eight times as likely to cause a fatal accident as the sober driver. With "blood alcohol above legally drunk," the ratio rises to 15 times. Alcohol use among both high school and college students also raises policy concerns. College students who drink have poorer academic attainment (Cook and Moore, 1993; Williams, Powell, and Wechsler, 2003). High school drinkers are more likely to drop out before graduation (Chatterji and DeSimone, 2005).

One economic approach is to assume that there are no grounds to intervene if the consumer chooses rationally and voluntarily, is reasonably informed of the risks, and creates no side effects for others. This view implicitly rejects all arguments not based on economic efficiency, including those grouped together as equity concerns. Furthermore, the view typically rejects other grounds as paternalistic. However, because alcohol and cigarette consumption are addictive, the issues of rationality, volition, and information take on closer scrutiny.

Models of Addiction

Models of addiction come out of both psychology/medicine and economics. Chaloupka and Warner (1999) identify three types.

Imperfectly Rational Addiction Models

These models propose that the addict has stable but inconsistent preferences in the short run as opposed to the long run. As Schelling (1978) described this person:

> Everybody behaves like two people, one who wants clean lungs and long life and another who adores tobacco. . . . The two are in a continual contest for control. (p. 290)

Are people really like this? Regret, in fact, is fairly common. In film, there is even the cliché of the hero in comedy who enters the tiger's cage telling the bystanders to ignore him should he change his mind and even scream for help. Of course, he changes his mind. Is he two different people at those two moments?

Myopic Addiction Models

Nearsightedness about the future harmful effects of the ingested drug provides a variant of the imperfectly rational model. Here, the individuals don't see the facts clearly; they

[1]In addition, cigarettes are implicated in low birth weights (Rosenzweig and Wolpin, 1995), and alcohol use by college-age youth has been shown to reduce educational attainment (Cook and Moore, 1993).

are naïve about the nature of the drug and its side effects. One may imagine someone easily persuaded by cigarette-smoking friends who may denigrate the societal information about cigarettes. One may see the teenager who only dimly perceives the realities of distant future health events, including cancers, and perhaps fails to connect the experience of smokers in older generations with his or her own behaviors and prospects.

Rational Addiction

Can addiction in some cases be a rational choice? Becker and Murphy (1988) discarded myopic models and investigated addiction by assuming that people incorporate rationally all information, past, present, and future, into their utility calculations. They showed that rationally choosing to ingest an addictive drug was possible under restrictive yet plausible conditions. The discussion here is developed from work by Becker and Murphy (1988); Becker, Grossman, and Murphy (1991); and MacDonald (2004).

Addiction researchers usually speak of "reinforcement" and "tolerance."

Reinforcement means that greater past consumption of addictive goods, such as drugs or cigarettes, increases the desire for present consumption. In short, smoking more now may make us smoke more later.

Tolerance occurs if the utility from a given amount of consumption is lower when past consumption is greater. This suggests that the future impacts of smoking or drinking or ingesting drugs decrease, when we consume more now. A single glass of wine may make someone tipsy the first time he or she drinks. Over time, with more drinking experience, the first glass of the evening may have little or no impact. We will use smoking to illustrate important model relationships, although drinking, illicit drugs, or even common substances such as caffeine, can provide similar examples.

Becker, Grossman, and Murphy introduce the construct of "addictive capital stock" S. For example, with more smoking experience the smoker's attitude toward cigarette consumption is likely to change. We assume therefore that addictive stock "reinforces" cigarette consumption, C, meaning that the more stock, the more one will smoke, leading to curves A^1 and A^2 in Figure 23-1. Though not shown in the figure, the utility function shows the smoker as gaining utility from cigarette consumption C, from the addictive stock S, as well as from income, which allows the purchase of other goods in addition to cigarettes.

The important questions in the model deal with what happens over time. For example, current consumption increases the addictive stock. Listening to Mozart at age 21 will likely increase our enjoyment of Mozart at age 22, thus increasing our musical "capital stock." Most smokers will remember how bad the first cigarette tasted, but similarly smoking or drinking at age 21 may increase enjoyment of smoking or drinking in subsequent years. So, a larger addictive stock makes future consumption more pleasurable.

A myopic, or near-sighted, addict looks solely at the reinforcement effect. A rational addict, however, also considers the future harmful consequences of current addictive behavior. The rationally addicted smoker weighs the present pleasure against both the future health consequences and the beneficial impact of current consumption on future consumption enjoyment.

The rational addiction theorists have drawn several further implications from their analyses.

- Addiction is more likely for people who discount the future heavily since they pay less attention to the potential adverse consequences.
- Addiction is more likely when the effects of past consumption depreciate more rapidly.
- Expected rises in future prices will have a dampening effect on current consumption, much like increases in current prices.

FIGURE 23-1 Rational Addiction Model

Models that examine people's behavior over time typically search for a "steady state", an equilibrium where all "outflows" and "inflows" maintain the system, like the equilibrium of a well-run fish tank. In the steady state equilibrium proposed here, the system will be maintained over time provided that current cigarette smoking adds exactly enough C to the addictive stock to replace the depreciation δS of that stock during the period. Mathematically, $C = \delta S$, where δ is the constant depreciation rate. The $C = \delta S$ line in Figure 23-1 depicts all the combinations of C and S that yield a steady state equilibrium.

Reviewing the elements of the model, we see:

1. *Consumption of cigarettes as a function of addictive stock.* Curve A^1 relates smoking to addictive stock for a person with a given rate of time preference (relating future utility to present utility) and a given level of wealth, and who faces a set of prices for cigarettes and nonaddictive goods. We can think of curve A^1 as a cigarette consumption curve, so the more stock S, the more consumption C. In other words, any given stock S is just sufficient to maintain consumption level C.

2. *Cigarette consumption needed to maintain addictive stock.* The stock of addictive capital depreciates at a rate of δ (between 0 and 1) per year. This suggests that the more stock we have, the more we will smoke. The ray from the origin, $C = \delta S$ is the *steady state line* where current cigarette consumption just offsets the depreciation of the stock of smoking capital.

The model provides a convenient way to see what happens to the rational addict over time. Consider a smoker who is on consumption curve A^1 (as an exercise, explain why a price increase from "low" to "high" would shift the consumption curve from A^1 to A^2) with addictive stock S_1. This stock implies a cigarette consumption of C_1, or point B. Notice, however, that consumption, C_1, will more than replace the depreciation in S_1 during the period (point B lies above the steady state line, $C = \delta S$). It follows that addictive stock will grow and exceed S_1 in the next period; for example it may rise to S_2

at point B'. Continuing this logic, it follows that whenever consumption, C, lies above the steady state line, the addictive stock, S, will grow. Finally, stock S_3 and consumption C_3 give a steady state equilibrium for case A^1. We label this equilibrium point as D.

Compare steady state equilibrium D, with another place where the two curves cross, point E. Notice that D is like a magnet; any stock near S_3 is pulled toward D. That is any stock a bit to the left of S_3 will bring growth in stock up to S_3; any stock to the right will depreciate down to S_3. Point D represents a "stable equilibrium." Try the same experiment with the equilibrium at point E, and see that it is unstable. Any stock slightly to the left of E will be pulled further to the left; any stock slightly to the right will eventually increase all the way to S_3.[2]

This model provides important policy implications about impacts of price changes, often induced through tax policies. Starting at point D consider a rise in price so that the cigarette consumption curve shifts from A^1 to A^2. With the price rise, smoking decreases at first from C_3 (at point D), to point D'. It then falls further over time since D' is below the steady-state line. Equilibrium smoking level falls to C_4 at point D''. This shows the model to be consistent with our prior conceptions about price and quantity demanded. The higher the price, all else equal, the lower the quantity demanded.

Moreover, the long-run responses to price changes *exceed* short-run responses. Initial decreases in smoking cause a subsequent decrease in the stocks of addictive capital, which then stimulate further smoking decreases.

Second, at some point, a rising price will cause all equilibria to disappear. Starting from point D'' and letting the price rise even more, a new A^3 curve will be everywhere below the $C = \delta S$ steady state line. This prediction is unique to the rational addiction model, the prediction that some cigarette smokers quit "cold turkey," without gradually reducing consumption down to zero, landing at a point similar to F where consumption equals 0.

It also follows that expectations about future prices of cigarettes will affect the addicts' current decisions about smoking. In Figure 23-1, we would interpret this by saying that a permanent price increase shifts the consumption curve downward farther than a temporary price increase. Both the price effect and the probability of going cold turkey are enhanced by permanent price increases. Likewise permanent restrictions on the advertising of cigarettes would have more effect than temporary ones.

Rationales for Public Intervention

Are cigarette smokers well-informed about the risks of smoking so they can make rational choices? Some economists (Lundborg and Lindgren, 2004; and Viscusi (1995) have challenged the common wisdom that smokers are ill-informed, reporting smokers' knowledge and responses to risk to be similar to that of nonsmokers. Findings from various fields regarding smoker- and nonsmoker behavior more generally suggest that smokers differ from nonsmokers on these bases.

Consider nonsmokers first. We mentioned that another justification for intervention is that smoking has detrimental side effects on others, or "external costs." Much then depends on the size of these costs. These externalities come from two principal sources the passive smoking incurred by people nearby, and all the various external costs caused by health hazards to the smoker. Manning et al. (1991) estimated the external costs at the equivalent of $0.33 per pack for a new smoker evaluated in 1995 dollars, though passive smoking costs were omitted. Viscusi (1995) also estimated the external costs per pack to be in this range, though lower than Manning's, and near zero under some scenarios.

[2]It can be shown that the A curve must cross the C line from above for an equilibrium to be stable. This occurs at point D. It does not occur at point E.

Because economic efficiency is only one economic criterion (the other is equity), because data issues can be disputed, and because economics is not the only basis to consider, many choose to intervene in tobacco and alcohol use. Economics offers two major tools that may be effective in curbing consumption of a targeted bad: restrictions on advertising and imposition of excise taxes. Advertising can be restricted by tax code revisions, but most often the public issue is whether to restrict advertising by selective or total bans. The excise tax tool is theoretically effective to the degree that demand is more elastic for a given supply. These two principal tools of intervention form the subject of our next investigations. First, however, consider why we have chosen not to address the several other tools that might be used.

Other Interventions

Two other potential forms of intervention are prohibitions on the consumption of the product and penalties for consumption or misuse of the product. Outright prohibition of cigarettes is unlikely to occur in the United States. Accounts of the period when alcohol became illegal in the 1920s seem to point to that clear conclusion. Furthermore, alcohol prohibition of that era probably was not even effective in reducing alcohol consumption (Miron, 1999; Dills, Jacobson, and Miron, 2005; Miron 2005). Studies, however, also find that more limited prohibitions, such as bans on smoking in public places, are effective in reducing both the intensity of smoking and the person's propensity to smoke.

Lesser prohibitions, however, often have been accepted and proven effective. These include the effect of lower speed limits on rates of fatal accidents involving alcohol, as well as bans on smoking in public places.[3] Many countries, especially in Scandinavia, apply much more severe penalties for drunk driving than does the United States. These include stiff jail sentences for alcohol offenses, offenses that many Americans regard as less serious. That legal penalties affect drunken-driving behavior was shown by Mullahy and Sindelar (1994) for U.S. data in which increased fines and license revocations were highly significant in models of the individual's probability to drive drunk.

Regulation has a mixed history according to researchers, although some estimate significant reductions in smoking followed by the clean air restrictions. It may even be as they claim, that the tax effects are overestimated to the extent that part of the "tax effect" is really due to unmeasured local clean air restrictions. However, most price and tax effect studies do not consider it necessary to incorporate such indicators of regulations. A recent study on regulation in Canada finds it to be relatively ineffective (Lanoie and Leclair, 1998).

Advertising Restrictions on Cigarettes and Alcohol

We begin with the role of advertising. At issue is whether advertising can increase the total consumption of bads, like cigarettes. The issues we will address are ones on which people differ and hold strong views. In a report on cigarettes, the Surgeon General (1989) concluded at one point that:

> There is no scientifically rigorous study available to the public that provides a definitive answer to the basic question of whether advertising and promotion affect the level of tobacco consumption. Given the complexity of the issue, none is likely to be forthcoming in the foreseeable future. (pp. 516–517)

[3]See Chaloupka and Saffer (1992) and McCarthy (1993).

Even this conclusion is disputed by parties to both sides of the issue.

Economists understand that well-intentioned interventions often have unintended consequences. Before blaming advertising for our ills, we should inquire into the nature of advertising.

Theories of Advertising

Three main theories have developed about how advertising works and what it does for or to the community. Advertising alternatively is a form of information, a tool for persuasion, or a complementary good. The first two of these represent an old battle in advertising theory with contrasting villains and heroes: Information is generally beneficial, while persuasion is at least more questionable. The most recent addition treats advertising as a complementary good. Finally, Box 23-2 visits the advertisement of worthless goods—patent medicines.

Advertising as Information

Nelson (1970, 1974) studied the implications of advertising as information. Viewed as information, advertising can be seen to lower equilibrium prices, create better access to the market for new entrants, and provide better matches of consumer preferences with

BOX 23-2

Can Advertising Lead Patients Astray? The Case of Medical Quackery

Excepting the medical heroes of history, such as Hippocrates and Galen, few doctors offered a scientific practice until the twentieth century. Modern medical science did not begin until the mid-nineteenth century and that the typical patient confronting the typical physician did not attain even a fifty-fifty chance of getting better until about 1900. Most early practitioners may have had strong faith in their practices, such as bleeding the patient or applying strong purgatives, but these often may have worsened a patient's chances for recovery.

Oddly, there have also been many doctors throughout history who knowingly advertised and sold a worthless bill of goods. These "quacks" brazenly promised marvelous healing powers for such oddities as "patent medicines." Such practices persist today mixed with generally innocent "alternative medicines," herbal treatments. However, there still are modernized equivalents to the magical electric boxes and oddly designed "magnetizations."

The audacity of the advertising medical quack was not lost on Gilbert and Sullivan, the noted creators of comic opera during the late nineteenth century. Their views on quacks were captured by:

Patent Medicines

Source: Photo by Scott Jordan.

Mikado:

My object all sublime
I shall achieve in time—
To let the punishment fit the crime,
The punishment fit the crime; . . .
The advertising quack who wearies
With tales of countless cures,
His teeth, I've enacted,
Shall all be extracted
By terrified amateurs.

feasible consumption bundles. Informed consumers find that their dependence on or loyalty to Brand A will be weakened by their improved knowledge of alternatives.

If it is easy to opt for another brand, then the consumer has flexibility, and a flexible consumer is more likely to resist undesirable changes in the brand, such as a drop in quality or an increase in price. This greater responsiveness to price implies a more elastic demand, and it makes possible lower market equilibrium prices. How can the firm's costly advertising activity help but be passed on to consumers in the form of higher prices? The mistake is that while the price at a given output must rise, the market equilibrium quantity may change due to competition, and the equilibrium price may fall.

Advertising as a Barrier to Entry

In contrast to advertising as information, Bain (1956) argued that advertising differentiates one brand from another, creating increased brand loyalty. By making consumers more resistant to price changes and demand, advertising can result in greater market power and higher equilibrium prices. Adding to this vision, Comanor and Wilson (1974) showed that the persuasive power of advertising may cause it to be asymmetrically effective for the incumbent versus potential new entrants. Consumers have greater experience with established firms and greater recognition of them. The next advertising dollar to be spent by the established firm will yield a greater return than the same dollar spent by the newcomer.

Advertising as a Complementary Good

Nobel laureate Gary Becker and colleague Kevin Murphy (1993) proposed a theory to account for these competing claims within a single model—one that appeals to an older theory of complements and substitutes. Let advertising be considered a good that is a complement to the good advertised. A consumer might wade through commercials with irritation during a ball game but enjoy the humorous one featuring a favorite beer. The commercial increases the consumer's marginal utility from consuming that brand and, under this theory, firm advertising will raise total consumption of the product, just as a reduction in the price of mustard will increase the consumption of hotdogs.

The Possible Effects of Brand Switching

When an imperfectly competitive firm advertises, it potentially improves its demand in part by inducing consumers to switch brands and in part by inducing consumers to consume more of the product in total. However, other firms also will advertise for these purposes, and the advertising among the firms may be partially or even totally offsetting. Advertising in the industry could have little or no effect on total industry demand, but it also could have a positive effect.

Laypeople often conclude mistakenly that the answer is obvious. Surely cigarette advertising must lead to more aggregate smoking or cigarette companies would not spend so much money on it. Cigarettes have been among the most heavily advertised products. A similar argument is made by some economists who note that the many available brands are really owned by a few companies and that the degree of brand switching (about 10 percent of smokers switch brands in a typical year) is not sufficient to justify the billions spent on advertising (Tye, Warner, and Glantz, 1987). Sales figures confirm that 80 to 90 percent of U.S. cigarette sales are generated by the top four firms.

Others argue that brand switching is a sufficient motivation for heavy advertising. Two points help explain this view: (1) the firm's decision to advertise is made ex ante with available information, and (2) the firm's decision criterion is what would happen

if it did not advertise. On the one hand, the firm commits money to advertising based on the effect it expects advertising to have. The firm may not have the econometric data published later, it may not believe what is published, or admittedly, it may have better information. On the other hand, the number of smokers who actually switch on average is less relevant than the unknown number who would switch if the firm did not advertise.

Increased Demand or Brand Switching?

To settle the question, we must examine the evidence. If we find that advertising increases total consumption, we could reduce consumption by restricting advertising. Studies suggest that cigarette advertising elasticities are very small. Research tends to find (Gallett, 2003; Baltagi and Levin, 1986) advertising has no significant marginal effect on cigarette demand. Where the ad effect is found to be significant, the reported elasticities are generally quite small.[4] These elasticities fall between 0.1 and 0.2, and the most common result falls around 0.1. The Toxic Substance Board of New Zealand (1989), a strong advocate of advertising bans, conservatively uses an advertising elasticity of 0.07 in estimating the effect of an advertising ban.

Suppose that the true advertising elasticity were 0.1 exactly, and we apply this figure to estimate the effect of a total ban on cigarette advertising. We would reduce cigarette consumption by 10 percent, which is the product of a 100 percent price reduction and the 0.1 elasticity. Even this crude estimate might raise an unusual controversy in that ban advocates (arguing that the ban was successful) and ban opponents (arguing that it didn't change much) both might claim that this evidence is support for their case.

The elasticity estimates often are drawn from time trends of aggregate data, sometimes aggregated to the national level. At this level, little variation in advertising expenditures is captured, and the massive advertising levels outside of the cigarette industry, though relevant to cigarette demand, usually are ignored (Saffer and Chaloupka, 1998). It is also econometrically unsafe to extrapolate this far out of sample so we must study the effects of actual advertising bans.

World experience with advertising bans is informative. Several countries have banned cigarette advertising outright, and the United States installed a partial ban (on broadcast media) in 1971. The picture is clear regarding the U.S. experience. The 1971 ban of cigarette advertising on television and radio somewhat paradoxically may have increased cigarette consumption. Hamilton's (1972) account illustrates this peculiar history. Prior to the 1971 ban, an FTC ruling on the Fairness Doctrine required television and radio stations to give equal time to antismoking messages.

The result was a flurry of memorable commercials showing the harm of smoking. In one, a father appears walking in the forest with his young son. They stop to rest, lean back against a tree trunk, and the father reaches for a cigarette. His son watches in admiration as his dad lights up, but the father sees this, thinks, and stops. He gets the message and so do the viewers. Hamilton showed that these antismoking messages were effective in reducing smoking in the population, while the advertising expenditures had small, if significant, marginal effects. Thus, when the ban eliminated both pro-cigarette and the mandatory anticigarette messages at the same time, the combined effect could have increased smoking.

Perhaps more important, the antismoking messages had a relatively greater effect on young, potential smokers. Lewit, Coate, and Grossman (1981) studied data on more

[4]McGuiness and Cowling (1975), Seldon and Doroodian (1989), and Tremblay and Tremblay (1995). Roberts and Samuelson (1988) simultaneously estimate brand switching and total consumption effects, concluding for their data that total consumption effects dominated.

than 6,000 youths. They found that television watching significantly increased the probability that a youth would start smoking, while the Fairness Doctrine ads reduced the probability that a youth would start smoking. Harris and Chan (1999) have also found the clear relation of price elasticity and age; from 15 to 17 year olds through 27 to 29 year olds, price elasticity in absolute value starts out high and continually declines.

For many years, the single cross-national study of the effect of advertising bans by Hamilton (1975) showed that the bans have no significant effect on cigarette consumption in the country. In a later study, incorporating many new years of data and experience with bans, Laugesen and Meads (1991) reported these bans to be effective. Studying data for 1960 to 1986 and developing an index measuring the advertising restrictions, their time series estimates showed that a country's banning tobacco advertising will reduce tobacco consumption by 6.8 percent. A recent study corroborates this result, though it warned that partial bans may invite tobacco firms to substitute advertising in unrestricted categories for banned advertising (Saffer and Chaloupka, 1998). Keeler and colleagues (2004) report that cigarette companies in the United States did exactly this in response to the U.S. tobacco settlement of 1998. Facing reduced revenues by 8.3 percent due to the consequent price increase, the companies offset about one-quarter to one-half of that through increased advertising.

Advertising and Alcohol Consumption

Although earlier studies reported no effect of advertising on alcohol consumption, Saffer (1991) found that such advertising was a significant factor in drinking. Similarly, Saffer and Dave (2003) found such advertising to be especially effective on youthful drinkers; they estimated that a complete ban on all alcohol advertising could reduce adolescent alcohol consumption by 24 percent with even stronger effects on binge drinking. Taking a different approach, Saffer (1997) found alcohol advertising levels to be correlated positively and significantly with motor vehicle fatalities, ceteris paribus. He estimated that partial bans (bans on broadcast advertising) would reduce annual fatalities by 2,000 to 3,000, while a total ban could reduce fatalities by up to 10,000 nationally.

Excise Taxes and Consumption of Cigarettes and Alcohol

The public commonly believes that taxes on products are always and fully passed on to the consumer, but this is not true. The irony is that if it were true, then cigarette and alcohol taxes would have no effect other than to raise money for the government coffers. By first examining the theory of excise taxation, we learn the importance of the price elasticity of demand and supply in determining the incidence of the tax and the degree to which consumption is reduced. With this understanding, we will examine the empirical knowledge regarding these elasticities.

The Consumption-Reducing Effects of Excise Taxes in Theory

Excise taxes form another major tool that can reduce consumption of bads in populations. Figure 23-2 depicts the supply and demand for alcoholic beverages. If a sufficient number of voters were to agree, the consumption of beer could be reduced from Q_E to Q_{E2} by imposing an excise tax increase of T dollars (recall that the tax shifts the supply curve vertically by the amount of the tax). The analysis also reveals that the tax would not fall entirely on the beer drinker, but the incidence would be shared. Assuming demand curve, D_0, because the consumer pays a higher price after the tax, we say that

the incidence on the consumer is $(P_{E2} - P_E)$. Because the producer pockets the lower amount, P_{S2}, we say that the incidence on the producer is $(P_E - P_{S2})$.

The research issue is illustrated by the alternative possibility that the demand curve for beer is D_1. The alternative equilibrium is at point A, at which the reduction in consumption (not shown) is less than the original reduction, $(Q_E - Q_{E2})$. Thus, the reduction in quantity demanded will depend on which curve represents the true demand curve, the relatively inelastic curve, D_1, or the more elastic curve, D_0. Generally, the more responsive demand is to price (the greater the demand elasticity in absolute value), the greater the corresponding reduction effected by the excise tax increase.

From models of the consumer's choice over bads, such as the rational addiction model, we know to distinguish between long-run and short-run effects of price changes. We also learned to distinguish youth from adult consumers, a distinction with important policy consequences. Box 23-3 provides a further discussion related to tobacco policy.

Excise Taxes and Cigarette Consumption in Practice

The importance of price elasticity is not lost on economists, and most econometric studies of cigarette consumption report price elasticity estimates. Over the history of these studies, the reported cigarette price elasticities in absolute value range rather widely, from as low as –0.2 to occasional estimates greater than –1.0. There is no doubt that cigarette demand responds significantly to price, but the response is generally inelastic. Building on the earlier work, more recent studies find short-run price elasticities in a narrower band, typical of which is the –0.3 to –0.5 band reported by Keeler et al. (1993).[5] The United States Tobacco Settlement of 1998 effected a rise in the price of cigarettes, and consequently it offered a natural experiment on the effects of price on consumption. The results show a decline in cigarette consumption of 8.3 percent, though increased advertising by cigarette companies offset this effect (Keeler et al., 2004). Sheu and colleagues (2004) estimated the price elasticity from these data to be in midrange, –0.46.

[5]See also Tremblay and Tremblay (1995). Smokeless tobacco demand also responds to price in econometric studies, both on price and the price of substitutes (Ohsfeldt, Boyle, and Capilouto, 1998).

BOX 23-3

Mind If I Smoke?

On a California billboard, the man's date responds to this question by asking: "Care if I die?" In a similar spirit, recent American films have depicted the inside of the tobacco industry as darkly menacing. The British news magazine, the *Economist*, ponders whether the tobacco industry has become "the new evil empire."

Meanwhile, other reports suggest that average smoking rates in the population continue to decline. The decline has also occurred among women, with an especially large drop in smoking among women of childbearing age. Tobacco companies generally have raised cigarette prices, and in California, the state legislature's cigarette sales tax increase at the beginning of 1999 was followed by an unexpectedly sharp decline in cigarette sales. The high level of legislative, activist, and consumer discussion and debate over tobacco continues throughout the country.

This scenario forms the backdrop for the tobacco companies' unprecedented November 1998 offer of $368 billion to the states in return for promises to limit further lawsuit activity. The American Cancer Society and the American Medical Association both gave their approval, albeit with some qualifications, and the settlement began with the highest hopes.

The legal theory applied in these contexts and to be used in future Department of Justice suits holds the tobacco companies liable for health costs incurred by the governments to provide care to cigarette-induced disease victims. The argument distinguishes cigarette issues from others involving voluntary risk taking, such as skydiving, alpine skiing, or work in risky occupations. An important legal question is whether the tobacco companies deliberately withheld critical health information.

Early research found that youth were much more responsive to price increases and more accessible to the excise tax tool. This is an attractive result for anyone wishing to deter youth from taking up the smoking habit: ". . . an excise tax increase . . . might continue to discourage smoking participation by successive generations of teenagers and young adults and gradually impact the smoking levels of older age groups as the smoking-discouraged cohorts move through the age spectrum" (Lewit and Coate, 1982, p. 143). Despite some contrary results in the literature, recent research tends to support the view that "price is a powerful determinant of smoking for high school seniors" (Gruber and Zinman, 2000); they estimate the cigarette price elasticity of these youths to be –0.67.

As predicted by some models, such as rational addiction, estimated long-run cigarette elasticities are larger than short-run elasticities in absolute value. Chaloupka (1991) applied the rational addiction framework and estimated long-run values approximately twice as large as for the short run. Keeler et al. (1993) found them to lie in a narrow range, –0.5 to –0.6. A more demanding test of the rational expectations model is one that takes seriously its claim that consumers make choices not only based on current cigarette prices but also on their ideas about future cigarette prices. The estimation process requires difficult econometrics, and ideal data sets are difficult to come by, but two recent studies confirm this forward-looking prediction (Baltagi and Griffin, 2001; and Gruber and Koszegi, 2000).

With the elasticity magnitudes reported in these various studies, what possible effects could excise tax increases be expected to generate? To focus the discussion, suppose that a tax increase has been installed of sufficient magnitude to double the price of cigarettes. Assuming an elasticity of –0.4, the 100 percent price increase, by simple extrapolation, would reduce cigarette consumption by 40 percent, a substantial reduction. As we discussed earlier, where a similar extrapolation for advertising bans

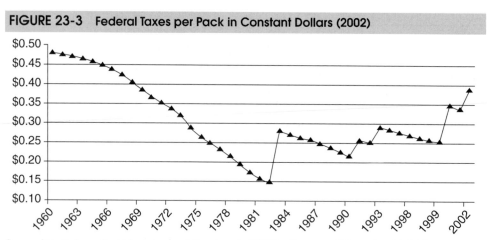

FIGURE 23-3 Federal Taxes per Pack in Constant Dollars (2002)

Source: http://tobaccofreekids.org/research/factsheets/pdf/0092.pdf, accessed November 25, 2005.

suggested a more modest reduction, such out-of-sample extrapolations are risky, but the example serves to illustrate the potency of the tax tool. Furthermore, the elasticity estimates for youth are large enough to double this effect for that age cohort. Likewise, the larger long-run elasticities suggest the greater policy effects as time passes.

Direct measures of the effect of cigarette taxes on mortality also show the effectiveness of tax policy. Michael Moore (1995) tested tax variables in equations to predict mortality from several smoking-related diseases. Higher taxes significantly reduce mortality from lung cancer, cardiovascular disease, and asthma. He reports that a 10 percent cigarette tax hike would save 3,700 lives per year in the United States. Evans and Ringel (1999) studied the effect of cigarette excise taxes on birth outcomes. Their research found the taxes effective in reducing smoking by expectant mothers and to generate better, higher birth weights in the newborns.

Although some countries have applied cigarette taxes vigorously to reduce population smoking, the United States has not done so until recently. In 1997, the U.S. average tax rate, at 35 percent of the average price of a pack, was the lowest among 29 countries in one study. The United Kingdom, Ireland, Germany, and all of Scandinavia ranged from 70 percent to 85 percent. The U.S. federal excise tax declined in real terms since the Surgeon General's mid-1960s announcement that cigarette smoking causes cancer until recent increases to $0.39 per pack (Figure 23-3). The tax rate fell over the years because a nearly constant nominal tax was eroded in percentage terms by the secular rise in price per pack.

Excise Taxes and Alcohol Consumption

Studies of alcohol consumption, price, and advertising have often focused on youth; these younger age groups exhibit the highest rates of alcohol abuse, such as binge drinking (Cook and Moore, 2000). The beer tax in Figure 23-2 was depicted as substantially effective in reducing consumption, but would this effect be experienced in real life? Grossman et al. (1998) find that young adults respond to beer price increases, and the elasticities range from –0.2 to –0.4 in the short run, with long-run elasticities 60 percent higher; other beer elasticity estimates have ranged even higher. Studies of wine and spirits yield elasticities ranging from –0.3 to –1.8 (Saffer and Chaloupka, 1998). The latter study also reports substantial, though inelastic, estimates for price elasticities of illicit drugs including marijuana, cocaine, and heroin. Thus, taxes should have major impacts on consumption of addictive substances.

Conclusions

This chapter examines the economic nature of health bads, and it studies the potential of curbs on advertising and increased excise taxes to reduce the consumption of bads. Econometric estimates of the effect of advertising for cigarettes tend to report small and sometimes insignificant elasticities. These are estimates of changes at the margin. In contrast, advertising bans entail by definition large reductions in advertising levels; while previous studies have suggested insignificant effects here as well, the most recent work reports that bans have some significant effect when studied on an international basis. Related studies on alcohol advertising also report statistically significant effects.

Excise taxes, however, appear to be more potent. Though cigarette and alcohol price elasticities are in the inelastic range, they are large enough in absolute value to have substantial potential as a curb to consumption if the public chooses to apply them. Consistent with rational addiction models, the long-run price elasticities are greater in absolute value than the short-run elasticities. Cigarette price elasticities for youth tend to be larger in absolute value than those for adults.

SUMMARY

1. The nature of addiction, though as yet unresolved, generates behaviors that appear generally consistent with a rational addiction model. Irrational or myopic addiction models provide viable alternatives.
2. Addictive behavior is usually assumed to involve both "reinforcement" and "tolerance." A myopic, or near-sighted, addict looks solely at the reinforcement effect. A rational addict, however, considers the future harmful consequences of current addictive behavior.
3. There are three contrasting theories of advertising. In one, advertising is primarily information, which leads to greater competition and possibly lower prices. The second describes advertising as a potential barrier to entry, which increases monopoly power and prices. The third describes advertising as a complement to the good advertised; it increases marginal utility of the product.
4. Advertising bans and related restrictions appear to have significant effects on consumption of cigarettes and alcohol. Though total effects of advertising are small in econometric studies, they are somewhat more substantial in a recent international study of total bans.
5. Excise taxes work to curb consumption in theory by increasing the price of the product. Then, the effect on consumption depends on consumer responsiveness to price, which is the price elasticity.
6. Increased excise taxes on cigarettes and alcohol appear to be more potent public policy tools for curbing the consumption of bads than are advertising bans. Though estimated price elasticities are small in absolute value, they can be combined with substantial price changes to result in correspondingly large reductions in consumption.

DISCUSSION QUESTIONS

1. Many students smoke, drink alcohol, or ingest other addictive substances, such as caffeine (in coffee, tea, or soft drinks). How do the addiction models that are presented relate to students' everyday habits?
2. Do cigarette and alcohol ads you have seen contain primarily informative content or persuasive content? What consequences would you predict from your finding?
3. Someone says: "The advertising elasticity of cigarette demand may be small, but it is big enough to warrant policy to ban cigarette advertising." What would "big enough" mean in this context?

4. What does the evidence on the effects of the partial U.S. ban on cigarette advertising suggest about the relative effectiveness of cigarette advertising versus antismoking advertising?
5. How does the responsiveness to cigarette advertising and price differ between youths and adults? Why is this important?
6. Explain how it is possible to advertise too little or too much.
7. Suppose it takes considerable time for the large majority of cigarette smokers to become fully informed about the fact that cigarette prices have risen all over. How would this matter to the effectiveness of a tax hike? What other effect of a cigarette tax hike may take considerable time?
8. How would an excise tax hike in Kansas be helped or harmed in its attempt to curb smoking among Kansans if the neighboring states (e.g., Missouri, Nebraska) did not also hike their cigarette excise taxes?
9. When all costs are considered, which public policy tool for curbing the consumption of bads would be the most costly to administer for a given amount of consumption reduction among consumers?

EXERCISES

1. The analysis accompanying Figure 23-1 investigates the impacts of an increase in cigarette prices. Use the figure to show both the short-run and the long-run impacts of a cigarette price decrease.
2. If the elasticity of aggregate cigarette demand with respect to advertising were 0.15, by extrapolation what effect on cigarette consumption would be caused by a 10 percent reduction in advertising? A 50 percent reduction? A 100 percent reduction? How and why does one's confidence in prediction change over this range of reductions?
3. Suppose the price elasticity of cigarette demand is –0.4. If we increased the prices of cigarettes by 50 percent, what would we expect to happen to the quantity purchased? To total expenditures on cigarettes?
4. In the discussion on rationales for intervention in markets, we note that Manning found external costs of $0.33 per pack of cigarettes.

$$\text{Demand: } Q = 1.45 - 0.19P$$
$$\text{Supply: } Q = 0.40 + 0.51P$$

 a. Draw a supply and demand diagram, and graph Manning's external costs of $0.33 (in 1995 dollars) based on a market price of $1.50 (in 1995 dollars) per pack.
 b. If a tax of $0.33 were imposed, what would happen to the market price, and to the equilibrium quantity?
5. Using Manning's estimate of external costs of $0.33 per pack of cigarettes:
 a. Calculate the new market price for cigarettes using a demand elasticity of –0.25. Would this be economically efficient?
 b. Calculate the government's revenue from a $0.33 tax on cigarettes in part a.

24

Epidemiology and Economics: HIV/AIDS in Africa

Concepts from Epidemiology

Economic Epidemiology

Case Study: HIV/AIDS in Africa

Conclusions

Infectious diseases have tormented human history, yet despite our great technological progress, many lethal epidemics remain with us, and some have arisen only recently. Analysts have long viewed the contact of an infecting agent and a human host as necessary for infection to incur. Recently, however, they have come to understand how crucial the behavior of the host is to this process. For example, the uninfected person's demand for prevention may affect choice of geographic location, social milieu, and health information, as well as demand for preventive goods and services. Economic theory shows how these economic behaviors can alter the course of the epidemic. In this chapter, we explain how theorists use economic principles to enrich understanding of epidemics. We then apply these and related economic ideas to one of the worst, the case of AIDS in Africa.

Concepts from Epidemiology

Analysts describe the magnitude of disease in society in a multitude of ways. The *incidence* rate is defined as the number of new cases for a defined population. The *hazard* rate, in comparison, is the instantaneous rate of new cases among the uninfected population in a given period of time. Like the incidence, it describes one's chances of getting the disease. "Instantaneous" refers to a time period that is arbitrarily short. The hazard rate is commonly used in models of epidemics, though it also applies to engineering, business, and economics. In our discussion, it represents the rate of new infections.

The fraction of the population that is currently infected is called the *prevalence* rate. Incidence contributes to prevalence like income contributes to wealth, in that incidence adds new cases to the total pool describing the prevalence of present cases. Entry and exit to this pool of the infected population are also defined by births and deaths, as in all population models, but also altered when people develop immunity or adapting behaviors. The dynamic process of a disease, its path through time, sometimes

shows the prevalence growing (perhaps even into a massive epidemic) or, one hopes, declining to a benign level.

Alleviating an epidemic can be achieved either by natural means or by public health measures, such as vaccinations. One of the most fundamental economic concepts helps to explain the problem of optimizing the use of vaccinations in a population. Figure 24-1 applies the concept of net benefit maximization by illustrating both the marginal social benefits and the marginal social costs of vaccination. As more people are vaccinated, it becomes more difficult and costly to search for people to get vaccinated; thus, the marginal costs will increase. In contrast, as more are vaccinated, the next vaccinated person provides a lesser external benefit to others (that is, his or her newly achieved immunity is less important to society). Consequently, the marginal benefits will tend to decrease. As we have seen throughout health economics, the maximum social benefit occurs where the marginal benefit equals the marginal cost. This is shown in Figure 24-1 as V_{opt}.

This process of vaccination succeeds by bringing immunity to the disease to the greater population. Immunity, however, can also be acquired through surviving an episode of the disease. It may seem odd to us, but parents in the past would often deliberately expose their children to an infectious disease so as to gain them immunity (see Box 24-1). For the less virulent diseases that plagued children in recent centuries, groups of young adults had often attained up to 95 percent immunity through surviving the disease. The remaining few young people still uninfected were often naturally immune and would remain so throughout their lives. For an epidemic to result from the process of infection and contagion, it must also be the case that the rate of new infections among the susceptible population be sufficiently high to overcome the healthful offsetting effects of vaccination, naturally acquired immunity, and other protections.

Though fighting infectious disease without the aid of modern medicine might appear to be a fruitless task, the evidence from medical historians shows that the prevalence of many infectious diseases declined substantially well before the discovery of modern, effective medicines (McKinlay and McKinlay, 1977). As was seen in Chapter 5, historians have shown that a good share of the reductions in infectious disease prevalence was due to the improved physical heartiness and resistance of the host, in turn, due especially to improvements in nutrition (McKeown, 1976; Fogel, 1986).

FIGURE 24-1 The Marginal Benefits and Costs of Vaccination

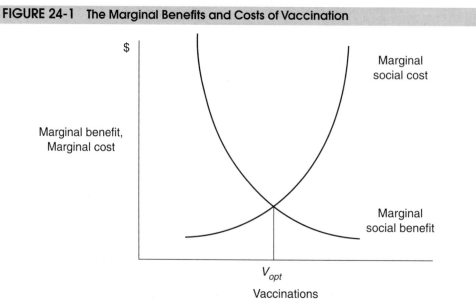

Wanting Your Children to Catch Chicken Pox

The world's first vaccination, for smallpox, was conducted by Edward Jenner in 1796. Jenner's vaccine, derived from cowpox, was different from the vaccine that by 1980 eradicated smallpox from the globe. Each vaccine contains some risk, however small; with eradication the vaccine was finally declared to have become more risky than the chance of contracting the disease. Forty other vaccines have come into use since Jenner's, though none have achieved the eradication success of the smallpox vaccine.

What did parents have at hand when no vaccines were available? How could they protect their children? The biggest part of the answer was "not much." Until well into the twentieth century, the typical child, often one of many, had roughly a fifty-fifty chance of surviving into adulthood.

One perhaps unusual and old-fashioned approach was nevertheless likely to be effective: Parents deliberately exposed their children to infectious diseases! Some held "measles parties" where the uninfected played in the same room with an infected child. Mumps and other childhood diseases came under the same method.

How could this possibly help? Many childhood diseases become more virulent as the child gets older, increasing the risks of bad consequences. The exposed younger children gained immunity and were safe through to their teens during which time susceptible children faced real dangers.

Boulier and colleagues examine the vaccination externality in more detail, starting with the Susceptible-Infective-Removed (SIR) model of epidemiology developed by Kermack and McKendrick (1927) and Hethcote (2000). This model relates to the infectiousness of the disease, the size of the population, and the percentage of the population that is susceptible to the disease.

They calibrate their model for influenza vaccination. As shown in Figure 24-2, from the first vaccination, the initial marginal private benefit is a little less than 0.6 cases of influenza prevented. The marginal external benefit is a little more than one additional case prevented, giving a marginal social benefit of 1.6 cases prevented. The marginal external benefit curve "balloons out" to be as high as 1.58, i.e. 1.77–0.19 additional cases prevented, before falling toward zero, as the number vaccinated increases, and the number who could catch the disease correspondingly falls.

This analysis suggests that while it is likely that there are externalities, analyses must be disease specific. They emphasize that using parallel shifts of demand curves, or simple multiples, is likely to provide seriously misleading results when used in measuring the benefits accruing to vaccination.

Economic Epidemiology

Economists have defined a new area of study described as "economic epidemiology." We will present these theoretical models and related empirical results. Then, we will examine how the world's worst present-day epidemic, the case of AIDS in Africa, can be better understood in light of economics. We seek to find how it came to be, and how it can be stopped.

Rational Epidemics

What would rational individuals (both those infected and uninfected) do in the face of an epidemic? Geoffard and Philipson (1996) incorporate the assumption of rational economic behavior into epidemiological models. Suppose both those who are uninfected

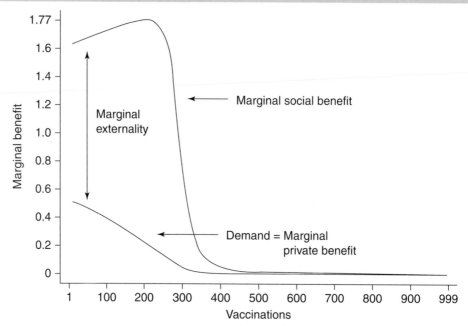

FIGURE 24-2 Vaccination Externalities

Source: Bryan L. Boulier, Singh Tejwant Datta, and Robert S. Goldfarb, "Vaccination Externalities," George Washington University, August 2003, Table 4, with permission from the authors.

and those who are infected seek to maximize their utilities. Realizing that one's customary behaviors entail a risk of infection, susceptible individuals will demand preventive care to some degree. Because preventive care entails costs, they will rationally choose less than the maximal amount of everyone getting preventive care.

At the same time, however, individuals may also demand risky experiences. For example, where the disease is transmitted sexually, the individuals' demand for sexual intimacy becomes a demand for risky experiences, a risk to which the individuals may be fully informed. In another context, suppose that a young grade-schooler wants very much to go to school, but her parents know that a measles epidemic has affected the school. The child's desire to go to school is a demand for a risky experience.

If fully informed, rational people seek to maximize utility, considering both costs and gains; people's behaviors may still lead to an epidemic. One special focus for economists is the responsiveness of prevention demand to new information regarding the prevalence of the disease.

The Prevalence Elasticity of Demand for Prevention

Assume that the susceptible population responds to information regarding an increased prevalence of the disease by demanding more preventive care. Further, define:

$$E_p = \text{Prevalence Elasticity of Demand for Preventive Care}$$

$$= \frac{\% \text{ Change in Prevention Demanded}}{\% \text{ Change in Disease Prevalence}} \tag{24.1}$$

If E_p is low (close to zero), only a small amount of prevention will be demanded, resulting in higher future prevalence. In contrast, if E_p is large (much greater than zero),

then a large amount of prevention (for example, vaccinations) will be demanded, resulting in lower future prevalence.

These demands for preventive care will, in turn, alter the prevalence rate of the disease and could dampen or reverse any further growth of prevalence. Philipson (2000) shows theoretically that a sufficiently elastic response (large E_p) leads to a decline in the prevalence rate, thus stemming the progress of the epidemic.

Do susceptible people respond in practice to the threat implied by an increased prevalence by demanding more prevention? Data for a recent measles epidemic were examined in two studies (Philipson, 1996; Goldstein et al., 1996). Both studies found evidence of a significant prevalence elasticity of demand for prevention. One found that the rate at which people got themselves "up-to-date" with the measles vaccine protection increased from 56 to 58 percent before a measles epidemic began, to 70 percent during the epidemic. Researchers found the same sort of demand behavior in a cross-state study of AIDS (Ahituv, Hotz, and Philipson, 1996). There, the use of condoms was quite responsive to the prevalence of AIDS. Thus, these data support the economic model, and imply that incorporating an economic response into the epidemiology model will better describe the course of epidemics.

Because people may respond to the threat, some epidemics will be self-limiting. Does this imply that we need not worry about rampant epidemics, such as the case of AIDS? No, this does not follow for at least two reasons. First, in some cases, the model predicts that an epidemic will continue to grow given no intervention. Second, the hoped-for behaviors can go awry. For example, given knowledge of high prevalence, people who customarily engage in high-risk activities may become more fatalistic (assuming that they will die anyhow), leading them to engage in yet more high-risk behaviors.

The Economic Consequences of Epidemics

An epidemic is potentially costly in several ways. Persons contracting the illness face direct costs, as do those who have as yet avoided it. Second, diseases potentially interact with the production of goods and service as well as the growth of the economy and its income per capita. We begin here with the costs to those current and potential sufferers.

If an epidemic comes, then what is its true cost to society? The orthodox approach is to estimate the cost of illness (COI) as the product of the prevalence times the per-illness cost (both treatment and foregone earnings) based on severity of the disease. Philipson (1995) shows that this approach neglects the cost of disease avoidance behaviors. We spend money, time, and effort in reducing the risk that we face from the disease.

We may choose to analyze a disease like a tax because the disease causes a loss of utility and naturally leads to efforts to avoid the disease. Treating an illness this way implies that the efforts at illness avoidance are costs, and these avoidance costs should become part of the cost of illness calculation. Tax avoidance costs are already treated as welfare loss, so why not illness avoidance costs?

The analysis of the relationships of epidemic illness to poverty, growth in GDP, and income per capita can be illustrated dramatically with the experience of AIDS in Africa. It is clear from available data of world experience that countries with lower income per capita experience greater HIV infection prevalence.

Thus, the experience of poverty and the related experience of AIDS are each more complex than is suggested by the world data. Poverty cuts two ways. The poor may be less well-informed about the dangers of HIV infection and how to avoid it. Also, when AIDS occurs, the poor experience a much greater proportional burden in caring for the ill person (Bloom and Sevilla, 2002). Whether AIDS epidemics have actually slowed the growth of real wages is not nearly as clear. Work by Bloom and Mahal

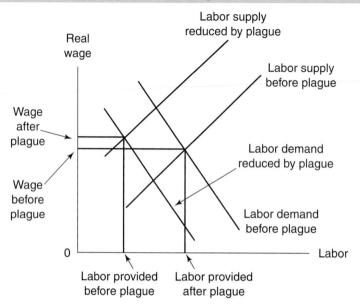

FIGURE 24-3 The Effect of Plague on Real Wage

(1997) finds that there is no significant empirical relationship between the prevalence of AIDS across 50 countries studied and the growth rate in real income per capita.

This result may be understood by analogy to the experience of Europeans with the black death, thought to have begun in 1348 and continuing for the next 200 years. The black death or "bubonic plague" spread a virus that was carried by rats; the infection was usually lethal. Consider Figure 24-3 with an initial demand and supply curve for labor. Before the plague, the various laborers of that time produced agricultural products and crafted other goods. The heightened mortality eliminated portions of the general population, including a share of those laborers. The plague's effect was to reduce the supply of labor and shift that curve to the left. The general population reduction, however, also reduced the demand for the products of labor, and the derived demand for labor, therefore, was reduced (shifted leftward) as well.

The result of the plague is that the equilibrium quantity of labor employed necessarily falls. However, we cannot determine from this analysis whether the real wage in equilibrium would necessarily rise or fall. The real wage here is analogous to the real income per capita, while the real output here is analogous to a country's real GDP. We have depicted the real wage as increasing, and the standard result for studies of the black death corresponds to this picture, as it is generally believed that the real wage rose. We note simply that neither a rise nor fall in the wage is a necessary result of the plague.

There is no doubt that an AIDS epidemic can and does retard a country's growth rate of GDP. While quandaries arise regarding the relation of total population to income per capita, it is clear that the massive loss of productive resources reduces total income. Similarly, there is no doubt that, should per capita income rise after a plague, it does so at huge and irretrievable expense in the suffering and loss of life that occurs.

The Difficulty of Eradicating Diseases

The excitement following the first report of the world eradication of smallpox was tempered by reports of the difficulty of achieving the same for other infectious diseases. Of about 40 vaccines available, only smallpox can claim this much success.

Complete eradication may often be an unwise goal. We earlier proposed that demand for prevention depends on prevalence. If so, the widespread application of an effective vaccine will reduce the prevalence of the disease, an essential step in the disease eradication process. However, when prevalence becomes sufficiently small, the demand for prevention may disappear. Why could this occur? What happens, in this theory, is that the benefits to vaccination can drop below any possible price of vaccination; the success of vaccination, somewhat ironically, will cause further vaccinations to lack sufficient benefits to cover the costs. The ensuing expansion of unvaccinated numbers, in turn, makes complete eradication unachievable.

Information

Controlling epidemics, such as AIDS, requires screening, tracing of partners, and education about the nature and transmission of the disease. The problem is one of incomplete information. Susceptible people will improve their chances when learning of effective ways to avoid infection. Knowledge of the available technologies improves the chances people will seek the appropriate care. In some cases, the technology that is most effective may be among the least costly, with lack of information itself being the key bottleneck.

Several interventions take their effect by shortening the incubation period of the infection. This period is defined as the time from the onset of the disease until the time it generates observable symptoms. Information provided through accurate testing, for example, provides an early warning and shortens the incubation period. This tends to generate beneficial results by speeding the process by which both the infected and the susceptible populations adopt protective and preventive behaviors.

The transmission of information can require the clash of two cultures, often one based more or less on scientific practices and the other on different and even questionable modes of choosing behaviors. The choice of whether to urge intervention may entail the question of whether imposing one's own culture is arrogant and interventionist, with the knowledge that suffering will continue, perhaps on a large scale, without such intervention.

The Role of Government in Battling Epidemics

The standard economic analysis proposes that collective action, generally involvement by government, may be justified when there is market failure or when issues of equity arise. Rationales of these kinds reasonably arise in the case of many epidemic diseases.

First, where immunity to the disease can be obtained through vaccination or other means, and where the disease is contagious, economists commonly recommend that vaccinations (for example) be encouraged either through provision or subsidies. The reason is that private pay vaccination will tend to underplay the external benefit of immunization; those immunized gain not only for themselves but also benefit others. By not becoming disease carriers, they reduce the risk to others. It is the classic example of an externality rationale for collective action.

Second, the optimality observed in models of competitive markets requires that information be adequate and symmetrically available to the market participants. Infectious disease commonly fails to fit this depiction. Even in sexually transmitted diseases (STD), the risks faced by each partner may not be fully known, and perhaps not known at all. While many examples in life exist where a person takes on a risk knowingly making a private rational decision, this picture is not as clear for AIDS and similar types of infections.

Third, an equity case could be made for some epidemic diseases. Equity may be violated, for example, should some segments of the populace suffer the disease more

than others. It might also apply if observers believe that the disease has been forced upon the sufferer in some sense, partly by public actions.

Fourth, Hilsenrath (1999) argues that the role of government in monitoring and controlling the overall economy forms an analogy to a potential role for government in epidemics like AIDS. Here, the government's role to encourage growth and stability takes on a public health aspect inasmuch as raging epidemics have macroeconomic consequences.

Fifth, as we saw in Chapter 13, health economists have pointed out the market failures entailed in the provision of charity. Millions of Americans may experience the charitable motivation to send money voluntarily to help halt AIDS in Africa, but the "free-rider effect" suggests that many of the potentially charitable people may choose not to donate, assuming that others will. The standard analysis here is that the potential donors gain from the healthful program in Africa even if they do not personally contribute.

The previous accounts explain that an economic rationale for government intervention can be provided on several grounds. These do not imply, however, that actual government interventions will be economically justified. For example, Philipson and Posner (1993) argue that the behaviors of epidemic sufferers matter substantially to the progress of an epidemic and to the wisdom of particular interventions. Should government encourage and provide AIDS testing? Intuition can run afoul with economic behavior here. Those testing negative may increase their risky behavior, or people testing positive may not care about infecting others. The examples add an extra condition to justifying government involvement—it must have a reasonable chance of being effective.

Philipson and Posner also argue that much of AIDS infection and contagion is conducted by personal choice, plausibly even rational choice. To understand, predict, and control the epidemic may require the understanding and manipulation of "prices" and benefits that those involved face when making their choices. We may find means to encourage the dampening of prevalence growth by understanding the role of this economic behavior.

Case Study: HIV/AIDS in Africa

HIV/AIDS[1]

The term *AIDS* (Auto-Immune Deficiency Syndrome) first appeared in the *Morbidity and Mortality Weekly Report (MMWR)* of the Centers for Disease Control (CDC) in 1982 to describe ". . . a disease, at least moderately predictive of a defect in cell-mediated immunity, occurring with no known cause for diminished resistance to that disease." AIDS is caused by infection with the human retroviruses HIV-1 or -2. These viruses are passed through sexual contact; through contact with blood, blood products, or other bodily fluids (as in drug abusers who share contaminated intravenous needles); intrapartum or perinatally from mother to infant; or via breast milk. There is no evidence that the virus can be passed through casual or family contact or by insects, such as mosquitoes.

By the end of 2003, almost 930,000 cumulative cases of AIDS had been reported in the United States. As noted in Table 24-1, over 525,000 had died, with the largest percentages between the ages of 35 and 44. However, the death rate from AIDS has

[1]Material in this section comes from Braunwald et al. (2001), develop.pbg.mcgraw-hill.com/medical/harrisons/downloads/manual_ch86.pdf, accessed November 16, 2005.

TABLE 24-1 Estimated Numbers of Deaths of Persons with AIDS, by Year of Death

Age at Death (yrs)	Year of Death					Cumulative Through 2003
	1999	*2000*	*2001*	*2002*	*2003*	*2003*
<13	97	51	48	35	29	5,103
13–14	18	8	4	11	8	252
15–24	232	216	270	199	229	9,789
25–34	3,258	2,823	2,512	2,143	1,928	142,761
35–44	7,706	7,138	7,525	6,896	6,970	216,093
45–54	4,994	5,203	5,548	5,737	5,964	104,064
55–64	1,556	1,631	1,873	1,840	2,146	33,717
>65	630	670	743	696	741	12,282
Total	18,491	17,741	18,524	17,557	18,017	524,060

Source: www.cdc.gov/hiv/stats/2003SurveillanceReport/table7.htm, accessed August 18, 2005.

decreased substantially due to the increased use of potent antiretroviral drugs. Major risk groups continue to be men who have had sex with men, and men and women injection drug users (IDUs); however, the number of cases that are transmitted heterosexually, particularly among women, has increased since the mid-1990s. The incidence of AIDS transmitted from women to their children has fallen dramatically, as has the risk of acquiring new infection through contaminated blood products.

Globally, HIV/AIDS is a pandemic, especially in developing countries. The current estimate of the number of cases of HIV infection worldwide is approximately 40 million, with over 25.4 million found in sub-Saharan Africa, and another 7.1 million in South and Southeast Asia. Of the worldwide cases, 45 percent are women.

Infections that take advantage of a weakened immune system include:

- Pneumocystis carinii pneumonia
- Toxoplasmosis
- Tuberculosis
- Extreme weight loss and wasting, exacerbated by diarrhea that can be experienced in up to 90 percent of HIV patients worldwide
- Meningitis and other brain infections
- Fungal infections
- Syphilis
- Malignancies, such as lymphoma and cervical cancer
- Kaposi's Sarcoma, which affects the skin and mouth and may spread to the lungs

Many of the economic theories just described take on a great reality in the context of the current African AIDS epidemic. While each continent has been infected, we will see that the epidemic in Africa is extraordinarily bad, making it a reasonable focus of policy by those intent on stopping the worldwide AIDS epidemic.

With over 20 million dead, projections of future human and material loss are disturbing and continue to worsen. Drugs and drug cocktails that stem the progress of the disease now exist. Human behavioral change, which might follow substantial improvements in the transmission of information, offers hope as well. The situation in Africa is so dire, however, that many propose that the response from the West must be stronger and sustained.

Costs of AIDS

Another way of assessing both the prevalence of AIDS and its consequences for human life is to assess its effect on life expectancy. Table 24-2 shows changes in life expectancy for the countries with the largest incidences of AIDS. Columns (1), (2), and (3) give the life expectancy with AIDS, the life expectancy without AIDS, and the difference. Note first that most, although not all, of the countries are in Africa.

TABLE 24-2 HIV/AIDS Annual Cost

Country	(1) Life Expectancy With AIDS	(2) Life Expectancy Without AIDS	(3) Difference	(4) % Decrease Labor Force	(5) Population Age 15–64	(6) Loss in $ × 1,000@$1/hr
Angola	44.6	46.5	1.9	6.0	6,323	286,040
Bahamas	69.1	72.8	3.7	6.4	198	9,506
Benin	53.5	55.0	1.5	3.8	4,071	114,497
Botswana	44.4	67.6	23.2	44.1	941	311,281
Brazil	67.2	67.6	0.4	0.8	126,390	720,856
Burkina Faso	45.3	53.4	8.1	21.1	6,828	1,080,211
Burundi	40.6	49.6	9.0	26.0	3,973	775,079
Cameroon	50.0	56.2	1.2	2.9	9,384	204,990
Central African Republic	44.3	52.9	8.6	22.7	2,271	386,489
Chad	45.2	47.2	2.0	6.2	4,759	221,693
Congo	50.9	56.9	6.0	14.3	30,361	3,260,728
Côte D'Ivoire	47.7	56.6	8.9	21.4	9,741	1,563,009
Dem. Republic of Congo	50.5	54.9	4.4	11.0	1,821	150,609
Djibouti	45.5	50.5	5.0	14.1	461	48,697
Dominican Republic	67.3	68.2	0.9	1.7	5,579	70,786
Eritrea	51.5	53.3	1.8	4.7	2,437	85,899
Ethiopia	44.5	50.6	6.1	17.1	38,978	5,009,111
Gabon	52.4	55.5	3.1	7.7	751	43,113
Gambia	45.4	47.0	1.6	5.0	842	31,575
Ghana	56.3	60.0	3.7	8.2	12,559	774,472
Guinea-Bissau	44.1	45.7	1.6	5.2	785	30,684
Guyana	63.7	65.4	1.7	3.4	524	13,256
Haiti	52.0	57.1	5.1	12.1	4,379	397,855
Honduras	65.6	67.1	1.5	2.9	4,027	86,955
India	62.3	62.8	0.5	1.0	690,215	5,414,867
Kenya	52.2	63.6	11.4	23.5	18,675	3,285,417
Lesotho	51.2	61.4	10.2	22.0	1,178	194,218
Liberia	48.1	51.8	3.7	10.1	1,583	119,370
Malawi	40.7	51.2	10.5	29.0	6,452	1,403,577
Mali	50.9	52.6	1.7	4.5	5,576	189,080
Mozambique	40.6	47.0	6.4	20.0	10,504	1,575,600
Myanmar	55.8	57.2	1.4	3.3	32,056	797,602

Namibia	45.1	62.1	17.0	36.1	1,172	317,261
Nigeria	51.3	55.6	4.3	10.6	70,328	5,586,399
Rwanda	39.4	49.2	9.8	28.7	4,687	1,007,294
Sierra Leone	37.3	39.0	1.7	7.1	3,046	161,819
South Africa	56.7	63.3	6.6	13.7	28,610	2,932,081
Swaziland	50.8	60.2	9.4	20.8	632	98,575
Thailand	69.6	71.4	1.8	3.2	44,791	1,072,125
Togo	51.3	57.1	5.8	13.8	2,958	305,637
Uganda	41.9	52.0	10.1	27.3	13,006	2,662,715
United Rep. of Tanzania	51.1	57.1	6.0	14.3	19,628	2,098,005
Zambia	40.5	57.6	17.1	40.1	5,751	1,731,375
Zimbabwe	42.9	66.5	23.6	45.8	7,160	2,460,816
Total						49,091,223

Sources: Life Expectancies: United Nations Population Division, *World Population Prospects: 2000 Revision Highlights*, February 28, 2001, p. 59; www.overpopulation.com/faq/health/infectious_diseases/aids/life_expectancy.html, accessed August 18, 2005; Population data from www.census.gov/ipc/www/idbsum.html.

While some countries have only small changes, Botswana shows a life expectancy decrease of 23.2 years and South Africa shows a decrease of 6.6 years.

The decrease in life expectancy implies a permanent decrease in the country's labor force, and it is an interesting exercise in applied economics to estimate the annual cost to the country's economy. Column (4) measures the percentage decrease in labor force in terms of years of labor that may be provided after the age of 15. For example, the 8.1 year decline in Burkina Faso, represents a 21.1 percent decline in labor force from the expected 38.4 years (i.e., 53.4 minus 15). These percentages are then multiplied by the 2005 populations between the ages of 15 and 64 (column 5), to give the number of person-years lost.

For a conservative measure of the loss, assume that half of the population would be working for 1,500 hours per year, at a wage of $1.00 per hour. Table 24-2 shows that the annual loss from HIV/AIDS for Burkina Faso, a tax on the country in foregone production, is over $1.08 billion! The countries with the largest losses include Ethiopia, Nigeria, and India (because its population is so large). Summing these losses for the countries in the table provides an annual HIV/AIDS productivity loss of $49.1 billion!

Fighting AIDS

Economic analysis can help to identify the reasons why halting this epidemic will benefit from strong responses from the private, the nonprofit, and the public sectors of these economies—. But it especially explains why private and voluntary market interactions will not stop AIDS in Africa, and why it has often made things much worse.

Sexual practices that were common and acceptable in the culture became deadly with the introduction of the AIDS virus. Similarly, common economic practices, such as traveling long distances to look for work or as a part of one's work, became ready means for the virus to travel. When local jobs disappear, sometimes due to side effects of the crisis, then the geographic search for work outside of the local area probably made the epidemic even worse.

A two-pronged attack on the problem can bring substantial success. Before 2001 drug treatments for HIV/AIDS were effective although extremely costly, with the annual cost of a three-drug combination antiretroviral (ART) regimen for a patient in a poor country approximately $10,000 to $25,000. As noted by Over (2004), only a few of the richest developing countries, such as Brazil and Thailand, could attempt to finance ART for their AIDS patients. In most developing countries, the only patients receiving ART were the very rich or those who had access to rationed, low-price supplies through a variety of pilot or research projects.

Since 2001, however, generic versions of ART medications have become available in poor countries at a cost of as little as $200 per year. In 2001, at the Doha round of World Trade Organization (WTO) discussions, both industrial and developing countries negotiated and signed a Declaration on Trade-Related Aspects of Intellectual Property Rights (TRIPs) and Public Health. This declaration confirmed provisions already implicit in earlier WTO agreements: a country would have the right to grant "compulsory licenses" to

FIGURE 24-4 Lowest World Prices per Patient per Year for Stavudine (d4T) + Lamivudin (3TC) + Nevirapine (NVP)

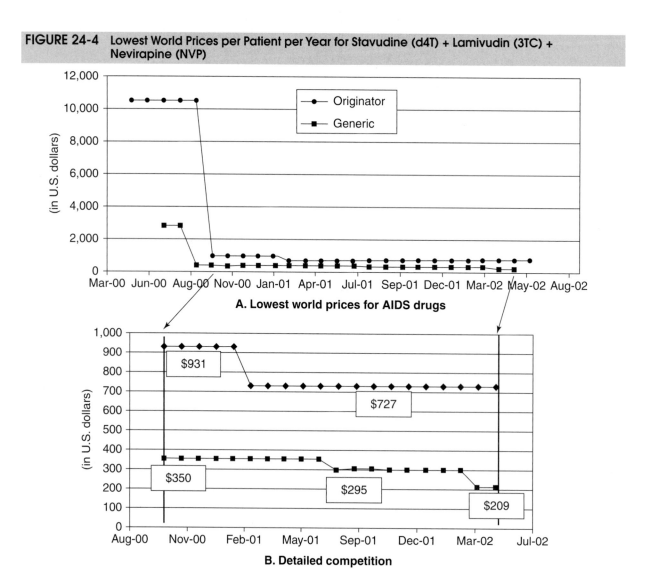

Source: Equitable Access: Scaling Up HIV/AIDS Treatment in Developing Countries, Medecins Sans Frontieres, www.msf.or.jp/access/pdf/a_021129-1.pdf, accessed December 2002.

a domestic pharmaceutical manufacturer to produce medications for domestic consumption when the national government decides there is a public health emergency. In 2003, further negotiation led to an extension of the declaration to permit countries without domestic pharmaceutical industries to import generic versions of patented drugs. Permission was made subject to the WTO's endorsement of the absence of domestic production capability, and generic manufacturers and exporters were required to ensure that the generic versions be easily distinguishable visually from the patented version.

To see how competition brought the treatment prices down, Figure 24-4 shows how the innovation of generic drugs brought down the cost of providing the triple combination of stavudine (d4T) + lamivudin (3TC)+ nevirapine (NVP) from over $10,000 per year to just over $200 per year for a generic equivalent. While such costs may still be very high for poor residents of poor countries, the 98 percent decline in treatment cost (Panel B) allows limited health care resources to go much further in treating HIV/AIDS.

Information forms the other major branch in the attack on AIDS in Africa. Low-cost prophylactic measures were not commonly used when the epidemic hit, nor were the causes of the epidemic widely known or understood.

Figure 24-5 demonstrates one of the key production processes that apply to stopping AIDS: the distribution and use of latex condoms. Individuals participate in the production of their own health. Many of the material inputs are simple and inexpensive, but it is the information that makes the health gain possible. The figure shows that increased condom usage in Thailand was accompanied by a decline in the incidence of STDs. The striking effectiveness of condom use in this case is a cause for optimism. However, Westerners attempting to help must confront local cultures and beliefs that may stand in the way of prevention. It is legitimate to ask whether they are justified in attacking "superstitions," in the means they use to attack the spreading virus?

The approach of providing scientifically valid information, however, has been applied in practice in Africa and with indigenous support. These two branches of the attack on AIDS in Africa suggest the need for collective action through government because information is substantially a public good, in which its marginal cost of transmission is extremely low once the infrastructure has been established. Furthermore, it is hard to sell information in a private market because it is economically infeasible to limit the information to those who pay.

A similarly important public role follows from an economic analysis of both the detrimental and the beneficial externalities involved. Risky sexual behaviors involve risks to more people than just the individual making the risky choice. Economic logic implies that

FIGURE 24-5 The Impact of Rising Condom Use in Thailand

Source: Confronting AIDS: Public Priorities in a Global Epidemic, World Bank, 1997.

the effective price of risky behaviors be raised, and government may be instrumental in doing so. The government can also intervene to reduce the effective price of safe sexual behavior, for example, by providing condoms freely yet with social discretion.

Also, a beneficial externality occurs to the millions of people worldwide who feel a charitable gain in the gains to Africans who keep or regain health. This charitable externality can in principle be expressed through voluntary charities, and we can hope that this proves an important source. However, free-riding behaviors can also be reduced through the collective provision of the aid to Africa. For an unusual example of aid to Africa, see Box 24-2.

Through the 1990s, foreign aid contributions from the United States to combat AIDS were not large. However, the unique present circumstances may require overriding that fear, at least in the view of the economist Jeffrey Sachs of Columbia

BOX 24-2

"The Right Man at the Right Time"

It has been said that some people begin to study economics when they come to believe that rock and roll isn't going to feed the hungry. Yet music superstars have frequently taken the forefront in teaching new generations about the world's problems, from the suffering millions in Ethiopia to the plight of farmers and farm workers. What made U2's world superstar musician, Bono, warrant the cover of *Time* magazine in March 2002 was his method for trying to "save the world." Bono successfully sought out the world's movers and shakers, from corporate giants to the U.S. Treasury Secretary to Pope John Paul II—people who were said to have found him surprisingly well-informed on the plight of Africans fighting the AIDS epidemic and hunger. *Time* called Bono "the right man at the right time."

When the rock star headed to Africa for rounds of talks and an economic summit, he first consulted with Jeffrey Sachs, famous for promoting debt relief for Bolivia and advising the transitional economies of Poland and Russia. Sachs has become one of his profession's leading advocates of aid and debt relief to an Africa in crisis.

It made good sense, too, for Bono to consult corporate leaders, who in some cases provide substantial funds to aid in Africa. Some criticize "tough love" via the American business style, yet others hope that it will be an approach that succeeds in an area in crisis.

Chris Hondros/Newmakers/Getty Images, Inc.

University. He has estimated that the United States would need to contribute $1 billion a year for a comprehensive plan to fight AIDS in a partnership with other industrialized nations (*Newsweek*, March 19, 2001). He points out that this is a small portion of U.S. Gross Domestic Product.

Economic Theory and African Reality

Two strands of health economic theory bear most critically on the African experience. The first among these must be the role of information. Affordable technologies, such as the use of condoms, are available in principle but they must be adopted to become effective. In many cases, the local cultural patterns in some African countries involve either a nonscientific understanding of AIDS or cultural relationships between the sexes that have minor effects during times when the risk of infection is low, but have potentially disastrous effects during an ongoing epidemic. To intervene with reliable, scientific information may be costly when it disturbs the local culture. In this sense, it could bear a cost similar to the costly AIDS drugs that must also play an important role. However, information has proved to be an effective weapon against AIDS in some cases where it is vigorously applied.

Secondly, the concept of prevalence elasticity of demand for preventive goods and services may also be very important in Africa. We have seen that a sufficiently large elasticity of demand for preventive care can result in a prevention response so large that growing prevalence of disease can result in a lower rate of new infections. Africans do not appear to have responded to growing evidence of the AIDS epidemic with behaviors that embrace preventive care. If, as this suggests, the prevalence elasticity of the demand for preventive care is very low, it portends a growing epidemic. Information could play a double role by encouraging the responsiveness of preventive demand to further evidence of a growing prevalence of the disease.

Conclusions

Economic epidemiology provides new theoretical ideas, speculative applications, and studies spurred on by a new urgency caused by the AIDS epidemic in progress across the world. Economic theory helps to inform epidemiological theory by developing the dynamic role of the elasticity of the demand for preventive care as it responds to a growing prevalence of the disease.

Epidemics have economic consequences most often found in the reduction of the growth rate of GDP, especially through the loss of manpower and the diversion of economic activity away from more productive efforts. It is unclear, however, whether an epidemic will tend to lower per capita income.

Information theory plays a critical role in epidemics in that the nature of the disease in scientific terms must become clear in order for the demand for prevention to overcome the progress of the disease. The chief technology is the vaccine. Where available, the vaccine must be seen as having benefits overcoming the costs.

Africa provides a sobering case study on the effects of the AIDS epidemic. Issues of information and the need to induce prevention responses among susceptible people are foci of attention, as is the treatment of AIDS sufferers. Changes in personal behaviors, such as the use of condoms, can involve small capital costs but have substantial effects. The epidemic meets the economic rationales for the involvement of collective action, and those speaking up most often about the problems of Africa usually emphasize the need for all three—government, private markets, and nonprofits—to play a part.

SUMMARY

1. Incidence is the number of new cases of the disease relative to the population. The hazard rate is the instantaneous rate of infection. Prevalence is the total number of cases per the population.
2. The prevalence elasticity of demand for preventive care is the percentage increase in the quantity of preventive care demanded per a percentage increase in the prevalence of the disease.
3. The standard epidemiological model predicts that an increase in the prevalence of an infectious disease will tend to result in an increase in the incidence rate of the disease.
4. In the economic model, a sufficiently high prevalence elasticity of demand for preventive care can lead to a decrease in the incidence of the disease.
5. Contracting an infectious disease is analogous to being affected by a tax in that it leads to costly responses to avoid the harm. These avoidance costs are logically part of the cost of illness.
6. The difficulty in eradicating an infectious disease can be explained by an economic model. When a sufficiently lowered prevalence of the disease leads people to demand zero preventive care, its benefits no longer outweigh its costs.
7. AIDS in Africa has reduced life expectancies in many countries. In some cases, the reduction has been from 10 to 20 years of life expectancy.
8. Methods to curb AIDS in Africa have included new drugs and efforts to get reduced prices for these drugs. It has also included effectively providing simple and inexpensive technologies such as the distribution of condoms.
9. Both the economic culture and the social culture revealed serious problems in dealing with the new epidemic.
10. Problems of information are central to most approaches toward stopping the AIDS epidemic in Africa.

DISCUSSION QUESTIONS

1. Identify several examples of preventive goods and services that are relevant to reducing the risk of infection from a disease that you name.
2. Philipson's model describes the role of the prevalence elasticity of demand for preventive care. Does this imply that the epidemic is "self-limiting" so that we need do nothing about it?
3. How might information regarding AIDS, its method of transmission, and the means to stop the epidemic be conveyed to people in Africa?
4. Is the complete eradication of all infectious diseases from the globe a wise objective? Is it a feasible objective?
5. What prices should drug companies charge for AIDS drugs for Africans? What the market will bear? At cost? Zero?

EXERCISES

1. Suppose that the prevalence elasticity of demand for prevention was 0.1. What would be the impact of a 10 percent increase in prevalence of a contagious disease? Why?
2. Provide an explanation for why increasing income inequality is associated with greater prevalence of HIV infection in Africa.
3. Suppose that the incidence of AIDS, I, is determined by the prevalence of AIDS, A, and the demand for preventive care, P, as in the equation:

$$I = kA^{0.03}P^{-0.01}$$

where k is a constant. Let preventive care demand, in turn, be a function of the prevalence of AIDS, so that $P = gA^{0.4}$. By substitution, find the incidence solely in terms of A, and determine from this whether incidence rises or falls with prevalence, A.

4. If asked to determine where the next million dollars to be spent on curbing AIDS in Africa should go, would you recommend high-tech drug treatments or relatively low-tech behavioral practices. Sketch out the categories of costs per case that will need to be measured to assess the problem in a cost-effectiveness format.

5. We have seen that there was a major decline in the price of drugs for HIV/AIDS between 2000 and 200?.
 a. Check various web sources to find what has happened to the prices since 2002.
 b. With the fall in the price of drugs, enumerate the other costs that stand in the way of larger scale treatment for HIV/AIDS in Africa.

Glossary

Actuarially Fair Insurance under which expected pay outs equal the premiums paid by beneficiaries.

Adverse Selection A situation often resulting from asymmetric information in which individuals are able to purchase insurance at rates that are below actuarially fair rates plus loading costs.

Agency Relationship A situation in which one person (agent) makes decisions on behalf of another person (principal).

Alternative Delivery System (ADS) Insurance and organizational arrangements for health care delivery that are alternatives to traditional fee-for-service (FFS) arrangements.

Asymmetric Information Situations in which the parties on the opposite sides of a transaction have differing amounts of relevant information.

Average Cost Total cost represents the sum of all fixed costs and variable costs in the short run. Average cost equals total cost divided by the quantity of output and also equals the sum of average variable cost (AVC) and average fixed cost (AFC). In the long run, average total cost represents the minimum possible cost per unit of producing any given level of output when there are no fixed costs.

Balance Billing The practice of collecting from the patient the difference between the charge and the insurance reimbursement.

Barrier-to-Entry Impediments to the unrestricted flow of factors into or out of an industry or occupation (e.g., control over natural resources, licensure, patents).

Budget Constraint The line that is the collection of points representing combinations of goods that the consumer is just able to afford.

Capitation A method of reimbursement in managed care plans in which a provider is paid a fixed amount per person over a given period regardless of the amount of services rendered.

Cardinal Utility A quantitative measure of the value of a good in terms of metrically measurable utility. It is used in the study of risk and insurance.

Case-Mix Index A numerical measure of the assortment of patient cases treated by a given hospital, so that a higher value indicates a greater average degree of complexity of the cases.

CAT (Computerized Axial Tomography) Diagnostic equipment which produces cross-sectional images of the head and/or body.

Centers for Medicare & Medicaid Services (CMS) An agency of the U.S. Department of Health and Human Services (DHHS). CMS is responsible for administering the financing and quality assurance programs for Medicare and the federal participation in Medicaid; formerly the Health Care Financing Administration (HCFA).

Certificate of Need (CON) Regulations that require health care providers to obtain approval from state planning agencies for capital expenditures that exceed various threshold levels (e.g., $500,000).

Ceteris Paribus Other things being held constant.

Coefficient of Variation A measure of dispersion equal to the standard deviation divided by the mean (and sometimes multiplied by 100).

Coinsurance (Rate) The share of costs that are paid by the beneficiary of a health policy (often after some deductible).

Community Rating The practice of setting insurance premiums based on the utilization pattern of a broad population in a region. This approach to rate setting contrasts with experience rating.

Comparative Statics The analysis that calculates the level of a new equilibrium given changed values of one or more economic parameters, such as prices or income.

Competition (See Perfect Competition)

Concentration Ratio The share of the market sales or production accounted for by a certain number of the largest firms. Often the four-firm ratio is used.

Consumer-Driven Health Plan (CDHP) A high-deductible health plan coupled with a tax-advantaged health spending account (HSA or HRA). Consumers are provided with information and tools to help with health care service and financing decisions.

Copayment Amounts paid by the insurance beneficiary as a result of coinsurance and deductibles.

Cost-Benefit Analysis (CBA) A method of comparing the monetary value of all benefits of a social project with all costs of that project.

Cost-Effectiveness Analysis (CEA) A method that tries to find the least cost method of achieving a desired objective(s) associated with a social project.

Cost Sharing (See also Copayment) Methods of financing health care that require some direct payments for services by patients.

Cost Shifting Increasing revenues from some payers to offset uncompensated care costs and lower net payments from other payers.

Cost-Utility Analysis (CUA) A form of cost-effectiveness analysis in which outcomes, such as quality-adjusted life years (QALYs), reflect the quantity and quality of life.

Cross (Price) Elasticity of Demand (See also Elasticity) The percentage change in the quantity demanded of one good resulting from a 1 percent change in the price of another good.

Crowd Out A response to the introduction or enhancement of public insurance, referring to the extent that those who have previously used private coverage now use public coverage.

Deductible The amount of health care charges for which a beneficiary is responsible before the insurer begins payment.

Demand Function The relationship between quantity demanded and price (and other independent variables, such as income and tastes). One could study individual demand as well as market demand.

Depreciation The change in the value of a good over time, due to deteriorating physical characteristics or technical obsolescence.

Diagnostic Related Groups (DRGs) A set of case types established under the prospective payment system (PPS) identifying patients with similar conditions and processes of care. There are currently 504 DRGs in Medicare's prospective payment system, each of which is assigned a relative weight that compares its costliness to the average for all DRGs.

Discount Rate The interest rate used when converting sums to be received at a future date to a present value.

Discounting The process of converting sums to be received at a future date to a present value.

Economic Profit (See also Monopoly Profit) The return over and above that which is necessary to keep the firm from exiting the market over the long run. These profits are also called above normal profits, excess profits, and supra normal profits.

Economies of Scale Situations in which the long-run average costs of a firm decline as output increases.

Economies of Scope Situations in which a firm can jointly produce two or more goods more cheaply than under separate production of the goods.

Edgeworth Box (in Consumption) A diagram that shows all possible allocations of fixed amounts of goods and services between two people.

Efficiency (See also Pareto Efficiency) Technical efficiency occurs when the firm produces the maximum possible sustained output from a given set of inputs. This idea is distinguished from allocative efficiency—situations in which either inputs or outputs are put to their best possible uses in the economy so that no further gains in output or welfare are possible. Both allocative and technical efficiency are prerequisites for Pareto efficiency.

Elasticity The percentage change in some dependent variable (e.g., quantity demanded) resulting from a 1 percent change in some independent variable (e.g., price). Elasticities that exceed 1 in absolute value are considered elastic; elasticities less than 1 are inelastic.

Elasticity of Substitution (See also Elasticity) The percentage change in the capital-labor ratio resulting from a 1 percent change in relative factor prices.

Equilibrium Price (Quantity) The price (quantity) at which the quantity demanded and the quantity supplied are equal.

Expected Value A measure used with a probability distribution of returns. The expected value is the sum of each probability multiplied by its corresponding return.

Experience Good A good for which evaluation is difficult prior to experience or purchase.

Experience Rating The practice of setting insurance premiums for an individual or group based on historical experience or risk associated with the individual or group.

Externality A case in which a consumer (producer) affects the utility (costs) of another consumer (producer) through actions that lie outside the price system.

Fee-for-Service (FFS) A method of payment under which the provider is paid for each procedure or service that is provided to a patient.

Fee Schedule A listing of fees by third-party payers showing the maximum amounts they will reimburse for specific services or procedures.

Firm Any entity that transforms inputs to some product or service that is sold in the marketplace.

First Fundamental Theorem of Welfare Economics The proposition that under specified conditions, competitive markets lead to Pareto efficient results.

Fixed Costs (TFC and AFC) Costs that do not vary with output. They are expressed either as total fixed cost (TFC) or average fixed cost (AFC).

Formulary A list of drugs developed by a managed care plan. Under a positive formulary, prescriptions on the list are covered. Under a negative formulary, prescriptions on the list are not covered.

Frontier Analysis A statistical analysis of firm efficiency that attempts to identify the best possible production practice and interprets firm inefficiency as a departure from the best possible production practice or frontier.

Game Theory A model that analyzes economic behavior as a series of strategic moves and countermoves by rival agents.

Gatekeeper The primary care provider who is responsible for coordinating a patient's care in a managed care plan. Often the gatekeeper must authorize referrals to specialists and nonemergency hospital admissions.

Gross Domestic Product (GDP) The market value of final goods and services produced within the borders of a country over a period of one year.

Group Insurance An insurance contract in which employees or members of a group are covered by a policy issued by their employer or group.

Hazard In epidemiology, the instantaneous rate of infection.

Health and Health Status (See also Morbidity Rate and Mortality Rate) The measures of the physical and emotional well-being of an individual or a defined population. Mortality and morbidity rates are often used to measure health status.

Health Care Goods and services used as inputs to produce health. In some analyses, one's own time and knowledge used to maintain and promote health are considered in addition to conventional health care inputs.

Health Maintenance Organization (HMO) A managed care plan that integrates financing and delivery of a comprehensive set of health care services to an enrolled population. HMOs may contract with or directly employ health care providers.

Health Savings Account (HSA) Introduced in 2003 as part of the Medicare prescription drug benefit legislation, the HSA is a less-restrictive medical savings account (MSA), owned by the employee, and open to anyone enrolled in a high-deductible health plan and not already covered by public or private insurance.

Health Plan Employer Data and Information Set (HEDIS) A set of standardized measures to evaluate health plan performance. HEDIS is used by the National Committee on Quality Assurance (NCQA) to accredit HMOs.

Health Reimbursement Account (HRA) An HRA is similar to a health spending account (HSA), but it is completely controlled by the employer and does not have to be linked to a high-deductible health plan. The HRA is used to pay for qualified medical expenses and can also be used to purchase health insurance.

Herfindahl-Hirschman Index (HHI) A measure of market concentration that incorporates the size distribution of firms. It is found by summing the squares of the market shares of each firm.

Human Capital A form of intangible capital that includes the skills and other knowledge that workers have or acquire through education, training, and health care that yields valuable productive services over time.

Incidence (See also Prevalence) In epidemiology, the number of new cases per a defined population.

Income Effect (See also Substitution Effect) The effect on quantity demanded that results from the change in real income associated with a relative change in the price of the good or service under study.

Income Elasticity of Demand (See also Elasticity) The percentage change in quantity demanded resulting from a 1 percent change in income.

Indemnity Insurance Traditional health insurance often associated with fee-for-service payments, fee schedules, and, which unlike managed care, places few restrictions on choice of providers.

Independent Practice Association (IPA) Physicians in independent, solo, or small group practices, who contract with a health maintenance organization to provide services to its members.

Indifference Curve Shows all combinations of goods that provide a constant level of satisfaction (utility) to the individual under study.

Inefficiency (See Efficiency and Pareto Efficiency)

Infant Mortality Rate The ratio of the number of deaths in infants age one year or less during a year divided by the number of live births during the year.

Inferior Good (See also Normal Good) A good or service for which demand decreases as income increases.

Internal Rate of Return The discount rate that will equate the time streams of costs and returns of an investment. It is a measure of the profitability of an investment.

Isoquant (Isoproduct Curve) All combinations of factors of production yielding a constant level of output.

Labor-Leisure Trade-off The line that is the collection of points representing the combinations of leisure time and earnings from work that are possible for a person.

Law of Demand There is an inverse relationship between price and quantity demanded, ceteris paribus.

Law of Diminishing Returns After some point, the marginal product of a variable input must diminish.

Loading Costs The administrative and other costs associated with underwriting an insurance policy.

Long Run (See also Short Run) A period of time sufficient to permit a firm to vary all factors of production.

Long-Term Care The ongoing health and social services provided for individuals who need assistance on a continuing basis because of physical or mental disability. Services can be provided in an institution, the home, or the community, and include informal services provided by family or friends as well as formal services provided by professionals or agencies.

Luxury Good A good that richer people tend to buy in greater proportions so that its income elasticity is greater than 1.

Managed Care Any payment or delivery arrangement used by a health plan or provider to control or to

coordinate use of health services to contain health expenditures, improve quality, or both.

Managed Care Organization (MCO) A general term referring to the various health plans that use managed care arrangements and have a defined system of selected providers that contract with them. The most common are health maintenance organizations (HMOs), preferred provider organizations (PPOs), and point-of-service (POS) plans.

Mandated Benefits The coverage in health insurance policies for certain services that are mandated by state insurance statutes.

Marginal Cost The increase in total cost resulting from a one-unit increase in output.

Marginal Labor (Factor) Cost The addition to total labor (factor) costs associated with an additional unit of labor (factor of production).

Marginal Product The addition to total output resulting from an additional unit of the variable input.

Marginal Rate of Substitution The amount of one commodity given up per unit increase in another commodity while maintaining the same level of satisfaction.

Marginal Rate of Technical Substitution The amount of one factor of production given up per unit increase in another factor of production while maintaining the same level of output.

Marginal Rate of Transformation The slope of the production possibilities curve, and the rate at which society can transform one good into another.

Marginal Revenue The addition to total revenue associated with a one-unit increase in output.

Marginal Revenue Product The addition to a firm's total revenue associated with employing one more unit of a variable input.

Marginal Utility The extra utility gained from consuming one more unit of a good holding others constant. Utility is a measure of the satisfaction from consuming goods.

Market Demand The total demand for a good by all consumers in the market.

Market Structure The structure relating to how an industry is organized in terms of the number and distribution of firms and how firms compete among themselves.

Medicaid The health insurance programs administered by the states for qualifying low-income beneficiaries. The federal government establishes minimum standards and provides matching grants. The program became law in 1965.

Medicare The federal health insurance program established in 1965 for the elderly and other selected groups.

Medical Savings Account (MSA) A limited health spending account (HSA) that was introduced on an experimental basis in the 1990s. MSAs were aimed at small businesses and individuals.

Medicare—Part A The Medicare Hospital Insurance that covers beneficiaries for inpatient hospital, home health, hospice, and limited skilled nursing facility services. Beneficiaries are responsible for deductibles and copayments.

Medicare—Part B The Medicare Supplementary Medical Insurance that covers Medicare beneficiaries for physician services, medical supplies, and other outpatient treatment. Beneficiaries are responsible for monthly premiums, copayments, deductibles, and balance billing.

Medicare—Part C (Medicare Advantage) An expanded set of options for the delivery of health care under Medicare. While all Medicare beneficiaries can receive their benefits through the original fee-for-service program, most beneficiaries enrolled in both Part A and Part B can choose to participate in a Medicare Advantage plan instead. Managed care or fee-for-service providers that seek to contract as Medicare Advantage plans must meet specific organizational, financial, and other requirements.

Medicare—Part D Beginning in 2006, Part D provides subsidized access to prescription drug insurance coverage on a voluntary basis, upon payment of a premium, to individuals entitled to Part A or enrolled in Part B, with premium and cost-sharing subsidies for low-income enrollees. Beneficiaries may enroll in either a stand-alone prescription drug plan (PDP) or an integrated Medicare Advantage plan that offers Part D coverage.

Medigap Policy A privately purchased insurance policy that supplements Medicare coverage and meets specified requirements set by federal statute and the National Association of Insurance Commissioners.

Monopoly Situations in which a firm faces a negatively sloped demand curve. In a pure monopoly, there is no other firm that produces a close substitute for the firm's product. Thus, the demand curve facing the monopolist is the market demand curve.

Monopoly Profit (Rent) The return over and above a normal profit resulting from monopoly.

Monopsony Situations in which a firm faces a positively sloped supply curve in the product or factor market because it is the only buyer.

Moral Hazard An insurance term that represents the disincentives created by insurance for individuals to take measures that would reduce the amount of care demanded. In the health services literature, it is more commonly used to express the additional quantity of health care demanded, resulting from a decrease in the net price of care attributable to insurance.

Morbidity Rate The rate of incidence of disease in a particular population.

Mortality Rate The death rate for a particular population. The crude death rate is the ratio of deaths during a year divided by mid-year population. Because age is

so important, the age-adjusted mortality rate is a measure that takes into account a population's age distribution.

Necessity A good whose consumption does not vary greatly with changes in peoples' incomes. More generally, a good with an income elasticity less than 1.

Nominal Value (See also Real Value) The money value measured in current dollars.

Nonprofit Firm A firm that is constrained by law from distributing any residual of income over costs to any party.

Normal Good (See also Inferior Good) A good or service for which demand increases as income increases.

Normal Return (Normal Profit) The return just sufficient to retain factors of production in an industry or an occupation in the long run. The return equal to the opportunity cost of a factor of production.

Nursing Facility An institution that provides skilled nursing care and rehabilitation services to injured, functionally disabled, or sick persons.

Offer Curve A set of points summarizing the amount of a good that an individual will offer for trade, given his or her preferences, endowment, and the prices of other goods.

Opportunity Cost The value of the best alternative that is forgone in order to get or produce more of the commodity under consideration.

Ordinal Utility Utility as evaluated through relative levels of satisfaction, when the particular unit of utility is not essential. Examples of ordinal numbers are first, second, and third.

Pareto Efficiency (Optimum) (See also Efficiency) A situation in which it is impossible to improve the level of welfare of one party without hurting the welfare level of another party. Situations in which the level of welfare of one or more parties can be improved without hurting any other party are Pareto improvements.

Pay-for-Performance (P4P) The effort by managed care organizations and other payers to reward providers who improve the quality of their care by meeting certain performance standards. Providers typically receive bonus payments for meeting the goals.

Participation/Assignment A situation in which a provider agrees to accept the third-party payer's payment in full, thereby relieving the patient of any balance (except for applicable patient copayments).

Peer Review Organization (PRO) An organization that contracts with the Centers for Medicare & Medicaid Services to investigate the quality of health care furnished to Medicare beneficiaries and to educate beneficiaries and providers. PROs also conduct limited review of medical records and claims to evaluate the appropriateness of care provided.

Perfect Competition A market structure in which there are (1) numerous buyers and sellers, (2) perfect information, (3) free entry and exit, and (4) a homogeneous product.

Play or Pay Insurance proposal that would require employers to either provide minimal levels of health insurance to their employees or pay into a fund that would be used to provide coverage.

Point-of-Service (POS) Plan A managed care plan that encourages patients to select a provider in a network. Members can select non-network providers but will incur higher out-of-pocket costs.

Preferred Provider Organization (PPO) An arrangement under which an enrollee is given financial incentives (e.g., no copayments) to seek care from selected physicians and hospitals with which the payer has contracted.

Prepaid Group Practice (PGP) A prepayment arrangement under which participating providers agree to provide services to eligible enrollees in return for a fixed capitated payment.

Prepayment (Prepaid Plans) Health insurance proposal that provides unlimited amounts of covered services in return for a fixed predetermined premium.

Present (Discounted) Value (PV or **PDV)** (See also Discounting) The value of a stream of returns to be received at future dates, which is discounted to the equivalent of present dollars.

Prevalence (See also Incidence) In epidemiology, the fraction of the population that is currently infected. Incidence adds new cases to the total pool describing the prevalence of present cases.

Price Discrimination The sale of goods or services to different individuals at different prices.

Price Elasticity of Demand (See also Elasticity) The percentage change in quantity demanded resulting from a 1 percent change in price.

Price Elasticity of Supply (See also Elasticity) The percentage change in quantity supplied resulting from a 1 percent change in price.

Price Index An index that expresses the current prices of a group of goods relative to the prices of these goods in a base year. A price index, often used to convert nominal values to real values, shows how much prices of those goods have changed since the base year.

Production Function The relationship between the maximum output that can be produced corresponding to any combination of factor inputs.

Production Possibilities Curve (Transformation Curve) A relationship showing all combinations of goods that an economy can produce with given amounts of input factors and the existing technology. The slope of the curve is the marginal rate of transformation showing the amount of one good that must be given up for a one-unit increase in the other good.

Prospective Payment System (PPS) The method of hospital reimbursement phased in by Medicare beginning in 1983 under which hospitals were reimbursed a fixed amount determined by the diagnostic related groups of their admissions.

Public Good (Pure) A good (e.g., national defense) that no one can be prevented from consuming, (i.e., nonexcludable), and that can be consumed by one person without depleting it for another (i.e., nonrival). The marginal cost of providing the good to another consumer is zero.

Quality-Adjusted Life-Year (QALY) A measure of health outcomes that incorporates quantity and quality of life. It uses a weighting system that assigns a value ranging from 1 (perfect health) to 0 (health state equivalent to death)

Rate Regulation (RR) Regulations administered largely at the state level that define the terms under which hospitals are reimbursed.

Real Value (See also Nominal Value) Monetary values that are adjusted for changes in the general level of prices relative to some arbitrarily selected base year.

Regression Analysis Statistical analysis that posits a linear relationship between a variable to be explained and one or more (in multiple regression) explanatory variables, in the form $y = a + bx$.

Reinforcement A characteristic of addictive behavior indicating that greater past consumption of addictive goods increases the desire for present consumption.

Relative Value Scale A system that assigns relative weights to health care procedures or services. These are sometimes used as guides by providers to price their services and by third-party payers to determine reimbursement levels.

Rent (Economic Rent) The remuneration to a factor of production, over and above that amount that is necessary to induce its supply in the market.

Reputation Good A good for which consumers rely on information provided by friends, neighbors, and others.

Resource-Based Relative Value Scale (RBRVS) A relative value scale used in Medicare reimbursement that is based on the resources involved in providing a service.

Risk Aversion The degree to which a certain income is preferred to a risky alternative with the same expected income.

Risk Selection The enrollment choices made by health plans or enrollees on the basis of perceived risk relative to the premium to be paid.

Roemer's Law The proposed positive relationship between the availability of hospital beds and a population's utilization of those beds. It is also referred to as Say's Law for hospital beds.

Search Good A good whose characteristics can be fully evaluated upon inspection.

Second Fundamental Theorem of Welfare Economics The proposition that any Pareto efficient outcome can, in principle, be achieved by competitive markets, given an appropriate initial endowment.

Short Run (See also Long Run) Situations in which the firm is not able to vary all its inputs. There is at least one factor of production that is fixed.

Selective Contracting The practice of a managed care organization (MCO) by which the MCO enters into participation agreements only with certain providers (and not with all providers who qualify) to provide health care services to health plan participants as members of the MCO's provider panel.

Small Area Variations The large variations in the per capita rates of utilization across small, homogeneous areas for many medical and surgical procedures.

Social Insurance Government insurance programs in which eligibility and premiums are not determined by the practices common to private insurance contracts. Premiums are often subsidized and there are typically redistributions from some segments of the population to others.

Social Welfare Function A decision rule under which society ranks all possible distributions of goods and services.

Staff Model HMO A health maintenance organization (HMO) in which physicians are directly employed by the HMO.

Substitutes The substitutes in consumption are goods that satisfy the same wants (e.g., beef and chicken) so that an increase in the price of one will increase the demand for the other. Substitutes in production are alternative goods that a firm can produce (e.g., corn and soybeans for a farmer) so that an increase in the price of one will lead to a decrease in the supply of another.

Substitution Effect (See also Income Effect) The change in quantity demanded resulting from a relative change in commodity prices, holding real income constant.

Supplier-Induced Demand (SID) The change in demand associated with the discretionary influence of providers, especially physicians, over their patients. Demand that is provided for the self-interests of providers rather than solely for patient interests.

Take Up A response to the introduction or enhancement of public insurance, referring to the extent that those who have previously been uninsured now use public coverage.

Target Income Hypothesis A model under which providers are thought to select a specified income level, and to adjust their amount of services provided or fees in order to reach this level.

Technical Efficiency (See Efficiency)

Technological Change A change in the process by which factors of production combine to produce outputs.

Theorem of the Second Best The economic theorem stating that the correction of some but not all market imperfections, in cases where there is more than one imperfection, will not necessarily improve society's welfare.

Time Costs The money value of the time lost through travel or waiting when consuming a product or service.

Tolerance A characteristic of addictive behavior indicating that the incremental utility from a given amount of consumption of the addictive good is lower when past consumption is greater. This suggests that the marginal future impacts of smoking or drinking or ingesting drugs decrease when we consume more now.

Uncompensated Care The care rendered by hospitals or other providers without payment from the patient or a government-sponsored private insurance program. It includes both charity care, which is provided without expectation of payment, and bad debts, for which the provider has made an unsuccessful effort to collect payment due from the patient.

Usual, Customary, and Reasonable (UCR) Reimbursement A system of insurance reimbursement under which the third-party payer restricts payment to the maximum of several limits (screens) that are established.

Utility and Utility Function Utility represents satisfaction or the level of welfare of an individual, measured in cardinal or ordinal utility terms. The utility function expresses the person's utility as a function of all possible combinations of goods and services.

Utilization Review (UR) The programs that attempt to determine whether specific services are medically necessary and delivered at an appropriate level and cost.

Variable Costs (TVC and AVC) Costs associated with variable factor(s) of production, often expressed as total variable cost (TVC) or average variable cost (AVC).

Welfare A measure of an individual's or a society's level of well-being.

Welfare Loss or **Deadweight Loss** A measure of the net loss of society's welfare resulting from a misallocation of resources, usually situations in which the marginal benefits of a good are not equal to marginal costs.

Yardstick Competition A regulatory pricing policy in which an average of the marginal costs of all competing firms is used as a standard of payment to induce the firm to engage in cost-cutting innovation.

References

Aaron, Henry J., "The Costs of Health Care Administration in the United States and Canada—Questionable Answers to a Questionable Question," *New England Journal of Medicine* (2003): 801–803.

Abbott, Thomas A., "Price Regulation in the Pharmaceutical Industry: Prescription or Placebo?" *Journal of Health Economics 14* (1995): 551–565.

Absolo, Ignacio, and Aki Tsuchiya, "Exploring Social Welfare Functions, and Violations of Monotonicity: An Example from Inequalities in Health," *Journal of Health Economics 23* (March 2004): 313–329.

Acton, Jan P., "Demand for Health Care Among the Urban Poor with Special Emphasis on the Role of Time," in *The Role of Health Insurance in the Health Services Sector*, Richard Rosett (ed.) (New York: Neal Watson, 1976).

Acton, Jan P., "Nonmonetary Factors in the Demand for Medical Services: Some Empirical Evidence," *Journal of Political Economy 83* (1975): 595–614.

Adamache, Killard W., and Louis F. Rossiter, "The Entry of HMOs into the Medicare Market: Implications for TEFRA's Mandate," *Inquiry 23* (1986): 349–364.

Adams, Scott J., "The Health Insurance-Wage Tradeoff: Evidence from Market Reform in the State of New York," March 2004, University of Wisconsin-Milwaukee.

Ahituv, Avner, V. Joseph Hotz, and Tomas Philipson, "The Responsiveness of the Demand for Condoms to the Local Prevalence of AIDS," *Journal of Human Resources 31* (4) (1996): 869–897.

Aigner, Dennis J., C. A. Knox Lovell, and Peter Schmidt, "Formulation and Estimation of Stochastic Frontier Production Function Models," *Journal of Econometrics 6* (1977): 21–37.

Akerlof, George A., "The Market for 'Lemons': Qualitative Uncertainty and the Market Mechanism," *Quarterly Journal of Economics 84* (1970): 488–500.

Albion, Mark S. and Paul W. Farris. *The Advertising Controversy: Evidence on the Economic Effects of Advertising.* (Boston: Auburn House, 1981).

Alchian Armen A. and Harold Demsetz, "Production, Information Costs, and Economic Organization," *American Economic Review 62* (1972): 777–795.

Alexander, Jeffrey A. et al., "Do Market-Level Hospital and Physician Resources Affect Small Area Variation in Hospital Use?" *Medical Care Research and Review 56* (1999): 94–117.

Altenstetter, Christa, "Health Care in Germany," prepared for distribution at the series Rekindling Reform: A Vision of Quality Health Care for All, New York, January 10–May 16, 2002, http://web.gc.cuny.edu/Eusc/activities/Paper/altenstetter2.htm. accessed July 19, 2002.

Altenstetter, Christa, and R. Busse "Health Care Reform in Germany: Patchwork Change Within Established Governance Structures," *Journal of Health Politics Policy and Law* (2005): 121–142.

Altman, Stuart H., and Marc A. Rodwin, "Halfway Competitive Markets and Ineffective Regulation: The American Health Care System," *Journal of Health Politics, Policy and Law 13* (1988): 323–339.

Alvarez-Dardet, Carlos and Maria Teresa Ruiz, "Thomas McKeown and Archibald Cochrane: A Journey Through the Diffusion of Their Ideas," *British Medical Journal 306* (May 8, 1993): 1252–1254.

Andermann, Anne Adina Judith, "Physicians, Fads, and Pharmaceuticals: A History of Aspirin," McGill University, mimeo and mjm.mcgill.ca/issues/v02n02/aspirin.html, accessed July 18, 2002.

Andersen, Ronald, and Lee Benham, "Factors Affecting the Relationship Between Family Income and Medical Care Consumption," in *Empirical Studies in Health Economics*, Herbert Klarman (ed.) (Baltimore: Johns Hopkins, 1970).

Anderson, Gerard F. and Jean-Pierre Poullier, "Health Spending, Access, and Outcomes, Trends in Industrialized Countries," *Health Affairs 18* (1999): 178–192.

Anderson, Gerard F., Peter S. Hussey, Bianca K. Frogner, and Hugh R. Waters "Health Spending in the United States and the Rest of the Industrialized World," *Health Affairs 24* (2005): 903–914.

Anderson, Gerard F., Uwe E. Reinhardt, Peter S. Hussey, and Varduhi Petrosyan, "It's The Prices, Stupid: Why the United States Is So Different from Other Countries," *Health Affairs 22* (3) (2003): 89–105.

Anderson, Keith B., "Regulation, Market Structure, and Hospital Costs: Comment," *Southern Economic Journal 58* (1991): 528–534.

Anderson, Odin W., *Health Services as a Growth Enterprise in the United States Since 1875*, 2nd ed. (Ann Arbor, MI: Health Administration Press, 1990).

Anderson, Patricia M., Kristin F. Butcher, and Phillip B. Levine, "Maternal Employment and Overweight Children," *Journal of Health Economics 22* (2003): 477–504.

Andreoni, James, "Impure Altruism and Donations to Public Goods: A Theory of Warm-Glow Giving," *The Economic Journal 100* (1990): 464–477.

Antel, John J., Robert L. Ohsfeldt, and Edmund R. Becker, "State Regulation and Hospital Costs," *Review of Economics and Statistics 77* (1995): 416–422.

Archibald, Robert, Clyde Haulman, and Carlisle Moody, "Quality, Price, Advertising, and Published Quality Ratings," *Journal of Consumer Research 9* (1983): 347–356.

Arnould, Richard J., Lawrence W. Debrock, and John W. Pollard, "Do HMOs Produce Specific Services More Efficiently?" *Inquiry 21* (1984): 243–253.

Arrow, Kenneth J. *Social Choice and Individual Values.* (New York: Wiley, 1975).

Arrow, Kenneth J., "Some Ordinalist-Utilitarian Notes on Rawls's Theory of Justice," *Journal of Philosophy 70* (1973): 245–262.

Arrow, Kenneth J., "Uncertainty and the Welfare Economics of Medical Care," *American Economic Review 53* (1963): 941–973.

Ash, Timothy Garton, *The Magic Lantern.* (New York: Vintage Books, 1993).

Associated Press, "Health Insurers Limit Access to New Health Advances," November 2, 1998.

Atkinson, Scott E. and Thomas Crocker, "Econometric Health Production Functions: Relative Bias from Omitted Variables and Measurement Error," *Journal of Environmental Economics and Management 22* (1992): 12–24.

Atkinson, Scott E. and Robert Halvorsen, "The Valuation of Risks to Life," *Review of Economics and Statistics 72* (1990): 133–136.

Auster, Richard D., Irving Leveson, and Deborah Sarachek, "The Production of Health, an Exploratory Study," *Journal of Human Resources 4* (1969): 411–436.

Bae, Jay P., "Drug Patent Expiration and the Speed of Generic Entry," *Health Services Research 22* (1997): 87–101.

Bain, Joe S. *Barriers to New Competition* (Cambridge, MA: Harvard, 1956).

Baker, Laurence C., "Managed Care and Technology Adoption in Health Care: Evidence from Magnetic Resonance Imaging," *Journal of Health Economics 2* (May 2001): 395–421.

Baker, Laurence C. and Kenneth S. Corts, "The Effects of HMOs on Conventional Insurance Premiums: Theory and Evidence," Working Paper 5356, National Bureau of Economic Research, November 1995.

Baker, Laurence C. and Kenneth S. Corts, "HMO Market Penetration and the Cost of Health Care: Market Discipline or Market Segmentation," *American Economic Review 86* (1996): 389–394.

Baker, Laurence C. and Joanne Spetz, "Managed Care and Medical Technology Growth," in *Frontiers in Health Policy Research, Volume 2*, Alan Garber (ed.) (Cambridge, MA: MIT Press, 2000).

Bala, Mohan V. and Gary A. Zarkin, "Are QALYs an Appropriate Measure for Valuing Morbidity in Acute Diseases?" *Health Economics 9* (2000): 177–180.

Ballou, Jeffrey P. and Burton A. Weisbrod, "Managerial Rewards and the Behavior of For-Profit, Governmental, and Nonprofit Organizations: Evidence from the Hospital Industry," *Journal of Public Economics 87* (2003): 1895–1920.

Baltagi, Badi H. and James M. Griffin, "The Econometrics of Rational Addiction: The Case of Cigarettes," *Journal of Business and Economic Statistics 19* (2001): 449–454.

Baltagi, Badi H. and Dan Levin, "Estimating Dynamic Demand for Cigarettes Using Panel Data: The Effects of Bootlegging, Taxation, and Advertising Reconsidered," *Review of Economics and Statistics 68* (1986): 148–155.

Barry, Michael J. et al., "Patient Reactions to a Program Designed to Facilitate Patient Participation in Treatment Decisions for Benign Prostatic Hyperplasia," *Medical Care 33* (1995): 771–782.

Barsky, Robert B. et al., "Preference Parameters and Behavioral Heterogeneity: An Experimental Approach in the Health and Retirement Study," *Quarterly Journal of Economics 62* (1997): 537–579.

Bator, Francis M., "The Simple Analytics of Welfare Maximization," *American Economic Review 47* (1957): 22–59.

Baumol, William J., "On the Social Rate of Discount," *American Economic Review 58* (1968): 788–802.

Baumol, William J., John C. Panzar, and Robert Willig. *Contestable Markets and the Theory of Industry* (San Diego: Harcourt Brace Jovanovich, 1982).

Bays, Carson W., "Why Most Private Hospitals Are Nonprofit," *Journal of Policy Analysis and Management 2* (1983): 366–385.

Beaulieu, Nancy D., "Quality Information and Consumer Health Plan Choices," *Journal of Health Economics 21* (2002): 43–63.

Becker, Gary S., Michael Grossman, and Kevin M. Murphy, "Rational Addiction and the Price on Consumption," *American Economic Review 81* (1991): 237–241.

Becker, Gary S., and Kevin M. Murphy, "A Simple Theory of Advertising as a Good or Bad," *Quarterly Journal of Economics 108* (1993): 941–964.

Becker, Gary S., and Kevin M. Murphy, "A Theory of Rational Addiction," *Journal of Political Economy 96* (1988): 675–700.

Behrman, Jere R. and Barbara L. Wolfe, "Does More Schooling Make Women Better Nourished and Healthier?: Adult Sibling Random and Fixed Effects Estimates for Nicaragua," *Journal of Human Resources 24* (1989): 644–663.

Benham, Lee, "The Effects of Advertising on the Price of Eyeglasses," *Journal of Law and Economics 15* (1972): 421–477.

Berger, Mark C. and J. Paul Leigh, "Schooling, Self Selection, and Health," *Journal of Human Resources 24* (1989): 433–455.

Bhattacharya, Jayanta, "Specialty Selection and Lifetime Returns to Specialization Within Medicine," *Journal of Human Resources 60* (2005): 115–143.

Bilodeau, David, Pierre-Yves Cremieux, and Pierre Oullette, "Hospital Technology in a Nonmarket Health Care System," *Southern Economic Journal 68* (2002): 511–29.

Bishop, Christine E., "Where Are the Missing Elders? The Decline in Nursing Home Use, 1985 and 1995," *Health Affairs 18* (1999): 146–155.

Blank, Rebecca M., "Can Equity and Efficiency Complement Each Other?" *Labour Economics 9* (4) (September 2002): 451–468.

Bleichrodt, Han, "Health Utility Indices and Equity Considerations," *Journal of Health Economics 16* (1997): 65–91.

Bleichrodt, Han and John Quiggin, "QALYs and Consumer Demand for Health Care," *Journal of Health Economics 18* (1999): 681–708.

Blendon, Robert J., Mollyann Brodie, and John Benson, "What Happened to Support for the Clinton Plan?" *Health Affairs 14* (1995): 7–23.

Blendon, Robert et al., "Common Concerns amid Diverse Systems: Health Care Experiences in Five Countries," *Health Affairs 22* (2003): 106–121.

Blomquist, Ake, "QALYs, Standard Gambles, and the Expected Budget Constraint," *Journal of Health Economics 21* (March 2002): 181–195.

Blomquist, Ake G. and R.A.L. Carter, "Is Health Care Really a Luxury?" *Journal of Health Economics 16* (1997): 207–230.

Blomquist, Ake and Pierre Thomas Leger, "Infomation Asymmetry, Insurance, and the Decision to Hospitalize," *Journal of Health Economics 24* (July 2005): 775–793.

Bloom, David F. and Ajay Mahal, "Does the AIDS Epidemic Threaten Economic Growth?" *Journal of Econometrics 77* (1997): 105–124.

Bloom, David E. and Jaypee Sevilla, "Health, Wealth, AIDS, and Poverty," mimeo, 2002.

Blundell, R., and F. Windmeijer, "Identifying Demand for Health Resources Using Waiting Time Information," *Health Economics 9* (2000): 465–474.

Bolin, Kristian, Lena Jacobson, and Bjorn Lindgren, "The Family as the Health Producer—When Spouses Act Strategically," *Journal of Health Economics 21* (2002): 475–495.

Bond, Ronald et al, *Staff Report on Effects of Restrictions on Advertising and Commercial Practice in the Professions: The Case of Optometry* (Federal Trade Commission, Washington, DC: Government Printing Office, 1980).

Borisova, Natalia, and Allen C. Goodman, "The Effects of Time and Money Prices on Treatment Attendance for Methadone Maintenance Clients," *Journal of Substance Abuse Treatment 26* (2004): 345–352.

Borjas, George J., H. E. Frech III, and Paul B. Ginsburg, "Property Rights and Wages: The Case of Nursing Homes," *Journal of Human Resources 17* (1983): 232–246.

Bosmans, Nathalie and Fabienne Fecher, "Performance of Belgian Hospitals: A Frontier Approach," *Health Economics 4* (1995): 389–397.

Bosworth, Barry and Gary Burtless, "Effects of Tax Reform on Labor Supply, Investment, and Saving," *Journal of Economic Perspectives 6* (1992): 3–25.

Boulier, Bryan L., Tejwant Singh Datta, and Robert S., Goldfarb, "Vaccination Externalities," George Washington University working paper, August 2003.

Braden, Bradley R. et al., "National Health Expenditures, 1997," *Health Care Financing Review 20* (1998): 83–110.

Braunwald, Eugene et al., "HIV Infection and AIDS," *Harrison's Manual of Medicine*, Chapter 86 (2001), www.harrisonsmed.com/downloads/manual_ch86, accessed January 16, 2003.

Brennan, Troyen A. et al., "Incidence of Adverse Events and Negligence in Hospitalized Patients," *New England Journal of Medicine 324* (1991): 370–376.

Brickley, James A. and R. Lawrence Van Horn, "Managerial Incentives in Nonprofit Organizations Evidence from Hospitals," *Journal of Law and Economics 45*, (2002): 227–249.

Brook, Robert H. et al., "Appropriateness of Acute Medical Care for the Elderly: An Analysis of the Literature," *Health Policy 14* (1990): 225–242.

Brook, Robert H. et al., "Does Free Care Improve Adults' Health?: Results from a Randomized Trial," *New England Journal of Medicine 309* (1983): 1426–1434.

Brouwer, Werner B. F. and Marc A. Koopmanschap, "On the Economic Foundations of CEA: Ladies and Gentlemen, Take Your Positions," *Journal of Health Economics 19* (2000): 439–460.

Brown, Douglas M., "Do Physicians Underutilize Aides?" *Journal of Human Resources 23* (1988): 342–355.

Brown, Lawrence D., "The National Politics of Oregon's Rationing Plan," *Health Affairs 10* (1991): 28–51.

Brown, Lawrence D. and Volker E. Amelung, "'Manacled Competition': Market Reforms in German Health Care," *Health Affairs 18* (1999): 76–91.

Browne, Mark J. and Helen I. Doerpinghaus, "Information Asymmetries and Adverse Selection in the Market for Individual Medical Expense Insurance," *Journal of Risk and Insurance 60* (1993): 300–312.

Buchanan, James, *The Limits of Liberty*. (Chicago: University of Chicago Press, 1975).

Bunker, John. P., Howard S. Frazier, and Frederick Mosteller, "Improving Health: Measuring Effects of Medical Care," *Milbank Quarterly 72* (1994): 225–258.

Burgess, James F. Jr. and Paul W. Wilson, "Variation in Inefficiency in U.S. Hospitals," *INFOR 36* (1998): 84–102.

Burstein, Philip L. and Jerry Cromwell, "Relative Incomes and Rates of Return for U.S. Physicians," *Journal of Health Economics 4* (1985): 63–78.

Busse, Reinhard and Annette Riesberg, *Health Care Systems in Transition: Germany* (Copenhagen, WHO Regional Office for Europe on behalf of the European Observatory on Health Systems and Policies, 2004).

Cady, John F., *Drugs on the Market*. (Lexington, MA: Lexington, 1975).

Cairns, John A. and Marjon M. van der Pol, "Saving Future Lives, A Comparison of Three Discounting Models," *Health Economics 6* (1997): 341–350.

Calem, Paul S. and John A. Rizzo, "Competition and Specialization in the Hospital Industry: An Application of Hotelling's Location Model," *Southern Economic Journal 61* (1995): 1182–1198.

Cameron, Sam, "Are Greek Smokers Rational Addicts?" *Applied Economics Letters 4* (1997): 401–402.

Cardon, James H. and Igal Hendel, "Asymmetric Information in Health Insurance: Evidence from the National Medical Expenditure Survey," *RAND Journal of Economics 23* (2001): 408–427.

Carey, Kathleen and James F. Burgess Jr., "On Measuring the Hospital Cost/Quality Trade Off," *Health Economics 8* (1999): 509–520.

Carlsen, Fredrik and Jostein Grytten, "Consumer Satisfaction and Supplier Induced Demand," *Journal of Health Economics 19* (2000): 731–783.

Carlson, Rick, *The End of Medicine*. (New York: Wiley Interscience, 1975).

Carroll, Norman V. and W. Gary Erwin, "Patient Shifting as a Response to Medicare Prospective Payment," *Medical Care 25* (1987): 1161–1167.

Casteneda, Laura, "'Viatical' Life Insurance Deals Get Tougher," *San Francisco Chronicle 10* (March 1997): E2.

Caudill, Stephen B., John M. Ford, and David L. Kaserman, "Certificate of Need Regulation and the Diffusion of Innovations," *Journal of Applied Econometrics 10* (1995): 73–78.

The Center for Evaluative Clinical Studies, *Dartmouth Atlas of Health Care* (Dartmouth Medical School, American Hospital Publications, Inc., 1996).

Chaloupka, Frank, "The Economics of Smoking," in *Handbook of Health Economics*, Anthony J. Culyer and Joseph P. Newhouse (eds.) (Elsevier Science B.V., 2000).

Chaloupka, Frank J., "Rational Addictive Behavior and Cigarette Smoking," *Journal of Political Economy 99* (1991): 722–742.

Chaloupka, Frank J. and Rosalie Liccardo Pacula, "An Examination of Gender and Race Differences in Youth Smoking Responsiveness to Price and Tobacco Control Policies," Working Paper 6541, National Bureau of Economic Research, April 1998.

Chaloupka, Frank J. and Henry Saffer, "Clean Indoor Air Laws and the Demand for Cigarettes," *Contemporary Policy Issues 10* (1992): 72–83.

Chaloupka, Frank J. and Kenneth E. Warner, "The Economics of Smoking," Working Paper 7047, National Bureau of Economic Research, March 1999.

Chang, Fwu-Ranq, "Uncertainty and Investment in Health," *Journal of Health Economics 15* (1996): 369–376.

Chatterji, Pinka and Jeff DeSimone, "Adolescent Drinking and High School Dropout," National Bureau of Economic Research Working Paper, 11337, 2005.

Chernew, Michael and Dennis P. Scanlon, "Health Plan Report Cards and Insurance Choice," *Inquiry 35* (1998): 9–22.

Chetty, V. K., "Stochastic Technology, Production Organization and Costs," *Journal of Health Economics 17* (1998): 187–210.

Chilingerian, Jon, "Evaluating Physician Efficiency in Hospitals: A Multivariate Analysis of Best Practices," *European Journal of Operations Research 80* (1995): 548–574.

Chiswick, Barry R., "The Demand for Nursing Home Care: An Analysis of the Substitution Between Institutional and Noninstitutional Care," *Journal of Human Resources 11* (1976): 295–316.

Christianson, Jon B. et al., "The HMO Industry: Evolution in Population Demographics and Market Structures," *Medical Care Review 48* (1991): 3–46.

Chou, Shin-Yi, "Asymmetric Information, Ownership and Quality of Care: An Empirical Analysis of Nursing Homes," *Journal of Health Economics 21* (2002): 293–311.

Clancy, Carolyn and Anne K., Gauthier, (eds.), "Consumer Driven Health Care: Beyond Rhetoric with Research and Experience," *Health Services Research 30* Suppl. (2004): 1049–1233.

Clark, Robert Charles, "Does the Nonprofit Form Fit the Hospital Industry?" *Harvard Law Review 93* (1980): 1417–1489.

Clarkson, Kenneth W., "The Effects of Research and Promotion on Rates of Return," in *Competitive*

Strategies in the Pharmaceutical Industry, Robert B. Helms (ed.) (Washington, DC: American Enterprise Institute, 1996) 238–268.

Cleverly, William O., "More Efficient Hospitals Are Closing," *Healthcare Financial Management 47* (1993): 82–85.

Cochrane, Archibald L., *Effectiveness and Efficiency: Random Reflections on Health Services.* (London: Nuffield Provincial Hospital Trust, 1972).

Cockburn, Ian, "The Changing Structure of the Pharmaceutical Industry," *Health Affairs 23* (2004):10–22.

Coddington, Dean C. et al., *The Crisis in Health Care: Costs, Choices, and Strategies.* (San Francisco: Jossey-Bass, 1990).

Coffey, Rosanna M., "The Effect of Time Price on the Demand for Medical Care Services," *Journal of Human Resources 18* (1983): 407–424.

Cogan, John F., R. Glenn Hubbard, and Daniel P. Kessler, *Healthy, Wealthy, & Wise: Five Steps to a Better Health Care System.* (Washington, DC: American Enterprise Institute and Stanford, CA: Hoover Institution, 2005).

Cohen, Harold A., "Variations in Cost Among Hospitals of Different Sizes," *Southern Economic Journal 33* (1967): 355–366.

Cohen, Joel W. and William D. Spector, "The Effect of Medicaid Reimbursement on Quality of Care in Nursing Homes," *Journal of Health Economics 15* (1996): 23–48.

Comanor, William S. and Thomas A. Wilson. *Advertising and Market Power.* (Cambridge, MA: Harvard, 1974).

Comanor, William S. and Thomas A. Wilson, "The Effect of Advertising on Competition: A Survey," *Journal of Economic Literature 17* (1979): 453–476.

Conover, Christopher J. and Frank A. Sloan, "Does Removing Certificate of Need Regulations Lead to a Surge in Health Care Spending?" *Journal of Health Politics, Policy and Law 23* (1998): 455–481.

Conrad, Robert F. and Robert P. Strauss, "A Multiple-Output Multiple-Input Model of the Hospital Industry in North Carolina," *Applied Economics 15* (1983): 341–352.

Cook, Philip J. and Michael J. Moore, "Alcohol," in *Handbook of Health Economics*, Anthony J. Culyer and Joseph P. Newhouse (eds.) (Elsevier Science B.V., 2000).

Cook, Philip J. and Michael J. Moore, "Drinking and Schooling," *Journal of Health Economics 12* (1993): 411–429.

Cook, Phillip J., Jan Orterman, and Frank A. Sloan, "Are Alcohol Excise Taxes Good for Us?: Short and Long Term Effects on Mortality Rates," National Bureau of Economic Research Working Paper 11139, 2005.

Cooper, Philip F. and Alan C. Monheit, "Does Employment-Related Health Insurance Inhibit Job Mobility?" *Inquiry 30* (1993): 400–416.

Cooper, Richard A. et al., "Economic and Demographic Trends Signal an Impending Physician Shortage," *Health Affairs 21* (2002): 140–154.

Corman, Hope and Michael Grossman, "Determinants of Neonatal Mortality Rate in the U.S.: A Reduced Form Model," *Journal of Health Economics 4* (1985): 213–236.

Corman, Hope, Theodore J. Joyce, and Michael Grossman, "Birth Outcome Production Function in the United States," *Journal of Human Resources 22* (1987): 339–360.

Cowing, Thomas G. and Alphonse G. Holtmann, "Multiproduct Short-Run Hospital Cost Functions: Empirical Evidence and Policy Implications from Cross-Section Data," *Southern Economic Journal 49* (1983): 637–653.

Cowing, Thomas G., Alphonse G. Holtmann, and Susan Powers, "Hospital Cost Analysis: A Survey and Evaluation of Recent Studies," *Advances in Health Economics and Health Services Research 4* (1983).

Coyle, Douglas, Martin J. Buxton, and Bernie J. O'Brien, "Stratified Cost-Effectiveness Analysis: A Framework for Establishing Efficient Limited Criteria," *Health Economics 12* (2003): 421–427.

Coyte, Peter et al., "The Relationship Between Variations in Knee Replacement Utilization Rates and the Reported Prevalence of Arthritis in Ontario, Canada," *Journal of Rheumatology 24* (1997): 2403–2412.

Cremieux, Pierre-Yves and Pierre Ouellette, "Omitted Variable Bias and Hospital Costs," *Journal of Health Economics 20* (2001): 271–282.

Cremieux, Pierre-Yves, Pierre Ouellette, and Caroline Pilon, "Health Care Spending as Determinants of Health Outcomes," *Health Economics 8* (November 1999): 627–639.

Cropper, Maureen L. et al., "The Health Benefit of Air Pollution Control in New Delhi," *American Journal of Agricultural Economics 79* (1997): 1625–1629.

Cubanski, Juliette, et al., *Medicare Chartbook, 3rd ed.,* (The Henry J. Kaiser Family Foundation, Summer 2005).

Culyer, A. J. "The Normative Economics of Health Care Finance and Provision," *Oxford Review of Economic Policy 5* (1989): 34–58.

Culyer, A. J., "The United Kingdom: Effective, Efficient, Equitable?" *Journal of Health Politics, Policy and Law 17* (1992): 667–688.

Culyer, A. J. and Adam Wagstaff, "Equity and Equality in Health and Health Care," *Journal of Health Economics 12* (1993): 431–457.

Culyer, A. J., Eddy van Doorslaer, and Adam Wagstaff, "Access, Utilisation and Equity: A Further Comment," *Journal of Health Economics 11* (1992a): 207–210.

Culyer, A. J., Eddy van Doorslaer, and Adam Wagstaff, "Utilisation as a Measure of Equity by Mooney, Hall, Donaldson and Gerard," *Journal of Health Economics 11* (1992b): 93–98.

Currie, Janet, "The Take up of Social Benefits," National Bureau of Economic Research Working Paper 10488, Cambridge MA, May 2004, http://

www.nber.org/papers/w10488, accessed August 10, 2005.

Currie, Janet and Nancy Cole, "Welfare and Child Health: The Link Between AFDC Participation and Birth Weight," *American Economic Review 83* (1993): 971–985.

Currie, Janet and Jonathan Gruber, "Saving Babies: The Efficacy and Cost of Recent Changes in the Medicaid Eligibility of Pregnant Women," *Journal of Political Economy 104* (1996): 1263–1296.

Currie, Janet and Patricia B. Reagan, "Distance to Hospital and Children's Use of Preventive Care: Is Being Closer Better, and for Whom?" *Economic Inquiry 41* (2005): 378–391.

Custer, W. S. and R. J. Willke, "Teaching Hospital Costs: The Effect of Medical Staff Characteristics," *Health Services Research 25* (1991): 831–857.

Cutler, David M., "The Economics of Better Health: The Case of Cardiovascular Disease," Harvard University, mimeo, February 2001.

Cutler, David M., *Your Money or Your Life* (Oxford: Oxford University Press, 2004).

Cutler, David M. and Jonathan Gruber, "Does Public Insurance Crowd Out Private Insurance," *Quarterly Journal of Economics 111* (1996): 391–430.

Cutler, David M. and Jonathan Gruber, "Health Policy in the Clinton Era: Once Bitten, Twice Shy," in *American Economic Policy in the 1990s*, Peter R. Orszag and Jeffrey A. Frankel (eds.) (MIT Press: Cambridge, MA, 2002).

Cutler, David M. and Jill R. Horwitz, "Converting Hospitals from Not-for-Profit to For-Profit Status: Why and What Effects?" Working Paper 6672, National Bureau of Economic Research, August 1998.

Cutler, David M. and Ellen Meara, "The Medical Costs of the Young and Old: A Forty-Year Perspective," Working Paper 6114, National Bureau of Economic Research, July 1997.

Cutler, David M., Mark McClellan, and Joseph P. Newhouse, "How Does Managed Care Do It?" *RAND Journal of Economics 31* (2000): 526–548.

Cutler, David M. and Sarah J. Reber, "The Trade-Off Between Competition and Adverse Selection," *Quarterly Journal of Economics 113* (1998): 433–466.

Cutler, David M. et al., "Pricing Heart Attack Treatments," Working Paper 7089. National Bureau of Economic Research, April 1999.

Daniels, Norman, "Equity of Access to Health Care: Some Conceptual and Ethical Issues," *Milbank Memorial Fund Quarterly/Health and Society 60* (1982): 51–81.

Daniels, Norman, "Health Care Needs and Distributive Justice," *Philosophy and Public Affairs 10* (1981): 146–179.

Daniels, Norman, *Just Health Care*. (Cambridge: Cambridge University Press, 1985).

Davis, Karen and Roger Reynolds, "The Impact of Medicare and Medicaid on Access to Medical Care," in *The Role of Health Insurance in the United States Health Services Sector*, Richard Rosett (ed.) (New York: Neal Watson, 1976).

Davis, Mark A., "On Nursing Home Quality: A Review and Analysis," *Medical Care Review 48* (1991): 129–166.

Deaton, Angus and Christina Paxson. "Mortality, Income, and Income Inequality over Time in Britain and the United States," Working Paper 8534, National Bureau of Economic Research, May 2001.

Deb, Partha M. and Ann M. Holmes, "Substitution of Physicians and Other Providers in Outpatient Mental Health Care," *Health Economics* (1998): 347–361.

Defelice, Lisa C. and W. David Bradford, "Relative Inefficiencies in Production Between Solo and Group Practice Physicians," *Health Economics 6* (1997): 455–465.

de Lissovoy, Gregory et al., "Preferred Provider Organizations One Year Later," *Inquiry 24* (1987): 127–135.

DesHarnais, Susan, James Chesney, and Steven Fleming, "Trends in Regional Variations in Hospital Utilization and Quality During the First Two Years of the Prospective Payment System," *Inquiry 25* (1988): 374–382.

DesHarnais, Susan et al., "The Early Effects of the Prospective Payment System on Inpatient Utilization and the Quality of Care," *Inquiry 24* (1987): 7–16.

Despotakis, Kostas A., "Economic Performance of Flexible Functional Forms," *European Economic Review 30* (1986): 1107–1143.

Deutsch, Larry, L., "Pharmaceuticals: The Critical Role of Innovation," in *Industry Studies,* 2nd ed., Larry L. Deutsch (ed.) (Armonk, NY: M.E. Sharpe, 1998).

Diehr, Paula et al., "What Is Too Much Variation: The Null Hypothesis in Small-Area Analysis," *Health Services Research 24* (1990): 741–771.

DiFranza, Joseph R. et al., "RJR Nabisco's Cartoon Camel Promotes Camel Cigarettes to Children," *Journal of the American Medical Association 266* (December 11, 1991): 3149–3153.

Dills, Angela K., Mirelle Jacobson, and Jeffrey A. Miron, "The Effect of Alcohol Prohibition on Alcohol Consumption: Evidence from Drunkenness Arrests," *Economics Letters 86* (2005): 279–284.

DiMasi, Joseph A., "New Drug Development in the United States from 1963 to 1999," *Clinical Pharmacology &Therapeutics 16* (5) (2001): 286–296.

DiMasi, Joseph A., Ronald W. Hansen, and Henry G. Grabowski, "The Price of Innovation: New Estimates of Drug Development Costs," *Journal of Health Economics 22* (2003): 151–185.

DiMasi, Joseph A., Ronald W. Hansen, and Henry G. Grabowski, "Reply: Extraordinary Claims Require

Extraordinary Evidence," *Journal of Health Economics 24* (2005): 1034–1044.

DiMasi, Joseph A. et al., "Cost of Innovation in the Pharmaceutical Industry," *Journal of Health Economics 10* (1991): 107–142.

Docteur, Elizabeth and Howard Oxley, "Health-Care Systems Reforms: Lessons from the Reform Experience," OECD Health Working Paper No. 9, OECD Publishing, 2003.

Donabedian, Avedis, *The Definition of Quality and Approaches to Its Assessment.* (Ann Arbor, MI: Health Administration Press, 1980).

Donabedian, Avedis, "Evaluating the Quality of Medical Care," *Milbank Memorial Fund Quarterly/Health and Society 44* (1966): 166–203.

Donaldson, Nancy et al., "Impact of California's Licensed Nurse-Patient Ratios on Unit-Level Nurse Staffing and Patient Outcomes," *Policy, Politics, & Nursing Practice 6* (2005): 198–210.

Donelan, Karen et al., "The Cost of Change: Public Discontent in Five Nations," *Health Affairs 18* (1999): 206–216.

Dong, Frederick et al., "Cost Effectiveness of ACE Inhibitor Treatment for Patients with Type 1 Diabetes Mellitus," *Pharmacoeconomics 22* (2004): 1015–1027.

Dor, Avi, "Non-Minimum Cost Functions and the Stochastic Frontier: On Applications to Health Care Providers," *Journal of Health Economics 13* (1994): 329–334.

Dorfman, Robert and Peter O. Steiner, "Optimal Advertising and Optimal Quality," *American Economic Review 44* (1954): 826–836.

Douglas, Stratford and Govind Hariharan, "The Hazard of Starting Smoking: Estimates from a Split Population Duration Model," *Journal of Health Economics 13* (1994): 213–230.

Dranove, David, "Demand Inducement and the Physician/Patient Relationship," *Economic Inquiry 26* (1988): 281–298.

Dranove, David, *The Economic Evolution of American Health Care.* (Princeton, NJ: Princeton University Press, 2000).

Dranove, David, "A Problem with Consumer Surplus Measures of the Cost of Practice Variations," *Journal of Health Economics 14* (1995): 243–251.

Dranove, David and Kenneth Cone, "Do State Rate Setting Regulations Really Lower Hospital Expenses?" *Journal of Health Economics 4* (1985): 159–165.

Dranove, David and David Meltzer, "Do Important Drugs Reach the Market Sooner?" *RAND Journal of Economics 25* (1994): 402–423.

Dranove, David, Carol J. Simon, and William D. White, "Is Managed Care Leading to Consolidation in Health-care Markets?," *Health Services Research 37* (2002): 573–594.

Dranove, David and Paul Wehner, "Physician Induced Demand for Childbirths," *Journal of Health Economics 13* (1994): 61–73.

Dranove, David and William D. White, "Agency and the Organization of Health Care Delivery," *Inquiry 24* (1987): 405–415.

Dranove, David, Carol J. Simon, and William D. White, "Determinants of Managed Care Penetration," *Journal of Health Economics 17* (1998): 729–745.

Drummond, Michael F. et al., *Methods for the Economic Evaluation of Health Care Programmes*, 2nd ed. (New York: Oxford University Press, 1997).

Dubos, Rene, *The Mirage of Health.* (London: George Allen and Unwin, Ltd., 1960).

Dunn, Daniel L. et al., "Economies of Scope in Physicians' Work: The Performance of Multiple Surgery," *Inquiry 32* (1995): 87–101.

Eakin, B. Kelly and Thomas J. Kniesner, "Estimating a Non-Minimum Cost Function for Hospitals," *Southern Economic Journal 54* (January 1988): 583–597.

Easley, David and Maureen O'Hara, "The Economic Role of the Nonprofit Firm," *Bell Journal of Economics 14* (1983): 531–538.

Economic Report of the President, transmitted to the Congress, February 1985. (Washington, DC: United States Government Printing Office, 1985).

Eddy, David M., "Clinical Decision Making: From Theory to Practice," *Journal of the American Medical Association 263* (January 19, 1990): 441–443.

Eisenberg, J. M., *Doctors' Decisions and the Cost of Medical Care* (Ann Arbor, MI: Health Administration Press, 1986).

Elixhauser, Anne, (ed.), "Health Care Cost-Benefit and Cost Effectiveness Analysis (CBA/CEA)," *Medical Care 31* (1993): JS1–JS150.

Elixhauser, Anne et al., "Health Care CBA and CEA from 1991 to 1996: An Updated Bibliography," *Medical Care 36* (1998): MS1–MS9.

Ellis, Randall P., "Creaming, Skimping and Dumping: Provider Competition on the Intensive and Extensive Margins," *Journal of Health Economics 17* (1998): 537–555.

Ellis, Randall P., "Hospital Cost Function Estimation When Firms May Not Try to Minimize Total Costs," mimeo. (Boston: Boston University, 1993).

Ellis, Randall P. and Thomas G. McGuire, "Provider Behavior Under Prospective Reimbursement," *Journal of Health Economics 5* (1986): 129–151.

Elzinga, Kenneth G. and T. F. Hogarty, "The Problem of Geographic Market Definition Revisited: The Case of Coal," *Antitrust Bulletin 23* (1978): 1–18.

Enthoven, Alain C., "National Health Service: Some Reforms That Might Be Politically Feasible," *The Economist 22* (1985): 61–64.

Ermann, Danny, "Hospital Utilization Review: Past Experience, Future Directions," *Journal of Health Politics, Policy and Law 13* (1988): 683–704.

Escarce, José J., "Explaining the Association Between Surgeon Supply and Utilization," *Inquiry 29* (1992): 403–415.

Escarce, José J., "Externalities in Hospitals and Physicians Adoption of a New Surgical Technology: An Exploratory Analysis," *Journal of Health Economics 15* (1996): 715–734.

Escarce, José J., "Would Eliminating Differences in Physician Practice Style Reduce Geographic Variations in Cataract Surgery Rates?" *Medical Care 12* (1993): 1106–1118.

Escarce, José J. and Mark V. Pauly, "Physician Opportunity Costs in Physician Practice Cost Functions," *Journal of Health Economics 17* (1998): 129–151.

Escarce, José J. et al., "Diffusion of Laparoscopic Cholecystectomy Among General Surgeons in the United States," *Medical Care 33* (1995): 256–271.

Eskin, Gerald J., "A Case for Test Marketing Experiments," *Journal of Advertising Research 15* (1975): 27–33.

Eskin, Gerald J. and Penny H. Barron, "Effect of Price and Advertising in Test-Market Experiments," *Journal of Marketing Research 14* (1977): 499–508.

Evans, Robert G., "Behavioral Cost Functions for Hospitals," *Canadian Journal of Economics 4* (1971): 198–215.

Evans, Robert G., "Supplier-Induced Demand; Some Empirical Evidence and Implications," in *The Economics of Health and Medical Care*, Mark Perlman (ed.) (London: Macmillan, 1974).

Evans, William N. and Diana S. Lien, "The Benefits of Prenatal Care: Evidence from the PAT Bus Strike," *Journal of Econometrics 125* (March 2005): 207–239.

Evans, William N. and Jeanne S. Ringel, "Can Higher Cigarette Taxes Improve Birth Outcome?" *Journal of Public Economics 72* (1999): 135–154.

Fare, Rolf and C. A. Knox Lovell, "Measuring the Technical Efficiency of Production," *Journal of Economic Theory 19* (1978): 150–162.

Farmer, Paul and Edward Nardell, "Editorial: Nihilism and Pragmatism in Tuberculosis Control," *American Journal of Public Health 88* (1998): 1014–1015.

Feinglass, Joe and James J. Holloway, "The Initial Impact of the Medicare Prospective Payment System on U.S. Health Care: A Review of the Literature," *Medical Care Review 48* (1991): 91–115.

Feinstein, Jonathon S., "The Relationship Between Socioeconomic Status and Health: A Review of the Literature," *Milbank Quarterly 71* (1993): 279–322.

Feldman, Roger and J. Begun, "Effects of Advertising: Lessons from Optometry," *Journal of Human Resources 13* (Supplement 1978): 247–262.

Feldman, Roger and Bryan Dowd, "Is There a Competitive Market for Hospital Services?" *Journal of Health Economics 5* (1986): 277–292.

Feldman, Roger and Bryan Dowd, "A New Estimate of the Welfare Loss of Excess Health Insurance," *American Economic Review 81* (1991): 297–301.

Feldman, Roger and Frank Sloan, "Competition Among Physicians Revisited," in *Competition in the Health Care Sector: Ten Years Later*, Warren Greenberg (ed.) (Durham, NC: Duke University Press, 1988).

Feldman, Roger et al., "The Effect of Premiums on the Small Firm's Decision to Offer Health Insurance," *Journal of Human Resources 32* (1998): 635–658.

Feldman, Roger et al., "Effects of HMOs on the Creation of Competitive Markets for Hospital Services," *Journal of Health Economics 9* (1990): 207–222.

Feldstein, Martin S., *Economic Analysis for Health Service Efficiency*. (Amsterdam: North-Holland, 1967).

Feldstein, Martin S., "Hospital Cost Inflation: A Study of Nonprofit Price Dynamics," *American Economic Review 61* (1971): 853–872.

Feldstein, Martin S., "The Rising Price of Physicians' Services," *Review of Economics and Statistics 52* (1970): 121–133.

Feldstein, Martin S., "The Welfare Loss of Excess Health Insurance," *Journal of Political Economy 81* (1973): 251–280.

Feldstein, Paul J., "The Emergence of Market Competition in the U.S. Health Care System. Its Causes, Likely Structure, and Implications," *Health Policy 6* (1986): 1–20.

Finkler, Merton D. and David D. Wirtschafter, "Cost Effectiveness and Data Envelopment Analysis," *Health Care Management Review 18* (1993): 81–88.

Fletcher, Suzanne W. and Graham A. Colditz, "Failure of Estrogen Plus Progestin Therapy for Prevention," *Journal of the American Medical Association 288* (3) (2002): 366–368.

Flexner, Abraham, *Medical Education in the United States and Canada, Bulletin No. 4*. (New York: Carnegie Foundation for the Advancement of Teaching, 1910).

Fogel, Robert W., "Nutrition and the Decline in Mortality Since 1700: Some Additional Preliminary Findings," Working Paper 1802, National Bureau of Economic Research, 1986.

Folland, Sherman T., "A Critique of Pure Need: An Analysis of Norman Daniels's Concept of Health Care Need," *International Journal of Social Economics 17* (1990): 36–45.

Folland, Sherman T., "Health Care in Small Areas of Three Command Economies: What Do the Data Tell Us?" *Eastern European Economics* (November–December, 2005): 31–52.

Folland, Sherman T., "The Quality of Mercy: Social Health Insurance in the Charitable Liberal State," *International Journal of Health Care Finance and Economics 5* 2005: 23–46.

Folland, Sherman T., "Value of Life and Behavior Toward Risk," *Health Economics* (2005): 159–171.

Folland, Sherman T., "Health Care Need, Economics, and Social Justice," *International Journal of Social Economics 13* (1986): 98–116.

Folland, Sherman T. and Richard A. Hofler, "How Reliable Are Hospital Efficiency Estimates?: Exploiting the Dual to Homothetic Production," *Health Economics 10* (2001): 683–698.

Folland, Sherman T. and Miron Stano, "Small Area Variations: A Critical Review of Propositions, Methods, and Evidence," *Medical Care Review 47* (1990): 419–465.

Folland, Sherman T. and Miron Stano, "Sources of Small Area Variations in the Use of Medical Care," *Journal of Health Economics 8* (1989): 85–107.

Fontana, John P., "Hospital Marketing Is Here to Stay," *Hospital Topics 62* (1984): 12–13.

Fournier, Gary M. and Jean M. Mitchell, "Hospital Costs and Competition for Services: A Multi-Product Analysis," *Review of Economics and Statistics 74* (1992): 627–634.

Fox, William F. and Richard A. Hofler, "Using Homothetic Composed Error Frontiers to Measure Water Utility Efficiency," *Southern Economic Journal 53* (1986): 461–477.

Frank, Richard G. "Editorial: New Estimates of Drug Development Costs," *Journal of Health Economics 22* (2003): 325–330.

Frank, Richard G. and David S. Salkever, "Generic Entry and the Pricing of Pharmaceuticals," *Journal of Economics and Management Strategy 6* (1997): 75–90.

Frank, Richard G. and David S. Salkever, "Nonprofit Organizations in the Health Sector," *Journal of Economic Perspectives 8* (1994): 129–144.

Frech, H. E. III, *Competition & Monopoly in Medical Care.* (Washington, DC: AEI Press, 1996).

Frech, H. E. III, "The Property Rights Theory of the Firm: Empirical Results from a Natural Experiment," *Journal of Political Economy 84* (1976): 143–152.

Frech, H. E. III, "The United States, Advances in Health Economics and Health Services Research Supplement 1: Comparative Health Systems." (Greenwich, CT: JAI Press, 1990): 43–75.

Frech, H. E. III and Paul B. Ginsburg, "Competition Among Health Insurers, Revisited," *Journal of Health Politics, Policy and Law 13* (1988): 279–291.

Frech, H. E. III and Richard D. Miller, Jr. *The Productivity of Health Care and Pharmaceuticals.* (Washington, DC: American Enterprise Institute, 1999).

Frech, H. E. III and Lee R. Mobley, "The Demsetz Hypothesis and Hospital Markets: An Empirical Analysis," Working Papers in Economics 5–96, Department of Economics, University of California, Santa Barbara, CA, 1996.

Frederick, Shane, George Loewenstein, and Ted O'Donoghue, "Time Discounting and Time Preference: A Critical Review," *Journal of Economic Literature 40* (2002): 351–401.

Frenk, Julio, "Editorial: Medical Care and Health Improvement: The Critical Link," *Annals of Internal Medicine 129* (1998): 419–420.

Friedman, Bernard and Claudia Steiner, "Does Managed Care Affect the Supply and Use of ICU Services?" *Inquiry 36* (1999): 68–77.

Friedman, Milton and Simon Kuznets, *Income from Independent Professional Practice* (New York: National Bureau of Economic Research, 1945).

Fries, James F., "Aging, Natural Death, and the Compression of Morbidity," *New England Journal of Medicine 303* (1980): 130–136.

Fuchs, Victor R., "The Clinton Plan: A Researcher Examines Reform," *Health Affairs 13* (1994): 102–114.

Fuchs, Victor R., "Economics, Health, and Post Industrial Society," *Milbank Memorial Fund Quarterly/Health and Society 57* (1979): 153–182.

Fuchs, Victor R., "Economics, Values, and Health Care Reform," Presidential Address to the American Economic Association, *American Economic Review 86* (1996): 11–24.

Fuchs, Victor R., "Health Care for the Elderly: How Much? Who Will Pay for It?" *Health Affairs 18* (1) (1999): 11–21.

Fuchs, Victor R., "Medicare Reform: The Larger Picture," *Journal of Economic Perspectives 14* (2) (2000): 57–70.

Fuchs, Victor R., "The Supply of Surgeons and the Demand for Operations," *Journal of Human Resources 13* (Supplement 1978): 35–56.

Fuchs, Victor R., "Time Preference and Health: An Exploratory Study," in *Economic Aspects of Health*, Victor R. Fuchs (ed.) (Chicago: The University of Chicago Press, 1982): 93–120.

Fuchs, Victor R., *Who Shall Live?* (New York: Basic Books, Inc., 1974).

Fuchs, Victor R. and James S. Hahn, "How Does Canada Do It? A Comparison of Expenditures for Physicians' Services in the United States and Canada," *New England Journal of Medicine 323* (1990): 884–890.

Fuchs, Victor R. and Marcia J. Kramer, "Determinants of Expenditures for Physicians' Services in the United States 1948–68," Publication No. (HSM) 73–3013, National Bureau of Economic Research, National Center for Health Services Research and Development, DHEW, December 1972.

Fuhrman, Vanessa, "Insurer Reveals What Doctors Really Charge," *Wall Street Journal*, August 18, 2005, D1.

Gabel, Jon and Dan Ermann, "Preferred Provider Organizations: Performance, Problems, and Promise," *Health Affairs 4* (1985): 24–40.

Gabel, Jon and Gail A. Jensen, "The Price of State Mandated Benefits," *Inquiry 26* (1989): 419–432.

Gagne, Robert and Pierre Thomas Leger, "Determinants of Physicians' Decisions to Specialize," *Health Economics 14* (2005): 721–735.

Galbraith, John K., *The Affluent Society.* (Boston: Houghton Mifflin, 1958).

Gallett, Craig A., "Advertising and Restrictions in the Cigarette Industry: Evidence of State-by-State Variation," *Contemporary Economic Policy 21* (2003): 338–348.

Garbacz, Christopher, "Smoke Detector Effectiveness and the Value of Saving a Life," *Economic Letters 31* (1989): 281–286.

Garber, Alan, "Advances in Cost-Effectiveness Analysis of Health Interventions," in *Handbook of Health Economics, Volume 1*, A. J. Culyer and Joseph P. Newhouse (eds.) (Elsevier Science B.V., 2000).

Garber, Alan M. and Charles E. Phelps, "Economic Foundations of Cost-Effectiveness Analysis," *Journal of Health Economics 16* (1997): 1–31.

Gaumer, Gary L., "Regulating Health Professionals: A Review of the Empirical Literature," *Milbank Memorial Fund Quarterly/Health and Society 62* (1984): 380–416.

Gaynor, Martin and Gerard F. Andersen, "Uncertain Demand, the Structure of Hospital Costs, and the Cost of Empty Beds," National Bureau of Economic Research Working Paper 4460, 1995.

Gaynor, Martin and Mark V. Pauly, "Compensation and Productive Efficiency in Partnerships: Evidence from Medical Group Practice," *Journal of Political Economy 98* (1990): 544–573.

Gaynor, Martin and Solomon Polachek, "Measuring Information in the Market: An Application to Physician Services," *Southern Economic Journal 60* (1994): 815–831.

Gaynor, Martin and William B. Vogt, "Antitrust and Competition in Health Care Markets," in *Handbook of Health Economics*, Anthony J. Culyer and Joseph P. Newhouse (eds.) (Elsevier Science B.V., 2000).

Gaynor, Martin and William B. Vogt, "Competition Among Hospitals," *RAND Journal of Economics 34* (2003): 764–785.

Gaynor, Martin, Deborah Haas-Wilson, and William B. Vogt, "Are Invisible Hands Good Hands? Moral Hazard, Competition, and the Second Best in Health Care Markets," *Journal of Political Economy* (2000): 992–1005.

Gegax, Douglas, Shelby Gerking, and William Schulze, "Perceived Risk and the Marginal Value of Safety," *Review of Economics and Statistics 73* (1991): 589–596.

Geoffard, Pierre-Yves and Tomas Philipson, "Rational Epidemics and Their Public Control," *International Economic Review 37* (3) (1996): 603–624.

Gerdtham Ulf-G, and M. Johannesson, "New Estimates of the Demand for Health: Results Based on a Categorical Health Measure and Swedish Micro Data," *Social Science and Medicine 49* (1999): 1325–1332.

Gerdtham, Ulf-G. et al., "An Econometric Analysis of Health Care Expenditure: A Cross-Section Study of the OECD Countries," *Journal of Health Economics 11* (1992): 63–84.

Gertler, Paul J., "Subsidies, Quality, and the Regulation of Nursing Homes," *Journal of Public Economics 38* (1989): 33–52.

Gertler, Paul J. and Donald M. Waldman, "Quality Adjusted Cost Functions and Policy Evaluation in the Nursing Home Industry," *Journal of Political Economy 100* (1992): 1232–1256.

Getzen, Thomas E., "Health Care Is an Individual Necessity and a National Luxury," *Journal of Health Economics 19* (2) (2000): 259–270.

Getzen, Thomas E. and Jean-Pierre Poullier, "International Health Spending Forecasts: Concepts and Evaluation," *Social Science and Medicine 34* (9) (1992): 1057–1068.

Gibson, Robert M. and Marjorie Smith Mueller, "National Health Expenditures, Fiscal Year 1976," *Social Security Bulletin 40* (1977): 3–32.

Gibson, Teresa R., Ronald J. Ozminkowski, and Ron Z. Goetzel, "The Effects of Prescription Drug Cost Sharing: A Review of the Evidence," *American Journal of Managed Care 11* (2005): 730–740.

Gillum B. S., E. J. Graves, and E. Wood, *National Hospital Discharge Survey: Annual Summary, 1995*, National Center for Health Statistics, Vital Health Statistics 13 (1998).

Ginsburg, Paul B. and Grossman, Joy M., "When The Price Isn't Right: How Inadvertent Payment Incentives Drive Medical Care," *Health Affairs*, http://content.healthaffairs.org/cgi/content/abstract/hlthaff.w5.376v1, accessed August 15, 2005.

Glick, Peter and David E. Sahn, "Health and Productivity in a Heterogeneous Urban Labor Market," *Applied Economics 30* (1998): 203–216.

Glied, Sherry, "Managed Care," in *Handbook of Health Economics, Volume 1A*, Anthony J. Culyer and Joseph P. Newhouse (eds.) (Elsevier Science, B.V., 2000).

Goddeeris, John H., "Economic Forces and Hospital Technology: Lessons from the United States Experience," *International Journal of Technology Assessment in Health Care 3* (1987): 223–240.

Goddeeris, John H., "Insurance and Incentives for Innovation in Medical Care," *Southern Economic Journal 51* (1984a): 530–539.

Goddeeris, John H. "Medical Insurance, Technological Change, and Welfare," *Economic Inquiry 22* (1984b): 56–67.

Goddeeris, John H. and Thomas P. Bronken, "Benefit-Cost Analysis of Screening," *Medical Care 23* (1985): 1242–1255.

Goddeeris, John H. and Burton A. Weisbrod, "Conversion from Nonprofit to For-Profit Legal Status: Why Does It Happen and Should Anyone Care?" *Journal of Policy Analysis and Management 17* (1998): 215–233.

Gold, Marthe R. et al. (eds). *Cost Effectiveness in Health and Medicine* (New York: Oxford University Press, 1996).

Goldberg, Lawrence G. and Warren Greenberg, "The Effect of Physician-Controlled Health Insurance," *Journal of Health Politics, Policy and Law 2* (1977): 48–78.

Goldberg, Theodore et al., "Evaluation of Economic Effects of Drug Product Selection Legislation," *Medical Care 17* (1979): 411–419.

Goldman, Dana P. et al., "Pharmacy Benefits and the Use of Drugs by the Chronically Ill," *Journal of the American Medical Association 291* (2004): 2344–2350.

Goldman, Dana P., "Pressure from Rising Health-Care Costs: How Can Consumers Get Relief?" www.rand.org/commentary/102305PE.html.

Goldman, Dana P. et al., "Redistributional Consequences of Community Rating," *Health Services Research 32* (1997): 71–86.

Goldstein, Karen P. et al., "The Effect of Epidemic Measles on Immunization Rates," *Journal of the American Medical Association 276* (1) (1996): 56–58.

Goodman, Allen C., "Estimation of Offset and Income Effects on the Demand for Mental Health," *Inquiry 26* (1989): 235–248.

Goodman, Allen C. and Miron Stano, "HMOs and Health Externalities: A Local Public Good Perspective," *Public Finance Review 28* (May 2000): 247–269.

Goodman, Allen C., Miron Stano, and John M. Tilford, "Applications and Extensions of the Grossman Health Care Model," *Southern Economic Journal 65* (1999): 791–806.

Goodman, Clifford S., "Healthcare Technology Assessment: Methods, Framework, and Role in Policy Making," *American Journal of Managed Care 4* (1998: Special Issue): SP200–SP213.

Gordon, Margaret S, *Social Security Policies in Industrial Countries*. (Cambridge: Cambridge University Press, 1988).

Gornick, Marian et al., "Twenty Years of Medicare and Medicaid: Covered Populations, Use of Benefits, and Program Expenditures," *Health Care Financing Review, Annual Supplement 6* (1985): 13–59.

Grabowski, Henry G. and John M. Vernon, "Brand Loyalty, Entry, and Price Competition in Pharmaceuticals After the 1984 Drug Act," *Journal of Law and Economics 35* (1992): 331–350.

Grabowski, Henry G. and John M. Vernon, "Prospects for Returns to Pharmaceutical R&D Under Health Care Reform," in *Competitive Strategies in the Pharmaceutical Industry*, Robert B. Helms (ed.) (Washington, DC: American Enterprise Institute, 1996): 194–207.

Grabowski, Henry G. and John M. Vernon, "Returns to R&D on New Drug Innovations in the 1980s," *Journal of Health Economics 13* (1994): 383–406.

Graddy, Elizabeth, "Interest Groups or the Public Interest—Why Do We Regulate Health Occupations?" *Journal of Health Politics, Policy and Law 16* (1991): 25–49.

Grannemann, Thomas W., Randall S. Brown, and Mark V. Pauly, "Estimating Hospital Costs: A Multiple-Output Analysis," *Journal of Health Economics 5* (1986): 107–127.

Green, Lee A. and Mark P. Becker, "Physician Decision Making and Variation in Hospital Admission Rates for Suspected Acute Cardiac Ischemia," *Medical Care 32* (1994): 1086–1097.

Grosskopf, Shawna and Vivian Valdmanis, "Measuring Hospital Performance: A Non-Parametric Approach," *Journal of Health Economics 6* (1987): 89–107.

Grossman, Michael, *The Demand for Health: A Theoretical and Empirical Investigation*. [New York: Columbia (for the National Bureau of Economic Research), 1972a].

Grossman, Michael, "On the Concept of Health Capital and the Demand for Health," *Journal of Political Economy 80* (1972b): 223–255.

Grossman, Michael and Theodore J. Joyce, "Unobservables, Pregnancy Resolutions, and Birth Weight Production Functions in New York City," *Journal of Political Economy 98* (1990): 983–1007.

Grossman, Michael, Frank J. Chaloupka, and Ismail Sirtalan, "An Empirical Analysis of Alcohol Addiction: Results from the Monitoring the Future Panels," *Economic Inquiry 36* (1998): 39–48.

Gruber, Jonathan, "The Incidence of Mandated Maternity Benefits," *American Economic Review 84* (1994): 622–641.

Gruber, Jonathan, "Medicaid," in *Means-Tested Transfers in the U.S.,* Robert A. Moffit (ed.) (Chicago: University of Chicago Press, 2002).

Gruber Jonathan and Botond Köszegi, "Is Addiction 'Rational'? Theory and Evidence," *The Quarterly Journal of Economics 116* (2001): 1261–1303.

Gruber, Jonathan and Alan B. Krueger, "The Incidence of Mandated Employer Provided Health Insurance: Lessons from Workers' Compensation Insurance," in *Health Benefits and the Workforce*, David Bradford (ed.) (Washington, DC: U.S. Government Printing Office, 1992).

Gruber, Jonathan and Brigitte C. Madrian, "Health Insurance, Labor Supply, and Job Mobility: A Critical Review of the Literature," National Bureau of Economic Research, Working Paper 8817, March 2002.

Gruber, Jonathan and Maria Owings, "Physician Financial Incentives and the Diffusion of Cesarean Section Delivery," *RAND Journal of Economics 27* (1996): 99–123.

Gruber, Jonathan and Jonathan Zinman, "Youth Smoking in the U.S.: Evidence and Implications," National Bureau of Economic Research Working Paper, 8872, 2002.

Grytten, Jostein and Rune Sørensen, "Supplier Inducement in a Public Health Care System," *Journal of Health Economics 14* (1995): 207–229.

Grytten, Jostein and Rune Sørensen, "Type of Contract and Supplier-Induced Demand for Primary Physicians in Norway," *Journal of Health Economics 20* (2001): 379–393.

Gully, O. David and Rexford E. Santerre, "The Effect of Tax Exemption on the Market Share of Nonprofit Hospitals," *National Tax Journal 46* (1993): 477–486.

Haas-Wilson, Deborah, "Consumer Information and Providers' Reputations: An Empirical Test in the Market for Psychotherapy," *Journal of Health Economics 9* (1990): 321–333.

Hadley, Jack, "Medicare Spending and Mortality Rates of the Elderly," *Inquiry 25* (1988): 485–493.

Hadley, Jack, *More Medical Care, Better Health?* (Washington, DC: Urban Institute, 1982).

Hadley, Jack and John Holahan, "How Much Medical Care Do the Uninsured Use and Who Pays for It?" *Health Affairs*, Web Exclusive, February 12, 2003, http://content.healthaffairs.org/cgi/reprint/hlthaff.w3.66v1, accessed September 4, 2005.

Hadley, Jack and John Holahan, "Covering the Uninsured: How Much Would It Cost?" *Health Affairs*, Web Exclusive, June 4, 2003, http:// content.healthaffairs.org/cgi/reprint/hlthaff.w3.250v1, accessed September 4, 2005.

Hadley, Jack and Stephen Zuckerman, "The Role of Efficiency in Hospital Rate Setting," *Journal of Health Economics 13* (1994): 335–340.

Hall, Mark A. and Christopher J. Conover, "The Impact of Blue Cross Conversions on Accessibility, Affordability, and the Public Interest," *The Milbank Quarterly 81* (2003): 509–542.

Hall, Thomas D. and Cotton M. Lindsay, "Medical Schools: Producers of What? Sellers to Whom?" *Journal of Law and Economics 23* (1980): 55–80.

Hamilton, James L., "The Demand for Cigarettes: Advertising, the Health Scare, and the Cigarette Advertising Ban," *Review of Economics and Statistics 54* (1972): 401–411.

Hamilton, James L., "The Effect of Cigarette Advertising Bans on Cigarette Consumption," Proceedings of the Third World Conference on Smoking and Health (Washington, DC: U.S. DHEW, 1975).

Hamilton, Vivian, "The Medicare Hospice Benefit: The Effectiveness of Price Incentives in Health Care Policy," *RAND Journal of Economics 24* (1993): 605–624.

Hansen, Ronald W., "Costs and Benefits of Cost Benefit Analysis in Pharmaceutical Promotion and Utilization Decisions," in *Competitive Strategies in the Pharmaceutical Industry*, Robert B. Helms (ed.) (Washington, DC: American Enterprise Institute, 1996): 322–336.

Hansen, W. Lee, "Shortages and Investment in Health Manpower," in *The Economics of Health and Medical Care: Proceedings of the Conference* on *the Economics of Health and Medical Care*, May 10–12, 1962. (Ann Arbor, MI: University of Michigan, 1964).

Hansmann, Henry, Daniel Kessler, and Mark McClellan, "Ownership Form and Trapped Capital in the Hospital Industry," Yale Law & Economics Research Paper No. 266, New Haven, CT, 2002.

Hansmann, Henry B., "The Effect of Tax Exemption and Other Factors on the Market Share of Nonprofit Versus For-Profit Firms," *National Tax Journal 40* (1987): 71–82.

Hansmann, Henry B., "The Role of Nonprofit Enterprise," *Yale Law Journal 89* (1980): 835–901.

Harrington, Charlene, James H. Swan, and Leslie A. Grant, "Nursing Home Bed Capacity in the States, 1978–86," *Health Care Financing Review 9* (1988): 81–97.

Harris, Jeffrey E., "The Internal Organization of Hospitals: Some Economic Implications," *Bell Journal of Economics 8* (1977): 467–482.

Harris, Jeffrey E. and Sandra W. Chan, "The Continuum-of-Addiction: Cigarette Smoking in Relation to Price Among Americans," *Health Economics Letters 2* (1998): 3–12.

Harris, Jeffrey E. and Sandra W. Chan, "The Continuum-of-Addiction: Cigarette Smoking in Relation to Price Among Americans Aged 15–29," *Health Economics 8*, (1999): 81–86.

Hassan, Mahmud, Gerard Wedig, and Michael A. Morrisey, "Charity Care by Non-Profit Hospitals: The Price of Tax-Exempt Debt," *International Journal of the Economics of Business 7* (2000): 47–62.

Hay, Joel W. and Gerard Anderson, "The Hospital Services Market: A Disequilibrium Analysis," *Southern Economic Journal 54* (1988): 656–665.

Hayek, Frederich, *The Constitution of Liberty* (Chicago: The University of Chicago Press, 1960).

Headen, Alvin E., Jr., "Wages, Returns to Ownership, and Fee Responses to Physician Supply," *Review of Economics and Statistics 72* (1990): 30–37.

Heffler, Stephen et al., "U.S. Health Spending Projections For 2004–2014," *Health Affairs*, February 23, 2005, http://content.healthaffairs.org/cgi/content/abstract/hlthaff.w5.74, accessed October 29, 2005.

Heffley, Dennis R. and Thomas J. Miceli, "The Economics of Incentive-Based Health Plans," *Journal of Risk and Insurance 65* (1998): 445–465.

Hellerstein, James K., "The Importance of the Physician in the Generic Versus Trade-Name Prescription Decision," *RAND Journal of Economics 29* (1998): 108–136.

Henderson, Rebecca and Iain Cockburn, "Scale, Scope, and Spillovers: The Determinants of Research Productivity in Drug Discovery," *RAND Journal of Economics 27* (1996): 32–59.

Henke, Klaus-Dirk, Margaret A. Murray, and Claudia Ade, "Global Budgeting in Germany: Lessons for the United States," *Health Affairs 13* (1994): 7–21.

Hethcote, Herbert W., "The Mathematics of Infectious Diseases," *SIAM Review 42* (4) (2000): 599–653.

Hill, Steven C. and Barbara L. Wolfe, "Testing the HMO Competitive Strategy: An Analysis of Its Impact on Medical Care Resources," *Journal of Health Economics 16* (1997): 261–286.

Hilsenrath, Peter, "Fiscal Policy Dilemmas and Health Spending in South Africa," *Journal of Health and Human Services Administration 21* (1999): 310–324.

Hirsch, Barry T. and Edwin J. Schumaker, "Classic or New Monopsony? Searching for Evidence in Nursing Labor Markets," *Journal of Health Economics 24* (2005): 969–989.

Hirsch, Barry T. and Edward Schumacher, "Monopsony Power and Relative Wages in the Labor Market for Nurses," *Journal of Health Economics 14* (1995): 443–476.

Hirsch, Barry T. and Edward Schumacher, "Union Wages, Rents, and Skills in Health Care Labor Markets," *Journal of Labor Research 19* (1998): 125–147.

Hirshleifer, Jack and Amihai Glazer, *Price Theory and Applications*, 5th ed. (Upper Saddle River, NJ: Prentice Hall, 1992).

Hirth, Richard A., "Consumer Information and Competition Between Nonprofit and For-Profit Nursing Homes," *Journal of Health Economics 18* (1999): 219–240.

Hirth, Richard A., Michael E., Chernew, and Sean M. Orzol, "Ownership, Competition, and the Adoption of New Technologies and Cost Saving Practices in a Fixed-Price Environment," *Inquiry 37* (2000): 282–294.

Hitiris, Theo and John Posnett, "The Determinants and Effects of Health Expenditure in Developed Countries," *Journal of Health Economics 11* (1992): 173–181.

Hodgkin, Dominic and Thomas G. McGuire, "Payment Levels and Hospital Response to Prospective Payment," *Journal of Health Economics 13* (1994): 1–29.

Hodgson, Thomas A., "Cigarette Smoking and Lifetime Medical Expenditures," *Milbank Quarterly 70* (1992): 81–125.

Hoerger, Thomas J., "Profit Variability in For-Profit and Not-for-Profit Hospitals," *Journal of Health Economics 10* (1991): 259–289.

Hoff, Timothy J., "Doing the Same and Earning Less: Male and Female Physicians in a New Medical Specialty," *Inquiry, 41* (Fall 2004): 301–315.

Hoffman, Catherine, Alicia Carbaugh, and Allison Cook, *Health Insurance Coverage in America, 2003* (Kaiser Family Foundation, November 2004) Table 7.

Hoge, Patrick, "BART, Unions Clash on Health Benefits," *San Francisco Chronicle*, June 26, 2005, http://www.sfgate.com/cgi-bin/article.cgi?f=/c/a/2005/06/26/BART.TMP, accessed August 1, 2005.

Holahan, John and David Liska, "Variations in Medicaid Spending Among States," *Assessing New Federalism: Issues and Options for States*, A–3. (Washington, DC: Urban Institute, January 1997).

Holahan, John and Mary Beth Prohl, "Changes in Insurance Coverage: 1994–2000 and Beyond," *Health Affairs Web Exclusive* (April 3, 2002), www.healthaffairs.org/WebExclusives/Holahan_Web_Excl_040302.htm, accessed June 18, 2002.

Holahan, John, Joshua Wiener, and Susan Wallin, "Health Policy for the Low-Income Population: Major Findings from the Assessing the New Federalism Case Studies." Washington, DC: Urban Institute, November 1998.

Holtmann, Alphonse G., "Theories of Non-Profit Institutions," *Journal of Economic Surveys 2* (1988): 29–45.

Holtmann, Alphonse G., "A Theory of Non-Profit Firms," *Economica 50* (November 1983): 439–449.

Holtmann, Alphonse G. and Todd L. Idson, "Wage Determination of Registered Nurses in Proprietary and Nonprofit Nursing Homes," *Journal of Human Resources 28* (1993): 55–79.

Hopkins, Carol, "Appeals Court Allows Hospitals to Expand," *Oakland Press*, March 24, 2005, www.theoaklandpress.com/stories/032405/loc_20050324011.shtml, accessed August 25, 2005.

Hornbrook, Mark C. and Alan C. Monheit, "The Contribution of Case-Mix Severity to the Hospital Cost-Output Relation," *Inquiry 22* (1985): 259–271.

Hsiao, William C., "Resource-Based Relative Value Scale: An Option for Physician Payment," *Inquiry 24* (1987): 360–361.

Hsiao, William C., Daniel L. Dunn, and Diana K. Verrilli, "Assessing the Implementation of Physician-Payment Reform," *New England Journal of Medicine 328* (1993): 928–933.

Hughes, David and Alistair McGuire, "Stochastic Demand, Production Responses and Hospital Costs," *Journal of Health Economics 22* (November 2003): 999–1010.

Hughes, Susan L. et al., "Impact of Home Care on Hospital Days: A Meta Analysis," *Health Services Research 32* (1997): 415–432.

Hurd, Michael D. and Kathleen McGarry, "Medical Insurance and the Use of Health Care Services by the Elderly," *Journal of Health Economics 16* (1997): 129–154.

Hurley, Jeremiah, "An Overview of the Normative Economics of the Health Sector," in *Handbook of Health Economics*, Volume I, A. J. Culyer and J. P. Newhouse (eds.) (Elsevier Science B.V., 2000).

Hurst, Jeremy, W., "Reform of Health Care in Germany," *Health Care Financing Review 12* (1991): 73–86.

Hurwitz, Mark A. and Richard E. Caves, "Persuasion or Information? Promotion and the Shares of Brand Name and Generic Pharmaceuticals," *Journal of Law and Economics 31* (1988): 299–320.

Huttin, Christine, "Drug Price Divergence in Europe: Regulatory Aspect," *Health Affairs 18* (1999): 245–249.

Iglehart, John K., "An Interview with Leonard D. Schaefer." *Health Affairs 14* (1995): 131–142.

Illich, Ivan, *Medical Nemesis* (New York: Bantam Books, 1976).

Illife, Steve and Sasha Shepperd, "What Do We Know About Hospital At Home: Lessons From International Experience," *Applied Health Economics and Health Policy 1* (2002): 141–147.

Institute of Medicine, *Crossing the Quality Chasm: A New Health System for the 21st Century* (Washington, DC, 2001).

Institute of Medicine, *To Err Is Human: Building a Safer Health System* (Washington, DC, 1999).

International Health, *How Australia Compares,* www.aihw.gov.au/publications/health/ihhac, 2002.

Ippolito, Pauline M. and Richard A. Ippolito, "Measuring the Value of Life Saving from Consumer Reactions to New Information," *Journal of Public Economics 25* (1984): 53–81.

Jacobson, Peter D., Louise E. Parker, and Ian D. Coulter, "Nurse Practitioners and Physician Assistants as Primary Care Providers in Institutional Settings," *Inquiry 35* (1998/99): 432–446.

Jaegher, Kris De and Marc Jegers, "A Model of the Physician with Demand Inducement," *Journal of Health Economics 19* (2000): 231–258.

Jantzen Robert and Patricia R. Loubeau, "Hospital Selection by Managed Care Insurers," *Health Care Management Review 25* (2000): 93–102.

Jensen, Gail A. and Allen C. Goodman, "The Economics of Gynecology and Obstetrics," in *Practical Strategies in Obstetrics and Gynecology,* Scott B. Ransom (ed.) (New York: W. B. Saunders, 1999): 719–733.

Jensen, Gail A. and Michael A. Morrisey, "Employer Sponsored Health Insurance and Mandated Benefit Laws," *Milbank Quarterly 77* (1999): 425–459.

Jensen, Gail A. and Michael A. Morrisey, "Endogenous Fringe Benefits, Compensating Wage Differentials and Older Workers," *International Journal of Health Care Finance and Economics 1* (2001): 203–226.

Jensen, Gail A. and Michael A. Morrisey, "Group Health Insurance: A Hedonic Price Approach," *Review of Economics and Statistics 72* (1990): 38–44.

Jensen, Gail A. and Michael A. Morrisey, "The Role of Physicians in Hospital Production," *Review of Economics and Statistics 68* (1986): 432–442.

Jha, Ashish K. et al., "Care in U.S. Hospitals—The Hospital Quality Alliance Program," *New England Journal of Medicine 353* (2005): 265–274.

Joesch, Jutta M., Thomas M. Wickizer, and Paul J. Feldstein, "Does Competition by Health Maintenance Organizations Affect the Adoption of Cost-Containment Measures by Fee-for Service Plans?" *American Journal of Managed Care 4* (1998): 832–838.

Johnston, Jack, "Advertising and the Aggregate Demand for Cigarettes: A Comment," *European Economic Review 14* (1980): 117–125.

Jondrow, James et al., "On the Estimation of Technical Inefficiency in the Stochastic Frontier Production Function Model," *Journal of Econometrics* (1982): 233–238.

Jones, Andrew M., "Smoking Cessation and Health: A Response," *Journal of Health Economics 15,* (December 1996): 755–759.

Jones, Chuck, "Despite Tax Break, Group LTC Market Stalls," *Life Association News 94* (1999): 32–35.

Jones, Robert F. et al., "Review of U.S. Medical School Finances, 1996–1997," *Journal of the American Medical Association 280* (1998): 813–818.

Jorgenson, Dale W., "Capital Theory and Investment Behavior," *American Economic Review 53* (1963): 247–259.

Joskow, Paul L., "The Effects of Competition and Regulation on Hospital Bed Supply and the Reservation Quality of the Hospital," *Bell Journal of Economics 11* (1980): 421–447.

Joyce, Geoffrey F. et al., "Employer Drug Benefit Plans and Spending on Prescription Drugs," *Journal of the American Medical Association 288* (14) (2002): 1733–1739.

Joyce, Theodore, "Impact of Augmented Prenatal Care on Birth Outcomes of Medicaid Recipients in New York City," *Journal of Health Economics 18* (1999): 31–67.

Joyce, Theodore, Andrew D. Racine, and Naci Mocan, "The Consequences and Costs of Maternal Substance Abuse in New York City: A Pooled Time-Series, Cross-Section Analysis," *Journal of Health Economics 11* (1992): 297–314.

Juba, David A., *Price Setting in the Market for Physicians' Services: A Review of the Literature*, U.S. Department of Health, Education and Welfare, Health Care Financing Administration, HEW Publication No. (HCFA) 030129-79, GPO 1979.

Jung, Ki-Taig, "Influence of the Introduction of a Per-Visit Copayment on Health Care Use and Expenditures: The Korean Experience," *Journal of Risk and Insurance 65* (1998): 35–56.

Kaestner, Robert, Theodore Joyce, and Hassan Wehbeh, "The Effect of Maternal Drug Use on Birth Weight: Measurement Error in Binary Variables," *Economic Inquiry 34* (October 1996): 617–629.

Kaiser Family Foundation, "Myths About The Uninsured," www.kff.org/uninsured/upload/Myths-about-the-Uninsured-Fact-Sheet.pdf, accessed August 17, 2005.

Kaiser Family Foundation, *Trends and Indicators in the Changing Health Care Marketplace*, 2004. Available at: www.kff.org/about/marketplace.cfm.

Kamien, Morton I. and Nancy L. Schwartz, *Market Structure and Innovation* (Cambridge: Cambridge University Press, 1982).

Kaplan, Robert M. and John P. Anderson, "A General Health Policy Model: Update and Applications," *Health Services Research 23* (1988): 203–235.

Keeler, Emmett B. and John E. Rolph, "The Demand for Episodes of Treatment in the Health Insurance Experiment," *Journal of Health Economics 7* (1988): 333–367.

Keeler, Emmett B., Willard G. Manning, Jr., and Kenneth B. Wells, "The Demand for Episodes of Mental Health Services," *Journal of Health Economics 7* (1988): 369–392.

Keeler, Theodore E. et al., "Taxation, Regulation, and Addiction: A Demand Function for Cigarettes Based on Time-Series Evidence," *Journal of Health Economics 12* (1993): 1–18.

Keeler, Theodore E. et al, "The U.S. National Tabacco Settlement: The Effects of Advertising and Price Changes on Cigarette Consumption," *Applied Economics 36* (2004): 1623–1629.

Kenkel, Donald S., "The Demand for Preventive Medical Care," *Applied Economics 26* (1994): 313–325.

Kermack, William O. and Anderson G. McKendrick, "Contributions to the Mathematical Theory of Epidemics," *Proceedings of the Royal Society A 115* (1927): 700–721.

Kessel, Reuben, "Price Discrimination in Medicine," *Journal of Law and Economics 1* (1958): 20–53.

Kessides, Ioannis N., "Advertising, Sunk Costs, and Barriers to Entry," *Review of Economics and Statistics 68* (1986): 84–95.

Kessler, Daniel and Mark McClellan, "The Effect of Hospital Ownership on Medical Productivity," National Bureau of Economic Research Working Paper 8537, 2001.

Kessler, Daniel P. and Mark B. McClellan, "Is Hospital Competition Socially Wasteful?," *Quarterly Journal of Economics 115* (2000): 577–615.

Klausen, Liv Marit, Trand E. Olsen, and Alf Erling Risa, "Technological Diffusion in Primary Health Care," *Journal of Health Economics 13* (1994): 439–452.

Kniesner, Thomas J. and John Leeth, "Compensating Wage Differentials for Fatal Injury Risk in Australia, Japan, and the United States," *Journal of Risk and Insurance 4* (1991): 75–90.

Kooreman, Peter, "Data Envelopment Analysis and Parametric Frontier Estimation: Complementary Tools," *Journal of Health Economics 13* (1994): 345–346.

Kooreman, Peter, "Nursing Home Care in the Netherlands: A Nonparametric Efficiency Analysis," *Journal of Health Economics 13* (1994): 301–316.

Krasny, Jacques and Ian R. Ferrier, "A Closer Look at Health Care in Canada," *Health Affairs 10* (1991): 152–158.

Krishnan, Ranjani, "Market Restructuring and Pricing in the Hospital Industry," *Journal of Health Economics 20* (2001): 213–237.

Kristof, Kathy M., "How Does a Viatical Settlement Work?" *Los Angeles Times*, December 9, 1999.

Kronick, Richard, Louis Olsen, and Todd Gilmer, "The Response of Small Businesses to Variation in the Price of Insurance: Evidence from a Randomized Trial," www.academyhealth.org/2004/ppt/kronickprice.ppt, accessed August 24, 2005.

Krueger, Alan B. and Uwe E. Reinhardt, "The Economics of Employer Versus Individual Mandates," *Health Affairs 13* (1994): 34–53.

Kwoka, John E. Jr., "Advertising and the Price and Quality of Optometric Services," *American Economic Review 74* (1984): 211–216.

Labelle, Roberta, Gregg Stoddard, and Thomas Rice, "A Re-Examination of the Meaning and Importance of Supplier-Induced Demand," *Journal of Health Economics 13* (1994): 347–368.

Lakdawalla, Darius and Tomas Philipson, "Nonprofit Production and Competition," Working Paper 6377, National Bureau of Economic Research, January 1998.

Lalonde, Marc, *A New Perspective on the Health of Canadians*, Office of the Canadian Minister of National Health and Welfare, Ottawa, 1974.

Lamberton, C. E., W. D. Ellington, and K. R. Spear, "Factors Determining the Demand for Nursing Home Services," *Quarterly Review of Economics and Business 26* (1986): 74–90.

Lambin, J. J., *Advertising, Competition and Market Conduct in Oligopoly over Time*. (Amsterdam: North-Holland, 1976).

Lane, Julia and Stephan Gohmann, "Shortage or Surplus: Economic and Noneconomic Approaches to the Analysis of Nursing Labor Markets," *Southern Economic Journal 61* (1995): 644–653.

Langwell, Kathryn M. and Lyle M. Nelson, "Physician Payment Systems: A Review of History, Alternatives and Evidence," *Medical Care Review 43* (1986): 5–58.

Lanoie, Paul and Paul Leclair, "Taxation or Regulation: Looking for a Good Anti-Smoking Policy," *Economics Letters 58* (1998): 85–89.

Laugesen, Murray and Chris Meads, "Tobacco Advertising Restrictions, Price, Income, and Tobacco Consumption in OECD Countries, 1960–1986," *British Journal of Addiction 86* (1991): 1343–1354.

Le Grand, Julian, "Further Tales from the British National Health Service," *Health Affairs 21* (3) (2002): 116–128.

Lee, Dwight R., "Why Workers Should Want Mandated Benefits to Lower Their Wages," *Economic Inquiry 34* (1996): 401–407.

Lee, L. F., M. R. Rosenzweig, and M. M. Pitt, "The Effects of Improved Nutrition, Sanitation, and Water Quality on Child Health in High Mortality Populations," *Journal of Econometrics 77* (1997): 209–235.

Lee, Maw L., "A Conspicuous Production Theory of Hospital Behavior," *Southern Economic Journal 38* (1971): 48–58.

Lee, Robert H. and Jack Hadley, "Physicians' Fees and Public Medical Care Programs," *Health Services Research 16* (1981): 185–203.

Lee, Roger I. and Lewis W. Jones, *The Fundamentals of Good Medical Care*. Publication of the Committee on the Costs of Medical Care. (Chicago: University of Chicago, 1933).

Lee, Young Hoon and Peter Schmidt, "A Production Frontier Model with Flexible Temporal Variation in Technical Efficiency," in *Measurement of Production Efficiency*, Harold O. Fried, C. A. Knox Lovell et al. (eds.) (New York: Oxford University Press, 1993).

Leffler, Keith B., "Persuasion or Information? The Economics of Prescription Drug Advertising," *Journal of Law and Economics 24* (1981): 45–74.

Leffler, Keith B., "Physician Licensure: Competition and Monopoly in American Medicine," *Journal of Law and Economics 21* (1978): 165–186.

Leffler, Keith B. and Cotton M. Lindsay, "Student Discount Rates, Consumption Loans, and Subsidies to Professional Training," *Journal of Human Resources 16* (1981): 468–476.

Legnini, Mark W. et al., "Changes in Connecticut Hospital Use Rates: Have Small-Area Variations Been Affected?" *Inquiry 27* (1990): 51–60.

Lehner, Laura A. and James F. Burgess, "Teaching and Hospital Production: The Use of Regression Estimates," *Health Economics 4* (1995): 113–125.

Leibenstein, Harvey, "Allocative Efficiency vs. 'X Efficiency,'" *American Economic Review 56* (1966): 392–415.

Leibenstein, Harvey, "Aspects of the X-Efficiency Theory of the Firm," *Bell Journal of Economics 6* (1975): 580–606.

Leibenstein, Harvey, *General X-Efficiency Theory and Economic Development*. (New York: Oxford University Press, 1978).

Leibowitz, Arlene A., "The Demand for Health and Health Concerns after 30 Years," *Journal of Health Economics 23* (2004): 663–671.

Leibowitz, Arlene A., "An Economic Perspective on Work, Family and Well-Being," in S.M. Bianchi, L.M. Casper, and R.B. King, (eds.) *Work, Family, Health, and Well-Being* (Mahwah, New Jersey: Lawrence Erlbaum, 2005).

Leigh, J. Paul, "Gender, Firm Size, Industry, and Estimates of the Value-of-Life," *Journal of Health Economics 6* (1987): 255–273.

Leonard, Kenneth L. and Joshua Graff Zivin, "Outcome Versus Service Based Payments in Health Care: Lessons from African Traditional Healers," *Health Economics 14* (2005): 575–593.

Lerner, Abba P., "The Concept of Monopoly and the Measurement of Monopoly Power," *Review of Economic Studies 11* (1943): 157–175.

Lerner, Arthur N., "Federal Trade Commission Anti-Trust Activities in the Health Care Services Field," *Antitrust Bulletin* (1984): 205–224.

Levit, Katherine et al., "Health Spending Rebound Continues in 2002," *Health Affairs 23* (2004): 147–150.

Levitt, Steven D. and Jack Ray Porter, "Estimating the Effect of Alcohol on Driver Risk Using Only Fatal Accident Statistics," NBER working paper series no. 6944.; National Bureau of Economic Research, 1999.

Lewin, Lawrence, Timothy J. Eckels, and Linda B. Miller, "Setting the Record Straight: The Provision of Uncompensated Care by Not-for Profit Hospitals," *New England Journal of Medicine 318* (1988): 1212–1215.

Lewit, Eugene M. and Douglas Coate, "The Potential for Using Excise Taxes to Reduce Smoking," *Journal of Health Economics 1* (1982): 121–145.

Lewit, Eugene M., Douglas Coate, and Michael Grossman, "The Effects of Government Regulation on Teenage Smoking," *Journal of Law and Economics 24* (1981): 545–569.

Li, Tong and Robert Rosenman, "Estimating Hospital Costs With a Generalized Leontief Function," *Health Economics 10* (2001): 523–538.

Liang, J. Nellie and Jonathon D. Ogur, *Restrictions on Dental Auxiliaries: An Economic Policy Analysis* (Washington, DC: Federal Trade Commission, 1987).

Lichtenberg, Frank R., "Pharmaceutical Innovation, Mortality Reduction, and Economic Growth," Working Paper 6569, National Bureau of Economic Research, May 1998.

Light, Donald W. and Rebecca N. Warburton, "Extraordinary Claims Require Extraordinary Evidence," *Journal of Health Economics 24* (2005): 1030–1033.

Lindrooth, Richard C., Anthony T. LoSasso, and Gloria J. Bazzoli, "The Effect of Urban Hospital Closure on Markets," *Journal of Health Economics 22* (September 2003): 691–712.

Linet, Martha S. et al., "Residential Magnetic Field Exposures and Childhood Acute Lymphoblastic Leukemia," *New England Journal of Medicine 337* (July 3, 1997): 1–7.

Linn, Margaret W., Lee Gurel, and Bernard S. Linn, "Patient Outcome as a Measure of Quality of Nursing Home Care," *American Journal of Public Health 4* (1977): 337–344.

Liu, Zhimei, William H. Dow, Edward C. Norton, "Effect of Drive-Through Delivery Laws on Postpartum Length of Stay and Hospital Charges," *Journal of Health Economics 23*(2004): 129–155.

Lleras-Muney, Adriana, "The Relationship Between Education and Adult Mortality in the United States," Working Paper 8986, National Bureau of Economic Research, June 2002.

Locke, John, *Epistola de Tolerantia, John Locke Bibliography*, www.libraries.psu.edu/iasweb/ locke/ ch0b.htm, July 1, 2002.

Locke, John, *On the Poor Law and Working Schools* (1697) eco.utexas.edu/~hmcleave/350k PEELocke Poor Ed Table. pdf, accessed May 14, 2006.

Locke, John, *Two Treatises of Government* (Cambridge: Cambridge University Press, 1960).

LoGerfo, James P. et al., "Rates of Surgical Care in Prepaid Group Practices and the Independent Setting: What Are the Reasons for the Differences?" *Medical Care 17* (1979): 1–10.

Long, Stephen H., Russell F. Settle, and Charles W. Wrightson Jr., "Employee Premiums, Availability of Alternative Plans, and HMO Disenrollment," *Medical Care 26* (1988): 927–938.

Lovell, C. A. Knox, and Shelton S. Schmidt (eds.), *The Measurement of Productive Efficiency*. (Oxford: Oxford University Press, 1993).

Lu, John Z. and William S. Comanor, "Strategic Pricing of New Pharmaceuticals," *Review of Economics and Statistics 80* (1998): 108–117.

Luft, Harold S., "Health Maintenance Organizations and the Rationing of Medical Care," *Milbank Memorial Fund Quarterly/Health and Society 60* (1982): 268–306.

Luft, Harold S., *Health Maintenance Organizations: Dimensions of Performance*. (New York: John Wiley & Sons, 1981).

Luft, Harold S., "How Do Health-Maintenance Organizations Achieve Their 'Savings'?" *New England Journal of Medicine 298* (1978): 1336–1343.

Lundborg, Petter and Bjorn Lindren, "Do They Know What They Are Doing? Risk Perception and Smoking Behavior Among Swedish Teenagers," *Journal of Risk and Uncertainty 28* (May 2004): 261–286.

MacDonald, Ziggy, "What Price Drug Use? The Contribution of Economics to an Evidence-Based Drugs Policy," *Journal of Economic Surveys 18* (2004): 113–152.

Madrian, Brigitte C., "Employment-Based Health Insurance and Job Mobility: Is There Evidence of Job-Lock?" *Quarterly Journal of Economics 109* (1994): 27–54.

Magnusson, Jon, "Efficiency Measurement and the Operationalization of Hospital Production," *Health Services Research 31* (1996): 21–37.

Maioni, Antonia, "Nothing Succeeds Like the Right Kind of Failure: Postwar National Health Insurance Initiatives in Canada and the United States," *Journal of Health Politics, Policy and Law 20* (1995): 5–30.

Manning, Willard G. and M. Susan Marquis, "Health Insurance: The Tradeoff Between Risk Pooling and Moral Hazard," *Journal of Health Economics 15* (1996): 609–639.

Manning, Willard G. et al., "A Controlled Trial of the Effect of a Prepaid Group Practice on Use of Services," *New England Journal of Medicine 310* (1984): 1505–1510.

Manning, Willard G. et al., *The Costs of Poor Health Habits*. (Cambridge, MA: Harvard University Press, 1991).

Manning, Willard G. et al., "Health Insurance and the Demand for Medical Care: Evidence from a Randomized Experiment," *American Economic Review 77* (1987): 251–277.

Mansfield, Edwin, "Patent Innovation: An Empirical Study," *Management Science 32* (1986): 173–181.

Mansfield, Edwin et al., *Managerial Economics: Theory, Applications, and Cases* (New York: Norton, 2002).

Mark, Tami L., "Analysis of the Rationale for, and Consequences of, Nonprofit and For-Profit Ownership Conversions," *Health Services Research 34* (1999): 83–101.

Mark, Tami L., "Psychiatric Hospital Ownership and Performance: Do Nonprofit Organizations Offer Advantages in Markets Characterized by Asymmetric Information?" *Journal of Human Resources 31* (1996): 631–649.

Marquis, M. Susan, Jeannette A. Rogowski, and Jose Escarce, "The Managed Care Backlash: Did Consumers Vote with Their Feet?" *Inquiry 41* (2004/2005): 376–390.

Massaro, Thomas A. and Yu-Ning Wong, "Positive Experience with Medical Savings Accounts in Singapore," *Health Affairs 14* (1995): 267–271.

Mather, Dell, B., "Incorporating Clinical Outcomes and Economic Consequences into Drug Formulary Decisions: A Practical Approach," *American Journal of Managed Care 5* (1999): 277–285.

Maynard, Alan, "The United Kingdom," in *Advances in Health Economics and Health Services Research, Supplement 1: Comparative Health Systems*, Jean-Jacques Rosa (ed.) (Greenwich, CT: JAI Press, 1990), 1–26.

Mayo, John W. and Deborah A. McFarland, "Regulation, Market Structure, and Hospital Costs," *Southern Economic Journal 55* (1989): 559–569.

Mayo, John W. and Deborah A. McFarland, "Regulation, Market Structure, and Hospital Costs: Reply," *Southern Economic Journal 57* (1991): 535–538.

McCarthy, Patrick S., "The Effect of Higher Rural Interstate Speed Limits in Alcohol-Related Accidents," *Journal of Health Economics 12* (1993): 281–299.

McCarthy, Thomas R., "The Competitive Nature of the Primary-Care Physician Services Market," *Journal of Health Economics 4* (1985): 93–117.

McClellan, Mark and Douglas Staiger, "Comparing Hospital Quality at For-Profit and Not-For-Profit Hospitals," National Bureau of Economic Research Working Paper 7324, 1999.

McGuinness, Tony and Keith Cowling, "Advertising and the Aggregate Demand for Cigarettes," *European Economic Review 6* (1975): 311–328.

McGuire, Thomas G., "Physician Agency," in *Handbook of Health Economics*, Volume 1A, Anthony J. Culyer

and Joseph P. Newhouse (eds.) (Elsevier Science B.V., 2000).

McGuire, Thomas G. and Mark V. Pauly, "Physician Response to Fee Changes with Multiple Payers," *Journal of Health Economics 10* (1991): 385–410.

McKay, Niccie L., "The Prisoner's Dilemma: An Obstacle to Cooperation in Health Care Markets," *Medical Care Review 51* (1994): 179–204.

McKeown, Thomas, *The Modern Rise of Population* (New York: Academic Press, 1976).

McKinlay, John B. and Sonja M. McKinlay, "The Questionable Contribution of Medical Measures to the Decline of Mortality in the United States in the Twentieth Century," *Milbank Memorial Fund Quarterly/Health and Society 55* (1977): 405–428.

McLaughlin, Catherine G., "The Dilemma of Affordability: Health Insurance for Small Business," in *American Health Policy: Critical Issues for Reform*, Robert B. Helms (ed.) (Washington, DC:AEI Press, 1993, 152–166).

McLaughlin, Catherine G., "Market Responses to HMOs: Price Competition or Rivalry?" *Inquiry 25* (1988): 207–218.

McLaughlin, Catherine G. and Wendy K. Zellers, "Small Business and Health Care Reform," The University of Michigan School of Public Health, 1994.

McPherson, Klim et al., "Small-Area Variations in the Use of Common Surgical Procedures: An International Comparison of New England, England, and Norway," *New England Journal of Medicine 307* (1982): 1310–1313.

Medicare and Medicaid, Prospective Payment Assessment Commission, *Medicare and the Health System, Report to Congress*. (Chicago: Commerce Clearing House, Inc., 1991).

Medicare Payment Advisory Commission (MedPAC), *Report to Congress, Medicare Payment Policy*, March 1999: ch. 7, app. D.

Medicare Payment Advisory Commission (MedPAC), *Report to Congress, Medicare Payment Policy*, March 2001: ch. 2.

Medicare Payment Advisory Commission (MedPAC), Report to Congress, *Medicare Payment Policy*, March 2002: ch. 4.

Medicare Payment Advisory Commission (MedPAC), *Report to Congress: Selected Medicare Issues*, June 1999, ch. 1, p. 6.

MedPAC, *Report to the Congress: Physician-Owned Specialty Hospitals* (Washington: MedPAC, March 2005), Table 10.

Melnick, Glen A. et al., "The Effects of Market Structure and Bargaining Position on Hospital Prices," *Journal of Health Economics 11* (1992): 217–233.

Miles, J. J., *Health Care and Antitrust Law*. (St. Paul, MN: West Group, 1998).

Miller, Rebecca S., Harry S. Jonas, and Michael E. Whitcomb, "The Initial Employment Status of Physicians Completing Training in 1994," *Journal of the American Medical Association 275* (1996): 708–712.

Miller, Richard D. Jr. and H.E. Frech III, *Health Care Matters: Pharmaceuticals, Obesity, and the Quality of Life* (Washington, D.C.: American Enterprise Institute, 2004).

Miller, Robert H. and Harold S. Luft, "Does Managed Care Lead to Better or Worse Quality of Care?" *Health Affairs 16* (1997): 7–25.

Miller, Robert H. and Harold S. Luft, "HMO Plan Performance Update: An Analysis of the Literature: 1997–2001," *Health Affairs 21* (4) (2002): 63–86.

Miller, Robert H. and Harold S. Luft, "Managed Care Plan Performance Since 1980: A Literature Analysis," *Journal of the American Medical Association 271* (May 18, 1994): 1512–1519.

Miron, Jeffrey A., "The Effect of Alcohol Prohibition on Alcohol Consumption," Working Paper 7130, National Bureau of Economic Research, May 1999.

Mitchell, Janet B. and Jerry Cromwell, "Impact of All-or-Nothing Assignment Requirement Under Medicare," *Health Care Financing Review 4* (1983): 59–78.

Mitchell, Janet B. and Jerry Cromwell, "Physician Behavior Under the Medicare Assignment Option," *Journal of Health Economics 1* (1982): 245–264.

Mobley, Lee Rivers and W. David Bradford, "Behavioral Differences Among Hospitals: Is It Ownership, or Location?" *Applied Economics 29* (1997): 1125–1138.

Monroe, Kent B., "Buyers Subjective Perceptions of Price," *Journal of Marketing Research 10* (1973): 70–80.

Montagne, C., "Bargaining Health Benefits in the Workplace: An Inside View," *Milbank Quarterly 80*, (3) (2002): 547–567.

Montgomery-Karp, Beverly, "Market Demands Call for New Treatment," *Advertising Age 54* (September 26, 1983): M9–11.

Mooney, Gavin et al., "Reweighing Heat: Response to Culyer, van Doorslaer, and Wagstaff," *Journal of Health Economics 11* (1992): 199–205.

Mooney, Gavin et al., "Utilisation as a Measure of Equity: Weighing Heat?" *Journal of Health Economics 10* (1991): 475–480.

Moore, Michael J., "Death and Tobacco Taxes," Working Paper 5153, National Bureau of Economic Research, June 1995.

Moore, Michael J. and W. Kip Viscusi, "Doubling the Estimated Value of Life: Results Using New Occupational Fatality Data," *Journal of Policy Analysis Management 7* (1988): 476–490.

Morgan, Eleanor J., "Innovation and Merger Decisions in the Pharmaceutical Industry," *Review of Industrial Organization 19* (2) (2001): 181–197.

Morrisey, Michael A., "Why Do Employers Do What They Do? Compensating Differentials" *International Journal of Health Care Finance and Economics 1* (2001a): 195–201.

Morrisey, Michael A., "Competition in Hospital and Health Insurance Markets: A Review and Research Agenda," *Health Services Research 36* (2001b): 191–222.

Morrisey, Michael A., "Movies and Myths: Hospital Cost Shifting," *Business Economics 30* (1995): 22–25.

Motheral, Brenda R., and Rochelle Henderson, "The Effect of a Copay Increase on Pharmaceutical Utilization, Expenditures, and Treatment Continuation," *American Journal of Managed Care 5* (1999): 1383–1394.

Mueller, Curt D. and Alan C. Monheit, "Insurance Coverage and the Demand for Dental Care," *Journal of Health Economics 7* (1988): 59–72.

Mukamel, Dana B. and William D. Spector, "The Competitive Nature of the Nursing Home Industry: Price Mark Ups and Demand Elasticities," *Applied Economics 34* (March 2002): 413–420.

Mullahy, John and Jody L. Sindelar, "Alcoholism, Work, and Income," *Journal of Labor Economics 11* (1993): 494–520.

Mullahy, John and Jody Sindelar, "Do Drinkers Know When to Say When? An Empirical Analysis of Drunk Driving," *Economic Inquiry 22* (1994): 383–394.

Murphy, Kevin M. and Robert H. Topel, "The Value of Health and Longevity," National Bureau of Economic Research Working Paper 11405, 2005.

Mushkin, Selma J., *Biomedical Research: Costs and Benefits.* (Cambridge, MA: Ballinger, 1979).

National Association of Home Care, "Basic Statistics About Hospice," www.nahc.org/consumer/hpcstats, 1999.

Naylor, C. David, "Health Care in Canada: Incrementalism Under Fiscal Duress," *Health Affairs 18* (1999): 9–26.

Nelson, Phillip, "Advertising as Information," *Journal of Political Economy 82* (1974): 729–754.

Nelson, Phillip, "Information and Consumer Behavior," *Journal of Political Economy 78* (1970): 311–329.

Newbold, Paul, *Statistics for Business and Economics*, 4th ed. (Upper Saddle River, NJ: Prentice Hall, 1995).

Newhouse, Joseph P., *The Economics of Medical Care* (Reading, MA: Addison-Wesley, 1978a).

Newhouse, Joseph P., "Why Is There a Quality Chasm?" *Health Affairs 21* (4) (2002): 13–25.

Newhouse, Joseph P., "Medicare Policy in the 1990s," Working Paper 8531, National Bureau of Economic Research, October 2001.

Newhouse, Joseph P., "Frontier Estimation: How Useful a Tool in Health Economics?" *Journal of Health Economics 13* (1994): 317–322.

Newhouse, Joseph P., "Medical Care Costs: How Much Welfare Loss?" *Journal of Economic Perspectives 6* (1992): 3–21.

Newhouse, Joseph P., "Has the Erosion of the Medical Marketplace Ended?" *Journal of Health Politics, Policy and Law 13* (1988): 263–277.

Newhouse, Joseph P., "The Structure of Health Insurance and the Erosion of Competition in the Medical Marketplace," in *Competition in the Health Care Sector: Past, Present and Future*, W. Greenberg (ed.) (Germantown, MD: Aspen Systems, 1978b).

Newhouse, Joseph P., "Medical-Care Expenditures: A Cross-National Survey," *Journal of Human Resources 12* (1977): 115–125.

Newhouse, Joseph P., "Toward a Theory of Nonprofit Institutions: An Economic Model of a Hospital," *American Economic Review 60* (1970): 64–74.

Newhouse, Joseph P. and Charles E. Phelps, "New Estimates of Price and Income Elasticities of Medical Care Services," in *The Role of Health Insurance in the Health Services Sector*, Richard Rosett (ed.) (New York: Neal Watson, 1976).

Newhouse, Joseph P., Geoffrey Anderson, and Leslie L. Roos, "Are Fee-for-Service Costs Increasing Faster Than HMO Costs?" *Medical Care 23* (1985): 960–966.

Newhouse, Joseph P., Geoffrey Anderson, and Leslie L. Roos, "Hospital Spending in the United States and Canada: A Comparison," *Health Affairs 7* (1988): 6–16.

Newhouse, Joseph P. et al., *Free for All? Lessons from the RAND Health Insurance Experiment.* (Cambridge MA: Harvard University Press, 1993).

Nguyen, Nguyen X. and Frederick W. Derrick, "Physician Behavioral Response to a Medicare Price Reduction," *Health Services Research 32* (1997): 283–298.

Nichols, Len M., Paul B. Ginsburg, and Robert A. Berenson et al., "Are Market Forces Strong Enough to Deliver Efficient Health Care Systems? Confidence is Waning," *Health Affairs 23* (March/April 2004): 8–21.

Niskanen, William A., *Bureaucracy and Representative Government* (Chicago: Aldine, Atherton, 1971).

Nord, Erik, "Health State Values from Multi-Attribute Utility Instruments Need Correction," *Annals of Medicine 33* (2001): 371–374.

Norton, Edward C., "Long-Term Care," in *Handbook of Health Economics*, Volume 1B, Anthony J. Culyer and Joseph P. Newhouse (eds.) (Elsevier Science B.V., 2000).

Norton, Edward C. and Douglas O. Staiger, "How Hospital Ownership Affects Access to Care for the Uninsured," *RAND Journal of Economics 25* (1994): 171–185.

Nozick, Robert, *Anarchy, State, and Utopia.* (New York: Basic Books, 1974).

Nyman, John A., "The Economics of Moral Hazard Revisited," *Journal of Health Economics 18* (1999): 811–824.

Nyman, John A., "Testing for Excess Demand in Nursing Home Markets," *Medical Care 31* (1993): 680–693.

Nyman, John A. and Daniel L. Bricker, "Profit Incentives and Technical Efficiency in the Production of Nursing Home Care," *Review of Economics and Statistics 71* (1989): 586–594.

Nyman, John A. et al., "Changing Physician Behavior: Does Medical Review of Part B Medicare Claims Make a Difference?" *Inquiry 27* (1990): 127–137.

O'Brien, Jack, Borje O. Saxberg, and Howard L. Smith, "For-Profit or Not-for-Profit Nursing Homes: Does It Matter?" *The Gerontologist 23* (1983): 341–348.

Ohsfeldt, Robert L., Raymond G. Boyle, and Eli I. Capilouto, "Tobacco Taxes, Smoking Restrictions, and Tobacco Use," Working Paper 6486, National Bureau of Economic Research, March 1998.

Okun, Arthur, *Efficiency and Equity: The Big Tradeoff* (Washington, DC: Brookings, 1975).

Okunade, Ablert A. and Chutima Suraratdecha, "Cost Efficiency, Factor Interchange, and Technical Progress in U.S. Specialized Hospital Pharmacies," *Health Economics 7* (1998): 363–371.

Olden, Peter C., Susan D. Roggenkamp, and Roice D. Luke, "A Post-1990s Assessment of Strategic Hospital Alliances and their Marketplace Orientations: Time to Refocus," *Health Care Management Review 27* (2002): 33–49.

Olesen, Ole B. and Niels C. Petersen, "The Use of Data Envelopment Analysis with Probablistic Assurance Regions for Measuring Hospital Efficiency," *Journal of Productivity Analysis 17* (2002): 83–109.

Olkin, Ingram and Jerome Sacks, "Cross-Disciplinary Research in the Statistical Sciences," Hayward, CA: Institute of Mathematical Statistics, September 1988.

Olsen, Jan Abel, "But Health Can Still Be a Necessity. . . . ," *Journal of Health Economics 12* (1993): 187–191.

Olsen, Jan Abel, "Theories of Justice and Their Implications for Priority Setting in Health Care," *Journal of Health Economics 16* (1997): 625–639.

Olsen, Jan Abel and Richard D. Smith, "Theory Versus Practice: A Review of 'Willingness-to Pay' in Health and Health Care," *Health Economics 10* (2001): 39–52.

Oregon Health Services Commission, State of Oregon, *Prioritization of Health Services: A Report to the Governor and Legislature*, May 1991.

Ozanne, Larry, "How Will Medical Savings Accounts Affect Spending?" *Inquiry 33* (1996): 225–236.

Ozcan, Yasar A., Roice D. Luke, and Cengiz Haksever, "Ownership and Organizational Performance: A Comparison of Technical Efficiency Across Hospital Types," *Medical Care 30* (1992): 781–794.

Parker-Pope, Tara, "Antismoking Sentiment Flares in Europe's Smoke-Filled Cafes," *Wall Street Journal*, August 28, 1995, sec. B1.

Parkin, David, Alistair McGuire, and Brian Yule, "Aggregate Health Care Expenditures and National Income: Is Health Care a Luxury Good?" *Journal of Health Economics 6* (1987): 109–128.

Paul, Chris, "Physician Licensure and the Quality of Medical Care," *Atlantic Economic Journal 12* (1984): 18–30.

Pauly, Mark V., *Health Benefits at Work: An Economic and Political Analysis of Employment-Based Health Insurance* (Ann Arbor, MI: The University of Michigan Press, 1997).

Pauly, Mark V., "Editorial: A Re-Examination of the Meaning and Importance of Supplier-Induced Demand," *Journal of Health Economics 13* (1994a): 369–372.

Pauly, Mark V., "Making a Case for Employer Enforced Individual Mandates," *Health Affairs 13* (1994b): 21–33.

Pauly, Mark V., "A Primer on Competition in Medical Markets," in *Health Care in America*, H. E. Frech III (ed.) (San Francisco: Pacific Research Institute for Public Policy, 1988a).

Pauly, Mark V., "Is Medical Care Different? Old Questions, New Answers," *Journal of Health Politics, Policy and Law 13* (1988b): 227–237.

Pauly, Mark V., *Doctors and Their Workshops* (Chicago: University of Chicago Press, 1980).

Pauly, Mark V., "Is Medical Care Different?" in *Competition in the Health Care Sector*, Warren Greenberg (ed.) (Germantown, MD: Aspen Systems, 1978).

Pauly, Mark V., "The Economics of Moral Hazard: Comment," *American Economic Review 58* (1968): 531–537.

Pauly, Mark V., *Medical Care at Public Expense* (New York: Praeger, 1971).

Pauly, Mark V. and Michael Redisch, "The Not-for-Profit Hospital as a Physician's Cooperative," *American Economic Review 63* (1973): 87–100.

Pauly, Mark V. and Mark A. Satterthwaite, "The Pricing of Primary Care Physicians' Services: A Test of the Role of Consumer Information," *Bell Journal of Economics 12* (1981): 488–506.

Payne, Abigail A., "Does the Government Crowd Out Private Donations? New Evidence from a Sample of Non-Profit Firms," *Journal of Public Economics 69* (1998): 323–345.

Pear, Robert, "Policy Changes Fail to Fill Gaps in Health Coverage" *New York Times*, August 9, 1998, sec. A1, A18.

Peden, Edgar A. and Mark S. Freeland, "Insurance Effects on U.S. Medical Spending (1960–1993)," *Health Economics 7* (1998): 671–687.

Peltzman, Sam, "Regulation of Pharmaceutical Innovation: The 1962 Amendments," American Enterprise Institute, Washington, DC, 1974.

Peltzman, Sam, "Toward a More General Theory of Regulation," *Journal of Law and Economics 19* (1976): 211–248.

Pernick, Martin S., "The Cultural Ecology of Health: Science, Values, and Society in the History of American Medicine," manuscript of book in progress, 1991.

Peterson, Mark A. (ed.), "Special Issue: Kenneth Arrow and the Changing Economics of Health Care," *Journal of Health Politics, Policy and Law 26* (5) (October 2001).

Petroshius, Susan M. and Kent B. Monroe, "Effect of Product Line Pricing Characteristics on Product Evaluations," *Journal of Consumer Research 13* (1987): 511–519.

Pharmaceutical Research and Manufacturers of America (PhRMA), *Pharmaceutical Industry Profile 2005*, www.phrma.org/publications/publications/17.03.2005.1142.cfm, accessed November 19, 2005.

Phelps, Charles E., "Good Technologies Gone Bad: How and Why the Cost-Effectiveness of a Medical Intervention Changes for Different Populations," *Medical Decision Making 17* (1997): 107–117.

Phelps, Charles E., *Health Economics* (New York: Harper Collins, 1992).

Phelps, Charles E., *Health Economics*, 2nd ed. (Reading, MA: Addison-Wesley, 1997).

Phelps, Charles E., "Induced Demand—Can We Ever Know Its Extent?" *Journal of Health Economics 5* (1986): 355–365.

Phelps, Charles E., "Information Diffusion and Best Practice," in *Handbook of Health Economics*, Volume I, Anthony J. Culyer and Joseph P. Newhouse (eds.) (Elsevier Science, B.V., 2000).

Phelps, Charles E., "Welfare Loss from Variations: Further Considerations," *Journal of Health Economics 14* (1995): 253–260.

Phelps, Charles E. and Cathleen Mooney, "Correction and Update on 'Priority Setting in Medical Technology Assessment,'" *Medical Care 30* (1992): 744–751.

Phelps, Charles E. and Stephen T. Parente, "Priority Setting in Medical Technology and Medical Practice Assessment," *Medical Care 28* (1990): 703–723.

Philipson, Tomas, "Economic Epidemiology and Infectious Diseases," in *Handbook for Health Economics*, Volume I, Anthony J. Culyer and Joseph P. Newhouse (eds.) (Elsevier Science, B.V., 2000).

Philipson, Tomas, "Private Vaccination and Public Health: An Empirical Examination for U.S. Measles," *Journal of Human Resources 31* (3) (1996): 611–630.

Philipson, Tomas, "The Welfare Loss of Disease and the Theory of Taxation," *Journal of Health Economics 14* (1995): 387–395.

Philipson, Tomas J. and Richard Posner, *Private Choices and Public Health: The AIDS Epidemic in Economic Perspective* (Cambridge: Harvard University Press, 1993).

Phlips, Louis, *The Economic of Imperfect Information* (Cambridge: Cambridge University Press. 1988).

Picone, Gabriel A. et al, "Does Higher Hospital Cost Imply Higher Quality of Care?" *Review of Economics and Statistics 85* (2003): 51–62.

Picone, Gabriel A., Martin Uribe, and R. Mark Wilson, "The Effect of Uncertainty on the Demand for Medical Care, Health Capital and Wealth," *Journal of Health Economics 17* (1998): 171–185.

Picone, Gabriel, Shin-Yi Chou, and Frank Sloan, "Are For-Profit Hospital Conversions Harmful to Patients and to Medicare?" *RAND Journal of Economics 33* (2002): 507–523.

Pindyck, Robert S. and Daniel L. Rubinfeld, *Microeconomics*, 4th ed. (Upper Saddle River, NJ: Prentice Hall, 1998).

Pitt, Mark M., "Estimating the Determinants of Child Health When Fertility and Mortality Are Selective," *Journal of Human Resources 32* (1997): 129–58.

Pollard, Michael R. and Robert F. Leibenluft, *Antitrust and the Health Professions*, Office of Policy and Planning, Federal Trade Commission, 1981.

Polsky, Daniel and Sean Nicholson, "Why Are Managed Care Plans Less Expensive: Risk Selection, Utilization, or Reimbursement?" *Journal of Risk and Insurance 71* (2004): 21–40.

Porell, Frank et al., "A Longitudinal Analysis of Nursing Home Outcomes," *Health Services Research 33* (1998): 835–865.

Portney, Paul R., "Housing Prices, Health Effects and Valuing Reduction in Risk of Death," *Journal of Environmental Economic Management 8* (1981): 72–78.

President of the United States, *The President's Comprehensive Health Reform Program*, February 6, 1992.

Pritchett, Lant and Lawrence H. Summers, "Wealthier Is Healthier," *Journal of Human Resources 31* (1996): 841–868.

Prospective Payment Assessment Commission, *Annual Report to Congress*, April 5, 1995.

Prospective Payment Assessment Commission, *Annual Report to Congress*, April 11, 1997.

Prospective Payment Review Commission, *Medicare Prospective Payment and the American Health Care System*, Report to Congress, June 24, 1991. (Chicago: Commerce Clearing House, Inc., 1991).

Quick, Jonathan D., M. R. Greenlick, and K. L. Roghmann, "Prenatal Care and Pregnancy Outcome in an HMO and General Population: A Multivariate Cohort Analysis," *American Journal of Public Health 71* (1981): 381–390.

Raffel, Marshall W. and Norna K. Raffel, *The U.S. Health System: Origins and Functions*, 4th ed. (Albany, NY: Delmar, 1994).

Rawls, John, *A Theory of Justice*. (Cambridge, MA: Belnap Press of the Harvard University Press, 1971).

Register, Charles A. and Edward R. Bruning, "Profit Incentives and Technical Efficiency in the Production of Hospital Care," *Southern Economic Journal 53* (1987): 899–914.

Reinhardt, Uwe E., "Germany's Health Care System: It's Not the American Way," *Health Affairs 13* (1994): 22–24.

Reinhardt, Uwe E., "A Production Function for Physician Services," *Review of Economics and Statistics 54* (1972): 55–65.

Rellman, Arnold S. and Marcia Angell, "America's Other Drug Problem," *The New Republic* (December 16, 2002): 27–41.

Renn, Steven C. et al., "The Effects of Ownership and System Affiliation on the Economic Performance of Hospitals," *Inquiry 22* (1985): 219–236.

Rhee, Sang-O et al., "USMGs Versus FMGs: Are There Performance Differences in the Ambulatory Setting?" *Medical Care 24* (1986): 248–258.

Rice, Dorothy, *Estimating the Cost of Illness*, U.S. Public Health Service Publication No. 947-6. (Washington, DC: U.S. Government Printing Office, May 1966).

Rice, Thomas, *The Economics of Health Reconsidered* (Chicago: Health Administration Press, 1998).

Rice, Thomas H., "The Impact of Changing Medicare Reimbursement Rates on Physician-Induced Demand," *Medical Care 21* (1983): 803–815.

Rice, Thomas H. and Roberta J. Labelle, "Do Physicians Induce Demand for Medical Service?" *Journal of Health Politics, Policy and Law 14* (1989): 587–600.

Ried, Walter, "QALYs Versus HYEs—What's Right and What's Wrong: A Review of the Controversy," *Journal of Health Economics 17* (1998): 607–625.

Rifkind, Basil M. et al., "Distribution of High Density and Other Lipoproteins in Selected LRC Prevalence Study Populations: A Brief Survey," *Lipids 14* (1979): 105–112.

Rizzo, John A., "Are HMOs Bad for Health Maintenance?" *Health Economics 13* (2005): 1117–1131.

Rizzo, John A., "Physician Advertising Revisited," *Medical Care 26* (1988): 1238–1244.

Rizzo, John A. and David Blumenthal, "Is the Target Income Hypothesis an Economic Heresy?" *Medical Care Research and Review 53* (1996): 243–266.

Rizzo, John A. and Richard J. Zeckhauser, "Advertising and Entry: The Case of Physician Services," *Journal of Political Economy 98* (1990): 476–500.

Rizzo, John A. and Richard J. Zeckhauser, "Advertising and the Price, Quantity, and Quality of Primary Care Physician Services," *Journal of Human Resources 27* (1992): 381–421.

Rizzo, John A. and Richard J. Zeckhauser, "Income Targets, Loss Aversion, and Physicians' Behavior," Working Paper, October 1998.

Rizzo, John A. and Richard Zeckhauser, "Reference Incomes, Loss Aversion and Physician Behavior," *Review of Economics and Statistics 85* (2003): 909–922.

Roberts, Mark J. and Larry Samuelson, "An Empirical Analysis of Dynamic, Nonprice Competition in an Oligopolistic Industry," *RAND Journal of Economics 19* (1988): 200–220.

Robinson, James C., "The End of Asymmetric Information," *Journal of Health Politics, Policy and Law 26* (2001): 1045–1053.

Rochaix, Lise, "Information Asymmetry and Search in the Market for Physicians' Services," *Journal of Health Economics 8* (1989): 53–84.

Roemer, Milton I. and William Shonick, "HMO Performance: The Recent Evidence," *Milbank Memorial Fund Quarterly/Health and Society 51* (Summer 1973): 271–317.

Roos, N. P. and L. L. Roos, Jr., "Surgical Rate Variations: Do They Reflect the Health or Socioeconomic Characteristics of the Population?" *Medical Care 20* (1982): 945–958.

Rosen, Harvey S., Chairman, Council of Economic Advisers, "Comments on Health Care at the Conference of the National Association of Business Economics," March 21, 2005, www.whitehouse.gov/cea/nabe-healthcare032105.pdf.

Rosen, Sherwin, "Theory of Equalizing Differences," in *Handbook of Labor Economics*, Volume 1, Orley Ashenfelter and Richard Layard (eds.) (New York: North-Holland, 1986, 641–692).

Rosenzweig, Mark R. and T. Paul Schultz, "Estimating a Household Production Function: Heterogeneity, the Demand for Health Inputs, and Their Effects on Birth Weight," *Journal of Political Economy 91* (1983): 723–746.

Rosenzweig, Mark R. and Kenneth I. Wolpin, "Sisters, Siblings, and Mothers: The Effect of Teen-Age Childbearing on Birth Outcomes in a Dynamic Family Context," *Econometrica 63* (1995): 303–326.

Rosett, Richard N. and Lien-fu Huang, "The Effect of Health Insurance on the Demand for Medical Care," *Journal of Political Economy 81* (1973): 281–305.

Rosko, Michael D. and Robert W. Broyles. *The Economics of Health Care* (New York: Greenwood, 1988).

Rotfeld, Herbert J. and Kim B. Rotzoll, "Advertising and Product Quality: Are Heavily Advertised Products Better?" *Journal of Consumer Affairs 10* (1976): 37–47.

Ruffin, Roy J. and Paul R. Gregory. *Principles of Economics*, 7th ed. (New York: Addison Wesley, 2001).

Ruffin, Roy J. and Duane E. Leigh, "Charity, Competition, and the Pricing of Doctors' Services," *Journal of Human Resources 8* (1973): 212–222.

Russell, Louise B., "The Diffusion of Hospital Technologies: Some Econometric Evidence," *Journal of Human Resources 12* (1977): 482–502.

Russell, Louise B., *Educated Guesses: Making Policy About Medical Screening Tests* (Berkeley, CA: University of California Press, 1994).

Russell, Louise B. et al., "The Role of Cost Effectiveness in Health and Medicine," *Journal of the American Medical Association 276* (1996): 1172–1177.

Saffer, Henry, "Alcohol Advertising and Motor Vehicle Fatalities," *Review of Economics and Statistics 79* (1997): 431–442.

Saffer, Henry, "Alcohol Advertising Bans and Alcohol Abuse: An International Perspective," *Journal of Health Economics 10* (1991): 65–79.

Saffer, Henry, "Alcohol Consumption and Alcohol Advertising Bans," National Bureau of Economic Research, Working Paper 7758, 2000.

Saffer, Henry and Frank Chaloupka, "Demographic Differentials in the Demand for Alcohol and Illicit Drugs," Working Paper 6432, National Bureau of Economic Research, February 1998.

Saffer, Henry and Dhaval Dave, "Alcohol Advertising of Alcohol Consumption by Adolescents," National Bureau of Economic Research Working Paper 9676, 2003.

Safriet, Barbara J., "Impediments to Progress in Health Care Workforce Policy: License and Practice Laws," *Inquiry 31* (1994): 310–317.

Salkever, David S., "Regulation of Prices and Investment in Hospitals in the United States," in *Handbook of Health Economics*, Volume 1B, Anthony J. Culyer and Joseph P. Newhouse (eds.) (Elsevier Science B.V., 2000).

Salkever, David S. and Thomas W. Bice, *Hospital Certificate-of-Need Controls: Impact on Investment, Costs, and Use.* (Washington, DC: American Enterprise Institute, 1979).

Salvatore, Dominick, *Schaum's Outline Series: Microeconomic Theory*, 2nd ed. (New York: McGraw-Hill, 1983).

Santerre, Rexford E. and John A. Vernon, "Hospital Ownership Mix Efficiency in the U.S.: An Exploratory Study," National Bureau of Economic Research Working Paper 11192, 2005.

Sasser, Alicia C., "Gender Differences in Physician Pay: Tradeoffs Between Career and Family," *Journal of Human Resources 60* (2005): 477–504.

Satterthwaite, Mark A., "Consumer Information, Equilibrium Industry Price, and the Number of Sellers," *Bell Journal of Economics 10* (1979): 483–502.

Scanlon, Dennis P. et al., "Competition and Health Plan Performance: Evidence from Health Maintenance Organization Insurance Market," *Medical Care 43* (2005): 338–346.

Scanlon, Dennis P. et al., "The Impact of Health Plan Report Cards on Managed Care Enrollment," *Journal of Health Economics 21* (2002): 19–41.

Scanlon, William J., "A Theory of the Nursing Home Market," *Inquiry 17* (1980): 25–41.

Schaefer, Mark E., "Demand Versus Need for Medical Services in a General Cost Benefit Setting," *American Journal of Public Health 65* (1975): 293–295.

Scheffler, Richard M., "The United Mine Workers' Health Plan: An Analysis of the Cost-Sharing Program," *Medical Care 22* (1984): 247–254.

Schelling, Thomas, "Ergonomics: The Art of Self Management," *American Economic Review 68* (1978): 290–294.

Scherer, F. Michael., *Innovation and Growth: Schumpeterian Perspectives.* (Cambridge, MA: MIT. 1984).

Schieber, George J. and Jean-Pierre Poullier, "International Health Spending: Issues and Trends," *Health Affairs 10* (1991): 106–116.

Schieber, George J. and Jean-Pierre Poullier, "Overview of International Comparisons of Health Care Expenditures," *Health Care Financing Review 10* (Annual Supplement 1989): 1–7.

Schmalensee, Richard, *The Economics of Advertising* (Amsterdam: North-Holland, 1972).

Schmalensee, Richard, "A Model of Advertising and Product Quality," *Journal of Political Economy 86* (1978): 485–503.

Schmidt, Peter and Robin Sickles, "Production Frontiers and Panel Data," *Journal of Business and Economic Statistics 2* (1984): 367–374.

Schnelle, John F. et al., "Relationship of Nursing Home Staffing to Quality of Care," *Health Services Research 39* (2004): 225–250.

Schneyer, Solomon, J. Steven Landefeld, and Frank H. Sandifer, "Biomedical Research and Illness: 1900–1979," *Milbank Memorial Fund Quarterly Health and Society 59* (1981): 44–58.

Schoen, Cathy et al., "Taking the Pulse of Health Care Systems: Experiences of Patients with Health Problems in Six Countries," *Health Affairs*, Web Exclusive, November 3, 2005: W509–525.

Schwartz, Joel and Douglas W. Dockery, "Increased Mortality in Philadelphia Associated with Daily Air Pollution Concentrations," *American Review of Respiratory Diseases 145* (1992): 600–604.

Schwartz, Michael et al., "Small Area Variations in Hospitalization Rates: How Much You See Depends on How You Look," *Medical Care 32* (1994): 189–201.

Schwartz, William B., "In the Pipeline: A Wave of Valuable Medical Technology," *Health Affairs 13* (1994): 70–79.

Schwartz, William B. and Daniel N. Mendelson, "Eliminating Waste and Inefficiency Can Do Little to Contain Costs," *Health Affairs 13* (1994): 224–238.

Schweitzer, Stuart O., *Pharmaceutical Economics and Policy* (New York: Oxford University Press, 1996).

Scitovsky, Anne A., "Changes in the Costs of Treatment of Selected Illnesses, 1971–1981," *Medical Care 23* (1985): 1345–1357.

Scitovsky, Anne A. and Nelda McCall, "Changes in the Costs of Treatment of Selected Illnesses, 1951–1964–1971," National Center for Health Services Research, DHEW Publication No. (HRA) 77-3161, 1977.

Seldon, Barry J. and Khowsrow Doroodian, "A Simultaneous Model of Cigarette Advertising: Effects on Demand and Industry Response to Public Policy," *Review of Economics and Statistics 71* (1989): 673–677.

Seldon, Barry J., Chulho Jung, and Roberto J. Cavazos, "Market Power Among Physicians in the U.S., 1983–1991," *Quarterly Review of Economics and Finance 38* (1998): 799–824.

Shalit, Sol S., "A Doctor-Hospital Cartel Theory," *Journal of Business 50* (1977): 1–20.

Shaw, James W., William C. Horrace, and Ronald J. Vogel, "The Determinants of Life Expectancy: An Analysis of the OECD Health Data," *Southern Economic Journal 71* (April 2005): 768–783.

Sherman, H. David, "Hospital Efficiency Measurement and Evaluation," *Medical Care 22* (1984): 922–935.

Sheu, Mei-ling et al., "The Effect of a Major Cigarette Price Change on Smoking Behavior in California: A Zero-Inflated Negative Binomial Model," *Health Economics 13* (2004): 781–791.

Shleifer, Andrei, "A Theory of Yardstick Competition," *RAND Journal of Economics 16* (1985): 319–327.

Short, Pamela F. and Peter Kemper, "Nursing Home Financing Reform: How Would It Affect Expenditures for Nursing Home Care?" *Inquiry 31* (1994): 141–152.

Shortell, Stephen M., *A Model of Physician Referral Behavior: A Test of Exchange Theory in Medical Practice* (Chicago: Center for Health Administration Studies, 1973).

Shortell, Stephen M., Robin R. Gillies, and David A. Anderson, "The New World of Managed Care: Creating Organized Delivery Systems," *Health Affairs 13* (1994): 46–64.

Sickles, Robin C. and Abdo Yazbeck, "On the Dynamics of Demand for Leisure and the Production of Health," *Journal of Business and Economic Statistics 16* (1998): 187–197.

Siegel, Joanna E. et al., "Recommendations for Reporting Cost-Effectiveness Analyses," *Journal of the American Medical Association 276* (1996): 1339–1341.

Silver, Morris, "An Economic Analysis of Variations in Medical Expenses and Work-Loss Rates," in *Empirical Studies in Health Economics*, Herbert Klarman (ed.) (Baltimore: Johns Hopkins, 1970).

Silverman, Elaine and Jonathan Skinner, "Are For Profit Hospitals Really Different? Medicare Upcoding and Market Structure," National Bureau of Economic Research (NBER), Working Paper 8133, Cambridge, MA, 2001.

Silverman, Elaine and Jonathan Skinner, "Medicare Upcoding and Hospital Ownership," *Journal of Health Economics 23* (2004): 369–389.

Simon, Carol J., David Dranove, and William White, "The Effect of Managed Care on the Incomes of Primary and Specialty Physicians," *Health Services Research 33* (1998): 549–569.

Sindelar, Jody, "The Declining Price of Health Insurance," in *Health Care in America*, H. E. Frech III (ed.). (San Francisco: Pacific Research Institute for Public Policy, 1988).

Sinjay, Ugur A. and Claudia R. Campbell, "Scope and Scale Economies in Merging Hospitals Prior to Merger," *Journal of Economics and Finance 19* (1995): 107–123.

Skinner, Jonathon, "What Do Stochastic Cost Functions Tell Us About Inefficiency?" *Journal of Health Economics 13* (1994): 323–328.

Skocpol, Theda, "The Rise and Resounding Demise of the Clinton Plan," *Health Affairs 14* (1995): 66–87.

Sloan, Frank A., et al., "Does Where You Are Admitted Make a Difference? An Analysis of Medicare Data," National Bureau of Economic Research (NBER), Working Paper 6896, Cambridge, MA, 1999.

Sloan, Frank A., "Not-For-Profit Ownership and Hospital Behavior," in *Handbook of Health Economics*, Volume I, Anthony J. Culyer and Joseph P. Newhouse (eds.). (Elsevier Science B.V., 2000).

Sloan, Frank A. et al., "Hospital Ownership and Cost and Quality of Care: Is There a Dime's Worth of Difference?" *Journal of Health Economics 20* (2001): 1–22.

Sloan, Frank A., "Property Rights in the Hospital Industry," in *Health Care in America*, H. E. Frech III (ed.). (San Francisco: Pacific Research Institute for Public Policy, 1988).

Sloan, Frank A., "Rate Regulation as a Strategy for Hospital Cost Control: Evidence from the Last Decade," *Milbank Memorial Fund Quarterly/Health and Society 61* (1983): 195–221.

Sloan, Frank A. and Edmund R. Becker, "Internal Organization of Hospitals and Hospital Costs," *Inquiry 28* (1981): 224–239.

Sloan, Frank A. and A. Bruce Steinwald, "Effects of Regulation on Hospital Costs and Input Use," *Journal of Law and Economics 23* (1980): 81–109.

Sloan, Frank A., Roger D. Feldman, and A. Bruce Steinwald, "Effects of Teaching on Hospital Costs," *Journal of Health Economics 3* (1983): 1–28.

Sloan, Frank A., Michael A. Morrisey, and Joseph Valvona, "Effects of the Medicare Prospective Payment System on Hospital Cost Containment: An Early Appraisal," *Milbank Quarterly 66* (1988a): 191–219.

Sloan, Frank A., Michael A. Morrisey, and Joseph Valvona, "Medicare Prospective Payment and the Use of Medical Technologies in Hospitals," *Medical Care 26* (1988b): 837–853.

Sloan, Frank A. et al., "The Demise of Hospital Philanthropy," *Economic Inquiry 28* (1990): 725–743.

Sloan, Frank A. et al., "Diffusion of Surgical Technology: An Exploratory Study," *Journal of Health Economics 5* (1986): 31–61.

Smith, Adam, *An Inquiry into the Nature and Causes of the Wealth of Nations* (Chicago: University of Chicago Press, 1976).

Smith, Cynthia et al., "Health Spending Growth Slows in 2003," *Health Affairs 24* (2005): 185–194.

Smith, Cynthia et al., "National Health Spending in 2004: Recent Slowdown Led By Prescription Drug Spending," *Health Affairs 25* (2006): 186–196.

Smith, Francis B, *The Retreat of Tuberculosis 1850–1950.* (London: Croom Helm, 1988).

Smith, James P., "Socioeconomic Status and Health," *American Economic Review 88* (1998): 192–196.

Smith, Sheila et al., "The Next Ten Years of Health Spending: What Does the Future Hold?" *Health Affairs 17* (1998): 128–140.

Solberg, Leif I. et al., "Is Quality Free? The Relationship Between Cost and Quality Across 18 Provider Groups," *American Journal of Managed Care 8* (2002): 413–422.

Sonnenfeld, Sally T. et al., "Projections of National Health Expenditures Through the Year 2000," *Health Care Financing Review 13* (1991): 1–27.

Sørenson, Rune and Jostein Grytten, "Competition and Supplier Induced Demand in a Health Care System with Fixed Fees," *Health Economics 8* (1999): 497–508.

Spence, A. Michael, "Monopoly, Quality, and Regulation," *Bell Journal of Economics 6* (1973): 417–429.

Sprang, Heather R., Gloria Bazzoli, and Richard Arnould, "Hospital Mergers and Savings for Consumers: Exploring New Evidence," *Health Affairs 20* (2001): 150–158.

STAKES, www.stakes.fi/english/facts/index.html, 2002.

Stano, Miron, "An Analysis of the Evidence on Competition in the Physician Services Markets," *Journal of Health Economics 4* (1985): 197–211.

Stano, Miron, "A Further Analysis of the Physician Inducement Controversy," *Journal of Health Economics 6* (1987): 227–238.

Stano, Miron, "Individual Health Accounts: An Alternative Health Care Financing Approach," *Health Care Financing Review 3* (1981): 117–125.

Stano, Miron and Sherman Folland, "Variations in the Use of Physician Services by Medicare Beneficiaries," *Health Care Financing Review 9* (1988): 51–58.

Stano, Miron et al., "The Effects of Physician Availability on Fees and the Demand for Doctors' Services," *Atlantic Economic Journal 13* (1985): 51–60.

Starr, Paul, "Health Care for the Poor: The Past Twenty Years," in *Fighting Poverty: What Works and What Doesn't*, Sheldon Danziger and Daniel Weinberg (eds.). (Cambridge: Harvard, 1986).

Starr, Paul, *The Social Transformation of American Medicine*. (New York: Basic Books, 1982).

Steinberg, Richard, "Charitable Giving as a Mixed Public/Private Good: Implications for Tax Policy," *Public Finance Quarterly 14* (1986): 415–431.

Steinberg, Richard, "Voluntary Donations and Public Expenditures in a Federalist System," *American Economic Review 77* (1987): 24–36.

Steinfels, Peter, "Oregon Medicaid's Doctor-Assisted Suicide," *New York Times*, March 7, 1998, national/metro sec.

Steinmann, Lukas and Peter Zweifel, "On the [In]effi-ciency of Swiss Hospitals-English Summary," *Ifo Studien 46* (2000): 197–217.

Stigler, George J., "The Economics of Information," *Journal of Political Economy 69* (1961): 213–225.

Stigler, George J., "The Theory of Economic Regulation," *Bell Journal of Economics 2* (1971): 3–21.

Stiglitz, Joseph E., *Economics of the Public Sector*, 2nd ed. (New York: Norton, 1988).

Strauss, John et al., "Gender and Life-Cycle Differentials in the Patterns and Determinants of Adult Health," *Journal of Human Resources 28* (1993): 791–837.

Street, Andrew, "How Much Confidence Can We Have in Hospital Efficiency Estimates?" *Health Economics 12* (2003): 896–907.

Succi, Melissa J., Shoou-Yih Lee, and Jeffrey A. Alexander, "Effects of Market Position and Competition on Rural Hospital Closures," *Health Services Research 31* (1997): 679–699.

Sullivan, Daniel, "Monopsony Power in the Market for Nurses," *Journal of Law and Economics 32* (1989): S135–S179.

Surgeon General of the United States, *Reducing the Health Consequences of Smoking: 25 Years of Progress, Executive Summary*. U.S. Department of Health and Human Services, Public Health Service, Office on Smoking and Health, Rockville, MD, 1989.

Svorny, Shirley, "Should We Reconsider Licensing Physicians?" *Contemporary Policy Issues 10* (1992): 31–38.

Tauras, John A. and Frank J. Chaloupka, "Price, Clean Indoor Air, and Cigarette Smoking: Evidence from the Longitudinal Data for Young Adults," National Bureau of Economic Research Working Paper 6937, 1999.

Tay, Abigail, "Assessing Competition in Hospital Care Markets: The Importance of Accounting for Quality Difference," *Rand Journal of Economics 34* (2003): 786–814.

Telser, Lester G., "Advertising and Competition," *Journal of Political Economy 72* (1964): 537–562.

Temin, Peter, "An Economic History of American Hospitals," in *Health Care in America*, H. E. Frech III (ed.). (San Francisco: Pacific Research Institute for Public Policy, 1988).

Tengs, Tammy O. et al., "Five Hundred Life-Saving Interventions and Their Cost-Effectiveness," *Risk Analysis 15* (1995): 369–390.

Teplensky, Jill D. et al., "Hospital Adoption of Medical Technology: An Empirical Test of Alternative Models," *Health Services Research 30* (1995): 437–466.

Thaler, Richard and Sherwin Rosen, "The Value of Saving a Life: Evidence from the Labor Market," in *Household Production and Consumption*, Nestor E. Terleckyi (ed.) (New York: National Bureau of Economic Research, 1975): 265–297.

Thomas, Lewis, *The Lives of a Cell* (New York: Viking, 1974).

Thornton, James, "Estimating a Health Production Function for the U.S.," *Applied Econometrics 34* (2002): 59–62.

Tilford, John M. et al., "Response to Health Insurance by Previously Uninsured Rural Children," *Health Services Research 34* (3) (1999): 761–775.

Tinbergen, Jan, *On the Theory of Economic Policy*. (Amsterdam: North-Holland Pub. Co., 1952).

Torrance, George W., "Preferences for Health Outcomes and Cost-Utility Analysis," *American Journal of Managed Care 3* (1997 Supplement): S8–S20.

Toxic Substances Board, *Health or Tobacco: An End to Tobacco Advertising and Promotion*, Department of Health, Wellington, New Zealand, May 1989.

Tremblay, Carol Horton and Victor J. Tremblay, "The Impact of Cigarette Advertising on Consumer Surplus, Profit, and Social Welfare," *Contemporary Economic Policy 13* (1995): 113–124.

Trigg, Andrew B. and Nick Bosanquet, "Tax Harmonisation and the Reduction of European Smoking Rates," *Journal of Health Economics 11* (1992): 329–346.

Tsuchiya, Aki, "QALYs and Ageism: Philosophical Theories and Age Weighting," *Health Economics 9* (2000): 57–68.

Tumlinson, Anne et al., "Choosing a Health Plan: What Information Will Consumers Use?" *Health Affairs 16* (1997): 229–238.

Tye, Joe B., Kenneth E. Warner, and Stanton A. Glantz, "Tobacco Advertising and Consumption: Evidence of a Causal Relationship," *Journal of Public Health Policy 8* (1987): 492–508.

United Kingdom Commission for Healthcare Audit and Inspection, *State of Healthcare 2005*, www. healthcare-commission.org.uk/NationalFindings/StateOfHealthcare/fs/en?CONTENT_ID=4006361&chk=sNVkqk, accessed November 15, 2005.

United Nations, "World Population from Year 0 to Stabilization," www.gopher.undp.org:70/00/ungophers/popin/wdtrends/history, 1996.

U.S. Department of Commerce. Statistical Abstract. Washington, DC, various years.

U.S. Department of Health and Human Services, National Institute of Allergies and Infectious Diseases, "The Relationship Between the Human Immunodeficiency Virus and the Acquired Immunodeficiency Syndrome," www.niaid.nih.gov/publications/hivaids/14.htm, accessed January 16, 2003.

U.S. Department of Health and Human Services, Public Health Service. *Health United States*, various years.

U.S. Department of Health and Human Services, Public Health Service. *Seventh Report to the President and Congress on the Status of Health Personnel in the United States*. DHHS Publication No. HRS-P-OD-90-1, March 1990.

U.S. Department of Health and Human Services, *Report of the Expert Panel on Population Strategies for Blood Cholesterol Reduction*. NIH Publication No. 90-3046, November 1990.

U.S. Department of Health and Human Services, *Understanding Estimates of the Uninsured: Putting the Differences in Context*, http://aspe.os.dhhs.gov/health/reports/hiestimates.htm, accessed March 17, 2003.

U.S. Department of Labor, Bureau of Labor Statistics, *Occupational Outlook Handbook*, 1990–1991 edition, April 1990.

Valdez, R. Burciaga et al., "Consequences of Cost Sharing for Children's Health," *Pediatrics 75* (1985): 952–961.

Valdmanis, Vivian G., "Ownership and Technical Efficiency of Hospitals," *Medical Care 28* (1990): 552–561.

van Doorslaer, Eddy and Adam Wagstaff, "Equity in the Delivery of Health Care: Some International Comparisons," *Journal of Health Economics 11* (1992): 389–411.

van Houten, Courtney and Edward C. Norton, "Informal Care and Health Use of Older Adults," *Journal of Health Economics 23* (2004): 1159–1180.

van Lear, William and Lynette Fowler, "Efficiency and Service in the Group Home Industry," *Journal of Economic Issues 21* (1997): 1039–1050.

Vehorn, Charles L., J. Steven Landefeld, and Douglas P. Wagner, "Measuring the Contribution of Biomedical Research to the Production of Health," *Research Policy 11* (1982): 3–13.

Viscusi, W. Kip, "Age Variations in Risk Perceptions and Smoking Decisions," *Review of Economics and Statistics 73* (1991): 577–588.

Viscusi, W. Kip, "Cigarette Smokers and the Social Consequence of Smoking," *Tax Policy and the Economy 9* (1995): 51–101.

Viscusi, W. Kip, "Promoting Smokers' Welfare with Responsible Taxation," *National Tax Journal 57* (1994): 547–558.

Viscusi, W. Kip, "Risk Equity," *Journal of Legal Studies 29* (June 2000): 843–871.

Viscusi, W. Kip, "The Value of Risks to Life and Health," *Journal of Economic Literature 31* (1993): 1912–1946.

Viscusi, W. Kip, John M. Vernon, and Joseph E. Harrington, Jr., *Economics of Regulation and Antitrust*, 2nd ed. (Cambridge, MA: MIT Press, 1995).

Vita, Michael G., "Exploring Hospital Production Relationships with Flexible Functional Forms," *Journal of Health Economics 9* (1990): 1–21.

Vitaliano, Donald F., "On the Estimation of Hospital Cost Functions," *Journal of Health Economics 6* (1987): 305–318.

Vitaliano, Donald F. and Mark Toren, "Cost Efficiency in Nursing Homes: A Stochastic Frontier Approach," *Journal of Health Economics 13* (1994): 281–300.

Vitaliano, Donald F. and Mark Toren, "Hospital Cost and Efficiency in a Regime of Stringent Regulation," *Eastern Economic Journal 22* (1996): 161–175.

Wagstaff, Adam, "Estimating Efficiency in the Hospital Sector: A Comparison of Three Statistical Cost Frontier Models," *Applied Economics 21* (1989): 659–672.

Wagstaff, Adam, "QALYs and the Equity-Efficiency Trade-Off," *Journal of Health Economics 10* (1991): 21–41.

Wagstaff, Adam and Guillem Lopez, "Hospital Costs in Catalonia: A Stochastic Frontier Analysis," *Applied Economics 3* (1996): 471–474.

Waldmann, Robert J., "Income Distribution and Infant Mortality," *Quarterly Journal of Economics 107* (1992): 1283–1302.

Walsh, Tom, "Hospital Fight Is Heading to West Oakland County," *Detroit Free Press*, May 23, 2003, www.freep.com/money/business/walsh23_20030523.htm, accessed August 25, 2005.

Warner, Kenneth E. and Linda M. Goldenhar, "The Cigarette Advertising Broadcast Ban and Magazine Coverage of Smoking and Health," *Journal of Public Health Policy 10* (1989): 32–42.

Warner, Kenneth E. et al., "Promotion of Tobacco Products: Issues and Policy Options," *Journal of Health Politics, Policy and Law 11* (1986): 367–392.

Wedig, Gerard J., "Health Status and the Demand for Health: Results on Price Elasticities," *Journal of Health Economics 7* (1988): 151–163.

Weiner, Jonathon P., "Forecasting the Effects of Health Reform on U.S. Physician Workforce Requirement," *Journal of the American Medical Association 272* (1994): 222–230.

Weinstein, M. A., "The Sum of Values from a Normal and a Truncated Normal Distribution," *Technometrics 6* (1964): 104–105.

Weinstein, Milton C. and Willard G. Manning, Jr., "Theoretical Issues in Cost-Effectiveness Analysis," *Journal of Health Economics 16* (1997): 121–128.

Weinstein, Milton C. et al., "Recommendations of the Panel on Cost-Effectiveness in Health and Medicine," *Journal of the American Medical Association 276* (1996): 1253–1258.

Weisbrod, Burton A., "Costs and Benefits of Medical Research: A Case Study of Poliomyelitis," *Journal of Political Economy 79* (1971): 527–544.

Weisbrod, Burton A., "The Health Care Quadrilemma: An Essay on Technological Change, Insurance, Quality of Care, and Cost Containment," *Journal of Economic Literature 29* (1991): 523–552.

Weisbrod, Burton A., *The Nonprofit Economy*. (Cambridge, MA: Harvard, 1988).

Weisbrod, Burton A., "Toward a Theory of the Voluntary Non-Profit Sector in a Three-Sector Economy," in *Altruism, Morality, and Economic Theory*, Edmund S. Phelps (ed.) (New York: Russell Sage Foundation, 1975).

Wells, William, John Burnett, and Sandra Moriarity. *Advertising: Principles and Practice*. (Upper Saddle River, NJ: Prentice Hall, 1989).

Wennberg, John E., "Dealing with Medical Practice Variations: A Proposal for Action," *Health Affairs 3* (1984): 6–32.

Wennberg, John E., "Population Illness Rates Do Not Explain Population Hospitalization Rates," *Medical Care 25* (1987): 354–359.

Wennberg, John E., "Small Area Analysis and the Medical Care Outcome Problem," in *Research Methodology: Strengthening Causal Interpretation of Non-Experimental Data*, E. Perrin and J. Bunker (eds.) Rockville: Department of Health and Human Services, PHS 90-3454, 1990: 177–213.

Wennberg, John E. and F. J. Fowler, "A Test of Consumer Contribution to Small Area Variations in Health Care Delivery," *Journal of the Maine Medical Association 68* (1977): 275–279.

Wennberg, John E. and Alan Gittelsohn, "Small Area Variations in Health Care Delivery," *Science 182* (1973): 1102–1108.

Wennberg, John E. and Alan Gittelsohn, "Variations in Medical Care Among Small Areas," *Scientific American 246* (1982): 120–134.

Wennberg, John E., B. A. Barnes, and M. Zubkoff, "Professional Uncertainty and the Problem of Supplier-Induced-Demand," *Social Science and Medicine 16* (1982): 811–824.

Wennberg, John E. et al., "Changes in Tonsillectomy Rates Associated with Feedback and Review," *Pediatrics 59* (1977): 821–826.

Wennberg, John E. et al., "Hospital Use and Mortality Among Medicare Beneficiaries in Boston and New Haven," *New England Journal of Medicine 321* (1989): 1168–1173.

Wheeler, Benedict W., "Health-Related Environmental Indices and Environmental Equity in England and Wales," *Environment and Planning A 36* (2004): 803–822.

Wickizer, Thomas M. and Paul J. Feldstein, "The Impact of HMO Competition on Private Health Insurance Premiums, 1985–92," *Inquiry 32* (1995): 241–251.

Wickizer, Thomas M., John R. C. Wheeler, and Paul J. Feldstein, "Does Utilization Review Reduce Unnecessary Hospital Care and Contain Costs?" *Medical Care 27* (1989): 632–647.

Wickizer, Thomas M., John R. C. Wheeler, and Paul J. Feldstein, "Have Hospital Inpatient Cost Containment Programs Contributed to the Growth in Outpatient Expenditures?" *Medical Care 29* (1991): 442–451.

Wiggins, Steven N. and Robert Mannes, "Price Competition in Pharmaceuticals: The Case of Anti-Infectives," *Economic Inquiry 42* (2004): 247–262.

Wilensky, Gail R. and Louis F. Rossiter, "Economic Advantages of Board Certification," *Journal of Health Economics 2* (1983): 87–94.

Williams, Alan, "Intergeneration Equity: An Exploration of the 'Fair Innings' Argument," *Health Economics 6* (1997): 117–132.

Williams, Alan and Richard Cookson, "Equity in Health," *Handbook of Health Economics*, Volume I, A. J. Culyer and J. P. Newhouse (eds.) (Elsevier Science, B.V., 2000).

Williams, Jenny, Lisa M. Powell, and Henry Wechsler, "Does Alcohol Consumption Reduce Human Capital Accumulation? Evidence from a College Alcohol Study," *Applied Economics* (2003): 1227–1239.

Williams, Scott C. et al., "Quality of Care in U.S. Hospitals as Reflected by Standardize Measures, 2002–2004," *New England Journal of Medicine 353* (2005): 255–264.

Williamson, Oliver E., *The Economics of Discretionary Behavior: Managerial Objectives in the Theory of the Firm* (Upper Saddle River, NJ: Prentice Hall, 1964).

Wilson, George W. and Joseph M. Jadlow, "Competition, Profit Incentives, and Technical Efficiency in the Provision of Nuclear Medicine Services," *Bell Journal of Economics 13* (1982): 472–482.

Wittink, Dick R., "Advertising Increases Sensitivity to Price," *Journal of Advertising Research 17* (1977): 27–33.

Wittman, Donald, "Efficient Rules in Highway Safety and Sports Activity," *American Economic Review 72* (1982): 78–90.

Wolfe, Barbara L., "Health Status and Medical Expenditures: Is There a Link?" *Social Science and Medicine 22* (1986): 993–999.

Wolfe, Barbara L. and Jere R. Behrman, "Women's Schooling and Children's Health: Are the Effects Robust with Adult Sibling Control for the Women's Childhood Background?" *Journal of Health Economics 6* (1987): 239–254.

Wolfe, John R. and John H. Goddeeris, "Adverse Selection, Moral Hazard, and the Wealth Effects in the Medigap Insurance Market," *Journal of Health Economics 10* (1991): 433–459.

Woods, Robert and P. R. Andrew Hinde, "Mortality in Victorian England: Models and Patterns," *Journal of Interdisciplinary History 18* (1987): 27–54.

Woolhandler, Steffie, Terry Campbell, and David U., Himmelstein, "Costs of Health Care Administration in the United States and Canada," *New England Journal of Medicine 349* (2003): 768–775.

World Bank Datasite, www.worldbank.org/data/databytopic/class.htm, accessed April 29, 2002.

World Health Organization, *Vital Statistics*, various years.

Writing Group for the Women's Health Initiative Investigators, "Risks and Benefits of Estrogen Plus Progestin in Healthy Postmenopausal Women," *Journal of the American Medical Association 288* (3) (2002): 321–333.

Yip, Winnie C., "Physician Response to Medicare Fee Reductions: Changes in the Volume of Coronary Bypass Graft (CABG) Surgeries in the Medicare and Private Sectors," *Journal of Health Economics 17* (1998): 675–699.

Yoo, Byung-Kwang et al., "Impacts of Informal Caregiver Availability on Long-term Care Expenditures in OECD Countries," *Health Services Research 39* (2004): 1971–1992.

Zeckhauser, Richard J. and D. Marks, "Sign-Posting Selected Product Information and Market Function," manuscript, John F. Kennedy School of Government, 1989.

Zipkin, Amy, "The Concierge Doctor is Available (at a Price)," *New York Times*, July 31, 2005, www.nytimes.com/2005/07/31/business/your_money/31doctor.

Zuckerman, Stephen, Jack Hadley, and Lisa Iezzoni, "Measuring Hospital Efficiency with Frontier Cost Functions," *Journal of Health Economics 13* (1994): 255–280.

Zwanziger, Jack and Adam Meirowitz, "Strategic Factors in Hospital Selection for HMO and PPO Networks," in *Managed Care and Changing Health Markets*, Michael A. Morrisey (ed.) (Washington, DC: AEI Press, 1998).

Zwanziger, Jack and Glen A. Melnick, "The Effects of Hospital Competition and the Medicare PPS Program on Hospital Cost Behavior in California," *Journal of Health Economics 7* (1988): 301–320.

Zwanziger, Jack and Cathleen Mooney, "Has Competition Lowered Prices?" *Inquiry 42* (2005): 73–85.

Name Index

Subject Index